ALSO BY IVAN DOIG

FICTION

Prairie Nocturne
Mountain Time
Bucking the Sun
Ride with Me, Mariah Montana
Dancing at the Rascal Fair
English Creek
The Sea Runners

NONFICTION

Heart Earth
Winter Brothers
This House of Sky

RIDE WITH ME, MARIAH MONTANA

IVAN DOIG

SCRIBNER

New York · London · Toronto · Sydney

SCRIBNER
1230 Avenue of the Americas
New York, NY 10020

First Scribner trade paperback edition 2005

SCRIBNER and design are trademarks of Macmillan Library Reference USA,
Inc., used under license by Simon & Schuster, the publisher of this work.

For information about special discounts for bulk purchases,
please contact Simon & Schuster Special Sales: 1-800-456-6798
or business@simonandschuster.com

DESIGNED BY LAUREN SIMONETTI

Manufactured in the United States of America

7 9 10 8 6

Library of Congress Control Number: 2005046551

ISBN-13: 978-0-689-12019-0
ISBN-10:   0-689-12019-2
ISBN-13: 978-0-7432-7126-4 (Pbk)
ISBN-10:   0-7432-7126-2 (Pbk)

To Wallace Stegner
one in a century

. . . I determined to give it a name and in honour of Miss Maria W——d called it Maria's River it is true that the hue of the waters of this turbulent and troubled stream but illy comport with the pure celestial virtues and amiable qualifications of that lovely fair one; but on the other hand it is a noble river . . .

Meriwether Lewis, June 8, 1805

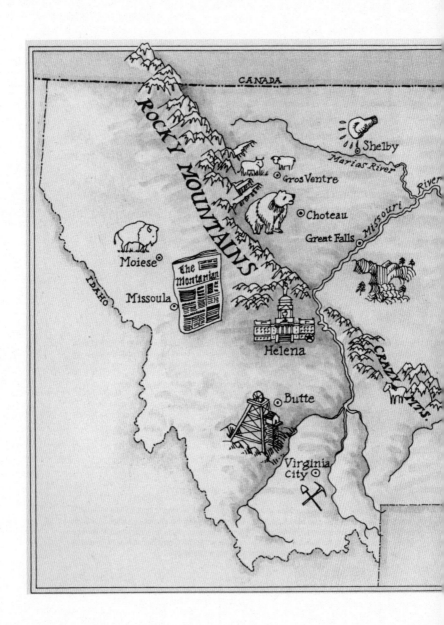

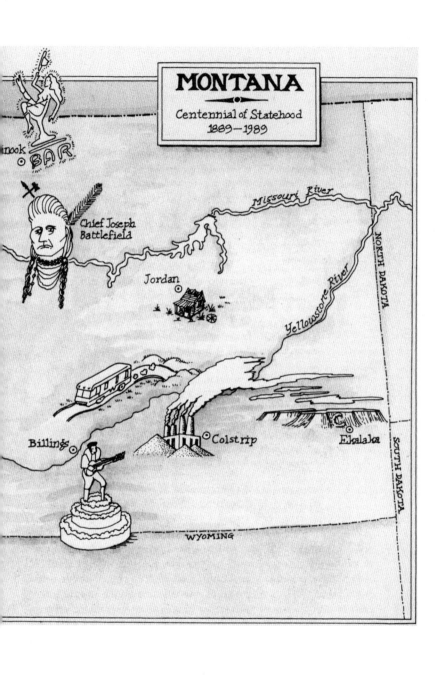

THE END TOWARD IDAHO

Well, old buddies out there the other side of the ink, I am not a happy camper this Fourth of July morn. What we've got here is the hundredth time the grandandglorious has turned up on the calendar since the U. States of A. decided to let Montana in, so wouldn't you think we could do the holiday with some hiss and vinegar by now? But no, it's going to be more of the lame old usual. From Yaak to Ekalaka today, we Montanans will bake our brains in the sun at rodeos, meanwhile consuming enough beer and fried chicken to cholesterate a vegetarian convention, waiting for dark so we can try to burn down our towns with fireworks. A centennial Fourth of the same old guff: hip-hip-hoorah, flap-the-flag-and-pass-the-swag. Maybe it is an American condition, in this strange nation we have become, all helmet and wallet and no brain or heart. But does Montana have to be in a patriotic coma too? Take it from Riley, friends: the calendar this morning says "Independence Day," but you can look high and low in the doings of this centennial year and nowhere find a really independent idea—like changing the name of this state of ours to something more appropriate, such as Destitution.

—*"WRIGHT ANGLES" COLUMN,*
MISSOULA MONTANIAN, JULY 4, 1989

CLICK. From where I was sitting on the bumper of the Winnebago I was doing my utmost to outstare that camera of hers, but as usual, no such luck. You would think, wouldn't you, that a person with a whole rodeo going on around her could come up with something more highly interesting to spend film on than me. Huh uh, not this cameraperson. No more than an arm's reach away she was down on one knee with the gizmo clapped to her eye like she couldn't see without it, and as soon as she'd shot she said as if it was something the nation was waiting to hear, "You're not such a bad-looking old coot, you know that?"

"The old part I do, yeah."

CLICK. Her next snap of the shutter caught me by surprise as it always did. After all this while, why didn't I know that the real picture Mariah wanted was ever the unexpected one, the one after you'd let your guard down.

She unfolded up out of her picture-taking crouch and stood there giving me a gotcha grin, her proud long mane of hair deeper than red—the double-rich color that on a fine horse is called blood bay—atop the narrow but good enough face and the figure, lanky but not awkwardly so, that somehow managed to be both long-legged and thoroughly mounded where the female variety is supposed to be mounded; one whole hell of a kit of prime woman suddenly assembled. I just sat there like a bumper ornament of the motorhome. What's a guy supposed to say, thanks ever so much for doing exactly what I wish to hell you would cut out doing?

Just then a sleepy *bleah* issued out of a Hereford calf unconcernedly trotting past us into the catch pen at the end of the arena. "AND KEVIN FREW HAS MISSED WITH HIS SECOND LOOP!" the announcer recited the obvious in that tin voice we'd had to hear all afternoon. By habit Mariah twirled a long lens onto her camera and in a couple of quick pulls climbed atop the arena fence to aim out at the horseback subject who was disgustedly coiling his pair of dud lariats, but then didn't bother to snap the scene. "FOLKS, WHAT DO YOU SAY WE GIVE THIS HARDLUCK COWBOY A BIG HAND OF APPLAUSE! IT'S THE ONLY PAY HE'S GOING TO TAKE HOME FROM HERE TODAY!" My thumb found the Frew boy on the program. Christamighty, he was only the first contestant in the third section of calf roping. Down through all the Fourths of July, if I had a dollar for every guy who entered the Gros Ventre rodeo under the impression he was a calf roper I could buy up Japan.

Mariah was staying perched on the top fence pole while she scanned through that telescope of a lens at the jampacked grandstand crowd across the arena. Involuntarily I found myself seeing the surroundings in the same bit by bit way she was through her picture-taking apparatus. What this was, the woven wire between the posts and poles of the arena fence sectioned everything in front of my eyes into pieces of view about the size of postcards. So when I gazed straight across, here would be a wire-rimmed rectangle of the rows of rodeo-goers in dark glasses and their best Stetsons. Seek a little higher and the green tremble of the tall cottonwoods along Gros Ventre's streets was similarly framed; like the lightest of snowfall, wisps of cotton loosed from the trees slowly posed in one weave of wire and floated on into the next. Farthest beyond, there hung the horizon rectangle, half sky and half cliffwall of Roman Reef and its companion mountains, up over English Creek where it all began. Where I began. Where she'd begun.

Everything of life picture-size, neatly edged. Wouldn't that be handy, if but true.

I shook my head and spat sourly into the dirt of the rodeo grounds. Blaze of the July afternoon notwithstanding, this was yet another of those days, half a year's worth by now, when my shadow would have frozen any water it passed over.

Naturally Mariah had come to the attention of young Frew, who halted his horse, doffed his rodeoing hat and held it over his heart in a mock pretty way while he yelled across to her, "Will this smile do?" Mariah delivered back to him, "The calf had a better one, Kevin," and kept on scoping the crowd. Young Frew shrugged mournfully and went back to winding up his spent ropes.

I regarded her there above me on the fence. That pert behind of hers nicely enhanced by bluejeans, and her snapbutton turquoise-colored western shirt like some runaway blossom against the sky. Mariah on high. Up there in sight of everybody for a mile, but oblivious to all as she waited for the next picture to dawn. Not for the first time, more like the millionth, I wondered whether her behavior somehow went with her name. That *eye* sound there in Mariah, while any other of the species that I'd ever encountered was always plain *ee* Maria. She was a singular one in every way I could see, for sure.

I stood up, partly to unstiffen but mainly to turn it into the opportunity to announce, "I've had about enough of this." Of course my words meant the all-afternoon rodeo and this perpetual damn calf-roping, but more than that, too.

Mariah ignored the more. "What's your big rush?" she wanted to know, all innocent, as she alit from the fence and turned to face me. She made that gesture of swinging her hair out of her eyes, the same little sudden tossing way she always did to clear her view into the camera. As always too, that sway of her head fired off a flash of earrings, silver today, against the illustrious hair. As if just the motion of her could strike sparks from the air. No wonder every man afoot or horseback who ever saw her sent his eyes back for a second helping.

"Jick, somebody's going to use you for a doorstop if you keep on the way you've been," she started right in again as if I was running a want ad for advice. "I had to half-drag you here today and now you can't wait to mope off home to the ranch and vegetate some more. I mean, what is this, suicide by boredom? Before, you were never the type to sit around like you got your tail caught in a crack." Before.

"You know as well as I do that you've got to get yourself going again," she supplied in the next breath. "That's why I want you to pack your socks and come along with me on this."

I'd already told her no. Three times, N-O. Actually I guess it must have been four, because Mariah never starts to really listen until you say a thing the third time.

"Sitting sounds good enough to me," I tried on her now. "The world can use more people who stay sat."

Wouldn't you know, all that drew me was the extended comment that if such was the case then I might just as well plop my butt behind a steering wheel where I'd at least be doing somebody a minimal amount of good, hadn't I. She let up just long enough to see if any of that registered on me. Judging not, she switched to: "I don't see how you can afford not to come. The whole trip gets charged off to the newspaper, the use of your rig and everything, didn't I tell you that already? And if you think that isn't a real deal you don't know the bean counters they've got running the *Montanian* now." Before I could point out to her that free stuff is generally overpriced, she was tying the whole proposition up for me in a polka dot bow. "So all you've got to do is bring the motorhome on over and meet the scribbler and me Monday noon, is that so tough?"

Tough, no; impossible, yes. How could I make her savvy the situation? Before, I'd have said I could shoulder whatever was asked of me, this included. But everything changed for me on that night six months ago, none of it for the better. You can be told and told it will all heal, but that does not make it happen any faster.

Mariah wasn't waiting for my deep thoughts to swim ashore. Gathering her gear into her camera bag, a lightweight satchel made of some kind of synthetic but painted up to resemble Appaloosa horsehide, complete with her initials as if burnt in by a branding iron, she simultaneously was giving the rodeo a final scan to make sure there wasn't some last-minute calf roping miracle to be recorded and saying over her shoulder as if it was all settled: "See you in Missoula on Monday, then."

"Like hell you will. Listen, petunia—if it was just you involved, I'd maybe see this different. But goddamn it, you know I don't even want to be in the same vicinity as that Missoula whistledick, let alone go chasing around the whole state of Montana with him."

"Jick. If I can put up with Riley for a couple of months, it shouldn't be that big a deal for you to."

She had me there. Of all the people who'd gladly buy a ticket to Riley Wright's funeral when the time came, Mariah was entitled to the head of the line.

"You and him, that's up to you," I answered as I had any number of times before. "Though for the life of me I can't see why you'd hang around that joker Riley any longer than it takes to cuss him out, let alone all the way from now until the celebrating gets over." The rest of July, August, September, October, the first week of November: four entire months, Mariah's version of "a couple."

"Because this centennial series is a chance that'll never come again." She still was working me over with those digging gray eyes. "Or anyway not for another hundred years, and I'm not particularly famous for waiting, am I?"

"Christamighty, Mariah." How many ways did I have to say no to this woman? "Just take the rig yourself, why don't you?" I fished into my pocket for the Winnebago keys and held them out to her. "Here. The Bago is yours for however long you want it and I don't give a good goddamn how poor a specimen of mankind you take along with you. Okay?"

She didn't take the keys, she didn't even answer my offer of them. No, all she did was that little toss of her head again, as if clearing her firecloud of hair out of the way would clarify me somehow too. People either side of us on their perches of bumpers and fenders were watching the pair of us more than the rodeo. Swell. See the world champion moper Jick McCaskill and his girl while they duke it out on the glorious Fourth; we ought to be selling ringside tickets. I started to turn away and do what I should have done long since, stick the key in the ignition of the Winnebago and head home to the ranch. Try that, though, when the next thing you hear is Mariah saying ever so slowly, in a voice not her usual bulletproof one:

"Jick. Jick, I need to have you along."

Damn. Double damn.

Going Winnebagoing around the countryside with her and the other one was still the last thing on this earth I wanted to do. But *need* instead of *want*. Do people really know what they are trying to reach for with that word? I wasn't sure I could tell, any more.

I scrutinized Mariah. Her, too? Her own wound not yet scarred over, either?

Our eyes held each other for a considerable moment. Until I had to ask her outright:

"You're not just saying that, are you?"

A kind of crinkle, or maybe tiniest wince, occurred in her expression. Then she gave me that all-out grin of hers, honest as the sun, and said: "If I was it'd be the first time, wouldn't it?"

God, that grin. That world-by-the-tail grin that brought back with fresh ache what I was missing, these months since.

In back of Mariah, out in the arena dirt a grunting guy was kneeling on a calf, trying to collect three of its legs to tie together. I knew how that caught calf felt.

Christamighty. Four entire months of letting myself get just exactly where I knew not to get, between the pair of them. Mariah the newspaper picture-taker, my headlong daughter. And writing Riley Wright, my goddamn ex-son-in-law.

Missoula was sizzling. *93,* the temperature sign on top of the *Montanian* building kept spelling out in blinking lights, as if it needed any spelling out.

I still had the majority of an hour before noon when Mariah and Riley were to present themselves and I'd already used up the scenery from the parking lot. The *Montanian* offices fronted onto the Clark Fork River, in a building that looked as though it had been installed before the river—a gray stone heap with an odd pointy-topped round tower, turret I guess it'd be, bellying out over its front entrance. When the rooftop temperature sign wasn't broadcasting a terrible number, it recited in spurts. Or tried to. First:

IF IT'S N WS

Next:

THEN IT' IN

And lastly:

THE MONTA IAN

Over and over again. I had to wonder what they thought about that gaptoothed brag across the river where the other newspaper, the *Missoulian,* was headquartered in a new low building like a desert fort. Mariah had told me it is rare to have two papers in one town any more, but who ever said Missoula is your average place.

I'd acquired a discarded copy of today's *Montanian* when I stopped at Augusta to coffee up before coming over Rogers Pass, but purposely wasn't reading it because that'd have seemed like giving in to the blinking sign. I figured it wouldn't count if I just leafed through to see whether Mariah had any photos in. The picture with her credit under it, though, I almost missed, not expecting to find her handiwork in the sports section. A balding softball player gasping on third base after running out a triple, his stomach pooching out under a T-shirt which read KEEP MONTANA GREEN. SHOOT A DEVELOPER.

Since I had the newspaper open anyway, I took a peek at Riley's column next. Same as ever, the *Wright Angles* heading and the all too familiar Riley mug, so favorable a picture of him it surely had not come from Mariah's camera, and then the day's dose of words.

The year: back there somewhere. The season: youth. We are six in number, three of each and much aware of that arithmetic.

Curlicues of drawl from the car radio. The girls sing along, and prairie hills squat all around the endless highway. We are, as the road-restless word that year says it, motating. Our green Studebaker coupe motates to the music of time, "melodied radio-special" for us, announces the disc jockey, "by the one and only Mr. Hank Williams."

Fast miles of lost romance banner behind us, who still think high school is the world. The gold-haired girl leans softly nearer the radio and hums at the hills easing past. Mr. Hank Williams echoes the wail life made as it happened to him, and might to us.

And some more like that. Riley was working himself up into a road mood, was he. Probably he never had to exert himself to be in a girling mood.

What roused me from Riley, not that it would have taken much, was the heavy whump of a car door against the passenger-side of the Bago. A brand new Bronco had pulled into the parking space there, and a guy with a California look to him was squeezing out and frowning down at his door edge and what must have been the first paint chip out of his previously virgin vehicle. My sympathy was not huge. I cast him a go-eat-a-toad-why-don't-you glance to let him know so, then stuck my head back in the newspaper while he gave the dusty put-putting Bago—naturally I had the generator on to run the air conditioning—and me some eyeball time before he vanished into a side door of the *Montanian* building. I figured he must be a bean counter. During the energy boom when there were some actual dollars in this state, a big California newspaper named the *Globe*—unfondly referred to by Mariah and for that matter Riley as the *Glob*—bought up the *Montanian*. A person has to wonder: is everything going to be owned by somebody somewhere else? Where does that eventually end up, in some kind of circle like a snake eating its tail?

I checked the dashboard clock again; still half an hour till noon. Well, hell. Given that I'd already made a five-hour drive from the Two Medicine country to get here and there was no telling what corner of the state Mariah and Riley would want to light off to when they showed up, it seemed only prudent to stoke myself up a little. I went back to the middle of the Winnebago to the gas stove and refrigerator there and from what was available began scrambling a batch of eggs with some slices of baloney slivered into them for body.

To combat the stovetop warmth I put the air conditioner up another notch. Pretty slick, if I do say so myself; one apparatus of the motorhome putting forth hot and another one canceling it out with cold. Next I nuked myself a cup of coffee by spooning some instant into a mug of water and giving it a strong minute in the microwave. Looking around for anything else to operate, I flipped the radio on for dining company. And about lost my hand to the ruckus of steel guitars and a woman semishouting:

> *"Somewhere south of Browning, along Highway 89!*
> *Just another roadkill, beside life's yellow line!*

But morning sends its angel
in a hawk-quick flash of light!
Guiding home forever
another victim of the night!"

Some angel, her. Leaving the music on but considerably toned
down, I seated myself to do justice to my plateload of lunch and the
question of what I was doing sitting here in a Missoula parking lot eating eggs a la baloney.

Every family is a riddle, or at least any I have ever heard of. People on
the outside can only glimpse enough to make them wonder what in the
name of Jesus H. Christ is going on in there behind the doors of their neighbors and friends, while those inside the family have times, sometimes lifetimes, of being baffled with one another. "Can this one really be *mine*?"
parent and child think back and forth, eyeing each other like foreign species.
Knots in the bloodline. The oldest story there is, and ever the freshest.

We McCaskills are far from immune. I still wished mightily that I
had stuck with my original inclination and kept saying no, daughter or
not, to Mariah's big thee-and-me-and-he-in-a-Winnebago idea. If that
daughter of mine didn't want to ram around the countryside alone with
Riley Wright while Montana went through its centennial commotion,
let the newspaper dig down and hire her a bodyguard, why not. Preferably one with experience as a coyote hunter, so that he could recognize
what he was dealing with in Riley.

"Up along the High Line, on Route 2 east of Shelby!
The guardian in action is Angel Number Three!
Now chrome collides with pheasant,
sending feathers in the air!
But heaven's breeze collects them
with a whisper of a prayer!"

"That was another oldie but goodie from Montana's homegrown
C-and-W group, The Roadkill Angels doing their theme song for you
here on Melody Roundup," the radio voice chirped. "The time now is
eleven forty-seven. In the weather outlook, temperatures east of the
Divide will hit the upper eighties the rest of this week, and in western
Montana they'll continue to climb into the nineties. So, hot *hot* HOT
is going to be the word . . ."

I shut the voice off. The hell with the radio guy and his word. I hate heat. Although, a week of scorchers would provide me a way to tackle Mariah about getting out of this trip, wouldn't it: "Sorry, petunia, but I'm allergic to any weather over ninety above—it makes me break out in a sweat."

But when I came right down to it, I knew I could not call things off that easily. Digest all my reasoning along with the pan of lunch and there still was the fact of Mariah and myself alone with each other, so to speak, from here on. She and I are the only Montana McCaskills there are now. God, it happens quick. My other daughter, Lexa, lives up in Sitka, married to a fellow with the Fish and Game Department there, both of them as Alaskan as you can get without having been conceived in an igloo. And Marcella, my wife . . .

I swallowed on the thought of her again and sat staring out the motorhome side window to Mount Sentinel and the University of Montana's big pale M up there, branded onto the mountain's grassy flank in white-painted rocks. Already the slope of Sentinel looked tan and crisp. By this time next week, wherever the Winnebago and I and Mariah and goddamn Riley might be, haying was going to have to get under way at my ranch by my hired couple, Kenny and Darleen. There was that whole situation, too. Even yet, in the worst of the nights when the question of what to do with the ranch was afire in my mind, I would turn in bed to where she ought to be and begin. "Marce . . ."

Her at every window of my mind. Ghosts are not even necessary in this life. It is hard facts that truly haunt.

I was not supposed to outlive Marcella. In just that many words, there is the history of my slough of mood, the brown trance that Mariah kept telling me and telling me I had to pull out of. But how do you, when the rest of a life together suddenly turns out backwards. Not that it ever can be a definite proposition, but any couple in a long marriage comes to have a kind of assumption, a shared hunch about who will die first, which is maybe never said out loud yet is thoroughly there. Our own fund of love, Marcella's and mine, seemed to have its eventual sum clearly enough set. My father died at sixty-five, and his father must have been a whole lot younger than that when the labors of his Scotch Heaven homestead did him in. In both of them, the heart simply played out. So, you didn't need to be much of a betting person to figure I'd go off the living list considerably before Marcella.

But cancer.

Only a year or so ago the two of us thought we were on the verge of getting life pretty well solved. By then we had adjusted, as much as parents ever do, to the breakup of Mariah and Riley's marriage. We'd hired a young couple from down at Choteau, Kenny and Darleen Rice, to take the worst of the ranch work off our hands from here on. And we'd bought the Winnebago, secondhand but with under fifty thousand miles on it, to do the traveling we had always promised ourselves— Alaska to see Lexa and Travis, and then somewhere away from Montana winter, maybe Arizona or New Mexico or even California. The brunt of our forty years of effort daylight to dark on the ranch seemed to be lifted at last, is what I am saying. And so when Marcella went in to the Columbus Hospital in Great Falls for that examination and there on the X-rays was the mortal spot on not just one lung but both, it was one of those can't-happen situations that a person knows all too well is actual. Six months before this Missoula forenoon—six months and six days, now—the air of life went out of my wife, and the future out of me. Her death was as if I'd been gutted, the way a rainbow trout is when you slit his underside all the way to the gills and run your thumbnail like a cruel little plow the length of the cut to shove the insides out.

An eruption of light where the side door of the Winnebago had been. I jerked back, blinking and squinting into the bright of noon.

"Hi, how many days you been here?" swept in Mariah's voice and swiftly the rest of the swirl of her, led by the ever present camera bag she hoisted with both hands. "You're the only person left in America who's always early."

"Gives people something to say about me, at least," I fended.

"You've got this place like an icebox, you know that?" As usual, her attention was in several directions at once, roving the inside of the motorhome as if she only had sixty seconds to memorize it. Today she was equipped with two or three more cameras and other gizmos than usual slung across her shadowplaid blouse, evidently loaded for the road. None of it seemed to weight her down any. A mark of Mariah was that she always held herself so straight, as if parting a current with her breastbone.

Her flying inspection lit on the frying pan with its evidence of recent scrambled eggs, and that brought out her grin. Which is to say, it brought Marcella into human face suddenly again, as if my thoughts of her were rendered visible. In most other ways Mariah was built McCaskill, but like her mother she grinned Withrow. So many times I saw it originate on old

Dode Withrow whenever he and my father talked sheep in the high summer pastures of the Two Medicine National Forest, and it awaited me on his daughter Marcella my first day in the first grade with her at the South Fork schoolhouse—that grin, one hundred percent pure, which seemed to reach out from all the way behind the eyes, to tell the world *Pretty good so far, what else you got up your sleeve?*

Trying desperately to get myself off that remembering train of thought, I put into voice: "I wasn't actually all that hungry, but—"

"—you figured you'd better eat before you got that way," Mariah melodically finished for me with a laugh. With a quick step she closed the distance between us and leaned down and provided me a kiss on the cheek. Another of the things about Mariah was that she closed her eyes to kiss. I always thought it was uncharacteristic of her, but I suppose kissing has all its own set of behavior.

Her lips sampled my cheek only an instant. She pulled back and stared at me.

After considerable scrutiny of the scissor-eyed kind only a daughter or wife can deliver, she asked: "What, did you fall face down on a porcupine?"

"You never seen a beard before?" I said in innocence. I suppose maybe that was a generous description of the not quite week of snowy stubble on my face; but I was growing the whiskers as fast as I could.

"Beard?!? Jick, *beard* has always been next thing to a cussword with you! What brought this on?"

"What do you think did, the centennial, of course. They're having a beard contest for it, up home. I figured I'd get in the spirit of things." Actually I didn't know why, after 64¾ years, I suddenly was letting my face grow wild. All I can report is that the morning after the Fourth of July I took stock at the mirror and thought to myself, hell with it, let her sprout.

"Jick, you look like what's left of a wire brush."

"It'll get to looking better."

"I guess it's bound to." She gave me another stare almost strong enough to wipe whiskers away, then shook her head and said, "Listen, I just came to say I'm not really here yet." My impulse was to retort that I knew she wasn't *all* here or the two of us wouldn't be about to go gallivanting around the state of Montana with that Riley dingbob, but I abstained. "To stay, that is," she more or less explained. "I've got a shoot I have to do. The Rotary Club speaker. Big fun," she droned in a contrary voice. By now she was fiddling with the middle camera around her neck as if the orator already was barreled in her lens. "How about if you stock us up on food while I'm doing that, okay? Riley's finishing up another of those thumbsucker columns of his and he's supposed to be done about the time I am. He better be, the turkey." Mariah hefted her photographic warbag and spun for the door. "See you."

Off she vanished Rotaryward, and I drove the Winnebago over to the big Buttrey's store at the east end of town. One thing about having spent a lifetime tending camp for sheepherders is that you don't dilly-dally in the presence of acres of groceries. Pushing the cart up one aisle and down the next, I tossed in whatever I came to that I figured we might conceivably need in Bago living. Supper of course was closest on my mind, and at the meat counter I contemplated pig liver until I remembered Mariah's golden words: "The whole trip gets charged off to the newspaper." I threw back the liver in favor of the three biggest ribeye steaks I could find.

All the checkout lines were busy—I guessed this was city living, people buying scads of stuff in the middle of the day—so I parked my cart at the end of a line of four other carts at least as heaped as mine and settled to wait.

I didn't stay settled long.

Only the moment or so it took to study idly along my neighbors in front of me in the grocery line until my eyes arrived at the woman, about my age, being waited on by the clerk at the cash register. I was viewing her in profile and that snub nose told me with a jolt.

Holy H. Hell, it couldn't be her, out of a past that seemed a thousand years distant. But yet it indubitably was. I mean, I know what is said about why coincidences so often happen: that there actually are only twelve people in the world and the rest is done with mirrors. But magic dozen or no, this was her for real. Shirley. My first wife.

For the next several eternal seconds I wondered if I was having some kind of attack. My knees went flimsy, as if something was pushing into them from behind, so that I had to put a hand to the grocery cart to steady myself. Simultaneously my heart seemed stopped yet I could almost hear it butting against my breastbone. My guts felt snaky, my blood watery. Normally I do not consider myself easy to spook. But where was there any normal in this, coinciding in a checkout line hundreds of miles from home with somebody you mistakenly barged into marriage with so long ago?

That marriage had been committed right here in Missoula. I was at the university on the GI bill, my last year in forestry school when Shirley and I connected. Shirley Havely, as she was then, from the town of Hamilton down toward the south end of the Bitterroot Valley. In that college time her figure was more on the tidy side than generous and her head was actually a bit big for the rest of her, but it was such a terrific head no male ever cared: a black cloud of hair that began unusually high on her forehead, creating a perfectly straight line across there like the top of a full-face mask; then black eyebrows that curved winningly over her bluebird-blue eyes; then that perky nose; then a smile like a lipstick advertisement. She was a Theta and a theater major and ordinarily our paths would not have crossed in a hundred years, but Shirley had a taste for life on the edge of campus. As did I, in those afterwar years. I hung around with some of the married veterans who lived and partied in prefab housing called Splinterville and at one Saturday night get-together there the two of us found ourselves at the keg of Highlander beer at the same time and she tested me out in a voice as frisky as the rest of her, "You're the smokejumper, aren't you." I surprised myself by smiling a smile as old as creation and giving her back, "Yeah, but that ain't all I'm up to." It happened fast after that, beginning with an indelible weekend when a Splinterville buddy and his wife were away and Shirley and I had the privacy of their place. Then the day after graduation in 1949, we were married. We stayed on in Missoula while I smokejumped that summer, that wicked fire season; on the Mann Gulch blowup in August, thirteen smokejumpers burned to death when the flames ran them down one after another on a tinder-dry grassy slope; and ever after I carried the thought that I could have been one of them if I hadn't been out of reach of the muster telephone on a trail maintenance project that day. Whether it was the fever of living with danger or it simply was the temperature of being young, whenever I got home from a parachute trip to a forest fire, whatever time of day, Shirley and I plunged straight to bed.

When that wore off, so did our marriage. After I passed the U.S. Forest Service exam and was assigned onto the Custer National Forest over in eastern Montana, Shirley did not last out our first summer there. It tore us both up pretty bad. Divorce was no everyday thing then.

That was then and this was now, me standing in the land of groceries gaping at some grayhaired lady with whom I'd once popped into bed whenever it crossed either of our minds. I still was totally unlaced by coinciding with Shirley here. What was going through me was like—like a storm of time. A kind of brainfade, I can only say, in and out, strong and soft, like the surprise warm gusts that a chinook wind hurls down from the mountains of the Two Medicine country: a far-off roar, a change in atmosphere, a surge of thaw where solid winter had been minutes ago, but the entire chinook rush taking place inside me, forcing through the canyon country of the mind. Right then and there, I'd have stopped all remembering that the sight of Shirley was setting off in me if I could have; don't think I didn't try. But I couldn't make my brain perform that at all, not at all. Even the familiar way she was monitoring the clerk at his tillwork, keenly counting her change as he drew it out before he in turn would count it into her hand, I recognized all the way to my bones. Shirley always not only dotted every *i* and crossed every *t*, she crossed every *i* and dotted every *t*, too, just in case. With but one monumental exception; me.

I caught my breath and tried to think of anything adult to step forward and say to her. *Remember me?* logically invited some response along the lines of *I sure do, you parachuting sonofabitch.* Or *How you been?* was equally meaningless, for although Shirley was still attractive in a stringent way it was plain that the same total of forty years had happened to her as to me since that altar mistake we'd made with each other. No, search as I did in myself, there seemed nothing fitting to parley to each other now. While I was gawking and trying not to seem to be, Shirley did give me one rapid wondering glance; but with my everyday Stetson on and sunglasses and the struggling whiskers, I must have looked more like a blind bum wanting to sell her a pencil than like anybody she'd ever been at all interested in.

"There you go, Mrs. Nellis," the clerk said cheerily as he positioned the final sack of groceries in her cart, and away Shirley went, one more time.

"Get everything at Buttrey's?" Mariah asked when she and I reconvened in the *Montanian* parking lot.

"Uh, yeah." Plenty. My mind still racing with it all as I stowed canned goods and other belly ammunition in the Bago's warren of compartments. Why were those married youngsters, Shirley and me, back into my life? It wasn't as if I hadn't had better sense since. After I found my way out of the Forest Service and into ranching on the same land where I was born, after I mustered myself and married Marcella in the springtime of 1953, I put that failed first try with Shirley out of memory. But now right here within sight of where that mutual wrong guess began, where education took on a darker meaning than a dramatic girl or a green punk of a smokejumper ever bargained for, that long-ago error insisted on preening its profile to me. What right, even, did that episode have to come swarming back at me again? Doesn't time know any statute of limitations, for Christ's sake?

Out of memory. Suddenly it chilled me, there in the blaze of that Missoula day, suddenly to be aware that there may be no such place.

"I can tell by looking that you're antsy to get going," Mariah was saying over her shoulder as she busily stacked film into the refrigerator. I admit I was about half tempted to respond, just to see the effect on her beaverish activity, *By the way, I just met up with the woman who could have been your mother.*

But the day had already had sufficient complication and so I kept on with my storekeeping and just conversed, "How was your Rotary shoot?"

"Same as a kabillion others. God, I can't wait to get going on the centennial. Something realer than lunch faces."

This time she had shown up loaded for bear, equipmentally speaking. As she continued to move gear in—black hard-sided cases somewhat like those that hold musical instruments but in this instance I knew contained her camera lights and stands, then a suitcase-looking deal that she said was a Leafax negative transmitter, which told me nothing, and another case with portable "soup," as she called her stuff for developing proof sheets of her pictures, then a cargo of ditty bags which must have held all other possible photographic dealies—I was starting to wonder whether there was going to be room in the motorhome for human occupancy.

When she at last ran out of outfit to stash, Mariah gave a quick frown in the direction of the *Montanian* building and the prominently absent Riley Wright, then in the next second I and my unshaven condition were under her consideration again. Oh sure, you bet. Up to her eye leapt a camera.

"Mariah, don't start," I warned. "I am not in a photogenic mood."

She dropped the camera to the level of her breastbone, holding it in both hands while she gazed at me as if she couldn't understand what I could possibly be accusing her of. With a honey of a grin she asked, "Don't you think you're being unduly suspicious?" and right there under the sound of *icious* I heard the telltale *click*.

"Hey, damn it! I just told you—"

"Now, now," she soothsoaped me. "Don't you want the history of that beard recorded? If the world's supply of film holds out, maybe I'll eventually get a picture of you looking presentable."

I kept a wary eye on her, but apparently she was through practicing camera aggravation on me for a while. Now impatience simply was making her goosier second by second. Her hair swung restlessly. Today's earrings were green-and-pink half moons which I gradually figured out represented watermelon slices. "All we need is the scribbler," her one-way conversation rattled on, "but you know him, you'd have to pay him to be late to get him to be on time."

"The slanderous McCaskill clan," in through the motorhome's doorway arrived the voice, still as satisfied with itself as a purring cat. "Ever ready to take up the bagpipes against a poor innocent ex-husband."

So here he was, Mister Words himself. I had not laid eyes on him in, what, the three years since he and Mariah split the blanket. But ducking into the Bago now the sonofabitch didn't look one eyeblink older. Same slim tall build, an inch, maybe two, shorter than I am. But notably wide and square at his shoulders, as if he'd forgotten to take the hanger out of his shirt. Same electric hair, wild and curly in that color that wasn't quite blond and wasn't quite brown; more like applesauce, which I considered appropriate. Same foxtail mustache, of the identical color as his hair. A person's first glimpse of this character, hair seemed to be the main agenda of his head, the face and anything behind it just along for the ride. But the guy was slyer than that, a whole hell of a lot. I have seen him talk to people, oh so casually asking them this or that, and before they knew it they'd been interviewed and were about to be served up with gravy on them in the next day's newspaper.

He was studying me now. I stonily met his nearest eye, surprisingly akin to Mariah's exact gray, and waited for something wisemouthed from him, but all he issued was, "Managed to find your way to civilization from Noon Creek, hmm?" which was only average for him. Even so, up in me came the instantaneous impulse to snap at him, let him know nothing was forgotten, not a thing mended between us. Instead, for Mariah's sake I just uttered the one flat word of acknowledgment: "Riley."

Meanwhile Mariah looked as if there was a dumpload she wanted to deliver onto him, but instead she expelled a careful breath and only asked: "Did the BB have any last words of wisdom for us?"

"You bet. I quote exactly: 'Make our consumers sit up and take notice.'" Riley swung back to the doorway, stuck his head out and intoned to Missoula at general in a kind of robot voice: "CONSUMERS OF NEWSPAPERS. IT HAS COME TO THE ATTENTION OF OUR LEADER, THE INCREDIBLE BB, THAT YOUR POSTURE LEAVES SOMETHING TO BE DESIRED. SO SIT UP AND TAKE NOTICE." He pulled back inside with us and said with a sense of accomplishment, "There, that ought to do it."

Mariah regarded him as if she was half-terminally exasperated, half-helplessly ready to laugh. "Riley, one of these days he's going to hear you mouth off like that."

Riley widened his eyes under applesauce-colored eyebrows. "And demote me to a photographer maybe even? Shit oh dear!" Next thing, he was at the doorway again, sending the robot voice out again: "BB, I DIDN'T MEAN IT. MARIAH MONTANA MADE ME DO IT."

"Demote?" Mariah pronounced in a tone full of barbwire. "Listen, mittenhead. You can barely handle the crayons you write with, let alone a camera."

Uh huh. We hadn't so much as turned a wheel yet and the road war was already being declared by both sides. The two of them faced each other across not much distance there in the middle of the motorhome, Mariah standing straight yet curved in that wonderful womanly way, Riley cocking a gaze down at her from that wilderness of hair. An outside soul couldn't help but wonder how they could stand to work under the same roof, even though Mariah had explained to me that they didn't really need to cross paths all that much at the newspaper, Riley's column appearing as it did without photos except his own perpetual smartass one. So imagine the mutual nasty surprise when Mariah unbeknownst put in her suggestion to do a series of photographs around the state during its centennial celebration and Riley in equal ignorance put in his suggestion to write a series of stories about same, and their editor the BB—his actual name was Baxter Beebe—decreed that they were going to have to do their series together, make a mix. Likely that's how gunpowder got discovered, too.

Which of them relented now I couldn't really tell, but it was Riley who turned a little sideways from Mariah and delivered to me as if we were in the middle of a discussion of it:

"Still hanging onto the ranch, hmm, Jick?"

To think that he would even bring that subject up.

"How's that going?" he pressed, blue eye fixed steadily on me.

Him and his two colors of eyes. I don't know what that particular ocular condition is called, maybe Crayola in the genes, but on Riley the unmatched hues were damn disconcerting—his way of looking at you in two tones, flat gray from one side and bright blue the other. Rampant right up to his irises.

I returned his gaze squarely and gave the ranch answer I'd heard Marcella's father Dode Withrow give whenever my own father asked him that question during the Depression, the selfsame answer that Montana ranchers and farmers must have given when times turned rocky for them in 1919 and the early twenties, and probably back before that in the crash of 1893. "Doing good, if you don't count going broke."

Brisk, or maybe the better spelling is brusque, Mariah passed between us toward the front of the motorhome, saying, "This isn't getting anything done. Let's head out."

"Mariah, you keep forgetting," Riley spouted in her wake. "Your license to boss me expired three years ago." At some leisure he proceeded to give himself a tour of the layout of the motorhome. The gateleg table where he'd have to write on his computer or whatever it was in the case he was carrying. The bathroom with its chemical toilet and the shower just big enough for a person the height of us to duck into. The kitchenette area with its scads of built-in cupboards all around the little stove and sink and refrigerator and microwave. Riley of course recognized the derivation of that condensed kitchen and delivered me one of his sly damn grins. "Jick, I didn't know you sheepherders have engines in your wagons these days." No, there was just a hell of a lot he didn't know. One silo after another could be filled with what this yoyo did not know, even though he did go through life as if it was all being explained through him.

"Tight goddamn outfit," I heard Riley mutter as he finished nosing around. I flared, thinking he was referring to the Winnebago, which was as capacious as Marcella and I had been able to afford; but then I realized from the note of resignation in his voice that he meant the management of the *Montanian,* who utterly would not hear of four months of travel expenses for Mariah and Riley until she came up with the frugal notion of using my Bago.

Something other than the fact that the newspaper's bean counters would sooner open their veins than their wallets seemed to be bugging Riley, though. He fixed a long look onto Mariah's camera bag as if the fake white hide with brown spotted pattern was in fact the rump of an Appaloosa. He'd had that equine paint job done and given her that bag the first Christmas they were married. I wondered if during the breakup of their marriage it ever occurred to Mariah to tell him he was the resident expert about a horse's ass, all right. Now he prowled some more, nosing into one end of the motorhome and then the other, until finally he turned to Mariah and asked: "Well, where do we sort out?"

"Sort out what?"

"Our bodies, Little Virgin Annie," Riley enunciated so elaborately you could all but hear his teeth click on that second word. "Where do we all sleep in this shoebox?"

Mariah sent him a satisfied glint that said she'd been waiting several thousand whetted moments for a chance like this. "I sleep here," she indicated the couch along the wall opposite the dinette area. Then with a toss of her head she aimed his attention, and mine, to the bed at the very rear of the motorhome, scrunched in behind the toilet amid closets and overhanging storage compartments. "You two," she gladly informed Riley, "sleep there."

"Oh, come on!" Riley howled, honestly aggrieved. "This wasn't in the deal, that I'd have to bed down with Life's Revenge here!" indicating none other than me.

"It sure as hell wasn't anywhere in my plans either," I apprised him.

"Then one of you delicate types sleep on the pulldown instead," said Mariah, which Riley and I both instinctively knew was a worse proposal yet. Guys our size, only a bare majority of the body would fit into the bunk that pulled down above the driver's and passenger's seats and the rest of our carcass would have to be folded up like an accordion some way.

"I wonder if it's too late to volunteer for the South Dakota centennial," Riley grumbled, but tossed a knapsack onto the rear bed as if deciding to stay for a while.

By default then, the wordbird and I unhappily resigned ourselves to being bedmates, and once Riley got his laptop computer and a fannypack tape recorder and a dictionary and a slew of other books and a bunch more kit and caboodle aboard, it finally looked like the historic expedition could strike off across Montana. Something was yet tickling at my mind, though. Here we were into the afternoon already and nobody had mentioned the matter of destination. Thus I felt compelled to.

"How far do we have to get to today, anyway?"

"Moiese," Mariah proclaimed, as if it was Tierra del Fuego.

She and Riley kept going on about their business as if that wasn't some kind of Missoula joke, so I had to figure it wasn't. "Now wait a goddamn minute here, am I right that Moiese is just up the road a little ways?"

"About an hour, yeah," Riley assessed, helping himself to a handful of the Fig Newtons he'd discovered in a cupboard. "Why?"

"Are you telling me I got up before daylight and drove my butt off for half a day in this rig just to chauffeur you two somegoddamnwhere you could get to and back in a couple of hours yourselves?"

It was Riley and Mariah's turn to look at each other, accomplices unhappily harnessed together. Riley shrugged and chewed a cookie. "Having you along as chaperone is strictly Mariah's idea," he pointed out. "I wanted Marilyn Quayle to come, myself."

"Shove it, Riley," he was instructed by Mariah. To me, she stated: "Moiese is where we both think the series ought to start. Begin the world at the right end, as somebody always said to me when I was growing up."

In the face of being quoted back to myself I surrendered quick and fished out the Bago's ignition key. "Okay, okay, Moiese it is. But how come there?"

Riley's turn to edify me. "Jick, companion of my dreams, we are going to see the ideal Montanans," he announced as if he was selling stuff on TV. "The only ones who were ever able to make a decent living in this state, before the rest of us came along and spoiled it for them."

Since I'd never been up into the Moiese country, I didn't have a smidgen of an idea what he was yammering about.

"Meaning who?"

Riley, damn him, gave me another sly grin.

"The buffalo."

Tracking buffalo from a motorhome the size of a small boxcar was an occupation I had never done, and so when we rumbled across the cattleguard—buffaloguard, I guess it'd be in this case—into the National

Bison Range at Moiese, I didn't know how things were going to go. Especially when the Range turned out to be what the word said, a big nice stretch of rolling rangeland that included Red Sleep Mountain sitting fat and slope-shouldered across the southern end of the Flathead Valley, enough country for livestock of any kind to thoroughly hide away in. The best I could imagine was that we'd need to creep the Winnebago along the gravel road until maybe eventually some dark dots might appear, far off across the prairie. About as thrilling as searching for flyspecks, probably.

For once, I was short of imagination. Just a couple of hundred yards beyond the Park Service visitor center, all of a sudden here were a dozen or so buffalo lolling around like barnyard cows.

"How's this for service?" I couldn't resist asking Mariah and Riley as I braked the Bago to a stop within fly-casting distance of the buffalo bunch. But he already was intent on them, leaning over my shoulder with notebook and pen ready for business, and she long since had rolled down her window and connected her camera to her eye.

Their goatees down in the grass, the miniature herd methodically whisked at flies with their short tasseled tails. Huge-headed. Dainty-legged. Dark as char. I knew buffalo only from the stories which the oldest of Two Medicine oldtimers, Toussaint Rennie, held me hypnotized with when I was a boy, and so it was news to me that a buffalo up close appears to be two animals pieced together: the front half of a shaggy ox and the rear of a donkey. There is even what seems like a seam where the hairy front part meets the hairless rear half. But although they are a cockeyed-looking creature—an absentminded family where everybody had put on heavy sweaters but forgot any pants, is the first impression a bunch like this gives—buffalo plainly know what they're on the planet for. Graze. Eat grass and turn it into the bulk of themselves. Protein machines.

These munched and munched while we gawked. Digestion of both sorts until suddenly an old bull with a head big as a mossy boulder began butting a younger male out of his way, snorting ominously to tell the rest of creation he was on the prod, and of course at that exact same moment came the sound of the passenger-side door as Mariah went out it.

"Hey, don't get—" I started to yelp and simultaneously bail out of my side of the Bago to head her off, but was halted by the grip of Riley's paw on my upper arm.

"Far be it from me to poke my nose into McCaskill family affairs"—

oh, sure—"but she generally knows what she's doing when she has a camera in her hand, Jick."

True, Mariah so far had only slipped her way in front of the Bago to where she could sneak shots at the bulls doing their rough stuff. But I was staying leery about how she was going to behave with that camera. Long lens or not, she had a history of getting right on top of whatever she was shooting. Years ago at a Gros Ventre rodeo, Marcella and I heard the announcer yap out, "FOLKS, HERE'S SOMETHING A LITTLE BIT DIFFERENT! MARIAH MCCASKILL WILL NOW . . ." and we looked up to see this daughter of ours hanging sideways off a running horse, snapping the view a bulldogger would have as he leaned off to jump onto the steer. We counted ourselves lucky that at least she didn't jump.

These buffalo now were not anything to fiddle around with. Compact though they were, some of them weighed as much as a horse, a *big* horse; couple all that muscle and sinew to those wicked quarter-moon horns and you have a creature that can hook and rip open a person. The reputation of buffalo is that even a grizzly bear will back off from them, and for once I vote with the bear. My buffalo unease was not helped any by their snorelike grunts, *umhh . . . umhh,* which somehow kind of hummed on in the air after you heard them. I noticed even Riley keeping half an eye on Mariah despite his unsought advice that there wasn't anything in her picture-taking behavior to sweat about.

She did nothing too suicidal, though, in firing off her *click* as a pony-sized calf suckled on its mama or the proddy old bull laid down and vigorously rolled, kicking all four legs in the air as he took his dust bath. Up until the point where she climbed onto the top of the Winnebago to see how the buffalo scene registered from up there.

My heart did some flutters as Riley and I listened to her prowling around on that slick metal roof. I mean, oughtn't there be some kind of hazard rule that a photographer never do anything a four-year-old kid would have the sense not to?

My flutters turned into genuine internal gyrations as the old bull shook off the last smatters of his dust refreshment, stood for a minute with his half-acre head down as if pondering deeply, then began plodding directly toward the motorhome.

"It must take nerves of utter steel," Riley observed to me.

"What, to be a photographer?"

"No, to be Mariah's father."

Riley's mouthery wasn't my overriding concern by now, though.

The buffalo bull continued toward us in a belligerently businesslike way, horned head growing huger with every undeviating step.

"Hey, up there," I leaned out the Bago window and called nervously to Mariah on the roof. "How about coming down in? This old boy looks kind of ornery."

Answer from on high consisted of a sudden series of *whingwhing-whings,* like a little machine going. It took me a bit—about four more paces by the inexorable buffalo—to figure out the blurty *whing* sounds, which kept on and on, as being the noise of a motorized camera Mariah resorted to when she wanted to fire the shutter fast enough to capture every motion. As now. "You've got to be kidding," her voice eventually came down but of course none of the rest of her. "When am I ever going to get closer buffalo shots than this?"

Only when skewered on a buffalo horn if she happened to slip off that roof. I had my mouth open to roar her some approximate version of that when I became aware of two dull pebbly eyes regarding me out of a mound of dense crinkly hair, around the front end of the motorhome. I yanked my head inside at record speed, but the buffalo was nearsightedly concentrating on the vehicle anyway. Experimentally he shifted his full weight sideways against the grillwork below the hood and began to rub.

The motorhome began to shake rigorously.

"I figured this rig must be good for something," Riley contributed as the buffalo settled into using the grill for a scratching post. Jesus, the power of that itch. The poor old Bago was rocking like an outhouse in an earthquake. *Umhh . . . umhh,* the three-quarter-ton beast grunted contentedly as he scraped and scraped. To look at up close, the hide on a buffalo is like a matted mud rug that hasn't been shaken out for many seasons, so there was no telling how long this bison version of house-cleaning was going to go on. From my perch in the driver's seat, every sway of the Bago brought into view those up-pointing horns, like bent spikes thick as tree limbs. *Whingwhing whingwhingwhing* from above told me Mariah still was merrily in action, but my jitters had had enough. Without thinking I asked over my shoulder to Riley: "If you know so goddamn much about buffalo, how do we get rid of an itchy one?"

"A little noise ought to make him back off," Riley diagnosed with all the confidence of an expert on large mammals and reached past me and beeped the horn.

The honk did send the buffalo scrambling away, but only far enough to whirl around. Those dancy little legs incredibly maneuvered the top-heavy bulk of the creature, then propelled it head-on at us. Squarely as a pointblank cannon shot, the buffalo butted the grill of the Bago with a crunching *Bam!*

"Shit oh dear!" Riley expressed in something like awe.

"Hey, quit, you sonofabitch!" I shouted. Properly that utterance would have been in the plural, for I was including in it both the horn-throwing buffalo and goddamn hornblowing Riley.

Overhead there had been the sound of a bellyflop, a person hitting the deck. At least there hadn't been a photographer's body flying past.

"Mariah?!" I squalled next, mesmerically watching the buffalo back off with exact little steps, as if pacing off for another go at the grill. "Will you get yourself down here now, for Christ's sake!?" Riley was poking the upper half of himself out the passenger-side window to try and locate her, for all the good that did.

"No way," arrived the reply from the roof. "I know that buffalo can't climb up here. But into the cab with you two lamebrains, I'm not so sure."

"Then can you at least hang onto something while I back us out of here? I'll take it as slow as I can, but . . ." Butt was still the topic on the buffalo bull's mind too, from the look of him. As I eased the Bago into reverse and we crept backwards down the road with Mariah prone on the roof, he lumbered toward us at the same gait as ours, patient as doomsday. Not until the motorhome at last bumped across the hoof-catching metal rods of a buffaloguard and we were safely on the other side of that barrier and the massive fence, did our pursuer relent.

When we halted and Riley and I piled out, that daughter of mine relinquished her armhold around the rooftop air conditioning unit and climbed down perfectly unscathed. The Winnebago, though: its grill had a squashed-in dent as big around as a washtub. The abused vehicle looked as if a giant fist had punched it in the snoot.

Luckily the hood would still open, just, and as far as I could tell the radiator had survived. "How, I don't know," I stormily told the *Montanian* perpetrators and punctuated by slamming the hood back down.

"Honking the horn was a perfectly dumb-ass idea," Mariah rendered.

"Riley's who did it," I self-defended.

"Then that explains it."

"Don't get your kilts flapping," Riley told us soothingly. "A little flexible arithmetic is all we need." He flipped open his notebook and jotted the reminder to himself. "I'll just diddle the expense account for the cost of fixing the grill when we get a chance. The bean counters will never know they've been in the Winnebago repair business."

"Speaking of," I gritted out. "Now that the two of you are done with your goddamn buffalo business, let's get the hell out of—"

Riley stirred in a suddenly squirmy way, like a kid who's had an icicle dropped down the back of his neck.

Mariah jumped him. "You haven't got what you need for a story yet, have you."

He grounded her with an appraising look and the rejoinder, "And you've just been burning film without getting the shot you want yet, haven't you."

Christamighty, all that uproar and neither one of them had anything printable to show for it? They called this newspapering? I suggested coldly to the pair of them, "How about reporting a buffalo attack on an innocent motorhome?"

"BUFFALO BONKS BAGO," Riley considered. "Naw, the BB would only give that story two inches on the pet care page."

Their stymied mood prevailed until Mariah proposed, "Let's go up Red Sleep for a look around, how about." Riley said with shortness, "Good as any."

Red Sleep Mountain is not hospitable to long-chassised motorhomes, and so as far as I was concerned it was up to Riley and Mariah to hitchhike us a ride up the steep one-lane road with a bison ranger. Rather, it was mostly up to Mariah, because any ranger with blood in him would be readier to take along a red-haired woman of her calibre than mere Riley and me.

Shortly we were in a ranger's van, rising and rising, the road up Red Sleep coiling back and forth and around, toward the eventual summit of the broad gentle slopes. Although no more buffalo, other game more than abounded. We drove past antelope curious about us and elk wary of us and every so often sage chickens would hurl up into a flock of flying panic at our coming. At least here on Red Sleep my eyes could enjoy what my mind couldn't. I was thoroughly ticked off yet, of course, about the Bago's bashed-in condition. But more was on me, too. The morning's encounter out of nowhere with Shirley. The firefly thoughts of the mind. Why should memory forever own us the way it does? That main heavy mood I'd been in ever since Marcella's death now had the Shirley layer of bad past added onto it. Was I radically imagining or did life seem to be jeering under its breath to me *is that all you can do, lose wives?*

I shook my head against that nagging theme and while Mariah and Riley carried on a conversation with the ranger I tried to make myself concentrate on the land spreading away below our climb of road. Montana west of the Continental Divide, the end toward Idaho, always feels to me as if the continent is already bunching up to meet the Pacific Ocean. But even though this was not my preferred part of the state I had to admit that the scene of the moment was A-number-1 country. North from the buffalo preserve the Flathead Valley stretched like a green tile floor, farms and ranches out across the level earth in highly orderly fashion, while to the west the silverblue Flathead River curved back and forth broad and casual, and to the east the Mission Mountains tepeed up prettily in single long slants of slope from the valley floor to peaks a mile and a half high. Extreme, all of it, to an east side of the Divide inhabitant like me accustomed to comfortable intermediate geography of foothills and buttes and coulees and creeks. But extremely beautiful too.

The federal guy dumped us out at the top of Red Sleep where there was a trail which he said led shortly to a real good viewpoint. While he drove off to check on the whereabouts of some mountain sheep, the three of us began hoofing.

Out in the tall tan grass all around, meadowlarks caroled back and forth. Here atop Red Sleep the afternoon sunshine felt toasty without being overwhelming. I'd begun to think life with Riley could even prove bearable, if it went on like this, but I had another think coming. We were in sight of the little rocky outcrop of viewpoint when he stopped in the middle of the trail, swung around to me and asked right out of nowhere:

"What do you say, rancher? Could you get grass to grow like this on that place of yours?"

Well, hell, sure. I thought so, anyway. What was this yoyo insinuating, that I hadn't paid any attention to the earth under me all my life? Riley was truly well-named; he could rile me faster than anybody else ever could. I mean, I saw his point about the wonderful grass of this buffalo preserve. Knee-high, thick as a lawn, it was like having a soft thicket beneath your feet. Originally this must have been the way prairie America was, before farming and ranching spread over it.

"Yeah, my place could likely be brought back to something like this," I responded to goddamn Riley. One thing for sure, that mustache wasn't a latch on his mouth. The ranch. Why did the SOB have to keep bringing up that tender topic? On this grass matter though, I finished answering him with "All it'd take is fantastic dollars" and indicated around us to the tremendous miles of tight ten-foot-high fence, the elaborate system of pastures, the just-so balancing of how much grazing the buffalo were allowed to do before the federal guys moved them to fresh country. Sure, you bet, with an Uncle Sam–financed setup like this I or just about anybody else above moron could raise sheep or cattle or any other known creature and still have knee-deep grass and songbirds too, but—

The *but* was Riley's department. "But in the good old U. States of A., we don't believe in spending that kind of money on anything but the defense budget, do we. The death sciences. Those are what get the fantastic dollars, hmm, Jick old buddy?"

Having delivered that, wherever it flew into the pigeonhole of his brain from, Riley spun around again and went stalking off down the trail. He all but marched over the top of Mariah where she knelt to try a shot of how a stand of foxtail was catching the sunlight—sprays of purplish green, like unearthly flame, reflecting out of the whisks of grass.

Riley, typical of him, had freshened another bruise inside of me with his skyblue mention of my ranch. What in the name of hell was I going to do with the place? I trudged along now trying to order myself, Don't think about the ranch. Like that game that kids play on each other: don't think about a hippopotamus, anything but a hippopotamus is okay to think about, but if you think about a hippopotamus you get a pinch, are you by any chance thinking about a hippopotamus?

I am not as zippy on a trail as I once was, but before too long I caught up with Mariah and Riley at the rock finger of viewpoint. Below, Red Sleep Mountain divided itself judiciously into two halves of a V, letting a small stream and its attending trees find their way down between. Then beyond, through the split of the V the neatly tended fields of the miniature Jocko River valley could be seen, and immediately over the Jocko, mountains and timber accumulated into long, long rising lines of horizon. By all evidence, the three of us were the only onlookers in this whole encompassing reach of planet.

Picturing that moment in the mind, it would seem a scene of thoroughest silence. But no. Warbles and trills and solo after solo of *sweet sweet* and *wheeep wheeep* and *deedeedee:* the air was magically busy.

None of us spoke while the songs of the birds poured undiluted. I suppose we were afraid the spate of loveliest sound would vanish if we broke it with so much as a whisper. But after a bit came the realization that the music of birds formed a natural part of this place, constant as the glorious grass that made feathered life thrive.

I take pride that while we three filled our ears, I was the one who detected the promising scatter of dark specks on the big slope to the west; at least my eyes aren't lame. After I wordlessly pointed them out to the newspaper whizzes, those dots grew and grew to become a herd of a couple hundred buffalo. Bulls, cows, calves, by the tens and dozens, spread out in a nice graze with one of the stout pasture fences blessedly between us and them so Mariah couldn't caper out there and invite a stampede onto herself. Of course, even this pepper pattern of a herd across an entire mountainslope amounted only to a fingernailful compared to the buffalo millions back in the last century. But I thought them quite the sight.

Mariah broke the spell. "Time for a reality check," she levied on Riley. "So what are you going to do in your Great Buffalo Piece?"

Riley's pen stopped tapping his notebook. "I won't know that until I sit down and do the writing, will I."

"Come off it, Tolstoy," Mariah said as if telling him the time of day. "Since when don't you have an angle to pull out of storage? Here's-my-ever-so-clever-idea-about-buffalo, and then plug in the details."

"Oh, it's that christly easy, is it," he retorted, starting to sound steamed.

Mariah sailed right on. "So, what can I best shoot to fit with your part of the piece? Buffalo, or country, or grass, or what?"

He gave her a malicious grin. "The birdsong. Get me that, that'll do."

For half an instant, that put me on his side. I wished they'd both can the argument or discussion or whatever kind of newspaperperson conversation this was, and let the air music stream on and on.

But Mariah had on her instructive voice now, not a good sign. "Don't freak, Riley. All I'm asking is for some idea of what you're going to write."

"Buy a Sunday paper and find out."

"How crappy are you going to be about this? Let's just get down to work, okay?"

"I *am* working! At least when you're not yapping at me."

"Then let's hear some of those fabulous words. What's your buffalo angle going to be?"

"I'm telling you, I don't know yet!"

"Tsk," she tsked briskly. "A tiny wee bit rusty out here in the real world after all that sitting around the office dreaming up columns, are you?"

"Mariah, ring off. Shoot whatever the fuck you want and they'll slap it on the page next to whatever the fuck I write and that'll be that. Simplissimo."

"Two half-assed pieces of work don't equal one good one," she said, all reasonableness.

"We are not going to be Siamese twins for the next four months!" he informed her. "You do your job your way and I'll do mine mine!"

With equal beat she responded, "No! The series won't be worth blowing your nose in if we do it that way!"

It must have been some marriage, theirs. By now I'd gone off a ways to try and not hear anything but the birds and the breeze in the grass, but I'd have had to go into the next county to tune those two out. Quite a day for the *Montanian* task force, so far. Newspapering is nothing I have ever done, but I have been around enough work to know when it is not going right. Here at the very start of their centennial series, Mariah and Riley both were spinning their wheels trying to get off high center.

Does time make fancy knots to entertain itself this way, as sailors did when ships were vessels of wind and rope? Cause to wonder, for a centennial started all of this of Mariah and Riley. Not this one of Montana's statehood, of course, but a number of years ago when the town of Gros Ventre celebrated a hundred years of existence. That day Mariah was on hand in both her capacities, so to speak; as somebody who was born and raised locally, and for the *Gros Ventre Weekly Gleaner* as its photographer, there at the start of her career of clicking. Thus she was in natural orbit on the jampacked main street of Gros Ventre that centennial day, and it was Riley who ricocheted in—I would like to say by blind accident but there was more to it than that, as I suppose there ever is. Riley's mother's side of the family was from Gros Ventre originally and so it could be said he was only being a dutiful son by coming with her to the reunion. My suspicion, though, is that he was mainly fishing for something to write in his column. When was he ever not?

In any case, I was witness to the exact regrettable minute when Riley Wright hooked up with Mariah. Late in the afternoon, after the parade and the creek picnic, with everybody feeling gala and while the street was clogged with people catching up on years of news from each other, extra commotion broke out at the Medicine Lodge saloon. Young Tim Kerz, who never could handle his booze, had passed out drunk and his bottle buddies decided a ceremony was called for to commemorate the first casualty of the day. Scrounging up a sheet of thick plywood, they laid out Tim on it as if ready for the grave—*his beer bier,* Riley called it in the column he wrote—to the point, even, of folding his hands on his chest with a purple gladiolus clutched in them. Then about a dozen of the unsoberest ones began tippily pallbearing Tim out of the Medicine Lodge over their heads, the recumbent body on high like a croaked potentate. Somehow Mariah seems to sense stuff like this before it can quite happen. She had raced up into a third-story window of the old Sedgwick House hotel with a panoramic view down onto the scene by the time the plywood processional erupted out of the Medicine Lodge, singing and cussing.

And then and there I noticed the tall shouldery man with the notebook and pen, one intent eye gray and the other blue, lifting his gaze over the tableau of Tim and the tenderly held gladiolus to Mariah above there as she worked her camera.

I had skyhigh hopes for Riley Wright originally. What daddy-in-law wouldn't? Oh, true, matters between him and Mariah had taken a couple of aggravatingly slow years to progress toward marriage. First the interval until a photographer's job at the *Montanian* came open for her. Then after she moved to Missoula for that, a span when carefully nothing was said by either us or them but Marcella and I knew that Mariah and Riley were living together. On their wedding day in 1983 we were glad to have that loose situation ended. So then here Riley was, in the family. An honorary McCaskill, so to speak. In his own right a semi-famous person because of his newspaper column, although some of that fame was a grudging kind from people who yearned to give him a knuckle sandwich for what he wrote. Just for instance, a few years ago when agriculture was at its rockbottom worst and corporations got busy taking each other over and hemorrhaging jobs every time they did, Riley simply ran a list of the counties in Montana that had voted for Reagan and put at the end, *How do you like him now?* Or the time he wrote about a big farming operator who was plowing up thousands of acres of virgin grassland in a time of roaring crop surpluses—farming the farm program, it's called—and then letting that broken earth sit fallow and victim to the wind, *When he becomes dust himself, the earth will spit him back out.*

But when Riley wasn't armed with ink, he truly looked like a prime son-in-law. Oh sure, even in his nonwriting mode, any moment of the day or night he was capable of being a smart aleck. But better that than a dumb one, I always figured. No, exactly because Riley was the kind of sassypants he was toward life, his natural Rileyness, call it, I made my offer. An afternoon in April three years ago, in the middle of lambing time, this was. He and I were sharing coffee from my thermos outside along the sunny south wall of the lambing shed. Bold black and white of a magpie strutted the top of a panel gate, and Noon Creek rippled and lulled, but otherwise just we two. A few minutes earlier when I'd seen Mariah and Riley arrive in his old gunboat Buick I momentarily thought it interesting that after we waved hello mutually, he headed straight down here to the shed while she went into the house to Marcella. Nothing major suggested itself from that, however, and so far as I knew, father- and son-in-law were sipping beanjuice companionably amid the finest of scenery. Spring can be an awful flop in the Two Medicine country. Weeks of mud, every step outdoors taken in overshoes weighted with the stuff. Weather too warm for a winter coat but cool enough to chill you into a cold. Then out pops a day such as this to make up for it all. Just west of us, seemingly almost within touch, the midair skyline of the Rockies yet had white tips of winter, sun-caught snow on the peak of Phantom Woman Mountain and the long level rimrock of Jericho Reef, but spring green colored all the country between us and the foot of the mountains—the foothill ridges where my lamb bunches were scattered, the alfalfa meadows pocketed away in the willow bends of Noon Creek, the arcing slope of Breed Butte between our ranch and those of English Creek, green all.

I recall that Riley looked a little peaked, like he was in need of a fresh turn of season right that moment. But then the stuff he and Mariah dealt with in their news life would make anybody ready for some recuperation by week's end, wouldn't it: a schoolbus wreck, or a guy getting high on something and blowing his wife and kids away with a deer rifle—Christ only knew what messes he and she just averagely had to write about and take pictures of, any given week. So Riley's expression of having been through the wringer bolstered my decision to speak my piece now. I mean, when better? Any number of times he had been heard to grouse about newspaper life and how he ought to just chuck it and go off and write the book he wanted to do about Montana, and equally often Mariah would wish out loud that she could do her own idea of photography instead of the *Montanian*'s, so I honestly and utterly believed that Marcella and I were handing them their chance.

The ranch was theirs to have, I told Riley on that pivotal day. Marce and I wanted the place to be his and Mariah's as soon as they liked. Maybe not the biggest ranch there ever was, but every acre of it financially clear and aboveboard; perfectly decent grazing land, a couple of sections of it still the original native prairie grasses that were getting to be rare, plus the new summer range we'd just bought on the North Fork of English Creek; every bit of it strongly fenced, which was needed when you neighbored onto a grass-sneaking cow outfit such as the Double W; irrigation ditches already installed to coax maximum hay from those creekside meadows; haying equipment that maybe was a little old but at least was paid for; decent enough sheepshed and other outbuildings, brand new house. Here it all sat for the taking, and at their ideal age, old enough to mostly know what they were doing and young enough that they still had the elbowgrease to do it, Riley and Mariah could run this place with a dab of hired help and still find time to work on their own words and photos, couldn't they? A golden chance for the two of them to try, at the very least.

But do you think goddamn Riley would see it that way?

"Jick, I can't."

"Aw, sure you can. I know this isn't your country up here"—Riley was originally off a ranch down in the southern part of the state, on the Shields River near the Crazy Mountains; the father in the family died some years ago but the Wright cattle outfit still was in operation, run by Riley's brother—"but the Two has got some things to recommend it, now doesn't it?" I held my thermos cup out in a salute to the royal Rockies and the sheep-specked foothills and the fluid path of Noon Creek. I don't care who you are, you cannot doubt the earth's promise on such a spring day.

"If it's the sheep that're bothering you, that's fixable," I splurged on. "This place has put up with cattle before." And for that matter horses, the original livestock my grandfather Isaac Reese brought onto this Noon Creek grass almost a hundred years before; and hoofless commodities such as hay, those beautiful irrigated meadows created by my uncle Pete Reese before he passed the ranch to me. I am on record as having declared that in order to keep the ranch going I would even resort to dude ranching, although as the joke has it I still don't see why they're worth fattening. In short, three generations of us had contrived, and every once in a while maybe even connived, to keep this Noon Creek ranch alive, and all the logic in me said Riley was the purely obvious next candidate.

"It's not the sheep."

"Well, okay, the money then," I hurried to assure him. "That's no big deal either. Marce and I have hashed it over a lot and we figure we can all but give you two the place. We'll need to take out enough to buy some kind of house in town, but hell, the way things are in Gros Ventre these days, that can't cost—"

"Money either," Riley cut me off. He had a pale expression on him like he'd just learned he was a stepchild. Pushing away from the warm wall of the shed, he turned toward me as if the next had to be said directly. "You're a contradiction in terms, Jick. A Scotchman too generous for his own good."

"In this case, I got my reasons," I said while trying mightily to think what was the unseen problem here. It's not every day a guy turns down a functioning ranch.

Riley flung the cold remains of his coffee, almost the cupful, to the ground. "You really want to hear some advice about this place?"

"Yeah, sure, I guess."

"Sell it to the Double Dub," he stated.

I felt as if I'd been slugged behind the ear.

Offer after offer had been made to me by Wendell Williamson when he was alive and snapping up smaller ranches everywhere to the east of me into his Double W holdings; the Gobble Gobble You is the nickname that own-everything penchant so rightly earned for the Williamson outfit. The same appetite in my direction was being continued as WW, Incorporated, part of a big land conglomerate back east, now that the Double W and the rest of the lower Noon Creek valley with it was theirs, courtesy of a buyout of the Williamson heirs. Every one of those offers I had always told Williamson and the corporaiders to go stuff.

"Jesus, Riley! That's what I've spent the majority of my life trying not to do!"

"Jick, get out while you can. Ranchers like you aren't going to have a prayer. The pricks running this country are tossing you guys to the big boys like flakes of hay to the elephants."

I still didn't tumble. "I know I'm pretty close to being history, but that's just exactly why the place ought to go to somebody younger like you," I argued back to him. "You and Mariah could have quite a setup here, and the Double Dub and the rest of the world go chase their tails. Why the hell won't you give it a try, at least?"

He and I stood staring at each other as if trying to get through to each other from different languages.

"Jick," Riley blurted it, "Mariah and I are splitting up."

Whatever is the biggest size of fool, that was me, there in the spring sunshine of the ranch I had just tried to give him, as Riley dropped the end of their marriage on me.

I turned away from him toward the mountains, my eyes stinging. By God, at least I would not bawl in front of this person.

Three years that had been now, since everything went crash. And the memory of it festered just as painfully even yet, here on Red Sleep Mountain.

"What, you want to give the BB the satisfaction of telling us he knew all along we couldn't manage to team up for this?" Mariah's latest interrogation of her fellow employee pierced across the grass to me.

Riley delivered in turn, "If the choice is one honeybucket-load of 'I told you so' from the BB or four months of this kind of crap from you—"

Just then the federal guy beeped the horn of his van, signal for our ride back down the mountain with him. Off we trooped to the trailhead, each of those two in their separate mads and me perturbed at them both. Was this what they called getting the job done, throwing snits?

Back at the Winnebago, silence now as sourly thick as their argument had been, I decided to use the chance to fill the air with what was on my mind.

"Too bad you two weren't hatched yet when there were people around who had really seen some buffalo."

As fresh as ever to me were those tales from Toussaint Rennie when I was but a shavetail kid, fourteen or fifteen years old, of having viewed buffalo in their original thousands and thousands when he himself alit in Montana as a youngster. "Before Custer," as Toussaint dated it, a chuckle chasing his words out his crinkled tan face. "Before those Indians gave Georgie his haircut, Jick. I was like you, young. My family came in from Dakota. We saw the end of it, do you know. Buffalo, then no buffalo."

"Yeah," I kept on remorselessly as I drove toward the original dozen dark grazers we'd encountered, who by now had drifted around a corner putting the high fence between us and any more possible butting of the Bago, "Toussaint said the Two Medicine country was absolutely buffalo heaven at first." I guess I was pouring it on a little, dwelling on Toussaint and what a sight the buffalo were to his fresh eyes, but damn it all, I did feel justifiably ticked off about having been enlisted into this big centennial journey that had petered out here in its first day.

Mariah eyed me severely from the passenger seat as if about to say something, thought better of it, then resumed a fixed gaze out the window. Behind her on the sidecouch where he was staring into his notebook as if it was in Persian, Riley stirred a little. "Geography time, class," he announced in a singsong schoolma'am voice. Then in his ordinary annoying one: "If this peerless pioneer of yours came from Dakota Territory, how come he was called Tucson?"

"That was the way it was pronounced, but spelled T-O-U-S-S-A-I-N-T," I took pleasure in setting him straight. "Nobody could ever get it out of him just what he was, but maybe French Cree. He's buried under a Cree cross up home, anyway."

"Métis," said Riley.

I glanced at him from the corner of my eye. The sonofagun did know some things. The Métis were Canadian French Crees who came to grief in 1885 when the Riel rebellion in Manitoba and Saskatchewan was put down and their leader, Louis Riel, was hung. Out of that episode, several Métis families fled south across the border into our Two Medicine country. But as I started to point out to Riley in case he thought he knew more than he did, "Yeah, but you see, by Riel's time Toussaint already had been in the Two—"

"Your guy Toussaint," Riley butted in on me. "How did he talk?"

"What the hell do you mean, how did he talk? Like any of the rest of us."

"Jick, I bet if you think about it, he didn't." Quick as this, Riley was in his persuading mode. "Do something for me a minute. Pretend you're him, tell me what Toussaint told you about the buffalo in just the words he said."

I gave the scribbler an X-raying look now. Which did everloving Riley want, a driver or somebody to play Let's Pretend?

"Stop! Right here!"

Mariah's urgent shout made me slam on the brakes, at the same time wildly goggling around and trying to brace myself for whatever national disaster this was.

After the scrushing noise of tires stopping too fast on gravel, in drifted the fluting notes of a meadowlark, answered at once by Mariah's quick *click*.

Daughter of my own loins notwithstanding, I could have throttled her. Here I figured the Winnebago was on fire or some such and she'd only wanted a picture stop.

I blew out the breath I'd been holding and with the last patience in me sat and waited for Hurricane Mariah to climb out and trigger off a bunch more shots at whatever she'd spied, but no. Our dust hadn't even caught up with us before she announced, "Okay," meaning *drive on.*

Meanwhile Riley wasn't paying her and our emergency landing any attention at all, but was back at me about how Toussaint talked. "Just in the way he said it, try to tell that story of him seeing those buffalo, hmm? No, wait." He scrabbled around, swapping his notebook and pen for his laptop computer. "From your lips to those of the *Montanian's* readers, Jick. Ready?"

My God, life with these people was herky-jerky.

It is true that I have always been able to remember. I could all but see Toussaint Rennie of fifty years before, potbellied and old as eternity, by profession the ditch rider of the Blackfeet Reservation's Two Medicine irrigation project and by avid avocation the most reliable conductor in the Two country's moccasin telegraph of lore and tale. Could all but hear as real as the meadowlark's notes the Toussaint chuckle at life.

" 'I was young then, I wanted to see,' " I began, to the *pucka pucka* accompaniment of Riley typing or whatever it's called these days. Mariah for a change quit fiddling with her camera and just listened. The sentences surprised me with their readiness, as if I was being told word by word right then instead of all those decades ago when Toussaint was yet alive. As if the telling was not at my own instigation. " 'When it came the season to hunt, I rode to the Sweetgrass Hills. From up there, the prairie looked burnt. Dark with buffalo, here, *there, everywhere. It was the last time. Nobody knew so, but it was. The buffalo were so many, the tribes left each other alone. No fighting. Each stayed in place, around the buffalo. Gros Ventres and Assiniboines at the northeast. Piegans at the west. Crees at the north. Flatheads at the south. For seven days, there was hunting. The herd broke apart in the hunting. I rode west, home, with the Piegans. They drove buffalo over the cliffs, there at the Two Medicine River. That, now. That was something to see."*

It was not seen again, by Toussaint's young eyes or any others. Killed for their hides or killed off by disease caught from cattle, the buffalo in their millions fell and fell as the cutting edges of the American frontier swathed westward into them. That last herd, in the last west called Montana, was followed by summers of scant and scattered buffalo, like crumbs after a banquet. Then came the Starvation Winter of 1883, hundreds of the Piegan Blackfeet dying of deprivation and smallpox in their creekside camps. A hunting society vanished there in the continent-wide shadow of a juggernaut society.

Say the slaughter of the buffalo, then, for what it was: they were land whales, and when they were gone our sea of life was less rich. The herds that took their place were manmade—ranch aggregates of cattle, sheep, horses—and to this day they do not fit the earth called Montana the way the buffalo did. In the words of the old man the color of leather:

"Those Indians, they said the buffalo best. They said, when the buffalo were all here the country looked like one robe."

This buffalo stuff of Riley's when it showed up in the *Montanian*, I read with definite mixed emotions.

I was pretty sure Toussaint would have gotten a chuckle out of seeing his words in the world, outliving him. That about the manmade herds, though. What, did goddamn Riley think I ought to have been in the buffalo business instead of the sheep business all these years? And Pete Reese before me? And my McCaskill grandfather, who withdrew us from Scotland and deposited us in Montana, before Pete? I mean, you come into life and livelihood with some terms set, don't you? The

Two Medicine country already was swept clear of buffalo and thick with sheep and other livestock by the time I came along. So why did I feel the prod of Riley's story?

And, yes, of Mariah's photo along with. That one she'd shot, sudden as a fingersnap, out the window of the motorhome in our slam-on stop while Riley was trying to persuade me to Toussaintize. A high thick fencepost of the buffalo range enclosure, a meadowlark atop. The beautiful black V dickey against his yellow chest, his beak open to the maximum, singing for all he was worth. Singing out of the page to the onlooker. And under and behind the songbird, within the fence enclosing that wonderful restored grass, dark hazes of form which the eye took the merest moment to recognize as buffalo, dim but powerful, indistinct but unmistakable.

The next day after Moiese the famous newspaper pair had me buzz us back down the highway to Missoula and keep right on going—when I asked if they wanted to stop at the *Montanian* for anything, Mariah and Riley both looked at me as if I'd proposed Russian roulette—south through the Bitterroot Valley. Well, okay, fine; as we drove along beside its lofty namesake mountains and their attendant canyons, even I could see that here was a piece of country well worth shooting and writing about, fertile valley with ranches and residential areas nervously crowding each other for possession of it, and any number of times in our Bitterroot route I figured my passengers would want to pull over and start picture-taking and scribbling in earnest.

Wrong a hundred percent. "Old news," Mariah and Riley chorused when at last I politely inquired whether they were ever going to get their butts into gear at chronicling the Bitterroot country's highly interesting rancho de la suburbia aspect. Old news? If I was translating right, the Bitterroot and the way it was populating was just too easy a story for these two. I couldn't help but think to myself, what kind of line of work was this story stuff, that it was hard to get anything done because it was too easy to bother with?

The next thing I knew, the Bago and we in it were across Chief Joseph Pass and over into the Big Hole. Well, okay, etcetera again. Now here was a part of Montana I had always hungered to see. The Big Hole, which is actually a high basin so closely ringed with mountains that it seems like a sudden grassy crater, has a reputation as a hay heaven and in fact the ranch crews were putting up that commodity fast and furious as we drove past hayfield after hayfield where beaverslide stackers, big wooden ramplike apparatuses which elevated the loads and dropped them like green avalanches onto the tops of haystacks, were studiously in action. Blindfolded, I could have told you what was going on just from the everywhere smell of new hay. You don't ordinarily see haymaking of that old sort any more, and I'd like to have pulled the motorhome over onto the side of the road and watched the scene of the Big Hole for a week steady—the new haystacks like hundreds of giant fresh loaves of bread, the jackstay fences marching their long XXXXXX lines of crossed posts between the fields, the timbered mountains like a decorated bowl rim around it all.

Yet the one blessed time we did stop so Mariah could fire off camera shots at a beaverslide stacker ramping up into the Big Hole's blue loft of sky, Riley chewed the inside of his mouth dubiously and asked her if she was sure she wasn't just jukeboxing some scenery. "Doesn't work," he dispatched her beaverslide idea. By the same token, when we hit the small town of Wisdom, far famous in the old horseworking days for the army of teamsters who jungled up in the creek willows there while waiting for the haying season to start, and Riley proposed doing a Wisdom piece of some kind, Mariah suggested he check the little filing cabinet he had up there instead of a brain and count how many *wistful little town off the beaten path that, lo, I will now discover for you* versions he'd churned out in that column of his. "Doesn't work," she nullified Wisdom for him.

So that was that for the Big Hole, too. Zero again on the Mariah-Riley centennial scoreboard.

Ditto for the Beaverhead Valley after that, nice substantial-looking westerny country that anybody with an eye in his or her head ought to have been able to be semi-poetic about.

Ditto after the Beaverhead for the beautiful Madison River, a murmuring riffle in its every droplet, classic water that was all but singing *trout trout trout.*

—

Ditto in fact for day after day of traipsing around southwestern Montana so that he or she but more usually both could peer out of the Winnebago, stew about whether the scene was the one that really truly ultimately ought to be centennialized, and decide, "Doesn't work." Doesn't work? Holy J. Christ, I kept thinking to myself, don't you pretty soon get to the point in any pursuit where you have to *make* it work? At this rate it was going to take them the next hundred years to get anything told about Montana's first hundred. Their weekly deadline was marching right at them and increasingly Riley was on the phone to the BB, assuring him that worldbeating words and pictures were just about on their way into the *Montanian,* you bet. Why, I more and more wondered, did Mariah want to put herself through this? Riley in and of himself was rough enough on the nerves. Add on the strain of both him and her breaking their fannies trying to find ultraperfect topics for the series, and this daughter of mine had let herself in for a whole hell of a lot.

It showed. We were down near Yellowstone Park at Quake Lake, where the earthquake in 1959 sloughed a mountainside down onto a campground of peaceful sleepers, when Riley prowled off by himself into the middle of a rockslide slope. I'd just caught up with Mariah after remembering to go back and lock up the rig as we all had to make a habit of because of her camera gear, and happened to comment that if Riley didn't muster what little sense he had and watch his footing up there, we'd be shipping him home to his momma in a matchbox. That was all it took for her to answer with considerable snap:

"Dad, I know your opinion of Riley by heart."

She hardly ever slipped and called me Dad. Mariah arrived home at Christmas from her first quarter away at college calling her mother and me by our given names. Maybe because she'd been somewhat similarly rejigged herself, back east in Illinois, where the nickname "Mariah Montana" was fastened onto her by her college classmates for her habit of always wearing blue jeans and a Blackfeet beaded belt and I suppose generally looking like what people back there figured a daughter of Montana must look like. Or maybe being on a first-name basis with her own parents had simply been Mariah's way of saying, I'm as grown as you are now. Even as a little girl she had seemed like a disguised adult, in possession of a disconcerting number of the facts of life. Our other daughter, Lexa, was a real ranch kid, always out with me among the sheep, forever atop a horse, so much like Marcella and I had been in our own growing up that it was as if we'd ordered Lexa from the catalogue.

Mariah, though, ever seemed to be the only author of herself. Almost before we could catch our breath about having this self-guided child, she discovered the camera and was out in the arena dirt locally at Gros Ventre or down at Choteau or Augusta as a rodeo photographer, wearing hightop black basketball shoes for quick footing to dodge broncs. Tall colt of a girl she was by then, in one glance Mariah there in the arena would seem to be all legs. Then in some gesture of aiming the camera, she would seem entirely arms. Then she would turn toward you and the fine high breasts of the woman-to-be predominated. Next it would be her face, the narrow length of it as if even her smile had to be naturally lanky. And always, always, her mane of McCaskill red hair, flowing like the flag of our tribe. Even then guys were of course eyeing her madly, and by the time she was home from college for summers on the bucking circuit, the rodeo romeos nearly stared the ring finger off her left hand trying to see if she was carrying any gold. But a wedding band was not the circle that interested Mariah. Throughout high school and those college years of hers at the Illinois Institute of the Arts, a place her mother and I had never even heard of before she chose it for its photography courses, and on into her first job of taking pictures for the *Gros Ventre Weekly Gleaner,* only the camera lens cupped life for Mariah.

Until Riley.

That marriage and its breakup should have been sufficient cure of Riley for her, it seemed to me. Yet here she was, putting up with him for the sake of doing this centennial series. Here he was, as Riley as ever, like whatever king it was who never forgot anything but never learned anything either. And here I was, half the time aggravated by the two of them for letting themselves wallow around the countryside together this way and the other half provoked at myself for being ninny enough to be doing it along with them.

All in all, I was just this side of really peeved when we pulled into Virginia City, which Mariah and Riley had taken turns giving a tense pep talk about on our way up from Quake Lake, each needlessly reminding the other that this was it, this was the place, they had to do some fashion of story here or perish trying.

Not a town to improve my mood much, either, old Virginiapolis. Sloping down a brown gulch, one deliberately museumy street—sort of an outdoor western dollhouse, it struck me as—crammed with tourists like sheep in a shearing pen. But I determinedly kept my mouth shut, even about having to navigate the Bago in that millrace of people and rigs for half an hour before a parking spot emptied, and we set off on foot for whatever it was that these two figured they were going to immortalize here.

All the rest of the day, another scorching one, we touristed around like everybody else, in and out of shacky old buildings from the 1860s when Virginia City was both a feverish goldstrike town and the capital of brand-new Montana Territory and up onto Boot Hill where vigilantes did their uplifting ropework on a crooked sheriff's gang, and I myself utterly could not see the attraction of any of it. More than that, something about our tromping through town like a Cub Scout troop fresh off a yellow bus wore on my nerves more and more. Riley, you might know, seemed to be writing an encyclopedia about Virginia City in his notebook. And Mariah was in her surveying mood; today she was even lugging around a tripod, which made her look like a one-person surveyor crew, constantly setting up to sweep her camera with the long lens along the streetful of sightseers below us from where we stood hip-deep in sagebrush on Boot Hill, or aiming out across the dry hogback ridges all around. This was tumbled country. Maybe it took convulsed earth of this kind to produce gold, as had been the case in the Alder Gulch treasure rush here. Now that I think it over, I suppose some of what was grating on me is what a wreck the land is after mining. Miners never put the earth back. At the outskirts of Virginia City are miles of dishwater-colored gravel heaps, leavings of hydraulic and dredge mining like monstrous mole burrows. Or scratchings in the world's biggest cat box, whichever way you want to put it. If Mariah's camera or Riley's pen could testify to that ruination, well, okay, I had to figure that the day of lockstep sightseeing was maybe worth it. Maybe.

So I was somewhat mollified, the word might be, as the three of us at last retreated into a bar called The Goldpanner for a drink before supper, Riley rashly offering to buy.

Inside was not quite the oasis I expected, though. As we groped toward a table, our eyes still full of the long summer sunlight, Riley cracked in a falsetto tone, "Basic black, very becoming." Indeed the bar's interior was about as dark as a moviehouse, with flickery little bulbs in phony gas lamps on the walls, but a person probably couldn't do any better in a tourist town.

Out of the gloom emerged a strapping young bartender wearing a pasted-on handlebar mustache and a full-front white apron the way they used to.

"Gentlemen and lady," he orated to us. "How may I alter your consciousness?"

It took me aback, until I remembered where we were. The Virginia City Players do summer theater here, and this fellow must be either an actor or desperately wanting to be. He was going to need a more receptive audience than Mariah, who took no notice of either his spiel or his get-up while specifying a Lord ditch for herself. I told the young Hamlet, "You can bring me a scotch ditch, please." It occurred to me that I still had to get through supper with Riley, so I added: "Go light on the irrigating water, would you." Then I remembered he was buying and tacked on, "Make the scotch Johnny Red, how about."

Riley was regarding the pasted-together bartender as if he constituted the world's greatest entertainment. All the knothead said, though, in a movie cowboy voice, was, "Pilgrim, I'm gonna cut the dust of the day with a G-ball."

When the drinks came and Mariah and I began paying our respects to Lord Calvert and Johnnie Walker—respect was right; Holy Jesus, in this joint the tab for drinks was $2.50 *apiece;* I could remember when it only took 25¢ to look into a glass—I glanced across and wondered disgustedly how we had ever, even temporarily, let into the family a guy who would sabotage his whiskey with ginger ale. But I suppose it couldn't really be said Riley was a G-ball drinker then. It was hard to know just what to call him. The very first night of this excursion of ours, in St. Ignatius after the buffalo range, he had studied the bottles behind the bar for about an eon and eventually asked the bartender there what he sold the most seldom of. "Water," the St. Ignatian cracked, but then pondered the inventory of bottles himself a while and nominated "Sloe gin, I guess it'd have to be." Whereupon Riley ordered one. Our night in Dillon, he'd taken another long gawk behind the bar and ordered an apricot brandy. In Monida, it'd been a Harvey Wallbanger. In Ennis, a benedictine. Evidently he was even going to drink goofy this whole damn trip.

But Riley's style of imbibing, or lack of one, was not what surprised me worst here. No, what got me was that I noticed he was holding his notebook up right in front of his eyes, trying to catch any glimmer of light from the sickly wall lamps, while he thumbed through page by page, shaking his head as he did and at last asking Mariah hopefully, "Got anything that works?"

She shook her head too, halfmoon earrings in and out of the red cloud of her hair as she did. "Still zippo."

This was just about it for me. An entire damn day of touristing this old rip-and-run gold town and not a particle of picture or print to show for it? After having chased all over this end of Montana? Little kids could produce more with fingerpaint than these two were.

I opened my mouth to deliver the message that the Bago and I had had enough of this centennial futility and in the morning would head ourselves home toward the Two Medicine country and sanity, thank you very goddamn much just the same, when instead an electronic chicklike *peep peep peep* issued from Riley's wrist.

"Shit oh dear," he uttered and shut off his wristwatch alarm. "I've got to call the BB about the teaser ad. He's going to be pissed when I tell him it'll just have to say 'Virginia City!' and then as vague as possible." As he groped off in search of a phone, Mariah too looked more than a little apprehensive.

Civilly as I could, I asked her: "Have you ever given any thought to some other line of work?"

"I know, the way Riley and I have been going about this must seem kind of strange to you." Kind of? "But," she hurried on, "we both just want this centennial series to be really good. Something different from the usual stuff we each end up doing. It's, well, it's taking a little time for the two of us to hit our stride, is all."

Despite her words her expression stayed worried. Tonight this was not at all the bossypants daughter who'd gotten me into this dud of a trip. This was a woman with something grinding on her.

"Maybe it's Riley," I diagnosed.

That got a rise out of her I hadn't expected. "Maybe what's Riley?" she demanded as if I'd accused her of orphanage arson.

"Well, Christ all get out, isn't it obvious? Riley goes through life like he's got a wild hair. Don't you figure that's going to affect how you're able to work, being around a walking aggravation like him?" What did it take to spell it out to Mariah? Riley flubbed the dub in that marriage to her, he turned down my ranch and as much as told me straight to my face that I was a dodo to try to keep the place going, not exactly the most relaxing soul to have around, now was he?

Speak of the devil. Riley returned out of the gloaming, appearing somewhat the worse for wear after the phone call.

"So how ticked off is he?" Mariah asked tautly as he plunked himself down.

"Considerably. This is about the time of day anyway he wakes up enough to get mean. The bewitching BB and his wee bitching hour. But he was shittier than average, I'd say." Riley fingered his mustache as if making sure it had survived the withering phone experience. "What he suggested was that instead of the teaser ad, he just leave a blank space in the paper all the time with a standing headline over it: WATCH THIS SPACE—MARIAH AND RILEY WILL EVENTUALLY THINK OF SOMETHING."

That plunged them both into a deep brood.

Oh, sure, Riley surfaced long enough to say as though it were a thought that was bothering him: "You know, every now and again that tightass SOB can be surprisingly subtul." But otherwise, these were two people as silent as salt.

The stumped look on the pair of them indicated they didn't need to hear trouble from me at that very moment. Besides, the Johnny Red was the pleasantest thing that had happened all day and it was soothing me sufficiently to begin what I thought amounted to a pretty slick observation. "I don't know all that much about newspapering, but—"

"—that's not going to keep you off the topic anyway, hmm?" Riley unnecessarily concluded for me. "What's up, Jick? You've had something caught crosswise in you all day here."

"Yeah, well, I'm just kind of concerned that you two didn't get anything today," I nicely didn't include *again, yet,* or *one more goddamn time,* "for your series."

By now Mariah seemed almost terminally lost in herself, tracing her camera trigger finger up and down the cold sweating glass in front of her. I could tell that she was seeing the day again shutter click by shutter click, sorting over and over for the fretful missing picture of the essence of Virginia City. For his part, Riley swirled his G-ball and took a major gulp as if it was soda pop, which it of course virtually was. Then he grinned at me in that foxy way, but he seemed interested, too. "And?"

"And so I just wondered if you'd maybe thought about some kind of story about the mining here. How it tore up the land like absolute hell and all."

Riley nodded acknowledgment, but said: "Mining has got to be Butte, Jick, when we get there in a couple of days. What the gold miners did here isn't a shovelful compared to Butte."

At least agreement could be reached about another round of drinks, and after those were deposited by the handlebar bartender I tackled Riley again. "Just tell me this then. What kind of stuff is it you're looking for to write about, exactly?"

In what seemed to be all seriousness, he replied:

"Life inside the turtle."

"Riley," I said, "how do you say that in American?"

"It takes a joke to explain it, Jick. So here you go, you lucky man." Riley was relishing this so much it all but puddled on the floor. "The world's greatest expert on the solar system was giving a talk, see. He tells his audience about the planets being in orbit around the sun, how the force of gravity works, and all of that. So then afterwards a little old lady comes up"—Riley caught a feminist glint from Mariah—"uhmm, a big young lady comes up to him and says, 'Professor, that was real interesting, but you're dead wrong. Your theory of gravity just doesn't make a lick of sense. The earth isn't a ball hanging out in thin air at all. What it is is a great big turtle and all of us live on top of its back, don't you see?'

"The scientist figures he's got her, right there. He says, 'Oh, really, madam? Then what holds the turtle up?'

"She tells him, 'It's standing on the back of a bigger turtle, what did you think?'

"He says, 'Very well, madam.' Now he knows he's got her nailed. He kind of rocks back on his heels and asks her: 'Then what can that second turtle possibly be standing on?'

"She gives him a look that tells him how pitiful he is. 'Another even bigger turtle, of course.'

"The scientist can't believe his ears. 'What!? *Another* turtle?'

" 'Naturally,' she tells him. 'It's turtles all the way down.' "

So, okay, I laughed in appreciation of Riley's rendition and Mariah surfaced out of her deep think enough to chuckle at the back of her throat, too.

But Riley was just getting wound up. Now he crossed his arms on the table and leaned intently at me from that propped position, his shoulders square as the corners of a door, his voice suddenly impassioned.

"See, Jick, that's the way something like this centennial usually gets looked at. Turtles all the way down. Hell, it starts right here in Virginia City—the turtle of brave pioneers, like the vigilantes here making windchimes out of outlaws. And next the cattle kingdom turtle." Riley put his hands side by side on the table and pretended to type with his eyes shut: *Montana as the last grass heaven, end of the longhorn trail. It* takes a little more effort with sheepherders than it does with cowboys, no offense intended, Jick, but there can be the sheep empire turtle too, woollies on every sidehill from hell to breakfast. And don't forget the Depression turtle, hard times on good people. Come all the way to today and there's the dying little town turtle. Or the suffering farmer turtle. Or the"—my distinct hunch is that he was about to say something like "the obsolete rancher turtle" but caught himself in time— "the scenic turtle, Montana all perfect sky and mountains and plains, still the best place to lay your eyes on even after a hundred years of hard use."

Riley finally seemed to be turtled out, and in fact declared: "I am just goddamn good and tired of stacking up turtles, in what I write. It's time, for me anyway," here he laid a gaze on Mariah, who received it with narrowed eyes but stayed silent, "to junk the old usual stuff I do. If my stories in this series are going to be anything, I want them to be about what goes on inside that usual stuff. Inside the goddamn turtle shell."

For me, this required some wrinkling inside the head. Granted that Riley's writing intentions were pure, which is a major grant from someone as skeptical toward him as I was, how the dickens was he going to go about this inside-the-turtle approach? Just for instance, I still was perturbed that the Big Hole haying, say, had been bypassed. To Riley and evidently Mariah as well, the Big Hole as an oldfangled hay kingdom qualified as usual stuff, known like a catechism from one end of Montana to the other. Yet not nearly a worn-out topic to me, who first heard of it before either of them was ever born. My first wages in life were earned as a scatter raker for my uncle Pete Reese, in the hayfields of the ranch I now owned. Those summers, when I was fourteen and fifteen and sixteen, daydreams rode the rake with me. The most persistent one was of traveling to the storied Big Hole, hiring on to a haying crew there, spending a bunkhouse summer in that temporary nation of hayhands and workhorses. Quite possibly take a summer name for myself; even there in Pete's little Noon Creek crew you might put up hay with a guy called Moxie or Raw Bacon Slim or Candy Sam all season, then when he was paid off find out that the name on his paycheck was Milton Huttleby or some such. Sure as hell take a different summer age for myself, older than my actual years—although it is hard now to remember that seething youngster urge for more age—and then do my utmost to live up to the job of Big Hole scatter raker there in the mighty fields ribbed to the horizon with windrows, hay the universe around me and even under me as the stuffing in the gunny sack cushion which throned my rake seat, the leather reins in my hands like great kite lines to the pair of rhythmically tugging horse outlines in front of me.

As I say, the Big Hole and its storied haying was a dream, in the sense that a world war and other matters claimed the summers when I might have gone and done. But that dream was a seed of who I am, too, for imagination does not sprout of nothing.

My haydream reverie was abruptly ended when I heard a bump behind me as someone stumbled into a chair and then a corresponding bump a little farther away, evidently a couple of customers finding their way to the table next to ours.

"It's even darker in here than it looks, Henry. How do they do that?" a female whisper inquired.

"They must use trick lighting somehow," came the male reply in an undervoice.

Meanwhile Mariah was staying cooped up with whatever was on her picture-taking mind while Riley was gandering off into the domain of the bartender behind her and me. Unusually thinkful, for a guy as wired up as him.

It didn't seem to me silence was normal for either of these two, so I was about to try and jog Mariah by asking if her notion about photographs was the same as Riley's about words, internal turtle work, when suddenly Riley's face announced inspiration. Quick as that, the sonofagun looked as if he had the world on a downhill pull.

"I see the piece!" he divulged.

Mariah sat up as if she'd just been shaken awake and peered at him through the bar gloom. "Where?"

"Here." He whomped his hand on the table. "This."

I squinted at the shellacked surface. "What, you're going to write about this table?"

"Gentleman and lady, you mistake me," Riley let us know in the bartender's Shakespeare tone of voice. "Not this table. This bar, and its innumerable ancestors the width and breadth, nay, the very depth, of our parched state. A piece about bars and bartenders! What do you say to that, Mariah Montana?"

Mariah took the last swig of her Calvert as if to strengthen herself, then studied Riley. What she said to it was, "This place? Get real."

He only mm-hmmed and rubbernecked past us to the bartender's domain as if trying to read the small print on the bottles. I could see Mariah gathering to jump him some more about this bar brainstorm of his, demand to know how the hell she was supposed to take a picture in here that wouldn't look like midnight in a coal bin. Myself, I thought Riley had finally hatched a halfway decent idea. There is just no denying that bars seem as natural to a lot of Montanans as caves to bears.

"Why don't we have another round," Riley was all sweet persuasion to Mariah now, "and talk it over," meaning his piece notion. Figuring that anything which might conceivably steer the two of them back on the track of their series was all to the good, I swung around in my chair to signal for the further round of drinks.

The bartender had changed sex.

That is to say, the handlebar specimen was gone and the 'tender now was a young woman—I say young; they all look young to me any more—in a low-cut red velvet outfit and brunette hair that lopped down on both sides long and crinkly like the ears of a spaniel and with a smile you could see from an airplane.

Need I say, it was a short hop to the conclusion that Riley's story idea about bars and their 'tenders had been fostered with the change of shifts which brought this female version onto the Goldpanner scene. Be that as it may, the velvet smiler was in charge of our liquid. I held up an indicative glass and called over, "We'll have another round of jelly sandwiches here, please, Miss," a word which brought Mariah's head sharply around.

I thought the new mode of bartender blinked at Riley a little quizzically when he beamed up at her and specified another G-ball, but maybe she was just that way, because when she brought the drinks her comment came out, "There you go?" and when she stated the damages, that too had a question curl on the end of it: "That'll be seven dollars and fifty cents?"

I don't know, is it possible that the more teeth there are in your smile, the less of anything you have higher up in your head? Watching Riley and this young lady exchange dental gleams, the theory did occur to me.

No sooner had Miss Bliss departed from us than Riley was onto his feet saying: "Actually, maybe I better go talk to her while she's not busy and find out how she goes about it." He gave Mariah a look of scrubbed innocence. "Bartending, that is."

"Riley," Mariah said too quietly, "you can go spread yourself on her like apple butter for all I care. I had my lifetime share of your behavior when we were married."

"Behavior?" Surprise and worse now furrowed the brow under his curly dance of hair. "What the hell is that supposed to mean, behavior? You never had any cause to complain about other women during our marriage."

"Oh, right," she said caustically. "What about that blond in Classified?"

"That doesn't count!" he answered, highly offended. "You and I were already separated then!"

With deadly evenness Mariah told him, "It all counts."

Riley seemed honestly baffled as he stared down at her. "What's got you on the prod? If it bothers you to see me have a"—he gave a quick glimpse in my direction—"social life, then look the other way."

"It wouldn't work," she levied on him next. "I'd just see you circling around to your next candidate to fuck."

Right there on the ef word my daughter's voice changed from anger to pain. And as if that kind of anguish is catching, Riley's tone sounded as afflicted as hers when he responded:

"Goddamn it, Mariah, you know I never played around while we were married. You know that." Silence was the best he could get from her on that. "What I do now is my own aff—business."

Mariah rattled the ice in her glass like a castanet. "Not if it interferes with the series. We were going to talk over your piece idea, you said."

"All right, let's talk and get it over with."

"Not with you standing there hot to trot."

Riley abruptly sat.

"You're rushing into this stupid bartender idea," Mariah began.

"My bartender idea is the best shot we've got," Riley began simultaneously.

"I think they're having a fight," the next-table woman whispered.

"I think you're right," the male undertone subscribed.

I would have refereed if I had known where to start. Riley, though, wasn't going to sit still for Mariah to pull his inspiration out from under him. "All righty right, you stay here and stew," he left her with as he scraped his chair back from the table. "I'll be over there doing the piece." With that he was away, taking up residence at the cash register end of the bar where the brunette item of contention had stationed herself. The solar increase of her smile showed that she didn't at all mind being Riley's topic.

I was beginning to see why Mariah had wanted me along as an ally against this guy. A paratroop battalion was about what it would take to jump on Riley adequately.

"Mariah, petunia," I tried to assuage, "that mophead is not worth—"

"It's okay, it's okay," she said in that too quiet way again. A sipping silence was all that followed that, from either of us. Spark patterns of light from the tiny bulbs trembled on the dim walls. Twinkle, twinkle, little bar. I watched Mariah watch Riley. He was right in one respect, she ought not to care how he conducted his life now that they were split. All too plainly, she cared with her every fiber. I don't know. Maybe a person simply cannot help getting the willies about what might have been.

Riley's sugared conversation with his story topic was going on and on and on. At last, though, here he came sashaying back to our table and in a not very good imitation of a matter of fact voice, wanted to know:

"What about a picture?"

Mariah eyed him as if he had slithered up through a crack in the floor.

"What about one, cradle robber?"

"Come on, Mariah, don't be that way. Honest to Christ, I was going to do a bartender piece even before Kimi just happened to come on shift."

"*Kimi!?*" Mariah voiced disbelievingly. "Riley, the only taste you've got is in your mouth."

Riley rolled his eyes and stared at the barroom ceiling as if the letters p-a-t-i-e-n-c-e were inscribed up there. "Just out of curiosity. Flash, what're you going to tell the BB when my written part lands in there and no picture with it?"

Mariah gave him a world record glower. Then she all but leapt out of the chair, tornadoed over to the end of the bar, began exhuming electrical cords and lightstands out of her camera baggage, and proceeded to aim into the targeted area of the bartending brunette. Next she pulled out what looked alarmingly like a quiver for arrows, but proved to be full of small white reflecting umbrellas which she positioned various whichways to throw more light on Kimi. *Prang prang prang,* Mariah yanked the legs of her tripod into extension.

"Henry, look at those people now!" from the lead whisperer.

"Isn't this something?" murmured its chorister.

"Kimi, sweetie, give us your biggest smile, if you know which one that is," Mariah directed in a kind of gritted tone as she aimed her light meter pistola at the bar maiden. Riley was hanging around right there handy, but she called out to me, "Jick, could you come hold this?"

I gingerly went over to the action area. Mariah thrust me an empty beer glass. "Hold it steady right there," she decreed, positioning the glass about nose-high out in the air in front of me and then stepping back behind the tripod and sighting her camera through the glass at Kimi.

Being in the shine of all the lights was making Kimi positively incandescent. Through her smile she emitted, "This is totally, like, exciting?"

Click, and some more quick triggerings of the shutter, and Mariah was icily informing Riley the picture of the piece was achieved and the rest was up to him, then unplugged and dismantled the lights and the rest of the paraphernalia in about a second and a half and rampaged back to our table and her Calvert and water.

I joined her, but of course Riley stayed hovering at the bar. I will say, he was laying it on thicker with his tongue than I could have with a trowel. He would mouth something sparkling, Kimi would mouth something, he would laugh, she would laugh—after a bit, Mariah declared: "If I have to watch any more of this I'll turn diabetic." Out she went to the Winnebago.

I am not naturally nocturnal. Not enough to sit around in a tourist bar into the whee hours while watching Riley lay siege to Kimi, at least. I drained the last of my drink and headed to the bar.

As I approached, Kimi was wanting to know where he got such a wild pair of contact lenses—"You can, like, color each eye different, I mean?"—and with a straight face Riley drawled that they were a hard-to-find kind called *aw, natural.* Then he was inquiring of her in a confidential way, "Okay now, Kimi, serious question. If I just came in here from Mars and asked for a drink, what would you give me?" Granted, he did have the notebook open in front of him. Maybe he was mixing business with pleasure, a little.

Kimi smiled a mile and said, "Oh, wow, I guess maybe a slow comfortable screw?"

Riley looked as if his ears could not believe their good fortune. My God, I thought to myself, does it just jump into his lap this way?

Kimi kept the smile beamed on him as she asked, "You know what that is, don't you?" Before Riley could muster an answer, which would have been highly interesting to hear, she was explaining: "It's sloe gin, Southern Comfort, and orange juice, like in a screwdriver? Get it? A Sloe Comfortable—"

"Got it," Riley vouched, trying not to look crestfallen. He downed a long restorative drag of his G-ball, evidently thinking furiously about how to get past that smile of Kimi's. Now he noticed me and frowned. "Something on your mind besides your hat, Jick?"

Something was, yes. A couple of somethings. How Riley and Mariah behaved toward each other wasn't any of my business, theoretically. Yet if you don't feel strongly enough about it to take sides with your own offspring, what in the hell did you spend the years raising the kid for? So on Mariah's behalf my intention had been to deliver some snappy comment to Riley that would let him know what a general louse he was being. But instead I seemed to be seeing myself, from the outside—I know that sounds freaky; it *was* freaky—standing there in a remembered way. As if I had stepped into a moment where I'd already been once: a waiting man beside me, his arm on the bar, a woman equally near: myself somehow suspended in the polar pull between them. Or was I imagining. Three scotch and waters will start the imagination going, I suppose. Whatever it swam in, the strange is-this-then-or-now remembering suddenly became not this bar but the Medicine Lodge, not this Riley-Kimi recipe but Stanley Meixell and Velma Simms. Velma in that long-ago time had been Gros Ventre's divorce champion, thrice married in an era that believed once ought to be plenty for anybody. That Fourth of July and others of the Depression years, she in her slacks of magical tightness served as timekeeper at the Gros Ventre rodeo, in charge of the whistle that signaled *time's up* during bronc rides; as one of the yearning hangers-on around the bucking chutes pointed out, "Think of all the pucker practice she's had." Stanley was . . . Stanley. The original forest ranger of the Two Medicine National Forest, who forfeited that million-acre job when his oldest friend, my father, turned him in for his hopeless drinking. Stanley who came back out of nowhere into our lives that summer of 1939 and freed our family of as much pain as he could. Who perched on that Medicine Lodge bar stool timelessly, the back of his neck lined and creased as if he'd been sleeping on chicken wire but the front of him durable enough to draw Velma Simms snuggling onto the bar stool close beside him. And there in the heat field between that woman and that man after I had popped in innocent as a day-old colt to discuss a matter with Stanley, I was the neutral element. The spectating zero rendered neutral by circumstances. Circumstantial youth, in that fifteenth summer of my life. Circumstantial widowerhood now.

"Jick?" Riley was asking. "Jick, are you okay?"

"Uh, you bet," I answered although I could feel that the backs of my hands were sweating as they do when my nerves are most upset. Spooky, how utter and complete, how faithful, that spasm of memory had seemed. As if there were furrows behind my brow, interior wrinkles to match the tracks of age across my forehead, and that memory out of nowhere clicked exactly into those grooves. I drew a breath and managed, "As good as a square guy can be in a round world, anyway. Just wanted to tell you, I'm calling it a night."

"Good idea," Riley said.

"Going on out to the Winnebago," I said.

"Yeah, fine," he said.

"Mariah's already out there," I said.

"Is she," he said.

"Morning will be here before we know it," I said.

Riley, still considerably furrowed up himself, studied me. Then he glanced at Kimi, who was giving us both a smile we could almost see our reflections in. When Riley turned back to me, his frown was severe. But to my surprise, he closed up his notebook, said a regretful thanks to Kimi for her inspiration, and accompanied me out into the night and the Winnebago.

Sure enough, readers of the *Montanian* were treated to Riley's dissertation about bartenders, that their wares were as integral to a citizenry such as ours as food and water, and that ever since the first saloons of Virginia City and the other goldstrike towns, a considerable portion of Montana's history could be measured the way irrigation is, by the liquid acre-foot. And of course: *These nights, if you hold your mouth right, the moisture of mercy may be dispensed to you by a Kimi Wyszynski . . .* At least a Sloe Comfortable You Know What was nowhere in it.

Mariah's picture had caught the smiling countenance of Kimi in the beer glass where the top portion begins to bulge out of the slender base. The woozy distortion puffed Kimi's cheeks out like a squirrel loaded for winter, made her teeth enormous, and squinched her eyes together. She resembled a nearsighted beaver looking at itself in a crazyhouse mirror.

We were camped that night on the Jefferson River just out of Silver Star, bracing for Butte the next day. Riley was in the shower at the back of the Bago, singing over and over: *"Oh, the moon still shines, on the moonshine stills, in the hills where the lupine twiiines!"* Conspicuously ignoring the melody of Riley, Mariah was across the dinette table from me fussing with one camera after another, whisking invisible dust off their lenses with the daintiest brush I'd ever seen.

I again studied the newsprint version of Kimi spread in front of me. I had to ask. "Mariah, is the newspaper really going to keep paying you and Riley for going around the state doing stuff like this?"

Without looking up she said, "We'll find out."

> *They named the place Butte, in the way that the night sky's button of light acquired the round sound of moon or the wind took to itself its inner sigh of vowel. Butte was echoingly what it was: an abrupt upshoot of earth, with the namesake city climbing out of its slopes.*
>
> *Beneath Butte's rind of sagebrush and rock lay copper ore.*
>
> *That red earth of Butte held industrial magic: telephone lines, radio innards, the wire ganglia of stoves and refrigerators, everything that made America electric began there in copper.*
>
> *The red copper earth drew other red to it. Bloody Butte, with its copper corpuscles. A dozen miners died underground in 1887, the early days of more muscle than machinery. In 1916, as the machine drill and the steam-hoisted shaft cage pressed the implacable power of technology against flesh and bone, Butte's underground toll for the year was 65 miners. The next year, a fire in the Speculator Mine killed 164. All the while, the greater killer quietly destroyed men's lungs: silicosis, 675 dead of it between 1907 and 1913.*

On its earth and its people of the mines, then, Butte's history of scars. Badges of honor, too, as scars sometimes are? It depends on how much blood you mind having in your copper. Maybe less arguable is Butte's history of chafe. "This beautiful copper collar, that the Company gave to me" became Butte's—Montana's—wry anthem of life under the Anaconda Copper Mining Company, a.k.a. William Rockefeller and Henry Rogers and others of Wall Street. The Butte miner was consistently the best paid workman in Montana. The ACM Company also saw to it that he was the most harnessed. Strikebreakers and Company police. The Company-imposed "rustling card" you had to carry to rustle up a job in the mines. The Montana National Guard stationed in the streets of Butte after dynamite punctuated the labor struggle in 1914. In its streets and its wallets and its caskets, Butte was its own kind of example of how a copperwired society works.

Enormous above Riley's words, Mariah's Butte photo was of the Berkeley Pit, the almost unbelievable open-pit mine which took the copper role from the played-out mineshafts everywhere under the streets of the city: a bulldozed crater a mile wide and deeper than the Empire State Building is tall. Ex-mine, it too now was, having been abandoned in favor of cheaper digging in South America.

"Quite the Butte story," I observed to the newspaper hotshots shortly after perusing it in that day's *Montanian*. "Who's going to deal?"

"I will," stated Mariah, plucking up the deck of cards and shuffling them with a fluent riffle which drew her a glance from Riley. We had pulled in at the Missouri Headwaters RV Park in Three Forks for the night. By now it had been most of a week since the Virginia City situation got so drastically Kimied, but conversation between Mariah and Riley still was only on the scale of "pass the ketchup, would you" and "here, take it." Thus an evening of playing pitch was my bright idea for cheering up Bago life. Of course I'd had to bribe Riley into it by letting him off the dishwashing for the next three nights, but well worth it.

"The Butte piece was just a thumbsucker," Riley took care to let me know as Mariah whizzed out six cards apiece to us.

I can put up with a lot while playing pitch, which to my way of thinking is the only card game worth sitting up to, and so I responded to Riley's latest codegram: "How do you mean? What's a thumb-sucker?"

"A think piece. When a writer sticks a thumb in his mouth and thinks he's on the tit of wisdom," Riley said moodily.

"No way was that Butte story of his a thumbsucker," Mariah informed me past Riley as if he was not at the table with us. "He wrote what needed saying. Now he's just having one of those oh-my-God-I-shot-my-wad spasms writers get."

Damned with faint praise or praised with a faint damn or wherever it was Mariah's backhanded defense had left him, Riley only snorted and concentrated fiercely on the cards in his hand.

Mariah fanned her own cards out, gave them a quick pinched appraisal and asked, "Who dealt this mess?"

"You did, butterfly," I informed her.

"Oh. Then it's up to you to bid first."

"I know. I am. Give a person time." I mulled what I held, primarily the king and jack of diamonds and then a bunch of junk like the seven of hearts and three even littler clubs. "I'll say two."

"Three," Riley grandly upped.

Mariah passed, and Riley led out with the queen of hearts, which she unhappily had to top with her king, and now it was my play. This is what's nice about pitch: the strategy needed right from the first card. By making hearts trump, Riley transformed my jack of diamonds into the jick, which is to say, the off card of the same color as the jack of trump. That, incidentally, is where my nickname springs from, the pronouncement by a family friend back when my folks were trying to fit the solemn given name John and then the equally unright Jack onto the child me that "He looks to me more like the jick of this family." Nomenclature aside, though, the rule in pitch is that jack takes jick but jick takes joker, and so here I could either mandatorily follow suit, hearts, with my seven and hope to take some later trick and maybe even somebody's joker or tenspot with my jick, or, since Mariah's king was taking this trick, I could forthwith sluff the jick to her so she would gain the point instead of the bidder, Riley. See what I mean about what a strategic marvel pitch is?

I sluffed my jick, drawing me a grin from Mariah and a dirty look from Riley. Which got another load of topsoil added to it after he trumped in on the next trick to regain the lead, led back with his invincible ace of hearts and instead of capturing a jack or joker or even a tenspot to count toward game, received an out-of-trump spade from Mariah and my seven of hearts, equally worthless to him.

Of his three bid, Riley so far only had one, that unlosable trump ace he'd just played. He now was pondering so deep you could almost hear his brain throb. His choices were perfectly clear, really—lead with his next strongest card and try to clean us out of any nontrump face cards or tens that would count toward game, or lead something weak and keep back his strong card to capture any of our face ones etcetera on the final trick—and so I helped him employ his time by asking him, "Well, then, Wordsworth, what kind of a Butte story would you rather have done than the one you did?"

"You saw those faces in the M & M yesterday," Mariah enlightened me as Riley tried to glower at each of us and study his cards at the same time. "What the scribbler wants is for those old Butte guys to read his stuff and fall off their barstools backwards and kick their legs in the air while they shout, 'That's me! Riley Wright told my whole life in that piece of his!'"

Riley clutched his cards rigidly and asked her with heat, "What the fuck's wrong with that?"

"Not a thing," she told him as if surprised at his utter density. "Don't you know a fucking compliment when you get one?"

Yesterday's Butte faces, yes. We'd begun on Butte by stopping in the old uptown area for lunch at the M & M, an enterprise which is hard to pin down but basically includes a fry kitchen and counter on one side and a serious bar along the other and sporting paraphernalia such as electronic poker machines in the entire back half of the building, and within it all a grizzled clientele who appeared to be familiar with most of life's afflictions, plus a few younger people evidently in the process of undergoing that same set of travails. All my life until actually coming there with the newspaper pair I had been leery of Butte. Of its molelike livelihood, as mining seemed to us surface-of-the-earth types. Of THE COMPANY, as the Anaconda Copper Mining Company was known in big letters in the Montana of my younger days, because Butte and its ore wealth were why THE COMPANY took the trouble to run everything it could think of in the state. Of, yes, younger incarnations of the rugged clientele around the three of us at that moment, for in its heyday of nine thousand miners Butte was famously a drinking whoring fistfighting place; when you met up with someone apt to give you trouble from his knuckles, the automatic evaluation was "too much Butte in him." But now with the M & M as a kind of comfortable warehouse of so much that had been Butte, and replete with the highly delicious lunch—a pork chop sandwich and a side dish of boiled cabbage with apricot pie for dessert had done nicely for me—I'd been quite taken with the hard-used old city. Until I happened to glance at the latest case of thirst barging in the door of the M & M, and it was the ghost of Ed Heaney nodding hello to me.

Bald as glass, with middle age living up to its name by accumulating on his middle, Ed was owner of the lumber yard in Gros Ventre and the father of my best friend in my growing-up years. An untalkative man whose habits were grooves of behavior the town could have told time by, nonetheless he had pieces of life that spoke fascination to me; his own boyhood in unimaginable Butte, his medals from Belleau Wood and other battles of the First World War tucked away in a dresser drawer. As I stared across the M & M at Ed's reincarnation, there where I'd been sure that the past could find no reason to swoosh out all over me, my mind split again. The everyday part knowing full well that Ed Heaney was many years gone to the grave and that probably half of male Butte resembled Ed. The remembering remnant of me, though, abruptly seeing a front lawn at dusk, during a town trip when I had swung by to quick-visit my friend Ray, and as we gab there on the grass the front porch screen door swings open and Ed Heaney stands in its surprise frame of light, as his lookalike did now in this Butte doorway, the radio news a murmur steady as a rumor behind Ed. "Ray, Mary Ellen," Ed calling out into the yard to his son and small daughter that first evening of September of 1939, "you better come in the house now. They've started another war in Europe."

The *whap* of Riley's finally chosen card on the table brought me back from Butte and beyond. He'd decided to lead an inconsequential five of clubs, which Mariah nonchalantly stayed under with the trey, so I ended up taking the trick with my mere six of clubs. I at once led back with my king of diamonds, which sent Riley into ponder again.

Mariah decided to employ this waiting period by working on me. "You know, you'd have plenty of time to shave before Riverboat Wright here plays his next card."

Before I could come up with a dignified reply, Riley surprised me by rapping out to her on my behalf: "What the hell, the beard gives him a hobby where there's not much danger he'll saw his fingers off."

I knew, though, he wasn't so much sticking up for me and my whisker project as he was jabbing it to Mariah. He could have chosen a better time to do it; when he finally played he still didn't use his strong card, whatever it was, and merely followed suit on my king with a lowly diamond. Mariah immediately gave him a wicked grin and sluffed me the ten of spades. Hoo hoo. Riley was a screwed monkey, and by now even he knew it. Sure enough, for the final trick he'd been saving the jack of hearts, the highest trump card left, but all it earned him was my deuce of clubs and Mariah's eight of spades, neither worth anything.

I cheerfully scorekept. One wooden match to Mariah for the jick I'd sluffed her, two to myself—besides my having the highest count for game, courtesy of the tenspot she'd sluffed me, my seven of hearts proved to be the low of trump—and three broken-backed matches to Riley to indicate he'd gone set and now was three points in the hole.

"My God!" he uttered when the game concluded several hands later with me at twenty-one, Mariah hot behind me at nineteen, and him still three in the hole. "Playing pitch with you two is like trying to eat a hamburger in the middle of a wolfpack."

Nor, despite being called a quitter every way Mariah and I could think of, and between us, that was quite a few, would Riley risk his neck any further in more pitch that evening. He took his mood off to bed at the back of the Bago, and while he got himself installed there I helped Mariah make up her couch bed per usual. Per usual she gave me a goodnight-in-spite-of-the-stickery-on-your-face kiss. Per usual I headed back to scrunch into bed beside Riley and speculate.

Nights with Riley were an ordeal. He dropped off to dreamville the moment he was horizontal, but before long the commotion would begin. There alongside of me he'd start to shimmy in his sleep, little jerky motions of his shoulders and arms and spasmy tiny kicks of his legs and ungodly noises from his throat. *Hnng. Nnhnng. Nnguhh!* Actually it was kind of fascinating in a way, like watching a spirited dog napping beside a stove, whimpering and twitching as he runs a dream rabbit. But as Riley's bed fuss went on and on I'd need eventually to whisper sharply, "hey, come out of it!" *Mmm,* he would acknowledge, almost agreeably, and I would try to rush to sleep before his next conniption.

I do my dreaming awake, and so the uproar going on in Riley in his zoo of sleep I could not really savvy. Was he writing, his mind restlessly sorting words there in the dark? Or yearning, his body at least, for the Kimies of the world . . . or remembering when Mariah's was the warm form beside him? Or was this merely something like an electrical storm in the night of the brain? Whatever was occurring, Riley Wright evidently paid for his days in the quivering of his nights.

Lewis and Clark had preceded Riley and Mariah a bit to this Three Forks area, discovering here in 1805 that a trio of rivers came together to make the source of the Missouri. Grandly christening every trickle of water they encountered all the way across the Dakotas and Montana, those original explorers nonetheless were smart enough to save up the names of their bosses, Jefferson, Madison and Gallatin, for these main tributaries, which I thought was more than passingly interesting. It didn't register so with the subsequent newspaper pair, however, and after a fruitless day of traipsing around the headwaters area they decided they wanted to go on to Helena for the night—but by back-tracking through Butte instead of the only-half-as-long route through Townsend.

"Butte? Hold on a minute here. You did Butte."

"Our Lady of the Rockies," explained Mariah abstractedly.

"Who's she?"

"Jesus's mom," Riley put in with equal unhelpfulness.

"Riddle me no newspaper lingo riddles, you two. All I want to know is—"

"The Mary statue," Riley intoned with awful patience. "Up on the Divide, over Butte. Ninety feet tall, shiny white. Maybe you happened to notice it?"

"Oh. *That* Lady of the Rockies."

But even the Madonna, giant robed figure who seemed to have popped over the mountaintop and stopped short in surprise at the sight of Butte, didn't provide any miracle for these two. Or as they of course put it to one another: "Doesn't work."

Thus we were finally Helena-bound on the freeway, just getting rolling atop the rise north of Butte, when the steering wheel wobbled significantly in my hands. I gave the news, "We've got ourselves a flat," and pulled the Winnebago off onto the shoulder of the freeway.

"At least this goes real nice with the rest of the day," Riley groused as we all three climbed forth into the dusk and I went to get the spare tire out. "Stuff it, Riley," Mariah told him, and from her tone she quite possibly meant the entire spare tire.

"Do you suppose you two could manage to quit the bloodletting long enough to—" I began, but was interrupted by a car horn's merry *beep beepitybeepbeep beep beep!*

Shave and a haircut, six bits, my rosy rear end. I irritatedly waved the approaching car past us but no, here it gaily pulled off onto the side of the road in front of us, an '84 ketchup-red Corvette driven by an old guy wearing a ballcap. As I was about to shout to him that we had the situation under control, thanks anyway, there came the winding-down sound of another slowing car, and an '81 white Buick LeSabre, another ballcapped grayhead at the wheel, beeped past and ground to a stop on the shoulder gravel in front of the Corvette.

Riley and Mariah and I turned our heads to the highway behind us as if we were on one swivel.

A cavalcade of cars was approaching, every one of them slowing. Already we were being given the beepitybeepbeep by the next about-to-pull-over vehicle, an elderly purple Cadillac.

Funeral procession, maybe? No, I'd never seen a funeral procession where everybody was wearing a ballcap. By now the first of what seemed to be geezerville on wheels, the Corvette pilot, was gimping his way along the barrow pit to us. "Got some trouble?" he called out cheerfully.

"We do now," muttered Riley. *Click,* I heard Mariah's camera capture our Corvette samaritan.

"Just a flat," I called back as the line of pulled-over vehicles built and built in front of us. "We appreciate your stopping and all. But honest, we can handle—"

"Aw hell, no problem," I was assured by Corvette, "we're plenty glad to help."

"Gives us somethin' to do," sang out LeSabre coming up at a stiff but hurried pace behind him.

"Yeah," I said slowly, looking at the long file of parked cars, each with its trouble blinkers winking on and off, like a line of Christmas lights. As if in rhythm with the trouble lights, Mariah's camera was clicking quick and often. Old men were hobbling out of the dusk toward us, two here, three there—they seemed to be a total of seven.

A long-haul truck thundered past, its transcontinental hurry accentuating the reposeful roadside caravan. "What are you guys," I felt the need to ask, "some kind of car club?"

"We're the Baloney Express riders," the Corvettier answered with a grin that transmitted wrinkles throughout his face.

"The who?"

"What happens, see, is that we ride around taking used cars where dealers need them," the explanation arrived. "Say for instance a used-car lot in Great Falls has got more vehicles than it wants, but a dealer down in Butte or over in Billings or somewhere ain't got enough. Well, see, the bunch of us drive a batch of cars down to the one who's short of them, and then go back home to the Falls in the van there." Sure enough, a windowed van such as is used for a small bus had ended up at the head of the parked procession. "Or like now," my tutor continued, "it's the other way around, the Butte guy got too many cars on hand and so he called up for us to come down and fetch these back to the Falls. The idea is, it's cheaper for the car dealers than hiring trucks to pack these cars around and besides it gives us," he jerked his head to indicate the further half dozen oldtimers now clustering around us like cattle at a salt lick, "a way to pass some time. Oh sure, we maybe like to gab a little, too, riding together in the van—one of our wives says the Pony Express had nothing on us, we're the Baloney Express. But see, we're all retired. If we wasn't doing this, we'd just be setting around being ornery."

Mariah was working her camera and Riley was staring at the ball-caps, all of which read *I ??? bowling. Where else can you get a pair of shoes so cheap?* and so the conversational role seemed to be up to me. "Quite the deal," I more or less congratulated the assemblage on their roadlife-in-retirement. Now that I had a closer look at these geezers, most of them, although stove-up and workworn, didn't appear as ancient as I'd originally thought; somewhere into their seventies. Which meant that these retired specimens weren't that much older than me, I had to admit with a pang. The one exception was a stooped long-faced fellow, about half-familiar to me, who either was a lot farther along in years than the others or had led a more imaginative life. He in fact spoke up now.

"Only thing wrong with this car setup we got is that the speed limit needs an adjustment. What we figure, there ought to be a law that a person can't drive faster than what age he is. If you're nineteen, say, you could only go nineteen miles an hour. That'd give us a little leeway to try out our speedometers."

I chuckled and admitted the plan sounded highly logical. Meanwhile a subdelegation of Baloney Expressers was curiously inspecting the caved-in nose of the Bago where the Moiese buffalo had butted it. "What happened to your grill, you hit a helluva big deer?"

"Uh, not exactly."

"As much as I hate to break up this soiree," Riley announced in a contrary tone, "that tire still needs changing. Against my better judgment, I'll even pitch in. Jick, where's the jack?"

"Right there in the rear compartment. The lug wrench is there too," I tacked on as a hint.

Riley gave me a barbed look, then one at the motionless Baloney Express bunch, and off he stalked. The next sound out of him was as he began grunting away at loosening the lug nuts of the flat tire.

Throughout that effort and then as he undertook to jack up the motorhome so the tire could come off, Riley's every move was watched by our clot of visitors, the whole bunch of them bent over intently with hands on knees like a superannuated football huddle. They in turn were watched by Mariah through her camera as she moved in behind them, sighted, frowned at the line of hunched-over backs, dropped to one knee, grinned and shot.

Evidently irked by his silent jury, none of whom yet had done a tap of work in the changing of the tire, Riley now indicated a nearby NO STOPPING roadsign and pointed out, "If a highway cop comes along and finds this congregation, he'll write tickets on you characters all night."

"No problem," Riley was assured by '83 Ford Fairlane, a scrawny guy about shoulder-high to the rest of us. "My nephew's the highway patrol along this stretch of road. If he comes along we'll just have him turn his siren on and make things official."

The Baloney Expressers all considered that a hilarious prospect, and a number of them gandered up and down the highway in hope of Fairlane's patrolman nephew.

I have to say, I was beginning to enjoy this myself, Riley doing all the work and these guys providing me sevenfold company. My original partner in conversation introduced himself, Jerome Walker, and cited among the spectators one who resembled him—"My brother Julius; he's older and smarter but I got the good looks"—and then the scrawny guy—"Another thing we call ourselves is The Magnificent Six and a Half, on account of Bill here"—and I handshook my way on down the line. The final guy Roger Tate, the stooped elderly-looking one, thought I looked as familiar as I thought he did. In Montana you only have to talk to a person for two minutes before you find you know them some way or another. But I wasn't able to place Roger, nor he me, until we both admitted lifetimes in the sheep business. Then he broke out with:

"By the God, now I know you! That herder I found up under Roman Reef that time, he was yours! What was his name again?"

Pat Hoy. Pat the pastor of pasture, Pat the supreme pilot of sheep, unfazed by mountain timber and bear and coyotes and July snowstorms, who in a dozen years of herding for me always grazed his band in the exact same slowgoing scatter-them-twice-as-wide-as-you-think-you-dare-to style which he enunciated as: "Sheep don't eat with their feet, so running will never fatten them." I had inherited him, so to speak, from my father-in-law Dode Withrow when Dode at last declared himself too old for the sheepraising life. Thus I acquired not only a matchless herder but Pat's twice a year migrations into spree as well. How many times I made that journey to First Avenue South in Great Falls and fetched Pat out of one saloon or another, flat broke and shakily winding down from his two-week binge of at first whiskey and then beer and at last cheap wine. But for all the aggravation his semiannual thirsts provided, how much I would give to wipe out the day when I arrived to tend his camp and saw that Pat's sheepdog was there at the wagon but Pat and sheep were nowhere in sight. That sent an instant icicle through me, dog but no herder, and while I found the sheep scattered over half of Roman Reef, there still was no sign of Pat. The next day a Forest Service crew and ranchers from English Creek and Noon Creek and the Teton country helped me to search, and so it came to be Roger Tate of the Teton contingent who rode onto the scene of Pat's corpse near a big lone rock outcropping, the kind that draws down lightning. The lightning bolt had struck Pat in the head and followed the zipper of his coat down the body, searing as it went.

I remembered staring down at Pat before we loaded him onto the packhorse. Since the time of my boyhood, lightning has always been one of my dreads, and here was what it looked like.

"Right you are. Pat Boyd. That was the fellow," Roger Tate was saying over Riley's lug wrench grunts. "Sure was a terrible thing. But it happens."

What also happens, I realized, is a second obliteration, the slower kind that was occurring now. Pat Hoy had been as good at what he did as any of us ever can be. But Dode Withrow, who knew that and joyously testified to it at the drop of a hat in his countless yarns about Pat, Dode too was dead. Pat's favorite denizens of First Avenue South, Bouncing Betty and Million Volt Millie and other companions of his sprees and megaphones of his reputation betweentimes, were gone to time now too. Even Roger here, original witness of Pat passing into the past, by now was losing grasp of that struck-down sheepherder's name; and Roger's remaining years as a memory carrier of any sort could not be many. It hit me out of nowhere, that I very nearly was the last who knew anything of the wonders of Pat Hoy.

"How about yourself?" one of the group in the barrow pit asked me. I blinked at that until I managed to backtrack and savvy that he meant what was the purpose of my own travels in the motorhome here.

"Just, uh, out seeing the country." All I'd need would be to tell these guys what Riley and Mariah were up to, and there'd doubtless be a long choirsing from them about what was wrong with newspapers these days. Mariah by now had moved off into the sagebrush and was shooting shots of the whole blinking fleet of vehicles. "My daughter there kind of likes to take pictures. And the other one"—how was I going to put this? that Riley was her ex-husband but still tagging around with her?—"is a guy in the paper business we been letting ride with us. Kind of a glorified hitchhiker."

Riley by now had the spare tire on and the Bago jacked back down. All that remained was for him to take the lug wrench and reef down hard in a final tighten of the lug nuts, but his audience showed no sign of dispersing until the performance was utterly over. Mariah materialized at my side, camera still busy, just as the voice of Roger the van driver resumed what must have been a perpetual conversation among the Baloney Express riders.

"By the God, you just never know about these cars. Back in 1958 I paid a guy to haul away five Model T's just to get them off the place, *paid the guy!* And now what the hell wouldn't they be worth, the way people are fixing old cars up and using them in these centennial parades and all."

Riley did a final contortion over a lug nut, then headed stormily over to Mariah and me. "Okay, the goddamn tire's changed," he muttered, "let's abandon the Grandpa Club and—" then he went *oomp* as Mariah nudged him ungently in the ribs with her elbow. "Mariah, what the f—"

"Riley," she half-whispered, "will you shut your face long enough to look at what we've got here?"

"So you figure we just better hang onto these clunkers instead of turning them over to the dealer, do you, Rog?" one of the others was responding to the saga of the lost treasure of Model T's. "Make rich guys out of ourselves at the next centennial, huh?"

"Sounds good to me," chimed in another voice. "A hundred years from now, I'll still only be thirty-nine by then."

A round of laughter, which multiplied when somebody else put in on him. "Nick, we're talking age here, not IQ."

By now Riley had his notebook out. "Five hundred years' worth of geezers in one bunch," his mutter changed to murmur. "Could work," he acknowledged, almost as much to himself as to Mariah. He turned to her, doubtless to ask if she had a decent picture for the piece, thought better of it from the expression on her face, and headed over to talk the Baloney Expressers into more talking.

They listened silent as fenceposts as Riley told them who he and Mariah were and what they were up to, Mariah backing him with an encouraging encompassing grin. Then the seven oldsters cast glances at each other without a word. Incipient fame seemed to have taken their tongues.

Finally one of them broached: "You gonna put all of us in the paper? It wouldn't be too good if just some of us was in and not others, if you see what we mean."

"Every mother's child," Riley grandly assured them of inclusion. "Now here's how we're going to have to do this." He scooted off into the Bago and was back immediately with his mini tape recorder. I was wondering myself how Riley was going to conduct a sevenway interview. We couldn't stay camped on the shoulder of the highway forever; every couple of minutes now a pickup or car was pulling in at the head of the line of ferried cars and a voice calling down the barrow pit in the dusk, "Everything okay there?" and one or the other of the Baloney Expressers would cup his hands to his mouth and cheerfully shout back, "No problem."

Riley's program turned out to be as simple as leapfrog. He would ride with the first driver at the head of the cavalcade for ten minutes, then that car would pull over and he would hop back to the second car, which in turn would become the lead car and interviewee for ten minutes, and on back through the seven drivers that way by the time we all reached Helena. "You guys are going to have to tell fast," Riley warned as he set the beeper on his wristwatch. "No room for hooey." The Baloney Expressers looked collectively offended at that word, but tagteam storytelling plainly appealed to them. They didn't budge yet, though, all standing trying to look innocently hopeful in regard to a certain red-headed young woman.

"Ride with me, Mariah, would you?" I asked, breaking seven geezer hearts simultaneously. Away the Expressers gimped to their vehicles, Riley heading for the lead van with its driver.

> *They have seen the majority of Montana's century, each of these seven men old in everything but their restlessness, and as their carefully strewn line of taillights burns a route into the night their stories ember through the decades.*
>
> *"I'm Roger Tate. I seem to be the oldest of this gang, if the truth be told. Maybe that's why they let me drive the van. Or maybe it's the fact that it's my van. Anyway, what I'd tell you about is my dad and those Model T's. Back in the twenties we raised sheep out a hell of a ways from town, west from Choteau there, and when my dad bought his first Model T he figured it was a wonderful advance, you know. Any time he wanted now he could scoot into town and get lit up. Only thing was, every time he came home from a spree like that he'd never bother to open a gate. Drive right through all the barbwire gates between town and our place, four of them. I was misfortunate enough to be the only boy in the family, so the next day he'd send me out to fix those doggone gates. I must have mended those four gates forty times apiece. That habit of his was kind of hard on cars, too, which was how we ended up with five Model T's. Eventually my dad gave out before the world supply of whiskey did, and it fell to me to build the ranch back up. But I've often thought, you know, thank the Lord that the old boy had gone into sheep instead of anything else. Not even he could entirely drink up the wool money each year before the lamb money came."*

This spell of driving time alone with Mariah I figured I had better make use of. I started off conversationally, "These pictures you're breaking your fanny on, petunia. What is it you're trying to do in them, that inside-the-turtle kind of stuff Riley was talking about?"

From the corner of my eye I saw her give that little toss of head, her hair surging back over her shoulder. "Something like, I suppose. But the way I think of it is that I'm trying to do cave paintings."

I nodded and mmhmmed. She'd taken the next summer after she and Riley split up, and gone to Europe to get over him. When her mother and I asked what she'd seen, her answer was caves. In France and Spain she had crouched and crawled through tunnel after tunnel into the past to see those deep walls with their paintings of bison and horses and so on from Stone Age times. Maybe ten thousand years, she said, those bison had been grazing and those horses running there in the stone dark.

> *The warning wink of brake lights. Like a flexible creature of the night, the chain of cars compresses itself to a halt on the shoulder of the freeway, then moves on.*
>
> *"Bill Bradley, I am. Not the long tall basketball senator, as you maybe already noticed. I guess I would want to tell about the grasshoppers. My folks and I was farming over towards Malta there in the Depression and just when we figured things couldn't get any worse, here came those 'hoppers and cleaned us out of our crop worse than any hailstorm ever could of. An absolute cloud of grasshoppers. You just can't believe how those buggers were. They sounded bad enough in the air, that sort of whirring noise the way sage chickens make when they take off, only a thousand times louder. But on the ground was worse. You could actually hear those things eating. Millions of grasshoppers and every last one of them chewing through a stem of wheat. I left my coat hanging on the door handle of the pickup and they even ate that to shreds. It still makes me about half sick to remember the sound of those grasshoppers eating, eating, eating."*

"Lascaux and Altamira," Mariah spoke the cave names as if talking of friends we both knew. "That's what I want my work to be like." Her voice came low and lovely, remembered tone of another woman I had loved, her mother.

"Do you see what I mean, Jick?" This next part she seemed to want me to particularly understand. "Something people can look back at, whenever, and get a grasp of our time. Another hundred years from now, or a hundred thousand—the amount of time between shouldn't make any difference. If my pictures are done right, people whenever ought to be able to say, 'oh, that's what was on their minds then.'"

And I think I did savvy what Mariah was getting at, that in a way— the waiting, the watching, the arrowing moment—she with her camera was in that cavewall lineage of portrait-painting hunters as patient as stone.

Down the long slope ahead of us, the car at the front of the cavalcade delivered its brakelight signal of stopping, *blink blinketyblinkblink blink blink.*

> *"My name is Nick Russo. I came into this country after the Second World War. Oh, I'd been west before, kind of. See, when I went into the Civilian Conservation Corps in '34, just a punk kid from an alley in Philadelphia, the next thing I knew I was on a fireline in that big Selway forest fire in Idaho. Then I went from the CCC straight into the Army, so I was already a sergeant when the war hit. I saw Montana from a troop train and that was it for me. Little towns with all that land and sky around them. Right there I told myself that when my military time was in, if I lived to get my time in, I'd come out here and see if I could make something of myself."*

On our minds. I could agree with Mariah there. We wear what has happened to us like a helmet soldered on.

Off the freeway to our right, the lights of the town of Boulder, which signaled the caravan's next stop and swap of Riley.

> *The used cars, a used man in each, move on.*
> *"My name is Bud Aronson and I was a packer until I got too stove up to do it any more. What you maybe want to hear from me happened when I was pretty much in the prime of life, back about 1955, and figured I could handle just about anything that came along, until this did. That hunting season I was running a pack string into the Bob Marshall Wilderness, so when there was a plane crash way*

back in there, I was the guy the search party sent for to bring the two bodies out. The plane had slammed into a mountain, pretty high up, and so the first thing I did was wrap the bodies in a tarp apiece just as they were and then we slid them on the snow down the mountain to the trailhead where we had to camp that night. See, my intention was to fold each body facedown across a packsaddle the next morning. But that night turned clear and cold, and in the morning we could not get those bodies to bend. Of all the packing I had ever done, this was a new one on me, how to fit those stiff bodies onto packhorses. What I finally did was take the biggest packhorse I had and sling both bodies onto it in a barrel-hitch tie, one lengthwise along each side for balance like you would with sides of meat. But that was the worst I ever handled, balancing that cargo of what had been men."

On a straight stretch where the Bago's headlights steadily fed the freeway into our wheels, I cast another quick glance over at Mariah. The interiors of the two of us inside this chamber of vehicle; caves within the cave of night. What does it take to see the right colors of life? Whether or not that was on her mind as on mine, Mariah too was intent. She sat staring straight ahead through the windshield as though she could pierce the night to that frontmost car where Riley was listening and recording.

The night flew by the motorhome's windows as I thought over whether to say the turbulence in me or to keep on trying not to.

"I'm Julius Walker. This is tough to tell. But if you want to know the big things about each of our lives, this has got to be mine. Quite a number of people lost a son over there in Vietnam. But my wife and I lost our daughter Sharon. All through high school in Dutton, what she wanted most was to be a nurse. She went on and took the nursing course at Columbus Hospital there in Great Falls and then figured she'd get to see some of the world by going into the Army. I kick myself every day of my life since, that I didn't try to talk her out of that. She ended up at the evacuation hospital at a place called Cu Chi. Sharon was killed right there on the base, in a mortar attack. They eventually found out there were tunnels

*everywhere under Cu Chi. The Americans were right on top
of a whole nest of Viet Cong. Good God Almighty, what were
those sonsabitches Johnson and Nixon thinking about, getting
us into something like that?"*

"Mariah," it broke out of me, "I don't think I can go on with this."

In the dimness of the Bago's cab her face whitely swung around to me, surprise there I more could feel than see.

A minute of nothing said. The pale glow of the dashlights seemed a kind of visible silence between us.

Then she asked, her eyes still steady on me: "What brought this on?"

Here was opportunity served up under parsley, wasn't it. Why, then, didn't I speak the answer that would have included her situation with Riley and my own with the memory flood unloosed by the sight of Shirley in Missoula, the sound of Toussaint's voice ventriloquizing in me at the buffalo range, the war report of bald ghost warrior Ed Heaney, the return of Big Hole longings across fifty years, the ambush of Pat Hoy's lonesome death, the poised-beside-the-bar sensation again of Stanley Meixell and Velma Simms and the mystery of man and woman; the answer, simply but totally, "All this monkeying around with the past."

Instead I said, "I'm not sure I'm cut out for this rambling life, is all. With you newspaper people, it's long days and short nights."

"There's more to it than that, though, isn't there," Mariah stated.

"Okay, so there is," I admitted, wondering how to go on with the confession that I was being spooked silly by things out of the past. "It's—"

"—the ranch, isn't it," she helpfully spliced on for me. "You worry about the place like you were a mother cat and it was your only kitten."

"Well, yeah, sure," I acknowledged. "I can't help but have the place on my mind some."

*The caravan resumes speed, into a curve of the highway,
another bend toward the past.*

*"And I'm Jerome Walker. If there's one thing in my life
that surprises me, it's that I've ended up in a city. Yeah, yeah,
I know Great Falls isn't Los Angeles or New York. But pretty
damn near, compared to how Julius and me grew up out in
the hills between Cascade and Augusta on our folks' cow
outfit. The home place there had been our granddad's home-*

stead, and I suppose I grew up thinking the Walkers were as natural to that country as the jackrabbits. But I turned out to be the one who cashed it all in, back in 1976, when the wife and I moved in to the Falls to live on our rocking chair money. I suppose in earlier times we'd have just moved to town, Cascade or Augusta either one. A lot of towns in those days had streets of retired ranchers they'd call something like Horse Thief Row, you know. But our kids were already in the Falls, in their jobs there, and naturally the grandkids were an attraction. So we went in, too. It's still kind of like being in another country. I about fell over, the first time I went downtown in the Falls and heard a grown man in a suit and tie say, 'Bye bye.'"

"I'll make you a deal," this Mariah Montana daughter of mine resorted to. "If you want to check on the place so bad, we'll all three go on up to the ranch just as soon as we're done in Helena, how about. Riley and I have got to do some pieces along the High Line anyway, and there's no real reason why we can't swing through the Two country getting there. How's that sound?"

Sweet enough to whistle to. I kept my eyes on the dark unfolding road while I asked: "And then?"

"Then you decide. After you've looked things over at the ranch, if you still think you'd rather be on your lonesome than . . ." she let the rest drift.

I sat up straighter behind the steering wheel. Maybe I was going to be able to disengage from this traveling ruckus fairly simply after all. "You got yourself a deal," I told Mariah with fresh heartiness.

Ahead of us the signal of blinks danced out of the night one more time. As the entire series of cars pulled over to stop again, Roger Tate's van now had become the last in line in front of us. In our headlights the sticker on Roger's rear bumper declared: DIRTY OLD MAN, HELL—I'M A SEXY SENIOR CITIZEN.

Mariah mused, "We ought to get a bumper sticker of some kind for the Bago."

Driver seven, the last who has become first.
"My name is Dale Starr. What I want to talk about is, am I losing my g.d. mind or are things repeating theirselves?

I've tried to do a little thinking about it. The way all the bad I've seen in my lifetime and figured we'd put behind us seems to be coming around again now. People losing their farms and ranches. Stores out of business. All the country's money being thrown around like crazy on Wall Street. How come we can't ever learn to do better than that? Of course we know the weather has got some kind of a more or less basis of repeating itself. Nature does have its son-of-a-bitch side too, doesn't it. Like the big thirty-year winters, 1886 and 1919 and 1948 and 1978. And the drought just after the First World War and again in the thirties and again these past years now. But I guess what I keep wondering is, shouldn't human beings have a little more control over theirselves than the weather does over itself?"

As he finishes, into view glow the lights of Helena, thousands of gemmed fires, each a beacon of some life young or old.

Dawn is when I have always liked life most, the forming hour or so before true day, and that next morning at the Prickly Pear RV Park, with Mariah up extra early to develop her shots of the Baloney Express contingent, I went out to sit on a picnic table and watch Helena show off its civic ornaments in the daybreak light. The dark copper dome of the state capitol. The Catholic Cathedral's set of identical twin steeples. The pale Arabianlike spire of the Civic Center. My favorite, though, stood perched on the high side of Last Chance Gulch, above the historic buildings downtown; the old fire watchtower up on four long legs of strutwork. Like a belltower carefully brought to where it could sound alarm into every street when needed. What a daystarting view it must be from there, out over the spread city and this broad shallow bowl of cultivated valley and the clasping ring of mountains all around.

In what seemed just another minute, the sun was up. That's the trouble with dawn, it doesn't last.

A joggedy-joggedy sound interrupted the quiet morning. Riley was out for his run. Mariah had already done her Jane exercises on the floor of the Bago. These two kept everything about themselves toned up except their heads. I watched as Riley rounded the endmost motorhome and cantered along the loop road toward the Bago and myself. He ran in a quick pussyfoot style, up on his toes as if dancing across hot coals.

"Feel better?" I greeted him as he trudged into our site, gulping air into his heaving chest.

"There's nothing like it," he panted, "except maybe chasing cars."

For a change, I didn't feel on the outright warpath against the guy, pacified as I was with the prospect of getting home to Noon Creek later today and not budging from there when Mariah and him set out to invade the rest of Montana. Let history whistle through their ears all it wanted. Mine were ready for a rest. So it was without actual malice, just kind of clinically, that I pointed out the bare wheelhub where the hubcap had flown off after Riley's tire-changing job of last night, and he gave a wheezing sigh and a promise to add a new hubcap onto the expense account along with the buffalohead dent in the hood. He'd regained some oxygen by now and started to take himself into the Bago for a shower.

"Whup, off limits yet," I warned. "Mariah's souping film."

Riley nodded to save precious breath. As he dragged over and draped onto the picnic table beside me to wait, I couldn't help but notice his running costume. Skintight and shiny, it made him look like he'd had a coat of black paint applied from the waist down to just above his knees. I let my curiosity ask: "What's that Spandex stuff made of?"

"Melted money," Riley formulated. "It'd be a whole lot cheaper to just do a Colter, I do admit."

As John Colter was the mountain man who was stripped naked and barefoot by the Blackfeet and given a few hundred yards headstart before they began chasing him over the prairie with murderous intent—talk about a marathon—I pleasantly enough passed the time imagining Riley in nude version hotfooting it across this valley going *oo! ow!* on the prickly pear cactuses.

But shortly the side door of the Bago opened and Mariah poked her head out and gave the all clear. She studied Riley in his running getup. "Good morning, Thunder Thighs."

In actual fairness, Riley's legs were not truly scrawny; but sectioned as they were into the top portion of pore-hugging black fabric and the elongation of contrasting skinwhite below, they did kind of remind a person of the telescoped-out legs on Mariah's tripod. But she'd said what she said with a grin, and although Riley gave her a considerable look, he decided not to go into combat over his lower extremities and instead asked, "How'd your geezer shots come out?"

"Show you after breakfast," she said, and somewhat to my surprise they both kept to their best behavior through that meal. Oh, still several tastes short of being sweet to each other, but civil, ever so carefully civil. Who knows, maybe it was only the temporary influence of my cheffing of venison sausage patties and baking powder biscuits swimming in milk gravy, or that Riley still was feeling sunny due to his epic of the Baloney Expressers, but in any event he perused Mariah's exactly apt photographic rendition of those seven bent-over elderly behinds judiciously clustered around the flat tire, seats of wisdom if there ever were, then he actually said: "Helluva picture, shooter. How good are you going to get?"

The little toss of her head, which stayed cocked slightly sideways as she eyed back at him. "How good is there?"

I honestly figured I was contributing to the general civility with my question. True, there was the consideration that the sooner I could get these two budged from Helena, the quicker we could motate to the ranch and I could see what that situation was. In any case, I asked: "So what kind of piece are you two going to do here today?"

Mariah looked brightly across at Riley. "We were just about to talk that over, weren't we."

"Ready when you are," Mister Geniality confirmed.

Her gaze at him stayed determinedly unclouded. "Mmm hmm. Well, I wondered if you had anything for here squirreled away in your notes."

"Actually, I did jot down one idea," he granted, spearing another biscuit.

"Trot it on out."

"I just absolutely think it captures the essence of early Helena."

"Sounds good. What is it?"

"You maybe won't be real keen on it."

"Why won't I? Come on, let's hear it."

"Promise not to get sore?"

"Riley, will you quit dinking around and just tell me what the fuck it is? I promise I'm not going to get sore, cross-my-heart-and-hope-to-die, will that do? Now then. What's this great Helena idea of yours?"

"Whores."

"*What?*"

"See, you're sore. I knew you would be."

Mariah expended a breath that should have swayed the trees outside. "I. Am. Not. Sore. But here we need some humongous idea for Helena and you come up with—"

"Pioneer businesswomen. Is that better?"

"Not hardly," she spoke the words like two cubes of ice. "Riley, take a reality check on yourself, will you? I am not going to burn film for that old half-assed male fantasy of prostitutes who just happen to be selling their bodies so they can save up to go to ballet school."

"That's just it. The wh— prostitutes here in Helena weren't. They were hard-headed real estate investors."

Mariah eyed Riley without mercy, trying to see if he was on the level. I have got to say, from the expression on his face his motive seemed purely horizontal. After a long moment she told him: "Say more."

Boiled down, Riley's discourse was about how, for a while back in the last century, the really quite extensive red-light district of Helena generated the funds for some of its, uhmm, practitioners to buy their own places of enterprise and that, whether you approved of their profession or not, their sense of local investment made them civic mothers just as much as any downtown mercantilist was a civic father. It of course didn't last, he said; that self-owned tenderloin trade went the way of other small frontier capitalists, done in by bigger market forces. But why shouldn't he and Mariah tell the story of those women, who'd tried to hold onto some financial independence in their desperate lives, just as readily as they would the one of some pioneer conniver who'd made his pile selling dry goods? I had to admit, it was something to think about. Who qualifies when it comes to history. Mariah too seemed to be mulling pretty hard by the time Riley got done dissertating.

From some distance off came the sound of someone opening the side door of a rig and announcing, "Going to be another hot one today, Hazel."

Mariah at last granted that Riley's idea was maybe worth a try but-he'd-better-know-what-he-was-talking-about-and-not-make-this-just-some-dippy-piece-about-whores-with-hearts-of-gold et cetera and when the newspaper aces went up to the state historical society to search out old photos of that domestically owned red-light district, I decided to tag along.

I ought to have known better than to hope that the two of them would get their photographic digging over with in a hurry and we could head to the Two country while the day was yet young, though. After some hours of killing time in the historical society I had all but memorized the countless exhibits about Montana's past. I had squinted at every everloving piece of the cowboy art of Charley Russell, reminded all the while of what Riley had said in one of his most notorious columns, that Montanans were as proud of the guy as if he had been Bertrand or Jane. By then my feet were like walking on a pair of toothaches and so I trudged upstairs one more time to check the place's library, where Mariah and Riley had said they'd meet me as soon as they surfaced from the photograph archives. Naturally, no trace of either of them. But this time I decided I would just find a place to sit until they eventually presented themselves.

Yet sitting doing nothing is not my best pastime either. Particularly not in a library, for it brought to mind Marcella, the winter we started going together when she was the librarian in Gros Ventre and I was conspicuously her most frequent patron.

No, I told myself, don't let it happen, don't get yourself swept up in one of those memory storms. My mind determinedly in neutral, I watched the library traffic. Over behind the librarian's desk was a distinguished guy wearing a tie and a mustache both, and though he was no Marcella he looked more or less civil. People came up to ask him various things, but I could hear that about every second one of them was pursuing genealogy.

Which set me to thinking. Family tree is nothing it ever occurred to me to shinny up very far, but with time to spend anyhow, why shouldn't I? Maybe that was the way: see what our past looked like in an official place such as this, instead of letting it ambush me barehanded as it kept doing. Of course, not even try to trace back more than the couple of generations to the other side of the Atlantic, that risky hidden territory of distant ancestors; just see what I could find of the Montana McCaskills and my mother's side of the family, the Reeses, by the time Mariah and Riley ever decided to show up.

I stepped over to the librarian, and in gentlemanly fashion he gave me what must have been his patented short course in ancestor-seeking, which card catalogue to use when looking for what, and so on.

"Any luck?" the library man asked on his next errand past me.

None. I told him I guessed I wasn't really surprised, as we're not particularly a famous family. Actually it is somewhat spooky to learn that so far as the world at large knows, your people are nonexistent.

"You might try over here." He ushered me to what he called the Small Collections shelf. "To be honest with you, this category is holdings we don't quite know what else to do with. Reminiscences people have written for their grandkids, and short batches of letters, and so on."

It makes you wonder, whether you really want to find anything about your family in the stray stuff. But I plucked out the thick name index binder labeled *Ma* through *Me* and took a look. The volume listed a world of *Mc*s, but no McCaskills. Which again didn't overly surprise me. As far as I knew, the only real skein of writing either of my parents did was my father's forest ranger diary, and a lot of that I did for him, when I rode with him as a boy on our sheep-counting trips into the mountains of his Two Medicine National Forest. Now that would have been something: nose around here in search of the past and find my own words coming out at me.

R had a binder all its own and half a dozen *Reese*s had pages in it, all right, but none of them my mother's parents Isaac and Anna. So much for—

Then it came to me. The old family story of the immigration officer who decided to do some instant Americanizing on my Danish grandfather when he stepped off the boat.

I thumbed a little deeper into the *R*s and just past *Rigsby*, would you believe, there was my mother's father in his original form, *Riis, Isak.*

"Noon Creek, Montana, rancher and horse dealer," the entry stated. *"Letters to his sister in Denmark, Karen Riis Jorgensen, 1886–1930. Originals at the Danish Folklore Archives, Copenhagen; translation by Centennial Ethnicity Study Project, with funding from Montana Committee for the Humanities. 27 items."*

And so. When the library man brought out the long thin box of them to me, the letters were the farthest thing from what I had expected.

Kæreste Søster Karen—

Amerika og Montana er altid en spændende Oplevelse . . . The handwriting on the photocopied pages was slanting but smooth, no hesitation to it. Isaac's penmanship in Danish, though, was not the real surprise. The typed translation. The man of these words was the only one of my grandparents I held any memory of, him sitting gray-mustached and bent but still looking thoroughly entertained by life, there at the head of our table some long ago Sunday dinner when I could barely peek over that table. Old Isaac's family fame was for chewing his way through English as if it was gristle. My father always told of the time Isaac was asked which of his roan saddle horses was for sale, the one out in the pasture with a herd of other ponies or the one alone in the corral, and the old boy answered, "De vun in a bunch by hisself."

But the Isaac of these letters my eyes listened to in amazement, if it can be said that way.

8 November 1889

Dearest sister Karen—
America and Montana are ever an adventure. Today I journeyed into the community of Gros Ventre for provisions and found there a proud new municipal adornment; beside the dirt of the village's main and only street, a flagpole of peeled pine with a fresh American flag bucking in the wind. Pole and flag were but hours old, as was the news that Montana has advanced from a type of colonial governance to become a fully equal state of the United States. In all truth, the celebratory merriment of Gros Ventre this day was so infectious it could not be resisted; but your Montanian brother nonetheless was truly moved by this fledging of his adopted land. DV, Montana and we in it shall ride the future as staunchly as that flag in the wind. . . .

12 June 1892
. . . The time is not far, my Karen, when I will have crews of teamsters at earnful labor throughout this Two Medicine country, and DV, I shall be able to stand about with my hands on my back, looking on like a baron. Streets, roads, reservoirs, all are to be built here in young Montana and the demand for my workhorses is constant. . . .

I carried these first few of the translated letters over to show the librarian. "This DV he sticks in every so often—do you happen to know where that comes from?"

"Deo volente, that'd be," he provided at once.

My high school Latin was quite a ways behind me. Oh, sure, like anybody I could dope out Deo as meaning God, deity, all that. But the other word . . .

" 'God willing,' it means," the librarian rescued me. "You find it a lot in letters of people who had some education back then."

Huh. Another surprise out of my horsetrading grandfather: I hadn't known there was an ounce of religion anywhere in our family line.

I went back to the table and resumed reading.

> *30 September 1897*
>
> *. . . No doubt, dearest sister, you will notice a shine in the ink of these words, for I write to you as a freshly married man. Before she took mine, her name was Anna Ramsay—a lovely, lively woman, Scotland-born, who arrived here last spring as the new teacher at our Noon Creek school. . . .*

After that sunburst of marriage Isaac's pages breathed to life *our much wished for child, Lisabeth*—my mother, born in 1900 on the first of April, and although we kidded her about it nobody was ever less of an April fool—and a few years later her brother *Peter, a fine squalling boy who seems determined to visit the neighbors all along Noon Creek with his voice.* The early ups and downs of the ranch I now owned were traced here. The doings of neighbors were everlastingly colored in ink. The steady pen brought the familiar snow of Two Medicine winter, and transformed it into the green of spring. Letter after letter I read as if old Isaac, strangulated by spoken language but soliloquizing with the best of them here on paper, somehow had singled me out for these relived times.

> *25 June 1914*
>
> *. . . I write you this from amid scenery that would put Switzerland in the shade. Our work camp this summer is at St. Mary Lake while my teamsters are building roads of the new Glacier National Park. Towering over us are mountains like castles of gray and blue, as if kings had come down from the sky to live even more royally at the top of the earth. Quite to my surprise, I was visited here this past week by Anna and the children; she took the impulse to come by wagon even though it is a tedious three-day journey from Noon Creek. Ever her own pilot through life, is my Anna. . . .*

You want not to count on history staying pleasant or even civil, though.

I have been so numb with grief, dearest Karen, that not until now have

I had the heart to write about . . . Anna. About her death, ten days before, in the influenza epidemic of 1918.

I pinched the bridge of my nose and swallowed hard to go on from that aching message of the loss of a wife. Isaac's Anna. My Marcella. The longest epidemic of all, loss.

Isaac too now seemed to falter, the letters foreshortened after that, even the one the next year telling of the wedding of my mother and father there at the Noon Creek ranch. Nor were there any more invocations of DV.

I was thumbing through the final little batch of translated pages, about to admit that Isaac and I both seemed to be out of steam for this correspondence, when my eye caught on the *McC* at the start of a name.

> *In the valley next over from this one, Lisabeth's father-in-law Angus McCaskill has died. The report is that he was fixing a fence after supper when his heart gave out. Such a passing I find less than surprising, for Angus was a man whose hands were full of work from daylight to last light. Still, although we know that all things find their end, it is sobering to me that he has gone from life at an age very like my own, neither a young man nor an old.*
>
> *His leaving of life has brought various matters to the front of my mind. At the funeral of Angus, when I went to speak consolation to his wife and now widow Adair, I was much startled to learn that she is removing herself to Scotland. "To visit, you surely mean." "No, to stay," she had me know. She will wait to see Varick and Lisabeth's child, soon due, into the world. But after greeting that grandchild with her eyes, then she will go. I was, and am, deeply baffled that a person would take such a step. You know that Denmark will never leave my tongue, but this has become the land of my heart. Not so, however, for Adair McCaskill. She has a singular fashion of referring to herself by name, and thus her requiem for the life she is choosing to depart from was spoken as: "Adair and Montana have never fitted together."*

Those two paragraphs held me. I reread and re-reread. My rightful name is John Angus McCaskill. Christened so for this other grand-

father who abruptly was appearing out of the pen of my grandfather
Isaac. My father's father, so long gone, I had never really given any
thought to. A shadow in other time. My main information on him was
the remark one or the other of my parents made every so often when
Mariah was growing up, that her rich head of hair came from her great-
grandfather Angus, of the deep shade the Scotch claim is the color of
their fighting blood. Yet here in ink Angus McCaskill suddenly was,
right out of nowhere, or at least the portion of him that echoes in my
own birth certificate. And with him, but evidently on her own terms,
was my grandmother I knew even less of. So scant was any mention of
Adair McCaskill by my parents that I sensed she and my mother had
been in-laws at odds, but that was all. I'd always assumed the North
Fork homestead claimed her as it did Angus. Willing reversal to Scotland was new lore to me.

I read on.

> Until now I have forborne from any mention of Angus
> McCaskill to you in my letters, dearest sister, because I
> believed the time would come when I would need to tell you
> the all. You will see that while my pen was quiet about Angus
> my mind rarely was, for his life made a crossroad with my
> own almost from the first of our days here in the Two
> Medicine country, some 35 years ago. He too was but young,
> new and green to this America, this Montana, when I sold
> him the first substantial horse he ever owned, a fine tall
> gelding of dark brown with the lively name of Scorpion. In the
> years that came, Angus cut an admired figure in the
> community, not only as an industrious homesteader and
> sheepman but also as teacher at the South Fork school. A man
> with poetry on his tongue and decent intentions in his heart,
> was Angus. The word "neighbor" has no better definition than
> the life he led. To me, however, Angus was more than simply a
> neighbor, more than a familiar face atop a strong horse which
> I had provided him. Greatly more, for the matter is, Angus
> was in love with my Anna all the years of our marriage.
>
> He manfully tried not to show his ardor for my wife, and
> never did I have cause to believe anything improper took place
> between the two of them. But his glances from across the room
> at her during our schoolhouse dances and other gatherings

*(how many glances that adds up to in 21 years!) told me
louder than words that he loved her from afar in a helpless
way. What must have been even worse a burden on the heart
of Angus was that he won Anna's affections before I did, or so
he had every cause to believe. He was the first to ask her to
marry; Anna being Anna, she delayed answer until after the
ensuing summer; and that was the summer of 1897 when I
hired her to cook for my crew during the plowing of fireguards
along the Great Northern railway and her life and mine were
joined. After we were married that autumn, I tried never to
show Angus that I knew of Anna's spurning of him, believing
that when she chose me over him the bargain was struck and
we all three could but live by it. Yet, even after his own
marriage, I could not help but feel pity for Angus, unable to
have Anna in his life.*

*Yet again—only now, dearest sister, and only to you on this
unjudging paper, can I bring myself to say this—I know with
all that is in me that if Anna had lived, she would have left
me for Angus McCaskill. I could see it coming in her. She had
a nature all her own, did my Anna; as measured as a judge in
making her mind up, but passionate in her decision once she
had done so. And so the moment merely waited, somewhere
ahead in time, when Anna would have decided that she and I
had had all of life together we could, and then she would have
turned to Angus. I believe she was nearing that moment just
before she died. Lisabeth was grown by then, Peter nearly so;
consequences of ending our marriage no longer would fall
directly on our children. I have spent endless nights wondering
what would have ensued. Surely, if her mother had gone with
Angus, Lisabeth would not then have married a McCaskill;
strong-minded as she is, she would have spoken her vow to the
Devil first. From that it follows that Lisabeth and Varick's
little boy Alec, and the other child on the way, those existences
come undone, do they not? As the saying is, all the wool in the
world can be raveled sooner than the skein of a single life.*

*As for myself, my debate in the hours of night is whether it
is more bearable to have become a widower than a rejected
husband. It is a question, I am discovering, that does not want
to answer itself.*

By the time I was done reading this the first time, the backs of my hands were pouring sweat. Jesus H. Christ, what we don't know about how things were before they got to us.

Over and over I read that letter, but the meaning did not change in any way, the words would not budge from Isaac Reese's unsparing rendering of them. My father's father had been in love with my mother's mother. And she more or less with him. In love but married to others.

And not just that. August 12, 1924, the date on this letter in which Isaac told all; the other child on the way, less than a month from being born, the one whose existence would have been erased if Anna Reese had not died before she could take her future to waiting Angus McCaskill. That child was precisely me.

As if that child was suddenly six years old and yearning for the teacher to call rest period so that he could put his head down on his school desk into the privacy of closed eyes, I right then laid forward into my arms on the library table and cradled my head. I did not know the tears were coming until I felt the seep of them at my eyelids, the wet paths being traced over my cheekbones.

That quiet crying: who did I weep for? For Anna Reese? Did that woman have to die for me to happen? Become in death my grandmother, as she never would have in life? Alec and I, and by way of me, Mariah and Lexa; we were freed into life when the epidemic took her, were we? Or were my tears Isaac's, for his having lost a wife? Or for Angus McCaskill for twice having lost love; once at the altar and once at the grave? Or for Adair McCaskill, second-choice wife in a land, too, that was never her own? Or was this again my grief for Marcella, my tears the tide of her passing into the past with the rest of these?

I wept for them all, us all.

A hand cupped my shoulder. "Sir? Are you all right?" The library man was squatting down beside me, trying to peer in through my pillow of arms.

I lifted my head and wiped my eyes with both hands. Gaggles of genealogists around the room had put aside their volumes to watch me. "Uhm. I forgot . . . forgot where I was." Blew my nose. Tried to clear my throat. "Some things kind of got pent up in me. The stuff in these . . ." I indicated Isaac's letters.

"At least they mean something to you," the librarian said gently.

"Yeah. Yeah, they do."

—

The librarian having assured me he'd tell my daughter and any tall yay-hoo with her that I'd meet them outside, I snuffled my way out into the sunshine. Into noon hour for the state workers, for across the street from the Historical Society the capitol's copper dome was like a hive for busy humanity below, men and women in groups and pairs as they hurried off to restaurants or chose shaded spots on the capitol lawn for bag lunch on the ground.

I plugged along slowly through the blanketing heat toward the Bago, trying not to look like a guy who had just made a public spectacle of himself. Talk about self-pandemonium. This trip was doing it to me something fierce. How the hell to ward it off, though? The past has a mind of its own, I was finding out. Maybe my weepy spell was over but I still felt flooded with those torrents of Isaac's ink.

"Hi, did you manage to keep yourself entertained this morning?" Mariah's voice caught up with me from behind. Before I could manage a response to that, she was alongside me with her arm hooked with mine and already was skipping on to "Ready for lunch, do I even need to ask?"

"Where's your partner in crime?" I inquired, glancing around for Riley.

"He's calling the BB to make sure our geezer piece got there okay. I missed a bet when we divorced. I should have sued the telephone for alienation of affection."

She, at least, seemed in an improved mood, which I verified by asking her how the red-light real estate piece was coming. "I think it's going to work," she conceded. "You never quite know with Riley when he reaches into that pantry of a brain of his. But his idea this time looks real zammo." Nor could you predict this newspaper pair. Less than twenty-four hours ago they could barely tolerate each other and here all of a sudden they were on their best productive behavior.

At the motorhome Mariah and I flung open all the doors and windows to let the heat out, but sultry as the weather was maybe a hotter amount flowed in. We moved off into the shade of a tree on the capitol lawn while waiting for Riley. Right next to us was a big oblong flowerbed in a blossom pattern forming the word CENTENNIAL; my God, they were even spelling it out in marigolds now.

The sky, though, had turned milky, soiled-looking. "What the hell's happened to our day?" I asked Mariah.

"Smog," she said, squinting critically at the murk; only the very nearest mountains around the city could be seen through the damn stuff. "Smoke from the forest fires in Idaho, I guess, and when it's this humid . . ."

Smog? Shit, what next. Even the air was getting me down now. I wished to Christ the scribbler would haul his butt out here and we could head for—

"Here you go," I heard next out of Mariah. The camera lifted to her eye and pointed at me. "A chance to pose with a general." Behind me stood the statue of General Meagher on horseback with sword uplifted like he was having it out with the pigeons. After the Civil War he'd been made territorial governor of Montana, but disappeared off a Missouri River steamboat during a night of drinking blackberry wine. I suppose they couldn't show that in a statue so they put him on horseback.

"Speaking of general," I tried on this daughter of mine without real hope, "these pictures you perpetually want to take of me are a general nuisance, do you know that?"

"Thaaat's my guy, just be your natural self if you can stand to," she launched into her picture-taking spiel behind that damn camera, "and you—"

For once she brought the camera down without a click. "You look kind of under the weather, Jick." Mariah's gray eyes took stock of me. "Are you okay?"

"I been better," I admitted. The morning in the unexpected company of our own sources was more major than I could put into words for her right then. Nor were the tears very far behind my eyes. "Must be the smog, is all." I tried to move my mind from the past toward some speck of the future. "So. We can hit on toward the ranch this afternoon, huh? Leave right after lunch and we ought to be able to get there by about—"

"Mmm, not quite," Mariah disposed of that hope in nothing flat. "We're going to have to hang on here until tomorrow. Riley and I still have a load of old pictures to go through in there. This has got to be the most photographed red-light district anywhere, you wonder if they were putting it on postcards."

Right then Riley emerged from the Historical Society building, a frown on him you could have plowed a field with.

"The BB wants to see us," he told Mariah of the phone call without any fooling around at all. "Right now. If not sooner."

What, a detour all the hell way back west to Missoula? At this rate the only chance I had of making a trip home to the ranch was to keep going in the opposite direction until I circled the globe to it.

"Why's he want to see us?" Mariah was asking warily.

"He wouldn't say," Riley reported. "He sounded like he was too busy concentrating on being mad."

"Oh, horse pucky," Mariah let out in a betrayed tone. She drew herself up even more erect than usual, as if having put on an armor breastplate to do battle. "Riley, you swore to me, you absofuckinglutely *swore* to me you weren't going to diddle around with the expense account this time! You know how pissed off—"

"Goddamn it, I haven't been!" Riley defended.

"—the BB gets when—" She halted and looked at him differently. "You haven't been?"

"No, I have not," he maintained, pawing furiously at his cookie duster. "This whole frigging trip, the only invented arithmetic is going to be for those goddamn Bago repairs eventually. If the BB has been sniffing around in our expense account so far, all it'll tell him is that it's cheaper keeping us on the road than it is having us cause trouble around the office. Huh uh. It's got to be something else on his tiny mind."

The office of Baxter Beebe was in that turret of the *Montanian* building, with a spiffy outlook across the Clark Fork River to pleasant tree-lined Missoula streets.

The decoration of that round room, though, I would have done something drastic about. Currently the motif consisted of stuffed animal heads. They formed a staring circle around the room, their taxidermed eyes aimed inward at Mariah and Riley and me as we entered; an eight-point buck deer and an elk with antlers like tree limbs and a surprised-looking antelope and a moose and a bear and a bobcat and a number of African creatures I couldn't begin to name and, my God, even a buffalo. Many bars used to have head collections on their walls and at first I figured the BB simply had bought one of those zoos of the dead when a bar was turned into a fern cafe. But then I noticed there was a gold nameplate under each head, such as:

Bull Elk
shot by Baxter Beebe
in the Castle Mountains
October 25, 1986

He was a pale ordinary enough guy sitting there behind a broad desk, but evidently he did his own killing.

As the three of us walked in, Beebe plainly wondered who the dickens I was. Riley had just made that same point as we parked the Winnebago in the *Montanian* lot and I remarked that I'd be kind of interested to meet this famous boss of theirs. "Oh, just great," he'd grumbled, "your general enthusiasm will help us a whole fucking lot in handling the BB." But when Mariah introduced me, the editor automatically hopped up, gave me a pump-handle handshake—I suppose a person in his position gets paid by the handshake—and instructed, "Call me Bax."

Riley and Mariah both sat down looking exceedingly leery, as if the seats might be those joke cushions that go *pththbfft!* when sat on. I found a chair too and did what I could to make myself less than conspicuous.

The BB—Bax—sat with his hands folded atop a stack of letters on the desk in front of him and stared expressionlessly at Mariah and Riley for what he must have thought was the prescribed amount of bossly time. Then he intoned in a voice so deep it was almost subterranean:

"Let me put it this way. There has been a very interesting response to your centennial series. A record number of letters to the editor. For instance." He plucked the top letter off the stack and held it straight out to Mariah and Riley as if toasting a marshmallow on the end of a stick. The two of them reached for the sheet of paper simultaneously and ended up each holding a corner. I leaned over to peek along as they silently read:

> *Your so-called series on the centennial is downright*
> *disgusting. If Riley Wright, whose name by rights ought to be*
> *Riley Wrong, can't find anything better about Montana than*
> *the guff he has been handing us, he should be put to writing*
> *about softball instead.*
>
> *Also, the pictures in your paper are getting weird. Since*

when is the Berkeley Pit art? I can go out to the nearest gravel
pit with my Instamatic and do just as good.
                                    PO'd on Mullan Road

Mariah started to say something, which I knew would be relevant to the letter writer's photographic judgment and general ancestry, but then caught herself and just gritted. For his part, Riley was grinning down at the letter as if he'd just been awarded the world prize for smart aleckry. Eventually, though, he became aware of the BB's solid stare.

"Yeah, I see your point here, Bax," Riley announced thoughtfully, too thoughtfully it seemed to me. "Before you can print this one," he flapped the letter in a fond way, "we've got to solve the PO'd style question, don't we. Grammatically speaking, PO'd has to stand for Piss Offed. So you'd think Pissed Off ought to be P'd O, now wouldn't you? But nobody ever says it that way, so do we go with PO'd as common usage? Shame to lose that nice rhyme, too, 'PO'd on Mullan Road.'" Riley brightened like a kid remembering what nine times eight equals. "Here we go. If the guy would move across town to Idaho Street, we'd have it made—'P'd O on Idaho!' What do you think, Bax? You figure we can get him to agree to move if we promise to publish his dumbfuck letter?"

"Riley," Beebe uttered in his deepest voice yet, "what are you talking about?"

Riley never got the chance to retort anything further smart, because the editor now started giving him and Mariah undiluted hell. How come Riley's pieces were all about slaughtered buffalo and coppered-out miners and, it was incredible but the fact of the matter was inescapable, the angelic qualities of bartenders? And where was Mariah getting picture ideas like the fannies of geezers and, it was incredible but the fact of the matter was inescapable again, Kimi the bartender seen woozily through the beer glass?

Wow, I thought to myself, and he doesn't even know yet about the hardheaded whores of Helena.

Beebe paused long enough in his bill of particulars to slap a hand down onto the stack of letters, *thwap.* Then he announced: "In other words, the two of you are outraging our readers."

Mariah tried to point out, "Bax, in Missoula people will write a sackful of letters to the editor if they think a stoplight is a couple of seconds slow."

The BB was less than persuaded. "This is very serious," he stated in a funeral tone and proceeded to elaborate all over again on how the expectations of the *Montanian*'s readers, not to mention his own extreme forbearance, were being very abused by the way the pair of them were going about the centennial series.

I do have to admit, my feelings were radically more mixed than I expected, sitting there listening to their boss ream out Riley and Mariah. Oh sure, I was as gratified as I ought to have been by the perfectly evident oncoming fact that he was working around to the extermination of the centennial series and our Bago sojourn. And any time Riley got a tromping, it suited me fine. But I hated to see Mariah catch hell along with him. Then there was the, well, what might be called this matter of office justice. Put it this way: it really kind of peed me off, too, that this yoyo of a BB could sit here in his round office and prescribe to Mariah, or for that matter even Riley, what they were supposed to be seeing, when they were the ones out there in the daylong world trying to do the actual work.

The beleaguered pair of them now were attempting to stick up for their series while Beebe went on lambasting it and them. So while the three of them squawked at each other, I gandered around at the BB's stuffed trophies. Massive moose. Small bobcat. African something or other. That big elk. *Dead heads,* I could just hear Mariah steaming to herself, *symbolic.*

"Excuse my asking, Bax," I broke in on the general ruckus, "but where's your mountain goat?"

Everything stopped.

Then Beebe eyeballed me as steadily as if a taxidermist had worked on him too, while Riley, damn his hide, started gawking ostentatiously around the room as if the mentioned goat might be hiding behind a chair. For her part, Mariah was shaking her head a millimeter back and forth and imperatively mouthing *No, not now!* at me.

Beebe set to answering me in a frosty way, "If you do any hunting yourself, Jack—"

"Jick," I corrected generously.

"Whatever. If you do any hunting yourself—"

I shrugged and put in, "Not quite fifty years' worth yet."

The BB blinked a number of times, then amended his tone considerably. "Then you will know it is very hard to achieve a mountain goat. I have never been privileged to shoot one."

"The hell!" I exclaimed as if he'd confessed he'd never tasted chocolate ice cream. "Christamighty, I got them hanging like flies on the mountains up behind my place."

"Your place?"

"My ranch, up along the Rocky Mountain Front. Yeah, I can sit in my living room with a half-decent pair of binoculars and watch goats till I get sick of them."

He steepled his fingers and peered at me over his half-prayerfulness. "That is very interesting, ah, Jick. But I would imagine that getting within range of them is another matter."

"No problem. Anybody who's serious about his hunting," I nodded to the dead heads along the walls, "and I can see you definitely are, I usually let them onto the place, maybe even take them up one of the trails to those goats myself. Tell you what, whyn't you put in to draw for a permit, then come on up this fall and we'll find you a goat?" I gave the BB a look overflowing with nimrod enthusiasm. What fault was it of mine if the mountain goats in west of my ranch actually were unreachable on the other side of the sheer walls of Gut Plunge Canyon? The BB had only asked me whether it was possible to get within range of them, not whether it was feasible to fire off a shot.

I figured I'd better land him before my enthusiasm played out. "In fact, Bax, how about you coming on up to go goating right after these two," I indicated Riley and Mariah with the same kind of nod I'd given the stuffed trophies, "get done with this centennial stuff of theirs in November?"

He kept gazing at me from behind his finger steeple for a while. Then he gazed a further while at Mariah and Riley. All three of us could see him working on the choice. Sacrificial sheep or mountain goat.

At last Baxter Beebe announced, "That is a very, very interesting offer, Jick. I am going to take you up on that." He turned toward the other two. "Riley, as I was getting to, there has been some marked reaction among our readers to your centennial pieces. Of course, one way of viewing it is that you are provoking people's attention. The exact same can be said of your photos, Mariah. So, speaking as your editor, I will tell you what." We waited for what. "As you continue the centennial series, I would expect that your topics will become somewhat more, shall we say, traditional. Perhaps I should phrase it this way: tone things down." The BB sent a final gaze around to Mariah, then to Riley, and even to me. He concluded: "Anyway, I thought you would want to know you are being read, out there in readerland."

I give Mariah and Riley due credit, they both managed not to look mock astonished that newspaper readers were reading newspapers.

No, instead Riley said in a hurry "You can't know what an inspiration that is to us, Bax," and stood, and Mariah was already up and saying brightly "Well, we'll go hit the road again then, Bax," and even I found my feet and joined the exodus while the BB shuffled the letters to the editor together, squaring them into a neat pile which he put in his OUT basket.

MOTATING THE HIGH LINE

Centennialitis will break out in Gros Ventre again on Thursday night. A combined work party and meeting of the Dawn of Montana steering committee will be held at the Medicine Lodge, beginning at 8:30 p.m. "Everybody better come or they're going onto my list to sweep up the parade route after the horses," stated committee chairperson Althea Frew. Other members of the steering committee are Amber Finletter, J. A. "Jick" McCaskill, Howard Stonesifer, and Arlee Zane.

—*GROS VENTRE WEEKLY GLEANER, AUGUST 1, 1989*

B RRK BRRK.
My waking thought was that the guy who invented the telephone ought to have been publicly boiled in his own brainwater. Outside the bedroom window, dawn was just barely making headway against dark. If manufactured noise at such an hour isn't an offense against human nature, I don't know what is.

BRRK BRRK.

Christamighty, Mariah already, was my next realization. When I'd deposited her and Riley back in Helena the afternoon before to put the finishing touches on their masterpiece of mattress capitalism, that daughter of mine had told me she'd call me at the ranch today and let me know what time to come back and get her and her haywire companion. But *this* time of day, before there even properly was a day yet?

BRRK BRRK.

Maybe I would do that getting and maybe I just wouldn't. Late as

I'd gotten in after the drive from Helena to Noon Creek, I hadn't even had a chance yet to see Kenny and Darleen and gather any report on the ranch. And even in so milky a start of the day, I couldn't help but wonder what order of fool I was for turning the BB around with goat bait the way I had. What got into me, there in Missoula, not to let His Exterminatorship go ahead and kill off the centennial series and my unwanted part in it?

BRRK BR—

I *hello*ed and braced.

"Oh, Jick, I'm so glad I caught you before you got out and around, I know what an early bird you are," a woman's voice arrived at full gallop. Never Mariah, expending words wholesale like that.

I elbow-propped myself a little higher in bed. "Uh, who—"

"Oh, you're funning me, aren't you, pretending not to know this is Althea. Next thing, you'll be claiming you forgot all about tonight."

"Forgot what?"

"Jick, our centennial committee meets tonight," the phone voice perceptibly stiffened into that of Althea Frew, chairperson. "We've missed you at the meetings lately."

"Yeah, well, I been away. Unavoidably so." And it mystified me as much as ever, how she and undoubtedly the whole Two Medicine country knew that in the dark of last night I had come back. Did bunny-slipper telegraph even need the existence of the telephone or did they simply emanate bulletins out through the connecting air?

"All the nicer to have you home with us again, just in time for tonight," she informed me with conspicuous enthusiasm. "We have an agenda that I know you'll be interest—"

"Althea, I'm not real sure I'm going to be able to stick around until tonight. I—"

"You're turning into quite a gadabout, Jick. But I'm sure you can make time for one eensy committee meeting. Oh, and would you ask Mariah if she can come take pictures for our centennial album sometime? See you tonight," and Althea toodled off the line.

The burden of conversation with Althea thus lifted, I sat up in the big double bed and by habit took a meteorological look out the window to the west. A moon new as an egg rested in the weatherless sky above the mountains. So far so good on that front, anyway.

I was at least out of bed and had my pants halfway on before the phone rang again. Typical Mariah. I grabbed the instrument up, doubly

PO'd at her for calling before I even had any breakfast in me and for not calling before Althea did her crowbar work on me.

"Damn it, petunia, do you have some kind of sixth sense about doing things at exactly the wrong time?"

Silence, until eventually:

"Uhmm, Jick, was you going to line us out on haying the Ramsay place, before Darleen and me head up there?"

Kenny's voice, across the hundred feet between the old house and my and Marce's. Jesus, the day was getting away from me. Ordinarily I'd be over there by the time my hired couple finished up breakfast. Hurriedly I told Kenny, "Must've looked at the wrong side of the clock this morning. I'll be right over."

"Darleen's got the coffeepot on," he assured me as if that was foremost in my mind as well as his, and hung up.

> *"Sometimes you eat the bear,*
> > *sometimes the bear eats you.*
> *Sometimes you drink the flood,*
> > *sometimes you sip the dew.*
> *Sometimes you both are one,*
> > *sometimes you break in two."*

When I got there, Kenny was walking jerky little circles behind Darleen while she did the dishes, neither of them looking anywhere near at the other and the radio Roadkill bunch yowling right along with them. I know there is no one style for mating, but the fact that these two ended up with each other still confounded me. While Kenny was forever performing his conversational perambulation or bringing a hand up to rub the back of his neck or swinging his arms or craning a look out the nearest window to get his eyes fidgeting along with the rest of him, Darleen sloped along with no excess motion, and often no motion at all. Or was theirs what was meant by an average marriage, the way they so radically averaged each other out.

Right off I noticed that Kenny now sported muttonchop side-burns—they made him look like a shampooed lynx—for Gros Ventre's centennial beard contest. But the moment I stepped in the kitchen, it was my countenance that received a startled going-over from Kenny and Darleen both. I wondered what secret from myself was showing there, until I remembered my own accumulating snowy whiskers.

The two of them gave each other a side glance. Then Kenny felt the abrupt need to know, "Jick, how you doing this morning?" while Darleen matter of factly chipped in, "You must've seen a helluva swath of Montana by now."

"Okay" and "yeah" I recited to those and while we were getting coffeed up for the day, Kenny filled me in on ranch matters. Rather, he told me as much as he could think of and Darleen filled him in on all he forgot to tell. Haying was about a week behind because of breakdowns, but on the other hand Kenny did the repairing himself and avoided mechanics at multiple dollars per hour. For the first time in several summers Noon Creek was flowing a good head of water, but on the other hand the beavers were gaily working overtime on damming. A considerable stretch of fenceline had been mended, but on one more hand, the roof portions that blew off the lambing shed in the Alaskan Express storm of February hadn't been. A last prodding glance from Darleen further reminded Kenny that, uhmm, well, actually he hadn't got around to tending the sheepherder yet this week, either. All in all, things were not really any worse than I expected, nor a damn bit better.

Now came Darleen's turn, to give a cook's-eye view of how grocery prices were rocketing. As she recited a blow-by-blow of her latest bout with Joe Prentiss at his cash register in the Gros Ventre Mercantile, I nursed away at a second cup of Darleen's muscular coffee and tried to ponder how long I could operate this ranch by remote control through Kenny and her. How long did I want to keep trying? *You can't get decent help any more,* ran any rancher's chronic plaint; probably it went back to Abel's last recorded remark about Cain. But actually the pair here in this kitchen were as decent as I had any right to expect. Take Darleen, yakking away at a rate that had me thankful I wasn't paying her by the word. She was made of tough stuff, I always had to grant her that. When a foot of heavy wet snow hit on Memorial Day of this year, wonderful moisture for the grass but hell on young lambs and spring-shorn ewes, Darleen slaved side by side with Kenny and me through all that terrible day of fighting weakening sheep to shelter. And Kenny, although he couldn't manage his time even if you hung a clock on his nose, would whale away at any given task until he eventually subdued it; all you could ask of a person on the wages a rancher can pay, really. No, another Kenny, a different Darleen, would not inch my ranch situation toward solution.

" . . . Joe Prentiss goes, 'What do you want me to do, give this stuff away?'" Darleen at last was wrapping up her grocery tale, "and I go, 'You bet that's what I *want,* but I sure don't see any sign of it *happening.*'"

I did what I could to grin approval of Darleen's defense of our kitchen budget, but my result was probably thin. All at once, the three of us seemed to be out of conversation. Kenny squirmed into a new configuration in his chair. Darleen appeared to have plenty more to say but instead was silently watching Kenny contort. I took sipping refuge behind my coffee cup and watched them both. What the hell now? Something was missing from this morning's session about the ranchwork, something that wanted saying but was being held back, and the other two knew it just as well as I did. Whatever it was I was about to cover it over by supposing out loud that we had better get to getting toward the day's labor—by now I had it worked out in my head that I'd camptend the sheepherder, fix any downed fence while I was up there, then swing home by way of upper Noon Creek to attack the beaver dam problem; I knew it would take Kenny three separate trips to achieve the same—when Kenny crossed his arms and put his hands on his shoulders as if hugging himself and brought out:

"Uhhmm, Jick, I met up with Shaun Finletter along the east fence there a couple days ago and he said to tell you he'd like to talk to you about the place."

And here it was, yet and again. The missing. The first peep of it, anyway. Because, the fact was that though Shaun Finletter's tongue would do that talking, the throat under the words was WW, Incorporated. The everloving goddamn corporaiders. Not twenty minutes after that conglomerated outfit bought the big Double W ranch from Wendell Williamson's heirs—as a tax write-off, naturally—some guy in a tie was here to make me an offer for this ranch. Other Double Dubsters had tried me regularly the past half dozen years, and now that Shaun was their manager of the Double W, I evidently was in his job description too: buy out the old pooter at the head of the creek. I have to say, in a way I missed Wendell Williamson, whom I despised heartily when he was alive. At least with Wendell you knew directly who was trying to gobble you; not some distant multibunch who saw you as a scrap of acreage they could make tax arithmetic out of.

"Did he," I at last remarked as neutrally as possible about Kenny's relay from Shaun and brought my coffee cup to the ready position for one more refill that I did not want. But at the stove Darleen was waiting for my real answer before she would lift the coffeepot, as if my words might make the load too much to handle; and Kenny still was in his self-hug. Both of them watching me so closely it was as bad as being in Mariah's strongest lens. They had reason. For if I sold, this ranch would be folded into the Double W holdings as one more cow pasture, the way every other ranch along Noon Creek had been. WW, Inc. saw no need for the Kennys and Darleens of this world.

BRRK BRRK.

Kenny sprang to the phone on the wall. "Hullo? You bet, he's right here." Before I could gather myself, Mariah's voice was in my ear:

"Hi. You know what? You don't have to come back to Helena for us."

"I don't?"

"See what a terrific daughter I can be when I half try? Riley and I can't tell yet when we'll be done here today, so we'll rent a car and come up to the Two whenever we are. We need to get going on that part of the state next anyway. Think you can keep yourself occupied without us a little while? Gas up the Bago. Bye."

It was midmorning by the time the grocery boxes and I made our escape from the Gros Ventre Mercantile and Joe Prentiss's opinion of Darleen, and headed west out of town toward the sheep camp.

Remarkable how quiet and thought-bringing a pastime it is to drive along without a photographer blazing away beside you and a word-wright whanging his laptop behind you. This road I knew like the back of my hand and so I simply had to hold the motorhome away from the slidey gravel edges of the roadbank and let my mind do whatever solo it wanted, this cream-of-summer morning. Everywhere ahead the mountains, the jagged rim where the Two Medicine country joins onto the sky, today were clear and near. A last few desperate patches of snow still showed bright among the topmost clefts of Roman Reef's wall of rock, but their destiny was evaporation in another week or so. The benchlands on either side of the valley road already were beveled pastures of crisp grass; summer in the Two country always takes on a tan by August. Against the slope of the high ridge south of town, the big GV outline in rocks painted white by the Gros Ventre high school freshmen each fall was by now like a fading set of initials chalked onto leather.

Yet the land still was green where it counted: beside me as I drove, the column of tall old cottonwood trees extending west alongside the

county road, through hay meadow after hay meadow until at last thinning into a pair of willow lines that curved down out of the mountains—English Creek, its main channel and north and south forks like
a handle and tines uncovering my beginnings to me.

There is nothing left standing of my father's English Creek ranger
station. I inescapably know that, and could not help but see so, yet
again, as the Bago topped the rise of the county road and started down
the long slow slant of grade to the forks of the creek. But the absence
always registers hard on me. The station. The house behind it where we
lived from my fourth year of life through my fifteenth. Barn, corral,
sheds, flagpole. Not a stick of any of those is left. In one way of looking at things this is appropriate, really. The U.S. Forest Service extinguished that site from our lives in the winter of 1939 when it directed
my father, over his loudest kicks against the policy, to move his district
office of the Two Medicine National Forest into town in Gros Ventre,
and so the facade of that earlier English Creek time may as well have
taken its leave.

Its thoughts, though, do not go.

"Mac, if headquarters doesn't send us out some new oilcloth one of
these years, they are going to get A Piece of My Mind." My mother, Lisabeth Reese when she began life and Beth McCaskill from her nineteenth year to her eighty-fourth and final one, had a certain tone of
voice that signaled in high letters Watch Out. My father, officially Varick McCaskill but Mac to all who knew him in his lifetime of rangering, listened when he had to and otherwise went his way of simply
loving her beyond all the limits. They stand in my memory at English
Creek as if they were the highest two of those sky-supporting mountains. Her reminding him for the fourth time in as many days that his
ranger diary for the week thus far was a perfect blank, lifting her black
eyebrows significantly as she half-turned from the cookstove and sup-
per-in-the-making to inquire, "Are you trying for a new record, Mac?"
Him angling forward in his long-boned way as he peered out the west
window, restless under any roof, declaring of the perpetual paperwork,
"I tell you, Bet, USFS stands for just what it sounds like, Us Fuss. If
there's an outfit with more fussing around to it than the Forest Service,
I'd like to know where."

And the other echo. The one that clangs like iron against iron in my
remembering. That never-ended argument from an English Creek suppertime.

"You're done running my life," my brother flinging behind him as he stomped from that vanished house.

"Nobody's running it, including you," my father hurling after him.

The issue was warm and blond, her name Leona Tracy. A blouseful of blossom, seventeen years old and already eternal. She and Alec vowed they were going to get married, they would find a way of existence different from the college and career that my Depression-haunted parents were urging onto Alec, they would show the world what fireproof love was like. None of it turned out that way. By that autumn of 1939 Alec and Leona were split. Her life found its course away from the Two Medicine country. And Alec's—

"Goddamn Riley anyhow," I heard declared in an angry voice. Mine. A lot was working on me. It always did, here along English Creek. But right now Riley somehow represented the whole business, Alec and Leona and my amazed grief as a not-quite-fifteen-year-old watching them cut themselves off from my parents and me, every nick of that past like scars across my own skin. Why is a centennial supposed to be such potent arithmetic, will somebody just tell me that? I mean, you think about it, it always is a hundred years since one damn thing or another happened; the invention of the dental drill or the founding of junk mail or some such. But the *half* centuries, the fifty-year wedges that take most of our own lifetimes, those are the truly lethal pieces of calendar. Instead of chasing off after olden topics, what about those closer truths? Maybe I was not such a hotshot at history as Riley Wright was, but this I knew deep as the springs of my blood: in spite of ourselves, or because of ourselves—I still cannot judge which—the family we McCaskills had been here at the English Creek ranger station never truly recovered from the ruction between my parents and my brother when Alec declared himself against the future they hoped for him, and in favor of linkage with Leona, that summer of fifty years ago.

Yet—there always seemed to be a yet where the goddamn guy was involved—the one person on this green earth to whom I'd shown my feelings about our McCaskill family fracture was Riley.

He did not know the entirety, of course. Not nearly. But its topmost raw residue in me, he knew. Four, five years ago, that English Creek evening of Riley and myself? Whenever, it was back before his and Mariah's marriage went off the rails, when during one of their weekend visits to the ranch at Noon Creek he mentioned that he'd been going around to cemeteries, seeing what he could gather for a column on tombstone inscriptions sometime, and did I suppose the Gros Ventre cemetery would have anything worthwhile? "Oh hell yeah," I assured him, ever helpful me, and so before sundown I found myself there amid the graves with Riley. Just we two, as Marcella and Mariah had let us know a cemetery visit was not their idea of entertainment.

The lawned mound of the Gros Ventre cemetery stands above the edge of town and the treeline of English Creek as if the land has bubbled green there; one single tinged knoll against the eastward grainfield plains and the tan benchlands stretching west like platforms to the mountains. I am never there without thinking of the care that the first people of Gros Ventre put into choosing this endsite.

Riley took to the headstones in the old part of the cemetery like a bee to red clover. He immediately was down on one knee, dabbing inscriptions into his notebook, looking close, looking around. I could tell when a person was involved with his job, so I told him I'd wait for him up in the area where people were being buried currently. The active part of the cemetery, so to say.

There I knelt and did a little maintenance against weeds on my father's grave. Beside him the earth on my mother's was still fresh and distinct. While I weeded, other more desperate upkeep was occurring nearby where a sprinkler went *whisha whisha* as it tried to give the ground enough of a drink after the summer day's hours and hours of sun.

Riley read his way along the headstones toward me, every now and then stopping to jot furiously. I noticed him pausing to copy the old-country commemoration off one particular lichen-darkened tombstone:

LUCAS BARCLAY
born August 16, 1852
Nethermuir, Scotland
died June 3, 1917
Gros Ventre, Montana
IN THE GREEN BED 'TIS A LONG SLEEP
ALONE WITH YOUR PAST MOUNDED DEEP.

Then I was back into my own thoughts and lost track of Riley until he was almost to me, lingering at the grave just the other side of my parents'.

"Who's this one, Jick, an uncle of yours?"

"No." I got up and went slowly over to where Riley was, in front of the stone that read simply:

ALEXANDER STANLEY McCASKILL

"Mariah's uncle. My brother."

Riley gave me a sharp glance of surprise. "I never knew you even had one."

There's just a whole hell of a lot you don't know, I had the surging urge to cry out to him, but that was the pain of this place, these gone people, wanting to find a target.

I hunkered down to work on the chickweed on Alec's grave and managed to answer Riley only: "No, I don't guess you had any way of knowing. Alec was killed in the war. Although by now I suppose a person has to specify which one. The Second World War." The desert in Tunisia in 1943, the German plane slipping out of the low suppertime sun on its strafing run. The bodies, this one among them, in the darkening sand.

Whisha, the lawn sprinkler slung its arc of water down the cemetery knoll below us, then an arc back up the slope, *whisha.* After a minute I glanced at Riley; rare for him to be wordless that long. He was looking at me like a cat who'd just been given a bath. Which surprised me until I remembered: Riley had his own turn at war. Not that he ever would say much about it, but the once I had outright asked him what it had been like in Vietnam he answered almost conversationally: "Nam was a fucking mess. But what else would anybody expect it to be?" So it must have been the cumulative total of war, wars, that had him gazing into me and beyond to my destroyed brother.

"How old was he when—" Riley indicated with a nod of his head at Alec's grave.

"Twenty-two, a little short of twenty-three." Riley himself I knew was born in 1950; how distant must seem a life that ended seven years before his began, yet even now I thought of Alec as only newly dead.

Riley faintly tapped his notebook with his pen. He appeared to be thinking it over, whether to go on with the topic of Alec. Being Riley, he of course did. "You named Lexa after him."

"Kind of, yeah. That 'Alexander' has been in the family ever since they crossed the water from Scotland, and I guess maybe before. So

Marce and I figured we'd pass it on through one of the girls. You got it right, though—Lexa's full name is Alexandra."

Riley was listening in that sponge way he had, as if every word was a droplet he wanted to sop up. His eyes, though, never left Alec's headstone.

"His stone," he said after a little. "It's—different."

By that he meant what was missing. No epitaph, no pair of years summing the sudden span of life. As though even the tombstone carver wasn't sure Alec's story was over with.

"Yeah, well, I guess maybe the folks"—I indicated the side by side graves of my mother and father—"didn't feel they were entitled to any particular last word on Alec. What happened was, there was a family ruckus between them and him. Alec, see, was brighter than he knew what to do with. My folks figured he had a real career ahead of him, maybe as an engineer, once he got out of his cowboy mode. But then he came down with a bad case of what he thought was love and they considered infatuation. In any event, Alec was determined to give up his chance at college and whatever else for it." (My mother bursting out at his news of impending marriage and staying on as a rider for the Double W: *Alec, you will End Up as Nothing More Than a Gimped-Up Saddle Stiff, and I for one Will Not*—) "The girl"—I swallowed hard, thinking of smiling lovely Leona and grinning breakneck Alec, the couple too pretty to last in a hard-edged world—"the girl changed her mind, so all the commotion was over nothing, really. But by then it was too late, too much had been said." (Alec at the other end of the phone line when I tried, beseeched, a summer-end mending between him and our parents: *Jicker, it's—it's all complicated. But I got to go on with what I'm doing. I can't*—Alec's voice there veering from what he was really saying, *I can't give in.*) Riley was watching me a lot more intently than I was comfortable with as I concluded both the weeding of the grave and the remembrance of Alec. "It was just one of those situations that turned out bad for everybody concerned, is all."

"Including you, from the sound of it."

"That is true." Unexpectedly the poisoned truth was rising out of me in flood, to Riley of all people. "I was only a shavetail kid at the time, trying to be on everybody's side and nobody's. But Alec and I somehow got crosswise with each other before that summer was over. It sure as hell wasn't anything I intended, and I think him neither. But it happened. So our last words ever to each other were an argument. By goddamn telephone, no less. The war came, off Alec went, then I did too. And then—" I indicated the tombstone and had to swallow hard to finish. "I have always hated how this turned out. Us ending as brothers with bad feelings between. Over somebody . . . something that didn't amount to all that much."

I could still feel Riley silently watching me. I cleared my throat and looked off to the sharp outline of the mountains against the dusk sky. "Getting dark. You got the epitaphs you wanted?"

Riley glanced at the remainder of unread headstones, then at me. "Enough," he said.

The Bago rumbled across the plank bridge of English Creek and I steered off the county road to head up the North Fork, past the distinctive knob overlooking that smaller valley.

In front of me now stood Breed Butte, whose slow arc of rise divides the watersheds of English Creek and Noon Creek beyond. I concentrated on creeping the motorhome along the rough road track, all the while watching and watching the grassy shoulders of Breed Butte and other hillsides for any sign of the North Fork's current residents, my sheep. I can probably never justify it in dollars, but midway through the ungodly dry summer of '85 I bought this North Fork land so as not to overgraze the short grass crop of my Noon Creek pastureland. As the drought hung on, every year perilous until finally this good green one, the North Fork became my ranch's summer salvation. This handful of valley with its twining line of creek had its moment during the homesteading era, when the North Fork was known as Scotch Heaven because of all the families—McCaskills, Barclays, Duffs, Frews, Findlaters, others—who alit in here like thistledrift from the old country, but the land had lain all but empty since. Empty but echoing. As I knew now from those letters in Helena, one of these Scotch Heaven homesteads harbored a silent struggle within it—*the matter is, Angus was in love with my Anna all the years of our marriage.* My grandfather Angus and the loved Anna he never attained. My grandmother Adair, in exile from Scotland and her own marriage as well. The first McCaskill battleground of the heart.

No sheep either. The only telltale splotch of light color was the herder's canvas-roofed sheepwagon high on the nearest shoulder of Breed Butte and so I veered the Bago from the creekside route to the sidetrack leading up to there, really no more than twin lines of ruts made long ago. Geared down, the Bago steadily growled its way up the slope, the dark timbered summit of the butte above to the west. The sheepwagon stood amid the buildings, what was left of them now that roofs had caved in and century-old corners were rotting out, of Walter Kyle's old place. I guess more truly the Rob Barclay place, as my father had always called it, for the original homesteader here—a nephew or some such of the Lucas Barclay with the grandly proclaiming tombstone. This Barclay must have been a stubborn cuss, to cocklebur himself so high and alone on Breed Butte for the sake of its lordly view. Like him, though, my current herder preferred to have the wagon up here even though it meant hauling water from the North Fork; a dusty reservoir about a quarter of a mile west of the falling-down buildings testified that there'd once been a spring there but it long since had dried up. I unloaded the groceries in the wagon and climbed back into the Winnebago to resume the search for the sheep and their keeper.

On impulse I drove to the brow of the slope above the buildings instead of back down to the creek road immediately. As a rancher trying to make a living from this country I subscribe to the reminder that view is particularly hard to get a fork into. Yet I somehow didn't want to pass up this divideline chance to sightsee. Onward east from where I was parked on Breed Butte now, a kind of veranda of land runs parallel between English Creek and Noon Creek, a low square-edged plateau keeping their valleys apart until they at last flow into the Two Medicine River. In boyhood Julys, I rode horseback across that benchland at dawn to help with the haying on Noon Creek. When the sun rose out of the Sweetgrass Hills and caught my horse and me, our combined shadow shot a couple of hundred feet across the grassland, a stretched version of us as if the earth and life had instantly wildly expanded.

But for once my main attention was ahead instead of back. Between the benchlands of the Blackfeet Reservation in the distance and my vantage point there on Breed Butte the broad valley of Noon Creek could be seen, the willowed stream winding through hay meadows and past swales of pasture, a majority of it the Double W's holdings. Of that entire north face of the Two Medicine country I was zeroed in on the corner of land directly below toward the mountains, my ranch. The old Reese house that was now the cookhouse. The new house, all possible windows to the west and the mountains, that Marcella and I had built. The line of Lombardy poplars marking our driveway in from the Noon

Creek road. The lambing shed. Even the upstream bend of hayfield where Kenny and Darleen were baling. Every bit of it could be enumerated from here.

Enumerating is one thing and making it all add up is a hell of another. Oh, I had tried. I'd even had the ranch put through a computer earlier this year. A Bozeman outfit in the land analysis business programmed it all for me and what printed out was that, no, the place couldn't be converted into a dude ranch because with the existing Choteau dudity colonies in one direction and Glacier National Park in the other, Noon Creek was not "destination-specific" enough to compete; that maybe a little money could be made by selling hay from the ranch's irrigated meadows, if the drought cycle continued and if I wanted to try to live on other people's misfortune; that, yes, when you came right down to it, this land and locale were best fitted to support Animal Units, economic lingo for cattle or the band of sheep I already had on the place (wherever the hell they were at the moment). In short, the wisdom of the microchips amounted to pretty much the local knowledge I already possessed. That to make a go of the ranch, you had to hard-learn its daily elements. Pace your body through one piece of work after another, paying heed always to the living components—the sheep, the grass, the hay—but the gravitational wear and tear on fences and sheds and roads and equipment also somehow attended to, so that you are able to reliably tell yourself at nightfall, that was as much of a day as I can do. Then get up and do it again 364 tomorrows in a row. Sitting there seeing the ranch in its every detail, knowing every ounce of work it required, Jesus but how I right then wished for fifteen years off my age. I'd have settled for five. Yet truth knows every way to nag. Even if I had seen that many fewer calendars, would it do any good in terms of the ranch ultimately? Maybe people from now on are going to exist on bean sprouts and wear polyester all over themselves, and lamb and wool belong behind glass in a museum. Maybe what I have known how to do in life, which is ranching, simply does not register any more.

It took considerable driving and squinting, back down to the creek road and on up the North Fork toward the opposite shoulder of Breed Butte, before I spotted the sheep fluffed out across a slope. Against the skyline on the ridge above them was the thin, almost gaunt figure of my herder, patchwork black and white dog alongside.

The sight of the sheep sent my spirits up and up as I drove nearer. In a nice scatter along the saddleback ridge between Breed Butte and the foothills, their noses down in the business of grazing, the ewes were a thousand daubs of soft gray against the tan grass and beside them their lambs were their smaller disorderly shadows. As much as ever I looked forward to moseying over and slowly sifting through the band, estimating the lambs' gain and listening to the clonking sound of the bellwether's bell, always pleasure. But the iron etiquette between camptender and sheepherder dictated that I must go visit with the herder first. I climbed out of the Bago and started up the slope to her.

Helen Ramplinger was my herder this summer and the past two. Tall for a woman, gawky really; somewhere well into her thirties, with not a bad face but strands of her long hair constantly blowing across it like random lines of a web. I was somewhat bothered about having so skinny a sheepherder, for fear people would blame it on the way I fed. But I honestly did provide Helen whatever groceries she ordered—it was just that she was a strict vegetarian. She had come into the Two country to join up with some back-to-the-earth health-foody types, granolas as they were locally known, out of a background of drugs and who knew what else. I admit, it stopped me in my tracks when Helen learned I needed a herder and came and asked for the job. Marcella, too; as she said, she figured that as Dode Withrow's daughter she'd listened to every issue involving sheepherders that was possible but now here was gender. It ended up that Marce and I agreed that although Helen's past of drugs had turned her into a bit of a space case, she seemed an earnest soul and maybe was only just drifty enough to be in tune with the sheep. So it had proved out, and I was feeling retroactively clever now as I drew near enough to begin conversation with her.

"Jick, I'm quitting," Helen greeted me.

I blanched, inside as well as out. Across the years I had been met with that pronouncement from sheepherders frequently and a significant proportion of the time they meant it. If they burned supper or got a pebble in their shoe or the sky wasn't blue enough to suit them, by sheepherder logic it was automatically the boss's fault, and I as boss had tried to talk sweetness to sour herders on more occasions than I cared to count. Here and now, I most definitely did not want to lose this one. With herders scarcer than hen's teeth these days and Kenny and Darleen tied up in haying and me kiting around the state with Mariah and Riley, what in the name of Christ was I going to do with this band of sheep if Helen walked off the job?

"Aw, hell, Helen. You don't want to do that. Let's talk this over, what do you say." I made myself swallow away the usual alphabet of sheep-herder negotiation—fancier food, a pair of binoculars, a new dog—and go directly to Z: "If it's a matter of wages, times are awful tough right now, but I guess maybe I could—"

"Hey, I didn't mean now." Helen gave me an offended look. "I mean next summer. I've had some time"—she gestured vaguely around us, as if the minutes and hours of her thinking season were here in a herd like the sheep—"to get my head straight, and I've decided I'm not going to be a herder any more. I'll miss it, though," she assured me.

Momentarily relieved but still apprehensive, I asked: "What is it you're going to do, then?"

"Work with rocks."

"Huh?"

"Sure, you know. Rocks. These." She reached down between the bunchgrass and picked up a speckled specimen the size of a grapefruit. The dog looked on with interest. "Don't you ever wonder what's in them, Jick? Their colors and stuff? You can polish them up and really have something, you know." Helen peered at me through flying threads of her hair. "Gemology," she stated. "That's what I want to do. Get a job as a rock person, polishing them up and fitting them into rings and belt buckles and bolo ties. I heard about a business out in Oregon where they do that. So I'm gonna go there. Not until after we ship the lambs this fall, though."

Helen gently put the young boulder down on the ground between the inquisitive dog and me, straightened to her full height, then gazed around in wistful fashion, down into the valley of the North Fork, and north toward Noon Creek, and up toward the dark-timbered climb of Breed Butte between the two drainages, and at last around to me again. "This is real good country for rocks, Jick," she said hopefully.

It was my turn to gesture grandly. "Helen, any rocks in my posses-sion"—and on the land we stood on I had millions of them—"you are absolutely welcome to."

My sheepherder's change of career to rocks had not left my mind by that evening, but it did have to stand in line with everything else.

Kenny and Darleen and I were just done with supper when some-thing about the size of a red breadbox buzzed into the yard and parked in the shadow of the Bago. Some dry-fly fisherman wanting to see how Noon Creek trout react to pieces of fuzz on the end of a line, was our unanimous guess, but huh uh. Doors of the squarish little red toy opened and out of it unfolded Mariah and Riley.

"It's a Yugo," Mariah informed us before I could even open my trap to ask, once she'd pecked me a kiss and said hi to Kenny and Darleen and they'd had the dubious pleasure of meeting Riley. "As close as the *Montanian*'s budget will ever come to Riley's dream of renting a Buick convertible."

"She just has no concept of what an expense account is for," Riley confided to Kenny and Darleen as if they were his lifelong co-conspirators. "I could have done arithmetic camouflage on that Buick so easy."

"Oh, sure, I can see it now—*'pencils and paper, $97.50 a day,'*" Mariah mocked him right back but with most of a grin. "Send the BB a signed confession while you're at it, why don't you."

Well, well, well. Positively sunny, were they both, after their Helena delving. That was one thing about Mariah—putting herself to work always improved her mood. Apparently the same was true of goddamn Riley. They seemed to have found their writing and picture-taking legs. Until one of them next delivered the other a kick with a frozen overshoe again, anyway.

"Darleen, don't you think travel agrees with him?" my newly zippy daughter turned her commentary onto me. "Except for his facial grooming." It was something, how Mariah could be bossy and persuasive at the same time. Yet I didn't even bristle at that, appreciably, because I was too busy noticing how much she looked in her element here. In this kitchen, this house—this ranch—where she had grown up. She moved as if the air recognized her and sped her into grooves it had been saving for her, as she crossed the kitchen and planted her fanny against the sink counter in the perfect comfortable lean to be found there, reaching without needing to look into the silverware drawer for forks for Riley and her when Darleen tried to negotiate supper into them and they compromised with her on monstrous pieces of rhubarb pie. Every motion, as smooth as if she knew it blindfolded. Then it struck me. Mariah *was* the element here. The grin as she kept kidding with Darleen and Kenny and Riley was her mother's grin, Marcella's quick wit glinting in this kitchen once again. The erectness, the well-defined collarbones that stated that life was about to be firmly breasted through—those were *my* mother's, definitive Beth McCaskill who had been born on this ranch as a Reese. Born of Anna Ramsay Reese, *ever her own pilot through life, is my Anna.* And on the Scotch Heaven side, the McCaskill side, Adair odd in her ways but persevering for as long as there was anything to persevere for. Mariah: as daughter, granddaughter, great-granddaughter, the time-spun sum of them all? Yet her own distinct version as well. The lanky grace that begins right there in her face and flows down the longish but accomplished geometries of her body, the turn of mind that takes her into the cave of her camera, those are her own, Mariah rara.

And couple Riley with her, the set of shoulders that had shrugged off my offer of this ranch. Right now he was as electric as that commotion of hair of his, regaling Kenny and Darleen with the time he'd written in his column that *some of the Governor's notions are vast and some are half-vast* and the BB didn't get it until the Guv's press secretary angrily called and suggested he try reading it out loud. I had to grant, there was a mind clicking behind that wiseacre face. There were a lot of places in the world where they would license Riley's head as a dangerous weapon. I eyed him relentlessly while the general chitchat was going on, wanting to see some sign of regret or other bother show up in him here on the ranch he had rejected, here across the kitchen from the woman he could have made that future with. I might as well have wished for him to register earthquakes in China.

"I gotta see what's under the hood of that Hugo," Kenny soon exclaimed, squirming up out of his chair. "You want to come take a look, Darleen?"

"Thanks just the same," demurred Darleen placidly. "Don't look too long, hon. We've got to get to Choteau. My folks' anniversary," she explained to the rest of us. "We hate like anything to miss the centennial shindig in town tonight, but you can tell us all about it in the morning, Jick."

This caused me to ponder Darleen and whether there was some kind of secret sisterhood by which she had become an ally of Althea Frew, but I ultimately dismissed the suspicion. Darleen isn't your ally type. Anyway I now had to tell Mariah what my centennial involvement was all about—Riley had his ears hanging out too—and transmit the request for her to take some commemorative pictures for Gros Ventre posterity. She rolled her eyes at the mention of Althea, but concluded as I did that we might as well go in tonight and get it over with.

"Mind if I tag along?" Riley asked in a supersweet way.

"Yeah," I confirmed. "But I imagine you will anyway, huh?"

"No problem," he asserted, which had become a major part of his vocabulary since we met up with the Baloney Expressers. "I'll be next thing to invisible."

The sun was flattening down behind Roman Reef for the night as the three of us left for town. Behind us the peaks and crags of the Rocky Mountain Front were standing their tallest there at the deepening of evening, while the Two Medicine country around us rested in soft shadows unrolling under that sunset outline of the mountains. This may be my own private theory about such summer evenings but it has always seemed to me that lulls of this sort are how a person heals from the other weather of this land, for the light calmly going takes with it the grievances that the Two is a country where the wind wears away at you on a daily basis, where drought is never far from happening, where the valley bottoms now in the perfect shirtsleeve climate of summer dusk were thirty-five degrees below zero in the nights of February.

The Bago kept pace with that pretty time between day and night as the road swung up onto the benchland between Noon Creek and English Creek. Until, of course, Riley set things off. Maybe a genealogist could trace whether his talent for aggravation ran in the family for hundreds of generations or whether the knack was a spontaneous cosmic outbreak with him like, say, sunspots. Either way, there on the road into town he apparently did not even need to try, to succeed in ruffling my feathers. Merely gawked ahead at the strategic moment and declared, "I'll be damned. Ye Olde Wild West comes to Noon Creek, hmm?"

"Aw, that bastardly thing," I murmured in disgust. "If they want something weird hung, they ought to hang themselves up by their—"

But he'd roused Mariah and her camera. In the passenger seat she suddenly spoke up. "No, wait, Riley's right." Since when? The next was inevitable. "Pull over," she directed, "and let me get some shots of that against those clouds."

The summer sky, with a couple of hours of evening light yet to be eked out, was streaked with high goldenish strands, the decorative dehydrated kind called mare's tail. Clouds are one matter and what's under them is another. Beside us where I had reluctantly halted the motorhome stood the main gate into the Double W. A high frame made of a crosspiece supported by posts big as telephone poles and almost as tall, it had loomed in the middle of that benchland for as long as I could remember. Until not so many years ago the sign hanging from the crosspiece had proclaimed the Williamsons as owners of everything that was being looked at. Now it read:

WW RANCH
INCORPORATED

More than that, though. Just under the sign, a steer skull swung in the breeze where it was hung on a cable between the gateposts. Weather-bleached white as mica, short curved Hereford horns point- ing, eye sockets endlessly staring.

That skull locket against the Double W sky was the idea of one of the managers who'd been sent out before Shaun Finletter was installed in the job a year or so ago. Goddamn such people. I drove past that dangling skull whenever I went to or from town and it got my goat every single time. That skull, I knew, was from a boneyard in a coulee near my east fenceline with the Double W, where there were the car- casses of hundreds of head of Double W cattle that piled up and died in the blizzard of 1979. Even the Williamsons, who always had more cattle than they had country for and took winter die-offs as part of their way of business, never used the skulls as trinkets.

"Guess what, I need somebody in the foreground for scale," Mariah called over from where she was absorbedly sighting through her cam- era. "Somebody real western. Jick, how about if you and your Stetson come stand there under the—"

"I will not."

The flat snap of refusal, in my tone of voice as much as my words— hell, in *me*—startled her. She whirled around to me, her hair swinging, with an odd guilty look.

"Sorry," Mariah offered, rare enough for her, too. "But it's a shot I ought to take. The way it looms there over everything, it makes a state- ment."

"I know what it makes."

In my mind's eye I saw how I would like to do the deed. Wait until dark. Nothing but blackness on either side of this benchland road until the Double W gateframe comes into the headlights. I flip onto bright, for all possible illumination for this, and stop the Bago about seventy- five feet from the gateway, its sign and the skull under swaying slightly in the night breeze that coasts down along Noon Creek. I reach to the passenger seat where the shotgun is riding, step out of the motorhome and go in front of the headlights to load both barrels of the weapon. Bringing the butt of the shotgun to my shoulder I sight upward. Do I imagine, or does the steer skull seem to sway less, quiet itself in the breeze, as I aim? I fire both barrels at once, shards and chunks of the skull spraying away into the night. One eye socket and horn dangle from the wire. Close enough. I climb back in the Bago and head toward a particularly remote sinkhole I know of to dispose of the shotgun.

I brought myself back from that wishdream, to Mariah, to what we were saying to each other. "Take a picture of the goddamn thing if you think you have to," I finished to her, "but it's going to be without me in it."

All was as silent as the suspended clouds for a long moment. Then Riley came climbing over the gearbox hump of the Bago past me and out the passenger door. Without a word he strode across the road and centered himself in the gateway for my daughter.

One whole hell of a promising evening, then, by the time we hit Gros Ventre and were heading into the Medicine Lodge Bar. Bar and Cafe, I'd better get used to saying, for the enterprise took on a split personality when Fred Musgreave bought it a few years ago. The vital part, the bar, was pretty much the same as ever, a dark oaken span polished to a sacred shine by generations of elbows, its long mirror and shelves of bottles and glasses a reflective backdrop for contemplation. But the other half of the wide old wooden building, where there likely were poker tables in the early days and in more recent memory a lineup of maroon booths which were rarely patronized, Fred had closed off with a divider and turned that outlying portion into an eatery. ("Can't hurt," his economic reasoning ran. "Could help.") By this time of evening, though, tourists sped on through to Glacier Park for the night and anybody local who was going to eat supper out would have done so a couple of hours ago, and thus Fred didn't mind providing the Medicine Lodge's dining side as the meeting place on centennial committee nights.

He must have had his moments of wishing these were paying customers, however. Through the cafe window we could see the place was pretty well jammed. Ranchers and farmers in there jawing at each other about crops and livestock prices, all trademarked with summer-tanned faces and pale foreheads as if bearing instructions *fit hat on at this line.* Of the women, a dressy few were in oldfangled centennial raiment, but most had restrained themselves. Beside me as we headed in I heard Mariah already grappling camera gear out of her Appaloosa bag.

The three of us stopped instantly inside the cafe door. We had to. Our feet were in a tangle of power cords, as if we'd gotten ensnared in some kind of ankle-high electrification project.

"Aw, crud," Riley uttered, grimacing up from the mess we'd stepped in to its source just inside the entryway. "Tonsil Vapor Purvis."

"There goes the neighborhood," agreed Mariah grimly.

Actually the television camera and tripod and lights and other gear were being marshaled by a pair of guys, but I did not have to be much of a guesser to pick out the one Riley and Mariah were moaning about. An expensive head of hair that was trying to be brown and red at the same time—Riley ultimately identified the shade for me as Koppel-tone—atop not nearly that boyish a face atop a robin's egg blue sport jacket; below the torso portion that fit on a television screen, bluejeans and jogging shoes.

"Well!" the figure let out in a whinnying way that turned the word into *weh-heh-heh-hell!* "Rileyboy!"

"And you managed to say that without a cue card," Riley answered in mock admiration. Tonsil Vapor Purvis didn't seem to know Mariah or even to care to, but his cameraman and her exchanged frosty nods.

"I haven't noticed you at any of the official centennial events," Tonsil Vapor informed Riley in a voice that rolled out on ball bearings. "Where are you keeping yourself?"

"Working," Riley stated as if that was a neighborhood the televi-sioneer naturally wouldn't be anywhere around.

"Isn't this centennial fantastic though?" declared Tonsil Vapor. "Have you had a chance to watch my Countdown 100 series?" When Riley shook his head, Tonsil Vapor rotated toward me. When I shook my head, he turned toward Mariah but she already had slid away and was taking pictures of people, cajoling and kidding with them as you can only when you've known them all your life.

"One hundred nightly segments on the centennial," Tonsil Vapor enunciated to the remaining captive pair of us to make sure we grasped the arithmetic.

"No kidding," Riley responded, gazing at Tonsil Vapor with

extreme attention as if the centennial was the newest of news and then jotting something down. When he turned the notepad so I could see it, it read: *A $25 haircut on a 25¢ head.*

"Builders of Montana, this week," the TVster was spelling out for us next. "We"—the royal We from the sound of it; the cameraman was showing no proprietary interest whatsoever—"are interviewing people about their occupational contribution to our great state. It occurred to me that an occasion like this, with oldtimers on hand," he sent me a bright smile, damn his blow-dried soul, "would turn up a fascinating livelihood of some kind."

"I don't have a paying occupation," I hastened to head off any interest in me as a specimen, "I'm a rancher."

"What do these epics of yours run, a minute forty?" asked Riley drily.

"No, no, the station is going all out on this. I'm doing *two-and-a-half-minute* segments, would you believe."

Riley let out a little cluck as if that was pretty unbelievable, all right, then sardonically excused himself to go get to work lest television leave him even farther back in the dust. Still leery of being a candidate for oldtimer of the night, I closely tagged off after Riley. We left Tonsil Vapor Purvis fussing to his cameraman, "This doesn't make it for my opening stand-up. Let's set up over there instead."

"Fucking human gumball machine," Riley was muttering as we rounded the partition between the cafe counter and the dining area in back. "Fucking television has the attention span of a—"

He halted so abruptly I smacked into his back. Riley, though, never even seemed to notice, in the stock-still way he was staring toward the rear of the cafe.

"WHAT is *that?*" his eventual question piped out in a three-note tune.

Golden as the light of the dawn sun, the cloth creation emblazoned the entire back wall of the cafe and then some. That is, the roomwide cascade of fabric flowed down from where it was tacked on lath along the top of the wall and surged up like a cresting molten wave at the worktables and quilting frames where stitchery was being performed on it, then spilled forward onto the floor in flaxen pools of yet to be sewn material.

Add in all the people bent over sewing machines or plucking away with needles or just hovering around admiring and gabbing, and I suppose you could think, as Riley obviously did, that the town of Gros Ventre had gone on a binge and decided to tent itself over.

"Just what it looks like," I enlightened the scribbler. "Our centennial flag."

Mariah whizzed past us.

"Looks like they're getting ready to declare independence, doesn't it," she appraised the room-swallowing flag and kept right on going to zero in on the sewing battalion.

Riley still stood there gawking like a moron trying to read an eye-chart, although the flag didn't seem to me all that tough to decipher. Plain as anything, the line of designs spaced across its top like a border pattern was livestock:

And down the sides the motifs were homestead cabins and ranch houses:

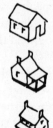

And although the sewing brigade had a way to go to get there, it only took the least imagination to see that the bottom border needed to be forest and stream:

In extenuation of Riley, it was true that the flag's full effect would not register until all the other elements were in place on it. The project the Heart Butte schoolkids were doing, for instance, of a Blackfeet chief's headdress in black and white cloth to resemble eagle feathers—rampant, as is said in flag lingo. And the combined contribution of the English Creek and Noon Creek ranch families, one entire cloth panel—the flag was so big it was being done in lengthwise sections, which were then quilted together—which was going to be a sawtooth pattern of purple-blue embroidery all the way across, signifying the mountains across the Two country's western skyline. Then at the hem of the mountains would come a cluster of buildings, being sewn away at by several townspeople even as Riley and I watched, to represent Gros Ventre: the spiked helmet outline of the Sedgwick House hotel, the sharp church steeples, the oldstyle square front of the Medicine Lodge itself, and so on. Finally, to top it all off, so to speak, for actually this constituted the very center of the whole flag scheme: the sun. Atop a dark seam of horizon the molten arc of it, spiffily done in reddish orange fabric that even looked hot, just beginning to claim the sky for the day. And over, under, and around the sun, in mighty letters of black, the message:

THE TWO MEDICINE COUNTRY

1889   1989

GREETS THE DAWN OF MONTANA

Riley at last managed to show some vital signs. He wondered out loud, plenty loud:

"Who thought up this sucker?"

That particular question I was not keen to deal with because, when you traced right back to it, the party who brought up the flag idea in the first place was more or less me. History's jukebox, John Angus McCaskill. It had been last fall when our steering committee was flummoxing around for some event worthy of marking Montana's centennial with, when Althea Frew pined what a shame it was that we didn't know what had gone on in Gros Ventre that epic day of statehood a hundred years ago. All the cue needed, of course, for me to spout off what I'd so long ago heard from Toussaint Rennie, that the 1889 citizenry of Gros Ventre, such as there was of it back then, took it into their collective head to be the very first to fly the revised American flag when

Montana came onto it as the forty-first star and so got up early enough to do that municipal flag-hoisting at the exact crack of day. Which inspired some other member of our committee to suggest that we simply emulate our forebears by raising a forty-one-starred flag at dawn on Centennial Day. But that was objected to as a backward step, nine of them in fact, in stars-and-stripes history. Okay, somebody else proposed, then let's put up a present-day American flag but a monumentally big one. But somebody yet again made the point that there were already in existence flags damn near as big as America itself—weren't we seeing Bush practically camped out in front of a whopper of a one during the presidential election campaign?—and we didn't have a prayer of competing in size. You might know it would be Althea who hatched the plan of making our own flag. Contrive our version as big as we could without smothering ourselves in it, sure, but most of all, design and fabricate the whole thing ourselves and hoist the Two Medicine country and Gros Ventre's own heralding banner at dawn on the centennial.

"It just kind of occurred," I summarized in answer to Riley and moved on into the needlery scene, tagged after by him. Primarily the women were getting things accomplished there at the sewing machines and worktables while the men mostly were standing around looking wise, both sets being duly chronicled by Mariah and her camera. Being greeted by the dozens and greeting back in equal number, I wound my way through the assemblage until I reached the quilting frame which held the panel our English Creek–Noon Creek mountain panorama was being embroidered on.

Lifelong familiar outlines met me there. Roman Reef's great bow of rimrock. The tall slopes of Phantom Woman Mountain. The Flume Gulch canyonline where Noon Creek has its source, and opposite that the comblike outcropping of Rooster Mountain. Really quite beautiful, how all the high skyline of the Two Medicine was transposed there onto the flag in heaviest darning yarn. All, that is, except the finale. The northmost mountain form, Jericho Reef's unmistakable wall-like silhouette, was sketched in pencil on the golden cloth for the next seamstress to follow.

Seamer, rather, for on the Jericho sketch was a pink paper stick-on with Althea's loopy but firm handwriting, which read:

Jick McCaskill—please stitch here!

So if Jericho was going to get sewn it was up to me, and there was no time like the present. "Got any socks you want darned, you should have brought them," I notified Riley and seated myself to perform fancywork.

"You know how to do that?" he asked skeptically as I plucked up the waiting needle and started trying to match the kind of stitches on the other thread mountains.

"Close enough," I said. "I've sewed shut more woolsacks than you can count."

Whether it was my example of industry or not, Riley suddenly snapped out of his tourist mode. "This night might actually turn into something. Hold the fort, Jick, I'm going out to the Bago for my listening gear."

Nature never likes a vacuum. No sooner was I shed of Riley than Howard Stonesifer happened by and stopped to spectate my labors. Which probably was good for my stitching because it lent a little feeling of scrutiny by posterity, Howard being the undertaker.

"Where you been keeping yourself?" Howard asked.

"Out and around," I summarized. "How's the burying business?"

"Mortally slow," he answered as he always did. "Isn't that Riley Wright I just bumped into?"

"I'm sorry to report, it is."

"Mariah and him are back together, eh?"

"They are not. They're just doing a bunch of these centennial stories togeth—with each other, is all. I'm traveling around with them while they do."

He studied down at me. "All three of you are together?"

"Well, yeah, together but not *together*. Thrown in with one another, more like. Howard, it's kind of complicated."

"I imagine it is," Howard said and departed.

My next visitor was none other than Mariah, who by now had cut her photographic swath across the room to those of us at the sewing frames and tables.

"I bet you never knew Betsy Ross had a beard," I addressed to her, jabbing my needle elegantly into the flagcloth as she neared.

It didn't even register on her. She wore a puzzled frown and even more uncharacteristically had dropped the camera from her eyes and was drilling a snake-killing gaze across the room.

I leaned out and saw for myself what was bugging her. Our centennial bunch was not exactly a youth group and wherever there was a Gros Ventrian wearing glasses, which was to say virtually everywhere, bright points of light glittered off both lenses. Or if a person happened to be anywhere near a wall, his or her skin was paled out and huge shadows were flung up behind the wan spectre. Any shot by Mariah was going to look like fireflies flitting through a convalescent ward.

Perfectly unconcerned about dazzling the populace, Tonsil Vapor had decided our centennial flag was a backdrop worthy of him and was having his cameraman move the lightstands here and there in front of the sewing tables. What astounded me was that everybody was pretending to be unaware they were being immersed in a pool of television light. Squint and bear it, was the code of the televised.

Not with Mariah. Under the pressure of her glower, the TV cameraman roused himself enough to shrug and indicate with a jerk of his head that Tonsil Vapor was the impresario here. Tonsil Vapor meanwhile was holding his sport-jacket sleeve against the wall of flag to make sure robin's egg blue went well with golden.

Mariah marched on him.

"Hey, I'm getting bounce from your lights in every shot I try. How about please holding off for a couple of minutes until I'm done back here?"

"We're setting up for my opening stand-up," Tonsil Vapor informed her.

"I can tell you are. How-about-turning-off-your-lights-for-two-minutes-while-I-finish-shooting-here."

"Television has every right to be here," Tonsil Vapor huffed. "This is a public event."

"That's the whole fucking point," Mariah elucidated. "It's not yours to hog."

"Let's do my stand-up," Tonsil Vapor directed past her to his cameraman and focused his concern on whether his tie was hanging straight.

"Whoa," Mariah told the TV pair. "If you're so determined to shoot, we'll all shoot."

She reached in her gear bag and pulled out a fresh camera, aiming it into the pleasantly surprised visage of Tonsil Vapor. I was more than surprised: it was the motorized one she'd used to take the rapid-fire photographs of the marauding buffalo bull at Moiese. Tonsil Vapor Purvis didn't look to me like he was that much of a mobile target.

With the bright wash of light on him, he fingered the knot of his tie. Brought his microphone up. Aimed his chin toward the lens of the

TV camera. "Ready?" he asked his cameraman, although with a little peek out the corner of his eye at Mariah to make sure she was set to shoot, too. The TV cameraman echoed "Ready" flatly back.

"This is Paul *whingwhingwhing* Purvis, bringing you another Countdown 100 *whingwhingwhing* moment from here in *whingwhing*—"

"Cut!" yelped the cameraman, pulling the earphones out away from his ears. Mariah quit firing the motorized shutter and the ricochet sounds stopped.

Tonsil Vapor swiveled his head toward her. "Your camera. We're picking up the noise."

"That's okay, no charge," Mariah answered calmly, keeping the offending camera zeroed into Tonsil Vapor's face. "You've been donating all kinds of light into my photography."

"Seriously, here," Tonsil Vapor said, a bit pouty. "We have an opening stand-up to do."

"Up you and your stand-up both," Mariah told him. "This is a public event and my gear has every right to be here."

Tonsil Vapor stared at her. Uncertainly he edged the microphone up toward his mouth. Mariah triggered off a couple of *whing*s and he jerked the mike back down.

With a scowl, Tonsil Vapor swiveled his head the other direction and addressed his cameraman. "Can we edit out her noise?" The cameraman gave him the French salute, shrugging his shoulders and raising the palms of his hands at the same time.

Tonsil Vapor visibly thought over the matter. Mariah did not bring the commotional camera down from her eye until he announced, "Actually, the bar is a more picturesque spot to do my opening stand-up."

Riley, prince of oblivion, sashayed back in from the Bago with his tape recorder as TVdom was withdrawing to the bar and Mariah was setting to work again on the sewing scene at the far end of the flag. He made a beeline to me.

"Quite a turnout, Jick," he observed brilliantly.

"Mmhmm," I replied and sewed onward.

"Lots of folks," he said as if having tabulated.

"Quite a bunch," I confirmed.

"I was wondering if you could kind of sort them out to me, so I can figure out good ones to talk to," he admitted, indicating to the tape recorder as if this was the machine's idea rather than his. "You know more about everybody here than they do about themselves."

"Gee, Riley, I wouldn't know where to start." I did a couple more stitches before adding: "Everybody in the Two country is equally unique."

Had I wanted, I indeed could have been Riley's accomplice on almost anyone in that filled room, for the Two Medicine country was out in force tonight. These are not the best of times for towns like Gros Ventre or the rural neighborhoods they are tied to. The young go away, the discount stores draw shopping dollars off to bigger places, the land that has always been the hope of such areas is thinner and thinner of people and promise. Yet, maybe because the human animal cannot think trouble all the time, anybody with a foot or wheel to get here had come tonight to advance the community's centennial rite. All the couples from the ranches along English Creek: Harold and Melody Busby, Bob and Janie Rozier, Olaf and Sonia Florin. From up the South Fork, Tricia and Gib Hahn, who ran the old Withrow and Hahn ranches combined. My longtime Noon Creek neighbor Tobe Egan, retired to town now. A number of the farm families from out east of town, Walsinghams and Priddys and Van Der Wendes, Tebbetses and Kerzes and Joneses. Townspeople by battalions: Joe and Myrna Prentiss from the Merc, the Muldauers who ran the Coast-to-Coast hardware store, Jo Ann and Vern Cooder from the Rexall drugstore. Riley's infinite faith in me to the contrary, one pair I didn't know the names of yet—the young couple who had opened a video parlor where The Toggery clothing store used to be. The bank manager Norman Peyser and his wife Barbara. Flo and Sam Vissert from the Pastime Bar three doors down the street. Others and others—not least, the new Gros Ventrian whom I addressed now as he bustled past Riley and me carrying a coffee urn as big as he was. "Nguyen, how you doing?"

"Doing just right!" Nguyen Trang Hoc and his wife Kieu and their three kids were being sponsored by a couple of the churches there in town. They were boat people, had come out of Vietnam in one of those hell voyages. Nguyen worked as a waiter here in the Medicine Lodge cafe, already speaking English sentences of utmost enthusiasm: "Here is your menu! I will let you look! Then we will talk some more!"

Naturally Riley was scanning the night's civic outpouring in his own cockeyed way. "Who's the resurrection of Buffalo Bill over there?" he asked, blinking inquisitively toward the figure hobbling ever so slowly through the front door.

"Aw," I began, "that's just—" and then the brainstorm caught up with me.

I identified the individual to Riley with conspicuous enthusiasm. "Been here in the Two country since its footings were poured. You might find him highly interesting to talk to. Garland's kind of a shy type, but I bet if you tell him you're from the newspaper that would encourage him a little."

"History on the hoof, hmm?" Riley perked right up and headed toward the front. "You're starting to show real talent for this centennial stuff, Jick."

While it is true I was the full length of the cafe away from Riley's introduction to the arrivee, there was no lack of volume to hearing what followed.

"NEWSPAPER! JUST THE GUY I WANT TO SEE! YOUNG FELLOW, WHAT YOU OUGHT TO BE WRITING A STORY ABOUT IS ME! YOU KNOW, I WAS BORN WITH THE GOSHDAMN CENTURY!"

Eyes rolled in all of us who were within earshot, which was to say everybody in the Medicine Lodge. Multiply the crowd of us by the total of times we had each heard the nativity scene of Good Help Hebner and you had a long number. Riley didn't seem grateful to be the first fresh listener of this eon, either. The look he sent me still had sting in it after traveling the length of the cafe. I concentrated on needlework and maintaining a straight face. "BY NOW HALF THIS COUNTRY IS HEBNERS, YOUNG FELLOW! AND I STARTED EVERY ONE OF THEM OUT OF THE CHUTE!"

Riley had no way of knowing it but that particular procreatorial brag was as close to the truth as Good Help was ever likely to come. Which made me shake my head all the more at the fact that it had taken the old so-and-so until his eighty-ninth year to start looking paternal, let alone patriarchal. For as long as I could remember, Good Help—need I say, that nickname implied the exact opposite—had lazed through life under about a week's grayish grizzle of whiskers; never enough to count as an intentional beard, never so little as to signify he had bothered to shave within recent memory. But now for the centennial he somehow had blossomed forth in creamy mustache and goatee. To me it still was a matter of close opinion whether Good Help more resembled Buffalo Bill or a billy goat, but definitely his new facial adornment was eyecatching.

"YOU GOT TO GO DO WHAT, YOUNG FELLOW? SPEAK UP, I'M GET-
TING SO DEAF I CAN'T HEAR MYSELF FART!" I couldn't actually hear
either the excuse Riley was employing to extricate himself, but Good
Help provided everybody in town the gist of it: "GOT TO GO SEE A MAN
ABOUT A DOG, HUH? YOU KNOW WHAT THEY SAY, STAND UP CLOSE
TO THE TROUGH, THE NEXT FELLOW MIGHT BE BAREFOOT!"

While Riley now tried to make an invisible voyage to the men's
room in the bar half of the Medicine Lodge, I chuckled and checked on
Mariah's doings. Easily enough done. She was wearing the turquoise
shirt she'd had on at the Fourth of July rodeo and you could see her
from here to Sunday. As she gravitated through the crowd, ever scouting for the next camera moment, it struck me what a picture she made
herself.

"Oh, Jick, I'm so relieved to see you here," Althea Frew pounced in
on me out of nowhere. In her centennial getup of a floor-length ging-
ham dress with a poke bonnet, she looked as if she'd just trundled in by
prairie schooner. "We were afraid you'd given up on the committee."

"Would I do that?" I denied, right then wishing I had.

"It's nice to see you back in the swim of things," she assured me and
patted my arm. Althea was the kind of person full of pats. "Can't I bring
you a cup of coffee?" she offered avidly.

Only if it is big enough for me to torpedo you in, I thought to
myself. Dave Frew had died of emphysema a year or so ago and all too
evidently Althea had formed the notion that because she was a widow
and I now was a widower, we were going to be an ordained pair at gatherings such as this. My own notion was, like hell we were. Already I had
dodged her on card parties and square dancing at the Senior Citizens'
Center. Althea seemed to regard me as an island just waiting to have her
airdropped onto it. Let her land and there'd be an instant new civilization, activities for all my waking hours. Christamighty, I more than
anybody knew that I needed refurbishing of some kind from my grief
for Marcella. But to put myself up for adoption by Althea . . .

"You take it with just a dab of cream, don't you?" Uh oh. She'd already
started to catalogue me. I knew where that would go. If she inkled out the
dosage in my coffee, as the night follows the day it would lead to how
crisp I like my fish fried and from there onward to my favorite piece of
music, on and on until she would know my underwear size.

"Black," I lied. "Don't bother, I'll get myself a cup, I was about to
head that direction anyhow."

As I recessed from my sewing and tried to tactically retreat to the coffee urn, Althea fell in step as if I'd invited her along. Wasn't this just ducky, now. She had us in motion in tandem in public, a hearts-and-flowers advertisement for the whole town to see. I craned around for Mariah's reaction to this. For once I was thankful to have her immersed in her picture-taking, across the room with her back to Althea and me as she immortalized Janie Rozier zinging a seam of the flag through her sewing machine.

I will swear on any Bible, I did not have anything major against Althea Frew. But I had nothing for her, either. True, Marcella and I had known her and Dave ever since we were young ranch couples starting out. Neighbors, friends, people who partnered each other a few times a night at dances, but not more than that. You cannot love everyone you know. Love isn't a game of tag, now you're it, now she's it.

I sipped at the plastic cup of coffee Althea bestowed on me and tried not to wince at its bitter taste. For that matter, I had no illusions that Althea was after me for my irresistible romantic allure. Simply put, pickings were slim in the Two Medicine country for women who outlived their husbands, as most of them showed every sign of doing. Here tonight for instance, Howard Stonesifer was one of those mother-smothered bachelors; Althea knew that even if old lady Stonesifer ever passed on, there was no denting Howard's set of habits. Tobe Egan over in the corner was a widower but his health was shot, and why should Althea take on another ill case after the years she had spent with Dave's emphysema? Go through this entire community and the actuarial tables were pretty damn bare for Althea's brand of husband-looking. Which was why yours truly was about to be the recipient of a whopping piece of the *Happy Birthday, Montana!* cake Althea was now adoringly cutting.

Right then Riley re-emerged from the direction of the men's room, cautiously checking around for the whereabouts of Good Help Hebner. I was not keen on fending with him just then, particularly if he was going to notice the close company Althea was keeping me, but it turned out Riley was pointedly ignoring my existence and instead migrated directly to Mariah.

Whatever he was saying to her, for once it seemed to be in earnest. She listened to him warily, but listened. Then came her speaking turn, and he nodded and nodded as if he couldn't agree more. It dawned on me that they must be conferring about whether to do a piece about tonight. I willed Mariah to tell him to go straight to hell, that their mutual woe of ending up in marriage had started here when she shot and he wrote that earlier Gros Ventre centennial shindig. Instead she studied him with care, then turned and pondered the cafeful of people as if taking inventory. While Althea yattered at me and I took solace in cake, Mariah led Riley over near us where Nan Hill, snow-haired and tiny with age, was sitting sewing.

"Nan, this man would like to talk to you for a story in the newspaper. How about telling him about doing the washing at Fort Peck while I take a picture, would you mind?" As Riley moved in with his tape recorder and a smile that would make you want to take him home and give him a bed by the fire, Mariah checked her light meter, then stood back, biting her lower lip as she held the camera up under her neck, lens pointing up, waiting. Waiting. Then ahead of the moment but somehow having seen it on its way, she swiftly but unobtrusively shifted the camera over to her eye as the old woman warmed into the telling.

> *Age is humped on her small back. It began to descend there in 1936 in daily hours over a washboard, scrubbing at the Missouri-mudded clothing of the men at labor on the biggest earthen dam in the world, Fort Peck. "We went there with just nothing and J. L. got on as a roustabout. I wanted to find some way of earning, too, so I put up a sign Laundry Done Here. I charged 15¢ for shirts—and that was washed, ironed, mended and loose buttons sewed on—and 10¢ for a pair of shorts, another 10¢ for an undervest, 5¢ for a handkerchief, and 10¢ for a pair of socks. Any kind of pants was 25¢ for washing and pressing. I had the business, don't think I didn't. Those three years at Fort Peck, I always had six lines of clothes hanging in the yard."*

The waltz of the camera, Riley following, led on from Nan to the Hoc family, Mariah poising in that long-legged crouch of hers while focusing on the little Hoc girl, her left hand under the camera cupping it upward in an offering way, right hand delicately fingering the lens setting, her shoulderlong flow of hair behind the camera like an extravagant version of the hood a photographer of old would hide his head under, and her voice going through a repertoire of coaxes until one brought out on the little Hoc girl what was not quite a smile but an expression more beautiful than that, Mariah telling her as if they had triumphed together, "Thaaat's what I want to see."

> *They are Asian delta people, newly come to American mountain headwaters. Their immense journey pivots on the children, especially on the lithe daughter made solemnly older by the presence of two cultures within her. Driver's license, income tax, television, food budget, rock music, all the reckless spill of America must come to her family through the careful funnel of this ten-year-old woman who is now the mother of words to her own parents.*

Althea was saying in my ear now, "It's so nice to see Riley back in your family. He and Mariah make such a wonderful couple."

"They are not—"

"People their age, they should take happiness while they can, don't you think?"

What I thought was that people any age shouldn't be trying to fool one another. That I should be able to say flat out to Althea, "Look, terms have not changed between us even though our lives have. I am not second-husband material for you, so kindly just put the pattern away, please."

But that was blunter than can be spoken in a room crowded with everyone who knew us. Even so, Althea didn't take the chance that I might blurt the impolite truth. "Oh foo, look what time it's gotten to be already. I'd better go look over the agenda for our meeting. It'll seem so much more like a committee now that you're back, Jick," she left me with, but not before a last fond assault on my arm, pat pat.

My ears got the next unwelcome traffic, a mimicking voice approaching fast: "He's kind of a shy type, but I bet if you tell him you're from the newspaper . . ."

Innocence seemed the best tack to take with Riley right then. "Get a lot of fascinating stuff out of Good Help, did you?"

"Gobs and gobs," he replied sardonically. "I figured I'd write that he's as intrinsically American as the Mississippi River."

"Oh yeah?"

"Yeah. A mile wide at the mouth."

"Gee," I said, genuinely interested in the prospect, "if you say that in the newspaper about a guy, won't he sue your nuts off?"

"Put your mind at ease," Riley told me. "Jick, damn you, you know that old codger could talk for a week and only ever tell the truth by accident. Even the BB would recognize it as the rankest kind of bullshit." Riley's two-toned gaze left me and went to the wall of fabric behind me. "The real story here is that humongous flag. If you characters ever manage to get it in the air." Riley scanned the room as if in search of anyone capable of that feat. He got as far as Althea, busy in her bonnet, and inquired: "By the way, who's your ladyfriend?"

"She is not—"

"Bashful never won the bushelful," he trilled out, god damn him. "Don't worry, I won't snitch to Mariah that you're busy girling behind her back. So, what's next in this festive evening?"

Barbecuing a fatmouthed newspaper guy over a slow fire, was what I wished could be next on the agenda. But instead I told Riley I had my needlework to tend to, in a tone that let him know it was a pursuit preferable to conversation with him, and headed myself from the coffee urn toward the Two Medicine mountainline panel of the flag.

I wasn't much more than in motion before a voice called out:

"Talk to you a minute can I, Jick?"

I was beginning to wonder: was there a procession all the way out into the street of people lined up to take aim on me?

This voice was that of Shaun Finletter from the Double W and so I at least knew what the sought minute of talk was going to be about. I turned around to Shaun's faceful of blondish fuzz—some of these beardgrowers were maybe going to need a deadline extension to Montana's *bi*centennial—and responded as civilly as I could manage: "How's tricks?"

"Oh, not bad, Jick. Yourself?"

"Just trying to stay level."

Shaun then plunged right down to business, which was the way Finletters were.

"Jick, I been hearing from headquarters. They're still real interested in making you an offer on your place."

"Are they." I felt like adding, are you sure that was headquarters making itself heard instead of hindquarters? But Shaun was a neighbor, even if I did wish his bosses in big offices would take a long walk off a short balcony.

Shaun rattled it off to me. "It's nothing against you at all, Jick . . . just a matter of big-scale economics . . . better able to put maximum animal units on that land . . ." The Double Dub had a great history of that, all right. Running more cattle than it had country for. The original Williamson, Warren, had practically invented overgrazing, and his son Wendell got in on buying up bankrupt smaller ranches during the Depression and *really* sandwiched cattle along Noon Creek from hell to breakfast, and now the corporation computers doubtless were unitizing cows and calves onto every last spear of grass.

Yet it was their business and none of my own, how the Williamsons or the corporaiders comported themselves on WW land they had title to. The patch of earth *I* held title to was the matter here, and Shaun now stated the dollars per acre, a damn impressive sum of them, that WW, Inc. would pay to take the ranch off my hands. "You know that's top dollar, the way things are, Jick."

Shaun was a nice enough human being. Someone who would look you square in the eye, as he was now while I scanned back at him and noticed he was growing beefier, a little more face, a bit more belly, than since I'd last seen him. Actually just a year or so older than Mariah, he and she had gone together a while in high school. My God, the way things click or don't. If that had worked out into marriage instead of her going on to photography and him to an ag econ degree at Bozeman, Shaun might well have been the answer to run my ranch; might have become the one to perpetually tell the Williamsons and WW, Inc. of the world to go to hell, instead of being their errand boy to me.

If I had pounds more of brains I might be smarter, too. I struggled to get myself back on the necessary train of thought. How to reply to the dollar sign. It wasn't as if I hadn't had practice closing one or both eyes to money. The first corporate guy, who'd acted as if he already owned my ranch and me as well, I'd told to stick his offer where the sun doesn't shine. All the others since, one or two every year, I'd just told nothing doing. But now here I was being perfectly polite with Shaun because even though he was the current factotum, I had known his family and him from when he was a waggy pup. Even I had to admit I seemed to be trending away from that original stick-it stance.

Click.

Shaun gave a little jump as if he'd been goosed. For once I didn't even mind that Mariah included me in her picture ambush. It was worth it to see the caught-while-sucking-eggs expression on Shaun.

"Don't let me interrupt Noon Creek man talk," Mariah put forth coolly with the camera still up to her eye. This was a different one than

I'd yet seen her use tonight. Did she possibly have a calibre for every occasion?

"It'll keep," said Shaun, wincing at the next *click*. Maybe it had been purely coincidental but after splitting up with Mariah he all but instantly married Amber, who notably stayed home and raised kids. "Think the proposition over and let me know, Jick. Mariah, it's always an event to see you," and he headed rapidly off out of pointblank range.

"He always was about halfway to being a dork," Mariah mentioned as we watched Shaun retreat. "He even necked like he was doing math."

"Yeah, well, he's maybe getting better at his calculations," I let her know. "You sure you don't want a ranch?"

"You saw how far I've gotten from the place," Mariah answered after a moment. "On the way into town."

It took me a moment, too, to discard that incident at the Double W gate. "I guess when you get to my age you're a little touchy about skulls."

"Quit that," she directed quickly. "You're much too young to be as old as you are."

Didn't I wish. But I let that pass and instead took Mariah by the elbow and turned her around to the golden flood of flag cloth. "Something I need you to do." I indicated to the panel where I'd sewn Jericho Reef halfway to completion; the panel for the McCaskills to have their stitches ride the wind on. "Sit down there and immortalize yourself."

"You promise I won't get a reputation for domesticity?" she kidded, but I could see she was tickled pink to be included in the centennial stitchwork.

"Probably not much danger," I said, and we laughed together as we hadn't for a long time.

So Mariah sat and had at it, the needle disappearing and then tugging through another dark dash of the mountainline above the ranch earth where we were both born. "It's like putting ourselves on a quilt, isn't it," her similar thought came out quietly.

"Kind of, yeah." I stood and watched her neat intense work with the needle. "But the next hundred years don't look that simple."

She knew I meant the ranch and whether to sell now or stagger on. "How are you leaning?"

"Both directions. Any advice from somebody redheaded would be a whole lot welcome."

Mariah crinkled a little face and I thought she'd stuck herself. But it turned out to be the topic that was sharp.

"You know I couldn't wait to get off the place when I was growing up," she mused. "Away to college. Away to—where I've been. I got over that and before I knew it I was fond of the place again. The ranch meant, well, it meant you and Mother, in a way. As if it was part of you—some member of the family you and she made out of the land." Now Mariah addressed downward as if reasoning to the sliver of metal passing in and out of the cloth. "But it'll never be part of me in that same way. It hurts to say, but I'm just a visitor at the ranch any more. Lexa and I dealt ourselves out of it by going off to our own lives. That's what happens. You and Mother maybe didn't know you were raising an Alaskan and a Missoulian, but that's how we turned out, didn't we. So it has to be up to you what to do with the place, Dad. It's yours. Not ours in any way that we should have a say."

"You want me to walk over there and tell Shaun the Double Dub's got itself a deal, is that it?"

Mariah swallowed, but both the tug of her needle and the look she sent me stayed steady. "It's up to you," she stood by.

Maybe I would have made that journey across the room to Shaun, right then and there, if Mariah had not abruptly put down her needle in exchange for her camera, twirled a lens on, and aimed in sudden contemplation of something occurring behind me. In curiosity, not to mention self-defense, I shifted half-around to see.

Riley at work. He had sicced his tape recorder onto the lawyer Don Germain, who for once had the quite unlawyerly look that he wasn't sure how he got into this but didn't know how to get out either. Without being able to hear the words, I could tell by the carefully innocent way Riley asked his questions and Don's pursed lips as he cogitated his answers that the interview topic must be something fundamental.

How and when should we lift our own roots? Or as we more usually ask it in this spacious nation, how many times? His were temporarily shifted for him from Rhode Island after law school, when his military stint put him at Malmstrom Air Force Base in Great Falls. Malmstrom made him a galvanized westerner, the shirts with pearlescent snap buttons and the brass belt buckle proclaiming THE BUCKAROO STOPS HERE *on his outside but the original element underneath, so he chose a place (Gros Ventre, but it could have been any of a thousand others) to try this trafficless wide-sky life. He him-*

*self tells the joke that the town is too small for one lawyer but
big enough for two. Readily enough, too, he reveals his snug fit
into his generation's statistics: a second wife, two children,
considerable tonnage of vehicles-TVs-VCR-snowmobile-gas
barbecue-power tools-satellite dish. It is his wife, though, who
teasingly tells that he has been struggling with the decision of
whether to keep his centennial contest beard or not, because of
the gray showing up in it.*

*So, he meets middle age in the mirror these mornings
and they debate. "I've really liked living here, don't get me
wrong. Cathy and I both would hate to leave Montana. But
the money is better almost anywhere else you can name.
Sure, this has been a good place to raise the kids. But
whether to spend the rest of my life here . . ."*

Ever so casually I said to Mariah, "I see you and Riley are piecing up
a storm."

"We're managing to," she said, and picked up where she had left off
in her stitching.

While Mariah completed Jericho Reef, I decided I had better seize that
opportunity to heed a certain call of nature—damn Althea and her
loveydovey cups of coffee anyway—and headed myself into the bar
toward the men's room.

And popped around the corner into light so extreme it set me back
on my heels. Tonsil Vapor and accomplice had Good Help Hebner sitting there posed against the dark oaken bar.

Not even a TV guy would voluntarily go near Good Help if he
knew what he was getting himself into, would he? During my business
in the men's room I worked out what must have taken place: after his
opening stand-up Tonsil Vapor had poked his head back into the supper club, discerned Riley getting both ears loaded by Good Help, and
figured there was his ripe interview subject.

When I emerged, Fred Musgreave was behind the near end of the
bar, ever so slowly wiping the wood with a dish towel as he eyed the
million-watt spectacle. Fred by nature was so untalkative it was said of
him that he was an absentee owner even when he was here on the
premises of the Medicine Lodge, so I merely walked my fingers along

the bar top to indicate to him that this was a night that needed some Johnny and propped myself there to spectate, on the chance that television might be more interesting outside the box than in.

Poised beside Good Help, Tonsil Vapor gave a royal nod, the camera's red light lit up, and he intoned into his microphone: "Here with us now is tonight's builder of Montana, Gros Ventre's own Garland Hebner—born, as he likes to say, with the century. Mr. Hebner, first off let me ask you, what was your line of work?"

"I have did it all," our new TV star airily assured his interlocutor.

"I'm sure you have," emitted Tonsil Vapor with a chuckle that sounded a trifle forced. "But what I meant was, what did you do for a living?"

"I was what you call self-employed."

Self-unemployed was more like it. Garland Hebner's only known activity had been that one that produces children, and as soon as they were big enough to be sent out to herd lamb bunches in the spring or drive a stacker team in haying, Hebner child after Hebner child brought home the only wages that tatterdemalion household ever saw.

"Cut," called out Tonsil Vapor, looking nonplussed. "But Mr. Hebner, this is an interview about how you helped to build Montana. Isn't there *some* interesting job you held, sometime or another?"

This did stump Good Help. He sat there blinking as if each of his eighty-nine years was being projected one after another onto the inside of his eyelids. Until:

"By the Jesus, I remember now! Sure, I had a job! Goshdamn interesting one, too! What it was, I—"

"No, no, wait until we roll and tell me then. Spontaneity is the lifeblood of television, Mr. Hebner. Now, then. Ready?" The cameraman minimally indicated he was, and Good Help appeared to be absolutely primed and cocked. The instant the line-of-work question had been recited again, Good Help got hold of Tonsil Vapor's mike hand, drew the instrument almost into his mouth and pronounced in a kind of quavery roar:

"I was the pigfucker! One entire summer! Ought to been the summer of 19-and-18, no, was it 19-and—"

"Cut!" squawked Tonsil Vapor as if he just had been.

The TV maestro stepped back a large pace, his mouth twice as far open as it had been yet tonight. Holding the microphone protectively against his sport jacket, he took stock of Good Help.

Eventually he managed, "Mr. Hebner, I'm afraid you misheard my question. What I asked you was what you did for a *living*, not—"

"I just was telling you! Don't you hear good? I was the pigfucker! Over across the mountains in that white pine country, in them big woods! Best goshdamn job I ever—"

While Tonsil Vapor expelled in a rapidly rising voice, "But we can't let you say that *on the AIR!*" I took a contemplative sip of my scotch ditch. Riley and Mariah's story on the red-light duchesses of Helena and now Good Help's unexpected occupation; kind of a rough day for history.

"He's trying to tell you the truth for once," I called down the bar.

Good Help squintly glared my way while Tonsil Vapor's coiffure rotated toward me. My own startlement had not been at the nature of Good Help's job but that he'd ever held one at all. 1918, though, explained it: enlistment into employment rather than the war in Europe.

Tonsil Vapor approached me, trailed by his electronic Siamese twin. He wore an expression as concerned as his cameraman's was languid. Leaning close, Tonsil Vapor asked me in a hushed tone:

"You mean to tell me that your town's historic citizen had sexual congress with—" and twirled his index finger in the corkscrew pattern of a pig's tail.

"Well, I can't testify one way or the other on that," I hedged. "But what he's trying to tell you about here is something else. One of the jobs on those logging crews over west of the mountains was, uh, like he says."

Tonsil Vapor peered at me in even more perplexity.

"Pigfucker," I clarified. "See, in those days when they'd go to skid logs out of the woods they'd string them together end to end with eye-bolt hitches, sort of like links of sausage. And the last log they'd hitch on was a hollowed-out one called the pig. After all the other logs were snaked out of the woods, then the eye-bolts and tools and anything else got thrown in the pig—I guess that's maybe why they called it that, you could toss anything into it—and it'd be skidded back into the timber for the next string of logs, same again. Anyway, the guy, usually he was just a punk of a kid," although it was at least as hard to think of Good Help Hebner young as it was to imagine him employed, "who threw the stuff into the pig was called the—"

"Pigfucker," intoned Tonsil Vapor, gazing down the bar to where

Good Help was passing the time by grooming his goatee with his fingers. "But wasn't that job ever called anything *nicer*?"

I shrugged. "Not that I ever heard of. Lumberjacks tend not to be dainty talkers."

The bored cameraman shifted his feet as if settling down for another wait, and he and Fred and I watched Tonsil Vapor chew the inside of his mouth as he continued staring down the bar at Good Help.

At length the cameraman suggested, "Let's just bleep out the mothering word."

"Shit, that just *emphasizes* it," Tonsil Vapor let out peevishly. "No, we've got to get our historic citizen to talk about the job without . . . Wait, I know!" His face lit up as if the camera and lights were on him. "I'll just say, 'Mr. Pigner, I—'"

"Hebner," I prompted.

" 'Mr. Hebner, I understand you once worked in a logging crew, quite a number of years ago in this Montana of ours. Would you please share with our viewing audience what you did in that job?' That way, he won't need to say—"

"Pigfucker," Good Help recited before the TVing was to commence again, "is what I ain't supposed to say on the television but just tell what that job with the pig was?" He squinted anxiously up at Tonsil Vapor, wanting to make sure he had the new ground rules straight.

"Perfect!" Tonsil Vapor pronounced. He turned to the cameraman one more time, got one more bored nod, aimed his chin into the lens and the bright lights came on again.

The Here-with-us-now part and so on went along fine, and I had to admit, Good Help Hebner ensconced there with the carved dark oak of the Medicine Lodge's ancient bar behind him looked amply historical. And I could tell by his squint of concentration that he had Tonsil Vapor's cue about his logging job clamped in mind.

"—share with our viewing audience that experience in the woods?" Tonsil Vapor got there as smooth as salve from a new tube and held the microphone in front of Good Help's venerable lips.

Good Help craned forward and carefully brayed:

"What I done was, I fucked the pig! One whole summer! Best gosh-damn job—"

—

I left the TV perpetrator staring in despair at Good Help and took my restored good humor back into the cafe. Only to be met by Althea shooing the crowd into chairs. "Oh, Jick, you're just in time, we're about to have the committee meeting."

Riley already had gone over and propped himself along the wall where he could study sideways into either the audience or our committee, dutiful nuisance that he was. Mariah meanwhile was signifying by pointing urgently to my chair at the pushed-together cafe tables where the committee members were supposed to sit that she wanted me up there for a group picture. No rest for the civic.

On my way to my seat, though, I paused at the end of the committee table to say brightly to Amber Finletter, who had been a wonderful neighbor to us when Marcella fell sick, "How you doing, Amber?" And wordlessly got back the merest little picklepuss acknowledgment.

Oh, horse pucky. Amber had her nose out of joint, McCaskillwise, because she figured Mariah was making a play for Shaun during that picture-taking of him and me. Jealousy has more lives than Methuselah's cat.

Then no sooner was I sat than I was afflicted with Arlee Zane. Arlee and I have known each other our entire lives and disliked each other that same amount of time.

Leaning over from his chair next to mine, Arlee now hung his fat face almost into mine and slanted his eyes in the direction of Althea at her speaking stand. Grinning like a jackass eating thistles he semiwhispered, "Jick, old son, are you getting any?"

I cast a glance of my own across the room toward Arlee's wife Phoebe and asked in turn, "Why? Have you noticed some missing?"

That settled the Arlee situation for a while, and I was able to direct my attention to Howard Stonesifer seated on the other side of me. "Catch me up on what's been happening here, Howard."

"Shaun Finletter and Mike Sisti rounded up a flagpole," he reported. "They went all the way across the mountains to Coram for the tree, to get one big enough to take this flag. Other than that, everybody's just sewing"—he cast a look at my chin shrubbery—"or growing."

With a soft *raprap raprap raprap* of her gavel—would you believe, even her hammering sounded like pats—Althea was commencing to officiate.

"The meeting will please come to order, everybody, including you,

Garland Hebner." Good Help had spied Riley at his listening post there along the wall and doubtless was creaking his way over to deliver an hour or two of autobiographical afterthought, but Althea's injunction halted the old boy as if he'd been caught slinking into the henhouse.

"It's so wonderful to see so many of you being so public spirited here tonight," Althea proceeded on. "I won't have to go door to door around town handing out pushbrooms after all." She smiled sweetly in saying that, but testimony could have been elicited in that audience from any number of persons who were choosing to put up with an evening of committee crap rather than risk Althea putting them in the wake of our centennial parade's horse version.

Under Althea's generalship we whipped right through Howard's minutes of the last meeting and Amber's treasurer's report, and when we got to the first order of business, guess whose it was.

"We need to give some thought to our flag-raising ceremony," Althea informed all and sundry. "It would be nicest, wouldn't it, if we could re-enact that dawn just the way it happened a hundred years ago, when our Gros Ventre forebears flew Montana's very first flag of statehood. But of course we don't know what was said on that wonderful occasion."

The funny thing was, I did know. To the very word, I possessed the scene that ensued that exact morning of a century ago. I had heard it from Toussaint Rennie, who inevitably was on hand at the occasion. The gospel according to Toussaint was that Lila Sedgwick had officiated. Strange to think of her, a mind-clouded old woman wandering the streets of Gros Ventre conversing with the cottonwood trees when I was a youngster, as ever having been vital and civic. But there in her young years Lila and the handful of others this community was composed of in 1889 had mustered themselves and made what ceremony they could. "Way before dawn," Toussaint's purling voice began to recite in me again now, there, at that committee table. "Out to the flagpole, everybody. It was still dark as cats, but—"

I had an awful moment before I could be sure Toussaint's words weren't streaming out through my mouth. Another spasm of the past, and this one as public as hell. It was one thing to have my memory broadcast out loud around Mariah and Riley and totally another to blab out here in front of everybody who knew me. I tried to fix an ever so interested stare on Althea as she continued to preside out loud and meanwhile clenched my own lips together so tightly I must have looked like a shut purse. But these cyclones out of yestertime into me: what was I going to do about them? I mean, when you come right down to it, just where is the dividing line between reciting what the past wants you to and speaking gibberish? Was I going to be traipsing around blabbering to the cottonwoods next?

"A ceremony isn't really a ceremony unless it has a speech, now is it?" Althea asked and answered simultaneously. "So, before our wonderful flag is hoisted Centennial morning, we really should have someone say a few words, don't you all agree?"

I wholly expected her to go into full spiel about what the speech ought to be about, and then somebody, quite possibly even me, could stick a hand up and suggest that she spout all of it again on Centennial morning and that would constitute the speech, but no, oh hell no. All Althea trilled forth next was:

"I nominate Jick McCaskill as our speaker."

From the various compass points of the committee table, Howard's hearty voice and Arlee's malicious voice and Amber's vindictive voice chorused: "I second the motion."

"Whoa, hold on a minute here," I tried to get in, "I'm not your guy to—" but do you think Althea would hear of it?

"Oh foo, Jick, you're entirely too modest. If you're stuck for what to say I'll be more than glad to help out, you always know where to find me. Now then, all in favor of Jick McCaskill . . ."

"Tell me, Mariah Montana," goddamn Riley started in, doing a syrup voice like that of TV Purvis, on our way home to the ranch. "When did you first realize your father is in the same oratorical league with Lincoln, Churchill, and Phil Donahue?"

"Oh, I always knew he was destined for public speaking because of how he practiced on the sheep," Mariah ever so merrily got into the spirit with a Baby Snooksy tone of her own. "He just has this wonderful talent for talking to sheep"—here she expertly made with her tongue the *prrrrr prrrrr prrrrr* call half-purr, half-coo, that I had taught her to coax sheep with almost as soon as she could toddle—"and so people are probably easy for him."

"Up yours, both of you," I stated wearily.

—

Maybe it was the prospect of chronic aid from Althea, from then until I had to get up in front of everyone on Centennial dawn and insert my foot into my mouth. Maybe it was that I did not see my presence could cure the ranch situation any, just then; Kenny and Darleen and Helen were going to keep on being Kenny and Darleen and Helen, whether or not I hovered over them, and so I might as well wait until they had the hay up and the lambs fattened for shipping before I faced what to do with the place. Maybe it was hunch. Or its cousin curiosity, after Mariah and I emerged from the house the next morning and encountered Riley, daisyfresh from solitary sleep in the motor-home, who told her he'd already been to the cookhouse and made the phone call and it was all set, and she in turn gazed at him and then for some reason at me, before saying solemnly, "Heavy piece, Riley."

So, yes, the three of us applied ourselves to the road again. Mariah and I in the Bago trailed Riley and the rental Yugo to town to turn the thing in at Tilton's garage, then I pointed the motorhome toward Choteau, as the *Montanian* pair had informed me that this next piece of work of theirs awaited there in the Teton River country.

"Has this got to do with dinosaur eggs, I hope?" In that vicinity, out west of Choteau, lay Egg Mountain—no more than a bit of a bump in the prairie, really, but where whole nests laid by dinosaurs had been found, and while I can't claim to know much more about paleontology than how to spell it, any scene where creatures of eighty million years ago hatched out their young like mammoth baby chicks sounded to me highly interesting.

"Umm, not exactly. Here's your turn coming up," Mariah busily pointed out, "that sign, there where it says—"

"Yeah, I can see that far," I said and gave her a look. What, did she figure I'm getting so decrepit I couldn't read the obvious roadside sign, which directed in perfectly clear lettering:

PINE BUTTE SWAMP PRESERVE
established 1978
protected and maintained by
The Nature Conservancy
14mi.———————⟶

The Teton country is quite the geography. Gravelroading straight west as the Bago now was, we had in front of us the rough great wall of the Rockies where gatelike canyons on either side of Indian Head Rock let forth the twin forks of the Teton River. The floorlike plain that leads to the foot of the mountains is wet and spongy in some places, in others bone-dry, in still others common prairie. And even though I usually only remark it from a distance when I'm driving past on a Great Falls trip, Pine Butte itself seems like a neighbor to me. It and its kindred promontories make a line of landmarks between the mountains and the eastward horizon of plains—Heart Butte north near the Two Medicine River, Breed Butte of course between Noon Creek and English Creek, Pine Butte presiding here over the Teton country like a surprising pine-topped mesa, Haystack Butte south near Augusta. Somehow they remind me of lighthouses, spaced as they are along the edge of that tumult of rock that builds into the Continental Divide. Lone sentinel forms the eye seeks.

We drove in sunny silence until I said something about how surprising it was to have a swamp out on a prairie, causing Riley to get learned and inform me that the Pine Butte swamp actually was underlain with so much bog it qualified as a fen.

"That what you're going to do here, some kind of an ecology piece?" I asked.

"Sort of," Mariah said.

"Sounds real good to me," I endorsed, gandering out at the companionable outline of Pine Butte drawing ever nearer and the boggy bottomland—in Montana you don't see a fen just every day—and the summits of the Rockies gray as eternity meeting the blue August sky. This area a little bit reminded me of the Moiese buffalo range where we'd started out, nice natural country set aside, even though I knew the Pine Butte preserve wasn't that elaborate kind of government refuge but simply a ranch before the land was passed on to the Conservancy outfit, which must have decided to be defender of the fen. I couldn't help but be heartened, too, that the news duo at least had progressed from getting us butted by buffalo to moseying through a sweet forenoon such as this. "Great day for the race," I chirped, even. Oh, I knew full well Mariah had heard that one a jillion times from me, but I figured maybe Riley would fall for it by asking "What race?" and then I'd get him by saying "The human race"—but huh uh, no such luck. Instead

Riley busied up behind me and announced, "Okay, gang, we've got to start watching along the brush for the state outfit. Should be easy enough to see, there's a crane on the truck they use to hoist the—"

"I'll watch out this side," Mariah broke in on him and proceeded to peer out her window as if she'd just discovered glass is transparent.

Dumb me. Even then I didn't catch on until another mile or so down the road when I happened to think out loud that even though we were going to be with ecology guys we'd all need to watch a little bit out in country like this, because the Pine Butte area is the last prairie habitat of—

The stiffening back of that daughter of mine abruptly told it.

"*Grizzlies?*" I concluded in a bleat. "Has this got to do with *grizzlies?*"

"Just one," said Mariah, superearnestly gazing off across the countryside away from my stare.

"That's way too damn many! This isn't going to be what I'm afraid it is, is it? Tell me it isn't."

Of course neither of this pair of story-chasing maniacs would tell me any such thing and so the nasty hunch that had been crawling up the back of my neck pounced.

"Bear moving!" I slammed on the brakes and right there in the middle of the county road swung around in my seat, as mad as I was scared—which is saying a lot—to goggle first at Mariah who ought to have known better than this and then at Riley whose goddamn phone call this morning all too clearly led into this. "Jesus H. Christ, you two! Anybody with a lick of sense doesn't want to be within fifty miles of moving a grizzly!"

"I reckon that's why the job falls to us," Riley couldn't resist rumbling in one of his mock hero voices. "What's got you in an uproar, Jick? The good news is you don't have to chauffeur the bear in the Bago. The state Fish and Game guys load him into a culvert trap."

I didn't give a hoot if they had portable San Quentin to haul a grizzly in, I wanted no part of it and I then and there let Mariah and Riley know exactly that. Didn't they even read their own newspaper, for Christ's sake? Only days ago a hiking couple in Glacier Park had encountered a sow grizzly and her two cubs, and survived the mauling only because they had the extreme guts and good sense to drop to the ground and play dead. And not all that far from where we right now sat, several—*several*—grizzlies lately kept getting into the geese and ducks at the Rockport Hutterite Colony until the Hutterites managed to run them off with a big tractor. The Bago, I emphasized, was no tractor.

Which did me about as much good with those two as if I'd said it all down a gopher hole.

Riley was mostly the one who worked on me—Mariah knew good and well how ticked off I was at her for this—and of course argument might as well have been his middle name. "The bear is already caught in a steel cable snare, the state guys will conk him out with a tranquilizer gun, and then they'll haul him in a chunk of culvert made of high tensile aluminum he'd have to go nuclear to get out of. Where's the problem?" he concluded, seeming genuinely puzzled.

The rancher portion of me almost said back to him, the problem is the grizzly, you Missoula ninny.

Instead, in spite of myself, my eyes took over from my tongue. They scrutinized the brush-lined creek as if counting up its willows like a tally with wooden matchsticks, they probed each shadowed dip of the Pine Butte fen, they leapt to every ruffle of breeze in the grass. Seeking and seeking the great furry form.

All the while, Riley's bewilderment was stacking up against the silent bounds of me and Mariah, who was keeping ostentatiously occupied with her camera gear. "Gang, I don't know what the deal is here," the scribbler owned, "but we can't just sit in the middle of this road watching the seasons change."

"Are you two going to this bear whether or not I'm along?" I managed to ask.

Say for Riley that he did have marginally enough sense to let Mariah do the answering on that one.

"Yes," she said, still without quite ever looking at me. "The Fish and Game guys are waiting for us."

I jammed the Bago into gear and we went on down the road for, oh, maybe as much as a quarter of a mile before Riley's bursting curiosity propelled out the remark, "Well, just speaking for myself, this is going to be something to remember, getting a free look at a grizzly, hmm?"

When neither of us in the cab of the motorhome responded, he resorted to: "You, ah, you ever seen one before, Jick?"

"Yeah."

"But up close?"

"Close enough." I glanced over at Mariah. Her face carefully showed nothing, but I knew she was replaying the memory, seeing it all again. Who could not? "I killed one once."

"The hell!" from Riley in his patented well-then-tell-me-all-about-it tone. "There on Noon Creek, you mean?"

"In the mountains back of the ranch, yeah." As sudden as that, the site near Flume Gulch was in my mind, as if the earth had jumped a click in its rotation and flung the fire-scarred slope, the survivor pine tree with its claw-torn bark, in through my eyes.

Greatly as I wished he would not, Riley naturally persisted with the topic. "You run across him by accident or track him down?"

"Neither."

"Then how'd you get together with Brother Griz?"

"I baited him."

Strong silence from behind me.

At last Riley said: "Did you. My dad did some of that, too, whenever he'd lose a calf. But black bear, those were. We didn't have grizzlies in the Crazy Mountains any more." Those last two words of his said the whole issue. Originally the West had been absolutely loaded with grizzly bears, but by now they were on the endangered species list.

"I'm not one of those Three S guys, if that's what you're thinking," I told Riley stonily. Law on the side of the grizzly notwithstanding, there still were some ranchers along these mountains who practiced the policy of shoot, shovel and shut up. Better a buried bear who'd be no threat to livestock or the leasing of oil rights than a living exemplification of wilderness, ran that reasoning.

"Riley never said you were," Mariah put in her two bits' worth.

Actually, except for her contribution being on his behalf it was just as well she did ante herself into this discussion, for my ultimate say on the grizzly issue needed to be to her rather than to some scribbler. I spoke it now, slowly and carefully:

"I don't believe in things going extinct. But that includes me, too."

I knew Riley was grinning his sly grin. "A grizzly couldn't have said it any better, Jick," issued from him. I didn't care. From the tight crinkle that had taken over her expression I could see that my words had hit home in Mariah, complicating what she had been remembering, what we both were remembering, of that time of the grizzly twenty-five years before.

It started with a paw mark in the pan of the slop milk Mariah had given the chickens.

Why that pan caught her eye so soon again after she'd done her morning chore of feeding the poultry flock, I do not know. Maybe even at ten years old as she was then, Mariah simply was determined to notice everything. When she came down to the lambing shed to find me I was surprised she and Lexa hadn't left yet for school, but nowhere near so surprised as when she told me, "You'd better come see the bear track."

I dropped to one knee there in the filth of the chicken yard, mindful only of that pale outline in the pan. My own hand was not as steady as I would have liked when I measured the bear's print with it. The width of the palmlike pad was well over six inches, half again wider than my hand. That and the five clawmarks noticeably off the toes distinguished what kind of bear this was. Not just a grizzly but a sizable one.

Considerations of all kinds swarmed in behind that pawprint. No sheep rancher has any reason to welcome a grizzly, that I know of. A grizzly bear in a band of sheep can be dynamite. So my mind flew automatically to the bunches of ewes and lambs scattered across the ranch—late April this was, the tail end of lambing season—like clusters of targets. But before that thought was fully done, the feel of invasion of our family was filling me. The creature that slurped the chickens' milk and tromped through the still-damp pan had been here astride the daily paths of our lives. Marcella merely on her way out to the clothesline, Mariah simply on her way to the chicken house, Lexa kiting all over the place in her afterschool scampers—their random goings surely crisscrossed whatever route brought the grizzly, coming out of hibernation hungry and irritable, in to the ranch buildings. Nor was I personally keen to be out on some chore and afterward all they'd ever find of me would be my belt buckle in a grizzly turd.

So when I phoned to the government trapper and his wife said he was covering a couple of other counties for the rest of the week, I did not feel I could wait.

It was the work of all that day to pick and prepare the trap site. Up toward Flume Gulch I was able to find the grizzly's tracks in the mud of the creek crossing, and on the trail along the old burn area of the 1939 forest fire I came across what in every likelihood was the same bear's fresh dropping, a black pile you'd step in to the top of your ankle. I chose the stoutest survivor pine there at the edge of the old burn and used the winch of the Dodge power wagon to snake a long heavy bullpine log in beside the base of the tree. Around the tree I built a rough pen of smaller logs to keep any stray livestock from blundering in, and even though the other blundersome species wasn't likely to come sashaying past I nonetheless nailed up a sign painted in red sheep paint to tell people: LOOK OUT—BEAR TRAP HERE. Then I bolted the chain of the trap to the bullpine log and set the trap, ever so carefully using screw-down clamps to cock its wicked steel jaws open, in the middle of the pen and covered it with pine swags. Finally, from the tree limb directly over the trap I hung the bait, a can of bacon grease.

One thing I had not calculated on. The next day was Saturday, and I got up that next morning to two schoolless daughters who overnight had caught the feverish delusion that they were going with me to check the bear trap.

They took my "No" to the court of appeal, but even after their mother had upped the verdict to "You are not going and let's not hear one more word about it," their little hearts continued to break loudly. All through breakfast there were outbreaks of eight-year-old pouts from Lexa and ten-year-old disputations from Mariah. As the *aws* and *why can't we*'s poured forth, I was more amused than anything else until the older of these caterwauling daughters cut out her commotion and said in a sudden new voice:

"You'd take us if we were boys."

Mariah should have grown up to be a neurosurgeon; she always could go straight to a nerve. Right then I wanted to swat her precocious butt until she took that back, and simultaneously I knew she had spoken a major truth.

"Mariah, that will do!" crackled instantly from her mother, but by Marcella's frozen position across the table from me I knew our daughter's words had hit her as they had me. Mariah still was meeting our parental storm and giving as good as she got, at risk but unafraid. Beside the tense triangle of the other three of us, Lexa's mouth made an exquisite little O in awe of her sister who scolded grownups.

That next moment of Marcella and I convening our eyes, voting to each other on Mariah's accusation, I can still feel the pierce of. At last I said to my fellow defendant, "I could stand some company up there. How would you feel about all of us going?"

"It's beginning to look like we'd better," Marcella agreed. "But you two"—she gave Lexa a warning look and doubled it for Mariah—"are staying in the power wagon with me, understand?"

When we got up to Flume Gulch, we had a bear waiting.

Its fur was a surprisingly light tan, and plenty of it loomed above the trap pen; this grizzly more than lived up to the size of his tracks. The impression the caught animal gave, which shocked me at first, was that it was pacing back and forth in the trap pen, peering over the stacked logs as if watching for our arrival. Then I realized that the bear was so angrily restless it only seemed he was moving freely; in actuality he was anchored to the bullpine log by the chain of the trap and could only maneuver as if on a short tether. I will tell you, though, that it dried my mouth a little to see how mobile a grizzly was even with a hind leg in a steel trap biting to its bone.

We must have made quite a family tableau framed in the windshield of the power wagon. Lexa so little she only showed from the eyes up as she craned to see over the dashboard. Mariah as intent as an astronomer in a new galaxy. Their mother and I bolt upright on either side trying not to look as agog as our daughters.

"I better get at it," I said as much to myself as to Marcella. Something bothered me about how rambunctious the bear was managing to be in the trap. Not that I was any expert on grizzly deportment nor wanted to be. Quickly I climbed out of the power wagon and reached behind the seat for the rifle while Marcella replaced me behind the wheel and kept watch on the grizzly, ready to gun the engine and make a run at the bear in event of trouble. Mariah craned her neck to catalogue my every move as I jacked a shell into the chamber of the rifle and slipped one into the magazine to replace it and for good measure dropped a handful of the .30-06 ammunition in my shirt pocket. "Daddy will show that bear!" Lexa piped fearlessly. Daddy hoped she was a wise child.

Armed and on the ground I felt somewhat more businesslike about the chore of disposing of the bear. Habits of hunting took over and as if I was skirting up the ridge to stay above a herd of deer below, in no time I had worked my way upslope from the trap tree and the griz, to where my shot would be at a safe angle away from the spectating trio in the power wagon. All the while watching the tan form of trapped anger and being watched by it. Great furry block of a thing, the grizzly was somehow wonderful and awful at the same time.

I drew a breath and made sure I had jacked that shell into the chamber of the .30-06. All in a day's work if this was the kind of work you were in, I kept telling myself, aim, fire, bingo, bruin goes to a honey cloud. Hell, other ranchers who had grazing allotments farther up in the Two Medicine National Forest, where there was almost regular traffic of grizzlies, probably had shot dozens of them over the years.

Abruptly and powerfully the bear surged upright and lurched toward the standing pine tree, as if to shelter behind it from me and my rifle. The chain on the trap was only long enough for the bear to get to the tree, not around it. But as the animal strained there I saw that only its toes of the left rear foot were clamped in the jaws of the trap, not the rear leg itself, which awfully suddenly explained why the bear seemed so maneuverable in the trap pen. *Next thing to not caught,* the trapper Isidor Pronovost used to say of a weasel or a bobcat toe-trapped that way, barely held but unable to escape, and such chanciness seemed all the mightier when the caught creature was as gargantuan as this grizzly.

I will swear on all the Bibles there are, I was not intentionally delaying the bear's execution. Rather, I was settling the barrel of the .30-06 across a silvered stump for a businesslike heart shot when instead the grizzly abruptly began climbing the tree. Attacking up the tree, erupting up the tree, whatever way it can strongest be said, branches as thick as my arm were cracking off and flying, widowmakers torn loose by the storm of fur. The dangling bait can sailed off and clanked against a snag not ten feet from me. The fantastic claws raking furrows into the wood, the massively exerting hulk of body launching and launching itself into that tree. The trap dangling from the bear's rear toes was coursing upward too, tautening the chain fastened into the bullpine log.

Awful turned even worse now. The log lifted at its chained end and began to be dragged to the tree, the bear bellowing out its pain and rage at the strain of that taut pull yet still mauling its way up the tree. I stood stunned at the excruciating tug of war; the arithmetic of hell that was happening, for the log's deadweight on those toes could—

Then I at last realized. The grizzly was *trying* to tear its toes off to get free.

All prescribed notions of a sure heart shot flew out of me. I fired at the bear simply to hit it, then blazed away at the region of its shoulders again, again, as it slumped and began sliding down the tree trunk, claws slashing bark off as they dragged downward, the rifle in my arms speaking again, again, the last two shots into the animal's neck as it crumpled inside the trap pen.

All those years after, I could understand that Mariah was uneasy about that memory of the toe-caught but doomed grizzly. What the hell, I was not anywhere near easy about it myself, even though I yet believed with everything in me that that particular bear had to be gotten rid of. I mean, six-inch-wide pawprints when you go out to feed the chickens? But I knew that what was bugging Mariah was not just the fate that bear had roamed into on our ranch. No, her bothersome remembering was of us, the McCaskills as we were on that morning. Of the excitement that danced in all four of us after I had done the shooting—Marcella with her worldbeating grin, Lexa hopping up and down as she put out her small hand to touch the pale fur, Mariah stock-still but fever-eyed with the thrill of what she'd witnessed, myself breaking into a wild smile of having survived. Of our family pride, for in honesty it can be called no less, about the killing of the grizzly, with never a thought that its carcass was any kind of a lasting nick out of nature. Late now, though, to try to tack so sizable an afterthought into that Flume Gulch morning.

Clearly this day's grizzly already knew that matters had become more complicated. The snared bear stood quiet but watchful in a pen of crisscrossed logs—much like the one I built—under a big cottonwood, a respectful distance between it and the two state men beside their truck when the motorhome and the three of us entered the picture.

Riley forthwith introduced himself and then Mariah and me to the wildlife biologist, and the biologist in turn acquainted us with his bear-management assistant, a big calm sort who apparently had been hired for both his musclepower and disposition. After we'd all handshook and murmured our hellos, the immediate next sound was Mariah's camera catching the stare of the bear. Inevitably she asked, "How close can I go?"

No sooner was the utterance out of her mouth than the grizzly lunged through the side of the pen, lurching out to the absolute end of the cable it was snared by. That cable was of steel and anchored to the tree and holding the bear tethered a good fifty yards away from the five of us, but even so . . .

"Right where you are is close enough until we get the tranquilizer in him," the biologist advised. He gave a little cluck of his tongue. "I've been at this for years and my heart still jumps out my throat when the bear does that."

Mine was halfway to Canada by now. I got calmed a little by

reminding myself that the assistant bear mover had in hand a .12-gauge semi-automatic shotgun with an extended magazine holding seven slugs, armament I was glad enough to see.

Riley went right on journalizing. With a nod toward the bear he asked, "What have we got here?" I sent him a look. *We?*

"A sub-adult, probably about a two-year-old," the biologist provided and went on to explain that a young bear like this one was a lot like a kid on the run, no slot in life yet and getting into trouble while it poked around. More than probably it had been one of the assailants on the Hutterites' fowl. Mischief this time was spelled v-e-a-l, a white-faced calf killed in the fence corner of the rancher's pasture we were now in.

> *This contest too is tribal. Ignore the incidental details that one community is four-footed and furred and the other consists of scantily haired bipeds, and see the question as two tribes in what is no longer enough space for two. Dominion, oldest of quarrels. The grizzly brings to the issue its formidable natural aptitude, imperial talent to live on anything from ants to, as it happens, livestock. But the furless tribe possesses the evolutionary equivalent of a nuclear event: the outsize brain that enables them to fashion weapons that strike beyond the reach of their own bodies.*

Riley did a bunch more interviewing of the biologist and the biologist talked of the capture event and the relocation process and other bear-management lingo, Mariah meanwhile swooping around with her camera doing her own capturing of the bear-moving team and Riley and for whatever damn reason, even me. Even she couldn't help generally glancing at the snared grizzly, as we all kept doing. Yet somehow the bear's single pair of eyes watched us with greater total intensity than our five human pair could manage in monitoring him. And a grizzly's eyes are not nearly its best equipment, either. Into that black beezer of a nose and those powerful rounded-off ears like tunnels straight into the brain, our smells and sounds must have been like stench and thunder to the animal.

The majority of my own staring went to the rounded crown of fur atop the bear's front quarters, the trademark hump of the grizzly. Not huge, just kind of like an extra biceps up there, an overhead motor of muscle that enabled the grizzly to run bursts of forty-five miles an hour or to break a smaller animal's neck with one swipe. Or to rip off its own trapped toe.

My throat was oddly dry when the question came out of me. "What do you bait with?"

The biologist turned his head enough to study me, then sent Riley an inquiring look. Who, goddamn his knack for aggravation, gave a generous okaying nod. Just what my mood needed, the Riley Wright seal of approval.

"Roadkills," the biologist told me. "I collect them. Heck of a hobby, isn't it? This one's a deer, good bear menu."

Now that he'd obliged Riley's notebook and Mariah's camera, the biologist said "We'd better get this bear underway. First we dart him off."

With doctor gloves on, he used a syringe to put the tranquilizer dose into a metal dart and then inserted the dart into what looked almost like a .22 rifle. The assistant hefted the shotgun and with their respective armaments the two bear men edged slowly out toward the grizzly, the biologist saying to us in reluctant tone of voice, "This is always a fun part."

When the pair neared to about thirty yards from him the bear *really* lunged now. At the end of the cable tether it stood and strained. My God, even the fur on the thing looked dangerous; this griz was browner than the tan one I'd shot, and the wind rippled in that restless dark field of hair.

Clicking and more clicking issued from Mariah's camera while the biologist and his guardian eased another ten yards closer to the bear. Riley alternately jotted in his notebook and restlessly tapped his pen on it. I wonder now how I was able to hear anything over the beating of my heart.

When he was no more than twenty yards from the bear, the biologist raised his dart rifle, leveled it for what seemed a long time, then fired, a compressed air *pfoop*. The dart hit the grizzly high in the hind quarters. As the Fish and Game men rapidly walked backwards to where we were, the bear reared up behind, thrashed briefly, then went down, lying there like a breathing statue as the paralyzing drug gripped it.

The bear men stood and waited, the shotgunner never taking his eyes off the bear, the biologist steadily checking his watch and the animal's vital signs. After about ten minutes the biologist said, "Let's try him."

He reached in the back of the truck for a long-handled shovel. Going over beside the hairy bulk with a careful but steady stride while the helper trailed him, shotgun at the ready, the biologist took a stance and rapped the near shoulder with the end of the shovel handle, not real hard but probably plenty to start a fight if the other party is a grizzly.

When the bear just lay there and took that, the biologist announced: "Okay, he's under."

Christamighty, I hadn't known there was even going to be any doubt about it or I for sure would have watched this part of the procedure from inside the metal walls of the motorhome.

There was a surprising amount of business to be done to the sedated bear. Weighing it in a tarp sling and scale that the state pair rigged from the stoutest branch overhead. Checking its breathing rate every few minutes. Fastening a radio collar—surveillance to see whether this was going to be a repeat offender—around its astonishing circumference of neck. Putting salve into its eyes to keep them from drying out during this immobilization period. And of course as the biologist said, "the *really* fun part," loading the thing into the culvert cage. All of us got involved in that except Mariah. For once I was thankful for her camera-mania as she dipped and dove around, snapping away at the two state guys and Riley and me huffing and puffing to insert the three-hundred-pound heap of limp grizzly into the tank-like silver trap. Every instant of that, remembering the fury exploding up that tree of twenty-five years ago, claws slashing bark into ribbons and broken branches flying, I was devoutly hoping this bear was going to stay tranquil. Sure, you bet, no question but that it was snoozing as thoroughly as drug science could make it do. Yet this creature in our hands felt hotblooded and ungodly strong, and all this time its eyes never closed.

Heaven's front gate could never sound more welcome than that clang of the door of the trap dropping shut when we at last had the bear bedded inside. "Nothing much to this job, hmm?" the panting Riley remarked to the biologist.

The state men then employed their crane to lift the cage onto the flatbed truck and soundly secured it with a trucker's large tie-down strap.

"Well, there," I declared, glad to be done with this bear business.

Almost as one, Mariah and Riley looked at me as if I was getting up from supper just as the meat and potatoes were put on the table.

Good God, how literal could they get, even if they were newspaper people. I mean, the movers had the bear all but underway. Did we need to watch every revolution of the truck's wheels, tag along like the Welcome Wagon to the grizzly's new home, to be able to say we'd seen bear moving?

By Mariah and Riley's lights, indubitably. Out our caravan proceeded to Highway 89 and then south and west down thinner and thinner roads, to a distant edge of the Bob Marshall Wilderness. As we went and went, maybe the bear was keeping his bearings but I sure as hell couldn't have automatically found my way back to the Pine Butte country.

Exile is the loser's land. Others set its borders, state its terms, enforce the diminishment as only the victors know how; the outcast sniffs the cell of wilderness.

The motorhome had been growling in low gear for what seemed hours, up and up a mountain road which had never heard of a Bago before, until at last the truck ahead swung into a sizable clearing.

"Here's where we tell our passenger adios," the biologist came over to us to confirm that this at last was the release site, sounding several hundred percent more cheerful than he had all day. The idea now, he told Riley and Mariah, was to simply let the bear out of the culvert, watch it a little while to be sure the tranquilizer was wearing off okay, and allow it to go its wildwood way, up here far from tempting morsels of calf etcetera.

He could not have been any readier than I was to say goodbye to the grizzly. The back of my neck was prickling. And though I couldn't see into the culvert trap, I somehow utterly knew, maybe the memory of the bear I had killed superimposing itself here, that the ruff of hair on the young grizzly's hump was standing on end, too.

"You folks stay in your vehicle," the biologist added, somewhat needlessly I thought, before heading back to the truck. The state pair themselves were going to be within for this finale of bear moving, for they could operate the crane from inside the cab of the truck to lift the trap door. Except for rolling her window down farther than I liked, even Mariah showed no great desire to be out there to greet the bear and instead uncapped a long lens and fitted it onto her camera.

The remote control debarkation of the bear began, the state guys peering back through the rear window of the truck cab to start the crane hoisting the culvert door so the bear could vamoose. We waited. And waited.

It was Mariah, scoping over there with her lens, who said it aloud. "Something's fouled up."

The truck doors opened and the two bear movers stepped out, the helper carefully carrying the shotgun. Reluctantly but I suppose necessarily, I rolled my window down and craned my head out, Riley practically breathing down the back of my neck.

"Equipment," the biologist bitterly called over to us as if it was his personal malady. "Murphy's Law seems to have caught up with the crane—probably some six-bit part gave out. This won't be as pretty but we can do the release process manually."

The pair of men climbed onto the flatbed of the truck. The shotgun guard stationed himself back by the truck cab while the biologist carefully climbed atop the trap and began the gruntwork of lifting the aluminum door up out of the slotted sides.

From the trap there was the sound of great weight shifting as the grizzly adjusted to the fact of freedom out there beyond the mouth of daylight. The big broad head poked into sight, then the shoulders with the furred hump atop them. I breathed with relief that we were about to be through with that haunting passenger.

The bear gathered itself to jump down to the ground but at the same time aggressively bit at the edge of the trap door above it. By reflex the biologist's hand holding that edge of the door jerked away.

The grizzly was all but out of the trap when the heavy door slammed down on its tailbone.

As instantly as the grizzly hit the ground it whirled against what it took to be attack, snarling, searching. The men on the truck froze, not to give the bear any motion to lunge at.

With suddenness again, the bear reared up on its hind legs to sense the surroundings. It saw the man on top of the culvert trap.

The grizzly dropped and charged, trying to climb the side of the truck to the men.

"Don't, bear!" the biologist cried out.

BWOOMWOOM, the rapid-fire of the shotgun blasted, and within the ringing in my ears I could hear the deep peals of echo diminish out over the mountainside.

> *Both shotgun slugs hit the grizzly in the chest. Stopping-power, the human tribe calls such large calibre ballistics, and it stopped the life of the bear the instant the twin bolts of lead tore into his heart and lungs. The bear slumped side-ways, crumpled, and lay there in the clearing. Above the sudden carcass the two bear men stood rooted for a long moment. For one or maybe both of them, the shotgun had bought life instead of death by mauling.*

Of all of Mariah's pictures of that day, here was the one that joined into Riley's words.

> *But as the shotgunner still held the gun pointing toward the grizzly, these survivors, too, seemed as lifeless as the furred victim.*

Normally I do not consider myself easy to spook. But that bear episode, close cousin to the outcome of my own grizzly encounter at Noon Creek, jittered me considerably. All this that was marching around in review in my head and then, kazingo, storming out in fresh form in the pieces Mariah and Riley found to do: I couldn't keep the thought from regularly crossing my mind—was I somehow an accomplice to occurrences? What was it that had hold of me, to make memory as intense as the experiences themselves? Maybe I was given somebody else's share of imagination on top of my own, yet tell me how to keep matters from entering my mind when they insist on coming in. Don't think I didn't try, day and night. But I could not get over wondering how contagious the past is.

Nor was I the only one with a mind too busy. The first several nights after the grizzly episode, Riley was as restless in bed beside me as if he was on a rotisserie. I laid there next to him as he sloshed around, wondering why I was such a glutton for punishment, until I just could not take it any longer and would give him a poke and call him a choice name, which might settle him down for maybe half a minute. Mariah was the opposite case on her couch at the other end of the Bago; too lit-tle movement could be heard from her, no regular breathing or other rhythms of sleep, and so I knew she was stark awake and seeing her photos of that Pine Butte day over and over. And if I was this well informed on the night patterns of those two I wasn't exactly peacefully slumbering myself, was I.

The day the *Montanian* duo decided to try their luck in the High Line country was one of those newmade ones after a night of rain. At the Hill 57 RV Park in Great Falls a lightning storm had crackled through about ten o'clock the night before, white sheets of light followed by a session of stiff windgusts that made me wonder why recreational vehicle parks are always in groves of big old brittle cottonwood trees, then the steady drum of rain on the motorhome roof which at last escorted me, and for all I knew Mariah and Riley as well, off to sleep. Out around us now as we drove north up Interstate 15 were wet grainfields and nervous farmers. After deathly drought the previous year, they finally had a decent crop and now August was turning so rainy they couldn't get machinery into those fields to do the round dance of harvest.

Maybe the rain-induced sleep was a tonic, maybe the road hymn of the tires was comfortably taking me over, but I felt a little bolstered this morning. Interested in the freeway community of traffic as cars and trucks and other rigs walloped along past the Bago. A venerable Chrysler LeBaron slid by with pots of little cactus in the hothouse sunshine of its rear window. A pickup pulling a horse trailer whipped past, bumper sticker saying CALF ROPERS DO IT IN FRONT OF THEIR HORSES.

Beyond the Valier turnoff the freeway traffic thinned away and I put our own pedal to the metal. I had the rig rolling right along at a generous sixty-five—which is the spot on the speedometer just beyond seventy—when I noticed a speck in the sideview mirror. Steadily and promptly it grew into a motorcycle, one of those sizable chromed-up ones with handlebars like longhorns. The rider rode leaning back, arms half-spread as if resting his elbows on the wind. That would be highly interesting, I thought, to cross the country that wide-open way, hurtling along directly on top of an engine, like saddling a peal of thunder and letting it whirl you over the land.

This skein of thought took my eyes off the sideview mirror longer than I realized, because when I glanced there again the motorcycle was gone. Vanishimo. Which puzzled me because I couldn't account for any exit where the thunder rider could have left the freeway.

Then there was a knocking on the Bago's door beside me.

I about rocketed up through the roof. In that erect new posture, though, I could see that the motorcyclist was right there alongside the front wheel of the Bago, directly under the side mirror. Kind of a wind-mussed guy, as I suppose was to be expected, he had an unlit cigarette in his mouth. Taking one hand off the handlebars he indicated toward the cig with a pointing forefinger.

Mariah had been catnapping in the passenger seat until the *knock knock knock* on my door brought her eyes open wide. Riley, dinking around on his laptop back at the nook table where he couldn't see what was happening, assumed the noise was the doing of one of us and figured he was being funny by asking, "Who wants in?"

"Guy on a motorcycle here," I reported, oh so carefully keeping the Bago at a constant speed and not letting it wander sideways into the visiting cyclist. One nudge from the motorhome and he'd be greasing a mile of Interstate 15 with his brains. "I guess maybe he wants a light for his cigarette."

Mariah scrambled out of the passenger seat, camera already up and aimed down across me at the motorcyclist while Riley yelped out, "Holy Christ, Mariah, the photo chance of a lifetime! A guy lighting a match in a seventy-mile-an-hour wind! The BB'll be so fucking proud of us he'll put us up for a Pulitzer! Get ready to shoot when I hand this nut a matchbook, okay?!"

"Riley, get stuffed," Mariah told him but only in an automatic way. She took time out from her clicking—the motorcyclist with his cigarette cocked expectantly was frowning in at us like he wondered what was taking so long—to reach down to the dashboard and shove in the cigarette lighter. "But Jick," Mariah went on as she clapped the camera back up to her eye, "you really ought to tell him it's a bad habit."

Whether she meant the smoking or pulling up companionably alongside rapidly moving large vehicles I am still not clear. Anyway, I rolled down the window and when the lighter popped out ready, I gingerly reached across and then handed it down into the windstream in the direction of the motorcyclist. His fingers clasped it from mine, then in a moment returned it. Satisfactorily lit, he veered away from the side of the Bago, waved thanks, and drew rapidly away down the gray thread of the freeway. As we watched him zoom toward the horizon, Riley said: "Is this a great country, or what."

Soon we were crossing the clear water of the Marias, literally Mariah's river. Oh, the name *Maria's* applied by Meriwether Lewis in 1805 to honor a lady of his acquaintance did not have the *h* on the end but it's said the same, the lovely lilting *rye* rising there in the middle. Midbridge of this lanky river that gathered water from the snows of the Continental Divide and looped it across the plains into the Missouri, I sneaked a quick look to the passenger seat and the firehaired daughter there. Whatever Marcella and I expected, our Mariah definitely had a hue all her own.

A quick handful of miles beyond the Marias put us at our noontime destination. To me the town of Shelby is the start of the High Line country, the land by now leveling eastward after all its geographical stairsteps down from the Divide seventy miles to the west. To look at, Shelby isn't particularly surprising, yet I always think of it as a place with more ambition than its situation warrants. Even now the town is best known for having put up a fat guarantee to lure the heavyweight championship fight between Jack Dempsey and Tommy Gibbons in 1923. Shelby took a bath in red ink but the fight gave it something to talk about ever since. Indeed, when Mariah and Riley and I stashed the Bago and went in the Sweetgrass Cafe for lunch, a lifesize blowup of Dempsey with his mitts up, maybe demanding his money, challenged us from the wall.

"There you go," I found myself saying as we awaited our grilled cheese sandwiches. "How about a piece on that fight?"

"Mmm," was all that drew from Mariah.

"Naw," came the instant verdict from Riley, although he did turn and contemplate the businesslike scowl of the pugilist. "The Manassas Mauler or the Molasses Wallower or whatever he was, Dempsey's been written about by the ton."

Mariah and I had the thought at the same instant. Riley must have wondered what sudden phase of the moon had the two of us grinning sappily at each other.

Heritage demanded that the family bywords be said in a woman's voice, and so Mariah tossed the hair out of her eyes and cocked her head around to deliver to Riley: "What about The Other Man."

"The other man?" Riley blinked back and forth between Mariah and me. "Who, Gibbons?" He quit blinking as the idea began to sink in. "Gibbons. What about him?"

Over lunch Mariah told him the tale just as I had told it to her, just as I had heard it from my mother.

When she'd finished, Riley expelled:

"Jesus H. Christ, that's a better idea for a piece than we've been able to think up all week! Maybe we ought to buy a Ouija board and let your grandmother do this whole series."

He glanced from one to the other of us as though deciding whether to say something more. And at last said it, quite quietly. "I wish Granda would have ever let me interview her."

Surprising to hear him speak her nickname within our family, as if he and Mariah still were married. As if Beth McCaskill still were alive.

Then the two of them headed off to the Marias Museum to get going on Gibbons.

> The morning of the day he had spent his life fighting to get to, Tommy Gibbons disappeared.
>
> He slipped out of the hotel at dawn while his wife and children still slept and walked up onto the treeless bench-land above Shelby. The town was encased by its land, the rimming benchlands as straight and parallel as the railroad steel below. But here above the boomtown splatter of hasty buildings and tents and Pullman cars, another view awaited: the Sweetgrass Hills, five magical dunes of earth swooping up out of that ledger-straight northern horizon.
>
> Equally unlikely, the forty-thousand-seat arena of fresh lumber sprawled below Gibbons as he roamed the ridgeline, trudging and pausing, trudging and pausing. Shelby was losing its shirt on promotion of the fight, yet its dreamday of making this oil-sopped little town known to the world was about to actually happen. A matter of hours from now Jack Dempsey would arrive on his royal train from Great Falls. Dempsey had taken the heavyweight championship of the world four years ago to the day, on another July Fourth, by pounding Willard senseless in three rounds. Two Julys ago, Dempsey the champion had demolished Carpentier in four rounds the way a butcher uses a cleaver on a side of beef.
>
> Tommy Gibbons was a thirty-two-year-old journeyman boxer. It had taken him eighty-eight fights to reach today. His distinction was that he had never been knocked out, never even knocked down. This afternoon he faced fifteen rounds in that prairie arena against the hugely favored Dempsey.

*Gibbons went back down the slope into Shelby. He said
something to his alarmed family and entourage about not
being able to sleep and having just wanted a walk. Then he
sat down to breakfast.*

She'd have eaten willows, my mother, in preference to being interviewed by Riley Wright. I'd had to talk like a good fellow even to get her
to let the young new *Gros Ventre Gleaner* editor do his piece on her
eighty-fourth birthday—the last of her life, it proved to be—about the
fact that she was born, with utmost inappropriateness, on April Fool's
Day of 1900. No sooner had the *Gleaner* man gone out the door than
she let me know she was chalking him onto the roster of the world's
fools. She said severely, "I wonder why that young man didn't ask me
about The Shelby Fight."

"How was he supposed to know to?"

"Jick, anybody with a Lick Of Sense At All knows that fight was a
big doings. That's why your father and I and Stanley were there."

"*You* were there?" I let out before I thought.

She gave me that look of hers labeled Of Course, You Ninny. "Your
father or Stanley neither one told you about The Bet?"

My sixty years of close acquaintanceship with my mother still had
given no guide as to whether silence or daylong interrogation was the
wiser lubricant to get her to talking. This time I tried a dumb shake of
my head.

"Well, I'm not surprised. It certainly wasn't anything for the two of
them to brag about." She unfastened her gaze from me and seemed to
be focusing off into a distance. "We saw the other man that morning
just after dawn, you know."

No, I didn't. "Saw who?"

"The man Jack Dempsey was going to fight, of course. He came
walking up over the brow of the hill ordinary as anything, right past our
tent." I must have looked as though I'd missed the conversational train
by some miles, because she deigned to circle back and explain. "We
camped that night, your father and Stanley and I, up on the bench
there above Shelby. With everybody who'd come to see the fight, you
couldn't get a room in town for love nor money." She paused ever so
briefly, then gave a glint of smile: "Well, for love, maybe. Anyway, we'd
simply brought a ridgepole tent—a lot of others did the same, it was a
regular tent town there the night before the fight. Your father and I

woke up at dawn, out of habit. Stanley was still fast asleep out under our Model T—there'd been a dance the night before and he'd gotten pretty well oiled—and so maybe there was some excuse for him. But your father saw the man as plain as I did. We both knew him right away, his picture and Dempsey's had been in every newspaper for months. He went right past our open tent flap and said, 'Good morning, quite a morning.' We watched him for, oh, most of an hour after that, walking around here and there on top of the bench. Your father figured the man must be worried half to death, to be out wandering around that early on the morning of a fight. I pointed out to him how silly an idea that was. We were up that early every blessed morning of our lives, weren't we?

"Your father and Stanley," my mother stated conclusively as if citing the last two mysteries of the universe. "How they ever thought Jack Dempsey would knock the other man out, I will never understand."

"Maybe because Dempsey knocked out almost everybody he fought?"

"All your father and Stanley had to do was use their eyes," she went right on. "Jack Dempsey was like somebody trying to hit a bee with a sledgehammer." To my startlement, she balled up her hands and swung a roundhouse right and then a matching orbit of left haymaker in the air between us. Even at age eighty-four, Beth McCaskill in fists was something to pay notice to.

"Just like that," she emphasized. "Sometimes he missed by only a little, other times by a lot. But he kept missing. Jick, anyone with a brain bigger than a cherry pit could savvy that there were only two possible reasons. Either Jack Dempsey was missing the other man on purpose, or he just could not manage to hit him squarely. Either way, it came to the same."

"But as I heard it, Gibbons was getting the cr— pudding beat out of him all through the whole fight."

"Oh, he was. Especially in the third round. That's when we started The Bet."

> *Dempsey pounded at Gibbons' body, trying to make him lower his jaw-guarding gloves. With a dozen rounds to go, Gibbons already was breathing heavily. Dempsey missed with a whistling uppercut. He resumed on the body, hitting Gibbons harder and harder until the bell.*

"Your father of course set it all off," my mother declared. "Can't you just hear him—'Jack Dempsey is eventually going to connect with one of those and knock that guy into the middle of next week, I'd bet anybody.'"

I could hear that, yes, and also the ominous ruffle of what was on its way to my father.

"Naturally," my mother said imperially, "I told him I would bet him a month of my filling the woodbox against a month of his doing the supper dishes, that the other man wouldn't be knocked out." My mother's turn to shake her head, but with incredulity. "Then Stanley had to get into it."

I believe it is not too strong to say that my family loved Stanley Meixell, almost as you are meant to love the person beside you at the altar when the bands of gold fasten your lives together. My father was but a redtopped sprig of a homestead boy the day he saw Stanley arrive, a ranger atop a tall horse, sent to create the Two Medicine National Forest. That day set the course of my father's life. Just as soon as he was big enough he was at the English Creek ranger station in the job of flunky that Stanley contrived for him, and as soon as he entered manhood he emulated Stanley by joining the U.S. Forest Service. By then my mother had come into the picture, and brisk as she was about the shortcomings of the world and particularly its male half, Beth McCaskill adopted that bachelor ranger Stanley Meixell, fussing over him when he shared our supper table as though he were her third small son beside Alec and me. Stanley eventually drank himself into blue ruin, a crash of career and friendship that was to haunt my parents until he righted himself, in their eyes and his own, a full ten years after. But at that earlier point he still had the bottle more or less under control and so the fondness was as thick as the exasperation in my mother's voice as she told me of Stanley's Shelby role.

" 'Aw, Beth, you're letting this sharpster husband take advantage of you,'" she quoted Stanley's Missouri drawl with deadly precision. "So of course I bet him too, that I would cook whatever he wanted for Sunday dinners for a month, against his bringing me a batch of fish every week for a month." She scanned me as if there must somewhere be an explanation of male gullibility. "They were so sure of that Jack Dempsey."

They sure must have been sure. I recalled that Stanley Meixell actively despised fishing, and dishwater was not my father's natural element.

The seventh round ended with Gibbons bleeding from nose and mouth and over an eye. In the eighth, Dempsey staggered him with a punch that found the jaw. The fighters traded jabs and hooks, clinched, sparred again. Dempsey swung again for the jaw but missed, swung with his other hand and missed again, then methodically hit Gibbons over the heart. They clinched until the bell.

"The other man was not a pretty sight, I do have to say," my mother acknowledged. "With the fight only half over, your father was grinning like a kitten in cream. Which must have been what inspired me to up our bet, don't you think?" I nodded instantly. "A month of my taking out the stove ashes," she proclaimed as if the upping was occurring again, "against a month of his washing the parts of the cream separator."

I flinched for my father. Washing the many discs and fittings of a cream separator was one of the snottiest jobs ever.

"Stanley of course couldn't stand prosperity either," my mother continued, "so I bet him a gallon of chockecherries every week—I pointed out that he could pick them while he was doing all that fishing—against my keeping him in pie and cake for a month."

Gibbons looked like a drowning man clinging to a rock as he clinched with Dempsey in the twelfth round, taking repeated punishment in the body. In the thirteenth, Dempsey almost wrestled him off his feet in a clinch, then threw a hook which Gibbons blocked with an elbow. At close quarters, Gibbons hit Dempsey twice, then a swing from Dempsey grazed his chin. Dempsey aimed for the jaw again, and missed. Gibbons struck him with one hand and then the other. They backed off and sparred until the bell.

Did she have it in mind from the start, hidden and explosive there in the ante? Or did it arrive to her as pure inspiration, Madame Einstein suddenly divining the square root of the universe? There between rounds thirteen and fourteen, my mother coolly bet those two rubes of hers the task of plucking her fifty spring chickens for canning, against a pair of handstitched deerhide dress-up gloves she would make for each of them if she lost.

And there my father and Stanley dangled in the noose of their own logic. Dempsey was whaling the ribcage off Gibbons with those body blows. Surely Gibbons' mitts had to drop, inevitably one of Dempsey's smashing tries had to find an open jaw. Not to mention the mutual vision of two forest rangers arriving at community dances with their workday hands princely in soft yellow deerskin, handstitched. But the plucking of fifty chickens . . .

By then the heat in the Shelby arena was tropical. People had draped handkerchiefs under their hats down the back of their sun-hit heads and necks so that the scene resembled Arabia, remembered my mother. Probably not all the sweat on my father and Stanley Meixell was solar, for now my mother was making philosophical remarks to Shelby at large about the surprising number of pikers in the ranks of the U.S. Forest Service.

Stanley and my father turned to each other.

One gritted out, "In for an inch, in for a mile, I guess, huh?" The other nodded painfully.

> When Gibbons survived the fourteenth round, the crowd threw seat cushions into the ring in exultation. The boxers shook hands as the final round began.
>
> Dempsey crowded Gibbons, Gibbons held onto Dempsey. Dempsey hit Gibbons in the body with each hand, then missed with a punch at the jaw. Gibbons reeled out of range, accepted two blows, and held onto Dempsey. Dempsey pulled back and fired a fist at Gibbons' jaw. It sailed over Gibbons' neck as the final bell rang.
>
> The referee, who was also the only fight judge, raised Dempsey's hand to signal that he was winner and still champion.
>
> Gibbons had the victory of the solitary, of the journeyer alone beyond what we had been—he was not destroyed.

Thus the stew of dishwater and fishline and chokecherries and chicken feathers that my father and Stanley Meixell existed in for the rest of the summer of 1923.

"The melodious thunk of Thelonious Monk, the razzmatazz of the snazziest jazz, is the tuuune my heart beattts for youuu . . ."

From Riley's merry uproar in the shower that evening, you'd have thought he had just gone fifteen rounds in the ring himself cleaning Jack Dempsey's clock. Mariah too looked almost ready to purr, and for my part I was glad enough to have been the inspiration, by proxy of Beth McCaskill, for their "other man" tale. Yet something uneasy kept tickling at me after supper there in the Bago as Mariah and I waited for Sinatra to finish his shower so that the three of us could head uptown and see what was what in Shelby after they turned the night on. Was I imagining, or did it seem that day by day where she and Riley were concerned, corners came off a little more? That the way they were managing to merge in their work was maybe causing them to creep beyond that? That the two of them had begun showing such civil tendencies toward each other that if you didn't know there had been a bloodthirsty divorce between them you would think they were companionably, uhm, merged?

Yet again, Mariah on the other side of the table nook from me did not appear particularly smitten with anybody except possibly the inventor of the camera. She was intent at marking up contact sheets of her day's Shelby photos with a grease pencil, and simultaneously eating a microwarmed apple turnover for dessert. With the same hand. Employing the utensil while holding the grease pencil tucked at a writing angle between her index and second fingers looked like there was every risk of forking her contact sheets or crayoning her pastry, but that was Mariah for you.

Conversational me, I waxed: "So, did you get the picture you wanted today?"

"I never do quite get that one," she responded between some slashes of cropping marks and a bite of turnover. "But maybe today's is a little closer to it." That chosen picture when it appeared with Riley's story extended all the way across the newspaper page: the wide, wide tan northern horizon as Gibbons would have seen it on his fight day dawn, absolute rim of the world blade-straight across human eyespan, but on that line of earth the bits of promontory that are the Sweetgrass Hills— a cone of dune, space, a blunter humped swell, space, another dune. As if saying no brink, even the planet's, stays so severe if taken one strip at a time.

By now Riley was trying the monkey-thunky stanza about the seventeenth different way and still didn't sound to me within hailing distance of any tune. Meanwhile Mariah had polished off both dessert and contact sheets and gone to putting on earrings for the evening, dangly hoops festooned with tiny pewter roses. Doing so, she remarked: "I always have wondered why he never goes on to the rest of a song."

"Yeah, well, this rig doesn't hold enough hot water for him to think his way past the first verse, is my guess." Her raised arms as she fastened the earrings brought up a point I would rather not have noticed. Two points, actually, making themselves known where the tips of her breasts tested the fabric of her green blouse. Mariah had showered before supper and pretty plainly her bra went missing in the aftermath. Be damned, though, if I was going to tell a thirty-five-year-old daughter how to dress herself.

The laundered Riley at last appeared, declaring Mariah and I had kept him waiting long enough. Any social suspicion I had was not borne out by him either, for although he gave Mariah a commendatory glance he passed up the chance to say anything flirty and just ushered us out into the night by yapping out a ring announcer's announcement of round sixteen.

We went north of the railroad tracks to a bar called the Whoop-Up, on Riley's insistent theory that the places across the tracks are always more interesting.

More interesting than what, I should have asked him the instant we set foot inside the sorry-looking enterprise.

Floor that must have been mopped annually whether it needed it or not. Orangish walls. Pool table, its green felt standing out like a desperate sample patch of lawn. Total crowd of three, one of them the bartender pensively hunched over a chess board at the near end of the bar. Nobody was smoking at the moment, but the barroom had enough accumulated tobacco smell to snort directly.

Perhaps symptomatically, bar stools were few and we ended up perched right next to the extant two customers, beer drinkers both, the beef-faced variety who still look like big kids even though they're thirty-some. Riley and me they gave minimum nods, Mariah and her blouse they gave maximum eyeballing. With distinct reluctance the bartender left his chess cogitation long enough to produce my scotch ditch and Mariah's Lord ditch, Riley meantime whistling tunelessly as he did his habitual shopping of the bottles behind the bar. "Lewis and Clark blackberry brandy," he eventually specified. "Always a good year."

The bartender went back to staring at his chess board. The two beer consumers resumed muttering to each other about how life was treating them. The three of us sipped. The most activity was generated by the clock above the cash register, one of those just barely churning ones that flops a new advertising placard at you about every half minute. Before long I was forcing myself not to count the number of times the ad for DEAD STOCK REMOVAL, with a cartoon drawing of a cow with a halo, 24-HOUR SERVICE, flopped into view.

"I'm trying to remember," Riley murmured to Mariah after a spell of this whoopee in the Whoop-Up. "Did we live this nerve-tingling kind of life before we were divorced?"

"Every night was an extravaganza," she assured him with almost a straight face.

Any fitting response to that seemed to elude Riley, and he focused off toward the bartender who was staying as motionless as his chess pieces. Riley of course grew curious. The two at the end of the bar near us did not look like chess types. Ever interrogative, Riley put forth to the bartender: "Where's your other player?"

"Sun City, Arizona. Take turns calling each other every fifteen minutes with a move."

That floored even Riley, at least briefly. But sure enough, on the dot when a quarter past came the bartender reached to the phone, punched a bunch of digits, rattled off what sounded like pawn to queen four, and hung up.

Activity picked up too at my ear nearest the beer pair. "Tell you, Ron, I don't know what you got going with Barbara Jo, but don't let her get you in front of no minister. This marriage stuff is really crappy. You take, Jeannie's mom is always on my back about why don't we come over more. But we go over there and the stuff she cooks, she never salts anything or anything, and I don't eat that crap without no salt on it. Last time she called up and asked Jeannie why we weren't coming over, I told Jeannie to tell her I had to lay down and rest. Then there's Jeannie's dad, he just got dried out down at Great Falls. Cranky old sonofabitch, I think they ought to let him have a few beers so he wouldn't be so much of a craphead, is what I think. And you know what else, Jeannie's brother and sister-in-law had a Fourth of July picnic and didn't even invite us. That's the kind of people they are. Jeannie and I been talking a lot lately. I told her, I about had it with her crappy family. Soon as the first of the year and I get enough money ahead to buy my big bike, I'm heading out to the coast and go to school somewhere."

"Yeah?" Ron responded. "What in?"

"Social work."

Our sipping went on as if we had glassfuls of molasses, so I admit it was an event out of the contagiously drowsy ordinary when Mariah took herself off to the ladies' room. She didn't realize it but she had company all the way, the double sets of bozo eyeballs from beside me. "Divorced, did I hear them say?" the nearer of the two, the Ron one, checked with the other in a muffled tone.

"Yeah, I heard the word," confirmed the other bar stool resident. "A free woman. Always the best price."

"She looks sweet enough to melt in your mouth, don't she," said the first.

"I'd sure like to give that a try," pined the other.

"Like to, hell. I'm gonna. You just watch."

I had turned and was sending them a glower which should have melted their vocal cords shut, but it is difficult to penetrate that much haze of beer and intrinsic lard. Nor was goddamn Riley any help. "Don't look at me," he murmured. "She was only ever my wife. You're stuck with her as a daughter permanently."

All too soon Mariah was emerging from the ladies' room, to the tune of the under-the-breath emission beside me, "Look at the local motion in that blouse." Ron the Romancer was applying a companionable leer all over her as she came back to the bar. If called into court, his defense could only have been that at no time did his eyeballs actually leave his body.

"Hey you, yayhoo," I began to call him down on his behavior just as Mariah gave him a look, then a couple of sharper glances as it dawned on her where his interest lay. But her admirer continued to spoon her up with his gaze even after she reached the bar and us again. Then, as if in a staring contest with what were standing sentinel in Mariah's blouse, the would-be swain swanked out to her: "That green sure brings out your best points."

I brightly suggested we call it a night.

"Ohhh, not till I finish this," Mariah said, and picked up her drink but didn't sit down with it. Instead she delivered me a little tickle in the ribs and said, "Trade places with me, how about."

That would put her directly next to the pair of shagnasties, removing me as a barrier of at least age if not dignity. "Uh, actually I'm just real comfortable where I am."

The tickle turned into an informative pincer on my rib. "Riley needs the company," she let me know. I flinched and made the trade.

Sidling onto the stool where I'd been, Mariah remarked to the staring bozo, "You seem pretty interested in what I'm wearing."

He looked like he'd been handed candy. "Yeah, I like what you haven't got on."

"Aw, crud," Riley uttered wearily and began to get off his stool in the direction of combat.

Mariah halted him with a stonewall look and a half-inch of headshake. Riley considered, shrugged, sat back down.

Turning around to her unremitting spectator again, who now seemed hypnotized by her earring dealybobs, she said in a way that left spaces in the air where her words had been: "Well then now—what's on your mind besides what's on my chest?"

He blinked quite a number of times. Then: "I was wondering if you'd, er, want to go out."

Mariah presented him what I recognized as her most dangerous grin. "Now doesn't that sound interesting," she assessed. "I'll bet you're the kind of guy who shows up for a date in your ready-to-go tuxedo."

"Er, I'm not sure I've got—what's a ready-to-go tuxedo?"

Mariah swirled her Calvert and water, took a substantial swig, then delivered in a tone icier than the cubes in her glass:

"A ten-gallon hat and a hard-on."

Into our drinks Riley and I simultaneously snorted aquatic laughs, which doubtless would have drawn one or the other of us the wrath of the red-faced bozo, except that his buddy on the other side of him gave out a guffaw that must have been heard in northernmost Canada and then crowed, "He can at least borrow the hat someplace, lady!"

"Screw you, Terry," the still-red shagnasty gritted out, in a 180-degree turn of his attentions. Then he swung around on his stool with his right fist in business, socking Terry in the middle of his hilarity and sending him sailing off backwards.

Terry rebounded off the pool table and with a roar tackled Mariah's suitor off his stool. The locked pair of them swooshed past us in midair, landed colossally and then rolled thumpedy-thump-thump across the floor in a clinch, cussing and grunting.

"Maybe I missed a chance there," Mariah reflected as the bartender whipped out a Little League baseball bat and kept it within quick reach while phoning the town marshal. She cast a last glance at the tornado of elbows and boots and *oofs* and *ooghs* as it thrashed across the floorboards. "He does seem to be a person who cares a lot."

Leaving the second battle of Shelby behind, we truly began tooling along the High Line, eastward on Highway 2 across that broad brow of Montana.

The Bago purred right along but the other three of us seemed to have caught our mood from the weather, which had turned hazy and dull. No trace whatsoever of the hundred-mile face of the Rockies behind us to the west, and on the northern horizon the Sweetgrass Hills were blue ghosts of themselves. With only the plains everywhere around I began to feel adrift, and Mariah and Riley too seemed logy and out of their element. As far as we were concerned this highway had been squeezed out of a tube of monotony. I wished the day could be rinsed, to give the High Line country a fairer chance with us.

Soon we were in the wheat sea. Out among the straw-toned fields occasional round metal bins and tall elevators bobbed up, but otherwise the only color other than basic farming was the Burlington Northern's roadbed of lavender gravel, brought in from somewhere far. That railroad built by Jim Hill as the transcontinental Great Northern route—farthest up on the American map and hence its Montanized designation "the high line"—cleaved open this land to settlement in the first years of this century and even yet the trackside towns are the only communities in sight. One after another as you drive Highway 2 they come peeping over the lonely horizon, Dunkirk, Devon, Inverness, Kremlin . . . a person would think he really was somewhere. Which can only have been the railroad's idea in naming these little spots big.

Our destination today was Havre, which didn't reassure me either. I'd been there a number of times before when livestock business compelled me to and knew it wasn't the kind of place I am geared for, out as the town is like a butter pat in the middle of a gigantic hotcake. So any conversation was something of a relief, even when Mariah caught sight of a jet laying its cloud road, the contrail stitching across a break in the sky's thin murk ahead of us, and said in disgruntled photographer fashion, "The Malmstrom flyboys have got the weather I want, up there."

That roused Riley to poke his head between us and peer through the windshield at the white route of the bomber or fighter or whatever the plane from the Great Falls air base was. "Another billion-dollar sil-ver bullet from Uncle Sam," he preached in a gold-braid voice. "Take that, you enemy, whoever the hell you are any more."

"Reminds me of your ack-ack career, petunia," I contributed to the aerial motif.

"Mmm, that time." The start of a little grin crept into Mariah's tone.

"Old Earlene." I couldn't help but follow the words with a chuckle.

"Brainpain Zane." Mariah escalated both of us into laughter with that.

Riley had sat back into his dinette seat. "I knew I should have brought a translator along when I hooked up with you two."

"This goes back to when I was a freshman in high school," Mariah took over the telling of it to him. "Initiation Day—you remember how dumb-ass those were anyway. This one, the seniors had us all carry brooms and whenever one of them would catch us in the hallway between classes and yell 'Air raid!' we were supposed to flop on our back and aim the broom up like an antiaircraft gun and go *'ack-ack-ack-ack.'* Cute, huh? Somehow I went along with the program until Earlene Zane, the original brainpain as we called her, caught me walking across the muddy parking lot to the schoolbus and yelled out, 'Air raid, McCaskill! Dump your butt in that mud, freshie!' I looked down at that mud and then I looked at Earlene, and the next thing I knew I'd swept the broom through the gloppiest mudhole, right at her. Big globs flew onto the front of her dress, up into her face, all over her. So I did it a bunch more times."

"Hey, don't leave out the best part," I paternally reminded her as Riley chimed in with our chortling.

"Oh, right," Mariah went on in highest spirit. "Every time I swat-ted a glob onto old Earlene, I'd go: *ack-ack-ack-ack.*"

By the time we'd laughed ourselves out at that, we were beyond Kremlin, with only another ten minutes or so of hypnotic highway to put us into Havre. I figured we had this High Line day made, whatever the rest of them were going to be like, when abruptly a spot of colors erupted at the far edge of the road.

Like a hurled mass the flying form catapulted up across the highway on collision course with the windshield in front of my face. Before it could register on me that I'd done any of it, I yelled "Hang on!" and braked the motorhome and swerved it instinctively toward where the large ringneck had flown up from, trying to veer over just behind the arc of its flight. The body with its whirring wings, exquisitely long feathered tail, even the red wattle mask of its head and the white circle around the bird's neck, all flashed past me, then sickly thudded against the last of the uppermost corner of the windshield where the glass meets the chrome fitting, on Mariah's side of the Bago. She ducked and flung up both arms in a horizontal fence to protect her face, the way a person automatically desperately will, as the web of cracks crinkled down from the shatterpoint.

By the time any of this was clear to me, the pheasant was a wad of feathers in the barrow pit a hundred yards behind us.

"You all right?" I demanded of Mariah as I got the Bago and myself settled back down into more regular road behavior. "Any glass get you?"

"Huh uh." She was avidly studying the damage pattern zigzagged into the upper corner of the windshield in front of her. "Damn, I wish I'd caught that with the camera."

"How about you, Riley?" I called over my shoulder. "You come through that okay?"

"Yeah," the scribbler answered in an appreciative voice. "Fine and dandy, Jick."

"Good. Then open that notebook of yours to the repairs page."

The next morning there in Havre was the fourth of September, which also happened to be Labor Day—always the message that summer is shot and winter is at the door—and two full months since Mariah cornered me into the centennial trip. Sure, I thought to myself while easing out of bed onto my tender leg, which was feeling the change in weather, why not lump all dubious anniversaries into one damn Monday and frost it with Havre.

Mariah mentioned nothing at breakfast—not even my hotcakes alBago, doily-size but by the dozens—she and Riley poring over a map spread between them, him listing off towns ahead of us on Highway 2 and jotting them into his notebook with question marks after them while she cogitated out loud about photographic prospects, so I ended the meal fed up in more ways than one. A High Line breeze whined insistently in the overhead vent of the motorhome. Riley's pen tippy-tapped monotonously in his notebook. I peered out to see what kind of weather was in store, but no luck there either, Havre being down in a hole so much you can't even begin to see to any significant horizon. The day had me disturbed, even I will admit. Try as I did to rein in my mood, I suppose a bit of it worked loose in my general remark:

"Whatever in hell you two eventually manage to come up with, I hope to Christ it's got some mountains somewhere around for a change. This country where there's nothing to lean your eyes on is getting me down."

Riley's pen quit tapping the notebook, and when I glanced over at the unaccustomed welcome silence, he had the pen angled like a pointer onto a spot on the map. Mariah's index finger was there from the opposite direction. Both their faces were lit up as if they had hit the same socket at the same time.

It was Mariah who gave me a thankful grin and said, "Great minds run on the same track."

"What, me and you two?" I said skeptically.

"Better than that," Riley chimed in. "You and Chief Joseph."

On the map, out beyond Havre a backroad dangles lonesomely south from the little town of Chinook. Down it, across miles and miles of grassland being swept by the wind and at last almost into the Bearpaw Mountains, we pulled in at the Chief Joseph Battleground.

The Joseph story, actually the Nez Percé story because he was but one of several chiefs who led their combined bands—not just their fighting men but women, children, their old people, their herd of horses, the whole works—out of the Wallowa Mountains in Oregon in flight from the push of whites on their land, I'd of course read the basics of: that after a dodging route of seventeen hundred miles and several successful battles, the Indians were cornered into surrender here only a few more days' march to sanctuary in Canada. What I saw now, at history's actual place, was that the Nez Percé in that autumn of the last century had two more horizons to get over. Up onto the brief rise above this Snake Creek bottomland where they'd pitched camp. Then over the wider rim of skyline ridge to the north and across the boundary into Canada. The small horizon, suddenly deadly with cavalry and infantry, had been the one that doomed them.

Our threesome sat within the protection of the motorhome and studied the ground of battle, across the somehow wicked-looking little creek of wild rose brambles and stunted willows.

After a bit, Riley tested the air with his cocked-to-one-side tone of voice. "Custer was a loser, and he's famous as hell. Chief Joseph fought longer and harder and didn't get his people killed wholesale, and all he's got is that plaque on a rock over there. Why'd it turn out that way?"

Whether or not Riley really expected an answer, I turned and gave him the one that needed no words—simply rubbed the back of my hand, the skin there.

We stepped from the Bago into a wind just short of lethal, Mariah and I stepping right back in and swapping our hats for winter caps and pulling on heaviest coats. But Riley must have been in some kind of writing fever because he braved the wind in just a jacket to hustle over for a look at the Joseph plaque. By the time we joined him at that— there actually proved to be three memorial markers, a plaque apiece in honor of the U.S. soldiers, the Indians, and the Chinook townsman who'd helped preserve the battlefield; about as democratic as you can get about a combat site, I suppose—gusts were whistling even harder out of the west and Riley had to give up on his polar bear act. Borrowing the Bago keys from me, along with my look that said I hoped he wasn't going to keep diddling around in this fashion in weather like this, he scooted back to the motorhome to don a saner coat while Mariah and I ducked behind a little wall of shelter put up to keep visitors from being spun away like tumbleweeds.

Hunched in out of the gale, she blew on her fingers to get ready for shutter action. I blew on mine simply because they were cold. Both of us scanned the battleground in front of us across the brambles of Snake Creek. Everywhere out there the dead grass flowed identically in the wind, coulees and brief benchlands merging into each other as just slightest dents and bulges in the grass-color of everything.

"What year was the battle?" I asked above the whoosh of the wind.

"1877," Mariah raised her voice in turn.

"This place still is in a bad mood," I observed.

Mariah said an eloquent nothing. I recognized why. I am not a cameraperson but even I could see that for her photography purpose, this site was hiding its face.

"Not nice," Riley reported meteorologically as a gust propelled him behind the windbreak wall with us.

"In more ways than one," Mariah shared with him out of her contemplation of the tan smudge of battlefield. "This is going to take some real figuring out to shoot." So saying, she automatically reached up and reset her winter cap with the bill backwards now over the neckfall of her hair, to keep the brim out of the way of her camera.

"I sympathize," the scribbler responded. Not in any smartass way, but as if he might actually mean it, which made me wonder what was getting into Riley Wright lately. "I need to tromp around out there a while myself," he sped on. "The wind just lends a little atmosphere, hmm?"

Atmosphere was one way of putting it. I expected prickles at a place like this, and they came at once. Spirits hovering in their old neighborhood are not something I can bring myself to believe in. But I do figure there could be sensations left over in us—the visitors, the interlopers—from tribal times, from cave times; maybe our hair roots go deep into that past and it rises up out of us as the prickles at such a site as this battlefield.

Wanting to stay out of the way of Mariah and her lens as she bowed her neck and started stalking for any photo chance, I stuck with Riley when he began his own prowl along the little ridge at the south edge of the battle site. Up as we were, I could see that the country here was higher than the Milk River Valley where Chinook lay, these surroundings gradually stairstepping into the rounded small summits of the Bearpaw Mountains. The nicest ranching country I'd seen yet on the High Line, actually; snowdrifts would last and last in the gullies on these north slopes, and other water surely awaited in springs tucked here and there. For livestock, a promising enough place. For a life-or-death encampment, no. As we tromped around, hunching in that wind, every sense told me what nasty country this was to fight in—the creek bottomland dangerously unsheltered yet all different levels of land around the site like crazy stairs and hideyholes.

Riley had the order of battle, to call it that, down pat from his research while we were driving from Havre. The slightly higher ground we were on was where the Nez Percé had been able to flop down in cover and drive back the white soldiers' first attack. The U.S. troops lost an immediate twenty-two men and two officers in that opening charge against the ridge, and about twice that many wounded. Some of the Nez Percé were killed that night by their own warriors who mistook them for Cheyennes allied with the white soldiers. Both sides dug in and it dragged on into a kind of sniping marathon from trenches and rifle pits. In all. Riley said, five days of such mauling took place. Near where we stood Chief Looking Glass was the last man killed, picked off by an army scout. Over there, Riley pointed out, the body of Chief Toohoolhoolzote had lain unburied because of the field of fire from the white soldiers. Down here below us, a howitzer shell caved in a shelter pit on a Nez Percé woman and her child.

In no time at all of that chilly trudging and standing, my achy shin felt like fire. Yet it never crossed my mind to retreat to the Bago.

Even the clouds were askew here, scattered fat cottonwad ones with perfectly flat bottoms as if skidding on the top of the wind. Every so often, a floe of cloudshadow would blot across the battlefield and I would see Mariah frown upward from her camera.

Riley was spieling something I had wondered about, how the Indians kept track of their casualties. *"Alahoos, an oldlike man who was still strong, made announcement of all incidents and events each day,"* he read off what he'd copied in his notebook earlier. *"All knew him and reported to him who had been wounded or killed in battle, who was missing or had disappeared."*

I'd stayed silent until something made me ask. "What was the weather like during the fighting here?"

"Cold, rainy, windy, generally shitty," Riley named off. "It ended up snowing about half a foot." This quicksilver battlesite in white, a first sift of snowfall halfway up the long grass, the bald brows of the hills showing through, I could readily see.

Then I recognized this day's weather. As much so as if the wind had put on a uniform and the chilly air assumed a familiar mask of ice.

It was blowing from May 18, 1943. I was eighteen and supposedly a soldier. After enlistment and basic training I was shipped to find my war in a part of the world I had barely even heard of, the Aleutian islands. If you look hard enough at a map they are a line of stepping stones in the North Pacific between Asia and Alaska, and the Japanese were using them in just that way in World War Two. In the fighting on the island of Attu my platoon was sent out hours before daylight the morning of our attack on Cold Mountain. We were to sneak into position where we could work over a Japanese emplacement of heavy machine guns, at least three of the goddamn things. That mountain was cold, all right. Ice on the tundra as we climbed the slope, and the wind trying to swat us off the face of the earth. Just in the earliest minute or so when it was getting light enough to see we spotted the first enemy, a sentry about fifty yards away. I guess he was not the greatest of sentries, because he was standing up there against the skyline shaking out a grass mat. Our lieutenant motioned the rest of us to take cover under a cutbank. Then he laid down in firing-range position with his legs carefully spraddled and shot the sentry. I have wondered ever since if that is pretty much what war is: some ninny stands up when he shouldn't and some other ninny shoots him when he shouldn't. What I do know for definite is that our prescribed plan of attack, to grenade those machine guns, was now defunct before it even started because we were way too far away to throw. Yet, for whatever reason, all at once here came four or five Japanese soldiers and an officer with a sword, kiyi-ing down in a bayonet attack on us. Our BAR man opened up, the Browning Automatic making that kind of regretful *tuck tuck tuck* sound as it fired, and that took care of the bayonet proposition. While the Japanese were thinking matters over, our lieutenant's next brain-storm was to send some of us out around to a little knoll so we could pinch in on the machine gun position. I was the third guy who had to scramble across there, running hunched down for maybe forty feet from the end of the cut bank to the cover of the knoll, and I was only a step from having it made when a bullet smashed my left leg not far above the ankle. I fell and rolled a long way down the mountainside. Not that I know an awful lot about it, except for the skinned up and bruised places all over my body later, because I'd immediately lost con-sciousness, but the other men of the platoon assured me I'd been the deadest-looking guy they ever saw, flopping down the slope like a rag doll.

That was my combat career, quick. Over with except for the piece of my leg where the ache lay under the bullet scar, my Attu tattoo. I—

No. Not over with. Not here, not this day. Peace of mind was splin-tered too by that bullet of forty-six years ago.

With a gulp I reached down and wildly rubbed my shin, trying to scrub away so much more than that boneload of pain. Oh sure, it served me right for traipsing around to these sorrowspots with this duo of Montanologists. Maybe my herder Helen had the right idea: go and live with rocks. Goddamn it all to hell anyway, how long did we have to stay here being augured by the wind? Mariah, I saw, had finally sorted her way across the deceptive levels of the battlefield and was at the far side marshaling a picture of the bust of Chief Joseph within an iron spike fence. I turned to strongly urge Riley too into finishing up this yowling site.

Riley was gone.

Gone where, gone how, there was no sign whatsoever.

I squinted against the wind and tried to get a grip on why he would up and vanish. My swoon back to the Aleutians surely hadn't taken long enough for him to walk off over any of the ridges or back to the Bago. And I could see along the entire creek and all the battlefield to where Mariah was working. But abruptly only the two of us in this welter of geography.

A new crop of prickles broke out on me. Aggravating as Riley could be with his presence, to have him subtracted this way was uncommonly spooky. As if my Attu memory of brushing against oblivion had brushed Ri—

Not forty feet from me, his tall figure suddenly rose from the ground. Oh sure, scribbling. Where the hell else would Riley be extant? He had lain down in a little dip, most likely a rifle pit dug by one of the Nez Percé, to belly into that sense of concealment and now here he stood again, telling his everlasting notebook about it all.

> . . . *in a pock in the earth. In a disease scar older than smallpox or any other.*
>
> *But craters of war heal over, don't they? Why else the bronze calm of plaques, the even-handed attestations to both sides who fought here in the narrow bottomland of Snake Creek in 1877? The grass has grown back as thick as flame. The brow of the hill to the east wears strips of farming like a cheerful striped cap. Sunshine dodges the clouds, uncurls flags of light on the hills.*
>
> *By now the only echoes at this battlesite are poetry. The sentences of surrender by Joseph, just the surviving chief of several who jointly led the Nez Percé almost magically through seventeen hundred miles of hostile territory and several battles before Snake Creek, were interpreted by one of General Howard's staff, transcribed by another; scrawled in a report to the Secretary of War, the surrender speech was merely a knell for one more band of outgunned Indians. But Joseph's words want to be more than that.*
>
> *I am tired of fighting.*
> *Our chiefs are killed.*
> *The old men are all killed.*

> It is cold and we have no blankets.
> My people have run to the hills,
> and have no blankets.
>
> Perhaps I shall find them among the dead.
>
> I am tired: my heart is sick and sad
> rom where the sun now stands,
> I will fight no more forever.

> Combat pits nowadays are greatly deeper in the prairie
> south of the Bearpaws, where the Nez Percé ghosted across
> the center of Montana on their route to defeat. Concrete
> burrows, complete arsenals underground. Missile silos, we
> let the Department of Defense (née the Department of War,
> 1789–1947) call these most deliberate of craters, as if what
> they store is lifegiving. Two hundred Minuteman missile
> silos across Montana. More of these fields of nuclear war-
> heads in the Dakotas and Wyoming, Nebraska and Col-
> orado and Missouri. Enough gopherholed megatonnage to
> incinerate people by the million.
> So, no, warpox does not heal. It merely scabs over with
> the latest materiel. And so we are still pitted, now with
> nuclear snipers' burrows. Maybe the one nearest you is for
> Kiev; if Mutual Assured Destruction has been calibrated
> cleverly enough, maybe the one siloed in Kiev is for here. (It
> is cold and we have no blankets.) In any case, the combat
> pits still are dutifully manned. On highways crisscrossing the
> heart of the West today, you can meet the next shift-change
> of missile crews in their Air Force vans, blue taxis to
> Armageddon.

So time came and went, there along Snake Creek. On Aleutian
wind agitating battle earth in Montana. Through summer into colder
calendar. Into Mariah's camera and Riley's notebook and out as scene
and story.

In me. In the arithmetic that if you add to an eighteen-year-old
wounded soldier the years now since his bullet, my birthday—this
day—was my sixty-fifth.

—

"Got it finally," Mariah declared, ruddy from the wind but an exultant grin on her, as she coalesced with Riley and me at the footbridge. She'd earned grinning rights, because what she'd done in her picture to go with Riley's piece was put that weather to work—the flat-bottomed clouds, each drifting separate against the sky, in the same sad lopped way that the sculpture of Chief Joseph's head seemed based in the air amidst them. Mariah hugged herself for warmth. "Brrr, let's get in out of this."

The wind put up a final struggle as we trudged head-on into it the last couple of hundred yards to the motorhome, which I forthwith went to unlock. Then remembered. "Oh yeah, I gave the keys to you, Riley."

"Hmm? So you did." He reached a hand into the side pocket of his coat and froze in that position. Next he cast an uh-oh look at Mariah where she was jigging in place trying to keep warm, then finally one toward me.

"Christamighty!" I yelped. "What'd you go and do now, lose the goddamn keys?"

"No, no, of course not," Riley piped with a swallow. "They're, ah, just in one of my other pockets, is all."

"So dig them out," I urged with vigor. "It's colder than the moon's backside out here."

Riley's gaze at me turned sickly. "The pocket of *that* jacket," he admitted, indicating toward the Bago. The jacket he'd changed for a heavier one. The jacket he'd left in the Bago. The jacket he'd locked in the Bago.

Right then I could have gladly mangled him. Riley Wright Ground Sausage, Handmade on Snake Creek. But Mariah put herself between us and headed me off with multiple adjurations of "Whoa now, that isn't going to get us anywhere!" and eventually I cooled down—in that wind it didn't take all that long—enough to agree we had to do something drastic.

And it is a drastic amount of effort to break out a motorhome's safety-glassed rear sidewindow, above head height, with a rock at the cold blowy end of a miserable day, just as it is an even more aggravating chore to pluck and dig all the shards of glass out of the windowframe, as we stretched and shivered and did until at last the frame was safe for Riley and me to boost Mariah up to shinny through.

After she unlocked the doors and the keys were retrieved and I'd revved the heater up to full blast to start thawing us out, Riley assured me he knew precisely what to do next.

"Do you," I said icily. "Isn't it kind of late in life for you to start in on growing a brain?"

"We'll just swing by the hardware store in Chinook and patch some weather glazing over the window until we can get it fixed," he outlined. Under my continued stare he added, "Ah, which reminds me," and flipped open his notebook to the page of the buffalo-bashed grill, the AWOL hubcap, the pheasant-cracked windshield and dented chrome, and added the rear sidewindow to Accounts Outstanding.

When we reached Chinook, Riley's bright weatherizing idea proved to have missed only one detail: the hardware store was closed up tight for the holiday.

"Pull in here," Mariah directed before I could start on Riley again, pointing with great definiteness at the IGA foodstore. In she marched while the window assassin and I sat in mutual polar silence, although the wind howled merrily in through the surprise aperture it found at the rear corner of the Bago, and in a jiffy she was back with a roll of freezer tape and a box of bags made out of some kind of clear crinkly material, remarkably stout. Riley and I piled out to help her tape the bags over the window. I can testify there is some justice in life, because he was the one who gave in to curiosity and asked her, "What are these anyway?"

"Turkey basting bags," Mariah told him.

Then she surprised the daylights out of me.

"Your main present is that I held off mentioning what day this is until right now," she addressed to me as soon as we were back inside the bandaged Bago, "knowing how owly you always get about your birthday. And now that we've faced the issue, I'm taking you out to birthday supper. And here's a little something to add to that, even."

Mariah produced out of one of her ditty bags a small package with a major bow on it and delivered it to me with a kiss, without even any daughterly comment about the risk her lips were taking on my whiskers.

This was more like it and I was much touched, sure, but could easily have stood not to have Riley within a hundred miles of our family moment. He too looked as if he wished himself absent, but contributed a semigruff "At least you picked a day with enough wind to help you with the candles."

A western tie, one of those bolo ones that hangs like a large locket, lay in the small box I'd unwrapped. Its centerpiece was a polished oval of stone set in a broochlike clasp. The stone was darkest green, so intensely so it approached black, but full of sparks of color, reds, golds, grays; like a night sky of stars of hues never seen before.

"Isn't this nifty," I not much more than whispered, overcome with the star-specked beauty of the gift after this mortally awful day. "Thank you, honey, my God, thank you." I breathed tenderly on the gem and rubbed it on the sleeve of my shirt, brightening the amulet's constellations of sparks even more. "What kind of stone—?"

"It's jasper," Mariah said, her gray eyes bright. "Helen found it for me on the North Fork, in that coulee that leads down to the McCaskill homestead. You really like it?"

"Do I ever."

"Then let's dude you up in it." Mariah came over and slipped the bolo loop over my head and critically slid the oval gem into place at the base of my throat; most painless way in the world to dress up, all right. "There now, look at you."

And for once she even asked. "How much would you mind having your picture taken, just for the occasion?"

"I guess it wouldn't necessarily be fatal," I allowed. "Bang away."

She shot a variety of me in my new neck adornment feeling swave and looking debonure, but didn't radically prolong this camera session. "Okay, you both got your faces set for supper?" she asked with the last *click.*

"Why don't you two go ahead," Riley suggested, reason personified for once. "I'll stay here and write the piece from today, get it on in to the evil elf."

"If you do that, I have to race back here and run film through the Leafax yet tonight," Mariah objected as if Riley had peed in the path of her parade. "What about that back-up piece you sneaked in? What does that need on it, anything I can send in quick?"

Even I admit, Riley was showing the frazzle of the day as much as any of us and obviously could stand a square meal and a night off. He rubbed his eyes one at a time, first the blue one left showing and then the gray, like he was dimming down even as we watched. "Let me think. Yeah, it's just a thumbsucker, any number of your shots of country you've already sent in will go okay with that one."

"Then come on," Mariah urged. "Let's go birthdaying."

—

So we were not spared Riley for the occasion, but all else seemed auspicious enough at the moment, Mariah's thoughtfulness, my new jasper dazzler, evening dining ahead along the Milk River. Chinook was a tidy town, some nice logic to it—its block of bars, just for example, was a concentrate of western oasis nomenclature: Mint, Stockman, Elk, right there door by door by door. Where we headed, though, was out to the edge of town to a blue-painted rambly enterprise Mariah had singled out for this birthday shindig of mine. By now the day was losing the last of its light, so the place's high old neon sign out front was like electric paint against the onset of night: a giant long-stemmed glass, in which was seated the representation of a curvy woman in fringed skirt and bandanna and high-heeled boots—she too was long-stemmed, one shapely leg cocked over the edge of the martini glass and the other extended fully into the air—with her head thrown back and her arm up, tossing her cowgirl hat into the sky. When the sign blinked, the leg kicked in frolicsome fashion and the hat sailed high.

THE LASS IN A GLASS, the red-tubed wording underneath I guess not unexpectedly said, and spaced beneath that ran the enumeration of *Bar, Lounge, Supper Club, Coffee Shop, Bus Depot* and *Motel.* Riley evidently figured he was back in my good graces now that we were amid my birthday celebration—he could not have been more mistaken—and gandering up at those neon announcements he commented: "Wouldn't you think they'd go all the way and add a maternity ward and a funeral parlor?"

As soon as we were inside, Riley did the dutiful and employed the lobby phone long enough to coax some functionary in Missoula—despite that earlier elf crack, the BB naturally was nowhere to be found on the newspaper premises over a holiday—into just going with the back-up piece and picking a nice one of Mariah's file photos to illustrate it with, happy fucking Labor Day to him too. The day's wind must have sharpened all our appetites, for without even any debate we then bypassed the bar and lounge and set ourselves for supper.

Our exit occurred a considerable while later, the three of us stuffed with soup, salad, fondue and breadsticks, prime rib, baked potato, two or three vegetables, and chocolate cake—when this place said supper club it meant it—but Mariah lighter by quite a few dollars. I thanked her a kabillion for the birthday feast, but if I thought I'd had an eventful enough day to hold me for another sixty-five years, I had another think coming.

Riley of course was the culprit. We were harmlessly on our way out of The Lass in a Glass enterprise, headed for the motorhome ready to tuck in for the night, when he made the uncharacteristic error of trying to be nice.

"Tell you what, Jick. Just to show you my heart's in the right place," patting his rump pocket where his billfold resided, "I'll buy you a birthday drink."

"Naw," I demurred as civilly as I could, "it's been kind of a hefty day. I think I'll turn in early."

Say for Riley, he didn't smart off with anything about somebody my age needing his sleep. Instead, worse, he turned to Mariah and invited, "At least I can keep my reckless generosity in the family. Buy you a round, can I, Mariah Montana?"

"Best offer I've had since Shelby," she responded, surprisingly full of cheer. Then to me: "You don't mind if we hang on in here a little while, do you? We'll let ourselves in the Bago quiet as we can."

"Actually, the night is still a pup, isn't it," I resorted to, letting my gaze rest on Riley. "Where's that drink you're financing?"

The bar of this Lass in a Glass emporium was an average enough place. A Hamm's clock above the cash register, Budweiser lampshades on the dangling overheads, other beer signs glowing here and there for general decor. The jukebox had Willie Nelson and Waylon Jennings singing to each other about various toots they'd been on. Wherever the Labor Day crowd was, it wasn't here; only a handful of customers in ballcaps and straw Stetsons, plus a wide young woman behind the bar who looked like she could handle any of them with one hand. Remembering the floor warriors of the Whoop-Up in Shelby, I hoped that was the case.

Mariah and I each ordered our usual and Riley put in for his usual unusual, you might say, by summoning up a Harvey Wallbanger.

"Whup, wait a minute here!" I jumped him triumphantly. "You already had one of those on the trip. In Ennis or Dillon or someplace back there."

"Jick, a man never wants to let himself get reliably unpredictable," he told me, whatever that meant.

No sooner were Willie and Waylon done songstering than a color television started droning in the corner. I wonder if someday somebody will invent silence.

It for sure won't be Riley. He started right in yammering to Mariah about what piece they—*we,* he kept phrasing it with what he must have figured was a generously inclusive glance at me—ought to press on to next, Fort Peck dam maybe? I'd for damn sure press him onward, I thought to myself, right out of the vicinity of the McCaskills if I but could.

Fort Peck I knew a little something about from when I was a kid during the Depression and construction of that earthen dam across the Missouri River was a relief project which Montanans believed Franklin Delano Roosevelt had sent from heaven. Enough to inquire innocently, "Doesn't the dam kind of look like a big ditch bank about four miles long?"

Riley cut me a look, not the inclusive sort this time. "That's one way of putting it."

"Sounds real photogenic," Mariah met that with. "Riley, don't you know any history that isn't horizontal?"

She said it in a way that could be taken as teasing, though, instead of lighting into him like I'd hoped she would. By the time the bar lady brought our fluids, Riley was right back to being his obstreperously curious self.

"That's some sign out front," he broached to her. "How'd this place get its name?"

"You don't know the half of it. Everybody here in town calls her"— the bar lady indicated out into the night where the neon maiden was kicking up her heels—"The Lass with Her Ass in a Glass. Story is, the guy who opened this place was from back east somewhere. He liked his martinis and he liked a girl he met out here, so he put them together on his sign."

"Eat your heart out, Statue of Liberty," Riley said over his shoulder eastward after the bar lady trod off.

"Don't ever say they aren't poetic souls in this town," Mariah reflected. "Anyway, on to celebration." She hoisted her glass to me, and I automatically reciprocated with mine, and Riley had to clink in too. My daughter flashed the grin her mother customarily had at so many of my birthdays, but the words of her toast were Mariah's own. "Mark this day with a bright stone."

All in all, then, as we settled into sipping and conversing—most of it back and forth between them, who seemed to have discovered they had a surprising amount to say to each other tonight—my evening of entry into senior citizenship could have been a whole lot worse thus far. I was going to have to cash us in early for the night to keep Mariah and Riley from getting too frisky with one another, and toward that end I yawned infectiously every so often. But all seemed under control until a funny impression came over me, the feeling that the three of us were about to be joined by somebody else, even though nobody had newly come into the bar. I could have sworn I kept hearing a half-familiar voice. None of the few partakers strung along the bar was anyone I recognized, though, nor did they look like logical discussants of . . .

" . . . eating dust and braving the elements," a tone like that of God's older brother resounded in a break in the bar conversation.

Mariah and Riley and I swiveled simultaneous heads toward the corner television.

Sure enough, Tonsil Vapor Purvis was in the tube in living color, not to mention a high-crowned cowboy hat.

"This centennial cattle drive is a true taste of the Old West," Tonsil Vapor was declaiming. "Twenty-seven hundred head of cattle are being driven by twenty-four hundred riders on horseback, while the world watches." The television picture changed from the mob of beeves and drovers to a traffic jam of communications ordnance, rigs with TV uplinks on top and all-terrain vehicles ridden by cameramen and reporters jabbering into cellular telephones. Abruptly the screen filled with a close-up of a bandannaed rider going *hyaah!*, either at a recalcitrant longhorn or Tonsil Vapor. The next instant, though, our news host was back, full-face-and-hat. "This trail drive means long hours in the saddle for these hardy cowpokes, but—"

At least Riley and Mariah's two-member reunion had been put on hold while they gawked disbelievingly at Tonsil Vapor in his buckaroo regalia and the rest. Indeed, I figured this was a heaven-sent, or at least beamed down by satellite, chance to further divert.

"Somebody tell me this," I postulated. "One sheepherder can handle a thousand sheep easy, but here they got a cowboy for every cow and a fraction. So if they call sheepherders dumb, where does that leave cowboys?"

"Now, now," Mariah purred as if running over with sympathy for television's mounted horde. "Don't be mean to those poor cowpokers."

"Hey, better to be a poker than a pokee," Riley got into the spirit by drawling in a croaky trailhand voice.

Mariah returned him a mock sultry grin, or maybe not so mock. "Oh, I don't know. We pokees figure there's a lot less strain involved for us."

Really great job there, Jick, of heading off the flirty-flirty stuff. Curfew seemed the only recourse. I cleared my throat and said, "If you two are done talking nasty, how about we head out to the Bago?"

"Jesus Christ!" Riley let out and sat straight up, gawking at the Hamm's clock and then back at Tonsil Vapor, who was going on and on. "They're giving him half an hour of airtime on this cattle drive! It's the *War and Peace* of cows' asses!"

"Horses', too," Mariah pointed out with photographic precision as Tonsil Vapor's visage again filled the screen, and I couldn't help but hoot along with my two tablemates.

Then before I could bring up the matter of adjournment again, the bar lady was serving us a reload on the drinks. "Who ordered these?" I inquired at large.

"I did," Mariah flourished a ten-dollar bill. "Anesthesia for watching Tonsil Vapor."

"You know, maybe this actually is a historic event," marveled Riley, critically cocking an ear as Tonsil Vapor intoned over pictures of cows, horseback riders, more cows, more horseback riders. "The biggest herd of clichés that ever trampled the mind. Bet you a jukebox tune he even manages to get in *ridin' 'em hard and puttin' 'em away wet* before he's done."

"You're on," Mariah took him up on it quick as that. I couldn't blame her. There wasn't much any of us would put past T. V. Purvis, but even he would need to outdo himself to call what was on the television screen heated cowboying. The way the mass of animals was strolling along through its media coverage, the only sweat that could pop out on the riders' ponies would have to be from stage fright.

So of course we had to watch the whole thing, during which another round of drinks evolved out of the residue of Mariah's tendollar bill, and wouldn't you know, just before the half hour was up and Tonsil Vapor was due to vanish into a blip, out spieled his observation that these Big Sky cowhands were ridin' 'em you-know-how and puttin' 'em away you-know-what.

"Hey, have you been moonlighting scripts for that bozo?" Mariah demanded of Riley with a nudge, although not as suspiciously as I would have.

"Faith is justified once every hundred years, is all that proves," Riley murmured becomingly of his powers of prediction. "Somebody owes me a serenade, though. Something besides Willin' and Waily for a change, okay?"

Mariah swigged the last of her current Calvert, fished out of her pile of change whatever coin a jukebox takes these days, and started to slide out of the booth to go pay off. But at the edge she paused, as if needing to make sure. "Vocal only?"

Riley blinked. Then said as if it was a new thought: "Doesn't have to be, far as I'm concerned."

I sat right there and watched as Mariah motated across the room to the jukebox and Riley unlimbered out of the booth after her and called over to the bar, "Okay if we dance, is it?"

The wide bar lady shrugged. "A lot worse than that's happened in here."

Mariah punched a button on the jukebox. Steel guitars reported. But after an overture or whatever it was, voice rode equal to the sound of the instruments, a slow song yet urgent, the woman singer of the Roadkill Angels confiding into the world's every ear.

> *"King's X," you said the last time*
> *we played this lovers' game.*

Mariah and Riley fashioned themselves to each other as those who've danced together do, her thumb hooked in a remembered kidding way into one of his rear belt loops, his spread hand in the natural place low in the narrow of her back.

> *"Time out," you called just when*
> *I'd chosen you by name.*

Both tall, both more lithe-legged than you'd expect of a lanky couple, they circled together in the slow repeating spin of the song.

> *"No fair," I called out after*
> *you changed the loving rules.*

Mariah's shoulder-long hair moved with the action of their bodies, now touching one blade of her back, now the other. Riley held his head in slightly tilted orbit as if accommodating down to hers.

"Don't cheat," you heard the warning,
that's just the game of fools.

What true dancers know is to never forget each other's eyes. Mariah and Riley read there as if they'd been to the same school for it as they drifted with the music.

Marcella in my arms. Not many years into the past, yet forever ago. We had just finished whirling the night away, the Labor Day dance at the old Sedgwick House hotel in Gros Ventre. Now we were home after the early a.m. drive to the ranch, the dark already beginning to thin toward dawn. The music or the delicious sense of each other—perhaps it is the same flame—still had hot hold of us, wrapping us to one another as we reached our bedroom. Marcella moved first, as soon as my fingers alit at her top button; snap buttons, they sassily proved to be, her western shirt pulling all the way open *plick plick plick plick plick* when my glorious wife laughed and took that single slow essential half-step backward as if dancing yet. Then Marce moved to me again.

This time when we cross our fingers
Let's make it for luck,
Let's break the old hex,
Let's take back those words, "King's X."

With the tune's conclusion, Mariah and Riley separated orderly enough, but there still was a kind of cling between them as they came back to the booth. She startled me with a wink and the avowal, "I promise you the next dance, birthday kid," but established herself in the booth somewhat closer to Riley than she was before. He in the meantime was enthusiastically summoning to the bar for yet another visit by Lord Calvert and Harvey Wallbanger and Johnny Walker.

Talk about wanting to call time out. I'd have crossed all my fingers and toes too if that would have put a King's X of delay into the way this pair was romping. They showed every sign of spending the night on the town, cozier and cozier with each other, and where that led I didn't even want to—

The bar lady sang out, "Anybody named Wright Riley? Phone call."

"Can't the world let a man enjoy his Wallbanger in peace?" Riley said plaintively, but took himself off to the phone in the lobby.

He was back quick, with an odd expression on his face. "Actually it's for you, Jick."

Oh, swell. I figured it had to be Kenny, telling me some catastrophe on the ranch. Even the phone earpiece didn't sound good, full of those frying sounds of distance. Apprehensively I said into the mouth part, "'Lo?"

"Hi, Dad. Happy birthday! If you'd stay home once in a while instead of gallivanting around, I'd have sent you a salmon."

"Lexa! Christamighty, petunia, it's good to hear you!" What I *could* hear of my younger daughter, that is, through all the swooshes and whishes across the miles to Sitka. "How'd you track me down?"

"I figured the newspaper would be keeping an eye on Riley wherever he was. Just where are you, anyway?"

I had to think a moment, which town by now. "In Chinook. In The Lass with Her A— uh, kind of an everything place. Riley broke down and bought me a birthday drink, would you believe."

Lexa gave a short snort of laughter, the proper response from a McCaskill at any notion of civility in the Wright brigade. Not that the one of us where it counted most, Mariah, was showing any similar sign of recognizing the ridiculous; from the phone I could see to the booth where she and Riley were paying each other necky attention. What differentiates how our children become? Take Lexa at the distant end of this phone line. Smaller, built more along her mother's lines than the lankiness of Mariah and me. Her hair more coppery than Mariah's, her face not so slimly intent, her chosen life more snug, moored. Yet those were the idlest of differences between my two daughters, they did not even begin to describe the distinction. I had not seen Lexa since she and Travis flew down for Marcella's funeral in February, yet I knew if she stepped out of that phone mouthpiece right then I would be surer of her actions than I was of any of Mariah's even after spending night and day of the last two months in her immediate vicinity.

"What's it like traveling with those two," Lexa was asking now, "the Civil War?"

"More like watching a bad dream start itself all over."

Distance hummed to itself while Lexa took in my news. Then she was exclaiming: "Mariah isn't falling for that mophead again? After the way they tore each other up in that divorce? She can't be."

"Honey, I wish you were right. But she shows every sign of doing just that."

"Tell her for me she needs her brain looked at. Tell her to go take up with the nearest sheepherder instead. I can't believe anybody, even that sister of mine, would—" Lexa's incredulity made way for a logical suspicion. "Dad, how many of those birthday drinks have you had?"

"I'm sober. All too."

And then wordlessness hung on the line between us, the audible ache of the miles between Montana and Alaska. Not just measurable distance was between us, but Mariah and Riley, the capacity for catastrophe the two of them represented. I remembered the expression on Riley when he said the call was for me. "Lexa, what was it you said to Riley when he answered the phone?"

"I just asked if he still was carrying a turkey around under his arm for spare parts."

Why couldn't that skeptical attitude toward Riley Wright be grafted onto Mariah? Judging from the ever closer conversation they were having in the booth, the sooner the better.

"I'm going to have to tackle Mariah in the morning about this Riley situation," I concluded to Lexa. "I'll keep you posted." I remembered that my son-in-law who hadn't turned out to be a dud was on the cleanup of last spring's *Exxon Valdez* oilspill. "How's Travis doing?"

"Sick at heart," Lexa reported in her own pained tone. "The whole wildlife crew at Prince William Sound is. New dead species all the time—the oil is up the food chain into the eagles now."

"I wish that surprised me." Where wouldn't that oilspill spread to, before things were done.

"Mm. Know what you get when you cross an oil executive and a pig?"

"No, what?"

"Nothing. There are some things a pig won't do."

Her bitter joke wasn't the best note to end on, but I didn't have any better. "Well, this is your nickel. Lexa, thanks for calling. It helps."

"Love you plenty. So long, Dad."

When I got back to the spooning booth, matters had quieted down, I was thankful to find. Mariah's arms were crossed in front of her with one hand up at the throat of her blouse, contemplatively fingering the point of her collar there. Riley was ever so lightly tapping the edge of the table with just the tips of his fingers, as if patting out some rhythm softly enough not to be heard. I had a moment of wondering how far gone they were; they'd each disposed of the drinks they were working on when I went to the phone, yet really neither one looked swacked. Quite the reverse. They both suddenly seemed keyed up and super attentive as I plunked myself down and passed along a few words of report about the Alaska wing of the family. What do they call a chance like this any more, window of opportunity? In any case, right now appeared to be the propitious opening for herding my birthday party-givers back to the Bago and letting things settle down overnight, and so I drank up fast before another round could happen or more dancing and carrying on, and gave the evening as casual an amen as I could.

"I'm gonna call it a day. You two look like you could stand to turn in, too. Ready?"

The gaping silence answered that before Mariah began to try.

"Jick. You go ahead. We, Riley and I, we're not going to be back at the Bago tonight."

I had a furious flaring instant of wanting to ask her, demand of her, where they were going to be instead; but that was senseless. I all too well knew. It was right out front, up in neon: M-o-t-e-l.

Once the desiring begins, all other laws fall. You know that whether you are fifteen or sixty-five or both added together. There in the motorhome the remainder of that night, I tried to fight through to longer thoughts than that first alarm about Mariah and Riley's craving for each other. Judiciousness. Forbearance. Parental declaration of neutrality. All had hearings with me, chorused their verdict over and over that whosever's affair this coupling night was, it was not mine. My stiff exit from the supper club had been correct deportment, giving the pair of them something to think over yet not making too much of what I was leaving behind. Definitely those two were adults, not to say veterans of each other. So what, if Riley was horny. All right, so what if Mariah was in that same condition. This happens and ever will, wherever people grasp enough about one another to fit onto and into.

And as regular as the basting bags taped over the Bago window flapped in the wind, I accepted every iota of their No Tell Motel linkup and still I sorrowed, fretted, all but wept.

Tonight, a single lightning night of them together, was no cause for bonedeep concern. Tomorrow and its cousins were. Any of the time ahead, the rest of this centennial journey or beyond, when Mariah might paradoxically backslide to Riley; with all the life that ought to be ahead of her, trapping herself into that again. I hoped against hope that what I was picturing was not about to happen. But as searingly clear as the flashes that had been coming to me from the gone years, I could see ahead to her and him failing with each other again. Their mutual season would not last, the solitude in each of them would win out, and they would break apart in anger and grief and worse again.

Some graft of time, I yearned for. Some splint of cognizance by which Mariah, Riley, the both, could be shown how not to repeat defeat. But all that was left of me seemed too used and brittle for any of that. Sixty-five years before, union between my parents passed existence along to me. On the Aleutian mountain battlefield in 1943, the poor aim of an enemy soldier lent me life from then until now. But what next. Or was this already the next. People do end up this way, alone in a mobile home of one sort or another, their remaining self shrunken to fit into a metal box.

I put my face in my hands and as if she could still be reached by such a clasp, I cried out:

"Marcella? Marce, what the hell am I going to do?"

Bread and ink making their morning rounds woke me.

The Eddy's Bakery truck looming in front of the windshield of the Bago took a minute to register on me when I foggily craned up out of bed to see what all the traffic at this campsite was. Everything came back too fast after that, however. This campsite the Lass in a Glass parking lot, Mariah and Riley inside between the sheets, the whole mess. By the time the news agent pulled up to replenish the newspaper boxes outside the motel and had let the lids drops, *kachunk kachunk kachunk,* I had some clothes and a mood on. Such sleep as I'd managed to get was ragged, tossful. All over I felt bony and bruised, as if I'd been slumbering on a sack of doorknobs. Oldlike. And the main matter still awaited with the daylight which was just starting to find Chinook, planetary capital of romance: how to induce a thirty-five-year-old headstrong daughter to take a reality check on herself.

Even the interior of the Bago seemed foreign this morning. Strange as hell, how a domicile so empty could feel so mussed. I shook my head in a yawn or at least some kind of a groggy gawp and gimped up front to an unbagged window for a peek at the day. If there was any balance at all to things, at least the weather would have to have improved.

The meteorological outlook, though, was not what hooked my gaze.

I did not want it to be what it was. I looked long and hard across the thirty or so feet from the motorhome to the newsboxes. I tried telling myself, huh uh, naw, they wouldn't, must be some other—yet newsprint does not lie, does it, at least not in this fashion.

Slowly I went out and dropped a quarter and a dime in the middle newspaper box. On either side of it the Great Falls *Tribune* and the Havre *Daily News* were reciting developments in Poland. The *Montanian* I plucked out hit closer to home than I'd ever dreamed print and picture could.

Center page, mighty, in splendid color, the photo of course was Mariah's. Of the Double W gateframe, tall thick poles and crosspiece in angular outline like a doorway slashed into the sky. Under and around the flagrant gateway, the Two Medicine country of that month-ago evening on our way in to the centennial committee meeting: the night-rumple of mountains where the sun had just departed, the thin strokes of clouds still glowing above. One mercy—standing so stark and dark, the gateframe's lettered sign announcing WW, Inc. ownership could not be read. But the steer skull dangling just beneath more than made up for it, declaring there against the Noon Creek sky like a horned ghost.

TWILIGHT OF THE RANCHER? epitaphed the headline beneath.

And beneath that, the words of Riley.

> *From a life spent under a Stetson, he has his divided mind written on his forehead, the tanned lower hemisphere where wind and sun and all other weathers of the ranch have reached and then above the hatline equator an oddly shy indoor paleness. When he was younger, that band of pearly forehead made him stand out at the Saturday night dances, as if a man needed to be bright-marked at the top to be able to schottische and square dance so nimbly. When he was that young, the fingers of his children traced there above his brow in wonder at the border between the ruddy skin and the protected zone of white. Now worry fits on at that line.*

The rancher starts his day as usual now with a choice of frets. Looks at the weather and plays the endless guessing game of climate—an open winter coming, or another Alaskan Express? the droughtiness of the 1980s at last over (the numerals in his grandfather's identical thought were the skein from 1917 into the mid-1920s, in his father's they were the 1930s) or only stoking up for more years of grass-shriveling heat? Checks the commodities page and calculates one more time what the latest disappointment in livestock prices is going to cost him. (Of all of Montana's hard weather, the reliably worst has been its economic climate.) He plots out all that needs immediate doing and tries to figure out why hired help has become the rarest commodity of all. Runs on through the wish list to where he always ends up, damning his bones for their increasing complaint against the daylight-to-dark ranch life, yearning with everything in him for someone to shoulder all this after he soon can't.

If the legends of his landed occupation are to be believed, a century and more ago Montana ranching began heroically, almost poetically, splendid in the grass. Yet even then, here and there a rancher twinged with the suspicion that legends are what people resort to when truth can't be faced. In 1882, cattleman Charles Anceny contemplated himself and his neighbors in Montana's new livestock industry with just such skepticism: "Our good luck consists more in the natural advantages of our country than in the scale of our genius."

Old Anceny portended even more than he knew. Natural advantages have a habit of eroding away under spirited exploitation. And the spirit of the West, of Montana, of America, has been what the legends speak of as grand and truth has to call aggrandizing. The consolidating, the biggening, goes on yet and with consequences below; as economic structures become more global somebody has to become more granular, and the rancher is among those. The marketplace that is the land is slipping out from under him. If you possess your own television network or have the spare change to own a professional football team or are paid an anchorman's salary for your face or are commensurately compensated for your appearance on the big screens of the movies, yes, you can maybe compete with corporations and foreign buyers to own enough ground to be a Montana squire. But this rancher born on a few thousand family acres doesn't have those infinite pockets. Instead what he owns is a penchant for counting too much on next year, and the notion that he's not actually working himself to death because he's doing it outdoors. Well, those are possessions too. But not the marketplace kind.

The rancher goes back and forth in his mind—give it up, tough it out. The past stretches from him like a shadow, recognizable but perplexing in the shapes it takes. He knows too well he is alone here in trying to look from those times to this. He rubs at that eclipse-line across his forehead and wonders how he and his way of life have ended up this way, forgotten but not gone.

I felt as if I'd been stripped naked, painted rainbow colors, and paraded across the state.

I spun from the newsbox and went to search the building.

He was established at a window table in the not yet open coffee shop, tippetytapping words into his processor. Flexing his fingers for his next character assassination, no doubt.

The newspaper page still was in my hand. Not for long. I wadded it up and hurled it in Riley Wright's face.

He flinched, but let it bounce off him without otherwise moving.

"The latest reader survey shows that the *Montanian* draws considerable reaction from sheep ranchers with a Scottish surname," the sonofabitch droned in the BB's tone of voice.

My fury was compounded of what he'd written about me, of how he'd resumed with Mariah, of everything this Wright character represented. Hours, years, could have been spent in the telling. But it shot out hard and quick.

"The stuff you do to people would gag a maggot."

"Jick, I think if you'd just simmer down—"

"I don't that much care a shit what you think. Just tell me this. Why do you keep giving the McCaskills so much grief?"

That got to him. At least something could. Dreadful squintlines of what I took to be anger pulled the skin white and webbed at the corners of his eyes. The torn look of a man seeing something he had hoped to avoid.

For once Riley searched a while to find anything to say. When he did, his voice was surprisingly husky, as if he was having trouble down in his throat, too.

"I'm not going to debate Mariah with you—that's between her and me, even if you don't want it to be. So let's just talk ranch."

"Yeah, let's," I snapped. "Now that you've written me up as such a supreme failure."

The goddamn guy would not give in to my gaze. He folded his arms across his chest and sighed. "Honest to Christ, it never dawned on me they'd slap that Double W picture on the ranch piece. As soon as I saw it this morning, I knew you'd come in here pissing fire. The only people who don't react to being written about are in the obituaries. But you're taking it entirely too personal. Jick, you're not the only one in that piece. Anybody trying to run a family ranch or farm, maybe any kind of a family outfit, is in that situation."

"Anybody, my rosy rear end. You might as well have plastered my name all over that description of—"

I stopped. The only face Riley had described was that of the situation, just as he claimed. Try mightily as I did, except for the universal hatline I could not point to where it wore a single identifiable feature of myself.

Riley said quietly, "Jick, there are only four of us in the world who know that piece fits you at all."

Himself and Mariah and . . . "Who're the other two?"

"You are. One version of you is as mad as if you'd found flyshit in your pepper. The other one of you knows what I wrote is the absogoddamnlute truth."

Right then I ached, in mind, in heart, worse than my Attu shin ever could. "You figure you even have the right to do my epitaph, don't you," I spat out at him. " 'Here lie the collected versions of Jick McCaskill.'"

Riley bailed out of his chair so abruptly I figured we were proceeding to fists, which suited me fine. By God, that suited me just fine. Sixty-five sonofabitching years old notwithstanding, extinction ordained for me in every goddamn copy of that morning's *Montanian* be as it may, I could still plant a few knuckles before Riley did me in.

But the slander merchant was snapping the screen down on his laptop and stepping back from the table carrying it at his side like the most innocent of appliances. See how the guy can't even be counted on to erupt when he ought to? Riley only said, "Not that this'll improve your disposition any, but I've got to get to a phone and send in this Chief Joseph piece. I'm sorry that other one happened to hit the paper today. If I'd done the Chief Joseph one last night instead of—well, just instead of, I'd have modemed it in then and the ranch piece wouldn't have run. But I guess that'd just be postponing the inevitable, hmm?" And with that he walked away, squaring those broadloom shoulders, out of the coffee shop toward the mutual motel room.

I slumped into a chair at the abandoned table. How long I stared out along Highway 2 at the Lass in a Glass sign, extinguished now, I do not know, but she found me there after the morning light had flattened into that of day.

"Hi. Up early, same as ever, I see," Mariah imparted too brightly, swinging her camera bag down and herself into the chair opposite me that Riley had vacated.

When I made no response, she took in a breath and tried some more of the obvious: "I was out shooting the country while the nice light lasted. The Bearpaws are a different set of mountains today."

"I imagine."

She glanced at me, then down at the table, then off into various corners of the comatose coffee shop. "They ought to be opening up here pretty quick and we can get some breakfast."

"Swell."

"How about a machine cup of coffee until then?"

"Why not."

On her way back from the coffee machine in the lobby she managed balance all the way to the table before the two Styrofoam cups slopped. "Shit," she said. Then while she was mopping at the spill with napkin after napkin, her voice took on another rare tone, a tinny one of every word having been rehearsed. *Mariah, Mariah,* ran in my mind, *what you're doing to yourself.* What she was letting be known now was:

"Actually, you were right about that deal you tried to make with me at the start. We can just borrow the rig to do the rest of the series and you can be shed of us, how about. I can drive you home to the ranch this morning, right now, while Riley pokes around town."

"Naw, that's okay," I said pleasant as pie but thinking, to hell with this noise, daughter of mine. No way are you going to cut me out of the picture so you can fall heart over head for Mr. Wrong again. Overnight is one thing, every night is another. "I'm kind of growing used to the Bago life. I'll just stick with you and Romeo until you're done. No problem."

Mariah swung her head the little bit to sway her hair away and clear a look at me. "No, really, we—I can get by okay."

"Mariah, I wouldn't dream of leaving you in the lurch. Besides, there's a lot of Montana left to be seen, isn't there, which I'd hate to miss, wouldn't I." I gave her a steady gaze before adding, "Then there's the other thing."

"Which other thing?"

"That if you're going to make a fool of yourself over Riley a second time in the same life, you're goddamn well going to have to do it in front of me."

Mariah reddened as if my words were a slap. But I kept on, I had to. "That's what you originally brought me along for, isn't it? To ride shot-gun against your inclinations to regard Riley Wright as a worthwhile human being? So that's exactly what I'm going to do."

"Jick . . . Dad . . ." she sorted nervously. "That, last night. Riley and I were just . . . feeling frisky."

I continued to look squarely at her. I hadn't thought it was a mutual yen for a night's deep sleep.

She moved her eyes from the path of mine and tried to maintain, "I don't know that I'm making a fool of myself over Riley."

"You're giving quite an imitation of it."

"This isn't like what happened before," she essayed in what was sur-prisingly like a plea but failed to convince me one least bit. "Riley and I, this time we're not, mmm"—to my horror, she was conscientiously sorting out in that flaming head of hers which way to translate to me the fact that they were scratching the bed itch; my God, I thought, does their generation have an entire warehouse of expressions for it?—"tak-ing up with each other. We're just seeing each other."

Speak of the devil, Riley right then stalked back into the coffee shop, spied Mariah and marched grimly over, calling out:

"That'll teach me ever to go near a fucking telephone. Can you believe this, that sonofabitching—"

Tension must have grown pretty dense in the vicinity of Mariah and me, because Riley stopped as if he'd walked into a glass wall.

"Uh *huh*," he evaluated. "A family conference. I'll just wait outside until the blood quits flowing."

"Why don't you hang around?" I offered. "You might learn something definitive about yourself."

"Depends on the source," he replied with extreme wariness as he regarded me and then my daughter the paramour.

"He thinks we're crazy to . . . be with each other," Mariah minimally summed up my views for him.

"Never heard of try, try again, hmm?" Even though the words pittered out of him as syruplike as ever, Riley looked drastically serious. "Jick, it wasn't anything intentional, last night. You know better than anybody that Mariah and I both came into this despite each other."

"Then why in goddamn hell didn't you keep it that way?" I erupted. The majority of parents my age were wildly worried about their married kids breaking up. Why was I the one to have to throw a fit that mine were getting back together? "You both were managing to get done what you wanted to, without having to tumble"—into bed, into the jungles between the legs, into an old fever newly risked—"all over each other just the way you originally did. I don't understand why you're willing to set each other up for grief again."

"Last night didn't remake the world," Mariah protested in a perplexed tone, drawing a startled glance from Riley. "I don't know that we're—"

Riley held up both hands as if stopping a shove. "This must be the ultimate definition of the morning after," he growled to Mariah. "We've got Cupid's conscience right here on our case and the BB waiting his turn."

"The BB," Mariah echoed, her perplexity giving way to something a lot worse.

"The very guy," Riley exhaled wearily. "He wants to see us back in Missoula again. Yet today."

Missoula was a whale of a drive from Chinook. What did this Beebe so-and-so think, that he could just reel us in whenever he felt like it? Or as I stated it now: "Can't that guy ever say what he wants to say on the telephone?"

Mariah and Riley exchanged cloudy looks. He was the one who at last said, "The BB is a Bunker Hill type of boss. He likes to see the whites of the eyes before he fires."

—

Past lunchtime but still lunchless, the roadweary three of us trooped into the *Montanian* building.

A ponytailed young man carrying camera gear similar to Mariah's slouched out of the BB's office as we approached it. He looked like he'd recently been pinched in a tender part. Mariah greeted him and asked how the BB's mood was. Ponytail responded, "He's chewing sand and shitting glass, if that gives you some idea," and stalked off.

So, braced is the basic description for the *Montanian* centennial task force as we entered the presence of Baxter Beebe. All during our drive from Chinook, Mariah and Riley had tried to think of how to save their skins this time. Without any result, for as Mariah put it, "We don't even know if this is a fresh mad or the same one he was in last time." I'd been bending my brain to the BB problem too, for the one thing I didn't want now was Riley and Mariah cast loose into the world together, without a chance for me to somehow cure her of him. I mean, this just really frosted my ass; finally wanting the centennial trip to careen onward and here the BB was about to grant my original wish and X-out the expedition.

The BB or Bax or whatever sent the two of them his average steely stare as we filed in, but in my case he bounced out of his chair and came and gave me the pump-handle handshake while declaring, "Great to see you again, Jiggs. I wanted you to hear this, too." Huh. Maybe they were fired and I was hired.

With that, Beebe circled back to his chair, seated himself again, clasped his hands as if glad to meet himself, and gazed at us ranked across the desk from him. When he figured enough time had passed, he pronounced:

"I have bad news for us all."

He eyeballed the trio of us as if he'd always known three was an unlucky number. Then he shook his head gravely and said:

"I lost out on a goat permit in the state drawing."

Mariah and Riley swallowed in chorus. For my part, I looked carefully around the tower walls at the dead menagerie again, trying to think of any other animal to ante in, but no luck.

All three of us waited for the BB to lower the boom on the centennial series. Instead he again singled me out for his approximation of pleasantry.

"But that's all right. We can try again next year, Chick."

Now I didn't know which to be more of, puzzled or alarmed. Nor it seemed did the pair beside me. If I was bonded to the BB as hunting crony for another year, where then did that leave Mariah and Riley? Did this mean he hadn't even hauled us in here to ream out about—

"The centennial series."

The depth of the BB's tone dashed all hope there. "I have something to tell you about that."

He gave us another going-over with his gaze, one by one by one. Then intoned very deeply:

"It's a bull's-eye."

The identical thought was in all three of us who heard this: hadn't the BB gotten his mouth mixed up, actually intending to tell us the centennial series was some other bull stuff than the ocular part? But no, huh uh, he was going on and on about how Mariah and Riley were finding the true grit of Montana and what a service to readers to provide them something more flavorful than the usual newsprint diet.

Now this was news. The letters to the editor that had been showing up in the *Montanian* were saying pretty much the same as when our buddy Bax here was chewing the inside of his mouth to tatters over them. Only a few days ago there'd been one that started off, *Why does your so-called writer Riley Wright dig up old bones like the Dempsey-Gibbons prizefight when the Real Issue is taxes?* and signed, *Mad As The Dickens On Southwest Higgins.* I noticed that Mariah and Riley, though both surprised within an inch of their capacity, were staying on their guard. Riley in a funny way even looked a little disappointed, I suppose at having his work so palatable to the BB.

After a lot more salve of that sort, the BB focused on Mariah and, to my surprise again, me.

"In other words, I just wanted you to know what a very good job you've been doing. Now, Mariah and Nick, if you would excuse us, there's something I have to convey to Riley."

As soon as Mariah and I were out of the tower, I asked: "What the hell is that little scissorbill up to?"

"Don't I wish I knew," said she is bewilderment. It wasn't like Mariah to look left out, but right then she seemed the occupational equivalent of orphaned.

"Maybe he just wanted us out of there so he could stuff Riley and put him on the wall," I speculated. "Which would be the best use of—"

"Why don't you wait here," she stated rapidly, "while I go check my mailbox," and all but galloped off out of range of further conversation.

Mariah was back a lot quicker than I expected, though, with one piece of mail sorted out of the sheaf of memos in her other hand. "For yoo-ou," she singsonged, holding the envelope out to me with her pinky suggestively up.

The handwriting with merry little o's dotting all the i's probably rated that, but I tried to make it look like a business matter as I thumbed open the flap thinking, what the hell now?

It was one of those greeting cards showing two little creatures, mice or rodents of some kind, wearing great big sombreros and doing, what else, a goddamn hat dance. Inside, the printed message was:

SO NOW YOU'RE A 'SENIOR' CITIZEN! COME JOIN THE FUN!

The one in the giddy handwriting below was:

Happy birthday, Jick! Everybody *misses you! Affectionately, Althea.*

"So?" my snoopy daughter asked with an eyebrow up. "You got a secret admirer, birthday boy?"

"Uh, Howard Stonesifer," I alibied casually and jammed the card in my hip pocket.

Mariah's other eyebrow now was up too, just as if she'd never heard of an undertaker dispatching birthday greetings to prospective customers. Right then, though, the door of the BB's office sprang open and out shot Riley grinning like a million dollars.

By now even I was plenty curious, not merely about how the BB had taken a shine to Riley but how anybody could. The sly so-and-so warded off even Mariah's intense questions, insisting "This is so terrific, we've got to go make an occasion of it. I'll tell you over lunch. I'll even buy. Even yours, Jick."

Depend on Riley, the lunch place was called Gyp's and was just big enough for a counter and a fry grill. I ever so imperviously slid onto the stool that put me between Mariah and Riley. Behind the counter was a bony cook who, according to the wall's autographed photos of him posing with Mike Mansfield and Kim Williams, was Gyp himself.

"Ain't seen you for a while, Riley," Gyp said affably. "Been nice."

"Hi, Gyp. The Health Department hasn't had you assassinated yet, hmm?" responded Riley as he plucked up a menu, opened it and slapped it closed without having looked at it. "White cheeseburger, fries, and an Oly."

"Same," said Mariah, eyes fixed on Riley.

"Same again," I said, eyes fixed on her.

Our beers came instantaneously, but before I could get mine lifted Mariah was leaning a bit in front of me to look with exceeding directness at Riley and he was peeking around me with a sweetheart grin at her. I felt like a sourball salesman at a Valentine party.

Mariah broached it first. "Okay, Chessy cat. What was that all about, the BB wanting to see you alone?"

Riley somehow increased that grin, his mustache almost tickling his earlobes. He announced:

"They want me in California."

At first I thought it was sarcasm of some kind. In the pause after Riley's words, I took a drag of my beer and inquired in kind, "What for, rubber checks? Or just general personality flaws?"

Then I noticed how utterly still Mariah had fallen, frozen in that same position of peering around me at him. As still as if gone brittle; as if the flick of a fingernail would crack her to smithereens.

In a stunned tone she finally managed to say: "At the *Glob,* you mean."

"The *Globe,* yeah," Riley responded.

"A column?"

"Yeah, a column."

Was it possibly so easy? Abracadabra or whatever the California equivalent is, and Riley vanishes off into the palm trees? A fatherly fraction of me felt bad about Mariah looking so stricken. But the overwhelming majority of me wanted to turn absolute handsprings.

Gyp slapped down our cheeseburgers in front of us. I spooned piccalilli on mine in celebratory fashion while Riley began ingesting french fries.

Mariah, though, pressed the question that I figured Riley had as much as answered with his proud announcement of California's desire for him. She choked it out as, "So what did you tell the BB?" Really, it was a crying shame she had to be put through this from the absconder, but how else would it ever get hammered home to her that Riley Wright's only lasting partner in passion was himself?

"This seems to be getting kind of personal," I noted. "Do you two want me out of here?"

"Sure do, just like always," vouched Riley in what was maybe a half-assed attempt to be funny.

"No," said Mariah in her same tight voice.

206 · Ivan Doig

"Tie vote," I interpreted to Riley. "Guess I'm staying."

"Suit yourself." He took his time about eating a fry, then washed it down with a long guzzle from his beer. "I told the BB yes, naturally, but that we don't want to until after the centennial series is done. He phoned down there and the *Globe* agreed to stagger along until then."

"Who's 'we'? You got a frog in your pocket?" It was the most elderly of jokes, but the way Mariah said it, it carried all the seriousness in the world. And not just for her. I put my swissburger down on the plate and began wiping away the piccalilli I'd squeezed out all over my hand when I heard that pronoun of Riley's.

The incipient Californian was gazing steadily back at her, past me. "Mariah Montana, my notion is for you to come too. As my wife again."

EAST OF CRAZY

... Wind is the ventriloquism of Montana's seasons. In utter summer it can blow in from the west, the mountains, and convince you November is here. The other way around, the truly world-changing recital: the chinook breathing springtime into deadest winter. In just such a toasting wind-from-another-time we found my father, slumped onto the steering wheel of his pickup after the exertion of putting on chains to navigate the instant new mud from the Shields River calving shed to home. ...

—RILEY WRIGHT'S NOTES, EN ROUTE
TO CLYDE PARK, SEPTEMBER 6, 1989

IT HIT ME LIKE a kick in the heart.

What is the saying?—life is one damn thing after another, and love is two damned things after each other. Both parts pertained in the instant after Riley's double-barreled ambush, oh, did they ever. Bad enough to me, the prospect of Mariah going into marriage misadventure with Riley again. But on top of that, the searing feeling of simply her *going*. California is the American word for away, and I knew perfectly well the declension of it. As if by rote, a time or two a year a visit would be staged, daughter dutifully back for some ration of days or father descending south to clutter up the routine there for a mutually uncomfortable span. Periodic phone calls, *Hi there, how you doing?—Good enough, how about yourself?*, because letters are not habit any more. But beyond such dabs of keeping in touch, absence across distance. The formula of the young for moving a life from what it came into the world attached to. No parent can say it is anything but the history of the race, tidally repeating, yet each time the pain comes new.

At least I wasn't alone in being caught off guard in the cardio quadrant. Mariah stared lidlessly past me and my strangled cheeseburger at the author of this remarriage proposal or marriage reproposal or whatever it constituted.

"I suppose this is a little bit of a surprise," Riley said around me to her in his ever sensitive fashion. Still leaning far forward onto the counter, he seemed poised to plunge as far as it would take to convince Mariah. Cupid's own daredevil, all of a goddamn sudden. "But why wait with it?" he charged onward. "Mariah, this *Globe* job is just what we want to make a fresh go at life. It's like winning the lottery when we didn't even know we had a ticket."

Blinking at last, Mariah made herself respond. "Quite a change of geography you've got in mind." Quite, yeah. Somehow Mariah California didn't have the same ring to it.

"But don't you see, that's just exactly why we ought to do it," Riley hurried to expound. "New territory, new jobs. New—"

"Job*uh*," she placed into the record to rectify the *s* he'd plotched onto the word. "You're forgetting, the *Glob* only invited you."

"A shooter like you," Riley assured her in revivalist style but obviously also meant it, "can latch on in no time, at the *Globe* or somewhere else if you want. Or if you want a chance to freelance, or to just do your photography for the sheer utter fun of it for a change, that's in the cards now too. Bless their sunglassed little heads, the *Globe*'s going to be paying me more than enough for both of us to live on. How's that for a deal, hmm?"

He paused to see how that went down with her. I eyed her too, but with a different question in mind. How Mariah could even entertain the notion of retying the knot with Riley was beyond me. I mean, after our too-green marriage blew up, you could not have paid me enough to get me to marry Shirley a second time. Talk about double jeopardy. Yet here was this otherwise unfoolable daughter of mine, sitting there not saying no to this human bad penny, which pretty much amounted to a second yes by default.

By now Riley had backtracked to where he'd been heading before her reminder of job singularity. He could get wound up when he half tried.

"New us again, Mariah, and I don't only mean being married another time. By the time we get through with this series we'll have done about everything we can, and maybe then some, at the *Montanian*. First thing it'll be right back to me trying not to write the identical columns I did a year ago or five years ago or ten, and you'll be back at shooting Rotarians and traffic lights being fixed. The Zombies Return to the Dead Zone, is what it'll be."

A would-be luncher came in the door, took one look at the madly gesticulating figure with a different color in each eye, and went right back out.

"You know as well as I do it's a fucking wonder that the BB and the bean counters let us do something like these centennial pieces even once in a hundred years," Riley resumed. "I've—"

"What about your perpetual book about Montana?" I thrust in on him.

"I was coming to that. I've finally savvied there isn't going to be any book. Every motherloving thing I know how to say about Montana, I've already put into the column or will put into this series." Back to his main audience, Mariah. "Okay, I grant that it's not quite the same for you and your camera. The one thing this state is always good for is to sit and have its picture taken. Photogenic as a baby's butt, that's ol' Montan'. But think what a change of scene would do for your work too, Mariah, hmm? Everygoddamnwhere we look here," Riley made a wild arms-wide gesture as if to grasp Montana at each end and hold it steady for us to see, "somebody or someplace is just trying to hang on by the fingernails, trying to figure out how to make some kind of a go of it against all the odds—a climate that's forever too cold or too hot or too dry or too fucking something else, and never enough jobs and wages that're always too low and somebody else always setting the prices on crops and livestock, and the place full of bigshot assholes like the BB who think the state is their personal shooting gallery, and people like us can't even do our work right without having to beg help from our relatives, and—"

The expression on me stopped him. "Look, Jick, if you don't want to hear this—"

"Who says I don't want to hear it? Rant on."

He did worse, though. He looked squarely at Mariah and as if breaking the news to her said quietly:

"Montana is a great place to live, but it's no place to spend a life."

I couldn't just sit there and take that. "What, you for Christ's sake think California *is* the—"

"California," Riley overrode me, "is America as it goddamn is, like it or don't. Nutso one minute and not so the next. Mariah, this is a chance to go on up, in what we do. I know you want to be all the shooter you can, just as I want to be all the writer I can. To do that we've got to get out of a place that has as many lids on it as this one does." Ardent as a smitten schoolboy, he reached for what to say and found: "There's just more, well, hell, more California than there is Montana to the world any more."

"We'll count up after the earthquake and see," I put in just as rabidly.

Riley's eyes and mine held. Good God Almighty, how had I misread him yet again these past weeks? All the while I was fretting about Mariah drifting toward him, he was cascading back into infatuation with her. He hadn't been just having a randy night in Chinook, he was all too genuinely putting himself into that motel prance with Mariah. This goddamn Wright. You couldn't even rely on him to be deceitful.

From my other hemisphere Mariah was saying: "Riley, are you really sure about all this, I mean, California and . . . all? An hour ago we were both scared to a dry pucker that the BB was going to can us, and now you're—we're the ones deciding to pack up and pull out?"

"Life happens fast when it gets rolling," Riley coined. "And we can't possibly go as wrong the second time married as we did the first, right?" He must have noticed me opening my mouth to say not necessarily— World War Two had followed World War One, hadn't it?—for he rapidly resorted to: "Or maybe let's just start the count from now instead of then." He dropped his voice into the rich tone of an announcer: "Together again, for the first time!"

There was a moment of threefold silence then, the two of them regarding each other past me as I perched there stewing.

"So?" Riley at last inquired. He gawked at the floor ostentatiously enough to draw the cafe owner's attention. "Do I have to get down on one knee? I kind of hate to, given Gyp's housekeeping."

"No," Mariah answered tightly. "I heard it all right from where you are." She put her hand on my arm as if to say *wait, don't go,* as though I was the one invited off to the land of quakes and flakes instead of her. Then she went around me and gave Riley a kiss that would have fused furnace metal.

—

The Bago by now could almost guide itself in the groove it had worn into this part of the universe, to Missoula and from Missoula, and the next day I drove rather absently, letting the motorhome and the freeway hum away the miles together while everything else was on my mind.

In the passenger seat Mariah too seemed to be on automatic, watching the weather—more rain; the spigot this year seemed to be stuck open instead of closed—and the country as we headed east, past Drummond, past Garrison, the twin paths of the freeway swinging south through the tan Deer Lodge valley and then reverting east again, halving Butte into its old hillside mining section and the shopping malls on the flats below, all the route until then a running start up to the Continental Divide; and quickly across and down to the headwaters of the Missouri, past Three Forks, and onward through the fine fields of the Gallatin Valley, past Bozeman, past the Bridger Mountains. I noticed that all the while her camera stayed inactive.

Those road hours Riley spent at writing something—not a *Montanian* piece, because he and Mariah hadn't talked one over—the *pucka pucka* rhythm of his laptop as intermittent as the mileposts rolling past.

> . . . *In the seasons before the chinook, hunting magpies with our .22s my brother and I played at being Lewis and Clark along the swift small river they named for one of the enlisted men of their expedition. A captaincy apiece, we insisted on—neither of us ever bothering to imagine back into 1806 to be a startled and proud Private Shields putting his footprints beside water that still carries his name—for boys settle for momentary glory.* . . .

Not until just beyond Livingston, when he let me know "It's this exit" and I swung the Bago north onto the suddenly thinner route of Highway 89 up the Shields River, did Riley put aside his wordbox and join the other two of us in watching the land.

The Shields River country was a new Montana to me. Accustomed as I was to the Two country's concentrated force of the Rocky Mountain Front along a single skyline, here I was surprised by piles of mountain ranges in all directions: the Absarokas to the south, the Castle range to the north, both the Bridger and the Big Belt ranges to the west and northwest, and to the east, over Riley's home ground, the high and solitary range called the Crazy Mountains.

My pair of passengers stayed as mute as the ranges of stone. Neither Riley nor Mariah looked forward to this chore, as I could readily understand. I was not, however, what could be called sympathetic. This reunification notion they had mutually lapsed into still seemed to me as crazy as those mountains up there. My one ray of hope was that the two of them at least hadn't hotfooted it off from Gyp's lunch counter yesterday to the marriage license bureau. "If we're going to go through with this California business," Mariah had managed to stipulate when the kissing let up, "let's do it all new down there. Get married there, I mean."

Riley pretended to count the weeks to *Glob*hood on his fingers, then consented. "I guess I can stand that. Maybe a change of preachers is a good idea anyway."

There in Missoula when the love doves eventually had to find their way back to the matter of the centennial series, something did develop that made me perk up.

After a final swig from his beer bottle and futile reconnaissance for any more french fries, Riley popped out with: "I dread to, but you know what I better do? Swing by the home place on our way east and break the news there."

Mariah gave her head a little toss and regarded him with extreme steadiness. "Break the news? You make it sound like a car accident."

"Joke, J-O-Q-U-E, *joke*!" Riley protested, but I had my doubts and quite possibly Mariah did too. However, there in Gyp's she let him get away with the explanation that he'd of course meant the news of the California job, the kind of thing that took a little getting used to for parents, sorry to say, with an ever so innocent glance in my direction.

Now Riley had me turn east off 89 at Clyde Park and head dead-on for the Crazies. The Shields River valley must have been a kind of geographical basket of good ground, because there was farming right up to the base of the mountains. Nice tidy ranches, of the cattle variety, were regular along the road.

The Wright family's ranch was up on a last ledge of fields before the Crazy Mountains stood like vast long tents of white. The place could be read at a glance as prosperous; the original clapboard house with a pleasant porch all the way across its front, the newer lower domicile where Riley's brother's family lived, the white-painted cattle sheds and pens, the nice grass of the tightly fenced pastures beyond. Country this orderly, you did wonder how it produced a guy like Riley.

Who, as we approached the driveway, cleared his throat and suggested to Mariah, "It might be best if you let me break the—tell about us."

She said with forced brightness, "Okay, sure, words are your department, aren't they."

I became aware of a heavy stare from Riley. "Who, me? I wouldn't even dream of depriving you of the chance to make the same wedding announcement twice in the same lifetime," I reassured him. "Besides, it ought to be highly interesting to hear."

A yappity pup careened across the yard to challenge the Bago. I braked just in time to keep him from becoming a pup pancake.

The canine commotion brought a woman out onto the porch of the older house. Plentiful without being plump, in blue jeans ageworn to maximum comfort and a red-checked shirt with a yoke of blue piping in emphasis across the chest, she still was wearing her hair in a summer hank—it sheened whiter than gray, grayer than white—more abbreviated than a ponytail, to keep it off her neck in back. Somewhat leathered and weathered, she nonetheless had a well-preserved appearance; time simply paid its respects to a face like that. She stood deliberating at the motorhome while the kiyi chorus of the pup reached new crescendos, until Riley slid back the sidewindow and yelled out, "Call off your dogpack, Mother, we're relatively peaceful."

"Here, Manslaughter," she spoke to the barking guardian and patted a denim thigh for him to come to her. By now the woman had recognized Mariah's red hair as well as Riley's vocal presence and she came down off the porch striding quickly, in a kind of aimed glide, toward the Winnebago as if she had something vital to deliver. But when the *Montanian* duo stepped out of the motorhome, followed by me, Riley's mother halted a good distance away and somehow managed to gaze from one to the other of them and both of them at once while saying diagnostically, "I saw by your performances in the paper that you two are tangled together again."

Riley, trust him, cupped a hand to his ear and asked, "Did I hear a 'hello' or was that thunder?" Then he brassed on over as if doing a major favor by delivering a kiss to his matriarch.

"It would help, Riley, it really would, if you'd keep me informed as to when you're on speaking terms with her," his mother gazed indicatively straight at Mariah, "so I can stay in step. Couldn't you have it announced on the radio or something?"

A watcher of this didn't have to be rocket-swift to pretty speedily realize that Riley's mother had as much peeve built up at Mariah as I did at Riley and for the one and same reason, the crash of their marriage. Why this surprised me any I don't know—just one more case of an in-law flopped into an outlaw—but it did.

Mariah looked like she'd rather be juggling hot coals, but she said to the silver-haired woman, "We maybe both better get in practice on our terms, how about."

Riley's mother eyed my daughter skeptically. Then perhaps registering the echo of McCaskill boneline in Mariah's form and my own over Mariah's shoulder, she cast her first full look at me. A moment was required to decipher me under the beard and then her eyes went wide.

"Jick!" she let out with her blaze of smile. "Hello again."

"'Lo, Leona."

Half a century it had been, since I first said that. Since Leona Tracy, as she was then, all but married my brother Alec.

I cannot say that oldest storm from the past swept through me again, as I stood now in the yard of Leona Wright's ranch, because the memory of that summer of 1939 has never really been out of me. The June evening it began, when just at suppertime at our English Creek ranger station Alec and Leona rode in, I can recall to the very sound of the quick extra stick of firewood being rattled into the stove by my mother as she set at generating an already-cooked meal for three into ample for five. Looking up from the Forest Service paperwork he'd been trying to contend with, my father watched through the window as my brother and the goldhaired girl, the fondest of arms around each other as they ambled, crossed the yard from their saddle horses. "Glued together at the hip, those two," he reported.

"Safer that way than face to face," my mother stated.

He looked around at her, startled. She always could surprise him more than he cared to admit. Then Alec and Leona arrived, more like alit, into the kitchen with the other three of us, and the summer of war began. For it was during that suppertime, well before the butterscotch meringue pie that I'd been dreamily counting on for dessert, when Alec announced that he and she intended to be married, that the college years and engineering career my parents had foreseen for him were nowhere in his picture, that he was staying on as a wage hand at the Double W until he and Leona could afford a preacher and a bed that fall. Nineteen years old, him, and seventeen, her, and they believed they had all the answers to my father's increasingly biting questions, to my mother's clamped silence which was worse than her saying something. Admittedly, that was not the first blowup ever to occur within our family, but the one that happened that night with the TNT of Leona added in knocked the absolute socks off us all. In my not quite fifteen years of life until then, there had been what I assumed was the natural McCaskill order of behavior; occasional eruption under our roof but always followed by a cooling down, a way found to overlook or bypass or amend, to go on in each other's company, which seemed to me the root definition of a family. But then and there, with lightning suddenness my brother had gone into bitter exile. And never lived long enough, due to war, to retrace his way from it.

The preamble to all that was Leona. I suppose her beauty simply ran away with itself, spun beyond the control of the teen girl she was. That spring of 1939 she'd dropped Earl Zane—not that I can fault anyone for choosing a McCaskill over a Zane any day of the week—and her romance with Alec got hot and heavy in a hurry. Maybe he was overly taken with the, what can they be called, natural resources of a seventeen-year-old beauty. But there was always this about it: Leona could have switched Alec onto simmer merely by telling him she wanted to finish high school that next year, that they'd do well to see how their passion stood up across a couple of seasons. She did not say such, or at least did not say it until late in the summer—too late—after Alec had declared independence from our family and could not bring himself to retreat. Shape it as fairly as I can and it still comes out that my brother got hit coming and going by Leona Tracy, first bowled over by her and then left flat in the dust of her change of mind.

Leona Wright, as she faced me now. It costs nothing to be civil and I had managed to be so the time or two I'd crossed paths with her in our grown lives, at Gros Ventre's town centennial where Mariah and Riley first veered to each other, then at their eventual wedding, and did again here, to the best of my power, as she said how sorry she'd been to hear about Marcella's death. That over, I drew into the background—Riley and Mariah were all but tooting with impatience—but couldn't help studying the once girl of gold who had gone silver. As the younger onlooker during Alec's courtship, I'd regarded the Leona of then as the bearer of the eighth and ninth wonders of the world. Now she was stouter with the years, weatherlines at her eyes and mouth, but still a highly noticeable woman.

And still a formidable smiler. Her face stayed wreathed in what seemed utmost pleasure even as she swiftly got down to basics with her visitational son. "What's the occasion? Have you used up all the rest of Montana in what you've been writing?"

The pup was running himself dizzy in circles around us. For his part, Riley looked like he was being rushed to his own hanging. Nor did confession seem to be good for the soul in this case, for he didn't appear any less uncomfortable after his recital of: "Mother, I'm switching jobs. They're giving me a column."

Leona lifted one silver eyebrow. "I thought you already have a column."

"This one's located in California."

Had the mother of Riley deigned to glance in the direction of her ex-daughter-in-law just then, the expression on Mariah would have told the rest of it, somewhat to the tune of *And if you think that's something to swallow, chomp on the news that your son and I are going to get married again, you old bat.* But Leona only gazed at Riley and switched to another smile, a measure of sadness in this one, before saying:

"In California? Riley, is that supposed to be an advancement?"

An evening such as this, with the peaks and fields of the Shields River country as fetching as Switzerland, a person did have to be more than a little screwloose to talk about living anywhere else. Riley drew in a mighty breath and performed his explanation to Leona that at the *Globe* he'd have twice as many readers as the entire population of Montana, that the salary there made the *Montanian* look like the two-bit outfit it was—I waited for him to get to the part about California being a better Petri dish of the world than Montana is, but he never did.

Mariah most notably was waiting too, for her rebetrothed to find his way around to that other announcement. Her earrings, sizable silver hoops, swung constantly, as if sieving the air, while she intently followed

Riley's words and Leona's if-a-mother-won't-be-kind-about-this-who-will? mode of listening.

The declaimant still was on California and not yet even in the remote vicinity of matrimony, however, when ecstatic yips from the Manslaughter pooch directed attention to a heftier version of Riley making his way across the yard from the new house to our powwow.

"Hey there, Morg, you're just in time for the family reunion," Riley greeted him in what was at least distraction if not relief.

Giving Mariah a nod of surprised recognition and me a more general one, the other responded in a tone that eerily echoed Riley's voice, "What's going on, Riler?"

I could see Riley barely resisting some crack such as *Don't beat around the bush that way, Morg, just come right out and ask.* He somehow forbore and resorted to manners instead. "Jick, you ever meet my brother Morgan? This is none other."

Morgan Wright and I shook hands and mutually murmured, "How you doing?" As soon as that was accomplished, Riley repeated his bulletin about going to the job in sunfunland.

Morgan stood spraddled, thumbs alone showing from the weather-worn hands parked in his front pockets, as though it might take all the time in the universe to hear this matter out. Then he asked Riley with concern, "Has California voted on this statewide yet?" which proved to me they were full-blooded brothers.

With a merry growl the pup at this point attacked a cuff of Mariah's bluejeans in a spontaneous tug of war. Standing on the besieged leg as methodically as a heron, Mariah lifted her other foot behind her and gave Manslaughter a firm crosskick in his furry little ribs. The pup let out a surprised *wuh!* and backed off to regard her with abrupt respect.

The Wright family conclave didn't even notice, what with Riley giving Morgan the whys and wherefores of California while Leona took it all in again with the same regretful smile. Suddenly she turned toward Mariah and me as if utmost revelation had hit home. Mariah tensed defiantly, and I confess even I braced a little in genetic sympathy, before Leona said urgently:

"Have you had supper?"

For whatever reason, Leona addressed that straight to me, as though the two of us were still responsible for the care and feeding of these giant tykes, her Riley and my Mariah.

"Naw, but that's okay, we'll nuke us up some frozen dinners in the Bago, it'll only take—"

"You will not, John Angus McCaskill," she said in the distinctive Leona voice. "You'll come in the house and have something decent."

I do have to say, the venison steaks and new potatoes with milk gravy and fresh biscuits with honey and garden-pea salad with tiny dices of cheese that Leona served up to us will never be equaled by anything under tinfoil.

During food, which I have always liked to believe is inspirational, I finally figured out Riley's case of topical lockjaw. The expression on him, which I can only liken to the look of the proverbial man in such crisis he didn't know whether to shit or go blind, I knew I had seen before, but when? Twice, actually. Most recently, there in the Medicine Lodge at the centennial committee meeting when he realized I'd sprung Good Help Hebner on him. But more vitally, that day of spring three years ago, when Riley palely delivered himself to the sheepshed beside Noon Creek to tell me he and Mariah had broken up.

Could it be, though? Such a garden-variety emotion behind Riley's evidently extreme quandary? A diagnosis can be simple yet complete. No, I now knew: more than anything, more than fear, fire, flood or blood, Riley Wright hated to look like a sap.

Hoo hoo hoo. Because that condition inevitably awaited him here whichever guise he chose to put on. Trotting around with an ex-wife, as though he couldn't get away from the situation Mariah represented, plainly stood out to Leona as highly sappy. But the instant he tried explaining that Mariah and he now saw the error of their divorce, Leona naturally enough would want to know why they wadded up their marriage in the first place then—and what answer was there to that but sappiness?

Meanwhile as Riley in his flummoxed state awaited some magical moment when Leona would welcome a defunct daughter-in-law back to her homey bosom, Mariah maintained a silence astonishing to me. I would have bet hard money this daughter of mine could not keep her lips hermetically sealed for this length of time under this amount of provocation.

By the time we had supped and pied and coffeed and been shooed into the living room by Leona, quite a number of moments passed but none of them were noticeably magical between Leona and Mariah. The closest came when Leona said with extreme neutrality, "I've been seeing your pictures in the paper. What was that one of the girl's head in a beer glass?"

Oh, for the simple green jealousy of that Kimi night, hmm, Mariah? She stiffly informed her once and future mother-in-law, "That's what's called an interpretive shot."

Leona looked as if she agreed that it needed interpretation, all right.

I was having to divide my attention between the living room contestants and outside, because through the big picture window toward the Crazy Mountains I could see a palomino mare frisking in a pasture next to the cattle lot. Beautiful lightish thing there in the dusk, its mane blowing like flax. Morgan Wright long since had excused himself from us by saying that as much as he hated to miss any further details of Riley's future, he and his Mrs. had to go in to a centennial committee meeting tonight in Clyde Park. (I told him there was an awful epidemic of that going around.) Even if that ostensible master of this ranch had been on hand, Morgan was not the one I would have asked about that horse. Somehow I knew that lovely bright mare could only be Leona's.

"So do you still ride?" I inquired, then wished I had the sentence back to makings, because that way of putting it also asked *or has age caught up with you too much?*

"Some," Leona replied, her eyes following the path of mine to the palomino but no smile finding her face this time, just a considering look. "When we're moving cattle I still help out. I tell Morgan that when I can't ride any more he may as well haul me to the dump."

The entire fifty years previous I would have thought, of course that is the case; Leona Tracy Wright was put into this world to enhance its saddle ponies with her golden—and later, silver—form, and when time ended that it indeed might as well conclude her, too. Life is temporary, after all, and the girl version of Leona had gone down its road at full gallop. But here on this ranch, on Leona's earned earth, I was beginning to see what more there was to her than that. The perfection of fence-lines and thrifty pastures and leisurely cattle in the dusk, butterpat fat—she and the late Herb Wright must have worked like twin furies to build such an enterprise. And she had stayed on in evident working partnership with Morgan. And she had endured a decade or so of aloneness since her husband's death, a sum I found enormous after my, what, eight or nine months since Marcella's passing.

Still. Her icepick treatment of Alec, and all it led to. Would some version of our McCaskill civil war have happened anyway, between

Alec and my parents, between Alec and me—a brother outgrowing the other or one staying with the logic of bloodline while the second felt the need to yank free—even if Leona had not been blondly there to precipitate it? Possibly, quite possibly. We are a family that can be kind of stiffbacked. But Leona was who precipitated it, and the best I have ever been able to do with that fact is to keep a silence about it. Plainly enough Leona, by lack of mention to Riley and Mariah when they first met, when it would have been the easiest chance ever to say *Isn't this funny, now? I used to go with a McCaskill myself, but we . . .* , she herself wanted nothing said of that long-ago fling with Alec, of the McCaskill family mess it caused.

My pondering along these lines was interrupted by simultaneous blurts:

"Leona. Riley and I—"

"Mother. Mariah and I—"

The annunciatory duo also halted in the same breath, each tongue waiting for the other to do the deed.

"Maybe you want to take turns at it," I suggested, "a syllable or so at a time."

Riley scowled at me and huffed that that wouldn't be necessary, and as if he was reciting from memory a manual on dismantling bombs, he apprised his mother that he and Mariah had nuptial intentions again.

Even Leona couldn't come up with any kind of smile to cover her reaction to this.

"But then why ever did you—" she of course launched, causing Mariah and Riley to concurrently roll their total of three gray eyes and one blue one. I'd already done the route Leona was raking them along, so I gazed again at the outer world. The pup Manslaughter went tearing across the yard in pursuit of a magpie fifty feet above his head.

When his mother's invocation of their breakup was completed, Riley in turn lodged the protest, "That's neither here nor there." Which when you think about it was a sappy remark even for Riley. The point exactly was the attempted union of him and Mariah *there,* in the none too distant past, and now *here* again; the two of them just would not let the goddamn notion go away.

"Okay, now everybody knows," Mariah surprisingly broke her self-imposed silence to summarize. "Why don't we talk about religion, sex, or baseball instead?"

"California," Leona uttered, as if that fit the bill for an extreme topic. "I have trouble imagining you there, Mariah."

"Maybe I'll get used to it," Mariah answered edgily.

"Neither one of you got used to your marriage the first time, though," Leona essayed. "I'm curious. Aren't you, Jick?" Downright purple with it, although I didn't say anything because Leona was doing just fine. I could see where Riley got his knack for getting under the skin. Leona studied the uneasy pair of intendeds with boundless interest and concern as she asked, "What's going to be different this time?"

"This time we'll know better than to both get mad for more than a month at a time," Riley floundered out.

"Leona," Mariah decided she'd better try, "maybe Riley and I did go ape, a little bit, in that divorce. You're welcome to blame me, if you want." At least that would balance things across family lines, given my attitude toward Riley. "But that doesn't change our getting back together," Mariah went on at a rattling pace. "This centennial trip has made us feel we want to stay that way." She snapped her head around to Riley so quick her earrings blurred. "Right?"

"Could scarcely have said it better myself," the wordsmith corroborated.

All of a sudden, from somewhere rang out a little *ding* and then a man's voice, as cultured as caviar, intoning: *"Kahk vasheh eemya ee otchestvo?"*

Riley, pretty much goosed up anyway even before this vocal development, catapulted out of his chair. "Who the f—?"

His mother flapped a hand at him and instructed, "Shush now, Riley, I've only got ten seconds to answer in."

Now Leona could be seen to be concentrating with every mental fiber, her thumb and forefinger pinching together in an intent little *o* as if practicing to pluck from the air. Then she threw her head back and recited firmly: *"Ya Leeona Meekhylovna."*

"The question in Russian was," the celestial male voice resumed, *" 'What is your first name and your patronymic?' If you were not able to translate it and answer in the allotted ten seconds, please do so now."*

Leona smiled triumphantly and marched across the room to snap off a tape player and a gizmo plugged in beside it. "I set the lessons on a timer," she explained, "to catch me by surprise. It seems more lifelike, that way."

Riley gazed at her as if counting slowly to himself. After what maybe was an allotted ten seconds, he began: "Mother—"

"*Mahts,*" she promptly identified for him.

"Whatever. In plain English, in little words so I can try to get this—what are you doing studying Russian?"

"We're Sisters of Peace," Leona informed her son. He continued to look at her as if she'd declared she was Queen of the Williewisps. "Our women's club here along the valley, it's our centennial project," Leona went on. "We're a sister group to women like ourselves in Moscow. *Muskvah.*"

Kind of needlessly, it seemed to me, Riley did check: "I take it you don't mean the one in Idaho."

"Spoof if you want," Leona responded in a style that suggested he'd be better off not to. "I just thought it would be nice. To know how they talk. We're going to send them a videotape of the Clyde Park centennial day doings. Jeff is going to be our cameraman." Leona looked over at Mariah as if just remembering her existence. "Cameraperson." I was recalling that Jeff must be Morgan's son, hard to think of anybody having Riley for an uncle. "I volunteered to learn enough to say a few things to them in Russian, on it," Leona went on as if Cyrillic from Clyde Park made perfect sense. I confess, in spectating Riley's reaction to his mother the sexagenarian rookie linguist and Mariah's reaction to her *and* him, I'd lost track—maybe it did.

"My mother the peacenik!" Riley gabbled to Mariah in some mix of being perplexed and resigned and wary and proud.

"Mmm," Mariah responded ever so neutrally.

"I might as well be doing something with myself," Leona concluded. "I have the time, after all." She smiled around at the three of us in equal allotments, her blue eyes steady within the fine wrinkles reaching in at their corners, then soberly focused on Riley and Mariah again. "Where are you headed next?" Her inquiry could just as well have meant what next plateau of folly they aspired to after rematrimony and California, but that son of hers chose to answer in Bagonaut terms, that we'd wheel east from here, out into the big open of Montana away from the ranges of the Rockies. Both he and Mariah, I was sorry to see, were beginning to look like they might come out of this evening intact after all.

I let Riley finish with the travel orientation and start to make what he obviously hoped were evening-ending indications. Then I spoke what I hoped were going to be the magical seven words.

"Whyn't you ride along with us, Leona?"

Leona looked pleasantly startled. Mariah looked as if I'd invited a Tartar into the tent. Riley looked as if I'd poleaxed him.

"I mean it," I went on cheerfully. Did I ever. There was no forgiving Leona that hurtful yearling romance with Alec and the consequences it walloped the McCaskills with, but this was no time to be pouty about that. What needed priority was the situation here in the room with us. Riley already was plainly provoked; he was in for a lot more aggravation if I had anything to do with it. I'd had my say, such as it was, to Mariah and this secondhand swain of hers after their Chinook night of ecstacy, hadn't I? A steady stout dose of Leona couldn't hurt as the next remedy to try on them, could it? "Come see some country," I spieled to her with enthusiasm. "I can guarantee you this about it, traveling with Riley and Mariah is the kind of experience you never even dreamed of before. Besides," I couldn't help giving Mariah an innocent look, "you can't beat the price. The newspaper's paying for it all."

"What a kind offer, Jick. But I'd just be in the way," Leona demurred with a dazzling thanks-anyway smile.

I assured her, "No more so than me." Quite possibly more effectively so, though. "These offspring of ours keep awful busy with each other," I sped on. "At what they're doing, I mean. Majority of the time, Leona, the two of them more than likely won't even notice you're around." Interesting that my tongue was capable of stretching itself so. The last person not to notice Leona must have been blind, deaf and on the other side of a lead door.

"You wouldn't mind, really?" Leona swung like a turret to the newspaper pair.

"No, no, no," Mariah managed with a swallow. "Not a bit."

"Entirely up to you and the Bagomaster, Mother," Riley got out, cutting me a *now you've gone and done it* glare from the corner of his blue eye.

"Jick?" Leona addressed me as if I was the next question. "This will teach you to make an offer like that."

"Snoose Syvertsen," Leona announced out of nowhere as the Bago purred past the Crazy Mountains and eastward along the Yellowstone River. "You remember him, don't you, Riley?"

Directly behind me at his writing station in the dinette where his laptop output was sounding slim this morning, Riley grumpily confirmed he remembered.

McCaskills in the forward seats and Wrights amidship, we had embarked down the Shields River valley from Leona's ranch an hour or so before. Outside, the day for once was rainless and fresh, the clawed-out peaks of the Crazies as clear as could be in dazzling first snow. Weather within the motorhome, though, was heavy and electrical, just as I'd hoped. In the passenger seat Mariah was noticeably squirmy and kept her eyes resolutely on the Yellowstone River as if seeking a spot deep enough to sink a mother-in-law in while Riley, as I say, was promisingly grumpy.

"Snoose was our choreboy a while, years back," Leona not unnaturally chose me as audience, "until he started herding sheep for a Big Timber outfit out on these flats. He'd go in to Livingston a couple of times a year to drink up his wages and whenever anybody asked him where he herded, he'd point off in this direction past the mountains and say, 'East of Crazy.'"

I chuckled and commentated, "At least the guy had his bearings," as if there were others in our vicinity, such as directly behind me and immediately beside me, who did not.

"I didn't get around to asking last night, Jick," Leona's words kept wafting distinctively to me as I drove. Hers was what I can only call a woodsmoke voice. It came as if tracing its way through the air to you, certain wisps more pungent than others. A voice, it had always seemed to me, that perfectly well knew it could embody as casually as it cared to because main attention would ever be on Leona's fierier attractions. So in essence, the listening side of a conversation with Leona was a matter of catching her drift. "Sheep," I heard loft from her now. "You're still running them, are you?"

"Still am," I admitted. "After about forty years they kind of get to be a habit."

"Morgan has us running breeds of cattle I've hardly even heard of," came her comparable report. "Red Angus, and some Simmentals. He figures we've got to try different kinds every so often to see how they'll do."

Yes, I thought savagely, that is the very thing a ranch needs: a Morgan Wright to dab around with new notions, to try out new fashions of livestock and crops. To put fresh muscle into the land. Which is exactly what my ranch has had no prospect of ever since Leona's other son, the knotheaded one behind me at that moment, turned down my offer.

"I'm surprised Riley hasn't brought you home some buffalo from Moiese to raise for hood ornaments," I lobbed over my shoulder.

"Buffalo?" Leona asked, puzzled, looking back and forth from me to her determinedly utterly silent progeny.

"Riley can explain it to you sometime when he's got his tongue along with him," I said. "Rest area coming up," I noted the announcing blue sign ahead by the side of the Interstate, "everybody get in the mood."

Riley was so ticked off at me that he violated the first principle of freeway lavatories: don't pass up any chance to go. I hummed off by myself to the men's side and on into the stall while Mariah and Leona, as silent toward each other as nuns with a vow, betook themselves into their side of the pleasant bungalow-size brick convenience. So far, so good, on this Leona deal. Riley already was significantly twitching. Keep applying his mother to one end of him and his ex-wife fiancée to the other and maybe he'd bail out to California early just to rescue his nerves. My definite hunch was that nothing, no known force, could peel Mariah away from finishing the centennial series; so if Riley called it quits, while she refused to—second thoughts about mushing their lives together again might be seeded right there, mightn't they? At least it gave me a somewhat promising prospect to mull while I had to be sat.

Walls in a public facility have their own topics they're insistent on, though. I could not help but notice, in fairly neat small penciling directly in front of me on the stall door, one lone unillustrated epistle. Leaning forward as much as was prudent, I just could read:

THE DEBRIS OF HUBRIS IS THE CHASSIS OF GENESIS.

I was contemplating my way through that when footsteps arrived.

"What'd we ever do before all these rest areas?" came a voice entering. "Just turn loose alongside the road? You know what they say, though. 'Pee by the side of the road and you get a sty in your eye.' But I don't remember that many styes, do you?"

"What all I don't remember would fill Hell's phone book," testified the other. As the duo zeroed in on the urinals, peeking under the stall wall as best I could I saw identical sets of streamline-striped jogging shoes—both pair of which, I would bet, were off the same sale table at the K Mart—blossoming out the bottom of very veteran bluejeans; by the sounds of their voices, these guys aged radically pore by pore upward from those zippy shoes.

"Hullo, what've we got here?" the first voice was saying. "Somebody left us a love note."

"I hope like the dickens it don't say, 'Smile, you're on Candid Camera.'"

"No. Huh. Huh. I'll be damned."

"Ain't that something, though? How do you suppose people get theirselves into the fixes they manage to?"

Whatever they were reading above the waterworks had not caught my eye on my way in, but it seemed to be something fairly sensational, because now several other guys were arriving—they were all of a group, at least from the evidence of universal speedstreak jogging shoes—and the note was the immediate topic of roundhouse debate.

"It says *what?* I never heard of no such thing." "Take a look for yourself, would you." "Let me get my reading specs on here. Any more I can't tell whether I'm on page nine or it's something by Paganini." "Suppose the guy who wrote this is on the level? What do you think, Bill?" "What am I, the expert on lying? Don't answer that." More reading, to the accompaniment of assorted trickles. "Hell if I know. Funny damn kind of a situation he claims he's got himself into." "I can see how it could happen." "I don't." "There's this much for sure. These days, anybody'd who'd pick up a hitchhiker ought to know better." "Ought to, yeah, but maybe he was trying to do somebody some good. You can't fault a man on that, can you?"

I emerged from the stall into the debating group. There in a cluster, seven familiar faces and I gawked at each other.

"We come across you in the goddamnedest places!" exclaimed Roger Tate, who I remembered was the seniormost of the Baloney Express car corps. "How you doing, Jick?" All the others heartily chimed in their greetings, old home week to the point where little Bill Bradley gestured in the pertinent direction and asked, "You seen this note on the wall here?"

"No," I admitted, "but I been hearing a lot about it." I moved up close enough to take my turn at examining the document.

BROKE AND BAREFOOT
Mine is a long story, but to put it short as can be, I picked up a hitchhiker yesterday when I left Coeur d'Alene, and after we reached here, and I got too sleepy to drive any more, I told him he had to get out, and go on on his own, while I

caught some sleep. He did, get out that is, and I locked myself in the pickup, and stretched out on the seat, but when I woke up this morning, my shoes that I had taken off, and all my money, were gone. I am stuck here, until somebody can help me out. Any money you can loan me, would help me buy gas and food to get home to Fargo, and I will take your name, and address, and mail it back to you, quick as I can. I am in the GMC pickup, red in color, at the east end of the parking lot. Thank you.

You hear all kinds of stories of people begging in wheelchairs or whatever, then as soon as you're out of sight they hop up and stroll off to buy drugs with the money you just gave them. Evidently what people won't resort to hasn't been thought of yet. Naturally my mental question was the same as the Baloney Expressers: was this broke-and-barefoot note the newest kind of cheat?

Another round of democratic Roger-Bill-Nick-Bud-Julius-Jerome-Dale debate produced the idea of actually going and taking a look at the guy in the red pickup. I was either born curious or became that way a minute later, so off I set with the investigating committee.

As we were cutting across the parking lot past the fleet of clunkers my companions were ferrying to a used car lot in Billings, Riley popped around the hood of an idling Continental Freightways semi. "The women were starting to wonder if you fell in," the knothead loudly addressed to me as he strode up. Then he recognized the company I was in. "Don't tell me. The Methuselah Hot Rod Club is on the loose again. Watch out, world."

Inevitably the Baloney Express gang greeted Riley with verdicts on his piece about them that, coming from them, he regarded as high praise. Then I explained to him our mission to the east end of the parking lot and he glanced nervously over his shoulder in the direction where his mother and Mariah were waiting for us in the Bago, precisely as the two women emerged around the semi in search of the searcher they'd sent scouting for me.

The sight of the seven geezers whose collective rumps she had presented to the reading public made it Mariah's turn for wariness, but they unanimously assured her that photograph of hers had presented their best side to the world. Her first grin of the past forty-eight hours broke out on Mariah as she asked what the occasion here was. Leona meanwhile was in an all-purpose smile while trying to get a handle on any of this, and after the Baloney Expressers' sevenfold explanation about the *Broke and Barefoot* note and I'd introduced Leona to each of them in gallant turn and the entire general scrimmage of us had started moving toward the pickup in question, she dropped back beside me and wondered in a whisper, "Jick, do you know everybody in Montana?"

"That's pretty much getting to be the case," I acknowledged.

"You want to watch out," she whispered again, "or you'll end up as Governor."

The vehicular description "red in color" proved to be a wishful memory of the beat-up pickup's faded appearance, and the young guy in it didn't look like much either. When our delegation drew up around him and he cranked down the window on the driver's side, the face framed there was one of those misfitting ones with not enough chin or mouth but a long thin nose and a wispy blond mustache, scraggly, really. His eyes were red-rimmed and darted around miserably among what must have looked to him like a posse from an old folks' home. Treed in a sapling about to snap, was the impression he gave.

But any con man worth the name would know precisely how to appear so simultaneously victimized and embarrassed, wouldn't he. The Baloney Expressers clustered around the driver's side window, as attentive a jury as they had been while watching Riley wrestle the Bago tire two months ago.

Roger Tate spoke the doubt of everybody. "One thing that's hard to savvy, Mister, is how somebody could get at you that way in a locked pickup."

"For the longest time I couldn't figure that out either," the young guy confessed tiredly. "I knew goddamn good and well I'd locked both doors. But what the bastard did, I finally caught on, was he unlocked his wing window while I wasn't looking"—the pickup was so old it did have those vent windows with a little catchlock that moved about half an inch for opening them—"and after I fell asleep he must've snuck back and reached in through it and got that door open. And took off with my money and shoes." The guy swallowed and looked like he was about to bawl, but seemed to feel he had to tell it all: "Didn't even leave me my socks."

The congress mulled that testimony. One of the Walker brothers, Julius, remarked: "You're quite a sleeper."

"Mister, I know it sounds fishy. I almost can't believe it myself, what happened. And nobody until you guys would even come near me to hear about it. But jeez, it's the truth," he concluded, his face saying the awful realization of how much predicament his life's quota was.

Nor was his situation eased any when two or three Expressers simultaneously asked whether he'd called the highway patrol or sheriff yet. The young guy squirmed and looked away from all our eyes, down at the steering wheel. "Can't do that. My license plates are out of date. Couldn't afford this year's." A majority of the Baloney Expressers at once investigated at the rear of the pickup and verified that the North Dakota *Peace Garden State* license plate was 1988's.

In the kind of tone a district attorney would use on a pickup thief, Bill Bradley wanted to know: "You say you're from Fargo, what were you doing all the way over in Coeur d'Alene?"

"Looking for work. I come from Coeur d'Alene originally. When there wasn't any jobs there, I got on driving tractor for my wife's uncle outside of Fargo. But he got droughted out again this summer, same like last summer, and he had to let me go." This chapter of his story poured out of him, either well-rehearsed or from the heart. "I hoped something maybe'd opened up, back home there. But jeez, all there is in Coeur d'Alene any more is changing bedsheets for tourists and they don't want people like me for that. Logging's down. Mining's gone to hell. Farmers and ranchers can't afford to hire. What am I supposed to do?" That last word broke out as a rising note toward wail, do*oo?*

I stood staring past the silent elderly heads at the wispy-whiskered specimen of woe and his faded illegitimate pickup. Curious no longer, I now was furious. When I was not much younger than him, other pickups were on the road, passing through the Two Medicine country from the droughted-out farms of the High Line with the bitter farewell GOODBY OLD DRY painted across their boxboards, and families of the Depression crammed aboard with whatever last desperate possessions they had managed to hang on to. The human landslide set loose by auction hammers cracking down. Two rages balanced in me: that here fifty years later there still was no goodbye to that grief of being driven from the land, or that a clever beggar would play on that memory of misery to coax money from us.

Out of that bloodsurge of the past, I called sharply to the pitiful or conniving face in the pickup window:

"There in Coeur d'Alene, did you ever know somebody named

Heaney?" Leona was a little distance from me, and out the side of my eye I saw her stir at that remembered name.

"Mister Heaney? Sure." The young guy lost a little of his complexion of despair as he found something definite to offer. "I used to mow his lawn. Ray Heaney? In the insurance business?"

The Baloney Express totality swiveled to watch my reaction. In my mind now was the Heaney house on St. Ignatius Street in Gros Ventre, Ray and I sprawled beneath tall cottonwoods on that lawn of another time, our boyhood best friendship now thinned to lines jotted on Christmas cards exchanged from his insurance agency to my ranch . . .

I nodded, which brought a chorus of "Well, hell, okay then" and "Good enough" from the group awaiting my verdict. Roger Tate swung around and told the young guy, "We got to have a little conference over here. You just sit tight."

Eagle-beaked old Dale Starr proved to be the fiscal lobe of Baloney Express. While the others looked to him to decree a sum that would get a man enough gasoline and meals to carry him from the middle of Montana all the way across North Dakota to Fargo, plus putting something on his feet, Dale in turn squinted at Riley and asked, "You in, Shakespeare?" Riley said he supposed he was. It seemed to be just assumed I was a donor, so Dale inquired next: "Ladies?" Without looking at each other, Mariah and Leona each nodded inclusion into the ante. Dale promptly announced, "Okay then, nine bucks a head."

After we'd all dug down in wallets or pockets or purses for Dale, he in turn riffle-counted the sheaf of bills, nodded, and handed the money to Roger Tate. Who led us back to the pickup and told the young guy, "Here's $99 to see you home. Take care."

The guy choked out several versions of thanks and promises to repay, then started the clattery pickup and headed out onto the Interstate. None of the eleven of us said anything as we watched him go. He had a lot of miles ahead of him yet to Fargo, and still faced walking into a shoe store in Billings barefoot.

After that not particularly restful stop, we let the freeway go on to Boston while we sideroaded north. Naturally I reverted to watching our retread lovers deal with Leona's flagship presence. Jangled but not yet to the point of disintegration, was my reading of Mariah and Riley's mutual mood so far. They were taking refuge in their work insofar as they could. True, no *Montanian* piece came to light from our excursioning through Rapelje and Harlowtown and Shawmut and Judith Gap. But shooter and scribbler kept reminding each other in earnest that they absolutely utterly just could not afford to flummox around the way they had at the outset of the trip; as one or the other of them phrased it at least once a day, "We don't have time for a scavenger hunt." And it sounded to me as if both Mariah and Riley actually grasped that, this time; these two were educable about anything but themselves.

It wasn't many days into this Leona phase of the trip before we came to an intersection, close to the exact middle of the state, where the sign pointing south said one hundred miles to Billings and the sign pointing east said one hundred miles to Jordan. The *Montanian* twosome chose east, and so we Bagoed onward into country where a hundred miles to anywhere seemed a highly conservative estimate.

Keep your eyes on the horizawn was in a song that came around fairly often on Melody Roundup on the Bago's radio and the landscape surrounding us now was much like that, a kind of combination of horizon hypnotically the same and the earth letting out a stretching yawn as it drew its edgeline against the sky. The Big Dry, this prairie region out ahead of us was called, partly because Big Dry Creek traces across it but also for the general precipitation picture. Not this year, though. After the drought of the past couple of summers, even this gaunt midriff of the state had received decent rain this year. I would bet that it was green years of this sort which fooled the homesteaders into settling out here in the first place. This was a neighborhood where I had never set foot but yet felt I knew something of. When I was a kid during the Depression, one of the country school systems somewhere out east here got so strapped for funds that the only musical instruments that could be afforded were harmonicas, and so harmonica bands were formed. Fourth of July solemnity, graduation day, any of those type of functions featured mouth organ musicians en masse and for a few years there I devoutly wished our own Gros Ventre high school would either go broke enough or sensible enough to forget about stuff like trumpets and put us all on harmonicas. I mean, wouldn't it be something to hear *Pompous Circumstances,* as my father called it, orchestrated by a schoolful of harmonica kids?

People were not many out here any more. Now that it was after Labor Day, as we drove we regularly saw the bumblebee colors of schoolbuses moving along rural roads. But even that scene scarcened here at the onset of the Big Dry country.

Pucka pucka pucka, Riley's wordbox began to tune up as we rolled on.

> *In the red schoolhouse of his head, Jefferson, great Tom, calculated the doubling of America westward. He knew that miles in chunks could be whittled into dreams, farms, nation, and out of that Jeffersonian box of mind came an orderly arithmetical survey system which put the pattern of mile-square sections on the land; came his 1803 bargain with France for the Louisiana Purchase, the frontier expanse all the way from the Mississippi Valley to the western side of what is now Montana; came his instructions to his enigmatic young personal secretary Meriwether Lewis to find a cohort—the steady William Clark, he turned out to be— and explore up the Missouri River into this new dreamscape.*
>
> *In the presidency of Lincoln, Abe who had built farm fences, came the Homestead Act. That broadstroke of legislation in 1862 and its cousin laws proclaimed: come west, come into the Jeffersonian vision, come gain yourself a piece of the earth by putting your labor—your life—into it for this little sum of years.*
>
> *Into Montana, mostly in the first fraction of the twentieth century, came scores of thousands of homesteaders in the greatest single spate of agricultural migration in American history. . . .*

We pulled into Winnett for the night. A grocery store. A couple of bars, one doubling as a cafe. A gas station out by the highway. Highway sheds, grain elevator. A school, nice and modern. Some houses that were being lived in, but not as many as there were empty ones and vacant lots. What was saddest to see, though, was not just the proverbial grass growing in the street but little jungles of morning glory vines snaking out.

And that was pretty much the town except for the courthouse. You might not ever think so if you didn't know, but Winnett, population two hundred, is the county seat of Petroleum County.

"Which," Riley announced out of the books he'd been looking stuff up in as I drove us along the scanty main street, "has a total population of—brace yourselves, gang—*six* hundred, in an area, hmm, bigger than the Los Angeles Basin."

"There he is on California again, Jick," Leona shared with me as if we were on a mutual quest for an antidote. She had taken off her Walkperson headset that had been reciting Russian into her and was gazing around Winnett as if she'd always been meaning to pay it a visit.

"Maybe you two want to put some of this elbow room in your suitcases for *Glob*land," I in turn suggested to Mariah and Riley as I aimed the Bago into the otherwise empty Petrolia RV Park. "Sounds like you could sell it by the inch down there."

The *Montanian* team ignored our parental remarks and scanned out the window at trafficless and pedestrianless Winnett. "Let me guess," Mariah eventually intoned to Riley. "What we need here is a photo of Jefferson rolling over in his grave, right?"

I will say for Riley that he was bright enough to immediately pack himself off uptown, so to speak, out of range of Mariah's photothinking mood. Myself, I figured she and her camera would charge right out and tackle the challenge of Winnett, but this daughter of mine could still surprise me. When Leona offered to come out and help me hook up the utilities, Mariah slick as a wink told her no, no, she'd be more than glad to help me at that herself, she knew Leona had lots and lots of Russian to pipe into her head yet.

So out we went, Mariah and I, around to the side compartments of the Bago. She had been waiting her chance to get hold of me alone. "Thanks a whole hell of a bunch, Daddio," she let me know in a tone that would have peeled paint.

"What, for my general sainthood or something specific?"

"You know goddamn good and well," she said, yanking the electrical hook-up cable out of its cubbyhole a mile a minute. "For inviting the Duchess of Moscow along."

"Figured you'd appreciate having some female company on the trip for a change," I responded with an extreme poker face. "The benefit of an older wiser woman and all that."

"Benefit, sure, you bet," Mariah bobbed her head as if bouncing each word at me. "Now any time I get a craving for it I'll know how to order borscht."

"In California," I cautioned, "they probably call it liquid essence of beet."

That headed her off on Leona, at least. Mariah eyed me as if debating whether this next issue was worth taking to war. "You really don't want me to go to California, do you."

I bent to fasten the Bago's water intake hose into the campground spigot. Not that I'd entirely intended it, but this left Mariah with the honey hose—the toilet drain—to gingerly drag out and handle.

"What I really don't want, Mariah, is for you and Riley to carve grief into each other, the way you did the first time. California is only the wrapper that comes in."

McCaskills, daughter and father, looked at each other over the utility hookups. We both were so taut that a breeze would have twanged notes out of us.

Mariah at last shook her head.

"Nice try, but this," she indicated with a lift of her chin toward Leona's chesty silhouette in the Bago sidewindow, "isn't going to change anything between Riley and me."

"Then you got nothing to worry about, do you," I asserted back to her. "You and Riley can practice at marriage again by each having a beloved in-law around."

In this promising outlook for disruption, that night after supper I figured a game of pitch might be just the thing to help matters along.

Remembering his trouncing when we'd played at Three Forks, Riley sent me a narrow look and stated: "Huh uh. I don't participate in blood sports."

But just as I'd hoped, Leona was not about to let him squirm out of it. "I don't see any competing nightlife in Winnett, do you?"

It didn't take much doing on my part to contrive the next, either.

"Why don't you and me take them on, Leona? Show these heirs of ours how the game is played, why not."

Riley of course had things so backwards he was actually relieved to be partnered with Mariah rather than me or his mother; it was Mariah who twitched at the generational pairing, but what could she say? No way around it for her, which T-totally suited me. If she figured she was going to remake life with this Wright guy, first let her consider the mess he could make of merely a hand of cards.

Pearl Harbor with playing cards instead of bombs, is the nearest description I can give of what ensued. Leona and I played circles around the other two. Mariah bid tersely and Riley extravagantly and by the end of the second hand we led them six to one in the hole. I had to start to worry a little that Leona and I would have the game won before Mariah's agony of playing partners with Riley had been sufficiently prolonged.

Leona, though, helped. While Riley was deep in ponder of an untakable trick, she maternally observed to him:

"You must have left your luck outside tonight."

"Hmm? Oh. Right, Mother."

Riley's problem was, he thought through the cards and out their other side. When he should have been calculating trump, he was off beyond in contemplation of whether the queen of diamonds had her hair in a wimple or a snood, and why jacks came to be called jacks instead of knaves, on and on until he was somewhere out in the forest that surrendered the woodpulp that the cards were made from. I suppose that is the literary mind, but it is pitiful to see in a game of pitch.

It was during the next hand, while we once again waited for Riley to play a card, that Leona remarked she had something she'd been wondering about.

"How do you two," she coolly included Mariah in her inquiring gaze, "decide on what story you're going to do?"

Riley stroked his mustache rapidly. "It varies, Mother," he said and tried to run his jack of trumps past me, which I had saved my queen precisely for.

"I've been trying to watch how you work together," Leona went on, "but I guess I don't quite savvy it yet. Do you match the pictures to the words or the words to the pictures?"

Mariah blinked as if she'd been asked to explain nuclear physics. "Uhmm, both, kind of."

And often neither, I felt like adding about their periodic dry spells on the centennial series. Instead I observed to Leona, "You know they warn a person about ever watching sausage being made. It's a little bit like that with this newspaper stuff."

Leona just smiled. I'd begun to notice, though, that she had different calibres of smiles. The broad beaming expression that seemed to welcome all of life—the Alectric smile, I thought of it as, for I had first seen it on her when she and Alec were sparking each other, that summer of fifty years ago—shined out most naturally. You could read a newspaper by the light of that facial glow. But there was also a Leona smile

236 · IVAN DOIG

that her eyes didn't quite manage to join in; the smile muscles performed by habit, but there was some brainwork going on behind that
one. And then there was one that can only be called her foolkiller smile;
when you got it, you wondered if you'd been eating steak with a spoon.
Mariah got that one a lot.

With Mariah nicely on low boil, the next logical mission of the
evening was to lend Riley some aggravation. As a former child and now
an all-too-veteran parent, I pretty much instinctively knew what would
do the job.

"I bet you're like me, Leona—never imagined, when he was a snip
of a kid, Riley would grow up to be such a leading citizen. I know with
Mariah, there were times when I wondered how the world was ever
going to be ready for her." From the corner of my eye I knew Mariah
was giving me a murderous stare, perfect to my purpose. Riley was just
pulling his head out of his latest mystical contemplation of his hand of
cards when I delivered the opening to Leona. "Funny to think back to
what they put us through when they were little, huh?"

"Funny is the word for it," Leona brightly informed us as Riley
uneasily held his cards in front of him like a tiny shield. "He was a holy
terror when he was little. The summer he was four, his dad started taking him with, out to the cattle. Here the next thing I knew, Riley was
refusing to pee in the bathroom. The only way he'd go was outside—
his little legs spraddled like he'd seen his dad do out on the range." She
looked fondly at Riley as if exhibiting him at the county fair. "He killed
off my entire bed of daisies that summer."

"Mother, will you for God's sake lay off my urinary history and—"

"Must be something about their generation, Leona," I put in
remorselessly. "Maybe the doctors in those days fed them orneriness pills
before they sent them home with us as babies from the hospital, you suppose? Mariah now, the story on her is—" and I of course proceeded to tell
about the time she was in grade school and every recess Orson Zane
would pester the daylights out of her but always was sneaky enough to get
away with it until finally the day Mariah carefully spit down the front of
her own dress, presented the damp evidence to the teacher as Orson's,
and got him the curative spanking he was overdue for.

Leona laughed as mightily over that as I had over Riley taking a
cowboy pee in the posies, our offspring meanwhile stewing in silence.
Eventually, though, Riley glumly thought out loud for our benefit:
"You know, folklorists just put numbers on stories that crop up time

and again. Number 368, The-Chihuahua-Who-Took-One-Nap-Too-Many-in-the-Microwave-Oven. Parents ought to do that. Just call out the numbers. Save yourselves the trouble of doing the telling."

"But Riley, hon, the telling is the fun of it," Leona told him instructively.

"Besides, numbers don't go high enough for all the stories parents save up as blackmail," Mariah noted with a censorious glance my direction.

"Speaking of numbers," I glided to, for we'd played out the hand in the course of the conversation, "what'd we make, partner?"

Leona turned over the tricks she and I had taken and counted out high, low, and jack. *"Tree,"* she reported with satisfaction, which by now we all knew was Russian for three.

"We treed them again, did we?" I thought that was pretty good, but nobody else seemed to catch it. Mariah was intent on my scorekeeping from the treasury of kitchen matches, to see how bad her and Riley's situation was by now. They'd actually scored a point, which wiped out their deficit—Leona's and my total now had reached nine—and I congratulated Mariah on their advance up to nothing.

"Gosh, Dad, just what I always wanted, a goose egg," she said in a dripping voice. "When I get done with it, what part of the goose do I stick it back in?"

Riley had gravitated off to the refrigerator and fetched a can of beer for each of us, plus his latest inspiration. "You ever hear that old Country-and-Western sermon about how a deck of cards stands for life?" He dropped into a deep drawl. *"Thurr're fifty-two cards in the deck, don't yuh see, one fer every week a the year. The four suits, hearts an' diamonds an' clubs an' spades, reperzents the four seasons a the year. They also mean the seasons a the human heart, love an' wealth an' war an' death. Add up all the spots a all the cards, along with the ever-prezent joker of life, an' they come out to three hundred sixty-five, one fer every day a the . . ."*

He paused at the expression on the other three of us. "You heard it?"

"Yes," stated Leona.

"Lots and lots of times," said I.

"Mmm hmm," even Mariah put in delicately.

"Oh." Riley busied himself picking up the cards he'd long since been dealt. "Whose bid?"

—

Now that there were four of us, commotion kicked off each morning in the Bago. The minute there was enough dawn, Riley was Spandexed up and out running the ridgeline. Mariah got down and Janed on the floor between the cab and the kitchen nook. Leona tucked herself behind the table there in the dinette, put her headset on like a tiara, and ingested Russian. I meanwhile did breakfast duty and tried to stay out of the various lines of fire.

Funny, what will bug a person. So as not to fill the ears of the rest of us with constant Moscowese, Leona performed silent recitation; that is, simply moved her lips in Russian to answer the headset questions. Myself, I considered it downright thoughtful of her and probably so would have Mariah, if she hadn't had to pop up in her exercise repetitions and every time see Leona wordlessly mouthing something—one exertion by Mariah would meet with a mute appeal about the way to the train station, her next contortion would have as backdrop a request to pass the salt. I noticed Mariah's workouts grow grimmer until she finally had to stop in midtummywork and ask:

"Mmm—Leona?"

The older woman blinked down at her, lifted off the headset and automatically palavered: "*Puhzhahlistah, puhftuhreetyeh vahpros yeshcho ras.* 'Please repeat the question again.'"

"Uh huh, right," Mariah said with a careful breath. "What I'm wondering is, how can you learn to say a word without *saying* it?"

Leona smiled interestedly while she considered. Then unloaded: "I suppose the same way you can put yourself through Jane Fonda's exercises without being Jane Fonda."

> *. . . The voices remember and remember. It was the second summer on the homestead, one of the early innocent years before the dry part of the weather cycle scythed across these arid plains, and the June rain had granted them a blue lake of crop, the blossoming flax that homesteaders sometimes resorted to until they could work the sod sufficiently to attempt wheat on it. The husband was out and away on some chore, as he always seemed to be, and the wife was at the stove, as she always seemed to be, when the three-year-old daughter called from just outside the door of the shanty.*
>
> *"See my snake, mommy."*
>
> *"Janie, hon, I don't have ti— See what? Janie, show me!"*

"My snake. He mine. I killded him."
There in the yard the child had taken the garden hoe
and hoed the rattlesnake in half. . . .

Road, road, and more road was the menu of this day as we headed east toward Jordan.

We passed prairie creeks in their deep troughs of flood-cut banks.

Dome formations poked up on the horizon like clay bowls upside down.

Fenceposts became more spindly and makeshift, crooked and thin as canes out here so far from forest.

Between Mosby and Sand Springs we met a Bluebird Wanderlodge with Minnesota plates and I could imagine that motorhome coming on a straight line, on cruise control, the 750 miles from the Twin Cities.

"A jackrabbit must have to pack a lunch through this country," I eventually couldn't help but observe as we went on through more miles of scantness.

"Those bunnies better put on their helmets and flak jackets," Riley said from his perch behind me. "The latest notion of what to do with this out here is to bombard the living shit out of it."

"Why's that?" I asked in honest surprise. A glance over my shoulder showed Leona looking at him with her eyebrows raised, too. "Montana isn't at war with anybody I know of."

"Tell it to the Pentagon, Jick." I heard him flipping in his notebook. "The military wants eight million more acres in the western states for tank maneuvers and artillery and bombing ranges. A million of those acres are up here around Glasgow. The other day an Undersecretary of Defense said—how's this for using the language bass ackwards?—these open spaces out here are 'a national treasure.' What he means is, they'll make terrific target practice."

The slap of Riley closing his notebook was the only sound for a while. His news about forthcoming bombs and tanks and artillery shells bugged the hell out of me. This country of the Big Dry did not appeal to me personally. Yet why couldn't it be left alone? Left be empty? Instead of the human creature finding one more way to beat up on the land.

Gas stations had grown so scarce that I pulled in at the one at Sand Springs—the gas station pretty much was Sand Springs—and crammed every drop of fuel I could into the Bago and religiously checked the tires and the air in the spare. Out on these extreme empty roads, you could die of car trouble.

The station attendant and I had been gabbing wholeheartedly—people out here in eastern Montana were as open as their plains—and while we did he noticed Mariah and Leona and Riley one after another emerge from the motorhome to stretch their legs or utilize the restroom or, in Mariah's case, just unlimber her camera on Sand Springs. When we settled up, along with my change he handed me:

"Traveling with your whole family, eh? That's nice to see, these days."

It surprised the daylights out of me, the notion of the four of us as a brood. I was briefly tempted to tell the stationman that yeah, we were just your normal vanilla American household these days; the silver-haired lady and I weren't married, at least to each other, but she'd once almost married my brother before thinking better of it, whereas the younger two, she mine (by my second wife) and him hers, *had* been married to one another but weren't any more, although they intended to be again. Family tree, hell. We were our own jungle.

Mariah found her picture that afternoon. Leona was the one, as we roved down from Jordan toward Cohagen, who noticed that some of the sheds on the ranches we were passing had chimneys and window sashes and for that matter, regular front doors: homestead houses that had been jacked up and moved after the sodbuster families "took the cure" and abandoned their claims in some final dry year. Mariah pored over one of those old shanties for what must have been an hour, and the photo she finally chose was a close-up of its siding, the wood weathered to the rich brown of a relic.

As long a day as it had been, prowling around the Big Dry country for Mariah and Riley to work on their piece, that night after we pulled into the campground on the outskirts of Jordan, pop. 450, I simply nuked up some frozen dinners.

Leona tasted the first forkful of hers and asked clinically:

"Excuse my asking, but what is this guck?"

Mariah was in her absent rhythm of tackling the food with a utensil in one hand while she messed around in a stack of proof sheets with the other, and Riley and I pretty much per usual were mauling away at our plates without much thought either, I suppose.

"Soybeans Incognito, would be my best guess," I theorized to Leona, although the label announced veal patties a la something-or-other.

"You people," she uttered more in sorrow than in anger, "eat like Gypsies."

"That's funny," Riley answered and gawked out at bare gray hills beyond the campground, ashen distance surrounding us everywhere. This will sound like I'm pouring it on, but honest to God, out there at the side of the road was a sign that read: HELL CREEK, 15 MILES. "You suppose maybe it might be because we *live* like Gypsies, Mother?"

Protocol when four people are packed into a motorhome and none of them are married to any of the others is tricky. Leona was up to it, though. She smiled from Riley to Mariah to me, then simply proposed it at large:

"Would anybody mind overly much if I took on the cooking?"

Our next encampment was at Circle, which Riley couldn't resist pointing out was a bigger dot on the map than we were used to; the town had about 800 population. This particular morning, while Leona and I held the fort at the Redwater RV Park, he and Mariah had gone downtown to the Big Sheep Mountains Retirement Home in search of more rememberers for their homestead piece. Old folks' home, such places used to be called. I wondered if I was going to end up in one of those. I hoped not. I hoped to Christ not.

For the time being, I actually had the Bago to myself while Leona was out doing her daily walk for exercise. The motorhome seemed suddenly expanded, big as an empty bus. Just me and a third cup of coffee and the rattle of the pages of the day's *Montanian* I had settled down with. EASTERN EUROPE in one headline, COCAINE in another. What the news seemed to add up to was that people were evaporating out of East Germany as fast as they could, leaving everything behind to bravely try to better their lives, while a sizable proportion of this country sat around trying to figure new ways to put conniption powder up its collective nose. I don't know. I try to be as American as anybody, but the balance of behavior looked pretty far out of whack at our end.

It was a relief, then, when Leona came back in from her constitutional and mentioned that she'd stopped by the phone box and called Morgan to see how things were at the ranch, and I said yeah, I was going to have to do the same to Noon Creek pretty quick, and we made conversation along that line for a while.

Leona hesitated, but then brought it up.

"Riley tells me you're thinking about selling your ranch."

I managed not to say he'd be the one to know, he was a major reason for that. Instead: "Thinking about is as far as I seem to get."

"It's always hard, isn't it," she answered. "When Herb and I married in '44 he'd already taken over the place from his folks, so all those years until Herb died, our ranch just always seemed to me as permanent as the Crazy Mountains. But that's not really the case any more. Morgan will run the place until his last breath. But after him, I just don't know. Jeff"—by now I knew that was her only grandchild, in college at Bozeman—"doesn't seem that interested. He's a quiet boy. So far, he won't even look at a girl." Leona turned aside to glance at her reflection in the window above the nook table, as if the answer to young Jeff might be there. "No, I'm not at all sure the ranch is in his future. He maybe takes after Riley." She swung a smile my way. "Don't even say it, Jick."

In truth, it was hard not to burst out at the contradiction of a nephew emulating Riley yet not chousing after the female of the species. But the eventuality in what Leona had just told me was outechoing that. So even the prospering Wrights were only postponing, staving off for one more generation, the question of what would become of their ranch.

Suddenly the ranch topic lost its appeal for both of us and Leona said she'd better put in a session on her Russian flashcards. I offered my services, figuring I could riffle cards in any language, and she brightened right up. "*Spaseebo.* Thank you. It'll make the situation seem more real to have you trying me out on the words instead of doing it myself."

I flicked and flipped to the best of my ability, springing stuff like *What time is it now, please?* on her until she said that was about enough vocabulary for any one day.

The topic that had been in my own mind while she'd been practicing *pah rooskee* had to come out. "Something you mentioned earlier, Leona. I'd kind of like to talk to you about it, if you wouldn't mind too much. All those years you spent with Herb—a lot like what I spent with Marce." I worked my throat overtime but managed to get the next words out. "What can you tell me about—this."

She knew what I meant. About being a widow, a widower. About being the one who lives on alone.

Leona's hands fiddled with the box of flashcards. The same little crimp of concentration she'd shown while I quizzed her on vocabulary appeared again between her silvered eyebrows, but her eyes stayed steady into mine. "You still miss Marcella something fierce, don't you."

I swallowed heavily and said, "That's still the case, yeah. I guess really that's what I'm wondering from you. Does it ever get any easier?"

"In some ways." Leona paused. "Maybe it has to, or we wouldn't be able to stand it. We'd crush down until there wasn't anything left of us either. But it . . . the grief, the worst of it anyway, eventually does"—I could see her search as she sometimes did for a Russian phrase—"space itself out some. Every now and again, something pops into memory that hurts as much as ever. And there are days you wish you could take off the calendar forever. Herb's birthday is always hard for me. And our anniversary. And the start of calving time, because that's the time of year he died. But," she found a smile to encourage me, "that leaves a majority of days when a person can get by okay, I suppose is how I look at it."

"Leona, if this is too damn personal, just up and say so and we'll skip it. But—how come you never remarried?"

She flushed a little and looked down at the table, but did tackle my question. "I've had a couple of chances. Not as many as you maybe think. But every time it seemed like such an effort. To get used to some-one all over again. I suppose I'm set in my ways, and at this—stage of life, the other person is bound to be, too."

"Yeah, I seem to be finding that out in myself. Old dogs bark the loudest." Immediately I wished that hadn't spouted out. Leona was, what, two years further into age than I was.

That inadvertent crack put her to looking squarely across at me again. She said, though, as if going right on with her catalogue of why she hadn't gone the matrimonial route with anybody in the years since Herb Wright's death: "Besides, you know my history, Jick. I don't seem to marry easily."

Huh. So she would at least allude in that direction. To Alec. Her jilt of him. The blond bolt of lightning she was for the McCaskills, back there half a century ago.

I didn't want to get into that with her now, given the missionary work she and I had ahead on Mariah and Riley and their marriage propensity.

244 · IVAN DOIG

Instead I kept on the course I'd started with the remarrying question. "There's a real reason I'm trying to get a line on this. See, one thing I'll be going home to, after our newspaper aces finish off the centennial, is somebody who's got herself convinced she and I ought to get together." Althea Frew probably right at that moment was humming around Gros Ventre red-circling on every calendar in town November 8, Centennial Day and the return of widower/bachelor/eligible-male-at-loose-ends-and-not-yet-utterly-decrepit, one J. A. McCaskill. "And at honest to Christ moments I wonder if she might just be right." Or as the Althea matter formed itself in the whispers in my mind, *My God, am I going to end up having to do that? If I am, I've got some overhauling to do on my thinking about that woman.* And soon. Centennial Day was not that far down the pike now, life beyond Mariah and Riley and the steering wheel of the Bago was fast coming at me, and if I was going to try and follow widower logic—admittedly, it was there—then pairing up with Althea would at least cure what loomed ahead of me at Noon Creek after that eighth morning of November, the aloneness. Loneliness.

"Oh, sure, she has plenty of things about her that kind of bug me," I summed Althea to Leona's smile of encouragement, "but she can probably double that in spades about me. We could likely iron each other out enough to make a marriage work, more or less, if it came to that. And that's what I'm wondering. Whether it's maybe worth it, not to have to try the rest of life"—the last of, we both knew I was saying— "all alone. But pretty plainly you've decided it's not worth it, huh? From your side of things, I mean."

That other side of things, I genuinely did have a long curiosity about. In the skin of a woman, how does life seem? I could remember speculating that about my mother, when I was still only a shavetail kid, fifteen or so; ranching and the Forest Service, male livelihoods both then—what did Beth McCaskill think of her existence in that largely man-run scheme of things? Certainly I'd had the occasions to mull McCaskill women since, too. Lexa, taking herself off to Alaska. Mariah—God, you bet, Mariah. And even though I felt we knew each other to the maximum, sometimes even Marcella had stirred that skin-whisper question.

"Maybe it's not just a matter of that," Leona was saying now, "the worth-it part, that is. Maybe it's more a matter of getting up enough nerve for it. I seem to have spent my nerve formating, whatever you'd say, on Herb."

Thinking how complete my version with Marcella had been, I could understand that too. "Uh huh. Could be that our share of enthusiasm for hearing wedding bells over and over again got parceled out to these kids of ours instead."

She laughed, looking a little relieved at the excuse to. I figured now was as logical a time as any, to start putting our heads together about Mariah and Riley and the flopperoo marriage they were determined to repeat.

"That's something I been wanting to get to with you, too, Leona. I don't have a whole lot of sway with Mariah, where Riley is concerned. But I wondered if there's any way you can work on him—or hell, *her*, for that matter—to keep them from going off the deep end again."

Leona gave me a smile, of a calibration I hadn't seen before. And delivered:

"Jick, you couldn't be more wrong. I think Riley and Mariah should get married again."

My ears about fell off.

While I was gaping at the woman, trying not to believe I'd heard what I'd heard, she was piling more on. "You're looking at me *kahk Srehdah nah Pyahtnyeetsoo*. Like Wednesday looks at Friday. But I'd think you, as Mariah's father and all, would be the first person in the world to want them back together."

"Togeth—? Leona, that first marriage of theirs didn't just come apart! Pieces of it are still flying through the air, it blew up so goddamn bad! Why in the name of anything holy should they make the exact identical mistake again?"

"Maybe they've learned how to do better."

"Or maybe they're only going to be better at how to make each other miserable. They weren't a couple of skim-milk kids when they got married, that first time. Now they're even more—well, indegoddamn-pendent, is about the most polite way to put it, the both of them."

She still toyed with a small smile, which did nothing to improve the rotten humor this suddenly had me in.

"So you're not really for people remarrying either?" she tried on me, I suppose apropos of the Althea theorizing I'd been doing.

"I'd be a thousand percent happy to see Mariah and Riley remarried," I protested. "Just not to each other."

"Jick, it's their choice."

"I *know* it's their choice." If it was mine, there'd have been no chance of a repeat performance by those two. "I also know neither one of them is dealing with a full deck when it comes to deciding about the other one." How to render this politely. No, to hell with polite. "They get hot to trot, out on their job all the time like they are without any other candidates around to button their bellybuttons to, and then while they're at it, so to speak, they figure hey, wow, they're magically back in love. But Leona, that'll only last as long as the bedsprings squeak. Then they'll be dishing out hurt to each other again, which is what I dread for them. And I don't see why you aren't leery of that, too. For Riley's sake, if nothing else. Maybe I've been misreading, but I somehow got the impression Mariah is not your favorite person in the universe."

Leona stood her territory.

"I have my difference with Mariah, that's all too true. We all side with our own children when a marriage of theirs breaks up. After all, we're parents, aren't we, Jick, not neutral peacekeeping forces. But I'm not the one who wants to try married life with Mariah again, am I. Riley is. I know you think he's gone loco about this"—understatement of the century—"but Riley's instincts are generally right. Usually more right than mine." Her expression suggested the not remote possibility that they might be righter than my own, too.

If she expected that to get a rise out of me, it did.

"Let's back up here a goddamn minute. Didn't I just hear you putting remarrying out of your own picture? If that's true for you, why in all hell isn't it true for Mariah and Riley after they've already flubbed the dub with each other once?"

"A difference in Vitamin G level, I suppose," wafted across the table from her to me.

"Huh?"

"In guts, Jick. I said 'nerve' before, but I guess we're into speaking plain, aren't we. My time of life, my way of—getting through, isn't anywhere near the same as Riley and Mariah's. Their generation has its own agenda and it should have. I know you can't help but feel Riley and Mariah are being scatty about this, but Jick, they've got so many more years ahead of them they can afford to take those chances, can't they? If they possess the guts to try to make a go of life with each other again, good for them."

Like the kid starting his third year in the second grade, it was beginning to dawn on me how much ground I was losing. Good God in sweet heaven. Here I'd invited Leona Tracy Wright along as an ally against the tendency of our offspring to get dangerously smitten with each other and she turns out to be their head cheerleader.

So I wasn't one bit better at getting through to her at this farther end of life than I'd been at the early part, was I. The realization knocked every blossom off me. Why was it, the consequence always had to be the same where this person was concerned? I had believed I was putting aside the past between Leona and the McCaskills, shelving that oldest grudge of her having been too good for my brother, spending these Bago hours getting to know her as she was now instead of a disruptive memory, but no. I still didn't have the shadow of a clue to the real Leona, any more than that other time I had tried to be at my social utmost with her.

Probably she wouldn't even remember that time; there wasn't any great reason for her to. The Fourth of July rodeo, that summer when Leona and Alec were going at romance hot and heavy. I could see Leona yet, her silver hair returned to gold, the half-century gone to leave her magically at seventeen again, there in a clover-green blouse with good value under it, perched on a car fender by the arena fence. Alec was entered in the calf roping and he glommed on to me to go over and entertain his lady love while he spruced up to compete. It promptly emerged, though, that besides keeping her company Alec wanted me to keep her occupied; he didn't want Earl Zane, Arlee's equally bigheaded older brother, to come strutting around and cut in on his progress with Leona.

I was just in the midst of telling Alec nothing doing, that my not-quite-fifteen-year-old-yet repertoire of life didn't include anything on how to handle hearts and hand-to-hand combat, when Leona revolved in our direction, patted the car fender beside her, and of course beamed me in with a smile the way a moth would head for a lamp.

Well, okay, maybe, I thought to myself as I zombied over to her leading my horse. The horse, my father's big gray saddle mount named Mouse, which he'd grandly lent me for the holiday, actually was my best hope with Leona, for she was such an avid rider she definitely knew horseflesh.

In one way of looking at it, my subsequent brief stay with Leona on that fender did serve Alec's purpose of repulse: Earl Zane never showed his ugly face, nor did any saber-toothed tigers. On the other hand, entertaining Leona was an uphill battle every moment. Things reached their ultimate dead end just after I had told her a joke she didn't get, which is infinitely worse than no joke at all, when Mouse chose that moment to unroll his business end and proceed to take a world-record leak in front of my horrified eyes and Leona's evidently interested ones. Honest to God, the tallywhacker on that horse looked like a firehose in action and Leona studied it like it was the newest thing in hydraulics. Mouse's golden stream washed away what little composure I had left, and by the time Alec showed up and asked Leona how I did as company, she in all too much truth reported: "He's a wonder."

Her current opinion of me probably wasn't even ankle-high to that. She was the same calm Leona, dentproof as her smile, but her voice had a different bearing than when we'd been rushing Russian into her.

"Jick, really, I'm sorry we don't see the same way on Riley and Mariah getting together again, but—"

"Forget it. I need some weather in me." I quickly got up and jammed on my hat and coat and went out the Bago door.

Wouldn't you know, the afternoon had turned as blustery outside as in. Clouds needed to come a long way to these eastern Montana plains and they always seemed to mean business by the time they got here. There already was rain monkeying around to the west and a gusty wind was clearing the way for it into Circle. I wished I'd grabbed my winter cap instead of my Stetson. Not that I've had that much experience at domestic strife, but one of its drawbacks evidently was being dressed wrong for stomping out.

Misery and company. I was forging past the RV park office, head down, when the manager pottered out and called to me.

"You're site five, aren't you? Mr."—he checked the sheet of paper in his hand—"McCaskill?"

When I said I supposed I was, he handed me the piece of paper. "This just came in for you."

"Came in?"

"Sure, by fax. Got our machine right there in the office, in case you want to send something back."

By now I had taken a look at the last line of the facsimile, *Yours with every fond thought* followed by the emphatic signature *Althea,* and in my current mood the reply that popped to mind was the legendary telegram to headquarters we used to joke about in the Forest Service, the fed-up ranger wiring his forest supervisor: *Fuck you. Strong letter to follow.*

However, not knowing the law on transmitting imaginative language by fax, I declined the campground manager's eager offer and dragged a lawn chair over behind a Lombardy poplar for a bit of shelter from the wind and sat to see what was to be contended with in Althea's missive.

> *Jick, dear—*
>
> *Not that I ever need an excuse to keep in touch with you, but those of us on the committee who are not off glamorously wandering the world (just joking! you know me!) have been arranging our Dawn of Montana ceremony, and as you are our orator I'm sure you will appreciate knowing the schedule.*
>
> > *5:00–5:30 a.m. Gather at the Medicine Lodge; musical interlude*
> > *5:30–6:00 Pancake breakfast*
> > *6:00–6:45 Dawn dance*
> > *6:45–6:50 Assemble at the centennial flagpole*
> > *6:50–6:52 Introduction of centennial speaker Jick McCaskill (Penciled in: by you know who!)*
> > *6:52–7:10 Centennial speech by Jick McCaskill*

There was more, you bet there was—Althea could have given lessons to Cape Canaveral on countdown—but I skipped past the rest of the schedule to see what she'd tamped in to her last pair of paragraphs.

> *It's hard to believe our centennial celebration is almost here. I'll have to find something to do with myself after November 8. But then I'm not the only one in that situation, am I?*
>
> *Kenny, who of course kindly told me where you are at this very moment (isn't fax such an advance!), says he'll see you in a day or two when you ship your lambs. I'll give you a jingle.*

In Glasgow the day after, Riley and I went to a car agency so he could jimmy onto the expense account a rental means of transportation for me—I made damn good and sure it was going to be a Ford Taurus instead of a Yugo—and I scorched road home to the ranch. That next morning at Noon Creek, events kept on at about the pace of a catfight in a rolling barrel. Typical of shipping days, a bonechilling squall swirled down off the mountains and we didn't even have the lambs started into the trucks before Shawn Finletter drove up and said his bosses back east just could not understand why I wasn't ready to sell. Right then, with sleet sifting down the back of my neck and a thousand lambless ewes blatting and Helen's dogging in the lamb pen rending the air with barks and Kenny profanely trying to fill the loading chute with lambs who had decided they were afraid of the color of the truck, I could not understand why either. At suppertime, Darleen informed me she and Joe Prentiss of the Gros Ventre Mercantile were no longer on speaking terms, even to argue, but before achieving that state of affairs Joe made it known that the Merc would no longer carry us on a monthly credit account and all groceries hereafter were strictly cash basis. I was still digesting that fiscal turn when Althea Frew was on the line—plain telephone, this time—offering herself as audience for me to rehearse my centennial speech on, and I had to freehand invent that I'd left my only copy back in the Bago, which even as we spoke was being driven by Mariah and Riley to a remote site on the Missouri River where Lewis and Clark had once camped, thus regrettably out of range of fax.

And the morning after we shipped the lambs, Helen departed from her herding years with me, riding beside me in the rental car as far as the Amtrak station in Shelby where she gave me a last remembering look through the blowing web of her hair and boarded the train for Oregon and gemology.

Back at Glasgow, at my earliest chance I innocently asked Mariah how everybody had gotten along in my absence.

She retorted with her camera, saying as she snapped me for the kabillionth time on the trip: "Riley would be easier to remarry if he were an orphan, I'll say that much."

Toward me, Leona behaved as if we'd never been at loggerheads at all, asking how my lambs had weighed out and how the grass prospect looked in the Two Medicine country now that some rain finally had found Montana, ranch talk that was our equivalent of church Latin.

Yeah, well, sure, I told myself, she'd had lifelong practice at sailing smoothly on, hadn't she. Yet I was surprised to find that my snit at her kept cooling off and off, I suppose because I didn't have time to maintain a mad; there was the hour-by-hour matter of the centennial trip and getting done what we were supposed to, all four. What a size life was these days. A person had to get up twice in the morning to begin to fill it. Across county after county I put on the miles, Leona put on the meals, and Mariah and Riley kept on scouring that upper righthand corner of the state. All navigation was straight on those roads, one dead-ahead run after another. The gray grain elevators of town after town we passed—Culbertson, Froid, Scobey, Flaxville—with the high plains all around farmed in brown plowed strips next to straw-colored fallow ones. Sometimes the yield of our miles would be a picture of Mariah's—the water tower of the town of Frazer hanging just above the planetary rim of the plains like a tiny balloon on a string. Sometimes what worked was a scene Riley and his tape recorder found in someone.

> *"We had to pack up and pull out of here in '32," the woman remembers while revisiting Plentywood for the centennial celebration. "Just walked away from our place, that summer, and never came back. It was so dry the corn didn't sprout, the potatoes barely came up, the pasture was awful short. My dad and older brother had gone on ahead out to the Coast, to Everett, Washington, where we had relatives and tried to get any work they could there. Then while my mother went around the countryside until she finally found somebody to trade our farm machinery to for a secondhand Model T Ford, my younger brother and I—I was thirteen at the time—we got on our horses and started moving our handful of cattle to the stockyard here in Plentywood. It was an overnight trip, Millard and I slept on the ground, then the next morning the cattle were anxious for water because they hadn't had any since noon the day before. But Big Muddy Creek here was so low there was deep mud and Millard said, 'Mary, we've got to push them on past that water or they'll bog down in there and we'll be in trouble.' I was almost in tears to leave our cows so thirsty, but Millard was right.*
>
> *"When we got home to the farm we loaded the Model*

> *T—Mother, Millard and I, and a yellow cat—and started*
> *for the Coast. We lost the cat on the way but the rest of us*
> *made it.*
> *"Our horses we just left there on the range."*

Miles City. By now we had roved into October. Mapwise, we were back south out of the farmed plains into cattlegrowing country again and Miles, as the pleasant brick-faced little city was called by ranchers who described their places as "forty miles from Miles," came as a kind of oasis to us all, the big cottonwoods at the Roche Jaune RV Park greeting the Bago like a home grove every time we drove in from one of Mariah and Riley's daily delvings.

This day, though, Leona and I had set them off afoot downtown— the *Montanian* pair had come up with the bright idea of studying what Riley called "bucklelaureate ceremonies" and so they were at a western-wear store seeing just what belt buckles, cowboy boots, rangerider big hats and other regalia walked out of the store in the course of a business day—and she and I headed on toward what she'd spied in a Miles City *Star* ad, a horse auction at the CMR Livestock Auction Yard. Myself, I could take or leave horses, but I knew Leona's interest in them—did I ever—and so I figured, well, hell, what's a few hours of horseflesh to put up with.

The auction sale ring was actually a half-circle, a tier of seats for those of us in the audience arcing around it, with the auctioneer's pulpit centered there against the wall where the livestock was hazed in through one gate, had its moment of being bid on, and hazed out the other gate back into the stockyard. FRIDAY—FEEDER CALVES SATURDAY—SLAUGHTER ANIMALS announced a large red sign above the auctioneer but a person pretty much knew by nose the livestock traffic through here: the mingled smell of cattle and horses was heavier, less pungent than the iodine-and-lanolin fragrance of sheep that I was used to.

Regular buyers had front row moviehouselike seats with their nameplates on them, but Leona and I tucked ourselves onto an ordinary bench high at the back of the arena. As usual I looked the crowd over for anybody I might know but the only such spotting this time was by Leona.

"I see Ozzie Breckenridge is here," she pointed out a long-drink-of-water guy about our age perched at the far end of the arena arc. "He runs a dude ranch, down by Absarokee. Herb and I used to deal horses with him a little." The dude herder noticed Leona too, traded her a nod and obviously wondered who the Methuselah in a Stetson next to her was.

"And ready and we go," the auctioneer chanted and the hazers brought the horses on, one at a time. Roans, pintos, piebalds, Appaloosas, bays, duns, you name it, the equine parade went on for a couple of hours. It seemed to me there was a serious oversupply of horses in the Miles City country and the bidding reflected that too, the auctioneer about having to work himself into a lather to get each animal sold off. In fact, the auction wound down to the point where the regular buyers had got up and left and the rest of the crowd was thinning rapidly too. Throughout it all, though, Leona was rapt.

As we still had chores to do around town, grocery shopping and so on, I finally suggested we stir. But Leona said, "Let's just watch this one last one, Jick. That's not a badlooking horse."

Neither was it a goodlooking horse. At best the thing was only about okaylooking, a sorrel gelding no more than fourteen hands high, shaggy and a little swaybacked, with the scar of a bad barbwire cut across its chest; the one pleasant distinction was a nice blaze of white on its face. Obviously Leona saw more in the animal than I could, and I sat back to learn.

"All right, folks," the auctioneer began as the blazeface trotted a tight circle in the sale ring, "we're here to sell. Who'll give me six fifty to start it off? Six hundred fifty, fifty, fifty, anybody six fifty? Six hundred then, anybody six, six, six, who'll say six, horsehorsehorse helluvahorse swelluvahorse horsehorse gottasellthishorse, six hundred, anybody?"

"It's a crime," Leona said softly to me, referring to the fact that the horse would be cut back into the cannery slaughter herd, which meant his destiny was to become dogfood, if nobody bid on him. "He's no canner. Look how he handles himself in all this commotion." True enough; the sorrel seemed alert to its weird confinement without getting panicky. Leona went on in the same soft tone: "That old fool Ozzie could use him in his dude string, if he just would."

Thinking of horses I had known, particularly an assassin packhorse named Bubbles, I started to nod in agreement that this one by comparison might be a decent equine citizen, but caught myself just in time. The auctioneer was spieling so desperately that I figured if I so much as twitched, I'd have bought myself a steed.

"Folks, remember, you're getting the whole horse here," the auctioneer admonished, "so isn't that worth at least five hundred fifty dollars? You can barely buy a big dog for that. Five fifty will start it off, five hundred fifty, fifty, fifty, ponyponypony onlypony nothingphonypony ponypony ownthepony, five hundred then, five, five, anybody, five? Where's the money, folks, where's the money? Will anybody bid five hundred dollars for this animal?"

Nobody would. The auctioneer's microphone voice took on a sweet fresh reasonableness. "All right, where do you want to start it then?"

Silence ensued. The only motion in the auction house was the blazeface slowly moving his head in wariness of the audience.

"Just one donor of green blood, that's all we need," the auctioneer sounded desperate again. "How about four fifty? Anybody, body, body, any bid, bid, bid?"

Leona had been fingering the top button of her blouse as if to make sure it was secure. Now she tapped the button with her index finger, just obviously enough that it was not missed by the auctioneer.

Oh, swell. Just what every motorhome household needs, an auxiliary horse.

But if Leona's signal alarmed me, it translated immediate new life into the auctioneer.

"Four fifty, I see bid! All right, it's more than I had. Now who'll say four hundred seventy-five, seventy-five, seventy-five, five, five, five—I have four seventy-five!"

More by osmosis than anything I could actually discern, I somehow knew that competing bid had come from Ozzie Breckenridge. He seemed to be casually eyeing in our direction, but I was pretty damn sure those gimlet eyes had taken in Leona's bidding method.

"Five now," the auctioneer raced on, "anybody, five hund-"—Leona tapped her button—"I have five hundred!"

Expensive as those taps were getting to be, I figured I'd better alert her to oculatory Ozzie. "Uh, Leona, that other guy can see you bid."

"I know," she said, finger delicately on button. "I want him to."

"Five fifty? Five fifty?" The auctioneer was putting it to Breckenridge, who was rubbing the back of his neck uneasily while he studied the sorrel from withers to nethers. "Five fifty? It's only double nickels. Five fifty?" Breckenridge continued to inspect the horse as if it was some hitherto unknown species. "It's a nifty for five fifty. Damn near a gifty. Why not bid a thrifty five fif— I have five fifty!"

Breckenridge's movement had looked to me more like a squirm than a bid, but maybe it was both.

"I have five fifty, now seventy-five, sev— I have five seventy-five!" Again Leona had wasted no time with her fingertap.

"Now six hundred, anybody six, six, six, who's say six?" I saw Breckenridge sneak a look at Leona to make sure she still was eagerly fingering that blouse button. By now he had the appearance of a man who'd sooner give up several of his teeth, but at last he made whatever indication it took and bid the six hundred dollars.

Instantly the auctioneer launched his spiel anew, but Leona just as promptly had dropped her finger from the button and was shaking her head no, with a little smile. Within seconds the auctioneer banged his hammer down *whammo,* declared "It's all done, it's a sold one!" and the considerably startled Oz Breckenridge was in possession of a horse.

Riley, though. I had to admit he was more immune to his mother than I'd hoped.

Try as I did to find signs that life with Leona was making him unravel, he seemed pretty much the selfsame goddamn specimen. Take the very next morning, when I innocently pulled into a gas station to feed the Bago on our way out of Miles City. Mariah and Riley were in a mutual work trance, finishing up their westernwear piece to transmit into the *Montanian,* and Leona had retreated into earset Russian, so I climbed out to do the gassing up by myself. I was topping up the air in the tires when Riley stuck his head out the side door of the Bago, to clear his so-called brain I guess, peering over me and the airhose while he did.

"Shit oh dear!" he let out in an old maidy voice. "Everybody knows that's only the half of it! Two elements short is a lot even for Montana. Those old Greeks would be ashamed to death of us, Jick buddy."

From where I was kneeling at the front tire I glanced up and down the main street of Miles City for anybody who looked approximately Greek. "What the hell are you yakking about now?" I addressed Riley, but he had pulled back into the motorhome, where I could hear him asking Mariah for something.

Next thing, he bounced out and past me, and I was happy to have him out of my hair while I finished tending to the tires.

Not until I went to hang the airhose back onto its stanchion at one side of the service station did I discover that where the sign there read

AIR & WATER

Riley had just finished block-lettering beneath with Mariah's biggest blackest grease pencil:

EARTH & FIRE

"Jesus H.—Riley, you want to get us all thrown in the clink?" I wildly checked around for the service station owner.

"Hmm?" Riley stepped back to admire his handwork. "Naw, we're doing this guy a favor. See, now all he has to do is hang up a new logo under his gas sign: NATURAL PHILOSOPHY WHILE YOU FILL."

"If they hang anything around here it's liable to be us, because of you, goddamn it. Come on, climb in the Bago and let's get the hell out of here."

> *A hundred coal cars on a railroad siding, today's resource wagontrain from the prairie to elsewhere. . . .*

As early as Plentywood, it had become a common sight for us to see oil pumps working away in the farmed fields. The rocking-beam kind, that were like washerwomen dipping and rising as they scrubbed clothes on a washboard. But when Leona had cited them to Mariah and Riley once and wondered if they were ever going to do a piece about the energy business in this end of the state, the two of them simply shook their heads and chorused: "Colstrip."

> *The gigantic draglines skin the soil away to get at the coal. Longnecked, mammoth, lumbering, they are oddly technological mirages of the dinosaurs who earlier roamed these plains. . . .*

Even the weather was getting to me, on that drive from Miles City down to Colstrip. Warmish and heavy, considerably too much so for this time of year. About the time you think you have seen everything this climate can possibly do, some new wrinkle comes along. Snow for the Fourth of July, or April hailstones big enough to knock out chickens. And now a sultry day in the middle of October, when the year ought to be gearing down toward winter.

"Must be getting into the banana belt," I commented.

"Tropical southern Montana, sure, you bet," Mariah more or less automatically responded from her watchful gaze out at the passing countryside.

Leona came in late on the conversation, just having shed her headset. "Isn't this nice-looking grassland, though?" she appraised the broad swales we'd been driving through for most of an hour.

"Now you've done it, Mother," Riley quit tapping at his laptop and pointed into the sky ahead.

Mariah had seen it too and already had her camera up.

Riley went on in his Movietone voice: "See there—the Power God heard that and is throwing thunderbolts at us."

The aircraft warning strobe lights on the smokestacks of the Colstrip power plants did seem like steady blinks of lightning in our direction. Even before I'd seen anything of this coal-stripping enterprise, I didn't like what I was seeing.

> There is no muss to the town of Colstrip. Everything looks laid out according to plan, all the neighborhoods new, the downtown area that was installed with the power plants sprigged up with trees and lawn and other landscaping.
>
> Talk about landscape work, though. Just out from Colstrip, the strip-mining takes hundreds of acres at a time and sorts that ground into towering heaps, the grayish overburden of soil and stone clawed aside from the pits in dunelike processions and the black pile of coal so high that a bulldozer atop it looks the size of a hornet. The extracted coal is carried for miles by a huge pipeline-like conveyor to the power plants in town, where electricity is generated and then goes into the transmission lines to VCRs, Jacuzzis, neon signs, all the rest. The smokestacks here above the mined prairie are the tailpipes of our electrical luxury.

A day of contemplating coal-stripping put all four of us ready for a drink before supper, you can bet. On Riley's insistence that the places on the edge of town are always more interesting, we pulled in at the Rosebud Bar just off the highway before Colstrip. "We get in on the indigenous this way, too, gang," he maintained as we trooped up to the door of the enterprise, by which I guess he meant that Rosebud Creek was just about within shouting distance.

Inside, the decor was relentlessly roses. Color photos of them beaded with dew. Vasefuls of red fabric versions on every table. A blimp shot of a stadium, which it didn't take me too long to figure out as the Rose Bowl. A very nearly life-size picture of Gypsy Rose Lee stripping for action, so to speak. Standing in a corner was a kid's sled with a you-know-what decal on it.

"Who do you suppose got hold of this place," Mariah wondered, "Gertrude Stein?"

"All right, tell me," Riley implored, stopping just inside the doorway with his back to it and covering his eyes with a hand. "There's a varnished plaque over the door that says *Gather ye rosebuds while ye may,* isn't there."

The other three of us turned and gawked up. Sure enough, there it posed: in fancy script with painted roses twining out the ends of each *y*, no less.

See what I mean about goddamn Riley—he could even floor his own mother. While Mariah whooped and gave him a vigorous tickle in the ribs, Leona perplexedly looked back and forth from the quotation to her son and asked, "How'd you ever know that?"

"Just unlucky, I guess."

A barmaid considerably beyond the bloom of youth came over as soon as we'd established ourselves at a table. "Hi, kids. What's it gonna be?"

I observed to her, "Quite the scheme of decoration."

"Isn't it, though," she said with a sigh. "They absolutely ruined this place when they went and redid it. They ought to be taken out and shot."

"What was it like before?"

"It looked like a whorehouse. The walls were red, all the chairs and booths were red velvet—we even had red lampshades. It was real pretty."

When we managed to get down to the business of drinks, Mariah of course had her usual Lord C and I my Johnny, and Leona's version had turned out to be forthright Jack Daniels and water. As the three of us entered the company of those gentlemen, though, Riley was brought a white production in a clear glass goblet.

"What in the name of hell are you drinking now?" I had to ask. "Rattlesnake milk?"

"Naw, it's a White Moccasin. Want a sip?"

"I'd rather parch," I let him know.

"Honestly, Jick, he was raised better than that," Leona frowned in reproof at her son's frippy concoction.

The barmaid saw it was six o'clock and turned the television set behind the bar on. If it proved to be T. V. Purvis I damn well was going to ask her to click it right back off, but the commercials eventually gave way instead to sportscasters, who seem to come in triplets.

"Well, well," Mariah contributed after craning around to check the screen scene as the players came on, "a bunch of high-paid hot dogs showing us their buns. My God, are they *still* playing that stuff?"

"You bet," I said. "The World Series, petunia."

"Or at least the California one," Leona said with a least little smile as the Oakland and San Francisco lineups electronically materialized on the screen.

"It comes to the same, I'm sure, Mother," maintained Riley, who I knew didn't give a hoot about sports except for cantering across the countryside.

"What beats me about having three guys on there to tell us what we're looking at, though," I started in, "is—"

"THERE'S AN EARTH—" one of the sportscasters declaimed and the television picture went blooey.

You didn't have to be a seismic scientist to fill in the rest of the word. For the next hours, when the TV people found a way to get back on the air, the four of us sat fascinated watching what the earthquake had done to the San Francisco Bay area. The collapse of that freeway, motorists crushed under slabs the size of aircraft carriers; the broken Bay Bridge; fallen buildings in Santa Cruz; all of San Francisco spookily lightless in the night except for the one neighborhood where apartment houses were burning; my God, I felt as sorry for people in that quake zone as if they had been bombed. And along with it, the overwhelming thought of how much worse it could have been. Candlestick Park with the World Series crowd of sixty thousand in it had not crumbled.

"Holy shit, think of it!" Riley said in genuine awe as a blimp camera panned down on Candlestick. "Fifteen hundred sportswriters at that ballgame and every one of them trying to transmit the same lead: *On this beautiful afternoon beside San Francisco Bay, God chose to shake the 'Stick.*"

"Helicopters," Mariah uttered wistfully, like a kid pointing out toys in a catalogue, as pictures of the gap in the Bay Bridge taken from midair came onto the screen. Both she and Riley erupted every time the coverage cut away from on the scene. "You fucking talking heads!" Riley roared at the set when a guy at a network desk somewhere began speaking with the Governor of California who had been caught on a sojourn in Germany. "Piggyback on what KGO is showing! You bunch of dumbfucks, let the local guys do the story in the streets!"

Eventually earthquake experts began coming on and saying this wasn't the Big One but it was a Pretty Big One. By then Leona and I had looked at each other a number of times with new understanding. A new feel for the distance between us and this avid pair glued to the coverage, maybe say. Neither she nor I would have willingly lived where such quakes kept happening if you deeded the whole of California to us. But if Riley and Mariah could have hopped on a plane and joined the newsgatherers right in the middle of all that earthquake mess, they instantly would have.

Billings begins a long way out from itself. Scatterings of housing developments and roadside businesses and billboards full of promises of more enterprises to come began showing up miles ahead of the actual city. The Bago and we four were rolling in on the freeway that runs shoulder to shoulder with the Yellowstone River, then the Yellowstone shied out of the picture and snazzy profiles of hotels and banks against the rimrocks became the feature.

"The Denver of the north," Riley crooned in an oily voice as downtown Billings came up on us. "The Calgary of the south." He waited until we were wheeling past a petroleum refinery that was obviously functioning much below capacity. "The Butte of tomorrow?"

"Mmm, though, look what the light is doing," Mariah put in. There in the late afternoon sunlight, the cliffs rimming the city were changing from baked tan to a honeyed color. Then and there I formed the opinion that held for the rest of our time in Billings, that if you had to have a city this was an interesting enough place to put it.

"No, honest to Pete, it's the truth, Jick, if I can call you that. Just about the highest place you can drive in Delaware is the overpass on Route 202 where it goes into Pennsylvania."

"Aw, come on, Carl. How do you keep your heads above water back there?"

We'd been in the Energy City RV Park most of a week while Mariah and Riley were out toiling away at the implications of Billings—not to any avail that I could see yet—and Leona and I were getting to know the couple in the Bago next door. Retirees from Wilmington, Carl and Harriet DeVere were out here tasting mountain country, and inasmuch as they were going to drive the alpine Cooke City highway into Yellowstone Park this afternoon, by nightfall they might have their fill of mountains, all right.

The DeVeres now said they hated to break up our coffeeklatch but they had to go food shopping, did we want to come along? It was a handy chance to do so because they towed behind their rig a Honda Civic—*Winnebago Shopping Cart,* a carved wooden sign on it said—and Leona volunteered while I said I had something else I'd better get at.

The shopping expedition hadn't much sooner gone out, though, than Riley came in. He plopped the Sunday editions of the *Montanian* and the Billings *Gazette* on the dinette table. "Holding down the Bago all by your lonesome?"

"Yeah. Nothing injurious seems to happen to it when I'm here by myself."

He gave me a two-toned look but let that pass. Before he could start pawing through the Sunday papers, I asked: "Where's Mariah?"

"Shooting my mother," he reported absently. "The DeVeres, too. They are kind of cute, the three of them peeling off out of here aboard their Japanese skateboard." He noticed my own endeavor. "What've you got there, your prayer book?"

"Aw, an old paperback I bought in Wolf Point. Figured I better get going on that centennial speech or—what the hell you looking at me like that for?"

"You do it deliberately, don't you."

"Do what?"

"Oh, come on!" He aimed a finger at the title of the book I was holding. *The Collected Eloquence of Winston Churchill.* Riley actually looked a little wild-eyed, in both separate-hued eyes. "*Winnie,* in the *Bago?* If that isn't a weird sense of—"

"Riley, a walking word game like you doesn't have any right to—"

The side door popped open, and the camera bag and then Mariah alit inside with us. She stood there a moment, straight as a willow, and studied Riley and me. "Sipping herbal tea and discussing Zen, guys?"

"Just practicing for the union of our families again," I let her have.

"Actually, our agenda at the moment is to just read the Sunday papers," Mariah addressed back to me. "Do you suppose that can be accomplished without hand-to-hand combat?"

Riley still looked snorty and I maybe was a little that way myself, but we clammed up. They put their noses into their literature and I into mine.

Never in the field of human conflict was so much—Churchill was hard to keep concentration on, though. I was bothered, not to say baffled. My eyes kept drifting first to Mariah, then to Riley, each of them busily mauling through a newspaper. Was that love? If so, how had it come out of the ash and salt of their first try together? Was I ever going to savvy what, when, how, why? Some great record so far, mine. Plainly I had underestimated Riley. I had misestimated Leona and what I figured would be her natural reaction against our offspring falling for each other again. And after my thirty-five years as her father, Mariah still went up, down, and sideways in my estimation practically all day long. Maybe reading other people's heads was not my strong suit.

I shut Churchill. Newsprint was more my speed at the moment, too. All that was left of the Sunday *Gazette* from the rummaging those two were doing of it was the section with astrology, crossword, and wedding couples. A little leery of learning what I might be on the cusp of, and not much one for killing time crosswording either, I examined the fresh faces of the couples, each wearing the smile of a lifetime. *Kimberlee This and Chad That said their vows to each other at the . . .* There were seven or eight such enraptured pairs pictured and I read the particulars on each, trying to divine any logic in Mariah and Riley repeating this process of matrimony. Pretty hard to make parse: *Mariah McCaskill and Riley Wright have announced their betrothal, again. Parents of the couple are Mrs. Leona Wright of the Shields River country and, against his will, Mr. Jick McCaskill of the Two Medicine country. The bride-to-be graduated from Gros Ventre High School and Illinois Institute of the Arts, and is a photographer who does not have a lick of sense beyond her camera. The incipient groom graduated from Clyde Park High School and the University of Montana and has been a Missoula inmate ever since. Ms. McCaskill will retain her maiden name, just as she did the first time they attempted the wedded state and royally screwed it up. Upon saying their vows one more time, the rewedded couple will go to California to have permanent lunch with the future.* No, try as I might, I couldn't credit these two with as much perspicacity as the eighteen- and twenty-year-olds radiating out of the wedding pictures.

"Funny place they pick to do it, though," I thought out loud.

"Who do what?" Mariah asked from where she was competitively sizing up a *Gazette* color photo of a Crow Indian fancy-dancer.

"Newlyweds."

Both she and Riley shot quick hard looks at me.

"Where they get married, I mean," I hastened to explain. "Not much church to it any more, I guess, huh?"

Now they glanced at each other. On their established principle that each of them was the wartime ambassador to his or her respective parent, it was Mariah who inquired of me in a combat tone:

"Is this leading up to another sermon against our getting married again? Because if it is . . ."

"It is not," I answered chillily. "I am only making the observation that it's kind of interesting that of this week's wedding crop here in the paper, three of the couples got hitched in one church or another, but there's four other pair who went and did it at—"

The Holiday Inn was quite the extravaganza, whether or not you were about to get your nuptial knot tied there.

Walk in as the four of us were doing and the lobby vastly soared all around you; in fact, that cubic center of the enterprise at first encounter seemed to be universally lobby, a hollow square the entire six stories to the roof and equally out to the perimeters of the half-acre carpeted-and-plantered space. You had to wonder whether the architect remembered to put on motel rooms, until you discerned that the half dozen beige facings that ran all the way around this atrium at equal heights apart like the ribcage of the building were actually balconies, with room doors off them. The place had a lot of other ruffles, too. Up one side of the whole deal shot a glassed-in elevator shaft outlined with sparkly dressingroom-like lights the full altitude to the ceiling. There, natural light descended through a skylight, I suppose for the sake of the trees—some of them fairly lofty—in eight-sided containers, beige, plunked near the middle of the atrium. At the far end of the expanse was a waterfall, no less.

I fingered my bowtie. A tuxedo was a new sensation for me. Beside me as we trailed the Mariah-Riley vanguard into the assemblage, Leona behaved like she went to weddings in the atrium of the Holiday Inn every day of her life.

True, she had been a little surprised to come into the Bago with the groceries and be informed by Riley we were going to a matrimonial function. "But I thought you two were waiting for the privacy of California. I don't have a thing to wear and—"

"Mother, it's not Mariah and me, it's"—he consulted his notebook—"Darcy and Jason."

Which didn't help Leona get her bearings any. "Do we know them?"

"That never matters with these two," I edified her about journalism.

Riley now did bring us to a halt at the edge of where the guest chairs and the altar and the food tables and all the rest were set up for the wedding and the reception after, the first sign of restraint he'd shown in any of this. That Leona and I were here at all was due to his cockeyed inspiration that this could serve as a kind of substitute function—a surrogate wedding, to quote him exactly—for our not being on hand whenever he and Mariah did their deed in California. Next he must have used a chisel instead of a pen to get the rental of formalwear for Leona and me as well as for him and Mariah onto the expense account. I do have to say, on Riley the money looked well spent. Those wide level shoulders of his filling out the fit of the tuxedo like a ship under full sail, his mustache and curly spill of hair a handsome topping to the regalia below, the guy looked slick as an ambassador. Hard to believe this was the identical yayhoo who once cracked to me, back in that living-together period of theirs before he and Mariah got married the first time, "Jick, in the immortal words of Robert Louis Stevenson, marriage is a sort of friendship recognized by the police."

"Okay, crew, people are going to be gathering for a while yet," he was briefing Leona and me currently, "and I've got to go locate the bride and groom, see what their last words are." Meanwhile Mariah was chewing the inside of her mouth as she gauged the airy acreages of the atrium, so it was plain that finding a photo was going to occupy her for some time to come. That left two of us at loose ends, and when I questioned Riley about what role Leona and I were supposed to perform here where we were perfect strangers to everybody, his set of directions was, "Mingle."

As the *Montanian*eers invaded the wedding party, Riley off to corner the wedding couple and Mariah just off, I admitted to Leona: "I don't really feel like wading right in. I'll just hang on here and watch things for a while. You go ahead and circulate, why don't you." With a quick understanding smile she said yes, she'd wander and see who was who, until it came time for the ceremony.

Is it just me, or does such an occasion inevitably prompt a lot to think about? Oh, sure, Mariah and Riley's forthcoming repeat performance—what do you suppose the California custom is, holding the wedding in a swimming pool?—was prominent in those thoughts, but so was the wife I wished was beside me. I hadn't missed Marcella so much in weeks and weeks. Anybody's start of married life I suppose can't help but remind you of your own. Up toward the altar, where there was an archway of flowers, I could see Riley was now interrogating today's nuptial couple. The bride Darcy was a looker, a dark-haired young woman with an outdoor tan that set off priceless teeth and quick eyes. The groom Jason, there was hope for; he was at that boy-man age that teeters on the Adam's apple and perhaps before he quite knew it he'd be a full-throated husband and father. Even though the two of them had agreed happily when Riley phoned about him and Mariah doing a piece on their great day, I hoped they had some inkling of what they were in for when put in print. But probably not even Riley Wright could dent them today.

"Sir?" I heard and realized it referred to me. What this was, a waitress had come by to prime me with a cup of punch or a glass of champagne, and of course punch wasn't even in the running. I sipped at the bubble stuff and as a I did, the tail of my eye caught a motion down behind where my elbow had been.

Taking a peek over my shoulder, I discovered a bronze statue about a foot and a half high levitating past. Then another appeared and vanished, and by the time I'd blinked at that, a third one silently circled in.

I backed off to where I could view the entire revolving trio. Huh. Elvis Presley, all three of him. Coming and going as a slowly spinning turntable revolved the triplet statuary. Huh again: in each stage Elvis was in full pelvic deployment, but otherwise these were three distinct ages of him, at the guitar-whanging start of his career, then in summit, and lastly in pudgy decline. Hound dog, top dog, and pound dog, I guess could be said.

The Elvi in orbit behind me, I was just getting my attention back onto the wedding crowd when Leona detoured out of it toward me.

"See what you think of this," she instructed and handed me a dainty cracker loaded with a tapioca-looking substance.

I tried it. "Not bad," I assessed, "particularly with a chaser of champagne."

"*Montahnskaya eekrah!*" Leona reported in jubilation. "Montana caviar!"

"Yeah? Where's it come from, up on the High Line by Kremlin?" I asked, which I thought was pretty good.

But Leona only shook her head seriously and informed me, "Over by Glendive. It's sturgeon eggs, out of the Yellowstone River." Having imparted that, she swept back to the crowd to delve further into wedding matters.

I supposed it was time I got into motion a little, too. So my champagne and I took a stroll around the outside of the throng, nodding when nodded to, sizing people up without being over-obvious about it. Everybody was dressed to the hilt, gabbing in knots of relatives or friends. I wouldn't have predicted so, but the young men displayed higher fashion than the young women. A number of groomsmen had those porcupine styles of hair they fuss together with gel someway. Highly interesting. As to the other hair situation among the males, a few mustaches besides Riley's could be counted but mine was the only beard in evidence. He and I were safely in the spectrum with our formal apparel, though; starting with the groom, every man there was tuxedoed up in some shade between maroon and purple like ours. I wondered whether Althea Frew knew of this current color scheme. Doubtless she already had the matter planned out, me in a plum-colored bib and tucker, she in exquisite mauve tulle, tweeting out vows to each other in the flower-arched foyer of the Medicine Lodge.

Uneasily I shook off the thought of Althea, and checked around to see how my *Montanian* companions were progressing here.

Riley, the damn chameleon, appeared to be utterly in his element at this event, cruising through the crowd as if personally fond of every cummerbund and pleat. Leona, too, with her freshly done-up silver hair and a blending dress looked classily in place.

Mariah, though. Mariah was in—well, I believe the term for what she was in is hot pink.

Against the general maroon of the tuxedo populace and, for that matter, the similar rich tone of the atrium rug, she looked like something that had ignited. At the formalwear rental shop that morning I hadn't paid any real attention to the women's end of things, the prospect of myself in soup-and-fish duds already plenty on my mind, but I did notice Leona a couple of times open her mouth as if to say something and then not. At the time I figured she was just running Russian through her head. But I now knew that those unvoiced remarks had to do with Mariah's selection—too strong a word, honestly, because shopping was nowhere on Mariah's list of priorities and she had simply grabbed out a dress and tried it on enough to be sure it wouldn't fall off her and said "Okay, this'll do, let's go"—of an eye-stinging pink outfit. I wonder, what is the Moscow phrase for *If that color was any louder it'd be audible.*

Nor for that matter was any other woman at the wedding carrying an Appaloosa camera bag the size of a satchel as an accessory to her outfit. Really, to capture the main sensation of these nuptials Mariah should have been shooting herself, for in those high heels and her pink number and her deeper-than-red hair she stalked among the wedding-going youngsters trailing every kind of reaction behind her. Multiply Kevin Frew's calfish gape at her atop the rodeo arena fence, back there on the Fourth of July, by about twenty and you have the general expression of the groom corps. The bride's maidens on the other hand seemed divided between disgust at such electric fashion and wishing they'd thought of it themselves.

After Mariah had parted the crowd waters all the way across the room and ended up at the revolving Elvi, I felt so sorry for her I sifted over to try and hearten her.

"I haven't seen you so dolled up since your high school prom, petunia."

"This get-up." She kicked off a high heel and massaged that foot against the other one. "I feel like a pink flamingo on stilts."

"Well, you look like society to me."

She fired a glance to the far end where a particular regal silver head and complementing aquamarine dress stood out resplendent against the atrium's cascade, as if Leona had magically enclouded there out of the sprays of blues and silvers off the spilling wall of water.

Mariah said with more rue than she probably wanted to admit to, "Not nearly as much as some. How did she manage to coordinate her dress with that goddamn waterfall, I ask you."

"Leona would look dressed to the teeth with nothing on but her birthday suit," I attested, which drew Mariah's eyes immediately back to me.

Well, I had given words a try. "How about a snifter of this seasoned water?" I offered her my champagne glass.

She considered it longingly, but shook her head. "Thanks, but not until I figure out some kind of a picture of this circus. Then I'll be ready for a swimming pool of that stuff."

"So," strolled up a swank specimen of plummy tuxedo which of course was Riley. "Quite a shindig, hmm?"

Mariah put her hand on his elegant shoulder to steady herself while she shed her other high heel shoe and massaged that foot. "My God, this is a tough sucker of a shoot," she let out along with her breath. "Everybody keeps looking right at me, right down the old lens hole. It's all going to come out like driver's license photos."

"Maybe you should have worn blue suede and a guitar and blended in as Elvis Number Four," I suggested to her.

"Come on, shooter, you can do it," Riley dismissed her photographic fret with the world's most unworried smile and leaned in and gave her a smoochy kiss alongside one ear. At first I figured he'd been too deep into the champagne, but no, this beamy kissy version was merely Riley rediscovering wedded bliss, even when it wasn't his own, quite yet.

I yearned for the old days of Moiese and Virginia City when Mariah would have handed him his head for that kind of canoodling. The worst she could summon currently was to cock a look at him and ask with just enough of a point on it, "How're you coming with your part of the piece?"

"Got it writ," Riley said to her surprise and mine too. "I've turned Biblical."

> *. . . Let him kiss me with the kisses of his mouth . . .*
> *She wanted him ever since Algebra. Alphabetized beside each other there in third period desks, x and y doing their things on the blackboard, maybe it simply was a case of possibilities put side by side. From day one she knew he spent that class hour peeking sideways at her results—not just the paper kind—but she didn't quite know why she one day was fond of that angle of gaze on her and wanted it forever.*
> *He wanted her in every one of the eternal ways of the Song of Solomon. But along other Bible lines too, of course. Those that say things like dwell. Abide, which seems to be a little bit different but no less awesome. Esteem. Worship.*

Beget. Words that send you a little dizzy, thinking about all they promise and ask.

. . . Honey and milk are under thy tongue . . .

Her favorite is anticipation. All her life she has liked to plan, imagine ahead, see how it turns out. It has just always seemed to her that's the way to make matters come out right, especially the big steps. Like getting married.

His is the avalanche approach. Now is timelier than later, you gain a lot of ground if you don't put off and put off but just up and do it. That way, you're sure you aren't wasting life on the small stuff but are honed in on what counts. Like getting married.

. . . His left hand is under my head, and his right hand doth embrace me . . .

He's a little spoiled, she grants that, coming from the mother he does. And she wishes the little thinning place in his crownhair didn't mark the spot where his father is as bald as a dead lightbulb. But genes aren't everything. (Are they?) She still feels right, too, about deciding to keep her own name, even though his mother told her she'll give up on that after the first time of having to do Christmas cards with their two separate names. (Will she?)

She's swifter than he is, he knows that much, and there's always been a breath-catching little lag between when she says something funny and when he gets it. But women are like that. Okay, okay, he realizes you can get the pud beat out of you for saying stuff like that these days. But isn't it some kind of biological fact? That girls, women that is, grow up faster and all of a sudden—well, develop into Amazonian princesses?

. . . There will I give thee my loves . . .

They don't give a fig, this wedding couple, about odds or obstacles or second thoughts or a million possible frets, is what it always comes down to. Not this day, not at this altar, which is an old, old word for a place of fire.

. . . For love is strong as death.

Riley still had something monumental on his mind as Mariah balanced against him to grimly work her feet back into high heelery. The moment she was shod again, he gave out another big goofy smile and said:

"You know, we could make this a doubleheader."

Witless witness though I was to Riley's sudden new shenanigan, I caught his drift before Mariah did, her photographic attention already focused back into the wedding throng like a riverjack trying to figure out just where to dynamite a logjam. *Doubleheader, hell,* the recognition hit my dismayed brain, *there went the ballgame.*

The object of Riley's intentions tumbled rapidly enough, however, to what had just been put to her. Her head jerked around, eyelids fanning, as she a little wildly sought verification in his face. "Get married, you mean? Here and now?"

"Yup, now and here," he corroborated with utmost good cheer. "All we'd have to do is arrange for the minister to hang around until Darcy and Jason scoot off to their honeymoon. Why, we've even got dear loving family on hand," he dispensed along with a generous wag of his head toward me and then one in the general direction of wherever his mother was mingling. "How about it, Mariah Montana?"

I honest to God had the impression, right then, that even Elvis in triplicate stopped spinning, for that longest of moments, to watch whether Mariah was going to endorse Riley's inspiration to hightail to the altar. So much for my campaign against. No, reason and history and minimum common sense never stand much chance against the human impulse to dart off and do it.

"N-No, no I don't think this is the time and place," Mariah declined nervously, to my surprise, not to mention Riley's. "Getting married in this"—her eyes did a loop-the-loop to indicate the infinite reaches of the Holiday Inn lobby—"while we're doing a piece here would seem kind of, mmm, tacked on, don't you think?"

What *I* thought, not that anybody was running a poll for my opinion, was that now they could derive a sample of what they were letting themselves in for by remarrying. Blow up at her, left, right, and sideways, I mentally urged goddamn Riley: insist it's now or never, matrimonially, because that way you'll come in for a nice reminder of the spikes that spring out when Mariah stiffens her back. Jump him, the dressed-up motel romeo, for treating marriage like the decision to go get an ice cream cone, I similarly brainwaved Mariah. Get out the big augur, each of you, and remind the other of how you caused the wind to whistle through the holes of that first marriage.

But see how Riley can't even be trusted to be his normal aggravating self? He fixed his two-tone gaze on Mariah and, in the same soapy mood as when he'd strolled up, grandly allowed: "A woman who knows her own mind, just what I've always wanted. California is fine by me, for us to get official." And off he went to sop up some more mood of the occasion, humming a little Mendelssohn.

For her part, Mariah threw me a don't-think-this-changes-anything-just-because-I-don't-want-to-get-married-wearing-hot-pink-in-a-glorified-blimp-hangar look, shouldered her camera bag purposefully, and headed out to do lens war with the weddinggoers again.

With the help of a sip of champagne I assessed where I had come out at from this Riley-Mariah close call: gained nothing, but lost none either. Could have been worse. Probably would be.

"Sir, would you care for some?" a waitress made a courtesy stop at me with a platter of hors d'oeuvre tidbits.

"No thanks," I explained, "I prefer big food."

I still can't account for the next event. I mean, there I was, dutifully keeping my nose out of Darcy and Jason's event, trying to blend my plum-tuxed self into the maroon backdrop of the atrium rug, when the bald guy emerged from the crowd and came straight at me as if he was being led by a dowsing stick.

Actually, the guiding instrument sat on his shoulder. The videocam in fact might have been mounted permanently there, the way it led the guy shoulder-first as if he was doing some kind of walking tango across the floor.

"Hi, I'm Jason's uncle, Jim Foraker. You must be from Darcy's side of the family."

"Just mildly acquainted, is all."

"I'm making a video for the kids," he said, bombardiering through the camera eyepiece onto my visage. "When Jason and Darcy get up into the years a little, it'll be kind of a kick for them to look back and see who all was at their wedding, don't you think?"

Especially when they try to figure out who the hell I am. Before I could retrieve my tuxedoed bearded self from posterity's lens, however, Jason's videoing uncle let drop: "I've got the sound package on this machine too, so how about saying something? Just act real natural. Tell the kids maybe what it was like at your own wedding?"

Which one? tore through my mind first. Shirley, when our young blood was on perk day and night. Marcella, everlasting but lost to me now too. My God, it gets to be a lot, to have to publicly pick and choose among sorrows. Darcy and Jason replaying on their golden anniversary in the year 2039 will have to be the ones to report whether I flinched, tottered, trembled, or just what. But whatever was registered by the videotape constituted only an emotional fraction. I felt as if I was coming apart, the pieces of my life I most prized—Marcella, the ranch, our life there together, our astonishing offspring Mariah and Lexa— cracking from me like streambanks being gashed away by rising water: yet at the same time I needed to hold, to not buckle under even to those heaviest thoughts, to somehow maintain myself in the here and now. Atrium extravaganza or not, other people's occasions deserve their sorrowless chance.

So. I had it to do, didn't I. Squaring myself in Jim Foraker's frame of lens to the extent I could, I began.

"Every wedding is the first one ever invented, for the couple involved. So I won't go into any comparison of this one with my own. But I can tell you a little something about after. I don't know whether a shivaree is still the custom"—some manner of mischief was; out in the parking lot I could see young guys tying a clatter of tin cans on behind a car with JUST MARRIED! DARCY ??? JASON soaped all over it—"but after Marcella and I got hitched, everybody in the Two Medicine country who was mobile poured in to the ranch that night."

Cars and pickups all with horns honking, it was like a convoy from the loony bin. People climbed out pounding on dishpans and washtubs and hooting and hollering; you could have heard them all the way onto the other side of Breed Butte. Of course the men laid hands on me and the women on Marcella, and we each got wheelbarrowed around the outside of the house clockwise and tipped out ceremoniously at the front door. Then it was incumbent on us to invite everybody in for the drinking and dancing, all the furniture in the living room pushed along one wall to make enough floor for people to foot to the music.

Luckily there is no limit to the congratulations that can be absorbed, and Marce and I were kept giddily happy by all the wellwishers delivering us handshakes and kisses on the cheek. Leave it to our fathers, though, to carry matters considerably beyond that. Lambing was just starting, and under the inspiration of enough wallops of scotch, Dode Withrow and Varick McCaskill formed the notion to go check on the drop band for me; as Dode declared, "Mac and me all but invented the sonofabitching sheep business." It was a mark of the occasion that Midge Withrow and my mother did not forthwith veto that foray, but just gave their spouses glances that told them to come back in somewhat more sober than they were going out. First Dode and my father had to flip a coin as to which of them got my working pair of overshoes to wear to the shed and who got stuck with two left ones from the discards in the corner of the mud porch, and then there was considerable general razzing from the rest of us about how duded up they were to be lamb lickers, but eventually the two of them clopped off, unbuckled but resolute, toward the lambing shed. Busy as we were with our houseful, Marce and I lost track of the fact of our sires traipsing around out there in the Noon Creek night, until we heard the worried blats of a ewe. Coming nearer and nearer. Then the front door flung open and there stood the volunteer overshoe brigade, muck and worse shed-stuff up the front of both of them to their chins—Dode had been the one who drew the two left overshoes, and it had been that awkward footwear that sent him sprawling face-first; my father, it developed, simply fell down laughing at Dode—and a highly upset mother sheep skittishly trailing them and stamping a front hoof while they wobbled in the doorway declaring, "By God, Jick and Marce, you can't afford not to hire us," each man with a lamb held high, little tykes still yellow and astonished from birth: the first twins of that lambing season.

Finishing that telling, I sought how to say next what it still meant to me, that shivaree of almost forty years before.

"I suppose there must have been a total of a couple of thousand years of friends under our roof, Marcella's and mine, that shivaree night. A lot has happened since; the toughest part being that Marcella isn't in this life with me, any more. But that shouldn't rob what was good at the time. Our shivaree was utmost fun, and by Christ," I nodded emphatically to make sure the lens picked up this part, "so is the remembering of it. Darcy, Jason," I lifted my champagne glass, just a hummingbird sip left in it by now but any was plenty to wish on, "here's to all you'll store up together, starting now."

Jason's uncle thanked me for my videocam soliloquy and I told him it'd been my pleasure, and next thing, it was ceremony time. I found where Leona and Riley were saving a seat for me. No sooner was I sat than

Riley said, "Here you go," and proffered me a little packet of the sort I
saw everybody had.

"What've we got here?"

"Birdseed," he defined. "You throw it at the bride and groom when
they head out the door to their honeymoon these days—it's better for
the birds than rice is."

Take progress any time you can find it, I guess, so I tucked away the
birdseed for later flinging and sat back to watch matrimony happen.
The waterfall had been switched off so that it wouldn't drown out the
minister's performance. For that matter, the entire huge cube of the
atrium had quieted down. Arriving guests and the desk clerks stopped
in midtransaction to watch. Waitresses paused lest a swinging door
emit a sound. By the time the groom was escorted by his best man
down the ramp past the glass elevator and the bride made her entrance
from the videogames area, you could have heard a Bible page drop.

The wedding was almost to climax in rings and kisses before I realized. I leaned toward Riley and whispered, "What became of Mariah?"

He murmured back, "She's shooting this."

I inspected every farflung corner of the atrium and behind the pot-
ted trees and even cast a glance under the grand piano, but no Mariah.

I whispered again, "Where the hell from?"

This time Riley's murmur was forceful. "You don't want to know."

With that I did know, though. Which is why, in the *Montanian*'s
photo of the Darcy-Jason wedding taken from overhead, the bride a
white blossom and the groom a plum sprig beside her and the minister's
open book and the dot rows of the heads of the wedding-goers as if seen
from the ceiling of a cathedral, the solo face gaping directly upward six
stories to the atrium skylight—and Mariah and her camera—is my
bearded one.

That was Billings, and the day directly after the wedding experience our
trend was east again, one last time, another three-hundred-miler to
somewhere that hadn't realized it'd been waiting a century for Mariah
and Riley.

And so even after we had reversed the long angling freeway journey
along the Yellowstone River all the way to Glendive, this time we still
continued east, as if pellmell to see North Dakota.

Shortly before the Dakota line, though, at Wibaux, behind me

Riley announced "Make a right here and keep on going until you hit the South Pole" and although he overstated it a bit, I aimed us down the quantity of miles ahead to Montana's southeastern corner.

Away from the green settled valley of the Yellowstone, counties in this part of the state are whopping maps with a single pin of town in each. The fact was, this was almost off the map of any of the four of us. I was the only one who had ever been anywhere into this emptiest corner, and that a long time ago. We might as well have been a carload of Swiss trying to sightsee Mongolia. Grassland with sage low and thin on it ran to all the horizons—cattle in specks of herds here and there—and a surprising number of attempts had been made to scratch some farming into this barebone plain, but what grew here mostly was distance. Except for an occasional gumbo butte or a gully full of tumbleweeds, out here there were no interruptions of the earth extending itself until bent by the weight of the sky.

Really pretty quiet all four of us stayed, throughout this long country. Leona spent time cramming Russian through her headset. Mariah mostly appraised the horizontal endlessness outside, occasionally fiddling with an earring, today white daisies as if this vicinity could stand a bit of bouquet. I idly wondered how I'd gotten so expert at miscalculation; if anything, Mariah and Riley acted more allied, alloyed, whatever, than before I'd applied Leona to this journey to split them. Mariah's only rival in the cosmos seemed to be Riley's word processor, going *pucka pucka* now but only sporadically, none of his long runs that said he was getting somewhere with the words.

> *The terrasphere now . . . space travel, this, except it's on the ground . . . the highway the orbit . . .*

Running down, maybe we all were. The centennial was only a handful of days away now. This had to be Mariah and Riley's last piece until they hit Gros Ventre for our dawn ceremony. Between now and then, once they finished in this final reach of the state, I was to drop them in Billings so they could rent a car and scoot to Missoula to begin closing down their lives there, then I'd leave Leona off at her ranch and hustle myself home to the Two country. Humongous agenda, as Mariah would have put it. So, maybe ahead preoccupied us. Maybe we were each a little hypnotized by the capacities of the plains; the full eighty miles down from the Wibaux turnoff, this road lined away as straight as the drop of a plumb bob. The only hint of deviation came after we passed through Baker, when the land began to rumple just enough to make the ride like a long slow roller coaster.

Even the roadkills were different from what we four mountain Montanans were used to; over the crest of any of the little rolly humps, the Bago was apt to intersect the angular length of a run-over rattlesnake.

Ekalaka has had to declare itself as best it can in such a circle of horizon. The little town is beside as much of a hill as it could find and has put a big definitive white letter of initial on that promontory. But what interested me as we gradually—everything out here seemed gradual—drew closer to our destination was that instead of the E a person would naturally expect for some place named Ekalaka, this civic monogram unmistakably read C.

"What, are they working their way up through the alphabet?" I prodded Riley, as my chances to do so were about to run out.

Ever clever, he explained the landmark C had to be for Carter County. Indeed, Ekalaka as we pulled in demonstrated itself even more as a conscientious county seat. Unusual for a Montana community, it possessed a town square, made up of a white-painted wooden courthouse, a jail, and a funeral parlor. Maybe you had to travel a ton of miles to reach this town but basics were here when you needed them.

So were three bars, not bad for a populace of 632, and a couple of grocery stores, and a hospital, and a small motel, and a Wagon Wheel Cafe, and an enterprise that declared it was a clothing store *and* a liquor store, and a bank and a propane plant and so on. By description alone, I know it does not sound like enough of a place to willingly make a six-hundred-mile roundtrip to visit. But not so, at least for me. I couldn't have said why, because Ekalaka tucked as it was into the southeast corner of the state was literally the farthest remove from Gros Ventre, and the two communities didn't bear any ready resemblance. But something about this hunkered little town quite appealed to me in the same way that Gros Ventre's concentrated this-is-what-there-is-of-it-and-we-think-it's-enough presence always had.

Now what? was always the question after Mariah and Riley hit a locale, and after a cruise of town and figuring out where to site the motorhome overnight—anywhere—we held a four-way conference on strategy for the rest of the day. Riley had spotted a Bureau of Land Management office and said he'd better get up there before closing time and find somebody to talk to about this area's yawning surpluses of, well, land. Leona said she wanted to stretch her legs and so she'd go with him and shop around town some while he gabbed. Mariah had her camera eye on the courthouse with its cupola that sat atop like a little party hat, but would stay and take stock of things until the afternoon light deepened better for shooting. For my part, I sighed and decided I'd better stay planted in the Bago too, needing to get myself organized toward my now not very distant centennial oration. So off Riley and Leona went, Mariah and I warning them not to get lost in the six-block-square expanse of Ekalaka.

For the first time in a long time, then, we were separated into the Wrights and the McCaskills, and maybe it was this almost inadvertent siding up into families that finally did it.

I admit I was a bit keyed up, with a speech to put together and all. It didn't take much of that to give me a sneaking admiration for Riley, even; this jotting stuff down wasn't as simple as it looked. Still, if Mariah hadn't done what she did, I would not have flown off the handle, now would I? All in the world I intended was to take a little break and administer some caffeine for inspiration. So, as I was about to nuke a cup of coffee in the microwave, I turned my head to ask if she wanted one too and found myself gazing into an all too familiar *click.*

"Mariah, goddamn that camera! You've about worn the face off me with it! You must have a jillion sonofabitching pictures of me by now, what the hell do you keep shooting them for?"

She of course could not resist snapping yet another one while I was right in the middle of that. Probably she captured me looking mad as a wet hen: white-bearded kid in a tantrum.

But then the camera did come down from her eye, and Mariah was giving me her own straight gaze. But through a glisten.

I blinked, dumbfounded. There was no mistaking. Her gray eyes were verging on tears.

Then Mariah said:

"Because I won't always have you."

That dropped on me like a Belgian brick. It had never occurred to me—how could it?—to regard myself as some kind of memory album for Mariah. Photographic shadows of myself that would pattern across her days after I no longer do.

I managed to say, "Petunia, I don't figure on checking out of life for a while yet."

"No, and don't you dare," she instructed me fiercely. Like mine, her voice was having trouble finding footing in the throat.

Talk about earthquakes being abrupt. Daughter and father, we this suddenly stared across the shaken up air between us.

"Mariah. I didn't know, it just never occurred to me that—that was on your mind." The way her mother was on mine; the way the ones we love ever are.

"I suppose really that's why I dragged you into this trip," she said with an alarming quiver in her voice. "And now we're about out of trip, aren't we."

"All good things must you-know-what," I tried, to see if I could jack her out of this choked-up mood. And won the booby prize at consoling, for now two distinct tears carried the glistening down Mariah's cheeks.

This was the exact pain I had wanted to keep her from. Loss. The gouge it tears through you. What I had been so sure would be incurred in her by Riley Wright, incurring instead from me.

Hard to know, though, how to be reassuring about your own time ahead in the green bed. I knew nothing to do but gulp and try from a new direction.

"I'll tell you what. When the time comes for me to go to the marble farm, you and Lexa just give me the Scotch epitaph, how about. The one I read about in trying to come up with something for this goddamn centennial speech. They used it there in the old country when somebody special to them went out of the picture ahead of time, so to speak. What they'd do was put on the stone: 'Here lies all of him that could die.'"

The words hung as clear between us as if spelled out in sharpest black and white of one of Mariah's photos. Our eyes held. After a bit I was able to provide what I knew from the storms of memory these past months. "Mariah. Just because I'm going to be dead someday doesn't mean I won't be available."

Mariah blinked hard, then gave a shaky grin. "You've got a deal, Daddio. I'll scratch that epitaph of yours into the rock with my fingernails if I have to." Her voice firmed as she went into stipulations: "But not until a long time from now, you hear? You at least have to match that old fart Good Help Hebner."

"Gives me something to shoot for," I agreed with an answering grin and figured we had come out of it to the good. Mariah, though, gave her hair a toss and looked at me in her considering-the-picture way— her eyes were thinking—but without her camera in between and I knew better.

"That's in the long run," she delineated. "Now what about your immediate future, Mister Jick."

"Well," I said in what I hoped she would think was earnest, "I was going to have a cup of coffee and then try to write a speech."

"I don't mean this very minute," she overinformed me. "What I do mean is the ranch and you and your mood when you get back to the Two country for good in a couple of days. The deciding you've got to do about things." Things, yeah. She hadn't even counted Althea Frew into the enumeration.

"Depends."

"On what?"

"Lots of things."

"Name a few."

"Don't you have something to go take a picture of?"

"That can wait. Right now I'm trying to talk to my father about the rest of his life."

"Let's find some prettier topic."

"No, let's don't. For a change, let's try to look at Jick McCaskill after this trip is over. After you make your speech. After you decide about the ranch."

"If you're going to be in the business of afters, Mariah, don't leave out the main one."

That threw her off, for a few seconds. Then she took a monumental breath. "All right then. After Riley and I—"

"Mariah, it's okay." I had to attempt this, finally, even if I didn't know how to say it, maybe never would know the right words for it. Nothing ever prepares you for speaking what you most need to, does it. "What I mean, it's all right about Riley and you. About you and him and marrying again and California, the whole works. It's okay with me now."

"Since when?" shot out of her in astonishment.

"If it needs a birth certificate, how about from right now," I told her and more than meant it.

It cost me a lot of my heart, but this needed doing. No time like—when you're about to run out of time. Minutes ago I had tried my utmost to show Mariah how to make loss into change, to accept that they for a while will seem to be the same, until a healing, a scarring over, whatever works, can manage to happen. Now to make it begin on myself, where my unholdable daughter was concerned.

"Christ knows, I can't guarantee I can always act as if Riley as a retread son-in-law is just fine and dandy with me," I set forth to her. "But I've played out the calendar on trying to change your mind or his. People can regulate each other only so far, huh?" And then they must do what I was now, gaze acceptingly at Mariah in what she chose for herself and tell myself without flinch, *This is how she is.*

"I suppose I've had some help realizing that, lately," I had to go on, my voice thinner than I wanted it to be. If I forced myself to do this I could. I would. I did. "Leona wouldn't give you the sweat off her saddle, yet it's fine by her for Riley to marry you again as many goddamn times as he can manage to. So if she can think that way from her side of things, why can't I from mine, right?"

Now Mariah really blinked. "You keep on and you're going to have me telling her thanks. *Spassyveebo* or whatever the cockeyed Russian for it is."

"Yeah, well, you're maybe better off in English."

My daughter studied me. She said at last: "What I can tell you is, I appreciate this. All of it. Even the hard time you gave me over Riley. I can see why you did it. Riley and I aren't exactly a prescription pair, are we."

"No, but I guess there are other kinds to be."

She pulled her camera to her abruptly, but just when I was resigned to being fired away at, she went to the side door of the Bago instead and peered out. "The light's nice now," she reported huskily. "I'd better go get shots of the courthouse."

"Before you do," I said. "What you were asking about me in—the short run. I'm working on it all, Mariah. Honest to Christ, I am working on it."

"I figured you were," she said and now gave me the full grin, the Mariah and Marcella grin. "You're entitled to a cup of coffee first, though."

Morning brought the next. Morning and Riley.

We were supposed to pull out of Ekalaka by midmorning, which would just get us to where we each were supposed to be that night; Mariah and Riley relaying on into Missoula from Billings by rental car, myself home to the Two country after dropping Leona off at her ranch. Quite a number of miles ahead for all involved and no time for dilly-dallying. Which Riley now came down with a severe case of.

He broke out with it to Mariah when we were amid breakfast in the Wagon Wheel Cafe, first putting down his coffee cup as delicately as if it contained nitroglycerin. "Got a little confession to make, shooter. I don't have my part of the piece yet."

"Mmm," she responded and stabbed up a next bite of hotcake. "Well, that's okay, isn't it? There's time yet. You can finish it up before we pull out." Leona and I attended to our food. Actually the listening I wanted to do was to the next table, where a habitual bunch of town guys were gabbing and coffeeing up for the day. "This Eastern Europe thing is a growing thing, I'm telling you," one with a *Sic 'em, Carter County Bulldogs* ballcap told the others. "See, what I'm saying is, what the hell is old Gorbachev gonna do if those countries keep this up, if you see what I'm saying." Even locutions seemed long in this stretched part of the state.

Not Riley's. "I don't have the piece started yet."

Mariah and Leona and I all looked at him.

"You mean," Mariah said as you would to an invalid, "really not started yet, not even anything jotted down?"

"Oh fuck yes," he responded, drawing a wince out of his mother. "I've got stuff jotted down until it won't quit. But I don't have the piece. The idea." He reflected. "Even any idea about the idea."

At any point in the trip until then I would have lit into Riley unmercifully. I mean, Christamighty, he had picked one hell of a place to be skunked. It was just about shorter to the moon than what we had to drive yet that day, and for him to do any dithering would just royally screw—but I kept my peace.

For a mother with a California-bound son who didn't seem to know how to aim himself out of downtown Ekalaka, Leona too was comparatively restrained. "Are we talking hours or days, that it's going to take you to think up something?"

But Mariah still was Riley's point of focus.

"I want to get this piece right," he said quite quietly to her. "This last couple of pieces, here and Gros Ventre, before we quit Montana— I want to do them up the way they deserve to be." He gave Mariah the diamond-assessing look he'd done in Helena when he saw her fresh print of the Baloney Express bunch and asked, *How good are you going to get, shooter?*

Breakfast dishes between and spectating parents on either side notwithstanding, I more than half expected Mariah to go straight across the table and kiss him his reward. The way Riley would tackle anything and anybody in his work was something terrific, even I had to admit. Mariah as much as said so with the savvying grin she gave him now, but she only reached for her camera bag and agreed in teammate fashion, "Okay, word guy, let's go find out how good there is."

"Jick?" Leona asked with surprising shyness when she and I were back in the Bago waiting for Mariah and Riley to finish rummaging Ekalaka for their piece. "Would you mind, do you think—could I practice my talk to the Sisters of Peace on you?"

I assured her I didn't overly mind. "As long as there's nothing physical or mental to the job, I'm probably capable." Besides, who knew, maybe some of her Centennial Day spiel to Moscow would rub off on me.

Across the dinette table from me, Leona drew herself up, the piping across the chest of her yoke shirt squaring itself impressively, and gazing at me as if I was the video camera, she broke out with an international smile and spouted:

"*Zdrahstfooyte, Syohstrih Meerah!* Greetings, Sisters of Peace. *Mwih ochen rahdih bwit vahsheemee droozyahmee.* We are very glad to be your friends. *Myehnyah zahvoot Leeona Meekhylovna Riyt.* My name is Leona Michaelovna Wright . . ." Gorbachev ought to have signed her up on the spot.

During one of her pauses to linguistically regroup, I asked something I'd been curious about, even a little leery for Leona's sake. "This sister group—I don't imagine they're ranch women, there in Moscow. So just who are they, do you know?"

"They're wives of soldiers killed in Afghanistan," Leona said in a voice carefully level.

My eyes followed hers, out and away from that mention of dying young in a war, to the hill with the big white C. Figuring we could contemplate the general landscape out around Ekalaka only so long without becoming too obviously oblivious to each other, I rose and headed for the jar of instant coffee and the microwave. "Get you something from the nuclear samovar here, can I?"

Both Leona and I jumped when the motorhome's side door opened and that son of hers yelped in, "Got it!"

I appraised Riley as he bounded in but confined my response. "Yeah? Where?"

"There." He nodded to the window his mother and I had just been scrupulously attentive to.

We swiveled to see what we'd missed.

"The C hill," said Riley. "The white alphabet."

> *White shadows of the towns, these initials on the nearest hill, trying to imprint community, constancy. To cry out in a single capital letter that these painted stones are not yet as abstractly abandoned as tepee rings. . . .*

And from that C hill I did see. In my mind, I saw all the way to white letters above English Creek, the outlines in painted rock on the benchland south of another hunkered town, my own town: GV, for Gros Ventre. For more than that. The devout abbreviation my grandfather Isaac Reese made sure to sprinkle through his letters to Denmark had been DV, the express wish of his world and time: *Deo volente,* God willing. These little towns of the land, the Ekalakas and the Gros Ventres, I believe are written onto time in letters that similarly say their hope and fate. GV. *Geo volente,* The earth willing.

Mariah was the next one to bollix up the departure plan. At least she spilled it right out:

"Riley and I have to stay."

Leona and I looked at each other, then at our contributions to journalism. Mariah had brought it out, so I was the one to inject: "What, are you two going to take up residence here?"

"Just overnight," Mariah maintained and explained her desire for morning light tomorrow to shoot the best picture of the C hill. "But you two don't have to stay just because we are," she summed up, sweet reason personified. "We've got it all worked out, huh, Riley?"

He now had the same cloud-of-bliss atmosphere he'd had throughout the nuptial event in the Holiday Inn. "Huh? Right, yeah, all worked out. Here's the deal."

What it amounted to was that the local BLM man had to go into Billings for a bureaucrat meeting the next day and he'd gladly drop Riley and Mariah there, to continue their trip to Missoula by a rental. Twenty-four hours more or less, they claimed, probably wouldn't make much difference one way or another with the BB at this late point in their *Montanian* careers. So, no problem, Leona and I could hit on down the road without them, right now.

"But if Jick and I go in the Bago," Leona lobbed into that, "where'll you stay?"

"There's a, uh, place at the edge of town," Mariah replied sunnily.

A place. Right. You bet. Also known as a motel. Chinook, Ekalaka; these two were original in their romantic venues, at least.

The C hill and our theoretically adult children behind us, Leona and I scooted for home. Eyebrows had gone up a notch, Leona's among them, when I said before leaving that I guessed she and I might as well head west out of Ekalaka on the back road to Broadus and on across the Northern Cheyenne and Crow reservations instead of retracing all the way north to Wibaux and the freeway. Mariah and Riley of course had to put in their combined four bits' worth that driving back up to Wibaux was maybe longer but definitely a more major road, but Leona rose to the occasion. "If Jick wants to go this other way, that's jake with me," and that settled that.

West we went, then, for once in this centennial trip traveling in as straight a line as possible instead of a journalistic curlicue, across country new to Leona and so far into my past as to be almost new. When we pretty soon passed by a parcel of the Custer National Forest that consisted of chalk buttes and some scattered ponderosa pine, something telling did come back to me from that early time of mine as a shavetail assistant ranger in this corner of the world: how those of us stationed out here used to joke that maybe the Custer wasn't the biggest national forest we could be on but it sure as hell was the longest. Across about seven hundred miles, from the Beartooth District midway in Montana to the Sheyenne District on the far side of North Dakota, the Custer was a scatter of administrative islands of dry stands of forest or grasslands. This afternoon in the Bago, with the teeny Ekalaka swatch of federal forest fading behind us and sixty or seventy prairie miles ahead of us to the next district of the Custer, that joke seemed still valid.

You might think Leona and I would be talked out, after a couple of months of motorhome life together. But we did find things to say, whenever one or the other felt like it. She was good to visit with that way. I let her know that Mariah and Riley now had, if not my blessing, at least my buttoned lip. She smiled and said that was probably as much as they had a right to expect. After a while she wondered how I was coming on my centennial morn speech and I said fine, except for not knowing what the hell I was going to say. " *'Ostahlos nahchahts, dah koncheets,'* the Russian saying is," she provided me. " 'All there is left to do is begin and finish.' "

That first hour or so went that way, nicely, on the surface. But after we buzzed through Broadus, Leona seemed to sense that my mind was on something else than talk and we let conversation lapse. I drove remembering. Places coming back to me, places over here—communities that now probably were ghosts of themselves—that I'd never even heard of in my Two country upbringing, and I'd always thought I was good in geography. Sonnette, Otter, Quietus. The look of this terrain odd to me too in comparison with the Two Medicine land. No real elevation here but constant little rises. Bumpy country, it still seemed to me. The road, the arid hills; probably the lives of the people around.

I recognized King Mountain, ten or a dozen miles to the southwest, its hatcrown summit in the middle of flattish timbered ridges. It was all I could do to keep the Bago on the galloping highway and gawk at that odd but remembered country. Ever since the four of us headed into eastern Montana, I had hoped Mariah and Riley would not zero in on this particular area for one of their pieces. More of the fact is, I hadn't known how I could handle myself if they dropped a finger onto the map just here and said, let's go. And so, now that I was free of that, how do I account for having chosen this route myself? For what I all at once blurted?

"Leona, would you mind a little sidetrip? Just down the country here a ways. It won't take long."

Leona looked at me from the passenger seat as if wondering where in an outback like this it was possible to go on a sidetrip. Whatever was in my voice must have said more than my words. She immediately answered, "If you want to, Jick, that'd be fine."

286 · IVAN DOIG

I recognized the turnoff surprisingly well, although I remembered not a single one of the rancher names on their signboard that soberly listed extensive mileages to their places. The road south off the highway was another plummet-line route, cleaving across the terrain as straight and quick as possible.

Leona stayed quiet as we drove. My mind did not. The young man I had been, I met here behind my eyes, seeing again with him. The badlands here along Otter Creek had always spooked him, me. Dry gulches and stark buttes and the odd reddish tone of the ground might be expected in the honest deserts of Arizona or New Mexico, but to find country of that kind here, showing through the grass like the bones of the earth, made the younger me feel like a stranger in my home state.

Three Mile Creek we passed, then Ten Mile, then Fifteen Mile, with cattleguards marketing the trafficless road between those streams. Then with a last *brrrump* the Bago rumbled across the cattleguard just before our destination, and I pulled into the driveway and shut the engine off.

The Fort Howes Ranger Station was little changed. The stockade-fence of pointed posts that had been out front was gone, replaced by a rail fence that looked more peaceable but less like the place's historic namesake, and some equipment sheds had been added, but the main buildings were the same as forty years ago, the ranger station like a shingle-sided cottage, the house its longer but similar mate. Their low-held roofs still were covered with fist-size rocks to absorb the heat of the sun, for it could get utterly broiling here in summertime.

Leona took it all in, the huddle of buildings each painted with the same federal red brush, the surrounding badlands with gray lopped-off slopes that duned down almost into the back doors. The rockfield roofs that even in the November afternoon chill looked like beds of rosy coals. "Different country," she said, with extreme curiosity in the gaze she turned toward me.

"Different guy, I guess I was, the last time I was here." She knew none of the particulars of my three-year career in the Forest Service here; nor, gone from the Two Medicine country into her own life with Herb Wright, had she ever heard of my first marriage. I told her it all. Of myself and Shirley, when I was assigned as assistant ranger here at the Fort Howes station and Shirley found herself in the unexpected role of Forest Service wife in what seemed the bare middle of nowhere—two Missoula campus hotshots abruptly out into the real world of rocks and routine. Of how, despite my determination to stand up under whatever job the Forest Service saddled me with, I never for a minute felt at home here; to me then, these encompassing buttes and rimrocks were as if the land had been cut down and these were the stumps. And of how, if I was uneasy here at Fort Howes, Shirley was entirely unhinged. *Quo vadis, hell,* was her reaction to my being assigned here.

Leona was listening as intently as I was telling it. I went on to the finale:

"As I remember it, Shirley and I passed the time by fighting. In those days we didn't have air conditioning and everything, and it could get pretty tough here in summer. I know the last time we got to arguing, Shirley pointed straight up at the roof and shouted at the top of her voice, *'Only snakes and bugs were meant to live under rocks!'*"

It had taken forty years, but I laughed at that memory. Leona gave a kind of elegant giggle as if trying to contain herself, but then burst into outright laughing too. Which set me off all the more, happy with the surprise that I was at last able to do so, and that really got us going, a genuine fit of laughing, Leona and I infectious back and forth, snorting to each other and then at the hilarious accused rocks atop the ranger house and convulsing off into new gales. Rollicking applause, four decades overdue, for Shirley for that exit line from our marriage.

"And I can't say I blame her," I brought out when Leona and I at last managed to slow our chortling enough to get some breath back. "Not one damn bit. It was a case of double behavior. Both of us flung our way into that marriage. It wasn't just her doing."

In record time Leona's face went from the glee we'd been sharing to deathly sober.

She gazed at me, her eyes working to take in the recognition as they'd done that first full moment of look at me in the yard of the Wright ranch. I could see how much it took for her now to manage the words:

"You're saying that about another case too, aren't you."

"Yeah, I am." I made a half-fist and gently tapped the steering wheel of the Bago as I thought of just how to put it. "It's probably past time I should've said something of the sort about you and Alec. But that old stuff dies hard, doesn't it." I studied the ranger house, the now-quiet combat zone of Shirley and my younger self, for a moment more and then shifted around to face Leona. "I don't know what the hell it is, whether it's just easier to keep on being half mad than it is to ever get over it, or what. But anyway, I need you to know, Leona—I don't hold you responsible any more for what happened between Alec and the rest of us in the family." For both her and me, I lightened it as much as I possibly could. "Probably you didn't have to hold a gun on him to keep him occupied with you."

She took her eyes from me and looked off at the chalk butte beyond the ranger station. Even yet, even sad, Leona's face fully hinted of the beautiful girl she was in those days. "No," she said as if from a distance. "No, I didn't have to."

The rest of the ride with Leona was a cruise across silk, as far as I was concerned. Ahead of me from Fort Howes, the landscapes and the moments unrolled as if carrying the Bago, bearing us like first guests across the miles, the autumn afternoon. Beyond the Tongue River and then the redstone hills of the Northern Cheyenne Reservation; at Lame Deer an Indian father in a down vest and big black hat was loping his horse in the barrow pit beside the pony of his maybe eight-year-old daughter, this evidently her saddleback lesson, the two of them watching each other without seeming to as they kept their easy but steady gait. Then mountains beginning to the south, the Rosebud and Bighorn ranges. Another hour of quiltpatch road and we were passing the Custer Battlefield, monument, straggle of Seventh Cavalry graves, wrought-iron cemetery fence. Studying the terrain chopped up by small coulees—you would have to go some to invent worse country for cavalry—Leona shook her head and said she never would understand what all the fuss over Custer was about. "A lot of better people have died in wars." I only made an agreeing noise in my throat, those World War Two storms of thought behind me too on the trip now, and headed us on. After Crow Agency the road sledding down into nice irrigated bottomland, sudden treeline at the far side of it, the Bighorn River hugging below benchland in a way to remind me of the valley of English Creek. Now through the western half of the Crow Reservation, long rolling miles toward Pryor while daylight went, before long the Bago's headlights picking out plywood signs with the spray-painted message CATTLE AT LARGE ON ROAD. No more so than me. Into full night before ever reaching the freeway at Laurel and then the twin lanes beside the Yellowstone River again, the motorhome and I and our passenger as if on comfortable automatic now, until Big Timber where we late-suppered in the Country Pride cafe. From there we had only the easy last hour home for Leona.

—

So I was surprised, to say the least, at how she spoke up after we were onto the ridge road from Clyde Park out toward the Crazy Mountains, minutes from the Wright ranch.

"Jick," she said in a strained voice. "Pull over. Please."

What, could she be carsick, now after damn near two months of Bago motion? Dashlight was all I had to diagnose by, but my instant glance across at her told me Leona most definitely looked peaked.

Making the best version of emergency landing I could, I nosed the motorhome onto an approach leading into a field and cut the motor.

She did not open the passenger door and bail out into the night air for recuperation as I expected she was going to. Instead Leona faced around to me and spoke beyond the capacity of expectations.

"That time. The night of that supper with your folks and you."

Of my brother Alec declaring as if it was the world's newest faith, *We got something to tell you, we're going to get married.* Of Leona wielding her smile that proclaimed *And nothing can dent us, we're magical at this age.* Of my mother and father as unmoving as the supper plates, more than half knowing the next to come, that Alec was going to say a college ladder into the future was not for him, now that he'd have a wife to support. I sat startled to be simultaneously at that supper scene again and in the halted motorhome. The woman of silver here who had been that invincibly smiling girl said:

"I'd told Alec I was pregnant."

"But then—"

"I . . . I wasn't."

She was having hard going, her voice throatier than in the most straining Russian lesson.

"But a girl could say that then and be believed," she managed to get it out, "before the pill and the foam and the whatever else they have these days. Men then didn't much understand female plumbing. Whether they do now, I wouldn't know."

Leona turned her head toward the windshield, as if the reflections of each of us in the night-backed glass needed to hear this too.

"In those days, we counted the days of the month," she kept on. At least that much I knew. Shirley and I had our own few months of calendar nerves, that long ago springtime in Missoula before we got married. "We'd been meeting out along the creeks, Alec and I," Leona's words remembered. "The old Ben English place right there across English Creek was standing empty then, that was one we met at. But it was awfully close to town, we had to be too careful there. Noon Creek was better for our purpose, all those ranches standing empty after the Double W bought them up—Fain's, the Eiseley place, the Nansen place. Alec and I both lived on horseback in those days and there wasn't any shortage of places to ride to and make love." Still facing ahead, she stopped and swallowed. Then resumed. "So it fit with—the way we'd been with each other, my telling him the calendar had played a surprise on us."

Sometimes you know a thing because even invisible it fills a gap. I asked anyway. "On the ride out from town that night, wasn't it. When you told Alec that."

Surprised herself, Leona swung to look directly at me again. "Yes. Jick, did Alec . . . have you always . . . ?"

"No, he never said a word of any of this to me. To any of us. I just remember there was something about you two when I watched you come over the rise." Alec with his head up even more than his customary proud riding style, Leona golden and promising even at too great a distance for details. Their perfect gait, horseman and horsewoman, down from outline against the June sky as I crossed the yard from a boyhood chore to that suppertime. One of those moments that is a seed of so much else.

"Alec was both scared to death and as happy as he could be," Leona spoke now as if we were both watching that saddle-throned figure of my nineteen-year-old brother. "You can be that way, when you're young and convinced you're in love. Right then and there, on the county road before we came into sight of the ranger station, he wanted to know if it was safe for me to be on horseback, would it hurt the baby? I laughed and told him he was getting away ahead of the game, worrying about that already." But that was Alec, wasn't it. All go and no whoa, as my mother always said of him. Beside me Leona was saying now: "It was happening sooner than he'd wanted, in one way—we still couldn't get married for a few months, until he'd saved up his wages and talked the Double W into some kind of living quarters for us. And in another way, he was thrilled pink with the idea he and I were going to have a child. I hope you see, Jick. It decided for us. A baby then meant the pair responsible had to get married, there wasn't just . . . living together. That was the thing about it: my telling Alec settled so much we were still trying to figure out. It made life seem so much—safer. And he wanted some kind of sure path as much as I did, something he could just latch on to and go with. You know how Alec was."

Yes. Alec McCaskill and Leona Tracy, I knew how they both were then. In memory the perfect two of them, another month into that summer of 1939, at the after-rodeo dance in Gros Ventre when Alec won the calf roping, my brother tall and alight with the fact that he was astraddle of the world, beside him Leona golden-haired in a white taffeta dress that flounced intriguingly with her every step. His armful of her as Alec advised my friend Ray Heaney and me, enough younger that the only company we kept at dances yet was the wall, *You guys better think about getting yourselves one of these.* That was the appearance, royal Alec and priceless Leona. In actuality, both before and after Leona, my brother stubborned his way into a life that did not lead to much of anywhere. And Leona there at seventeen, who looked like her life was on clockwork—smile; let her hair gleam in the sun; beautify whatever scene she found herself in, on the back of a horse or twirling in taffeta at a Fourth of July dance—in actuality, a seventeen-year-old head on a body with the collected urges of centuries in it, on it. No more than the figurehead is steering the ship under full sail was Leona Tracy in charge of herself then.

This next I didn't ask. Why the episode with Alec didn't come out the way she'd set it in motion. This she owed herself to tell.

"I couldn't go through with it," the Leona of now was saying as if still in accusation against herself. Her voice had the same crimp of hard—hurtful—concentration that I knew was pierced in between her eyes. "Pretty soon after the Fourth, I told him that . . . it was a false alarm, that I was . . . back in step with Mother Moon. Oh, I think Alec more than half knew what I'd done. Started to do. Especially when I went on and said I thought we had better hold off on marriage entirely, that I'd decided to finish high school and take a look at life then."

A person tends to think that the past has happened only to himself. That it's his marrow only, particular and specific; filling his bones one special way. The anguished look on Leona disabused me of that forever.

"It's there, isn't it, Jick. If I'd kept matters that Alec and I simply were going together, that I didn't want to get serious about marriage right then, he might've eventually listened to what your folks wanted for him." And gone to college and made the life that education could have brought him, I mentally finished the fifty-year-old family accusation against her. "Or if I'd gone ahead and shotgunned him into marrying me, we in all likelihood really would have had a child by the time the war came." And Alec would not have charged off and enlisted the week after Pearl Harbor, this new burden of proof against Leona ran. "Either way," she finished with difficulty, "Alec might not have . . . ended up as he did."

I felt a sting at my eyes, but Leona was nowhere near crying. There is a dry sorrow beyond tears.

She waited, there in the almost-dark of the motorhome cab.

Life is choices. I could go back to the long McCaskill grudge against her, fortified now by knowing that my parents and ultimately I were righter than we had even imagined, about her effect that family-tearing summer. Or. Or I could make as much of a start as I could in the other direction.

By saying, as I now did:

"Leona Tracy was somebody the McCaskills never knew how to contend with. So I think we're lucky to have Leona Wright take sides with us."

We pulled in to the Wright ranch at close to midnight, the yard light illuminating the tidy buildings and the cow corrals and a Chevy pickup with a considerable portion of the ranch on it as mud. Out from under the pickup materialized a half-grown dog letting out a nightsplitting woof.

"Morgan and Kathy will be wondering what Manslaughter has got treed," Leona said. "I'll go across and let them know I'm back in one piece." She sounded strangely shy, tentative, with the next: "You want to come with, come in for a little while?"

"Naw, I'm going to turn in pretty quick, thanks anyhow."

"I guess it's a rare chance in this rig"—she cast a memorizing look around in the motorhome, which suddenly was seeming as empty as an unloaded moving van—"to have some sleeptime all to yourself."

"Yeah, I guess," I managed to semichuckle.

"You'll have breakfast with us, surely," she stipulated.

"Actually I can't. I've got to pull out for the Two Medicine country real early. I need to get home and sort out the situation there."

"Then I'd better say thanks now, for bringing me back. And for everything else you did today, Jick."

"That's okay, thanks for riding along. Been nice having some company. Been interesting."

Leona leaned across from the passenger seat and gave me a no-nonsense kiss, surprisingly like Mariah's version, on my approximate cheek. She smiled, maybe still a little sadly, before she opened the passenger door of the Bago. "With my background, would you believe it's taken me sixty-seven years to kiss a man with a beard?"

DAWN ARTICULATING

When asked what he thought of today's centennial celebration, 89-year-old Garland Hebner, odds-on winner of the beard contest, declared: "A time was had by all."

—*GROS VENTRE WEEKLY GLEANER, NOVEMBER 8, 1989*

A HUNDRED HOURS LATER, which had seemed like a century, the Noon Creek road was a dike through the dark as I headed the Bago in from my ranch toward Gros Ventre and centennial morning.

The only other creature up this early was at the crest of the benchland, a jackrabbit that leapt in panic and ricocheted back and forth in the tunnel of light cut by the motorhome's bright beams. I switched onto dim and the skittering jack managed to dart free into the barrow pit.

Otherwise, nothing but before-dawn blackness on either side of the gravel embankment of road until the gateframe at the turnoff into the Double W, high and logthick, came into the headlights.

I flipped onto bright again, as if the increased wash of light would bleach away that triumphal WW sign and the cable-strung cow skull swaying beneath in the wind. Still no such luck. Nearer and nearer the gateway drew, the motorhome's headlights leveled steady on it; my trigger finger itching as ever here, both of my gripping hands feeling the shotgun rise in aim at the hated goddamn fancy transom, my eyes sighting in on the welcome vision of putting an end to that plaything skull by blasting it to bits.

But by now other conclusions, this final nightful of thinking them through, shouldered that one away and I drove past.

Life was definitely awake when I reached town. The Medicine Lodge was as lit up as boxed lightning. Switched on in more ways than one, too, for music was blaring out of the radiant old saloon as I climbed down from the Bago. The municipal serenade hit a crescendo that sounded like a truckload of steel guitars rolling over and over and then a woman's voice boomed in amplification: "That was a little tune we picked up from a rock group called Drunks With Guns. So now you've had your wake-up music and can tackle the pancake breakfast these nice folks have got ready for you, and we'll be back shortly."

Yeah, well, I guess there are all different ways of feeling gala, and musical commotion of their sort must be one of them. I started to cross the street to the site of rumpus, not to mention breakfast, but had to wait for traffic, one lone van toodling through town from the south. I stood impatiently for it to pass, more than ready to scoot across and get myself in out of the chilly wind; November is not much of a pedestrian season in the Two Medicine country. The leisurely vehicle at last reached me and I started to get my thoroughly cooled heels into motion again. But right in front of me the van pulled up, blockading my path, and the driver tapped out on his horn *beep beepitybeepbeep beep beep!*

I remained there with my jaw on my shoetops while geezers in dress-up stockman Stetsons, the dapper low-crowned kind you don't see often any more, came stiffly climbing out both sides of the van. "How you doing, Jick? All revved up to go through this again in 2089?" "Jick, you Two Medicine people get up before God sends Peter out to the Gate." "Got your speechmaking pants on this morning, have you, Jick?"

The Baloney Express gang and I shook hands and slapped shoulders and conducted general hubbub there in the middle of the street until I managed to ask, "What, you mean to tell me you guys got up before the chickens and drove all the hell the way up here from Great Falls just for our ceremony?"

"How could we stay away?" Roger Tate responded from behind the steering wheel of the van. "Ain't we all been waiting most of a hundred years for this?"

"Besides, it's only ninety miles back to the Falls," Julius Walker chipped in. "The way Roger drives, it'll only take us half an hour to get home."

"Had to deliver this anyway," Dale Starr declared and presented me a five-dollar bill and four ones.

"What's this, you guys running a lottery now too?"

"Compliments of our Shoeless Joe from Fargo," explained Dale, about our broke-and-barefoot casualty in the rest area a couple of months ago. "Wrote that things are still pretty tough with him, but he's trying to scout up enough odd jobs to get by on."

Then the other Walker, Jerome, had me by an elbow and was steering me back to the side of the street I'd started from. "We got something to show you over here, too. Don't look so alarmed, we didn't bring none of those used cars with us."

He headed me toward the rear of my Winnebago, where a couple of the more nimble members somehow had slipped away to and already were standing there with full moon grins. Gingerly I stepped around to peer at the rear of the Bago, and there on the bumper blazed a sticker in Day-Glo orange:

HONORARY BALONEY EXPRESS RIDER

"We had it made up special," announced Bill Bradley, rocking back on his tiny heels as if nearly bowled over with pride.

I didn't know whether to laugh or bawl, and so likely did a mix of the two.

After I had thanked them sevenfold, the bunch said they realized I needed to gather my mind toward the speech I was going to make— "Say what you're gonna say good and loud, or at least loud," ran the general tenor of their advice—and off they hobbled toward the Medicine Lodge and pancakes and coffee.

A minute to compose myself was definitely required, and I moved to the side of the Bago that was out of the wind and stood looking at Gros Ventre. Like other Montana towns, no Easy Street anywhere in it. Instead this highway main street, born wide because freight wagons and their spans of oxen or workhorses had needed maneuvering room, the twin processions of businesses, dead and alive, now aligned along that original route, the high lattice of cottonwood limbs above the sidewalks. With all the cars and pickups parked downtown at this usually empty hour and only one building alight, Gros Ventre looked busy in an odd concentrated way, as if one behavior had entirely taken over and shoved all other concerns out of the way. Maybe that is what a holiday is. The dark up there beyond the cottonwoods was just beginning to soften, the first of the hourlong suggestion of light before actual sunrise. I gazed across the street at the crowd of heads behind the plate glass window on the cafe side of the Medicine Lodge. Bobbing amid them, in a rhythm of choosing and coaxing and focusing and clicking, was a fireball of hair deeper than red. Mariah riding the moments as they came. Riley was not in action yet. I could see him propped against the cafe wall, arms folded, not even wielding his notebook yet.

I squared myself, ready at last to go across and be part of the occasion. I wish you were here for this, Marcella. But you are not. And so I hope I bring to this day the strength of what we were together.

Gros Ventre entire seemed to be within the straining walls of the Medicine Lodge when I entered. Never in the field of human jubilee had so many so voluntarily got up so early. Some were history-costumed, here and there frock coats and Lillian Russell finery, elsewhere cowboy and horsewoman outfits complete with hats of maximum gallonage; even occasional fringed leather trapper getups. Others were in common clothes. In whatever mode, conversation was epidemic, people yakking and visiting back and forth in a mass from one end of the cafe to the other. The back wall was startlingly bare, the centennial flag down now and in folded repose across a number of long tables like a golden tarpaulin, ready to be taken out for hoisting when the time shortly came. All other tables of the Medicine Lodge and a borrowed bunch more had been pushed together in spans devoted to pancake consumption.

But my policy had to be first things first, even ahead of breakfast, so I made my way over to her.

Naturally Mariah was in midshoot of Amber Finletter, who was wearing big goony glasses with blunked-out lenses like Orphan Annie's eyes and a housenumber "1" attached off the side to make the eyerig read as a 100. Such centennial embodiment notwithstanding, I got Mariah aside and had the talk with her I needed to have.

To my news she simply gave me a ratifying buzz on the cheek and added: "What can I say? I was the one who kept at you to get yourself going again, wasn't I. You don't vegetate worth a damn, Jick."

Then it was her turn, of telling me what she needed to.

Four months' worth of words with this daughter of mine dwindled to basics. I only asked:

"You're real sure?"

"I finally am," said Mariah.

Away she flew, back to work, and myself to breakfast. Sleepy 4-H kids were ladling out the food. I negotiated a double plateload of pancakes and swam them in syrup, further fortified myself with a cup of Nguyen's coffee, then went over and found a seat across from Fred Musgreave, who had surrendered his bar domain to the music posse.

Fred appraised my hotcake stack and asked, "Gonna build a wind-break inside yourself?"

"Uh huh," I acknowledged cheerfully and began forking.

A fresh gust rattled the plate glass window. "At least it isn't snowing," Fred granted.

"Shhh," I cautioned him against hexing the weather.

After pondering me and my steady progress through the pancakes, Fred concluded: "I gather you're saving up your inventory of words for your speech."

I suppose I was. But also, by now a lot of the essential had been said. Said and done. I forked on and watched Mariah aiming her camera at Bill Rides Proud, his Blackfeet braids spilling down his back.

When pats descended on my off arm, the noneating one, I didn't even need to look. "Morning, Althea."

"Oh, Jick. It's so nice to see you back for good."

A Mariah-style "mmm" was all I was willing to give that until I had the last of the hotcakes inside me. In something close to alarm, Fred Musgreave abandoned the chair across from me to Althea and she took it like a throne. This morning her sense of occasion featured turn-of-the-century regalia, a sumptuous velvet bustle-dress with matching feathered hat; it broke my eating rhythm a moment to realize that, feathers excluded, the plum color of everything on Althea Frew exactly matched that of my Billings wedding motif.

"What a nice bolo tie," she found to compliment on me after considerable inspection. I only *mmm*ed that too, all the help really that Althea needed with a conversation. Pleasant as fudge, she proceeded to give me a blow-by-blow account of our centennial committee's doings in my lamented absence and then on into every jot and tittle of this dawn event and beyond. "Then we'll have more dancing, then when the bells ring all over the state at 10:41, we'll start our parade. Then—" You could tell she could hardly wait to get going on the next hundred years; for that matter, Althea would be gladly available by seance when Montana had to gird up for its millennium.

Suddenly music met its makers in the bar half of the Medicine Lodge, the band tuning up thunderously cutting off Althea in midgush.

"Interesting chamber orchestra," I remarked for her benefit.

Althea flinched the least little bit as a new chorus of whangs and clangs ensued. "I put Kevin in charge of hiring the music. He told me they're a dance band."

"Depends on the dance, I guess."

Over the throb of the music she swung back onto that ever favorite topic of hers, me. "We're all so anxious to hear your speech."

I grinned, by far the fondest I'd ever given her, making her bat her eyes in surprise, before I said: "I kind of feel that way myself."

Mood music was not the term I ordinarily would have applied to whatever the band was performing, yet somewhere behind my grin was the amplified tune beating through my body in an oddly familiar way. Then the voice of the woman singer resounded:

"Somewhere south of Browning, along Highway 89!"

The singer interrupted herself to announce it was action time, everybody better find their feet and stomp a quick century's worth. Even without that I was already up, needing to go see, assuring Althea I'd connect with her at speech time. And yes, as I passed I gave her a pat.

"Just another roadkill, beside life's yellow line!"

National anthems I can take or leave, but the music put out by these Roadkill Angels now drew me as if it was the strongest song of the human clan. And was drawing everybody else in the Two Medicine country, judging by how jampacked the bar side of the Medicine Lodge suddenly was with dancers and onlookers. The players in the band, mostly armed with guitars of colors I didn't even know they made them in, held forth on a temporary stage that had been carpentered across the far end of the bar. Behind and a little higher sat a drummer in a black plug hat with an arrow through it.

Amid this onstage aggregation the woman singer didn't look like much—chunky, in an old gray gabardine cattledealer suit, her blond hair cut in an approximate fringe—but her voice made maximum appearance, so to speak. She sang, my God, she sang with a power and a timbre that pulled at us just short of touch, as when static electricity makes the hair on an arm stand straight when a hand moves just above it. Holding the microphone like she was sipping from it, she sent that voice surging and tremoring, letting it ride and fall with the cascades of the instruments but always atop, always reaching the words out and out to the crowd of us. She activated the air of the Medicine Lodge: the floorful of solos being danced in front of the Roadkill Angels band was magnificent, the 4-H kids especially shining at the quick-limbed undulations this music wanted.

Up near the bandstand I spotted Mariah and Riley in conference, I assumed about their coverage of this spree. But then he looked at her for a moment, smoothed his mustache before nodding, and stuck his notebook in his pocket while she went over along the wall to where Howard Stonesifer and his ancient mother were sitting, Howard watching the dancers, and his mother watching the dancers and Howard. To old Mrs. Stonesifer's astonishment and Howard's blushing agreement, Mariah with royal fuss hung her cameras one after another around Howard's neck for safekeeping. He sat there proudly sashed and bandoliered with her photographic gear as she and Riley found space on the dance floor.

This was not the slow clinging spin in each other's arms as it had been at The Lass in a Glass. But even while dancing apart as they now were, the two of them responded to each other like partners who have heard all possible tunes together. Again, as that night in Chinook, their eyes steadily searched each other's.

When the song ended, they headed toward me.

I favored Riley with the question, "So how would you describe this band?" He responded, "It definitely isn't elevator music."

Mariah, though, was the one with something on her mind. She stood in front of me, a bit flushed from her round on the floor with Riley. "Dad," she said, "how about dancing with me?"

"Mariah, I can't dance to this stuff. Parts of my body would fall off."

She gave me a monumental grin and said, "I'll bet they can tone the music down just enough to keep you in one piece," and she flashed away to the bandstand to put in her request to the singer.

I started to take this chance to say to Riley what I needed to, but he beat me to the draw by digging into the front pocket of his pants. "Before I forget, here," and he handed me a folded wad of money.

Inquiry must have been written on me as large as the bankroll I was gaping down at.

"For Bago repairs, courtesy of the expense account," Riley droned in what was probably a bean counter voice.

At that I rapidly performed finger arithmetic on the currency and sure enough, dented grill–lost hubcap–assorted ailing windows–and what all, it was the whole damages. All this and the surprise remuneration delivered by Baloney Express. By God, business was finally picking up as Montana approached its second hundred years.

I had to ask. "What'd you make up to charge this much off to?"

"Helicopter rental," said the scribbler nonchalantly.

"Heli—? Christamighty, how are you ever going to get the BB to believe *that*?"

"By the note I stuck on that says we also used the flight to spot mountain goats up behind your ranch."

After that, I almost hated to give him my news. And at first it did stupefy him. Riley was resilient, though, and by the time Mariah got back to tow me onto the dance floor, we left him looking only somewhat fogged over.

> *"So we've survived*
> *the nicks of time . . ."*

The music still had enough steel in it to be sold by the metric ton, but the woman singer was almost gentle now.

> *"Done our best against*
> *the tricks of time . . ."*

Whatever Mariah and I may have lacked in grace as a dance team we made up for in tall, our long McCaskill legs putting us at an eyelevel above almost all the other couples'. There was a privileged feeling in this, like being swimmers through water controlling itself into small bobbing waves, hundreds of them but each one head-size. I started to say something to Mariah about the specialness of this a.m. guitar cotillion scene, but she was immersed in it too, her eyes alight as our slow tour of the floor in each other's arms brought us past what seemed the entire community of the Two Medicine country.

> *"They'll say of us that*
> > *we had a past . . ."*

Elbow to elbow, wall to wall, the Medicine Lodge was a rainbow swirl of twined couples. Dancers came in all varieties. A tall young woman with a ponytail stared soulfully over the hairline of her partner half a head shorter than her. Of the English Creek contingent, plaid-shirted Harold Busby, with an Abe Lincoln beard since I'd last seen him, twirled by with his wife Melody in a swishing black skirt with white fringe.

> *"But we know our way*
> > *to now at last . . ."*

Althea Frew freighted me a chiding look as she steered an apprehensive Fred Musgreave by us. I felt a rump bump and glanced back to find it was Kenny, his jeans tucked in the tops of his boots, earnestly waltzing with his arms cocked wide and his behind canted out, as if about to grapple with Darleen as she tried to match steps with him.

But of them all, people in costumes of the past century, people dressed in everyday, people with generations behind them in the Two country, people newer to its demanding rhythm of seasons—of them all, I concentrated on Mariah, her lanky form perfectly following mine as we danced, her face intent on mine, on this time together. I could not but think to myself, how did Marce and I ever do it, give the world this flameheaded woman?

After the music, we rejoined Riley. He and Mariah talked matters over a last time as I just listened. Before any too much could be said, though, marching orders for all of us came from Althea, commandeering the singer's mike: "It's time, everyone! Out, out, out!"

True to her words, the crowd did begin to sluice out of the Medicine Lodge into the street, Amber Finletter and Arlee Zane at the door handing out to everybody, man woman child whatever, gold-colored ballcaps with DAWN OF MONTANA printed on the front. Arlee and I somehow managed to thoroughly ignore each other even while he held out a cap which I took. Behind me Riley of course wanted to know if there were any with earflaps for the Two Medicine climate, but then clapped a cap onto his frizzhead insofar as it would go and trooped on out with the rest of us.

It was breezy and then some, I will say. Quite a swooshing overhead as the wind gusted around in the tops of the cottonwoods. But Two Medicine people are born recognizing the nearest windbreak, and the centennial crowd now divided almost exactly to bunch in front of either the Mercantile or the *Gleaner* office, the empty lot with the flagpole between them, in a way that reminded me of sheep on either side of a fast creek. Meanwhile Riley for once had an idea that was useful as well as bright. I reluctantly loaned him the keys and he hustled off and moved the Bago around to the alley behind the Merc and the *Gleaner,* parking it broadside across the back of the flagpole lot to block at least a fraction of the wind.

Before I quite knew it, Althea had herself and me up into the back of Arlee Zane's auctioneering pickup, our vehicular speaking stand for the occasion. Above, the ropes still sang in their pulleys on the flagpole, but Althea seemed to regard it as the most refreshing weather of the entire century as she bustled forward to the microphone setup to introduce me.

I only half-heard her toasty testimonial to me, occupied as I was with my own words to come, the shapes and shadows of all I had to try to articulate. When is a person ever fit to speak for his native patch of ground? Old Churchill must have been something beyond a human being. Too quickly, Althea's pertinent part was ringing out—"and it's my deep personal pleasure to present to you our Dawn of Montana speaker, Jick McCaskill!"—and I was up there peering out over the loudspeaking apparatus atop the pickup cab and having the microphone bestowed on me reverently by Althea.

There in the half-light, sunrise impending only a number of minutes away, I could make out individual faces of the crowd. I could see Mariah's Dawn of Montana cap, backward on her head to keep the bill out of the way of her camera. I could pick out the screen glow of Riley's word processor where he'd perched it on the pickup fender down in front of me. For the first time, it struck me that words of mine here might pass into print via Riley. The *Montanian*'s last centennial story, me at his laptop mercy. The thought of that once would have scared me spitless, but now I simply smiled at it as fact. Ink outlasts blood.

So I began.

"I don't really have the best feet for it, but I'm following in my mother's footsteps here. Hers was a Fourth of July speech, back when Montana was only half this old—and some of us were as young as it was possible to be, it seems now. The idea, there at that holiday gathering of the Two Medicine country in 1939, was for her to commemorate the pioneer Ben English and the creek that carries his name for us."

> *Silent this morning within the greater rush of the wind,*
> *English Creek flowed at the edge of the town, of the crowd,*
> *of the amplified reach of the speaker's voice.*

I held the pages of my speech firmly in both hands against the zephyrs both outside and within me. "Most of you knew my mother, at least in her last years, so you know that from Beth McCaskill you customarily got more of what was on her mind rather than less. I suppose it shouldn't have been any surprise"—although it mightily had been; I could yet see my father in breathless freeze beside me on the picnic grass as we heard her multiply that occasion up from mere ritual—"when she began to speak not only about English Creek, where my father's ranger station was at the time, but of Noon Creek, where she was born on the ranch I have operated for the past forty years."

I drew a breath and made it into those words of my mother's:

" 'Two creeks, two valleys, two claims on my heart,' she said on that day in 1939. And being Beth McCaskill she was not about to stop at that. No, she proceeded to call the roll of dead ranches along Noon Creek. Of the families who had to leave those places during the Depression with the auction hammer echoing in their ears. The Torrance place, the Emrich place, the Chute place, old Thad Wainwright's place. The Fain place, the Eiseley place, the Nansen place." Places, all, she knew as vacant and doomed; but where my hotblooded brother and the Leona of then found spring shelter for what their bodies wanted. "Places that are still being added to, yet today, across the emptying parts of this state. A little while back you maybe read, as I did, how Riley

Wright summed up a lot of this: 'Of all of Montana's hard weather, the reliably worst has been its economic climate.'"

Only the sound of the wind making the cottonwoods give followed into the pause of his words.

"There are goodbyes to be said today besides our farewell to Montana's original century," I spoke it out while watching the writing figure. "The person down here doing the story of our ceremony, the selfsame Riley Wright, is one of those who is leaving for a life elsewhere. What he's going to find to say about us this morning, heaven only knows and even it usually has to guess, where Riley is concerned." For that he cocked an applesauce eyebrow at me but kept typing. "Riley and I have not always seen eye to eye. But I'll say this for him: life never looks quite the same after Riley Wright has shown it to you."

I paused and peeked down at him as the crowd clapped a sendoff for Riley. It was hard to be sure under partial light, but the sonofagun may have blushed.

I made myself resume.

"The other leave-taking, the one that makes today's goodbyes plural, is geographically closer to home. This one—no offense to Riley, but this other one knocks an even bigger hole in me. This other one is my—"

My throat caught, and I looked out at my daughter in the crowd, Mariah with her camera down, giving me her validating grin; I swallowed as hard as I ever have and finished the saying of it:

"—self."

There was a stir at that. Of all the honors there are, that moment of the Two country's twinge toward me is what I will take.

"My leaving is of my ranch," I went on. "The Reese place, as it began. Part of it also the Ramsay place, the homestead of my grandmother's side of the family. The McCaskill place, I guess since I had a moment of sanity about forty years ago and came back to the Two country from other pursuits and married Marcella and we settled in to work the place, our place. Now, though. Now like so many others I've had to face the day when the land and the McCaskill family no longer match up. It is no easy thing to admit"—all of them within listening range knew so, yet I had to tell them the specific hardness of it—

"because I have always believed, as the people before us did and as I'm sure you have, that he who owns the soil owns up to the sky."

His words climbed as he threw his head back to outspeak a gust that rattled his pages, to send his voice higher, stronger. Language is the light that comes out of us. Imagine the words as if they are our way of creating earthlight, as if what is being spoken by this man in a windswept dawn is going to carry everlastingly upward, the way starshine is pulsing constantly across the sky of time to us. Up through the black canyons of space, the sparks we utter; motes of wordfire that we glimpse leaving on their constellating flight, and call history.

"So, when you've got it to do," I resumed like a man resolved, "you wrestle the question until you see where it falls. The automatic answer is to let my ranch follow all the others on Noon Creek. Go the way"— the Double W way, the conglomerate way, I did not even need to say— "that such places economically have to go, we all know."

I took an even firmer grip on the pages of my talk and headed into what I had to say next.

"However."

Funny, how that lone word made Shaun Finletter suddenly look as if his arithmetic had been smudged.

"The automatic way of doing things isn't necessarily mine, any more," I kept at the matter. "I've maybe learned a little something about being usefully ornery, from the company I've been keeping these past few months." Mariah only paused for a half-second in biting off the leader of an exposed roll of film in her lightning reload of the camera. Riley gave me a gaze of kitten innocence. "Anyway," I delivered the rest of it, "I'm leaving my ranch, yes. But leaving it to . . ."

The Nature Conservancy guy on the other end of the phone the night before had sounded simultaneously enthused and curious, as if he wished he could peer across the distance from Helena to Noon Creek and gauge me face to face.

"Naturally we're interested in a piece of country like yours, Mr.

McCaskill. We try to keep real track of what's left of the original biology there along the Rocky Mountain Front, and those native grasses on the prairie part of your place qualify for the kind of preservation we want to do. We know how you've taken care of that land. What, ah, did you have in mind?"

When I told him for comparison what the Double Dub through Shaun was offering me, he responded: "We don't always have the dollars to pay market value like that, but there's a way of doing it called a bargain sale. What that is, the differential between the market value of a ranch such as yours and what the Conservancy can afford to pay qualifies as a charitable gift; it comes off your income tax load, you net out on it. Let me run some numbers by you, okay?"

After that trot across the calculator, I said to him:

"Good enough. The outfit is yours, if you can do a couple of other things for me."

"And those are?"

I laid it on him that Kenny and Darleen had to be kept for at least a year, given a chance to perform the upkeep or caretaking or whatever on the place. "They aren't either one exactly whiz kids, but they're hell for work." My figuring was that the two of them would be able to show their worth okay within a year, but also that it conceivably might take every minute of that span.

"We can stand them, it sounds like," the Conservancy director granted in a dry tone. "And the other thing?"

When I told him, his voice sat up straighter.

"Actually, we've been thinking about a preserve for those someplace on this side of the mountains, if we could manage to get enough land together out north from Pine Butte."

"It's got to be part of the deal," I made good and sure. "The name and everything."

Through the phone earpiece I could all but hear the land preservation honcho thinking *Holy smoke, we don't get many ranchers who are such a big buddy of . . .* Then with determination he said: "We'll do it."

I took a pleasant moment to cast a gaze east from the ranch house, out across the moonlit hay meadows and grass country between there and my fenceline with the Double W. If Pine Butte could be kept a fen, this ranch could be kept a range. After all, WW Inc. wanted to see maximum animal units on this piece of land, didn't it? It was about to have them. Buffalo. A whole neighboring ranchful. Right in here next to a corporate cow pasture would now be the Toussaint Rennie Memorial Bison Range, original inhabitants of this prairie, nice big rambunctious butting ones. Let the sonofabitching Double W tend *its* fences against those, for a change.

The Nature Conservancy headman, trying to keep delight out of his tone, carefully checked to see that we were really concluded. "That's all the details of our transaction then, Mr. McCaskill? We sure appreciate your doing this."

"One more thing," I said into the phone. "Happy next hundred years."

"I guess I see this as giving back to the earth some of the footing it has given to me and mine," I told the intent crowd now. "If we McCaskills no longer will be on that particular ground, at least the family of existence will possess it. That kind of lineage needs fostering too, I've come to think—our kinship with the land."

Mariah, of course operating as if she and I and the camera were the only three for miles around, had come climbing up over the bumper onto the other front fender of the auctioneering pickup and was kneeling there for a closeup of me framed between the loudspeaker horns.

"Speaking of lineage . . ." I resorted to with a rueful glance down at this ambushing daughter.

When the audience had its laugh at that, I looked from the impervious lens of Mariah to them and back to her again before I could resume.

"Mariah here is going into the next hundred years in her own style, as you might expect. She begins it immediately after our ceremony today. With Riley leaving—our loss and California's gain, but they need all they can get—maybe the *Montanian* figured it might as well trade in Mariah's job too. In any case, her new arrangement is—I don't know what something like this is actually called, but Mariah is being turned loose on this state as the *Montanian*'s photographer at large."

When she and I came off the dance floor to him this morning, Riley looked at her as if he was seeing the last one of a kind. "I still think we could've made it work this time, Mariah Montana."

"I don't," Mariah said gently but firmly, "and that'd have been a fatal start right there."

"You know, that's the trouble with reality checks," Riley said as if he'd been asked for a diagnosis. "They fuck up the possibilities of imagination."

"Better that than us," she gave him back, keeping her tone as deliberately light as his. "Riley, you know what?"

"I hope you're not going to tell me this builds character," he said in the voice of a man somewhere between keeping his pride and facing loss.

"Huh uh, worse. What I finally figured out is that you and I love just some of each other, mostly the job parts. We collaborate like a house afire. If the centennial trip went on forever maybe we could too. But that's just it—beyond our work, we make trouble for each other. We didn't manage to wear any of the rough edges off each other in three years of being married, and trying it again would be just more of the same. New try, new place, new whatever, but we'd be the same." Mariah cocked her head as if it was her turn to diagnose. "We're each in our own way so ungodly focused."

"Spoken like a photographer," he couldn't resist intoning.

"What it is, Riley," she said as quietly as before, "we can't keep up with each other. I don't know anything to be done about that and I think you don't either." Still looking at Riley, Mariah inclined her head toward me. "Jick McChurchill here would probably say we're geared too different. You've got a definite direction of what you want to do, and it turns out I've got mine."

"I've got to point out, Mariah," Riley said with care, "staying put is a funny kind of direction."

"Mmm. I know. I'm maybe a funny kind." She looked at me in a way that made Riley do the same. "I come by it honestly, huh?" But then she turned to him again, her gray eyes delivering quietly but definitely to his gray and blue. "If I go to California because of your chance there, I'm tagging after. If you stay here in Montana because of me, you're tagging after. Riley, neither one of us is cut out for that, are we."

Riley had known ever since the motel in Ekalaka; Mariah was distinctive even in fashioning a goodbye. After that, the BB was undoubtedly the easier case, Mariah letting him blab on about how very unique her photowork in the centennial series had been until he found himself agreeing that her best use of talent would be to keep on picturing Montana as it struggled with Century Number Two, wouldn't it.

And so Riley for once didn't argue. There in the Medicine Lodge, waiting to do their last piece before it became Mariah's job to rove and his to transplant himself to the *Globe* column, he managed at least a semblance of his sly look as he said to her: "You may be right—we're maybe a little advanced to be playing tag." But for half a moment I felt sorry for Riley, going off to California with just his mustache for company.

"The last some months," the microphone carried my words, "I've been on the go in parts of this state of ours that I'd scarcely even heard of. A lot of my daily reading since the Fourth of July has been roadmaps, and it eventually dawned on me that Montana is the only state of the continental forty-eight that is a full time zone wide. Where the Clark Fork River crosses into Idaho it gains into Pacific time, and when the Missouri River flows across into North Dakota an hour is adjusted onto life from there to the Great Lakes—while we here beside the Continental Divide that sends those rivers on their way exist on Mountain time. And I wonder whether Montana maybe fills a span of time all to itself in more than just that map sense.

"An awful amount of what I saw across this state, what Riley wrote of and Mariah caught in her pictures, does raise the question of what we've got to celebrate about. Montana has a tattered side. You look at the blowing away prairies that never should have been cut by a plow and the little towns they are taking with them, you look at the dump heaps and earth poisons left by mining, you look at so many defeated lives on the Indian reservations, you look at a bottom wage way of life that drives our young people generation after generation to higher jobs elsewhere, you look at the big lording it over the little in so much of our politics and economy and land—you look at these warps in Montana and they add up in a hurry to a hundred years of pretty sad behavior.

"Then you draw a deep breath, get a little of this endemic fresh air sweeping through your brain"—the wind surged stronger than ever through the treetops, and members of the audience made sure they weren't beneath cottonwood limbs that could crash down—"and you look at the valleys that are the green muscles on the rock bones of this state, you look at the last great freeflowing river in the continental U.S., the Yellowstone; you look at people who've been perpetually game to outwork the levels of pay here because they can love a mountain with their eyes while doing it, you look at the unbeatable way the land latches into the sky here atop the Rocky Mountain Front or on the curve of the planet across the eastern plains—and you end up calculating that our first hundred years could have been spent worse.

"So, what I've come to think is that Montana exists back and forth that way. That this wide state is a kind of teeter-totter of time. Maybe that expanse, and our born-into-us belief here that life is an up and down proposition, are what give us so much room and inclination to do both our worst and our best."

> *Do they hear us yet, the far suns of the night? A hundred years may be only enough to start the waft of our words, the echo chorus of what we have been like. The voices wing up and up, trying to clock us into the waiting sum of time. A man on the roof of the Helena Herald that morning an exact century ago, shouting down into the streets the telegraph news: "Statehood!" The accented cluck of a Danish-born teamster reining his horses around as they grade the roadbed of the Great Northern railway. A homestead wife weeping alone in her first days of cabined isolation, saying over and over "I will not cry, I will not" until at last she does not. The potentates of Anaconda Copper calculating the profits of extraction and the social costs of it not at all. Congresswoman Jeannette Rankin's unique double "No!" in the stampede votes for war, spaced apart by the years between World War One and World War Two. Grudges and fears, our tellings carry starward. Doubts and dreams and hopes. Eloquence of loss, a Montana specialty. Love's whisperings . . .*

Sounds of distance have changed with the years. I found so when I placed the other call last night, after settling the ranch matter with the Conservancy. No longer comes the silent stretch of time as you wait for the other person to be summoned to the phone. The phone miles now have a kind of fizz to them, a restless current of connection as if the air is being held apart to make way for the words back and forth. I have made other calls in my life that I thought were vital—Christamighty, I had just done one—but what I said into the phone now pulsed out of me as if I had been rehearsing for it forever. Maybe a person at last knows when he is ready. Maybe he simply can't stand being unready any longer. Whichever, I spoke it all into the humming listening miles.

"Jick, I didn't expect . . . isn't this sort of—quick?" Leona said at the other end.

"Not if you count from fifty years ago. I'd say we better get started and make up for lost time."

"Is this a proposal? Because you know I haven't been able to bring myself to remarry . . . and you said you aren't really sure eith—"

"A kind of one. Enough of one to get us started, how about."

At that, she was nowhere near as overcome with surprise as a certain son of hers had been. This morning when Mariah had gone off to the bandstand to modulate the music and I'd used that opportunity to tell Riley what Leona and I intended, he looked at me like Wednesday looks at Friday. Then asked in a stupefied way:

"Wait, wait, let me get this straight. Are you telling me you're marrying my mother?"

I couldn't resist. Actually, I didn't try overly hard.

"Who said anything about marrying? We figure we'll just see how things go."

Even over the phone I'd been able to feel the smile that came into Leona's tone after I suggested we simply try life together, preacherless. The two of us, spend some time here in Gros Ventre in the house I'd be buying with the ranch money, some time there on the Wright ranch if I solemnly promised to Morgan not to get in the way—or whenever we felt like it, do some Bago travel.

"Without being chaperoned by Riley and Mariah?" she came back at me with a laugh.

"We outlasted them fair and square, so here's our chance," I advocated.

She had to turn serious, though. We both did. Leona phrased it slowly, still more than a little afraid of it.

"Jick, is this because of Alec in some way?"

I wanted that said, I needed for her to know the full terms. It freed me to state the new truth:

"No. Finally, it isn't because of that."

The rest of my phone performance tumbled out fast. I told my intent listener that the stirrings I felt were for her, Leona Wright as she now was, and not some vanished girl who never married my brother. That I knew we were both shaky about defining love all over again at our age but I hoped she felt enough toward me to give this a try. That the time we had already spent together justified sharing some more, that we needed to see whether it could extend into years. Into lasting together. The gold ring kind of lasting if it developed that way, but any kind that proved enduring was worth a whirl. That—

Leona quit listening and spoke back across the miles.

"Yes," she magically said. "Yes to it all. Let's be together, Jick, and see from there."

We spent a delicious excited minute working out how and when to start, then each fell silent, not wanting the goodbye. After a bit Leona said in that woodsmoke voice of hers:

"Jick?"

"Yeah?"

"You are a wonder."

> *All, all the spoken sparks we are capable of kindling, try-*
> *ing to pattern us against the nightdrop. And reflecting back*
> *into us, as this man is saying in the Gros Ventre near-dawn,*
> *as the afterglint we know as memory.*

"Memories are stories our lives tell us," I went to now, seeing Althea check her watch meaningfully. "I believe that you can't come to a day such as this one, a gathering such as we all are, without hearing those murmurs from within ourselves. One such, in me this moment, is of see-ing Lila Sedgwick on these streets, when she was as old as I was young. Lila's own mind by then had some better days than others, but no days were clear, any more. Yet it was because of Lila, the unclouded Lila when she was young in 1889, that we are at this ceremony this dawn. When Lila's mind no longer could tell her the story of that morning a hundred years ago, it lived on in another memory. Toussaint Rennie told it to me, and I want to speak it now, to pass it into your memories."

The cadences of Toussaint, the rememberer of the earlier Two coun-try, began in me now.

" 'Way before dawn. Out to the flagpole, everybody. It was still dark as cats, but Dantley from the livery stable had a lantern. Lila says, "This is the day of statehood. This is Montana's new day." Sedge puts up the new flag, there it was.' "

Then in my own refound voice:

"As those first Montanans did, let's now put up our flag and, for as long as our eyes or our memories hold out, see what we can make our days bring."

As the applause resounded the flag-raising team set to business, the furled cylinder of fabric being carried to them at the base of the pole by many arms . . .

The next thing was, I was blindsided by Mariah, hugging and kissing me and declaring I had an entire new career ahead as a public spieler. I told her I hoped to Christ not, then held her just far enough away to gauge as I said: "Petunia, I hope you're ending up out of all this okay. I mean, without any—company?"

Mariah performed the little sidetoss of her head, the proud cascade of hair clearing away from her gray eyes as if offering me the clearest possible look into them, into her.

"You know how Missoula is," she stated with a grin. "Somebody interesting will come along." She swung her gaze just for a moment past me to the figure scrutinizing the flag ceremony and tapping steadily into his writing machine, soldiering on. "Riley did."

Now ready to hoist, four men take grips on the lariat-thick lanyard . . .

"So when do you have to head down the road?" Mariah issued next, her camera up and ready but not yet firing as we turned to watch the flag-raising.

"Right after this." By afternoon the Bago and I would be there at the other ceremony, when Leona and her women's club videoed the Crazy Mountains country for their Sisters of Peace to see.

"Tell your sweetie for me I hope her Russian pronunciation knocks their garters off in Moscow," Mariah instructed.

"I surely will."

The flag-raisers had their hands full. Shaun Finletter and Joe Prentiss and Kevin Frew and Larry Van Der Wende, strong men all, were hefting down hard on the rope, but only slowly did the flag do any significant unfolding, the attached end streaming up in a draggy thin triangle as more and more of the tremendous bundle lifted out of the holders' arms. They were going to have to go some to get it all the way aloft by sunrise.

Then, though. Then the streamer was high enough to reach the full wind, funneling over the Bago between the buildings, and the golden cloth caught at that force, bellying like a boatsail. The men pulled and pulled, the giant flag billowing out and out, writhing up through the air.

"Christamighty, listen to that!"

Why I let that out I don't know, for Mariah beside me plainly was hearing the same astounding thing. Everybody in Gros Ventre was, maybe everybody period. Now snugged against the top of the pole, up in that storm of air the blowing flag was making a sound that filled the sky, a roaring crackle like a vast fire blazing. Blizzard, chinook, squall, gale, I thought I had heard them all but never this. Ultimate Montana wind and great field of cloth, they were creating thunderous melody of flow over our heads.

The central emblem panel of THE TWO MEDICINE COUNTRY 1889 1989 GREETS THE DAWN OF MONTANA shimmered, as if in emphasis, every time the wind powerfully snapped the flag into another loud rumple.

But suddenly there was a new, quicker, dancier snap of rhythm within the flag roar.

The upper border of the flag, the sheep-cow-horse repeating design, was flying on its own, as if the livestock were bucking free of the heavier fabric beneath.

Then the panel below that, with the sewn-on representation of a Blackfeet chief's headdress, tore free and similarly flew from the flag rope on its own.

The crowd, stunned, awed, whatever, gaped up in silence until there came the vexed voice of Althea Frew:

"Oh, foo."

One by one the other sewn seams were freeing themselves there in the wild ride of the wind, the bottom border of forest and stream abruptly a separate wing of banner, next the stitchwork panel of Gros Ventre's buildings undulating independently as if the wind had lifted the entire town.

"Every part up there's got a mind of its own!" a voice—odds were it was one of the Baloney Express bunch—called out, setting off laughter.

"By God, this'll give us something to remember!" someone else shouted, and the laughter grew.

"Yeah, hell, we're getting all different kinds of flags out of this, for the same price as one!" issued from someone else, which set the crowd to really cheering and clapping, waves of sound to match the flapping symphony above.

Mariah had been clicking the overhead parade of banners as if motorized, but she stopped now and jiggled me in the ribs.

"What a zammo morning. We're next, Jick," she announced as keenly as if she and I were ticketed on the next ascension of wind.

So to speak, so we were: the mountainline of the Two country up over English Creek and Noon Creek that the two of us had stitched on came flapping free, Roman Reef and Phantom Woman Mountain and Flume Gulch and Jericho Reef dancing in the sky. I had to chuckle at that, the geographical pennant of the McCaskills, as Mariah

> *swiftly moved low to one side of him and captured the pic-*
> *ture to go with these words, of Jick with his bearded head*
> *thrown back as he laughed upward at the multiplying ban-*
> *ners of the centennial. As she clicked, day's arrival was defi-*
> *nite, the sun articulating its long light onto the land.*

ACKNOWLEDGMENTS

MY GROUND RULES FOR myself in this novel have been the same as in the first two books of this trilogy, *English Creek* and *Dancing at the Rascal Fair:* the heartland of the McCaskill family is the Rocky Mountain Front near what is actually Dupuyer, Montana, but the specific places and people are of my own invention. Similarly, except for a handful of irresistibly emblematic Montana institutions—the M & M in Butte, the Country Pride cafe in Big Timber, the Wagon Wheel cafe in Ekalaka, and the sign on the Elk Bar in Chinook—the RV parks, bars, eating places and so on that are my Bago travelers' ports of call across the state are not actual.

Again, too, a community of friends and acquaintances unflinchingly lent themselves to me and the making of this book these past three years: Mike Olsen, Ann McCartney, earring consultants Bryony Angell and Gilia Angell, Bob Simmons, Liz Darhansoff, Jud Moore, Laird Robinson, Michael Korn, Marshall Nelson, Lee Goerner, Sharon Waite, Richard Maxwell Brown, Barry Lippman, Hazel and Gene Bonnet, Barbara A. Niemczyk, Sue Lang, Pete Steen, Joy Hamlett and two generations of Bradley Hamletts, Bill Robbins, Merrill Burlingame, Ted and Jean Schwinden, Laurie Paris, Dorothy LaRango, Sven H. Rossel, Dore Schwinden, Thomas Blaine, Germaine Stivers, Marsha Hinch, Barbara Arensmeyer, Laura McCann, Tom Chadwick, Herb Griffin, Tom Stewart, Jim Castles, Brian Kahn of the Montana Nature Conservancy, Nancy McKay, Jean Roden, John Roden, Jim Norgaard, Vern Carstensen, Peter Haley, Dave Carr, Linda Foss, and Elizabeth Simpson.

Nor could a book of this sort have been done without these libraries and their helpful staffs: Great Falls Public Library; the Montana Historical Society at Helena; the Mansfield Library of the University of Montana at Missoula; the Parmly Billings Library; the Renne Library of Montana State University at Bozeman; the Shoreline Community College Library at Seattle; and the University of Washington Library at Seattle.

Throughout the decade of research I've spent on these books, I was rescued time and again by the extraordinary skills of Dave Walter, reference librarian of the Montana Historical Society. Among other things, this trilogy is a monument to Dave's patience.

My, and Riley's, versions of history have been derived and inspired from numerous sources, these perhaps main among them. The Indian quote about buffalo that "the country was one robe" is from *The Last of the Buffalo,* by George Bird Grinnell. For historical backdrop of Virginia City and the Alder Gulch mining era, and much else in Montana's past, I've gratefully relied on *Montana: A History of Two Centuries,* by Michael P. Malone and Richard B. Roeder. Butte's story is voluminously told, but specifics about mining fatalities were drawn from the annual reports of the Montana Inspector of Mines and "The Perils of Working in the Butte Underground: Industrial Fatalities in the Copper Mines, 1880–1920," Brian Shovers, *Montana: The Magazine of Western History,* Spring. 1987; about the Montana National Guard's 1914 occupation of the city from "Butte: A Troubled Labor Paradise." Theodore Wiprud, *Montana: The Magazine of Western History,* Oct., 1971; and about the Company's use of "rustling cards" from *The Gibraltar,* by Jerry W. Calvert. Detailed research on women's exigencies in the frontier environment is in Paula Petrik's chapter, "Capitalists with Rooms: Prostitution in Helena, 1865–1900," and elsewhere in her book *No Step Backward.*

My version of the process of relocating a grizzly bear is an amalgam of techniques and circumstances; I'm greatly indebted to wildlife biologist Michael Madel for his painstaking advice on my grizzly scene. It should be noted that according to the best available figures from the Montana Department of Fish, Wildlife and Parks, there have been two fatalities of grizzlies in more than two hundred bear relocations by that Department. Riley's account of the Dempsey-Gibbons fight in Shelby is drawn from avid coverage by national newspapers, and valuable background was provided to me during my Shelby visit by Theo Bartschi, Mabel Iverson, and the Marias Museum of History and Art. The detail of Tommy Gibbons disappearing to walk the hills at dawn is in a sidebar in *The New York Times*. July 5, 1923. In the scenes at the Chief Joseph Battlefield and the town of Chinook, the quote about Alahoos being told the Nez Percé casualties of each day is in *Hear Me, My Chiefs*, by L. V. McWhorter, and Charles Anceny's observation about luck-over-genius in the pioneer cattle industry of Montana can be found in the *Rocky Mountain Husbandman*, Feb. 9, 1882. *A Traveler's Companion to Montana History*, by Carroll Van West, was especially helpful in my sojourns into eastern Montana. For purposes of plot I've sometimes changed the locales, but I'm much indebted for quintessential episodes of the homestead and Depression eras to Mary Dawson, once of Sumatra; Fern Eggers, once of Vananda; and Lucy Olds of Butte. For historic photos and background before my visit to the Fort Howes Ranger Station, I wish to thank the Custer National Forest headquarters and Dr. Wilson F. Clark, author of *Custer National Forest Lands: A Brief History*.

The *Montanian* and the freewheeling way Mariah and Riley go about their journalism are a figment of my imagination, as much a vehicle for this novel as the Bago they resort to. But for basic lore and lingo of newspapering today; I was greatly helped by feature writer Kathleen Merryman, and by Steve Wainwright's tutoring of me in the newspaper technology of the moment. As for Mariah's habits of the camera, some are Carol Doig's, a few are even my own, and I learned bundles from the splendid lensman Chris Bennion letting me watch some of his shoots.

Kudos to Zoe Kharpertian, copy-editing virtuoso, for finding a way to keep the lilt of westernisms amid the logic of style.

To Linda Bierds, my deep thanks for looking over this manuscript chapter-by-chapter with her unique combination of ever-encouraging friendship and poet's insight.

Similar gratitude to Bill Lang, former editor of *Montana: The Magazine of Western History* and still a polymath of Montana and Western history.

Finally, all ultimate thanks to my wife Carol, for her photography from Moiese to Ekalaka and for her confidence and care toward this book from A to Z.

A SCRIBNER
READING GROUP GUIDE

RIDE WITH ME, MARIAH MONTANA

"We are a family that can be kind of stiffbacked," Jick McCaskill reflects with a characteristic sense of life's complications as he narrates this final novel of the classic Two Medicine trilogy. In *English Creek*, Ivan Doig gave us the West of the 1930s; in *Dancing at the Rascal Fair*, the alluring Rocky Mountain frontier of the late nineteenth century. Now, by way of Jick again and another cast of ineffably believable characters, he brings the story forward to 1989, Montana's centennial summer. Jick, facing age and loss, is jump-started back into adventure and escapade by his red-headed and headlong daughter Mariah, a newspaper photographer. "Pack your socks and come along with me on this," she directs. The grand tour she has in mind is centenary Montana by Winnebago, but the drawback is the reporter assigned with her, restless-minded Riley Wright. "Listen, petunia . . ." says Jick, "I don't even want to be in the same vicinity as that Missoula whistledick, let alone go chasing around the whole state of Montana with him."

But chase around they do, in beguiling encounters with the American road and all the rewards and travails this can bring—among them, a charging buffalo, a senior citizens' used-car caravan, astounding bartenders, obtuse admonitions from the home office, and blazing arguments (and a surprising alliance of convenience) between Mariah and Riley. And just as the centennial is a cause for reflection as well as jubilation, the exuberant travels of this trio bring on "memory storms" that become occasions for reassessment and necessary accommodations of the heart.

DISCUSSION QUESTIONS

1. At one point in *Ride With Me, Mariah Montana,* Jick muses, "Everything of life picture-size, neatly edged. Wouldn't that be handy, if but true." In one sense, Doig does tie the lives of his characters to the art of photography. Explore the ocular imagery in the novel, particularly as related to Jick and Mariah. How much of the novel is about learning to readjust your eyes to new light?

2. Why is the newspaper business, a vagrant occupation reliant on waves of inspiration, so appealing to Mariah and Riley? Study the articles in the centennial series and compare/contrast how Mariah

with her camera and Riley with his pen respond to the challenge of portraying the West. Why do they steer away from romanticizing the "wistful little town off the beaten path" in their depiction of Montana?

3. Jick remarks that the buttes rising from the heart of Montana's earth are "lone sentinel forms the eye seeks." Why does the eye seek them? How do they inform Jick's invisible landscape, and to what extent is the ranch (also a kind of sentinel) a part of Jick's mental dwelling place?

4. Doig, through the persona of Riley, flexes his storytelling muscles when describing the Baloney Express. Riley writes, "They have seen the majority of Montana's century, each of these seven men old in everything but their restlessness, and as their carefully strewn line of taillights burns a route into the night their stories ember through the decades." Discuss the significance of the encounter with these colorful old men and how their tales prove to be a turning point in the centennial series.

5. Having read his ancestors' letters with surprise and sorrow, Jick becomes acutely vulnerable. He reflects about Mariah and Riley, "Let history whistle through their ears all it wanted. Mine were ready for a rest." Why does Jick resist reminiscence?

6. Compare the scene at the Nez Perce grave site with the scene at the grave site where Alec is buried. Which is harder for Jick to bear— the recollection of his own experience at war or his recollection of the "battle" Alec waged with his family?

7. At the height of his depression, Jick wryly regrets, "People do end up this way, alone in a mobile home of one sort or another, their remaining self shrunken to fit into a metal box." After an exasperated cry for help to his late wife, where, then, does Jick turn? What events, people, and thoughts lead him out of his sense of abandonment and urge him to grasp at life with both vigor and calm resolve?

8. In "East of Crazy," Doig describes the wind with subtle imagery. How does the image of the Chinook complement the plot of Mariah and Riley venturing into a questionable second relationship?

9. Jick sums up Riley's character as the king "who never forgot anything but never learned anything either." Explain why Mariah is initially willing to overlook Riley's impenetrable hardheadedness and reenter a marriage with him. Does Doig lead us to side with Mariah in her final decision?

10. What effect does Leona's revelation of the events leading to her breakup with Alec have on Jick? Could we attribute his subse-

quent, even stronger desire for her to the fact that he, too, has felt her "dry sorrow beyond tears," and finds consolation in knowing she can relate to his sense of loss. How does this feeling of loss both include and transcend the loss of Alec?

11. In his stories and memoirs, Doig depicts the historic struggle to keep Montana's working ranches alive. Contrast Riley's cynical attitude toward the fate of the Montana ranch with Jick's initial idealism about his own sheep ranch. How does Jick come to terms with the reality of losing what he had worked so hard for?

12. As he did in *English Creek*, Doig incorporates a dancing scene and a moving speech at the end of *Ride With Me, Mariah Montana* to frame the emotional development of his characters, Jick and Mariah. Discuss how the style of writing in these passages elevates the reader's attitude toward Jick as father and rancher and Mariah as daughter and photographer.

BACKGROUND NOTES

Completing a Voyage Around a Century

When I set out to put a century of the American West into my Two Medicine trilogy of novels, the past was almost too cooperative. As I crisscrossed Montana in ten years of research and writing, the cycle of drought and hard times that I was exploring in the homesteaders' era of *Dancing at the Rascal Fair* and the Depression years of *English Creek* struck the state again. People I talked to there in the 1980s echoed what their parents said about the hardships of the 1930s and their grandparents said after the terrible winter of 1919; again and again I was reminded that the past has its own undying voice.

The rigors and splendors of traveling the West competed during my writing of this finale of the trilogy, as I traced out my characters' reportorial "circumnavigation" of Montana's landscape and history during the state's centennial year of 1989. At the National Bison Range at Moiese, a buffalo herd grazed past my car so close the swish of their tails could be heard. At the Chief Joseph Battlefield, while changing to a heavier coat as night and cold descended, I locked myself out of my rental car, fifteen miles from anywhere—a bonehead maneuver I immediately foisted off onto one of my characters. The summer before, Montana was being scorched by record heat as my photographer wife, Carol, and I drove a newly rented motor home out onto the prairie expanses east of Billings. When the temperature hit 105, the motor home conked out on a remote road. Miraculously, with maybe a few cusswords thrown in, the vehicle was coaxed back to life, only to suffer system failures of one kind or another in each day's extreme heat until the ultimate meltdown, the air conditioner. Our final recourse: a bedtime visit to a swimming pool and then sleeping in wet bathing suits. Clamminess never felt better.

Finishing up that novel and the decade of creating people and past akin to my own—I'm the grandson of Montana homesteaders and the son of Montana ranch workers—I let the book have the last word on my belovedly difficult home country:

> You look at the unbeatable way the land latches into the sky atop the Rocky Mountain Front or on the curve of the planet across the eastern plains—and you end up calculating that our first hundred years could have been spent worse.

ENGLISH CREEK

IVAN DOIG

SCRIBNER

New York · London · Toronto · Sydney

Again for Carol

SCRIBNER
1230 Avenue of the Americas
New York, NY 10020

First Scribner trade paperback edition 2005

SCRIBNER and design are trademarks of Macmillan Library Reference USA, Inc., used under license by Simon & Schuster, the publisher of this work.

For information about special discounts for bulk purchases, please contact Simon & Schuster Special Sales: 1-800-456-6798 or business@simonandschuster.com

DESIGNED BY LAUREN SIMONETTI

Manufactured in the United States of America

10

Library of Congress Control Number: 2005046550

ISBN-13: 978-0-689-11478-6
ISBN-10:   0-689-11478-8
ISBN-13: 978-0-7432-7127-1 (Pbk)
ISBN:10:   0-7432-7127-0 (Pbk)

"You got to make your way in this old pig iron world."

Miss Rose Gordon (1885–1968)

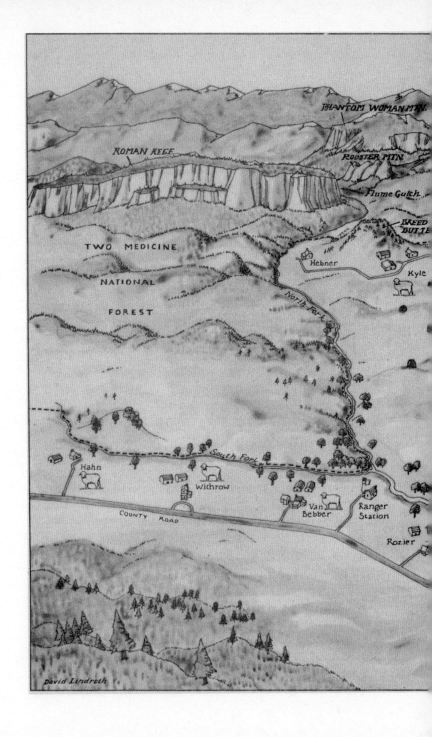

PHANTOM WOMAN MTN

ROMAN REEF

ROOSTER MTN

Flume Gulch

BREED BUTTE

TWO MEDICINE

Hebner

Kyle

NATIONAL

North Fork

FOREST

South Fork

Hahn

Withrow

Van Bebber

Ranger Station

COUNTY ROAD

Rozier

David Lindroth

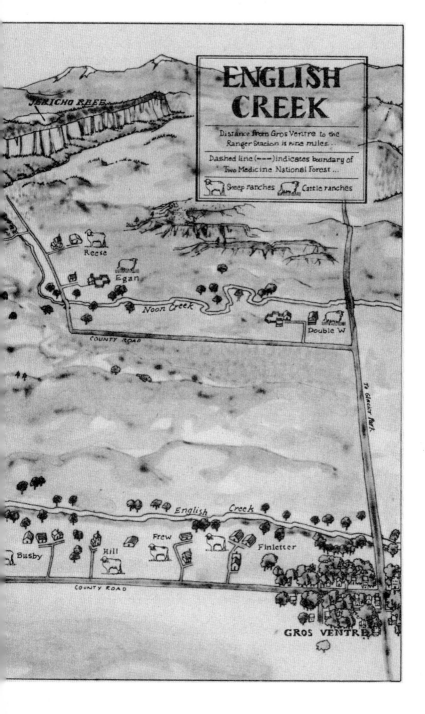

ENGLISH CREEK

Distance from Gros Ventre to the
Ranger Station is nine miles...

Dashed line (---) indicates boundary of
Two Medicine National Forest...

🐑 Sheep ranches   🐄 Cattle ranches

JERICHO REEF

Reese

Egan

Noon Creek

COUNTY ROAD

Double W

To Glacier Park

English Creek

Busby

Hill

Frew

Finletter

COUNTY ROAD

GROS VENTRE

ONE

This time of year, the report from the dust counties in the northeastern part of the state customarily has it that Lady Godiva could ride through the streets there without even the horse seeing her. But this spring's rains are said to have thinned the air sufficiently to give the steed a glimpse.

—*GROS VENTRE WEEKLY GLEANER, JUNE 1*

THAT MONTH OF JUNE swam into the Two Medicine country. In my life until then I had never seen the sidehills come so green, the coulees stay so spongy with runoff. A right amount of wet evidently could sweeten the universe. Already my father on his first high patrols had encountered cow elk drifting up and across the Continental Divide to their calving grounds on the west side. They, and the grass and the wild hay meadows and the benchland alfalfa, all were a good three weeks ahead of season. Which of course accounted for the fresh mood everywhere across the Two. As is always said, spring rain in range country is as if halves of ten-dollar bills are being handed around, with the other halves promised at shipping time. And so in the English Creek sheepmen, what few cowmen were left along Noon Creek and elsewhere, the out-east farmers, the storekeepers of Gros Ventre, our Forest Service people, in just everyone that start of June, hope was up and would stay strong as long as the grass did.

Talk could even be heard that Montana maybe at last had seen the bottom of the Depression. After all, the practitioners of this bottomed-out notion went around pointing out, last year was a bit more prosperous, or anyway a bit less desperate, than the year before. A nice near point of measurement which managed to overlook that for the several years before last the situation of people on the land out here had been godawful. I suppose I ought not to dwell on dollar matters when actually our family was scraping along better than a good many. Even though during the worst years the Forest Service did lay off some people—Hoovered them, the saying went—my father, ranger Varick McCaskill, was never among them. True, his salary was jacked down a couple of times, and Christ only knew if the same wasn't going to start happening again. But we were getting by. Nothing extra, just getting by.

It gravels me every time I read a version of those times that makes it sound as if the Depression set in on the day Wall Street tripped over itself in 1929. Talk about nearsighted. By 1929 Montana already had been on rocky sledding for ten years. The winter of 1919—men my father's age and older still just called it "that sonofabitch of a winter"— was the one that delivered hard times. Wholesale. As Dode Withrow, who had the ranch farthest up the south fork of English Creek, used to tell: "I went into that '19 winter with four thousand head of ewes and by spring they'd evaporated to five hundred." Trouble never travels lonesome, so about that same time livestock and crop prices nosedived because of the end of the war in Europe. And right along with that, drought and grasshoppers showed up to take over the dry-land farming. "It began to be just a hell of a situation," my father always said of those years when he and my mother were trying to get a start in life. "Anyplace you looked you saw people who had put twenty years into this country and all they had to show for it was a pile of old calendars." Then when drought circled back again at the start of the thirties and joined forces with Herbert Hoover, bad progressed to worse. That is within my own remembering, those dry bitter years. Autumn upon autumn the exodus stories kept coming out of the High Line grain country to the north and east of us, and right down here on the highway which runs through the town of Gros Ventre anybody who looked could see for himself the truth of those tales, the furniture-loaded jitney trucks with farewells to Montana painted across their boxboards in big crooked letters: GOODBY OLD DRY and AS FOR HAVRE YOU CAN HAVE 'ER. The Two country did have the saving grace that the price for lambs and wool recovered somewhat while other livestock and crops stayed sunk. But anybody on Two land who didn't scrape through the early thirties with sheep likely didn't scrape through at all. Cattle rancher after cattle rancher and farmer after farmer got in deep with the banks. Gang plow and ditcher, work horses and harness, haymow and cream separator: everything on those places was mortgaged except the air. And then foreclosure, and the auctioneer's hammer. At those hammer sales we saw men weep, women as stricken as if they were looking on death, and their children bewildered.

So it was time hope showed up.

"Jick! Set your mouth for it!"

Supper, and my mother. It is indelible in me that all this began there right at the very outset of June, because I was working over my saddle and lengthening the stirrups again, to account for how much I was growing that year, for the ride up with my father on the counting trip the next morning. I can even safely say what the weather was, one of those brockled late afternoons under the Rockies when tag ends of storm cling in the mountains and sun is reaching through wherever it can between the cloud piles. Tell me why it is that details like that, saddle stirrups a notch longer or sunshine dabbed around on the foothills some certain way, seem to be the allowance of memory while the bigger points of life hang back. At least I have found it so, particularly now that I am at the time where I try to think what my life might have been like had I not been born in the Two Medicine country and into the McCaskill family. Oh, I know what's said. How home ground and kin together lay their touch along us as unalterably as the banks of a stream direct its water. But that doesn't mean you can't wonder. Whether substantially the same person would meet you in the mirror if your birth certificate didn't read as it does. Or whether some other place of growing up might have turned you wiser or dumber, more contented or less. Here in my own instance, some mornings I will catch myself with a full cup of coffee yet in my hand, gone cold while I have sat here stewing about whether my threescore years would be pretty much as they are by now had I happened into existence in, say, China or California instead of northern Montana.

Any of this of course goes against what my mother forever tried to tell the other three of us. That the past is a taker, not a giver. It was a warning she felt she had to put out, in that particular tone of voice with punctuation all through it, fairly often in our family. When we could start hearing her commas and capital letters we knew the topic had become Facing Facts, Not Going Around with Our Heads Stuck in Yesterday. Provocation for it, I will say, came from my father as reliably as a dusk wind out of a canyon. Half a night at a time he might spend listening to Toussaint Rennie tell of the roundup of 1882, when the cowmen fanned their crews north from the elbow of the Teton River to the Canadian line and brought in a hundred thousand head. Or the tale even bigger and earlier than that, the last great buffalo hunt, Toussaint having ridden up into the Sweetgrass Hills to see down onto a prairie that looked burnt, so dark with buffalo, the herd pinned into place by the plains tribes. Strange, but I can still recite the tribes and where they pitched their camps to surround those miles of buffalo, just as Toussaint passed the lore of it to my father: Crows on the southeast, Gros Ventres and Assiniboines on the northeast, Piegans on the west, Crees along the north, and Flatheads here to the south. "Something to see, that must've been," my father would say in his recounting to the rest of us at supper. "Mac, somebody already saw it," my mother would come right back at him. "What you'd better Put Your Mind To is the Forest Supervisor's Visit Tomorrow." Or if she didn't have to work on my father for the moment, there was Alec when he began wearing a neck hanky and considering himself a cowboy. That my own particular knack for remembering, which could tuck away entire grocery lists or whatever someone had told me in innocence a couple of weeks before, made me seem likely to round out a houseful of men tilted to the past must have been the final stem on my mother's load. "Jick," I can hear her yet, "there isn't any law that says a McCaskill can't be as forward-looking as anybody else. Just because your father and your brother—"

Yet I don't know. What we say isn't always what we can do. In the time after, it was her more than anyone who would return and return her thoughts to where all four of our lives made their bend. "The summer when . . ." she would start in, and as if the three-note signal of a chickadee had been sung, it told me she was turning to some happening of that last English Creek summer. She and I are alike at least in that, the understanding that such a season of life provides more than enough to wonder back at, even for a McCaskill.

"JICK! Are you coming, or do the chickens get your share?" I know with all certainty too that that call to supper was double, because I was there at the age where I had to be called twice for anything. Anyway, that second summons of hers brought me out of the barn just as the pair of them, Alec and Leona, topped into view at the eastern rise of the county road. That is, I knew my brother as far as I could see him by that head-up way he rode, as if trying to see beyond a ridge-line in front of him. Leona would need to be somewhat nearer before I could verify her by her blouseful. But those days if you saw Alec you were pretty sure to be seeing Leona too.

Although there were few things more certain to hold my eyes than a rider cresting that rise of road, with all the level eastern horizon under him as if he was traveling out of the sky and then the outline of him and his horse in gait down and down and down the steady slow slant toward the forks of English Creek, I did my watching of Alec and Leona as I crossed the yard to our house behind the ranger station. I knew better than to have my mother call me time number three.

I went on in to wash up and I suppose was a little more deliberately offhand than I had to be by waiting until I'd dippered water into the basin and added hot from the kettle before announcing, "Company."

The word always will draw an audience. My father looked up from where he was going over paperwork about the grazers' permits, and my mother's eyebrows drew into that alignment that let you know you had all of her attention and had better be worth it.

"Alec and Leona," I reported through a face rinse. "Riding like the prettiest one of them gets to kiss the other one."

"You seem to know a remarkable lot about it," my mother said. Actually, that sort of thing was starting to occur to me. I was fourteen and just three months shy of my next birthday. Fourteen, hard on to fifteen, as I once heard one of the beerhounds around the Medicine Lodge saloon in Gros Ventre describe that complicated age. But there wasn't any of this I was about to confide to my mother, who now instructed: "When you're done there you'd better bring in that spare chair from your bedroom." She cast the pots and pans atop the stove a calculating look, then as if having reminded herself turned toward me and added: "Please." When I left the room she already had rattled a fresh stick of wood into the kitchen range and was starting in on whatever it is cooks like her do to connive food for three into a supper for five.

"Remind me in the morning, Bet," I could overhear my father say, "to do the rest of this Uncle Sam paper."

"I'll serve it to you with breakfast," promised my mother.

"Fried," he said. "Done to a cinder would suit me, particularly Van

Bebber's permit. It'd save me arguing the Section Twenty grass with him one goddamn more time."

"You wouldn't know how to begin a summer without that argument with Ed," she answered. "Are you washed?"

By the time I came back into the kitchen with the spare chair which had been serving as my nightstand Alec and Leona were arriving through the doorway, him inquiring "Is this the McCaskill short-order house?" and her beaming up at him as if he'd just recited Shakespeare.

They were a pair to look on, Alec and Leona. By now Alec was even taller than my father, and had the same rich red head of hair; a blood-bay flame which several hundred years of kilts and skirts being flung off must have fanned into creation. Same lively blue eyes. Same straight keen McCaskill nose, and same tendency to freckle across it but nowhere else. Same deep upper lip, with the bottom of the face coming out to meet it in stubborn support; with mouth closed, both Alec and my father had that jaw-forward look which meets life like a plow. Resemblance isn't necessarily duplication, though, and I see in my mind's eye that there also was the message of that as promptly as my brother and my father were in the same room that evening. Where my father never seemed to take up as much space as his size might warrant, Alec somehow took up his share and then some. I noticed this now, how Alec had begun to stand in that shambly wishbone way a cowboy adopts, legs and knees spraddled farther apart than they need to be, as if hinting to the world that he's sure longing for a horse to trot in there between them. Alec was riding for the Double W ranch, his second summer as a hand there, and it had caused some family ruction; his going back to cowboying instead of taking a better-paying job, such as driving a truck for Adam Kerz as my mother particularly suggested. But the past year or so Alec had had to shut off his ears to a lot of opinions my parents held about this cowboy phase of his. Last Fourth of July, when Alec showed up in rodeo clothes which included a red bandanna, my father asked him: "What, is your Adam's apple cold?"

Not that you could ever dent Alec for long. I have told that he had a head-up, nothing-in-life-has-ever-slowed-me-up-yet way of riding. I maybe should amend that to say that on horseback Alec looked as if he was riding the world itself, and even afoot as he was here in the kitchen he seemed as if he was being carried to exactly where he wanted to go. Which, just then, I guess you would have to say he was. Everything was coming up aces for Alec that year. Beating Earl Zane's time with Leona.

Riding for the Double W in a green high-grass summer. And in the fall he would head for Bozeman, the first McCaskill to manage to go to college. Launching Alec to college from the canyon of the Depression was taking a mighty exertion by our whole family, but his knack for numbers plainly justified it; we none of us held a doubt that four years from now he would step out of Bozeman trained in mechanical engineering. Yes, Alec was a doer, as people said of him. My own earliest memory of this brother of mine was the time, I must have been four and him eight, when he took me into the pasture where the ranger station's saddle horses were grazing and said, "Here's how you mooch them, Jick." He eased over to the nearest horse, waited until it put its head down to eat grass, then straddled its neck. When the horse raised its head Alec was lifted, and slid down the neck into place on its back and simultaneously gripped the mane to hang on and steer by. "Now you mooch that mare," Alec called to me and I went beside the big chomping animal and flung my right leg over as he had, and was elevated into being a bareback rider the same as my brother.

"'Lo, Jicker," Alec said across the kitchen to me now after his greeting to my mother and father. "How's the world treating you?"

"Just right," I said back automatically. "'Lo, Leona."

Leona too was a horseperson, I guess you'd call it these days. When Tollie Zane held his auction of fresh-broke saddle horses in Gros Ventre every year he always enlisted Leona to ride them into the auction ring because there is nothing that enhances a saddle pony more than a good-looking girl up there on his back. Right now, though, as she entered my mother's kitchen Leona's role was to be milk and honey. Which she also was first-rate at. A kind of pause stepped in with Leona whenever she arrived somewhere, a long breath or two or maybe even three during which everyone seemed to weigh whether her hair could really be so gold, whether her figure actually lived up to all it advertised on first glance. I managed to notice once that her chin was pointier than I like, but by the time any male looked Leona over enough to reach that site, he was prepared to discount that and a lot more.

Anyhow, there in the kitchen we went through that pause period of letting Leona's looks bask over us all, and on into some nickel and dime gab between Alec and my father—

"Working hard?"

"Well, sure, Dad. Ever see me do anything different?"

"Just times I've seen you hardly working."

"The Double W makes sure against that. Y'know what they say. Nobody on the Double W ever gets a sunburn, we don't have time."

—and an old-as-womankind kitchen ritual between Leona and my mother—

"Can I help with anything, Mrs. McCaskill?"

"No, probably it's beyond help."

—until shortly my mother was satisfied that she had multiplied the food on the stove sufficiently and announced: "I expect you brought your appetites with you? Let's sit up."

I suppose every household needs some habited way to begin a meal. I have heard the Lord thanked in some of the unlikeliest of homes, and for some of the unholiest of food. And seen whole families not lift a fork until the patriarch at the head of the table had his plate full and his bread buttered. Ours, though, said grace only once every three hundred sixty-five days, and that one a joke—my father's New Year's Eve invocation in that Scotch-preacher burr he could put on: "We ask ye on this Hogmanay, gi' us a new yearrr o' white brread and nane o' yourrr grray."

Other than that, a McCaskill meal started at random, the only tradition to help yourself to what was closest and pass the food on clockwise.

"How's cow chousing?" My father was handing the mashed potatoes to Leona, but looking across at Alec.

"It's all right." Alec meanwhile was presenting the gravy to Leona, before he realized she didn't yet have spuds on her plate. He colored a little, but notched out his jaw and then asked back: "How's rangering?"

When my father was a boy a stick of kindling flew up from the ax and struck the corner of his left eye. The vision was saved, but ever after that eyelid would droop to about half shut whenever amusement made him squint a little. It descended now as he studied the meal traffic piling up around Leona. Then he made his reply to Alec: "It's all right."

I had the bright idea this conversation could benefit from my help, so I chimed in: "Counting starts tomorrow, Alec. Dode's sheep, and then Walter Kyle's, and then Fritz Hahn's. Dad and I'll be up there a couple, three days. Remember that time you and I were along with him and Fritz's herder's dog Moxie got after a skunk and we both—"

Alec gave me a grin that was tighter than it ought to have been from a brother. "Don't let all those sheep put you to sleep, sprout."

Sprout? Evidently there was no telling what might issue from a person's mouth when he had a blond girl to show off in front of, and the look I sent Alec told him so.

"Speaking of counting," Alec came up with next, "you got your beavers counted yet?" Here he was giving my father a little static. Every so often the Forest Service regional headquarters in Missoula—"Mazoola," all of us pronounced it my father's way, "emphasis on the zoo"—invented some new project for rangers to cope with, and the latest one we had been hearing about from my father was the inventory he was supposed to take of the beaver population on the national forest portion of English Creek. "Christamighty," he had grumped, "this creek is the beaver version of New York City."

Now, though, with Leona on hand—this was the first time Alec had brought her out for a meal; the rest of us in the family recognized it as an early phase, a sort of curtain-raiser, in the Alec style of courting—my father just passed off the beaver census with: "No, I'm waiting for policy guidance from the Mazoola inmates. They might want me to count only the tails and then multiply by one, you never know."

Alec didn't let it go, though. "Maybe if they like your beaver arithmetic, next summer they'll have you do fish."

"Maybe." My father was giving Alec more prancing room than he deserved, but I guess Leona justified it.

"Who's this week's cook at the Double W?" My mother, here. "Leona, take some more ham and pass it on to Jick. He goes through food like a one-man army these days." I might have protested that too if my plate hadn't been nearly empty, particularly of fried ham.

"A Mrs. Pennyman," Alec reported. "From over around Havre."

"By now it's Havre, is it. If Wendell Williamson keeps on, he'll have hired and fired every cook between here and Chicago." My mother paused for Alec's response to that, and got none. "So?" she prompted. "How does she feed?"

"It's—filling." The question seemed to put Alec a little off balance, and I noticed Leona provide him a little extra wattage in her next gaze at him.

"So is sawdust," said my mother, plainly awaiting considerably more report.

"Yeah, well," Alec fumbled. I was beginning to wonder whether cowboying had dimmed his wits, maybe driven his backbone up through the judgment part of his brain. "You know. It's usual ranch grub." He sought down into his plate for further description and finally proclaimed again: "Filling, is what I'd call it."

"How's the buttermilk business?" my father asked Leona, I suppose to steer matters off Alec's circular track. Her parents, the Tracys, ran the creamery in Gros Ventre.

"Just fine," Leona responded along with her flash of smile. She seemed to be on the brink of saying a lot more, but then just passed that smile around to the rest of us, a full share to my father and another to my mother and then one to me that made my throat tighten a little, then letting it rest last and coziest on Alec. She had a natural ability at that, producing some pleasantry and then lighting up the room so you thought the remark amounted to a whole hell of a lot more than it did. I do envy that knack in a person, though likely wouldn't have the patience to use it myself even if I had it.

We still were getting used to the idea of Leona, the three of us in the family besides Alec. His girls before her were from the ranch families in here under the mountains or from the farm folks east of Gros Ventre. Nor was Leona in circulation at all for the past few years, going with Tollie Zane's son Earl as she had been. But this past spring, Alec's last in high school and Leona's next-to-last, he somehow cut Earl Zane out of the picture. "Swap one cowboy for another, she might as well have stayed put," my mother said at the time, a bit perturbed with Alec anyway about his intention for the Double W summer job again.

—"All right, I guess," Alec was answering profoundly to some question of my father's about how successful the Double W's calving season had turned out.

How's this, how's that, fine, all right, you bet. If this was the level of sociability that was going to go on, I intended to damn promptly excuse myself to get back to working on my saddle, the scenic attractions of Leona notwithstanding. But then just as I was trying to estimate ahead to whether an early piece of butterscotch meringue pie could be coaxed from my mother or I'd do better to wait until later, Alec all at once put down his fork and came right out with:

"We got something to tell you. We're going to get married."

This kicked the conversation in the head entirely.

My father seemed to have forgotten about the mouthful of coffee he'd just drunk, while my mother looked as if Alec had announced he intended to take a pee in the middle of the table. Alec was trying to watch both of them at once, and Leona was favoring us all with one of her searchlight smiles.

"How come?"

Even yet I don't know why I said that. I mean, I was plenty old enough to know why people got married. There were times recently, seeing Alec and Leona mooning around together, when I seemed to savvy more than I actually had facts about, if that's possible.

Focused as he was on how our parents were going to respond, the philosophy question from my side of the table jangled Alec. "Because, because we're—we love each other, why the hell do you think?"

"Kind of soon in life to be so certain on that, isn't it?" suggested my father.

"We're old enough," Alec shot back. And meanwhile gave me a snake-killing look as if I was going to ask old enough for what, but I honestly didn't intend to.

"When's all this taking place?" my father got out next.

"This fall." Alec looked ready to say more, then held on to it, finally just delivered it in one dump: "Wendell Williamson'll let us have the house on the Nansen place to live in."

It was up to my mother to cleave matters entirely open. "You're saying you'll stay on at the Double W this fall?"

"Yeah," Alec said as if taking a vow. "It's what I want to do."

The unsaid part of this was huge, huger than anything I had ever felt come into our kitchen before. The financing to send Alec to Bozeman my parents had been gathering like quilt pieces: whatever savings the household managed to pinch aside, plus a loan from my mother's brother Pete Reese, plus a part-time job which my father had set up for Alec with a range-management professor at the college who knew us from having spent time up here studying the Two, plus of course Alec's own wages from this summer, which was another reason why his choice of the Double W riding job at thirty dollars a month again was less than popular—Christ-amighty, since my own haying wages later this summer would go into the general household kitty, even I felt I had a stake in the Bozeman plan. And now here was Alec choosing against college. Against all the expectation riding on him. Against—

"Alec, you will End Up as Nothing More Than a Gimped-Up Saddle Stiff, and I for one Will Not—"

More out of samaritan instinct than good sense my father headed my mother off with a next query to Alec: "How you going to support yourselves on a cow chouser's wages?"

"You two did, at first."

"We starved out at it, too."

"We ain't going to starve out." Alec's grammar seemed to be cow-boyifying, too. "Wendell'll let me draw ahead on my wages for a few heifers this fall, and winter them with the rest of the outfit's. It'll give us our start."

My father finally thought to set down his coffee cup. "Alec, let's keep our shirts on here"—language can be odd; I had the vision just then of us all sitting around the table with our shirts off, Leona across from me in full double-barreled display—"and try see what's what."

"I don't see there's any what's what about it," Alec declared. "People get married every day."

"So does the sun rise," my mother told him, "without particular participation by you."

"Mom, now damn it, listen—"

"We all better listen," my father tried again. "Leona, we got nothing against you. You know that." Which was a bit short of true in both its parts, and Leona responded with a lower beam of smile. "It's just that, Godamighty, Alec, cattle have gone bust time after time these last years. That way of life just has changed. Even the Double W would be on hard times if Wendell Williamson's daddy hadn't left him such deep pockets. Whether anybody'll ever be able to start off from scratch in the cow business and make a go of it, I don't see how."

Alec was like any of us, he resisted having an idea pulled from under him. "Rather have me running sheep up on one of your allotments, is that it? There'd be something substantial to look forward to, I suppose you think, sheepherding."

My father seemed to consider. "No, most probably not, in your case. It takes a trace of common sense to herd sheep." He said it lightly enough that Alec would have to take it as a joke, but there was a pok-ing edge to the lightness. "Alec, I just think that whatever the hell you do, you need to bring an education to it these days. That old stuff of banging a living out of this country by sheer force of behavior doesn't work. Hasn't for almost twenty years. This country can outbang any man. Look at them along the creek here, even these sheepmen. Hahn, Ed Van Bebber, Pres Rozier, the Busbys, Dode Withrow, Finletter, Hill. They've all just managed to hang on, and they're as good a set of stock-men as you'll find in the whole goddamn state of Montana. You think any of them could have got under way, in years like there've been?"

"Last year was better than the one before," Alec defended with that litany of the local optimists. "This one looks better yet."

I saw my father glance at my mother, to see if she wanted to swat down this part of Alec's argument or whether he should go ahead. Even I could tell from the held-in look of her that once she got started there'd be no stopping, so he soldiered on. "And if about five more come good back to back, everybody'll be almost to where they were fifteen or twenty years ago. Alec, trying to build a living on a few head of stock is a dead end these days."

"Dad—Dad, listen. We ain't starting from fifteen or twenty years ago. We're starting from now, and we got to go by that, not whatever the hell happened to—to anybody else."

"You'll be starting in a hole," my father warned. "And an everlasting climb out."

I say warned. What rang through to me was an alarm different from the one in my father's words; an iron tone of anger such as I had never heard out of him before.

"That's as maybe." Alec's timbre was an echo of the anger, the iron. "But we got to start." Now Alec was looking at Leona as if he was storing up for the next thousand years. "And we're going to do it married. Not going to wait our life away."

If I ever get old enough to have brains, I will work on the question of man and woman.

All those years ago, the topic rode with me into the next morning as my father and I set off from the ranger station toward the mountains. Cool but cloudless, the day was a decent enough one, except for wind. I ought to have been in a topnotch mood, elevated by the anticipation that always began with my father's annual words, "Put on your mountain clothes in the morning."

Going along on one of these start-of-June rides with my father as he took a count of the sheep summering on the various ranchers' range allotments in the national forest was one of the awaited episodes of life. Better country to look ahead to could not be asked for. Kootenai, Lolo, Flathead, Absaroka, Bitterroot, Beaverhead, Deerlodge, Gallatin, Cabinet, Helena, Lewis and Clark, Custer, Two Medicine—those were the national forests of Montana, totaling dozens of ranger districts, but to our estimation the Two Medicine was head and shoulders above the other forests, and my father's English Creek district the topknot of the Two. Anybody with eyes could see this at once, for our ride this morning led up the North Fork of English Creek, which actually angles mostly west and northwest to thread between Roman Reef and Rooster Mountain to its source, and where the coulee of the North Fork opened ahead of us, there the first summits of the Rockies sat on the horizon like stupendous sharp boulders. Only when our first hour or so of riding carried us above that west edge of the coulee would we see the mountains in total, their broad bases of timber and rockfall gripping into the foothills. And the reefs. Roman Reef ahead of us, a rimrock half a mile high and more than three long. Grizzly Reef even bigger to the south of it, smaller Jericho Reef to the north. I don't know, are mountain reefs general knowledge in the world? I suppose they get their name because they stand as outcroppings do at the edge of an ocean, steady level ridges of stone, as if to give a calm example to the waves beyond them. Except that in this case the blue-gray billow up there is not waves but the Continental Divide against the sky. The name aside, though, sections of a fortress wall were what the three reefs reminded me of, spaced as they were with canyons between them and the higher jagged crags penned up behind. As if the whole horizon of the west had once been barricaded with slabs of rock and these were the mighty traces still standing. I must not have been the only onlooker this occurred to, as an even longer barrier of cliff farther south in the national forest was named the Chinese Wall.

The skyline of the Two. Even here at the outset the hover of it all always caused my father to turn and appreciatively call over his shoulder to Alec and me something like "Nothing the matter with that." And always Alec and I would chorus "Not one thing" both because we were expected to and because we too savored those waiting mountains.

Always was not in operation this year, however. My father did not pause to pronounce on the scenery, I had no chance to echo him, and Alec—Alec this year was on our minds instead of riding between us.

So our first stint on the road up the North Fork was broken only by the sound of our horses' hooves or one or the other of us muttering a horse name and urging a little more step-along in the pace. Even those blurts of sound were pretty pallid, because where horse nomenclature was concerned my father's imagination took a vacation. A black horse he invariably named Coaly, a white one always Snowball. Currently he was riding a big mouse-colored gelding who, depend on it, bore the title of Mouse. I was on a short-legged mare called Pony. Frankly, high among my hopes about the business of growing up was that I would get a considerably more substantial horse out of it. If and when I did, I vowed to give the creature as much name as it could carry, such as Rimfire or Chief Joseph or Calabash.

Whether I was sorting through my horse hopes or the outset of this counting trip without Alec weighed more heavily on me than I realized, I don't know. But in either case I was so deep into myself that I was surprised to glance ahead and learn that Mouse and my father were halted, and my father was gandering back to see what had become of me.

I rode on up and found that we had arrived to where a set of rutted tracks—in flattery, it could have been called almost a road—left the North Fork roadbed and crossed the coulee and creek and traced on up the side of Breed Butte to where a few log buildings could be seen.

Normally I would have been met with some joke from my father about sunburning my eyeballs if I went around asleep with my eyes open like that. But this day he was looking businesslike, which was the way he looked only when he couldn't find any better mood. "How about you taking a squint at Walter's place," he proposed. "You can cut around the butte and meet me at the road into the Hebner tribe."

"All right," I of course agreed and turned Pony to follow the ruts down and across the North Fork swale. Walter Kyle always summered in the mountains as herder of his own sheep, and so my father whenever he rode past veered in to see that everything was okay at the empty ranch. This was the first time he had delegated me, which verified just how much his mind was burdened—also with that question of man and woman? at least as it pertained to Alec McCaskill and Leona Tracy?—and that he wanted to saunter alone awhile as he sorted through it all.

As soon as my father had gone his way and I was starting up Breed Butte, I turned myself west in my saddle to face Roman Reef, tapped the brim of my hat in greeting, and spoke in the slow and distinct way you talk to a deaf person: "'Lo, Walter. How's everything up on the reef?"

What was involved here was that from Walter Kyle's summer range up there in the mountains, on top of Roman Reef a good five miles from where I was, his actual house and outbuildings here on Breed Butte could be seen through Walter's spyglass. Tiny, but seen. Walter had shown Alec and me this stunt of vision when we took some mail up to him during last year's counting trip. "There ye go," he congratulated as each of us in turn managed to extend the telescope tube just so and sight the building specks. "Ye can see for as long as your eye holds out, in this country." Walter's enthusiasm for the Two was that of a person newly smitten, for although he was the most elderly of all the English Creek ranchers—at the time he seemed to me downright ancient, I suppose partly because he was one of those dried-up little guys who look eternal—he also was much the most recent to the area. Only three or four years ago Walter had moved here from down in the Ingomar country in the southeastern part of the state, where he ran several bands of sheep. I have never heard of a setup like it before or since, but Walter and a number of other Scotch sheepmen, dedicated bachelors all, lived there in the hotel in Ingomar and operated their sheep outfits out of their back pocket and hat, you might say. Not one of them possessed a real ranch, just grazing land they'd finagled one way or another, plus wagons for their herders, and of course sheep and more sheep. Away each of those old Scotchies would go once a week, out from that hotel with boxes of groceries in the back of a Model T to tend camp. For whatever reason, Walter pulled out of hotel sheep tycooning—my father speculated that one morning he turned to the Scotchman beside him at the table and burred, "Jock, for thirrty yearrs ye've been eating yourrr oatmeal aye too loud," got up, and left for good—and bought the old Barclay place here on Breed Butte for next to nothing.

Pony was trudging up the butte in her steady uninspired way, and I had nothing to do but continue my long-distance conversation with Walter. Not that I figured there was any real chance that Walter would be studying down here exactly then, and even if he was I would be only a gnat in the spyglass lens and certainly not a conversationalist on whom he could perform any lip reading. But I went ahead and queried in the direction of the distant reef: "Walter, how the hell do people get so crosswise with one another?"

For last night's rumpus continued to bedevil me from whatever angle I could find to view it. The slant at which Alec and my parents suddenly were diverging from each other, first of all. In hindsight it may not seem such an earthquake of an issue, whether Alec was going to choose college or the wedding band/riding job combination. But hindsight is always through bifocals; it peers specifically instead of seeing whole. And the entirety here was that my father and my mother rested great hopes on my brother, especially given all that they and others of their generation had endured in the years past, the Depression years they had gotten through by constantly saying within themselves "Our children will know better times. They've got to." Hopes of that sort only parents can know. That Alec seemed not to want to step up in life, now that the chance at last was here, went against my parents' thinking as much as if he'd declared he was going to go out on the prairie and dig a hole and live a gopher's existence.

Walter Kyle had seen a lot of life; his mustache, which must have been sandy in his youth, now was as yellow-white as if he'd been drinking cream from a jar. "What about that, Walter? From your experience, has Alec gone as goofy as my folks think?" And got back instead of Walter's long Scotch view of life my father's briefer Scotch one, his last night's reasoning to Alec: "Why not give college a year and then see? You got the ability, it's a crime not to use it. And Bozeman isn't the moon. You'll be back and forth some times during the year. The two of you can see how the marriage notion holds up after that." But Alec wasn't about to have time bought from him. "We're not waiting our life away," ran his constant response. "Our life": that convergence of Alec and Leona and the headlong enthusiasm which none of the rest of us had quite realized they were bringing to their romance. Well, it will happen. Two people who have been around each other for years and all of a sudden find that nobody else in history has ever been in love before, they're inventing it themselves. Yet apply my mind to it in all the ways I could, my actual grasp of their mood wasn't firm, for to me then marriage seemed about as distant as death. Nor did I understand much more about the angle of Leona and—I was going to say, of Leona and my parents, but actually of Leona and the other three of us, as I somehow did feel included into the bask she aimed around our kitchen. Leona, Leona. "Now there is a topic I could really stand to talk to you about, Walter." Yet maybe a bachelor was not the soundest source either. Perhaps old Walter Kyle knew only enough about women, as the saying goes, to stay immune. Anyhow, with all care and good will I was trying to think through our family situation in a straight line, but Leona brought me to a blind curve. Not nearly the least of last evening's marvels was how much ground Leona had been able to hold with only a couple of honest-to-goodness sentences. When my father and mother were trying to argue delay into Alec and turned to her to test the result, she said just "We think we're ready enough." And then at the end of the fracas, going out the door Leona turned to bestow my mother one of her sunburst smiles and say, "Thank you for supper, Beth." And my mother saying back, just as literally, "Don't mention it."

The final line of thought from last night was the most disturbing of all. The breakage between my father and Alec. This one bothered me so much I couldn't even pretend to be confiding it to Walter up there on Roman Reef. Stony silence from that source was more than I could stand on this one. For if I'd had to forecast, say at about the point Alec was announcing marriage intentions, my mother was the natural choice to bring the house down on him. That would have been expected. It was her way. And she of course did make herself more than amply known on the college/marriage score. But the finale of that suppertime was all-male McCaskill: "You're done running my life," flung by Alec as he stomped out with Leona in tow, and "Nobody's running it, including you," from my father to Alec's departing back.

Done running my life. Nobody's running it, including you. Put that way, the words without the emotion, it may sound like something concluding itself; the moment of an argument breaking off into silence, a point at which contention has been expended. But I know now, and I somehow knew even then, that the fracture of a family is not a thing that happens clean and sharp, so that you at least can calculate that from here on it will begin to be over with. No, it is like one of those worst bone breaks, a shatter. You can mend the place, peg it and splint it and work to strengthen it, and while the surface maybe can be brought to look much as it did before, the deeper vicinity of shatter always remains a spot that has to be favored.

So if I didn't grasp much of what abruptly was happening within our family, I at least held the realization that last night's rift was nowhere near over.

Thinking heavily that way somehow speeds up time, and before I quite knew it Pony was stopping at the barbwire gate into Walter Kyle's yard. I tied her to the fence on a long rein so she could graze a little and slid myself between the top and second strands.

Walter's place looked hunky-dory. But I did a circle of the tool shed and low log barn and the three-quarter shed sheltering Walter's old Reo Flying Cloud coupe, just to be sure, and then went to the front of the house and took out the key from behind the loose piece of chinking which hid it.

The house too was undisturbed. Not that there was all that much in it to invite disturbance. The sparse habits of hotel living apparently still were in Walter. Besides the furniture—damn little of that beyond the kitchen table and its chairs of several stiff-back varieties—and the open shelves of provisions and cookery, the only touches of habitation were a drugstore calendar, and a series of coats hung on nails, and one framed studio photograph of a young, young Walter in a tunic and a fur cap: after Scotland and before Montana, he had been a Mountie for a few years up in Alberta.

All in all, except for the stale feel that unlived-in rooms give off, Walter might just have stepped out to go down there on the North Fork and fish a beaver dam. A good glance around was all the place required. Yet I stood and inventoried for some minutes. I don't know why, but an empty house holds me. As if it was an opened book about the person living there. Peruse this log-and-chinking room and Walter Kyle could be read as thrifty, tidy to the verge of fussy, and alone.

At last, just to stir the air in the place with some words, I said aloud the conclusion of my one-way conversation with the mustached little sheepman up on the Reef: "Walter, you'd have made somebody a good wife."

Pony and I now cut west along the flank of Breed Butte, which would angle us through Walter's field to where we would rejoin the North Fork road and my father. Up here above the North Fork coulee the outlook roughened, the mountains now in full rumpled view and the foothills bumping up below them and Roman Reef making its wide stockade of bare stone between the two. On this part of our route the land steadily grew more beautiful, which in Montana also means more hostile to settlement. From where I rode along this high ground, Walter Kyle's was the lone surviving ranch to be looked back on between here and the English Creek ranger station.

The wind seemed to think that was one too many, for it had come up from the west and was pummeling everything on Walter's property, including me. I rode now holding on to my hat with one hand lest it skitter down to the North Fork and set sail for St. Louis. Of all of the number of matters about the Two country that I never have nor will be able to savvy—one life is not nearly enough to do so—a main one is why in a landscape with hills and buttes and benchlands everywhere a person is so seldom sheltered from the everlasting damn wind. I mean, having the wind of the Two forever trying to blow harmonica tunes through your rib cage just naturally wears on the nerves.

The Two, I have been saying. I ought to clarify that to us the term meant both the landscape to all the horizons around—that is pretty much what a Montanan means by a "country"—and the national forest that my father's district was part of. In those days the six hundred square miles of the Two Medicine National Forest were divvied into only three ranger districts: English Creek; Indian Head, west of Choteau; and Blacktail Gulch, down by Sun River at the south end of the forest. Actually only my father's northmost portion of the Two Medicine National Forest had anything at all to do with the Two Medicine River or Two Medicine Lake: the vicinity where the forest joins onto the south boundary of Glacier National Park and fits in there, as a map shows it, like a long straight-sided peninsula between the park and the Continental Divide and the Blackfeet Indian Reservation. So the Two Medicine itself, the river that is, honestly is in sight to hardly any of the Two country. Like all the major flows of this region the river has its source up in the Rockies, but then the Two Medicine promptly cuts a sizable canyon east through the plains as it pushes to meet the Marias River and eventually the Missouri. Burrows its way through the prairie, you might almost say. It is just the ring of the words, Two Medicine, that has carried the name all the way south along the mountains some thirty miles to our English Creek area. The derivation as I've heard it is that in distant times the Blackfeet built their medicine lodge, their place for sacred ceremony, two years in a row at a favorite spot on the river where buffalo could be stampeded over nearby cliffs, and the name lasted from that pair of lodges. By whatever way Two Medicine came to be, it is an interesting piece of language, I have always thought.

My father was waiting at another rutty offshoot from the North Fork road. This one had so many cuts of track, some of them dating from the era of wagon wheels, that it looked like a kind of huge braid across the grassland. My father turned his gaze from the twined ruts to me and asked: "Everything under control at Walter's?"

"Uh huh," I affirmed.

"All right." His businesslike expression had declined into what I think is called dolor. "Let's go do it." And we set off into the weave of tracks toward the Hebner place.

—

No matter what time of day you approached it, the Hebner place looked as if demolition was being done and the demolishers were just now taking a smoke break. An armada of abandoned wagons and car chassis and decrepit farm equipment—even though Good Help Hebner farmed not so much as a vegetable garden—lay around and between the brown old buildings. A root cellar was caved in, a tool shop had only half a roof left, the barn looked distinctly teetery. In short, not much ever functioned on the Hebner place except gravity.

Out front of the barn now as we rode in stood a resigned-looking bay mare with two of the littler Hebner boys astraddle her swayed back. The pair on the horse must have been Roy and Will, or possibly Will and Enoch, or maybe even Enoch and Curtis. So frequent a bunch were they, there was no keeping track of which size Hebner boy was who unless you were around them every day.

I take that back. Even seeing them on a constant basis wouldn't necessarily have been a foolproof guide to who was who, because all the faces in that Hebner family rhymed. I don't know how else to put it. Every Hebner forehead was a copy of Good Help's wide crimped-in-the-middle version, a pale bony expanse centered with a kind of tiny gully which widened as it went down, as if the nose had avalanched out of there. Across most of the left side of this divided forehead a hank of hair flopped at a crooked angle. The effect was as if every male Hebner wore one of those eye patches shown in pictures of pirates, only pushed up higher. Then from that forehead any Hebner face simply sort of dwindled down, a quick skid of nose and a tight mouth and a small ball of chin.

The tandem horsebackers stared us the length of the yard. It was another Hebner quality to gawp at you as if you were some new species on earth. My father had a not entirely ironic theory to explain that: "They've all eaten so goddamn much venison their eyes have grown big as deers'." For it was a fact of life that somewhere up there in the jackpines beyond the Hebner buildings would be a woolsack hanging from a top limb. The bottom of the sack would rest in a washtub of water, and within the sack, being cooled nicely by the moisture as it went wicking up through the burlap, would be a hindquarter or two of venison. Good Help Hebner liked his deer the same way he preferred his eggs—poached.

"Actually, I don't mind Good Help snitching a deer every so often," my father put it. "Those kids have got to eat. But when the lazy SOB starts in on that goddamn oughtobiography of his—how he ought to have been this, ought to have done that—"

"Morning, Ranger! Hello there, Jick!"

I don't know about my father, but that out-of-nowhere gust of words startled me just a little. The greeting hadn't issued from the staring boys on the mare but from behind the screen door of the log house. "Ought to have been paying attention to the world so I'd seen you coming and got some coffee going."

"Thanks anyway, Garland," said my father, who had heard years of Good Help Hebner protocol and never yet seen a cup of coffee out of any of it. "We're just dropping off some baking Beth came out long on."

"We'll do what we can to put it to good—" Commotion in front of the barn interrupted the voice of Good Help. The front boy atop the old horse was whacking her alongside the neck with the reins while the boy behind him was kicking the mount heartily in the ribs and piping, "Giddyup, goddamn you horse, giddyup!"

"Giddyup, hell!" Good Help's yell exploded across the yard. It was always said of him that Good Help could talk at a volume which would blow a crowbar out of your hand. "The pair of you giddy off and giddy over to that goshdamn woodpile!"

We all watched for the effect of this on the would-be jockeys, and when there was none except increased exertion on the dilapidated mare, Good Help addressed my father through the screen door again: "Ought to have taken that pair out and drowned them with the last batch of kittens, way they behave. I don't know what's got into kids any more."

With the profundity of that, Good Help materialized from behind the screening and out onto the decaying railroad tie which served as the front step to the Hebner house. Like his place, Good Help Hebner himself was more than a little ramshackle. A tall yet potbellied man with one bib of his overalls usually frayed loose and dangling, his sloping face made even more pale by a gray-white chevron of grizzle which mysteriously never matured into a real mustache. Garland Hebner: nicknamed Good Help ever since the time, years back, when he volunteered to join the Noon Creek cattlemen when they branded their calves and thereby get in on a free supper afterward. In Dill Egan's round corral, the branding crew at one point looked up to see Hebner, for no reason that ever became clear, hoisting himself onto Dill's skittish iron-gray stud. Almost before Hebner was truly aboard, the gray slung him off and then tried to pound him apart while everybody else bailed out of the corral. Hebner proved to be a moving target; time and again the hooves of the outraged horse missed the rolling ball of man, until finally Dill managed to reach in, grab hold of a Hebner ankle, and snake him out under the corral poles. Hebner wobbled up, blinked around at the crowd, then sent his gaze on to the sky and declared as if piety was natural to him: "Well, I had some Good Help getting out of that, didn't I?"

Some extra stickum was added to the nickname, of course, by the fact that Good Help had never been found to be of any use whatsoever on any task anybody had been able to think up for him. "He has a pernicious case of the slows," Dode Withrow reported after he once made the error of hiring Good Help for a few days of fencing haystacks.

"Ranger, I been meaning to ask if it mightn't be possible to cut a few poles to fix that corral up with," Good Help was blaring now. The Hebner corral looked as if a buffalo stampede had passed through it, and translated out of Hebnerese, Good Help's question was whether he could help himself to some national forest pine without paying for it. "Ought to have got at it before now, but my back . . ."

His allergy to work was the one characteristic in which the rest of the family did not emulate Good Help. They didn't dare. Survival depended on whatever wages the squadron of Hebner kids could earn by hiring out at lambing time or through haying season. Then at some point in their late teens each Hebner youngster somehow would come up with a more serious job and use it as an escape ladder out of that family.

Alec and I had accidentally been witnesses to the departure of Sanford, the second oldest Hebner boy. It occurred a couple of springs before when Ed Van Bebber came by the ranger station one Friday night and asked if Alec and I could help out with the lambing chores that weekend. Neither of us much wanted to do it, because Ed Van Bebber is nobody's favorite person except Ed Van Bebber's. But you can't turn down a person who's in a pinch, either. When the pair of us rode into Ed's place early the next morning we saw that Sanford Hebner was driving the gutwagon, even though he was only seventeen or so, not all that much older than Alec at the time. And that lambing season at Van Bebber's had been a rugged one; the hay was used up getting through the winter and the ewes thin as shadows and not particularly ready to become mothers. Ed had thrown the drop band clear up onto the south side of Wolf Butte to provide any grass for them at all, which meant a tough mile and a half drive for Sanford to the lambing shed with each gutwagon load of ewes and their fresh lambs, and a played-out team of horses by the time he got there. With the ewes dropping eighty and ninety lambs a day out there and the need to harness new horses for every trip, Sanford was performing about two men's work and doing it damn well. The day this happened, dark had almost fallen, Alec and I were up on the hillside above the lambing shed helping Ed corral a bunch of mother ewes and their week-old lambs, and we meanwhile could see Sanford driving in with his last load of lambs of the day. We actually had our bunch under control just fine, the three of us and a dog or two. But Ed always had to have a tendency toward hurry. So he cupped his hands to his mouth and yelled down the hill:

"HEY THERE YOU HEBNER! COME UP HERE AND HELP US CORRAL THESE EWES AND LAMBS!"

I still think if Ed had asked properly Sanford probably would have been fool enough to have climbed up and joined us, even though he already had put in his workday and then some. But after the season of man's labor he had done, to be yelled at to come up and help a couple of milk-tooth kids like us chase lambs: worse than that, to not be awarded even his first name, just be shouted to the world as a Hebner—I still can see Sanford perched on the seat of that gutwagon, looking up the slope to us, and then cupping his hands to his mouth the same way Ed had, and hear yet his words carry up the hill:

"YOU GO PLUMB TO HELL YOU OLD SON OF A BITCH!"

And he slapped his reins on the rumps of the gutwagon team and drove on to the lambing shed. At the supper table that night, Sanford's check was in his plate.

Sanford and that money, though, did not travel back up the North Fork to this Hebner household. When Alec and I headed home that night Sanford rode double behind me, and when we dismounted at the ranger station he trudged into the dark straight down the English Creek road, asking at every ranch on the way whether a job of any sort could be had. "Anything. I'll clean the chicken house." The Busby brothers happened to need a bunch herder, and Sanford had been with them ever since; this very moment, was herding one of their bands of sheep up in the mountains of the Two. To me, the realization of Sanford's situation that evening when Ed Van Bebber canned him, Sanford knocking at any door rather than return home, having a family, a father that he would even clean chicken houses to be free of; to me, the news that life could deal such a hell of a situation to someone about the age of Alec and me came as a sobering gospel.

"Missus!" Having failed to cajole my father out of free timber, Good Help evidently had decided to settle for the manna we'd come to deliver. "Got something out here."

The screen door opened and closed again, producing Florene Hebner and leaving a couple of the very littlest Hebners—Garlena and Jonas? Jonas and Maybella?—gawping behind the mesh. Since the baked goods were tied in a dish towel on my saddle, I did the courteous thing and got off and took the bundle up to Florene. Florene was, or had been, a fairly good-looking woman, particularly among a family population minted with the face of Good Help. But what was most immediately noticeable about her was how worn she looked. As if she'd been sanded down repeatedly. You'd never have guessed the fact by comparing the two, but Florene and my mother went through grade school at Noon Creek together. Florene, though, never made it beyond the second year of high school in Gros Ventre because she already had met Garland Hebner and promptly was pregnant by him and, a little less promptly on Garland's part, was married to him.

She gave a small downcast smile as I handed her the bundle, said to me, "Thank your ma again, Jick," and retreated back inside.

"Funny to see Alec not with you," Good Help was declaiming to my father as I returned from the doorway to Pony. "But they do grow and go."

"So they do," my father agreed without enthusiasm. "Garland, we got sheep waiting for us up the mountain. You ready, Jick?" My father touched Mouse into motion, then uttered to Good Help in parting, purely poker-faced: "Take it easy."

The route we rode out of the Hebner place was a sort of topsy-turvy L, the long climbing stem of ruts and then the brief northwestward leg of the North Fork trail where it tops onto the English Creek–Noon Creek divide. Coming onto that crest, we now would be in view of the landmarks that are the familiar sentries of the Two country. Chief Mountain; even though it is a full seventy miles to the north and almost into

Canada, standing distinct as a mooring peg at the end of the long chain of mountains. Also north but nearer, Heart Butte; no great piece of geography, yet it too poses separate enough from the mountain horizon that its dark pyramid form can be constantly seen and identified. And just to our east the full timber-topped profile of Breed Butte, a junior landmark but plainly enough the summit of our English Creek area.

With all this offered into sight I nonetheless kept my eyes on my father, watching for what I knew would happen, what always happened after he paid a visit to the Hebner place.

There at the top of the rise he halted his horse, and instead of giving his regard to the distant wonders of Chief Mountain and Heart Butte, he turned for a last slow look at the Hebner hodgepodge. Then shook his head, said, "Jesus H. Christ," and reined away. For in that woebegone log house down there, and amid those buildings before neglect had done its handiwork on them, my father was born and brought up.

Of course then the place was the McCaskill homestead. And the North Fork known by the nickname of Scotch Heaven on account of the several burr-on-the-tongue-and-thistle-up-the-kilt families who had come over and settled. Duffs, Barclays, Frews, Findlaters, Erskines, and my McCaskill grandparents, they lit in here sometime in the 1880s and all were dead or defeated or departed by the time the flu epidemic of 1918 and the winter of '19 got done with them. I possessed no first-hand information on my father's parents. Both of them were under the North Fork soil by the time I was born. And despite my father's ear to the past, there did not seem to be anything known or at least fit to report about what the McCaskills came from in Scotland. Except for a single scrap of lore: the story that a McCaskill had been one of the stonemasons of Arbroath who worked for the Stevensons—as I savvy it, the Stevensons must have been a family of engineers before Robert Louis cropped into the lineage and picked up a pen—when they were putting the lighthouses all around the coast of Scotland. The thought that an ancestor of ours helped fight the sea with stone meant more to my father than he liked to let on. As far as I know, the only halfway sizable body of water my father himself had ever seen was Flathead Lake right here in Montana, let alone an ocean and its beacons. Yet when the fire lookout towers he had fought for were finally being built on the Two Medicine forest during these years it was noticeable that he called them "Franklin Delano's lighthouses."

Looking back from now at that matter of my McCaskill grandparents I question, frankly, whether my mother and father would or could have kept close with that side of the family even if it had still been extant. No marriage is strong enough to bear two loads of in-laws. Early on the choice might as well be made, that one family will be seen as much as can be stood and the other, probably the husband's, shunted off to rare visits. That's theory, of course. But theory and my mother together—in any case, all I grew up knowing of the McCaskills of Scotch Heaven was that thirty or so years of homestead effort proved to be the extent of their lifetimes and that my father emerged from the homestead, for good, in the war year of 1917.

"Yeah, I went off to Wilson's war. Fought in blood up to my knees." As I have told, the one crack in how solemn my father could be in announcing something like this was that lowered left eyelid of his, and I liked to watch for it to dip down and introduce this next part. "Fact is, you could get yourself a fight just about any time of day or night in those saloons outside Camp Lewis." That my father's combat had been limited to fists against chins in the state of Washington seemed not to bother him a whit, although I myself wished he had some tales of the actual war. Rather, I wished his knack with a story could have illuminated that war experience of his generation, as an alternative to so many guys' plain refrain that I-served-my-time-over-in-Frogland-and-you-by-God-can-have-the-whole-bedamned-place. But you settle for what family lore you can.

My father's history resumes that when he came back from conducting the war against the Camp Lewis saloonhounds, he was hired on by the Noon Creek cattle ranchers as their association rider. "Generally some older hand got the job, but I was single and broke, just the kind ranchers love to whittle their wages down to fit"—by then, too, the wartime livestock prices were on their toboggan ride down—"and they took me on."

That association job of course was only a summer one, the combined Noon Creek cattle, except those of the big Double W ranch, trailing up onto the national forest grass in June and down out again in September, and so in winters my father fed hay at one cow ranch or another and then when spring came and brought lambing time with it he would hire on with one of the English Creek sheepmen. I suppose that runs against the usual notion of the West, of cow chousers and mutton conductors forever at odds with each other. But anybody who grew up around stock in our part of Montana knew no qualm about working with either cattle or sheep. Range wars simply never were much the Montana style, and most particularly not the Two Medicine fashion. Oh, somewhere in history there had been an early ruckus south toward the Sun River, some cowman kiyiing over to try kill off a neighboring band of sheep. And probably in any town along these mountains, Browning or Gros Ventre or Choteau or Augusta, you could go into a bar and still find an occasional old hammerhead who proclaimed himself nothing but a cowboy and never capable of drawing breath as anything else, especially not as a mutton puncher. (Which isn't to say that most sheepherders weren't equally irreversibly sheepherders, but somehow that point never seemed to need constant general announcement as it did with cowboys.) By and large, though, the Montana philosophy of make-do as practiced by our sizable ranching proportion of Scotchmen, Germans, Norwegians, and Missourians meant that ranch people simply tried to figure out which species did best at the moment, sheep or cows, and chose accordingly. It all came down, so far as I could see, to the doctrine my father expressed whenever someone asked him how he was doing: "Just trying to stay level."

In that time when young Varick McCaskill became their association rider there still would have been several Noon Creek cattle ranchers, guys getting along nicely on a hundred or so head of cows apiece. Now nearly all of those places either were bought up by Wendell Williamson's Double W or under lease to it. "The Williamsons of life always do try to latch on to all the land that touches theirs" was my father's view on that. What I am aiming at, though, is that among those Noon Creek stockmen when my father was hired on was Isaac Reese, mostly a horse raiser but under the inspiration of wartime prices also running cattle just then. It was when my father rode in to pick up those Reese cattle for the drive into the mountains that he first saw my mother. Saw her as a woman, that is. "Oh, I had known she had some promise. Lisabeth Reese. The name alone made you keep her somewhere in mind."

Long-range opportunities seemed to elude my father, but he could be nimble enough in the short run. "I wasn't without some practice at girling. And Beth was worth some extra effort."

The McCaskill-Reese matrimony ensued, and a year or so after that, Alec ensued. Which then meant that my father and mother were supporting themselves and a youngster by a job that my father had been given because he was single and didn't need much wage. This is the brand of situation you can find yourself in without much effort in Montana, but that it is common does not make it one damn bit more acceptable. I am sure as anything that the memory of that predicament at the start of my parents' married life lay large behind their qualms about what Alec now was intending. My father especially wanted no repeat, in any son of his, of that season by season scrabble for livelihood. I know our family ruckus was more complicated than just that. Anything ever is. But if amid the previous evening's contention my father and Alec could have been put under oath, each Bibled to the deepest of the truths in him, my father would have had to say something like: "I don't want you making my mistakes over again." And Alec to him: "Your mistakes were yours, they've got nothing to do with me."

My brother and my father. I am hard put to know how to describe them as they seemed to me then, in that time when I was looking up at them from fourteen years of age. How to lay each onto paper, for a map is never the country itself, only some ink suggesting the way to get there.

Funny, what memory does. I have only a few beginning recollections of the four or so years we spent at the Indian Head ranger station down there at the middle of the Two Medicine National Forest, where my father started in the Forest Service. A windstorm one night that we thought was going to take the roof off the house. And Alec teaching me to mooch my way onto the back of a grazing horse, as I have told about. But clearest of all to me is a time Alec and I rode double into the mountains with our father, for he took us along on little chore trips as soon as we were big enough to perch on a horse. How can it be that a day of straddling behind the saddle where my brother sat—my nose inches from the collar of Alec's jacket, and I can tell you as well as anything that the jacket was green corduroy, Alec a greener green than the forest around us—is so alive, even yet? Anyway, after Indian Head came our move to English Creek and my father's rangering of the north end of the Two ever since. Now that I think on all this, that onset of our English Creek life was at the start of Alec's third school year, for I recall how damn irked I was that, new home or not, here Alec was again riding off to school every morning while I still had a whole year to wait.

Next year did come and there we both were, going to school to Miss

Thorkelson at the South Fork schoolhouse, along with the children of the ranch families on the upper end of English Creek, the Hahn boys, a number of Busbys and Roziers, the Finletter twins, the Withrow girls, and then of course the Hebner kids, who made up about half the school by themselves. Alec always stood well in his studies. Yet I can't help but believe the South Fork school did me more good than it did him. You know how those one-room schools are, all eight grades there in one clump for the teacher to have to handle. By a fluke of Hebner reproductive history Marcella Withrow and I were the only ones our age at South Fork, so as a class totaling two we didn't take up much of Miss Thorkelson's lesson time and she always let us read extra or just sit and partake of what she was doing with the older grades. By the time Marcella and I reached the sixth grade we already had listened through the older kids' geography and reading and history and grammar five times. I still know what the capital of Bulgaria is, and not too many people I meet do.

Stuff of that sort I always could remember like nobody's business. Numbers, less so. But there Alec shined. Shined in spite of himself, if such is possible.

It surprised the hell out of all of us in the family. I can tell you the exact night we got this new view of Alec.

It had been paper day for my father, the one he set aside each month to wrestle paperwork asked for by the Two Medicine National Forest headquarters down in Great Falls, and more than likely another batch wanted by the Region One office over in Missoula as well. The author of his sorrow this particular time was Missoula, which had directed him to prepare and forward—that was the way Forest Service offices talked—a report on the average acreage of all present and potential grazing allotments in his English Creek ranger district. "Potential" was the nettle in this, for it meant that my father had to dope out from his maps every bit of terrain which fit the grazing regulations of the time and translate those map splotches into acreage. So acres had been in the air that day in our household, and it was at supper that Alec asked how many acres there were in the Two Medicine National Forest altogether.

Alec was twelve at the time. Which would have made me eight, since there were four years between us. Three years and forty-nine weeks, I preferred to count it, my birthday being on September fourth and Alec's the twenty-fifth of that same month. But the point here is that we were both down there in the grade school years and my father didn't particularly care to be carrying on a conversation about any more acreage, so he just answered: "Quite a bunch. I don't know the figure, exactly."

Alec was never easy to swerve. "Well, how many sections does it have?" You likely know that a section is a square mile, in the survey system used in this country.

"Pretty close to 600," my father knew offhand.

"Then that's 384,000 acres," imparted Alec.

"That sounds high, to me," my father responded, going on with his meal. "Better get a pencil and paper and work it out."

Alec shook his head against the pencil and paper notion. "384,000," he said again. "Bet you a milkshake."

At this juncture my mother was heard from. "There'll be no betting at the supper table, young man." But she then got up and went to the sideboard where the mail was put and returned with an envelope. On the back of it she did the pencil work—600 times 640, the number of acres in a section—and in a moment reported:

"384,000."

"Are you sure?" my father asked her.

My mother in her younger days had done a little schoolteaching, so here my father simply was getting deeper into the arithmetic bog. "Do you want to owe both Alec and me milkshakes?" she challenged him back.

"No, I can do without that," my father said. He turned to Alec again and studied him a bit. Then: "All right, Mister Smart Guy. How much is 365 times 12?"

This too took Alec only an instant. "4,380," he declared. "Why? What's that?"

"It's about how many days a twelve-year-old like you has been on this earth," my father said. "Which is to say it's about how long it's taken us to discover what it is you've got in that head of yours."

That, then, was what might be called the school year portion of Alec. An ability he couldn't really account for—"I don't know, Jicker, I just can," was all the answer I could ever get when I pestered him about how he could handle figures in his head like that—and maybe didn't absolutely want or at least welcome. The Alec of summer was another matter entirely. What he didn't display the happy knack of, in terms of ranch or forest work that went on in the Two country at that season of year, hadn't yet been invented. Fixing fences, figuring how to splice in barbwire and set new braceposts, Alec was a genius at; anytime an English Creek rancher got money enough ahead for fence work, here he came to ask Alec to ride his lines and fix where needed. When Alec, at age thirteen, came to his first haying season and was to drive the scatter rake for our uncle Pete Reese, after the first few days Pete put him onto regular windrow raking for a while instead. As a scatter raker Alec was working the job for more than it was worth, trotting his team of horses anywhere in the hayfield a stray scrap of hay might be found; the regularity of making windrows, Pete said, slowed him down to within reason. That same headlong skill popped out whenever Alec set foot into the mountains. On our counting trips before this year, he perpetually was the first to see deer or elk or a red-tailed hawk or whatever, before I did and often before our father did.

The combination of all this in Alec, I am sure as anything, was what inspired my father and mother to champion college and engineering for him. They never put it in so bald a way, but Alec's mathematical side and his knacky nature and his general go-to-it approach seemed to them fitted for an engineer. A builder, a doer. Maybe even an engineer for the Forest Service itself, for in those New Deal times there were projects under way everywhere a place could be found for them, it seemed like. The idea even rang right with Alec, at first. All through that winter of his last year in high school Alec kept saying he wished he could go right now, go to the college at Bozeman and get started. But then Leona happened, and the Double W summer job again, and the supper ruckus about marriage over college.

Well, that was a year's worth of Alec, so to speak. His partner in ruckus, my father up there on the horse in front of me, can't be calendared in the strictly regular fashion either. Despite the order of months printed and hung on our wall at the English Creek ranger station, a Varick McCaskill year began with autumn. With Indian summer, actually, which in our part of Montana arrives after a customary stormy turn of weather around Labor Day. Of course every ranger is supposed to inspect the conditions of his forest there at the end of the grazing season. My father all but X-rayed his portion of the Two Medicine National Forest. South Fork and North Fork, up under the reefs, in beyond Heart Butte, day after day he delved the Two almost as if making sure to himself that he still had all of that zone of geography. And somehow when the bands of sheep trailed down and streamed toward the railroad chutes at Blackfoot or Pendroy, he was on hand there too to look them over, gossip with the herders, the ranchers, the lamb buyers, join in the jackpot bets about how much the lambs would weigh. It was the time of year when he could assess his job, see right there on the land and on the hoof the results of his rangering and give thought to how to adjust it. A necessary inventory season, autumn.

He never wintered well. Came down with colds, sieges of hacking and sniffing, like someone you would think was a permanent pneumonia candidate. Strange, for a man of his lengthy strength and one otherwise so in tune with the Two country. "Are you *sure* you were born and raised up there on the North Fork?" my mother would ask, along with about the third mustard plaster she applied onto him every winter. "Maybe a traveling circus left you."

More than likely, all of my father's winter ailments really were symptoms of just one, indoorness. For stepping out a door somehow seemed to extend him, actually tip his head higher and brace his shoulders straighter, and the farther he went from a house the more he looked like he knew what he was doing.

Does that sound harsh? It's not meant to. All I am trying to work into words here is that my father was a man born to the land, in a job that sometimes harnessed him to a desk, an Oliver typewriter, a book of regulations. A man caught between, in a number of ways. I have since come to see that he was of a generation that this particularly happens to. The ones who are firstborn in a new land. My belief is that it will be the same when there are births out on the moon or the other planets. Those firstborn always, always will live in a straddle between the ancestral path of life and the route of the new land. In my father's case the old country of the McCaskills, Scotland, was as distant and blank as the North Pole, and the fresh one, America, still was making itself. Especially a rough-edged part of America such as the Montana he was born into and grew up in. All my father's sessions with old Toussaint Rennie, hearing whatever he could about the past days of the Two Medicine country, I think were due to this; to a need for some footing, some groundwork of the time and place he found himself in.

The Forest Service itself was an in-between thing, for that matter. Keeper of the national forests, their timber, grass, water, yet merchant of those resources, too. Anybody local like my father who "turned green" by joining the USFS now sided against the thinking of a lot of people he had known all his life, people who considered that the country should be wide open, or at least wider open than it was, for using.

And even within all this, ranger Varick McCaskill was of a betwixt variety. A good many of the guys more veteran than my father dated back to the early time of the Forest Service, maybe even to when it originated in 1905; they tended to be reformed cowboys or loggers or some such, old hands who had been wrestling the West since before my father was born. Meanwhile the men younger than my father were showing up with college degrees in forestry and the New Deal alphabet on their tongues.

So there my father was, between and between and between. My notion in all this is that winter, that season of house time and waiting, simply was one more between than he could stand.

When spring let him out and around, my father seemed to green up with the country. In the Two, even spring travels in on the wind; chinooks which can cause you to lean into them like a drunk against a lamppost while they melt away the snowbanks of winter. The first roar of a chinook beginning to sweep down off the top of the Rockies signaled newness, promise, to my father. "The wind from Eden," he called the chinook, for he must have read that somewhere. Paperwork chores he had put off and off now got tackled and disposed of. He and his assistant ranger gave the gear of the English Creek ranger district a going-over; saddles, bridles, pack saddles, fire equipment, lookout phone lines, all of it. With his dispatcher he planned the work of trail crews, and the projects the Civilian Conservation Corps boys would be put to, and the deployment of fire guards and smokechasers when the fire season heated up.

And from the first moment that charitably might be classified as spring, my father read the mountains. Watched the snow hem along the peaks, judging how fast the drifts were melting. Cast a glance to English Creek various times of each day, to see how high it was running. Kept mental tally of the wildlife; when the deer started back up into the mountains, when the fur of the weasel turned from white to brown, how soon the first pile of coal-black droppings in the middle of a trail showed that bears were out of hibernation. To my father, and through him to the rest of us in the family, the mountains now were their own calendar, you might say.

And finally, spring's offspring. Summer. The high season, the one the rest of my father's ranger year led up to. Summer was going to tell itself, for my father and I were embarking into it now with this counting trip.

—

"—a gander. Don't you think?"

My father had halted Mouse and was swiveled around looking at me in curiosity. Sometimes I think if I endure in life long enough to get senile nobody will be able to tell the difference, given how my mind has always drifted anyway.

"Uh, come again?" I mustered. "I didn't quite catch that."

"Anybody home there, under your hat? I was saying, it's about time you checked on your packslinging. Better hop off and take a gander."

Back there on the subject of our horses I should have told too that we were leading one pack horse with us. Tomorrow, after we finished the counting of the Kyle and Hahn bands of sheep, we were going on up to Billygoat Peak where Paul Eliason, the junior forester who was my father's assistant ranger, and a couple of trail men were building a fire lookout. They had gone in the previous week with the pre-cut framework and by now likely had the lookout erected and shingled, but the guywire had been late in coming from Missoula. That was our packload now, the roll of half-inch galvanized cable and some eyebolts and turnbuckles to tie down the new lookout tower. You may think the wind blows in the lower areas of the Two, but up there on top it really huffs.

This third horse, bearer of the load whose lash rope and diamond hitch knot I now was testing for tautness, was an elderly solemn sorrel whom my father addressed as Brownie but the rest of us called by the name he'd been given before the Forest Service deposited him at the English Creek station: Homer. Having Brownie né Homer along was cause for mixed emotions. One more horse is always a nuisance to contend with, yet the presence of a pack animal also made a journey seem more substantial; testified that you weren't just jaunting off to somewhere, you were transporting.

Since the lookout gear and our food only amounted to a load for one horse it hadn't been necessary to call on my father's packer, Isidor Pronovost, and his eight-mule packstring for this counting trip of ours. But even absent he had his influence that morning as I arranged the packs on Brownie/Homer under my father's scrutiny, both of us total converts to Isidor's perpetual preachment that in packing a horse or a mule, balance is everything. One of the best things that was ever said to me was Isidor's opinion that I was getting to be a "pretty daggone good cargodier" in learning how to fit cargo onto a pack animal. These particular Billy Peak packs took some extra contriving, to make a roll of heavy guywire on one side of the pack saddle equivalent to some canned goods on the other side of it and then some light awkward stuff such as our cooking utensils in a top pack, but finally my father had proclaimed: "There, looks to me like you got it Isidored."

Evidently I had indeed, for I didn't find that the packs or ropes had shifted appreciably on our ride thus far. But I went ahead and reefed down on the lash rope anyway, snugging my diamond hitch even further to justify the report to my father: "All tight as a fiddle string."

While I was cross-examining the lash rope my father had been looking out over the country all around. Roman Reef predominated above us, of course. But just across the gorge of the North Fork from it another landmark, Rooster Mountain, was starting to stand over us, too. Its broad open face of slope was topped with an abrupt upshoot of rock like a rooster's comb, which gave it the name.

"Since we're this far along," my father decided, "maybe we might as well eat some lunch."

The view rather than his stomach guided him in that choice, I believe.

By now, late morning, we were so well started into the mountains above the English Creek–Noon Creek divide that we could see down onto both drainages and their various ranches, and on out to where the farm patterns began, east of the town of Gros Ventre. To be precise, on a map our lunch spot was about where the east-pointing panhandle of the Two Medicine National Forest joins onto the pan—the pan being the seventy-five-mile extent of the forest along the front of the Rockies, from East Glacier at the north to Sun River at the south. Somehow when the forest boundary was drawn the English Creek corridor, the panhandle route we had just ridden, got included, and that is why our English Creek ranger station was situated out there with ranches on three sides of it. That location like a nest at the end of a limb bothered some of the map gazers at Region One headquarters over in Missoula. They'd have denied it, but they seemed to hold the theory that the deeper a ranger station was buried into preposterous terrain, the better. Another strike was that English Creek sat nearly at the southern end of my father's district, nothing central or tidy about the location either. But the Mazoola inmates had never figured out anything to do about English Creek, and while the valley-bottom site added some riding miles to my father's job, the convenience of being amid the English Creek ranch families—his constituents, so to speak—was more than worth it.

My mother had put up sandwiches for us; slices of fried ham between slabs of homemade bread daubed with fresh yellow butter. You can't beat that combination. Eating those sandwiches and gazing out over the Two country mended our dispositions a lot.

If a person can take time to reflect on such a reach of land other matters will dim out. An area the size of the Two is like a small nation. Big enough to have several geographies and an assortment of climates and an appreciable population, yet compact enough that people know each other from one end of the Two to the other.

A hawk went by below us, sailing on an air current. A mark of progress into the mountains I always watched for, hawks and even eagles now on routes lower than our own.

Mostly, however, as my father and I worked our way through sandwiches and a shared can of plums, I simply tried to store away the look of the land this lush June. Who knew if it would ever be this green again? The experience of recent years sure as hell didn't suggest so. For right out there in that green of farmland and prairie where my father and I were gazing, a part of the history of the Depression began to brew on a day of early May in 1934. Nobody here in the Two could have identified it as more than an ordinary wind. Stiff, but that is never news in the Two country. As that wind continued east, however, it met a weather front angling down out of Canada, and the combined velocity set to work on the plowed fields along the High Line. An open winter and a spring of almost no rain had left those fields dry; brown talcum waiting to be puffed. And so a cloud of wind and topsoil was born and grew. By the time the dirt storm reached Plentywood in the northeastern corner of the state the grit of it was scouring paint off farmhouses. All across the Dakotas further dry fields were waiting to become dust. The brown storm rolled into the Twin Cities, and on to Chicago, where it shut down plane flights and caused streetlights to be turned on in the middle of the day. I don't understand the science of it, but that storm continued to grow and widen and darken the more it traveled, Montana dirt and Dakota dirt and Minnesota dirt in the skies and eyes of Illinois, Indiana, Ohio. And on and on the storm swept, into New York City and Washington, D.C., the dust of the West fogging out the pinnacle of the Empire State building and powdering the shiny tabletops within the White House. At last the dirt cloud expended itself into the Atlantic. Of course thereafter came years of dust, particularly in the Great Plains and the Southwest. But that Montana-born blow was the Depression's great nightmare storm; the one that told the nation that matters were worse than anyone knew, the soil itself was fraying loose and flying away.

In a way, wherever I scrutinized from the lunch perch of that day I was peering down into some local neighborhood of the Depression. As if, say, a spyglass such as Walter Kyle's could be adapted to pick out items through time instead of distance. The farmers of all those fields hemming the eastern horizon. They were veterans of years of scrabbling. Before WPA relief jobs and other New Deal help began to take hold, many a farm family got by only on egg money or cream checks. Or any damn thing they could come up with. Time upon time we were called on at the ranger station by one overalled farmer or another from near Gros Ventre or Valier or even Conrad, traveling from house to house offering a dressed hog he had in the trunk of his jalopy for three cents a pound. Believe it or not, though, those farmers of the Two country were better off than the ones who neighbored them on the east. That great dust storm followed a path across northern Montana already blazed by drought, grasshoppers, army worms, you name it. Around the time the CCC, the Civilian Conservation Corps, was being set up, my father and other rangers and county agents and maybe government men of other kinds were called to a session over at Plentywood. It was the idea of some government thinker—the hunch was that it came down all the way from Tugwell or one of those—that everybody working along any lines of conservation ought to see Montana's worst-hit area of drought. My father grumbled about it costing him three or four days of work from the Two, but he had no choice but to go. I especially remember this because when he got back he said scarcely anything for about a day and a half, and that was not at all like him. Then at supper the second night he suddenly looked across at my mother and burst out, "Bet, there're people over there who're trying to live on just potatoes. They feed Russian thistles to their stock. Call it Hoover hay. It— I just never saw such things. Never even dreamed of them. Fencelines pulled loose by the wind piling tumbleweeds against them. When a guy goes to drive a fencepost, he first has to punch holes in the ground with a crowbar and pour in water to soften the soil. And out in the fields, what the dust doesn't cover, the goddamn grasshoppers get. I tell you, Bet, it's a crime against life, what's happening."

So that was the past that came to mind from the horizon of green farms. And closer below us, along the willowed path of Noon Creek, the

Depression history of the cattlemen was no happier memory. Noon Creek is the next drainage north of English Creek, swale country without as much cottonwood and aspen along its stream banks. Original cattle country, the best cow-grazing land anywhere in the Two. But what had been a series of about ten good ranches spaced along Noon Creek was dwindled to three. Farthest west, nearest our lunch perch, the Reese family place now run by my mother's brother Pete, who long ago converted to sheep. Just east from there Dill Egan's cow outfit with its historic round corral. And everywhere east of Dill the miles of Double W swales and benchland and the eventual cluster of buildings that was the Double W home ranch. Dill Egan was one of those leery types who steered clear of banks, and so had managed to hold his land. The Williamsons of the Double W owned a bank and property in San Francisco or Los Angeles, one of those places, and as my father put it, "When the end of the world comes, the last sound will be a nickel falling from someplace a Williamson had it hid." Every Noon Creek cowman between the extremes of Dill Egan and Wendell Williamson, though, got wiped out when the nation's plunge flattened the cattle market. Places were foreclosed on, families shattered. The worst happened at a piece of Noon Creek I could not help but look down onto from our lunch site; the double bend of the stream, an S of water and willows like a giant brand onto the Noon Creek valley. The place there had belonged to a rancher who, on the day before foreclosure, told his wife he had some things to do, he'd be a while in the barn. Where he tacked up in plain sight on one of the stalls an envelope on which he had written I CANT TAKE ANY MORE. I WONT HAVE MY EARS KNOCKED DOWN BY LIFE ANY MORE. And then hung himself with a halter rope.

The name of the rancher was Carl Nansen, and that Nansen land was bought up by the Double W. "Wendell Williamson'll let us have the house on the Nansen place to live in" had been Alec's words about the domestic plan after he and Leona became Mr. and Mrs. this fall.

The thought of this and the sight of that creek S were as if wires had connected in me, for suddenly I wanted to turn to my father and ask him everything about Alec. What my brother was getting himself into, sashaying off into the Depression with a saddle and a bridle and a bride. Whether there was any least chance Alec could be headed off from cowboying, or maybe from Leona, since the two somehow seemed to go together. How my father and my mother were going to be able to reason in any way with him, given last night's family explosion. Where we

40 · IVAN DOIG

stood as a family. Divided for all time? Or yet the unit of four we had always been? Ask and ask and ask; the impulse rose in me as if coming to percolation.

My father was onto his feet, had pulled out his pocket watch and was kidding me that my stomach was about half an hour fast as usual, it was only now noon, and I got up too and went with him to our horses. But still felt the asking everywhere in me.

No, I put that wrong. About the ask, ask, ask. I did not want to put to my father those infinite questions about my brother. What I wanted, in the way that a person sometimes feels hungry, half-starved, but doesn't know exactly what it is that he'd like to eat, was for my father to be answering them. Volunteering, saying "I see how to bring Alec out of it," or "It'll pass, give him a couple of weeks and he'll cool off about Leona and then . . ."

But Varick McCaskill wasn't being voluntary; he was climbing onto his horse and readying to go be a ranger. And to my own considerable surprise, I let him.

We tell ourselves whatever is needed to go from one scene of life to the next. Tonight in camp, I told myself, as we ended that June lunchtime above the English Creek–Noon Creek divide. Tonight would be early enough to muster the asking about Alec. What I was temporarily choosing, with silence, was that my father and I needed this trail day, the rhythm or ritual or whatever it was, of beginning a counting trip, of again fitting ourselves to the groove of the task and the travel and the mountains. Of entering another Two summer together, I might as well say.

Dode Withrow's sheep were nowhere in evidence when we arrived at the counting vee an hour or so after our lunch stop. A late start by the herder might account for their absence, or maybe it just was one of those mornings when sheep are poky. In either case, I had learned from my father to expect delay, because if you try to follow some exact time when you work with sheep you will rapidly drive yourself loony.

"I might as well go up over here and have a look at that winter kill," my father decided. A stand of pine about a mile to the north was show-ing the rusty color of death. "How about you hanging on here in case the sheep show up. I won't be gone long." He forced a grin. "Think about how to grow up saner than that brother of yours."

"This whole family's sanity could stand some thinking about" crossed my mind in reply but didn't come out. My father climbed on Mouse and went to worry over winter kill on his forest.

I took out my jackknife and started putting my initials into the bare fallen log I was sitting on. This I did whenever I had time to pass in the forest of the Two, and I suppose even yet up there some logs and stumps announce *J McC* to the silent universe.

The wind finally had gone down, I had no tug at my attention except for the jackknife in my hand. Carving initials as elaborate as mine does take some concentration. The *J* never was too bad to make and the *M* big and easy, but the curves of the *C*s needed to be carefully cut. Thanks to the tardy Withrow sheep I had ample leisure to do so. I suppose sheep have caused more time to be whiled away than any other creatures in the world. Even yet on any number of Montana ridgelines there can be seen stone cairns about the height of a man. Sheepherders' monuments they are called and what they are monuments to is monotony. Just to be doing something a herder would start piling stones, but because he hated to admit he was out there hefting rocks for no real reason, he'd stack up a shape that he could tell himself would serve as a landmark or a boundary marker for his allotment. Fighting back somehow against loneliness. That was a perpetual part of being a sheepherder. In the wagons of a lot of them you would find a stack of old magazines, creased and crumpled from being carried in a hip pocket. An occasional prosperous herder would have a battery radio to keep him company in the evenings. Once in a while you came across a carver or a braider. Quite a few, though, the ones who give the herding profession a reputation for skewed behavior, figured they couldn't be bothered with pastimes. They just lived in their heads, and that can get to be cramped quarters. Those religions which feature years of solitude and silence I have grave doubts about. I believe you are better off doing anything rather than nothing. Even if it is only piling stones or fashioning initials.

In any event, that jackknife work absorbed me for I don't know how long, but to the point where I was startled by the first blats of the Withrow sheep.

I headed on down through the timber on foot to help bring them to the counting vee. A sheepman could have the whole Seventh Cavalry pushing his band along and he'd still seem glad of further help.

Dode Withrow spotted me and called, "Afternoon, Jick. That father of yours come to his senses and turn his job over to you?"

"He's patrolling to a winter kill. Said he'd be back by the time we get up to the vee."

"At the rate these sonsabitches want to move along today he's got time to patrol the whole Rocky Mountains."

This was remarked loud enough by Dode that I figured it was not for my benefit alone. Sure enough, an answer shot out of the timber to our left.

"You might just remember the sonsabitches ARE sheep instead of racehorses."

Into view over there between some trees came Dode's herder, Pat Hoy. For as long as I had been accompanying my father on counting trips, and I imagine for years before, Dode and Pat Hoy had been wrangling with each other as much as they wrangled their sheep. "How do, Jick. Don't get too close to Dode, he's on the prod this morning. Wants the job done before it gets started."

"I'm told you can tell the liveliness of a herder by how his sheep move," Dode suggested. "Maybe you better lay down, Pat, while we send for the undertaker."

"If I'm slow it's because I'm starved down, trying to live on the grub you furnish. Jick, Dode is finally gonna get out of the sheep business. He's gonna set up a stinginess school for you Scotchmen."

That set all three of us laughing as we pushed the band along, for an anthem of the Two was Dode Withrow's lament of staying on and on in the sheep business. "In that '19 winter, I remember coming into the house and standing over the stove, I'd been out all day skinning froze-to-death sheep. Standing there trying to thaw the goose bumps off myself and saying, 'This is it. This does it. I am going to get out of the sonofabitching sheep business.' Then in '32 when the price of lambs went down to four cents a pound and might just as well have gone all the way to nothing, I told myself, 'This is really it. No more of the sonofabitching sheep business for me. I've had it.' And yet here I am, still in the sonofabitching sheep business. God, what a man puts himself through."

That was Dode for you. Poet laureate of the woes of sheep, and a sheepman to the pith of his soul. On up the mountain slope he and Pat Hoy and I now shoved the band. It took a while, because up is not a direction sheep particularly care to go, at least at someone else's suggestion. Sheep seem perpetually leery of what's over the hill, which I suppose makes them either notably dumb or notably smart.

Myself, I liked sheep. Or rather I didn't mind sheep as such, which is the best a person can do towards creatures whose wool begins in their brain, and I liked the idea of sheep. True, sheep had to be troubled with more than cattle did, but the troubling was on a smaller scale. Pulling a lamb from a ewe's womb is nothing to untangling a leggy calf from the inside of a heifer. And a sheep you can brand by dabbing a splot of paint on her back, not needing to invite half the county in to maul your livestock around in the dust of a branding corral. Twelve times out of a dozen, in the debate of cow and ewe I will choose sheep.

For a person partial to the idea of sheep I was in the right time and place. With the encouragement of what the Depression had done to cattle prices the Two Medicine country then was a kind of vast garden of wool and lambs. Beginning in late May, for a month solid a band of sheep a day passed through the town of Gros Ventre on the way north to the Blackfeet Reservation, band after band trailing from all the way down by Choteau, and other sheep ranchers bringing theirs from around Bynum and Pendroy. (Not without some cost to the civic tidiness of Gros Ventre, for the passage of a band of a thousand ewes and their lambs through a town cannot happen without evidence being left on the street, and occasionally the sidewalks. Sheep are nervous enough as it is, and being routed through a canyon of buildings does not improve their bathroom manners any. Once, Carnelia Muntz, wife of the First National banker, showed up in the bank and said something about all the sheep muss on the streets. I give Ed Van Bebber his full due. Ed happened to be in there cashing a check, and he looked her up and down and advised: "Don't think of them as sheep turds, Carnelia. Think of them as berries off the money tree.") This was a time on the reservation when you could see a herder's wagon on top of practically every rise: a fleet of white wagons anchored across the land. Roy Cleary's outfit up around Browning in itself ran fifteen thousand head of ewes or more. And off to the east, just out of view beyond the bench ridges, the big sheep outfits from over in Washington were running their tens of thousands, too. And of course in here to the west where we were working Dode Withrow's sheep to the counting vee, my father's forest pastured the English Creek bands. Sheep and their owners were the chorus in our lives at the English Creek ranger station, the theme of every season and most conversation.

———

At the counting vee my father was waiting for us. After greetings had been said all around among him and Dode and Pat, Dode handed my father a gunny sack with a couple of double handfuls of cottoncake in it, said, "Start 'em, Mac," and stepped around to his side of the counting gate.

Here on the spread-out English Creek range the tally on each grazing allotment was done through a vee made of poles spiked onto trees, the sheep funneling past while my father and the rancher stood alongside the opening of the narrow end and counted.

Now my father went through the narrow gate into the vee, toward the leery multitude of ewes and lambs. He shook the sack in front of him where the sheep could see it and let a few cottonseed pellets trickle to the ground.

Then it came, that sound not even close to any other in this world, my father's coax to the sheep: the tongue-made *prrrrr prrrrr prrrrr,* remotely a cross between an enormous cat's purr and the cooing of a dove. Maybe it was all the R's built into a Scotch tongue, but for whatever reason my father could croon that luring call better than any sheepman of the Two.

Dode and Pat and I watched now as a first cluster of ewes, attentive to the source of the *prrrrrs,* caught the smell of the cottoncake. They scuffled, did some ewely butting of each other, as usual to no conclusion, then forgot rivalry and swarmed after the cottoncake. As they snooped forward on the trail of more, they led other sheep out the gate and started the count. You could put sheep through the eye of a needle if you once got the first ones going so that the others could turn off their brains and follow.

My job was at the rear of the sheep with the herder, to keep the band pushing through the counting hole and to see that none circled around after they'd been through the vee and got tallied twice—or, had this been Ed Van Bebber's band, I would have been back there to see that his herder, on instructions from Ed, didn't spill some sheep around the wing of the corral while the count was going on, so that they missed being tallied.

But since these were Dode's sheep with Pat Hoy on hand at the back of them I had little to add to the enterprise of the moment and was there mostly for show. I always watched Pat all I could without seeming to stare, to try to learn how he mastered these woolies as he did.

Some way, he was able just to *look* ewes into behaving better than they had in mind. One old independent biddy or another would step out, size up her chance of breaking past Pat, figure out who she was facing, and then shy off back into the rest of the bunch. This of course didn't work with lambs, who have no more predictability to them than hens in a hurricane. But in their case all Pat had to do was say "Round 'em, Taffy" and his caramel-colored shepherd dog would be sluicing them back to where they belonged. A sheep dog as good as Taffy was worth his weight in shoe leather. And a herder as savvy as Pat knew how to be a diplomat toward his dog, rewarding him every now and then with praise and ear rubbing but not babying him so much that the dog hung around waiting to be complimented rather than performing his work. That was one of my father's basic instructions when I first began going into the mountains with him on counting trips, not to get too affectionate with any herder's dog. Simply stroke them a time or two if they nuzzled me and let it go at that.

Taffy came over now to see if I had any stray praise to offer, and I just said, "You're a dog and half, Taffy."

"Grass gets much higher up here, Jick, I'm liable to lose Taffy in it," Pat called over to me. "You ever see such a jungle of a year?"

"No," I confessed, and we made conversation for a bit about the summer's prospects. Pat Hoy looked like any of a thousand geezers you could find in the hiring bars of First Avenue South in Great Falls, but he was a true grassaroo; knew how to graze sheep as if the grass was his own sustenance as well as theirs. No herder in all of the Two country was more highly prized than Pat the ten months of the year when he stayed sober and behind the sheep, and because this was so, Dode put up with what was necessary to hang on to him. That is, put up with the fact that some random number of times a year Pat proclaimed: "I quit, by damn, you can herd these old nellies your own self. Take me to town." Dode knew that only two of those quitting proclamations ever meant anything: "The sonofagun has to have a binge after the lambs are shipped and then another one just before lambing time, go down to Great Falls and get all bent out of shape. He's got his pattern down like linoleum, Pat has. For the first week he drinks whiskey and his women are pretty good lookers. The next week or so he's mostly on beer and his women are getting a little shabby. Then for about two weeks after that he's on straight wine and First Avenue squaws. That gets it out of his system, and I go collect him and we start all over."

—

You can see how being around Dode and Pat lifted our dispositions. When the count was done and we had helped Pat start the sheep on up toward the range he would summer them on—the ewes and lambs already browsing, taking their first of however many million nibbles of grass on the Two between then and September—Dode stayed on with us awhile to swap talk. "What's new with Uncle Sam?" he inquired.

"Roosevelt doesn't tell me quite everything, understand," my father responded. "We are going modern, though. It has only taken half of my goddamn life, but the Billy Peak lookout is about built. Paul will have her done in the next couple days. This forest is finally going to have a goddamn fire tower everyplace it ought to have one. Naturally it's happening during a summer when the forest is more apt to float away than burn down, but anyway." Dode was a compact rugged-faced guy whose listening grin featured a gap where the sharp tooth just to the left of his front teeth was missing, knocked out in some adventure or another. A Dode tale was that when he and Midge were about to be married he told her that he intended to really dude up for the wedding, even planned to stick a navy bean in the tooth gap. But if Dode looked and acted as if he always was ready to take on life headfirst, he also was one of those rare ones who could listen as earnestly as he could talk.

"Alec still keeping a saddle warm at the Double W?" Dode was asking next.

"Still is," my father had to confirm.

Dode caught the gist behind the tight pair of words, for he went on to relate: "That goddamn Williamson. He can be an overbearing sonofabitch without half trying, I'll say that for him. A while back I ran into him in the Medicine Lodge and we sopped up a few drinks together, then he got to razzing me about cattle being a higher class of animal than sheep. Finally I told him, 'Wendell, answer me this. Whenever you see a picture of Jesus Christ, which is it he's holding in his arms? Always a LAMB, never a goddamn calf.'"

We hooted over that. For the first time all day my father didn't look as if he'd eaten nails for breakfast.

"Anyway," Dode assured us, "Alec'll pretty soon figure out there are other people to work for in the world than Wendell goddamn Williamson. Life is wide, there's room to take a new run at it."

My father wagged his head as if he hoped so but was dubious. "How about you, you see a nickel in sight anywhere this year?" So now it was

Dode's turn to report, and my father just as keenly welcomed in his information that down on the Musselshell a wool consignment of thirty thousand fleeces had gone for twenty-two cents a pound, highest in years, encouragement that could "goddamn near make a man think about staying in the sheep business," and that Dode himself didn't intend to shear until around the end of the month "unless the weather turns christly hot," and that—

I put myself against a tree and enjoyed the sight and sound of the two of them. All the English Creek sheepmen and my father generally got along like hand and glove, but Dode was special beyond that. I suppose it could be said that he and my father were out of the same bin. At least it doesn't stretch my imagination much to think that if circumstances had changed sides when the pair of them were young, it now could have been Dode standing there in the employ of the U.S. Forest Service and my father in possession of a sheep ranch. Their friendship actually went back to before either of them had what could be called a career, to when they both were bronc punks, youngsters riding in the Egans' big round corral at Noon Creek every summer Sunday. My father loved to tell how Dode, who could be a snazzy dresser whenever there was any occasion, would show up to do his bronc-riding in a fancy pair of corduroy pants with leather trim. "To look at him, it was hard to know how much was Dode and how much was dude. But he was the best damn rider you'd ever see, too."

By this time of afternoon a few clouds had concocted themselves above the crest of the mountains and were drifting one after another out over the foothills below us. Small fleecy puffs, the kind which during the dry years made people joke in a disgusted way, "Those are empties from Seattle going over." This fine green year it did not matter that they weren't rainbringers, and with the backdrop of my father and Dode's conversation I lost myself in watching each cloud shadow cover a hill or a portion of a ridgeline and then flow down across the coulee toward the next, as if the shadow was a slow mock flood sent by the cloud.

"I hear nature calling," Dode now was excusing himself. He headed off not toward the timber, though, but to a rock outcropping about forty yards away, roughly as big and high as a one-story house. When Dode climbed up onto that I figured I had misunderstood his mission; he evidently was clambering up there to look along the mountain and check on Pat's progress with the sheep.

But no, he proceeded to do that and the other too, gazing off up the mountain slope as he unbuttoned and peed.

Do you know, even as I say this I again see Dode in every particular. His left hand resting on his hip and the arm and elbow kinked out like the handle on a coffee cup. His hat tilted back at an inquiring angle. He looked composed as a statue up there, if you can imagine stone spraddled out in commemoration of that particular human function.

My father and I grinned until our faces almost split. "There is only one Dode," he said. Then he cupped his hands and called out in a concerned tone: "Dode, I hope you've got a good foothold up there. Because you sure don't have all that much of a handhold."

By the time Dode declared he had to head down the mountain toward home, pronto, or face consequences from Midge, I actually was almost in the mood that a counting trip deserved. For I knew that traveling to tomorrow's sheep, those of Walter Kyle and Fritz Hahn, would take us up onto Roman Reef, always topnotch country, and after that would come the interesting prospect of the new Billy Peak lookout tower. It had not escaped me either that on our way to that pair of attractions we would spend tonight at a camping spot along the North Fork under Rooster Mountain, which my father and I—and, yes, Alec in years past—considered our favorite in the entire Two. Flume Gulch, the locale was called, because an odd high gully with steep sides veered in from the south and poured a trickle of water down the gorge wall into the North Fork. If you had to walk any of that Flume Gulch side of the creek, you would declare the terrain had tried to stand itself on end and prop itself up with thick timber and a crisscross of windfalls. But go on the opposite side of the creek and up onto the facing and equally steep slope of Rooster Mountain and you would turn around and say you'd never been in a grassier mountain meadow. That is the pattern the seasons make in this part of the Two, a north-facing slope bursting with trees and brush because snow stays longest there and provides moisture, while a south-facing slope is timberless but grassy because of all the sun it gets. Anyway, wild and tumbled country, Flume Gulch, but as pretty as you could ask for.

By just before dusk my father and I were there, and Mouse and Pony and Homer were unsaddled and tethered on the good grass of the Rooster Mountain slope, and camp was established.

"You know where supper is," my father advised. By which he meant that it was in the creek, waiting to be caught.

This far up the North Fork, English Creek didn't amount to much. Most places you could cross it in a running jump. But the stream was headed down out of the mountains in a hurry and so had some pretty riffles and every now and again a pool like a big wide stairstep of glass. If fish weren't in one of those waters, they were in the other.

Each of us took his hat off and unwound the fishline and hook wrapped around the hatband. On our way up, we had cut a pair of willows of decent length and now notched the wood about an inch from the small end, tied each fishline snug into each notch so it couldn't pull off, and were ready to talk business with those fish.

"Hide behind a tree to bait your hook," my father warned with an almost straight face, "or they'll swarm right out of the water after you."

My father still had a reputation in the Forest Service from the time some Region One headquarters muckymuck who was quite a dry-fly fisherman asked him what these English Creek trout took best. Those guys of course have a whole catechism of hackles and muddlers and goofus bugs and stone flies and nymphs and midges. "Chicken guts," my father informed him.

We didn't happen to have any of those along with us, but just before leaving home we'd gone to the old haystack bottom near the barn and dug ourselves each a tobacco can of angleworms. Why in holy hell anyone thinks a fish would prefer a dab of hair to something as plump as a stack-bottom worm I never have understood the reasoning of.

The fish in fact began to prove that, right then. I do make the concession to sportsmanship that I'll fish a riffle once in a while, even though it demands some attention to casting instead of just plunking into the stream, and so it pleased me a little that in the next half hour or so I pulled my ten fish out of bumpy water, while at the pool he'd chosen to work over my father still was short of his supper quota.

"I can about taste that milkshake," I warned him as I headed downstream a little to clean my catch. Theoretically there was a standing bet in our family, that anybody who fished and didn't catch ten owed the others a milkshake. My father had thought this up some summers ago to interest Alec, who didn't care anything for fishing but always was keen to compete. But after the tally mounted through the years to where Alec owed my father and me eight milkshakes each, during last year's counting trip Alec declared himself out and left the fishing to us.

And the two of us were currently even-stephen, each having failed to hook ten just once, all of last summer.

"I'm just corraling them first," my father explained as he dabbed a fresh worm to the pool. "What I intend is to get fish so thick in here they'll run into each other and knock theirselves out."

The fish must have heard and taken pity, because by the time I'd gutted mine here he came with his on a willow stringer.

"What?" I inquired as innocently as I could manage. "Did you decide to forfeit?"

"Like hell, mister. Ten brookies, right before your very eyes. Since you're so advanced in all this, go dig out the frying pan."

Even yet I could live and thrive on that Flume Gulch meal procedure: fry up both catches of fish, eat as many for supper as we could hold, resume on the rest at breakfast. Those little brookies, Eastern brook trout about eight inches long, are among the best eating there can be. You begin to taste them as quick as they hit the frying pan and go into their curl. Brown them up and take them in your fingers and eat them like corn on the cob, and you wish you had the capacity for a hundred of them.

When we'd devoured four or so brookies apiece we slowed down enough to share out a can of pork and beans and some buttered slices of my mother's bread, then resumed on the last stint of our fish supper.

"That hold you?" my father asked when we each had made seven or eight trout vanish.

I bobbed that I guessed it would, and while he went to the creek to rinse off our tin plates and scour the frying pan with gravel, I set to work composing his day's diary entry.

That the U.S. Forest Service wanted to know, in writing, what he'd done with his day constituted my father's single most chronic bother about being a ranger. Early on, someone told him the story of another rider-turned-ranger down on the Shoshone National Forest in Wyoming. "Trimmed my horse's tail and the wind blew all day," read the fellow's first diary try. Then with further thought he managed to conclude: "From the northeast." My father could swallow advice if he had to, and so he did what he could with the perpetual nag of having to jot his activities into the diary. When he did it was entirely another matter. Two or three weeks he would stay dutiful, then came a Saturday morning when he had seven little yellow blank pages to show for his week, and the filling in had to start:

"Bet, what'd I do on Tuesday? That the day it rained and I worked on Mazoola paperwork?"

"That was Wednesday. Tuesday you rode up to look over the range above Noon Creek."

"I thought that was Thursday."

"You can think so if you like, but you'd be wrong." My mother was careful to seem half-exasperated about these scriving sessions, but I think she looked forward to the chance to set my father straight on history, even if it was only the past week's. "Thursday I baked, and you took a rhubarb pie for the Bowens when you went to the Indian Head station. Not that Louise Bowen is capable of recognizing a pie."

"Well, then, when I rode to the Guthrie Peak lookout, that was—only yesterday? Friday?"

"Today is Saturday, yesterday most likely was Friday," my mother was glad to confirm for him.

When I became old enough to go into the mountains with him on counting trips my father perceived relief for his diary situation. Previously he had tried Alec, but Alec had the same catch-up-on-it-later proclivity as his. I think we had not gone a mile along the trail that very first morning when he reined up, said as if it had just occurred to him out of nowhere, "Jick, whyn't you kind of keep track of today for me?" and presented me a fresh-sharpened stub pencil and a pocket notebook.

It did take a little doing to catch on to my father's style. But after those first days of my reporting into my notebook in the manner of "We met up with Dill Egan on the south side of Noon Creek and talked with him about whether he can get a bigger permit to run ten more steers on" and my father squashing it down in his diary to "Saw D. Egan about steer proposition," I adjusted.

By now I was veteran enough that the day came readily to the tip of my pencil. "Patroled"—another principle some early ranger had imparted to my father was that if you so much as left the station to go to the outhouse, you had patroled—"Patroled the n. fork of English Creek. Counted D. Withrow's sheep onto allotment. Commenced packing bolts and turnbuckles and cable to Billy Peak lookout site."

My father read it over and nodded. "Change that 'bolts and turn-buckles and cable' just to 'gear.' You don't want to be any more definite than necessary in any love note to Uncle Sam. But otherwise it reads like the very Bible."

So the day was summed and we had dined on trout and the campfire was putting warmth and light between us and the night, and we had nothing that needed doing except to contemplate until sleep overcame us. My father was lying back against his saddle, hands behind his head and his hat tipped forward over his forehead. Ever since a porcupine attracted by the salt of horse sweat had chewed hell out of Alec's saddle on the counting trip a couple or three years ago, we made it a policy to keep our saddles by us.

He could make himself more comfortable beside a campfire than anybody else I ever knew, my father could. Right now he looked like he could spend till dawn talking over the Two country and everything in it, if Toussaint Rennie or Dode Withrow had been on hand to do it with.

My thoughts, though, still circled around Alec—well, sure, somewhat onto Leona too—and what had erupted at supper last night. But again the reluctance lodged itself in me, against outright asking my father what he thought the prospect was where Alec was concerned. I suppose there are times a person doesn't want to hear pure truth. Instead, I brought out something else that had been dogging my mind.

"Dad? Do you ever wonder about being somebody else?"

"Such as who? John D. Rockefeller?"

"What I mean, I got to thinking from watching you and Dode together there at the counting vee. Just, you know, whether you'd ever thought about how he could be in your place and you in his."

"Which would give me three daughters instead of you and Alec, do you mean? Maybe I'll saddle up Mouse and go trade him right now."

"No, not that. I mean life generally. Him being the ranger and you being the sheepman is what I had in mind. If things had gone a little different back when you guys were, uh, younger." Were my age, was of course what was hiding behind that.

"Dode jaw to jaw with the Major? Now I know I'm going to head down the mountain and swap straight across, for the sake of seeing that." In that time the regional forester, the boss of everybody in the national forests of Montana and northern Idaho, was Evan Kelley. Major Kelley, for he was like a lot of guys who got a big army rank during the war, hung on to the title ever afterward as if it was sainthood. The Major's style of leadership was basic. When he said frog, everybody better jump. I wish I had a nickel for every time my father opened his USFS mail and muttered: "Oh, Jesus, another kelleygram. When does he ever sleep?" Everybody did admit, the Major at least made clear the gospel in his messages to his Forest Service men. What he prescribed from his rangers was no big forest fires and no guff. So far, my father's slate was clean of both. In those years I didn't give the matter particular thought, but my father's long stint in charge of the English Creek district of the Two Medicine National Forest could only have happened with the blessing of the Major himself. The Pope in Missoula, so to speak. Nobody lower could have shielded ranger Varick McCaskill from the transfers that ordinarily happened every few years or so in the Forest Service. No, the Major wanted that tricky northmost portion of the Two, surrounded as so much of it was by other government domains, to be rangered in a way that wouldn't draw the Forest Service any bow-wow from the neighboring Glacier Park staff or the Blackfeet Reservation people; and in a way that would keep the sheepmen content and the revenue they paid for summer grazing permits flowing in; and in a way that would not repeat the awful fires of 1910 or the later Phantom Woman Mountain burn, right in here above the North Fork. And that was how my father was rangering it. So far.

"I guess I know what you're driving at, though." My father sat up enough to put his boot against a pine piece of squaw wood and shove it farther into the fire, then lay back against his saddle again. "How come we do what we do in life, instead of something else. But I don't know. I do not know. All I've ever been able to figure out, Jick, is that no job fits as well as a person would like it to, but some of us fit the job better than others do. That sorts matters out a little."

"Yeah, well, I guess. But how do you get in the job in the first place to find out whether you're going to fit it?"

"You watch for a chance to try it, is all. Sometimes the chance comes looking for you. Sometimes you got to look for it. Myself, I had my taste of the army because of the war. And it took goddamn little of army life to tell me huh uh, not for me. Then when I landed back here I got to be association rider for Noon Creek by setting out to get it, I guess you'd say. What I did, I went around to Dill Egan and old Thad Wainwright and your granddad Isaac and the other Noon Creekers and asked if they'd keep me in mind when it came time to summer their cows up here. Of course, it maybe didn't particularly hurt that I mentioned how happy I'd be to keep Double W cows from slopping over onto the Noon Creek guys' allotments, as had been going on. Anyway, the job got to be mine."

"What, the Double W was running cattle up here then?"

"Were they ever. They held a permit, in the early days. A hellish big one. Back then the Williamsons didn't have hold of all that Noon Creek country to graze. So, yeah, they had forest range, and sneaked cows onto anybody else's whenever they could. The number one belief of old Warren Williamson, you know, was that other people's grass might just as well be his." I didn't know. Warren Williamson, father of the present Double W honcho, was before my time; or at least died in California before I was old enough for it to mean anything to me.

"I'll say this one thing for Wendell," my father went on, "he at least buys or rents the country. Old Warren figured he could just take it." He gave the pine piece another shove with his boot. "The everlasting damn Double W. The Gobble Gobble You, as the gent who was ranger when I was association rider used to call it."

"Is that—" I had it in mind to ask if that was why he and my mother were so dead set against Alec staying on at the Double W, those old contentions between the Williamsons' ranch and the rest of the Two country. But no, the McCaskill next to me here in the fireshine was a readier topic than my absent brother. "Is that how you got to be the ranger here? Setting out to get the job?"

He went still for a moment, lying there in that sloped position against the saddle, feet toward the fire. Then shook his head. "The Forest Service generally doesn't work that way, and the Major sure as hell doesn't. Point yourself at the Two and they're liable to plunk you down on the Beaverhead or over onto the Bitterroot. Or doghouse you in the Selway, back when there still was a Selway. No, I didn't aim myself at English Creek. It happened."

I was readying to point out to him that "it happened" wasn't a real full explanation of job history when he sat up and moved his hat back so as to send his attention toward me. "What about you, on all this if-I-was-him-and-he-was-me stuff? Somebody you think you'd rather be, is there?"

There he had me. My turn to be less than complete. I answered: "Not rather, really. Just might have been, is all."

An answer that didn't even start toward truth, that one was. And not the one I would have resorted to anytime up until supper of the night before. For until then if I was to imagine myself happening to be anybody else, who could the first candidate have been but Alec? Wasn't all the basic outline already there? Same bloodline, same place of growing up, same schooling, maybe even the same body frame if I kept growing at my recent pace. Both of us September arrivals into the world, even; only the years needed swapping. The remarkable thing to me was that our interests in life were as different as they were, and I suppose I had more or less assumed that time was going to bring mine around to about where Alec's were. But now, precisely this possibility was what was unsettling me. That previous night at the supper table when Alec made his announcement about him and Leona and I asked "How come?" what I intended maybe was something similar to what my parents were asking of Alec. Something like "Already?" What was the rush? How could marriage and all be happening this soon, to my own brother? Yes, maybe put it this way: what I felt or at least sensed and was trying to draw into focus was the suggestion that Alec's recent course of behavior in some way foreshadowed my own. It was like looking through the Toggery window in Gros Ventre at a fancy suit of clothes and saying, by the Christ, they'll never catch me dead in *those*. But at the same time noticing that they seem to be your exact fit.

"Like who?" my father was asking in a tone which signaled me that he was asking it for the second time.

"Who?" I echoed, trying to think of anything more.

"Country seems to be full of owls tonight," he observed. Yet he was still attentive enough in my direction that I knew I had to come up with something that resembled an answer.

"Oh. Yeah. Who." I looked at the fire for some chunk that needed kicking farther in, and although none really did, I kicked one anyway. "Well, like Ray. That's all I had in mind, was Ray and me." Ray Heaney was my best friend at high school in Gros Ventre. "Us being the same age and all, like you and Dode."

This brought curiosity into my father's regard of me. "Now that takes some imagination," he said. "Dode and me are Siamese twins compared to you and Ray."

Then he rose, dusting twigs and pine needles off the back of him from where he had lain. "But I guess imagination isn't a struggle with you. You maybe could supply the rest of us as well, huh? Anyway, let's give some thought to turning in. We got a day ahead of us tomorrow."

If I was a believer in omens, the start of that next morning ought to have told me something.

The rigamarole of untangling out of our bedrolls and getting the campfire going and making sure the horses hadn't quit the country during the night, all that went usual enough.

Then, though, my father glanced around at me from where he had the coffeepot heating over a corner of the fire and asked: "Ready for a cup, Alec?"

Well, that will happen in a family. A passing shadow of absentmindedness, or the tongue just slipping a cog from what was intended. Ordinarily, being miscalled wouldn't have riled me. But all this recent commotion about Alec, and my own wondering about where anybody in this family stood anymore, and that fireside spell of brooding I'd done on my brother and myself, and I don't know what the hell all else—it now brought a response which scraped out of me like flint:

"I'm the other one."

Surprise passed over my father. Then I guess what is called contrition.

"You sure as hell are," he agreed in a low voice. "Unmistakably Jick."

About my name. John Angus McCaskill, I was christened. As soon as I began at the South Fork school, though, and gained a comprehension of what had been done to me, I put away that Angus for good. I have thought ever since that using a middle name is like having a third nostril.

I hadn't considered this before, but by then the John must already have been amended out of all recognition, too. At least I can find no memory of ever being called that, so the change must have happened pretty early in life. According to my mother it next became plain that "Johnnie" didn't fit the boy I was, either. "Somehow it just seemed like calling rhubarb vanilla," and she may or may not have been making a joke. With her you couldn't always tell. Anyhow, the family story goes on that she and my father were trying me out as "Jack" when some visitor, noticing that I had the McCaskill red hair but gray eyes instead of everybody else's blue, and more freckles than Alec and my father combined, and not such a pronouncement of jaw as theirs, said something like: "He looks to me more like the jick of this family."

So I got dubbed for the off card. For the jack that shares only the color of the jack of trumps. That is to say, in a card game such as pitch, if spades are led the jack of clubs becomes the jick, and in the taking of tricks the abiding rule is that jack takes jick but jick takes joker. I explain this a bit because I am constantly dumbfounded by how many people, even here in Montana, no longer can play a decent hand of cards. I believe television has got just a hell of a lot to answer for.

Anyway, Jick I became, and have ever been. An odd tag, put on me out of nowhere like that. This is part of the pondering I find myself doing now. Whether some other name would have shifted my life any. Yet, of what I might change, I keep deciding that that would not be among the first.

This breakfast incident rankled a little even after my father and I saddled up and resumed the ride toward the Roman Reef counting vee where we were to meet Walter Kyle's sheep at around noon. Nor did the weather help any. Clouds closed off the peaks of the mountains, and while it wasn't raining yet, the air promised that it intended to. One of those days too clammy to go without a slicker coat and too muggy to wear one in comfort.

To top it all off, we now were on the one stretch of the trail I never liked, with the Phantom Woman Mountain burn on the slope coming into sight ahead of us. Everywhere over there, acre upon acre upon acre, a gray cemetery of snags and stumps. Of death by fire, for the Phantom Woman forest fire had been the one big one in the Two's history except for the blazing summer of 1910.

Ahead of me, my father was studying across at the burn in the gloomy way he always did here. Both of us now moping along, like sorrow's orphans. If I didn't like the Phantom Woman neighborhood, my father downright despised it. Plainly he considered this gray dead mountainside the blot on his forest. In those times, when firefighting was done mainly by hand, a runaway blaze was the bane of the Forest Service. My father's slate was as clean as could be; except for unavoidable smudges before lightning strikes could be snuffed out, timber and grass everywhere else on his English Creek ranger district were intact, even much of the 1910-burnt country restoring itself by now. But the awful scar here was unhealed yet. Not that the Phantom Woman fire was in any way my father's own responsibility, for it happened before this district was his, while he still was the ranger at Indian Head rather than here. He was called in as part of the fire crew—this was a blaze that did run wild for a while, a whole hell of a bunch of men ended up fight-

ing Phantom Woman before they controlled it—but that was all. You
couldn't tell my father that, though, and this morning I wasn't in a
humor to even try.

When time has the weight of a mood such as ours on it, it slows to
a creep. Evidently my father figured both the day and I could stand
some brightening. Anyway it was considerably short of noon—we were
about two thirds of our way up Roman Reef, where the North Fork
hides itself in a timber canyon below and the trail bends away from the
face of Phantom Woman to the other mountains beyond—when he
turned atop Mouse and called to me:

"How's an early lunch sound to you?"

"Suits me," I of course assured him.

Out like this, my father tended to survive on whatever jumped out
of the food pack first. He did have the principle that supper needed to
be a cooked meal, especially if it could be trout. But as for the rest of
the day, if leftover trout weren't available he was likely to offer up as
breakfast a couple of slices of headcheese and a can of tomatoes or green
beans, and if you didn't watch him he might do the exact same again
for lunch. My mother consequently always made us up enough slab
sandwiches for three days' worth of lunches. Of course, by the second
noon in that high air the bread was about dry enough to strike a match
on, but still a better bet than whatever my father was apt to concoct.

We had eaten an applebutter sandwich and a half apiece and were
sharing a can of peaches for dessert, harpooning the slices out with our
jackknives to save groping into the pack for utensils, when Mouse suddenly snorted.

"Stand still a minute," my father instructed, which I already was
embarked on. Meanwhile he stepped carefully backward the three or
four paces until he was beside the scabbard on Mouse, with the .30-06
rifle in it. That time of year in the Two, the thought was automatic in
anybody who at all knew what he was doing: look around for bears, for
they are coming out of hibernation cantankerous.

What Mouse was signaling, however, proved to be a rider appearing
at the bend of the trail downhill from us. He was on a blaze-face sorrel,
who in turn snorted at the sight of us. A black pack mare followed into
sight, then a light gray pack horse with spots on his nose and his neck
stretched out and his lead rope taut.

"Somebody's new camptender, must be," my father said and
resumed on our peaches.

The rider sat in his saddle that permanent way a lot of those old-timers did, as if he lived up there and couldn't imagine sufficient reason to venture down off the back of a horse. Not much of his face showed between the buttoned-up slicker and the pulled-down brown Stetson. But thinking back on it now, I am fairly sure that my father at once recognized both the horseman and the situation.

The brief packstring climbed steadily to us, the ears of the horses sharp in interest at us and Pony and Homer and Mouse. The rider showed no attention until he was right up to my father and me. Then, though I didn't see him do anything with the reins, the sorrel stopped and the Stetson veered half out over the slickered shoulder nearest us.

"Hullo, Mac."

"I had half a hunch it might be you, Stanley. How the hell are you?"

"Still able to sit up and take nourishment. Hullo, Alec or Jick, as the case may be."

I had not seen him since I was, what? four years old, five? Yet right then I could have tolled off to you a number of matters about Stanley Meixell. That he was taller than he looked on tat sorrel, built in the riderly way of length mostly from his hips down. That he had once been an occasional presence at our meals, stooping first over the washbasin for a cleanse that included the back of his neck, and then slicking back his hair—I could have said too that it was crow-black and started from a widow's peak—before he came to the table. That unlike a lot of people he did not talk down to children, never delivered them phony guff such as "Think you'll ever amount to anything?" That, instead, he once set Alec and me to giggling to the point where my mother threatened to send us from the table, when he told us with a straight face that where he came from they called milk moo juice and eggs cackleberries and molasses long-tailed sugar. Yet of his ten or so years since we had last seen him I couldn't have told you anything whatsoever. So it was odd how much immediately arrived to mind about this unexpected man.

"Jick," I clarified. "'Lo, Stanley."

It was my father's turn to pick up the conversation. "Thought I recognized that black pack mare. Back up in this country to be campjack for the Busby boys, are you?"

"Yeah." Stanley's yeah was that Missourian slowed-down kind, almost in two parts: yeh-uh. And his voice sounded huskier than it ought to, as if a rasp had been used across the top of it. "Yeah, these times, I guess being campjack is better than no jack at all." Protocol was back to him now. He asked my father, "Counting them onto the range, are you?"

"Withrow's band yesterday, and Kyle's and Hahn's today."

"Quite a year for feed up here. This's been a million dollar rain, ain't it? Brought the grass up ass-high to a tall Indian. Though I'm getting to where I could stand a little sunshine to thaw out with, myself."

"Probably have enough to melt you," my father predicted, "soon enough."

"Could be." Stanley looked ahead up the trail, as if just noticing that it continued on from where we stood. "Could be," he repeated.

Nothing followed that, either from Stanley or my father, and it began to come through to me that this conversation was seriously kinked in some way. These two men had not seen each other for the larger part of ten years. So why didn't they have anything to say to one another besides this small-change talk about weather and grass? And already were running low on that? And both were wearing a careful look, as if the trail suddenly was a slippery place?

Finally my father offered: "Want some peaches? A few in here we haven't stabbed dead yet."

"Naw, thanks. I got to head on up the mountain or I'll have sheepherders after my hide." Yet Stanley did not quite go into motion; seemed, somehow, to be storing up an impression of the pair of us to take with him.

My father fished out another peach slice and handed me the can to finish. Along with it came his casual question: "What was it you did to your hand?"

It took me a blink or two to realize that although he said it in my direction, the query was intended for Stanley. I saw then that a handkerchief was wrapped around the back of Stanley's right hand, and that he was resting that hand on the saddle horn with his left hand atop it, the reverse of usual procedure there. Also, as much of the handkerchief as I could see had started off white but now showed stains like dark rust.

"You know how it is, that Bubbles cayuse"—Stanley tossed a look over his shoulder to the gray pack horse—"was kind of snaky this morning. Tried to kick me into next week. Took some skin off, is all."

We contemplated Bubbles. As horses go, he looked capable not just of assault but maybe pillage and plunder and probably arson, too. He was ewe-necked, and accented that feature by stretching back stubbornly against the lead rope even now that he was standing still. "A dragger," the Forest Service packer Isidor Pronovost called such a creature. "You sometimes wonder if the sunnabitch mightn't tow easier if you was to tip him over onto his back." The constellation of dark nose spots which must have given Bubbles his name—at least I couldn't see anything else nameable about him—drew a person's attention, but if you happened to glance beyond those markings, you saw that Bubbles was peering back at you as if he'd like to be standing on your spine. How such creatures get into packstrings I just don't know. I suppose the same way Good Help Hebners and Ed Van Bebbers get into the human race.

"I don't remember you as having much hide to spare," my father said then to Stanley. During the viewing of Bubbles, the expression on my father's face had shifted from careful. He now looked as if he'd made up his mind about something. "Suppose you could stand some company?" Awful casual, as if the idea had just strolled up to him out of the trees. "Probably it's no special fun running a packstring one-handed."

Now this was a prince of an offer, but of course just wasn't possible. Evidently my father had gone absent-minded again, this time about the counting obligation he'd mentioned not ten sentences earlier. I was just set to remind him of our appointment with Walter's and Fritz's sheep when he added on: "Jick here could maybe ride along with you."

I hope I didn't show the total of astonishment I felt.

Some must have lopped over, though, because Stanley promptly enough was saying: "Aw, no, Mac. Jick's got better things to do than haze me along."

"Think about morning," my father came back at him. "Those packs and knots are gonna be several kinds of hell, unless you're more lefthanded than you've ever shown."

"Aw, no. I'll be out a couple or three days, you know. Longer if any of those herders have got trouble."

"Jick's been out that long with me any number of times. And your cooking's bound to be better for him than mine."

"Well," Stanley began, and stopped. Christamighty, he seemed to be considering. Matters were passing me by before I could even see them coming.

I will always credit Stanley Meixell for putting the next two questions in the order he did.

"It ought to be up to Jick." Stanley looked directly down at me. "How do you feel about playing nursemaid to somebody so goddamn dumb as to get hisself kicked?"

The corner of my eye told me my father suggested a pretty enthusiastic response to any of this.

"Oh, I feel fine about—I mean, sure, Stanley. I could, uh, ride along. If you really want. Yeah."

Stanley looked down at my father now. "Mac, you double sure it'd be okay?"

Even I was able to translate that. What was my father going to face from my mother for sending me off camptending into the mountains with Stanley for a number of days?

"Sure," my father stated, as if doubt wasn't worth wrinkling the brain for. "Bring him back when he's dried out behind the ears."

"Well, then." The brown Stetson tipped up maybe two inches, and Stanley swung a slow look around at the pines and the trail and the mountainslope as if this was a site he might want to remember. More of his face showed. Dark eyes, blue-black. Into the corners of them, a lot of routes of squint wrinkles. Thin thrifty nose. Thrift of line at the mouth and chin, too. A face with no waste to it. In fact, a little worn down by use was the impression it gave. "I guess we ought to be getting," Stanley proposed. "Got everything you need, Jick?"

I had no idea in hell what I needed for going off into the Rocky Mountains with a one-handed campjack. I mean, I was wearing my slicker coat, my bedroll was behind my saddle, my head was more or less on my shoulders despite the jolt of surprise that all of this had sent through me, but were those nearly enough? Anyway, I managed to blurt:

"I guess so."

Stanley delivered my father the longest gaze he had yet. "See you in church, Mac," he said, then nudged the sorrel into motion.

The black pack horse and the light gray ugly one had passed us by the time I swung onto Pony, and my father was standing with his thumbs in his pockets, looking at the series of three horse rumps and the back of Stanley Meixell, as I reined around onto the trail. I stopped beside my father long enough to see if he was going to offer any explanation, or instructions, or edification of any damn sort at all. His face, still full of that decision, said he wasn't. All I got from him was: "Jick, he's worth knowing."

"But I already know him."

No response to that. None in prospect. The hell with it. I rode past my father and muttered as I did: "Don't forget to do the diary."

"Thanks for reminding me," my father said, poker-faced. "I'll give it my utmost."

The Busby brothers, I knew, ran three bands of sheep on their forest allotment, which stretched beneath the cliff face of Roman Reef. Stanley had slowed beyond the first bend of the trail for me to catch up, or maybe to make sure I actually was coming along on this grand tour of sheepherders.

"Which camp do we head for first?" I called ahead to him.

"Canada Dan's, he's the closest. About under that promontory in the reef is where his wagon is. If we sift right along for the next couple hours or so we'll be there." Stanley and the sorrel were on the move again, in that easy style longtime riders and their accustomed horses have. One instant you see the pair of them standing and the next you see them in motion together, and there's been no rigamarole in between. Stopped and now going, that's all. But Stanley did leave behind for me the observation: "Quite a day to be going places, ain't it."

"Yeah, I guess."

It couldn't have been more than fifteen minutes after we left my father, though, when Stanley reined his horse off the trail into a little clearing and the pack horses followed. When I rode up alongside he said: "I got to go visit a tree. You keep on ahead, Jick. I'll catch right up."

I had the trail to myself for the next some minutes. Just when I was about to rein around and see what had become of Stanley, the white of the sorrel's blaze flashed into sight. "Be right there," Stanley called, motioning me to ride on.

But he caught up awfully gradually, and in fact must have made a second stop when I went out of sight around a switchback. And before long he was absent again. This time when he didn't show up and didn't show up, I halted Pony and waited. As I was about to go back and start a search, here Stanley came, calling out as before: "Be right there."

I began to wonder a bit. Not only had I been volunteered into this expedition by somebody other than myself, I sure as the devil had not signed on to lead it.

So the next time Stanley lagged from sight, I was determined to wait until he was up with me. And as I sat there on Pony, firmly paused, I began to hear him long before I could see him.

> *"My name, she is Pancho,*
> *I work on a rancho.*
> *I make a dollar a day."*

Stanley's singing voice surprised me, a clearer, younger tone than his raspy talk.

So did his song.

> *"I go to see Suzy,*
> *She's got a doozy.*
> *Suzy take my dollar away."*

When Stanley drew even with me, I still couldn't see much of his eyes under the brim of the pulled-down hat, although I was studying pretty hard this time.

"Yessir," Stanley announced as the sorrel stopped, "great day for the race, ain't it?"

"The race?" I gaped.

"The human race." Stanley pivoted in his saddle—a little unsteadily, I thought—enough to scan at the black pack mare and then the gray one. He got a white-eyed glower in return from the gray. "Bubbles there is still in kind of an owly mood. Mad because he managed to only kick my hand instead of my head, most likely. You're doing fine up ahead, Jick. I'll wander along behind while Bubbles works on being crabby."

There was nothing for it but head up the trail again. At least now I knew for sure what my situation was. If there lingered any last least iota of doubt, Stanley's continued disappearances and his ongoing croon dispatched it.

> *"My brother is Sancho,*
> *he try with a banjo*
> *to coax Suzy to woo."*

I have long thought that the two commonest afflictions in Montana—it may be true everywhere, but then I haven't been everywhere—

are drink and orneriness. True, my attitude has thawed somewhat since I have become old enough to indulge in the pair myself now and again. But back there on that mountain those years ago, all I could think was that I had on my hands the two worst of such representations, a behind-the-bush bottle tipper and a knot-headed pack horse.

> *"But she tell him no luck,*
> *the price is an extra buck,*
> *him and the banjo make two."*

I spent a strong hour or so in contemplation of my father and just what he had saddled me with here. All the while mad enough to bite sticks in two. Innocent as a goddamn daisy, I had let my father detour me up the trail with Stanley Meixell. And now to find that my trail compadre showed every sign of being a warbling boozehound. Couldn't I, for Christ's sake, be told the full extent of the situation before I was shoved into it? What was in the head of that father of mine? Anything?

After this siege of black mull, a new thought did break through. It occurred to me to wonder just how my father ought to have alerted me to Stanley's condition beforehand. Cleared his throat and announced, "Stanley, excuse us but Jick and I got something to discuss over here in the jackpines, we'll be right back"? Worked his way behind Stanley and pantomimed to me a swig from a bottle? Neither of those seemed what could be called etiquette, and that left me with the perturbing suggestion that maybe it'd been up to me to see the situation for myself.

Which gave me another hour or so of heavy chewing, trying to figure out how I was supposed to follow events that sprung themselves on me from nowhere. How do you brace for that, whatever age you are?

Canada Dan's sheep were bunched in a long thick line against a stand of lodgepole pine. When we rode up a lot of blatting was going on, as if there was an uneasiness among them. A sheepherder who knows what he is doing in timber probably is good in open country too, but vice versa is not necessarily the case, and I remembered my father mentioning that Canada Dan had been herding over by Cut Bank, plains country. A herder new to timber terrain and skittish about it will dog the bejesus out of his sheep, keep the band tight together for fear of losing some. Canada Dan's patch-marked sheepdog looked weary, panting, and I saw Stanley study considerably the way these sheep were crammed along the slope.

"Been looking for you since day before yesterday," Canada Dan greeted us. "I'm goddamn near out of canned milk."

"That so?" said Stanley. "Lucky thing near isn't the same as out."

Canada Dan was looking me up and down now. "You that ranger's kid?"

I didn't care for the way that was put, and just said back: "Jick McCaskill." Too, I was wondering how many more times that day I was going to need to identify myself to people I'd had no farthest intention of getting involved with.

Canada Dan targeted on Stanley again. "Got to bring a kid along to play nursemaid for you now, Stanley? Must be getting on in years."

"I bunged up my hand," Stanley responded shortly. "Jick's been generous enough to pitch in with me."

Canada Dan shook his head as if my sanity was at issue. "He's gonna regret charity when he sees the goddamn chore we got for ourselves up here."

"What would that be, Dan?"

"About fifteen head of goddamn dead ones, that's what. They got onto some deathcamas, maybe three days back. Poisoned theirselfs before you can say sic 'em." Canada Dan reported all this as if he was an accidental passerby instead of being responsible for these animals. Remains of animals, they were now.

"That's a bunch of casualties," Stanley agreed. "I didn't happen to notice the pelts anywhere there at the wag—"

"Happened right up over here," Canada Dan went on as if he hadn't heard, gesturing to the ridge close behind him. "Just glommed onto that deathcamas like it was goddamn candy. C'mon here, I'll show you." The herder shrugged out of his coat, tossed it down on the grass, pointed to it and instructed his dog: "Stay, Rags." The dog came and lay on the coat, facing the sheep, and Canada Dan trudged up the ridge without ever glancing back at the dog or us.

I began to dread the way this was trending.

The place Canada Dan led us to was a pocket meadow of bunch grass interspersed with cream-colored blossoms and with gray mounds here and there on it. The blossoms were deathcamas, and the mounds were the dead ewes. Even as cool as the weather had been they were bloated almost to bursting.

"That's them," the herder identified for our benefit. "It's sure convenient of you fellows to show up. All this goddamn skinning, I can stand all the help I can get."

Stanley did take the chance to get a shot in on him. "You been too occupied the past three days to get to them, I guess?" But it bounced off Canada Dan like a berry off a buffalo.

The three of us looked at the corpses for a while. There's not all that much conversation to be made about bloated sheep carcasses. After a bit, though, Canada Dan offered in a grim satisfied way: "That'll teach the goddamn buggers to eat deathcamas."

"Well," Stanley expounded next, "there's no such thing as one-handed skinning." Which doubled the sense of dread in me. I thought to myself, But there is one-handed tipping of a bottle, and one-handed dragging me into this campjack expedition, and one-handed weaseling out of what was impending here next and—

All this while, Stanley was looking off in some direction carefully away from me. "I can be unloading the grub into Dan's wagon while this goes on, then come back with the mare so's we can lug these pelts in. We got it to do." We? "Guess I better go get at my end of it."

Stanley reined away, leading the pack horses toward the sheep-wagon, and Canada Dan beaded on me. "Don't just stand there in your tracks, kid. Plenty of these goddamn pelters for both of us."

So for the next long while I was delving in ewe carcasses. Manhandling each rain-soaked corpse onto its back, steadying it there, then starting in with that big incision from tail to jaw, which, if your jackknife slips just a little deep there at the belly, brings the guts pouring out onto your project. Slice around above all four hooves and then down the legs to the big cut, then skin out the hind legs and keep on trimming and tugging at the pelt, like peeling long underwear off somebody dead. It grudges me even now to say so, but Stanley was accurate, it did have to be done, because the pelts at least would bring a dollar apiece for the Busby brothers and a dollar then was still worth holding in your hand. That it was necessary did not make it less snotty a job, though. I don't know whether you have ever skinned a sheep which has lain dead in the rain for a few days, but the clammy wet wool adds into the situation the possibility of the allergy known as wool poisoning, so that the dread of puffed painful hands accompanies all your handling of the pelt. That and a whole lot else on my mind, I slit and slit and slit, straddled in there over the bloated bellies and amid the stiffened legs. I started off careful not to work fast,

in the hope that Canada Dan would slice right along and thereby skin the
majority of the carcasses. It of course turned out that his strategy was
identical and that Canada Dan had had countless more years of practice
at being slow than I did. In other circumstances I might even have
admired the drama in the way he would stop often, straighten up to ease
what he told me several times was the world's worst goddamn crick in
his back, and contemplate my scalpel technique skeptically before finally
bending back to his own. Out of his experience my father always testified that he'd rather work any day with sheepherders than cowboys. "You
might come across a herder that's loony now and then, but at least they
aren't so apt to be such self-inflated sonsabitches." Right about now I
wondered about that choice. If Canada Dan was anywhere near representative, sheepherders didn't seem to be bargains of companionship
either.

Finally I gave up on trying to outslow Canada Dan and went at the
skinning quick as I could, to get it over with.

Canada Dan's estimate of fifteen dead ewes proved to be eighteen.
Also I noticed that six of the pelts were branded with a bar above the
lamb number, signifying that the ewe was a mother of twins. Which
summed out to the fact that besides the eighteen casualties, there were
two dozen newly motherless lambs who would weigh light at shipping
time.

This came to Stanley's attention too when he arrived back leading
the black pack mare and we—or rather I, because Stanley of course
didn't have the hand for it and Canada Dan made no move toward the
task whatsoever—slung the first load of pelts onto the pack saddle.
"Guess we know what all that lamb blatting's about, now," observed
Stanley. Canada Dan didn't seem to hear this, either.

Instead he turned and was trudging rapidly across the slope toward
his sheepwagon. He whistled the dog from his coat and sent him polic-
ing after a few ewes who had dared to stray out onto open grass, then
yelled back over his shoulder to us: "It's about belly time. C'mon to the
wagon when you get those goddamn pelts under control, I got us a
meal fixed."

I looked down at my hands and forearms, so filthy with blood and
other sheep stuff I didn't even want to think about that I hated to touch
the reins and saddlehorn to climb onto Pony. But climb on I did, for it
was inevitable as if Bible-written that now I had to ride in with Stanley
to the sheepwagon, unload these wet slimy pelts because he wasn't able,

ride back out with him for the second batch, load them, ride back in and unload—seeing it all unfold I abruptly spoke out: "Stanley!"

"Yeah, Jick?" The brown Stetson turned most of the way in my direction.

All the ways to say what I intended to competed in my mind. Stanley, this just isn't going to work out. . . . Stanley, this deal was my father's brainstorm and not mine; I'm heading down that trail for home. . . . Stanley, I'm not up to—to riding herd on you and doing the work of this wampus cat of a sheepherder and maybe getting wool poisoning and— But when my mouth did move I heard it mutter:

"Nothing, I guess."

After wrestling the second consignment of pelts into shelter under Canada Dan's sheepwagon I went up by the door to wash. Beside the basin on the chopping block lay a sliver of gray soap, which proved to be so coarse my skin nearly grated off along with the sheep blood and other mess. But I at least felt scoured fairly clean.

"Is there a towel?" I called into the sheepwagon with what I considered a fine tone of indignation in my voice.

The upper part of Canada Dan appeared at the dutch door. "Right there in front of your face." He pointed to a gunny sack hanging from a corner of the wagon. "Your eyes bad?"

I dried off as best I could on the burlap, feeling now as if I'd been rasped from elbow to fingertip, and swung on into the sheepwagon.

The table of this wagon was a square of wood about the size of a big checkerboard, which pulled out from under the bunk at the far end and then was supported by a gate leg which folded down, and Stanley had tucked himself onto the seat on one side of our dining site. Canada Dan as cook and host I knew would need to be nearest the stove and sit on a stool at the outside end of the table, so I slid into the seat opposite Stanley, going real careful because three people in a sheepwagon is about twice too many.

"KEEYIPE!" erupted from under my inmost foot, about the same instant my nose caught the distinctive smell of wet dog warming up.

"Here now, what the hell kind of manners is that, walking on my dog? He does that again, Rags, you want to bite the notion right out of him." This must have been Canada Dan's idea of hilarity, for he laughed a little now in what I considered an egg-sucking way.

Or it may simply have been his pleasure over the meal he had concocted. Onto the table the herder plunked a metal plate with a boiled chunk of meat on it, then followed that with a stained pan of what looked like small mothballs.

"Like I say, I figured you might finally show up today, so I fixed you a duke's choice of grub," he crowed. "Get yourselves started with that hominy." Then, picking up a hefty butcher knife, Canada Dan slabbed off a thickness of the grayish greasy meat and toppled it aside. "You even got your wide choice of meat. Here's mutton."

He sliced off another slab. "Or then again here's growed-up lamb."

The butcher knife produced a third plank-thick piece. "Or you can always have sheep meat."

Canada Dan divvied the slices onto our plates and concluded: "A menu you don't get just everywhere, ain't it?"

"Yeah," Stanley said slower than ever, and swallowed experimentally.

The report crossed my mind that I had just spent a couple of hours elbow deep in dead sheep and now I was being expected to eat some of one, but I tried to keep it traveling. Time, as it's said, was the essence here. The only resource a person has against mutton is to eat it fast, before it has a chance for the tallow in it to congeal. So I poked mine into me pretty rapidly, and even so the last several bites were greasy going. Stanley by then wasn't much more than getting started.

While Canada Dan forked steadily through his meal and Stanley mussed around with his I finished off the hominy on the theory that anything you mixed into the digestive process with mutton was probably all to the good. Then I gazed out the dutch door of the sheepwagon while waiting on Stanley. The afternoon was going darker, a look of coming rain. My father more than likely was done by now with the counting of Walter Kyle's and Fritz Hahn's bands. He would be on his way up to the Billy Peak lookout, and the big warm dry camp tent there, and the company of somebody other than Canada Dan or Stanley Meixell, and probably another supper of brookies. I hoped devoutly the rain already had started directly onto whatever piece of trail my father might be riding just now.

Canada Dan meanwhile had rolled himself a cigarette and was filling the wagon with blue smoke while Stanley worked himself toward the halfway point of his slab of mutton. "Staying the night, ain't you?" the herder said more as observation than question. "You can set up the tepee, regular goddamn canvas hotel. It only leaks a little where it's ripped in that one corner. Been meaning to sew the sumbitch up."

"Well, actually, no," said Stanley.

This perked me up more than anything had in hours. Maybe there existed some fingernail of hope for Stanley after all. "We got all that pack gear to keep dry, so we'll just go on over to that line cabin down on the school section. Fact is"—Stanley here took the chance to shove away his still-mutton-laden plate and climb onto his feet as if night was stampeding toward him—"we better be getting ourselves over there if we're gonna beat dark. You ready, Jick?"

Was I.

The line cabin stood just outside the eastern boundary of the Two forest, partway back down the mountain. We rode more than an hour to get there, the weather steadily heavier and grimmer all around us, and Stanley fairly grim himself, I guess from the mix of alcohol and mutton sludging around beneath his belt. Once when I glanced back to be sure I still had him I happened to see him make an awkward lob into the trees, that exaggerated high-armed way when you throw with your wrong hand. So he had finally run out of bottle, and at least I could look forward to an unpickled companion from here on. I hoped he wasn't the kind who came down with the DTs as he dried out.

Our route angled us down in such a back and forth way that Roman Reef steadily stood above us now on one side, now on our other. A half-mile-high stockade of gray-brown stone, claiming all the sky to the west. Even with Stanley and thunderclouds on my mind I made room in there to appreciate the might of Roman Reef. Of the peaks and buttresses of the Two generally, for as far as I'm concerned, Montana without its mountain ranges would just be Nebraska stretched north.

At last, ahead of us showed up an orphan outcropping, a formation like a crown of rock but about as big as a railroad roundhouse. Below it ran the boundary fence, and just outside the fence the line cabin. About time, too, because we were getting some first spits of rain, and thunder was telling of lightning not all that far off.

The whole way from Canada Dan's sheepwagon Stanley had said never a word nor even glanced ahead any farther than his horse's ears. Didn't even stir now as we reached the boundary fence of barbwire. In a hurry to get us into the cabin before the weather cut loose I hopped off Pony to open the gate.

My hand was just almost to the top wire hoop when there came a terrific yell:

"GODAMIGHTY, get AWAY from that!"

I jumped back as if flung, looking crazily around to see what had roused Stanley like this.

"Go find a club and knock the gatewire off with that," he instructed. "You happen to be touching that wire and lightning hits that fence, I'll have fried Jick for supper."

So I humored him, went off and found a sizable dead limb of jackpine and tapped the hoop up off the top of the gate stick with it and then used it to fling the gate to one side the way you might flip a big snake. The hell of it was, I knew Stanley was out-and-out right. A time, lightning hit Ed Van Bebber's fence up the South Fork road from the English Creek ranger station and the whole top wire melted for about fifty yards in either direction, dropping off in little chunks as if it'd been minced up by fencing pliers. I knew as well as anything not to touch a wire fence in a storm. Why then had I damn near done it? All I can say in my own defense is that you just try going around with Stanley Meixell on your mind as much as he had been on mine since mid-morning and see if you don't do one or another thing dumb.

I was resigned by now to what was in store for me at the cabin, so started in on it right away, the unpacking of the mare and Bubbles. Already I had size, my father's long bones the example to mine, and could do the respected packer's trick of reaching all the way across the horse's back to lift those off-side packs from where I was standing, instead of trotting back and forth around the horse all the time. I did the mare and then carefully began uncargoing Bubbles, Stanley hanging on to the halter and matter-of-factly promising Bubbles he would yank his goddamn spotty head off if the horse gave me any trouble. Then as I swung the last pack over and off, a hefty lift I managed to do without bumping the pack saddle and giving Bubbles an excuse for excitement, Stanley pronounced: "Oh, to be young and diddling twice a day again."

He took notice of the considerable impact of this on me. "'Scuse my French, Jick. It's just a saying us old coots have."

Nonetheless it echoed around in me as I lugged the packs through the cabin door and stashed them in a corner.

By now thunder was applauding lightning below us as well as above and the rain was arriving in earnest, my last couple of trips outside considerably damp. Stanley meanwhile was left-handedly trying to inspire a fire in the rickety stove.

The accumulated chill in the cabin had us both shivering as we lit a kerosene lantern and waited for the stove to produce some result.

"Feels in here like it's gonna frost," I muttered.

"Yeah," Stanley agreed. "About six inches deep."

That delivered me a thought I didn't particularly want. "What, ah, what if this turns to snow?" I could see myself blizzarded in here for a week with this reprobate.

"Aw, I don't imagine it will. Lightning like this, it's probably just a thunderstorm." Stanley contemplated the rain spatting onto the cabin window and evidently was reminded that his pronouncement came close to being good news. "Still," he amended, "you never know."

The cabin was not much of a layout. Simply a roofed-over bin of lodgepole logs, maybe fifteen feet long and ten wide and with a single window beside the door at the south end. But at least it'd be drier than outside. Outside in fact was showing every sign of anticipating a night-long bath. The face of the Rocky Mountains gets more weather than any other place I know of and a person just has to abide by that fact.

I considered the small stash of wood behind the stove, mostly kindling, and headed back out for enough armfuls for the night and morning. Off along the tree line I found plenty of squaw wood, which already looked soused from the rain but luckily snapped okay when I tromped it in half over a log.

With that provisioning done and a bucket of water lugged from a seep of spring about seventy yards out along the slope, I declared myself in for the evening and shed my wet slicker. Stanley through all this stayed half propped, half sitting on an end of the little plank table. Casual as a man waiting for eternity.

His stillness set me to wondering. Wondering just how much whiskey was in him. After all, he'd been like a mummy on the ride from Canada Dan's camp, too.

And so before too awful long I angled across the room, as if exercising the saddle hours out of my legs, for a closer peek at him.

At first I wasn't enlightened by what I saw. The crowfoot lines at the corners of Stanley's eyes were showing deep and sharp, as if he was squinched up to study closely at something, and he seemed washed out, whitish, across that part of his face, too. Like any Montana kid I had seen my share of swacked-up people, yet Stanley didn't really look liquored. No, he looked more like—

"How's that hand of yours?" I inquired, putting my suspicion as lightly as I knew how.

Stanley roused. "Feels like it's been places." He moved his gaze past me and around the cabin interior. "Not so bad quarters. Not much worse than I remember this pack rat palace, anyway."

"Maybe we ought to have a look," I persisted. "That wrapping's seen better times." Before he could waltz off onto some other topic I stepped over to him and began to untie the rust-colored wrapping.

When I unwound that fabric, the story was gore. The back of Stanley's hand between the first and last knuckles was skinned raw where the sharp calk of Bubbles' horseshoe had scraped off skin: raw and seepy and butchered-looking.

"Jesus H. Christ," I breathed.

"Aw, could be worse." Even as he said so, though, Stanley seemed more pale and eroded around the eyes. "I'll get it looked at when I get to town. There's some bag balm in my saddlebag there. Get the lid off that for me, would you, and I'll dab some on."

Stanley slathered the balm thick across the back of his hand and I stepped over again and began to rewrap it for him. He noticed that the wrapping was not the blood-stained handkerchief. "Where'd you come up with that?"

"The tail off my shirt."

"Your ma's gonna like to find that."

I shrugged. Trouble was lined up deep enough here in company with Stanley that my mother's turn at it seemed a long way off.

"Feels like new," Stanley tried to assure me, moving his bandaged hand with a flinch he didn't want to show and I didn't really want to see. What if he passed out on me? What if—I tried to think of anything I had ever heard about blood poisoning and gangrene. Supposedly those took a while to develop. But then, this stint of mine with Stanley was beginning to seem like a while.

I figured it was time to try to get Stanley's mind, not to say my own, off his wound, and to bring up what I considered was a natural topic. So I queried:

"What are we going to do about supper?"

Stanley peered at me a considerable time. Then said: "I seem to distinctly remember Canada Dan feeding us."

"That was a while back," I defended. "Sort of a second lunch."

Stanley shook his head a bit and voted himself out. "I don't just feel like anything, right now. You go ahead."

So now things had reached the point where I had lost out even on my father's scattershot version of cooking, and was going to have to invent my own. I held another considerable mental conversation with U.S. forest ranger Varick McCaskill about that, meanwhile fighting the stove to get any real heat from it. At last I managed to warm a can of provisions I dug out of one of the packs of groceries for the herders, and exploring further I came up with bread and some promising sandwich material.

An imminent meal is my notion of a snug fortune. I was even humming the Pancho and Sancho and Suzy tune when, ready to dine, I sat myself down across the table from Stanley.

He looked a little quizzical, then drew in a deep sniff. Then queried: "Is that menu of yours what I think it is?"

"Huh? Just pork and beans, and an onion sandwich. Why?"

"Never mind."

Canada Dan's cooking must have stuck with me more than I was aware, though, as I didn't even think to open any canned fruit for dessert.

Meanwhile the weather was growing steadily more rambunctious. Along those mountainsides thunder can roll and roll, and constant claps were arriving to us now like beer barrels tumbling down stairs.

Now, an electrical storm is not something I am fond of. And here along the east face of the Rockies, any of these big rock thrusts, such as that crown outcropping up the slope from the cabin, notoriously can draw down lightning bolts. In fact, the more I pondered that outcropping, the less comfortable I became with the fact that it neighbored us.

In my head I always counted the miles to how far away the lightning had hit—something I still find myself doing—so when the next bolt winked, somewhere out the south window, I began the formula:

One, a-mile-from-here-to-there.

Two, a-mile-from-here-to-there.

Three . . . The boom reached us then; the bolt had struck just more than two miles off. That could be worse, and likely would be. Meanwhile rain was raking the cabin. We could hear it drum against the west wall as well as on the board roof.

"Sounds like we got a dewy night ahead of us," Stanley offered. He looked a little perkier now, for whatever reason. Myself, I was beginning to droop, the day catching up with me. I did some more thunder-counting whenever I happened to glimpse a crackle of light out the window, but came up with pretty much the same mileage each time and so began to lose attention toward that. Putting this day out of its misery seemed a better and better idea.

The cabin didn't have any beds as such, just a cobbled-together double bunk arrangement with planks where you'd like a mattress to be. But anyplace to be prostrate looked welcome, and I got up from the table to untie my bedroll from behind my saddle and spread it onto the upper planks.

The sky split white outside the cabin. That crack of thunder I honestly felt as much as heard. A jolt through the air, as if a quake had leapt upward out of the earth.

I believe my hair was swept straight on end, from that blast of noise and light. I know I had trouble getting air into my body, past the block-ade where my heart was trying to climb out my throat.

Stanley, though, didn't show any particular ruffle at all. "The quick hand of God, my ma used to say."

"Yeah, well," I informed him when I found the breath for it, "I'd just as soon it grabbed around someplace else."

I stood waiting for the next cataclysm, although what really was on my mind was the saying that you'll never hear the lightning bolt that hits you. The rain rattled constantly loud now.

At last there came a big crackling sound quite a way off, and while I knew nature is not that regular I told myself the lightning portion of the storm had moved beyond us—or if it hadn't, I might as well be dead in bed as anywhere else—and I announced to Stanley, "I'm turning in."

"What, already?"

"Yeah, already," a word which for some reason annoyed me as much as anything had all day.

Leaning over to unlace my forester boots, a high-topped old pair of my father's I had grown into, I fully felt how much the day had fagged me. The laces were a downright chore. But once my boots and socks were off I indulged in a promising yawn, pulled out what was left of my shirttail, and swung myself into the upper bunk.

"Guess I'm more foresighted than I knew," I heard Stanley go on, "to bring Doctor Hall along for company."

"Who?" I asked, my eyes open again at this. Gros Ventre's physician was Doc Spence, and I knew he was nowhere near our vicinity.

Stanley lanked himself up and casually went over to the packs. "Doctor Hall," he repeated as he brought out his good hand from a pack, a brown bottle of whiskey in it. "Doctor Al K. Hall."

The weather of the night I suppose continued in commotion. But at that age I could have slept through a piano tuners' convention. Came morning, I was up and around while Stanley still lay flopped in the lower bunk.

First thing, I made a beeline to the window. No snow. Not only was I saved from being wintered in with Stanley, but Roman Reef and all the peaks south beyond it stood in sun, as if the little square of window had been made into a summer picture of the Alps. It still floors me, how the mountains are not the same any two days in a row. As if hundreds of copies of those mountains exist and each dawn brings in a fresh one, of new color, new prominence of some feature over the others, a different wrapping of cloud or rinse of sun for this day's version.

I lit a fire and went out to check on the horses and brought in a pail of fresh water, and even then Stanley hadn't budged, just was breathing like he'd decided on hibernation. The bottle which had nursed him into that condition, I noticed, was down by about a third.

Telling myself Stanley could starve to death in bed for all I cared, I fashioned breakfast for myself, heating up a can of peas and more or less toasting some slices of bread by holding them over the open stove on a fork.

Eventually Stanley did join the day. As he worked at getting his boots on I gave him some secret scrutiny. I couldn't see, though, that he assayed much better or worse than the night before. Maybe he just looked that way, sort of absent-mindedly pained, all the time. I offered to heat up some breakfast peas for him but he said no, thanks anyway.

At last Stanley seemed ready for camptending again, and I figured it was time to broach what was heaviest on my mind. The calendar of our continued companionship.

"How long's this going to take, do you think?"

"Well, you seen what we got into yesterday with Canada Dan. Herders have always got their own quantities of trouble." Stanley could be seen to be calculating, either the trouble capacities of our next two sheepherders or the extent of my impatience. "I suppose we better figure it'll take most of a day apiece for this pair, too."

Two more days of messing with herders, then the big part of another day to ride back to English Creek. It loomed before me like a career.

"What about if we split up?" I suggested as if I was naturally businesslike. "Each tend one herder's camp today?"

Stanley considered some more. You would have thought he was doing it in Latin, the time it took him. But finally: "I don't see offhand why that wouldn't work. You know this piece of country pretty good. Take along the windchester," meaning his rifle. "If any bear starts eating on me he'll pretty soon give up on account of gristle." Stanley pondered some more to see whether anything further was going to visit his mind, but nothing did. "So, yeah. We got it to do, might as well get at it. Which yayhoo do you want, Gufferson or Sanford Hebner?"

I thought on that. Sanford was in his second or third summer in these mountains. Maybe he had entirely outgrown the high-country whimwhams of the sort Canada Dan was showing, and maybe he hadn't. Andy Gustafson on the other hand was a long-timer in the Two country and probably had been given the range between Canada Dan and Sanford for the reason that he was savvy enough not to let the bands of sheep get mixed. I was more than ready to be around somebody with savvy, for a change.

"I'll take Andy."

"Okey-doke. I guess you know where he is, in west of here, about under the middle of Roman Reef. Let's go see sheepherders."

Outside in the wet morning I discovered the possible drawback to my choice, which was that Andy Gustafson's camp supplies were in the pack rig that went on Bubbles. That bothered me some, but when I pictured Stanley and his hamburgered hand trying to cope with Bubbles for a day, I figured it fell to me to handle the knothead anyway. At least in my father's universe matters fell that way. So I worked the packs onto the black mare for Stanley—she was so tame she all but sang encouragement while the load was going on her—and then faced the spotty-nosed nemesis. But Bubbles seemed not particularly more snorty and treacherous than usual, and with Stanley taking a left-handed death grip on the halter again and addressing a steady stream of threats into the horse's ear and with me staying well clear of hooves while getting the packsacks roped on, we had Bubbles loaded in surprisingly good time.

"See you back here for beans," Stanley said, and as he reined toward

Sanford's camp Pony and I headed west up the mountain, Bubbles grudgingly behind us.

I suppose now hardly anybody knows that horseback way of life on a trail. I have always thought that horseback is the ideal way to see country, if you just didn't have to deal with the damn horse, and one thing to be said for Pony was that she was so gentle and steady you could almost forget she was down there. As for the trail itself; even in the situation I was in, this scene was one to store away. Pointed west as I was the horizon of the Rockies extended wider than any vision. To take in the total of peaks I had to move my head as far as I could to either side. It never could be said that this country of the Two didn't offer enough elbow room. For that matter, shinbone and cranium and all other kind, too. Try as you might to be casual about a ride up from English Creek into these mountains, you were doing something sizable. Climbing from the front porch of the planet into its attic, so to speak.

Before long I could look back out onto the plains and see the blue dab of Lake Frances, and the water tower of Valier on its east shore— what would that be, thirty miles away, thirty-five? About half as far off was the bulge of trees which marked where the town of Gros Ventre sat in the long procession of English Creek's bankside cottonwoods and willows. Gros Ventre: pronounced *Grove*-on, in that front-end way that town names of French origin get handled in Montana, making Choteau *Show*-toh and Havre *Hav*-er and Wibaux *Wee*-boh. Nothing entertained residents of Gros Ventre more than hearing some tourist or other outlander pop out with *Gross Ventree*. My father, though, figured that the joke was also on the town: "Not a whole hell of a lot of them know that Gros Ventre's the French for Big Belly." Of course, where all this started is that Gros Ventre is the name of an Indian tribe, although not what might be called a local one. The Gros Ventres originally, before reservation days, were up in the Milk River country near the Canadian line. Why a place down here picked up that tribe's name I didn't really know. Toussaint Rennie was the one who knew A to Why about the Two country. Sometime I would have to ask him this name question.

Distant yet familiar sites offering themselves above and below me, and a morning when I was on my own. Atop my own horse and leading a beast of burden, even if the one was short-legged and pudgy and the other one definitely justified the term of beast. Entrusted with a Winchester 30.30 carbine, not that I ever was one to look forward to shooting it out with a bear. A day to stand the others up against, this one. The twin feelings of aloneness and freedom seemed to lift and lift me, send me up over the landscape like a balloon. Of course I know it was the steady climb of the land itself that created that impression. But whatever was responsible, I was glad enough to accept such soaring.

Quite possibly I ought to think about this as a way of life, I by now was telling myself. By which I didn't mean chaperoning Stanley Meixell. One round of that likely was enough for a lifetime. But packing like this, running a packstring as Isidor Pronovost did for my father; that was worth spending some daydreams on. Yes, definitely a packer's career held appeal. Be your own boss out on the trail. Fresh air, exercise, scenery. Adventure. One of the stories my father told oftenest was of being with Isidor on one of the really high trails farthest back in these mountains of the Two, where a misstep by one horse or mule might pull all the rest into a tumble a few thousand feet down the slope, when Isidor turned in his saddle and conversationally said: "Mac, if we was to roll this packstring right about here, the buggers'd bounce till they stunk."

Maybe a quieter mountain job than packing. Forest fire lookout, up there in one of Franklin Delano's lighthouses. Serene as a hermit, a person could spend summers in a lookout cabin atop the Two. Peer around like a human hawk for smoke. Heroic work. Fresh air, scenery, some codger like Stanley to fetch your groceries up the mountainside to you. The new Billy Peak lookout might be the prime job. I'd be finding that out right now if my father hadn't detoured me into companioning damn old Stanley. Well, next year, next counting trip . . .

Up and up I and my horses and my dreams went, toward the angle of slope beneath the center of Roman Reef. Eventually a considerable sidehill of timber took the trail from sight, and before Pony and Bubbles and I entered the stand of trees, I whoaed us for a last gaze along all the mountains above and around. They were the sort of thing you would have if every cathedral in the world were lined up along the horizon.

Not much ensued for the first minutes of the forested trail, just a sharpening climb and the route beginning to kink into a series of switchbacks. Sunbeams were threaded down through the pine branches and with that dappled light I didn't even mind being in out of the view for the next little while.

A forest's look of being everlasting is an illusion. Trees too are mortal and they come down. I was about to face one such. In the middle of a straight tilt of trail between switchbacks, there lay a fresh downed lodgepole pine poking out over my route, just above the height of a horse.

On one of my father's doctrines of mountain travel I had a light little cruising ax along with me. But the steep hillside made an awkward place to try any chopping and what I didn't have was a saw of any sort. Besides, I was in no real mood to do trail maintenance for my father and the United States Forest Service.

I studied the toppled lodgepole. It barriered the trail to me in the saddle, but there was just room enough for a riderless horse to pass beneath. All I needed to do was get off and lead Pony and Bubbles through. But given the disposition of Bubbles, I knew I'd damn well better do it a horse at a time.

I tied Bubbles's lead rope to a middle-sized pine, doubling the square knot just to be sure, and led Pony up the trail beyond the windfall. "Be right back with that other crowbait," I assured her as I looped her reins around the leftover limb of a stump.

Bubbles was standing with his neck in the one position he seemed to know for it, stretched out like he was being towed, and I had to haul hard on his lead rope for enough slack to untie my knots.

"Come on, churnhead," I said as civilly as I could—Bubbles was not too popular with me anyway, because if he originally hadn't kicked Stanley I wouldn't have been in the camptending mess—and with some tugging persuaded him into motion.

Bubbles didn't like the prospect of the downed tree when we got there. I could see his eyes fixed on the shaggy crown limbs overhead, and his ears lay back a little. But one thing about Bubbles, he didn't lead much harder when he was being reluctant than when he wasn't.

I suppose it can be said that I flubbed the dub on all this. That the whole works came about as the result of my reluctance to clamber up that sidehill and do axwork. Yet answer me this, was I the first person not to do what I didn't want to? Nor was goddamn Bubbles blameless, now was he? After all, I had him most of the way past the windfall before he somehow managed to swing his hindquarters too close in against the hillside, where he inevitably brushed against a broken branch dangling down from the tree trunk. Even that wouldn't have set things off, except for the branch whisking in across the front of his left hip toward his crotch.

Bubbles went straight sideways off the mountain.

He of course took the lead rope with him, and me at the end of it like a kite on a string.

I can't say how far downslope I flew, but I was in the air long enough to get good and worried. Plummeting sideways as well as down is unnerving, your body trying to figure out how to travel in those two directions at once. And a surprising number of thoughts fan out in your mind, such as whether you are most likely to come down on top of or under the horse below you and which part of you you can best afford to have broken and how long before a search party and why you ever in the first place—

I landed more or less upright, though. Upright and being towed down the slope of the mountain in giant galloping strides, sinking about shin-deep every time, the dirt so softened by all the rain.

After maybe a dozen of those plowing footfalls, my journey ended. Horse nostrils could be heard working overtime nearby me, and I discovered the lead rope still was taut in my hands, as if the plunge off the trail had frozen it straight out like a long icicle. What I saw first, though, was not Bubbles but Pony. A horse's eyes are big anyway, but I swear Pony's were the size of Terraplane headlights as she peered down over the rim of the trail at Bubbles and me all the way below.

"Easy, girl!" I called up to her. All I needed next was for Pony to get excited, jerk her reins loose from that stump and quit the country, leaving me down here with this tangled-up pack horse. "Easy, Pony! Easy, there. Everything's gonna be—just goddamn dandy."

Sure it was. On my first individual outing I had rolled the packstring, even if it was only one inveterate jughead of a horse named Bubbles. Great wonderful work, campjack McCaskill. Keep on in this brilliant fashion and you maybe someday can hope to work your way up to moron.

Now I had to try to sort out the situation.

A little below me on the sidehill Bubbles was floundering around a little and snorting a series of alarms. The favorable part of that was that he was up on his feet. Not only up but showing a greater total of vigor than he had during the whole pack trip so far. So Bubbles was in one piece, I seemed to be intact, and the main damage I could see on the packs was a short gash in the canvas of the top pack where something snagged it on our way down. Sugar or salt was trickling from there, but it looked as if I could move a crossrope over enough to pinch the hole shut.

I delivered Bubbles a sound general cussing, meanwhile working along the lead rope until I could grab his halter and then reach his neck. From there I began to pat my way back, being sure to make my cussing sound a little more soothing, to get to the ruptured spot on the pack.

When I put my hand onto the crossrope of the diamond hitch to tug it across the gash, that top pack seemed to move a bit.

I tugged again in a testing way, and the summit of the load on Bubbles's back definitely moved, more than a bit.

"Son of a goddamn sonofabitch," I remember was all I managed to come out with to commemorate this discovery. That wasn't too bad under the circumstance, for the situation called for either hard language or hot tears, and maybe it could be pinpointed that right there I grew out of the bawling age into the cussing one.

Bubbles's downhill excursion had broken the last cinch, the one the lash rope ties into to hold the top pack into place on a horse's back. So I had a pack horse whole and healthy—and my emotions about Bubbles having survived in good fettle were now getting radically mixed— but no way to secure his load onto him. I was going to have to ride somewhere for a new cinch, or at the very least to get this one repaired.

Choices about like Canada Dan's menu of mutton or sheep meat, those. Stanley by now was miles away at Sanford Hebner's camp. Besides, with his hand and his thirst both the way they were, I wasn't sure how much of a repairer he would prove to be anyway. Or I could climb on Pony, head back down the trail all the way to the English Creek station, and tell that father of mine to come mend the fix he'd pitched me into.

This second notion held appeal of numerous kinds. I would be rid of Stanley and responsibility for him. I'd done all I could; in no way was it my fault that Bubbles had schottisched off a mountaintop. Most of all, delivering my predicament home to English Creek would serve my father right. He was the instigator of all this; who better to haul himself up here and contend with the mess?

Yet when I came right down to it I was bothered by the principle of anyone venturing to my rescue. I could offer all the alibis this side of Halifax, but the truth of it still stood. Somebody besides myself would be fishing me out of trouble. Here was yet another consequence of my damned in-between age. I totally did not want to be in the hell of a fix I was. Yet somehow I just as much did not relish resorting to anybody else to pluck me out of it. Have you ever been dead-centered that way?

Hung between two schools of thought, neither one of which you wanted to give in to? Why the human mind doesn't positively split in half in such a situation I don't know.

As I was pondering back and forth that way I happened to rub my forehead with the back of my free hand. It left moisture above my brow. Damn. One more sign of my predicament: real trouble always makes the backs of my hands sweat. I suppose nerves cause it. Whatever does, it spooks a person to have his hands sweating their own worry like that.

"That's just about enough of all this," I said out loud, apparently to Pony and Bubbles and maybe to my sweating hands and the mountainside and I suppose out across the air toward Stanley Meixell and Varick McCaskill as well. And to myself, too. For some part of my mind had spurned the back-and-forth debate of whether to go fetch Stanley or dump the situation in my father's lap, and instead got to wondering. There ought to be some way in this world to contrive that damn cinch back together. "If you're going to get by in the Forest Service you better be able to fix anything but the break of day," my father said every spring when he set in to refurbish the English Creek equipment. Not that I was keen on taking him as an example just then.

No hope came out of my search of Bubbles and the packs. Any kind of thong or spare leather was absent. The saddlestrings on my saddle up there where Pony was I did think of, but couldn't figure how to let go of the horse at hand while I went to get them. Bubbles having taken up mountaineering so passionately, there was no telling where he would crash off to if I wasn't here to hang on to him.

I started looking myself over for possibilities.

Hat, coat, shirt: no help.

Belt: though I hated to think of it, I maybe could cut that up into leather strips. Yet would they be long enough if I did.

No, better, down there: my forester boots, a bootlace; a bootlace just by God might do the trick.

By taking a wrap of Bubbles's lead rope around the palm of my left hand I was more or less able to use the thumb and fingers to grasp the lash cinch while I punched holes in it with my jackknife. All the while, of course, talking sweetly to Bubbles. When I had a set of holes accomplished on either side of the break, I threaded the bootlace back and forth, back and forth, and at last tied it to make a splice. Then, Bubbles's recent standard of behavior uppermost in my mind, I made one more set of holes farther along each part of the cinch and wove in the remainder of the bootlace as a second splice for insurance. In a situation like this, you had better do things the way you're supposed to do them.

I now had a boot gaping open like an unbuckled overshoe, but the lash cinch looked as if it ought to lift a boxcar. I did some more brow-wiping, and lectured Bubbles on the necessity of standing still so that I could retie his packs into place. I might as well have saved my breath. Even on level ground, contriving a forty-foot lash rope into a diamond hitch means going endlessly back and forth around the pack horse to do the loops and lashes and knots, and on a mountainside with Bubbles fidgeting and twitching every which way, the job was like trying to weave eels.

At last I got that done. Now there remained only the matter of negotiating Bubbles back up to where he had launched from. Talk about an uphill job. But as goddamn Stanley would've observed to me, I had it to do.

Probably the ensuing ruckus amounted to only about twenty minutes of fight and drag, though it seemed hours. Right then you could not have sold me all the pack horses on the planet for a nickel. Bubbles would take a step and balk. Balk and take a step. Fright or exasperation or obstinacy or whatever other mood can produce it had him dry-farting like the taster in a popcorn factory. Try to yank me back down the slope. Balk again, and let himself slide back down the slope a little. Sneeze, then fart another series. Shake the packs in hope the splice would let go. Start over on the balking.

I at last somehow worked his head up level with the trail and then simply leaned back on the lead rope until Bubbles exhausted his various acts and had to glance around at where he was. When the sight of the trail registered in his tiny mind, he pranced on up as if it was his own idea all along.

I sat for a while to recover my breath—after tying Bubbles to the biggest tree around, with a triple square knot—and to sort of take stock. The pulling contest definitely had taken all the jingle out of me.

There's this to be said for exertion, though. It does send your blood tickling through your brain. When I was through resting I directly went over to Bubbles, addressed him profanely, thrust an arm into the pack with the canned goods and pulled cans out until I found the ones of tomatoes. If I ever did manage to get this menagerie to Andy Gustafson's sheep camp I was going to be able to say truthfully that I'd had lunch and did not need feeding by one more sheepherder.

I sat back down, opened two cans with my jackknife, and imbibed tomatoes. "One thing about canned tomatoes," my father had the habit of saying during a trail meal, "if you're thirsty you can drink them and if you're hungry you can eat them." Maybe, I conceded, he was right about that one thing.

By the time I reached Andy Gustafson's camp my neck was thoroughly cricked from the constant looking back over my shoulder to see if the packs were staying on Bubbles. They never shifted, though. Thank God for whoever invented bootlaces.

Andy's band was spread in nice fashion along both sides of a timbered draw right under the cliff of Roman Reef. If you have the courage to let them—more of it, say, than was possessed by a certain bozo named Canada Dan—sheep will scatter themselves into a slow comfortable graze even in up-and-down country. But it takes a herder who is sure of himself and has a sort of sixth sense against coyotes and bear.

I was greeted by a little stampede of about a dozen lambs toward me. They are absent-minded creatures and sometimes will glance up and run to the first moving thing they see, which was the case with these now. When they figured out that Pony and Bubbles and I were not their mommas, they halted, peered at us a bit, then rampaged off in a new direction. Nothing is more likeable than a lamb bucking in fun. First will come that waggle of the tail, a spasm of wriggles faster than the eye can follow. Then a stiff-legged jump sideways, the current of joy hitting the little body so quick there isn't time to bend its knees. Probably a bleat, *byeahhh,* next, and then the romping run. Watching them you have to keep reminding yourself that lambs grow up, and what is pleasantly foolish in a lamb's brain is going to linger on to be just dumbness in the mind of a full-size ewe.

Andy Gustafson had no trove of dead camased ewes, nor any particular complaints, nor even much to say. He was wrinkled up in puzzlement for a while as to why it was me that was tending his camp, even after I explained as best I could, and I saw some speculation again when he noticed me slopping along with one boot unlaced. But once he'd checked through the groceries I'd brought to make sure that a big can of coffee and some tins of sardines were in there, and his weekly newspaper as well—Norwegian sheepherders seemed to come in two varieties, those whose acquaintance with the alphabet was confined to the

X they used for a signature and those who would quit you in an instant if you ever forgot to bring their mail copy of *Nordiske Tidende*—Andy seemed perfectly satisfied. He handed me his list of personals for the next camptending—razor blades, a pair of work socks, Copenhagen snoose—and away I went.

Where a day goes in the mountains I don't know, but by the time I reached the cabin again the afternoon was almost done. Stanley's saddle sorrel and the black pack horse were picketed a little way off, and Stanley emerged to offer me as usual whatever left-handed help he could manage in unsaddling Bubbles.

He noticed the spliced lash cinch. "See you had to use a little wildwood glue on the outfit."

I grunted something or other to that, and Stanley seemed to divine that it was not a topic I cared to dwell on. He switched to a question: "How's old Gufferson?"

"He said about three words total. I wouldn't exactly call that bellyaching." This sounded pretty tart even to me, so I added: "And he had his sheep in a nice Wyoming scatter, there west of his wagon."

"Sanford's on top of things, too," Stanley reported. "Hasn't lost any, and his lambs are looking just real good." Plain as anything, then, there was one sore thumb up here on the Busbys' allotment and it went by the name of Canada Dan.

Stanley extended the thought aloud. "Looks like Dan's asking for a ticket to town."

This I didn't follow. In all the range ritual I knew, and even in the perpetual wrestle between Dode Withrow and Pat Hoy, the herder always was angling to provoke a reason for quitting, not to be fired. Being fired from any job was a taint, a never-sought smudge. True, Canada Dan was a prime example that even God gets careless, but—

The puzzle pursued me on into the cabin. As Stanley stepped to the stove to try rev the fire a little, I asked: "What, are you saying Canada Dan *wants* to get himself canned?"

"Looks like. It can happen that way. A man'll get into a situation and do what he can to make it worse so he'll get chucked out of it. My own guess is, Dan's feeling thirsty and is scared of this timber as well, but he don't want to admit either one to himself. Easier to lay blame onto somebody else." Stanley paused. "Question is whether to try disappoint him out of the idea or just go ahead and can him." Another season of thought. Then: "I will say that Canada Dan is not such a helluva human being that I want to put up with a whole summer of his guff."

This was a starchier Stanley than I had yet seen. This one you could imagine giving Canada Dan the reaming out he so richly deserved.

The flash of backbone didn't last long, though. "But I guess he's the Busby boys' decision, not mine."

Naturally the day was too far gone for us to ride home to English Creek, so I embarked on the chores of wood and water again, at least salving myself with the prospect that tomorrow I would be relieved of Stanley. We would rise in the morning—and I intended it would be an early rise indeed—and ride down out of here and I would resume my summer at the English Creek ranger station and Stanley would sashay on past to the Busby brothers' ranch and that would be that.

When I stumped in with the water pail, that unlaced left boot of mine all but flapping in the breeze, I saw Stanley study the situation. "Too bad we can't slice up Bubbles for bootlaces," he offered.

"That'd help," I answered shortly.

"I never like to tell anybody how to wear his boots. But if it was me, now . . ."

I waited while Stanley paused to speculate out the cabin window to where dusk was beginning to deepen the gray of the cliff of Roman Reef. But I wasn't in any mood for very much waiting.

"You were telling me all about boots," I prompted kind of sarcastically.

"Yeah. Well. If it was me now, I'd take that one shoestring you got there, and cut it in half, and lace up each boot with a piece as far as it'll go. Ought to keep them from slopping off your feet, anyhow."

Worth a try. Anything was. I went ahead and did the halving, and the boots then laced firm as far as my insteps. The high tops pooched out like funnels, but at least now I could get around without one boot always threatening to leave me.

One chore remained. I reached around and pulled my shirt up out of the back of my pants. The remainder of the tail of it I jackknifed off. Stanley's hand didn't look quite so hideous this time when I rewrapped it; in the high dry air of the Two, cuts heal faster than can be believed. But this paw of Stanley's still was no prizewinner.

"Well," Stanley announced now, "you got me nursed. Seems like the next thing ought to be a call on the doctor." And almost before he was through saying it, last night's bottle reappeared over the table, its neck tilted into Stanley's cup.

Before Stanley got too deep into his oil of joy, there was one more vital point I wanted tended to. Diplomatically I began, "Suppose maybe we ought to give some thought—"

"—to supper," Stanley finished for me as he dippered a little water into his prescription. "I had something when I got back from Sanford's camp. But you go ahead."

I at least knew by now I could be my own chef if I had to, and I stepped over to the packs to get started.

There a harsh new light dawned on me. Now that we had tended the camps the packs were empty of groceries, which meant that we— or at least I, because so far I had no evidence that Stanley ever required food—were at the mercy of whatever was on hand in Stanley's own small supply pack. Apprehensively I dug around in there, but all that I came up with that showed any promise was an aging loaf of bread and some Velveeta cheese. So I made myself a bunch of sandwiches out of those and mentally chalked up one more charge against my father.

When I'd finished, it still was only twilight, and Stanley just had applied the bottle and dipper to the cup for a second time. Oh, it looked like another exquisite evening ahead, all right. A regular night at the opera.

Right then, though, a major idea came to me.

I cleared my throat to make way for the words of it. Then:

"I believe maybe I'll have me one, too."

Stanley had put his cup down on the table but was resting his good hand over the top of it as if there was a chance it might hop away. "One what?"

"One of those—doctor visits. A swig."

This drew me a considerable look from Stanley. He let go of his cup and scratched an ear. "Just how old're you?"

"Fifteen," I maintained, borrowing the next few months.

Stanley did some more considering, but by now I was figuring out that if he didn't say no right off the bat, chances were he wouldn't get around to saying it at all. At last: "Got to wet your wick sometime, I guess. Can't see how a swallow or two can hurt you." He transferred the bottle to a place on the table nearer me.

Copying his style of pouring, I tilted the cup somewhat at the same time I was tipping the bottle. Just before I thought Stanley might open his mouth to say something I ended the flow. Then went over to the water bucket and dippered in a splash or so the way he had.

It is just remarkable how something you weren't aware of knowing can pop to your aid at the right moment. From times I had been in the Medicine Lodge saloon with my father, I was able to offer now in natural salute to Stanley:

"Here's how!"

"How," Stanley recited back automatically.

Evidently I swigged somewhat deeper than I intended. Or should have gone a little heavier on the splash of water. Or something. By the time I set my cup down on the board table, I was blinking hard.

While I was at this, Stanley meanwhile had got up to shove wood into the stove.

"So what do you think?" he inquired. "Will it ever replace water?"

I didn't know about that, but the elixir of Doctor Hall did draw a person's attention.

Stanley reseated himself and was gandering around the room again. "Who's our landlord, do you know?"

"Huh?"

"This cabin. Who's got this school section now?"

"Oh. The Double W."

"Jesus H. Christ." Accompanying this from Stanley was the strongest look he had yet given me. When scrutiny told him I was offering an innocent's truth, he let out: "Is there a blade of grass anywhere those sonuvabitches won't try to get their hands on?"

"I dunno. Did you have some run-in with the Double W too?"

"A run-in." Stanley considered the weight of the words. "You might call it that, I guess. I had the particular pleasure once of telling old Warren Williamson, Wendell's daddy, that that big belly of his was a tombstone for his dead ass. 'Scuse my French again. And some other stuff got said." Stanley sipped and reflected. "What did you mean, 'too'?"

"My brother Alec, he's riding for the Double W."

"The hell you say." Stanley waited for me to go on, and when I didn't he provided: "I wouldn't wish that onto nobody. But just how does it constitute a run-in?"

"My folks," I elaborated. "They're plenty piss—uh, peed off over it."

"Family feathers in a fluff. The old, old story." Stanley tipped a sip again, and I followed. Inspiration in a cup must have been the encouragement my tongue was seeking, for before long I heard myself asking: "You haven't been in the Two country the last while, have you?"

"Naw."

"Where you been?"

"Oh, just a lot of places." Stanley seemed to review them on the cabin wall. "Down in Colorado for a while. Talk about dry. Half that state was blowing around chasing after the other half. A little time in both Dakotas. Worked in the wheat harvest there, insofar as there was any wheat after the drouth and the grasshoppers. And Wyoming. I was an association rider in that Cody country a summer or two. Then Montana here again for a while, over in the Big Hole Basin. A couple of haying seasons there." He considered, summed: "Around." Which moved him to another drag from his cup.

I had one from mine, too. "What're you doing back up in this country?"

"Like I say, by now I been everyplace else, and they're no better. Came back to the everloving Two to take up a career in tending camp, as you can plainly see. They advertise in those big newspapers for one-handed raggedy-ass camptenders, don't you know. You bet they do."

He did seem a trifle sensitive on this topic. Well, there was always some other, such as the matter of who he had been before he became a wandering comet. "Are you from around here originally?"

"Not hardly. Not a Two Mediciner by birth." He glanced at me. "Like you are. No, I—"

Stanley Meixell originated in Missouri, on a farm east of St. Joe in Daviess County. As he told it, the summer he turned thirteen he encountered the down-row of corn: that tumbled line of cornstalks knocked over by the harvest wagon as it straddled its way through the field. Custom was that the youngest of the crew always had to be the picker of the down-row, and Stanley was the last of five Meixell boys. Ahead of him stretched a green gauntlet of down-row summers. Except that by the end of the first sweltering day of stooping and ferreting into the tangle of downed stalks for ears of corn, Stanley came to his decision about further Missouri life. "Within the week I was headed out to the Kansas high plains." If you're like me you think of Kansas as one eternal wheatfield, but actually western Kansas then was cattle country. Dodge City was out there, after all.

Four or five years of ranch jobs out there in jayhawk country ensued for Stanley. "I can tell you a little story on that, Jick. This once we were dehorning a bunch of Texas steers. There was this one ornery sonuvabitch of a buckskin steer we never could get corraled with the others. After enough of trying, the foreman said he'd pay five dollars to anybody who'd bring that sonuvabitching steer in. Well, don't you know, another snot-nose kid and me decided we'd just be the ones. Off we rode, and we come onto him about three miles away from the corral, all by hisself, and he wasn't about to be driven. Well, then we figured we'd just rope him and drag him in. We got to thinking, though—three miles is quite a drag, ain't it? So instead we each loosed out our lariat, about ten feet of it, and took turns to get out in front of him and pop him across the nose with that rope. When we done that he'd make a hell of a big run at us and we'd dodge ahead out of his way, and he choused us back toward the corral that way. We finally got him up within about a quarter of a mile of the dehorning. Then each of us roped an end and tied him down and went on into the ranch and hitched up a stoneboat and loaded him on and boated him in in high old style. The foreman was waiting for us with five silver dollars in his hand."

Cowboying in the high old style. Alec, I thought to myself, you're the one who ought to be hearing this.

As happens, something came along to dislodge Stanley from that cowboying life. It was a long bunkhouse winter, weather just bad enough to keep him cooped on the ranch. "I'd go give the cows a jag of hay two times a day and otherwise all there was to do was sit around and do hairwork." Each time Stanley was in the barn he would pluck strands from the horses' tails, then back he went beside the bunkhouse stove to braid horsehair quirts and bridles "and eventually even a whole damn lasso." By the end of that hairwork winter the tails of the horses had thinned drastically, and so had Stanley's patience with Kansas.

All this life history of Stanley's I found amazingly interesting. I suppose that part of my father was duplicated in me, the fascination about pawing over old times.

While Stanley was storying, my cup had drained itself without my really noticing. Thus when he stopped to tip another round into his, I followed suit. The whiskey was weaving a little bit of wooze around me, so I was particularly pleased that I was able to dredge back yet another Medicine Lodge toast. I offered it heartily:

"Here's lead in your pencil!"

That one made Stanley eye me sharply for a moment, but he said only as he had the first time, "How," and tipped his cup.

"Well, that's Missouri and Kansas accounted for," I chirped in encouragement. "How was it you got up here to Montana?"

"On the seventeenth of March of 1898, to be real exact," Stanley boarded the first train of his life. From someone he had heard about Montana and a go-ahead new town called Kalispell, which is over on the west side of the Rockies, about straight across from there in the cabin where Stanley was telling me all this. Two days and two nights on that train. "The shoebox full of fried chicken one of those Kansas girls fixed for me didn't quite last the trip through."

In Kalispell then, "you could hear hammers going all over town." For the next few years Stanley grew up with the community. He worked sawmill jobs, driving a sawdust cart, sawfiling, foremanning a lumber piling crew. "Went out on some jobs with the U.S. Geological Survey, for a while there." A winter, he worked as a teamster hauling lumber from Lake Blaine into Kalispell. Another spell, he even was a river pig, during one of the log drives on the north fork of the Flathead River. "It was a world of timber over there then. I tell you something, though, Jick. People kind of got spoiled by it. Take those fires—December of my first year in Kalispell. They burned along the whole damn mountains from Big Fork to Bad Rock Canyon and even farther north than that. Everybody went out on the hills east of town at night to see the fire. Running wild on the mountains, that way. Green kid I was, I asked why somebody didn't do something about it. 'That's public domain,' I got told. 'Belongs to the government, not nobody around here.' Damn it to hell, though, when I saw that forest being burned up it just never seemed right to me." Stanley here took stiff encouragement from his cup, as if quenching the distaste for forest fire.

"Damn fire anyhow," I seconded with a slurp of my own. "But what got you across the mountains, here to the Two?"

Stanley gave me quite a glance, I guess to estimate the state of my health under Dr. Al K. Hall's ministration. I felt first-rate, and blinked Stanley an earnest response that was meant to say so.

"Better go a little slow on how often you visit that cup," he advised. Then: "The Two Medicine country. Why did I ever kiss her hello. Good question. One of the best."

What ensued is somewhat difficult to reconstruct. The bald truth, I may as well say, is that as Stanley waxed forth, my sobriety waned. But even if I had stayed sharp-eared as a deacon, the headful of the past which Stanley now provided me simply was too much to keep straight.

Tale upon tale of the Two country; memories of how the range looked some certain year; people who passed away before I was born; English Creek, Noon Creek, Gros Ventre, the reservation; names of horses, habits of sheepherders and cowboys, appreciations of certain saloons and bartenders. I was accustomed to a broth of history from my father and Toussaint Rennie, some single topic at a time, but Stanley's version was a brimming mulligan stew. "I can tell you a time, Jick, I was riding along in here under the Reef and met an old Scotch sheepherder on his horse. White-bearded geezer, hadn't had a haircut since Christmas. 'Lad!' he calls out to me. 'Can ye tell me the elevation here where we are?' Not offhand, I say to him, why does he want to know? 'Ye see, I was right here when those surveyors of that Theological Survey come through years ago, and they told me the elevation, but I forgot. I'm pretty sure the number had a seven in it, though.'" The forest fires of 1910, which darkened daytime for weeks on end: Stanley helped combat the stubborn one in the Two mountains west of where Swift Dam now stood. The flu epidemic during the world war: he remembered death outrunning the hearse capacity, two and three coffins at a time in the back of a truck headed for the Gros Ventre town cemetery. The legendary winter of '19: "We really caught hell, that time. Particularly those 'steaders in Scotch Heaven. Poor snowed-in bastards." The banks going under in the early twenties, the tide of homesteaders reversing itself. "Another time I can tell. In honor of Canada Dan, you might say. Must of been the summer of '16, I was up in Browning when one of those big sheep outfits out in Washington shipped in five thousand ewes and lambs. Gonna graze them there on the north end of the Two. Those sheep came hungry from eighteen hours on the stock cars, and they hit the flats out there and got onto deathcamas and lupine. Started dying by the hundreds. We got hold of all the pinanginated potash and sulfate of aluminum there was in the drugstore at Browning, and sent guys to fetch all of it there was in Cut Bank and Valier and Gros Ventre too, and we started in mixing the stuff in washtubs and dosing those sheep. Most of the ones we dosed pulled through okay, but it was too late for about a thousand of them others. All there was to do was drag in the carcasses and set them afire with brush. We burned dead sheep all night on that prairie."

Those sheep pyres I believe were the story that made me check out of Stanley's companionship for the evening. At least, I seem to remember counseling myself not to think about deceased sheep in combination with the social juice I'd been imbibing, by now three cups' worth. Stanley on the other hand had hardly even sipped during this tale-telling spell.

"I've about had a day," I announced. The bunk bed was noticeably more distant than it'd been the night before, but I managed to trek to it.

"Adios till the rooster crows," Stanley's voice followed me.

"Or till the crow roosts," I imparted to myself, or maybe to a more general audience, for at the time it seemed to me an exceptionally clever comment.

While my tongue was wandering around that way, though, and my fingers were trying to solve the bootlace situation, which for some reason began halfway down my boots instead of at the top where I was sure they ought to be, my mind was not idle. Cowboying, teamstering, river pigging: all this history of Stanley's was unexpected to me. I'd supposed, from my distant memory of him having been in our lives when I was so small, that he was just another camptender or maybe even an association rider back when this range was occupied by mostly cattle instead of sheep. But riding along up here and being greeted by the elevation-minded sheepherder as an expert on the Two: that sounded like, what, he'd been one of the early ranchers of this country? Homesteader, maybe? Fighting that forest fire of '10: must have volunteered himself onto the fire crew, association rider would fit that. But dosing all those sheep: that sounded like camptender again.

Then something else peeped in a corner of my mind. One boot finally in hand, I could spare the concentration for the question. "Stanley, didn' you say you been to this cabin before? When we got here, didn' you say that?"

"Yessir. Been here just a lot of times. I go back farther than this cabin does. I seen it being built. We was sighting out that fenceline over there when old Bob Barclay started dragging in the logs for this."

Being built? Sighting the boundary fencelines? The history was skipping to the most ancient times of the Two forest now, and this turn and the whiskey together were compounding my confusion. Also, somebody had put another boot in my hand. Yet I persisted.

"What, were you up here with the Theologic—the Geologic—the survey crew?"

Stanley's eyes were sharp, as if a new set had been put in amid the webs of eyelines. And the look he fastened on me now was the levelest thing in that cabin.

"Jick, I was the ranger that set up the boundaries of the Two Medicine National Forest."

Surely my face hung open so far you could have trotted a cat through it.

In any Forest Service family such as ours, lore of setting up the national forests, of the boundary examiners who established them onto the maps of America as public preserves, was almost holy writ. I could remember time upon time of hearing my father and the other Forest Service men of his age mention those original rangers and supervisors, the ones who were sent out in the first years of the century with not much more than the legal description of a million or so acres and orders to transform them into a national forest. "The forest arrangers," the men of my father's generation nicknamed them. Elers Koch on the Gallatin National Forest, Coert duBois on the Lolo, other boundary men who sired the Beaverhead and the Custer and the Helena and so on; the tales of them still circulated, refreshed by the comments of the younger rangers wondering how they'd managed to do all they had. Famous, famous guys. Sort of combinations of Old Testament prophets and mountain men, rolled into one. Everybody in the Forest Service told forest arranger stories at any chance. But that Stanley Meixell, wrong-handed campjack and frequenter of Doctor Al K. Hall, had been the original ranger of the Two Medicine National Forest, I had never heard a breath of. And this was strange.

"My sister is Mandy,
she's got a dandy.
At least so the boys say."

I woke with that in my ears and a dark brown taste in my mouth.

The serious symptoms set in when I sat up in my bunk. My eyes and temples and ears all seemed to have grown sharp points inward and were steadily stabbing each other. Life, the very air, seemed gritty, gray. Isn't there one hangover description that your tongue feels like you spent the night licking ashtrays? That's it.

"Morning there, Jick!" Stanley sang out. He was at the stove. "Here, better wash down your insides with this." Stepping over to the bunk, he handed me a tin cup of coffee turned tan with canned milk. Evidently he had heated the milk along with the coffee, because the contents of the cup were all but aflame. The heat went up my nose in search of my brain as I held the cup in front of my lips.

"No guarantee on this left-handed grub," Stanley called over his shoulder as he fussed at something on the stove top, "but how do you take your eggs?"

"Uh," I sought around in myself for the information. "Flipped, I guess."

Stanley hovered at the stove another minute or two while I made up my mind to try the death-defying trip to the table.

Then he turned and presented me a plate. Left-handed they may have been, but the eggs were fried to a crisp brown lace at the edges, while their pockets of yolk were not runny but not solidified either. Eggs that way are perfection. On the plate before me they were fenced in by wide tan strips of sidepork, and within a minute or so Stanley was providing me slices of bread fried in the pan grease.

I am my mother's son entirely in this respect: I believe good food never made any situation worse.

I dug in and by the time I'd eaten about half the plateful, things were tasting like they were supposed to. I even managed to sip some of the coffee, which I discovered was stout enough to float a kingbolt.

Indeed, I swarmed on to the last bite or so of the feast before it occurred to me to ask, "Where'd you get these eggs?"

"Aw, I always carry a couple small lard pails of oats for the horses, and the eggs ride okay in the oats."

Breakfast made me feel restored. "Speaking of riding," I began, "how soon—"

"—can we head down the mountain." Stanley inventoried me. And I took the chance to get in my first clear-eyed look of the day at him. Stanley seemed less in pain than he had when we arrived to this cabin but less in grasp of himself than he had during last night's recounting of lore of the Two. A man in wait, seeing which way he might turn; but unfortunately, I knew, the bottle habit soon would sway his decision. Of course, right then who was I to talk?

Now Stanley was saying: "Just any time now, Jick. We can head out as soon as you say ready."

On our ride down Stanley of course was into his musical repertoire again, one minute warbling about somebody who was wild and woolly and full of fleas and never'd been curried above her knees and the next crooning a hymnlike tune that went *"Oh sweet daughters of the Lord, grant me more than I can afford."*

My mind, though, was on a thing Stanley said as we were saddling the horses. In no way was it what I intended to think about, for I knew fully that I was heading back into the McCaskill family situation, that blowup between my parents and Alec. Godamighty, the supper that produced all that wasn't much more than a half a week ago. And in the meantime my father had introduced Stanley and Canada Dan and Bubbles, not to mention Dr. Al K. Hall, into my existence. There were words I intended to say to him about all this. If, that is, I could survive the matter of explaining to my mother why the tops of my boots gaped out like funnels and how come my pants legs looked like I'd wiped up a mountainside with them and where the tail of my shirt had gone. Thank the Lord, not even she could quite see into a person enough to count three tin cups of booze in him the night before. On that drinking score, I felt reasonably safe. Stanley didn't seem to me likely to trouble himself enough to advertise my behavior. On the other hand, Stanley himself was a logical topic for my mother. More than likely my father had heard, and I was due to hear, her full opinion of my having sashayed off on this campjacking expedition.

A sufficiency to dwell on, and none of it easy thinking. Against my intentions and better interests, though, I still found myself going back and forth over the last scene at the cabin.

I had just handed the lead rope for the black mare and ever-loving Bubbles up to Stanley and was turning away to go tighten the cinch on Pony's saddle. It was then that Stanley said he hoped I didn't mind too much about missing the rest of the counting trip with my father, to the Billy Peak lookout and all. "I couldn't of got along up here without you, Jick," he concluded, "and I hope you don't feel hard used."

Which of course was exactly how I had been feeling. You damn bet I was, ever since the instant my father volunteered me into Stanley's company. Skinning wet sheep corpses, contending with a pack horse who decides he's a mountain goat, nursing Stanley along, lightning, any number of self-cooked meals, the hangover I'd woke up with and still had more than a trace of—what sad sonofabitch wouldn't realize he was being used out of the ordinary?

Yet right then, eighteen-inch pincers would not have pulled such a confession from me. I wouldn't give the universe the satisfaction.

So, "No," I had answered Stanley, and gone on over to do my cinching. "No, it's all been an education."

TWO

This will mark the fifteenth Fourth of July in a row that Gros Ventre has mustered a creek picnic, a rodeo and a dance. Regarding those festivities, ye editor's wife inquires whether somebody still has her big yellow potato-salad bowl from last year; the rodeo will feature $140 in prize money; and the dance music will again be by Nola Atkins, piano, and Jeff Swan, fiddle.

—*GROS VENTRE WEEKLY GLEANER, JUNE 29*

I HAVE TO HONESTLY say that the next few weeks of this remembered summer look somewhat pale in comparison with my Stanley episode.

Only in comparison, though.

You can believe that I arrived back to English Creek from the land of sheepherders and pack horses in no mood to take any further guff from that father of mine. What in Holy H. Hell was that all about, him and Stanley Meixell pussyfooting around each other the way they had when they met there on the mountain, then before it was over my father handing me over to Stanley like an orphan? Some counting trip, that one. I could spend the rest of the summer just trying to dope out why and what and who, if I let myself. Considering, then, that my bill of goods against my father was so long and fresh, life's next main development caught me by entire surprise. This same parent who had just lent me as a towing service for a whiskeyfield geezer trying to find his way up the Rocky Mountains—this identical father now announced that he would be off the English Creek premises for a week, and I hereby was elevated into being the man of the house.

"Your legs are long enough by now that they reach the ground," he provided by way of justification the suppertime this was unveiled, "so I guess that qualifies you to run this place, don't you think?"

Weather brought this about, as it did so much else that summer. The cool wet mood of June continued and about the middle of the month our part of Montana had its solidest rain in years, a toad-drowner that settled in around noon and poured on and on into the night. That storm delivered snow onto the mountains. Several inches fell in the Big Belts south beyond the Sun River, and that next morning here in the Two, along the high sharp parts of all the peaks a white skift shined, fresh-looking as a sugar sprinkle. You could bet, though, there were a bunch of perturbed sheepherders up there looking out their wagon doors at it and not thinking sugar. Anyway, since that storm was a straightforward douser without any lightning and left the forests so sopping that there was no fire danger for a while, the desk jockeys at the national forest office in Great Falls saw this as a chance to ship a couple of rangers from the Two over to Region headquarters for a refresher course. Send them back to school, as it was said. Both my father and Murray Tomlin of the Blacktail Gulch station down on the Sun River had been so assiduous about evading this in the past that the finger of selection now never wavered whatsoever: it pointed the pair of them to Missoula for a week of fire school.

The morning came when my father appeared in his Forest Service monkey suit—heather-green uniform, side-crimped dress Stetson, pine tree badge—and readied himself to collect Murray at the Blacktail Gulch station, from where they would drive over to Missoula together.

"Mazoola," he was still grumbling. "Why don't they send us to hell to study fire and be done with it? What I hear, the mileage is probably about the same."

My mother's sympathy was not rampant. "All that surprises me is that you've gotten by this long without having to go. Have you got your diary in some pocket of that rig?"

"Diary," my father muttered, "diary, diary, diary," patting various pockets. "I never budge without it." And went to try to find it.

I spectated with some anticipation. My mood toward my father hadn't uncurdled entirely, and some time on my own, some open space without him around to remind me I was half sore at him, looked just dandy to me. As did this first-ever designation of me as the man of the house. Of course, I was well aware my father hadn't literally meant that I was to run English Creek in his absence. Start with the basic that nobody ran my mother. As for station matters, my father's assistant ranger Paul Eliason was strawbossing a fire trail crew not far along the South Fork and the new dispatcher, Chet Barnouw, was up getting familiar with the lookout sectors and the telephone setup which connected them to the ranger station. Any vital forest business would be handled by one of those two. No, I had no grandiose illusions. I was to make the check on Walter Kyle's place sometime during the week and help Isidor Pronovost line out his packstring when he came to pack supplies up to the fire lookouts and do some barn cleaning and generally be on hand for anything my mother thought up. Nothing to get wild-eyed about.

Even so, I wasn't prepared for what lay ahead when my father came back from his diary hunt, looked across the kitchen at me, said, "Step right out here for some free entertainment," and led me around back of the ranger station.

There he went to the side of the outhouse, being a little gingerly about it because of his uniform. Turned. Stepped off sixteen paces— why exactly sixteen I don't know, but likely it was in Forest Service regulations somewhere. And announced: "It's time we moved Republican headquarters. How're your shovel muscles?"

So here was my major duty of "running" English Creek in my father's absence, Digging the new hole to site the toilet over.

Let me be clear. The job itself I didn't particularly mind. Shovel work is honest sweat. Even yet I would sooner do something manual than to diddle around with some temperamental damn piece of machinery. No, my grouse was of a different feather than that. I purely was perturbed that here was one more instance of my father blindsiding me with a task I hadn't even dreamt of. First Stanley, now this outhouse deal. Here was a summer, it was beginning to seem like, when every time I turned around some new and strange avenue of endeavor was already under my feet and my father was pointing me along it and chirping, "Right this way, Jick."

All this and I suppose more was on my mind as my father's pickup vanished over the rise of the Gros Ventre road and I contemplated my work site.

Moving an outhouse may not sound like the nicest occupation in the world. But neither is it as bad as you probably think. Here is the program: when my father got back from Missoula we would simply lever up each side of the outhouse high enough to slip a pole under to serve as a skid, then nail crosspieces to keep the pair of skids in place and, with a length of cable attached to the back of the pickup, snake the building over atop the new pit and let it down into place, ready for business.

So the actual moving doesn't amount to all that much. The new pit, though. There's the drawback. The pit, my responsibility, was going to take considerable doing. Or rather, considerable digging.

At the spot my father had paced to and marked, I pounded in four stakes with white kitchen string from one to another to represent the outhouse dimensions. Inasmuch as ours was a two-holer, as was considered good-mannered for a family, it made a considerable rectangle; I guess about half again bigger than a cemetery grave. And now all I faced was to excavate the stringed-in space to a depth of about seven feet.

Seven feet divided by, umm, parts of five days, what with the week's other jobs and general choring for my mother. I doped out that if I did a dab of steady digging each afternoon I could handily complete the hole by Saturday when my father was due back. Jobs which can be broken down into stints that way, where you know that if you put in a certain amount of daily effort you'll overcome the chore, I have always been able to handle. It's the more general errands of life that daunt me.

I don't mean to spout an entire sermon on this outhouse topic, but advancing into the earth does get your mind onto the ground, in more ways than one. That day when I started in on the outhouse rectangle I of course first had to cut through the sod, and once that's been shoveled out it leaves a depression about the size of a cellar door. A sort of entryway down into the planet, it looked like. Unearthing that sod was the one part of this task that made me uneasy, and it has taken me these years to realize why. A number of times since, I have been present when sod was broken to become a farmed field. And in each instance I felt the particular emotion of watching that land be cut into furrows for the first time ever—*ever;* can we even come close to grasping what that means?—and the native grass being tipped on its side and then folded under the brown wave of turned earth. Anticipation, fascination. Part of the feeling can be described with those words or ones close to them. It can be understood, watching the ripping plow cut the patterns that will become a grainfield, that the homesteaders who came to Montana in their thousands believed they were seeing a new life uncovered for them.

Yet there's a further portion of those feelings, at least in me. Uneasiness. The uneasy wondering of whether that ripping-plow is honestly the best idea. Smothering a natural crop, grass, to try to nurture an artificial one. Not that I, or probably anyone else with the least hint of a qualm, had any vote in the matter. Both before and after the Depression—which is to say, in times when farmers had money enough to pay wages—kids such as I was in this particular English Creek summer were merely what you might call hired arms; brought in to pick rocks off the newly broken field. And not only the newly broken, for more rocks kept appearing and appearing. In fact in our part of Montana, rock-picking was like sorting through a perpetual landslide. Anything bigger than a grapefruit—the heftiest rocks might rival a watermelon—was dropped onto a stoneboat pulled by a team of horses or tractor, and the eventual load was dumped alongside the field. No stone fences built as in New England or over in Ireland or someplace. Just raw heaps, the slag of the plowed prairie.

I cite all this because by my third afternoon shift of digging, I had confirmed for myself the Two country's reputation for being a toupee of grass on a cranium of rock. Gravel, more accurately, there so close to the bed of English Creek, which in its bottom was a hundred percent small stones. We had studied in school that glaciers bulldozed through this part of the world, but until you get to handling the evidence shovelful by shovelful the fact doesn't mean as much to you.

I am dead sure this happened on the third afternoon, a Wednesday, because that was the day of the month the English Creek ladies' club met. There were enough wives along the creek to play two tables of cards and so have a rare enough chance to visit without males cluttering up the scene. Club day always found my mother in a fresh dress right after our noon meal, ready to go. This day, Alice Van Bebber stopped by to pick her up. "My, Jick, you're growing like a weed," Alice crooned out the car window to me as my mother got in the other side. Alice always was flighty as a chicken looking in a mirror—living with Ed likely would do it to anybody—and away the car zoomed, up the South Fork road toward Withrows', as it was Midge's turn to be hostess.

I know too that when I went out for my comfort station shift, I began by doing some work with a pick. Now, I didn't absolutely have to swing a pick on this project. With a little effort the gravel and the dirt mixed with it were shovelable enough. But I simply liked to do occasional pickwork. Liked the different feel and rhythm of that tool, operated overhand as it is rather than the perpetual reach-down-and-heave of shoveling. Muscles too need some variety in life, I have always thought.

So I was loosening the gravelly earth at the bottom of the hole with swings of the pick, and on the basis of Alice Van Bebber's blab was wondering to myself why a grownup never seemed to say anything to me that I wanted to hear, and after some minutes of this I stopped for breath. And in looking up saw just starting down toward the ranger station from the rise of the county road a string of three horses.

Sorrel and black and ugly gray.

Or, reading back down the ladder of colors, Bubbles and the pack mare and the saddle horse that Stanley Meixell was atop.

I didn't think it through. I have no idea why I did it. But I ducked down and sat in the bottom of the hole.

The moment I did, of course, I began to realize what I had committed myself to. They say nine tenths of a person is above the ears, but I swear the proportion sometimes gets reversed in me. Not that I wasn't safely out of sight squatting down there; when I'd been standing up working, my excavation by now was about shoulder deep on me. No problem there. No problem so long as Stanley didn't get a direct look down into the hole. But what if that happened? What if Stanley stopped at the station, for some reason or other? And, say, being stopped anyway he decided to use the outhouse, and as he was headed out there decided to amble over to admire this pit of mine? What then? Would I pop up like a jack-in-the-box? I'd sure as the dickens look just as silly as one.

I was also learning that the position I had to squat in wasn't the world's most comfortable. And it was going to take a number of minutes for Stanley and company to saunter down from the rise and pass the station and go off up the North Fork road, before I could safely

stand up. Just how many minutes began to interest me more than anything else. Of course I had no watch, and the only other way I knew to
keep track of time was to count it off like each five-second interval
between lightning and thunder: one a-mile-from-here-to-there— But
the problem there, how much time did I have to count off? That I'd
have to work out in my head, Alec style. Let's see: say Stanley and his
horses were traveling 5 miles an hour, which was the figure Major Kelley was always raising hell with the Forest Service packers about, insisting they by God and by damn ought to be able to average that. But the
Major had never encountered Bubbles. Bubbles surely would slow
down any enterprise at least half a mile an hour, dragging back on his
lead rope like a tug of war contestant the way he did. Okay, 4½ miles
an hour considering Bubbles, and it was about a mile from the crest of
the county road to down here at the ranger station; then from here to
where Stanley would pass out of sight beyond the North Fork brush
was, what, another third of a mile, maybe more like half a mile. So now:
for Stanley to cover one mile at 4½ miles an hour would take—well,
5 miles an hour would be 12 minutes; 4 miles an hour would be 15
minutes; round the 4½ mile an hour pace off to say 13 minutes; then
the other one third to one half mile would take somewhere around
6 minutes, wouldn't it be? So, 13 and 6, 19 minutes. Then 19 times
60 (60 seconds to the minute), and that was, was, was . . . 1100-
something. And divide that by the five seconds it took to say each—

Never mind, I decided. This hunching down in a toilet hole was all
getting dismal enough without me trying to figure out how many *a-
mile-from-here-to-theres* there are in 1100-something. Besides, I had no
idea how much time I had already spent in the calculating.

Besides again, numbers weren't really what needed thinking on. The
point to ponder was, why was I hiding anyway? Why had I plunked
myself into this situation? Why didn't I want to face Stanley? Why had
I let the sight of him hoodoo me like this? Some gab about the weather,
inquire as to how his hand was getting along, say I had to get back to
digging, and that would have been that. But no, here I was, playing turtle to the bottom of an outhouse pit. Sometimes there's nobody
stranger in this world than ourselves.

So I squatted and mulled. There is this for sure about doing those
two together, they fairly soon convince you that you can think better
standing up. Hell with it, I eventually told myself. If I had to pop up
and face Stanley with my face all pie, so be it.

I unkinked and came upright with some elaborate arm-stretching, as if I'd just had a nice break from work down there. Then treated myself to a casual yawn and began eyeing around over the rim of the pit to determine which direction I had to face embarrassment from.

And found nobody.

No Stanley. No Bubbles. Nothing alive anywhere around, except one fourteen-year-old fool.

"So," my mother inquired upon return from her ladies' club, "everything peaceful around here?"

"Downright lonesome," I said back.

Now let me tell of my mother's contribution to that week.

It ensued around midday on Thursday. First thing that morning Isidor Pronovost showed up and I spent the front of the day working as cargodier for him, helping make up packs of supplies to take up to the fire lookouts.

"Balance," Isidor sermoned as he always did. "We got to balance the buggers, Jick. That's every secret of it." Harking back to my Bubbles experience I thought to myself, Don't I know it.

Then Isidor was not much more than out of sight with his pack-string when here came my mother's brother, Pete Reese. English Creek was getting about as busy as Broadway.

Pete had driven into town from his ranch on Noon Creek on one errand or another, and now was looping home by way of English Creek to drop off our mail and see how we were faring. He stepped over and admired my progress on the outhouse hole. "Everybody on the creek'll be wanting to patronize it. You thought of charging admission?" Then handed me the few letters and that week's *Gleaner*. His doing so reminded me I was the temporary host of the place and I hurriedly invited, "Come on over to the house."

We no sooner were through the door than my mother was saying to Pete, "You're staying for dinner, aren't you," more as declaration than question. So Pete shed his hat and offered that he supposed he could, "if it's going to be something edible." Pete got away with more with my mother than just about anyone else could, including my father. "Park your tongue then," she simply retorted, and went to work on the meal while Pete and I chinned about the green year.

That topic naturally was staying near the front of everybody's mind. By now the weather service was declaring this the coolest June in Montana since 1916 and the wettest in almost as long, news which was more than welcome. In Montana too much rain is just about enough. All the while the country had been greening and greening, the crop and livestock forecasts were flourishing, too. Pete imparted that Morrel Loomis, the biggest wool buyer operating in the Two country, had come up from Great Falls for a look at the Reese and Hahn and Withrow bands, and that Pete and Fritz and Dode all decided to go ahead and consign their wool to Loomis on his offer of twenty-one and a half cents a pound. "Enough to keep me floating toward bankruptcy," Dode had been heard to say, which meant that even he was pretty well pleased with the price.

"Beats last year by a couple of cents, doesn't it?" I savvily asked Pete.

"Uh huh, and it's damn well time. Montana has got to be the champion next-year country of the entire damn world."

"How soon did you say you'd be haying?" my mother interrogated without looking around from her meal work at the stove. I wish now that she had in fact been facing around toward Pete and me, for I am sure my gratitude for that question was painted all over my face. Whenever haying began I was to drive the scatter rake for Pete, as I had done the summer before and Alec had for the few summers before that. But getting a rancher to estimate a date when he figured his hay crop would be ready was like getting him to confess to black magic. The hemming and hawing did have the basis that hay never was really ready to mow until the day you went out and looked at it and felt it and cocked an eye at the weather and decided this was as good a time as any. But I also think ranchers cherished haying as the one elastic part of their year. The calendar told them when lambing or calving would begin, and shipping time loomed as another constant, so when they had a chance to be vague—even Pete, of the same straightforward lineage as my mother, now was pussyfooting to the effect that "all this rain, hay's going to be kind of late this year"—they clung to it.

"Before the Fourth?" my mother narrowed the specification.

"No, I don't suppose." It was interesting to see comments go back and forth between this pair; like studying drawings of the same face done by two different artists. Pete had what might be called the kernel of my mother's good looks. Same neat nose, apple cheeks, attractive Reese chin, but proportioned smaller, thriftier.

"The week after?"

"Could be," Pete allowed. "Were you going to feed us sometime today or what?"

Messages come in capsules as well as bottles. The content of "Could be" was that no hay would be made by Pete Reese until after the Fourth of July, and until then I was loose in the world.

There during dinner, it turned out that Pete now was on the question end of the conversation:

"Alec been around lately?"

"Alec," my mother reported in obituary tones, "is busy Riding the Range."

"Day and night?"

"At least. Our only hope of seeing him is if he ever needs a clean shirt."

My personal theory is that a lot of misunderstanding followed my mother around just because of her way of saying. Lisabeth Reese McCaskill could give you the time of day and make you wonder why you had dared to ask. I recall once when I was about eleven that we were visited for the morning by Louise Bowen, wife of the young ranger at the Indian Head district to the south of us. Cliff Bowen was newly assigned onto the Two, having held down an office job at Region head-quarters in Missoula all the time before, and Louise was telling my mother how worried she was that her year-old, Donny, accustomed to town and a fenced yard, would wander off from the station, maybe fall into the Teton River. I was in the other room, more or less reading a *Collier's* and minding my own business, but I can still hear how my mother's response suddenly seemed to fill the whole house:

"Bell him."

There was a stretch of silence then, until Louise finally kind of peeped: "Beg pardon? I don't quite—"

"Put a bell on him. The only way to keep track of a wandering child is to hear him."

Louise left not all too long after that, and that was the extent of our visits from her. But I did notice, when my father drove down to borrow a saw set from Cliff a month or so later and I rode along, that Donny Bowen was toddling around with a lamb bell on him.

Pete was continuing on the topic of Alec. "Well, he's at that age—"

"Pete," she headed him off, "I know what age my own son is."

"So you do, Bet. But the number isn't all of it. You might try and keep that in mind."

My mother reached to pass Pete some more fried spuds. "I'll try," she allowed. "I Will Try."

When we'd eaten and Pete declared, "It's time I wasn't here" and headed home to Noon Creek, my mother immediately began drowning dirty dishes and I meanwhile remembered the mail I'd been handed, and fetched it from the sideboard where I'd put it down. There was a letter to my mother from Mr. Vennaman, the Gros Ventre school superintendent—even though Alec and I were gone from the English Creek school my mother still was president of its board and so had occasional dealings with the education muckymucks in Gros Ventre and Conrad—and a couple of Forest Service things for my father, probably the latest kelleygrams. But what I was after was the *Gleaner,* thinking I'd let my dinner settle a little while I read.

As usual, I opened to page 5. The newspaper was always eight pages and page 5 was always the At Random page, carrying the editor Bill Reinking's own comments, and syndicated features about famous people or events, and local history, and even poetry or quotations if Bill felt like it. Random definitely was the right word for it, yet every week that page was a magnet for a mind like mine.

I'd been literary for maybe three minutes when I saw the names.

"Mom? You and Pete are in the paper."

She turned from where she was washing dishes and gave me her look that said, you had now better produce some fast truth.

I pinned down the newsprint evidence with my finger: "See, here."

25 YEARS AGO IN THE GLEANER
Anna Reese and children Lisabeth and Peter visited Isaac
Reese at St. Mary Lake for three days last week. Isaac is pro-

viding the workhorses for the task of building the roadbed from St. Mary to Babb. Isaac sends word through Anna that the summer's work on this and other Glacier National Park roads and trails is progressing satisfactorily.

As she read over my shoulder I thought about the journey that would have been in those days. Undoubtedly by democrat wagon, from the Reese place on Noon Creek all the way north almost to Chief Mountain, the last peak on that horizon. I of course had been over that total route with my father, but only a piece at a time, on various riding trips and by pickup to the northernmost part. But to do the whole journey at once, by hoof and iron wheel, a woman and two kids, struck me as a notable expedition.

"Sounds like a long time in a wagon," I prompted cannily. "You never told me about that."

"Didn't I." And she turned and went back to her dishpan.

Well, sometimes you could prompt my mother, and sometimes you might as well try conversing with the stove poker.

I retreated into my hole, so to speak. Yet, you know how it is when you're doing something your body can take care of by itself. Your mind is going to sneak off somewhere on its own. As the rest of me dug, mine was on that wagon journey with my mother and Pete and their mother.

There wouldn't have been the paved highway north to Browning and the Park then, just the old road as the wheels of the freight wagons had rutted it into the prairie. Some homesteads must have still existed between Gros Ventre and the Blackfeet Reservation boundary at Birch Creek, but probably not many. Those were the years when the Valier irrigation project was new and anybody who knew grain grew on a stem was over there around Lake Frances trying to be a farmer. Mostly empty country, then, except for livestock, all the way to Birch Creek and its ribbon line of cottonwoods. Empty again from there north to Badger Creek, where I supposed some of the same Blackfeet families lived then as now. There near Badger the Reese wagon would have passed just west of the place where, a century and some before, Meriwether Lewis and the Blackfeet clashed. That piece of reservation country to us was simply grass, until my father deduced from reading in a book of the Lewis and Clark journals that somewhere off in there near where Badger flows into the Two Medicine River was the place Lewis and his men killed a couple of Blackfeet over a stealing incident and began the long prairie war between whites and Indians. Passing that area in a pickup on paved highway never made that history seem real to me. I would bet it was more believable from a wagon. Then up from Badger, the high benches to where the Two Medicine trenched deep through the landscape. Maybe another couple of days of travel beyond that, through Browning and west and then north across Cut Bank Creek and through that up and down country above it, and over the divide to St. Mary, and there at the end of it all the road camp, its crews and tents and workhorses. In my imagination I saw it as somewhat like a traveling circus, but with go-devils and scrapers and other road machines instead of circus wagons. And its ringmaster, my grandfather, Isaac Reese. He was the only one of my grandparents yet alive when I became old enough to remember and I could just glimpse him in a corner of my mind. A gray-mustached man at the head of the table whenever we had Sunday dinner at the Reeses', using his knife to load his fork with food in a way which would have caused my mother to give Alec or me absolute hell if we had dared try it. I gather, though, that Isaac Reese got away with considerably more than that in life—I suppose any horse dealer worth his reputation did—and it was a thriving Reese ranch there on Noon Creek that Pete took over after the old man's death.

This Reese side of the family wandered into the conversation whenever someone would learn that my mother, although she was married to a man only a generation or so away from kilts, herself was just half Scottish. "The other half," my father would claim when he judged that she was in a good enough mood he could get away with it, "seems to be something like porcupine." Actually, that lineage was Danish. Isak Riis left Denmark aboard the ship *King Carl* sometime in the 1880s, and the pen of an immigration official greeted him onto American soil as Isaac Reese. In that everybody-head-west-and-grab-some-land period, counting was more vital than spelling anyway. By dint of what his eyes told him on the journey west, Isaac arrived to North Dakota determined on a living from workhorses. The Great Northern railroad was pushing across the top of the western United States—this was when Jim Hill was promising to cobweb Dakota and Montana with railroad iron—and Isaac began as a teamster on the roadbed. His ways with horses and projects proved to be as sure as his new language was shaky. My father claimed to have been on hand the famous time, years later, when Isaac couldn't find the words "wagon tongue" and ended up calling it "de Godtamn handle to de Godtamn vagon."

Within days after sizing up the railroad situation "the old boy was borrowing money right and left from anybody who'd take his note, to buy horses and more horses"—my father was always a ready source on Isaac, I guess greatly grateful to have had a father-in-law he both admired and got entertainment from—and soon Isaac had his own teams and drivers working on contract for the Great Northern.

When construction reached the east face of the Rockies, the mountains held Isaac. Why, nobody in the family ever could figure out. Certainly in Denmark he must never have seen anything higher than a barnyard manure pile. And unlike some other parts of Montana, this one had no settlement of Danes. (Though, as my father pointed out, maybe those *were* Isaac's reasons.) In any case, while his horses and men worked on west through Marias Pass as the railroad proceeded toward the coast, Isaac stayed and looked around. In a week or so he horsebacked south along the mountains toward Gros Ventre, and out of that journey bought a homestead relinquishment which became the start of the eventual Reese ranch.

Isaac Reese was either shrewd as hell or lucky as hell. Even at my stage of life I am not entirely clear whether there is any appreciable difference between the two. By whichever guidance he lit here in a region of Montana where a couple of decades of projects were standing in line waiting for a man with a herd of workhorses. The many miles of irrigation canals of the water schemes at Valier and Bynum and Choteau and Fairfield. Ranch reservoirs ("ressavoys" to Isaac). The roadbed when the branch railroad was built north from Choteau to Pendroy. Street grading when Valier was built onto the prairie. All those Glacier Park roads and trails. As each appurtenance was put onto the Two country and its neighboring areas, Isaac was on hand to realize money from it.

"And married a Scotchwoman to hang on to the dollars for him," my father always injected at this point. She was Anna Ramsay, teacher at the Noon Creek school. Her I knew next to nothing about. Just that she died in the influenza epidemic during the war, and that in the wedding picture of her and Isaac that hung in my parents' bedroom she was the one standing and looking in charge, while Isaac sat beside her with his mustache drooping whimsically. Neither my mother nor my father ever said much about Anna Ramsay Reese; which helped sharpen my present curiosity, thinking about her trundling off to St. Mary in that wagon. Like my McCaskill grandparents she simply was an absent figure back there, cast all the more into shadow by my father's supply of stories about Isaac.

In a sense, the first of those Isaac tales was the genesis of our family. The night my father, the young association rider, was going to catch Isaac by ambush and request my mother in marriage, Isaac greeted him at the door and before they were even properly sat down, had launched into a whole evening of horse topics, Clydesdales and Belgians and Morgans and fetlocks and withers and hocks. Never tell me a Scandinavian harbors no sense of humor.

When my father at last managed to wedge the question in, Isaac tried to look taken aback, eyed him hard and repeated as if he was making sure: "Marriage?" Or as my father said Isaac pronounced it: "Mare itch?"

Then Isaac looked at my father harder yet and asked: "Tell me dis. Do you ever took a drink?"

My father figured honesty was the best answer in the face of public knowledge. "Now and then, yes, I do."

Isaac weighed that. Then he got to his feet and loomed over my father. "Ve'll took one now, den." And with Mason jar moonshine reached down from the cupboard, the pairing that began Alec and me was toasted.

When I considered that I'd done an afternoon's excavating, physically and mentally, I climbed out and had a look at the progress of my sanitation engineering. By now the pile of dirt and gravel stood high and broad, the darker tone on its top showing today's fresh shovel work and the drier faded-out stuff the previous days'. With a little imagination I thought I could even discern a gradation, like layers on a cake, of each stint of my shovelfuls of the Two country, Monday's, Tuesday's, Wednesday's, and now today's light-chocolate top. Damn interesting, the ingredients of this earth.

More to the immediate point, I was pleased with myself that I'd estimated the work into the right daily dabs. Tomorrow afternoon was going to cost some effort, because I was getting down so deep the soil would need to be bucketed out. But the hole looked definitely finishable.

I must have been more giddy with myself than I realized, because when I went over to the chopping block to split wood for the kitchen woodbox, I found myself using the ax in rhythm with a song of Stanley's about the gal named Lou and what she was able to do with her wingwangwoo.

When I came into the kitchen with the armload, my mother was looking at me oddly.

"Since when did you take up singing?" she inquired.

"Oh, just feeling good, I guess," I said and dumped my cargo into the woodbox loud enough to try prove it.

"What was that tune, anyway?"

" 'Pretty Redwing,'" I hazarded. "I think."

That brought a further look from her.

"While I'm at it I might as well fill the water bucket," I proposed, and got out of there.

After supper, lack of anything better to do made me tackle my mother on that long ago wagon trip again. That is, I was doing something but it didn't exactly strain the brain. Since hearing Stanley tell about having done that winter of hairwork a million years ago in Kansas, I had gotten mildly interested and was braiding myself a horsehair hackamore. I was discovering, though, that in terms of entertainment, braiding is pretty much like chewing gum with your fingers. So:

"Where'd you sleep?"

She was going through the *Gleaner.* "Sleep when?"

"That time. When you all went up to St. Mary." I kept on with my braiding just as if we'd been having this continuing conversation every evening of our lives.

She glanced over at me, then said: "Under the wagon."

"Really? You?" Which drew me more of her attention than I was bargaining for. "Uh, how many nights?"

I got quite a little braiding done in the silence that answered that, and when I finally figured I had to glance up, I realized that she was truly studying me. Not just taking apart with a look: studying. Her voice wasn't at all sharp when she asked: "Jick, what's got your curiosity bump up?"

"I'm just interested, is all." Even to me that didn't sound like an overly profound explanation, so I tried to go on. "When I was with Stanley, those days camptending, he told me a lot about the Two. About when he was the ranger. It got me interested in, uh, old times."

"What did he say about being ranger?"

"That he was the one here before Dad. And that he set up the Two as a national forest." It occurred to me to try her on a piece of chronology I had been attempting to work out ever since that night of my cabin binge. "What, was Dad the ranger at Indian Head while Stanley still was the ranger here?"

"For a while."

"Is that where I remember Stanley from?"

"I suppose."

"Did you and Dad neighbor back and forth with him a lot?"

"Some. What does any of that have to do with how many nights I slept under a wagon twenty-five years ago?"

She had a reasonable enough question there. Yet it somehow seemed to me that a connection did exist, that any history of a Two country person was alloyed with the history of any other Two country person. That some given sum of each life had to be added into every other, to find the total. But none of which sounded sane to say. All I did finally manage was: "I just would like to know something about things then. Like when you were around my age."

No doubt there was a response she had to bite her tongue to keep from making: that she wasn't sure she'd ever been this age I seemed to be at just now. Instead came:

"All right. That wagon trip to St. Mary. What is it you want to know about it?"

"Well, just—why was it you went?"

"Mother took the notion. My father had been away, up there, for some weeks. He often was, contracting horses somewhere." She rustled the *Gleaner* as she turned a page. "About like being married to a ranger," she added, but lightly enough to show it was her version of a joke.

"How long did that trip take then?" Now, in a car, it was a matter of a couple or three hours.

She had to think about that. After a minute: "Three and a half days. *Three* nights," she underscored for my benefit, "under the wagon. One at Badger Creek and one on the flat outside Browning and one at Cut Bank Creek."

"How come outside Browning? Why not in town?"

"My mother held the opinion that the prairie was a more civilized place than Browning."

"What did you do for food?"

"We ate out of a chuck box. That old one from chuckwagon days, with all the cattle brands on it. Mother and I cooked up what was necessary, before we left."

"Were you the only ones on the road?"

"Pretty much, yes. The mail stage still was running then. Somewhere along the way I guess we met it."

She could nail questions shut faster than I could think them up. Not deliberately, I see now. That was just the way she was. A person who put no particular importance on having made a prairie trek and seen a stagecoach in the process.

My mother seemed to realize that this wasn't exactly flowering into the epic tale I was hoping for. "Jick, that's all I know about it. We went, and stayed a few days, and came back."

Went, stayed, came. The facts were there but the feel of them wasn't.

"What about the road camp?" I resorted to next. "What do you remember about that?" The St. Mary area is one of the most beautiful ones, with the mountains of Glacier National Park sheering up beyond the lake. The world looks to be all stone and ice and water there. Even my mother might have noticed some of that glory.

Here she found a small smile, one of her surprise sidelong ones. "Just that when we pulled in, Pete began helloing all the horses."

She saw that didn't register with me.

"Calling out hello to the workhorses in the various teams," she explained. "He hadn't seen them for a while, after all. 'Hello, Woodrow!' 'Hello, Sneezer!' Moses. Runt. Copenhagen. Mother let him go on with it until he came to a big gray mare called Second Wife. She never thought the name of that one was as funny as Father did."

There is this about history, you never know which particular ember of it is going to glow to life. As she told this I could all but hear Pete helloing those horses, his dry voice making a chant which sang across that road camp. And the look on my mother told me she could, too.

Not to be too obvious, I braided a moment more. Then decided to try the other part of that St. Mary scene. "Your own mother. What was she like?"

"That father of yours has been heard to say I'm a second serving of her."

Well, this at least informed me that old Isaac Reese hadn't gotten away with nearly as much in life as I'd originally thought. But now, how to keep this line of talk going—

"Was she an April Fool too?"

"No," my mother outright laughed. "No, I seem to be the family's only one of that variety."

Probably our best single piece of family lore was that my mother, our unlikeliest candidate for any kind of foolery, was born on the first of April of 1900. "Maybe you could get the calendar changed," I recall that my father joked this particular year, when he and Alec and I were spoofing her a little, careful not to make it too much, about the coincidence of her birthday. "Trade dates with Groundhog Day, maybe." She retorted, "I don't need the calendar changed, just slowed down." It sobers me to realize that when she made that plaint about the speed of time, she was not yet two thirds of the age I am now.

—"Why did I What?" The *Gleaner* was forgotten in front of her now, her gaze was on me: not her look that could skin a rock, just a highly surprised once-over.

I swear that what I'd had framed in mind was only further inquiry about my grandparents, how Anna Ramsay and Isaac Reese first happened to meet and when they'd decided to get married and so on. But somewhere a cog slipped, and what had fallen out of my mouth instead was "Why'd you marry Dad?"

"Well, you know," I now floundered, searching for any possible shore, "what I mean, kids wonder about something like that. How we got here." Another perilous direction, that one. "I don't mean, uh, *how,* exactly. More like why. Didn't you ever wonder yourself? Why your own mother and father decided to get married? I mean, how would any of us be here if those people back then hadn't decided the way they did? And I just thought, since we're talking about all this anyway, you could fill me in on some of it. Out of your own experience, sort of."

My mother looked at me for an eternity more, then shook her head. "One of them goes head over heels after anything blond, the other one wants to know the history of the world. Alec and you. Where did I get you two?"

I figured I had nothing further to lose by taking the chance: "That's sort of what I was asking, isn't it?"

"All right." She still looked skeptical of the possibility of common sense in me, but her eyes let up on me a little. "All right, Mr. Inquisitive. You want to know the makings of this family, is that it?"

I nodded vigorously.

She thought. Then: "Jick, a person hardly knows how to start on this. But you know, don't you, I taught most of that—that one year at the Noon Creek school?"

I did know this chapter. That when my mother's mother died in the flu epidemic of 1918, my mother came back from what was to have been her second year in college and became, in her mother's stead, the Noon Creek teacher.

"If it hadn't been for that, who knows what would have happened," she went on. "But that did bring me back from college, about the same time a redheaded galoot named Varick McCaskill came back from the army. His folks still were in here up the North Fork. Scotch Heaven. So Mac was back in the country and the two of us had known each other, oh, all our lives, really. Though mostly by sight. Our families didn't always get along. But that's neither here nor there. That spring when this Mac character was hired as association rider—"

"Didn't get along?"

I ought to have known better. My interruption sharpened her right up again. "That's another story. There's such a thing as a one-track mind, but honestly, Jick, you McCaskill men sometimes have no-track minds. Now. Do you want to Hear This, Or—"

"You were doing just fine. Real good. Dad got to be the association rider and then what?"

"All right then. He got to be the association rider and—well, he got to paying attention to me. I suppose it could be said I paid some back."

Right then I yearned for the impossible. To have watched that double-sided admiration. My mother had turned nineteen the first of April of that teaching year; a little older than Alec was now, though not a whole hell of a lot. Given what a good-looker she was even now, she must have been extra special then. And my father the cowboy—hard to imagine that—would have been in his early twenties, a rangy redhead who'd been out in the world all the way to Camp Lewis, Washington. Varick and Lisabeth, progressing to Mac and Bet. And then to some secret territory of love language that I couldn't even guess at. They are beyond our knowing, those once young people who become our parents, which to me has always made them that much more fascinating.

—"There was a dance, that spring. In my own schoolhouse, so your father ever since has been telling me I have nobody to blame but myself." She again had a glow to her, as when she'd told me about Pete helloing the horses. "Mac was on hand. By then he'd been hired by the Noon Creek ranchers and was around helping them brand calves and so on. That dance"—she shrugged, as if an impossible question had been asked—"that dance I suppose did it, though neither of us knew it right then. I'd been determined I was never going to marry into a ranch life. Let alone to a cow chouser who didn't own much more than his chaps and hat. And later I found out from your father that he'd vowed never to get interested in a schoolmarm. Too uppity to bother with, he always thought. So much for intentions. Anyway, now here he was, in my own schoolroom. I'd never seen a man take so much pleasure in dancing. Most of it with me, need I say. Oh, and there was this. I hadn't been around him or those other Scotch Heaveners while I was away at college, and I'd lost the knack of listening to that burr of theirs. About the third time that night he said something I couldn't catch, I asked him: 'Do you always talk through your nose?' And then he put on a *real* burr and said back, 'Lass, it saves wearr and tearrr on my lips. They'rrre in prrrime condition, if you'rrre everrr currrious.'"

My father the flirt. Or flirrrt. I must have openly gaped over this, for my mother reddened a bit and stirred in her chair and declared, "Well, you don't need full details. Now then. Is that enough family history?"

Not really. "You mean, the two of you decided to get married because you liked how Dad danced?"

"You would be surprised how large a part something like that plays. But no, there's more to it than that. Jick, when people fall in love the way we did, it's—I don't mean this like it sounds, but it's like being sick. Sick in a wonderful way, if you can imagine that. The feeling is in you just all the time, is what I mean. It takes you over. No matter what you do, what you try to think about, the other person is there in your head. Or your blood, however you want to say it. It's"—she shrugged at the impossible again—"there's no describing it beyond that. And so we knew. A summer of that—a summer when we didn't even see each other that much, because your father was up in the Two tending the association cattle most of the time—we just knew. That fall, we were married." Here she sprung a slight smile at me. "And I let myself in for all these questions."

There was one, though, that hovered. I was trying to determine whether to open my yap and voice it when she took it on herself. "My guess is, you're thinking about Alec and Leona, aren't you."

"Yeah, sort of."

"Lord knows, they imagine they're in a downright epidemic of love," my mother acknowledged. "Alec maybe is. He's always been all

go and no whoa. But Leona isn't. She can't be. She's too young and"—
my mother scouted for aptness—"flibberty. Leona is in love with the
idea of men, not one man. And that's enough on that subject." She
looked across at me in a way that made my fingers quit even pretending they were manufacturing a horsehair hackamore. "Now I have one
for you. Jick, you worry me a little."

"Huh? I do?"

"You do. All this interest of yours in the way things were. I just hope
you don't go through life paying attention to the past at the expense of
the future. That you don't pass up chances because they're new and
unexpected." She said this next softly, yet also more strongly than anything else I'd ever heard her say. "Jick, there isn't any law that says a
McCaskill can't be as forward-looking as anybody else. Just because
your father and your brother, each in his own way, looks to the past to
find life, you needn't. They are both good men. I love the two of
them—the three of you—in the exact way I told you about, when your
father and I started all this. But, Jick, be ready for your life ahead. It
can't all be read behind you."

I looked back at her. I wouldn't have bet I had it in me to say this.
But it did come out: "Mom, I know it all can't. But some?"

That next afternoon, Friday, was the homestretch of my digging. It
needed to be, with my father due home sometime the next morning. And
so once more unto the bowels of the earth, so to speak, taking down with
me into the outhouse pit an old short-handled lady shovel Toussaint Rennie had given my father and a bucket to pack the dirt out with.

My mood was first-rate. My mother's discourse from the evening
before still occupied my thinking. The other portion of me by now was
accustomed to the pit work, muscles making no complaint whatsoever,
and in me that feeling of bottomless stamina you have when you are
young, that you can keep laboring on and on and on, forever if need be.
The lady shovel I was using was perfect for this finishing-off work of
dabbing dirt into the bucket. To make it handy in his ditch-riding Toussaint always shortened the handle and then ground off about four
inches of the shovel blade, cutting it down into a light implement about
two thirds of a normal shovel but which still, he proclaimed, "carries all
the dirt I want to." And working as I had been for a while each day
without gloves to get some good calluses started, now I had full benefit

of the smooth old shovel handle in my bare hands. To me, calluses have always been one of the marks of true summer.

How long I lost myself to the rhythm of the lady shovel and the bucket I don't know. But definitely I was closing in on the last of my project, bottoming the pit out nice and even, when I stepped toward my ladder to heft up a pailful of dirt and found myself looking into the face of a horse. And above that, a hat and grin which belonged to Alec.

"Going down to visit the Chinamen, huh?"

Why did that get under my skin? I can run that remark of Alec's through my ears a dozen times now and find no particular reason for it to be rilesome. In my brother's lofty position I'd likely have commented in similar fashion. But there must be something about being come upon in the bottom of an outhouse hole that will unhinge me, for I snapped right back to Alec:

"Yeah, we can't all spend our time roosting on top of a horse and looking wise."

Alec let up on his grinning at that. "You're a little bit owly there, Jicker. You maybe got a touch of shovelitis."

I continued to squint up at him and had it framed in my mind to retort "Is that anything like wingwangwoo fever?" when it dawned on me that Alec was paying only about half attention to our conversation anyway. His gaze was wandering around the station buildings as if he hadn't seen them for a decade or so, yet also as if he wasn't quite seeing them now either. Abstracted, might be the twenty-five-cent word for it. A fellow with a lot on his mind, most of it blond and warm.

One thing did occur to me to find out:

"How much is 19 times 60?"

"1140," replied Alec, still looking absent. "Why?"

"Nothing." Damned if I was going to bat remarks back and forth with somebody whose heart wasn't in it, so I simply asked, "What brings you in off the lone prairie?" propped an arm against the side of my pit and waited.

Alec finally recalled that I was down there and maybe was owed some explanation for the favor of his presence, so he announced: "I just came by for that town shirt of mine. Need it for rodeo day."

Christamighty. The powers of mothers. Barely a full day had passed since Mom forecast to Pete that it would take the dire necessity of a shirt to draw Alec into our vicinity, and here he was, shirt-chaser incarnate.

It seemed to me too good a topic to let him have for free. "What, are you entering the pretty shirt contest this year?"

Now Alec took a squint down at me from the summit of the horse, as if I only then really registered on him. "No, wisemouth, the calf roping." Hoohoo. Here was going to be another Alec maneuver just popular as all hell with our parents, spending money on the entry fee for calf-roping.

"I guess that color of shirt does make calves run slower," I deadpanned. The garment in question was dark purplish, about the shade of chokecherry juice. Distinctive, to put it politely. "It's in the bottom drawer there in our—the porch bedroom." Then I figured since I was being helpful anyway, I might as well clarify the terrain for Alec. "Dad's in Missoula. But maybe you'd already heard that, huh?"

But Alec was glancing around in that absent-minded way again, which was nettling me a little more every time he did it. I mean, you don't particularly like to have a person choosing when to phase in and out on you. We had been brothers for about fourteen and five-sixths years, so a few seconds of consecutive attention didn't strike me as too awful much to expect of Alec.

Evidently so, though. He had reined his horse's head around to start toward the house before he thought to ask: "How's Mom's mood?"

"Sweet as pie. How's yours?"

I got nothing back from that. Alec simply passed from sight, his horse's tail giving a last little waft as if wiping clean the field of vision which the pit framed over me.

As I was reaching down to resume with my bucket of earth, though, I heard the hooves stop and the saddle creak.

"Jicker?" Alec's voice came.

"Yeah?"

"I hear you been running the mountains with Stanley Meixell."

While I knew you couldn't have a nosebleed in the English Creek valley without everybody offering you a hanky for a week afterward, it had never occurred to me that I too was automatically part of this public pageant. I was so surprised by Alec knowing of my Stanley sojourn that I could only send forth another "Yeah?"

"You want to be a little more choosy about your company, is all."

"Why?" I asked earnestly of the gape of the pit over me. Two days ago I was hiding out from Stanley in this very hole like a bashful badger, and now I sounded like he was my patron saint. "What the hell have you got against Stanley?"

No answer floated down, and it began to seem to me that this brother of mine was getting awful damn cowboyish indeed if he looked down on a person for tending sheep camp. I opened my mouth to tell him something along that line, but what leaped out instead was: "Why's Stanley got everybody in this damn family so spooked?"

Still nothing from above, until I heard the saddle leather and hooves again, moving off toward the house.

The peace of the pit was gone. Echoes of my questions to Alec drove it out. In its stead came a frame of mind that I was penned down here, seven feet below the world in a future outhouse site, while two members of this damn McCaskill family were resting their bones inside the house and the other one was gallivanting off in Missoula. To each his own and all that, but this situation had gotten considerably out of proportion.

The more I steamed, the more a dipper of water and a handful of gingersnaps seemed necessary to damper me down. And so I climbed out with the bucket of dirt, flung it on the pile as if burying something smelly, and headed into the house.

"Your mind is still set," my mother was saying as I came through the doorway into the kitchen.

"Still is," agreed Alec, but warily. Neither of them paid me any particular attention as I dippered a drink from the water bucket. That told me plenty about how hot and heavy the conversation was in here.

"A year, Alec." So she was tackling him along that angle again. Delay and live to fight again another day. "Try college for a year and decide then. Right now you and Leona think the world begins and ends in each other. But it's too soon to say, after just these few months."

"It's long enough."

"That's what Earl Zane likely thought, the day before Leona dropped him for you." That seemed to me to credit Earl Zane with more thought capacity than he'd ever shown. Earl was a year or so older than Alec, and his brother Arlee was a year ahead of me in school, and so far as I could see the Zane boys were living verifications that the human head is mostly bone.

"That's past history," Alec was maintaining.

I punctuated that for him by popping the lid off the Karo can the gingersnaps were kept in. Then there was the sort of scrabbling sound as I dug out a handful. And after that the little sharp crunch as I took a first bite. All of which Alec waited out with the too patient annoyance of somebody held up while a train goes by. Then declared: "Leona and I ain't—aren't skim milk kids. We know what we're doing."

My mother took a breath which probably used up half the air in the kitchen. "Alec. What you're doing is rushing into trouble. You can't get ahead on ranch wages. And just because Leona is horse happy at the moment doesn't mean she's going to stay content with a ranch hand for a husband."

"We'll get by. Besides, Wendell says he'll boost my wages after we're married."

This stopped even my mother, though not for long. "Wendell Williamson," she said levelly, "has nobody's interest at heart but his own. Alec, you know as well as anybody the Double W has been the ruin of that Noon Creek country. Any cattle ranch he hasn't bought outright he has sewed up with a lease from the bank—"

"If Wendell hadn't got those places somebody else would have," Alec recited.

"Yes," my mother surprised him, "maybe somebody like you. Somebody who doesn't already have more money than he can count. Somebody who'd run one of those ranches properly, instead of gobbling it up just for the sake of having it. Alec, Wendell Williamson is using you the way he uses a handkerchief to blow his nose. Once he's gotten a few years of work out of you"—another kitchen-clearing breath here—"and evidently gotten you married off to Leona, so you'll have that obligation to carry around in life, too—once he's made enough use of you and you start thinking in terms of a real raise in wages, down the road you'll go and he'll hire some other youngster—"

"Youngster? Now wait one damn min—"

"—with his head full of cowboy notions. Alec, staying on at the Double W is a dead end in life."

While Alec was bringing up his forces against all this, I crunched into another gingersnap.

My brother and my mother sent me looks from their opposite sides of the room, a convergence about as taut as being roped with two lassos simultaneously. She suggested: "Aren't you supposed to be shoveling instead of demolishing cookies?"

"I guess. See you around, Alec."
"Yeah. Around."

Supper that night was about as lively as dancing to a dead march.

Alec had ridden off toward town, Leona-ward, evidently altered not one whit from when he arrived, except for gaining himself the rodeo shirt. My mother was working out her mood on the cooking utensils. I was a little surprised the food didn't look pulverized when it arrived to the table. So far as I could see, I was the only person on the place who'd made any true progress that day, finishing the outhouse hole. When I came in to wash up I considered announcing cheerfully "Open for business out there" but took a look at my mother's stance there at the stove and decided against.

So the two of us just ate, which if you're going to be silent is probably the best thing to be doing anyway. I was doubly glad I had coaxed as much conversation out of her last night as I had. I sometimes wonder if life is anything but an averaging out. One kind of day and then its opposite.

Likely, though, the mother of Alec McCaskill would not have agreed just then that life has its own simple average. For by the time my mother washed the supper dishes and I was drying them, I began to realize she wasn't merely in a maternal snit. She was thinking hard about something. And if I may give myself credit, it occurred to me that her thinking deserved my absence. Any new idea anybody in the McCaskill family could come up with deserved all encouragement.

"Need me any more?" I asked as I hung the dish towel. "I thought I might ride up to check on Walter's and fish my way home till toward dark." The year's longest day was just past; twilight would go on for a couple or three hours yet.

"No. No, go ahead." Her cook's instinct roused her to add: "Your father will be home tomorrow, so catch us a big mess." In those times a person could; the legal limit was twenty-five fish a day.

And then she was back into the thinking.

Nothing was amiss at Walter Kyle's place. As I closed the door on that tidy sparse room, I wondered if Walter didn't have the right idea. Live alone and let everybody else knock bruises on one another.

The fishing was as close to a cinch as fishing can ever be. Since I was using an honest-to-God pole and reel and it was a feeding time of evening, the trout in those North Fork beaver dams all but volunteered. Do I even need to say out loud that I limited? One more time I didn't owe my father a theoretical milkshake, and there still was evening left when the gill of that twenty-fifth trout was threaded onto my willow stringer and I went to collect Pony from the tall meadow grass where she was grazing.

My mother still was in her big think when I came back into the ranger station toward the last of dusk. I reported that the mess of cleaned fish was in a pan of water in the spring house, then stretched myself in an obvious sort of way, kissed her goodnight, and headed for the north porch and my bed. I honestly didn't want to be around any more heavy cogitation that day.

The north porch, a screened-in affair, had been built to take advantage of the summer shade on that side of the English Creek ranger station house, but in late spring Alec and I always moved out there to use it as our bedroom. Now that he was bunking at the Double W, I of course had the room to myself, and I have to testify here that gaining a private bedroom goes far toward alleviating the absence of a brother.

Not just the privacy did I treasure, though. It seemed to me at the time, and still does, that a person could not ask for a better site than that one for day's end. The north porch made a sort of copperwire bubble into the night world. Moths would bat and bat against the screening, especially if I'd brought a coal oil lamp out with me. Mosquitoes, in the couple of weeks in early June when they are fiercest, would alight out there and try to needle their way in, and there's a real reward to lying there knowing that those little whining bastards can't get at you. Occasional scutterings and whishes in the grass brought news of an owl or skunk working on the field mouse population, out there beyond the lampshine. Many an evening, though, I would not even light the lamp, just use the moon when I went out to bed. Any bright night filled the width of that porch with the shaggy wall of English Creek's cottonwoods and aspen, and atop them like a parapet the blunt black line of the benchland on the other side of the water. Out the west end of the porch a swatch of the mountains stood: Roman Reef, and the peaks of Rooster Mountain and Phantom Woman behind it. With Alec's cot folded away I had room to move mine longways into the east end of the room, so that I could lie looking at the mountains, and enjoy the bonus too that, with my head there below the east sill, the sunrise would over-shoot me instead of beaming into my face.

I recall that this was a lampless night, that I was flopping into bed without even any thought of reading for a while, more tired from the day than I'd realized, when I heard my mother at the telephone starting a call.

"Max? This is Beth McCaskill. Can't you think of anybody better to do that?" A short space of silence, then she announced: "All right then. I'll do it. I still think your common sense has dried up and blown away. But I'll Do It." And whanged down the receiver as if her words might sneak back out of the telephone wire.

What that was about I had no clue. Max? The only Max I could conjure up was Max Devlin, the assistant supervisor at the Two Medicine forest headquarters down in Great Falls, and why she would be calling him up this time of night just to doubt his common sense I couldn't figure. But maybe the go-round with Alec had put her into her mood to deliver the Forest Service a little of what she considered it generally deserved. I definitely was not going back out there to inquire. Sleep was safer.

My father arrived home from Missoula full of sass and vinegar. He always came away from a Region headquarters session avid to get back to the real planet again.

Even the fact that it was Saturday and he had a blank week of diary entries to catch up on didn't dent his spirits. "Easy enough after one of these Mazoola schools. Let's see: Monday, snored. Tuesday, tossed and turned. Wednesday, another restless day of sleep. . . ."

As for my handiwork out back, he was duly impressed. "The entire Fort Peck dam crew couldn't have dug better."

What ought I to tell about the days between then and the Fourth of July? The outhouse got moved in good order, fitting over my pit like a hen onto a fresh nest, and I put in another shovel day of tossing the dirt into the old hole. My father combed the Two up, down, and sideways, checking on the fire lookouts and patrolling the allotments to see how the range was looking and siccing Paul Eliason and the CCC crews onto trail and road work and any other improvements that could be thought up. Shearing time came and went; I helped wrangle Dode Withrow's sheep in the pens the shearers set up at the foot of the South Fork trail to handle the Withrow and Hahn and Kyle bands, then Pete came and took me up to the Blackfeet Reservation for a couple more days' wrangling when his were sheared out there on the open prairie north of the Two Medicine River. Nothing more was seen of Alec at English Creek. My mother no doubt posted my father about the going-over she had given Alec when he came by for the shirt, although a reaming like that has to be seen and heard to be entirely appreciated.

Beyond that, I suppose the main news by the morning of the Fourth when the three of us began to ready to go to town for the holiday was that we *were* going. For my father didn't always get the Fourth of July off; it depended on fire danger in the forest. I in fact was getting a little nervous about this year. The cool summer turned itself around in the last week of June. Each day, a little hotter and stickier. Down in Great Falls they had first a dust storm—people trying to drive in from Helena reported hundreds of tumbleweeds rolling across the highway on Gore Hill—and after that about fifteen minutes of thunderstorm with rain coming down as if from faucets. But then, the Falls receives a lot of bastardly weather we don't. Particularly in summer, its site out there on the plains gives storms a chance to build and build before they strike the city. The mountain weather was our concern, and so much of May and June had been cool and damp that even this hot start of July wasn't really a threat, yet.

Final persuasion came from the holiday itself. That Fourth morning arrived as a good moderate one, promising a day warm enough to be comfortable but nowhere near sweltering, and my father said his decision as we sat down to breakfast. It came complete with a sizable grin, and the words of it were: "Watch out, Gros Ventre. Here we come."

I had a particular stake in a trouble-free Fourth and parental good humor. By dint of recent clean living and some careful asking, and I suppose the example of son-in-rebellion provided to my parents by Alec, I had won permission to make a horseback sojourn into town in order to stay overnight with my best friend from school, Ray Heaney.

As I cagily pointed out, "Then the morning after the Fourth, I can just ride back out here and save you a trip into town to get me."

"Strange I didn't see the logic of all this before," commented my mother. "You'll be saving us a trip we wouldn't have to make if you didn't stay in there in the first place, am I right?" But it turned out that was just her keeping in practice.

Of course, receiving permission from your parents is not the same as being able to hang on to it, and I was stepping pretty lightly that morning to keep from inspiring any second thoughts on their part. In particular, as much as possible I was avoiding the kitchen and my mother's culinary orbit. Which was sound Fourth of July policy in any case. A reasoning person would have thought she was getting ready to lay siege to Gros Ventre, instead of only going in there on a picnic.

My father ventured through for a cup of coffee and I overheard my mother say "Why I said I'd do this I'll never know" and him respond "Uh huh, you're certainly downright famous for bashfulness" and then her response in turn, but with a little laugh, "And you're notorious for sympathy."

As I was trying to dope that out—my mother bashful about a creek picnic?—my father poked his head into where I was and asked: "How about tracking down the ice creamer and putting it in the pickup?"

I did so, meanwhile trying to calculate how soon I could decently propose that I start my ride to town. I didn't want to seem antsy about it. On the other hand I sure desired to get the Fourth of July under way.

But here came my father out and over to me at the pickup. Then commemorated himself with me forever by saying, "Here. Better carry some weight in your pocket so you don't blow away." With which I was handed a half dollar.

I must have looked my startlement. Other Fourth of Julys, if there was any spending money bestowed on Alec and me it was more on the order of ten cents. If there was any.

"Call it shovel wages." My father stuck his hands in his hip pockets and studied the road to town as if he'd never noticed it before. "You might as well head on in. We'll see you there at the park." Then, as if in afterthought: "Why don't you ride Mouse, he can stand the exercise."

When you are fourteen you take a step up in life whenever you can find it and meanwhile try to keep a mien somewhere between "At last!" and "Do you really mean that?" I stayed adult and stately until I was behind the barn and into the horse pasture; then gave in to a grin the dimension of a jack-o-lantern's. A by God full-scale horse, mine for the holiday. In the corner of the pasture where Pony was grazing she lifted her head to watch me but I called out, "Forget it, midget," and went on over and bridled Mouse.

—

Mouse and I scooted right along that road toward Gros Ventre. He was a fast walker, besides elevating me and my spirits more than I'd been used to on Pony. The morning—mid-morning and past, by now—was full of sun, but enough breeze was following along English Creek for a person to ride in pure comfort. The country still looked just glorious. All the valley of English Creek was fresh with hay. Nobody was mowing quite yet, except for the one damp green swath around Ed Van Bebber's lower field where he had tried it a week too early as he did every year.

I was more than ready for the Fourth. A lot seemed to have happened since that evening back at the start of June when I looked up and saw Alec and Leona parading down the rise to join us for a family supper. One whole hell of a lot. No longer was I even sure that we four McCaskills quite were a family. It was time we all had something else on our minds besides ruckus. Alec plainly already did, the way he intended to trig up on behalf of Leona and a calf. And given how my mother was whaling into the picnic preparation and my father was grinning like a Chessy cat about getting the day off from rangering and I was strutting atop this tall horse with coinage heavy in my pocket, the Fourth was promising to do the job for the other three of us.

It is no new thought to say that life goes on. Yet that's where it does go.

In maybe an hour and a half, better time than I would have thought possible for that ride in from the English Creek station, Mouse and I were topping the little rise near the turnoff to Charlie Finletter's place, the last ranch before town.

From there a mile or so outside, Gros Ventre looked like a green cloudbank: cottonwood trees billowing so thick that it took some inspection to find traces of houses among them. Gros Ventre's neighborhoods were planted double with cottonwoods, a line of trees along the front yards and another between sidewalk and street. Then the same colonnade again on the other side of the street. All of this of course had been done fifty or more years before, a period of time that grows you a hell of a big cottonwood. Together with the original groves that already rose old and tall along English Creek before Gros Ventre was ever thought of, the streetside plantation produced almost a roof over the town. This cottonwood canopy was particularly wonderful just before a rain, when the leaves began to shiver, rattle in their papery way. The whole town seemed to tingle then, and the sound picked up when a gust of wind from the west ushered in the rain, and next the air was filled with the seethe of water onto all that foliage. In Gros Ventre even a dust-settler sounded like a real weather event.

The English Creek road entered town past the high school, one of those tan-brick two-story crates that seemed to be the only way they knew how to build high schools in those days, and I nudged Mouse into an even quicker pace so as not to dwell on that topic any longer than necessary. We were aiming ourselves across town, to the northeast end where the Heaneys' house stood.

Mouse and I met Main Street at the bank corner, alongside the First National, and here I can't help but pause for a look around Gros Ventre of that Fourth of July day, just as I did then before reining Mouse north along the street.

Helwig's grocery and merc, with its old-style wooden square front and the Eddy's bread sign in its window.

The Toggery clothing store, terra cotta along its top like cake frosting.

Musgrave's drugstore, with the mirror behind the soda fountain so that a person could sit there over a milkshake—assuming a person had the price of a milkshake, not always the case in those times—and keep track of the town traffic.

Grady Tilton's garage.

Dale Quint's saddlery and leather repair shop. Maybe a decent description of Gros Ventre of that time was that it still had a leather man but not yet a dentist. A person went to Conrad for tooth work.

Saloons, the Pastime and Spenger's, although Dolph Spenger was a dozen or more years dead.

The Odeon movie theater, the one place in town with its name in neon script. The other modern touch lent by the Odeon was its recent policy of showing the movie twice on Saturday night; first at seven-thirty, then the "owl show" at nine.

The post office, the only new building in Gros Ventre since I was old enough to remember. A New Deal project, this had been, complete with a mural of the Lewis and Clark expedition portaging around the Great Falls of the Missouri River in 1805. Lewis and Clark maybe were not news to postal customers of the Two country, but York, Clark's Negro slave standing out amid the portagers like a black panther in a snowfield, definitely was.

The little stucco-sided Carnegie library, with its flight of steps and ornamented portico as if a temple had been intended but the money gave out.

Across from the library the town's smallest storefront, where Gene Ladurie had his tailor shop until his eyes went bad; now the WPA sewing room was situated there.

The Lunchery, run by Mae Sennett. The occasional times when I would be with my father when he was on Forest Service meal money, the Lunchery was our place and oyster stew our order. It of course came from a can, but I see that bowl yet, the milk yellowing from the blob of butter melting in the middle of it, and if Mae Sennett was doing the serving herself she always warned, "Watch out for any oysterberries," by which she meant those tiny pearls that sometimes show up. I have to say, I still am not truly comfortable eating in any establishment that doesn't have that tired ivory look to its walls that the Lunchery did. A proof that the place has been in business longer than overnight and at least has sold decent enough food that people keep coming back.

Doc Spence's office. Across the empty lot from Doc's, the office of the lawyer, Eli Kinder. Who, strange to say, was a regular figure in the sheep traffic through this street, when the bands flowed through town on their way to the summer grass of the Blackfeet Reservation. Eli was a before-dawn riser and often would arrive downtown just as a band of sheep did. It was odd to see him, in his suit and tie, helping those woollies along Main Street, but Eli had been raised on a ranch down in the Highwood Mountains and knew what he was doing.

The sidestreet businesses, Tracy's creamery and Ed Heaney's lumber yard and hardware and Adam Kerz's coal and trucking enterprise.

The set of bank buildings, marking what might be called the down of downtown: the First National Bank of Gros Ventre in tan brick, and cattycorner from it the red brick of what had been the English Creek Valley Stockmen's Bank. The Valley Stockmen's went under in the early 1920s when half of all the banks in Montana failed, and the site now was inhabited, if not exactly occupied, by Sandy Staub's one-chair barber shop. The style in banks in those times was to have a fancy doorway set into the corner nearest the street intersection—Gros Ventre's pair of bank buildings stared down each other's throats in exactly this fashion—and when Sandy took over the Valley Stockmen's building he simply painted barber-pole stripes on one of the fat granite pillars supporting the doorway.

What have I missed? Of course; also there on the Valley Stockmen's block the newspaper office, proclaiming on a plate-glass window in the same typeface as its masthead: GLEANER. Next to that a more recent enterprise, Pauline Shaw's Moderne Beauty Shoppe. The story was that when Bill Reinking first saw his new neighboring sign, he stuck his head in the shop to ask Pauline if she was sure she hadn't left an "e" off Beauty.

I heard somebody say once that the business section of every Western town he'd ever seen looked as if it originated by falling out the back end of a truck. Not so with Gros Ventre. During those Depression years Gros Ventre did look roadworn. Weathered by all it had been through. But to me the town also held a sense of being what it ought to be. Of aptness, maybe is the term. Not fancy, not shacky. Steady. Settlement here dated back to when some weary freight wagoneer pulled in for the night at the nice creekside sheltered by cottonwoods. As the freighters' trail between Fort Shaw on the Sun River and southern Alberta developed, this site became a regular waystop, nicknamed The Middle since it was about midway between Fort Shaw and Canada—although some of us also suspect that to those early-day wagoneers the place seemed like the middle of nowhere. Gros Ventre grew to about a thousand people when the homesteaders began arriving to Montana in droves in the first decade of this century—my mother could remember in her childhood coming to town and seeing wagon after wagon of immigrants heading out onto the prairie, a white rag tied on one spoke of a wagonwheel so the revolutions could be counted to measure the bounds of the claimed land—and that population total never afterward varied more than a hundred either way.

This south to north route Mouse and I were taking through Gros Ventre, I now have to say, saved for the last what to me was the best of the town: a pair of buildings at the far end of Main Street, last outposts before the street/highway made its curve and zoomed from Gros Ventre over the bridge across English Creek.

The night during our campjacking trip when I was baptizing my interior with alcohol and Stanley Meixell was telling me the history of the Two Medicine National Forest from day one, a surprise chapter of that tale was about the hostelry that held the most prominent site in Gros Ventre. Stanley's arrival to town when he first came here to the Two was along the route Mouse and I had just done, from the south, and as Stanley rode along the length of Main Street, here at the far end a broad false-front with a veranda beneath it was proclaiming:

BEER   LIQUORS   CIGARS

MEALS AT ALL   **NORTHERN HOTEL**   LUNCHES

HOURS   PUT UP

C. E. SEDGWICK, PROP.

"Looks like it could kind of use a prop, all right," Stanley observed to a bib-overalled idler leaning against one of the porch posts. Who turned out to be the exact wrong person to make that joke to: C. E. Sedgwick himself.

"If my enterprise don't suit you," Sedge huffed, "you can always bunk down there in the diamond willows," indicating the brush at the bend of English Creek.

"How about," Stanley offered, "me being a little more careful with my mouth, and you giving me a second chance as a customer?"

Sedge hung his thumbs into his bib straps and considered. Then decided: "Go mute and I might adopt you into the family. Bring your gear on in."

The Northern burned in the dry summer of 1910. Although, according to old-timers, "burned" doesn't begin to say it. Incinerated, maybe, or conflagrated. For the Northern blaze took the rest of the block with it and threatened that whole end of town; if there had been a whisper of wind, half of Gros Ventre would have become ash and a memory. Sedge being Sedge, people weren't surprised when he decided to rebuild. After all, he went around in those overalls because what he really liked about being a hotelier was the opportunity to be his own maintenance man. But what Sedge erected still sat, this Fourth when I was atop Mouse, across the end of Main Street as a kind of civic astonishment. A three-story fandango in stone, quarried from the gray cliffs near where English Creek joins the Two Medicine River; half a block square, this reborn Sedgwick hostelry, with round towers at each corner and a swooping pointed ornament in the middle, rather like the spike on those German soldiers' helmets. Even yet, strangers who don't know that the Pondera County courthouse is twenty-two miles east in Conrad assume that Sedge's hotel is it. Sedge in fact contributed to the civic illusion by this time not daubing a sign all across the front of the place. Instead only an inset of chiseled letters rainbowing over the entranceway:

Sedge sold out in 1928, to a family from Seattle who seemed to somehow eke a living out of that big gray elephant of a hotel even after hard times hit. About 1931 Sedge died of pleurisy, and almost as if she'd been waiting just offstage, his widow emerged as one of Gros Ventre's most well-to-do citizens and certainly the looniest. Lila Sedgwick was a tall bony woman. Her build always reminded me of Abraham Lincoln. Almost any day she could be seen downtown three or four times, some days six or eight, for she no sooner would get home than she would forget about having just gone for the mail or on some other errand and would go for it again. In her long old-style dresses with those Lincoln arms and elbows poking out she inevitably was a figure of fun, although the one and only time I said something smart about her my mother's frown closed me down in a hurry.

"Lila Sedge is not to be laughed at," she said, not in her whetstoned voice but just sort of instructively. "The clouds have settled on her mind."

I don't know where my mother got that, but always after when I would see Lila Sedge, creeping along this street for the third time in an hour or gandering up at a cottonwood tree as if she'd never encountered one before, I would wonder about how it was to have a clouded mind. Somewhere in there, I supposed, a bruise-colored thunderhead that was Sedge's death. Maybe mares' tails high away in the past where she was a girl. Fluffs which carried faces—aunts, uncles, schoolmates, any of us she happened to meet on the street—in and out of her recognition. Until my mother's words about Lila Sedge I had never thought of the weather of the brain, but more and more I have come to believe in it.

But enough on that. The Sedgwicks and their namesake hotel provided Gros Ventre its one titanic building and its roving human landmark. The enterprise across the street from the Sedgwick House ministered to the town internally.

The Medicine Lodge saloon gave Gros Ventre its "rough" section of town in the thriftiest manner possible. I would calculate that in Great Falls it took about three blocks of First Avenue South to add up into a neighborhood of similar local notoriety. Actually, as with any pleasure emporium, the wickedest thing about the Medicine Lodge was its reputation.

The Medicine Lodge had waited out Prohibition behind boarded windows, but Tom Harry more than brought it back to light and life. Also, maybe after those dry years the town was thirsty for a saloon with a bit of flair. Tom Harry had come over from running a bar, and some said a taxi dance joint as well, at the Fort Peck dam project. Supposedly all he brought with him was a wad of cash and the picture of Franklin Delano Roosevelt which had adorned the wall of his Fort Peck enterprise. Be that as it may, in the Medicine Lodge FDR was promptly joined on the wall by a minor menagerie of stuffed animal heads Tom Harry acquired from somewhere. Several buck deer and an antelope and a mountain sheep and a bobcat snarling about the company he was in, not to mention the six-point elk head which set off arguments every hunting season about how much his absent body would weigh.

As matters proved out, along with Tom Harry also came a set of invisible rules of saloon behavior which every so often somebody would stray across. I think of the night when my father and I were entering the Medicine Lodge and met a stranger with a cigar in his mouth being forcibly propelled into the street. It turned out that although Tom Harry himself went around under a blue cigarette haze—tailormades; no Fort Peck bartender ever had time to roll his own—he would not tolerate cigar smoke.

In itself, the taxidermy herd populated the Medicine Lodge considerably. But the place also held a constant legion of the living, more or less. These setters, as my father called the six or eight guys who sat around in there—he was not above stepping in for a beer after our Lunchery meal, and if nobody official-looking was on hand Tom Harry didn't seem to mind my being with him—the setters always occupied the stools at the far end of the bar, and anybody who entered got long gazes from them as if they were cataloguing the human race.

Decapitated animals and owlish geezers do not, I realize, sound like much of a decor. And yet the Medicine Lodge did three times as much business as Spenger's or the Pastime, both much more "respectable" places back downtown. I suppose it is and ever will be the habit of the race: people gravitate to a certain place to do their drinking, and logic will never veer them. At least one night a week in the Medicine Lodge, gravitation amounted to something more like an avalanche. Saturday night, thirsts converged from everywhere in the Two country. Hay hands who had come in for a bath and haircut at Shorty Staub's but decided instead to wash down the inside of themselves. Shearing crews one time of year, lamb lickers (as guys who worked in lambing sheds were known) another. Any season, a sheepherder in from the mountains or the reservation to inaugurate a two-week spree. Government men from reclamation projects. Likely a few Double W cowpokes. Definitely the customary setters, who had been building up the calluses on their elbows all week just for this. Always a sufficient cast of characters for loud dialogues, occasional shoving matches, and eventual passing-outs. Maybe you couldn't get away with cigar smoke in the Medicine Lodge, but you could with what counted.

Turning east past the Sedgwick House and the Medicine Lodge, Mouse and I now were into the Heaneys' side of town. An early priest had persuaded the Catholic landowner who platted this particular neighborhood to name the streets after the first missions in Montana, which in turn bore the names of saints. This created what the current Gros Ventre postmaster, Chick Jennings, called "the repeater part of town," with mailing addresses such as St. Mary St., St. Peter St., and St. Ignatius St. It was at the end of St. Ignatius St. that the Heaney house stood, a white two-story one with sills of robin's egg blue. Ed Heaney owned the lumber yard, and so was the one person in town in those Depression years with some access to paint. The robin's egg blue had been a shipping mistake by the manufacturer; it is a shade pretty delicate to put up against the weather of Montana; and Ed lugged the can home and made the best of it.

The place looked empty as I rode up, which was as I expected. Rather than the creek picnic, the Heaneys always went out to a family shindig at Genevieve's parents' farm, quite a ways east of Gros Ventre on the Conrad road. So with Ray out there I wouldn't link up with him until the rodeo, and I simply slung my warbag inside the Heaneys' back porch and got on Mouse again, and went picnicking.

Cars and pickups and trucks were parked so thick that they all but swamped the creekside part of town. It is nice about a horse, that you can park him handily while Henry Ford still would be circling the block and cussing. I chose a stand of high grass between the creek bank and the big cottonwoods just west of the picnic and pastured Mouse on a tie of rope short enough that he couldn't tangle it around anything and long enough for him to graze a little. Then gave him a final proud pat, and headed off to enlist with the picnickers.

Some writer or another put down that in the history of Montana, the only definite example of civic uplift was when the Virginia City vigilantes hung the Henry Plummer gang in 1864. I think that overstates, a bit. You can arrive into the most scruffy of Montana towns and delve around a few minutes and in all likelihood find a public park, of some sort. In Gros Ventre's instance the park was a half circle of maybe an acre, fronting on English Creek just west of Main Street and the highway bridge, one last oasis before the road arrowed north into the plains and benchlands. In recent years WPA crews had made it a lot more of a park than it had been, clearing out the willows which were taking over the creek bank and then laying in some riprap to keep the spring runoff out. And someone during that WPA work came up with an idea I've not seen before or since. There near the creek where a big crippled cottonwood leaned—a windstorm had ripped off its main branches—a crew sawed the tree off low to the ground, leaving a broad stump about two feet high, then atop the stump was built a speaker's pulpit, a slatted round affair somewhat on the order of a ship's crow's nest. The one and only time I saw Senator Burton K. Wheeler, who some people thought might become president if Roosevelt ever stopped being, we were let out of school to hear him give a speech from this speaking stump.

From where I had left Mouse I emerged into the creekside corner of the park where the stump pulpit stood, and I stopped beside it to have a look around.

A true Two country Fourth of July. The trees were snowing.

Fat old cottonwoods stood all along the arc between the park and the neighborhood, while younger trees were spotted here and there across the rest of the expanse, as if they had been sent out to be shade-bearers. The day was providing just enough breeze into the treetops to rattle them a little and make them shed their cotton wisps out through the air like slow snow.

Through the cottonfall the spike of tower atop the Sedgwick House stuck up above one cottonwood at the far side of the park. As if that tree had on a party hat.

As for people, the park this day was a bunch of islands of them. I literally mean islands. The summer thus far had stayed cool enough that even a just warm day like this one was putting people into the shade of the cottonwoods, each gathering of family and friends on their specific piece of dappled shade like those cartoons of castaways on a desert isle with a single palm tree.

I had to traipse around somewhat, helloing people and being helloed, before I spotted my mother and my father, sharing shade and a spread blanket with Pete and Marie Reese and Toussaint Rennie near the back of the park.

Among the greetings, my father's predominated: "Thank goodness you're here. Pete's been looking for somebody to challenge to an ice-cream-making contest." So before I even got sat down I was off on that tangent. "Come on, Jick," Pete said as he reached for their ice-cream freezer and I picked up ours, "anybody who cranks gets a double dish."

We took our freezers over near the coffee and lemonade table where everybody else's was. This year, I should explain, was the turn of English Creek and Noon Creek to provide the picnic with ice cream and beverage. Bill Reinking, who despite being a newspaperman had some fairly practical ideas, was the one to suggest the system; that instead of everybody and his brother showing up at the Fourth armed with ice creamers and coffeepots and jugs of lemonade, each part of the community take a turn in providing for all. Now one year the families west of Main Street in Gros Ventre did the ice cream, coffee and ade, the next year the families east of Main Street, the one after that those of us from English Creek and Noon Creek, and then after us what was called "the rest of Creation," the farm families from east and south and north of town and anybody else who didn't fit some other category.

So for the next while Pete and I took turns with the other ice-cream manufacturers, cranking and cranking. Lots of elbow grease, and jokes about where all that fancy wrist work had been learned. Marie shortly came over on coffee duty—she was going to do the making, my mother would serve after everybody'd eaten—and brought along a message from my father and Toussaint: "They say, a little faster if you can stand it." Pete doffed his Stetson to them in mock gratitude. The holiday definitely was tuning up. And even yet I can think of no better way to begin a Fourth of July than there among virtually all of our English Creek neighbors. Not Walter Kyle, up on the mountain with his sheep; and not the Hebners, who never showed themselves at these creek picnics; and not the Withrows, who must have been delayed some way. But everybody else. The South Fork folks other than the Withrows: Fritz and Greta Hahn, Ed and Alice Van Bebber. Then the population of the main creek, those who merely migrated downstream here to the park, so to speak. Preston and Peg Rozier. Charlie and Dora Finletter. Ken and Janet Busby, and Bob and Arleta Busby; I had half wondered whether Stanley Meixell might show up with the Busbys, and was relieved that he hadn't. Don and Charity Frew. The Hills arrived last, while I was still inventorying the crowd; J.L. leaning shakily on his wife Nan. "Set her down, J.L.," somebody called, referring to the ice creamer the Hills had brought with them, "we'll do the twirling." "I get to shivering much more than this," J.L. responded, "and I can just hold the goddamn thing in my hands and make ice cream." In truth, J.L.'s tremble was constant and almost ague-like by now. It is terrible to see, an ailment fastened onto a person and riding him day and night. I hope not to end up that way, life over and done with before existence is.

But that was not the thought for this day. If a sense of life, of the blood racing beneath your skin, is not with you at a Fourth of July creek picnic, then it is never going to be.

When Pete and I finished ice-cream duty and returned to the blanket, my father had Toussaint on the topic of what the Fourth of July was like when Gros Ventre and he were young.

"Phony Nose Gorman," Toussaint was telling. "Is he one you remember?"

My father shook his head: "Before my time." Much of Toussaint's lore was before anyone's time.

"Tim Gorman," Toussaint elaborated, "Cox and Floweree's foreman awhile. Down on Sun River. Froze his nose in that '86 winter. Some doctor at Fort Shaw fixed him up. Grafted skin on. I saw him after, the surgery was good. But Phony Nose Gorman he was called. He was the one the flagpole broke with. There across from the Medicine Lodge, where that garage is now. He was climbing it to put Deaf Smith Mitchell's hat on top. On a bet. Those times, they bet on the sun coming up."

Toussaint Rennie this day looked maybe sixty-five years old, yet had to be at least a dozen beyond that. He was one of those chuckling men you meet rarely, able to stave off time by perpetually staying in such high humor that the years didn't want to interrupt him. From that little current of laugh always purling in him Toussaint's face had crinkled everywhere it could. Tan and wrinkled deep, that face, like a gigantic walnut. The rest of Toussaint was the general build of a potbelly stove. Girth and age and all, he still was riding the ditches of the Blackfeet Reservation's Two Medicine irrigation project, his short-handled shovel sticking out of a rifle scabbard as his horse plodded the canal banks. Allotting a foot-and-a-half head of water to each farm ditch; plugging gopher holes or muskrat tunnels in the canal bank with gunny sacks of dirt; keeping culverts from clogging; in a land of scarce water a ditch rider's job was vital above most others, and Toussaint apparently was going to hold his until death made it drop from his hand.

In about the way that shovel was carried in that scabbard, the history of the Two country rested there in Toussaint's memory, handy to employ. And sharpened by steady use. It never was clear to me how Toussaint, isolated way to hell and gone—he bached out there a few miles west of where the highway crossed the Two Medicine River, about fifteen miles from Browning and a good thirty from Gros Ventre— could know news from anywhere in the Two country as fast as it happened. Whatever the network was (my father called it moccasin telegraph) Toussaint was its most durable conductor. He came to the Two in the time of the buffalo, a boy eight or so years old when his family roved in from somewhere in the Dakotas. The Rennies were part French; my father thought they might have started off as Reynauds. But mostly tribal haze. Of their Indian background Toussaint himself was only ever definite in declaring himself *not* a Blackfeet, which had to do with the point that the Two Medicine woman he married, Mary Rides Proud, *was* one. The usual assumption was that the Rennie lineage was Métis, for other Métis families had ended up in this general region of Montana after the Riel rebellion in Canada was put down in 1885. But count back across the decades and you found that Toussaint already had grown to manhood here in the Two country by the time the Canadians were hanging Louis Riel and scattering his followers. Toussaint himself was worse than no help on this matter of origin, for all he would say was to claim pedigree from the Lewis and Clark expedition: "I come down from William Clark himself. My grandfather had red hair."

Thinking back on it now, I suspect the murk of Toussaint's lineage was carefully maintained. For the one thing unmistakable about the

Rennie family line was its knack for ending up on the side of the winners in any given contest of the Montana frontier. "The prairie was so
black with buffalo it looked burnt. I was with the Assiniboines, we
came down on the buffalo from the Sweetgrass Hills," one Toussaint
tale would relate, and the next, "The trader Joe Kipp hired me to take
cattle he was selling to the Army at Fort Benton. He knew I kept Indians from stealing them." Able to straddle that way, Toussaint had a view
into almost anything that happened in the early Two country. He was
with the bull teams that brought the building materials for the original
Blackfeet Reservation agency north of Choteau, before there was a
Choteau or a Gros Ventre. "Ben Short was the wagon boss. He was a
good cusser." After the winter of '86, Toussaint freighted cowhides off
the prairie by the thousands. "That was what was left in this country by
spring. More cowhides than cows." He saw young Lieutenant John J.
Pershing and his Negro soldiers ride through Gros Ventre in 1896,
herding a few hundred woebegone Crees north to push them back over
the line into Canada. "Each creek those soldiers crossed, English Creek
and Birch Creek and Badger Creek and all of them, some more Crees
leaked away into the brush." He saw the canals come to the prairie, the
eighty-thousand-acre irrigation project that built Valier from scratch in
1909 and drew in trainloads of homesteaders. "Pretty quick they wondered about this country. Dust blew through Valier there, plates were
turned facedown on the table until you turned them up to eat off of.
One tree, the town had. Mrs. Guardipee watered it from her wash
tubs." And the Two Medicine canal he himself had patrolled for almost
a quarter century, the ditch rider job he held and held in spite of being
not a Blackfeet: "It stops them being jealous of each other. With me in
the job, none of them is." The first blats of sheep into this part of Montana were heard by Toussaint. "I think, 1879. People called Lyons,
down on the Teton. Other sheepmen came fast. Charlie Scoffin, Charlie McDonald, Oliver Goldsmith Cooper." The first survey crews he
watched make their sightings. "1902, men with telescopes and Jacob's
staffs."

—"The first Fourth of July you ever saw here," my father was
prompting. "When was that, do you think?"

Toussaint could date it without thinking. "Custer's year. '76. We
heard just before the Fourth. All dead at the Little Bighorn. Everybody.
Gros Ventre was just only a hotel and saloon then. Men took turns,
coming out of the saloon to stand sentry. To look north." Here Tous-

saint leaned toward Pete's wife Marie and said in mock reproach: "For Blackfeet."

All of us echoed his chuckle. The tease to Marie was a standard one from Toussaint. Married to Pete, she of course was my aunt, and if I'd had a thousand aunts instead of just her she still would have been my favorite. More to the point here, though, Marie was Toussaint's granddaughter, and the only soul anywhere in that family who could get along with him. Most of Toussaint's sons wouldn't even speak to him, his daughters had all married out of his orbit as rapidly as they could, and down through the decades any number of his Rides Proud in-laws had threatened to shoot him. (Toussaint claimed he had a foolproof antidote to such threats: "I tell them bullets can fly more than one direction.") I myself remember that the last few years of her life, Toussaint and his wife Mary didn't even live under the same roof; whenever my father and I stopped by their place, Toussaint was to be found in residence in the bunkhouse. Thus all the evidence said that if you were a remove or two from him Toussaint could be a prince of the earth toward you, but anybody sharing the same blood with him he begrudged. Except Marie. Marie was thin and not particularly dark—her father was Irish, an office man at the agency in Browning—and only her black hair, which she wore shoulder-long, brought out the Blackfeet ancestry and whatever farther east Indian heredity it was that Toussaint transmitted. So her resemblance to Toussaint really was only a similar music in her voice, and the same running chuckle at the back of her throat when she was pleased. Yet be around the two of them together for only a minute and you knew without mistake that here were not merely natural allies but blood kin. There just was something unmistakably alike in how each of them regarded life. As if they had seen it all before and shared the amusement that things were no better this time around.

But Toussaint's story of the first Fourth wasn't quite done. "I took a turn at sentry. I was in there drinking with them. In the saloon. Already an old man, me. Fifteen."

"Ancient as Jick," Marie murmured with a smile in my direction. If she but knew. Maybe my toot with Stanley that night in the cabin didn't break any saloon records, but it was spree enough for a starter.

"Jick has a few months to go yet," my mother corrected Marie's observation.

"I'm getting there as fast as I can," I defended, drawing a laugh from our assemblage.

—

As you can see, an all but perfect Fourth of July picnic so far. I say all but, because the year before, Alec had been with us instead of off sparking Leona. The only awareness of him this year was the way people took some care not to mention him to my parents.

My mother turned to Marie and asked: "Do you suppose these scenery inspectors have earned any food?"

"We'll take pity on them," Marie agreed, and the picnic provisions began to emerge from the pair of grub boxes.

The blanket became like a raftload of food, except that such a cargo of eating likely would have sunk any raft.

There were the chickens my mother spent part of the morning frying. Delectable young spring fries with drumsticks about the thickness of your thumb. This very morning, too, Toussaint had caught a batch of trout in the Two Medicine and now here they beckoned, fried up by Marie. Blue enamel broilers of fish and fowl, side by side. The gateposts of heaven.

Marie's special three bean salad, the pinnacle of how good beans can taste. My mother's famous potato salad with little new green onions cut so fine they were like sparks of flavor.

New radishes, sweet and about the size of a marble, first of Marie's garden vegetables. A dozen and a half deviled eggs arrayed by my mother.

A jar of home-canned pickled beets, a strong point of my mother's. A companion jar of crabapple pickles, a distinction of Marie's.

A plate of my mother's corn muffins. A loaf of Marie's saffron bread. Between the two, a moon of Reese home-churned butter.

An angelfood cake by Marie. A chocolate sour cream cake from my mother.

My eyes feasted while the rest of me readied to. My father urged, "Dive in, Toussaint," and the passing of dishes got under way.

"Been a while since breakfast," Pete proclaimed when he had his plate loaded. "I'm so excited to see food again I'm not sure I'll be able to eat."

"Too bad about you," Marie said in that soft yet take-it-or-leave-it way so like Toussaint's. And my mother didn't overlook the chance to put in: "Wait, we'll sell tickets. People will line up to see Pete Reese not eat."

"Come on now, Bet," came the protest from Pete. "I have never eaten more than I could hold."

As they should do at a picnic, the conversing and the consuming cantered along together in this fashion. I think it was at the start of the second plateload, when we were all letting out-dubious hmmms about having another helping of this or that but then going ahead and having it, that Pete asked my father if fire school in Missoula had made him any smarter than he was before.

"Airplanes," my father announced. "Airplanes are the firefighting apparatus of the future, at least according to this one hoosier we heard from over there."

"The hell. How's that gonna work?"

"I didn't say it was going to work. I just said what the hoosier told us. They're going to try parachutists—like these guys at fairs?"

"Say on," urged Toussaint, squinting through a mask of eager puzzlement. Toussaint always was avid to hear developments of this sort, as if they confirmed for him the humorous traits of the human race. "That radio stuff," he had declared during the worst of the drought and the dust storms, "it monkeys with the air. Dries it out, all that electric up there."

"They're just now getting ready to test all this out," my father continued his report of latest up-in-the-air science. "Send an airplane with a couple of these parachutists over a mountain smoke and see if they can jump down there and tromp it out before it grows to a real fire. That's the cheery theory, anyhow."

Pete shook his head. "They couldn't pay me enough to jump out of one of those."

"Hell, Pete, the jumping would be easy money. The landing is the only drawback." My father readied to plow into another of Toussaint's trout, but first offered as if in afterthought: "Fact is, I told them I'd volunteer"—my mother's full skepticism sighted in on him now, waiting to see if there was any color of seriousness in this—"if the parachute was going to be big enough for my saddle horse and packstring too."

The vision of my father and assorted horses drifting down from the sky the way the cottonwood fluffs were floating around us set everybody to laughing like loonies.

Next it was Toussaint's inning again. The mention of horses reminded him of a long ago Fourth of July in Gros Ventre when everybody caught horse race fever. "How it happened, first they matched every saddle horse against every other saddle horse. Ran out of those by middle of the afternoon. Still plenty of beer and daylight left. Then somebody got the notion. Down to the stable, everybody. Brought out the stagecoach horses. Bridled them, put boys on them bareback. Raced them against each other the length of Main Street." The Toussaint chuckle. "It was hard to know. To bet on the horse, or how high the boy would bounce."

Which tickled us all again. Difficult to eat on account of laughing, and to laugh on account of eating. Give me that dilemma anytime.

All this horse talk did remind me about Mouse, and I excused myself to go picket him onto another patch of grass. Truth to tell, getting myself up and into motion also would shake down some of the food in me and make room for more.

Thinking back on that scene as I wended my way to the edge of the park where Mouse was tethered, I have wished someone among us then had the talent to paint the portrait of that picnic. A group scene that would have preserved those faces from English Creek and Noon Creek and Gros Ventre and the out-east farming country and, yes, Toussaint's from the Two Medicine. That would convey every one of those people at once and yet also their separateness. Their *selves,* I guess the word should be. I don't mean one of those phony-baloney gilt concoctions such as that one of Custer and all his embattled and doomed troopers there at the Little Bighorn, which hangs in three fourths of the saloons I have ever been in and disgusts me every single time. (To my mind, Custer can be done justice only if shown wearing a tall white dunce cap.) But once I saw in a magazine, *Look* or *Life* or one of those old every-week ones, what one painter tried in this respect of showing selves. He first painted little pictures of tropical flowers, in pink and other pastels; wild roses I guess would be our closest comparison flower here in the Two country. Some several hundred of those, he painted. Then when all these were hung together in the right order on the wall, the flower colors fit together from picture to picture to create the outline of a tremendously huge snake. In any picture by itself you could not see a hint of that snake. But look at them together and he lay kinked across the entire wall mightier than the mightiest python.

That is the kind of portrait I mean of the creek picnic. Not that very many of those people there in the park could be called the human equivalent of flowers, nor that the sum of them amounted to a colossal civic snake. But just the point that there, that day, they seemed to me all distinctly themselves and yet added up together too.

I have inquired, though, and so far as I can find, nobody ever even thought to take a photograph of that day.

When I came back from retethering Mouse, my parents and Pete and Marie were in a four-way conversation about something or other, and Toussaint was spearing himself another trout out of the broiler. His seemed to me the more sensible endeavor, so I dropped down next to him to inflict myself on the chicken supply. I was just beginning to do good work on my favorite piece of white meat, a breastbone, when Toussaint turned his head toward me. The potato salad had come to rest nearest my end of the blanket and I reached toward it, expecting that he was going to ask me to pass it to him. Instead Toussaint stated quietly: "You are a campjack these days."

Probably I went red as an apple. I mean, good Christamighty. Toussaint's words signaled what I had never dreamt of: moccasin telegraph had the story of my sashay with Stanley.

Everything that coursed through me in those moments I would need Methuselah's years to sort out.

Questions of source and quantity maybe hogged in first. How the hell did Toussaint know? And what exactly did he know? My dimwitted approach to a barbwire fence in an electrical storm? My tussle with Bubbles? My alcoholic evening in the cabin? No, he couldn't know any of those in detail. Could he?

The unnerving possibility of Toussaint having dropped some mention of that last and biggest matter, my night of imbibing, into the general conversation while I was off tending Mouse made me peer toward my mother.

No real reassurance there. Her mood plainly had declined since the parade of the food onto the blanket, she now was half listening to my father and Pete and half gazing off toward the ripples of English Creek. Whatever was occupying her mind, I could only send up prayers that it wasn't identical to the topic on mine.

Geography next. How far had the tale of Jick and Stanley spread?

Was I traveling on tongues throughout the whole damn Two country? "Hear about that McCaskill kid? Yeah, green as frog feathers, ain't he? You wonder how they let him out of the house by himself."

And beyond that, philosophy. If I was a Toussaint topic, just what did that constitute? The mix of apprehension and surmise was all through me. Plus a flavor of something which seemed surprisingly like pride. Better or worse, part of me now was in Toussaint's knowledge, his running history of the Two. In there with Phony Nose Gorman and the last buffalo hunt and the first sheep and the winter of '86 and Lieutenant Black Jack Pershing and the herded Crees and—and what did that mean? Being a part of history, at the age of fourteen years and ten months: why had that responsibility picked me out?

They say when a cat walks over the ground that will be your grave, a shiver goes through you. As I sat there that fine July noon with a breastbone forgotten in my hand, Toussaint again busy eating his trout after leaving the track of those six soft words across my life—"You are a campjack these days"—yes, I shivered.

My father's voice broke my trance. "If Toussaint and Jick ever would get done eating for winter, we could move along to the delicacy part of the meal. Some fancy handle-turning went into the making of that ice cream, you know. Or at least so I hear by rumor."

My mother was up, declaring she'd bring the cups of coffee if a certain son of hers would see to the dessert. Toussaint chuckled. And put up a restraining hand as I started to clamber to my feet, ready to bolt off to fetch dishes of ice cream, bolt off anywhere to get a minute of thinking space to myself.

"Do you know, Beth," Toussaint began, stopping her and my heart at the same time, "do you know—your potato salad was good."

A picnic always slides into final contentment on ice cream. All around us as each batch of people finished dessert and coffee, men flopped onto their backs or sides while the women sat up and chatted with one another.

I, though; I wasn't doing any sliding or flopping, just sitting there bolt upright trying to think things through. My head was as gorged as my stomach, which was saying a lot.

My father, though, acted as if he didn't have a thing in the world on his mind. To my surprise, he scootched around until he had room to lie flat, then sank back with his head in my mother's lap and his hat over his face.

"Pretty close to perfect," he said. "Now if I only had an obedient wife who'd relieve me of these dress shoes."

"If I take them off you," my mother vowed, "you'll be chasing after them as they float down the creek."

"This is what I have to put up with all the time, Toussaint," came his voice from under the hat. "She's as independent as the moon." My mother answered that by sticking out a thumb and jabbing it between a couple of his ribs, which brought a *whuw!* out of him.

Down at creekside, the school superintendent Mr. Vennaman was stepping up into the stump rostrum. Time for the program, evidently. I tried to contain at the back of my mind the cyclone of thoughts about Toussaint and moccasin telegraph and myself.

"—always a day of pleasure," Mr. Vennaman's voice began to reach those of us at the back of the park. "This is a holiday particularly American. Sometimes, if the person on the stump such as I am at this moment doesn't watch his enthusiasm, it can become a little too much so. I am always reminded of the mock speech which Mose Skinner, a Will Rogers of his day, proposed for this nation's one hundredth birthday in 1876: 'Any person who insinuates in the remotest degree that America isn't the biggest and best country in the world, and far ahead of every other country in everything, will be filled with gunpowder and touched off.'"

When the laughing at that died down, Mr. Vennaman went on: "We don't have to be quite that ardent about it, I think. But this is a day we can simply be thankful to be with our other countrymen. A day for neighbors and friends and family.

"Some of those neighbors, in fact, are here with a gift of song for us." Mr. Vennaman peered over toward the nearest big cottonwood. "Nola, can the music commence?"

This was interesting. For under that towering tree sat a piano. Who came up with the idea I never did know, but some of the Gros Ventre men had hauled the instrument—of course it was one of those old upright ones—out of Nola Atkins's front room, and now here it was on the bank of English Creek, and Nola on the piano bench readying to play. I'd like to say Nola looked right at home, but actually she was kept busy shooing cottonwood fluff off the keys and every so often there'd be a *plink* as she brushed away a particularly stubborn puff.

150 · IVAN DOIG

Nonetheless, Nola bobbed yes, she was set.

I think it has to be said that the singing at events such as this is usually a pretty dubious proposition, and that's more than likely why some out-of-town group was invited to perform at each of these Fourth picnics. That way, nobody local had anything to live down. This year's songsters, the Valier Men's Chorus, now were gathering themselves beside Nola and the piano. Odd to see them up there in that role, farmers and water company men, in white dress shirts and with the pale summits of their foreheads where hats customarily sat.

Their voices proved to be better than you might expect. The program, though, inadvertently hit our funny bones as much as it did our ears, because the chorus's first selection was "I Cannot Sing the Songs of Long Ago," and then, as if they hadn't heard their own advice, they wobbled into "Love's Old Sweet Song." The picnic crowd blossomed with grins over that, and I believe I discerned even a trace of one on Nola Atkins at the piano.

Mr. Vennaman came back up on the stump, thanking the Valierians "for that memorable rendition" and introducing "yet another neighbor, our guest of honor this day." Emil Thorsen, the sheepman and state senator from down at Choteau, rose and declared in a voice that could have been heard all the way downtown that in early times when he was first running for office and it was all one county through here from Fort Benton to Babb instead of being broken up into several as it is now, he'd have happily taken up our time; "but since I can't whinny any votes out of you folks any more, I'll just say I'm glad to be here among so many friends, and compliment you on feeding as good as you ever did, and shut myself up and sit down." And did.

Mr. Vennaman popped to his feet again, leading the hand-clapping and then saying: "Our next speaker actually needs no introduction. I'm going to take a lesson from Senator Thorsen and not bother to fashion one." Two traits always marked Mr. Vennaman as an educator: the bow tie he perpetually wore and the way, even saying hello on the street, he seemed to be looking from the front of a classroom at you. Now he peered and even went up on his tiptoes a bit, as if calling on someone in the back row of that classroom, and sang out: "Beth McCaskill?"

I knew I hadn't heard that quite right.

Yet here she was, getting up from beside my father and smoothing her dress down and setting off toward the speaker's stump, with folded sheets of paper clutched in her business hand. No doubt about it, I was the most surprised person in the state of Montana right then. But Pete and Marie were not far behind and even Toussaint's face was squinched with curiosity.

"What—?" I floundered to my father. "Did you know—?"

"She's been sitting up nights writing this," he told me with a cream-eating grin. "Your mother, the Eleanor Roosevelt of English Creek."

She was on the stump now, smoothing the papers onto the little stand, being careful the creek breeze didn't snatch them. She looked like she had an appointment to fight panthers, but her voice began steady and clear.

"My being up here is anybody's suggestion but my own. It was argued to me that if I did not make this talk, it would not get made. That might have been the better idea.

"But Maxwell Vennaman, not to mention a certain Varick McCaskill, has the art of persuasion. I have been known to tell that husband of mine that he has a memory so long he has to tie knots in it to carry it around with him. We'll all now see just how much my own remembering is made up of slip knots."

Chuckles among the crowd at that. A couple of hundred people being entertained by my mother: a minute before, I would have bet the world against it.

"But I do say this. I can see yet, as clearly as if he was standing in long outline against one of these cottonwoods, the man I have been asked to recall. Ben English. Many others of you were acquainted with Ben and the English family. Sat up to a dinner or supper Mary put on the table in that very house across there." Heads turned, nodded. The English place was directly before us, across the creek from the park. One of the Depression's countless vacant remnants, with a walked-away look to it. If you were driving north out of Gros Ventre the English place came so quick, set in there just past the highway bridge, that chances were you wouldn't recognize it as a ranch rather than a part of the town. But from the park, the empty buildings across there seemed to call their facts over to us. The Englishes all dead or moved away. The family after them felled by the Depression. Now the land leased by Wendell Williamson. One more place which had supported people, now populated by Double W cows.

"Or," my mother was continuing, "or dealt with Ben for horses or cattle or barley or hay. But acquaintance doesn't always etch deep, and so at Max Vennaman's request I have put together what is known of Ben English.

42

"His is a history which begins where that of all settlers of the West of America has to: elsewhere. Benson English was born in 1865 at Cobourg, in Ontario in Canada. He liked to tell that as he and his brothers one by one left home, their mother provided each of them with a Bible, a razor, whatever money she could, and some knitted underwear." My mother here looked as if she entirely approved of Ben English's mother. "Ben English was seventeen when he followed his brother Robert into Montana, to Augusta where Robert had taken up a homestead. Ben found a job driving freight wagon for the Sun River Sheep Company from the supply point at Craig on the Missouri River to their range in the mountains. He put in a year at that, and then, at eighteen, he was able to move up to driving the stage between Craig and Augusta." She lifted a page, went right on as if she'd been giving Fourth of July speeches every day of her life. "Atop there with four horses surging beneath him seemed to be young Ben English's place in the world. Soon, with his wages of forty dollars a month, he was buying his own horses. With a broke team in the lead and his green ones in the other traces, he nonetheless somehow kept his reputation as a driver you could set your clock by." Here she looked up from her sheets of paper to glance over to Senator Thorsen. "Ben later liked to tell that a bonus of stage driving was its civic opportunities. On election day he was able to vote when the stage made its stop at the Halfway House. Then again when it reached Craig. Then a third time when he got home to Augusta."

When the laughter of that was done, my mother focused back down to her pages. "There was a saying that any man who had been a stagecoach driver was qualified to handle the reins of heaven or hell, either one. But Ben English, as so many of our parents did, made the choice halfway between those two. He homesteaded. In the spring of 1893 he filed his claim southwest of here at the head of what is now called Ben English Coulee. The particulars of the English homestead on Ben's papers of proof may sound scant, yet many of us here today came from just such beginnings in this country: 'A dwelling house, stable, corrals, two and a half miles of wire fences, thirty acres of hay cut each season— total value, eight hundred dollars.'

"Around the time of his homesteading Ben English married Mary Manix of Augusta, and they moved here, to the place across the creek, in 1896. Their only child, Mary, was born there in 1901."

Here my mother paused, her look fastened over the heads of all of us on the park grass, toward the trunk of one of the big cottonwoods farthest back. As if, in the way she'd said earlier, someone was standing in outline against the gray bark. "A lot of you can remember the look of Ben English. A rangy man, standing well over six feet, and always wearing a black Stetson, always with a middle crimp. He sometimes grew a winter beard, and in his last years he wore a mustache that made him look like the unfoolable horse dealer he was. Across thirty-some years my father, Isaac Reese, and Ben English knew each other and liked each other and tried to best each other. Put the pair of them together, my mother used to say of their visits, and they would examine a horse until there was nothing left of it but a hank of tail hair and a dab of glue. Once when my father bought a horse with an odd stripe in its face, Ben told him he was glad to see a man of his age taking up a new occupation: raising zebras. My father got his turn back when Ben bought a dark bay Clydesdale that stood twenty-one hands high at the shoulder, very likely the hugest horse there ever has been in this valley, and, upon asking what the horse's name was, discovered it was Benson. Whenever my father saw Ben and the Benson horse together he called out, 'Benson andt Benson, but t'ank Godt vun of t'em vears a hadt.'"

Of all the crowd, I am sure my father laughed loudest at this Isaac Reese tale, and Pete was nodding in confirmation of that accent he and my mother had grown up under. Our speaker of the day, though, was sweeping onward. "Anyone who knew Ben English more than passingly will recall his knack for nicknames. For those of you old enough to remember them around town, Glacier Gus Swenson and Three Day Thurlow both were christened that way by Ben English." Chuckles of recognition spattered amid the audience. Glacier Gus was an idler so slow that it was said he wore spurs to keep his shadow from treading on his heels. Three Day Thurlow had an everlasting local reputation as a passable worker his first day on a job, a complainer on his second, and gone sometime during his third. "Ben's nicknaming had no thought of malice behind it, however. He did it for the pleasure it gave his tongue. In any event, in their pauper's graves Glacier Gus and Three Day each lie buried in a suit given by Ben English."

She put the page she had just finished beneath the others, and the next page she met with a little bob of her head, as if it was the one she'd been looking for all this time. "So it is a justice of language that a namer himself lives on in an extra name. Originally this flow of water was simply called Gros Ventre Creek, to go with the townsite. But it came to be a saying, as the sheepmen and other travelers would pass through here, that they would stop for noon or the night when they reached English's Creek. An apostrophe is not the easiest thing in the world to keep track of, and so we know this as English Creek."

She paused again and I brought my hands up ready to clap, that sounding to me like the probable extent of the Ben English history. But no, she was resuming. Do I never learn? My mother had her own yard-stick as to when she was done with a topic.

"I have a particular memory of Ben English myself. I can see him yet, riding past our ranch on Noon Creek on his way to his cattle range in the mountains, leading a string of cayuse pack horses carrying block salt. On his way back he would ride into our yard and pass the time of day with my father while still sitting in his saddle, but hardly ever would he climb down and come in. His customary explanation was that he had to get home and move the water. He seemed to feel that if he stayed in the saddle, he indeed was on his way to that irrigating task."

My father had his head cocked in a fashion as if what she was recit-ing was new to him. I figured that was just his pride in her perfor-mance, but yet . . .

"And that memory leads to the next, of Ben English in his fields across from us here, moving the water. Guiding the water, it might be better said. For Ben English used the water of his namesake creek as a weaver uses wool. With care. With respect. With patience. Persuading it to become a product greater than itself." Once more she smoothed the page she was reading from. "Greater than itself. As Ben English himself became, greater than himself. From the drudgery of a freight wagon to the hell deck of a stagecoach to a dry-land homestead to a ranch of green water-fed meadows that nicely supported a family, that was the Montana path of Ben English. Following his ability, trusting in it to lead him past the blind alleys of life. This is the day to remember a man who did it that way."

Was I the only one to have the thought brim up in me then? That suddenly, somehow, Alec McCaskill and the Double W had joined Ben English in this speech?

Whether or not, my mother had returned to the irrigation theme.

"Bill Reinking has been kind enough to find for me in the *Gleaner* files something which says this better than I can. It is a piece that I remembered was published when the first water flowed into the ditches of the Valier irrigation project. Who wrote it is not known. It is signed simply 'Homesteader.' Among the hundreds, no, thousands who were homesteading this country then, maybe 'Homesteader' isn't quite as anonymous as 'Anonymous.' But awfully close. It is titled 'The Lord of the Field.'" She drew a deep breath. "It reads:

" 'The irrigator is the lone lord of his field. A shovel is his musket, gumboots are his garb of office, shank's mare is his steed. To him through the curving laterals the water arrives mysteriously, without sign of origin or destination. But his canvas dam, placed with cunning, causes the flood to hesitate, seek; and with an eager whisper, pour over the ditch bank and onto the grateful land. The man with the shovel hears the parched earth drink. He sees its face of dusty brown gladden to glistening black. He smells the odor of life as the land's plants take the water in green embrace. He feels like a god, exalted by this power of his hand and brain to create manmade rain—yet humble as even a god must be under the burden of such power.' "

I honestly believe the only breath which could be discerned in that crowd after that was the one my mother let out. Now she locked her attention to her written sheets, and the words it gave her next were:

"Ben English is gone from us. He died in the summer of 1927, of a strained heart. Died, to say it plainly, of the work he put into this country, as so many have. My own father followed Ben English to the grave within three years. Some say that not a horse in the Two country has had a good looking-over since their passing." Which was one of the more barbed things she could have said to this audience, full as it was of guys who considered themselves pretty fancy horsemen. But she of course said it anyway and sailed on.

"Ben English is gone, and the English place stands empty across there, except for the echoes of the auctioneer's hammer." A comment with bigger barbs yet. Ted Muntz, whose First National Bank had foreclosed on the English place from the people Mrs. English sold it to, without doubt was somewhere in this audience. And all out among the picnic crowd I saw people shift restlessly, as if the memory of the foreclosure auctions, the Depression's hammer sales, was a sudden chafe.

My father by now was listening so hard he seemed to be frozen, an ice statue wearing the clothing of a man, which confirmed to me that not even he knew how far my mother was headed with this talk.

"English Creek is my second home," she was stating now as if someone was arguing the point with her, "for you all know that Noon Creek is where I was born and grew up. Two creeks, two valleys, two claims on my heart. Yet the pair are also day and night to me, as examples of what has happened to this country in my lifetime. Noon Creek now is all but empty of the families I knew there. Yes, there is still the Reese name on a Noon Creek ranch, I am proud as anything to say. And the Egan name, for it would be easier to dislodge the Rocky Mountains than Dill Egan. But the others, all the ranches down Noon Creek but one—all those are a roll call of the gone. The Torrance place: sold out at a loss, the family gone from here. The Emrich place: foreclosed on, the family gone from here. The Chute place: sold out at a loss, the family gone from here. Thad Wainwright's place, Thad one of the first cattlemen anywhere in this country: sold out at a loss, Thad passed away within a year. The Fain place: foreclosed on, the family gone from here. The Eiseley place: sold out at a loss, the family gone from here. The Nansen place." Here she paused, shook her head a little as if again disavowing Alec's news that this was where he and Leona would set up a household. "The Nansen place: foreclosed on, Carl dead by his own hand, Sigrid and the children gone from here to her parents in Minnesota."

What she was achieving was a feat I hadn't known could be done. While her words were expressing outright the fate of those Noon Creek ranching families, she was telling an equally strong tale with the unsaid. "All the ranches down Noon Creek but one" had been her phrase of indictment. Everybody in this park this day knew what "but one" meant; knew who ended up holding the land, by outright buy or by lease from the First National Bank of Gros Ventre, after each and every of those sales and foreclosures. A silent echo I suppose sounds like a contradiction in terms, yet I swear this was what my mother was ringing into the air: after every "sold—foreclosed—gone from here," the reverberating unspoken fact of that family ranch swallowed by the Double W.

"English Creek," she was going on, "thankfully has been spared the Noon Creek history, except once." We knew the next of her litany; it stared us in the face. "The English place. After Ben's death, sold to the Wyngard family who weren't able to make a go of it against the Depression. Foreclosed on, the Wyngards gone from here.

"A little bit ago, Max Vennaman said this is a day for friends and neighbors and families. So it is. And so too we must remember these friends and neighbors and families who are not among us today because they were done in by the times." This said with a skepticism that suggested the times had familiar human faces behind them.

"But an auction hammer can shatter only a household, not the gifts of the earth itself. While it may hurt the heart to see such places as the home of Ben English occupied only by time and the wind, English Creek is still the bloodstream of our valley. It flows its honest way"— the least little pause here, just enough to seed the distinction from those who prosper by the auction hammer—"while we try to find ours."

She looked up now, and out across us, all the islands of people. Either she had this last part by heart or was making it up as she went, because never once did she glance down at her sheaf of pages as she said it.

"There is much wrong with the world, and I suppose I am not known to be especially bashful about my list of those things. But I think it could not be more right that we honor in this valley a man who savvied the land and its livelihood, who honored the earth instead of merely coveting it. It could not be more right that tall Ben English in his black hat amid his green fields, coaxing a head of water to make itself into hay, is the one whose name this creek carries."

She folded her sheaf of papers once, then again, stuck them in the pocket of her dress and stepped down from the stump.

Everybody applauded, although a few a lot more lukewarmly than others. Under our tree we were all clapping hard and my father hardest of all, but I also saw him swallow in a large way. And when he realized I was watching him, he canted himself in my direction and murmured so that only I could hear: "That mother of yours."

Then she was back with us, taking compliments briskly. Pete studied her and said: "Decided to give the big boys some particular hell, didn't you?" Even Toussaint told her: "That was good, about the irrigating." But of us all, it was only to my father that she said, in what would have been a demand if there hadn't been the tint of anxiousness in it: "Well? What did you think?"

My father reached and with his forefinger traced back into place a banner of her hair that the creek breeze had lifted and lain across her ear.

"I think," he said, "I think that being married to you is worth all the risk."

I lead the world in respect for picnics, but I do have to say that one was enough to last me for a while.

Toussaint's murmur to me, my mother's speech to the universe. A person's thought can kite back and forth between those almost forever.

It was just lucky I now had specific matters to put myself to, fetching Mouse from where he was tethered and riding through the dispersing picnickers and heading on across the English Creek bridge to the rodeo grounds.

I was to meet Ray Heaney on the corral alongside the bucking chutes, the best seats in the arena if you didn't mind perching on a fence pole. Again this year my father drilled home to me his one point of rodeo etiquette. "Just so you stay up on that fence," he stipulated. "I don't want to see you down in there with the chute society." By which he meant the clump of fifteen or twenty hangers-on who always clustered around the gates of the bucking chutes, visiting and gossiping and looking generally important, and who regularly were cleared out of there two or three times every rodeo by rampaging broncs. When that happened, up onto anything climbable they all would scoot to roost, like hens with a weasel in their midst, and a minute or so after the bronc's passage they'd be right back in front of the chutes, preening and yakking again. I suppose the chute society offended my father's precept that a horse was nothing to be careless around. In any case, during the housecleanings when a bronc sent them scrambling for the fence it was my father's habit to cheer loudly for the bronc.

No Ray yet, at our fence perch. So I stayed atop Mouse and watched the world. In the pens behind the chutes the usual kind of before-rodeo confusion was going on, guys hassling broncs here and calves there, the air full to capacity with dust and bawling and whinnying. Out front, about half the chute society was already planted in place, tag-ends of their conversations mingling. "That SOB is so tight he wouldn't give ten cents to see Christ ride a bicycle backwards. . . . Oh hell yes, I'll take a quarter horse over a Morgan horse any time. Them Morgans are so damn hot-blooded. . . . With haying coming and one thing and another, I don't see how I'm ever going to catch up with myself. . . ."

I saw my mother and father and Pete and Marie and Toussaint—and Midge Withrow had joined them, though Dode wasn't yet in evidence—settling themselves at the far end of the grandstand, farthest from the dust the bucking horses would kick up.

Other people were streaming by, up into the grandstand or to sit on car fenders or the ground along the outside of the arena fence. I am here to recommend the top of a horse as an advantageous site to view mankind. Everybody below sees mostly the horse, not you.

Definitely I was ready for a recess from attention. From trying to judge whether people going by were nudging each other and whispering sideways, "That's him. That's the one. Got lit up like a ship in a storm, out there with that Stanley Meixell."

Keen as I could be, I caught nobody at it, at least for sure, and began to relax somewhat. Oh, I did get a couple of lookings-over. Lila Sedge drifted past in her moony way, spied Mouse and me, and circled us suspiciously a few times. And the priest Father Morrisseau knew me by sight from my stays with the Heaneys, and bestowed me a salutation. But both those I considered routine inspections, so to speak.

People kept accumulating, I kept watching. A Gros Ventre rodeo always is slower to get under way than the Second Coming.

Then I happened to remember. Not only was I royally mounted, I also was carrying wealth.

I nudged Mouse into action, to go do something about that four-bit piece my father had bestowed. Fifty whole cents. Maybe the Depression *was* on the run.

The journey wasn't far, just forty yards or so over to where, since Prohibition went home with Hoover, the Gros Ventre Rotary Club operated its beer booth. I swung down from Mouse and stepped to the plank counter. Behind it, they had several washtubs full of icewater and bottles of Kessler and Great Falls Select stashed down into the slush until only the brown necks were showing. And off to one side a little, my interest at the moment, the tub of soda pop.

One of the unresolved questions of my life at that age was whether I liked orange soda or grape soda better. It can be more of a dilemma than is generally realized: unlike, say, those picnic options of trout or fried chicken, you can't just dive in and have both. Anyway, I voted grape and was taking my first gulp when somebody inquired at my shoulder, "Jick, how's the world treating you?"

The inquirer was Dode Withrow, and his condition answered as to why he wasn't up in the grandstand with Midge and my folks and the others. As the expression goes, Dode had fallen off the wagon and was still bouncing. He was trigged out in a black sateen shirt and nice gray gabardine pants and his dress stockman Stetson, so he looked like a million. But he also had breath like the downwind side of a brewery.

"'Lo, Dode. You looking for Midge and the folks? They're down at the far end."

Dode shook his head as if he had water in his ears. "That wife of mine isn't exactly looking for me." So. It was one of the Withrow family jangles that Dode and Midge built up to about once a year. During them was the only time Dode seriously drank. Tomorrow there was going to be a lot of frost in the air between Midge and Dode, then the situation would thaw back to normal. It seemed to me a funny way to run a marriage; I always wondered what the three Withrow daughters, Bea and Marcella and Valerie, did with themselves during the annual temper contest between their parents. But this summer was showing that I had everything to learn about the ways of man and woman.

"Charlie, give me a couple Kesslers," Dode was directing across the beer counter. "Jick, you want one?"

"Uh, no thanks," dumbly holding up my grape soda the way a toddler would show off a lollipop.

"That stuff'll rot your teeth," advised Dode. "Give you goiter. St. Vitus' dance."

"Did you say two, Dode?" Charlie Hooper called from one of the beer tubs.

"I got two hands, don't I?"

While Dode paid and took a swig from one bottle while holding the other in reserve, I tried to calculate how far along he was toward being really drunk. Always tricky arithmetic. About all that could be said for sure was that of all the rodeo-goers who were going to get a skinful today, at this rate Dode was going to be among the earliest.

Dode tipped the Kessler down from his mouth and looked straight at me. Into me, it almost seemed. And offered: "Trade you."

I at first thought he meant his bottle of beer for my grape pop, and that befuddled me, for plainly Dode was in no mood for pop. But no, he had something other in mind, he still was gazing straight into my eyes. What he came out with next clarified his message, but did not ease my bafflement. "My years for yours, Jick. I'll go back where you are in life, you come up where I am. Trade, straight across. No, wait, I'll toss in Midge to boot." He laughed, but with no actual humor in it. Then shook his head again in that way as if he'd just come out from swimming. "That's in no way fair. Midge is okay. It's me—" he broke that off with a quick swig of Kessler.

What seemed needed was a change of topic, and I asked: "Where you watching the rodeo from, Dode? Ray and I are going to grab a fence place up there by the booth. Whyn't you sit with us?"

"Many thanks, Jick." He made it sound as if I had offered him knighthood. "But I'm going to hang around the pens awhile. Want to watch the broncs. All I'm good for any more. Watching." And off he swayed, beer bottle in each hand as if they were levers he was steering himself by. I hated to see Dode in such a mood, but at least he always mended quick. Tomorrow he would be himself, and probably more so, again.

Still no Ray on the fence. The Heaneys were taking their sweet time at the family shindig. When Ray ever showed up I would have to compare menus in detail with him, to see how the Heaneys could possibly outeat what we had gone through at the creek picnic.

By now my pop had been transferred from its bottle into me, and with time still to kill and figuring that as long as I had Mouse I might as well be making use of him, I got back up in the saddle.

I sometimes wonder: is the corner of the eye the keenest portion of the body? A sort of special sense, operating beyond the basic ones? For the corner of my right eye now registered, across the arena and above the filing crowd and top pole of the fence, a chokecherry-colored shirt; and atop that, a head and set of shoulders so erect they could not be mistaken.

I nudged Mouse into motion and rode around to Alec's side of the rodeo grounds.

When I got there Alec was off the horse, a big alert deep-chested blood bay, and was fussing with the loop of his lariat in that picky way that calf ropers do. All this was taking place out away from the arena fence and the parked cars, in some open space which Alec and the bay and the lariat seemed to claim as their own.

I dismounted too. And started things off with: "I overheard some calves talking, there in the pens. They were saying how much they admired anybody who'd rope them in a shirt like that."

"Jicker!" he greeted me back. "What do you know for sure?" Alec's words were about what they ever would have been, yet there hung that tone of absent-mindedness behind them again. I wanted to write it off to the fact that this brother of mine had calf roping on his mind just then. But I couldn't quite convince myself that was all there was to the matter.

It did occur to me to check whether Alec was wearing a bandanna this year, and he wasn't. Evidently my father at least had teased that off him permanently.

"Think you got a chance to win?" I asked, just to further the conversation.

"Strictly no problem," Alec assured me. All the fuss he was giving that rope said something else, however.

"How about Bruno Martin?" He was the young rancher from Augusta who had won the calf-roping the previous year.

"I can catch a cold faster than Bruno Martin can a calf."

"Vern Crosby, then?" Another quick-as-a-cat roper, who I had noticed warming up behind the chute pens.

"What, you taking a census or something?" Alec swooshed his lariat overhead, that expectant whir in the air, and cast a little practice throw.

I explored for some topic more congenial to him. "Where'd you get the highpowered horse?"

"Cal Petrie lent him to me." Cal Petrie was foreman of the Double W. Evidently Alec's ropeslinging had attracted some attention.

I lightly laid fingertips to the bay's foreshoulder. The feel of a horse is one of the best touches I know. "You missed the creek picnic. Mom spoke a speech."

Alec frowned at his rope. "Yeah. I had to put the sides on Cal's pickup and haul this horse in here. A speech? What about? How to sleep with a college book under your pillow and let it run uphill into your ear?"

"No. About Ben English."

"Ancient history, huh? Dad must have converted her." Alec looked like he intended to say more, but didn't.

There wasn't any logical reason why this should have been on my mind just then, but I asked: "Did you know he had a horse with the same name as himself?"

"Who? Had a what?"

"Ben English. Our granddad would say 'T'ank Godt vun of t'em vears a—'"

"Look, Jicker, I got to walk this horse loose. How about you doing me a big hairy favor?"

Something told me to be a little leery. "Ray's going to be waiting for me over on the—"

"Only take a couple minutes of your valuable time. All it is, I want you to go visit Leona for me while I get this horse ready."

"Leona? Where is she?"

"Down toward the end of the arena there, by her folks' car."

As indeed she was, when I turned to see. About a hundred feet from us, spectating this brotherly tableau. Leona in a clover-green blouse, that gold hair above like daybreak over a lush meadow.

"Yeah, well, what do you mean by visit?"

"Just go on over there and entertain her for me, huh?"

"Entert—?"

"Dance a jig, tell a joke." Alec swung into the saddle atop the bay. "Easy, hoss." I stepped back a bit and Mouse looked admiring as the bay did a little prance to try Alec out. Alec reined him under control and leaned toward me. "I mean it, about you keeping Leona company for me. Come get me if Earl Zane shows up. I don't want that jughead hanging around her."

Uh huh. Revelation, all twenty-two chapters of it.

"Aw, the hell, Alec. I—" was about to declare that I had other things in life to do than fetch him whenever one of Leona's ex-boyfriends came sniffing around. But that declaration melted somewhere before I could get it out, for here my way came one of those Leona smiles that would burn down a barn. Simultaneously she patted the car fender beside her.

While I still was molten in the middle of all that, Alec touched the bay roping horse into a fast walk toward some open country beyond the calf pens. So I figured there was nothing for it but go on over and face fate.

" 'Lo, Leona."

"Hello, John Angus." Which tangled me right at the start. I mean, think about it. The only possible way in this world she could know about my high-toned name was from Alec. Which meant that I had been a topic of conversation between them. Which implied—I didn't know what. Damn it all to hell anyway. First Toussaint, now this. I merely was trying to have a standard summer, not provide word fodder for the entire damn Two country.

"Yeah, well. Great day for the race," I cracked to recoup.

Leona smiled yet another of her dazzlers. And said nothing. Didn't even inquire "What race?" so I could impart "The human race" and thereby break the ice and—

"You all by your lonesome?" I substituted. As shrewd as it was desperate, this. Not only did it fill the air space for a moment, I would truthfully tell Alec I had been vigilant about checking on whether or not Earl Zane was hanging around.

She shook her head. Try it sometime, while attempting to keep a full smile in place on your face. Leona could do it and come out with more smile than she started with. When she had accomplished this facial miracle she leaned my way a little and nodded her head conspiratorially toward the other side of the car.

Holy Jesus. Was Earl Zane over there? Earl Zane was Alec's size and built as if he'd been put together out of railroad ties. Alec hadn't defined to me this possibility, of Earl Zane already being on hand. What was I supposed to do, tip my hat to him and merrily say "Hi there, Earl, just stand where you are, I'll go get my brother so he can come beat the living daylights out of you"? Or better from the standpoint of my own health, climb back on Mouse and retreat to my original side of the arena?

For information's sake, I leaned around Leona and peered over the hood of the car. And was met by startled stares from Ted and Thelma Tracy—Leona's parents—and another couple with whom they were seated on a blanket and carrying on a conversation.

"Your folks are looking real good," I mumbled as I pulled my head back to normal. "Nice to see them so."

Leona, though, had shifted attention from me to the specimen of horseflesh at the other end of the reins I was holding. "Riding in style, aren't you?" she admired.

"His name is Mouse," I confided. "Though if he was mine, I'd call him, uh, Chief Joseph."

Leona slowly revolved her look from the horse to me, the way the beam of a lighthouse makes its sweep. Then asked: "Why not Crazy Horse?"

From Leona that was tiptop humor, and I yukked about six times as much as I ordinarily would have. And in the meantime was readying myself. After all, that brother of mine had written the prescription he wanted from me: entertain her.

"Boy, I'll have to remember that. And you know, that reminds me of one. Did you ever hear the joke about the Chinaman and the Scotchman in a rowboat on the Sea of Galilee?"

Leona shook her head. Luck was with me. This was my father's favorite joke, one I had heard him tell to other Forest Service guys twenty times; the heaviest artillery I could bring to bear.

"Well, see, there was a Chinaman and a Scotchman together in a rowboat on the Sea of Galilee. Fishing away, there. And after a while the Chinaman puts down his fishing pole and he leans over and nudges the

Scotchman and says, 'Jock, tell me. Is is true what they say about Occidental women?' And the Scotchman says, 'Occidental, hell. I'm cerrtain as anything that they behave the way they do on purrpose!'"

I absolutely believed I had done a royal job of telling, even burring the R's just right. But a little crimp of puzzlement now punctuated Leona's smiling face, right between her eyes. She asked: "The Sea of Galilee?"

I cast a wide look around for Alec. Or even Earl Zane, whom I would rather fight with one hand in my pocket than try to explain a joke to somebody who didn't get it. "Yeah. But you see, that isn't—"

Just then, Mouse got into the act. Why he could not have waited another two minutes until I had found a way to dispatch myself from Leona; why it didn't come into his horse brain any other time of the day up until that very moment; why—but no why about it, he was proceeding, directly in front of where Leona and I were sharing the fender, to take his leak.

The hose on a horse is no small sight anyway during this process. But with Leona there six feet away spectating, Mouse's seemed to poke down, down, down.

I cleared my throat and examined the poles of the arena fence and then the posts that supported the poles and then the sky over the posts and then crossed and uncrossed my arms a few times, and still the downpour continued. A wild impulse raised in me: Mouse's everlasting whiz reminded me of Dode Withrow spraddled atop that boulder the second day of this unprecedented summer, and I clamped my jaw to keep from blurting to Leona that scene and the handhold joke. That would be about like you, John Angus McCaskill. Celebrate disaster with a dose of social suicide. Do it up right.

Meanwhile Leona continued to serenely view the spectacle as if it was the fountains of Rome.

"I'll take over now, Jicker." Alec's voice came from behind us; he had circled outside of the arena on the bay horse. Peals of angel song could not have come more welcome. "How'd he do as company, Leona?"

Leona shined around at Alec, then turned back to bestow me a final glint. And answered: "He's a wonder."

I mounted up and cleared out of there; Alec and Leona all too soon would be mooning over each other like I didn't exist anyway; and as promptly as I was out of eyeshot behind the catch pen at the far end of the arena I gave Mouse a jab in the ribs that made him woof in surprise. Chief Joseph, my rosy hind end.

But I suppose my actual target was life. This situation of being old enough to be on the edge of everything and too young to get to the middle of any of it.

"Hi," Ray Heaney greeted as I climbed onto the arena fence beside him. The grin-cuts were deep into his face and the big front teeth were out on parade. Ray could make you feel that your arrival was the central event in his recent life. "What've you been up to?"

"Oh"—summary seemed so far out of the question, I chose neutrality—"about the usual. You?"

"Pilot again." So saying, Ray held up his hands to show his calluses. One hard oblong bump across the base of each finger, like sets of knuckles on his palms. I nodded in commendation. My shovel calluses were mosquito bites in comparison. This made the second summer Ray was stacking lumber in his father's lumber yard—the "pile it here, pile it there" nature of that job was what produced the "pilot" joke—and his hands and forearms were gaining real heft.

Now Ray thrust his right mitt across to within reach of mine. "Shake the hand that shook the hand?" he challenged. It was a term we had picked up from his father—Ray could even rumble it just like Ed Heaney's bass-drum voice—who remembered it from his own boyhood in Butte when guys still went around saying "Shake the hand that shook the hand of John L. Sullivan," the heavyweight boxing champ of then.

I took Ray up on the hand duel, even though I pretty well knew how this contest of ours was going to turn out from now on. We made a careful fit of the handshake grip; then Ray chanted the start, "One, two, *three.*"

After about a minute of mutual grunted squeezing, I admitted: "Okay. I'm out-squoze."

"You'll get me next time," Ray said. "Didn't I see Alec riding around acting like a calf roper?"

Some years before, Ed Heaney had driven out from Gros Ventre to the ranger station one summer Saturday to talk forest business with my father. And with him, to my surprise and no little consternation, came his son my age, Ray. I could see perfectly damn well what was intended here, and that's the way it did happen. Off up the South Fork our fathers rode to eyeball a stand of timber which interested Ed for buck-rake teeth he could sell at his lumber yard, and Ray and I were left to entertain one another.

Living out there at English Creek I always was stumped about what of my existence would interest any other boy in the world. There was the knoll with the view all the way to the Sweetgrass Hills, but some-how I felt that might not hold the fascination for others that it did for me. Ordinarily horses would have been on hand to ride, the best solu-tion to the situation, but the day before, Isidor Pronovost and some CCC guys had taken all the spare ones in a big packstring to set up a spike camp for a tree-planting crew. Alec was nowhere in the picture as a possible ally; this was haying time and he was driving the scatter rake for Pete Reese. The ranger station itself was no refuge; the sun was out and my mother would never let us get away with lolling around inside, even if I could think up a reasonable loll. Matters were not at all improved by the fact that, since I still was going to the South Fork grade school and Ray went in Gross Ventre, we only knew each other by sight.

He was a haunting kid to look at. His eyes were within long deep-set arcs, as if always squinched the way you do to thread a needle. And curved over with eyebrows which wouldn't need to have been much thicker to make a couple of respectable blond mustaches. And then a flattish nose which, wide as it was, barely accommodated all the freck-les assigned to it. When Ray really grinned—I didn't see that this first day, although I was to see it thousands of times in the years ahead—deep slice-lines cut his cheeks, out opposite the corners of his mouth. Like a big set of parentheses around the grin. His lower lip was so full that it too had a slice-line under it. This kid looked more as if he'd been carved out of a pumpkin than born. Also, even more so than a lot of us at that age, his front teeth were far ahead of the rest of him in size. In any schoolyard there always were a lot of traded jibes of "Beaver tooth!" but Ray's frontals really did seem as if they'd been made for toppling willows.

As I say, haunting. I have seen grown men, guys who ordinarily wouldn't so much as spend a glance at a boy on the street, stop and study that face of Ray's. And here he was, thank you a whole hell of a lot, my guest for this day at English Creek.

So we were afoot with one another and not knowing what to do about it, and ended up wandering the creek bank north of the ranger station, with boredom building up pretty fast in both of us. Finally, I got the idea of showing him the pool a little ways downstream in English Creek where brook trout always could be seen, hanging there dark in the clear water. In fact, I asked Ray if he felt like fishing, but for some reason he looked at me a little suspiciously and mumbled, "Huh uh."

We viewed the pool, which took no time at all, and then thrashed on along in the creek brush for awhile, just to be doing anything. It was semi-swampy going, so at least we could concentrate on jumping across the wet holes. Ray was dressed in what I suppose his mother thought were old enough clothes to go into the country with, but his old clothes were so noticeably ritzier than my everyday ones that he maybe was embarrassed about that. Anyway, for whatever reason, he put up with this brushwhacking venture of mine.

Whacked was what he got. My mind was on something else, likely how much of the day still gaped ahead of us, and without thinking I let a willow spring back as I pushed past it. It whipped Ray across the left side of his face and drew a real yelp from him. Also a comment to me:

"Watch out with those, beetle brain."

"Didn't mean to," I apologized. Which most likely would have buried the issue, except for what I felt honor bound to add next: "Sparrow head."

You wonder afterwards how two reasonably sane people descend into a slanging match like that.

"Slobberguts," Ray upped the ante with.

"Booger eater," I promptly gave him back.

"Pus gut."

"Turd bird."

As I remember it, I held myself in admirable rein until Ray came out with "turkey dink."

For some reason that one did it. I swung on Ray and caught him just in front of the left ear. Unluckily, not quite hard enough to knock him down.

He popped me back, alongside the neck. We each got in a few more swings, then the fisticuffs degenerated into a wrestle. More accurately, a mud wallow.

We each were strong enough, and outraged enough, to be able to tip the other, so neither one of us ended up permanently on top. Simply, at some point we wore out on wanting to maul one another any further, and got to our feet. Ray's clothes looked as if he'd been rolled the length of a pig pen. Mine I guess weren't much better, but they hadn't started off as fancy and so I figured my muss didn't matter as much.

Of course, try convince my mother of that. Come noon we had to straggle in to get any dinner, and when she laid eyes on us, we were in for a scouring in more ways than one. Ray she made change into a set of my clothes—funny, how improved he looked when he was out of that town gear—and sat us at opposite ends of the table while we ate, then immediately afterward she issued two decrees: "Jick, I believe you would like To Read in the Other Room. Ray, I think you would like To Put Together the Jigsaw Puzzle I Am Going to Put Here on the Table for You."

When I started high school in Gros Ventre, Ray came over to me at noon hour the first day. He planted himself just out of arm's reach from me and offered: "Horse apple."

I balled up both my fists, and my tongue got ready the words which would fan our creekside battle to life again: "Beaver tooth." Yet the direction of Ray's remark caught my notice. "Horse apple" was pretty far back down the scale from "turkey dink."

For once in my life I latched on to a possibility. I held my stance and tendered back to Ray: "Mud minnow."

It started a grin on him while he thought up: "Slough rat."

"Gumbo gopher," I provided, barely managing to get it out before we were both laughing.

Within the week I was asking my mother whether I could stay in town overnight with Ray, and after that I made many a stay-over at the Heaneys' throughout the school year. Not only did I gain the value of Ray and me being the best of friends; it was always interesting to me that the Heaneys were a family as different from ours as crochet from oil cloth. For one thing they were Catholic, although they really didn't display it all that much. Just through a grace before every meal and a saint here and there on the wall and eating fish on Friday, which eventually occurred to me as the reason Ray had looked at me suspiciously there at the creek when I asked him about fishing. For another, in almost every imaginable way the Heaney family was as tidy as spats on a rooster. (The "almost" was this: Ray and his sister Mary Ellen, three years younger, were allowed liberties with their food that I'd never dreamt of. Take hotcakes as an example. Ray and Mary Ellen poured some syrup on, then rolled each hotcake up, then syruped the outside and began eating. A kind of maple syrup tamale, I now know enough to realize. When I first began overnighting with them they urged me to try mine that way, but the thought of my mother's response to something like that made me figure I might as well not get converted. At other meals too Ray and Mary Ellen squooged their food around in remarkable ways and ate only as much of it as they felt like. I tell you, it shocked me: people my own age leaving plates that looked more as if they'd been walked through than eaten from.) Ray's mother, Genevieve, kept that big two-story house dusted and doilied to a faretheewell. Mary Ellen already had her mind set on being a nurse—she was a kind of starchy kid anyway, so it was a good enough idea—and you couldn't scratch a finger around there without her wanting to daub it with Mercurochrome and wrap you up like a mummy.

Then there was Ray's father, Ed. You could hang your hat on Ed Heaney's habits. Every evening he clicked the lock on the door of the lumber yard office as if it was the final stroke needed to complete six o'clock, and if he wasn't walking in the kitchen door at five minutes after six, Genevieve started peering out the kitchen window to see what had happened to him. Another five minutes, Ed washing up and toweling down, and supper began. As soon as supper was over Ed sat at the kitchen table going through the Falls *Leader* and visiting with Genevieve while she did the dishes, his deep voice and her twinkly one, back and forth, back and forth. Then at seven straight up, Ed strode into the living room, planted himself in his rocking chair and clicked on the big Silvertone floor radio. He listened straight through until ten o'clock— if somebody spouting Abyssinian had come on the air, Ed would have sat there and listened—and then went up to bed. Thus everything in the Heaney household in the evening was done against the backdrop of Ed's Silvertone, and Genevieve and Ray and Mary Ellen had become so used to tuning out sound that you often had to say something to them a couple of times to make it register. In Ray, there was an opposite kind of consequence, too. Ray had heard so much radio he could mimic just about any of it, Eddie Cantor and Walter Winchell and Kaltenborn giving the news and all those.

But Ed, I was telling about. You couldn't know it to look at Ed Heaney, because the lumber yard life had put a middle on him, and he was bald as a jug, but he served in France during the war. In fact spent I don't know how much time in the trenches. Enough that he didn't want to squander one further minute of his life talking about it, evidently. Just once did I ever manage to get him going on that topic. That Ed won some medals over there I knew because Ray once sneaked them out of a dresser drawer in Ed and Genevieve's bedroom and showed them to me. You wouldn't expect medal-winning about Ed either. In any case, though, one Heaney suppertime when I was in to stay with Ray some topic came up that emboldened me to outright ask Ed what he remembered most about being in the war. Figuring, of course, I might hear tales that led to the medals.

"Shaving."

After a while Ed glanced up from his eating and realized that Ray and Mary Ellen and Genevieve and I were all regarding him in a stymied way.

"We had to shave every day," he elaborated. "Wherever we were. Belleau Wood, we only got a canteen of water per man per day. But we still used some of it to shave. The gas masks they gave us were a French kind. Sort of a sack that went over your face like this." Ed ran a hand around his chinline. "If you had whiskers it didn't fit tight enough. Gas would get in. You'd be a goner."

Ed began to take another bite of his supper, but instead repeated: "Belleau Wood. About midday there we'd be in our foxholes—graves, we called them—all of us shaving, or holding our shirts up to read them for lice. Thousands of us, all doing one or the other."

The other four of us waited, dumbstruck, to see where this sudden hallway of Ed's memory led.

But all he said more was "Pass the stringbeans, please."

Now that we were established atop the arena corral, I reported to Ray my chin session with Dode Withrow at the beer booth. Ray took what might be called a spectator interest in the Withrow family. He never came right out and said so, but his eye was on the middle Withrow girl, Marcella, who was in the same high school class we were. Marcella was trim in figure like Midge and had a world-by-the-tail grin like Dode's usual one. So far Ray's approach to Marcella was distant admiration, but I had the feeling he was trying to figure out how to narrow the distance.

Maybe the day would come when I was more interested in a Leona or a Marcella than in perching up there above general humanity, but right then I doubted it. I considered that the top-pole perch Ray and I had there next to the bucking chutes was the prime site of the whole rodeo grounds. We had clear view of every inch of the arena, the dirt oval like a small dry lake bed before us. And all the event action would originate right beside us, where even now the broncs for the first section of bareback riding were being hazed into the chutes alongside my corral spot. The particular Gros Ventre bucking chute setup was that as six broncs at a time were hazed in for their set of riders, pole panels were retracted between each chute, leaving what had been the half-dozen chutes as one long narrow pen. Then as the horses crowded in a single file, the panels were shoved in place behind them one by one, penning each bronc into the chute it would buck into the arena from. As slick a system as there is for handling rodeo broncs, I suppose. But what is memorable to me about it is the instant before the pole panels were shoved into place to serve as chute dividers: when the horses came swarming into the open chute pen, flanks heaving, heads up and eyes glittering. From my perch, it was like looking down through a transom into a long hallway suddenly filled with big perplexed animals. Not many sights are its equal.

Above and to the left of Ray and me was the announcing booth and its inhabitants, a nice proximity which added to the feeling that we were part of the inside happenings of the rodeo. To look at, the booth resembled a little woodshed up on stilts, situated there above and just in back of the middle of the bucking chutes. It held elbow room for maybe six people, although only three of the booth crowd did any actual rodeo work. Tollie Zane, if you could call his announcing work. Tollie evidently was in residence at the far end of the booth, angled out of view from us but a large round microphone like a waffle iron standing on end indicated his site. Then nearest to us was the scorekeeper, Bill Reinking, editor of the *Gleaner*, prominent with his ginger mustache and silver-wire eyeglasses. I suppose he did the scorekeeping on the principle that the only sure way for the *Gleaner* to get any accuracy on the rodeo results was for him to originate the arithmetic. Between Bill and Tollie was the space for the timekeeper, who ran the stopwatch to time the events and blew the whistle to signal when a bronc rider had lasted eight seconds atop a bareback or ten in a saddle ride. The timekeeper's spot in the booth was empty, but this was about to be remedied.

"Wup wup wup," some Paul Revere among the chute society cried. "Here she comes, boys! Just starting up the ladder!"

Heads swiveled like weathervanes hit by a tornado. And yes, Ray and I also sent our eyes around to the little ladder along the side of the announcing booth and the hypnotizing progress up it of Velma Simms.

"Tighter than last year, I swear to God," someone below us was contending.

"Like the paper fits the wall," testified another.

And yet another, "But I still need to know, how the hell does she get herself into those britches?"

Velma Simms came of Eastern money. Plumbing equipment I believe was its source; I have seen her family name, Croake, on hot-and-cold spigots. And in a community and era which considered divorce usually more grievous than manslaughter, she had been through three husbands. That we knew of. Only the first was local, the lawyer Paul Bogan. They met in Helena when he got himself elected to the legislature, and if my count is right, it was at the end of his second term when Velma arrived back to Gros Ventre and Paul stayed over there at the capital in some kind of state job. Her next husband was a fellow named Sutter, who'd had an automobile agency in Spokane. In Gros Ventre he was like a trout out of water, and quickly went. After him came Simms, an actor Velma happened across in some summer performance at one of the Glacier Park lodges. By February of his first Two country winter Simms was hightailing his way to California, although he eventually did show up back in Gros Ventre, so to speak, as one of the cattle rustlers in a Gene Autry movie at the Odeon. Lately Velma seemed to have given up marrying and instead emerged each Fourth with a current beau tagging along. They tended to be like the scissorbill following her up the ladder now, in a gabardine stockman's suit and a too clean cream Stetson, probably a bank officer from Great Falls. I cite all this because Paul Bogan, the first in the genealogy, always had served as rodeo timekeeper, and the next Fourth of July after his change of residence, here Velma presented herself, bold as new paint, to take up his stopwatch and whistle. It was her only instance of what might be called civic participation, and quite why she did it nobody had a clue. But Velma's ascension to the booth now was part of every Gros Ventre rodeo. Particularly for the male portion of the audience. For as you may have gathered, Velma on her Fourth appearances was encased in annual new slacks of stunning snugness. One of the theoreticians in the chute society just now was postulating a fresh concept, that maybe Velma heated them with an iron, put them on hot, and let them shrink down on her like the rim onto a wagon wheel.

I saw once, in recent years at the Gros Ventre rodeo, a young bronc rider and his ladyfriend watching the action through the pole arena gate. They each held a can of beer in one hand, and the rider's other hand was around the girl's shoulders. *Her* other hand, though, was down resting lightly on his rump, the tips of her fingers just touching the inseam of his Levis back there. I'll admit to you, it made my heart turn around and face north. That the women now can and will do such a thing seems to me an advance like radio. My awe of it is tempered only by the regret that I am not that young man, or any other. But let that go. My point here is just that in the earlier time, only rare self-advertised rumps such as that of Velma Simms were targets of public interest, and then only by what my father and the other rangers called ocular examination.

It registered on me there had been a comment from Ray's direction. "Come again?" I apologized.

"No hitch in Velma's gitalong," Ray offered one more time.

I said something equally bright in agreement, but I was surprised at Ray making an open evaluation of Velma Simms, even so tame a one as that. The matter of Marcella maybe was on his mind more than I figured.

Just then an ungodly noise somewhere between a howl and a yowl issued above us. A sort of high HHHRUNGHHH like a cat was being skinned alive. I was startled as hell, but Ray knew its source. "You see Tollie's loudspeaking getup?" he inquired with a nod toward the top of the announcer's booth. I couldn't help but have noticed such a rig. The contraption was a pyramid of rods, which held at its peak a half-dozen big metal cones like those morning-glory horns on old phonographs, pointing to various points of the compass. Just in case those didn't cover the territory, there was a second set of four more 'glory horns a couple of feet beneath. "He sent off to Billings for it," informed Ray, who had overheard this information when Tollie came to the lumber yard for a number of two-by-fours to help brace the contraption into place. "The guy who makes them down there told him it's the real deal to announce with."

We were not the only ones contemplating Tollie's new announcing machinery. "What the goddamn hell's Tollie going to do," I heard somebody say below us, "tell them all about it in Choteau?" Choteau was thirty-three miles down the highway.

"WELCOME!" crackled a thunderblast of voice over our heads. "To

the   Gros Ventre   rodeo!   Our   fifteenth   annual
show!   You folks   are wise   as hooty   owls   to roost
with us   here   today.   Yes   sir!   Some   of
everything   is liable   to happen   here   today   and—"
Tollie Zane, father of the famous Earl, held the job of announcing the
Gros Ventre rodeo on the basis by which a lot of positions of authority
seem to get filled: nobody else would be caught dead doing it. But
before this year, all that the announcing amounted to was shouting
through a megaphone the name of each bucking horse and its rider.
The shiny new 'glory horns evidently had gone to Tollie's head, or at
least his tonsils. "The Fourth   of   July   is called   the
cowboys'   Christmas   and our   festivities   here
today   will get   under way   in just—"

"Called what?" somebody yelled from the chute society. "That's
Tollie for you, sweat running down his face and he thinks it's
snowflakes."

"Santy Claus must have brought him that goddamn talking contraption," guessed somebody else.

"Naw, you guys, lay off now," a third one put in. "Tollie's maybe
right. It'd explain why he's as full of shit as a Christmas goose."

Everybody below us hee-heed at that while Tollie roared on about
the splendiferous tradition of rodeo and what heart-stopping excitement we were going to view in this arena today. Tollie was a kind of
plodding talker anyway, and now with him slowed down either out of
respect for the new sound system or because he was translating his
remarks from paper—this July Christmas stuff was originating from
somewhere; had a kit come with the 'glory horns and microphone?—
you could about soft-boil an egg between parts of his sentences.

"Anybody here   from   Great Falls?"

Quite a number of people yelled and waved their hands.

"Welcome   to   America!"

Out in the crowd there were laughs and groans. And most likely
some flinching in the Rotary beer booth; a real boon to business, Tollie
cracking wise at the expense of people who'd had ninety miles of driving time to wonder whether this rodeo was worth coming to.

But this seemed to be a day when Tollie, armed with amplification,
was ready to take on the world. "How about   North   Dakota?
Who's here   from   North   Dakota?"

Of course, no response. Tourists were a lot scarcer in those days, and the chances that anybody would venture from North Dakota just to see the Gros Ventre rodeo were zero and none.

"That's right!" blared Tollie. "If I   was you   ·   I wouldn't admit it   neither!"

Tollie spieled on for a while, actually drawing boos from the Choteau folks in the crowd when he proclaimed that Choteau was known as a town without a single bedbug: "No sir   they are   all married and have   big families!" At last, though, the handling crew was through messing with the chute alongside Ray and me, and Tollie was declaring "We are   just about   to get   the   pumpkin rolling.   Bareback   riding   will be   our first   event."

"Pumpkin?" questioned whoever it was in the chute society that was keeping tab of Tollie's excursions through the calendar. "Judy H. Christ! Now the whistledick thinks it's Halloween."

About all that is worth mentioning of the early part of the rodeo is that its events, a section of bareback riding and after that some steer-wrestling or mauling or whatever you want to call it, passed fairly mercifully. Ray and I continued to divide our time snorting laughs over something either Tollie or the chute society provided. Plus our own wiseacre efforts, of course. Ray nearly fell off the corral from cackling when I speculated whether this much time sitting on a fence pole mightn't leave a person with the crack in his behind running crosswise instead of up and down. You know how that is: humor is totally contagious when two persons are in the same light mood. And a good thing, too, for by my estimation the actual events of a rodeo can always use all the help they can get. Although like anybody out here I have seen many and many a rodeo, to me the arena events are never anything to write home special about. It's true that bareback riding has its interesting moments, but basically the ride is over and done with about as it's getting started. I don't know, a guy flopping around on the naked back of a horse just seems to me more of a stunt than a sport. As for steer-wrestling, that is an absolutely phony deal, never done except there in front of a rodeo crowd. Leaping onto a running steer has about as much to do with actual cattle ranching as wearing turquoise belt buckles does. And that calf-roping. Calf-roping I nominate as an event the spectators ought to be paid for sitting through. I mean, here'll come one yayhoo out after the calf swinging a community loop an elephant could trot through, and the next guy will pitch a loop so teeny that it bounces off the back of the calf's neck like a spitwad. Whiff whiff whiff, and then a burst of cussing as the rope-flinger's throw misses its mark: there is the essence of rodeo calf-roping. If I ran the world there'd be standards, such as making any calf-roping entrant dab onto a fencepost twenty feet away, just to prove he knows how to build a decent loop.

"Alec's bringing his horse in," Ray reported from his sphere of the arena. "Guess he's roping in this section."

"So's everybody else in the world, it looks like." Horsemen and hemp, hemp and horsemen. It was a wonder the combined swishing of the ropes of all the would-be calf ropers now assembling didn't lift the rodeo arena off the ground like an autogyro. As you maybe can tell, my emotions about having a brother forthcoming into this event were strictly mixed. Naturally I was pulling for Alec to win. Brotherly blood is at least that thick. Yet a corner of me was shadowed with doubt as to whether victory was really such a good idea for Alec. Did he need any more confirming in his cowboy mode? Especially in this dubious talent of hanging rope necklaces onto slobbering calves?

This first section of the calf-roping now proceeded about as I could have foretold, a lot of air fanned with rope but damn few calves collared. One surprise was produced, though. After a fast catch Bruno Martin of Augusta missed his tie, the calf kicking free before its required six seconds flat on the ground were up. If words could be seen in the air, some blue dandies accompanied Martin out of the arena.

The other strong roper, Vern Crosby, snagged his calf neatly, suffered a little trouble throwing him down for the tie, but then niftily gathered the calf's legs and wrapped the pigging string around them, as Tollie spelled out for us, "faster   than   Houdini   can   tie his   shoe   laces!"

So when the moment came for Alec to guide the blood bay roping horse into the break-out area beside the calf chute, the situation was as evident as Tollie's voice bleating from that tin bouquet of 'glory horns:

"Nineteen   seconds   by   Vern   Crosby   is still the time   to beat.   It'll take   some fancy   twirling by this   next   young   buckaroo.   One of   the hands   out at   the Double   W   he's getting   his-self   squared away   and   will be   ready   in just—"

The calf chute and the break-out area where each roper and his horse burst out after the creature were at the far end of the bucking chutes from us. Ray cupped his hands and called across to there: "Wrap him up pretty, Alec!"

Across there, Alec appeared a little nervous, dandling his rope around more than was necessary as he and the bay horse waited for their calf to emerge. But then I discovered I was half nervous myself, jiggling my foot on its corral pole, and I had no excuse whatsoever. You wouldn't catch me out there trying to snare a two-hundred-pound animal running full tilt.

The starter's little red flag whipped down, and the calf catapulted from the chute into the expanse of the arena.

Alec's luck. Sometimes you had to think he held the patent on four-leaf clovers and rabbit's feet. The calf he drew was a straight runner instead of a dodger. Up the middle of the arena that calf galloped as if he was on rails, the big horse gaining ground on him for Alec every hoofbeat. And I believe that if you could have pulled the truth from my father and mother right then, even they would have said that Alec looked the way a calf roper ought to. Leaning forward but still as firm in his stirrups as if socketed into them, swinging the loop of the lariat around and around his head strongly enough to give it a good fling but not overdoing it. Evidently there had been much practice performed on Double W calves as Alec rode the coulees these past weeks.

"Dab it on him!" I heard loudly, and realized the yell had been by me.

Quicker than it can be told Alec made his catch. A good one, where all the significant actions erupt together: the rope straightening into a tan line in the air, the calf gargling out a *bleahh* as the loop choked its neck and yanked it backward, Alec evacuating from the stirrups in his dismount. Within a blink he was in front of the tall bay horse and scampering beside the stripe of rope the bay was holding taut as fishline, and now Alec was upending the calf into the arena dust and now gathering calf legs and now whipping the pigging string around them and now done.

"The time   for Alec   McCaskill"—I thought I could hear gloom inside the tinny blare of Tollie's voice, and so knew the report was going to be good—"seventeen   and   a half   seconds."

The crowd whooped and clapped. Over at the far fence Leona was beaming as if she might ignite, and down at the end of the grandstand my parents were glumly accepting congratulations on Alec. Beside me Ray was as surprised as I was by Alec's first-rate showing, and his delight didn't have the conditions attached that mine did.

"How much is up?" he wondered. I wasn't sure of the roping prize myself, so I asked the question to the booth, and Bill Reinking leaned out and informed us, "Thirty dollars, and supper for two at the Sedgwick House."

"Pretty slick," Ray admired. I had to think so myself. Performance is performance, whatever my opinion of Alec's venue of it. Later in the afternoon there would be one more section of calf ropers, but with the main guys, Bruno Martin and Vern Crosby, already behind him, Alec's leading time looked good enough to take to the bank.

Tollie was bleating onward. "Now we turn to some prairie sailors and the hurricane deck," which translated to the first go-round of saddle bronc riding. I will say for saddle bronc riding that it seems to me the one rodeo event that comes close to legitimate. Staying on a mount that is trying to unstay you is a historic procedure of the livestock business. "The boys are hazing the ponies into the chutes and when we commence and get started the first man out will be Bill Semmler on a horse called Conniption. In this meanwhile though did you hear the one about the fellow who goes into the barber shop and—"

I never did get to hear Tollie's tonsorial tale, for I happened to glance down to my left into the bucking chutes and see disaster in a spotted horsehide charging full tilt at me.

"Hang on!" I yelled to Ray and simultaneously flipflopped myself rightward and dropped down the fence so that I had my arms clamped around both the top corral pole and Ray's hips.

Ray glommed tight to the pole with his hands. WHOMP! and a clatter. The impact of the pinto bucking horse slamming into the chute end where our section of corral cornered into it went shuddering through the pair of us, as if a giant sledgehammer had hit the wood; but our double gripping kept us from being flung off the top of the fence.

"Jesus!" Ray let out, rare for him. "There's a goosy one!"

Our narrow brush did not escape microphone treatment. "This little Coffee Nerves pinto down at chute six has a couple of fence squatters hugging the wood pretty good!" Tollie was alerting the world. "We'll see whether they go ahead and kiss it!"

"Numbnuts," I muttered in the direction of the Zane end of the announcing booth. Or possibly more than muttered, for when I managed to glower directly up there, Bill Reinking was delivering me a certifying wink and Velma Simms was puckered the way a person does to hold in a laugh.

Ray had it right, the pinto was truly riled and then some, as I could confirm while cautiously climbing back onto my perch and locking a firm arm around the corner post between chute and corral. No way was I going to take a chance on being dislodged down into the company of this Coffee Nerves bronc. The drawback of this flood-the-chutes-with-horses system was that the first horse in was the last to come out, from this end chute next to me. While the initial five horses were being bucked out Coffee Nerves was going to be cayusing around in chute six and trying to raise general hell.

The pinto looked more than capable. Coffee Nerves had close-set pointy ears; what are called pin ears, and indicate orneriness in a horse. Worse, he was hog-eyed. Had small darty eyes that shot looks at the nearest threat all the time. Which, given my position on the fence, happened to be me. I had not been the target of so much eyeball since the tussle to get that Bubbles pack horse up the side of the mountain.

Ray was peering behind me to study Coffee Nerves, so he was the one who noticed. "Huh! Look who must've drew him."

There in back of chute six, Earl Zane was helping the handlers try to saddle the pinto.

My session of watchdogging Leona for Alec of course whetted my interest in the matter of Earl Zane, whom I ordinarily wouldn't bat an eye to look at. Now here he loomed, not ten feet away from Ray and me, at the rear of Coffee Nerves' chute amid the cussing crew of handlers trying to contend with the pinto and the saddle that was theoretically supposed to go on its back. Earl Zane had one of those faces that could be read at a glance: as clear as the label on a maple sugar jug it proclaimed SAP. I suppose he was semi-goodlooking in a sulky kind of way. But my belief was that Earl Zane's one known ability, handling horses, derived from the fact that he possessed the identical amount of brain as the average horse did and they thus felt affinity with him. Though whether Coffee Nerves, who was whanging a series of kicks to the chute lumber that I could feel arrive up through the corral pole I was seated in, was going to simmer down enough to accommodate Earl Zane or anybody else remained an open question.

In any case, I was transfixed by what was brewing here. Alec looked likely to win the calf-roping. Coffee Nerves gave every sign of being the buckingest saddle bronc, if Earl could stay on him. Two winners, one Leona. The arithmetic of that was something to contemplate.

Various geezers of the chute society were peering in at Coffee Nerves and chiming "Whoa, hoss" and "Here now, knothead, settle down," which was doing nothing to improve the pinto's disposition. After all, would it yours?

Distracted by the geezer antics and the Earl-Alec equation, I didn't notice the next arrival until Ray pointed out, "Second one of the litter."

Indeed, Earl Zane had been joined in the volunteer saddling crew by his brother Arlee, the one a year ahead of Ray and me in school. Another horse fancier with brain to match. And full to overflowing with the Zane family swagger, for Arlee Zane was a big pink specimen: about what you'd get if you could coax a hog to strut around on its hind legs wearing blue jeans and a rodeo shirt. Eventually maybe Arlee would duplicate Earl, brawny instead of overstuffed. But at present there just was too much of all of him, up to and including his mouth. At the moment, for instance, Arlee had strutted around to the far side of the announcing booth and was yelping up to his sire: "Tell them to count out the prize money! Old Earl is going to set his horse on fire!" God, those Zanes did think they were the ding-dong of the world's bell.

"How about a bottle of something?" I proposed to Ray. The mental strain of being around three Zanes at once must have been making me thirsty. "I'm big rich, I'll buy."

"Ace high," Ray thought this sounded, and added that he'd hold our seats. Down I climbed, and away to the beer booth again. The tubs weren't showing many Kessler and Select necks by now. I half expected to coincide with Dode again, but didn't. But by the time I returned to Ray with our two bottles of grape, I was able to more or less offhandedly report that I had seen Marcella and the other Withrow daughters, in the shade under the grandstand with a bunch more of the girls we went to school with. Leona on one side of the arena, Marcella and the school multitude on the other, Velma Simms in the air behind us; I did have to admit, lately the world was more full of females than I had ever previously noticed.

"Under way   again." Tollie was issuing forth. "A   local buckaroo   coming out   of chute   number   one—"

Bill Semmler made his ride but to not much total, his bronc a straight bucker who crowhopped down the middle of the arena in no particularly inspired way until the ten seconds were up and the whistle blew.

"Exercise," commented Ray, meaning that was all Semmler was going to get out of such a rocking-horse ride.

At that, though, exercise was more than what was produced by the next rider, an out-of-town guy whose name I didn't recognize. Would-be rider, I ought to say, for a horse called Ham What Am sailed him onto the earth almost before the pair of them issued all the way out the gate of chute two. Ham What Am then continued his circuit of the arena, kicking dirt twenty feet into the air with every buck, while the ostensible rider knelt and tried to get any breath back into himself.

"Let's give   this   hard luck   cowboy   a—big hand!" Tollie advocated. "He sure   split a   long crack   in the air   that time."

"You guys see any crack out there in the air?" somebody below us inquired. "Where the hell is Tollie getting that stuff?"

"Monkey Ward," it was suggested. "From the same page featuring toilet paper."

But then one of the Rides Proud brothers from up at Browning, one or another of Toussaint's army of grand-nephews he wasn't on speaking terms with, lived up to his name and made a nice point total atop a chunky roan called Snuffy. Sunfishing was Snuffy's tactic, squirming his hind quarters to one side and then the other with each jump, and if the rider manages to stay in tune with all that hula wiggling it yields a pretty ride. This performance was plenty good enough to win the event, unless Earl Zane could do something wonderful on top of Coffee Nerves.

Following the Rides Proud achievement, the crowd laughed as they did each year when a little buckskin mare with a flossy mane was announced as Shirley Temple, and laughed further when the mare piled the contestant, some guy from Shelby, with its third jump.

"That Shirley   for a little   gal   she's got   a mind of her   own," bayed Tollie, evidently under the impression he was providing high humor. Then, sooner than it seemed possible for him to have drawn sufficient breath for it, he was giving us the next loud-speaker   dose.   "Now here   is a rider   I have   some acquaintance with.   Getting set   in chute   number five on Dust Storm   Earl Zane.   Show them   how   Earl!"

So much for assuming the obvious. Earl had not drawn the pinto; his and Arlee's participation in saddling it was only the Zane trait of sticking a nose into anything available.

The fact remained, though, that Alec's rival was about to bounce out into the arena aboard a bucking animal. I craned my neck trying to get a look at Leona, but she was turned in earnest conversation with a certain calf roper wearing a chokecherry shirt and I could only see a golden floss. Quite a wash of disappointment went through me. Somehow I felt I was missing the most interesting scene of the entire rodeo, Leona's face, just then.

"And here   he comes   a cowboying   sonofagun   and a son   of   yours truly—"

In fairness, I will say Earl Zane got a bad exit from the chute, the cinnamon-colored bronc he was on taking a little hop into the arena and stopping to gaze around at the world just as Earl was all primed for him to buck. Then as it sank in on Earl that the horse wasn't bucking and he altered the rhythm of his spurring to fit that situation, Dust Storm began to whirl. A spin to the left. Then one to the right. It was worth the admission to see, Earl's thought process clanking one direction and the horse's the other, then each reversing and passing one another in the opposite direction, like two drunks trying to find each other in a revolving door. The cinnamon bronc, though, was always one phase ahead of Earl, and his third whirl, which included a sort of sideways dip, caused Earl to lurch and lose the opposite stirrup. It was all over then, merely a matter of how promptly Earl would keep his appointment with the arena dirt.

"Blew a stirrup" came from the chute society as Earl picked himself up off the planet and the whistle was heard. "Ought've filled those stirrups with chewing gum before he climbed on that merry-go-round."

Tollie, however, considered that we had seen a shining feat. "Almost made it   to the   whistle   on that   rough one!   You can   still show   your face   around home,   Earl!"

Possibly the pinto's general irritation with the world rather than the diet of Tollie's voice produced it, but either way, Coffee Nerves now went into his biggest eruption yet. Below me in the chute he began to writhe and kick, whinnying awfully, and I redoubled my life grip on the corner post as the *thunk! thunk!* of his hooves tattooing the wood of the chute reverberated through the seat of my pants.

"Careful," Ray warned, and I suppose sense would have been to trade my perch for a more distant site. Yet how often does a person get to see at close range a horse in combat with mankind. Not just see, but feel, in the continuing *thunk*s; and hear, the pinto's whinny a sawblade of sound ripping the air; and smell, sweat and manure and animal anger in one mingled unforgettable odor.

Coffee Nerves' hammerwork with his hooves built up to a crash, a splay of splinters which sent the handlers tumbling away from the back of the chute, and then comparative silence. Just the velocity of air through the pinto bronc's nostrils.

"The sonofabitch is hung up," somebody reported.

In truth, Coffee Nerves was standing with his rear right leg up behind him, the way a horse does for a blacksmith to shoe him. Except that instead of any human having hold of that wicked rear hoof, it was jammed between a solid chute pole and the splintered one above it.

As the handling crew gingerly moved in to see what could be done about extrication, Tollie enlightened the crowd:

"This little pinto pony down in six is still proving kind of recaltrisant. The chute boys are doing some persuading and our show will resume in just a jiffy. In the meantime since this is the cowboys' Christmas so to say that reminds me of a little story."

"Jesus, he's back on to Christmas" issued from the chute society. "Will somebody go get Tollie a goddamn calendar?"

"Dumb as he is," it was pointed out, "it'll take two of us to read it to him."

"There was this little boy who wanted a pony for Christmas." Somebody had gone for a prybar to loosen the imprisoning poles and free the renegade pony of chute six, but in the meantime there was nothing to do but let Tollie wax forth. Even at normal, Tollie's voice sounded as if his adenoids had gotten twined with his vocal cords. With the boost from the address system, his steady drone now was a real ear-cleaner. "Well you see this little boy kept telling the other kids in the family that he had it all fixed up with Santa Claus. Santa Claus was going to bring him a pony certain sure. So when Christmas Eve came they all of them hung their stockings by the fireplace there."

"If I hang a woolsack alongside my stove," somebody in front of the chutes pined, "suppose I'd get Velma Simms in it?"

"And the other kids thought they'd teach this little boy a lesson. So after everybody had gone

to bed   they got   back up   again   and went   on out
to the barn   and   got some   ladies, excuse   my language,   horse manure."

"Quick, mark that down," somebody advised up to Bill Reinking.
"That's the first time Tollie's ever apologized for spouting horse shit."

"And filled   his stocking with it.   So the next   morning
they're all gathered   to look and see   what Santa   Claus
left   each one   of them.   Little Susie says 'Look, he   left
me   a   dollie   here in   my   stocking.'   And little
Tommy says   And look   he left me   apples and   oranges
in mine.'   And they turned   to the little   boy   and asked
'Well, Johnny   what did Santa   leave *you*?'   And
Johnny   looked   in his stocking   and said   'He   left
me   my pony   but he   got away!'"

There was that sickly laughter a crowd gives out because it's embarrassed not to, and then one of the chute men called up to the booth that
they had the goddamn bronc freed, get the rider on him before he
raised any more hell.

BACK TO BUSINESS!" Tollie blared as if he was calling elephants,
before Bill Reinking managed to lean across and shove the microphone
a little farther from Tollie's mouth. "Back to business. The   bronc
in chute   six   has consented   to rejoin   us. Next man up
last one   in this   go-round   on a horse called   Coffee
Nerves   will be   Dode Withrow."

I yanked my head around to see for sure. 11s. Dode was up top the
back of chute six, gazing at the specimen of exasperated horse below.
Dode did look a little soberer than when I met up with him by the beer
booth. He wasn't any bargain of temperance yet, though. His face
looked hot and his Stetson sat toward the back of his head in a dude
way I had never seen him wear it.

Ray was saying, "I never knew Dode to enter the bucking before."
Which coincided with what was going through my mind, that Dode
was the age of my father and Ray's. That his bronc-stomping had taken
place long years ago. That I knew for a certainty Dode did not even
break horses for his own use anymore but bought them saddle ready
from Tollie Zane.

"No," I answered Ray, "not in our time."

I had a clear view down into the chute as the bronc crew tried to
keep Coffee Nerves settled long enough for Dode to ease into the sad-

dle. The pinto went through another symphony of commotion, kicking and slamming sideways and whinnying that sawtoothed sound; but then hunched up motionless for a moment in a kind of sitting squat, contemplating what next to pull from its repertoire. In that moment Dode simply said "Good enough" and slid into the saddle.

As if those words of Dode's were a curfew, the gapers and gawkers of the chute society evaporated from the vicinity where Coffee Nerves would emerge into the arena, some of them even seeking a safe nest up on the corral.

"One of   our friends   and   neighbors   Dode   is. Rode   many   a bad one in   his time.   He'll be dancing out   on this   little pinto   in just   one minute."

It honestly occurred no more than a handful of seconds from then. Dode had the grip he wanted on the bucking rope and his arm was in the air as if ready to wave and he said in that same simple tone, "Open."

The gate swung, and Coffee Nerves vaulted into the arena.

I saw Dode suck in a fast breath, then heard it go out of him in a *huhhh* as the horse lit stiff-legged with its forefeet and kicked the sky with its hind, from both directions ramming the surprise of its force up through the stirrups into Dode. Dode's hat left him and bounced once on the pinto splotch across Coffee Nerves' rump and then toppled into the dust of the arena. But Dode himself didn't shake loose at all, which was a fortunate thing because Coffee Nerves already was uncorking another maneuver, this time swapping ends before crashing down in all stiff-legged style. Dode still sat deep in the saddle, although another *huhhh* reamed its way out of him. Maybe imagine you have just jumped from a porch roof to the ground twice in about five seconds, to give yourself some idea of the impact Dode was absorbing. He must have been getting Coffee Nerves' respect, for now the bronc exactly reversed the end-swapping he had just done, a trick almost guaranteed to catch the rider leaning wrong. Yet Dode still was up there astride the pinto.

I remember tasting dust. My mouth was open to call encouragement to Dode, but there was nothing that seemed good enough to call out for this ride he was making.

Now Coffee Nerves launched into the jump he had been saving up for, a real cloud-chaser, Dode at the same instant raking the horse's shoulders with his spurs, both those actions fitting together exactly as if animal and man were in rhythm to a signal none of the rest of us could hear, up and up the horse twisting into the air and the rider's free left arm high above that, Coffee Nerves and Dode soaring together while the crowd's urging cry seemed to help hold them there, a wave of sound suspending the pair above the arena earth so that we all could have time to fix the sight into memory everlastingly.

Somewhere amid it all the whistle blew. That is, off some far wall of my awareness echoed that news of Dode having ridden Coffee Nerves, but the din that followed flooded over it. I still believe that if Coffee Nerves had lit straight, as any sane horse would do descending from a moon visit like that, Dode would not have blown that left stirrup. But somehow Coffee Nerves skewed himself half sideways about the time he hit the ground—imagine now that the ground yanks itself to one side as you plummet off that porch—and Dode, who evidently did not hear the timer's whistle or was ignoring it, stayed firm in the right stirrup, nicely braced as he was, but the pinto's slewfoot maneuver jolted his boot from the left one. And now when Coffee Nerves writhed into his next buck, cattywampus to the left, he simply sailed away from under Dode, who dropped off him back first, falling like a man given a surprise shove into a creek.

Not water, however, but dust flew up around the form which thumped to the arena surface.

The next developments smudged together. I do know that now I was shouting out "Dode! Dode!" and that I lit running in the arena direct from the top of the corral, never even resorted to any of the poles as rungs to get down, and that Ray landed right behind me. As to what we thought we were going to accomplish I am not at all clear; simply could not see Dode sprawled out there by himself, I suppose.

The pickup man Dill Egan was spurring his horse between Dode and Coffee Nerves, and having to swat the pinto in the face with his hat to keep him off Dode. Before it seemed possible my father and Pete were out there too, and a half dozen other men from out of the grandstand and Alec and a couple of others from the far side of the arena, their hats thwacking at Coffee Nerves as well, and through all the commotion I could hear my father's particular roar of "HYAH! HYAH!" again and again before the bronc finally veered off.

"Fell off   the rainbow   on that one   right enough," Tollie was blaring. So that registered on me, and the point that the chute society, this once when they could have been useful out here in the arena, were dangling from various fence perches or peering from behind the calf chute. But the sprint Ray and I made through the loose arena dirt is marked in me only by the sound that reached us just as we reached Dode. The noise hit our ears from the far end of the arena: a tingling *crack!* like a tree breaking off and then crashing and thudding as it came down.

For a confused instant I truly thought a cottonwood had fallen. My mind tried to put together that with all else happening in this over-crowded space of time. But no, Coffee Nerves had slammed head-on into the gate of the catch pen, toppling not just the gate but the hefty gatepost, which crunched the hood of a parked car as it fell over. People who had been spectating along the fence were scattering from the prospect of having Coffee Nerves out among them.

The bronc however had rebounded into the arena. Piling into that gatepost finally had knocked some of the spunk out of Coffee Nerves. He now looked a little groggy and was wobbling somewhat, which gave Dill Egan time to lasso him and dally the rope around a corral post.

This was the scene as I will ever see it. Dode Withrow lying out there with the toes of his boots pointing up and Coffee Nerves woozy but defiant at the end of the lasso tether.

Quite a crowd encircled Dode, although Ray and I hung back at its outer edge; exactly what was not needed was any more people in the way. Doc Spence forged his way through, and I managed to see in past the arms and legs of all the men around him and Dode. And saw happen what I so desperately wanted to. When Doc held something under Dode's nose, Dode's head twitched.

Before long I heard Dode give a long *mmmm,* as if he was terrifically tired. After that his eyes came open and he showed that he was able to move, in fact would have tried to sit up if Doc Spence hadn't stopped him. Doc told Dode to just take it easy, damn it, while he examined Dode's right leg.

By now Midge and the Withrow girls had scurried out and Midge was down beside Dode demanding, "You ninny, are you all right?"

Dode fastened his look on her and made an *mmmm* again. Then burst out loud and clear, "Goddamn that stirrup anyway," which lightened the mood of all of us around him, even Midge looking less warpath-like after that. I could just hear the razzing Dode was going to take from his herder Pat Hoy about this forced landing of his: "Didn't know I was working for an apprentice bronc stomper, Dode. Want me to saddle up one of these big ewes, so's you can practice staying on?"

Relief was all over my father as he went over to the grandstand fence to report to my mother and Marie and Toussaint. Ray and I tagged along, so we heard it as quick as anybody. "Doc thinks it's a simple leg break," my father relayed. "Could have been a hell of a lot worse. Doc's going to take him to Conrad for overnight just to make sure."

My mother at once called out to Midge an offer to ride with her to the hospital in Conrad. Midge, though, shook her head. "No, I'll be all right. The girls'll be with me, no sense in you coming."

Then I noticed. Toussaint was paying no attention to any of this conversation, nor to the process of Dode being put on a stretcher over his protestations that he could walk or even foot-race if he had to, nor to Coffee Nerves being tugged into exit through what little was left of the catch pen gate. Instead he, Toussaint, was standing there gazing into the exact center of the arena, as if the extravaganza that Coffee Nerves and Dode had put on still was continuing out there. The walnut crinkles deepened in his face, his chuckle rippled out, and then the declaration: "That one. That one was a ride."

There of course was more on the schedule of events beyond that. Tollie inevitably thought to proclaim, "Well, folks   the show   goes on." But the only way for it to go after that performance by Coffee Nerves and Dode was downhill, and Ray and I retained our fence perch just through the next section of calf-roping to see whether Alec's seventeen and a half seconds would hold up. Contestant after contestant rampaged out, flailed some air with a lariat, and came nowhere close to Alec's time.

It had been a rodeo. English Creek had won both the saddle bronc riding and the calf-roping.

While the rodeo grounds emptied of crowd Ray and I stretched our attendance as long as we could. We watched the wrangling crew unpen the broncs and steers and calves. Listened to as much of the chute society's post mortem as we could stand. Had ourselves another bottle of pop apiece before the beer booth closed. Then I proposed that we might as well take a horse tour of Gros Ventre. Ray thought that sounded dandy enough, so I fetched Mouse and swung into the saddle, and Ray climbed on behind.

We had sightseen most of the town before wandering back past the Medicine Lodge, which by now had its front door propped open with a beer keg, probably so the accumulating fume of cigarette smoke and alcoholic breath wouldn't pop the windows out of the place. As Dode Withrow would have said, it sounded like hell changing shifts in there. The jabber and laughter and sheer concentration of humanity beyond that saloon doorway of course had Ray and me gazing in as we rode past, and that gaze was what made me abruptly halt Mouse.

Ray didn't ask anything, but I could feel his curiosity as to why we were stalled in the middle of the street. Nor was it anything I could put into words for him. Instead I offered: "How about you riding Mouse down to your place? I'll be along in a little. There's somebody I got to go see."

Ray's look toward the Medicine Lodge wondered "In there?" but his voice only conveyed, "Sure, glad to," and he lifted himself ahead into the saddle after I climbed down. Best of both worlds for him. Chance to be an unquestioning friend and get a horse to ride as well.

I went into the blue air of the saloon and stopped by the figure sitting on the second bar stool inside the doorway. The Medicine Lodge was getting itself uncorked for the night ahead. Above the general jabber somebody toward the middle of the bar was relating in a semishout: "So I told that sonofabitch he just better watch his step around me or there's gonna be a new face in hell for breakfast." My interest, though, was entirely here at the seated figure.

The brown hat moved around as he became aware of me.

"'Lo, Stanley," I began, still not knowing where I was going next with any of this.

"Well, there, Jick." The crowfoot lines clutched deeper at the corners of Stanley Meixell's eyes as he focused on me. He didn't look really tanked up, but on the other hand couldn't be called church-sober either. Someplace in between, as he'd been so much of our time together on the mountain. "Haven't seen you," he continued in all pleasantness, "since you started living aboveground."

Good Christ, Stanley had noticed my ducking act that day I was digging the outhouse hole and he rode by. Was my every moment visible to people anymore, like a planet being perpetually studied by one of those California telescopes?

"Yeah, well. How you been?"

"Fine as snoose. And yourself?"

"What I mean, how's your hand doing?"

Stanley looked down at it as if I was the first to ever point out its existence. He still had some doozies of scabs and major bruises there on the injury site, but Stanley didn't seem to regard this as anything but ordinary health. "It ain't bad." He picked up the bottle of beer from the counter before him. "Works good enough for the basics, anyway." And tipped down the last of that particular beer. "Can I buy you a snort?"

"No, no thanks."

"On the wagon, huh? I've clumb on it some times myself. All else considered, though, I'd just as soon be down off."

It occurred to me that since I was in this place anyway it didn't cost any more to be cordial. The stool between Stanley and the doorway was vacant—an empty mixed-drink glass testified that its occupant had traveled on—so I straddled the seat and amended: "Actually I would take a bottle of orange, though."

Stanley indicated his empty beer bottle to Tom Harry, the nearest of the three bartenders trying to cope with the crowd's liquid wants. "When you get time, professor. And a sunjuice for my nurse, here."

Tom Harry studied me. "He with you?" he asked Stanley.

"Closer than kin, him and me," Stanley solemnly vouched to the barman. "We have rode millions of miles together."

"None of it aged him that much," Tom Harry observed, nonetheless setting up a bottle of orange in front of me and a fresh beer for Stanley.

"Stanley," I started again. He was pushing coins out of a little pile, to pay for the latest round. Fishing up a five-cent piece, he held it toward me between his thumb and forefinger. "Know what this is?"

"Sure, a nickel."

"Naw, it's a dollar a Scotchman's been squeezing." The fresh beer got a gulp of attention. For the sake of the conversation I intended I'd like to have known how many predecessors that bottle had had, but of course Tom Harry's style of bartending was to swoop empties out of sight so no such incriminating count could be taken.

I didn't have long to dwell on Stanley's possible intake, for some out-of-town guy wearing a panama hat zigged when he meant to zag on his way toward the door and lurched into the pair of us. Abruptly the guy was being gripped just above the elbow by Stanley—his right hand evidently had recuperated enough from Bubbles for this, too—and was retargeted toward the door with advice from Stanley: "Step easy, buddy, so you don't get yourself hurt. In this county there's a five-dollar fine for drawing blood on a fool."

Mr. Panama Hat hastily left our company, and Stanley's handling of the incident reminded me to ask something. "How you getting along with Canada Dan these days?"

"Better," Stanley allowed. "Yeah, just a whole lot better." He paid recognition to his beer bottle again. "Last I heard, Dan was up in Cut Bank. Doing some town herding."

Cut Bank? Town herding? "What, did the Busby boys can him?"

"I got them to give Dan a kind of vacation." Then, in afterthought: "Permanent."

I considered this. Up there in the Two with Stanley those weeks ago, I would not have bet a pin that he was capable of rousing himself to do justice to Canada Dan. Yet he had.

"Stanley—"

"I can tell you got something on your mind, Jick. Might as well unload it."

If I could grapple it into position, that was exactly what I intended. To ask: what was that all about, when we first met you there on the mountain, the skittishness between you and my father? Why, when I ask anyone in this family of mine about Stanley Meixell, is there never a straight answer? Just who are you to us? How did you cross paths with the McCaskills in the past, and why are you back crisscrossing with us again?

Somebody just beyond Stanley let out a whoop, then started in on a twangy rendition of the song that goes: *I'm a calico dog, I'm a razorback hog, I'm a cowboy on the loose! I can drink towns dry, I can all but fly, I flavor my beans with snoose!* In an instant Tom Harry was there leaning over the bar and categorically informing the songster that he didn't care if the guy hooted, howled, or for that matter blew smoke rings out his butt, but no singing.

This, Stanley shook his head over. "What's the world coming to when a man can't offer up a tune? They ruin everything these days."

First Dode, now Stanley. It seemed my mission in life this Fourth of July to steer morose beer drinkers away from even deeper gloom. At least I knew which direction I wanted to point Stanley: back into history.

"I been trying to figure something out," I undertook honestly enough, one more time. "Stanley, why was it you quit rangering on the Two?"

Stanley did some more demolition on his beer, then cast a visiting glance around the walls at Franklin Delano Roosevelt and the stuffed herd, and eventually had to look at me and ask as if verifying:

"Me?"

"Uh huh, you."

"No special reason."

"Run it by me anyway."

"Naw, you'd be bored fast."

"Why'n't you let me judge that."

"You got better use for your ears."

"Jesus, Stanley—"

All this while I was attempting to pry sense out of Stanley, the tail of my eye was trying to tell me something again. Someone had come up behind me. Which wasn't particular news in the Medicine Lodge throng, except this someone evidently had no other site in mind; his presence stayed steadily there, close enough to make me edgy about it, sitting half braced as I was in case this guy too was going to crash in our direction.

I turned on the bar stool to cope with the interloper and gazed full into the face, not all that many inches away, of Velma Simms.

I must tell you, it was like opening a kitchen drawer to reach in for a jelly spoon and finding instead the crown jewels of England. For I had never been close enough, head-on, to Velma to learn that her eyes were gray. Gray! Like mine! Possibly our four were the world's only. And to garner further that her lipstick, on the very lips that ruled the rodeo whistle, was the beautiful dark-beyond-red of ripe cherries. And that she was wearing tiny pearl earrings, below the chestnut hair, as if her ears could be unbuttoned to further secrets even there. And that while the male population of northern Montana was focusing on the backside of Velma's renowned slacks, they were missing important announcements up front. Sure, there could be found a few lines at the corners of her eyes and across her forehead. But to me right then, they simply seemed to be affidavits of how imaginative a life this lady had led.

Unbelievable but so. Out of all the crowded flesh in the Medicine Lodge just then, solely onto me was fixed this attention of Velma Simms.

She just stood there eyeing me while I gaped, until the point of her attention finally prodded through to me.

"Oh. Oh, hello, Mrs.—uh, Velma. Have I got your seat?" I scrambled off the bar stool as if it was suddenly red-hot.

"Now that you mention it," she replied, and even just saying that, her words were one promissory note after another. Velma floated past me and snuggled onto the stool. A little extra of that snuggle went in Stanley's direction.

"Saw you there at the announcing booth," I reminisced brightly.

"Did you," said she.

I may be a slow starter, but eventually I catch up with the situation. My quick gawp around the saloon confirmed what had been trying to dawn on me. This year's beau in the gabardine suit was nowhere.

"Yeah, well," I began to extricate myself. "I got to be getting."

"Don't feel you need to rush off," said Stanley. As if God's gift to the male race wasn't enthroned right there beside him. "The night's still a pup."

"Uh huh. That's true, but—"

"When you got to go," put in Velma, twirling the empty mixed-drink glass to catch Tom Harry's attention for a refill, "you got to go."

"Right," I affirmed. "And like I say, I, uh, got to go."

What made me add to the total of my footprints already in my mouth I can't truly account for. Maybe the blockade I had hit again in wanting to ask all the questions of Stanley. In any case, the parting I now blurted out was:

"You two in a dancing mood tonight? What I mean, see you at the dance, will I?"

Stanley simply passed that inquiry to Velma with a look. In theory, Velma then spoke her answer to me, although she didn't unlock her gaze from him at all as she said it: "Stanley and I will have to see whether we have any spare time."

So. One more topic clambering aboard my already bent-over brain. Stanley Meixell and Velma Croake Bogan Sutter Simms.

"Ray? What kind of a summer are you having?"

We were up in the double window of his bedroom, each of us propped within the sill. A nice breeze came in on us there, the leaves of the big cottonwood in the Heaneys' front yard seeming to flutter the air our way.

Downstairs the radio had just been turned on by Ed Heaney, so it was seven o'clock. The dance wouldn't get under way for an hour or so yet, and as long as Ray and I were going to be window sitting anyway for the next while, I figured I'd broach to him some of all that was on my mind.

"Didn't I tell you? Pilot."

"No, I don't mean that. What it is, do things seem to you kind of unsettled?"

"How?"

"Well, Christ, I don't know. Just in general. People behaving like they don't know whether to include you in or out of things."

"What kind of things?"

"Things that went on years ago. Say there was an argument or a fight or something, people fell out over it. Why can't they just say, here's what it was about, it's over and done with? Get it out of their systems?"

"That's just grownups. They're not going to let a kid in on anything, until they figure it's too late to do him any good."

"But why is that? What is it that's so goddamn important back there that they have to keep it to themselves?"

"Jick, sometimes—"

"What?"

"Sometimes maybe you think too much."

I thought that over briefly. "What am I supposed to do about that? Christ, Ray, it's not like poking your finger up your nose in public, some kind of habit you can remind yourself not to do. Thinking is thinking. It happens in spite of a person."

"Yeah, but you maybe encourage it more than it needs."

"I what?"

"See, maybe it's like this." Ray's eyes squinched more than ever as he worked on his notion, and the big front teeth nipped his lower lip in concentration. Then: "Maybe, let's say maybe a thought comes into your head, it's only about what you're going to do next. Saddle up Mouse and take a ride, say. That's all the thought it really needs. Then put on the saddle and climb on. But the mood you're in, Jick, you'd stop first and think some more. 'But if I go for a ride, where am I going to go?'" Ray here went into one of his radio voices, the words coming clippity-clippity like old Kaltenborn's. " 'What is it I'll see when I get there? Did anybody else ever see it? And if anybody did, is it going to look the same to me as it did to them? And old Mouse here, is it going to look the same to Mouse as it does to me?'"

Raymond Edmund Heaney von Kaltenborn broke off, and it was just Ray again. "On and on that way, Jick. If you think too much, you make it into a whole dictionary of going for a ride. Instead of just going. See what I'm saying?"

"Goddamn it now, Ray, what I mean is more important than god-damn riding a horse."

"It's the same with anything. It'll get to you if you think about it too much, Jick."

"But what I'm telling you is, I don't have any choice. This stuff I'm talking about is on my mind whether or not I want it to be."

Ray took a look at me as if I had some sort of brain fever that might be read in my face. Then in another of his radio voices intoned: "Have you tried Vicks VapoRub? It sooooothes as it wooooorks."

There it lay. Even Ray had no more idea than the man in the moon about my perplexity. This house where we sat tucked in blue-painted sills, above its broad lawned yard and under its high cottonwoods, this almost second home of mine: it ticked to an entirely different time than the summer that was coursing through me. The Heaney family was in place in the world. Ed was going to go on exiting the door of his lumber yard at six every evening and picking up his supper fork at ten after six and clicking on that Silvertone radio at seven, on into eternity. Genevieve would go on keeping this house shining and discovering new sites for doilies. Mary Ellen would grow up and learn nursing at the Columbus Hospital in Great Falls. Ray would grow up and take a year of business college at Missoula and then join his father in the lumber yard. Life under this roof had the rhythm of the begattings in the Bible. The Heaneys were not the McCaskills, not even anywhere similar, and I lacked the language to talk about any of the difference, even to my closest friend.

> *"Swing, swing, and swing 'em high!*
> *Allemande left and allemande aye!*
> *Ingo, bingo, six penny high!*
> *Big pig, little pig, root hog or die!"*

The dance was under way, but only just, when Ray and I wandered down there to the Sedgwick House to it. Which is to say the hall—I suppose old C. E. Sedgwick or maybe even Lila Sedge conceived of it as a ballroom, but everybody else considered it the dance hall—was crammed to an extent that made the Medicine Lodge look downright lonely across the street, but not all that many people were dancing yet. Visiting, circulating, gathering an eyeful of everybody else, joking, trying to pry out of a neighbor how many bushels an acre his wheat looked like or what his lambs weighed by now, but only one square of actual dancers out there footing it to Jerome Satterlee's calling. Partly, everybody knew it took Jerome a little while (translate that to a few drinks) to get his tonsils limbered up. And then he could call dances until your shoes fell off your feet.

"A little thin out here on the floor, it looks to me like," Jerome was now declaring, preparatory to the next dance. "You know what I mean? Let's get one more square going here, make it look like we mean business. Adam, Sal, step on out here, you can stand around and grab any time. How about all you Busbys, you're half a square yourselves. Good, good. Come on now, one more couple. Nola plays this piano twice as good when we got two squares on the floor." At the upright, Nola Atkins sat planted as if they'd simply picked up the piano bench from the creek picnic with her on it and set them both down here on the band platform. Beside her, Jeff Swan had his fiddle tucked under his chin and his bow down at his side as if it was a sword he was ready to draw. "One more couple. Do I have to telephone to Valier and ask them to send over four left feet? Whup, here they come now, straight from supper, dancers if I ever saw any. Leona Tracy and Alec McCaskill, step right in there. Alec, you checked your horse and rope at the door, I hope? Now, this is somewhat more like—"

Stepping in from the Sedgwick House dining room, rodeo prize money in his pocket and free supper under his belt and a grin everywhere on his face there was any space for it, Alec looked like a young king coming home from his crowning ceremony.

Even so, to notice this glorious brother of mine you had to deliberately steer your eyes past Leona. Talk about an effort of will.

Leona took the shine in any crowd, even a dance hall full. The day's green blouse was missing. I mean, she had changed out of it. Now she wore a white taffeta dress, full and flouncy at the hem. In square dancing a lot of swirling goes on, and Leona was going to be a swirl worth seeing.

I shot a glance around the dance hall. My parents had missed this grand entry. They'd gone out to J. L. and Nan Hill's ranch, a couple of miles up English Creek, for supper and to change clothes, and were taking their own sweet time about getting back in. And Pete and Marie were driving Toussaint home to the Two Medicine, so they'd be even later arriving. I was the sole family representative, so to speak, to record the future Mr. and Mrs. Alec McCaskill come swanking in.

"Ready out there? Sure you are. You'll get to liking this so much, before the night is out you'll want to trade your bed for a lantern." Jerome, when he got to going good, put a lot of motion into his calling, using both arms to direct the traffic of dancers; kind of like a man constantly hanging things here and there in a closet. His gestures even now said he was entering into the spirit of the night. "All right, sonnies and honeys. Nola, Jeff, let's make 'em prance. Everybody, here we go:

> *"First four forward. Back to your places.*
> *Second four follow. Shuffle on back.*
> *Now you're getting down to cases,*
> *Swing each other till the floorbeams crack!"*

Here in the time I am now it seems hard to credit that this Fourth of July dance was the first I ever went to on my own. That is, was in company with somebody like Ray instead of being alone as baggage with my parents. Of course, without fully acknowledging it Ray and I also were well on our way to another tremendous night, the one when each of us would step through this dance hall doorway with a person neither parent nor male alongside. But that lay await yet. My point just now is that where I was in life this particular Fourth night, closing in on fifteen years of age, I had been attending dances since the first few months of that total. And Alec, the all-winning rodeo-shirted sashayer out there on the floor right now, the same before me. Each a McCaskill baby bundled in blankets and cradled in chairs beside the dance floor. Imbibe music along with mother's milk: that was the experience of a lot of us of Two country upbringing. Successors to Alec's and my floorside infancy were here in the Sedgwick House hall this very night: Charity Frew's half-year-old daughter, and another new Helwig baby, and a couple of other fresh ones belonging to farm folks east of town, a swaddled quartet with chairs fenced around them in the farthest corner of the dance hall.

> *"Salute your ladies, all together.*
> *Ladies, to the gents do the same.*

Hit the lumber with your leather.
Balance all, and swing your dame!"

It might be said that the McCaskill dancing history was such that it was the portion of lineage that came purest into Alec and me. Definitely into Alec. Out there now with that white taffeta back and forth to him like a wave of the sea, he looked like he could romp on forever. What little I knew of my father's father, the first McCaskill to caper on America's soil instead of Scotland's, included the information that he could dance down the house. Schottisches and Scotch reels in particular, but he also adopted any Western square dances. In his twinkling steps, so to speak, followed my mother and father. Dances held in ranch houses, my mother-to-be arriving on horseback with her party dress tied on behind the saddle, my father-to-be performing the Scotch Heaven ritual of scattering a little oatmeal on the floor for better gliding. Schoolhouse dances. In the face of the Depression even a hard times dance, the women costumed in gunnysack dresses and the men in tattered work clothes. And now Alec the latest McCaskill dancer, and me beginning to realize I was on my way.

"Bunch the ladies, there in the middle.
Circle, you gents, and dosie doe.
Pay attention to old Jeff's fiddle.
Swing her around and away you go!"

Can it be that all kinds of music speak to one another? For what I always end up thinking of in this dancing respect is a hymn. To me it is the one hymn that has ever seemed to make much sense:

"Dance, dance, wherever you may be,
I am the Lord of the dance," said he,
"And I'll lead you all, wherever you may be,
And I'll lead you all in the dance," said he.

I almost wish I had never come across those words and their tune, for they make one of those chants that slip into your mind every time you meet up with the circumstances they suggest. It was so then, even as Ray nudged me to point out the Busby brothers going through a fancy twirl with each other instead of with their wives and I joined Ray and everybody else in laughing, and it is so now. Within all else those musical words, a kind of beautiful haunting. But I suppose that is what musical words, and for that matter dances and dancers, are for.

> *"Gents to the center, ladies round them.*
> *Form a circle, balance all.*
> *Whirl your girls to where you found them.*
> *Promenade all, around the hall!"*

This concluding promenade brought Alec and Leona over toward where Ray and I were onlooking, and spying us they trooped right up. Leona in the flush of the pleasure of dancing was nearly more than the eyes could stand. I know Ray shifted a little nervously beside me, and maybe I did too.

"Mister Jick again," she greeted me. At least it wasn't "Hello, John Angus." "And Raymond Edmund Heaney," she bestowed on Ray, which really *did* set Ray to shifting around.

So high in flight was Alec tonight, though, that nobody else had to expend much effort. A lank of his rich red hair was down across his forehead from the dancing, and the touch of muss just made him look handsomer.

"Here's a pair of wall guards," he observed of Ray and me while he grinned mightily. "You guys better think about getting yourselves one of these things," giving Leona a waist squeeze.

Yeah, sure, right. As if Leonas were as plenty as blackberries. (I have wondered often. If Marcella Withrow had been on hand that night instead of at the Conrad hospital with her father, would Ray have nerved himself up and squired her out onto the floor?) But if you can't carry on conversation with your own brother, who can you? So to keep mouth matters in motion, I asked: "How was it?"

Alec peered at me and he let up on that Leona squeezing. "How was what?"

"Supper. The supper you won for handcuffing that poor little calf."

"Dandy," he reported, "just dandy." And now Leona awarded *him* a squeeze, in confirmation.

"What'd you have, veal?" Ray put in, which I thought was pretty good. But Alec and Leona were so busy handling each other's waists they didn't catch it, and Alec said, "Naw, steaks. Dancing fuel." He looked down at his armful of Leona. "Speaking of which—"

"TIMBERRR!"

I was not the only one whose ears almost dropped off in surprise. That cry was a famous one at any dance such as this. It dated back to Prohibition days, and what it signaled back then, whenever somebody stuck his head in through the dance hall doorway and cut loose the call, was the availability of Mason jar moonshine for anybody who cared to step outside for a sip.

So my surprise was double. That the cry resounded through the hall this night and that the timber crier there in the doorway, when I spun around to see, proved to be my father, with my mother on his arm.

He wore his brown pinstripe suit coat, a white shirt, and his newest Levis. She was in her blue cornflower frock with the slight V neckline; it was pretty tame by today's standards, but did display enough of throat and breastbone to draw second glances. Togged out that way, Varick and Lisabeth McCaskill made a prime pair, as rangers and wives often did.

Calls and claps greeted my father's solo.

"You'd be the one to know about timber, Mac!"

"Hoot mon, Scotch Heaven has come to town!"

"Beth, tell us fair and square: has he been up in the Two practicing that?"

Even Alec wagged his head in—admiration? consternation? both and more?—before declaiming to Leona, "There's dancing to be done. Let's get at it before the rowdy element cuts loose with something more."

Ray and I sifted over to my parents' side of the hall. My father was joshing Fritz Hahn that if Dode could still ride a bronc like that, it was Fritz's turn next Fourth to uphold the South Fork reputation. Greta and my mother were trading laughter over something, too. Didn't I tell you a dance is the McCaskill version of bliss?

"Here they are, the future of the race," my father greeted Ray and me. "Ray, how're you summering?"

"Real good," Ray responded, along with his parenthetical grin. "Quite a rodeo, wasn't it."

"Quite a one," my father agreed, with a little shake of his head which I knew had to do with the outcome of the calf-roping. But at once he was launched back into more visiting with Fritz and Ray, and I just parked myself and inventoried him and my mother. It was plain my father had timbered a couple of drinks; his left eyelid was down a little, as if listening to a nightlong joke. But no serious amount. My mother, though. My mother too looked bright as a butterfly, and as she and my father traded grab with the Hahns and other people who happened by to say good words about her Ben English speech or his timber whoop, both her and him unable to keep from glancing at the back-and-forth of the dancers more than at their conversationalists, a suspicion seeded in me. Maybe, more than maybe, my mother had a drink or two in her, too.

here you guys been?" I voiced when I got the chance.

And received what I deserved. "Places," stated my mother, then laughed.

Well, I'd had one escape this day. Getting in and out of the Medicine Lodge without coinciding with my own parents there.

Out on the floor, the swirl was dissolving as it does after the call and music have hit their climax, and Jerome was enlisting everybody within earshot for the next variety of allemande and dosie doe. "Now I can't call dances to an empty floor, can I? Let's up the ante here. Four squares this time, let's make it. Plenty of territory, we don't even have to push out the walls yet."

"The man needs our help," my father suggested to my mother and the Hahns, and off they all went, to take up places in the fourth square of dancers forming up.

The dance wove the night to a pattern all its own, as dances do. I remember the standard happenings. Supper hour was announced for midnight, both the Sedgwick House dining room and the Lunchery were going to close at one A.M. Ray and I had agreed that supper hour—or rather, an invitation to oyster stew at the Lunchery, as my parents were certain to provide—would be our personal curfew. Jerome at one point sang out, "Next one is ladies' choice!" and it was interesting to see some of the selections they made, Alice Van Bebber snagging the lawyer Eli Kinder and immediately beginning to talk him dizzy, pretty Arleta Busby putting out her hand to that big pile of guff Ed Van Bebber, of all damn people. My parents too made South Fork pairings, my mother going over to Fritz Hahn, Greta Hahn coupling onto my father's arm. Then after one particularly rousing floor session, Jerome announced that if anyone cared to pass a hat he and the musicians could manage to look the other way, and collection was taken to pay him and Nola and Jeff.

As I say, all this was standard enough, and mingled with it were

some particularities of this night. The arrival of Good Help and Florene
Hebner, magically a minute or so after the hat had been passed. Florene
still was a presentable-looking woman, despite a dress that had been
washed to half its original color. Good Help's notion of dressing up was
to top off his overalls with a flat cap. My mother once commented, "A
poor-boy cap and less under it." The departure of the grocery store
family, the Helwigs, with Luther Helwig wobbling under the load of
booze he had been taking on and his wife Erna beside him with the
bawling baby plucked from the far end chair corral. In such a case you
always have to wonder: was a strategic motherly pinch delivered to that
baby? And my eventual inspiration for Ray and me to kill off the last of
my fifty-cent stake with a bottle of pop apiece. "How about stepping
across for something wet?" was the way I proposed it to Ray. He took
on a worried look and began, "I don't know that my folks want me
going in that—" "Christ, not the Medicine Lodge," I relieved him, "I
meant the Lunchery." Through it all, dance after dance after dance, my
tall redheaded father and my white-throated mother in the musical
swim at one end of the hall, my tall redheaded brother and Leona star-
ring at the other end.

It was in fact when Ray and I returned from our pop stop that we
found a lull in the dancing and made our way over to my parents again,
to be as convenient as possible for an oyster stew invite.

"I suppose you two could eat if you had to?" my father at once settled that issue, while my mother drew deep breaths and cast a look
around the hallful.

"Having fun?" I asked her, just to be asking something, while my
father was joshing Ray about being girl-less on such a night.

"A ton," she confirmed.

Just then Jerome Satterlee appeared in our midst, startling us all a
little to see him up close instead of on the platform. "What, did you
come down for air, Jerome?" my father kidded.

"Now don't give an old man a hard time," responded Jerome. "Call
this next one, how about, Mac. Then we can turn 'em loose for midnight supper. Myself, I got to go see a man about a dog."

My father was not at all a square dance caller of Jerome's breadth.
But he was known to be good at—well, I will have to call it a sort of
Scotch cadence, a beat of the kind that a bagpipe and drum band puts
out. Certainly you danced smoother to Jerome's calling, but my father's
could bring out stamping and clapping and other general exuberation.

I think it is not too much to say that with my eyes closed and ears stuffed, I could have stood there in the Sedgwick House and told you whether it was Jerome or my father calling the dance, just by the feel of how feet were thumping the hall floor.

To make sure their smooth terms could stand his absence, my father looked the question at my mother, and she told him by a nod that he ought to go do the call. She even added, "Why don't you do the Dude and Belle? This time of night, everybody can stand some perking up."

He climbed onto the band platform. "'Lo, Nola, Jeff. This isn't any idea of mine, understand."

"Been saving you the best strings of this fiddle, Mac," Jeff answered. "When you're ready."

Nola nodded, echoed: "When you're ready."

"All right, then. Try to make me look like I know what I'm doing." My father tipped his left shoulder down, pumped a rhythm with his heel a number of times to get a feel of the platform. Then made a loud hollow clap with his hands which brought everybody's attention, and called out over the hall: "Jerome is taking a minute to recuperate. He said he hates to turn things over to anybody with a Scotch notion of music, but saw no choice. So you're in for it."

"What one we gonna do, Mac, the Two Medicine two-step?" some wit yelled out.

"No sir. I've got orders to send you to midnight supper in style. Time to do the Dude and Belle. And let's really do it, six squares' worth." My father was thinking big. Six squares of dancers in this hall would swash from wall to wall and end to end, and onlookers already were moving themselves into the doorway or alongside the band platform to grant space. "All right. You all know how it starts. Join hands and circle left."

Even yet I am surprised that I propelled myself into doing it. I stepped away from Ray, soldiered myself in front of my mother, and said:

"Mrs. McCaskill, I don't talk through my nose as pretty as the guy you usually gallivant around with. But suppose I could have this dance with you anyway?"

Her face underwent that rinse of surprise that my father sometimes showed about her. She cast a look toward the top of my head as if just realizing my height. Then came her sidelong smile, and her announcement:

"I never could resist you McCaskill galoots."

Arm in arm, my mother and I took a place in the nearest square. People were marshalling everywhere in the hall, it looked like a major parade forming up. Another thunderclap from my father's hands, Nola and Jim opened up with the music, and my father chanted us into action.

"First gent, swing the lady so fair.
Now the one right over there.
Now the one with the sorrel hair.
Now the belle of the ballroom.
Swirl and twirl And promenade all.

Second gent, swing the lady first-rate."

Besides my mother and me, our square was Bob and Arleta Busby, and the Musgreaves who ran the drugstore, and luck of luck, Pete and Marie, back from returning Toussaint to the Two Medicine and dancing hard the past hour or so to make up for time lost. All of them but me probably had done the Dude and Belle five hundred times in their lives, but it's a basic enough dance that I knew the ropes. You begin with everybody joining hands—my mother's firm feel at the end of one of my arms, Arleta's small cool hand at my other extreme—and circling left, a wheel of eight of us spinning to the music. Now to my father's call of "You've done the track, now circle back" the round chain of us goes into reverse, prancing back to where we started. Swing your partner, my mother's cornflower frock a blue whirlwind around the pair of us. Now the lady on the left, which in my instance meant hooking arms with Arleta, another first in my life. Now return to partner, all couples do some sashaying right and left, and the "gent" of this round steps forth and begins swinging the ladies in turn until he's back to his own partner. And with all gusto, swings her as the Belle of the Ballroom.

"Third gent, swing the lady in blue."

What I would give to have seen all this through my father's eyes. Presiding up there on the platform, pumping rhythm with his heel and feeling it multiplied back to him by the forty-eight feet traveling the dance floor. Probably if you climbed the helmet spike of the Sedgwick

House, the rhythm of those six squares of dancers would have come quivering up to you like spasms through a tuning fork. Figure within figure within figure, from my father's outlook over us, the kaleidoscope of six simultaneous dance patterns and inside each the hinged couple of the instant and comprising those couples friends, neighbors, sons, wife with flashing throat. The lord of the dance, leading us all.

"Fourth gent, swing the lady so sweet."

The fourth gent was me. I stepped to the center of our square, again made the fit of arms with Arleta Busby, and swung her.

"Now the one who looks so neat."

Marie glided forth, solemnly winked at me, and spun about me light as a ghost.

"Now the one with dainty feet."

Grace Musgreave, plump as a partridge, didn't exactly fit the prescription, but again I managed, sending her puffing out of our fast swirl.

"Now the belle of the ballroom."

The blue beauty, my mother. *"Swirl and twirl."* Didn't we though. *"Now promenade all."* Around we went, all the couples, and now it was the women's turn to court their dudes.

> *"First lady, swing the gent who's got sore toes.*
> *Now the one with the great big nose.*
> *Now the one who wears store clothes.*
> *Now the dude of the ballroom.*
>
> *Second lady, swing the gent in size thirteens.*
> *Now the one that ate the beans.*
> *Now the one in brand new jeans.*
> *Now the dude of the ballroom.*

> *Third lady, swing the gent with the lantern jaw.*
> *Now the one from Arkansas.*
> *Now the one that yells, 'Ah, hah!'*
> *Now the dude of the ballroom."*

So it went. In succession I was the one in store clothes, the one full of beans, and the lantern-jawed one—thankful there not to be the one who yells "Ah hah!" which Pete performed for our square with a dandy of a whoop.

> *"Fourth lady, swing the gent whose nose is blue."*

My mother and Bob Busby, two of the very best dancers in the whole hall.

> *"Now the one that spilled the glue."*

Reese reflections dancing with each other, my mother and Pete.

> *"Now the one who's stuck on you."*

My mother and sallow Hugh Musgreave.

> *"Now the dude of the ballroom."*

She came for me, eyes on mine. I was the proxy of all that had begun at another dance, at the Noon Creek schoolhouse twenty years before. My father's voice: *"Swirl him and twirl him."* My moment of dudehood was an almighty whirl, as if my mother had been getting up the momentum all night.

> *"All join hands and circle to the left,*
> *Before the fiddler starts to swear.*
> *Dudes and belles, you've done your best.*
> *Now promenade, to you know where."*

"Didn't know you were a lightfoot," Ray greeted me at the edge of the throng heading through the doorway to supper hour.

"Me neither," I responded, blowing a little. My mother was with Pete and Marie right behind me; we all would have to wait for my father to make his way from the band platform. "Let's let them catch up with us outside. I can use some air."

Ray and I squirmed along between the crowd and the lobby wall, weaseling our way until we popped out the front entry of the Sedgwick House.

I was about to say here that the next historic event of this Fourth of July, Gros Ventre category, was under way as the two of us emerged into the night, well ahead of my parents and the Reeses. But given that midnight had just happened I'd better call this the first occurrence of July 5.

The person most immediately obvious of course was Leona, white and gold in the frame of light cast onto the street by the Sedgwick House's big lobby window. And then Arlee Zane, also there on that raft of light; Arlee, ignorance shining from every pore.

Beyond them, a bigger two with the reflected light cutting a line across their chests; face to face in the dimness above that, as if they were carrying on the nicest of private chats. Except that the beam-frame build of one and the chokecherry shirt of the other showed them to be Earl Zane and Alec and therefore they were not chatting.

"Surprised to see you without a skim milk calf on the end of a string," Earl was offering up as Ray and I sidled over beside Leona and Arlee so as not to miss anything. Inspiring Arlee to laugh big as if Earl's remark deserved it.

"What, are you out here in the night looking for that cinnamon pony?" I give Alec credit for the easy way he said this, tossing it out as a joke. "He went thataway, Earl."

Earl proved not to be in the market for humor just now, however.

"I suppose you could have forked him any better?" You could all but hear the thick gears move in Earl's head to produce the next remark. "You likely had a lot of riding practice recently."

"Earl, you lardbrain," this drew from Leona.

But Alec chose to cash Earl's remark at face value. "Some of us do get paid to stay on horses instead of bailing off of them. Come on, Leona, let's go refuel before the dancing starts again."

Earl now had another brain movement. "Surprised you can dance at all these days, what with marriage on your mind." He leaned a little toward Alec to deliver the final part: "Tell me this, McCaskill. Has it ever climbed out the top of your pants yet?"

That one I figured was going to be bingo. After all, anybody who has grown up in Montana has seen Scotch lawsuits get under way for a lot less commentary than that. At dances the situation was common enough almost to be a regular feature. One guy with a few too many drinks in him calls some other guy a name none too fond, and that party responds with a fist. Of course the commotion was generally harsher than the combat, but black eyes and bent noses could result.

"Earl, you jugheaded—" Leona was responding, but to my considerable disappointment Alec interrupted her by simply telling Earl, "Stash it, sparrowhead. Come on, Leona, we got business elsewhere."

"I bet you got business all right," Earl adventured on. "Leona business. Snatch a kiss, kiss a snatch, all the same to you, McCaskill, ain't it?"

I can't truly say I saw it happen. Not in any way of following a sequence: this and then this and then this. No, the event simply arrived into my mind, complete, intact, engraved before its realization could make itself felt. Versions of anything of this sort are naturally suspect, of course. Like that time Dempsey fought Gibbons up at Shelby for the heavyweight championship. About ten thousand people were there, and afterward about a quarter million could provide you an eyewitness account. But I will relate just as much of this Earl and Alec episode as I can vouch for. One instant Earl was standing there, admiring the manufacture of his last comment, and then in the next instant was bent in half, giving a nasty tossing-up noise, *auheughhh,* that made my own stomach turn over.

What can have inspired Alec, given that the time-honored McCaskill procedure after loss of temper was to resort to a roundhouse right, to deliver Earl that short straight jab to the solar plexus?

That economical punch of Alec's produced plenty, though. Every bit of this I can see as if it were happening over again right now. Earl now in full light, doubled down as he was, Alec stepping around him to collect Leona, and the supper crowd in its long file out of the Sedgwick House stopping and gawking.

"God DAMN!" exploded between Ray and me, Arlee pushing through and combining his oath with the start of a haymaker targeted on Alec's passing jaw.

Targeted but undelivered. On the far side of Arlee's girth from me Ray reached up, almost casually it seemed, and latched onto Arlee's wrist. The intended swing went nowhere after that, Ray hanging on to the would-be swingster as if he'd just caught him with that hand in the cookie jar, and by the time Arlee squared around and managed to begin to tussle in earnest with Ray—thank heaven for the clomping quality of the Zane brain—I had awarded Arlee a bit of a shove to worry him from my side.

Where the ruckus would have progressed beyond that I have ever been curious about. In hindsight, that is. For if Arlee had managed to shake out of Ray's grip, he was elephant enough to provide us both some pounding.

But by now my father was on hand, and Pete and two or three other men soldiered out of the crowd to help sort us into order, and somebody was fetching Tollie Zane out of the Medicine Lodge on Earl's behalf.

"Jick, that's enough," my father instructed. "Turn him loose, Ray. It's over."

This too I am clear about. Those sentences to Ray and me were the full sum of what was said by any McCaskill here in this aftermath. What traveled to Alec from my father was a stare, a studying one there in the frame of hotel light as if my father was trying to be sure this was the person he thought it was.

And got back from Alec one of the identical caliber.

Then Leona was in the grasp of my brother, and my mother stepped out alongside my father, and each couple turned and went.

"Ray?"

"What?"

We were side by side in bed, in the dark of his room. Outside the open twin windows a breeze could be heard teasing its way through the leaves of the giant cottonwood.

"You helped a lot, there at the dance."

"That's okay."

"You'll want to watch out Arlee doesn't try get it back on you."

"Yeah."

There was silence then, and the dark, until Ray startled me with something between a giggle and a laugh. What the hell now? I couldn't see what he was doing, but as soon as words started issuing from him, I knew. He was pinching his nose closed.

"He wants   to watch out   around   me" came droning out in exact imitation of Tollie's rodeo announcing, "or I'll   cut his heart out   and drink   his blood."

That got me into the act. With a good grasp on my nose, I proposed in the same tinny tone:

"Yank off   his arm   and make him   shake hands with it."

Ray giggled and offered:

"Grab him   by the   epiglommis   until   his eyes pooch out."

"Sharpen   the point   on his   head"—I paused for my own giggles—"and   pound him   in   like a post."

"Kickenough   crap   out of   him   to daub   a log barn," Ray envisioned. "Goddamn   booger   eater   him anyhow."

With each atrocity on Arlee our laughing multiplied, until the bed was shaking and we tried to tone things down before Ray's folks woke up and wondered just what was going on.

But every time we got ourselves nearly under control, one or the other of us erupted again—"thump   old Arlee   as far   into hell"—on and on, laughing anew, snorting it out in spite of ourselves—"as a bird   can fly   in a   lifetime"—sides shaking and throats rollicking until we were almost sick, and then of course we had to laugh at the ridiculousness of that.

Nor, when Ray finally did play out and conked off to sleep, did that fever of humor entirely leave me. I would doze for a while and then be aware I was grinning open-eyed into the darkness about one or another moment of that immense day, that never-can-be-forgotten Fourth. Here I rest, world, as happy as if I had good sense and the patent on remembrance. My mother on the park stump giving her Ben English speech and Dode at the top of that leap by Coffee Nerves and my father calling out the Dude and Belle to the dancing crowd and my brother one-punching Earl Zane and Ray pitching in on Arlee and, you bet, Stanley Meixell collecting Velma Simms. Scene by scene they fell into place in me, smooth as kidskin and exact as chapter and verse, every one a perfect piece of that day and now of the night; a set of hours worth the price of the rest of the life.

THREE

The sun shines, hay is being made. All along English Creek and Noon Creek, mowing and raking and stacking are the order of the day. As to how this year's cutting compares with those of recent years—have you seen any rancher lately who wasn't grinning like a Christian holding four aces?

—GROS VENTRE WEEKLY GLEANER, JULY 20

"HAND ME A HALF-INCH, would you, Jick."

"Here you go." I passed the open-end wrench of that size to Pete beneath the power buckrake. There was a grunt of exertion, a flash of metal as the wrench flew and clattered off the chassis, and the news from Pete:

"Sonofabitch must be a three-eighths."

I had been here before. "Did you hit your knuckles?"

"Sure did."

"Did you round the head off the bolt?"

"Sure did."

"Are you sure you want to put up hay again this year?"

"Guess what, nephew. The next rusted-up sonofabitch of a bolt under here has got your name on it."

At noon of that first day of preparing Pete's haying machinery, when he and I came in to wash up for dinner Marie took one look at the barked knuckles and skin scrapes and blood blisters on the both of us and inquired: "Did you two count your fingers before you started all this?"

—

Despite what it took out of a person's hide I still look back on that as topnotch employment, my job of haying for Pete.

The Reese ranch was a beauty for hay. Pete inherited not only my grandfather Isaac Reese's acreage there along Noon Creek but old Isaac's realization that nurturing more than one source of income is as good an idea as you can have in Montana. Pete was continuing with the sheep Isaac had turned to after the crash of cattle prices and also was improving the ranch's hayfields, running ditches into the bottomland meadows of wild hay to irrigate them from Noon Creek. Even in the Depression's driest years, Pete always had hay to sell during the winter. This year it looked as if he would have a world of the stuff. Those wild meadows of timothy and wiregrass lay one after another along the creek like green pouches on a thong. Then there was the big field atop the Noon Creek–English Creek divide which grew dry-land alfalfa. In a wet year like this one, the alfalfa was soaring up more than knee high and that wide benchland field looked as green as they say the Amazon is.

Those first days after the Fourth of July, the hay was very nearly ready for us and I was more than ready for it. Ready to have the McCaskill family situation off my mind for the main part of each day, at least. It did not take a great deal of original thinking to realize that the deadlock between my parents and Alec now was stouter than it had been before. If Alec ever needed any confirming in his rooting tooting cowboy notion of himself, his rodeo day calf-roping and pugilistic triumph had more than done so. Both of those and Leona too. Alec's feet might not even touch the ground until about August. Anyway, I had spent so much thought on the Alec matter already that summer that my mind was looking around for a new direction. My father, my mother, my brother: let them do the sorting out of Alec's future. I now had an imminent one haying at Noon Creek—all my own.

I might have known. "The summer when," I have said my mother ever after called this one. For me, the summer when not even haying turned out as expected. The summer when I began to wonder if anything ever does.

To be quite honest, on a task like those first few days of readying the equipment for haying I provided Pete more company than help. I mean, I can fix machinery when I have to but I'd rather be doing anything else. My point of view is that I would be more enthusiastic about the machine era if the stuff healed itself instead of requiring all the damn repair it does. And Pete was much the same as me where wrench work was involved.

But I still maintain, companionship is no small thing to create. Amid all that damn bolting, unbolting, rebolting, bushing, shimming, washering, greasing, oiling, banging, sharpening, straightening, wouldn't you welcome a little conversation? And the farther removed from the mechanical chore at hand the better? At least my uncle and I thought so. I recall Pete, just right out of the blue, telling me about the Noon Creek Kee-Kee bird. "You never heard of the Kee-Kee bird we got around here? Jick, I am surprised at you. The Kee-Kee bird shows up the first real day of winter every year. Lands on top of the lambing shed over there and takes a look all around. Then he says, 'Kee-Kee-Keerist All Mighty, this is c-c-cold c-c-country!' and heads for California." I in return favored Pete with a few of the songs from Stanley's repertoire, starting with the one about the lady who was wild and wooly and full of fleas and never had been curried above her knees. He looked a little surprised at my musical knowledge, but was interested enough.

This sticks with me, too: how startling it was to hear, from a face so reminiscent of my mother's, the kind of language Pete unloosed on the haying equipment during those repair days. It also was kind of refreshing.

All in all, then, Pete and I got along like hand and glove. And I have already recited Marie's glories, back there at the Fourth of July picnic. If anybody in the Two country could cook in the same league as my mother, it was Marie. So my ears and the rest of me both were well nourished, that couple of days as Pete and I by main strength and awkwardness got the haying gear into running order. It never occurred to me at the time, but I suppose Pete welcomed having me around—and Alec in the earlier summers when he was in the raking job—because he and Marie were childless. Their son died at birth, and Marie very nearly died with him. Her health in fact had never been strong since. So for a limited time, at least, someone my age was a privileged character with the Reeses.

Even so, I held off until Pete and I were finishing up the last piece of equipment, replacing broken guards on the mowing machine, before I tried him on this:

"Pete, you know Stanley Meixell, don't you?"

"Used to. Why?"

"I'm just sort of curious. My folks don't say much about him."

"He's been a long time gone from this country. Old history."

"Were you around him when he was the English Creek ranger?"

"Some. When anybody on Noon Creek who could spell K-O-W was running cattle up there on the forest. During the war and just after, that was."

"How was he as a ranger?"

"How was he?"

"Well, yeah. I mean, did Stanley go about things pretty much the way Dad does? Fuss over the forest like he was its mother hen, sort of?"

"Stanley always struck me as more of a rooster than a mother hen." That, I didn't get. Stanley hadn't seemed to me particularly strutty in the way he went about life. "But I will say this," Pete went on. "Stanley Meixell and your father know these mountains of the Two better than anybody else alive. They're a pair of a kind, on that."

"They are?" That the bunged-up whiskey-sloshing camptender I had squired around up there in the Two was as much a master of the mountains as my father—all due respect to Pete, but I couldn't credit it.

Figuring maybe Pete's specific knowledge of Stanley was better than his general, I asked: "Well, after he was the English Creek ranger, where was his ticket to?"

"His ticket?"

"That's the saying Forest Service guys have about being transferred. After here, where'd Stanley get transferred to?"

"The Forest Service isn't my ball of string, Jick. How do you feel about sharpening some mower sickles? There's a couple against the wall of the shop somewhere."

"How's she going, Jick?"

The third morning I rode over to Pete and Marie's, the mower man Bud Dolson greeted me there at breakfast. Pete had gone into Gros Ventre to fetch him the night before, Bud having come up on the bus all the way from Anaconda. Ordinarily he was on the bull gang at the smelter there, a kind of roustabout's job as I understood it. "Good to get out in the real air for a change," Bud claimed was his reason for coming to mow hay for Pete summer after summer. Smelter fumes would be sufficient propulsion to anywhere, yes. But I have a sneaking hunch that the job as mower man, a month of being out here by himself with just a team of horses and a mowing machine and the waiting hay, meant a lot in itself to somebody as quiet as Bud.

The first genuine scorching day of summer arrived with Bud, and by about nine o'clock the dew was off the hay and he was cutting the first swath of the nearest of the Noon Creek meadows, a path of fallen green beside the standing green.

"How do, Jick."

While I was saddling Pony to go home to English Creek at the end of that afternoon, Perry Fox came riding in from Gros Ventre.

You still could find Perry's species in a lot of Montana towns then, old Texas punchers who rode north on a trail drive somewhere before the turn of the century and for this reason or that never found their way back to Texas. Much of the time when I was growing up, Gros Ventre had as many as three of them: Andy Cratt, Deaf Smith Mitchell, and Perry Fox. They had all been hands for the old Seven Block ranch when it was the cattle kingdom of this part of Montana, then afterward hung on by helping out the various small ranchers at branding time and when the calves were shipped, and in between, breaking a horse for somebody now and again. Perry Fox was the last of them alive yet. Into his seventies, I guess he had to be, for Toussaint Rennie told my father he could remember seeing both Perry and Deaf Smith Mitchell in the roundup of 1882, skinny youngsters aboard big Texican saddles. Now too stove-up for a regular ranch job, Perry spent his winters in Dale Quigg's saddle store helping out with harnessmending and other leather work and his summer job was on the dump rake for Pete.

As I responded to Perry's nod and drawl of greeting and watched him undo his bedroll and warbag from behind his saddle—like Bud, Perry would put up in the bunkhouse here at Pete's now until haying was done—I couldn't help but notice that he had a short piece of rope stretched snug beneath his horse's belly and knotted into each stirrup. This was a new one on me, stirrups tied like that. That night I asked my father about it.

"Come to that, has he," my father said. "Riding with hobbled stirrups."

I still didn't savvy.

"At his age Perry can't afford to get thrown any more," my father spelled it out for me. "He's too brittle to mend. So with the stirrups tied down that way, he can keep himself clamped into them if his horse starts to buck."

"Maybe he just ought to quit riding horseback," I said, without thinking it through.

My father set me straight on that, too. "Guys like Perry, if they can't ride you might as well take them out and shoot them. Perry has never learned to drive a car. The minute he can't climb onto a horse and keep himself there, he's done for."

The fourth morning, Pete had me harness up my team of horses and take my rake to the mowed field to help Perry get the dump-raking under way.

Truth be told, that day I was the one who did the majority of the dump-raking—scooping the hay into windrows, that was—while Perry tinkered and tinkered with his rake teeth and his dump lever and his horses' harness and so on. Right then I fully subscribed to what Pete said about his custom of hiring Perry haying after haying: "He's slow as the wrath of Christ, but he is steady." I suppose if my behind was as aged and bony as Perry's, I wouldn't have been in any hurry either to apply it to a rake seat for the coming four or five weeks.

At the end of that day of windrowing, when Perry and I had unhitched our teams and Pete was helping us look them over for any harness sores, up the road to the ranch buildings came the Forest Service pickup and in it my father and my mother as well. They'd been to Great Falls on a headquarters trip my father had to make and before starting home they swung by First Avenue South to chauffeur the last of the haying crew to Pete.

He tumbled out of the back of the pickup now. The stackman, Wisdom Johnson.

"Hey, Pete!" cried Wisdom. Even after the two-hour ride from Great Falls in the open breezes Wisdom was not what could be called even approximately sober. On the other hand he wasn't so swacked he had fallen out of the pickup on the way to the job, which was the hiring standard that counted. "Hey, Perry!" the greeting process went on. "Hey, Jick!" If the entire population of Montana had been there in the

Reese yard, Wisdom would have greeted every one of them identically. Wisdom Johnson's mind may not have been one of the world's broadest, but it liked to practice whatever it knew.

"As I savvy it, Wisdom," acknowledged Pete, "that's what you're here for all right. Hay."

"Pete, I'm ready for it," Wisdom testified earnestly. "If you want to start stacking right now, I am ready. You bet I am. How about it, ready to go?" Wisdom squinted around like Lewis and Clark must have. "Where's the field?"

"Wisdom, it's suppertime," Pete pointed out. "Morning will be soon enough to start stacking. You feel like having some grub?"

Wisdom considered. "No. No, I don't." He swallowed to get rid of the idea of food. "What I need to do is sort of sit down for a while."

Perry stepped forward. "I'll herd him to the bunkhouse. Right this way, Wisdom. Where'd you winter?"

"Out on the coast," reported Wisdom as he unsteadily accompanied Perry. "Logging camp, up north of Grays Harbor. Rain! Perry, do you know it'd sometimes rain a week steady? I just did not know it could rain that much."

Chin in hand and elbow propped on the doorframe, my mother skeptically watched all this out the rolled-down window of the pickup. Now she opened the door and stepped out. Not surprisingly, she looked about two-thirds riled. I don't know of any Montana woman who has never gritted her teeth, one time or another, over that process of prying men off bar stools and getting them launched toward whatever they're supposed to be doing in life. "I'll go in and visit Marie," she announced, which my father and Pete and I all were glad enough to have happen.

Pete made sure my mother was out of earshot, then inquired: "He in Sheba's place, was he?"

"No, in the Mint, though he did have Bouncing Betty with him. She wasn't about to turn loose of him as long as he had a nickel to his name." Upon study, my father looked somewhat peevish, too. Wisdom Johnson must have taken considerable persuading to part with Bouncing Betty. "So at least I didn't have to shake him directly out of a whore's bed. But that's about the best I can say for your caliber of employee, brother-in-law."

Pete broke a grin at my father and razzed: "I wouldn't be so damn hard up for crew if you'd paid attention to the example of Good Help Hebner and raised anything besides an occasional scatter raker."

Somehow Pete had known what the moment needed. Pete's kidding had within it the fact that the other of the rake-driving McCaskill brothers had been Alec, and he was not a topic my father particularly cared to hear about these days. Yet here it came, the half wink of my father's left eye and the answer to Pete's crack: "Scatter rakers were as good as I could do. Whatever that says about *my* caliber."

The fifth day, we made hay.

The windrows that Perry and I had raked formed a pattern I have always liked. A meadow with ribs of hay, evenly spaced. Now Perry was dump-raking the next field down the creek and Bud was mowing the one beyond that.

Those of us in the stacking crew began our end of the matter. We sited the overshot stacker toward the high edge of the meadow, so the haystack would be up out of the deepest winter snowdrifts along Noon Creek. With the power buckrake, Pete shoved several loads of hay into place behind the stacker. Then Wisdom maneuvered and smoothed that accumulation with his pitchfork until he had the base of his stack made the way he wanted it. An island of hay almost but not quite square—eight paces wide, ten paces long—and about chest high.

"You said last night you're ready, Wisdom," called Pete. "Here it comes." And he bucked the first load of hay onto the fork of the stacker. "Send it to heaven, Clayton."

The final man, or I should say member, of our haying crew was the stacker team driver, twelve-year-old Clayton Hebner. Pete always hired whichever Hebner boy was in the twelve-to-fourteen-year range for that stacker team job and they were pretty much interchangeable, a skinny kid with a forelock and nothing to say for himself; apparently the volume knob for that whole family was on Good Help Hebner. All that was really noticeable about Clayton was his Hebner way of always eyeing you, as if you were the latest link in evolution and he didn't want to miss the moment when you sprouted wings or fins. At Pete's words Clayton now started into motion his team of horses hitched to the cable which, through a tripod-and-pulley rig within the stacker, lifts the twin arms of the stacker and the hay-loaded fork, and the hay went up and up until—

It occurs to me: does everybody these days think that hay naturally comes in bales? That God ordained that livestock shall eat from loaves of hay tied up in twine by thirteen-thousand-dollar machinery? If so, maybe I had better describe the notion of haying as it used to be. All in the world it amounted to was gathering hay into stacks about the size of an adobe house; a well-built haystack even looks as solid and straightforward as an adobe structure, though of course stands higher and has a rounded-off top. But try it yourself sometime, this gathering of ten or twelve tons of hay into one stack, and you will see where all the equipment comes in. Various kinds of stackers were used in various areas of the West, beaver slides, Mormon derricks, two-poles, jayhawks, but Pete's preference was an overshot. An overshot stacker worked as its name suggests, tossing a load of hay up over a high wide framework which served as a sort of scaffolding for the front of the haystack. If, say, you hold your arms straight out in front of you, with your hands clutching each end of a basket with hay piled in it: now bring your arms and the basket straight up over your head with a little speed and you are tossing the hay exactly as an overshot does. In short, a kind of catapult principle is involved. But a calculated one, for it is the responsibility of the stacker team driver to pace his horses so that the overshot's arms and fork fling the hay onto whichever part of the stack the stackman wants it. Other than being in charge of the speed of the team, though, driving the stacker team is a hell of a dull job, walking back and forth behind the horses as they run the overshot up and down, all damn day long, and that's why a kid like Clayton usually got put on the task.

So hay was being sent up, and as this first haystack and the day's temperature both began to rise, Wisdom Johnson suffered. This too was part of the start of haying: Wisdom sweating the commerce of Great Falls saloons out of himself. Soaking himself sober, lathering into the summer's labor. We all knew by heart what the scene would be this initial morning, Wisdom lurching around up there atop the mound of hay as if he had a log chained to each leg. It was a little painful to watch, especially now that my camptending sojourn with Stanley Meixell had taught me what a hangover truly is.

Yet agonized as Wisdom looked, the stack was progressing prettily, as we also knew it would. The stackman, he was maestro of the haying crew. When the rest of us had done our mowing or raking or bucking or whatever, the final result of it all was the haystacks the stackman built. And Wisdom Johnson could build them, as he put it, "high and tall and straight." No question about it, Wisdom was as big and brawny as the ideal stackman ought to be; nine of him would have made a dozen. And he also just looked as if he belonged atop a haystack, for he was swarthy enough to be able to pitch hay all day up there without his shirt on, which I envied much. If I tried that I'd have burned and blistered to a pulp. Wisdom simply darkened and darkened, his suntan a litmus each summer of how far along our haying season was. As July heated up into August, more than once it occurred to me that with the sweat bathing Wisdom as he worked up there next to the sun, and his arm muscles bulging as he shoved the hay around, and that dark leathering of his skin, he was getting to look like the heavyweight fighter Joe Louis. But of course that wasn't something you said to a white person back then.

This was the second summer of Wisdom being known as Wisdom instead of his true name, Cyrus Johnson. The nickname came about because he had put up hay a number of seasons in the Big Hole Basin down in the southwestern part of the state, and according to him the Big Hole was the front parlor of heaven. The hay there was the best possible, the workhorses all but put their harnesses on themselves each morning, the pies of Big Hole ranch cooks nearly floated off into the air from the swads of meringue atop them. The list of glories ran on and on. Inasmuch as the Big Hole had a great reputation for hay even without the testimony of Cyrus Johnson, the rest of us at the Reese table tended to nod and say nothing. But then came one supper-time, early in the first summer I hayed for Pete, when Cyrus started in on a fresh Big Hole glory. "You take that Wisdom, now. There's my idea of a town. It's the friendliest, drinkingest, prettiest place—"

"Wisdom? That burg?" Ordinarily Bud Dolson was silence himself. But Anaconda where he was from was not all that far from the Big Hole town of Wisdom and Bud had been there. As Cyrus now had the misfortune of asking him.

"I think so," replied Bud. "I blinked. I might've missed most of it."

Cyrus looked hurt. "Now what do you mean by that?"

"Cy, I mean that the town of Wisdom makes the town of Gros Ventre look like London, England."

"Aw, come on, Bud. Wisdom is a hell of a nice town."

Bud shook his head in pity. "If you say so, Wisdom." And ever since, the big stackman was Wisdom Johnson to us.

—

This first stack was well under way, Pete having buckraked several windrows in to the stacker. Now began my contribution to the haying process. I went over and climbed onto my scatter rake.

If you happen never to have seen one, a scatter rake simply resembles a long axle—mine was a ten-foot type—between a set of iron wheels, high spoked ones about as big around as those you think of a stagecoach having, but not nearly so thick and heavy. The "axle," actually the chassis of the rake, carries a row of long thin curved teeth, set about a hand's width apart from each other, and it is this regiment of teeth that rakes along the ground and scrapes together any stray hay lying there. As if the hayfield was a head of hair and the scatter rake a big iron comb going over it, so to speak. Midway between the wheels a seat stuck up for the rake driver—me—to ride on, and a wooden tongue extended forward for a team of horses to be hitched to.

My team was in harness and waiting. Blanche and Fisheye. As workhorses go, they weren't too bad a pair; a light team, as you didn't need the biggest horses in the world just to pull a scatter rake, but more on the steady side than frisky. That Blanche and Fisheye were civilized at all was a relief to me, because you never know what you might get in a team of horses. One of them maybe can pull like a Percheron but is dumb, and the other one clever enough to teach geometry but so lazy he constantly lays back in the traces. Or one horse may be a kicker, and his mate so mild you could pass a porcupine under him without response. So except for Fisheye staring sideways at you in a fishy way as you harnessed him, and Blanche looking like she needed a nap all the time, this team of mine was better than the horse law of averages might suggest.

I believe I am right in saying Pete was the first rancher in the Two country to use a power buckrake: an old automobile chassis and engine with a fork mounted on it to buck the hay in from the field to the stack. Wisdom Johnson a few summers before had brought word of the invention of the power buckrake in the Big Hole: "I tell you, Pete, they got them all over that country. They move hay faster than you can see." That proved to be not quite the case, but the contraption could bring in hay as fast as two buckrakes propelled by horses. Thus the internal combustion engine roared into the Reese hayfields and speeded matters up, but it also left dabs of hay behind it, scatterings which had either blown off the buckrake fork or which it simply missed. The scatter raker was the gatherer of that leftover hay, which otherwise would be wasted. In place on my rake seat, I now clucked to Blanche and Fisheye, reined them toward the part of the meadow Pete had been bucking in loads from, and my second summer of scatter raking was begun.

I suppose I have to admit, anybody who could handle a team of workhorses could run a scatter rake. But not necessarily run it as it ought to be done. The trick was to stay on the move but at an easy pace. Keep the horses in mild motion and the rake teeth down there gathering leftover hay, instead of racing around here and yon. Roam and glean, by going freestyle over a field as a fancy skater swoops around on ice. Well, really not quite that free and fancy, for you do have to tend to business enough to dump your scatterings in some good place for the buckrake to get it, and not in a boggy spot or on top of a badger mound. But still I say, the more you could let yourself go and just follow the flow of the hayfield, so to speak—keep swooping back and forth where the power buckrake had recently been, even if there wasn't much spilled hay there—the better off you were as a scatter raker. A mind as loose as mine was about right for scatter raking.

"How did it go?" my mother asked, that first night of full haying. We were waiting supper for my father, who was somewhere up the North Fork inspecting the progress of a CCC trail crew there.

"A stack and a half," I reported offhandedly as if I had been a hayhand for centuries. "About usual, for first day."

"How did you get along with Blanche and Fisheye?"

"They're kind of a logy pair of sonsa—" I remembered in time to mend my mouth; the vocabulary I'd been using around Pete and the crew was a quick ticket to trouble here at home—"of so and sos. But they're okay."

She appraised me from where she was leaning against the kitchen sink, arms folded across her chest. Then surprised me with her smile and: "It's quiet around here, without you."

I chose to take that as a compliment. More than that, I risked ribbing her in return, a little. "Well, I guess I could call you up on the telephone every noon from Pete and Marie's, and sing you a song or tell you a joke."

"Never mind, Mister Imagination," she declined. "I'll adjust."

—

I didn't pay it sufficient mind at the time, but in truth my mother *did* have to adjust. Alec in exile. Me rationed between English Creek and the Noon Creek hayfields. My father beginning to be gone more and more as fire danger increased in the forest. The reverse of her usual situation of a houseful of male McCaskills, a genuine scarcity of us. There is another topic which occupies my mind these days. The way life sorts us into men and women, not on any basis of capability that I have ever been able to see. High on the list of questions I wish I'd had the good sense to ask, throughout that immense summer, is the one to my mother. Her view about being born as a woman into a region which featured male livelihoods.

"You finally starved out, did you," she now greeted my father's late arrival. "Wash up and sit up, you two; supper will be just a minute now."

"How'd it go today?" my father asked me, and I repeated my report of Reese haying. Through that and other supper conversation he nodded and said uh huh a lot, which signaled that he was only half listening. The symptom was annual. At this point of the summer, and hot as this one suddenly had turned, fire was forever on the mind of a forest ranger. The joke was told that when the preacher at a funeral asked if anyone wanted to memorialize the deceased, a ranger was the first one onto his feet and began: "Old Tom wasn't the worst fellow I ever knew. Now I'd like to add a few words about fire prevention."

When you think about it, my father's yearly deep mood about fire was understandable enough. He was responsible for an entire horizon. The skyline made up of peaks and reefs and timbered slopes and high grasslands: that conglomeration of nature was designated his district of the Two Medicine National Forest, and every blessed inch of it was prey to lightning storms and careless campfires and flipped cigarettes. His line of defense was a light thread of men across that mass of mountain and forest; the lookouts in the tall towers, and at this time of year, the fire guards and other smokechasers he would start hiring and stationing for quick combat against lightning strikes or smolders of any sort. My father entirely subscribed to the theory that the time to fight a forest fire was before it got going. True, the timber of the Two here on the east face of the Rockies was not as big and dense and incendiary as the forests farther west in Montana and Idaho. "But that doesn't mean they're made of goddamn asbestos either" ran the complaint of east-side rangers on the Two, the Lewis and Clark, the Custer and the Helena, against what they saw as a westward tilt in the thinking and the fire budget of Region One headquarters. It was a fact that the legendary fires occurred over there west of the Continental Divide. The Bitterroot blaze of 1910 was an absolute hurricane of flame. Into smoke went three million acres of standing trees, a lot of it the finest white pine in the world. And about half the town of Wallace, Idaho, burned. And this too: the Bitterroot fire killed eighty-five persons, eighty-four of them done in directly by the flames and the other one walked off a little from a hotshot crew on Setzer Creek and put a pistol to himself. The Forest Service, which was only a few years old at the time, was bloodied badly by the Bitterroot fire. And as recently as 1934 there had been the fiasco of the Selway fires along the Idaho-Montana line. That August, the Selway National Forest became the Alamo of Region One. Into those back-country fires the regional forester, Major Kelley, and his headquarters staff poured fifty-four hundred men, and they never did get the flames under control. The Pete King Creek fire and the McLendon Butte fire and about fifteen smaller ones all were roaring at once. The worst afternoon, ten square miles of the Selway forest were bursting into flame every hour. And when the fire at Fish Butte blew up, a couple of hundred CCC guys had to run like jackrabbits. Five fire camps eventually went up in smoke, both the Pete King and Lochsa ranger stations damn near did. Nothing the Forest Service tried on the Selway worked. Nothing could work, really. An inferno has no thermostat. The rains of late September finally slowed the Selway fires, and only weeks after that Major Kelley killed off the Selway National Forest, parceled out its land to the neighboring forests and scattered its staff like the tribes of Israel. The Selway summer sobered everybody working in Region One—that total defeat by fire and the Major's obliteration of a National Forest unit—and for damn sure no ranger wanted any similar nightmare erupting in his own district.

I stop to recount all this because of what happened now, as my father finished supper and thumbed open the day's one piece of mail, an official Forest Service envelope. "What've we got here," he wondered, "the latest kelleygram?"

His next utterance was: "Sonofabitch."

He looked as if he had been hit with a two-by-four, stunned and angry. Then, as if the words would have to change themselves when read aloud, he recited from the letter:

" 'Placement of manpower this fire season will be governed by localized fire danger measurements. An enforced lag of manning below current danger will eliminate over-manning designed to meet erratic peak loads and will achieve material decrease in FF costs over past years' expenditures. Organization on east-side forests in particular is to be held to the lowest level consistent with carefully analyzed current needs.' "

My mother oh so slightly shook her head, as if this confirmed her suspicions of brainlessness in the upper ranks of the U.S. Forest Service. My father crumpled the letter and crossed the kitchen to the window looking out on Roman Reef and Rooster Mountain and Phantom Woman peak and other of the profiles of the Two.

I asked, "What's all that mean?"

"No fire guards on our side of the Divide until things start burning," said my father without turning from the window.

Right up until the time haying started, I had been rehearsing to myself how to talk my parents into letting me live in the bunkhouse at Pete's with the rest of the hay crew. It was something I imagined I much wanted to do. Be in on the gab of Wisdom and Perry and Bud, hear all the tales of the Big Hole and First Avenue South and Texas and Anaconda and so on and so on. Gain one more rung towards being a grownup, I suppose was what was working on me. Yet when haying time arrived I did not even bring up the bunkhouse issue.

For one thing, I could anticipate my mother's enunciation about one shavetail McCaskill already living in a bunkhouse "and to judge by Alec's recent behavior One Is More Than Enough." For another, with my father on the go as much as he was this summer it seemed plain that he would prefer for me to be on hand at English Creek whenever he couldn't. But do you know, I actually made it unanimous against myself. What the matter came right down to was that I didn't want to give up the porch bedroom at English Creek for the dubious gain of bunking with hay hands.

Which is how I became a one-horsepower commuter. The one horse being Pony, whom I found I regarded with considerable more

esteem ever since Mouse decided to hose down the rodeo grounds that
time in front of Leona. Each morning now I got up at five, went out
and caught and saddled Pony outside the barn—quite a lot of light in
the sky that time of year—and the pair of us would head for the Reese
ranch.

Where morning is concerned, I am my father all over again. "The
day goes downhill after daybreak" was his creed. I don't suppose there
are too many people now who have seen a majority of the dawns of
their life, but my father did, and I have. And of my lifetime of early rising I have never known better dawns than those when I rode from English Creek to my haying job on Noon Creek.

The ford north of the ranger station Pony and I would cross; if there
was enough moon the wild roses along the creek could be seen, pale
crowds of them; and in a few minutes of climbing we came atop the
bench of land which divides the two creek drainages. Up there, at that
brink of dawn hour, the world revealed all its edges. Dark lines of the
tops of buttes and benches to the north, towards the Two Medicine
River and the Blackfeet Reservation. The Sweetgrass Hills bumping up
far on the eastern horizon like five dunes of black sand. The timbered
crest of Breed Butte standing up against the stone mountain wall of the
west. What trick of light it is I can't really say, but everything looked as
if drawn in heavy strokes, with the final shade of night penciled in
wherever there was a gulch or coulee.

The only breaks in the stillness were Pony's hooves against the earth,
and the west breeze which generally met us atop that broad benchland.
I say breeze. In the Two country any wind that doesn't lift you off your
horse is only a breeze. My mountain coat was on me, my hat pulled low,
my hands in leather work gloves, and I was just about comfortable.

Since Pete's haying season always lasted a month or a little more, I
rode right through the phases of the moon. My favorite you can guess
on first try. The fat full moon, resting there as if it was an agate marble
which had rolled into the western corner of the sky. During the early
half of my route the mountains still drew most of their light from the
moon, and I watched the reefs and other rock faces change complexion, from light gray to ever so slightly pink, as the sunrise began to
touch them. Closer to me, the prairie flowers now made themselves
known amid the tan grass. Irises, paintbrushes, bluebells, shooting
stars, sunflowers.

Then this. The first week or so of those daybreak rides, the sun was north enough that it came up between the Sweetgrass Hills. They stand sixty or seventy miles across the prairie from where I was riding, way over towards Havre, so there was a sense that I was seeing a sunrise happening in a far land. The gap between the mounded sets of hills first filled with a kind of orange film; a haze of coming light, it might be called. Then the sun would slowly present itself, like a big glowing coal burning its way up through the horizon.

Those dawns taught me that beauty makes the eyes greedy. For even after all this, mountains and moon and earth edges and the coming of the sun, I considered that what was most worth watching for was the first shadow of the day. When the sun worked its way about half above the horizon, that shadow emerged to stretch itself off from Pony and me—horse and youngster melded, into an apparition of leftover dark a couple of hundred feet in length. Drawn out on the prairie grass in that far-reaching first shadow, Pony and I loomed like some new creature put together from the main parts of a camel and a giraffe.

Is it any wonder each of these haying-time dawns made me feel remade?

Meanwhile it continued to be the damnedest summer of weather anybody could remember. All that rain of June, and now July making a habit of ninety degrees. The poor damn farmers out east of Gros Ventre and north along the High Line were fighting a grasshopper invasion again, the hot days hatching out the 'hoppers faster than the farmers could spread poison against them. And for about five days in the middle of July an epidemic of lightning storms broke out in all the national forests of Region One. A lookout reported a plume of smoke up the South Fork of English Creek, on a heavily forested north slope of Grizzly Reef. This of course caused some excitement in the ranger station, and my father hustled his assistant ranger Paul Eliason and some trail men and a nearby CCC brush crew up there. "Paul's used to those big trees out on the coast," my father remarked to my mother. "It won't hurt him to find out that the ones here are big enough to burn." That Grizzly Reef smoke, though, turned out to be a rotten log and some other debris smoldering in a rocky area, and Paul and his crew handled it without much sweat.

That mid-July dose of lightning and his dearth of fire guards to be smokechasers put my father in what my mother called "his prowly mood." But then on the morning of the twenty-first of July we woke up to snow in the mountains. Fire was on the loose elsewhere in Montana—spot fires across the Continental Divide in the Flathead country and others up in Glacier Park, and a big blaze down in Yellowstone Park that hundreds of men were on—while my father's forest lay snoozing under a cool sheet of white.

"How did you arrange that?" my mother mock-questioned him at breakfast. "Clean living and healthy thoughts?"

"The powerrr of Scotch prrayerrr," he rumbled back at her in his preacher voice. Then with his biggest grin in weeks: "Also known as the law of averages. Tough it out long enough in this country and a snowstorm will eventually happen when you actually want it to."

As I say, putting up Pete's hay always took about a month, given some days of being rained out or broke down. This proved to be a summer when we were reasonably lucky about both moisture and breakage. So steadily that none of us on the crew said anything about it for fear of changing our luck, day on day along Noon Creek our new stacks appeared, like fresh green loaves.

My scatter-raking became automatic with me. Of course, whenever my mind doesn't have to be on what I am doing, it damn well for sure is going to be on some other matter. Actually, though, for once in my life I did a respectable job of combining my task at hand and my wayfaring thoughts. For if I had a single favorite daydream of those hayfield hours, it was to wonder why a person couldn't be a roving scatter-raker in the way that sheep shearers and harvest hands moved with their seasons. I mean, why not? The principle seems to me the same: a nomad profession. I could see myself traveling through Montana from hay country to hay country—although preferably with better steppers than Blanche and Fisheye if there was much distance involved—and hiring on, team and rake and all, at the best-looking ranch of each locale. Maybe spend a week, ten days, at the peak of haying at each. Less if the grub was mediocre, longer if a real pie maker was in the kitchen. Dwell in the bunkhouse so as to get to know everybody on a crew, for somehow every crew, every hay hand, was discernibly a little different from any other. Then once I had learned enough about that particular country and earned from the boss the invite "Be with us again next year, won't you?" on I would go, rolling on, the iron wheels and line of tines of my scatter rake like some odd over-wide chariot rumbling down the road.

An abrupt case of wanderlust, this may sound like, but then it took very little to infect me at that age. Can this be believed? Except for once when all of us at the South Fork school were taken to Helena to visit the capitol, a once-in-a-while trip with my father when he had to go to forest headquarters in Great Falls was the farthest I had ever been out of the Two country. Ninety miles; not much of a grand tour. There were places of Montana I could barely even imagine. Butte. All I knew definitely of Butte was that when you met anyone from there, even somebody as mild as Ray Heaney's father Ed, he would announce "I'm from Butte" and his chin would shoot out a couple of inches on that up-sound of *yewt*. In the midst of all this wide Montana landscape a city where shifts of men tunneled like gophers. Butte, the copper kingdom. Butte, the dark mineral pocket. Or the other thing that was always said: "Butte's a hole in the ground and so's a grave." That, I heard any number of times in the Two country. I think the truth may have been that parts of Montana like ours were apprehensive, actually a little scared, of Butte. There seemed to be something spooky about a place that lived by eating its own guts, which is the way mining sounded to us. Butte I would surely have to see someday. And the Big Hole Basin. As Wisdom Johnson told it, as haying season approached in the Big Hole the hay hands—they called them hay-diggers down there, which I also liked—began to gather about a week ahead of time. They sifted in, "jungled up" in the creekside willows at the edge of town, and visited and gossiped and just lay around until haying started. I savored the notion of that, the gathering, the waiting. Definitely the Big Hole would be on my hay rake route. And the dry Ingomar country down there in the southeastern part of the state, where Walter Kyle had done his hotel style of sheep ranching. The town water supply was a tank car, left off on the railroad siding each week. Walter told of coming back to town from sheep camp one late fall day and seeing flags of celebration flying. His immediate thought was that somebody had struck water, "but it turned out to be just the armistice ending the war." Havre and the High Line country. Fork Peck dam. Miles City. Billings, Lewistown. White Sulphur Springs. Red Lodge. Bozeman and the green Gallatin Valley. For that matter, Missoula. Montana seemed to be out there waiting for me, if I only could become old enough to get there.

But. There's always a "but" when you think about going everywhere and doing everything. But how old *was* that, when I would be advanced enough to sample Montana to the full?

North of the ears strange things will happen. Do you know who kept coming to mind, as I thought my way hither and thither from those Noon Creek hay meadows? Stanley Meixell. Stanley who had gone cowboying in Kansas when he was a hell of a lot younger than I was. Stanley who there in the cabin during our camptending journey told me of his wanders, down to Colorado and Wyoming and over into the Dakotas, in and out of jobs. Stanley who evidently so much preferred the wandering life that he gave up being a forest ranger, to pursue it. Stanley who could plop himself on a bar stool on the Fourth of July and be found by Velma Simms. But Stanley who also looked worn down, played out and overboozed, by the footloose way of life. The example of Stanley bothered me no little bit. If the wanderer's way was as alluring as it seemed from my seat on the scatter rake, how then did I account for the eroded look around Stanley Meixell's eyes?

Almost before I knew it the first few weeks of haying were behind us and we were moving the equipment onto the benchland for the ten days or so of putting up the big meadow of dry-land alfalfa there. "The alfaloofee field," as Perry Fox called it. This was another turn of the summer I looked forward to with interest, for this alfalfa haying was far enough from the Reese ranch house that we no longer went in at noon for dinner. Now began field lunches.

My stomach aside, why did I look forward to this little season of field lunches? I think the answer must be that the field lunches on the bench constituted a kind of ritual that appealed to me. Not that I would want to eat every meal of my life in the stubble of a hayfield. But for ten days or so it was like camping out or being on an expedition; possibly even a little like "jungling up" the way the Big Hole hay hands started off. Whatever, the alfaloofee field lunch routine went like this. A few minutes before noon, here came Marie in the pickup. She had with her the chuckbox, the old Reese family wooden one with cattle brands burned everywhere on its sides, and when a couple of us slid it back to the tailgate and lifted it down and opened it, in there waited two or three kinds of sandwiches wrapped in dish towels, and a bowl of potato or macaroni salad, and a gallon jar of cold tea or lemonade, and bread and butter and jam, and pickles, and radishes and new garden carrots, and a pie or cake. Each of us chose a dab of shade around the power buckrake or the pickup; my preference was to sit on the running board of the pickup, somehow it seemed more like a real meal when I sat up to eat; and then we ploughed into the lunch. Afterward, which is to say the rest of the noon hour, Pete was a napper, with his hat down over his eyes. I never was; I was afraid I might miss something. Clayton too was open-eyed, in that silent sentry way all the Hebner kids had. Perry and Bud smoked, each rolling himself a handmade. This was the cue for Wisdom to pull out his own sack of Bull Durham, pat his shirt pocket, then say to Perry or Bud, "You got a Bible on you?" One or the other would loan him the packet of cigarette papers and he'd roll himself one. Strange how he could always have tobacco but perpetually be out of papers, which were the half of smoking that cost almost nothing. But that was Wisdom for you.

The womanly presence of Marie, slim and dark, sitting in the shade of the pickup beside the chuckbox and the dozing Pete, posed the need for another ritual. As tea and lemonade caught up with kidneys, we males one after another would rise, carefully casual, and saunter around to the far side of the haystack and do our deed. Then saunter back, trying to look like we'd never been away and Marie showing no least sign that we had.

Eventually Pete would rouse himself. He not only could nap at the drop of an eyelid, he woke up just as readily. "I don't suppose you characters finished this field while I was resting my eyes, did you?" Then he was on his feet, saying the rest of the back-to-work message: "Until they invent hay that puts itself up, I guess we got to."

Our last day of haying the benchland alfalfa brought two occurrences out of the ordinary.

The first came at once, when I headed Blanche and Fisheye to the southwest corner of the field to start the morning by raking there awhile. Maybe a quarter of a mile farther from where I was lay a nice grassy coulee, at the base of that slope of Breed Butte. The ground there was part of Walter Kyle's place, and with Walter summering in the mountains with his sheep, Dode Withrow always put up the hay of this coulee for him on shares. The Withrow stacking crew had pulled in and set up the afternoon before; I could pick out Dode over there, still with a cast on his leg, and I could all but hear him on the topic of trying to run a haying crew with his leg set in cement. If I hadn't been so content with haying for Pete, Dode would have been my choice of somebody to work for.

Maybe scatter rakers are all born with similar patterns of behavior in them, but in any case, at this same time I was working the corner of our field the Withrow rake driver was doing the nearest corner of theirs. Naturally I studied how he was going about matters, and a minute or so of that showed me that he wasn't a he, but Marcella Withrow.

I had no idea what the odds must be against a coincidence like that: Marcella and me having been the only ones in our class those eight years of grade school at South Fork, and now the only English Creek ones in our particular high school class in Gros Ventre, and this moment both doing the same job, in the same hay neighborhood. It made me grin. It also caused me to peek around with care, to make sure that I wouldn't be liable for any later razzing from our crew, and when the coast looked clear I waved to Marcella. She did the same, maybe even to checking over her shoulder against the razzing possibility, and we rattled past one another and raked our separate meadows. Some news to tell Ray Heaney the next time I got to town, anyway.

The other event occurred at noon, and this one went by the name of Toussaint Rennie.

He arrived in the pickup with Marie and the chuckbox of lunch. "I came to make sure," Toussaint announced, his tan gullied face solemn as Solomon. "Whether you men build haystacks right side up."

Actually the case was that Toussaint had finished ditch-riding for a while, with everybody harvesting now instead of irrigating, and Marie had driven up to the Two Medicine to fetch him for company for the day. What conversations went on between those two blood- and soul-mates I've always wished I could have overheard.

The gab between the hay crew and Toussaint was pretty general, though, until we were done eating. Pete then retired to his nap spot, and Perry and Bud and eventually Wisdom lit up their smokes, and so on. A little time passed, then Toussaint leaned from where he was sitting and laid his hand on the chuckbox. "Perry," he called over to Perry Fox. "We ate out of this, a time before."

"That we did," agreed Perry. "But Marie's style of grub is a whole helluva lot better."

Toussaint put his finger to the large F burnt into the end of the chuckbox. "Dan Floweree."

The finger moved to the 9R brand on the box's side. "Louis Robare." To the TL beside it: "Billy Ulm."

Then to the lid, where the space had been used to burn in a big D-S. "This one you know best, Perry."

I straightened up. It had come to me: where Perry and Toussaint would have first eaten out of this chuckbox. When those cattle brands were first seared into its wood. The famous roundup of 1882, from the elbow of the Teton River to the Canadian line; the one Toussaint told my father about, the one he said was the biggest ever in this part of Montana. Nearly three hundred men, the ranchers and their cowhands and horse wranglers and night herders and cooks; forty tents it took to hold them all. Each morning the riders fanned out in half circles of about a dozen miles' ride and rounded in the cattle for sorting. Each afternoon the branding fires of the several outfits sent smoke above the prairie as the irons wrote ownership onto living cowhide. When the big sweep was over, coulees and creek bottoms searched out over an area bigger than some Eastern states, it was said a hundred thousand head of cattle were accounted for.

"Davis-Hauser-Stuart," Perry was saying of the brand on the chuckbox lid. "My outfit at the time. DHS, the Damn Hard Sittin'."

Wisdom Johnson was beginning to catch up with the conversation. "Where was this you're talking about?"

"All in through here," Perry indicated with a slow swing of his head from shoulder to shoulder. "Roundin' up cattle."

"Cattle?" Wisdom cast a look around the benchland, as if a herd might be pawing out there this very moment. "Around here?" It did seem a lot to believe, that this alfalfa field and the farmland on the horizon east of us once was a grass heaven for cows.

"Everywhere from the Teton to Canada, those old outfits had cattle," Perry confirmed. "If you could find the buggers."

Bud Dolson spoke up. "When'd all this take place?"

Toussaint told him: "A time ago. '82."

"Eighteen *eighty-two?*" queried Wisdom. "Perry, how ungodly old *are* you?"

Perry pointed a thumb at Toussaint. "Younger'n him."

Toussaint chuckled. "Everybody is."

236 · IVAN DOIG

—

How can pieces of time leap in and out of each other the way they do? There I sat, that noontime, listening to Toussaint and Perry speak of eating from a chuckwagon box all those years ago; and hearing myself question my mother about how she and her mother and Pete were provisioned from the same chuckbox on their St. Mary wagon trip a quarter of a century ago; and gazing on Pete, snoozing there in the shade of the pickup, simultaneously my admired uncle and the boy who helloed the horses at St. Mary.

Toussaint and the history that went everywhere with him set me to thinking. Life and people were a kind of flood around me this summer, yet for all my efforts I still was high and dry where one point of the past was concerned.

When Toussaint climbed to his feet to visit the far side of the alfalfa stack, I decided. Hell, he himself was the one who brought the topic up, back at the creek picnic on the Fourth. *You are a campjack these days.* And an outhouse engineer and a dawn rider and a hay equipment mechanic and a scatter raker, and an inquisitive almost-fifteen-year-old. I got up and followed Toussaint around the haystack.

"Jick," he acknowledged me. "You are getting tall. Mac and Beth will need a stepladder to talk to you."

"Yeah, I guess," I contributed, but my altitude was not what I wanted discussed. As Toussaint tended to his irrigation and I to mine, I asked: "Toussaint, what can you tell me about Stanley Meixell? I mean, I don't know him real well. That time up in the Two, I was only lending him a hand with his camptending, is all."

"Stanley Meixell," Toussaint intoned. "Stanley was the ranger. When the national forest was put in."

"Yeah, I know that. But more what I was wondering—did he and my folks have a run-in, sometime? I can't quite figure out what they think of Stanley."

"But you," said Toussaint. "You do thinking, too, Jick. What is it you think of Stanley?"

He had me there. "I don't just know. I've never come up against anybody like him."

Toussaint nodded. "That is Stanley," he affirmed. "You know more than you think you do."

—

Well, there I was as usual. No more enlightened than when I started. The chronic condition of Jick McCaskill, age fourteen and eleven twelfths years, prospects for a cure debatable.

At least the solace of scatter-raking remained to me. Or so I thought. As I say, this day I have just told about was the one that finished off the benchland alfalfa. A last stint of haying, back down on the Noon Creek meadows, awaited. Even yet I go over and over in my mind the happenings which that last spell of haying was holding in store. Talk about a chain of events. You could raise and lower the anchor of an ocean liner on the string of links that began to happen now.

Our new venue for haying was the old Ramsay homestead. The "upper place," my mother and Pete both called it by habit, because it was the part of the Reese ranch farthest up Noon Creek, farthest in toward the mountains. The meadows there were small but plentiful, tucked into the willow bends of Noon Creek the way pieces of a jigsaw puzzle clasp into one another. Pete always left the Ramsay hay until last because its twisty little fields were so hard to buckrake. In some cases he had to drive out of sight around two or three bends of the creek to brink in enough hay for a respectable stack. "You spend all your damn time here going instead of doing" was his unfond sentiment.

For me on the scatter rake, though, the upper place was just fine. Almost any direction I sent Blanche and Fisheye prancing toward, there stood Breed Butte or the mountains for me to lean my eyes on. In this close to them, the Rockies took up more than half the edge of the earth, which seemed only their fair proportion. And knowing the reefs and peaks as I did I could judge where each sheep allotment was, there along the mountain wall of my father's forest. Walter Kyle atop Roman Reef with his sheep and his telescope. Andy Gustafson with one of the Busby hands, under the middle of the reef where I had camptended him: farther south, Sanford Hebner in escape from his family name and situation. Closer toward Flume Gulch and the North Fork, whatever human improvement had replaced Canada Dan as herder of the third Busby band. Lower down, in the mix of timber and grass slopes, Pat Hoy and the Withrow sheep; and the counting vee where my father and

I talked and laughed with Dode. Already it was like going back to another time, to think about that first day of the counting trip.

The upper place, the old Ramsay place, always presented me new prospects of thought besides its horizons, though. For it was here that I was born. Alec and I both, in the Ramsay homestead house that still stands there today, although abandoned ever since my father quit as the Noon Creek association rider and embarked us into the Forest Service life. I couldn't have been but a year or so old when we moved away, yet I felt some regard for this site. An allegiance, even, for a bond of that sort will happen when you have been the last to live at a place. Or so I think. Gratitude that it offered a roof over your head for as long as it did, this may be, and remorse that only emptiness is your successor there.

Alec and I, September children, native Noon Creekers. And my mother's birthplace down the creek at the Reese ranch house itself. Odd to think that of the four of us at the English Creek ranger station all those years, the place that answered to the word "home" in each of us, only my father originated on English Creek, he alone was our link to Scotch Heaven and the Montana origins of the McCaskills. We Americans scatter fast.

And something odder yet. In a physical sense, here at the upper place I was more distant from Alec than I had been all summer. The Double W lay half the length of Noon Creek from where my rake now wheeled and glided. Mentally, though, this advent to our mutual native ground was a kind of reunion with my brother. Or at least with thoughts of him. While I held the reins of Blanche and Fisheye as they clopped along, I wondered what saddle horse Alec might be riding. When we moved the stacker from one site to the next, I thought of Alec on the move too, likely patrolling Double W fences this time of year, performing his quick mending on any barbwire or post that needed it. By this stage of haying Wisdom Johnson a time or two a day could be heard remembering the charms of Bouncing Betty, on First Avenue South in Great Falls. I wondered how many times a week Alec was managing to ride into Gros Ventre and see Leona. Leona. I wondered— well, just say I wondered.

With all this new musing to be done, the first day of haying the Ramsay meadows went calmly enough. A Monday, that was, a mild day following what had been a cool and cloudy Sunday. Wisdom Johnson, I remember, claimed we now were haying so far up into the polar regions that he might have to put his shirt on. Anyway, a Monday, a getting-under-way day.

The morning of the second Ramsay day, though, began unordinary. I started to see so as soon as Pony and I were coming down off the benchland to the Reese ranch buildings. My mind as usual at that point was on sour milk soda biscuits and fried eggs and venison sausage and other breakfast splendors as furnished by Marie, but I couldn't help watching the other rider who always approached the Reeses' at about the time I did. This of course was Clayton Hebner, for as I'd be descending from my benchland route Clayton would be riding in from the Hebner place on the North Fork, having come around the opposite end of Breed Butte from me. Always Clayton was on that same weary bay mare my father and I had seen the two smaller Hebner jockeys trying to urge into motion, at the outset of our counting trip, and always he came plodding in at the same pace and maybe even in the same hooftracks as the morning before. The first few mornings of haying I had waved to Clayton, but received no response. And I didn't deserve any. I ought to have known Hebners didn't go in for waving.

But etiquette of greeting was not what now had my attention. This particular morning, Clayton across the usual distance between us looked larger. Looked slouchy, as if he might have nodded off in the saddle. Looked somehow—well, the word that comes to mind is dormant.

I had unsaddled Pony and was turning her into the pasture beside Pete's barn when it became evident why Clayton Hebner didn't seem himself this morning. He wasn't.

"Hello there, Jick!" came the bray of Good Help Hebner. "Unchristly hour of the day to be out and about, ain't it?"

"Clayton buggered his ankle up," Good Help was explaining in a fast yelp. Even before the sire of the Hebner clan managed to unload himself from the swaybacked mare, Pete had appeared in the yard with an expression that told me ranch house walls did nothing to dim the identification of Good Help Hebner. "Sprained the goshdamn thing when him and Melvin was grab-assing around after supper last night," Good Help sped on to the two of us. "I tell you, Pete, I just don't know—"

—what's got into kids these days, I finished for Good Help in my mind before he blared it out.

Yet just about the time you think you can recite every forthcoming point of conversation from a Good Help Hebner, that's when he'll throw you for a loop. As now, when Good Help delivered himself of this:

"Ought not to leave a neighbor in the lurch, though, Pete. So I'll take the stacker-driving for you a couple days till Clayton mends up."

Pete looked as though he'd just been offered something nasty on the end of a stick.

But there just was no way around the situation. Someone to drive the stacker team was needed, and given that twelve-year-old Clayton had been performing the job, maybe an outside chance existed that Good Help could, too. Maybe.

"Dandy," uttered Pete without meaning a letter of it. "Come on in and sit up for breakfast, Garland. Then Jick can sort you out on the horses Clayton's been using."

"Kind of a racehorsey pair of bastards, ain't they?" Good Help evaluated Jocko and Pep, the stacker team.

"These? Huh uh," I reassured him. "They're the oldest tamest team on the place, Garland. That's why Pete uses them on the stacker."

"Horses," proclaimed Good Help as if he had just been invited to address Congress on the topic. "You just never can tell about horses. They can look logy as a preacher after a chicken dinner and the next thing you know they turn themselves into goshdamn mustangs. One time I—"

"Garland, these two old grandmas could pull the stacker cable in their sleep. And just about do. Come on, I'll help you get them harnessed. Then we got to go make hay."

The next development in our making of hay didn't dawn on me for quite some time.

That is, I noticed only that Wisdom Johnson today had no cause to complain of coolness. This was an August day with its furnace door open. Almost as soon as all of us got to the hayfield at the upper place, Wisdom was stripping off his shirt and gurgling a drink of water.

How Wisdom Johnson did it I'll never know, but he drank water oftener than the rest of us on the hay crew all together and yet never got heatsick from doing so. I mean, an ordinary person had to be careful about putting cool water inside a sweating body. Pete and Perry and Clayton and I rationed our visits to the burlapwrapped water jug that was kept in the shade of the haystack. But Wisdom had his own waterbag, hung on the stacker frame up there where he could reach it anytime he wanted. A hot day like this seemed to stoke both Wisdom's stacking and his liquid consumption. He'd swig, spit out the stream to rinse hay dust from his mouth. Swig again, several Adam's apple swallows this time. Then, refreshed, yell down to Pete on the buckrake: "More hay! Bring 'er on!"

Possibly, then, it was the lack of usual exhortation from Wisdom that first tickled my attention. I had been going about my scatter raking as usual, my mind here and there and the other, and only eventually did I notice the unusual silence of the hayfield. Above the brushy bend of the creek between me and the stack, though, I could see the stacker arms and fork taking load after load up, and Wisdom was there pitching hay energetically, and all seemed in order. The contrary didn't seep through to me until I felt the need for a drink of water and reined Blanche and Fisheye around the bend to go in to the stack and get it.

This haystack was distinct from any other we had put up all summer.

This one was hunched forward, leaning like a big hay-colored snowdrift against the frame of the stacker. More like a sidehill than a stack. In fact, this one so little resembled Wisdom's straight high style of haystack that I whoaed my team and sat to watch the procedure that was producing this leaning tower of Pisa.

The stacker fork with its next cargo of hay rose slowly, slowly, Good Help pacing at leisure behind the stacker team. When the arms and the fork neared the frame, he idly called, "Whoap," eased Jocko and Pep to a stop, and the hay gently plooped onto the very front of the stack, adding to the forward-leaning crest.

Wisdom gestured vigorously toward the back of the stack. You did not have to know pantomime to decipher that he wanted hay flung into that neighborhood. Then Wisdom's pitchfork flashed and he began to shove hay down from the crest, desperately parceling it toward the lower slope back there. He had made a heroic transferral of several huge pitchforkfuls when the next stacker load hovered up and plooped exactly where the prior one had.

Entrancing as Wisdom's struggle was, I stirred myself and went on in for my slug of water. Not up to me to regulate Good Help Hebner. Although it was with difficulty that I didn't make some crack when Good Help yiped to me: "Yessir, Jick, we're haying now, ain't we?"

From there on Wisdom's sidehill battle was a lost cause. When that haystack was done, or at least Wisdom called quits on it, and it was time to move the stacker to the next site, even Perry stopped dump-raking in the field next door and for once came over to help.

The day by now was without a wisp of moving air, a hot stillness growing hotter. Yet here was a haystack that gave every appearance of leaning into a ninety-mile-an-hour wind. Poles and props were going to be necessary to keep this stack upright *until* winter, let alone *into* winter.

Wisdom glistened so wet with sweat, he might have just come out of swimming. Side by side Perry and I wordlessly appraised the catty-wampus haystack, a little like mourners to the fact that our raking efforts had come to such a result. Pete had climbed off the buckrake and gained his first full view and now looked like he might be coming down with a toothache.

"Pete," Wisdom started in, "I got to talk to you."

"Somehow that doesn't surprise me," said Pete. "Let's get the stacker moved then we'll gab."

After the stacker was in place at the new site and Pete bucked in some loads as the base of the next stack, he shut down the buckrake and called Wisdom over. They had a session, with considerable head-shaking and arm-waving by Wisdom. Then Pete went over to Good Help, and much more discussion and gesturing ensued.

Finally Good Help shook his head, nodded, spat, squinted, scratched, and nodded again.

Pete settled for this and climbed on the buckrake.

For the next little while of stacking hay there was slightly more snap to Good Help's teamstering. He now had Jocko and Pep moving as if they were only half asleep instead of sleepwalking. Wisdom managed to get his back corners of the stack built good and high, and it began to look as if we were haying semi-respectably again.

Something told me to keep informed as I did my scatter-raking, though, and gradually the story of this new stack became clear. Once more, hay was creeping up and up in a slope against the frame of the stacker. But that was not the only slope. Due to Wisdom's determined efforts to build up the back corners, the rear also stood high. Prominent behind, low in the middle, and loftiest at the front where Good Help again was dropping the loads softly, softly. Something new again in the history of hay, a stack shaped like a gigantic saddle.

Wisdom Johnson now looked like a man standing in a coulee and trying to shovel *both* sidehills down level.

My own shirt was sopping, just from sitting on the rake. Wisdom surely was pouring sweat by the glassful. I watched as he grabbed his waterbag off the frame and took a desperate swig. It persuaded me that I needed to come in and visit the water jug again.

I disembarked from my rake just as Wisdom floundered to the exact middle of the swayback stack and jabbed his pitchfork in as if planting a battle flag.

"Drop the next frigging load right on that fork!" he shouted down to Good Help. So saying, he stalked up to the back of the haystack, folded his arms, and glowered down toward the pitchfork-target he had established for the next volley of hay.

This I had to watch. The water jug could wait. I planted myself just far enough from the stack to take in the whole drama.

Good Help squinted, scratched, spat, etcetera, which seemed to be his formula of acknowledgment. Then he twirled the ends of the reins and whapped the rumps of Jocko and Pep.

I suppose the comparison to make is this: how would you react if you had spent the past hours peacefully dozing and somebody jabbed a thumb between your ribs?

I believe even Good Help was more than a little surprised at the flying start his leather message produced from Jocko and Pep. Away the pair of horses jogged at a harness-rattling pace. Holding their reins, Good Help toddled after the team a lot more rapidly than I ever imagined he was capable of. The cable whirred snake-like through the pulleys of the stacker. And the load of hay was going up as if it was being fired from one of those Roman catapults.

I spun and ran. If the arms of the stacker hit the frame at that runaway velocity, there was going to be stacker timber flying throughout the vicinity.

Over my shoulder, though, I saw it all.

Through some combination of stumble, lurch, and skid, Good Help at last managed to rare back on the reins with all his weight and yanked the horses to a stop.

Simultaneously the stacker arms and fork popped to a halt just inches short of the frame, the whole apparatus quivering up there in the sky like a giant tuning fork.

The hay. The hay was airborne. And Wisdom was so busy glowering he didn't realize this load was arriving to him as if lobbed by Paul Bunyan. I yelled, but anything took time to sink in to Wisdom. His first hint of doom was as the hay, instead of cascading down over the pitchfork Good Help was supposed to be sighting on, kept coming and coming and coming. A quarter of a ton of timothy on a trajectory to the top of Wisdom's head.

Hindsight is always twenty-twenty. Wisdom ought to have humped up and accepted the avalanche. He'd have had to splutter hay the next several minutes, but a guy as sturdy as he was wouldn't have been hurt by the big loose wad.

But I suppose to look up and see a meteorite of hay dropping on you is enough to startle a person. Wisdom in his surprise took a couple of wading steps backward from the falling mass. And had forgotten how far back he already was on the stack. That second step carried Wisdom to the edge, at the same moment that the hayload spilled itself onto the stack. Just enough of that hay flowed against Wisdom to teeter him. The teetering slipped him over the brink. "Oh, *hell*," I heard him say as he started to slide.

Every stackman knows the danger of falling from the heights of his work. In Wisdom's situation, earth lay in wait for him twenty feet below. This lent him incentive. Powerful as he was, the desperately grunting Wisdom clawed his arms into the back of the haystack as he slid. Like a man trying to swim up a waterfall even as the water sluices him down.

"Goshdamn!" Good Help marveled somewhere behind me. "Will you look at that!"

Wisdom's armwork did slow his descent, and meanwhile a sizable cloud of hay was pulling loose from the stack and coming down with him, considerably cushioning his landing. As it turned out, except for scratched and chafed arms and chest and a faceful of hay Wisdom met the ground intact. He also arrived to earth with a full head of steam, all of which he now intended to vent on Good Help Hebner.

"You satchel-ass old son of a frigging goddamn"—Wisdom's was a rendition I have always wished I'd had time to commit to memory. An entire opera of cussing, as he emerged out of the saddle-back stack. But more than Wisdom's mouth was in action, he was trying to lay hands on Good Help. Good Help was prudently keeping the team of horses between him and the stackman. Across the horses' wide backs they eyed one another, Wisdom feinting one way and Good Help going the other, then the reverse. Since the stacker arms and fork still were in the sky, held there only by the cable hitched to the team, I moved in and grabbed the halters of Jocko and Pep so they would stand steady.

By now Pete had arrived on the buckrake, to find his stacking crew in this shambles.

"Hold everything!" he shouted, which indeed was what the situation needed.

Pete got over and talked Wisdom away from one side of the team of horses, Good Help pussyfooted away from their opposite side, and I backed Jocko and Pep toward the stack to let down the arms and fork.

Diplomacy of major proportions now was demanded of Pete. His dilemma was this: if he didn't prune Good Help from the hay crew, Wisdom Johnson was going to depart soonest. Yet Pete needed to stay on somewhat civil terms with Good Help, for the sake of hanging on to Clayton and the oncoming lineage of Hebner boys as a ready source of labor. Besides all that, it was simply sane general policy not to get crosswise with a neighbor such as Good Help, for he could just as readily substitute your livestock for those poached deer hanging in his jackpines.

Wisdom had stalked away to try to towel some of the chaff off himself with his shirt. I hung around Pete and Good Help. I wouldn't have missed this for the world.

"Garland, we seem to have a problem here," Pete began with sizable understatement. "You and Wisdom. He doesn't quite agree with the way you drive stacker team."

"Pete, I have stacked more hay than that guy has ever even seen." By which Good Help must have meant in several previous incarnations, as none of us who knew him in this lifetime had ever viewed a pitchfork in his hands. "He don't know a favor when it's done to him. If he'd let me place the loads the way they ought to be, he could do the stacking while setting in a goshdamn rocking chair up there."

"He doesn't quite see it that way."

"He don't see doodly-squat about putting up hay, that fellow. I sure don't envy you all his haystacks that are gonna tip assy-turvy before winter, Pete."

"Garland, something's got to give. Wisdom won't stack if you're going to drive."

The hint flew past Good Help by a Texas mile. "Kind of a stubborn bozo, ain't he?" he commiserated with Pete. "I was you, I'd of sent him down the road long since."

Pete gazed at Good Help as if a monumental idea had just been presented. As, indeed, one had.

"I guess you're right. I'd better go ahead and can him," Pete judiciously agreed with Good Help. I gaped at Pete. But he was going right on: "I do need to have somebody on the stack who knows what he's doing, though. Lucky as hell you're on hand, Garland. Nobody else on this crew is veteran to the stacking job like you are. What we'll do, I'll put you up on the stack and we'll make some hay around here for a change, huh?"

Good Help went as still as Lot's wife, and I swear he even turned about as white.

"Ordinarily, now"—I didn't get to hear all of the ensuing catalogue of excuse, because I had to saunter away to keep my giggles in, but—"this goshblamed back of mine"—I heard more than enough—"if it'll help you out with that stubborn bozo I can just head on home, Pete"—to know that it constituted Good Help's adieu to haying.

That night at English Creek my father and mother laughed and laughed at my retelling of the saga of Wisdom and Good Help.

"A pair of dandies, they are," my father ajudged. Recently he seemed to take particular pleasure in any evidence that jugheaded behavior wasn't a monopoly of the Forest Service.

But then a further point occurred to him, and he glanced at my mother. She looked soberly back at him. It had occurred to her, too. She in fact was the one who now asked it: "Then who's going to drive the stacker team?"

"Actually," I confessed, "I am."

So that was how I went from haying's ideal job to its goddamn dullest.

Back and forth with that stacker team. All of haying until then I had idly glanced at those little towpaths worn into the meadow, out from the side of each stack we put up, identical routes the exact length of the stacker cable. Now it registered on me how many footsteps, horse and human, it took to trudge those patterns into creation. The scenery meanwhile constant: the rear ends of Jocko and Pep looming ahead of me like a pair of circus fat ladies bending over to tie their shoelaces. Too promptly I discovered a charm of Pep's, which was to hoist his tail and take a dump as soon as we were hitched up at a new stack site, so that I had to remember to watch my step or find myself shin deep in fresh horse apples.

Nor did it help my mood that Clayton with his tender ankle was able to sit on the seat of the scatter rake and do that job. *My* scatter rake. The first long hours of driving the stacker team I spent brooding about the presence of the Hebner tribe in this world.

I will say, the stacker team job shortly cured me of too much thinking. The first time I daydreamed a bit and was slow about starting the load up onto the stack, Wisdom Johnson brought me out of it by shouting down: "Hey, Jick! Whistle or sing, or show your thing!" I was tempted to part Wisdom's hair with that particular load of hay, but I forebore.

Maybe my stacker team mood was contagious. Suppertime of the second day, when I got back to English Creek I found my mother frowning over the week's *Gleaner*. "What's up?" I asked her.

"Nothing," she said and didn't convince me. When she went to the stove to wrestle with supper and I had washed up, I zeroed in on the article she'd been making a mouth at. It was one on the Random page:

PHANTOM WOMAN:
WHEN FIRE RAN
ON THE MOUNTAIN

Editor's note: The fire season is once again upon us, and lightning needs no help from the carelessness of man. It is just 10 years ago that the Phantom Woman Mountain conflagration provided an example of what happens when fire gets loose in a big way. We reprint the story as a reminder. When in the woods, break your matches after blowing them out, crush cigarette butts, and douse all campfires.

Forest Service crews are throwing everything in the book at the fire on Phantom Woman Mountain, but so far, the roar-

ing blaze has thrown it all back. The inferno is raging in up-and-down country near the headwaters of the North Fork of English Creek, about 20 miles west of Gros Ventre. Reports from Valier and Conrad say the column of smoke can be seen from those communities. How many acres of forest have been consumed is not known. It is certain the loss is the worst in the Two Medicine National Forest since the record fire season of 1910.

One eyewitness said the crews seemed to be bringing the fire under control until late yesterday afternoon. Then the upper flank of the fire broke loose "and started going across that mountain as fast as a man can run."

H. T. Gisborne, fire research specialist for the U.S. Forest Service at Missoula, explained the "blowup" phenomenon: "Ordinarily the front of a forest fire advances like troops in skirmish formation, pushing ahead faster here, slower there, according to the timber type and fuels, but maintaining a practically unbroken front. Even when topography, fuels, and weather result in a crown fire, the sheet of flames leaps from one tree crown to the next at a relatively slow rate, from one-half to one mile an hour. But when such 'runs' throw spots of fire ahead of the advancing front, the spots burn back to swell the main front and add to the momentum of the rising mass of heat. Literally, a 'blowup' of the front of the fire may then happen."

No word has been received of casualties in the Phantom Woman fire, although reports are that some crews had to flee for their lives when the "blowup" occurred.

When my father came in for supper, my mother liberated the *Gleaner* from me and handed it to him, saying: "Mac, you might as well see this." Meaning, you might as well see it before our son the asker starts in on you about it.

The headline stopped him. Bill Reinking always got in touch with him about any story having to do with the Two Medicine National Forest. "Why's this in the paper?" my father now demanded of the world at large.

"It's been ten years, Mac," my mother told him. "Ten years ago this week."

He read it through. His eyes were intent, his jaw was out, as if stubborn against the notion that fire could happen in the Two Medicine National Forest. When he tossed the *Gleaner* aside, though, he said only: "Doesn't time fly."

The next day, two developments.

I took some guilty pleasure at the first of these. Not long before noon, Clayton dropped one wheel of the scatter rake into a ditch that was closer than he'd noticed, and the impact broke one of the brackets that attaches the dumping mechanism to the rake frame. Clayton himself looked considerably jarred, although I don't know whether mostly by the jolt of the accident or the dread that Pete would fire him for it.

But Pete being Pete, he instead said: "These things happen, Clayton. We'll cobble it with wire until we can get a weld done on it." And once I got over my secret satisfaction about the superiority of my scatter-raking to Clayton's, I was glad Pete didn't come down hard on the boy. Being a son of Good Help Hebner seemed to me punishment enough for anybody.

Then at the end of the workday, as Pony and I came down the benchland to the ford of English Creek, I saw a second Forest Service pickup parked beside my father's outside the ranger station. I figured the visitor might be Cliff Bowen, the young ranger from the Indian Head district just south of us, and it was. When I stepped in to say hello, I learned Cliff had been to headquarters in Great Falls and had come by with some fire gear for my father. And with some rangerly gripes he was sharing as well. Normally Cliff Bowen was mild as milk, but his headquarters visit left him pretty well steamed.

"Mac, Sipe asked me how things are going." Sipe was Ken Sipe, the superintendent of the Two Medicine National Forest. "I told him, about as good as could be expected, but we're going to need more smoke-chasers." July and now August had stayed so hot and dangerous that east-of-the-Divide rangers had been permitted to hire some fire manpower, but only enough, as my father had said, "to give us a taste."

"How'd that go over with him?" my father wondered.

"About like a fart in church. He told me it's Missoula policy. Hold down on the hiring, on these east-side forests. Goddamn it, Mac, I don't know what the Major's thinking of. This forest is as dry as paper. We get one good lightning storm in the mountains and we'll have fires the whole sonofabitching length of the Two."

"Maybe the Major's got it all arranged with upstairs so there isn't going to be any lightning the rest of the summer, Cliff."

"Yeah, maybe. But if any does get loose, I hope to Christ it aims for the rivets on the Major's hip pocket."

My father couldn't help but laugh. "You think snag strikes are trouble. Figure how long the Major'd smolder."

Two developments, I said back there. Amend that to three. As I led Pony to her pasture for the night, the heat brought out sweat on me, just from that little walk. When I reached the house the thermometer in our kitchen window was catching the western sun. Ninety-two degrees, it read. The hot heavy weather was back. The kind of weather that invites lightning storms.

But all we got that night was a shower, a dab of drizzle. When I climbed out of bed in the morning I debated whether Pete's hay would be too wet to stack today. So that I wouldn't make my ride for nothing, I telephoned the Reese ranch.

"Pete thinks it'll be dry enough by middle of the morning," Marie's voice told me. "Come on for breakfast. I have sourdough hotcakes."

It turned out that the sourdough hotcakes were the only real gain of the morning for our hay crew. We took our time at the breakfast table and then did a leisurely harnessing-up of our teams and made no hurry of getting to the Ramsay place's hayfields, and still Perry and Bud and Wisdom had a lot of smoke time while Pete felt of the hay and gandered at the sky. Finally Pete said, "Hell, let's try it." We would do okay for a while, put up a dozen or so loads, then here would come a sun shower. Just enough moisture to shut us down. Then we'd hay a little more, and another sun shower would happen. For a rancher trying to put up hay, that is the most aggravating kind of day there can be. Or as Pete put it during one of these sprinkly interruptions: "Goddamn it, if you're gonna rain, *rain.*"

By about two o'clock and the fourth or fifth start-and-stop of our stacking, he had had enough. "The hell with it. Let's head for home."

I naturally anticipated an early return to English Creek, and started thinking about where I might go fishing for the rest of the afternoon. My theory is, the more rotten the weather, the better the fishing. But as I was unharnessing Jocko and Pep, Pete came out of the house and asked:

"Jick, how do you feel about a trip to town?"

Inasmuch as we were rained out anyway, he elaborated, I might just as well take the scatter rake in to Grady Tilton's garage and get the broken bracket welded, stay overnight at the Heaneys' and in the morning drive the repaired rake back here to the ranch. "I checked all this out with headquarters", meaning my mother, "and she said it'd be okay."

"Sounds good to me," I told Pete. The full fact was, after the days of trudging back and forth behind the stacker team it sounded like an expedition to Africa.

So I set off for Gros Ventre, about midafternoon. Roving scatter raker Jick McCaskill hitting the road, even if the route only was to town and back.

The first couple of miles almost flew by, for it was remarkable what a pair of steppers Blanche and Fisheye now seemed to me; speed demons in comparison to Jocko and Pep. My thoughts were nothing special. Wondering what Ray Heaney would have to report. Mulling the rest of the summer. Another week or so of haying. The start of school was—Christamighty, only thirty days away. And my fifteenth birthday, one day less than that. I ask you, how is it that after the Fourth of July each summer, time somehow speeds up.

I like to believe that even while curlicues of this sort are going on in my head, the rest of me is more or less on the job. Aiming that scatter rake down the Noon Creek road I took note of Dill Egan's haystacks, which looked to me like poor relations of those Wisdom built. Way over on the tan horizon to the northeast I could see specks that would be Double W cattle, and wondered where Alec was riding or fence-fixing today. And of course one of the things a person always does a lot of in Montana is watching other people's weather. All that sky and horizon around you, there almost always is some atmospheric event to keep track of. At the top of the country road's rise from Dill Egan's place, I studied a dark anvil cloud which was sitting over the area to the northwest of me. My father was not going to like the looks of that one, hovering along the edge of his forest. And our Ramsay hayfield is going to have itself a bath, I told myself.

In a few more minutes I glanced around again, though, and found that the cloud wasn't sitting over the Ramsay place. It was on the move. Toward Noon Creek and me. A good thing I was bright enough to bring my slicker along on the rake; the coat was going to save me from some wet.

But the next time I reconnoitered, rain was pushed off my mental agenda. The cloud was bigger, blacker, and closer. A whole hell of a lot closer. It also was rumbling now like it was the engine of the entire sky. That may sound fancy, but view it from my eyes at the time: a dark block of storm, with pulses of light coming out of it like flame winking from firebox doors. And even as I gawked at it, a jagged rod of lightning stabbed from the cloud to the earth. Pale lightning, nearer white than yellow. The kind a true electrical storm employs.

As I have told, I am not exactly in love with lightning anyway. Balling the reins in both my hands, I slapped Blanche and Fisheye some encouragement across their rumps. "Hyaah, you two! Let's go!" Which may sound drastic, but try sitting on a ten-foot expanse of metal rake with lightning approaching and then prescribe to me what you would have done.

Go we did, at a rattling pace, for the next several minutes. I did my best to count distance on the thunder, but it was that grumbling variety that lets loose another thump before you've finished hearing the one before. My eyes rather than my ears had to do the weather forecasting, and they said Blanche and Fisheye and the rake and I were not going as fast as the storm-cloud was traveling or growing or whatever the hell it was doing.

The route ahead stretched on and on, for immediately after coming up out of Dill Egan's place the Noon Creek road abandons the bottomland and arrows along the benchland between Noon Creek and English Creek until it eventually hits the highway north of Gros Ventre. Miles of country as exposed as a tabletop. I tell you, a situation like that reminds a person that skin is damn thin shelter against the universe.

One thing the steady thunder and the pace of the anvil cloud did tell me was that I somehow had to abandon that road. Find a place to pull in and get myself and my horses away from this ten-foot lightning rod on wheels. The question was, where? Along the English Creek road I'd have had no problem: within any little way there, a ranch could be pulled into for shelter. But around here the Double W owned everything, and wherever there did happen to be a turnoff into one of the abandoned sets of Noon Creek ranch buildings, the Double W kept the gate padlocked against fishermen. As I verified for myself, by halting my team for a quick scan at the gate into the old Nansen place.

A lack of choices can make your mind up for you in a hurry. I whapped Blanche and Fisheye again and on down the county road we clattered, heading for a high frame of gateposts about three quarters of a mile off. The main gate into the Double W.

It took forever, but at last we pulled up at that gateframe and the Double W turnoff. From the crosspiece supported by the big gateposts—the size and height of telephone poles, they really were—hung the sign:

WW RANCH
WENDELL & MEREDICE WILLIAMSON

The sign was creaking a little, the wind starting to stir in front of the storm.

Neither the sign nor the wind I gave a whit about just then. What I had forgotten was that this turnoff into the Double W had a cattleguard built in there between the gateposts. A pit overlaid with a grill of pipes, which vehicles could cross but hoofed creatures such as cattle couldn't. Hoofed creatures such as cattle and horses. To put Blanche and Fisheye through here, I would have to open the barbwire livestock gate beside the cattleguard.

You know what I was remembering. "GODAMIGHTY, get AWAY from that!"—Stanley's cry as I approached the wire gate at the cabin during our camptending trip. "You happen to be touching that wire and lightning hits that fence—" This coming rumblebelly of a storm made that June one look like a damp washcloth. Every time I glanced in its direction now, lightning winked back. And nowhere around this entrance to the Double W was there a stick of wood, not one sole single goddamn splinter, with which to knock the hoop off the gate stick and flip the wire gate safely aside.

Holy H. Hell. Sitting here telling this, all the distance of years between that instant and now, I can feel again the prickling that came across the backs of my hands, the sweat of dismay on its way up through my skin there. Grant me three moments which could be erased from my life, and that Double W gate scene would be one.

I wiped my hands against my pants. Blanche swished her tail, and Fisheye whinnied. They maybe were telling me what I already knew. Delay was my worst possible behavior, for that storm was growing nearer every second that I stood there and stewed. I wiped my hands again. And jumped at the gate as if in combat against it. One arm grappling around the gatepost, the other arm and hand desperately working the wire hoop up off the gatestick. Oh yes, sure, this gate was one of those snug obstinate bastards; I needed to mightily hug the stick and post together to gain enough slack for the hoop to loosen. Meanwhile everyplace my body was touching a strand of barbwire I could feel a kind of target line, ready to sizzle: as if I was trussed up in electrical wiring and somebody was about to throw the switch.

I suppose in a fraction of what it takes to tell about it, I wrestled that gate open and slung it wide. Yet it did seem an immense passage of time.

And I wasn't on easy street yet. Blanche and Fisheye, I have to say, were taking all of this better than I was, but even so they were getting a little nervous about the storm's change in the air and the loudening thunder. "Okay, here we go now, nothing to it, here we go," I soothed the team and started them through the gate. I could have stood some soothing myself, for the scatter rake was ten feet wide and this gate was only about eleven. Catch a rake wheel behind a gatepost and you have yourself a first-class hung-up mess. In my case, I then would have the rake in contact with the barbwire fence, inviting lightning right up the seat of my pants, while I backed and maneuvered the rake wheel out of its bind. Never have I aimed anything more carefully than that wide scatter rake through that just-wide-enough Double W gateway.

We squeaked through. Which left me with only one more anxious act to do. To close the gate, for there were cattle in this field. Even if they were the cattle of the damn Double W, even if it mattered nothing to me that they got out and scattered to Tibet; if you have been brought up in Montana, you close a gate behind you.

So I ran back and did the reverse of the wrestling that'd opened the gate. Still scared spitless about touching that wire. Yet maybe not quite as scared as when I'd first done it, for I was able to say to myself all the while, What in the hell have I done to deserve this dose of predicament?

Again on the rake, I broke all records of driving that Double W approach road, down from the benchland to where the ranch buildings were clustered on the north side of Noon Creek. Across the plank bridge the rake rumbled, my thunder against the storm's thunder, and I sighted refuge. The Double W barn.

In minutes I had my team unhitched—leaving the scatter rake out by a collection of old machinery, so that lightning at least would have to do some sorting to find it—and was ensconcing them in barn stalls. They were lathered enough that I unharnessed them and rubbed them dry with a gunnysack. In fact, I looked around for the granary, went over there, and brought back a hatful of Double W oats apiece to Blanche and Fisheye as their reward.

Now I could draw a breath and look around for my own benefit.

The Double W had buildings and more buildings. This barn was huge and the two-story white Williamson house across the yard could have housed the governor of Montana. You would think this was ranch enough for anybody, yet Wendell Williamson actually owned another one at least as big as this. The Deuce W—its cattle brand was 2w— down in the Highwood Mountains between Great Falls and Lewistown, a hundred or more miles from here. More distance than I'd been in my whole life, and Wendell goddamn Williamson possessed both ends of it.

Be that as it may, the Double W was now my port in the storm, and I had better make my presence known.

No one was in sight. It would take a little while for the rain to bring in Alec and the other riders and the hay crew from the range and the hayfield. But somebody was bound to be in the house, and I hurried over to there before I had to do it during the storm.

I knocked at the front door.

The door opened and Meredice Williamson was standing there smiling and saying: "Yes?"

"'Lo, Mrs. Williamson. I put Blanche and Fisheye in your barn."

That seemed to be double Dutch to her. But she smiled on and commended: "That was good of you. I'm sure Wendell will be pleased."

I sought to correct her impression that a delivery of Blanche and Fisheye was involved here. "Well, no, they'll only be there until it clears up. I mean, what it is, I was driving my scatter rake to town and the storm started coming and I had to head in here on account of lightning, so I unhitched my team and put them in the barn there, I hope that's all right?"

"I'm sure it must be," she acceded, pretty plainly because she had no idea what else to say. Meredice Williamson was a city woman—a lawyer's widow, it was said—whom Wendell met and married in California a few winters before. The unkind view of her was that she'd had too much sun on the brain down there. But I believe the case honestly was that because Meredice Williamson only came north to spend summers at the Double W, she never got clued in to the Two country; never quite caught up with its rhythms of season and livelihood and lore. At least, standing there within the weathered doorway in her yellow sun frock and with her graying hair in perfect marcelled waves, she looked much like a visitor to her own ranch house.

Yet maybe Meredice Williamson was not as vague as the general estimate of her, for she now pondered my face a moment more and then asked: "Are you Beth McCaskill's other boy?"

Which wasn't exactly my most preferred phrasing of it. But she did have genealogical fact on her side. So I bobbed yes and contributed: "Jick. Alec's brother."

"Wendell thinks highly of Alec," she confided, as if I gave a hoot in hell about Mr. Double W's opinion. So far as I could see Wendell Williamson was a main contributor to Alec's mental delinquency, encouraging him in his damn cowboy notions. The summer's sunder of my family followed a faultline which led to this doorstep. Fair is fair, though, and I couldn't really blame Meredice Williamson for Wendell's doings. Innocent as a bluebird on a manure pile, this lady seemed to be. Thus I only said back:

"Yeah. So I savvy."

Just then the leading edge of rain hit, splatting drops the size of quarters on the flagstones of the walk. Meredice Williamson peered past me in surprise at the blackening sky. "It looks like a shower," she mustered. "Wouldn't you like to step inside?"

I was half tempted. On the other hand, I figured she wouldn't have the foggiest notion of what to do with me once I was in there. Furnish me tea and ladyfingers? Ask me if I would care for a game of Chinese checkers?

"No, that's okay," I replied. "I'll wait in the bunkhouse. Alec likely will show up there pretty quick. I'll shoot the hooey with him until the rain's over and then head on to town." Here Meredice Williamson's expression showed that she was unsure what hooey was or why we would shoot it. In a hurry I concluded: "Anyway, thanks for the borrow of your barn."

"You're quite welcome, Jake," she was saying as I turned and sprinted across the yard. The rain was beginning to pelt in plentiful drops now, pocking the dust. Flashes of light at the south edge of the storm and the immediate rumbles made me thankful again that I was in off the rake, even if the haven was the Double W.

Strange, to be in a bunkhouse when its residents are out on the job. Like one of those sea tales of stepping aboard a ship where everything is intact, sails set and a meal waiting on the galley stove, but the crew has vanished.

Any bunkhouse exists only to shelter a crew. There is no feel of it as a home for anybody, although even as I say that I realize many ranch hands spent their lives in a bunkhouse. Alec himself was a full-timer here, and would be until he and Leona tied their knot. Even so, a bunkhouse to me seems a place you can put up with for a season but that would be enough.

If you are unaccustomed to a bunkhouse, the roomful of beds is a medley of odors. Of tobacco in three incarnations: hand-rolled cigarettes, snoose, and chewing tobacco. The last two, in fact, had a permanent existence in the spit cans beside about half the bunks. These I took special note of, not wanting to kick one of them over. Of too many bodies and not enough baths; yet I wonder why it is that we now think we have to deodorize the smell of humanness out of existence. Of ashes and creosote; the presence of an elderly stove and stovepipe. All in all, the scent of men and what it takes them to lead the ranch hands' life.

I glanced around to try and figure out which bunk was Alec's. An easy enough mystery. The corner bunk with the snapshot of Leona on the wall above the pillow.

Naturally the picture deserved a closer look.

It showed Leona on a horse in a show ring—that would be Tollie Zane's during one of his horse sales—and wearing a lady Stetson and leather chaps. And a smile that probably fused the camera. But I managed to get past the top of Leona, to where something else was tugging my eyes. Down the length of her chaps, something was spelled out in tooled letters with silver spangles between. I moved in for a closer look yet, my nose almost onto the snapshot, and I was able to make out:

M

*

O

*

N

*

T

*

A

*

N

*

A

Well, that wasn't the message that ordinarily would come to mind from looking along Leona's leg. But it was interesting.

I could hear voices, and men began trooping in. The hay crew. And at the tail end of them Alec, who looked flabbergasted to see me sitting on his bunk.

"Jicker, what in blazes—" he started as he strode over to me. I related to him my scatter rake situation and he listened keenly, although he didn't look perceptibly happier with my presence. "As soon as the rain lets up, I'll head on to town," I assured him.

"Yeah, well. Make yourself at home, I guess." Now, to my surprise, my brother seemed short of anything more to say. He was saved from having to, by the arrival of the Double W foreman Cal Petrie and the other two riders, older guys named Thurl Everson and Joe Henty. Both had leather gloves and fencing pliers, so I imagined they were glad to be in away from barbwire for a while, too.

Cal Petrie spotted me perched on the bunk aside Alec, nodded hello, and steered over to ask: "Looking for a job?" He knew full well I wasn't, but as foreman it was his responsibility to find out just what brought me here.

Again I explained the scatter rake–lightning situation, and Cal nodded once more. "A stroke of that could light you up like a Christmas tree, all right. Make yourself to home. Alec can introduce you around." Then Cal announced generally: "After supper I got to go to town for some sickle heads for the mowers, and I can take two of you jaspers in with me in the pickup. I'll only be in there an hour or so, and you got to be ready to come home when I say. No staying in there to drink the town dry, in other words. So cut cards or Indian rassle or compare dicks or however you want to choose, but only two of you are going." And he went off into the room he had to himself at the far end of the bunkhouse.

In a hay crew such as the Double W's there were ten or a dozen guys, putting up two stacks at once, and what struck me as Alec made me known to them was that three of the crew were named Mike. A gangly one called Long Mike, and a mower man naturally called Mike the Mower, and then one who lacked either of those distinctions and so was called Plain Mike. The riders who had come in with Cal Petrie I already knew, Thurl and Joe. Likewise the choreboy, old Dolph Kuhn, one of those codgers who get to be as much a part of a ranch as its ground and grass. So I felt acquainted enough even before somebody chimed out:

"What, are you another one of the famous fist-fighting McCaskills?" Alec's flooring of Earl Zane at the Fourth of July dance was of course the natural father of that remark.

"No, I'm the cut-and-shoot type," I cracked back. "When the trouble starts, I cut through the alley and shoot for home."

You just never know. That joke had gray whiskers and leaned on a cane, but it drew a big laugh from the Double W yayhoos even so.

There followed some more comment, probably for the fortieth time, about how Alec had whopped Earl, and innumerable similar exploits performed in the past by various of this crew. You'd have thought the history of boxing had taken place in that bunkhouse. But I was careful not to contribute anything further. The main rule when you join a crew, even if it's only for the duration of a rainstorm, is to listen more than you talk.

Alec still didn't look overjoyed that I was on hand, but I couldn't help that. I didn't order up the damn electrical storm, which still was rumbling and crashing around out there.

"So," I offered as an opener, "what do you know for sure?"

"Enough to get by on," Alec allowed.

"Been doing any calf-roping?"

"No."

That seemed to take care of the topic of calf-roping. Some silence, then Alec hazarded: "How's the haying going at Pete's?"

"We've pretty close to got it. A few more days left. How're they doing here?"

"More like a couple of weeks left, I guess."

And there went the topic of haying. Alec and I just sat back and listened for a little to where the discussion had now turned, the pair of slots for town. Some grumping was going on about Cal Petrie's edict that only two of the crew were going to get to see the glories of Gros Ventre on a Saturday night. This was standard bunkhouse grouse, though. If Cal had said the whole shebang of them could go to town with him there'd have been grumbling that he hadn't offered to buy them the first round of drinks as well. No, the true issue was just beginning to come out: more than half the hay crew, six or so guys, considered themselves the logical town candidates. The variety of reasoning—the awful need for a haircut, a bet to be collected from a guy who was going to be in the Medicine Lodge only this very night, even a potential toothache that necessitated preventive remedies from the drugstore—was remarkably well rehearsed. This Double W bunch was the kind of crew, as the saying went, who began on Thursday to get ready on Friday to go to town on Saturday to spend Sunday.

Long Mike and Plain Mike and a sort of a gorilla of a guy who I figured must be one of the two stackmen of this gang were among the yearners for town. Plain Mike surprised me by being the one to propose that a game of cards settle the matter. But then, you just never know who in a crew will turn out to be the tiger rider.

The proposal itself eliminated the big stackman. "Hell with it, I ain't lost nothing in that burg anyway." At the time I thought his sporting blood was awfully anemic. It has since dawned on me that he could not read; could not tell the cards apart.

Inasmuch as Plain Mike had efficiently whittled off one contender, the other four felt more or less obliged to go along with a card game.

"We need an honest banker," Plain Mike solicited.

"You're talking contradictions," somebody called out.

"Damn, I am at that. Honest enough that we can't catch him, will do. Hey there, Alec's brother! How about you being the bank for us?"

"Well, I don't know. What are you going to play?"

"Pitch," stipulated Plain Mike. "What else is there?"

That drew me. Pitch is the most perfect of card games. It excels poker in that there can be more than one winner during each hand, and cribbage in that it doesn't take an eternity to play, and rummy and hearts in that judgment is more important than the cards you are dealt, and stuff like canasta and pinochle can't even be mentioned in the same breath with pitch.

"I guess I could," I assented. "Until the rain lets up." It still was raining like bath time on Noah's ark.

"Pull up a stump," invited Plain Mike, nodding toward a spare chair beside the stove. "We'll show you pitch as she is meant to be played."

Uh huh, at least you will, I thought to myself as I added my presence to the circle of card players. But I will say this for the Double W yayhoos, they played pitch the classic way: high, low, game, jack, jick, joker. It would just surprise you, how many people go through life under the delusion that pitch ought to be played without a joker in the deck, which is a skimpy damned way of doing it, and how many others are just as dim in wanting to play with two jokers, which is excessive and confusing.

My job of banker didn't amount to all that much. Just being in charge of the box of Diamond wooden matches and paying out to each player as many matches as he'd made points, or taking matches back if he went set. Truth be told, I could have kept score more efficiently with a pencil and sheet of paper, and Alec simply could have done it in his head. But these Double W highrollers wanted to be able to squint around the table and count for themselves how much score everybody else had.

From the very first hand, when the other players were tuning up with complaints like "Is this the best you can deal, a mess like this?" and Plain Mike simply bid three, "in them things called spades," and led with the queen, it was worth a baccalaureate degree in the game of pitch to watch Plain Mike. He bid only when he had one sure point, ace for high or deuce for low, with some other point probable among his cards, so that when he *did* bid it was as good as made. But during a hand when anybody else had the bid, he managed to run with some point, jack or jick or joker, for himself, or at least—this, a real art of pitch—he managed to sluff the point to somebody besides the bidder. I banked and admired. While the other cardsters' scores gyrated up and down, with every hand Plain Mike added a wooden match or two to his total.

Around us the rest of the crew was carrying on conversation. If you can call it that. There is no place like a bunkhouse for random yatter. One guy will grouch about how the eggs were cooked for breakfast and another will be reminded of a plate of beans he ate in Pocatello in 1922. Harness the gab gas of the average bunkhouse and you'd have an inexhaustible fuel.

I was taking it all in, eyes and mind pretty much on the card game and ears shopping around in the crew conversation, when one of the pitch players popped out with:

"Aw hell, there goes Jick."

I blinked and sat up at that. Anybody would, wouldn't he? All right, so my attention was a bit divided: so what the hell business was it of some stranger to announce it to the world? But then I saw that the guy hadn't meant me, he was just bemoaning because he'd tried to run the jick past Plain Mike and Plain Mike had nabbed it with his jack of trump.

The only one to notice my peeved reaction was Plain Mike himself, who I would say did not miss many tricks in life as well as in cards. "A jick and a Jick we got here, huh?" he said now. "Who hung that nickname on you, that battling brother of yours?"

Actually my best guess was that it'd been Dode Withrow who suggested I looked like the jick of the McCaskills, but my parents were
vague about the circumstance. I mean, a person wants to know his own
history insofar as possible, but if you can't, you can't. So instead of trying to go into all that before this Double W crowd I just responded:
"Somebody with an imagination, I guess."

"Lucky thing he didn't imagine you resembled the queen of hearts,"
observed Plain Mike and turned his attention back to the pitch game.

By now Alec, looking restless and overhearing all this name stuff,
had come over and joined me in watching the card game. This was certainly a more silent brother than I'd ever been around before. Maybe it
had something to do with his surroundings, this hay crew he and the
other riders now had to share the bunkhouse with. Between checking
out the window on the progress of the rain and banking the pitch game,
I started mulling what it would be like to work in this hay crew instead
of Pete's. If, say, ranches were swapped under Alec and me, him up the
creek at the Reese place as he'd been at my age and me here at the Gobble Gobble You. Some direct comparison of companions was possible.
Wisdom Johnson was an obvious choice over the gorilla of a guy who
was one of the Double W stackmen, and a rangy man called Swede who
more than likely was the other one. A possible advantage I could see to
the gorilla was what he might have inflicted on Good Help Hebner for
trying to drown him in hay, but that was wishful thinking. Over on the
conversation side of the room, Mike the Mower looked somewhat
more interesting than Bud Dolson. He was paying just enough attention to the pair of stories not to seem standoffish. His bunk was the
most neatly made, likely showing he had been in the army. All in all,
though, Mike the Mower showed more similarity to Bud than difference. Mower men were their own nationality.

From how they had been razzing one another about quantities of
hay moved, three of the five pitch players—Plain Mike and Long Mike
and a heavy-shouldered guy—were the horse buck-rakers. I was pretty
sure how they shaped up on the job. The heavy-shouldered guy, who
looked like a horseman, was the best buckraker. Long Mike was the
slowest. And Plain Mike did just enough more work than Long Mike to
look better.

A couple of younger guys, around Alec's age but who looked about
a fraction as bright, likely were the stacker team drivers in this outfit.

Then a slouchy elderly guy in a khaki shirt, and a one-eyed one; I suppose it doesn't say much for my own haying status that I was working down through this Double W crew, getting to the bunchrakers and whoever the scatter raker was, when the telephone jangled at the far end of the room.

The ring of that phone impressed me more than anything else about the Double W had yet. I mean, there was no stipulated reason why there couldn't be a telephone in a bunkhouse. But at the time it seemed a fairly swanky idea.

Cal Petrie stepped out of his room to answer it. When he had listened a bit and yupped an answer, he hung up and looked over toward where Alec and I were on the rim of the card game.

"Come on up for supper with us," the foreman directed at me. "Give the mud a little more chance to dry out, that way."

Cal declaimed this as if it was his own idea, but I would have bet any money as to who was on the other end of that phone line. Meredice Williamson.

Not long after, the supper bell sounded the end of the card game. The heavy-shouldered guy had the highest score, and yes, Plain Mike had the next. Now that they were the town-bound pair they received a number of imaginative suggestions of entertainment they might seek in there, as the crowd of us sloshed over to the kitchen door of the house. While everybody scraped mud off his feet and trooped on in I hung back with Alec, to see what the table lineup was going to be.

"Jick," he began, but didn't go on with whatever he had in mind. Instead, "See you after supper," he said, and stepped into the house, with me following.

The meal was in the summer room, a kind of windowed porch along the side of the house, long enough to hold a table for a crew this size. I of course did know that even at a place like the Double W, family and crew ate together. If the king of England had owned Noon Creek benchland instead of Scottish moors, probably even he would have had to go along with the ranch custom of everybody sitting down to refuel together. So I wasn't surprised to see Wendell Williamson sitting at the head of the table. Meredice sat at his right, and the old choreboy Dolph Kuhn next to her. At Wendell's left was a vacancy which I knew would be the cook's place, and next to that Cal Petrie seated himself. All five of them had chairs, then backless benches filled the rest of both sides of the table, which was about twenty feet long.

I felt vaguely let down. It was a setup about like any other ranch's, only bigger. I suppose I expected the Double W to have something special, like a throne for Wendell Williamson instead of a straightback kitchen chair.

Alec and Joe and Thurl, as ranch regulars, took their places next to the head-of-the-table elite, and the hay crew began filling in the rest of the table to the far end. In fact, *at* the far end there was a kitchen stool improvised as a seat, and Meredice Williamson's smile and nod told me it was my place.

This I had not dreamt of. Facing Wendell Williamson down the length of the Double W supper table. He now acknowledged me by saying: "Company. Nuhhuh. Quite a way to come for a free meal, young fellow."

Before thinking I said back: "Everybody says there's no cooking like the Double W's."

That caused a lot of facial expressions along the table, and I saw Alec peer at me rather firmly. But Wendell merely said "Nuhhuh" again—that "nuhhuh" of his was a habit I would think anybody with sufficient money would pay to have broken—and took a taste of his cup of coffee.

To me, Wendell Williamson always looked as if he'd been made by the sackful. Sacks of what, I won't go into. But just everything about him, girth, shoulders, arms, even his fingers, somehow seemed fuller than was natural; as if he always was slightly swollen. Wendell's head particularly stood out in this way, because his hair had retreated about halfway back and left all that face to loom out. And the other odd thing up there was, what remained of Wendell's hair was thick and curly and coal-black. A real stand of hair there at the rear of that big moonhead, like a sailor might wear a watchcap pushed way back.

The cook came in from the kitchen with a bowl of gray gravy and handed it to Wendell. She was a gaunt woman, sharp cheekbones, beak of a nose. Her physiognomy was a matter of interest and apprehension to me. The general theory is that a thin cook is a poor idea.

Plain Mike was sitting at my left, and at my right was a scowling guy who'd been one of the losers in the pitch game. As I have always liked to keep abreast of things culinary, I now asked Plain Mike in an undertone: "Is this the cook from Havre?"

"No, hell, she's long gone. This one's from up at Lethbridge."

What my mother would have commented danced to mind: "So Wendell Williamson has to import them from Canada now, does he? I'm Not Surprised."

I kept that to myself, but the scowler on my right had overheard my question and muttered: "She ain't Canadian though, kid. She's a Hungrarian."

"She is?" To me, the cook didn't look conspicuously foreign.

"You bet. She leaves you hungrier than when you came to the table."

I made a polite "heh-heh-heh" to that, and decided I'd better focus on the meal.

The first bowl to reach me contained a concoction I've never known the actual name of but in my own mind I always dub tomato smush. Canned tomatoes heated up, with little dices of bread dropped in. You sometimes get this as a side dish in cafes when the cook has run out of all other ideas about vegetables. Probably the Lunchery in Gros Ventre served it four days a week. In any case, tomato smush is a remarkable recipe, in that it manages to wreck both the tomatoes and the bread.

Out of chivalry I spooned a dab onto my plate. And next loaded up with mashed potatoes. Hard for any cook to do something drastic to mashed potatoes. The gravy, though, lacked salt and soul.

Then along came a platter of fried liver. This suited me fine, as I can dine on liver even when it is overcooked and tough, as this was. But I have observed in life that there is no middle ground about liver. When I passed the platter to the guy on my right, he mumbled something about "Lethbridge leather again," and his proved to be the majority view at the table.

There was some conversation at the head of the table, mostly between Wendell and the foreman Cal about the unfairness of being rained out at this stage of haying. In light of what followed, I see now that the rainstorm was largely responsible for Wendell's mood. Not that Wendell Williamson ever needed a specific excuse to be grumpy, so far as I could tell, but this suppertime he was smarting around his wallet. If the rain had started before noon and washed out the haying, he'd have had to pay all this hay crew for only half a day. But since the rain came in the afternoon he was laying out a full day's wages for not a full day's work. I tell you, there can be no one more morose than a rancher having to pay a hay crew to watch rain come down.

Anyway, the bleak gaze of Wendell Williamson eventually found its way down the length of the table to me. To my surprise, since I didn't think anybody's welfare mattered to him but his own, Wendell asked me: "How's your folks?"

"Real good."

"Nuhhuh." Wendell took a mouthful of coffee, casting a look at the cook as he set down his cup. Then his attention was back on me:

"I hear your mother gave quite a talk, the day of the Fourth."

Well, what the hell. If Wendell goddamn Williamson wanted to tap his toe to that tune, I was game to partner him. The McCaskills of this world maybe don't own mills and mines and all the land in sight, as some Williamson back in history had managed to grab, but we were born with tongues.

"She's sure had a lot of good comments on it," I declared with enthusiasm. Alec was stirring in his seat, trying to follow all this, but he'd missed Mom's speech by being busy with his roping horse. No, this field of engagement was mine alone. "People tell her it brought back the old days, when there were all those other ranches around here. The days of Ben English and those."

"Nuhhuh." What Wendell would have responded beyond that I will never know, for Meredice Williamson smiled down the table in my direction and then said to Wendell: "Ben English. What an interesting name, I have always thought." Mr. Double W didn't conspicuously seem to think so. But Meredice sallied right on. "Was he, do you think?"

"Was he what?" retorted Wendell.

"English. Do you suppose Mr. English was of English extraction?"

"Meredice, how in hell—" Wendell stopped himself and swigged some more sour coffee. "He might've been Swedish, for all I know."

"It would be more fitting if he were English," she persisted.

"Fitting? Fit what?"

"It would be more fitting to the memory of the man and his times." She smiled toward me again. "To those old days." Now she looked somewhere over my head, and Plain Mike's, and the heads of all of us at our end of the table, and she recited:

"Take of English earth as much
As either hand may rightly clutch.
In the taking of it breathe
Prayer for all who lie beneath."

Then Meredice Williamson dipped her fork and tried a dainty bite of tomato smush.

All around the table, though, every other fork had stopped. Even mine. I don't know, maybe Kipling out of the blue would have that effect on any group of diners, not just hay hands. But in any case, there was a mulling silence as Wendell contemplated Meredice and the rest of us contemplated the Double W boss and his wife. Not even a "nuh-huh" out of Wendell.

Finally Cal Petrie turned toward me and asked, "How's that power buckrake of Pete's working out?"

"Real good," I said. "Would somebody pass the liver, please?" And that pretty much was the story of supper at the great Double W.

Alec walked with me to the barn to help harness Blanche and Fisheye. He still wasn't saying much. Nor for that matter was I. I'd had about enough Double W and brooding brother, and was looking forward to getting to town.

Something, though—something kept at me as we started harnessing. It had been circling in the back of my mind ever since the hay crew clomped into the bunkhouse that afternoon. Alec came in with them. Cal Petrie and the riders who had been fixing fence made their appearance a few minutes after that.

I may be slow, but I usually get there. "Alec?" I asked across the horses' backs. "Alec, what have they got you doing?"

On the far side of Blanche, the sound of harnessing stopped for an instant. Then resumed.

"I said, what have they—"

"I heard you," came my brother's voice. "I'm helping out with the haying."

"I figured that. Which job?"

Silence.

"I said, which—"

"Raking."

You cannot know with what struggle I resisted popping out the next logical question: "Dump or scatter?" Yet I already knew the answer. I did indeed. The old slouchy guy in the khaki shirt and the one-eyed one, they were plodding dump rakers if I had ever seen the species. And that left just one hayfield job unaccounted for. My brother the calf-roping caballero was doing the exact same thing in life I was. Riding a scatter rake.

I did some more buckling and adjusting on Fisheye. Debating with myself. After all, Alec was my brother. If I couldn't talk straight from the shoulder with him, who could I?

"Alec, this maybe isn't any of my business, but—"

"Jick, when did that detail ever stop you? What's on your mind, besides your hat?"

"Are you sure you want to stay on here? More than this summer, I mean? This place doesn't seem to me anything so special."

"So you're lining up with Mom and Dad, are you." Alec didn't sound surprised, as if the rank of opinion against him was like one of the sides in choosing up to play softball. He also didn't sound as if any of us were going to alter his thinking. "What, is there a law that says somewhere that I've got to go to college?"

"No, it's just that you'd be good at it, and—"

"Everybody seems awful damn sure about that. Jick, I'm already doing something I'm good at, if I do say so my own self. I'm as good a hand with cattle as Thurl or Joe or anybody else they ever had here. So why doesn't that count for anything? Huh? Answer me that. Why can't I stay on here in the Two country and do a decent job of what I want to, instead of traipsing off to goddamn college?"

For the first time since he stepped into the bunkhouse and caught sight of me, Alec came alive. He stood now in front of Blanche, holding her haltered head. But looking squarely at me, as I stood in front of Fisheye. The tall and blue-eyed and flame-haired Alec of our English Creek years, the Alec who faced life as if it was always going to deal him aces.

I tried again, maybe to see if I was understanding my brother's words. "Christamighty, though, Alec. They haven't even got you doing what you want to do here. You hired on as a rider. Why're you going to let goddamn Wendell do whatever he wants with you?"

Alec shook his head. "You do sound like the folks would."

"I'm trying to sound like myself, is all. What is it about the damn life here that you think is so great?"

My brother held his look on me. Not angry, not even stubborn. And none of that abstracted glaze of earlier in the summer, as though only half seeing me. This was Alec to the full, the one who answered me now:

"That it's my own."

"Well, yeah, I guess it is" was all I could manage to respond. For it finally had struck me. This answer that had popped out of Alec as naturally as a multiplication sum, this was the future. So much did my brother want to be on his own in life, he would put up with a bad choice of his own making—endure whatever the Double W heaped on him, if it came to that—rather than give in to somebody else's better plan for him. Ever since the night of the supper argument our parents thought they were contending with Alec's cowboy phase or with Leona or the combination of the two. I now knew otherwise. What they were up against was the basic Alec.

"Jick," he was saying to me, "do me a favor about all this, okay?"

"What is it?"

"Don't say anything to the folks. About me not riding, just now." He somewhere found a grin, although a puny one. "About me following in your footsteps as a scatter raker. They have a low enough opinion of me recently." He held the grin so determinedly it began to hurt me. "So will you do that for me?"

"Yeah. I will."

"Okay." Alec let out a lot of breath. "We better get you hooked up and on your way, or you'll have to roll Grady out of bed to do the welding."

One more thing I had to find out, though. As I got up on the seat of the scatter rake, the reins to Blanche and Fisheye ready in my hand, I asked as casually as I could:

"How's Leona?"

The Alec of the Fourth of July would have cracked "Fine as frog hair" or "Dandy as a field of dandelions" or some such. This Alec just said: "She's okay." Then goodbyed me with: "See you around, Jicker."

"Ray? Does it ever seem like you can just look at a person and know something that's going to happen to them?"

"No. Why?"

"I don't mean look at them and know everything. Just something. Some one thing."

"Like what?"

"Well, like—" I gazed across the lawn at the Heaney house, high and pale white in the dark. Ed and Genevieve and Mary Ellen had gone to bed, but Ray and I won permission to sprawl on the grass under the giant cottonwood until Ray's bedroom cooled down a bit from the sultry day. The thunderstorm had missed Gros Ventre, only left it its wake of heat and charged air. "Promise not to laugh at this?"

"You couldn't pay me to."

"All right. Like when I was talking to Alec out there at the Double W after supper. I don't know, I just felt like I could tell. By the look of him."

"Tell about what?"

"That he and Leona aren't going to get married."

Ray weighed this. "You said you could tell something that's going to happen. That's something that's *not* going to happen."

"Same thing."

"Going to happen and not going to happen are the same thing? Jick, sometimes—"

"Never mind." I stretched an arm in back of my head, to rub a knuckle against the cottonwood. So wrinkled and gullied was its trunk that it was as if rivulets of rain had been running down it ever since the deluge floated Noah. I drifted in thought past the day's storm along Noon Creek, past the Double W and Alec, past the hayfields of the Ramsay place, past to where I had it tucked away to tell Ray:

"Saw Marcella a while back. From a distance."

"Yeah?" Ray responded, with what I believe is called elaborate indifference.

The next morning I returned with the rake to the Reese place, confirmed with Pete that the hay was too wet for us to try, retrieved Pony, and by noon was home at English Creek in time for Sunday dinner. During which I related to my parents my visit to the Double W.

My father, the fire season always on his mind now, grimaced and said: "Lightning. You'd think the world could operate without the damn stuff." Then he asked: "Did you see your brother?" When I said I had, he only nodded.

Given how much my mother had been on her high horse against the Double W all summer, I was set to tell her of the latest cook and the tomato smush and the weakling gravy. But before I could get started she fixed me with a thoughtful look and asked: "Is there anything new with Alec?"

"No," came flying out of me from some nest of brotherly allegiance I hadn't been aware of. Lord, what a wilderness is the thicket of family. "No, he's just riding around."

This is what I meant, earlier, about the chain of events of that last spate of haying. If Clayton Hebner had not grab-assed himself into a twisted ankle, I would not now have been the sole depository of the news of Alec's Double W situation.

The second Saturday in August, one exact month since we started haying, we sited the stacker in the last meadow along Noon Creek.

Before climbing on the power buckrake Pete cast a long gaze over the windrows, estimating. Then said what didn't surprise anybody who'd ever been in a haying crew before: "Let's see if we can get it all up in one, instead of moving the stacker another damn time."

"If you can get it up here," vowed Wisdom, "we'll find someplace to put it."

So that final haystack began to climb. Bud Dolson, now that mowing was over, was on top helping Wisdom with the stacking. Perry too was done with his part of haying, no more windrows to be made. He tied his team in some shade by the creek and in his creaky way was dabbing around the stack with a pitchfork, carrying scraps of hay to the stacker fork. Clayton, I am happy to report, had mended enough to drive the stacker team again and I had regained my scatter rake.

Of course, it was too much hay for one stack. But on a last one, that never stops a hay crew. I raked and re-raked behind Pete's swoops with his buckrake. The stack towered. The final loads wouldn't come off the stacker fork by themselves, Wisdom and Bud pulled up the hay pitchforkful by pitchforkful to the round summit of the stack.

At last every stem of hay was in that stack.

"How the hell do we get off this thing?" called down Bud from the island in the air, only half joking.

"Along about January I'll feed from this stack," Pete sent back up to him. "I'll bring out a ladder and get you then."

In actuality, the descent of Wisdom and Bud was provided by Clayton running the stacker fork up to them, so they could grab hold of the fork teeth while they climbed down onto the frame.

Marie had driven up from the main ranch to see this topping-off of the summer's haying, and brought with her cold tea and fresh-baked oatmeal cookies. We stood and looked and sipped and chewed, a crew about to scatter. Perry to head back into Gros Ventre and a winter of leather work at the saddle shop. Bud tonight onto a bus to Anaconda and his smelter job. Wisdom proclaimed he was heading straight for the redwood logging country down in California, and Pete and Bud had worked on him until they got Wisdom to agree that he would ride the bus with Bud as far as Great Falls, at least getting him and his wages past the Medicine Lodge saloon. Clayton, over the English Creek–Noon Creek divide to the North Fork and Hebner life again. Pete and Marie, to fencing the haystacks and then shipping the lambs and then trailing the Reese sheep home from the reservation, and all too soon feeding out the hay we had put up. Me, to again become a daytime dweller at English Creek instead of a nightly visitor.

"Either this weather is Out Of Control," declared my mother, "or I'm Getting Old."

It can be guessed which of those she thought was the case. This summer did not seem to be aware that with haying done, it was supposed to be thinking about departure. The wickedest weather yet settled in, a real siege of swelter. The first three days I was home at English Creek after finishing at Pete's the temperature hit the nineties and the rest of the next couple of weeks wasn't a whole lot better. Too hot. Putting up with heat while you drive a scatter rake or work some other job is one thing. But having the temperature try to toast you while you're just hanging around and existing, that somehow seems a personal insult.

Nor, for all her lament about August's runaway warmth, was my mother helping the situation any. The contrary. She was canning. And canning and canning. It started each June with rhubarb, and then would come a spurt of cooking homemade sausage and layering it in crocks with the fat over it, and next would be the first of the garden vegetables, peas, and after them beets to pickle, and then the various pickings of beans, all the while interspersed with making berry jams, and at last in late August the arrival to Helwig's merc in Gros Ventre of the flat boxes of canning peaches and pears. We ate all winter on what my mother put up, but the price of it was that during a lot of the hottest days of summer the kitchen range also was blazing away. So whenever canning was the agenda I steered clear of the house as much as I could. It was that or melt.

In the ranger station as well, life sometimes got too warm for comfort, although not just because of the temperature reading.

"How's it look?" my father asked his dispatcher Chet Barnouw first thing each morning. This time of year, this sizzling August, Chet's reports were never good. "Extreme danger" was the fire rating on the Two Medicine National Forest now, day after day. There already were fires, big ones, on forests west of the Continental Divide; the Bad Rock Canyon fire in the Flathead National Forest was just across the mountains from us.

Poor Chet. His reward for reporting all this was to have my father say, "Is that the best news you can come up with?" My father put it lightly, or tried to, but both Chet and the assistant ranger Paul Eliason knew it was the start of another touchy day. Chet and Paul were young and in their first summer on the Two, and I know my father suffered inwardly about their lack of local knowledge. Except for being wet behind the ears, they weren't a bad pair. But in a fire summer like this, that was a big except. As dispatcher Chet was in charge of the telephone setup that linked the lookout towers and the guard cabins to the ranger station, and he kept in touch with headquarters in Great Falls by the regular phone system. His main site of operation, thus, was the switchboard behind a partition at one side of my father's office. I think my mother was the one who gave that cubbyhole the name of "the belfry," from all the phone signals that chimed in there. The belfry took some getting used to, for anybody, but Chet was an unhurryable type best fitted for the job of dispatcher.

Of the two, Paul Eliason gave my father more grief than Chet did. Paul did a lot of moping. You'd have thought he was born looking glum about it. Actually the case was that the previous winter, just before he was transferred to the English Creek district as my father's assistant ranger, Paul and his wife had gotten a divorce and she'd gone home to her mother in Seattle. According to what my father heard from Paul it was one of those things. She tried for a year to put up with being a Forest Service wife, but Paul at the time was bossing CCC crews who were building trail on the Olympic National Forest out in the state of Washington, and the living quarters for the Eliasons was a backcountry one-room cabin which featured pack rats and a cookstove as temperamental as it was ancient. Perfect circumstances to make an assistant ranger–city wife marriage go flooey if it ever was going to.

"He's starting to heal up," my father assessed Paul at this point of the summer. "Lord knows, I've tried to keep him busy enough he doesn't have time to feel sorry for himself."

If I rationed myself and didn't get in the way of business, my father didn't mind that I hung around in the ranger station. But there was a limit on how much I wanted to do that, too. Whenever something was happening—the lookouts up there along the skyline of the Two calling in their reports to Chet in the belfry, my father tracing his finger over and over the map showing the pocket fires his smokechasers already had dealt with—the station was a lively enough place to be. But in between those times, rangering was not much of a spectator sport.

Each day is a room of time, it is said. In that long hot remainder of August I knew nothing to do but go from one span of sun to the next with as little of rubbing against my parents as possible. My summer's work was done, they were at the zenith of theirs.

Consequently a good deal of my leisure or at least time-killing was spent along the creek. I called it fishing, although it didn't really amount to that. Fish are not dumb; they don't exert themselves to swallow a hook during the hot part of the day. So until the trout showed any signs of biting I would shade up under a cottonwood, pull an old magazine from my hip pocket, and read.

A couple of times each week I would saddle Pony and ride up to Breed Butte to check on Walter Kyle's place, then fish the North Fork beaver dams on my way home. Walter's place was a brief hermitage for me on those visits. The way it worked was this. We and Walter were in the habit of swapping magazines, and after I had chosen several to take from the pile on his shelf, I would sit at his kitchen table and think matters over for a while before heading down to the beaver dams.

That low old ranch house of Walter Kyle's was as private a place as could be asked for. To sit there at the table looking out the window to the south, down the slope of Breed Butte to the willow thickets of the North Fork and beyond to Grizzly Reef's crooked cliffs and the line of peaks into the Teton River country, was to see the earth empty of people. Just out of sight down the North Fork was our ranger station and only over the brow of Breed Butte the other direction was the old McCaskill homestead, now Hebnerized. But all else of this long North Fork coulee was vacancy. Not wilderness, of course. Scotch Heaven left traces of itself, homestead houses still standing or at least not quite fallen down, fencelines whose prime use now was for hawks to perch on. But any other breathing soul than me, no. The sense of emptiness all around made me ponder the isolation those early people, my father's parents among them, landed themselves into here. Even when the car arrived into this corner of the Two Medicine country, mud and rutted roads made going anywhere no easy task. To say nothing of what winter could do. Some years the snow here drifted up and up until it covered the fenceposts and left you guessing its depth beyond that. No, those homesteaders of Scotch Heaven did not know what they were getting into. But once in, how many cherished this land as their own, whatever its conditions? It is one of those matters hard to balance out. Distance and isolation create a freedom of sorts. The space to move in according to your own whims and bents. Yet it was exactly this freedom, this fact that a person was a speck on the earth sea, that must have been too much for some of the settlers. From my father's stories and Toussaint Rennie's, I knew of Scotch Heaveners who retreated into the dimness of their homestead cabins, and the worse darkness of their own minds. Others who simply got out, walked away from the years of homestead effort. Still others who carried it with them into successful ranching. Then there were the least lucky who took their dilemma, a freedom of space and a toll of mind and muscle, to the grave with them.

It was Alec who had me thinking along these heavy lines. Alec and his insistence on an independent life. Was it worth the toll he was paying? I could not give an absolute affidavit either way. What I did know for sure was that Alec's situation now had me in my own kind of bind. For if my parents could learn what a fizzle Alec's Double W job was, it might give them fresh determination to persuade him out of it. At very least, it might soften the frozen mood, put them and him on speaking terms again. But I had told Alec I'd say nothing to them about his situation. And his asking of that was the one true brother-to-brother moment between us since he left English Creek.

That's next thing to hopeless, to spend your time wishing you weren't in the fix you are. And so I fished like an apostle, and read and read, and hung around the ranger station betweentimes, and eventually even came up with something else I wanted to do with myself. The magazines must have seeded the notion in me. In any case it was during those hot drifting last of August days that I proposed to my mother that I paper my porch bedroom.

She still was canning. Pole beans by now, I think. She tucked a wisp of hair back from where it had stuck to her damp forehead and informed me: "Wallpaper costs money." I never did understand why parents seem to think this is such startling news, that something a kid wants costs money. Based on my own experience as a youngster, the real news would have been if the object of desire was for free.

But this once, I was primed for that response from my mother "I'll use magazine pages," I suggested. "Out of those old *Post*s and *Collier's*. There's a ton of pictures in them, Mom."

That I had thought the matter through to this extent told her this meant something to me. She quit canning and faced me. "Even so, it would mean buying the paste. But I suppose—"

I still had my ducks in a row. "No, it won't. The Heaneys have got some left over. I heard Genevieve say." Ray's mother had climaxed her spring cleaning that year by redoing the Heaney front hall.

"All right," my mother surrendered. "It's too hot to argue. The next time anybody makes a trip to town, we'll pick up your paste."

I can be fastidious when it's worth being so. The magazine accumulation began to get a real going-over from me for illustrations worthy of gracing my sleep parlor.

I'd much like to have had Western scenes, but do you know, I could not find any that were worth a damn. A story called "Bitter Creek" showed a guy riding with a rifle across the pommel of his saddle and some pack horses behind him. The pack horses were all over the scenery instead of strung together by rope, and there was every chance that the guy would blast his leg off by not carrying that rifle in a scabbard. So much for Bitter Creek. Then there was a story which showed a couple on horseback, which drew me because the pair made me think of Alec and Leona. It turned out, though, that the setting was a dude ranch, and the line under the illustration read: "One Dude Ranch is a Good Deal Like Another. You Ride Horseback and You Overeat and You Lie in the Sun and You Fish and You Play Poker and You Have Picnics." All of which may be true enough, but I didn't think it interesting enough to deserve wall space.

No, the first piece of art I really liked was a color illustration in *Collier's* of a tramp freighter at anchor. And then I found a *Post* piece showing a guy leaning on the railing of another merchant vessel and looking across the water to a beautiful sailing ship. "As the 'Inchcliffe Castle' Crawled Along the Coast of Spain, Through the Strait of Gibraltar, the Engineer Was Prey to a Profound Preoccupation." This was more like it. A nautical decor, just what the room could use. I went ahead and snipped out whatever sea story illustrations I could find in the stack of magazines. I could see that there wasn't going to be enough of a fleet to cover the whole wall, but I came across a Mr. Moto detective series that went on practically forever and so I filled in along the top of the wall with action scenes from that, as a kind of contrasting border.

When I was well launched into my paperhanging, Mr. Moto and various villains up top there and the sea theme beginning to fill in under, I called in my mother to see my progress.

"It does change the look of the place," she granted.

The evening of the twenty-fifth of August, a Friday, an electrical storm struck across western Montana and then moved to our side of the Continental Divide. It threw firebolts beyond number. At Great Falls, radio station KFBB was knocked off the air and power lines blew out. I would like to be able to say that I awoke in the big storm, so keen a weather wizard that I sat up in bed sniffing the ozone or harking to the first distant avalanche of thunder. The fact is, I snoozed through that electrical night like Sleeping Beauty.

The next morning, more than two hundred new lightning fires were reported in the national forests of Region One.

Six were my father's. One near the head of the South Fork of English Creek. One at the base of Billygoat Peak. Two in the old Phantom Woman burn, probably snags alight. One in northwest behind Jericho Reef. And one up the North Fork at Flume Gulch.

The McCaskill household was in gear before daybreak.

"Fire school never told us they come half a dozen at a time," muttered my father and went out to establish himself in the ranger station.

I stoked away the rest of my breakfast and got up to follow him. My mother half advised and half instructed, "Don't wear out your welcome." But she knew as well as anything that it would take logchains and padlocks to keep me out of the station with all this going on.

As soon as I stepped in I saw that Chet and Paul looked braced. As if they were sinners and this was the morning after, when they had to stand accountable to a tall red-haired Scotch preacher.

My father on the other hand was less snorty than he'd been in weeks. Waiting for the bad to happen was always harder for him than trying to deal with it once it did.

"All right," was all my father said to the pair of them, "let's get the guys to chasing these smokes." Chet started his switchboard work and the log of who was sent where at what time, Paul began assessing where he ought to pitch in in person.

The day was not August's hottest, but hot enough. It was vital that all six plumes of smoke be gotten to as quickly as possible, before midday heat encouraged these smudges to become genuine fires. The job of smokechaser always seemed to me a hellish one, shuffling along a mountainside with a big pack on your back and then, when you finally sighted or sniffed out the pocket of fire, using a shovel or a pulaski to smother it to death. All the while, dry trees standing around waiting to catch any embers and go off like Roman candles.

No, where firefighting of any sort was concerned I considered myself strictly a distant witness. Alec had done some, a couple of Augusts ago on the fireline against the Biscuit Creek blaze down on Murray Tomlin's ranger district at the south end of the Two, and as with everything else he showed a knack for it. But I did not take after my brother in that flame-eating regard.

It was mostly good news I was able to repeat to my mother when I visited the house for gingersnaps just past mid-morning. In those years the official Forest Service notion for fighting forest fires was what was called the ten A.M. policy: gain control of a fire by ten the morning after it's reported; if it's still out of hand by then, aim for ten the next morning, and so on. Chet had reported to headquarters in Great Falls, "We've got ten A.M. control on four of ours"—the South Fork, Billygoat, and the two Phantom Woman situations. All four were snag strikes, lightning gashing into a dead tree trunk and leaving it slowly burning, and the nearest fire guard had been able to put out the South Fork smolder, the lookout man and the smokechaser stationed on Billygoat Peak combined to whip theirs, while the Phantom Woman pair of smokes were close enough together that the smokechaser who'd been dispatched up there managed to handle both. So those four now were history. Jericho Reef and Flume Gulch were actual blazes; small ones, but still alive and trying. A fire guard named Andy Ames and a smokechaser named Emil Kratka were on the Flume Gulch blaze. Both were new to that area of the Two, but my father thought well of them. "They'll stomp it if anybody can." Jericho Reef, so much farther back in the mountains, seemed more like trouble. Nobody wanted a backcountry fire getting under way in weather like this. Paul had nibbled on the inside of his lips for a while, then suggested that he collect the CCC crew that was repairing trail on the North Fork and go on up to the Jericho Reef situation. My father told him that sounded right, and Paul charged off up there.

"Fire season in the Forest Service," said my mother. "There is nothing like it, except maybe St. Vitus' dance."

Ours was the only comparatively good news in the Two Medicine National Forest that Saturday. At Blacktail Gulch down by Sun River, Murray Tomlin was still scooting his smokechasers here and there to tackle a dozen snag strikes. The worst of the electrical storm must have dragged through Murray's district on its way to Great Falls. And on his Indian Head district south of us Cliff Bowen had a fire away to hell and gone up in the mountains, under the Chinese Wall. He'd had to ask headquarters for a bunch of EFFs, which were emergency firefighters the Forest Service scraped together and signed up in a real pinch, from the bars and flophouses of Clore Street in Helena and Trent Avenue in Spokane and First Avenue South in Great Falls and similar fragrant neighborhoods where casual labor hung out. It was going to take Cliff most of the day just to hike his EFFs up to his fire. "Gives me a nosebleed to think about fighting one up there," my father commiserated.

"Sunday, the day of rest" was the mutter from my father as he headed to the ranger station the next morning.

Had he known, he would have uttered something stronger. It turned out to be a snake of a day. By the middle of the morning, Chet was telling Great Falls about ten A.M. control on one of our two blazes—but not the one he and my father expected. Jericho Reef was whipped; Paul and his CCs found only a quarter-acre ground fire there and promptly managed to mop it up. "Paul should have taken marshmallows," my father was moved to joke to Chet. Flume Gulch, though, had grown into something full-fledged. All day Saturday, Kratka and Ames had worked themselves blue against the patch of flame, and by nightfall they thought they had it contained. But during the night a remnant of flame crawled along an area of rock coated with pine needles. Sunday morning it surfaced, touched off a tree opposite from where Kratka and Ames were keeping an eye on matters, and the fire then took off down a slant of the gulch into a thick stand of timber. In a hurry my father yanked Paul and his CCs back from Jericho Reef to Flume Gulch, and I was killing time in the ranger station, late that morning, when Chet passed along the report Paul was phoning in from the guard cabin nearest Flume Gulch.

Thus I was on hand for those words of Paul's that became fabled in our family.

"Mac," Chet recited them, "Paul says the fire doesn't look that bad. It just keeps burning, is all."

"Is that a fact," said my father carefully, too carefully. Then it all came. "Kindly tell Mr. goddamn Eliason from me that it's his goddamn job to see to it that the goddamn fire DOESN'T keep burning, and that I—no, never mind."

My father got back his breath, and most of his temper. "Just tell Paul to keep at it, keep trying to pinch it off against a rock formation. Keep it corraled."

Monday made Sunday look good. Paul and his CC crew still could not find the handle on the Flume Gulch fire. They would get a fireline almost built, then a blazing fir tree would crash over and come sledding down the gulch, igniting the next jungle of brush and windfall and tinder-dry timber. Or sparks would shoot up from the slope, find enough air current to waft to the other steep side of the gulch, and set off a spot fire there. Ten A.M. came and went, with Paul's report substantially the same as his ones from the day before: not that much fire, but no sight of control.

My father prowled the ranger station until he about had the floor worn out. When he said something unpolite to Chet for the third time and started casting around for a fresh target, I cleared out of there.

The day was another scorcher. I went to the spring house for some cold milk, then in to the kitchen for a doughnut to accompany the milk down. And here my father was again, being poured a cup of coffee by my mother. As if he needed any more prowl fuel today.

My father mimicked Paul's voice: " 'Mac, the fire doesn't look that bad. It just keeps burning, is all.' Jesus. How am I supposed to get through a fire season with help like that, I ask you."

"The same way you do every summer," suggested my mother.

"I don't have a pair of green peas as assistant and dispatcher, every summer."

"No, only about every other summer. As soon as you get them trained, Sipe or the Major moves them on and hands you the next fresh ones."

"Yeah, well. At least these two aren't as green as they were a month ago. For whatever that's worth." He was drinking that coffee as if it was going to get away from him. It seemed to be priming him to think out loud. "I don't like it that the fire outjumped Kratka and Ames. They're a real pair of smokehounds, those guys. It takes something nasty to be too much for them. And I don't like it that Paul's CCs haven't got matters in hand up there yet either." My father looked at my mother as if she had the answer to what he was saying. "I don't like any of what I'm hearing from Flume Gulch."

"I gathered that," she said. "Do you want me to put you up a lunch?"

"I haven't said yet I'm going up there."

"You're giving a good imitation of it."

"Am I." He carried his empty coffee cup to the sink and put it in the dishpan. "Well, Lisabeth McCaskill, you are famous the world over for your lunches. I'd be crazy to pass one up, wouldn't I."

"All right then." But before starting to make his sandwiches, my mother turned to him one more time. "Mac, are you sure Paul can't handle this?" Which meant: are you sure you shouldn't *let* Paul handle this fire?

"Bet, there's nothing I'd like more. But I don't get the feeling it's being handled. Paul's been lucky on his other fires this summer, they both turned out to be weinie roasts. But this one isn't giving up." He prowled over to the window where Roman Reef and Rooster Mountain and Phantom Woman peak could be seen. "No, I'd better go up there and have a look."

I didn't even bother to ask to go along. A counting trip or something else routine, that was one thing. But the Forest Service didn't want anybody out of the ordinary around a fire. Particularly if his sum of life hadn't yet quite made it to fifteen years.

"Mom? I was wondering—" Supper was in the two of us. She had washed the dishes and I had dried. I could just as well have abandoned the heat of the house for an evening of fishing. But I had to rid myself of at least part of what had been on my mind the past weeks. "I was wondering—well, about Leona."

Here was an attention-getter. My mother lofted a look and held it on me. "And what is it you've been wondering about Leona?"

"Her and Alec, I mean."

"All right. What about them?"

I decided to go for broke. "I don't think they're going to get married. What do you think?"

"I think I have a son in this kitchen who's hard to keep up with. Why are Alec and Leona tonight's topic?"

"It's not just tonight's," I defended. "This whole summer has been different. Ever since the pair of them walked out of here, that suppertime."

"I can't argue with you on that. But where do you get the idea the marriage is off?"

I thought about how to put it. "You remember that story Dode tells about Dad? About the first time you and Dad started, uh, going together? Dad was riding over to call on you, and Dode met up with him on the road and saw Dad's clean shirt and shined boots and the big grin on him, and instead of 'Hello' Dode just asked him, 'Who is she?'"

"Yes," she said firmly. "I know that story."

"Well, Alec doesn't look that way. He did earlier in the summer. But when I saw him at the Double W that time, he looked like somebody had knocked the blossom off him. Like Leona had."

My mother was unduly slow in responding. I had been so busy deciding how much I could say, without going against my promise to Alec not to tell what a botch his Double W job was, that I hadn't realized she too was doing some deciding. Eventually her thoughts came aloud:

"You may have it right. About Leona. We're waiting to see."

She saw that I damn well wanted a definition of "we."

"Leona's parents and I. I saw Thelma Tracy the last time I was in town. She said Leona's mind still isn't made up, which way to choose."

"Choose?" I took umbrage on Alec's behalf. "What, has she been seeing some other guy, too?"

"No. To choose between marrying Alec and going on with her last year of high school is what she's deciding. Thelma thinks school is gaining fast." She reminded me, as if I needed any: "It starts in a little over a week."

"Then what—what do you think will happen after that? With Alec, I mean. Alec and you and Dad."

"We'll just have to see in September. Your father still has his mad on about Alec throwing away college. For that matter, I'm not over mine either. To think, a mind like Alec's and all he wants to do Is Prance Around Like—" She caught herself. Then got back to her tone of thinking out loud: "And knowing Alec, I imagine he's still just as huffy as we are."

"Maybe"—I had some more careful deciding than ever, how to say this so as not to bring about something which would rile Alec even more—"maybe if you and Dad sort of stopped by to see Alec. Just dropped by the Double W, sort of."

"I don't see how it would help. Not until Leona and the college question are out of the way. Another family free-for-all won't improve matters. Your father and your brother. They'll have to get their minds off their argument, before anything can be done. So."

The "so" which meant, we have now put a lid on this topic. But she added, as if it would reassure me:

"We wait and see."

Say this for the Forest Service life, it enlarges your days. Not long after my mother and I were done with breakfast the next morning, the telephone rang. Everybody in a ranger's family knows the rings of all the lookout sites and guard cabins on the line. The signal was from the fire guard Ames's cabin, the one nearest to Flume Gulch.

"Rubber that, will you, Jick," called my mother from whatever chore she was on elsewhere in the house. "Please."

I went to the wall phone and put the receiver to my ear. Rubbering, which is to say listening in, was our way of keeping track of matters without perpetually traipsing back and forth between the house and the ranger station.

"Mac says to tell Great Falls there's no chance of controlling the fire by ten today," Paul was reporting to Chet. "If you want his exact words, he says there isn't a diddling deacon's prayer of whipping it today." Even on the phone Paul's voice sounded pouty. My bet was, when my father arrived and took over as fire boss, Paul had reacted like a kicked pup.

"Approximate words will do, given the mood Mac's been in," Chet told Paul. "Anything else new, up there?"

"No" from Paul and his click of hanging up.

I relayed this, in edited form, to my mother. She didn't say anything. But with her, silence often conveyed enough.

When the same phone ring happened in late morning, I called out, "I'll rubber."

This voice was my father himself.

"It is an ornery sonofabitch," he was informing Chet. "Every time a person looks at it, it looks a little bigger. We better hit it hard. Get hold of Isidor and have him bring in a camp setup. And tell Great Falls we need fifty EFFs and a timekeeper for them."

"Say again on that EFF request, Mac," queried Chet. "Fifteen or fifty? One-five or five-oh?"

"Five-oh, Chet."

Pause.

Chet was swallowing on the figure. With crews of emergency fire-fighters already on the Chinese Wall fire and the fires down in the Lewis and Clark forest, Two headquarters in Great Falls was going to greet this request for fifty more like the miser meeting the tax man.

"Okay, Mac," Chet mustered. "I'll ask for them. What else can I get you?" Chet could not have realized it, but this was his introduction to the Golden Rule of a veteran ranger such as my father when confronted with a chancy fire: always ask for more help than you think you'll need.

Or as my father said he'd once heard it from a ranger of the generation before him: "While you're getting, get plenty."

"Grub," my father was going on. "Get double lunches in here for us today." Double lunches were pretty much what they sound like: about twice the quantity of sandwiches and canned fruit and so on that a working man could ordinarily consume. Firefighters needed legendary amounts of food. "And get us a real cook for the camp by tonight. The CC guy we been using could burn water. I'm going to get some use out of him by putting him on the fireline."

"Okay," said Chet again. "The double lunches I'll get out of Gros Ventre, and I'll start working on Great Falls for the fifty men and a timekeeper and a cook. Anything else?"

"Not for now," allowed my father. Then: "Jick. You there?"

I jumped, but managed: "Yeah?"

"I figured you were. How's your fishing career? Owe me a milkshake yet?"

"No, I didn't go yesterday."

"All right. I was just checking." A moment, then: "Is your mother around there?"

"She's out in the root cellar, putting away canning."

"Is she. Okay, then."

"Anything you want me to tell her?"

"Uh huh, for all the good it'll do. Tell her not to worry."

"I will if I want to," she responded to that. "Any time your father asks Great Falls for help, it's worth worrying about." She set off toward the ranger station. "At least I can go into town for the double lunches. That'll keep Chet free here. You can ride in with me."

While she was gone to apprise Chet, the Flume Creek fire and my father filled my mind. Trying to imagine what the scene must be. That campsite where my father and I, and Alec in the other summers, caught our fill of brookies and then lazed around the campfire; flames now multiplied by maybe a million. In the back of all our minds, my father's and my mother's and mine, we had known that unless the weather let up it would be a miracle not to have a fire somewhere on the Two. Montana weather, and a miracle. Neither one is anything to rest your hopes on. But why, out of all the English Creek district of the Two

Medicine National Forest, did the fire have to be there, in that extreme and beautiful country of Flume Gulch?

I heard the pickup door open and my mother call: "Jick! Let's go."

I opened the screen door and stepped from the kitchen. Then called back: "No, I think I'll just stay here."

From behind the steering wheel she sent me a look of surprise. "Do you feel all right?" That I would turn down a trip to town must be a malady of some sort, she figured.

"Yeah. But I just want to stay, and do some more papering on my room."

She hesitated. Dinnertime was not far off, her cookly conscience now was siding with her motherly one. "I thought we'd grab a bite at the Lunchery. If you stay, you'll have to fix your own."

"Yeah, well, I can manage to do that."

As I was counting on, she didn't have time to debate with me. "All right then. I'll be back as soon as I can." And the pickup was gone.

I made myself a headcheese sandwich, then had a couple of cinnamon rolls and cold milk. All the while, my mind on what I had decided, my eyes on the clock atop the sideboard.

Each day a room of time. Now each minute as slow as the finding and pasting of another page onto my bedroom wall in there.

I waited out the clock because I had to. It at last came up on the noon hour. The time to do it.

Out the kitchen door I went, sprinting to the ranger station. Just before coming around to its front, I geared myself down to what I hoped was my usual walking pace.

Chet was tipped back in a chair in the shade of the porch while he ate his lunch, as I'd counted on. Dispatchers are somewhat like gophers: they're holed up indoors so much they pop out into the air at any least chance.

"Hey there, Jick," I was greeted by Chet as I sauntered onto the porch. "What's up? It's too blasted hot to move if you don't have to."

"I came to see if it's okay if I use the town line. I forgot to tell Mom something and I want to leave word for her at the Lunchery."

"Sure thing. Nothing's going on right now, you can help yourself. You should've just rung me, Jick. I'd have gone in and switched it for you." Uh huh, and more than likely have stayed on and listened, as was a dispatcher's habit. Rubbering was something that worked both directions.

"No, that's okay, I didn't want to bother you. I won't need the line long." In I went to the switchboard and moved the toggle switch that connected the ranger station to the community telephone line.

"When you're done," Chet said as I headed off the porch past him, "just ding the dealybob and I'll switch things back to our line."

"Right. Thanks, Chet. Like I say, I won't be long." I moseyed around the corner of the station out of Chet's sight, then sped like hell back to our house.

Facing the phone, I sucked in all the breath I could, to crowd out my puffing and my nervousness about all that was riding on this idea of mine. Then I lifted the receiver, rang central in Gros Ventre, and asked to be put through to the Double W.

Onto the line came a woman's voice: "Hello?"

Perfect again: Meredice Williamson. I hadn't been sure what I was going to resort to if Wendell answered.

"'Lo, Mrs. Williamson. Can I—may I speak to Alec McCaskill in the bunkhouse, please? That is, would you ask him to go to the phone out at the bunkhouse? This is, uh, personal."

Down the line came the silence of Meredice Williamson pondering her way through the etiquette of yet another Two country situation. Maybe I would have been better off with Wendell's straightforward bluster. At last she queried: "Who is this, please?"

"This is Alec's brother Jick. I put Blanche and Fisheye in your barn that time, remember? And I'm sorry to call but I just really need to talk to—"

"Oh yes. Jack. I remember you well. But you see, Alec and the other men are at lunch—"

"Yeah, I figured that, that's why I'm calling right now."

"Could I have him return your call afterward?"

"No, that'd be too late. I need to talk to him now, it's just that it's, like I said, private. Family. A family situation has come up. Arisen."

"I see. I do hope it's nothing serious?"

"It could get that way if I don't talk to Alec. Mrs. Williamson, look, I can't explain all this. But I've got to talk to Alec, while he's alone. Without the whole damn—without everybody listening in."

"I see. Yes. I think I see. Will you hold on, Jack?" As if from a great distance, I heard her say: "Alec, you're wanted on the phone. I wonder if it might be more convenient for you to answer it in the bunkhouse?"

Now a dead stretch of time. But my mind was going like a million.

All of the summer to this minute was crowded into me. From that sup-pertime when Alec stomped out with Leona in tow, through all the days of my brother going his stubborn way and my parents going their stubborn one, through my times of wondering how this had come to be, how we McCaskills had so tangled our family situation, to now, when I saw just how to unknot it all. At last it was coming up right, the answer was about to dance within this telephone line.

Finally a voice from across the miles. "Jick? Is that you? What in the holy hell—"

"Alec, listen, I know this is kind of out of the ordinary."

"You're right about that."

"But just let me tell you all this, okay? There's a fire. Dad's gone up to it, at Flume Gulch—"

"The hell. None of that country's ever burned before."

"Well, it is now. And that's why I got hold of you, see. Alec, Dad's only help up there is Paul Eliason, and Paul doesn't know zero about that part of the Two."

A void at the Double W bunkhouse. The receiver offered only the sounds within my own ear, the way a seashell does. At last Alec's voice, stronger than before, demanding: "Jick, did Dad ask you to call me? If so, why in all hell couldn't he do it him—"

"No, he didn't ask me. He's up on the fire, I just told you."

"Then who—is this Mom's idea?"

"Alec, it's nobody's damn idea. I mean, it's none of theirs, you can call it mine if it's anybody's. All that's involved, Dad needs somebody up there who knows that Flume Gulch country. Somebody to help him line out the fire crew."

"That's all, huh. And you figure it ought to be me."

I wanted to shout, Why the hell else would I be on this telephone line with you? But instead carefully stayed to: "Yeah, I do. Dad needs your help." And kept unsaid too: this family needs its logjam of quar-rel broken. Needs you and our father on speaking terms again. Needs this summer of separation to be over.

More of the seashell sound, the void. Then:

"Jick, no. I can't."

"Can't? Why not? Even goddamn Wendell Williamson'd let you off to fight a forest fire."

"I'm not going to ask him."

"You mean you won't ask him."

"It comes to the same. Jick, I just—"

"But why? Why won't you do this?"

"Because I can't just drop my life and come trotting home. Dad's got the whole damn Forest Service for help."

"But—then you won't do it for him."

"Jick, listen. No, I can't or won't, however you want to say it. But it's not because of Dad, it's not to get back at him or anything. It's—it's all complicated. But I got to go on with what I'm doing. I can't—" All these years later, I realize that here he very nearly said: "I can't give in." But the way Alec actually finished that sentence was: "I can't go galloping home any time there's a speck of trouble. If somebody was sick or hurt, it'd be different. But—"

"Then don't do it for Dad," I broke in on him, and I may have built up to a shout for this: "Do it because the goddamn country's burning up!"

"Jick, the fire is Dad's job, it's the Forest Service's job, it's the job of the whole crew they'll bring in there to Flume Gulch. It is not mine."

"But, Alec, you can't just—" Here I ran out of argument. The dead space on the telephone line was from my direction now.

"Jick," Alec's voice finally came, "I guess we're not getting anywhere with this."

"I guess we're not."

"Things will turn out," said my brother. "See you, Jick." And the phone connection ended.

It was too much for me. I stood there gulping back tears.

The house was empty, yet they were everywhere around me. The feel of them, I mean; the accumulation, the remembering, of how life had been when the other three of my family *were* three, instead of two against one. Or one against two, as it looked now. Alec. My mother. My father.

People. A pain you can't do without.

Eventually I remembered to ding the phone, signaling Chet that I was done with the town line. Done in, was more like it.

For the sake of something, anything, to do, I wandered to my bedroom and listlessly thumbed through magazines for any more sea scenes to put on the wall. Prey to a Profound Preoccupation, that was me.

—

At last I heard the pickup arrive. Nothing else I did seemed to be any use in the world, maybe I at least had better see if my mother needed any help with the fire lunches she was bringing.

I stepped out the kitchen door to find that help already was on hand, beside her at the tailgate of the pickup.

A brown Stetson nodded to me, and under it Stanley Meixell said: "Hullo again, Jick."

Civility was nowhere among all that crowded my brain just then. I simply blurted:

"Are you going up to the fire?"

"Thought I would, yeah. A man's got to do something to ward off frostbite."

My mother was giving Stanley her look that could peel a rock. But in an appraising way. I suppose she was having second thoughts about what she had set in motion here, by fetching Stanley from the Busby's ranch, and then third thoughts that any possible help for my father was better than no help, then fourth thoughts about Stanley's capacity to *be* any help, and on and on.

"Do you want some coffee?" she suggested to Stanley.

"I better not take time, Bet. I can get by without it." The fact was, it would take more than coffee to make a difference on him. "Who's this dispatcher we got to deal with?"

My mother told him about Chet, Stanley nodded, and she and he headed for the ranger station. Me right behind them.

"Getting those lunches up there'd be a real help, all right;" Chet agreed when my mother presented Stanley. But all the while he had been giving Stanley a going-over with his eyes, and it must be said, Stanley did look the worse for wear; looked as old and bunged up and afflicted as the night in the cabin when I was rewrapping his massacred hand. In this instance, though, the affliction was not Stanley's hand but what he had been pouring into himself with it.

Not somebody you would put on a fire crew, at least if your name was Chet Barnouw and the responsibility was directly traceable to you. So Chet now went on, "But beyond you taking those up for us, I don't see how we can use—"

"How're you fixed for a hash slinger?" Stanley asked conversationally.

Chet's eyebrows climbed. "You mean it? You can cook?"

"He's A-number-one at it," I chirped in commemoration of Stanley's breakfast the morning of my hangover.

Chet needed better vouching than my notorious appetite. He turned to my mother. If ever there was a grand authority on food, it was her. She informed Chet: "When Stanley says he can do a thing, he can."

"All right then," said Chet. "Great Falls more than likely would just dig out some wino fryhouse guy for me anyway." The dispatcher caught himself and cleared his throat. "Well, let's get you signed up here."

Stanley stepped over to the desk with him and did so. Chet looked down at the signature with interest.

"Stanley Kelley, huh? You spell it the same way the Major does."

My mouth flapped open. The look I received from my mother snapped it shut again.

All politeness, Stanley inquired: "The who?"

"Major Evan Kelley, the Regional Forester. The big sugar, over in Missoula. Kind of unusual, two E's in Kelley. You any relation?"

"None that I know of."

Chet went back in his belfry, and Stanley headed to the barn to rig up a saddle horse and Homer as the pack horse. Ordinarily I would have gone along to help him. But I was shadowing my mother, all the way back to the house.

As soon as we were in the kitchen I said it.

"Mom? I've got to go with Stanley."

The same surprise as when I'd stepped up and asked to dance the Dude and Belle with her, that distant night of the Fourth. But this request of mine was a caper in a more serious direction. "I thought you'd had enough of Stanley," she reminded me, "on that camptending episode."

"I did. But that was then." I tried, for the second time this day, to put into words more than I ever had before. "If Stanley's going to be any help to Dad, I'm going to have to be the help to Stanley. You know what he told me, after the camptending. When he said he couldn't have got along up there without me. The fire camp will be even worse for him. Paul's going to be looking down his neck the whole while and the first time he catches Stanley with a bottle he'll send him down the road." Plead is not a word I am ashamed of, in the circumstances. "Let me go with him, Mom."

She shook her head. "A fire camp is a crazyhouse, Jick. It wouldn't be just you and Stanley this time. They won't let you hang around—"

Here was my ace. "I can be Stanley's flunky. Help him with the cooking. That way I'd be right there with him all the time."

Serious as all this was, my mother couldn't stop her quick sideways grin at the notion of me around food full-time. But then she sobered. With everything in me, I yearned that she would see things my way. That she would not automatically tell me I was too young, that she would let me play a part at last, even just as chaperone, in this summer's stream of events.

Rare for Beth McCaskill, not to have an answer ready by now. By now she must have been on tenth and eleventh thoughts about the wisdom of having asked Stanley Meixell to go to Flume Gulch.

My mother faced me, and decided.

"All right. Go. But stay with Stanley or your father at all times. Do you Understand That? At All Times."

"Yes," I answered her. Any term of life as clear as that, even I could understand.

Stanley was my next obstacle.

"She said you can? C-A-N, can?"

"Yeah, she did. You can go on in and ask her." I kept on with my saddling of Pony.

"No, I'll take your word." He rubbed the back of his right hand with his left, still studying me. "Going to a fire, though—you sure you know what you're getting into?"

Canada Dan and Bubbles and Dr. Al K. Hall in a tin cup had come into my life at the elbow of this man and he could stand there and ask me that?

I shot back, "Does anybody ever?"

The squinch around Stanley's eyes let up a little. "There you got a point. Okey-doke, Jick. Let's get to getting."

Up the North Fork road the summer's second Meixell-McCaskill expedition set out, Stanley on a buckskin Forest Service gelding named Buck, leading the pack horse Homer with the load of lunches, and me behind on Pony.

—

I still don't know how Stanley managed the maneuver, but by the time we were past the Hebner place and topping the English Creek–Noon Creek divide, the smoke rising out of the canyon of the North Fork ahead of us, I was riding in the lead just as on our camptending expedition. That the reason was the same, I had no doubt. I didn't bother to look back and try to catch Stanley bugling a bottle, as that was a sight I did not want to have to think about. No, I concentrated on keeping us moving at a fast walk, at least as fast as I could urge Pony's short legs to go.

Something was different, though. This time Stanley wasn't singing. To my surprise I missed it quite a lot.

Smoke in a straight column. Then an oblong haze of it drifting south along the top of Roman Reef. The day's lone cloud, like a roll of sooty canvas on a high shelf.

A quantity of smoke is an unsettling commodity. The human being does not like to think its environs are inflammable. My mother had the memory that when she was a girl at Noon Creek the smoke from the 1910 fires brought a Bible-toting neighbor, a homesteader, to the Reese doorstep to announce: "This is the wrath of God. The end of the world is come." Daylight dimming out to a sickly green color and no distinct difference between night and day, I suppose it would make you wonder.

That same 1910 smoke never really left my father. He must have been about twelve or thirteen then, and his memory of that summer when the millions of acres burned in the Bitterroot while the Two had its own long stubborn fire was the behavior of the chickens there at the family homestead on the North Fork. "Christamighty, Jick, by about noon they'd go in to roost for the night, it got so dark." The 1910 smoke darkness, and then the scarred mountainside of Phantom Woman as a later reminder; they stayed and stayed in my father, smears of dread.

Stanley too had undergone the 1910 smoke. In the cabin he had told me of being on that fire crew on the Two fire west of Swift Dam. "Such as we were, for a crew. Everybody and his cousin was already fighting some other sonuvabitch of a fire, Bitterroot or somewheres else. We dabbed at it here as best we could, a couple of weeks. Yeah, and we managed to lose our fire camp. The wind come up and turned a flank of that fire around and brought it right into our camp. A thing I never will forget, Jick, all the canned goods blew up. That was about all that was left when the fire got done with that camp, a bunch of exploded goddamn tin cans."

All three of them, each with a piece of memory of that awful fire summer. Of how smoke could multiply itself until it seemed to claim the world.

Now that my father had stepped in as fire boss at Flume Gulch, Paul Eliason was the camp boss. I will say, Paul was marshaling things into good order. We rode in past a couple of CCs digging a toilet trench. A couple of others were setting up the fire boss tent, each of them pounding in tent pegs with the flat of an ax. The feed ground—the kitchen area—already was built, and there we encountered Paul.

Paul still had an expression as if somebody big was standing on his foot and he was trying to figure out what to say about it, but he lost no time in sending one of the CCs off with Homer and the lunches to the fire crew. "Late is better than never," he rattled off, as if he invented that. "Thanks for delivering, Jick," he next recited, awarded Stanley a nod too, and started back to his next target of supervision.

"Paul," I managed to slow and turn him, "somebody here you got to meet. This is Stanley, uh—"

"—Kelley. Pleased to know you, ranger."

"—and, he's here to—" I finally found the inspiration I needed: "Chet signed him on as your cook." Well, as far as it went, that was true, wasn't it?

Paul studied this news. "I thought Chet told me he was going to have to get one out of Great Falls, and the chances didn't look real good even there."

"He must have had his mind changed," I speculated.

"Must have," Paul conceded. He looked Stanley over. "Have you ever cooked for a fire camp before?"

"No," responded Stanley. "But I been in a fire camp before, and I cooked before. So it adds up to the same."

Paul stared. "For crike's sake, mister. Have you got any idea what it takes to cook for a bunch of firefighters? They eat like—"

"Oh yeah," Stanley inserted, "and I almost forgot to tell you, I also've ate fire camp grub. So I been through the whole job, a little at a time."

"Uh huh" emitted from Paul, more as a sigh than an acknowledgment.

Stanley swung his gaze around the camp in interest. "Have you got some other candidate in mind for cook?"

"No, no, I sure as the devil don't. I guess you're it. So the feed ground is yours, mister." Paul waved to the area where the cookstove and a work table and the big T table to serve from had been set up. "You better get at it. You're going to have CCs coming at you from down that mountain and EFFs coming up from Great Falls. Figure supper for about seventy-five." Paul turned to me. "Jick, I appreciate you getting those lunches up here. If you start back now, you'll be home well before dark."

"Well, actually, I'm staying," I informed Paul. "I can be Stanley's flunky. My mom said it's okay."

Possibly this was the first time a member of a fire crew ever arrived with an excuse from his mother, and it sure as hell was nothing Paul Eliason had ever dealt with before. Particularly from a mother such as mine. You could all but see the thought squatting there on his mind: what next from these damn McCaskills?

But Paul only said: "You sort that out with your father. He's the fire boss." And sailed off to finish worrying the camp into being.

Stanley and I began to tour our feed ground. The muleloads of groceries and cooking gear Isidor Pronovost had brought in by packstring. An open fire pit and not far from it the stove. Both were lit and waiting, as if hinting that they ought to be in use. A long work table built of stakes and poles. And about twenty feet beyond it, the much bigger T-shaped serving table. I could see the principle: tin plates and utensils and bread and butter and so forth were to be stacked along the stem of the T so the fire crew could file through in a double line, one along each side of the stem, to the waiting food at both arms of the T. The food, though. That I could not envision: how Stanley and I were going to manage, in the next few hours, to prepare a meal for seventy-five guys.

"So," Stanley announced. "I guess—"

This I could have completed in my sleep—"we got it to do."

The Forest Service being the Forest Service and Paul being Paul, there hung a FIRE CAMP COOK BOOK on a nail at the serving table. Stanley peered over my shoulder as I thumbed to the page titled "First Supper," then ran my finger down that page to where it was decreed: "Menu—beef stew."

"Slumgullion," Stanley interpreted. "At least it ain't mutton."

Below the menu selection, instructing began in earnest: "Place large wash boiler, half full of water, on fire."

"Christamighty, Stanley, we better get to—" I began, before noticing the absence at my shoulder.

Over beside the packs of groceries, Stanley was leaning down to his saddlebags. Oh, Jesus. I could forecast the rest of that movement before it happened, his arm going in and bringing forth the whiskey bottle.

I don't know which got control of my voice, dismay or anger. But the message was coming out clear: "Goddamn it all to hell, Stanley, if you start in on that stuff—"

"Jick, you are going to worry yourself down to the bone if you keep on. Here, take yourself a swig of this."

"No, damn it. We got seventy-five men to feed. One of us has got to have enough damn brains to stay sober."

"I know how many we got to feed. Take a little of this in your mouth, just enough to wet your whistle."

When things start to skid they really do go, don't they. It wasn't enough that Stanley was about to begin a bender, he was insisting on me as company. My father would skin us both. My mother would skin whatever was left of me after my father's skinning.

"Just taste it, Jick." Stanley was holding the bottle out to me, patient as paint.

All right, all goddamn right; I had run out of thinking space, all the foreboding in the world was in me instead; I would buy time by faking a little swig of Stanley's joy juice, maybe after putting the bottle to my lips like this I could accidentally on purpose drop the—

Water.

Yet not quite *only* water. I swigged a second time to be sure of the taste. Just enough whiskey to flavor it faintly. If I'd had to estimate, perhaps a finger's worth of whiskey had been left in the bottle before Stanley filled it with water.

"It'll get me by," Stanley asserted. He looked bleak about the prospect, and said as much. "It's worse than being weaned a second time. But I done it before, a time or two when I really had to. Now we better get down to cooking, don't you figure?"

"The Forest Service must of decided everything tastes better with tin around it," observed Stanley as he dumped into the stew boiler eight cans each of tomatoes and peas.

"Sounds good to me right now," I said from where I was slicing up several dozen carrots.

———

"You got time to slice some bread?" Stanley inquired from where he was stirring stew.

"Yeah." I was tending a round boiler in which twelve pounds of prunes were being simmered for dessert, but figured I could dive back and forth between tasks. "How much?"

"This is the Yew Ess Forest Service, remember. How ever much it says in the book."

I went and looked again at the "First Supper" page.

Twenty loaves.

"Jick, see what it says about how much of this sand and snoose to put in the stew," Stanley requested from beside the wash boiler, a big box of salt in one hand and a fairly sizable one of pepper in the other.

"It doesn't."

"It which?"

"All the cookbook says is 'Season to taste.'"

"Aw, goddamn."

My right arm and hand felt as if they'd been slicing for years. I remembered I was supposed to set out five pounds of butter to go with the bread. Stanley now was the one at the cookbook, swearing steadily as he tried for a third time to divine the proportions of salt and pepper for a wash boiler of stew.

"What's it say to put this butter on?"

His finger explored along the page. "Pudding dishes. You got time to start the coffee after that?"

"I guess. What do I do?"

"Fill two of them halfbreed boilers in the creek. . . ."

All afternoon Paul had been going through the camp at such a pace that drinks could have been served on his shirttail. But he gave Stanley and me wide berth until he at last had to pop over to tell us the fire crew was on its way in for supper.

He couldn't help eyeing us dubiously. I was sweaty and bedraggled, Stanley was parched and bedraggled.

"Mind if I try your stew?" Paul proposed. I say proposed, because even though Paul was camp boss it was notorious that a cook coming up on mealtime had to be handled with kid gloves.

This advantage must have occurred to Stanley, because he gave Paul a flat gaze, stated, "If you're starved to death, go ahead; I got things to do," and royally strode over to the work table where I was.

We both watched over our shoulders like owls, though. Paul grabbed a spoon, advanced on the stew tub, dipped out a dab, blew on it, tasted. Then repeated. Then swung around toward us. "Mister, you weren't just woofing. You *can* cook."

Shortly the CCs streamed into camp, and Stanley and I were dishing food onto their plates at a furious rate. A day on a fire line is ash and sweat, so these CCs were not exactly fit for a beauty contest. But they were at that brink of manhood—most of them about Alec's age—where energy recovers in a hurry. In fact, their appetites recuperated instantly. Some CCs were back on line for seconds before we'd finished serving everybody a first helping.

Paul saw how swamped Stanley and I were with the serving, and sent two of his CC camp flunkies to take over from us while we fussed with reheating and replenishment. The fifty emergency firefighters from Great Falls were yet to come.

So was my father. I had seen him appear into the far end of camp, conferring with Kratka and Ames, now his fireline foremen, and head with them to the boss tent. He wore his businesslike look. Not a good sign.

I was lugging a resupply of prunes to the T table when I glanced into the grub line and met the recognition of my father, his hand in mid-reach for a tin plate.

For a moment he simply tried to register that it was me standing before him in a flour sack apron.

"Jick! What in the name of hell are you doing here?"

"'Lo, Dad. Uh, I'm being the flunky."

"You're—" That stopped not only my father's tongue but all other parts of him. He stood rooted. And when I sunk in, so to speak, he of course had to get his mind to decide who to skin alive for this, Paul or Chet.

"Mom said I could," I put in helpfully.

This announcement plainly was beyond mortal belief, so now my father had definite words to express to me. "You're going to stand there with your face hanging out and tell me your mother—" Then the figure at the stove turned around to him and he saw that behind this second flour sack apron was Stanley.

"Hullo, Mac," Stanley called out. "I hope you like slumgullion. 'Cause that's what it is."

"Jesus H.—" My father became aware of the audience of CCs piling up behind him in the grub line. "I'm coming around there, you two. You better have a story ready when I arrive."

Stanley and I retreated to the far end of the kitchen area while my father marched around the T table to join us. He arrived aiming huffy looks first to one of us and then the other, back and forth as if trying to choose between targets.

"Now," he stated. "Let's hear it."

"You're kind of on the prod, Mac," observed Stanley. "You don't care that much for slumgullion, huh?"

"Stanley, goddamn you and your slumgullion. What in the hell are the pair of you doing in this fire camp?"

Stanley was opening his mouth, and I knew that out of it was going to drop the reply, "Cooking." To head that off, I piped: "Mom figured you could use our help."

"She figured what?"

"She wouldn't have sent us"—adjusting the history of my inception into the trip with Stanley and the lunches—"if she hadn't figured that, would she? And what's the matter with our cooking?" Some CCs were back in line for third helpings; *they* didn't seem to lack appreciation of our cuisine.

I noticed something else. My father no longer was dividing huffy looks between Stanley and me. He was locked onto Stanley. My presence in this fire camp was not getting my father's main attention.

As steadily as he could, after his afternoon of drought and wholesale cookery, Stanley returned the scrutiny. "Mac," he said, in that rasped-over voice from when my father and I first met him on the trail that day of June, "you're the fire boss. You can put the run on us any time you want. But until you do, we can handle this cooking for you."

My father at last said: "I'm not putting the run on anybody. Dish me up some of your goddamn slumgullion."

It was getting dusk when the EFFs arrived into camp like a raggle-taggle army. These men were drift, straight from the saloons and flophouses of First Avenue South in Great Falls, and they more than looked it. One guy even had a beard. Supposedly a person couldn't be hired for emergency firefighting unless he owned a stout pair of shoes, but of course the same passable shoes showed up on guy after guy in the sign-up line. Most of these EFFs now were shod in weary leather, and hard-worn blue jeans if they were ranch hands, and bib pants if they were gandy dancers or out-of-work smeltermen from Black Eagle. Motley as they looked from the neck down, I paid keener attention to their head-gear. There was a legend in the Forest Service that a fire boss once told his sign-up man in Spokane: "Send me thirty men if they're wearing Stetsons or fifty if they're wearing caps." Most of these EFFs at least were hatted; they were used to outdoor work, were not city guys except for recreational purposes.

I remember that this time, Stanley and I were lugging another boiler of coffee to the T table. For I damn near dropped my end when a big guy leaned out of the back of the grub line, peered woozily toward me, then yelled in greeting:

"Hey, Jick!"

Wisdom Johnson had not advanced conspicuously far on his plan to head for the redwood country for the winter. As soon as Stanley and I got the boiler situated on the table, I hustled to the back of the grub line to shake hands with Wisdom.

"That First Avenue South," he marveled. "That's just quite a place."

Uh huh, I thought. And Bouncing Betty is quite a guide to it.

What my first night in a fire camp was like I can't really tell you. For when Stanley and I at last were done washing dishes, I entered my sleeping bag and that is the last I know.

Breakfast, though. If you have not seen what six dozen firefighters will consume for breakfast, the devastation may shock you. It did me, after I awoke to the light of a gas lantern and Stanley above it half croaking, "Picnic time again, Jick."

Whack off a hundred and fifty slices of ham for frying. Mush: two sixteen-quart round boilers of water and four pounds of oatmeal into each. Milk for the mush, fifteen tall cans of Sego mixed with the same of water. Potatoes to make fried spuds—thank the Lord, we had just enough of the canned variety so that I didn't have to start peeling. Fill two more halfbreed boilers for coffee, slice another oodle of bread, open seven cans of jam.

Enough grub to feed China, it looked to me like. But Stanley viewed matters and shook his head.

"Better dig out a half dozen of those fruitcakes, Jick, and slice them up."

I still blink to think about it, but only crumbs of those fruitcakes were left when that crew was done.

That morning my father put his firefighters to doing everything that the Forest Service said should be done in such a battle. Fireline was being dug, snags were being felled, wherever possible the flames were being pinched against Flume Gulch's rocky outcroppings. One saving grace about a fire burning its way down a north slope is that it usually comes slowly, and my father's crews were able to work close, right up against the face of the fire. On the other hand, Flume Gulch truly was a bastardly site to have to tackle. The fire had started at the uppermost end of the gulch, amid a dry tangle of windfall, and was licking its way down through jungly stands of Douglas fir and alpine fir and an understory of brush and juniper and more windfall. "Heavy fuel," as it's called. Burning back and forth on the gulch's steep sides as a falling flaming tree or a shower of sparks would ignite the opposite wall of forest. So, in a sense, in a kind of slow sloshing pattern the fire was advancing right down the trough of nature's version of a flume, aiming itself into the creekside trees along the North Fork and the high grassy slope opposite the gulch. And all the forested country waiting beyond that slope.

To even get to the fire my father's men had to climb up the face of the creek gorge into the gulch, and once there they had to labor on ground which sometimes tilted sharply ahead of them and sometimes tilted sideways but always tilted. At breakfast I had heard one of the CCs telling the EFFs that Flume Gulch was a spraddledy-ass damn place.

Besides being high and topsy-turvy the fire battleground was hot and dry, and my father designated Wisdom Johnson to be the Flume Gulch water cow. What this involved was making trips along the fireline with a five-gallon water pack on his back, so that the thirsty men could imbibe a drink from the pack's nozzle—the tit. "I thought I had done every job there was," claimed Wisdom, "but I never hit this one."

About mid-morning, when he came down from the gulch to refill, Wisdom brought into camp my father's message for Paul. Paul read it, shook his head, and hustled down the trail to phone it on to Chet at the ranger station.

"What'd it say?" I pumped Wisdom before he could start back up with his sloshing water pack.

" 'No chance ten A.M. control today,' " Wisdom quoted. Then added his own view of the situation in Flume Gulch: "Suffering Jesus, they're a thirsty bunch up there."

"A lot of Great Fall nights coming out through the pores," Stanley put in piously from the work table where he and I next were going to have make double lunches for the seventy-five firefighters. Which, the cook book enlightened us, amounted to a hundred and fifty ham sandwiches, a hundred and fifty jam sandwiches, and seventy-five cheese sandwiches.

" 'Slice the meat about four slices to the inch,' " I read in a prissy voice. " 'Slice the bread about two slices to the inch.' Christamighty, they want us to do everything by the measurement and then don't provide us any damn thing to measure with."

"Your thumb," said Stanley.

"My thumb what?"

"Your thumb's a inch wide. Close enough to it, anyhow. Go by that. The Forest Service has got a regulation for everything up to and including how to swat a mosquito with your hat. Sometimes, though, it don't hurt to swat first and read up on it later."

My thumb and I set to slicing.

At noon Paul and his pair of camp flunkies and Stanley and Wisdom and I lugged the sandwiches and canned fruit and pork and beans up to the fireline.

I had grown up hearing of forest fires. The storied fire summers, Bitterroot, Phantom Woman, Selway, this one, they amounted to a Forest Service catechism. Yet here, now, was my first close view.

Except for the smoke boiling in ugly fashion into the sky, the scene was not as awful as you might expect. Orange flames were a dancing tribe amid the trees, and the firefighters were a rippling line of shovel-ers and axmen and sawyers as they tried to clear anything combustible from in front of the fire. But then when you got over being transfixed by the motions of flame and men, the sense of char hit you. A smell like charcoal, the black smudge of the burned forest behind the flames. And amid the commotion of the fireline work, the sounds of char, too—flames crackling, and continual snap of branches breaking as they burned, and every so often a big roar of flame as a tree crowned out.

What told me most about the nature of a forest fire was one single tree, a low scrawny young Douglas fir. It had managed to root high up within a crack in one of the gulch's rock formations, and as I was gawk-ing around trying to register everything, I saw that tree explode. Spon-taneously burst into flames, there on its stone perch so far from any other foliage or the orange feather-edge of the fire itself.

I found my father and read his face. Serious but not grim. He came over to my pack of sandwiches and plowed into one. I glanced around to be sure Paul wasn't within hearing, then said: " 'It doesn't look that bad. It just keeps burning, is all.' "

He had to grin at that. "That's about the case. But I think there's a chance we can kick it in the pants this afternoon. Those First Avenuers are starting to get their legs under them. They'll get better at fireline work as the day goes on." He studied the sky above Roman Reef as if it would answer what he said next. "What we don't need is any wind."

To shift himself from that topic, my father turned to me.

"How about you? How you getting along?"

"Okay. I never knew people could eat so much, though."

"Uh huh. Speaking of which, pass me another sandwich, would you." Even my father, conscientiously stoking food into himself. It was as if the fire's hunger for the forest had spread an epidemic of appetite among us as well.

My father watched Stanley divvy sandwiches out to a nearby bunch of EFFs. "How about your sidekick there?"

"Stanley's doing real good." Then the further answer I knew my father was inviting: "He's staying dry."

"Is he. Well, that's news. When he does get his nose in the bottle, you let me know. Or let Paul know if I'm not around. We got to have a cook. One'll have to be fetched in here from somewhere when Stanley starts a bender."

"If he does," I agreed because of all that was involved, "I'll say so."

—

Through the afternoon I flunkied for Stanley. Hot in that base camp, I hope never to suffer a more stifling day. It was all I could do not to wish for a breath of breeze.

Stanley too was sweating, his shirt dark with it.

And he looked in semi-awful shape. Agonized around the eyes, the way he had been when Bubbles butchered his hand. What bothered me more than his appearance, though, he was swigging oftener and oftener at the bottle.

As soon as Stanley went off to visit nature I got over there to his saddle pack, yanked the bottle out, and sipped.

It still was water with a whiskey trace. Stanley's craving thirst was for the trace rather than the water, but so far he hadn't given in.

This lifted my mood. As did the continuing absence of wind. I was predicting to Stanley, "I'll bet they get the fire whipped."

"Maybe so, maybe no," he responded. "Where a forest fire is concerned, I'm no betting man. How about peeling me a tub of spuds when you get the chance."

"Stanley, I guess this isn't exactly any of my business, but—have you seen Velma? Since the Fourth?"

"Now and then."

"Yeah, well. She's quite—quite a lady, isn't she?"

"Quite a one."

"Uh huh. Well. So, how are you two getting along?"

Stanley flexed his hand a time or two, then went back to cutting bacon. Tonight's main course was a casserole—if you can do that by the tubful—of macaroni and canned corn and bacon slices. "We've had some times," he allowed.

Times with Velma Simms. Plural. The gray eyes, the pearl-buttoned ears, those famous rodeo slacks, in multiple. Sweat was already rolling off me, but this really opened the spigots. I went over to the water bucket and splashed a handful on my face and another on the back of my neck.

Even so, I couldn't help resuming the topic. "Think anything will come of it?"

"If you mean permanent, nope. Velma's gave up marrying and I never got started. We both know there's a season on our kind of entertainment." Stanley slabbed off another half dozen slices of bacon, I peeled away at a spud. "But a season's better than no calendar at all, is what I've come to think." He squinted at the stacked results of his bacon slicing. "How many more hogs does that recipe call for?"

I was still peeling when the casualty came down from the gulch.

He was one of the CCs, half carried and half supported by two others. Paul hurried across the camp toward them, calling: "How bad did he get it?"

"His cawlehbone and awm," one of the helping CCs answered. New York? Philadelphia? Lord only knew what accent any of the CC guys spoke, or at least I sure didn't.

"Get him on down to the trailhead," Paul instructed the bearers. Then summoned the timekeeper: "Tony, you'll have to drive the guy in to the doc in Gros Ventre."

A limb of a falling snag had sideswiped the injured CC. This was sobering. I knew enough fire lore to realize that if the limb had found the CC's head instead of his collarbone and arm, he might have been on his way to the undertaker rather than to Doc Spence.

As yet, no wind. Calm as the inside of an oven, and as hot. I wiped my brow and resumed peeling.

"What would you think about going for a stroll?"

This proposal from Stanley startled me. By now, late afternoon, he looked as if it took ninety-nine percent of his effort to stay on his feet, let alone put them into motion.

"Huh? To where?"

His head and Stetson indicated the grassy slope of Rooster Mountain above us, opposite the fire. "Just up there. Give us a peek at how things are going."

I hesitated. We did have our supper fixings pretty well in hand. But to simply wander off up the mountainside . . .

"Aw, we got time," Stanley told me as if he'd invented the commodity. "Our stepdaddy"—he meant Paul, who was down phoning Chet the report of the injured CC—"won't be back for a while."

"Okay, then," I assented a little nervously. "As long as we're back here in plenty of time to serve supper."

I swear he said it seriously: "Jick, you know I'd never be the one to make you miss a meal."

I thought it was hot in camp. The slope was twice so. Facing south as it did, the grassy incline had been drinking in sun all day, not to mention the heat the forest fire was putting into the air of this whole area.

"Yeah, it's a warm one," Stanley agreed. I was watching him with concern. The climb in the heat had tuckered me considerably. How Stanley could navigate this mountainside in his bent-knee fashion—more than ever he looked like a born horseman, grudging the fact of ground—was beyond me.

Except for a few scrubby pines peppered here and there, the slope was shadeless until just below its summit where the forest overflowed from this mountain's north side. Really there weren't many trees even up there because of the rocky crest, the rooster comb. And Stanley and I sure as hell weren't going that high anyway, given the heat and steepness. So it was a matter of grit and bear it.

Stanley did lean down and put a hand flat against the soil of the slope as if he intended to sit. I was not surprised when he didn't plop himself down, for this sidehill's surface was so tropical I could feel its warmth through the soles of my boots.

"Looks to me like they're holding it," I evaluated the fire scene opposite us. Inasmuch as we were about halfway up our slope, we were gazing slightly downward on Flume Gulch and the fire crew. Startling how near that scene seemed; these two sides of the North Fork vee truly were sharp. Across there in the gulch we could see the smoke pouring up, a strange rapid creation to come from anything as deliberate as this downhill fire; and close under the smoke column, the men strung out along the fireline. Even the strip of turned earth and cleared-away debris, like a long wavery stripe of garden dirt, that they were trying to pen the fire with; even that we could see. In a provident moment I had snagged a pair of binoculars from the boss tent before Stanley and I set off on our climb, and with them I could pick out individuals. I found my father and Kratka in conference near the center of the fireline. Both of them stood in that peering way men do up a sidehill, one foot advanced and the opposite arm crooking onto a hip. They looked like they could outwait any fire.

The dry grass creaked and crackled under my feet as I stepped to hand the binoculars to Stanley. He had been gandering here, there and elsewhere around our slope, so I figured he was waiting to use the glasses on the actual fire.

"Naw, that's okay, Jick. I seen enough. Kind of looks like a forest fire, don't it?" And he was turning away, starting to shuffle back down to the fire camp.

When the first firefighters slogged in for supper, my father was with them. My immediate thought was that the fire was whipped: my father's job as fire boss was done.

As soon as I could see faces, I knew otherwise. The firefighters looked done in. My father looked pained.

I told Stanley I'd be right back, and went over to my father.

"It jumped our fireline," he told me. "Three places."

"But how? There wasn't any wind."

"Like hell. What do you call that whiff about four o'clock?"

"Not down here," I maintained. "We haven't had a breath all afternoon. Ask Stanley. Ask Paul."

My father studied me. "All right. Maybe down here there wasn't any. But up there some sure as hell came from somewhere. Not much. Just enough." He told me the story. Not long after Stanley and I took our look at things from the slope, with the afternoon starting to cool away from its hottest, most dangerous time, a quick south wind came along Roman Reef and caught the fire. "The whole east flank made a run like gasoline had been poured on it. Jumped our fireline like nothing and set off a bunch of brush. We got there and corraled it. But while we were doing that, it jumped in another place. So we got to that one, got that one held. And in the meanwhile, goddamned if it didn't jump one more time." That one flared and took off, a stand of fir crowning into orange flame. "I had to pull the crew away from that flank. Too damn dangerous. So now we've got ourselves a whole new fire, marching right down the mountain. Tomorrow we're going to have to hold the son-ofabitch here at the creek. Damn it all to hell anyway."

My father did fast damage to his plateful of supper and went back up to the fire. He was keeping Kratka's crew on patrol at what was left of fireline until the cool of the evening would damper the flames.

Ames's gang of CCs and EFFs meanwhile were ready to dine. Ready and then some. "Hey, Cookie!" one among them yelled out to Stanley. "What're you going to founder us on tonight?"

"Soupa de bool-yon," Stanley enlightened him in a chefly accent of some nature. "Three buckets of water and one on-yon." Actually the lead course was vegetable soup, followed by the baconized macaroni and corn, and mashed potatoes with canned milk gravy, and rice pudding, and all of it tasted just heavenly if I do say so myself.

Dark was coming on by the time Stanley and I went to the creek to fill a boiler with water as a headstart toward breakfast.

From there at creekside the fire lay above us to the west. A few times in my life I had seen Great Falls at night from one of its hills. The forest fire reminded me of that. A city alight in the dark. A main avenue of flame, where the live edge of the fire was advancing. Neighborhoods where rock formations had isolated stubbornly burning patches. Hundreds of single spots of glow where snags and logs still blazed.

"Pretty, ain't it," Stanley remarked.

"Well, yeah, I guess. If you can call it that."

"Tomorrow it'll be just an ugly sonuvabitch of a forest fire. But tonight, it's pretty."

My father had come back into camp and was waiting for Paul to arrive with the phone report from Chet. As soon as Paul showed up, my father was asking him, "How's Ferragamo?" Joseph Ferragamo was the CC the falling snag had sideswiped.

"The doc splinted him up, then took him to the hospital in Conrad. Says he'll be okay." Paul looked wan. "A lot better off than some, anyway."

"How do you mean?" my father wanted to know.

Paul glanced around to make sure none of the fire crew were within earshot. "Mac, there've been two CCs killed, over on the west-side fires. One on the Kootenai, and one on the Kaniksu fire. Snags got both of them."

My father said nothing for a little. Then: "I appreciate the report, Paul. Round up Ames and Kratka, will you. We've got to figure out how we're going to handle this fire tomorrow."

My father and Paul and the pair of crew foremen took lanterns and headed up the creek to look over the situation of tomorrow morning's fireline. My father of course knew the site backwards and forwards, but the hell of it was to try to educate the others in a hurry and in the dark. I could not help but think it: if Alec . . .

At their bed ground some of the fire crew already were oblivious in their sleeping bags, but a surprising many were around campfires, sprawled and gabbing. The climate of the Two. Roast you all day in front of a forest inferno, then at dark chill you enough to make you seek out fire.

While waiting for my father, I did some wandering and exercising of my ears. I would like to say here and now that these firefighters, from eighteen-year-old CCs to the most elderly denizen among the First Avenue South EFFs, were earnestly discussing how to handle the Flume Gulch fire. I would *like* to say that, but nothing would be farther from the truth. Back at the English Creek ranger station, on the wall behind my father's desk was tacked one of those carbon copy gags that circulate among rangers:

Subjects under discussion during one summer (timed by stopwatch) by U.S. Forest Service crews, trail, fire, maintenance and otherwise.

	PERCENT OF TIME
Sexual stories, experiences and theories	37%
Personal adventures in which narrator is hero	23%
Memorable drinking jags	8%
Outrages of capitalism	8%
Acrimonious remarks about bosses, foremen and cooks	5%
Personal adventures in which someone not present is the goat	5%
Automobiles, particularly Fords	3%
Sarcastic evaluations of Wilson's war to end war	2%
Sarcastic evaluations of ex-President Coolidge	2%
Sarcastic evaluations of ex-President Hoover	2%
Sears Roebuck catalogue versus Montgomery Ward catalogue	2%
The meteorological outlook	2%
The job at hand	1%

From what I could hear, that list was just about right.

—

Stanley I had not seen for a while, and it crossed my mind that he may have had enough of the thirsty life. That he'd gone off someplace to jug up from an undiluted bottle.

But no, when I at last spied my father and his fire foremen and Paul returning to camp and then heading for the tent to continue their war council, I found Stanley in that same vicinity. Looking neither worse nor better than he had during our day of cooking.

Just to be sure, I asked him: "How you doing?"

"Feeling dusty," he admitted. "Awful dusty."

My father spotted the pair of us and called over: "Jick, you hang on out here. We got to go over the map, but it won't take too long." Into the tent he ducked with Paul, Kratka and Ames following.

"You want me to get your sipping bottle?" I offered to Stanley, referring to the one of whiskey-tinged water in his saddlebag.

"Mighty kind," replied Stanley. "But it better wait." And before I could blink, he was gone from beside me and was approaching the tent where my father's war council was going on.

Stanley stuck his head in past the flap door of the tent. I heard:

"Can I see you for part of a minute, Mac?"

"Stanley, it's going to have to wait. We're still trying to dope out our fireline for the morning."

"That fireline is what it's about, Mac."

There was a moment of silence in the tent. Then Paul's voice:

"For crying out loud! Who ever heard of a fire camp where the cook gets to put in his two bits' worth? Mister, I don't know who the devil you think you are, but—"

"All right, Paul," my father umpired. "Hold on." There was a moment of silence, which could only have been a scrutinizing one. My father began to say: "Stanley, once we get this—"

"Mac, you know how much it takes for me to ask."

A moment again. Then my father: "All right. There's plenty of night ahead. We can stand a couple of minutes for me to hear what Stanley has to say. Paul, you guys go ahead and map out how we can space the crews along the creek bottom. I won't be long." And bringing one of the gas lanterns out he came, giving Stanley a solid looking-over in the white light.

Side by side the two of them headed out of earshot of the tent. Not out of mine, though, for this I was never going to miss. They had gone maybe a dozen strides when I caught up with them.

The three of us stopped at the west end of the camp. Above us the fire had on its night face yet, bright, pretty. No hint whatsoever of the grim smoke and char it showed by day.

"Mac, I'm sorry as all hell to butt into your war council, there. I hate to say anything about procedure. Particularly to you. But—"

"But you're determined to. Stanley, what's on your mind?"

"The idea of tackling the fire down here on the creek, first thing in the morning." Stanley paused. Then: "Mac, my belief is that's not the way to go about it."

"So where would you tackle it?"

Stanley's Stetson jerked upward, indicating the slope of grass across the North Fork from us. "Up there."

Now in the lantern light it was my father's eyes that showed the hurtful squint Stanley's so often did.

The thought repelled my father. The fire doubling its area of burn: both sides of the North Fork gorge blackened instead of one. More than that—

"Stanley, if this fire gets loose over the slope and up into that next timber, it can take the whole goddamn country. It can burn for miles." My father stared up at the dim angle of the slope, but what was in his mind was 1910, Bitterroot, Selway, Phantom Woman, all the smoke ghosts that haunt a fire boss. "Christamighty," he said softly, "it could burn until snowfall."

Jerking his head around from that thought, my father said: "Stanley, don't get radical on me here. What in the hell makes you say the fire-line ought to be put up there on the mountain?"

"Mac, I know you hate like poison to see any inch of the Two go up in smoke. I hated it, too. But if you can't hold the fire at the base of the gulch, it's gonna break out onto the slope there anyway."

"The answer there is, I'm supposed to hold it."

"Supposed to is one thing. Doing it's another."

"Stanley, these days we've got what's called the ten A.M. policy. The Forest Service got religion about all this a few years ago. The Major told us, 'This approach to fire suppression will be a dividend-payer.' So the rule is, try to control any fire by ten the next morning."

"Yeah, rules are rules," agreed Stanley. Or seemed to agree, for I had heard my father any number of times invoke the second part of this ranger station catechism: "And fools are fools."

My father pulled out a much-employed handkerchief, wiped his eyes, and blew his nose. Among the aggravations of his day was smoke irritation.

"All right, Stanley," he said at last. "Run this by me again. You're saying give the fire the whole damn slope of Rooster Mountain?"

"Yeah, more or less. Use the morning to backfire in front of that rocky top." Backfiring is when you deliberately burn an area ahead of a fire, to rob its fuel. It has to be done just right, though, or you've either wasted your time or given the fire some more flame to work with. "Burn in a fireline up there that hell itself couldn't jump." Stanley saw my father was still unconverted. "Mac, it's not as nasty a place as this gorge."

"Christamighty, I can't pick places to fight a fire by whether they're nasty or not."

"Mac, you know what I mean." Stanley spelled it out for my father anyway. "That slope is dry as a torch. If you put men down in this gorge and the fire sets off that slope behind them too, you're going to be sifting piles of ashes to find their buttons."

I could see my father thinking it: nothing in the behavior of the Flume Gulch fire to date supported Stanley's picture. If anything, this slow downhill fire was almost *too* slow, staying up there in wicked terrain and burning when and where it pleased. He and his crews had been able to work right up beside the fire; it was the geography they couldn't do anything about. True, the fire's behavior could all change when it reached the gorge, but—"I can't see how the fire could set off the slope across this much distance," my father answered slowly.

"I can," Stanley said back.

Still stubborn as a government mule against the notion of voluntarily doubling the size of the Flume Gulch burn, my father eyed back up at the slope of Rooster Mountain. "Hell, what if we're up there merrily backfiring and the fire doesn't come? Goes down this gorge instead, right through this camp and around that slope? Then's when we'll have a bigger mess on our hands."

"That's a risk," admitted Stanley. "But my belief is it's a worse risk to tackle that fire down in here, Mac. Up there you'd have a bigger fireline. And rocks instead of men to help stop it."

My father considered some more. Then said: "Stanley, I'd rather take a beating than ask you this. But I got to. Are you entirely sober?"

"Sorry to say," responded Stanley, "I sure as hell am."

"He is," I chimed in.

My father continued to confront Stanley. I could see that he had more to say, more to ask.

But there I was wrong. My father only uttered, "The slope is something I'll think about," and set off back to the boss tent.

Stanley told me he was going to turn in—"This cooking is kind of a strenuous pastime"—and ordinarily I would have embraced bed myself. But none of this was ordinary. I trailed my father to the war council once more, and heard him say as soon as he was inside the tent:

"Ideas don't care who their daddies are. What would you guys say about this?" And he outlined the notion of the fireline atop the slope.

They didn't say much at all about it. Kratka and Ames already had been foxed once by the Flume Gulch fire. No need for them to stick their necks out again. After a bit my father said: "Well, I'll use it all as a pillow tonight. Let's meet here before breakfast. Meantime, everybody take a look at that slope on the map."

Paul's voice finally came. "Mac, can I see you outside?"

"Excuse us again, gents."

Out came my father and Paul. Again I made sure to catch up before the walking could turn into talking.

At the west edge of the camp Paul confronted my father. "Mac, whichever way you decide on tackling this fire, I'll never say a word against you. But the fire record will. You can't get around that. If you don't have the crew down here to take the fire by its face in the morning, Sipe is going to want to know why. And the Major—if this fire gets away down the gorge and around that slope, they'll sic a board of review on you. Mac, they'll have your hide."

My father weighed all this. And at last said: "Paul, there's another if. If we can kill this fire, Sipe and the Major aren't going to give one good goddamn how we did it."

Paul peered unhappily from the flickering crack in the night on the Flume Gulch side of us, to the dark bulk of the Rooster Mountain slope on our other. "You're the fire boss," he said.

—

I am not sure I slept at all that night. Waiting, breath held, any time I imagined I heard a rustle of wind. Waiting for the morning, for my father's fireline decision. Waiting.

"Christamighty, Stanley. Twenty loaves *again?*"

"Milk toast instead of mush to start with this morning, Jick," confirmed Stanley from the circle of lantern light where he was peering down into the cookbook. "Then after the bread, it's 'Place twenty cans of milk and the same of water in a twenty-quart half-oval boiler.'"

"Yeah, yeah, yeah. Let me get the damn slicing done first."

My father and Ames were the first ones through the breakfast line. Ames's men had come off the fireline earliest last night, so they were to be the early ones onto it this morning. Wherever that fireline was going to be.

I was so busy flunkying that it wasn't until a little break after Ames's men and before Kratka's came that I could zero in on my father. He and Ames brought their empty plates and dropped them in the dishwash tub. My father scrutinized Stanley, who was lugging a fresh heap of fried ham to the T table. Stanley set down the ham and met my father's regard with a straight gaze of his own. "Morning, Mac. Great day for the race, ain't it?"

My father nodded to Stanley, although whether in hello or agreement it couldn't be told. Then he turned to Ames. "Okay, Andy. Take your gang up there to the top and get them started digging the control line for backfiring." And next my father was coming around the serving table to where Stanley and I were, saying: "Step over here, you two. I've got something special in mind for the pair of you."

Shortly, Wisdom Johnson came yawning into the grub line. He woke up considerably when my father instructed him that the tall, tall slope of Rooster Mountain, just now looming up in the approach of dawn, was where his water duty would be today.

"But, Mac, the fire's over here, it ain't up there!"

"It's a new theory of firefighting," my father told him. "We're going to do it by mail order."

Kratka's men were soon fed. It transpired that my father himself was going to lead this group onto the slope and supervise them in lighting the strips of backfires.

First, though, he called Paul Eliason over. I heard him instruct: "Have Chet tell Great Falls the same thing as yesterday—'No chance ten A.M. control today.'"

"Mac," Paul began. "Mac, how about if I at least wait until toward that time of morning to call it in? I don't see any sense in advertising what—what's going on up here."

My father leveled him a stare that made Paul sway back a little. "Assistant ranger Eliason, do you mean to say you'd delay information to headquarters?"

Paul gulped but stood his ground. "Yeah. In this case, I would."

"Now you're talking," congratulated my father. "Send it in at five minutes to ten." My father turned and called to the crew waiting to go up the mountain with him. "Let's go see a fire."

"Stanley, this makes me feel like a coward."

"You heard the man."

It was well past noon, the sweltering heart of so hot a day. The rock formation we were perched on might as well have been a stoked stove. Pony and the buckskin saddle horse were tethered in the shade of the trees below and behind us, but they stood there drooping even so.

Stanley and I were chefs in exile. This rock observation point of ours was the crown-shaped formation above the line cabin where the two of us sheltered during our camptending shenanigan. How long ago it seemed since I was within those log walls, bandaging Stanley's hand and wishing I was anywhere else.

I had heard the man. My father, when he herded the pair of us aside there at breakfast and decreed: "I want you two out of here this afternoon. You understand?" If we did, Stanley and I weren't about to admit it. My father the fire boss spelled matters out for us: "If the wind makes up its mind to blow or that fire takes a turn for some other reason, it could come all the way down the gorge into this camp. So when you get the lunches made, clear out of here."

"Naw, Mac," Stanley dissented. "It's a good enough idea for Jick to clear out, but I—"

"Both of you," stated my father.

"Yeah, well," I started to put in, "Stanley's done his part, but I could just as well—"

"Both of you," my father reiterated. "Out of here, by noon."

The long faces on us told him he still didn't have Stanley and me convinced. "Listen, damn it. Stanley, you know what happened the last argument you and I had. This time, let's just don't argue." Then, more mild: "I need you to be with Jick, Stanley."

Stanley shifted the way he was standing. Did so again. And finally came out with a quiet "Okey-doke, Mac," and headed back to his cookstove.

My father did not have to labor the point to me. I knew, and nodded it to him, that the other half of what he had just said was that I was needed to be with Stanley. But he stopped me from turning away to my flunky tasks.

"Jick," he said as if this had been stored up in him for some time. "Jick, I can't risk you." His left eyelid came down as he forced a grin to accompany his words: "You've earned a grandstand seat this afternoon. Lean back and watch the event."

Thus here we were. Simmering in safety on this rock outlook, barbecued toes our only peril. At our angle the fire camp at the mouth of the gorge was in sight but Flume Gulch and the fire itself were just hidden, in behind the end of Roman Reef that towered over us. The cloud of smoke, though, told us the fire was having itself a big time.

The grass slope of Rooster Mountain lay within clear view. A tan broad ramp of grass. If Pat Hoy had had Dode Withrow's sheep in a scattered graze there they would have been plain to the unaided eye. In fact, at first it puzzled me that although even my father agreed this rock site was a healthy enough distance behind the fire for Stanley and me, the slope seemed so close. Eventually I figured out that the huge dark dimension of the smoke made the distance seem foreshortened.

I had snagged the binoculars again from the boss tent, and every few minutes I would squat—as with the slope yesterday at this time, our island of stone was too damn hot to sit on—and prop my elbows on my knees to steady the glasses onto the fireline work.

The brow of the slope, between its rocky top and the grass expanse stretching down to the North Fork, by now resembled a reflection of the devastation in Flume Gulch opposite it. All morning until about ten o'clock, when the day began to get too hot for safe backfiring, my father's men little by little had blackened that area. First they trenched the control line along the ridgetop, then the careful, careful burning began. Four or five feet wide at a time, a strip of grass was ignited and let to burn back uphill into the bare control line. When it had burned itself out, the next strip below it was lit. Down and down, the barrier of scorch was built that way, the dark burn scar at last inflicted across the entire upper part of the slope. And even yet at the edge of the forest atop the skyline, crews were cutting down any trees which stood too close behind the backfired fireline, other teams were hauling the combustible foliage a safe distance into the rocks and timber. My father's men were doing their utmost up there to deny the Flume Gulch fire anything to catch hold and burn when it came. If it came.

Even Stanley now and again peered through the binoculars to the fireline preparation. He wasn't saying anything, though, except his appraisal when we climbed onto the sun-cooked rock: "Hotter than dollar chili, ain't it?"

The event, as my father called it. Can you believe: it took me by total surprise. After all that waiting. All that watching, anticipating. The human being is the world's most forecasting damn creature. Yes, my imagination had the scene ready as if it were a dream I'd had twenty nights in a row, how the fire at last would cross from Flume Gulch and pull itself up out of the gorge of the North Fork onto the slope, vagrant ribbons of flame at first and then bigger fringes and at last a great ragged orange length climbing toward the fireline where my father's men waited to battle it in any way they could.

Instead, just this. Nothing seemed imminent yet, the smoke still disclosed the fire as only approaching the creek gorge. Maybe just brinking down onto the height between the gulch and the gorge, would have been my guess. I deemed that the next little while would start to show whether the fire preferred the gorge or Stanley's slope. So I did not even have the binoculars to my eyes, instead was sleeving the sweat off my forehead. When Stanley simply said: "There."

From both the gorge and the bottom of the slope the fire was throwing up smoke like the chimneys of hell. So much smudge and smear, whirling, thickening, that the slope vanished behind the billowing cloud. It scared me half to death, this smoke eclipse.

The suck of fear that went through me, the sweat popping out on the backs of my hands as I tried to see through smoke with binoculars. I can never—I *want* never—to forget what went through me then, as I realized what would be happening to my father and his fire crew if they had been in the gorge as the avalanche of fire swooped into it. The air itself must be cooked, down in there.

Then this. The smoke, all of it, rose as if a windowblind was being lifted. Sixty, eighty feet, I don't know. But the whole mass of smoke lifted that much. Stanley and I could look right into the flames, abruptly they were as bright and outlined as the blaze in a fireplace. The fire already had swarmed across the gorge and was stoking itself with the grass of the lower slope. Just as clear as anything, that aggregation of flame with the smoke curtained so obligingly above it, as much fire as a person could imagine seeing at once. And then, it awes me to even remember it, the fire crazily began to double, triple—multiply impossibly. I was told later by Wisdom Johnson: "Jick, this is the God's truth, a cool wind blew over us right then, down into that fire." A wedge of air, it must have been, hurling itself under that furiously hot smoke and flame. And that air and those flames meeting. The fire spewed up across the slope in an exploding wave, a tide. The crisp tan grass of the slope, going to orange and black. In but a minute or two, gone.

The smoke closed down again, boiled some more in a gray heavy way. But then there began to be clefts in the swirl, thinnings, actual gaps. The binoculars now brought me glimpses of men spaced along the backfired fireline and the rock summit of the slope, stomping and swatting and shoveling dirt onto flame wherever it tried to find fuel enough to catch. But more and more sentrylike watching instead of fire combat. Watching the flamestorm flash into collision with the backfired barrier or the rock comb of Rooster Mountain, and then dwindle.

These years later, I wish I could have those next minutes back to makings. Could see again that slope battle, and our fire camp that the sacrifice of the slope had saved. Could know again the rise of realization, the brimming news of my eyes, that the Flume Gulch fire steadily was quenching itself against my father's fireline, Stanley Meixell's fireline.

I couldn't speak. For some time after, even. My mouth and throat were as dry as if parched by the fire. But finally I managed:

"You knew the slope would go like that."

"I had the idea it might" was as much as Stanley would admit. "Superheated the way it was, from both the fire and the sun."

He looked drained but satisfied. I may have, too.

"So," Stanley said next. "We better go get to work on goddamn supper."

Dusk. Supper now behind us, only the dishes to finish. My father came and propped himself against the work table where Stanley and I were dishwashing. "It went the way you said it would," he said to Stanley, with a nod. Which passed for thanks in the complicated system of behavior between these two men. Then my father cleared his throat, and after a bit asked Stanley if he could stand one more day of cooking while the fire crew policed smoking snags and smolder spots tomorrow, and Stanley replied yeah, cooking wasn't all that much worse anyway than dealing with sheepherders.

I broke in:

"Tell me the argument."

Nothing, from either of these two.

I cited to my father from when he directed Stanley and me to clear out of the fire camp: "The last argument you and Stanley had, whenever the hell it was." I had searched all summer for this. "What was that about?"

My father tried to head me off. "Old history now, Jick."

"If it's that old, then why can't I hear it? You two—I need to know. I've been in the dark all damn summer, not knowing who did what to who, when, where, any of it. One time you send me off with Stanley, but then we show up here and you look at him like he's got you spooked. Damn it all to hell anyway"—I tell you, when I do get worked up there is not much limit—"what's it all about?"

Stanley over his dishwater asked my father: "You never told him, huh?" My father shrugged and didn't answer. Stanley gazed toward me. "Your folks never enlightened you on the topic of me?"

"I just told . . . No. No, they sure as hell haven't."

"McCaskills," Stanley said with a shake of his head, as if the name was a medical diagnosis. "I might of known you and Bet'd have padlocks on your tongues, Mac."

"Stanley," my father tried, "there's no need for you to go into all that."

"Yeah, I think there is." I was in Stanley's gaze again. "Phantom Woman," he began. "I let that fire get away from me. Or at least it got away. Comes to the same. A fire is the fire boss's responsibility, and I was him." Stanley turned his head to my father. Then to me again. "Your dad had come up from his Indian Head district to be a fireline foreman for me. So he was on hand when it happened. When Phantom Woman blew up across that mountainside." Stanley saw my question. "Naw, I can't really say it was the same as happened on that slope today. Timber instead of grass, different this and that. Every goddamn fire. But anyhow, up she blew, Phantom Woman. Flames everywhere, all the crew at my flank of the fireline had to run out of there like singed cats. Run for their lives. It was just a mess. And then that fire went and went and went." Stanley's throat made a dry swallow. "Burned for three weeks. So that's the history of it, Jick. The blowup happened at my flank of the fireline. It was over that that your dad and I had our"— Stanley faced my father—"disagreement."

My father looked back at Stanley until it began to be a stare. Then asked: "That's it? That's what you call the history of it?"

Stanley's turn to shrug.

My father shook his head. Then uttered:

"Jick, I turned Stanley in. For the Phantom Woman fire."

"Turned him in? How? To who?"

"To headquarters in Great Falls. Missoula. The Major. Anybody I could think of, wouldn't you say, Stanley?"

Stanley considered. "Just about. But Mac, you don't—"

"What," I persisted, "just for the fire getting away from him?"

"For that and—" My father stopped.

"The booze," Stanley completed. "As long as we're telling, tell him the whole of it, Mac."

"Jick," my father set out, "this goes back a long way. Longer than you know about. I've been around Stanley since I was, what? sixteen? seventeen?"

"Somewhere there," Stanley confirmed.

"There were a couple of years in there," my father was going on, "when I—well, when I wasn't around home much. I just up and pulled out for a while, and Stanley—"

"Why was that?" This seemed to be my main chance to see into the McCaskill past, and I wanted all the view I could get. "How come you pulled out?"

My father paused. "It's a hell of a thing to have to say, after all this with Alec. But my father and I, your grandfather—we were on the outs. Not for anything like the same reason. He did something I couldn't agree with, and it was just easier all around, for me to stay clear of the homestead and Scotch Heaven for a while. Eventually he got over it and I got over it, and that's all that needs to be said about that episode." A pause. This one, I knew, sealed whatever that distant McCaskill father-son ruckus had been. "Anyway, Stanley took me on. Started me here on the Two, giving me any seasonal job he could come up with. I spent a couple of years that way, until we went into the war. And then after, when I was the association rider and your mother and I had Alec, and then you came along—Stanley suggested I take the ranger test."

I wanted to hear history, did I. A headful was now available. Stanley had been the forest arranger, the one who set up the Two Medicine National Forest. Stanley had stood in when my father was on the outs with his father. Stanley it had been who urged this father of mine into the Forest Service. And it was Stanley whom my father had—

"It never was any secret Stanley liked to take a drink," I was hearing the elaboration now. "But when I started as ranger at Indian Head and he still was the ranger at English Creek, I started to realize the situation was getting beyond that. There were more and more days when Stanley couldn't operate without a bottle at his side. He still knew more about the Two than anybody, and in the normal course of events I could kind of keep a watch on things up here and catch any problem that got past Stanley. We went along that way for a few years. Nobody higher up noticed, or at least minded. But it's one thing to function day by day, and another to have to do it during a big fire."

"And Phantom Woman was big enough," Stanley quietly dropped into my father's telling of it all.

Something was adding up in a way I didn't want it to. "After Phantom Woman. What happened after Phantom Woman?"

Stanley took his turn first. "Major Kelley tied a can to me. 'Your employment with the U.S. Forest Service is severed,' I believe is how it was put. And I been rattling around ever since, I guess." He glanced at my father as if he had just thought of something further to tell him. "You remember the couple times I tried the cure, Mac. I tried it a couple more, since. It never took."

"But you got by okay here," I protested. "You haven't had a real drink all the time we've been cooking."

"But I'll have one the first minute I get back to the Busbys'," Stanley forecast. "And then a couple to wash that one down. Naw, Jick. I know myself. I ought to, I been around myself long enough." As if to be sure I accepted the sum of him, Stanley gave it flatly: "In a pinch I can go dry for as long as I did here. But ordinarily, no. I got a built-in thirst."

Now my father. "I never expected they'd come down on Stanley that hard. A transfer, some rocking-chair job where the drinking wouldn't matter that much. Something to get him off the English Creek district. I couldn't just stand by and see both him and the Two country go to hell." The expression on my father: I suppose here was my first inkling that a person could do what he thought was right and yet be never comfortable about it. He shook his head over what had to be said next, erasing the inquiry that had been building in me. "You know how the Major is. Put up or shut up. When he bounced Stanley, he handed me English Creek. I wanted it run right, did I? Up to me to do it." My father cast a look around the fire camp, into the night where no brightness marked either Flume Gulch or the slope. "And here I still am, trying to."

Again that night I was too stirred up for sleep. Turning and turning in the sleeping bag; the question beyond reach of questioner; the two similar figures crowding my mind, they and my new knowledge of them as awake as the night.

Up against a decision, my father had chosen the Two country over his friend, his mentor, Stanley.

Up against a decision, my brother had chosen independence over my father.

Rewrite my life into one of those other McCaskill versions and what would I have done in my father's place, or my brother's? Even yet I don't know. I do not know. It may be that there is no knowing until a person is in so hard a place.

All that next morning my father had Kratka's crew felling suspicious snags in the burnt-over gulch and creek bottom, and Ames's men on the slope to patrol for any sign of spark or smudge amid that char which had been grass. Mop-up work was all this amounted to—a couple of days of it needed to be done after a fire this size, just to be on the safe side—and at lunch my father said he was thinking about letting half of the EFFs go back to Great Falls tonight. He predicted, "The thanks I'll get is that headquarters will want to know why in holy hell I didn't get them off the payroll *last* night."

Stanley and I recuperated from the lunch preparation and gradually started on supper, neither of us saying anything worthwhile.

When the hot part of the afternoon had passed without trouble, even my father was satisfied that the Flume Gulch fire was not going to leap from its black grave.

He came into camp early with the EFFs who were being let go. "Paul, the show is all yours," he delegated. "I'm going to head into Gros Ventre with one load of these guys, and Tony"—the timekeeper—"can haul the rest. Have Chet tell Great Falls to send a truck up and get them from there, would you. And Paul"—my father checked his assistant as Paul started off to phone the order to Chet—"Paul, it was a good camp."

I was next on my father's mental list. "Jick, you might as well come in with me. Stanley can leave Pony off on his ride home."

Plainly my father wanted my company, or at least my presence.

"Okay," I said. "Let me tell Stanley."

My father nodded. "I'll go round up Wisdom. He's somewhere over there bragging up Bouncing Betty to the CCs. Meet us down at the pickups."

The ride to town, my father driving and Wisdom and I beside him in the cab of one pickup and the other pickup load of EFFs behind us, was mostly nickel-and-dime gab. Our route was the Noon Creek one, a handier drive from the fire camp than backtracking over to English Creek. Reminiscent exclamations from Wisdom when we passed the haystacks of the Reese place. Already the stacks were turning from green to tan. Then my father eyeing around the horizon and thinking out loud that August sure as hell ought to be done with heat and lightning by now. More than that, I have no memory of. The fact may even be that I lulled off a little, in the motion of that pickup cab.

When we had goodbyed Wisdom and the other EFFs, my father and I grabbed a quick supper in the Lunchery. Oyster stew never tasted better, which is saying a lot. Before we could head home, though, my father said he had to stop by the *Gleaner* office. "Bill is going to want all the dope about the fire. It may take a little while. You want me to pick you up at Ray's after I'm done?" I did.

St. Ignatius St. was quiet, in the calm of suppertime and just after, except for one series of periodic *whirr*s. Which proved to be Ray pushing the lawn mower around and around the Heaney front yard. Behind him, Mary Ellen was collecting the cut grass with a lawn rake bigger than she was.

I stepped into the yard and propped myself against the giant cottonwood, in its shadowed side. Busy as Ray and Mary Ellen were, neither saw me. Myself, I was as tired as I have ever been, yet my mind was going like a million.

After a minute I called across the lawn to Ray: "A little faster if you can stand it."

His grin broke out, and from the far corner of the yard he came pushing the lawn mower diagonally across to me, somehow making in the back of his throat the *clackaclackaclackaclacka* sound of a horse-drawn haymower.

"Ray-AY!" protested Mary Ellen at his untidy shortcut across the lawn. But then here she came raking up after him.

"What do you think?" Ray asked when he reached the tree and me. "Had I better bring this out to Pete's next summer and make hay with you?"

"Sounds good to me," I said. "But that's next summer. I want to know where this one went to." The light in the Heaney kitchen dimmed out, another one came on in the living room, then the murmur of Ed's radio. Seven P.M., you could bank on it. I thought back to my last visit to this household you could set your clock by, when I pulled in from the Double W and the session with Alec that first Saturday night of the month. "It's been a real quick August."

"Quicker than you know," advised Ray. "Today is September. School's almost here."

"The hell. I guess I lost some days somewhere." Three more days and I would be fifteen years old. Four more days and Ray and Mary Ellen and I would be back in school. It didn't seem possible. Time is the trickiest damn commodity. The sound of Ed Heaney's radio in there should have been what I was hearing the night of the Fourth of July, not almost to Labor Day. Haying and supper at the Double W and the phone call to Alec and the forest fire and the revelations from Stanley and my father, all seemed as if they should be yet to happen. But they were the past now, in my mind like all that history in Toussaint's and Stanley's.

"Can we feed you something, Jick?" Ray asked in concern. "You look kind of hard-used."

"Dad and I ate uptown," I said. "And he'll be here any minute. But I suppose I could manage to—"

Just then the front porch screen door opened and Ed Heaney was standing there. We all three looked at him in curiosity because with the screen door open that way he was letting in moths, which was major disorderly conduct for him. I will always see Ed Heaney in that doorway of light, motionless there as if he had been pushed out in front of a crowd and was trying to think of what to say. At last he did manage to bring out words, and they were these:

"Ray, Mary Ellen, you better come in the house now. They've started another war in Europe."

FOUR

"We'll be in it inside of six months," was one school of thought when Europe went to war in September of 1939, and the other refrain ran, "It's their own scrap over there, we can just keep our nose out this time." But as ever, history has had its own say and in a way not foretold—at Pearl Harbor last Sunday, in the flaming message of the Jap bombs.

—*GROS VENTRE WEEKLY GLEANER, DECEMBER 11, 1941*

ALL THE PEOPLE OF that English Creek summer of 1939—they stay on in me even though so many of them are gone from life. You know how when you open a new book for the first time, its pages linger against each other, pull apart with a reluctant little separating sound. They never quite do that again, the linger or the tiny sound. Maybe it can be said that for me, that fifteenth summer of my existence was the new book and its fresh pages. My memories of those people and times and what became of them, those are the lasting lines within the book, there to be looked on again and again.

My mother was the earliest of us to get word of Pearl Harbor on that first Sunday of December, 1941. The telephone rang, she answered it, and upon learning that the call was from Two Medicine National Forest headquarters in Great Falls she began to set them straight on the day of the week. When told the news from Hawaii she went silent and held the receiver out for my father to take.

In a sense Alec already had gone to the war by then. At least he was gone, with the war as a kind of excuse. For when the fighting started in Europe and the prospect for beef prices skyrocketed, Wendell Williamson loaded up on cattle. Wendell asked Alec to switch to the Deuce W, his ranch down in the Highwood Mountains, as a top hand there during this buildup of the herd. Just after shipping time, mid-September of 1939, Alec went. It may come as no vast surprise that he and Leona had unraveled by then. She had chosen to start her last year of high school, Alec was smarting over her decision to go that way instead of to the altar, and my belief is that he grabbed the Deuce W job as a way to put distance between him and that disappointment.

I saw Leona the day of the Gros Ventre centennial, several years ago now. She is married to a man named Wright and they run a purebred Hereford ranch down in the Crazy Mountains country. The beauty still shines out of Leona. Ranch work and the riding she does have kept her in shape, I couldn't help noticing. But one thing did startle me. Leona's hair now is silvery as frost.

She smiled at my surprise and said: "Gold to silver, Jick. You've seen time cut my value."

Left to my own devices, I would not tell any further about Alec. Yet my brother, his decisions, the consequences life dealt him, always are under that summer and its aftermath like the paper on which a calendar is printed.

Before he enlisted in the army the week after Pearl Harbor, Alec did come back to Gros Ventre to see our parents. Whether reconciliation is the right amount of word for that visit I don't really know, for I was on a basketball trip to Browning and a ground blizzard kept those of us of the Gros Ventre team there overnight. So by the time I got back, Alec had been and gone. And that last departure of his from English Creek led to a desert in Tunisia. How stark it sounds; yet it is as much as we ever knew. A Stuka finding that bivouac at dusk, swooping in and splattering twenty-millimeter shells. Of the cluster of soldiers who were around a jerry can drawing their water rations, only one man lived through the strafing. He was not Alec.

So. My last words with my brother were those on the telephone when I tried to talk him into going to the Flume Gulch fire. I do have a hard time forgiving life for that.

Ray Heaney and I went together to the induction station at Missoula in September of 1942, about a week after my eighteenth birthday. And we saw each other during basic training at Fort Lewis out in Washington. In the war itself, though, we went separate ways. Ray spent a couple of years of fighting as a rifleman in Italy and somehow came through it all. These days Ray has an insurance agency over in Idaho at Coeur d'Alene, and we keep in touch by Christmas card.

I wound up in a theater of World War Two that most people don't even know existed, the Aleutians campaign away to hell and gone out in the Northern Pacific Ocean off Alaska. Those Aleutian islands made me downgrade the wind of the Two country. There is not a lot else worth telling in my warrior career, for early in our attack on Cold Mountain I was one of those who got an Attu tattoo—a Jap bullet in my left leg, breaking the big bone not far above the ankle. Even yet on chilly days, I am reminded down there.

When the army eventually turned me loose into civilian life I used my GI bill to study forestry at the university in Missoula. Each of those college summers I worked as a smokejumper for the Forest Service, parachuting out of more airplanes onto more damn forest fires than now seems sane to me. And in the last of those smokejumping summers I began going with a classmate of mine at the university, a young woman from there in the Bitterroot country. The day after graduation in 1949, we were married. That marriage lasted just a year and a half, and it is not something I care to dwell on.

That same graduation summer I took and passed the Forest Service exam and was assigned onto the Custer National Forest over in eastern Montana. I suppose one of the Mazoola desk jockeys thought it scrupulous, or found it in some regulation, that most of the state of Montana should be put between me and my father on the Two. But all that eastern Montana stint accomplished—hell, even the name got me down, that dodo Custer—was to cock me into readiness to shoot out of the Forest Service when the chance came.

Pete Reese provided the click. As soon as his lambs were shipped in the fall of 1952 Pete offered me a first crack at the Noon Creek ranch. Marie's health was giving out; she lived only a few more years, dark lovely doe she was; and Pete wanted to seize an opportunity to buy a sheep outfit down in the Gallatin Valley near Bozeman, where the winters might not be quite so ungodly. I remember every exact word from Pete in that telephone call: "You're only an accidental nephew, Jick, but I suppose maybe I can give you honorary son-in-law terms to buy the place and the sheep."

I took Pete up on his offer and came back to the Two Medicine country so fast I left a tunnel in the air.

On the twenty-first of March of 1953—we kidded that going through a lambing time together would tell us in a hurry whether we could stand each other the rest of our lives—Marcella Withrow and I were married. Her first marriage, to a young dentist at Conrad, had not panned out either, and she had come back over to Gros Ventre when the job of librarian opened up. That first winter of mine on the Reese place I resorted to the library a lot, and it began to dawn on me that books were not the only attraction. I like to think Marce and I are both tuned to an echo of Dode: "Life is wide, there's room to take a new run at it."

In any event, Marce and I seem to have gotten divorce out of our systems with those early wrong guesses, and we have produced two daughters, one married to a fish-and-game man up at Sitka in Alaska, the other living at Missoula where she and her husband both work for the newspaper. We also seem to be here on Noon Creek to stay, for as every generation ends up doing on this ranch we have lately built a new house. Four such domiciles by now, if you count the Ramsay homestead where I was born. It cost a junior fortune in double-glazing and insulation, but we have windows to the mountains all along the west wall of this place. These September mornings when I sit here early at the kitchen table and watch dawn come to the skyline of the Two, coffee forgotten and cold in my cup, the view is worth any price.

The thirty-plus years of ranching that Marce and I have put in here on Noon Creek have not been easy. Tell me what is. But so far the pair of us have withstood coyotes and synthetic fabrics and Two country winters and the decline of sheepherders to persevere in the sheep business, although we have lately diversified into some Charolais cattle and several fields of that new sanfoin alfalfa. I am never going to be red-hot about being a landlord to cows. And the problem of finding decent hay hands these days makes me positively pine for Wisdom Johnson and Bud Dolson and Perry Fox. But Marce and I are agreed that we will try whatever we have to, in order to hang on to this land. I suppose even dude ranching, though I hope to Christ it never quite comes to that.

Along English Creek, the main change to me whenever I go over there is that sheep are damn few now. Cattle, a lot of new farming; those are what came up on the latest spin of the agricultural roulette wheel. About half the families, Hahns, Frews, Roziers, another generation of Busby brothers, still retain the ranches their parents brought through the Depression. The Van Bebber ranch is owned by a North Dakotan named Florin, and he rams around the place in the same slambang fashion Ed did. Maybe there is something in the water there.

And Dode Withrow's place is run by one of Dode's other son-in-laws, Bea's husband Merle Torrance. Dode though is still going strong, the old boy. Weathered as a stump, but whenever I see that father-in-law of mine he is the original Dode: "What do you know for sure, Jick? Have they found a cure yet for people in the sonofabitching sheep business?"

Anyway, except for big aluminum sheds and irrigation sprinklers slinging water over the fields, you would not find the ranches of English Creek so different from the way they were.

The Double W now is owned by a company called TriGram Resources, which bought it from the California heirs after Wendell Williamson's death. As a goddamn tax writeoff, need I say.

How can it be twenty years since my father retired from the Forest Service? Yet it is.

After this summer I have told about, the next year was awful on him, what with Alec gone from us to the Deuce W and the decision from Mazoola in the winter of 1939 to move my father's district office from English Creek into Gros Ventre. Access realignment, they called it, and showed him on paper how having the ranger station in town would put him closer by paved road to the remote north portion of the Two. He kicked against it in every way he could think of; even wrote to the Regional Forester himself, the Major: "Since when is running a forest a matter of highway miles?" Before long, though, the war and its matters were on my father's mind and the mail was bringing Forest Service posters urging "LET'S DELIVER THE WOODS: SHARPEN YOUR AX TO DOWN THE AXIS."

The way the water of a stream riffles around a rock, the Forest Service's flow of change went past my father. Major Kelley departed Missoula during the war, to California to head up the government project of growing guayule for artificial rubber. "I'd rather take a beating than admit it," my father confessed, "but I was kind of getting used to those goddamn kelleygrams." The Two supervisor Ken Sipe was tapped for a wartime job at Forest Service headquarters in Washington, D.C., and stayed on back there. Their successors in Region One and the Two Medicine forest headquarters simply left my father in place, rangering the English Creek district. I have heard of a ranger out in the state of Washington who spent a longer career on a district, but my father's record wasn't far behind.

His first winter of retirement in Gros Ventre was a gloomy and restless time for him, although my mother and I could never tell for sure how much of that was retirement and how much just his usual winter. It was a relief to us all when spring perked him up. I had a call from him the morning of the first day of fishing season:

"Bet you a beer you've forgotten how to string ten fish on a willow."

"I can't get away," I had to tell him. "I've got ewes and lambs all over creation out here. You sure you wouldn't like to take up a career as a bunch herder?"

"Brook trout," he informed me, "are the only kind of herd that interests me. You're missing a free chance at a fishing lesson."

"I'll cash that offer next Sunday, okay? You can scout the holes for me today. I want Mom to witness your count when you get home, though. It's past time I was owed a beer, and it's beginning to dawn on me that your arithmetic could be the reason."

"That'll be the day," he rose to my joshing. "When I don't bring home ten fish on a willow. As will be shown to you personally next Sunday."

When he hadn't returned by dusk of that day, my mother called me at the ranch and I then called Tom Helwig, the deputy sheriff. I drove across the divide to English Creek and just before full dark found my father's pickup parked beside the North Fork, on Walter Kyle's old place. Tom Helwig and I and the men from the English Creek ranches searched and searched, hollering in the dark, until giving up about midnight.

With first light of the next morning I was the one who came onto my father. His body, rather, stricken by a heart attack, away back in the brush atop a beaver dam he'd been fishing. Nine trout on the willow stringer at his side, the tenth still on the hook where my father had dropped his pole.

"Jick, the summer when Alec left. Could it have come out different? If your father and I hadn't kept at him, hadn't had our notions of what he should do—would it all have been different?"

My mother brought this up in the first week after my father passed away. In a time like that, the past meets you wherever you turn. The days do not use their own hours and minutes, they find ones you have lived through with the person you are missing.

Only that once, though, in all the years from then to now, did she wonder that question aloud. The other incidents of the summer of 1939 we often talk over, when I stop by to see how she is doing. She has stayed on in her own house in Gros Ventre. "I'm sufficient company for myself," this mother of mine maintains. She still grows the biggest vegetable garden in town and is perpetual president of the library board. What irks her is when people regard her, as she puts it, "as if I was Some Kind of a Monument." I had to talk hard when her eighty-fourth birthday came this April and the new young editor of the *Gleaner* wanted to interview her. GROS VENTRE WOMAN HAS 'FOOLED' THE 20TH CENTURY was the headline. You know how those stories are, though. It is hard to fit such a life into mere inches of words.

I had never told her or my father of Alec's refusal, that noon when I phoned him about the Flume Gulch fire. And I did not when she asked could it, would it all have come out different?

But what I did say to her was the one truth I could see in that distant English Creek summer.

"If you two hadn't had the notions you did, you wouldn't have been yourselves. And if Alec hadn't gone his way, he wouldn't have been Alec."

She shook her head. "Maybe if it had been other times—"

"Maybe," I said.

—

And Stanley Meixell.

Stanley stayed on with the Busby brothers until their lambs were shipped that fall of 1939, then said he thought he'd go have a look at Oregon—"always did like that name." Early in the war the Busbys received word that he was working in a shipyard out there at Portland. After that, nothing.

So I am left with the last scene of Stanley after the Flume Gulch fire, before my father and I headed in to Gros Ventre. I went over to where Stanley was stirring a pot of gravy.

"Yessir, Jick. Looks like this feedlot of ours is about to close down."

"Stanley," I heard myself saying, "all that about the Phantom Woman fire—I don't know who was right or wrong, or if anybody was, or what. But I'm sorry, about the way things turned out back then."

"A McCaskill who'll outright say the word sorry," replied Stanley. He tasted the gravy, then turned to me, his dark eyes steady within the weave of squint lines. "I was more right than I even knew, that time."

"What time was that?"

"When I told your folks you looked to me like the jick of the family."

ACKNOWLEDGMENTS

THIS IS A WORK of fiction, and so English Creek, the Two Medicine National Forest, and the town of Gros Ventre exist only in these pages. Some of their geography is actual—the area of Dupuyer Creek and the Rocky Mountain Front, west of the town of Dupuyer, Montana. I'm afraid, though, that anyone who attempts to sort the real from the imagined in this book is in for confusion. In general I've retained nearby existing places such as Valier, Conrad, Choteau, Heart Butte and so on, but anything within what I've stretched geography to call the "Two Medicine country" I have felt free to change or invent. Thus my town of Gros Ventre, on Dupuyer's actual site, shares with Dupuyer only its origin as a stopover for freight wagons. That, and my love for the place.

Two persons I allude to were actual: Regional Forester Evan W. Kelley and pioneer Ben English. Insofar as possible I've sketched them from contemporary accounts or historical records. Where their lives coincide with those of my own characters, I've simply tried to do what seems to me the fiction writer's job—make the stuff up as realistically as I can. My particular thanks to Mary English Lindsey for sharing with me her memories of her father, and to Jack Hayne for contributing from his lode of knowledge about the Dupuyer area's pioneers.

I could not have created my version of the Two country in the period of this novel without the newspaper files and other local historical material of several northern Montana public libraries. I'm much indebted to Choteau Public Library and librarians Maureen Strazdas and Marian

Nett; Conrad Public Library and librarians Corleen Norman and Steve Gratzer, Great Falls Public Library, librarians Sister Marita Bartholome, Howard Morris, and Susan Storey, and library director Richard Gerken; Havre Public Library and librarian Bill Lisonby; Hill County Library and Dorothy Armstrong; Valier Public Library and librarian Sue Walley. And my appreciation as well to Harriet Hayne of Dupuyer, for sharing the taped interviews done for Dupuyer's remarkable centennial volume, *By Gone Days and Modern Ways.*

The Forest History Society provided many otherwise unavailable details of the lives led by U.S. Forest Service rangers and their families. Great thanks to my friends there for being so attentive to my needs, whether I happened to be on premises or at my typewriter in Seattle: Kathy and Ron Fahl, Mary Beth Johnson, and Pete Steen.

Much of the 1930s background for this book derives from the holdings of the three principal repositories of Montana history, and I'm grateful to the staff of each. The Renne Library of Montana State University at Bozeman; librarians Minnie Paugh and Ilah Shriver of Special Collections, and archivist Jean Schmidt. The Mansfield Library of the University of Montana at Missoula; librarian Kathy Schaefer of Special Collections, and archivist Dale Johnson. The Montana Historical Society at Helena; Bob Clark, Patricia Bick, Ellen Arguimbau—with particular thanks to reference librarian Dave Walter, who unflinchingly fielded query after query in the years I worked on this book.

For their generous encouragement and for rescuing me whenever I got lost in their specific fields of expertise, my thanks too to Montana's corps of professional historians, particularly Stan Davison, Bill Farr, Harry Fritz, Duane Hampton, Mike Malone, Rex Myers, and Rich Roeder. And I know of no other state with a published heritage of such quality and quantity as that of *Montana: The Magazine of Western History;* my gratitude to *Montana*'s editor, Bill Lang, for his skills as well as his friendship.

The University of Washington Library, my home base for this and my other books, again was an invaluable resource. I owe thanks to the Northwest Collection's Carla Rickerson, Andy Johnson, Dennis Andersen, Susan Cunningham, and Marjorie Cole; to Glenda Pearson of the Newspaper and Microcopy Center; and to Barbara Gordon of the Forest Resources library.

For vital guidance into the historical holdings of the U.S. Forest Service, I'm indebted to Maggie Nybo of Lewis and Clark National Forest headquarters in Great Falls and Raymond Karr and Jud Moore of the information office at Region One headquarters in Missoula. And I owe specific and special thanks to Charles E. "Mike" Hardy of Missoula, both for loaning me his personal collection of fireline notebooks, cookbooks, etc., and for his cataloguing of the papers of Harry T. Gisborne, long-time USFS forest fire researcher, at the University of Montana archives. I emphasize that while I have drawn from the fire descriptions of Gisborne, Elers Koch, and a number of other Montana foresters of their generation, the Flume Gulch fire is my own concoction.

I benefited greatly from listening to two career Forest Service men as they "pawed over old times": the late Nevan McCullough of Enumclaw, Washington, and Dahl Kirkpatrick of Albuquerque, New Mexico. My thanks to Mike McCullough for arranging that joint interview.

Many of the details of my Gros Ventre Fourth of July rodeo are due to the diligence of Kristine Fredriksson, registrar of collections and research at the ProRodeo Hall of Champions & Museum of the American Cowboy in Colorado Springs.

Vernon Carstensen, as ever a fund of ideas, brought to my attention the Montana origins of the famous dust storm of May, 1934, which I have appropriated for my Two Medicine country, and was a valuable sounding board about the Depression and the West.

Special thanks to my first and best friend in the Dupuyer country, Tom Chadwick; his driving skills delivered Carol and me to much of the landscape of this book.

My wife, Carol, has been the first reader of all my books. This time, camera ever in hand, she also became geographer of the Two country and architect of the town of Gros Ventre. My debt to her in all my work is beyond saying.

To my agent Liz Darhansoff, and my editor, Tom Stewart—thanks for making *English Creek* possible.

One of my first memories, a few months before my sixth birthday, is of hearing my parents and their neighbors discuss the radio news of the death of President Franklin Delano Roosevelt in April, 1945. Thus it is very nearly forty years now that I have been listening to Montanans. But never with more benefit than during the writing of *English Creek*. By interview or letter or phone, and in some instances by conversation and acquaintanceship down through the years, the following Montanans have lent me lore which in one way or another contributed to this book. My deep thanks to them all. *Bozeman:* Jake and Eleanor

Mast. *Butte:* Lucy Old. *Byunum:* Ira Perkins. *Choteau:* A. B. Guthrie, Jr.
Conrad: Albert Warner. *Corvallis:* Helen Eden. *Deer Lodge:* Frank A.
Shaw. *Dupuyer:* Lil and Tom Howe. *Flaxville:* Eugene Hatfield. *Forsyth:*
James H. Smith. *Frazer:* Arthur H. Fast. *Fort Benton:* Alice Klatte,
C. G. Stranahan. *Great Falls:* George Engler, Ted Fosse, Geoffrey
Greene, Bradley and Joy Hamlett. *Hamilton:* Billie Abbey, George M.
Stewart. *Havre:* Charles M. Brill, Edward J. Cook, Elmer and Grace
Gwynn, Frances Inman, Frank Lammerding, Howard Sanderson.
Helena: John Gruar, Eric White. *Hogeland:* Adrian Olszewski. *Jackson:*
Kenneth Krause. *Malta:* Fred Olson, Egil Solberg. *Missoula:* Henry J.
Viche. *Peerless:* Ladon Jones. *Superior:* Wally Ringer. *Valier:* Jim Sheble.
White Sulphur Springs: Joyce Celander, Tony Hunolt, Clifford Shearer.
Wisdom: Mr. and Mrs. Fred Else.

My inspiration for "The Lord of the Field" in Beth McCaskill's
Fourth of July speech was Montgomery M. Atwater's article "Man-
Made Rain," written for the Montana Writers' Project during the WPA
era. Similarly the "Subjects under discussion . . . by U.S. Forest Service
crews" was inspired by the versatile Bob Marshall, "A Contribution to
the Life History of the Lumberjack," *Pulp and Paper Magazine of
Canada,* May 21, 1931. The observation that a forest fire at night
resembles a lighted city is from Elers Koch, in *Early Days in the Forest
Service, Region One.* The theological survey joke is told by Hartley A.
Calkins in that same volume. The analogy of a wedge of cool air thrusting between a fire and its smoke, and other rare eyewitness descriptions
of a forest fire blowup, derive from H. T. Gisborne's article on the Half-
Moon fire in *The Frontier,* November 1929.

During three summer stints of research in Montana and throughout
the rest of those years of delving for and writing this book, many persons
provided me hospitality, information, advice, encouragement, or other
aid. My appreciation to Coleen Adams, Margaret Agee, Pat Armstrong,
Genise and Wayne Arnst, Robert Athearn, John Backes, Bill Bevis, Gene
and Hazel Bonnet, Merrill Burlingame, Harold and Maxine Chadwick,
Juliette Crump, H. J. Engles, Clifford Field, Howard and Trudy Forbes,
Glen Gifford, Sam Gilluly, Madeleine Grandy, Carol Guthrie, Vicki and
Chuck Hallingstad, Gary Hammond of the Nature Conservancy's Pine
Butte preserve, Eileen Harrington, John James, Carol Jimenez, Melvylei
Johnson, Pat Kelley, Bill Kittredge, Dr. Jim Lane, Sue Lang, Becky Lang
and Joel Lang, Marc Lee, Gail Malone, Elliot Marks of the Nature Con-
servancy, Sue Mathews, Ann McCartney, Nancy Meiselas, Horace Mor-

gan, Ann and Marshall Nelson, Ken Nicholson, Peggy O'Coyne, Bud and Vi Olson, Gary Olson, Judy Olson, Laura Mary Palin, Cille and Gary Payton, Dorothy Payton, Patty Payton, Dorothy and Earl Perkins, Jarold Ramsey, Bill Rappold, Marilyn Ridge, Jean and John Roden, Tom Salansky, Ripley Schemm, Ted and Jean Schwinden, Annick Smith, Gail Steen, Fay Stokes, Margaret Svec, Merlyn Talbot, Dean Vaupel; John Waldner and the other members of the New Rockport Hutterite colony; Irene Wanner, Donald K. Watkins, Lois and Jim Welch, Rosana Winterburn, Glen Gifford, Sonny Linger, Ken Twichel. And the people of Dupuyer, Montana.

A SCRIBNER
READING GROUP GUIDE

ENGLISH CREEK

DISCUSSION POINTS

1. Much of the success of *English Creek* stems from the credibility of the narrative voice. Show how Jick McCaskill's acute sensitivity and observant personality make him a prime candidate for creating a balanced narrative structure. How does Doig artistically meld Jick's psychological musings with his more historical accounts?

2. The novel is in great part about Jick's journey into maturity, into wisdom. How does Jick bridge the gap between boyhood and manhood? Who is particularly influential in his coming of age?

3. Laconicism is a common characteristic of the ranchers and mountain men in Western film and fiction. Jick inherits his father's wry wit; show how he uses it to deal with life's bitter situations.

4. Is Alec a foil to Jick? Are there key choices that Alec makes and particular events in his life that save him from being a flat character and make him, rather, someone worth serious consideration?

5. At the end of Chapter One, Jick says, "Skinning wet sheep corpses, contending with a pack horse who decides he's a mountain goat, nursing Stanley along, lightning, any number of self-cooked meals, the hangover I'd woke up with and still had more than a trace of—what sad sonofabitch wouldn't realize he was being used out of the ordinary?" Jick's pack trip with Stanley Meixell is a jolting thrust from innocence to experience. What prompts Jick to discard his first impressions of Stanley and delve deeper into the meaning of the man behind Dr. Al K. Hall?

6. Why is Beth eager to avoid looking back? Compare and contrast Jick's attitude toward the past and its stories with his mother's attitude. Do the deaths of Varick and Alec rattle Beth into retrospective musings, even regret about what might have been?

7. Discuss how the Double W embodies the characteristics of the classic villain of the West.

8. Consider Velma Simms and Leona Tracy and how Doig paints their entrance into a room full of males. Compare and contrast the adoration they receive with the more quiet acknowledgment Beth receives from the men who love her. Why is Leona so alluring to Alec, even Jick? Is her highly physical role in the novel, a role charged with sexual tension, somehow comparable to the role of Willa Cather's Lena Lingard in *My Antonía*?

9. The Fourth of July dance adds mystery and musicality to the novel. Discuss the imagery surrounding this "beautiful haunting" and how the scene helps Jick to see his parents in a way that illuminates "all that had begun at another dance, at the Noon Creek schoolhouse twenty years before."

10. Why does Varick McCaskill listen to Stanley's advice about the fire in Flume Gulch? Were Jick not "prey to a profound preoccupation," would the novel have turned out the way that it does?

11. Doig recognizes the danger of engaging in literary symbolism at the risk of adding pretense to a novel that aims to be more realistic. What literary devices does he use instead to enliven both the narrative and his characters' voices? Do you think the inclusion of these devices, particularly song lyrics, is Doig's attempt at a fusion of poetry and fiction?

BACKGROUND NOTES

THE PIECE OF THE WORLD I ADMIRE MOST

Am I Jick? People have asked me a thousand times whether the fourteen-year-old narrator of *English Creek,* in his pivotal summer of 1939, is my literary alter ego. No, not by a long shot, as Jick McCaskill himself would put it. But his homeland, the Two Medicine country of Montana and of my trilogy by that name, for an important time was mine.

English Creek and its valley are actually the Dupuyer Creek area of northern Montana, beneath the skyline of the Rocky Mountain Front. It's the region where I lived during high school and was a ranch hand and farm worker for several summers, the "Facing North" country in my memoir, *This House of Sky*, and it is big and hard and glorious—the piece of the world I admire most. It's a country of margin, of America changing, ascending from one geography to another, and of the sensation Isak Dinesen caught in *Out of Africa*: "In the highlands you woke up in the morning and thought: Here I am, where I ought to be."

Looking back on *English Creek,* the first of my fiction to be set in Montana, I see that it shares with *This House of Sky* an emphasis on landscape and weather and their effects on people's lives. In both books (all right, in all my books) I was trying to write about the grit of an America that even yet half-exists in the mountains-and-plains West: ranching, haying, fire-fighting, the Forest Service itself, all have their own techniques and lingo which make them vivid. What I deliberately made different from *This House of Sky* was the voice of this book—the narrative not as densely poetic as *Sky's*. Instead, I tried for a kind of idiomatic eloquence, a western cadence ruffled by turns of phrase. Jick, the narrator, is a man of today looking back on 1939, which gave him the angle of view I needed to hang the storyline on, and he has the love of sayings and stories that animates a lot of otherwise taciturn westerners. I remember, as I worked on the book, how Jick's voice, built as it was from my decades of file cards and notebook of dialogue and phrasing, excited me so much I hated to admit it, for fear of jinx. But that voice of his, from the opening line when he tells us "That month of June swam into the Two Medicine country," felt true to the time and country, and came more easily than the style of any of my books before or since.

ALSO BY IVAN DOIG

Fiction

Prairie Nocturne
Mountain Time
Bucking the Sun
Ride with Me, Mariah Montana
English Creek
The Sea Runners

Nonfiction

Heart Earth
Winter Brothers
This House of Sky

DANCING AT THE RASCAL FAIR

Ivan Doig

Scribner

New York London Toronto Sydney

SCRIBNER
1230 Avenue of the Americas
New York, NY 10020

First Scribner trade paperback edition 2003
SCRIBNER and design are trademarks of Macmillan Library Reference
USA, Inc., used under license by
Simon & Schuster, the publisher of this work.

For information about special discounts for bulk purchases, please
contact Simon & Schuster Special Sales:
1-800-456-6798 or business@simonandschuster.com

Manufactured in the United States of America

25   27   29   30   28   26   24

Library of Congress Cataloging-in-Publication Data
Doig, Ivan.
Dancing at the rascal fair / Ivan Doig.
p.   cm.
1. Montana—Fiction. 2. Scots—Montana—Fiction. 3. Frontier and
pioneer life—Montana—Fiction. I. Title.
PS3554.O415D36   1996
813'.54—dc20   96-23018
CIP

ISBN-13: 978-0-684-83105-3
ISBN-10:   0-684-83105-8

Scotchmen and coyotes was the only ones
that could live in the Basin,
and pretty damn soon the coyotes starved out.

    —CHARLES CAMPBELL DOIG (1901–71)

TO BLACKFEET
RESERVATION

NOON CREEK
SCHOOL

Egan

Noon Creek

Double W

A. Frew   Findlater

North

Erskine

Fork

Duff

South Fork

SOUTH FORK
SCHOOL

English Creek

TO GROS VENTRE
(9 miles)

SCOTLAND AND HELENA

Harbour Mishap at Greenock. Yesterday morning, while a horse and cart were conveying a thousand-weight of sugar on the quay at Albert Harbour, one of the cartwheels caught a mooring stanchion, which caused the laden conveyance and its draft animal to fall over into the water. The poor creature made desperate efforts to free itself and was successful in casting off all the harness except the collar, which, being attached to the shafts of the sunken cart, held its head under water until it was drowned. The dead animal and the cart were raised during the forenoon by the Greenock harbour diver.
—GLASGOW CALEDONIAN, OCTOBER 23, 1889

T O SAY the truth, it was not how I expected—stepping off toward America past a drowned horse.

You would remember too well, Rob, that I already was of more than one mind about the Atlantic Ocean. And here we were, not even within eyeshot of the big water, not even out onto the slow-flowing River Clyde yet, and here this heap of creature that would make, what, four times the sum total of Rob Barclay and Angus McCaskill, here on the Greenock dock it lay gawping up at us with a wild dead eye. Strider of the earth not an hour ago, wet rack of carcass now. An affidavit such as that says a lot to a man who cannot swim. Or at least who never has.

But depend on you, Rob. In those times you could make light of whatever. There was that red shine on you, your cheeks and jawline always as ruddy and smooth as if you had just put down the shaving razor, and on this largest day of our young lives you were aglow like a hot coal. *A stance like a lord and a hue like a lady.* You cocked your head in that way of yours and came right out with:

1

"See now, McAngus. So long as we don't let them hitch a cart to us we'll be safe as saints."

"A good enough theory," I had to agree, "as far as it goes."

Then came commotion, the grieved sugar carter bursting out, "Oh Ginger dear, why did ye have to tumble?" and dockmen shouting around him and a blinkered team of horses being driven up at full clatter to drag their dead ilk away. Hastily some whiskered geezer from the Cumbrae Steamship Line was waving the rest of us along: "Dead's dead, people, and standing looking at it has never been known to help. Now then, whoever of you are for the *James Watt,* straight on to the queue there, New York at its other end, step to it please, thank you." And so we let ourselves be shooed from the sight of poor old horsemeat Ginger and went and stepped onto line with our fellow steerage ticketholders beside the bulk of the steamship. Our fellow Scotland-leavers, half a thousand at once, each and every of us now staring sidelong at this black iron island that was to carry us to America. One of the creels which had held the sugar was bobbing against the ship's side, while over our heads deckhands were going through the motions of some groaning chore I couldn't begin to figure.

"Now if this was fresh water, like," sang out one above the dirge of their task, "I'd wager ye a guinea this harbor'd right now taste sweet as treacle."

"But it's not, ye bleedin' daftie. The bleedin' Clyde is tide salt from the Tail of the Bank the full way up to bleedin' Glasgow, now en't it? And what to hell kind of concoction are ye going to get when ye mix sugar and salt?"

"Ask our bedamned cook," put in a third. "All the time he must be doing it, else why's our mess taste like what the China dog walked away from?" As emphasis he spat a throat gob over the side into the harbor water, and my stomach joined my other constituent parts in trepidation about this world-crossing journey of ours. A week and a half of the Atlantic and dubious food besides?

That steerage queue seemed eternal. Seagulls mocked the line of us with sharp cries. A mist verging on rain dimmed out the Renfrewshire hills beyond Greenock's uncountable roofs. Even you appeared a least little bit ill at ease with this wait, Rob, squinting now and again at the steamship as if calculating how it was that so much metal was able to float. And then the cocked head once more, as if pleased with your result. I started to say aloud that if Noah had taken this much time to load the ark, only the giraffes would have lasted through the deluge, but that was remindful of the waiting water and its fate for cart horses and others not amphibious.

Awful, what a person lets himself do to himself. There I stood on that Greenock dock, wanting more than anything else in this life not to put foot aboard that iron ship; and wanting just as desperately to do so and do it that instant. Oh, I knew what was wrestling in me. We had a book—*Crofutt's Trans-Atlantic Emigrants' Guide*— and my malady was right there in it, page one. Crofutt performed as our tutor that a shilling was worth 24 American cents, and how much postal stamps cost there in the big country, and that when it came midnight in old Scotland the clocks of Montana were striking just five of the afternoon. Crofutt told this, too, I can recite it yet today: *Do not emigrate in a fever, but consider the question in each and every aspect. The mother country must be left behind, the family ties, all old associations, broken. Be sure that you look at the dark side of the picture: the broad Atlantic, the dusty ride to the great West of America, the scorching sun, the cold winter—coldest ever you experienced!— and the hard work of the homestead. But if you finally, with your eyes open, decide to emigrate, do it nobly. Do it with no divided heart.*

Right advice, to keep your heart in one pure piece. But easier seen than followed.

I knew I oughtn't, but I turned and looked up the river, east up the great broad trough of the Clyde. East into yesterday. For it had been only the day before when the pair of us were hurled almost all the way across Scotland by train from Nethermuir into clamorsome Glasgow. A further train across the Clyde bridge and westward alongside mile upon brown mile of the river's tideflats and their smell. Then here came Greenock to us, Watt's city of steam, all its shipyards and docks, the chimney stalks of its sugar refineries, its sharp church spires and high, high above all its municipal tower of crisp new stone the color of pie crust. A more going town than our old Nethermuir could be in ten centuries, it took just that first look to tell us of Greenock. For night we bedded where the emigration agent had advised, the Model Lodging House, which may have been a model of something but lodging wasn't it; when morning at last came, off we set to ask our way to the Cumbrae Line's moorage, to the *James Watt*, and to be told in a Clydeside gabble it took the both of us to understand:

"The *Jemmy*, lads? Ye wan' tae gi doon tae the fit of Pa'rick."

And there at the foot of Patrick Street was the Albert Harbor, there was the green-funneled steam swimmer to America, there were the two of us.

For I can't but think of you then, Rob. The Rob you were. In all that we said to each other, before and thereafter, this step from our old land to our new was flat fact with you. The Atlantic Ocean and the continent America all the way across to Montana stood as but the width of a cottage threshold, so far as you ever let on. No second guess, never a might-have-done-instead out of you, none. A silence too total, I realize at last. You had family and a trade to scan back at and I had none of either, yet I was the one tossing puppy looks up the Clyde to yesterday. Man, man, what I would give to know. Under the stream of words by which you talked the two of us into our long step to America, what were your deep reasons? I am late about asking, yes. Years and years and years late. But when was such asking ever not? And by the time I learned there was so much within you that I did not know and you were learning the same of me, we had greater questions for each other.

A soft push on my shoulder. When I turned to your touch you were smiling hard, that Barclay special mix of entertainment and estimation. We had reached the head of the queue, another whiskery geezer in Cumbrae green uniform was trumpeting at us to find Steerage Number One, go forward toward the bow, descend those stairs the full way down, mind our footing and our heads . . .

You stayed where you stood, though, facing me instead of the steamship. You still had the smile on, but your voice was as serious as I ever had heard it.

"Truth now, Angus. Are we both for it?"

Standing looking at it has never been known to help. I filled myself with breath, the last I intended to draw of the air of the pinched old earth called Scotland. *With no divided heart.*

"Both," I made myself say. And up the *Jemmy*'s gangplank we started.

Robert Burns Barclay, single man, apprentice wheelwright, of Nethermuir, Forfarshire. That was Rob on the passenger list of the *James Watt*, 22nd of October of the year 1889. Angus Alexander McCaskill, single man, wheelworks clerk, of Nethermuir, Forfarshire, myself. Both of us nineteen and green as the cheese of the moon and trying our double damnedest not to show it.

Not that we were alone in tint. Our steerage compartment within the *Jemmy* proved to be the forward one for single men—immediately the report went around that the single women were quartered farthest aft, and between them and us stood the married couples and a terrific populace of children—and while not everyone was young, our shipmates were all as new as we to voyaging. Berths loomed in unfamiliar tiers with a passageway not a yard wide between them, and the twenty of us bumped and backed and swirled like a herd of colts trying to establish ourselves.

I am tall, and the inside of the ship was not. Twice in those first minutes of steerage life I cracked myself.

"You'll be hammered down to my size by the time we reach the other shore," Rob came out with, and those around us hoohawed. I grinned the matter away but I did not like it, either the prospect of a hunched journey to America or the public comment about my altitude. But that was Rob for you.

Less did I like the location of Steerage Number One. So far below the open deck, down steep stair after stair into the iron gut of the ship. When you thought about it, and I did, this was like being a kitten in the bottom of a rainbarrel.

"Here I am, mates," recited a fresh voice, that of the steward. "Your shepherd while at sea. First business is three shillings from you each. That's for mattress to keep you company and tin to eat with and the finest saltwater soap you've ever scraped yourself with." Ocean soap and straw bed Rob and I had to buy along with everyone else, but on Crofutt's advice we'd brought our own trustworthy tinware. "Meals are served at midship next deck up, toilets you'll find in the deckhouses, and that's the circle of life at sea, mates," the steward rattled at us, and then he was gone.

As to our compartment companions, a bit of listening told that some were of a fifty embarking to settle in Manitoba, others of a fifty fixed upon Alberta for a future. The two heavenly climes were argued back and forth by their factions, with recitations of rainfall and crop yields and salubrious health effects and imminence of railroads, but no minds were changed, these being Scottish minds.

Eventually someone deigned to ask us neutral pair what our destination might be.

"Montana," Rob enlightened them as if it was Eden's best neighborhood. "I've an uncle there these seven years."

"What does the man do there," sang out an Alberta adherent, "besides boast of you as a nephew? Montana is nothing but mountains, like the name of it."

"He's the owner of a mine," Rob reported with casual grandness, and this drew us new looks from the compartment citizenry. Rob, though, was not one to quit just because he was ahead. "A silver mine at Helena, called the Great Maybe."

All of steerage except the two of us thought that deserved the biggest laugh there was, and for the next days we were known as the Maybe Miners. Well, they could laugh like parrots at a bagpiper. It was worth that and more, to have Lucas Barclay there in Montana ahead of us.

"Up?" offered Rob to me now, with a sympathetic toss of his head. Back to deck we climbed, to see how the *Jemmy*'s departure was done.

As I look on it from now, I suppose the others aboard cannot but have wondered about the larky companion beside me at the deck rail, dispensing his presiding smile around the ship as if he had invented oceangoing. The bearing of a bank heir, but in a flat cap and rough clothes? A mien of careless independence, but with those workworn wheelwright's hands at the ends of his young arms? And ever, ever, that unmatchable even-toothed smile, as though he was about to say something bright even when he wasn't; Rob could hold that smile effortlessly the way a horse holds the bit between his teeth. You could be fooled in a hurry about Rob, though. It maybe can be said my mind lacks clench. Rob had a fist there in his head. The smile gave way to it here when he spotted a full family, tykes to grandfolks, among us America-goers.

"They all ought've come, Angus. By damn, but they ought've. Am I right?" He meant all the rest of his own family, his father and mother and three older brothers and young sister; and he meant it hotly. Rob had argued for America until the air of the Barclay household was blue with it, but there are times when not even a Barclay can budge Barclays. Just thinking about it still made him tense as a harp. "They ought've let the damned 'wright shop go, let old Nethermuir doze itself to death. They can never say I didn't tell them. You heard."

"I heard."

"Lucas is the only one of the bunch who's ever looked ahead beyond his nose. See now, Angus, I almost wish we'd been in America as long as Lucas. Think of all he must've seen and done, these years."

"You'd have toddled off there when you were the age of Adair, would you?" Adair was Rob's sister, just twelve or so, and a little replica of Rob or at least close enough; tease her as I did by greeting her in gruff hard-man style *Hello you, Dair Barclay,* and she always gave me right back, snappy as beans, *Hello yourself, old Angus McCaskill.*

"Adair's the one in the bunch who most ought've come," Rob persisted. "Just look around you, this ship is thick with children not a minute older than Adair." He had a point there. "She'd positively be thriving here. And she'd be on her way to the kind of life she deserves instead of that"—Rob pointed his chin up the Clyde, to the horizon we had come from—"back there. I tried for her."

"Your parents would be the first to say so."

"Parents are the world's strangest commodity, haven't you ever noticed—Angus, forgive that. My tongue got ahead of itself."

"It went right past my ears. What about a walk around deck, shall we?"

At high tide on the Clyde, when the steam tug arrived to tow this behemoth ship of ours to deep water at the Tail of the Bank, Rob turned to me and lifted his cap in mock congratulation.

"We're halfway there," he assured me.

"Only the wet part left, you're telling me."

He gave my shoulder a push. "McAngus, about this old water. You'll grow used to it, man. Half of Scotland has made this voyage by now."

I started to retort that I seemed to belong to the half without webfeet, but I was touched by this, Rob's concern for me, even though I'd hoped I was keeping my Atlantic apprehensions within me. The way they resounded around in there—*Are we both for it? Both*—I suppose it was a wonder the entire ship wasn't hearing them like the thump of a drum.

We watched Greenock vanish behind the turn of the Firth. "Poor old River Carrou," from Rob now. "This Clyde makes it look like a piddle, doesn't it?"

Littler than that, actually. We from an inland eastern town such as Nethermuir with its sea-seeking stream Carrou were born thinking that the fishing ports of our counties of Fife and Forfar and Kincardine and Aberdeen must be the rightful entrances to the ocean, so Rob and I came with the natural attitude that these emigration steamships of Greenock and Glasgow pittered out the back door of Scotland. The Firth of Clyde was showing us otherwise. Everywhere around us the water was wider than wide, arms of it delving constantly between the hills of the shore, abundant islands were stood here and there on the great gray breadth as casually as haycocks. Out and out the *Jemmy* steamed, past the last of the beetle-busy packet boats, and still the Clyde went on carving hilly shores. Ayr. Argyll. Arran. This west of Scotland perhaps all sounded like gargle, but it was as handsome a coast as could be fashioned. Moor and cliff and one entire ragged horizon of the Highlands mountains for emphasis, shore-tucked villages and the green exactness of fields for trim.

And each last inch of it everlastingly owned by those higher than Angus McCaskill and Rob Barclay, I reminded myself. Those whose names began with Lord. Those who had the banks and mills. Those whitehanded men of money. Those who watched from their fat fields as the emigrant ships steamed past with us.

Daylight lingered along with the shore. Rain came and went at edges of the Firth. You saw a far summit, its rock brows, and then didn't.

"Just damp underfoot, try to think of the old ocean as," Rob put in on me.

"I *am* trying, man. And I'd still just as soon walk to America."

"Or we could ride on each other's shoulders, what if?" Rob swept on. "No, McAngus, this steam yacht is the way to travel." Like the duke of dukes, he patted the deck rail of the *Jemmy* and proclaimed: "See now, this is proper style for going to America and Montana."

America. Montana. Those words with their ends open. Those words that were ever in the four corners of my mind, and I am sure Rob's, too, all the minutes since we had left Nethermuir. I hear that set of words yet, through all the time since, the pronouncement Rob gave them that day. America and Montana echoed and echoed in us, right through my mistrust of journeying on water, past Rob's breeze of manner, into the tunnels of our bones. For with the *Jemmy* underway out the Firth of Clyde we were threading our lives into the open beckon of those words. Like Lucas Barclay before us, now we were on our way to be Americans. To be—what did people call themselves in that far place Montana? Montanese? Montanians? Montaniards? Whatever that denomination was, now the two of us were going to be its next members, with full feathers on.

My first night in steerage I learned that I was not born to sleep on water. The berth was both too short and too narrow for me, so that I had to kink myself radically; curl up and wedge in at the same time. Try that if you ever want to be cruel to yourself. Too, steerage air was thick and unpleasant, like breathing through dirty flannel. Meanwhile Rob, who could snooze through the thunders of Judgment Day, was composing a nose song below me. But discomfort and bad air and snores were the least of my wakefulness, for in that first grief of a night—oh yes, and the *Jemmy* letting forth an iron groan whenever its bow met the waves some certain way—my mind rang with everything I did not want to think of. Casting myself from Nethermuir. The drowned horse Ginger. Walls of this moaning ship, so close. The coffin confines of my bedamned berth. The ocean, the ocean on all sides, including abovehead. *Dark Neptune's labyrinthine lanes/'Neath these savage liquid plains.* I rose in heartrattling startlement once when I accidentally touched one hand against the other and felt wetness there. My own sweat.

I still maintain that if the Atlantic hadn't been made of water I could have gone to America at a steady trot. But it seems to be the case that fear can sniff the bothering places in us. Mine had been in McCaskills for some eighty years now. The bones of the story are this. With me on this voyage, into this unquiet night, came the fact that I was the first McCaskill since my father's grandfather to go upon the sea. That voyage of Alexander McCaskill was only a dozen miles, but the most famous dozen miles in Great Britain of the time, and he voyaged them over and over and over again. He was one of the stonemasons of Arbroath who worked with the great engineer Robert Stevenson to build the Bell Rock lighthouse. On the clearest of days I have seen that lighthouse from the Arbroath harbor and have heard the story of the years of workships and cranes and winches and giant blocks of granite and sandstone, and to this moment I don't know how they could do what was done out there, build a hundred-foot tower of stone on a reef that vanished deep beneath every high tide. But there it winks at the world even today, impossible Bell Rock, standing in the North Sea announcing the Firth of Forth and Edinburgh beyond, and my great-grandfather's toolmarks are on its stones. The generations of us, we who are not a sea people, dangle from that one man who went to perform stonework in the worst of the waters around Scotland. Ever since him, Alexander has been the first or second name of a McCaskill in each of those generations. Ever since him, we have possessed a saga to measure ourselves against. I lay there in the sea-plowing *Jemmy* trying to think myself back into that other manhood, to leave myself, damp sackful of apprehension that I was, and to feel from the skin inward what it would have been like to be Alexander McCaskill of the Bell Rock those eighty years ago. *A boat is a hole in the water,* began my family's one scrap of our historic man, the solitary story from our McCaskill past that my father would ever tell. In some rare furlough from his brooding, perhaps Christmas or Hogmanay and enough drinks of lubrication, that silence-locked man my father would suddenly unloose the words. *But there was a time your great-grandfather was more glad than anything to see a boat, I'm here to tell you. Out there on the Bell Rock they were cutting down into the reef for the lighthouse's foundation, the other stonemen and your great-grandfather, that day. When the tide began to come in they took up their tools and went across the reef to meet their boat. Stevenson was there ahead of them, as high as he could climb on the reef and standing looking out into the fog on the water. Your great-grandfather knew there was wrong as soon as he saw Stevenson. Stevenson the famous engineer of the Northern Lights, pale as the cat's milk. As he ought have been, for there was no boat on the reef and none in sight anywhere. The tide was coming fast, coming to cover all of the Bell Rock with water higher than this roof. Your great-grandfather saw Stevenson turn to speak to the men. "This I'll swear to, Alexander the Second," your great-grandfather always told me it just this way. "Mister Stevenson's mouth moved as if he was saying, but no words came out. The fear had dried his mouth so." Your great-grandfather and the men watched Stevenson go down on his knees and drink water like a dog from a pool in the rock. When he stood up to try to speak this time, somebody shouted out, "A boat! There, a boat!" The pilot boat, it was, bringing the week's mail to the workship. Your great-grandfather always ended saying, "I almost ran out onto the water to hail that boat, you can believe."*

"You ask was I afraid, Alexander the Second?" My father's voice became a strange, sad thunder when he told of my great-grandfather's reply to him. *"Every hour of those three Bell Rock years, and*

most of the minutes, drowning was on my mind. I was afraid enough, yes. But the job was there at the Bell Rock. It was to be done, afraid or no afraid."

The past. The past past, so to speak, back there beyond myself. What can we ever truly know of it, how can we account for what it passes to us, what it withholds? Employ my imagination to its utmost, I could not see myself doing what Alexander McCaskill did in his Bell Rock years, travel an extent of untrustable water each day to set Abroath stone onto reef stone. Feed me first to the flaming hounds of hell. Yet for all I knew, my ocean-defying great-grandfather was afraid of the dark or whimpered at the sight of a spider but any such perturbances were whited out by time. Only his brave Bell Rock accomplishment was left to sight. And here I lay, sweating steerage sweat, with a dread of water that had no logic newer than eighty years, no personal beginning, and evidently no end. It simply was in me, like life's underground river of blood. Ahead there, I hoped *far* ahead, when I myself became the past— would the weak places in me become hidden, too? Say I ever did become husband, father, eventual great-grandfather of Montana McCaskills. What were they going to comprehend of me as their firstcomer? Not this sweated night here in my midnight cage of steerage, not my mental staggers. No, for what solace it was, eventually all that could be known of Angus Alexander McCaskill was that I did manage to cross the Atlantic Ocean.

If I managed to cross it.

Through the night and most of the next day, the *Jemmy* steamed its way along the coast of Ireland to Queenstown, where our Irish came aboard. To say the truth, I was monumentally aware of Queenstown as the final chance to me to be *not* aboard; the outmost limb-end where I could still turn to Rob and utter, *no, I am sorry, I have tried but water and I do not go together.* So far I had managed not to let my tongue say that. It bolstered me that Rob and I had been up from Steerage Number One for hours, on deck to see whatever there was, blinking now against the sun and its sparkle on the blue Queenstown harbor. And so we saw the boats come. A fleet of small ones, each catching the wind with a gray old lugsail. They were steering direct to us and as the fleet neared we could make out that there was one man in each boat. No. One woman in each boat.

"Who are these, then?" I called to a deckhand sashaying past.

"Bumboats," he flung over his shoulder. "The Irish navy. Ye'll learn some words now."

Two dozen of the boats nudged against the steamship like piglets against a sow, and the deckhand and others began tossing down ropes. The women came climbing up like sailors—when you think of it, that is what they were—and with them arrived baskets, boxes, creels, buckets, shawls. In three winks the invaders had the shawls spread and their wares displayed on them. Tobacco, apples, soap. Pickled meat. Pinafores. Butter, hardbread, cheese. Pots of shamrock. Small mirrors. Legs of mutton. Then began the chants of these Irishwomen singing their wares, the slander back and forth between our deckhands and the women hawkers, the eruptions of haggling as passengers swarmed around the deck market. The great deck of the steamship all but bubbled over with people.

As we gaped at the stir of business Rob broke out in delight, "Do you see what this is like, Angus?" And answered himself by whistling the tune of it. I laughed along with every note, for the old verse thrummed as clear to me as an anthem.

> *Dancing at the rascal fair,*
> *devils and angels all were there,*
> *heel and toe, pair by pair,*
> *dancing at the rascal fair.*

From the time we could walk Rob and I had never missed a rascal fair together—that day of fest when Nethermuir farmers and farm workers met to bargain out each season's wages and terms and put themselves around a drink or so in the process. The broad cobbled market square of our twisty town, as abrupt as a field in a stone forest, on that one day of magic filled and took on color and laughter. Peddlers, traveling musicians, the Highland dancer known as Fergus the Dervish, whose cry of *hiiyuhh!* could be heard a mile, onlooking townfolk, hubbub and gossip and banter, and the two of us like minnows in that sea of faircomers, aswim in the sounds of the ritual of hard bargaining versus hard-to-bargain.

I see you wear the green sprig in your hat. Are you looking for the right work, laddie?

Aye, I am.

And would you like to come to me? I've a place not a mile from here, as fine a field as ever you'll see to harvest.

Maybe so, maybe no. I'll be paid for home-going day, will I?

Maybe so, maybe no. That locution of the rascal fair, up there with Shakespeare's best. I have wondered, trying to think back on how Rob and I grew up side by side, how the McCaskills and the Barclays began to be braided together in the generation before us, how all has happened between us since, whether those bargaining words are always in the air around us, just beyond our hearing and our saying, beyond our knowing how to come to terms with them. But that is a thought of now, not then. Then I knew of no maybes, for Rob was right as right could be when he whistled of the rascal fair there on the *Jemmy*'s deck; with these knots of dickering and spontaneous commotion and general air of mischief-about-to-be, this shipboard bazaar did seem more than anything like that mix of holiday and sharp practice we'd rambled through in old Nethermuir.

Remembered joy is twice sweet. Rob's face definitely said so, for he had that bright unbeatable look on him. In a mood like this he'd have called out "fire!" in a gunshop just to see what might happen. The two of us surged along the deck with everybody else of the *Jemmy*, soaking in as much of the surprise jubilee as we could.

"Have your coins grown to your pockets there in Scotland?" demanded the stout woman selling pinafores and drew laughing hoots from us all.

"But mother," Rob gave her back, "would any of those fit me?"

"I'd mother you, my milktooth boy. I'd mother you, you'd not forget it."

"Apples and more apples and more apples than that!" boasted the next vendor.

"Madam, you're asking twice the price of apples ashore!" expostulated a father with his wife and eager-eyed children in a covey around him.

"But more cheap, mister man, than the ocean's price of them."

"I tell ye," a deckhand ajudged to another, "I still fancy the lass there with the big cheeses—"

The other deckhand guffawed. "Cheese, do ye call those?"

"—and ye know I en't one that fancies just anyoldbody."

"No, just anybody born of woman."

"Muuuht'n, muuuht'n," bleated the sheep-leg seller as we jostled past.

"Green of the sod of Ireland!" the shamrock merchant advertised to us.

So this was what the world was like. I'd had no idea.

Then we were by a woman who was calling out nothing. She simply stood silent, both hands in front of her, a green ball displayed in each.

Rob passed on with the others of our throng, I suppose assuming as I first did that she was offering the balls as playthings. But children were rampant among this deck crowd and neither they nor their parents were stopping by the silent woman either.

Curiosity is never out of season with me. I turned and went back for a close look. Her green offerings were not balls, they were limes.

Even with me there in front of her, the woman said nothing. I had to ask. "Your produce doesn't need words, missus?"

"I'm not to name the ill they're for, young mister, else I can't come onto your fine ship."

Any schoolboy knew the old tale of why Royal Navy sailors came to be called limies, and so I grinned, but I had to let Madam Irish know I was not so easily gulled. "It takes a somewhat longer voyage than this to come down with scurvy, missus."

"Tisn't the scurvy."

"What, then?"

"Your mouth can ask your stomach when the two of them meet, out there on the herring pond."

Seasickness. Among my Atlantic thoughts was whether the crossing would turn me as green as the rind of these limes. "How can this fruit of yours ward off that, then?"

"Not ward it off, no. There's no warding to that. You only get it, like death. These fruit are for after. They clean your mouth, young mister. Scour the sick away."

"Truth?"

She nodded. But then, what marketeer wouldn't.

It must have been the Irish sun. I fished for my coins. "How much for a pocketful?"

Doubtful transaction done, I made my way along the deck to where Rob was. He and the majority of the other single men from our compartment had ended up here around the two youngest Irishwomen, plainly sisters, who were selling ribbons and small mirrors. The flirting seemed to be for free.

The sight of the saucy sisters elevated my mood some more, too, and so I stepped close behind Rob and caroled appropriately in his ear:

> *"Dancing at the rascal fair,*
> *show an ankle, show a pair,*
> *show what'll make the lasses stare,*
> *dancing at the rascal fair."*

"Shush, you'll be heard," he chided, and glanced around to see whether I had been. Rob had that prim side, and I felt it my duty every so often to tweak him on it.

"Confess," I urged him. "You'd give your ears for a smile from either of these lovelies."

Before he could answer me on that, the boatswain's whistle shrilled. The deck market dissolved, over the side the women went like cats. In a minute their lugsails were fanned against the sparkling water of Queenstown harbor, and the *Jemmy* was underway once more.

After Queenstown and with only ocean ahead for a week and a day, my second seagoing night had even less sleep in it than my first. Resolutely telling myself there was no back door to this ship now, I lay crammed into that stifling berth trying to put my mind anywhere—multiplication, verse, Irish sisters—other than Steerage Number One.

What I found I could spend longest thoughts on, between periodic groans from the *Jemmy* that required me to worry whether its iron was holding, was Nethermuir. Rascal fair town Nethermuir. Old grayrock town Nethermuir, with its High Street wandering down the hill the way a drowsy cow would, to come to the River Carrou. Be what it may, a fence, a house, a street, the accusing spire of a church, Nethermuir fashioned it of stone, and from below along River Street the town looked as though it had been chiseled out complete rather than erected. Each of the thousand mornings that I did my route to open the wheelwright shop, Nethermuir was as asleep as its stones. In the dark—out went the streetlights at midnight; a Scottish town sees no need to illumine its empty hours—in the dark before each dawn I walked up River Street from our narrow-windowed tenements past the clock tower of the linen mill and the silent frontages of the dye works and the paper mill and other shrines of toil. Was that the same me back there, trudging on stone past stone beneath stone until my hand at last found the oaken door of the 'wright shop? Climbing the stair to the office in the nail loft and coaxing a fire in the small stove and opening the ledger, pen between my teeth to have both hands free, to begin on the accounts? Hearing the workmen say their day-starting greetings, those with farthest to come arriving first, for wasn't that always the way? Was that truly me, identical with this steerage creature listening to a steamship moan out greetings to disaster? The same set of bones called Angus McCaskill, anyway. The same McCaskill species that the Barclays and their wheelwright shop were accustomed to harboring.

To see you here is to lay eyes on your father again, Angus, Rob's father Vare Barclay told me at least once a week. A natural pleasantry, but Vare Barclay and I equally knew it was nowhere near true. When you saw my father there over his forge in an earlier time, you were viewing the keenest of wheelsmiths; the master in that part of Scotland at making ninety pounds of tire-iron snugly band itself onto a wagon wheel and become its invincible rim. Skill will ask its price, though. The years of anvil din took nearly all of my father's hearing, and to attract his attention as he stood there working a piece of iron you would have had to toss a wood chip against his shirt. Do that and up he would glance from his iron, little less distant when he was aware of you than when he wasn't. Never did I make that toss of contact with him, when sent by my mother on errand to the 'wright shop, without wondering what it would take to mend his life. For my father had gone deaf deeper than his ears.

I am from a house of storm. My parents Alex and Kate McCaskill by the middle of their marriage had become baffled and wounded combatants. I was their child who lived. Of four. Christie, Jack and Frank, who was already apprenticing with my father at the Barclay 'wright shop—in a single week the three of them died of cholera. I only barely remember them, for I was several years the youngest— like Rob's sister Adair in the Barclay family, an "afterthought" child; I have contemplated since whether parents in those times instinctively would have a late last child as a kind of insurance—but I recall in all clarity my mother taking me to the farm cottage of a widow friend of hers when the killing illness began to find Nethermuir. When my mother came for me six weeks later she had aged twice that many years, and our family had become a husk the epidemic left behind. From then on my father lived—how best to say this?—he lived alongside my mother and me rather than with us. Sealed into himself, like someone of another country who happened to be traveling beside us. Sealed into his notion, as I grew, that the one thing for me was to follow into his smithy trade. *I'm here to tell you, it's what life there is for us and ours. A McCaskill at least can have an honest pair of hands.* Oh, there was war in the house about that. My father could not see why I ought to do anything but apprentice myself into hammer work in the Barclay wheelshop as he had, as my brother Frank had; my mother was equally as set that I should do anything but. His deafness made their arguments over me a roaring time. The teacups rattled when they went at it. The school-leaving age was thirteen, so I don't know how things would have gone had not my father died when I was twelve. My mother at once took work as a spinner in the linen mill and enrolled me with the 'venture schoolteacher Adam Willox. Then when I was sixteen, my mother followed my father into death. She was surprised by it, going the same way he had; a stroke that toppled her in the evening and took her in the early morning. With both of them gone, work was all the family I had. Rob's father put me on as clerk in the 'wright shop in the mornings, Adam Willox made me his pupil-teacher in the afternoons. Two half-occupations, two slim wages, and I was glad enough to have them, anything. Vare Barclay promised me full clerkwork whenever the times found their way from bad to good again, Adam Willox promised I could come in with him as a schoolkeeper whenever pupils grew ample enough again. But promises never filled the oatmeal bowl. So when Rob caught America fever, I saw all too readily the truth in what he said about every tomorrow of our Nethermuir lives looking the same. About the great American land pantry in such places as his uncle's Montana, where homesteads were given—given!—in exchange for only a few years of earnful effort. The power of that notion of homesteading in America, of land and lives that would be all our own. We never had known anything like it in our young selves. *America. Montana.* This ship to them. This black iron groaner of a ship that—

I was noticing something I devoutly did not want to. The *Jemmy* seemed to be groaning more often.

I held myself dead still to be sure.

Yes, oh sweet Christ and every dimpled disciple, yes: my berth was starting to sway and dive.

A boat is a hole in the water. And a ship is a bigger boat.

I heard Rob wake with a sleepy "What?" just before full tumult set in. The *Jemmy* stumbled now against every wave, conked its iron beak onto the ocean, rose to tumble again. The least minute of this behavior was more than enough storm for a soul in steerage, but the ruckus kept on and on. Oftener and oftener the ship's entire iron carcass shuddered as the propellor chewed air. Sick creatures shudder before they die, don't they. I felt each and every of these shakings as a private earthquake, fear finding a way to tremble not merely me but every particle of existence. Nineteen did not seem many years to have lived. *What if the old Bell Rock had drowned me?* my father remembered being asked in boyhood by Alexander McCaskill at the end of that floodtide tale. *Where would you be then, Alexander the Second?* What if, still the question.

Even yet this is a shame on me to have to say, but fear brought a more immediate question, too, insistent in the gut of me and below. I had to lay there concentrating desperately not to soil myself.

Amid it all a Highlands voice bleated out from a distant bunk, "Who'd ever think she could jig like this without a piper?" Oh, yes, you major fool, the ranting music of bagpipes was the only trouble we lacked just now. The Atlantic had its own tune, wild and endless. I tried to wipe away my sweat but couldn't keep up with it. I desperately wanted to be up out of Steerage Number One and onto deck, to see for myself the white knuckles of the storm ocean. Or did I. Again the ship shook; rather, was shaken. What was out there? My blood sped as I tried to imagine the boiling oceanic weather which could turn a steamship into an iron cask. Cloudcaps darker than night itself. High lumpy waves, foaming as they came. Wind straining to lift the sea into the air with it, and rain a downward flood determined to drown the wind.

The storm stayed ardent. Barrels, trunks, tins, whatever was movable flew from side to side, and we poor human things clung in our berths to keep from flying, too. No bright remarks about jigs and pipes now. The steerage bunks were stacked boxes of silence now. Alberta, Manitoba, Montana were more distant than the moon. I knew Rob was clamped solidly below me, those broad wheelwright hands of his holding to whatever they had met. The worst was to keep myself steady there in the bunk while all else roved and reeled. Yet in an awful way the storm came to my help; its violence tranced a person. From stem to stern the *Jemmy* was 113 of my strides; I spent time on the impossibility of anything that length not being broken across canyons of waves. The ship weighed more than two thousand tons; I occupied myself with the knowledge that nothing weighing a ton of tons could remain afloat. I thought of the Greenock dock where I ought to have turned back, saw in my closed eyes the drowned cart horse Ginger I was trying every way I knew not to see, retraced in my mind every stairstep from deck down into Steerage Number One; which was to say down into the basement of the titanic Atlantic, down into the country where horses and humans are hash for fish.

Now the *Jemmy* dropped into a pause where we did not teeter-totter so violently. We were havened between crags of the sea. I took the opportunity to gasp air into myself, on the off chance that I'd ever need any again. Rob's face swung up into view and he began, "See now, McAngus, that all could have been worse. A ship's like a wagon, as long as it creaks it holds, and—" The steamship shuddered sideways and tipped ponderously at the same time, and Rob's face snapped back into his berth.

Now the ship was grunting and creaking constantly, new and worse noises—you could positively feel the *Jemmy* exerting to drag itself through this maelstrom—and these grindstone sounds of its effort drew screams from women and children in the midship compartments, and yes, from more than a few men as well, whenever the vessel rolled far over. Someone among the officers had a voice the size of a cannon shot and even all the way down where we were could be heard his blasts of "BOS'N!" and "ALL HANDS!" Those did not improve a nonswimmer's frame of mind, either.

The *Jemmy* drove on. Shuddering. Groaning. Both. Its tremors ran through my body. Every pore of me wanted to be out of that berth, free from water. But nothing to do but hold onto the side of the berth, hold myself as level as possible on a crooked ocean.

Nothing, that is, until somebody made the first retching sound.

Instantly that alarm reached all our gullets. I knew by heart what Crofutt advised. *Any internal discomfort whilst aboard ship is best ameliorated by the fresh air of deck. Face the world of air; you will be new again.* If I'd had the strength I'd have hurled Crofutt up onto that crashing deck. As it was, I lay as still as possible and strove not think of what was en route from my stomach to mouth.

Steerage Number One's vomiting was phenomenal. I heaved up, Rob heaved up, every steerage soul heaved up. Meals from a month ago were trying to come out of us.

Our pitiful gut emptyings chorused with the steamship's groans

Our poor storm-bounced guts strained, strained, strained some more. Awful, the spew we have in us at our worst. The stench of it all and the foulness of my mouth kept making me sicker yet. Until I managed to remember the limes.

I fumbled them out and took desperate sucks of one. Another I thrust down to the bunk below. "Rob, here. Try this."

His hand found mine and the round rind in it.

"Eat at a time like now? Angus, you're—"

"Suck it. For the taste." I could see white faces in the two bunks across from us and tossed a lime apiece over there as well. The *Jemmy* rose and fell, rose and fell, and stomachs began to be heard from again in all precincts of the compartment. Except ours.

Bless you, Madam Irish. Maybe it was that the limes put their stern taste in place of the putrid. Maybe that they puckered our mouths as if with drawstrings. Maybe only that any remedy seemed better than none. Whatever effect it may have been, Rob and I and the other lime-juiced pair managed to abstain from the rest of the general gagging and spewing. I knew something new now. That simply being afraid was nowhere near so bad as being afraid and retching your socks up at the same time.

Toward dawn the Atlantic got the last of the commotion out of its system. The *Jemmy* ploughed calmly along as if it had never been out for an evening gallop at all. Even I conceded that we possibly were going to live, now.

"Mates, what's all this muss?" The steward put in his appearance and chivied us into sluicing and scrubbing the compartment and sprinkling chloride of lime against the smell, not that the air of Steerage Number One could ever be remedied much. For breakfast Rob and I put shaky cups of tea into ourselves and I had another lime, just for luck. Then Rob returned to his berth, claiming there was lost sleep to be found there, and I headed up for deck, anywhere not to be in that ship bottom.

I knew I still was giddy from the night of storm. But as I began to walk my first lap of the deck, the scene that gathered into my eyes made me all the more woolheaded.

By now the weather was clement, so that was no longer the foremost matter in me. And I knew, the drybrain way you know a map fact, that the night's steaming progress must have carried us out of

sight of land on all sides. But the ocean. The ocean I was not prepared for nor ever could be.

Anywhere my eyes went, water bent away over the curve of the
world. Yet at the same time the *Jemmy* and I were in a vast washbasin, the rims of the Atlantic perfectly evident out there over us.
Slow calm waves wherever I faced, only an occasional far one bothering to flash into foam like a white swimmer appearing and disappearing. No savage liquid plains these. This was the lyric sea,
absently humming in the sameness of the gray and green play of its
waves, in its pattern of water always wrinkling, moving, yet other
water instantly filling the place. All this, and a week of water extending yet ahead.

I felt like a child who had only been around things small, suddenly seeing there is such a thing as big. Suddenly feeling the
crawling fear I had known the past two nights in my berth change
itself into a standing fact: if the *Jemmy* wrecked, I would sink like a
statue, but nobody could outswim the old Atlantic anyway, so why
nettle myself over it? Suddenly knowing that for this, the spectacle
of the water planet around me, I could put up with sleepless nights
and all else; when you are nineteen and going to America, I learned
from myself in that moment, you can plunder yourself as much as is
needed. Maybe I was going to see the Atlantic each dawn through
scared red eyes. But by the holy, see it I would.

I made my start that very morning. Ocean cadence seemed to be
more deliberate, calmer, than time elsewhere, and I felt the draw of
it. Hour by slow hour I walked that deck and watched and watched
for the secret of how this ocean called Atlantic could endlessly go
on. Always more wrinkling water, fresh motion, were all that made
themselves discernible to me, but I kept walking and kept watching.

"How many voyages do you suppose this tea has made?"

"Definitely enough for pension."

"Mahogany horse at dinner, Aberdeen cutlet at supper." Which
was to say, dried beef and smoked haddock. "You wouldn't get
such food just any old where."

"You're not wrong about that."

"The potatoes aren't so bad, though."

"Man, potatoes are never so bad. That's the principle of potatoes."

"These ocean nights are dark as the inside of a cow, aren't they."

"At least, at least."

"We can navigate by the sparks." The *Jemmy's* funnel threw constant specks of fire against the night. "A few more times around the deck will do us good. Are we both for it?"

"All right, all right, both. Angus, you're getting your wish, back there on the Clyde."

"What's that, now."

"You're walking us to America."

"Listen to old Crofutt here, will you. *We find, from our experience, that the midpoint of the journey is its lowest mark, mentally speaking. If doubt should afflict you thereabout, remonstrate with yourself that of the halves of your great voyage, the emigration part has been passed through, the immigration portion has now begun. Somewhere there on the Atlantic rests a line, invisible but valid, like Greenwich's meridian or the equator. East of there, you were a leaver of a place, on your way FROM a life. West across that division, older by maybe a minute, know yourself to be heading TO a life.*"

"Suppose we're Papists yet?" Sunday, and the priest's words were carrying to us from the Irish congregation thick as bees on the deck's promenade.

"I maybe am. There's no hope whatsoever for you."

"This Continental Divide in Montana that old Crofutt goes on about, Angus. What is that exactly?"

"It's like, say, the roof peak of America. The rivers on this side of it flow here to the Atlantic, on the other they go to the Pacific."

"Are you telling me we're already on water from Montana, out here?"

"So to say."

"Angus, Angus. Learning teaches a man some impossible things, is what I say."

"Too bad they're not bumboats. I could eat up one side of a leg of mutton and down the other about now." Autumn it may have been back in Scotland, but there off Newfoundland the wind was hinting winter, and Rob and I put on most of the clothes we possessed to stay up and watch the fishing fleets of the Newfoundland coastal banks.

"And an Irish smile, Rob, what about. Those sisters you were eyeing at Queenstown, they'd be one apiece for us if my arithmetic is near right."

"Angus, I don't know what I'm going to do with you. I only hope for your sake that they have women in America, too."

"There's a chance, do you think?"

"Shore can't be all so far now."

"No, but you'll see a change in the color of the ocean first. New York harbor will be cider instead of water, do you know, and it'll start to show up out here."

Then came the day.

"Mates," the steward pronounced, "we're about to pass old Sandy Hook. New York will step right out and meet us now. I know you've grown attached to them, but the time is come to part with your mattresses. If you'll kindly all make a chain here, like, and pass them along one to the next to the stairway . . ." Up to deck and overboard our straw beds proceeded, to float off behind us like a flotilla of rafts. A person would think that mine ought to have stood out freshest among them, so little of the sleep in it had been used.

New York was the portal to confusion, and Castle Garden was its keyhole. The entire world of us seemed to be trying to squeeze into America through there. Volleys of questions were asked of us, our health and morals were appraised, our pounds and shillings slid through the money exchange wicket to come back out as dollars and cents. I suppose our experience of New York's hustle and bustle was every America-comer's: thrilling, and we never wanted to do it again. Yet in its way, that first hectic experience of America was simply like one of the hotting-up days back in the 'wrightshop, when the bands of tire iron were furnaced to a red heat and then made to encircle the newly crafted wagon wheels. Ultimately after the sweating and straining and hammering, after every kind of commotion, there was the moment as the big iron circle was cooling and clasping itself ever tighter around the wheel when you would hear a click, like a sharp snap of fingers. Then another, and another—the sound of the wheelspokes going the last fraction of distance into their holes in the hub and the rim, fitting themselves home. And if you listened with a bit of care, the last click of all came when the done wheel first touched the ground, as if the result was making a little cluck of surprise at its new self. Had you been somewhere in the throng around Rob and me as we stepped out of Castle Garden's workshop of immigration into our first American day, to begin finding our way through a city that was twenty of Glasgow, you might have heard similar sounds of readiness.

Then the railroad and the westward journey, oceanic again in its own way, with islands of towns and farms across the American prairie. Colors on a map in no way convey the distances of this earth. What would the place Montana be like? Alp after alp after alp, as the Alberta adherent aboard ship assured us? *The Territory of Montana,* Crofutt defined, *stands as a tremendous land as yet virtually untapped. Already planetarily famous for its wealth of ores, Montana proffers further potentialities as a savannah for graziers and their herds, and where the hoofed kingdom does not obtain, the land may well become the last great grain garden of the world. Elbow room for all aspirants will never be a problem, for Montana is fully five times the size of all of Scotland.* How was it going to be to live within such distances? To become pioneers in filling such emptiness? At least we can be our own men there, Rob and I had told each other repeatedly. And now we would find out what kind of men that meant.

America seemed to go on and on outside the train windows, and our keenness for Montana and Lucas Barclay gained with every mile.

"He'll see himself in you," I said out of nowhere to Rob. I meant his uncle; and I meant what I was saying, too. For I was remembering that Lucas Barclay had that same burnish that glowed on Rob. The face and force to go with it, for that matter. These Barclays were a family ensemble, they all had a memorable glimmer. Years and years back, some afterschool hour Rob and I were playing fox-chase in the woodyard of the wheelwright shop, and in search of him I popped around a stack of planks into my father and Lucas and Rob's father Vare, eyeing out oak for spokes. I startled both myself and them by whirling into the midst of their deliberation that way, and I remember as clear as now the pair of bright Barclay faces and my father's pale one, and then Lucas swooping on me with a laugh to tickle his thick thumb into my ribs, *I met a man from Kingdom Come, he had daggers and I had none, but I fell on him with my thumb, and daggered and daggered 'um!* Was that the final time I'd seen Lucas before his leaving of Scotland, that instant of rosy smile at a flummoxed boy and then the tickling recital? The lasting one, at least.

"I hope Lucas doesn't inspect too close, then," Rob tossed off. "Else we may get the door of the Great Maybe slammed in our faces."

"Man," I decided to tease, "who could ever slam a door to you? Shut with firmness and barricade it to keep you from their wives, daughters and maiden aunts, maybe, but—"

Rob gave my shoulder a push. "I can't wait to see the surprise on Lucas," he said, laughing. "Seven years. I can't wait."

"I wonder just what his life is like, there."

"Wonder away, until sometime tomorrow. Then you can see the man himself and know."

In truth, we knew little more than the least about Lucas Barclay in these Montana years of his. Rob said there had been only a brief letter from Lucas to Nethermuir the first few Christmases after he emigrated, telling that he had made his way to the city of Helena and of his mining endeavor there; and not incidentally enclosing as his token of the holiday a fine fresh green American banknote of one hundred dollars. You can be sure as Rob's family was that more than a greeting was being said there, that Lucas was showing the stay-at-homes the fruit of his adventure; Lucas's decision against the wheelwright shop and for America had been the early version of Rob's: too many Barclays and not enough wagon wheels any more. Even after his letters quit—nobody who knew Lucas expected him to spend time over paper and pen—that hundred dollars arrived alone in an envelope, Christmas after Christmas. *The Montana money,* Rob's family took to calling it. *Lucas is still Lucas,* they said with affection and rue for this strayed one of the clan; *as freehanded a man as God ever set loose.*

I won't bother to deny that in making our minds up for America Rob and I found it persuasive that money was sent as Christmas cards from there. But the true trove over across in Montana, we considered, was Lucas himself. Can I make you know what it meant to us to have this uncle of his as our forerunner? As our American edition of *Crofutt,* waiting and willing to instruct? Put yourself where we were, young and stepping off to a new world in search of its glorious packets of land called homesteads, and now tell me whether or not you want to have a Lucas Barclay ahead, with a generous side that made us know we could walk in on him and be instantly welcome; a Lucas who would know where the best land for homesteading beckoned, what a fair price was for anything, whether they did so-and-so in Montana just as we were accustomed to in Scotland, whether they ever did thus-and-such at all. Bold is one thing and reckless is another, yes? I thought at the time and I'll defend it yet, the steamship ticket could only take us to America and the railroad ticket could only deliver us across it—Rob and I held our true ticket to the Montana life we sought, to freedom and all else, in Lucas Barclay.

Helena had three times the people of Nethermuir in forty times the area. Helena looked as if it had been plopped into place last week and might be moved around again next week. Helena was not Hellenic.

A newcomer had to stand and goggle. The castellated edge of the city, high new mansions with sharp-towered roofs, processioned right up onto the start of the mountains around. Earth-old grit side by side with fresh posh. Then grew down a shambles of every kind of structure, daft blurts of shack and manor, with gaping spots between which evidently would be filled when new fashions of habitation had been thought up. Lastly, down the middle of it all was slashed a raw earthquakelike gash of gulch, in which nested block after block of aspiring red-brick storefronts.

"Quite the place," I said.

"So it is," said Rob.

Say for Helena, gangly capital city of the Territory of Montana and peculiar presbytery of our future with Lucas, it started us off with luck. After the Model Lodging House of Greenock, we knew well not to take the first roost we saw, and weary as we were, Rob and I trudged the hilly streets until we found a comparatively clean room at Mrs. Billington's, a few blocks away from Last Chance Gulch. Mrs. Billington observed to us at once, "You'll be wanting to wash the travel off, won't you," which was more than true.

Those tubbings in glorious hot water were the first time since Nethermuir that we had a chance to shed our clothes.

"Old Barclay? Oh hell yeah," the most veteran boarder at Mrs. Billington's table aided us. "He works down at the depot. Watch sharp or you'll trip right over him there."

Here was news, Lucas in a railroad career, and our jauntiness was tinged with speculation as to how that could have come about. Down the steep streets of Helena Rob wore the success of our journey as if it was a helmet. And when we came into sight of the depot, his triumphant face could not have announced us more if he'd had a trumpet in front of it. I was proud enough myself.

Until we stepped into the depot, asked a white-haired shrimp of a fellow in spectacles where we might find the railway clerk named Barclay, and got: "I'm him. Elmer W. Barclay. Who might you be?"

Elmer W. was nothing at all like Lucas, but he definitely was the Barclay everyone in Helena seemed to know about, in our next few hours of asking and asking. We found as well the owner of the Great Maybe mine, but he was not Lucas either. Nor were any of the three previous disgusted owners we managed to track down. In fact, Lucas's name was six back in the record of ownership the Second Deputy Clerk and Recorder of Lewis and Clark County grudgingly dug out for us, and there had been that many before Lucas. It grew clear to Rob and me that had the Great Maybe been a silver coin instead of a silver mine, by now it would be worn smooth from being passed around.

By that first night, Rob was thoughtful. "What do you suppose, Lucas made as much money from the Great Maybe as he thought was there and moved on to another mine? Or didn't make money and just gave the mine up?"

"Either way, he did move on," I pointed out.

"Funny, though," Rob deliberated, "that none of these other miners can bring Lucas to mind."

That point had suggested itself to me too, but I decided to chide it on its way. "Rob, how to hell could they all remember each other? Miners in Montana are like hair on a dog."

"Still," he persisted, "if Lucas these days is anything like the Lucas he was back in Nethermuir, somebody is bound to remember him. Am I right?"

"Right enough. We just need to find that somebody."

"Or Lucas. Whichever happens first."

"Whichever. Tomorrow we scour this Helena and make Lucas happen, one way or the other."

But the next day Helena provided us not Lucas, but history. Rob and I met our first Montana frost that November morning when we set out, and saw our breath all the way to the post office, where we asked without luck about Lucas. We had just stepped from there, into sunshine now, to go and try at the assay office when I saw the fellow and his flag on a rooftop across the street.

"Stay"-something, he shouted down into the street to us, "stay"-something, "stay"-something, and ran the American flag with 41 stars on it up a tall pole.

Cheers whooped from others in the street gaping up with us, and that in turn brought people to windows and out from stores. Abruptly civilization seemed to be tearing loose in Helena as the crowd flocked in a tizzy to the flag-flying edifice, the *Herald* newspaper building.

"What is this, war with somebody?" Rob asked, as flabbergasted as I.

"Statehood!" called out a red-bearded man scurrying past. "The president just signed it! It took goddamn near forever, but Montana's a state at last! Follow me, I'm buying!"

And so that eighth day of November arose off the calendar and grabbed Rob and me and every other Helena Montanian by the elbow, the one that can lever liquid up to the lips. Innocents us, statehood was a mysterious notion. However, we took it to mean that Montana had advanced out of being governed from afar, as Scotland was by the parliament in London, into running its own affairs. Look around Helena and you could wonder if this indeed constituted an improvement. But the principle was there, and Rob and I had to drink to it along with everyone else, repeatedly.

"Angus, we must've seen half the faces in Helena today," Rob estimated after we made our woozy way back to the lodging house. "And Lucas's wasn't among them."

"Then we know just where he is," I found to say. "The other half."

The day after that and the next several, we did try the assay office. The land office. The register of voters. The offices of the newspapers. The Caledonian Club. The Association of Pioneers. The jail. Stores. Hotels.

Saloons, endless saloons. The Grand Central or the Arcade or the Iroquois or the Cricket, the IXL or the Exchange or the Atlantic, it all ran the same:

"Do you know a man Lucas Barclay? He owned the Gre—a mine."

"Sometimes names change, son. What does he look like?"

"More than a bit like me. He's my uncle."

"Is he now. Didn't know miners had relatives." Wipe, wipe, wipe of the bartender's towel on the bar while he thought. "You do look kind of familiar. But huh-uh. If I ever did see your face on somebody else it was a time ago. Sorry."

Boarding houses.

"Good day, missus. We're trying to find the uncle of my friend here. Lucas Barclay is his name. Do you happen to know of him?"

"Barkler? No, never heard of him."

"Barclay, missus. B-A-R-C-L-A-Y."

"Never heard of him, either."

Finally, the Greenwood cemetery.

"You boys are good and sure, are you?" asked the caretaker from beside the year-old gravestone he had led us to.

We stood facing the stark chiseled name. "We're sure," said Rob.

The caretaker eyed us regretfully.

"Well, then," he declared, abandoning hope for this stone that read LEWIS BERKELEY PASSED FROM LIFE 1888, "that's about as close as I can come to it for you. Sorry."

"See now, we can't but think it would need to be a this year's burial," Rob specified to the caretaker, "because there's every evidence he was alive at last Christmas." He meant by this that the Montana money from Lucas had arrived as always to Nethermuir.

"B-A-R-C-L-A-Y, eh?" the caretaker spelled for the sixth time. "You're sure that's the way of it?" Rob assured him for the sixth time he was. The caretaker shook his head. "Nobody by that name among the fresh ones. Unless he'd be there." He nodded to the low edge of the graveyard, down near where the railroad right-of-way crossed the Fort Benton road. The grave mounds there had no markers.

Realization arrived to Rob and me at the same instant. The paupers' field.

Past a section of lofty monuments where chiseled folds of drape and tassels were in style, we followed the caretaker down to the poorfield.

"Who are these, then?" asked Rob.

"Some are loners, drifters, hoboes. Others we just don't know who the hell they are. Find them dead of booze some cold morning up there in the Gulch. Or a mine timber falls on them and nobody knows any name for them except Dutchy or Frenchy or Scotty." I saw Rob swallow at that. The caretaker studied among a dozen bare graves. "Say, last month I buried a teamster who'd got crushed when his wagon went over on him. His partner said the gent called himself Brown, but a lot of folks color theirselves different when they come west. Maybe he'd be yours?"

It did not seem likely to either Rob or me that Lucas would spurn a life of wagons in Nethermuir and adopt one here. Indeed, the more we thought, the less likely it seemed that Lucas could be down among the nameless dead. People always noticed a Barclay.

Discouragement. Perplexity. Worry. All those we found abundantly that first week in Helena but no Lucas.

Not one least little bit did Rob let go of the notion of finding him, though. By week's end he was this minute angry at the pair of us for not being bright enough to think where Lucas might be, the next at Lucas for not being anywhere. Then along came consternation—"Tell me truth, Angus, do you think he can be alive?"—and then around again to bafflement and irk: "Why to hell is that man so hard to find?"

"We'll find him," I said steadily to all this. "I can be stubborn and you're greatly worse than that. If the man exists in this Montana, we'll find him."

Yet we still did not.

We had to tell ourselves that we'd worn out all investigation for a Helena version of Lucas, so we had better think instead of other possible whereabouts. The start of our second week of search, we went by train to try Butte. That mining city seemed to be a factory for turning the planet inside out. Slag was making new mountains, while the mountains around stood with dying timber on their slopes.

The very air was raw with smelter fumes and smoke. No further Butte, thank you, for either Rob or me, and we came away somehow convinced it was not the place Lucas Barclay would choose either.

Back at Helena we questioned stagecoach drivers, asking if they had heard of Lucas at their destination towns, White Sulphur Springs and Boulder and Elkhorn and Diamond City. No and no and no and no. Meanwhile, we were hearing almost daily of some new silver El Dorado where a miner might have been drawn to. Castle. Glendale. Granite. Philipsburg. Neihart. We began to see that tracking Lucas to a Montana mine, if indeed he was still in that business of Great Maybes, would be like trying to find out where a Gypsy had taken up residence.

That week of search ended as empty as our first.

Sunday morning, our second Sabbath as dwellers of Helena, I woke before the day did, and my getting out of bed roused Rob. "Where're you off to?" he asked as I dressed.

"A walk. Up to see how the day looks."

He yawned mightily. "McAngus, the wheelwright shop is all the way back in Scotland and you're still getting out of bed to open it." More yawn. "Wait. I'll come along. Just let me figure which end my shoes fit on."

We walked up by the firebell tower above Last Chance Gulch. Except for the steady swimming flight of an occasional magpie, we were up before the birds. Mountains stretched high everywhere around, up in the morning light which had not yet found Helena. The business streets below were in sleeping gray. Over us and to the rim of the eastern horizon stretched long, long feathers of cloud, half a skyful streaked extravagantly with colors between gold and pink, and with purple dabs of heavier cloud down on the tops of the Big Belt Mountains. A vast sky tree of glow and its royal harvest beneath.

"So this is the way they bring morning into Montana," observed Rob. "They know their business."

"Now that I've got you up, you may as well be thoroughly up, what about." I indicated the firebell tower, a small open observation cabin like the top of a lighthouse but perched atop an open spraddle of supports.

Rob paused as we climbed past the big firebell and declared, "I'd like to ring the old thing and bring them all out into the streets. Maybe we would find Lucas then."

Atop the tower, we met more of dawn. The land was drawing color out of the sky. Shadows of trees came out up near the summit of Mt. Helena, and in another minute there were shawls of shadow off the backs of knolls. Below us the raw sides of Last Chance Gulch now stood forth, as if shoveled out during the night for the next batch of Helena's downtown to be sown in.

Rob pondered into the hundred streets below, out to the wide grassy valley beyond. Nineteen thousand people down there and so far not a one of them Lucas Barclay. A breeze lazed down the gulch and up the back of our necks. "Where to hell can he be, Angus? A man can't vanish like smoke, can he?"

Not unless he wants to, I thought to myself. But aloud: "Rob, we've looked all we can. There's no knowing until Christmas if Lucas is even alive. If your family gets the Montana money from him again, there'll be proof. But if that doesn't happen, we have to figure he's—" Rob knew the rest of that. Neither of us had been able to banish that Lewis Berkeley tombstone entirely from mind. I went on to what I had been mulling. "It's not all that far to Christmas now. But until then, we'd better get on with ourselves a bit. Keep asking after Lucas, yes. But get on with ourselves at the same time."

Rob stirred. He had that cocked look of his from when we stepped past the drowned horse on the Greenock dock, the look that said out to the world *surely you're fooling?* But face it, this lack of trace of Lucas had us fooled, fully. "Get on with ourselves, is it. You sound like Crofutt."

"And who better?" I swept an arm out over the tower railing to take in Helena and the rest of Montana. As full sunrise neared, the low clouds on the Big Belts were turning into gold coals. On such a morning it could be believed there was a paunch of ore on every Montana mountain. By the holy, this was a country to be up and around in. "Look at you here, five thousand miles from Scotland and your feet are dry, your color is bright, and you have no divided heart. Crofutt and McCaskill, we've seen you through and will again, lad. But the time has arrived to think of income instead of outgo. Are we both for that?"

He had to smile. "All right, all right, both. But tell me this, early riser. Where is it you'd see us to next, if you had your way?"

We talked there on the bell hill until past breakfast and received the scolding of our lives from Mrs. Billington. Which was far short of fair, for she gained profit for some time to come from that fire tower discussion of ours. What Rob and I chose that early morning, in large part because we did not see what else to decide, was to stay on in Helena until Christmas sent its verdict from Nethermuir.

Of course we needed to earn while we tried to learn Montana, and if we didn't have the guidance of Lucas Barclay we at least had an honest pair of hands apiece. I took myself down to a storefront noticed during our trekking around town, Cariston's Mercantile. An Aberdeen man and thus a bit of a conniver, Hugh Cariston; but just then it made no matter to me whether he was the devil's half-brother. He fixed a hard look on me and in that Aberdonian drone demanded:

"Can ye handle sums?"

"Aye." I could, too.

I am sure as anything that old Cariston then and there hired me on as a clerk and bookkeeper just so he could have a decent Scots burr to hear. There are worse qualifications.

In just as ready a fashion, Rob found work at Weisenhorn's wagon shop. "Thin stuff," he shook his head about American wheels, but at least they made a job.

So there is the sum we were, Rob, as our Scotland-leaving year of 1889 drew to a cold close in new Montana. Emigrants changed by the penstrokes of the Cumbrae Steamship Line and Castle Garden into immigrants. Survivors of the Atlantic's rites of water, pilgrims to Helena. Persons we had been all our lives and persons becoming new to ourselves. How are past and present able to live in the same instant, and together pass into the future?

You were the one who hatched the fortunate notion of commemorating ourselves by having our likenesses taken on that Hogmanay, New Year's Eve, as they tamely say it here in America. "Angus, man, it'll be a Hogmanay gift such as they've never had in Nethermuir," you proclaimed, which was certainly so. "Let them in old Scotland see what Montanians are." We had to hustle to get to Ball's Photographic Studio before it closed.

That picture is here on my wall, I have never taken it down. Lord of mercy, Rob. Whatever made us believe our new muttonchop sidewhiskers became us? Particularly when I think how red mine were then, and the way yours bristled. We sit there in the photograph looking as if the stuffing is coming out of our heads. Once past those sidewhiskers, the faces on us were not that bad, I will say. Maybe an opera house couldn't be filled on the basis of them, but still. Your wide smile to match the wide Barclay chin, your confident eyes. Your hair black as it was and more than boun- tiful, the part in it going far back on the right side, almost back even with your ear. It always gave you that look of being unveiled before a crowd, a curtain tugged aside and the pronouncement: *Here, peo- ple, is Robert Burns Barclay.* Then, odd—I know this is only tintype history, catching a moment with the head-rod in place on the back of the neck—but there is a face-width gap between us as we pose, Rob, as if the absence of Lucas fit there. And then myself, young as you. As for my own front of the head, there beside you I show more expanse of upper lip than I wish was so, but there is not much to be done about that except what I later did, the mustache. The mouth could be worse, the nose could be better, but they are what I was given from the bin. The jaw pushes forward a little, as if I was inspecting into the camera's lens tunnel. My eyes—my eyes in our photograph are watching, not proclaiming as yours are. Even then, that far ago, watching to see what will become of us.

GROS VENTRE

---

*We dislike to speak ill of any civic neighbor, yet it
must be said that the community of Gros Ventre is
gaining a reputation as Hell with a roof on it.
Their notion of endeavor up there is to dream of
the day when whiskey will flow in the plumbing. It
is unsurprising that every cardsharp and hardcase
in northern Montana looks fondly upon Gros Ventre as a second home. We urge the town fathers, if
indeed the parentage of that singular municipality
can be ascertained, to invite Gros Ventre's rough
element to take up residence elsewhere.*
— CHOTEAU QUILL, APRIL 30, 1890

WORD FROM Scotland reached us in early February, and it
was yes and then some. As regular as Christmas itself, the Montana money from Lucas had again wafted to Nethermuir; and together with it this:

Gros Ventre, Mont., 23 Dec. 1889

My dear brother Vare and family,
 *You may wonder at not hearing from me this long while. Some day
it will be explained. I am in health and have purchased a business.
This place Gros Ventre is a coming town. I remain your loving
brother,*

Lucas Barclay

"The man himself, Angus! See now, here at the bottom! Written
by our Lucas himself, and he's—"

"Rob, man, did I ever give up on a Barclay? It takes you people some time to find the ink, but—"

We whooped and crowed in this fashion until Mrs. Billington announced in through our door that she would put us out into the winter streets if we didn't sober up. That quelled our eruption, but our spirits went right on playing trumpets and tambourines. Weeks of wondering and hesitation were waved away by the sheet of paper flying in Rob's hand: Lucas Barclay definitely alive, unmistakably here in Montana, irrevocably broken out in penmanship—I managed to reach the magical letter from Rob for another look.

When Lucas finally put his mind to it, he wrote a bold hand. Bold scarcely says it, in fact. Each and every word was a fat coil of loops and flourishes, so outsize that the few sentences commanded the entire face of the paper. I thought I had seen among Adam Willox's pupils of the 'venture school all possible performances of pen, but here stood script that looked meant to post on a palace wall.

I said as much to Rob, but he only averred, "That would be like Lucas," and proceeded to read us the letter's contents aloud for the third time. "This place Graws Ventree. Ever hear of it, did you?"

Neither of us had word one of French, and the town name had never passed my ears before. "We can ask them at the post office where it is," I suggested. "A letter got from the place all the way to Scotland, after all."

He already was putting on his coat and cap and I mine. To see our haste, you'd have thought we had only to rush across the snowy street to be in Gros Ventre.

"Grove On," the postal clerk pronounced Lucas's town, which was instructive. So, in its way, was what he told us next. "It's quite a ways toward Canada, up in that Two Medicine country. Not a whole hell of a lot up there but Indians and coyotes. Here, see for yourselves."

What we saw on the map of post routes of Montana was that our first leg of travel needed to be by train north along the Missouri River to Craig, easy as pie. Then from Craig to Augusta by stagecoach, nothing daunting either. But from Augusta to the map dot Gros Ventre, no indication of railroad or stage route. No postal road. No anything.

The clerk did not wait for us to ask how the blank space was to be found across. "You'll need to hitch a ride on a spine pounder."

Rob and I were blanker than the map gap.

"A freight wagon," the clerk elaborated. "They start freighting into that country whenever spring comes."

And so we waited for spring to have its say. In Montana, that is most likely to be a stutter. By the time snow and mud departed and then abruptly came back, went off a second time and decided to recur again, I thought I might have to bridle Rob. He maybe thought the same about me. But the day at last did happen when we stepped off the train at Craig, wandered along the banks of the Missouri River flowing swift and high with first runoff, and presented ourselves at the stagecoach station. There we were looked over with substantial curiosity by the agent. Rob and I were topped off with Stetson hats now, but I suppose their newness, and ours, could be seen from a mile off.

At five minutes before scheduled departure and no sign of anyone but us and the spectating agent, Rob asked restlessly: "How late will the stage be?"

"Who said anything about late?" the agent responded. "Here's the fellow now who handles the ribbons." In strode a rangy young man, tall as myself, who nodded briskly to the agent and reached behind the counter to hoist out a mail sack. Likely the newcomer wasn't much older than Rob or I, but he seemed to have been through a lot more of life.

"Yessir, Ben," the agent greeted him. "Some distinguished passengers for you today, all both of them."

The stage driver gave us his brisk nod. "Let's get your warbags on board."

We followed him outside to the stagecoach. "Step a little wide of those wheelers," he gestured toward the rear team of the four stagecoach horses. "They're a green pair. I'm running them in there to take the rough spots off of them."

Rob and I looked at each other. *And how did you journey from Craig to Augusta, Mr. McCaskill and Mr. Barclay? Oh, we were dragged along behind wild horses.* There was nothing else for it, so we thrust our bedrolls and bags up top to the driver. When he had lashed them down, he pulled out a watch and peered at it. "Augusta where you gents are aiming for?"

"No," I enlightened him, "we're going on to Gros Ventre." Meanwhile Rob was scrutinizing the wheels of the stagecoach and I was devoutly hoping they looked hale.

The driver nodded decisively again. "You'll see some country, up there." He conferred with his pocket watch once more, then put it away. "It's time to let the wheels chase the horses. All aboard, gents."

No two conveyances can be more different, but that stagecoach day was our voyage on the *Jemmy* out the Firth of Clyde over again. It has taken me this long to see so, among all else that I have needed to think through and through. But my meaning here is that just as the Clyde was our exit from cramped Scotland to the Atlantic and America, now Rob and I were leaving one Montana for another. The Montana of steel rails and mineshafts and politics for the Montana of—what? Expanse, definitely. There was enough untouched land between Craig and Augusta to empty Edinburgh into and spread it thin indeed. Flatten the country out and you could butter Glasgow onto it as well. So, the widebrimmed Montana, this was. The Montana of plain arising to foothills ascending to mountains, the continent going through its restless change of mood right exactly here. And the Montana of grass and grass and grass and grass. Not the new grass of spring yet—only the south slopes of coulees showed a green hint—but I swear I looked out on that tawny land and could feel the growth ready to burst up through the earth. The Montana that fledged itself new with the seasons.

The Montana, most of all to us that wheel-voyaging day, of the world's Rob Barclays and Angus McCaskills. We had come for homestead land, had we? For elbow room our ambitions could poke about in? For a 160-acre berth in the future? Here began the Montana that shouted all this and then let the echoes say, come have it. If you dare, come have it.

The stagecoach ride was a continuing session of rattle and bounce, but we had no runaway and no breakdown and pulled into

Augusta punctual to the minute, and so Rob and I climbed down chipper as larks. Even putting up for the night at what Augusta called a hotel didn't dim us, cheered as we were by word that a freight wagon was expected the next day. The freighter had passed with supplies for a sheep ranch west of town and would need to come back through to resume the trail northward. "Better keep your eyes skinned for him," our stage driver advised. "Might be a couple weeks before another one comes through."

Toward noon of the next day, not only were our eyes still skinned but our nerves were starting to peel.

"He must've gone through in the night," Rob declared, not for the first time. "Else where to hell is he?"

"If he's driving a wagon through this country at night, we don't want to be with him anyway," I suggested. "The roads are thin enough in daylight."

"Angus, you're certain sure it was light enough to see when you first stepped out here?"

"Rob. A wagon as long as a house, and four horses, and a man driving them, and you're asking if they got past me? Now maybe they tunneled, but—"

"All right, all right, you don't have to jump on me with tackety boots. I'm only saying, where to hell—"

What sounded like a gunshot interrupted him. Both of us jumped like crickets. Then we caught the distant wagon rumble which defined the first noise as a whipcrack.

Rob clapped me on the shoulder and we stepped out into the road to await our freight wagon.

The freighter proved to be a burly figure with a big low jaw which his neck sloped up into, in a way that reminded me of a pelican. He rubbed that jaw assiduously while hearing Rob, then granted in a croaky voice that he could maybe stand some company, not to mention the commerce. We introduced ourselves to him, and he in turn provided: "Name's Herbert."

Rob gave him the patented Rob smile. "Would that be a first name, now? Or a last?"

The freighter eyed him up and down as if about to disinvite us. Then rasped: "Either way, Herbert's plenty. Hop on if you're coming."

We hopped. But while stowing our bags and bedrolls I took the chance to inventory the wagon freight. You don't work in a store such as Cariston's without hearing tales about wagonloads of blasting powder that went to unintended destinations.

Boxes of axle grease, sacks of beans, bacon, flour, coffee. Some bundles of sheep pelts, fresh enough that they must have come from the ranch where the freighter had just been. Last, a trio of barrels with no marking on them. Herbert saw me perusing these.

"Lightning syrup," he explained.

"Which?"

"Whiskey. Maybe they've heard of it even where you men come from?"

The first hours of that journey, Rob and I said very little. Partly that was because we weren't sure whether Herbert the freighter tolerated conversation except with his horses. Partly it was because nothing really needed speaking. Now that we were on our last lap to Lucas's town, Rob all but glittered with satisfaction. But also, we were simply absorbed in the sights of the land. A geography of motion, of endless ridges and knob hills and swales the wagon track threaded through. And instead of mountains equally all around as in Helena, here tiers of them were stacked colossally on a single horizon, the western. Palisades of rock, constant canyons. Peaks with winter still on them. As far ahead north as we could see, the crags and cliffs formed that vast tumbled wall.

I at last had to ask. "How far do these mountains go on like this?"

"Damn if I know," responded Herbert. "They're in Canada this same way, and that's a hundred fifty miles or so."

On and on the country of swales and small ridges rolled. Here was land that never looked just the same, yet always looked much alike. I knew Rob and I would be as lost out here as if we had been put on a scrap of board in the middle of the sea, and I was thanking our stars that we were in the guidance of someone as veteran to this trail as Herbert Whomever or Whoever Herbert.

Just to put some words into the air to celebrate our good fortune, I leaned around Rob and inquired of our shepherd: "How many times have you traveled this trail by now?"

"This'll make once."

The glance that shot between Rob and me must have had some left over for the freighter, because eventually he went on: "Oh, I've drove this general country a lot. The Whoop-up Trail runs along to the east of here, from Fort Benton on up there into Canada. I've done that more times than you can notch a stick. This trail meets up with that one, somewhere after this Gros Ventre place. All we got to do, men, is follow these here tracks."

Rob and I peered at the wheel marks ahead like two threads on the prairie. This time Rob did the asking.

"What, ah, what if it snows?"

"That," Herbert conceded, "might make them a little harder to follow."

After we stopped for the night and put supper in us, Herbert grew fidgety. Twice he got up from beside the campfire and prowled to the freight wagon and back, and then a third time. Maybe this was only his body trying itself out after the day of sitting lumplike on the wagon seat, but somehow I didn't think so.

Finally he peered across the fire, first at Rob, then at me.

"Men, you look like kind of a trustable pair."

"We like to think we're honest enough," vouched Rob. I thought I had better tack on, "What brings the matter up?"

Herbert cleared his throat, which was a lot to clear. "That whiskey in the wagon there," he confessed. "If you two're interested as I am, we might could evaporate a little of her for ourselves."

I was puzzling on "evaporate" and I don't know what Rob was studying, when Herbert elaborated: "It ain't no difference to the saloonkeeper getting those barrels, if that's what you're stuck on. He's just gonna water them up fuller than they ever was, you can bet your bottom dollar. So if there's gonna end up being more in those barrels than I started out with anyhow, no reason not to borrow ourselves a sip apiece, now is there? That's if you men think about this the way I do."

If Rob and I had formed a philosophy since stepping foot into Montana, it was to try to do as Montanians did, within reason. This seemed within.

Herbert grabbed the lantern and led as we clambered into the freight wagon. Rummaging beneath the seat, he came up with a set of harness awls and a hammer. Carefully, almost tenderly, he began tapping upward on the top hoop of the nearest whiskey barrel. When the barrel hoop unseated itself to an inch or so above its normal latitude, Herbert placed the point of a small awl there in a seam between staves and began zestfully to drill.

"That's a thing I can do," Rob offered as soon as the freighter stopped to rest fingers. Rob had hands quick enough to shoe a unicorn, and now he moved in and had the drilling done almost before he started.

This impressed even Herbert. "This ain't your profession, is it?"

"Not quite yet. Angus, have you found the one with the tune?"

A straw to siphon with was my mission, and from a fistful off the floor of the wagon I'd been busily puffing until I found a sturdy one that blew through nicely. "Here's one you could pipe the Missouri River through." Rob drew his awl from the hole and delicately injected my straw in its place. Herbert had his cup waiting beneath when the first drops of whiskey began dripping out. "She's kind of slow, men. But so's the way to heaven."

When each of our cups was about two inches moist and the barrel hole plugged with a match stick and the hoop tapped back into place to hide it, Herbert was of new manufacture. As we sat at the campfire and sipped, even his voice sounded better when he asked intently: "How's the calico situation in Helena these days?"

I had a moment of wondering what was so vital to him about that specific item of dry goods. Then it dawned on me what he meant. Women. And from there it took no acrobatics of logic to figure out what sort of women.

Rob raised his cup in a mock toast and left the question to me. Well, there was rough justice in that, you could say. I had been the first to investigate the scarlet district of Helena, with promptitude after I'd begun earning wages at the mercantile. Not that Rob was six counties behind me, for it had been the next time I said I was setting off up the gulch that he fidgeted, scratched an ear, cleared something major from his throat, then blurted: "You can stand company, can't you?" That too had been new of America, transit from the allure of the Nethermuir mill girls with the boldest tongues to those Helena brothel excursions of ours winterlong. Without ever saying so to each other—it was the side of life Rob did not like to be noticed in—we both well knew that among the deepest of the Nethermuir traps we were escaping from was one of those accident marriages. A wedding beside the cradle, as was said. It happened to so many we knew and it had been just as likely to happen to either of us sooner or later, by the nature of things probably sooner. So, yes, America, Montana, Helena had been new open terms of possibility in more ways than one.

"Worst thing about being a freighter," Herbert was proclaiming after my tepid report on Helena, "is how far she is between calico. Makes the need rise in a man. Some of these mornings, I swear to gosh I wake up and my blanket looks like a tepee."

From Herbert the rest of that evening, we heard of the calico situation at the Canadian forts he freighted to. (Bad.) The calico situation in New Orleans, where he'd been posted as a soldier in the Union army. (Astounding.) The calico situation at Butte as compared with anywhere else in Montana. (A thousand times better.) The calico situation among the Mormons, the Chinese, the Blackfeet, the Nez Perce, and the Sioux.

When we had to tell him no, we hadn't been to London to find out the English calico situation, he looked regretful, tipped the last of his cup of whiskey into himself, and announced he was turning in for the night. "Men, there's no hotel like a wagon. Warm nights your room is on the wagon, stormy nights it's under it." Herbert sniffed the air and peered upward into the dark. "I believe tonight mine's going to be under."

Herbert's nose knew its business. In the morning, the world was white.

I came out of my bedroll scared and stayed that way despite the freighter's assessment that "this is just a April skift, maybe." From Rob's blinking appearance, he, too, could have done without a fresh white surprise this morn. After Helena's elongated winter of snow flinging down from the Continental Divide, how was a person supposed to look at so much as a white flake without thinking the word *blizzard?* Nor was there any checking on the weathermaking intentions of the Divide mountains now, as they were totally gone from the west, that direction a curtain of whitish mist. Ridges and coulees nearest us still could be picked out, their tan grass tufting up from the thin blanket of freshfall. But our wagon trail, those thin twin wheel tracks—as far as could be told from the blank and silent expanse all around us, Herbert and Rob and I and the freight wagon and four horses had dropped here out of the sky along with the night's storm.

The snow had stopped falling, which was the sole hope I saw anywhere around. But was the sky empty by now? Or was more winter teetering where this plopped from?

Rob put his head back and addressed firmly upward into the murk: "Can't you get the stove going up there?" But he still looked as discomfited as I must have.

"She sure beats everything, Montana weather," Herbert acknowledged. "Men, I got to ask you to do a thing."

Rob and I took turns at it, one walking ahead of the wagon and scuffing aside the snow to find the trail ruts while the other rode the seat beside Herbert and tried to wish the weather into improvement.

"When do you suppose spring comes to this country?" Rob muttered as he passed me during one of our walking-riding swaps.

"Maybe by the end of summer," I muttered back.

Later: "You remember what the old spinster in the story said, when somebody asked her why she'd never wed?"

"Tell me, I'm panting to know."

"'*I wouldn't have the walkers, and the riders went by.*' Out here, she'd have her choice of us."

"She'd need to negotiate past Herbert first."

Later again: "Am I imagining or is Montana snow colder than snow ever was in Scotland?"

"If you're going to imagine, try for some sunshine."

Still later: "Herbert says this could have been worse, there could have been a wind with this snow."

"Herbert is a fund of happy news."

It was morning's end before Herbert informed us, "Men, I'm beginning to think we're going to get the better of this."

He no more than said so when the mist along the west began to wash away and mountains shouldered back into place here and there along that horizon. The light of this ghostly day became like no other I had ever seen, a silver clarity that made the stone spines of ridges and an occasional few cottonwood trees stand out like engravings in book pages. Any outline that showed itself looked strangely singular, as if it existed only right then, never before. I seemed to be existing differently myself. Again as it had happened on that first full Atlantic morning of mine when I watched and watched the ocean, I could feel a slowing of the day; a shadowless truce while light speaks to time.

At last the sun burned through, the snow began melting into patches, the wheel tracks emerged ahead of us like new dark paint. Our baptism by Montana spring apparently over, Rob and I sat in grateful tired silence on the freight wagon.

We were wagoneers for the rest of that day and the next, crossing the Teton River and observing some distant landmark buttes which Herbert said were near a settlement called Choteau. Then at supper on the third night Herbert reported, "Tomorrow ought to about get us there." In celebration, we evaporated the final whiskey barrel to the level of the two previous nights', congratulating ourselves on careful workmanship, and Herbert told us a number of chapters about the calico situation when he was freighting into Deadwood during the Dakota gold rush.

Not an hour after we were underway the next morning, the trail dropped us into a maze of benchlands with steep sides. Here even the tallest mountains hid under the horizon, there was no evidence the world knew such a thing as a tree, and Herbert pointed out to us alkali bogs which he said would sink the wagon faster than we could think about it. A wind so steady it seemed solid made us hang onto our hats. Even the path of wagon tracks lost patience here; the bench hills were too abrupt to be climbed straight up, and rather than circle around endlessly among the congregation of geography, the twin cuts of track attacked up the slopes in gradual sidling patterns.

Herbert halted the wagon at the base of the first long ruts angling up and around a benchland. "I don't think this outfit'll roll herself over, up there. But I thought wrong a time or two before. Men, it's up to you whether you want to ride her out or give your feet some work."

If Herbert regarded these slopes as more treacherous than the cockeyed inclines he had been letting us stay aboard for . . . Down I climbed, Rob prompt behind me.

We let the wagon have some distance ahead of us, to be out of its way in case of tumbling calamity, then began our own slog up the twin tracks. *And how did you journey from Augusta to Gros Ventre, Mr. McCaskill and Mr. Barclay? We went by freight wagon, which is to say we walked.* The tilted wagon crept along the slope while we watched, Herbert standing precariously on the lazyboard, ready to jump.

"Any ideas, if?"

"We're trudging now, I suppose we'd keep on. Our town can't be that far."

"This is Montana, remember. You could put all of Scotland in the watch pocket of this place."

"True enough. Still, Gros Ventre has to be somewhere near by now. Even Herbert thinks so."

"Herbert thinks he won't tip the wagon over and kill himself, too. Let's see how right he is about that, first."

The benchlands set us a routine much as the snow had done: trudge up each slope with the wind in our teeth, hop onto the freight wagon to ride across and down the far side, off to trudge some more. The first hour or so, we told ourselves it was good for the muscles. The rest of the hours, we saved our breath.

"Kind of slaunchwise country, ain't she?" remarked Herbert when we paused for noon. Rob and I didn't dare study each other. If Gros Ventre was amid this boxed-in skewed landscape; if this windblown bleakness was where we had plucked ourselves up across the world to find Lucas Barclay . . .

Mid-afternoon, though, brought a long gradual slope which the wagon could travel straight up in no peril, and we were able to be steady passengers again. By now Rob and I were weary, and wary as well, expecting the top of each new ridgeline to deliver us back into the prairie infantry. But another gradual slope and widened benchland appeared ahead, and a next after that. And then the trail took the wagon up to a shallow pass between two long flat ridges.

There in the gap, Herbert whoaed the horses.

What had halted him, and us, was a change of earth as abrupt as waking into the snow had been.

Ahead was where the planet greatened.

To the west now, the entire horizon was a sky-marching procession of mountains, suddenly much nearer and clearer than they were before we entered our morning's maze of tilted hills. Peaks, cliffs, canyons, cite anything high or mighty and there it was up on that rough west brink of the world. Mountains with snow summits, mountains with jagged blue-gray faces. Mountains that were free-standing and separate as blades from the hundred crags around them; mountains that went among other mountains as flat palisades of stone miles long, like guardian reefs amid wild waves. The Rocky Mountains, simply and rightly named. Their double magnitude here startled and stunned a person, at least this one—how deep into the sky their motionless tumult reached, how far these Rockies columned across the earth.

The hem to the mountains was timbered foothills, dark bands of pine forest. And down from the foothills began prairie broader than any we had met yet, vast flat plateaus of tan grassland north and east as far as we could see. Benchland and tableland countless times larger than the jumbled ridges behind us, elbow room for the spirit.

Finally, last in our looking, about a mile in front of us at the foot of the nearest of these low plateaus, a line of cottonwood trees along a creek made the graceful bottom seam across this tremendous land.

I just sat and let it all dazzle at me. Rob was equally stone-still at my side.

"Oh yeah, I see where we are now," contributed Herbert. "There's old Chief." He pointed out to us Chief Mountain, farthest north on the mountain horizon and a step separate, independent, from the rest of the crags. "She's Canada up beyond that. Between her and here, though, comes the Two Medicine River. Can't see that from where we're at, but this whole jography is called the Two Medicine country."

I so wish Rob and I right then had performed what we ought to: politely request Herbert to close his eyes and cover his ears, step off the wagon together, face ourselves to this Two Medicine country, and then leap high and click our heels in the air loud enough to be heard in Nethermuir. For every soul that has ever followed a notion bigger than itself, we ought to have performed that. To send our echo into the canyons of time: *here is Montana, here is America, here is all yet to come.*

Now Herbert was finding for us the Sweetgrass Hills, a cluster of bumps on the plains far northeast of us. "Men, unless I'm more

wrong than usual, those're about seventy-five miles from where
we're at." Montana distances made your head swim. "Then this
kind of a tit over here, Heart Butte." A dark breastlike cone that
rose northwest near the rougher Rockies. Much closer to us, west
along the line of creek trees, stood a smaller promontory like the
long aft sail of a windship, with a tree-dark top. "Don't know what
that butte is, she's a new one on me," Herbert confessed as our
wagon began to jostle down toward the creek's biggest stand of cottonwood trees. In this landscape of expanse the local butte did not
stand particularly high, it was not monumentally shaped, yet it
managed to speak prominence, separateness, managed somehow to
preside. A territory of landmarks as clear as towers was this Two
Medicine country. Already I felt able to find my way in this clean-
lined land.

Rob and I interrupted our gaping to trade mighty grins. All we
needed now was Lucas Barclay and his coming metropolis.

Herbert cleared his gallon of throat and gestured toward the cottonwood grove ahead. When we didn't comprehend, he said:

"Here she is, I guess."

Gros Ventre took some guessing, right enough.

Ahead of us under the trees waited a thin scatter of buildings, the
way there can be when the edge of town dwindles to countryside.
None of the buildings qualified as much more than an eyesore, and
beyond them on the far bank of the creek were arrayed several
picketed horses and a cook wagon and three or four tents of ancient
gray canvas, as if wooden walls and roofs hadn't quite been figured
out over there yet.

From the wagon seat Rob and I scanned around for more town,
but no. This raggle-taggle fringe of structures was the community
entire.

Rather, this was Gros Ventre thus far in history. Across the far
end of the single street, near the creek and the loftiest of the cottonwoods, stood a two-story framework. Just that, framework, empty
and forlorn. Yellow lumber saying, more like pleading, that it had
the aspiration of sizable enterprise and lacked only hundreds of
boards and thousands of nails to be so.

Trying to brighten the picture for Rob, I observed: "They, ah, at
least they have big plans."

Rob made no answer. But then, what could he have?

"Wonder where it is they keep the calico at," issued from Herbert. He pondered Gros Ventre a moment further. "Wonder if they *got* any calico."

Our wagon rolled to a halt in front of what I took to be a log barn and which proved to be the livery stable. Rob and I climbed down and were handed our luggage by Herbert. As we shook hands with him he croaked out companionably, "Might see you around town. Kind of hard to miss anybody in a burg this size."

Rob drew in a major breath and looked at me. I tried to give him a grin of encouragement, which doubtless fell short of either. He turned and went over to the hostler who had stepped out to welcome this upsurge of traffic. "Good afternoon. We're looking for a man Lucas Barclay."

"Who? Luke? Ain't he over there in the Medicine Lodge? He always is."

Our eyes followed the direction the stableman jerked his head. At the far end of the empty dirt street near the bright skeleton of whatever was being built, stood a building with words painted across the top third of its square front in sky blue, startling as a tattoo on a forehead:

MEdICINE

LOdGE

I saw Rob open his mouth to ask definition of a medicine lodge, think better of it, and instead bid the hostler a civil, "Thank you the utmost."

Gathering ourselves, bedrolls and bags, off we set along the main and only street of this place Gros Ventre. I was wrong about the street being empty; it in fact abounded with cow pies, horse apples, and other animal products.

"Angus," Rob asked low, as we drew nearer to the skelter of tents and picketed horses across the creek, "what, do they have Gypsies in this country?"

"I wish I knew just what it is they have here." The door into the Medicine Lodge whatever-it-was waited before us. "Now we find out."

Like Vikings into Egypt, we stepped in.

And found it to be a saloon. Along the bar were a half dozen partakers, three or four others occupied chairs around a greentop table where they were playing cards.

"Aces chase faces, Deaf Smith," said one of the cardsters as he spread down his hand.

"Goddamn you and the horse you rode in on, Perry," responded his opponent mildly, and gathered the cards to shuffle.

Of course Rob and I had seen cowboys before, in Helena. Or what we thought were. But these of Gros Ventre were a used variety, in soiled crimped hats and thick clothing and worn-down boots.

The first of the Medicine Lodge clientele to be aware of us was a stocky tan-faced man, evidently part Indian. He said something too soft for us to hear to the person beside him, who revolved slowly to examine us over a brownish longhorn mustache. I wish I could say that the mustached one showed any sign we were worth turning around to look at.

Had someone been counting our blinks—the Indian-looking witness maybe was—they'd have determined that Rob and I were simultaneous in spying the saloonkeeper.

He stood alone near one end of the bar, intently leaning down, busy with some task beneath there. When he glanced up and intoned deep, "Step right over, lads, this bunch isn't a fraction as bad as they look," there was the remembered brightness of his Barclay cheeks, there was the brand of voice we had not heard since leaving Nethermuir.

Lucas possessed a black beard now with gray in it like streaks of ash. The beard thickly followed his jaw and chin, with his face carefully shaved above that. Above the face Lucas had gone babe-bald, but the dearth of hair only emphasized the features of power dispersed below in that frame of coaly whiskers: sharp gray eyes under heavy dark eyebrows, substantial nose, wide mouth to match the chin, and that stropped ruddiness identical to Rob's.

Rob let out a breath of relief that must have been heard all the way to Helena. Then he smiled a mile and strode to the bar with his hand out as far as it could go:

"Mister Lucas Barclay, I've come an awful distance to shake your hand."

Did I see it happen? Hear it? Or sheerly feel it? Whichever the sense, I abruptly knew that now the attention of everyone in the saloon weighed on Rob and me. Every head had pivoted to us, every eye gauged us. The half-breed or whatever he was seemed to be memorizing us in case there was a bounty on fools.

The saloonkeeper himself stared up at us thunderous. If faces could kill, Rob and I would have been never born.

The two of us stared stunned as he glowered at Rob. At me. At Rob again. Now the saloonkeeper's back straightened as if an iron rod had been put in his spine, but he kept his forearms deliberately out of sight below the bar. My mind flashed full of Helena tales of bartenders pulling out shotguns to moderate their unruly customers. By the holy, though, could anyone with eyes think Rob and I were anything like unruly right then?

Finally the saloonkeeper emitted low and fierce to Rob what his face was already raging out: "Are you demented? Who to hell are you anyway, to come spouting that?"

"Rob!" from Rob the bewildered. "Lucas, man, I know you like myself in the mirror! I'm Rob, your nephew."

The saloonkeeper still stared at him, but in a new way.

Then:

"By Jesus, you are. Chapter and verse. By Jesus, you're Vare's lad Robbie, grown some."

The fury was gone from Lucas Barclay's face, but what passed into its place was no less unsettling. All emotion became unknown there now; right then that face of Lucas Barclay could have taught stoniness to a rock.

Still as baffled as I was, Rob blurted next: "Lucas, what is the matter here? Aren't we welcome?"

At last Lucas let out a breath. As if that had started him living again, he said as calm as cream to Rob: "Of course you're welcome. It's pure wonderful that you're here, lad. You've come late, though, to do any handshaking with me."

Lucas raised his forearms from beneath the bar and laid on the dark polished wood the two stumps of amputation where his hands had been.

I tell you true, I did not know whether to stare or look away, to stay or turn tail, to weep or to wail. There was no known rightness of behavior, just as there was no rightness about what had happened to Lucas. Like the clubs of bone and flesh he was exhibiting to us, any justice in life seemed ripped, lopped off. To this day the account of Lucas Barclay's mining accident causes my own hands to open and close, clench their fingernails hard against their palms, thankful they are whole. It happened after the Great Maybe and Helena, when Lucas had moved on to a silver claim called the Fanalulu in the outcropping country between Wolf Creek and Augusta. *My partner on that was an old Colorado miner Johnny Dorgan. This day we were going to blast. I was doing the tamping in, Johnny was behind me ready with the fuse. What made this worse was that I had miner's religion, I always made sure to use a wooden tamp on the powder so there'd be no chance of spark.* But this once, the blasting powder somehow did go off. Dorgan had turned to reach for his chewing tobacco in the coat behind him and was knocked sprawling, with quartz splinters up and down his back. He scrambled on all fours to where Lucas had been flung, a burned and bloody mass. The worst was what was left—what was gone—at the ends of Lucas's arms. Dorgan tied a tourniquet on each, then took Lucas, a wagonload of pain, to the Army post hospital at Fort Shaw. *Johnny thought he was delivering a corpse, I suppose. He very near was.* The surgeon there saved what he could of Lucas, starting at the wrists. *Did I want to die, at first? By Jesus, I wanted worse than that. I wanted the world dead. I hated everything above snake-high.* For months, Lucas was tended by the Fort Shaw surgeon. *I was his pastime, his pet. He made me learn to handle a fork and a glass with these stubs. He said if a man can do that, he can make himself a life.*

There in the Medicine Lodge, Lucas's maiming on show in front of him, Rob's case of stupefaction was even worse than mine. He brought his hand back to his side as if burned and stammered, "Lucas . . . I . . . we never—"

"Put it past, Robbie," his uncle directed. "Have a look at these to get used to them. Christ knows, I've had to."

While Rob's eyes still were out like organ stops, Lucas's powerful face turned toward me. "And who's this long one?"

Would you believe, I stupidly started to put my hand out for a shake, just as Rob had. Catching myself, I swallowed and got out: "Lucas, I'm Angus McCaskill. You knew my father, back—"

"You're old Alex's lad? By Jesus, they must have watered you. You've grown and then some." His gaze was locked with mine. "Is your father still the best wheelsmith in the east of Scotland?"

"No. He's, he's dead."

Lucas's head moved in a small wince of regret. "I'm sorry to hear so. Death is as thorough on the good as the bad." His arm stumps vanished briefly beneath the bar again and came up delivering a whiskey bottle clutched between. "Down here among the living we'd better drink to health, ay?"

Lucas turned from us to the line of glasses along the back bar shelf, grasped one between his stumps, set it in place in front of me, turned and did the same with one for Rob, a third time with a glass for himself. Next he clasped the whiskey bottle the same way and poured an exactly even amount in each glass. It was all done as neatly as you or I could.

"Sedge, Toussaint, you others," Lucas addressed the rest of the clientele, "line your glasses up here. You're not to get the wild idea I'm going to make a habit of free drinks. But it's not just any old day when a Barclay arrives to Gros Ventre."

Lucas poured around, lifted a glass of his own as you would if you had to do it only with your wrists, and gave the toast:

"Broth to the ill, stilts to the lame."

Our drink to health became two, then Lucas informed Rob and me he was taking us to home and supper and that he may as well show us the town while we were out and about. The half-breed, Toussaint, assured us, "This Gros Ventre, there never was one like it," and chuckled. The mustached man, called Sedge, stepped behind the bar to preside there, and Lucas led Rob and me out on tour.

Gros Ventre could be taken in with two quick glimpses, one in each direction along the street, yet it registered on me in a slow woozy way, like a dream of being shown somewhere at the far end of the world. Or maybe a dream of myself dreaming this, reality a phase or two away from where I was. At any rate, my mind was stuck on Lucas and his maiming and he was energetically intent only on showing us Montana's Athens-to-be. Rob and I did much nodding and tried to mm-hmm properly as Lucas tramped us past such sights as Fain's blacksmith shop, encircled by odds and ends of scrap iron. Kuuvus's mercantile, a long, low log building which sagged tiredly in the middle of its roofbeam. A sizable boarding house with a sign above its door proclaiming that it was operated by C.E. Sedgwick—which was to say, the mustachioed Sedge—and his wife Lila. Near the creek in a grove of cottonwoods, a tiny Catholic church with the bell on an iron stanchion out front. (A circuit-riding priest circulated through "every month or so," Lucas noted favorably.) Dantley's livery stable where Herbert the freighter had disembarked us. Next to it Gros Ventre's second saloon, Wingo's: a twin to the Medicine Lodge except it was fronted with slabs instead of boards. To our surprise—we now knew why Herbert hadn't materialized at the Medicine Lodge—we were informed in an undervoice by Lucas that the town did have a calico supply, ensconced here in Wingo's. "Two of them," Lucas reported with a disapproving shake of his head. "Wingo calls them his nieces."

We also became enlightened about the tents and picketed horses.

"That's the Floweree outfit, from down on the Sun River," Lucas told us. "Trailing a herd of steers north. These cattle outfits all come right through on their way up to borrow grass. I tell you, lads, this town is situated—"

"Borrow?" echoed Rob.

"From the Indians. Blackfeet. Their reservation is north there"—Lucas gestured beyond the creek with one of his stubs; would I ever get used to the sight of them?—"fifteen miles or so, and it goes all the way to Canada. Cattle everywhere on it, every summer."

And how did the municipality of Gros Ventre strike you, Mr. Mc-Caskill and Mr. Barclay? We found the main enterprise to be theft of grass, and our host had no hands.

Be fair, though. The fledgling town was not without graces. It proffered two. First and finest was its trees, cottonwoods like a towering lattice above the little collection of roofs. When their buds became leaf, Gros Ventre would wear a green crown, true enough. And the other distinction stood beside the Sedgwick boarding house: a tall slender flagpole, far and away the most soaring construction in Gros Ventre, with its somewhat faded 41-star American flag energetically flapping at the top. When Rob or I managed to remark on this public-spirited display, Lucas glanced upward and said there was a story to that, all right, but he marched us across to what he plainly considered the centerpiece of Gros Ventre, the building skeleton at the end of the street.

"Sedge's hotel," Lucas identified this assemblage of lumber and air for us. "I've put a bit of money into it too, to help him along. The Northern, he's going to call it."

Rob and I must have looked less comprehending than we already were, for Lucas impatiently pointed out that the hotel site was at the north end of town. "You'll see the difference this hotel will make," he asserted. "Sedge and Lila will have room for dozens here."

Thinking of what it had taken for Rob and me to reach this speck on the map, I did wonder how dozens at once were going to coincide here.

Lucas faced the pair of us as if he'd heard that. He thrust his stubs into his coat pockets and looked whole and hale again, a bearded prophet of civic tomorrows.

"Robbie, Angus. I know Gros Ventre must look like a Gypsy camp to you. But by Jesus, you ought've seen what a skimpy place it was when I came three years ago. You had to look twice to see whether anybody lived here but jackrabbits. The Sedgwicks and Wingo, Kuuvus and his wife and Fain and his, they've all come in since then. And they're just the start. This'll be a true town before you know it."

Evidently we did not manage to appear convinced. Lucas started anew.

"Lads, you have eyes in your heads. If you used them at all on your way here, you saw that there's land and more land and then more of more, just for the taking here in Montana. And by Jesus, people will take it. That's the history of the race, in so many words. They'll flock in here, one day, and that day not long from now. The railroad is being built, do you know, up north of the Two Medicine River. That's what'll bring them, lads. Steam and steel is the next gospel. And when people come, they'll need everything a town can furnish them," concluded the lord of the Medicine Lodge.

There was a brief silence, reverent on Lucas's part, dazed on ours. Then he did some more dream-building for us, in a confiding way:

"My belief is we'll see a railroad of our own here. After all, they talk of building one to that piddle spot beside the road, called

Choteau. A squeak of a place like Choteau gets a railroad, we ought to get a dozen, ay?"

Lucas gazed out the solitary street to the straight-topped benchland south of us, then past the flagpole to the jagged tumble of mountains along the west. Up came an armstub that thoughtfully smoothed the black-and-gray beard as he contemplated. "This is rare country," he murmured. "Just give our Gros Ventre a little time and it'll be a pure grand town."

"Whom never a town surpasses," issued from me, *"for honest men and bonny lasses."* I suppose I was thinking out loud. For the long moment Lucas contemplated me, I much wished I'd kept the words in me.

"Is that old Burns," he asked at last, "as in the middle of our Robbie's name?"

"The same," I admitted.

"Angus is a lad of parts," Rob roused himself to put in, "he can recite the rhyming stuff by the yard. See now, he was pupil teacher for Adam Willox."

"I knew Adam," recalled Lucas. "He had a head on his shoulders." Lucas eyed me again, as if hoping to see the start of one growing on me, then declared the next of Gros Ventre's matchless attractions was supper.

Past the rear of his saloon and across a wide weedy yard he led us toward a two-story frame house. The house needed paint—this entire town needed that—but it sat comfortably between two fat gray cottonwood trees, like a mantel clock between pewter candlesticks. Lucas related to us that the house had come with the Medicine Lodge, he'd bought both from the founder of Gros Ventre, named DeSalis. It seemed DeSalis had decided the begetting of Gros Ventre was not a sufficient source of support in life, and had gone back to Missouri. But we had the luck, Lucas pointed out, that DeSalis first sired five children here and so provided ample guest space for us.

As we reached the front porch, Lucas stopped as if he had suddenly butted up against a new fact.

"Now you'll meet Nancy," he said.

"Nancy?" I could see that Rob was buoyed by the sight of the considerable house, and now this news that Lucas at least had been fortunate enough to attain a mate in life. "The Mrs.! And doesn't that make her my aunt, I ask you? Lucas, man, why didn't you tell—"

Lucas's face underwent another change to stone. "Did you hear me say one goddamned thing about being married? Nancy is my—housekeeper."

Rob reddened until he looked like he might ignite. "Lead on, Lucas," I inserted in a hurry. "We're anxious to meet Nancy."

He manipulated the doorknob with his stubs and led us into the front parlor. "Nancy! We have people here."

From the kitchen doorway at the far end of the parlor stepped a young woman. Her dress was ordinary, but that made the only thing. Hair black as a crow's back. A figure tidily compact yet liberally curvaceous. A squarish face, the nose and cheekbones a bit broad; the upper lip surprisingly rising a bit in the very middle, revealing the first teeth in a way that seemed steadily but calmly questioning. None of this Nancy-the-housekeeper was lovely in any usual way but her each feature was more attractive on second notice, and even more so on a third. Remarkable dark, dark eyes, perhaps black, too. And her skin was brown as a chestnut, several shades darker than that of the half-Indian or whatever he was in the Medicine Lodge, Toussaint.

Rob was trying not to be frog-eyed, and failing. I suppose I was similar. Lucas now seemed to be enjoying himself.

Deciding the situation could stand some gallantry, I stepped toward the woman of the inquisitive lip and began, "How do you do, Miss—"

Lucas snorted a laugh, then called to me: "Buffalo Calf Speaks."

"Excuse me?"

"Buffalo Calf Speaks," Lucas repeated, more entertained than ever. "She's Blackfeet. Her Indian name is Buffalo Calf Speaks. So if you're going to call her Miss, that's what Miss she is."

"Yes, well." Strange sensation it is, to want to strangle a grinning handless man. I put myself around to the woman again and tried anew: "Nancy, hello. My name is Angus McCaskill." I forced a grin of my own. "I'm from a tribe called Scotchmen."

"Yes," she answered, but her eyes rapidly left me to look at Rob, his shining resemblance to Lucas. Lucas told her, "This is my brother's son. His name is Rob."

"Rob?" Her intonation asked how that word could be a name.

"Like Bob Wingo," Lucas instructed, "except Scotchmen say it Rob. They never do anything the way ordinary people do, right, lads?"

"Rob," Nancy repeated. "From Scot Land."

"That's him, Nancy. Rob and Angus are going to be with us for a while. Now we need supper." The woman's dark eyes regarded us a moment more, then Lucas, and she went back through the kitchen doorway.

So that was Nancy. Or at least the start of her.

"Don't stand there like the awkward squad," Lucas chafed us. "Come sit down and tell me news of Nethermuir. If the old place has managed to have any, that is."

That supper, and that evening, were like no other.

I am all too sure that neither Rob nor I managed to learn, at least on the first many tries, how to keep a face under control when a meat platter or a spud dish was passed to it between those bony stubs at the ends of Lucas's sleeves. What we did learn was that a person without hands needed to have his meat cut for him—Nancy sat beside Lucas and did the knifework before ever touching her own plate—but he then could manipulate a fork the way a clever bear might take it between its paws, and he could spoon sugar into his coffee without a spill and stir it efficiently. We learned by Lucas's telling of it that he could dress himself except for the buttoning; "I'd like to have my knee on the throat of the man who invented buttons." That he could wind his pocket watch by holding it against his thigh with one stub and rolling the stem with the other. That, what I had wondered most about, he had taught himself to write again by sitting down night after night, a pen between his stubs, and copying out of an old book of epitaphs. "*Stone Stories*, the title of it was. It fit my mood. I made myself work at a line a night, until I could do it first try. Then two lines a night, and four, on up to a page of them at a time. Not only did I learn writing again, lads, the epitaphs were a bit of entertainment for me. The Lillisleaf stee-plejack's one: *Stop, traveler, as you go by/I too once had life and breath/but I fell through life from steeple high/and quickly passed by death.* Angus, what would your man Burns think of that one, ay? Or the favorite of mine. *In the green bed 'tis a long sleep/Alone with your past, mounded deep.* By Jesus, that's entirely what I was, alone, after the accident to my hands. At least"—he indicated Nancy, buttering bread for him—"I'm over that now." We learned by Lucas's ironic telling that he had earned good money from the Fanalulu mine before the accident—"the great secret to silver mining, lads, is to quit in time; otherwise, the saying is that you need a gold mine to keep your silver mine going"—and we inferred from this house and its costly furnishings those were not the last dollars to find their way to Lucas. Where did this man get the sheer strength to wrestle the earth for its silver and then, when that struggle had done its worst to him, to wrestle a pen for the months of learning to write again?

We learned as much as he could bring himself to tell us about that letter that found its way to us in Helena. "Why did I write it, after these years?" Lucas lifted his coffee cup between his stubs and drank strong. "Matters pile up in a person. They can surprise you, how they want out. I must have wanted to say to old nose-in-the-air Nethermuir that I'm still living a life of my own. Even so, I couldn't bring myself yet to tell about the accident, about my—condition. How do you say to people, 'I'm a bit different these days than you remember, my hands are gone'?" Lucas gave us a gaze across the table, and Nancy added her dark one to it. A jury of two, waiting for no answer we could give.

After a moment, Lucas resumed: "And now that you lads are here, I know it'll get told without me. That's a relief. Why I don't know, but someway that's a relief."

Back in the saloon, when Lucas went to close up for the night and decided we needed one more drink to health and that happened to lead to another, we learned about Nancy.

"She came with, when I bought the Medicine Lodge and the house," Lucas imparted. "Lads, you're trying not to look shocked, but that's the fact of it. Nancy was living with the DeSalises—this all goes back a few years, understand—when I bought out old Tom. You met Toussaint Rennie, the half-breed or whatever arithmetic he is, in here when you came. Toussaint is married to Nancy's mother's sister, and that's all the family she has. The others died, up on the reservation in the winter of '83. The Starvation Winter, these Blackfeet call that, and by Jesus they did starve, poor bastards them, by the hundreds. Pure gruesome, what they went through. The last of the buffalo petered out that year, and the winter rations the Blackfeet were supposed to get went into some Indian agent's pocket, and on top of it all, smallpox. They say maybe a third of the whole tribe was dead by spring. Nancy was just a girl then, twelve or so, and Toussaint and his wife took her to raise. Then the winter of '86 came, a heavier winter than '83 ever thought of being, and Toussaint didn't know whether he was going to keep his own family alive up there on the Two Medicine River, let alone an extra. So he brought Nancy in here and gave her to the DeSalises. There's that shocked look again, lads." Himself, Lucas somehow appeared to be both grim and amused. "They say when Toussaint rode into town with her, the two of them wrapped in buffalo robes, they had so much snow on them they looked like white bears. When I came up here and bought the saloon and the house and DeSalis pulled out with his family for Missouri, Nancy stayed on with me. She can be a hard one to figure, Nancy can. By now she's part us and part them"—Lucas's nod north signified the reservation and its Blackfeet—"and you never quite know which side is to the front, when. But Nancy has always soldiered for me. By Jesus, she's done that. I need some things done, like these damn buttons and shaving and all little nuisances like that. She needs some place to be. So you see, it's an arrangement that fits us both." Lucas shrugged into his coat, thrust his arm ends into its pockets and instantly looked like a builder of Jerusalems again. "This isn't old Scotland, lads. Life goes differently here."

Differently, said the man. In the bedroom that night, I felt as if the day had turned me upside down and shaken me out. Lucas without hands. This end-of-nowhere place Gros Ventre. The saga of Nancy.

Rob looked as if he'd received double of whatever I had. "Christ of mercy, Angus. What've we gotten ourselves into here?"

It helped nothing to have the wind out of Rob's sails, too. I tried to put a little back in by pointing out: "We did find Lucas, you have to say that for us."

"Not anything like the one I expected. Not a—" He didn't finish that.

"The man didn't lose those hands on purpose, Rob."

"I never meant that. It's a shock to see, is all. How could something like that happen?"

"Lucas told. Tamping the blasting powder and someway—"

"Not that, Angus. What I mean, how could it happen to *him?*"
To a Barclay, he really meant. My own weary guess was that fate
being what it is, it keeps a special eye for lives the size of Lucas's. A
pin doesn't draw down lightning. But how say so to Rob this unearthly night and make any sense. He was rattling at top speed
now: "Lucas always was so good with his hands. He was Crack Jack
at anything he tried—and now look at him. I tell you, Angus, I
just—and Nancy Buffalo-whatever. There's a situation, now.
Housekeeper, he calls her. She must even have to help him take a
piddle."

"That's as maybe, but look at all Angus does manage to do."

"Yes, if it hadn't been for that damned letter he managed to
write—" Rob shook his head and didn't finish that either.

Well, I told myself, here is interesting. A Barclay not knowing
what to make of another Barclay. The history of the world is not
done yet.

From our bedroom window I could see the rear of the Medicine
Lodge and the patch of dirt street between the saloon and the forlorn hotel framework. Another whisper from Burns came to mind:
*Your poor narrow footpath of a street/where two wheelbarrows tremble
when they meet.* Those lines I had the sense to keep to myself and
said instead: "Anyway, here is where we are. Maybe Gros Ventre
will look more grand after a night's sleep."

Rob flopped onto his side of the bed but his eyes stayed open
wide. All he said more was, "Maybe so, maybe no."

And do you know, Gros Ventre did improve itself overnight, at
least in the way that any place has more to it than a first glimpse
can gather. In the fresh weather of dawn—Montana's crystal mornings made it seem we'd been living in a bowl of milk all those years
in Scotland—I went out and around, and in that opening hour of
the day the high cottonwoods seemed to stand even taller over the
street and its little scatter of buildings. Grave old nurses for a
foundling town. Or at least there in the daybreak a person had hope
that nurture was what was happening.

Early as the hour was, the flag already was tossing atop the Sedgwick flagpole. Beyond, the mountains were washed a lovely clean
blue and gray in the first sunlight. The peaks and their snow stood

so clear I felt I could reach out and run a finger along that chill rough edge. At the cow camp across the creek the cook was at his fire and a few of the cowboys, or riders, as Lucas referred to them, were taking down the tents. I heard one of the picketed horses whinny, then the rush of the creek where the water bumped busily across a bed of rocks.

"Angus, you are early," came a voice behind me. "Are you seeing if the sun knows how to find Gros Ventre?"

I turned around, to Toussaint Rennie. Lucas had said Toussaint was doing carpenter work for Sedge on the famous hotel. *Toussaint does a little of everything and not too much of anything. He's not Blackfeet himself—it is not just entirely clear what he is—but he has a front finger in whatever happens in this country. Has had for years, and it's not even clear how many years. A bit like a coyote, our Toussaint. Here and there but always in on a good chance. He comes down from the Two Medicine, works at a little something for a while, goes home long enough to father another child, comes down to work at whatever presents itself next.* And came once in a blizzard to deposit his wife's niece to the house I had just stepped from.

Was this person everywhere, every time? I managed to respond to Toussaint, "The day goes downhill after dawn, they say."

"I think that, too," he vouched. The strange lilting rhythm in his voice, whatever its origins; as if warming up to sing. "You live good at dawn." Toussaint nodded toward the flagpole and its flapping banner. "You ought to have been here then."

"Then?"

"That statehood. Sedge put up the flagpole in honor. Lila had the idea, fly the flag the first of anyone. We did, do you know. The first flag in Montana the state, it was ours. Here in Gros Ventre."

I thought of the flag unfurling atop the *Herald* building in Helena that November morning, of the other flags breaking out all over the city, of the roaring celebration Rob and I had enlisted in. "How are you so sure this one was the first?"

"We got up early enough," testified Toussaint. "Way before dawn. Sedge woke up me, I woke up Dantley, we woke up everybody. Wingo and his nieces, the Kuuvuses, the Fains, Luke and"—Toussaint glanced around to be sure we were alone—"that Blackfeet of his. Out to the flagpole, everybody. It was still dark as cats, but Dantley had a lantern. Lila says, 'This is the day of statehood. This is Montana's new day.' Sedge puts up the new flag, there it was. Every morning since, he puts it up." Toussaint chuckled. "That flag. The wind has a good time with it. Sedge will need a lot of flags, if he keeps on."

The morning was young yet when Fain of the blacksmith shop came to ask if Rob might help him with a few days of wheelwork. Rob backed and filled a bit but then concluded he supposed he could, and I was glad, knowing he was privately pleased to be sought out and knowing, too, that a chance to use his skill would help his mood. The two of us had decided we'd give our situation a few days and conclude then whether to go or stay. I say decided; the fact that we had to wait anyway for another freight wagon or some other conveyance out of Gros Ventre was the major voice in the vote.

When Rob went off with Fain, I offered to Lucas to lend a hand—just in time I caught myself from putting it that way—in the saloon.

The notion amused Lucas. "Adam Willox taught you how to swamp, did he?"

I said I didn't know about that, but people had been known to learn a thing if they tried.

"I've heard of that myself," Lucas answered dryly. "You at least don't lack attitude. Come along if you want, we'll show you what it's like to operate a thirst parlor."

Swamping was sloshing buckets of water across the floor and then sweeping the flood out the door, I learned promptly, and when the saloon had been broomed out, there were glasses to wash and dry, empty bottles to haul out and dump, beer kegs to be wrestled, poker tables and chairs to be straightened, spittoons to be contended with. Lucas meanwhile polished the bar from end to end, first one foreshortened arm and then the other moving a towel in caressing circles on the wood. I am not happy to have to say this, but as happened the evening before when he was showing off Gros Ventre to us, the person that Lucas was to me depended on whether his stubs were in the open or out of sight as they now were in the towel. Part of the time I could forget entirely that Lucas was maimed as he was. Part of the time there was nothing I was more aware of. I wondered what kind of courage it took to go on with life in public after damage such as Lucas's.

Eventually Lucas called a pause in our mutual neatening tasks. "Do you feel any thirst?" he asked. I did. He nodded and stated: "We can't have people thinking we sit around in here and drink. So we'll take a standing one, ay?"

I watched astounded as Lucas wrestled forth a small crock and poured us each a beerglass of buttermilk.

"Buttermilk until well into the afternoon, Angus," he preached. "The saloonman doesn't live who can toss liquor into himself all day long and still operate the place."

As we sipped the cow stuff and Lucas told me another installment of Gros Ventre's imminent eminence, my gaze kept slipping to his stubs. I needed to know, and since there was no good time to ask this it may as well be now as any.

"Lucas, would you mind much if I ask you a thing?"

He regarded me in the presiding way of Rob aboard the steam-ship. "About my hands, you mean. The ones I haven't got. It's pure wonderful how interesting they are to people. Everyone asks something eventually. All but Nancy. All the others—'But how do you tie your shoes,'" he mimicked. "'But how do you get your dohickey out to take a piddle.' Well? Bang away, Angus lad."

I gulped, not just on the taste of buttermilk. "Do they—does it ever still hurt, there?"

Lucas looked at me a very long moment, and then around the Medicine Lodge as if to be sure there were no listening ghosts in its corners. "Angus, it does. Sometimes it hurts like two toothaches at once. Those are the times when it feels as if I still have the hands but they're on fire. But I don't have them, do I, so where does that pain come from?" The asking of that was not to me, however, and Lucas went on: "There, then. That's one. Next question?"

"That one was all, Lucas."

After Lucas began to see that I could do saloon tasks almost half as well with two hands as he could with none, he made strong use of me. Indeed, by the second day I was hearing from him: "Angus, I've some matters at the house. You can preside here till I get back, ay?" And there was my promotion into being in charge of the Medicine Lodge during the buttermilk hours of the day.

"How do, Red."

The taller of the pair who were bowlegging their way to the bar gave me the greeting, while the short wiry one beside him chirped, "Pour us somethin' that'll cheer us up, professor."

In that order of presentation, Perry Fox and Deaf Smith Mitchell these were. Riders for the Seven Block cattle ranch, out near the Blackfeet reservation. Progeny of Texas who, to hear them tell it, had strayed north from that paradisiacal prairie and hadn't yet found their way back. The one called Deaf Smith was no more hard of hearing than you or I, but simply came from a Texas locality of that name. Not easy to grasp logically, was Texas.

In not much more time than it would have taken Lucas to serve an entire saloonful, I managed to produce a bottle and pour my pair of customers a drink.

They lifted a glass to each other and did honor to the contents, then Perry faced me squarely. "Red, we got somethin' to ask you."

This put me a bit wary, but I said: "I'm here listening."

"It's kind of like this. Luke's been tellin' us there's these Scotch soldiers of yours that put a dress on when they go off to war. Is he pullin' our leg, or is that the God's truth?"

"Well, the Highlanders, yes, they have a history of wearing kilts into battle. But Lucas and Rob and I come from the Lowlands, we're not—"

"Pay me," Perry drawled to Deaf Smith. "Told you I could spot when Luke is funnin' and when he ain't."

Deaf Smith grudgingly slid a silver dollar along the bar to Perry. To me, he aimed: "Just tell us another thing now, how the hell do you guys make that work, fightin' in dresses? What's the other side do, die of laughin'?"

The dilemma of the Lowlander. To venture or not into the Highlands thicket of kilts, bagpipes, the Clearances, clan quarrels, and all else, the while making plain that I myself didn't number among those who feuded for forty generations over a patch of heather. The voice of my schoolmaster Adam Willox despairing over the history of the Highlands clans swam to mind: *If it wasn't for the Irish, the Highlands Scotch would be the most pixied people on earth.* But Lucas's voice floated there in my head, too: *Conversation is the whetstone of thirst, Angus. These Montanans in their big country aren't just dry for the whiskey, they're dry for talk.*

"Gents, let's look at this from another way." Before going on, I nodded inquiringly toward the bottle. Perry and Deaf Smith automatically nodded in turn. Pouring them another and myself a buttermilk, I made change from Perry's fresh dollar and began: "As I hear it, this geezer Custer was more fully dressed than the Indians at the Little Big Horn. Am I right so far?"

"How do you suppose Lucas spends his afternoons?" Rob asked near the end of our arrival week in Gros Ventre, no freight wagon having reappeared nor news of any. We were waiting for Lucas to show himself and take over bar duty from me, so that we could go around to the house for our turn at supper.

"With Nancy on hand, how would you spend yours?" I asked back reasonably.

Rob looked at me with reproach and was about to say further when Lucas materialized, striding through the Medicine Lodge doorway as if entering his favorite castle. "Lads, sorry I'm late. Affairs of business take scrupulous tending, you know how it is. Carry yourselves over to the house now, Nancy has your feast waiting."

"She does put him in a good frame of mind," Rob mused as we went to the house.

"Man, that's not just a frame of mind, there are other compartments involved, too."

"You can spare me that inventory," he retorted with a bit of an edge, and in we went to eat. But I was impressed from then on with Rob's change of attitude about Nancy and her benefit to Lucas. Indeed, at supper he began the kind of shiny talk to her that for the first time since we landed in Gros Ventre sounded to me like the characteristic Rob.

The rumor is being bruited that a hotel, possibly of more than one story, is under construction in Gros Ventre. The notion of anyone actually desiring to stay overnight in that singular community: this, dear readers, is the definition of optimism.

Some such salvo was in each of the past issues of the Choteau newspaper I was reading through to pass time in the Medicine Lodge. But I thought little of them until the slow afternoon I came across the one:

Gros Ventre recently had another instance of the remarkably high mortality rate in that locale. Heart failure was the diagnosis. Lead will do that to a heart.

I blinked and read again. The saloon was empty, and in the street outside nothing was moving except Sedge's and Toussaint's hammers sporadically banging the hotel toward creation. Gros Ventre this day seemed so peaceful you would have to work for hours to start a dogfight. Even so, as soon as Lucas came in I pressed him about the *Quill* item.

"People die everywhere, Angus."

"As far as I know, that's so. But the *Quill* seems to say they have help here in Gros Ventre."

"You know how newspapers are."

"The question still seems to be how Gros Ventre is."

"Angus, you are your father's son, no mistake. Stubborn as strap iron and twice as hard to argue with. All right, then. A man or two died before his time here, the past year or so. But—"

"A man or two?"

"Three, if you must count. But what I'm saying if you'll listen, two of those would have gone to their reward wherever they were. Cattle thieves. Not a race known for living to old age, lad."

"What happened with them?"

Lucas stroked his beard with a forearm. "That is not just entirely clear. Williamson out at the Double W might know, or Thad Wainwright"—owners of big cattle ranches north of town, I had heard. "Or maybe even Ninian Duff." Evidently another lord of cattle, though this one I hadn't heard of before.

"And man three?"

"What would you say to a glass of buttermilk?" Lucas busily began to pour himself one. "It's good for all known ailments, and—"

"Lucas, I'm swimming in the stuff. The particular ailment we're talking about is man number three's."

"That one, now." A major gulp of buttermilk went down him. "That one, I do have to say was ill luck."

When nothing further seemed forthcoming from Lucas except continued attention to his buttermilk, I persisted: "Dying generally is ill luck, we can agree on that. But I still haven't heard the man's ailment."

"He was shot in an argument over cards."

"What, in here?"

"Don't be pure ridiculous, lad. In Wingo's, of course." Lucas looked at me with extreme reproach, but I held gaze with him. After a bit he glanced away. "Well, you may have a point. It would have happened in here if it hadn't been the gambler's week there instead. But after that, Wingo and I talked it over and we've given gamblers the bye. Pleasant games among local folk, now. A coming town like this has its good name to think of, you know."

Was it in spite of Gros Ventre's fresh reputation for excitement that the two of us the very next day let pass the chance to go on a freight wagon retracing our route toward Augusta and Helena? Or in hope of it? Either case, the notion grew on me now that maybe I might as well go ahead and try a bit of land-looking between intervals of helping Lucas in the saloon, just to be sure we weren't missing some undisclosed reason for hope here in Gros Ventre's neighborhood.

This supposition met no objection from Rob. He was staying in demand with Fain for as much wheelwork and other repair as any pair of hands could do, so there was sound sense in him earning while I scouted about. "It could be you'll find a Great Maybe for us," he said, though not within Lucas's hearing. "Have at it, McAngus, why not. I'll keep Gros Ventre in tune while you're out and around."

Lucas of course was several thousand percent in favor of my intention. "By Jesus, Angus, now you're talking. The best part of the world is right out there waiting for you and Robbie. Tell you what, I'll even make a contribution to your exploring. Follow me." I tracked after him to the shed room behind the saloon.

"There now," he plucked the peg from the door hasp with his stubs and grandly pushed the door open, "choose your choice."

Saddles were piled on other saddles, and the walls were hung with bridles as if it was raining leather. Seeing my puzzlement, Lucas spelled the matter out:

"Collateral. These cattle outfits seem to specialize in hiring men who are thirstier than they have money for. I'm not running the Medicine Lodge as a charity, and so my borrowers put up these, ay? Go ahead, have your pick."

Several of the saddles were larger than the others, large enough that they looked as if they would house a horse from his withers to his tail. "What're these big ones?"

"Lad, do you even need to ask? Those are Texas saddles."

Since Nethermuir, the progression had been train, steamship, stagecoach, freight wagon, and shoe leather, and to it I now added the plump little pinto mare named Patch, rented to me by the half-day by Dantley and saddled maximally with my new Texican saddle. The pony's gaily splotched colors made me feel as if I was riding forth into the country around Gros Ventre in warpaint, but I suppose the actuality is that I sallied out looking as purely green as I was.

The earth was mine to joggle over aboard Patch, at least until each midday. (Lucas was strict that he wanted me to continue my saloonkeeping afternoons so he could take care of what he termed "business at the house.") Now the question was the homestead-seeker's eternal one, where best to seek?

Whatever compass is in me said south first. Not south as a general direction of hope, for as Rob and I tramped through those steep treeless benchlands in the wake of Herbert's freight wagon ten days before, we had plenty of time to agree that living there would be like dwelling on top of a table. But south a mile or so from Gros Ventre, to the pass where Herbert had halted the wagon to give us our unforgettable first glimpse into the Two Medicine country, was where I felt I needed to start, up for a deeper look at it all.

Everything was in place. The continent's flange of mountain range along the west. The dark far butte called Heart and the nearer slow-sloping one like an aft sail. The grass plateaus beyond Gros Ventre and its cottonwood creek. The soft rumple of plains toward the Sweetgrass Hills and where the sun came from. Enough country that a century of Robs and Anguses would never fill it. As I sat awhile on Patch, above to my right a hawk hung on the wind, correcting, correcting. I let myself wish that I had that higher view, that skill to soar to wherever I ought to be. Then I reined Patch east, the hawk's direction.

Three mornings in a row I rode different tracts eastward of Gros Ventre, following along the creek and its fringe of willow and cottonwood until the land opened into leveler prairie, flattening and fanning into an even horizon which Lucas's maps showed were incised by the big rivers, the Marias, the Milk, and ultimately the Missouri. This prairie before the rivers, though, had no habitation nor showed much sign it wanted any. In that trio of mornings I met only one other human being, a rider named Andy Cratt who was another of the Seven Block ranch's Texans or Texicans or whatever they called themselves. He was suspiciously interested in the origin of my saddle until I invoked Lucas. When Cratt and I parted, it took the next half hour for his moving horseback figure to entirely dwindle from my over-the-shoulder looks. Noble enough country, this eastward prairie—Toussaint told me it had been thick with buffalo when he first came—but so broad, so open, so exposed, that I felt like a field mouse under the eye of the hawk out there.

North needed only a single morning. North was red cattle on buff hills, north was ranch after ranch already built along a twisty stream called Noon Creek—Thad Wainwright's large Rocking T, Pat Egan's sizable Circle Dot, three or four smaller enterprises upstream toward the mountains, and most of all, Warren Williamson's huge Double W, which held fully half of that Noon Creek country. General opinion I had overheard in the Medicine Lodge was that you could rake hell from corner to corner and not find a nastier item than Warren Williamson. Or, as was supposedly replied to a traveler who innocently wondered what the cattle brand WW stood for, Wampus Cat Williamson. I'd only glimpsed Williamson when he stepped into the Medicine Lodge to summon a couple of his riders, a thickset impatient man several shades paler than his weather-browned cowboys. Evidently those white-handed men of money were here as in Scotland, those whose gilt family crests properly translated would read something like, *Formerly robbers, now thieves*. There where the road ran along the benchland between Gros Ventre and Noon Creek, I gazed down at the fortlike cluster of Double W ranch buildings and wondered whether Rob and I would ever possess a fraction as much roof over us.

"You're becoming a regular jockey," Rob tossed cheerily as he came out from dinner and I rode up to grab a bite before spelling Lucas at the saloon.

"You're missing all the thrill of exploration," I replied as I climbed off Patch and stiffly tottered toward the house.

That evening in the Medicine Lodge I mentioned to Lucas that I thought I might ride west the next day by following the creek up from town toward the area that lay nestled under the mountains.

Lucas had not remarked much on my land-looking, maybe on the basis that he figured I ought to see plenty before making my mind up. But now he said:

"That'll be worth doing. That North Fork is pure handsome prospect. Plan to spend the full day at it, there are a lot of miles in that country up there." To my surprised look, Lucas cleared his throat and allowed: "Business at the house can rest for an afternoon."

"That's more than generous of you," I said with what I hoped was a straight face.

"Angus, here's a pregnant thought for you. While you're about it tomorrow, pay a visit to Ninian Duff. His is the first place up the North Fork, just there after the creek divides."

Here was a name Lucas had mentioned in connection with the vanishment of cattle rustlers. When I reminded him so, Lucas gave me one of his long perusals and instructed, "You'll remember, lad, I only said maybe. But you might do well to stay away from the man's cows."

Lucas paused, then added: "Don't particularly tell Ninian you're working here in the saloon with me. He and I are not each other's favorite, in that regard."

I thought that over. "If I'm to meet the man, I could stand to know something more about that, Lucas."

"Angus, you're one who'd want to know which way the rain falls from. I've nothing against Ninian Duff. It's just that he and his are more churchly folk."

Orthodox, orthodox/who believe in John Knox./Their sighing canting grace-proud faces/their three-mile prayers and half-mile graces. I knew the breed. Maybe I would pay a visit to some old holy howler and maybe I wouldn't, too.

Wind was my guide west, early the next morning. It met me face-first as soon as I rode around the creek bend where the big cottonwoods sheltered Gros Ventre. The stiff breeze required me to clamp my hat down tight and crinkle my eyes, but no cloud showed itself anywhere there in the Rockies where the wind was flowing from, and the first sunshine made a promise of comfort on my back. Who knew, maybe this was simply how a Two Medicine day whistled.

The road today wasn't honestly one, just twin prints of wheel marks such as those Herbert's freight wagon had tracked to Gros Ventre. Yet this was peopled land along the main creek, homesteads inserted into each of the best four or five meadows of wild hay. Here was handsome, with the steady line of grassed benchland backing the creek and the convenient hedge of willows and sturdy trees giving shelter all along the water. The long-sloped promontory butte with its timber top poked companionably just into sight over the far end of this valley of homesteaders, but beyond that butte where the tiers of mountains and forest began to show, it looked like tangled country. This was the best land I'd yet seen: any one of these established homesteads down here I would gladly own. Were Rob and I already latecomers?

The mare Patch of course decided to drink when we came to a crossing of the creek, and as usual in those first days of my horsemanship I of course forgot to climb off and have myself one before she waded in and muddied the water. Today, though, the streambed was thoroughly gravel, several-colored and bright under the swift clean flow as a spill of marbles, so Patch didn't roil the drinking site. I rode her on across before getting down and drinking the fresh brisk water from my hands.

Now that I was on that side of the crossing I could see past the willows to another creekline, coiling its way as if climbing leisurely, between the benchland I had followed all the distance from town and a knobby little pine ridge directly in front of me. Here I was, wherever I was: by Lucas's description that other water had to be the North Fork, this the South. To me the natural thing was to point Patch toward the top of the knob, for a scan around. Patch did not necessarily agree, but plodded us up the slope anyway.

You would imagine, as I did, that this climb to see the new country would bring anticipation, curiosity. And there you'd be as wrong as I was. For what I began to feel was a growing sense of familiarity. Of something known, making itself recognized. The cause of the feeling, though, I kept trying to place but couldn't. The wind, yes, that. Smell of new grass, which I had been among for several days of riding by now. A glimpse of a few grazing cattle below near that north creek branch, like stray red specks from the Double W's cow hundreds. Cold whiff from where a snowbank lay hidden in some north-facing coulee. All those but something more.

At the knob top, I saw. The earth's restless alteration of itself here. The quickening swells of plains into foothills and then the abrupt upward spill of the mountains. While Rob and I were aboard the stagecoach between Craig and Augusta we had watched this, the entire interior of America soaring through its change of mood. That same radical mood of terrain I was feeling here—the climb of the continent to its divide, higher, greater, more sudden than seemed possible; like a running leap of the land.

Here was magnificent. And here, just below me, one single calm green wrinkle amid the surrounding rumpus of surging buttes and tall timbered ridges and stone cliff skyline, lay the valley of the North Fork.

To say the truth, it was the water winding its way through that still valley—its heartstream, so to speak—that captured me then and there. When the summitline up along these mountains, the Continental Divide, halved the moisture of America's sky, the share beyond went west to the Pacific Ocean while that of this slope was destined to the Atlantic. *Are you telling me*, Rob shipboard, *we're already on water from Montana, out here?* Aye, yes and yea, Rob. This supple little creek below me, this North Fork, was the start of that water which eventually touched into the Atlantic. This was the first flowing root of that pattern of waves I watched and watched from the deck of the emigrant ship. But greatly more than that, too, this quiet creek. Here at last was water in its proper dose for me. Plentiful fluid fuel for grass and hay, according to the browsing cows and the green pockets of meadow between the creek's twists. Shelter from the wind and whatever rode it in winter stood in thick evidence, creekbank growth of big willows and frequent groves of quaking ash. The occasional ponds behind beaver dams meant trout, a gospel according to Lucas. And by its thin glitter down there and the glassy shallowness of the main creek back where the mare and I crossed, not any of this North Fork ran deep enough to drown more of me than my knees.

I sat transfixed in the saddle and slowly tutored myself about the join of this tremendous western attic to the rest of the Two Medicine country. No human sign was anywhere around, except for the tiny pair of homesteads just above the mouth of the North Fork, one of them undoubtedly that of the old Bible-banger Whoo-jamadinger whom Lucas mentioned to me. Other than those, wher-ever I looked was pure planet. There from the knob I could see eastward down the creek to where Gros Ventre was tucked away; for that matter, I could see all the way to the Sweetgrass Hills, what, more than eighty miles distant, that Herbert had pointed out to Rob and me. By the holy, this was as if stepping up onto the hill above the Greenock dock and being magically able to gaze across all of Scotland to Edinburgh. My eyes reluctant to leave one direc-tion for the next, nonetheless I twisted to scan each of them over and over: north, the broad patient benchland and the landmark butte that lifted itself to meet it; southward, the throng of big dry-grass ridges shouldering between this creek branch and the South Fork . . .

West. West, the mountains as steady as a sea wall. The most eminent of them in fact was one of the gray-rock palisades that lay like reefs in the surge of the Rockies, a straight up-and-down cliff perhaps the majority of a mile high and, what, three or more miles long. A stone partition between ground and sky, even-rimmed as though it had been built by hand, countless weathers ago. That rim-ming mountain stood nearest over the valley of the North Fork. A loftier darkly timbered peak loomed behind the northernmost end of the cliff rim, and between the pair a smaller mountain topped with an odd cockscomb rock formation fitted itself in. Close as I was now to these promontories, which was still far, for the first time since Rob and I came to Gros Ventre these seemed to me local mountains. They were my guide now, even the wind fell from mind in their favor. Seeing them carving their canyons of stone into the sky edge, scarps and peaks deep up into the blue, a person could have no doubt where he was. The poor old rest of the earth could hold to whatever habit of axis it wished, but this Two Medicine country answered to a West Pole, its own magnetic world top here along its wildest horizon.

Someway in the midst of all my gawking I began to feel watched myself. Maybe by someone at either of the homesteads along the creek, but no one was in view. By the cows then? No, they seemed all to have their noses down in their daydream fashion of eating. Nothing else, nobody, anywhere that I could find.

As much as I tried to dismiss the feeling, though, the touch of eyes would not leave me. Who knew, probably these seven-league mountains were capable of gazing back at me. Nonetheless I cast a glance behind me for surety's sake.

On a blood bay horse not much farther away than a strong spit sat a colossally bearded figure.

He was loose-made—tall, thin, mostly legs and elbows, a stick man. And that beard was a dark-brown feedbag of whiskers halfway down his chest. He also had one of those alarming foreheads you sometimes see on the most Scottish of Scots, a kind of sheer stark cliff from the eyes up. As if the skull was making itself known under there.

All of this was regarding me in a blinkless way. I gaped back at the whiskers and forehead, only gradually noticing that the horseman's hands were either side of his saddle horn, holding another lengthy stick of some sort across there and pointing it mostly towards me. Then I realized that stick was a rifle.

"You have business here, do you?" this apparition asked.

"I hope to," I answered, more carefully than I had ever said anything before. From the looks of him, the lightest wrong word and I was a gone geezer. "I'm, I'm looking for homestead land to take up."

"Ay, every man who can walk, crawl or ride is looking for that. But not many of them find here."

"That's their loss, I would say. This country"—I nodded my head cautiously to the North Fork and the butte—"is the picture of what I'd hoped for."

"Pictures are hard to eat," he gave me for that. Maybe I was hoping too much, but I thought his stare had softened a bit as he heard more of my voice. At least the rifle hadn't turned any farther in my direction. Any mercy there was to this situation, I would devoutly accept. He levied his next words: "You are new to here?"

"As the dew," I admitted, and told him in general but quick about Rob and myself and our homesteading intention, and that if we needed any vouching it could be obtained in full at the Medicine Lodge saloon from none other than Lucas Barc—

By the time I caught up with what my tongue was saying, His Whiskerness made up his mind about me. "Lucas Barclay has had a misfortunate life," he announced. "He can answer to God for it. Or knowing Lucas, more likely argue with Him about it until the cows

come home to Canaan. But so far as I can see, you are not Lucas."
He slid the rifle into its scabbard. "My name is Duff."

So. I could well believe that this personage and Lucas came keen
against each other, as iron sharpens iron.

I introduced myself and we had a handshake, more or less. Ninian Duff immediately turned to inquisition:

"You are from?"

"Nethermuir, in Forfar."

"Ay, I know of your town. Flora and I are East Neuk of Fife
folk. As are Donald and Jen Erskine, next along the creek here. We
made the journey together, three years since." People were leaving
even the fat farms of Fife, were they? Old Scotland was becoming a
bare cupboard.

As if he had run through his supply of words for this hour, Ninian
Duff was now gazing the length of the valley to where the far shoulder of the butte angled down to the North Fork. I kept a sideway
eye on him as much as I dared. Ninian Biblical Rifleman Duff,
scarecrow on a glorious horse. Was there no one in this Two Medicine country as normal as me? He sat silently studying the calm
swale of green beneath us as if making certain every blade of grass
was in place, as if tallying the logs in the two lonely homestead
houses. Abruptly:

"You are not afraid of work?"

"None that I've met yet."

The whiskers of Ninian Duff twitched a bit at that. "Homesteading has brands of it the rest of the world never heard of. But that is
a thing you will need to learn for yourself. Were I you"—a hypothesis I wasn't particularly comfortable with—"I'd have a look at the
patch of land there aneath Breed Butte, along the top of the creek.
Then you can dinner with us and we will talk." Ninian Duff started
his powerful red-brown horse down off the knob. "We eat at noon,"
he declared over his shoulder in a way that told me he did not mean
the first minute beyond twelve o'clock.

When I rode back into Gros Ventre it was nearly suppertime. I
was vastly saddle-tired—cowboys must have a spare pair of legs
they put on for riding, I was learning—but could feel the North
Fork, the future, like music under my skin. Could bring back into
my eyes that valley I rode up after encountering Ninian Duff, the

long green pocket of creekside meadow, the immense ridges that were timber where they weren't grass and grass where they weren't timber, the Montana earth's giant sawline of mountains against the sky beyond, the nearer gentler soar of the timber-topped prominence called Breed Butte. Could hear echo all of what Ninian told me at dinner: *I have found that cattle do well enough, but the better animal hereabout may be sheep. A person can graze five or six of them on the same ground it takes for one cow. Ay, these ridges and foothills, the mountains themselves, there is room up here for thousands and thousands of sheep. The Lord was the shepherd of us, so we have His example of extreme patience to go by, too. But nothing born with wool on its back can be as troublesome as we who weave it before wearing, I believe you will agree . . . Don't come thinking a homestead is free land. Its price is serious sweat, and year after year of it . . . But were I you, the one place I'd want to homestead is here along the North Fork while there is still the pick of the land . . .*

Too thrilled yet to settle into a chair, I decided instead I'd relieve Lucas in the saloon, let him have a long supper in preparation for a Medicine Lodge Saturday night. Then Rob and I could go together for our own meal and talk of our homesteads. By the holy, the two of us would be owners of Montana yet.

Stopping by the house to tell Nancy this calendar, I swung off the pinto horse like a boy who has been to the top of the world. The kitchen door was closest for my moment's errand. With my mind full of the day's discovery, in I sailed.

In on Rob and Nancy.

She was at the stove. He was half-perched, arms leisurely crossed, at the woodbox beside the stove. True, there was distance between them. But not quite enough. And they were too still. Too alike in the caught look each cast me.

All this might have been mistakable. It is no long jump to the nearest conclusion, ever. There was something more, though. The air in the room seemed to have been broken by me. I had crashed into the mood here as if it was a door of glass.

Rob recovered first. "McAngus, is there a fire?" he called out swift and smooth. "You're traveling like there's one in your hip pocket."

"The prospect of supper will do that to me." I almost added *You're in here amply early yourself,* but held it. "Nancy, I just came to say I'll go to the saloon for Lucas, then eat after he does, if you please."

Her dark eyes gave away nothing. "Yes," she acknowledged.

I turned to Rob again. "Get your eyes ready for tomorrow, so I can show you heaven."

"The homesteads? You've found a place?"

"I have, if you like the land there an inch as much as I do. Lord of Mercy, Rob, I just wish you'd been with me today to see it all. It's up the North Fork, good grass and water with trout in it and timber to build with and the mountains standing over it and—"

"I'll hope it doesn't blind me, all that glory," Rob broke in. "So tomorrow I need to hoist myself onto a horse, do I?"

"You do. Rob, you'll fall head over heels for this land as quick as you see it."

"I'd bet that I will." He came across the kitchen with a smile and clapped me on the shoulder. "Angus, you've done a rare job of work, finding us land already."

My riding muscles did not feel like already, but I let that pass. "Right now I'd better find Lucas for supper. Come along, can't you? I'll even serve you the first drink and keep the majority of my thumb out of it."

"This North Fork must be a place, it's sending you that giddy," Rob said back, still smiling in his radiating way. "But I'll stay on here to keep Lucas company for supper. You'll owe me that drink later."

Well, I thought as I crossed the space to the saloon, it's time to stir the blood around in our man Rob, and soonest best.

That evening in the Medicine Lodge I managed to put a few extra drinks into myself, and Rob followed without really noticing. As matters progressed, Lucas sent us a couple of looks but evidently decided we deserved to celebrate my discovery of our homesteads-to-be. He moved us down to the quiet end of the bar he called the weaning corner, set a bottle in front of us and went to tend some parched Double W riders who had just stormed in. After a bit, I proposed:

"Let's go see about the calico situation, why don't we. Those calico nieces of Wingo's down the street."

Rob looked surprised, and when he hesitated with an answer, I pressed:

"Man, haven't you noticed, the bedcovers on my side look like a tepee these mornings?"

He laughed loud and long over that. I was sober enough to notice, though, that he didn't make the logical joke in return about our bedding resembling a two-pole tent.

But he went with me, and the bottle came along, too.

On our way back from Wingo's belles, I was feeling exceptionally clever about having invented this mind-clearing evening for Rob, and we were both feeling improved for the other reason, so we halted ourselves in front of the hotel framework for nocturnal contemplation and a further drink or so. Not that we could hold many more without tamping them in.

A quarter moon lent its slight light into the Montana darkness. I commemorated dreamily, "It is the moon, I know her horn."

"This Montana even has its own moon," declared Rob in wonder, lurching against me as he peered upward. "You don't find a place like this Montana just any old where."

I chortled at how wise Rob was. Right then I couldn't see how life could be any better.

Rob tugged at my sleeve and directed my attention down the lonely single street of Gros Ventre. "See now, Angus. This is what a coming town looks like by night."

"Dark," I observed.

"But its day will dawn, am I right?" He made his voice so much like Lucas's it startled me. Now Rob straightened himself with extreme care and peered like a prophet along the dim street. "You'll see the day soon, lad, when the Caledonian Railway"—the line of our journey from Nethermuir to Greenock—"will run through the middle of this town Gros Ventre. By Jesus, I think I can hear it now! *Whoot-toot-toot! Whoot-toot-toot!*"

"The train will stop exactly here"—I made a somewhat crooked X in the dirt with my foot—"and Queen Victoria and the Pope of Rome will climb off and step into the Medicine Lodge for a drink with us."

"And I'll own all the land that way"—Rob pointed dramatically north—"and you'll own all the other"—now pointing south—"and we'll have rivers of red cattle we'll ship to Chicago on our train."

"And we'll have Texas cowboys," I threw in. "Thirteen dozen of them apiece."

Rob was laughing so hard I thought he would topple both of us into the dirt of the street. "Angus, Angus, Angus. I tell you, man, it'll be a life."

"It will," I seconded. And we lurched home to the house of Lucas and Nancy.

As clear as today, I remember how that next morning went. The weather was finer than ever and even had the wind tethered somewhere, the mountains stood great and near, and as Rob and I rode past my knob of yesterday onto Breed Butte to see straight down into the heart of the valley, I thought the North Fork looked even more resplendent than I had seen it the day before. We sat unspeaking for a while, in that supreme silence that makes the ears ring. Where the bevels of the valley met, the creek ran in ripples and rested in beaver ponds. A curlew made deft evasive flight across the slope below us as if revealing curlicues in the air. Everything fit everything else this day.

Rob too said how picture-pretty a patch of the earth this truly was. Then he started in with it.

"I don't just know, though. Maybe we ought to wait, Angus."

"Wait? Isn't that the thing that breaks wagons?" I tossed off, although I was stung. Wait for what, Eden to reopen? "Man, I've seen this country from here to there, these past days, and there's none better than this valley. It decides itself, as far as I'm concerned. This North Fork is head and shoulders over anything else we could choose. But if you want to ride with me around to where I've been and see for yourself, tomorrow we can—"

"Angus, I mean wait with this whole idea of homesteading."

I thought my ears were wrong. Then I hoped they were. But the careful look on Rob told me I'd heard what I'd heard.

"Rob, what's this about? We came half across the world to find this land."

"Homesteading would be a hard go," he maintained. "We'd better do some thinking on it before we rush in. See now, we're too late in the year to buy cattle and have calves to sell this fall. As to sheep, we'd need to bring sheep from Christ knows where and we don't have the money for that. Two houses to build, fences, everything to be done from the ground up—it'd be main sweat, all the way." As if our lives so far have been made of silk, do you mean,

Rob? But I was so dumbstruck that the words didn't find their way out of me. Rob gazed down at the North Fork and shook his head once as if telling it, sorry, but no.

And then he had a matter to tell me. "Angus, I'm thinking strong of going in with Fain. There's plenty of work for two in his shop. Everything in Montana with a wheel on it can stand repair. Fain's offered to me already, and it'd be a steady earn. And a chance to stay on in Gros Ventre, for a time at least." He glanced off at the North Fork again, this time not even bothering to dismiss it with a headshake. "I'd be nearer to Lucas that way."

"Lucas? Man, Lucas is managing in this life at least as well as either of us. He has—" It hit me before her name fell off my tongue. "Nancy." The mood I broke when I walked in on the two of them the evening before. The way Rob outshined himself at every meal. The change from his first night's distaste for Lucas's domestic arrangement. I almost somersaulted off my horse just thinking of how much more there was to this than I'd noticed. This was no routine rise of the male wand, this was a genuine case of Rob and Nancy, and maybe what would be greatly worse, of Nancy and Rob. Whoever the saint of sanity is, where are you when we need you?

"Angus, think it over," Rob was going on. "There's always a job for a schooled man like yourself in a growing town. When we see how things stand after we get some true money together there in Gros Ventre, well, then can be the time to decide about homesteading. Am I right?"

I answered only, "I'll need to think, you're right that far." Then I touched the pinto into motion, down off the butte toward the North Fork and Gros Ventre, and Rob came after.

I thought of nothing else but Rob and Lucas and Nancy the rest of that day and most of the next. I hadn't been so low in mood since those first Atlantic nights in the pit of the *Jemmy*'s stomach. Within my mind I looked again and again and again from one of these alarming people to the other to the third, as you would scan at the corners of a room you were afraid in.

Nancy seeing Rob as a younger Lucas. A Lucas fresh and two-handed. Nancy whose life had been to accept what came.

Lucas in his infatuation with town-building not seeing at all that under his own roof, trouble was about to grow a new meaning.

Rob—Rob unseeing too, not letting himself see the catastrophe he was tipping himself and Lucas and Nancy toward. Rob who could make himself believe water wasn't wet. Of his sudden catalog of excuses against the North Fork, not a one came anywhere close to the deep reason of why he wanted to stay in Gros Ventre. But if I knew that, I also knew better than to try to bend Robert Burns Barclay from something he had newly talked himself into. Take and shake Rob until his teeth rattled and they'd still be castanets of his same tune.

Here the next of life was, then. A situation not only unforeseen from the stone streets of Nethermuir or the steerage berth in the *Jemmy* or the fire tower hill of Helena or the freight wagon seat from which Rob and I first saw Gros Ventre, it couldn't have been dreamed of by me in thousands of nights. Rob coveting—not another's wife in this case, but close enough. There was an entire commandment on that and you didn't have to be John Knox to figure out why. Particularly if the one coveted from was not mere neighbor but of one's own blood.

Dampness in my eyes, the conclusion to the floodtide of all this. Normally I am not one to bathe in tears. But it ought to make the sea weep itself dry, what people can do to people. I had undergone family storm in Nethermuir and that was enough. I had not come to Montana to watch the next persons closest to me, Rob and Lucas, tear each other apart; in the pitting of a Barclay against a Barclay no one could ever win unripped. Even the North Fork, grandeur though it was, wasn't worth taking sides in this. Nothing was. Search myself and the situation in every way, this I could see nothing to do but leave from.

I said as much—just the leaving; I didn't want to be the one to utter more than that—to Lucas as soon as he strode humming into the saloon near the end of that second afternoon.

"Up to the North Fork already? Aren't you getting ahead of yourself? You and Robbie will need to file your homestead claims at the land office in Lewistown first, you know."

"No, leaving is what I mean. Away from here."

Lucas broke a frown and studied me, puzzled. "Not away from this Two Medicine country, you don't mean."

"Lucas, I do mean that. Away."

"Away where?" he erupted. "Angus, are you demented? You know there's no better country in all of Montana. And that's damn close to meaning all of the world. So where does leaving come in, sudden as this? Here, let's have some buttermilk and talk this over."

"Lucas, it's just that I've had—second thoughts."

"Your first ones were damn far better." Lucas had plunked down a glass of buttermilk apiece for us, instantly forgot them and now was violently polishing the bar I had just polished. "Leaving! By Jesus, lad, I don't know what can have gotten into you and Robbie. I have heard strange in my time, but you two take the prize. Now if the pair of you can just get enough of a brain together to think this through, you'll—"

"It's only me leaving. Rob intends to stay on with Fain."

"Robbie says that, after coming all the way from Nethermuir to get away from the wheel shop?" Lucas polished even more furiously. "Put a hammer in a Barclay's—" he stopped, then managed to go on—"a Barclay's hand and he doesn't know when to put it down, ay?"

I let silence answer that, and Lucas was immediately back at me: "Tell me this, now. If you're so set on leaving, what wonderful damn place is it you're going to?"

"I'll maybe go have another look at that Teton River country we came through on the freight wagon. Or around Choteau—"

"The Teton? Choteau?" I might as well have said the Styx and Hades to this man. "Angus, are you entirely sober?"

I assured him I was never more so. Lucas shook his head and tried: "Well, at least you can stay on for a bit, can't you?"

My turn to shake a head.

"Lad, what's your headlong hurry?" Lucas demanded, as peeved as one person could be. "Weary of my hospitality, are you?"

"Lucas"—I sought how to say enough without saying too much—"a welcome ought not be worn out, is all."

Lucas stopped wiping the bar and gazed at me. Abruptly his face had the same look of thunder as when Rob first stepped up to him asking for a handshake. What a thorough fool I was. Why had I said words with my real meaning behind them?

Lucas moved not at all, staring at me. Then with great care to say it soft, he said:

"I don't consider it's been worn out. Do you?"

"No, no, nothing of the sort. I just think I'd better be on my way before—it might."

At last Lucas unlocked his gaze from me. "I ought to have seen. I ought to have, ay."

He stared down at his stubs on the bar towel, grimacing to the roots of his teeth as he did, and I knew I was watching as much pain as I ever would. Hell itself would try to douse such agony. I reached across the bar and gripped Lucas halfway up each forearm, holding him solid while he strained against the invisible fire inside his sleeves.

Gradually Lucas's breath expelled in a slow half-grunt. At last he swallowed deep and managed: "Any sense I ever had must've gone with my hands."

I let go my grasp of the stubbed arms. "Lucas, listen to me. There's nothing happened yet, I swear it. I—"

He shook his head, swallowed trouble one more time, and began randomly swiping the bar with the relentless towel again even though each motion made him wince. "Not with you, no. You I can believe, Angus. You're in here telling me, and that's truth in itself."

So I had said all, and he had heard all, without the names of Rob and Nancy ever being spoken. More than ever, now, I felt the need to be gone from Gros Ventre. I wished I already was, and far.

Lucas swabbed like a man possessed until he reached the two glasses of buttermilk, glowered at them and tossed their contents into the swill pail. In an instant he had replaced them with glasses of whisky and shunted mine along the bar to me with his forearm.

"Here's to a better time than this," he snapped out, and we drank needfully.

Still abrupt, he queried: "Have you told our Robbie you're leaving?"

"Not yet, but I'm about to, when he comes off work."

"Hold back until tonight, why not." Lucas gazed out across the empty Medicine Lodge as if daring it to tell him why not. "I'll get Sedge to take the saloon for a while and the three of us at least can have a final supper together. We may as well hold peace in the family until then, don't you think?"

I thought, peace is nowhere in the outlook I see among the Barclays. But aloud I agreed.

When Lucas and Rob and I went around to the house that evening, supper already waited on the table, covered with dish towels. Three places were set, with the plates turned down.

"We're on our own for a bit," Lucas announced. "Nancy has gone home with Toussaint, up to the reservation to visit her aunt. So tonight, lads, it's a cold bite but plenty of it." He sat down regally, reached his right stub to the far edge of his plate and nudged the dish toward him until it lipped over the edge of the table; that lip he grasped with both stubs and flipped the plate over exactly in place. *"Turn up your plates and let's begin/Eat the meat and spit the skin,"* he recited tunefully. "Most likely *not* old Burns, ay, Angus?"

Dismay and concern and suspicion had flashed across Rob's face rapidly as a shuffle of cards and now he was back to customary confidence again. I could see him wanting to ask how long an absence "a bit" amounted to, but he held that in and said instead, "Angus and I can be bachelors with the best of them. We've been practicing at it all our lives. Here, I can do the carving," and he reached over to cut Lucas's cold beef for him.

My meal might as well have been still on the cow, I had so little enthusiasm for it. Rob jabbed and chewed with remarkable concentration. Lucas fed himself some bites in his bearlike way. Then he began out of nowhere:

"I've been thinking how to keep you two out of mischief."

My heart climbed up my throat, for I thought he meant what the two on my mind, Rob and Nancy, were heading headlong into. This would teach me to keep my long tongue at home.

But Lucas sailed on: "When you lads take up your land, I mean."

I gave him an idiot's stare. Had he forgotten every word I said in the Medicine Lodge this afternoon?

"It can be a hard go at first, homesteading," Lucas imparted as if from God's mountaintop. I caught a didn't-I-say-so glance from Rob, but we both stayed quiet, to find out whatever this was on Lucas's mind. "Hard," repeated Lucas as if teaching us the notion. "Nobody ever has enough money to start with, and there's work to be done in all directions at once, and then there's the deciding of what to raise. The North Fork there, that's sinfully fine country but it'd be too high to grow much of anything but hay, do you think?"

I recited yes, that was what I thought. Rob offered nothing.

"So the ticket up there will need to be livestock, ay?" Ay and amen, Lucas. "Cattle, though, you're late to start with this year, with calving already done. You'd be paying for both the cows and their calves and that's a pure dear price. And horses, this country is swimming in horses, the Indians have them and Dantley deals in them and there's this new man Reese with them on Noon Creek. No sense in horses. But I'll tell you lads what may be the thing, and that's sheep. This Two Medicine country maybe was made for sheep. As sure as the pair of you are sitting here with your faces hanging out, sheep are worth some thinking about. Say you had some yearling ewes right now. You'd have the wool money this summer, and both lambs and wool next year. Two revenues are better than one," he informed us. "It's more than interesting, Angus, Ninian Duff saying to you that he's thinking of selling his cattle for sheep. Ninian is a man with an eye for a dollar." Tell us too, Lucas, does a fish swim and will a rock sink and can a bird fly? Why be trotting out this parade of homestead wisdom, when Rob wants none and I've already told you I'm leaving?

Sermon done, we finished eating, or in my case gave up on the task. Lucas swung his head to me and requested: "Angus, would you mind? My chimney."

I fetched his clay pipe, tobaccoed it, and held it to him as he took it with his mouth. After I lit it and he puffed sufficiently, he used a forearm to push it to the accustomed corner of his mouth, then quizzed: "What do you lads think of the sheep notion?"

Rob looked at me but I determinedly kept my mouth clamped. He was the one bending the future to awkward angles, let him be the one to describe its design to Lucas.

Instead, Rob bought himself another minute by jesting, "Sheep sound like the exact thing to have. Now if we only had sheep."

Lucas deployed a pipe cloud at us, and with it said:

"I'll go with you on them."

Neither Rob nor I took his meaning.

"The sheep!" Lucas spelled out impatiently. "I'll partner the two of you in getting sheep. A band of yearling ewes, to start you off with."

Rob sat straight up. Probably I rose some myself. Lucas puffed some more and went right on: "I can back you a bit on the homestead expenses, too. Not endlessly, mind you; don't get the wild idea I'm made of money. But to help you get underway. You pair are going to need to dive right to work, Montana winters come before you know it. I'd say tomorrow isn't too soon for starting. But spend the rest of spring and summer up there at it, and the North Fork will have to make room for you two."

"Lucas, man," Rob burst out, "that's beyond generous." Hesitation was gone from him. This again was the Rob I had come from Nethermuir and Helena with.

"You're for it, Robbie, are you?" Lucas made sure.

"Who wouldn't be? A chance like this?" Somewhere in his mind Rob had to adjust about Nancy. But with her absent to Toussaint's household and Lucas's offer laying like money to be picked up, you could all but hear Rob click with adjustment.

I knew Lucas had one more piece to put into place, and it came, it came.

"There's still one constituency to be heard from," he dispatched benignly around his pipe to me. "What do you say to the idea, Angus? Can I count on you both?"

Lucas Barclay, rascal that you knew how to be even without hands. Your bearded face and Rob's bare bright one waited across that supper table. Waited while my mind buzzed like a hive. *This isn't old Scotland, lads.* Waited for the one answer yet to come, the last answer of that evening and of the time that has ensued from it. *Life goes differently here.* The answer, Lucas, that you and I knew I could not now avoid saying, didn't we?

And say it I did.

"Both."

SCOTCH HEAVEN

Prophetic indeed was the man who uttered, "You can fight armies or disease or trespass, but the settler never." Word comes of yet another settlement of homesteaders in this burgeoning province of ours. Who can ever doubt, with the influx which is peopling a childless land and planting schools by the side of sheep sheds and cattle corrals, that Choteau County is destined to be the most populous in Montana? Of this latest colony, situated into the foothills a dozen or so miles west of Gros Ventre, it is said so many of the arrivees originated in the land of the kilt and the bagpipe that Gros Ventrians call the elevated new neighborhood Scotch Heaven.

—CHOTEAU QUILL, JULY 3, 1890

"HOTTER'N NOT, said the Hottentot."

"And what else do you expect, man. Montana is up so high it's next door to the sun."

"Speaking of high, your lifting muscles are ready, are they?"

"As ready as they'll ever be." We each grasped an end of the next log.

"Then here it comes, house. Up she goes. Tenderly, now. Up a bit with your end. Up up up, that's the direction. A hair more. Almost there. There. Ready to drop?"

"Let's do."

With a sound like a big box lid closing, the log fell into place, its notched ends clasping into those of the cabin's side walls.

DANCING AT THE RASCAL FAIR

"Well?" demanded Rob the log hewer. "Does your end fit?"

I squinted dramatically at the wink of space between the log we had just placed and the one below. "Snug enough. You'll barely be able to toss your cat through the crack."

That brought him in a rush. He eyed along the crevice—which would vanish easily enough when chinked—and lamented, "A tolerant tolerance, my father and Lucas would have called that in the wheelshop. See now, these Montana trees have more knots in them than a sailor's fingers."

"Lucky thing we're just practicing on this house of yours," I philosophized for him. "By the time we build mine, now—"

"Lucky thing for you I'm so much a saint I didn't hear that."

God proctored poor dim old Job about how the measures of the earth were laid. Had Job but been a homesteader, he could have readily answered that the government of the United States of America did it.

The vast public domain westward of the Mississippi River, as Crofutt put the matter for us when Rob and I were somewhere back there on his oceanic border from emigration to immigration, *where the stalwart homesteader may obtain legal title to his land-claim by five years of living upon it and improving it with his building and husbandry labors, has been summed in an idea as simple as it is powerful: the land has been made into arithmetic. This is to say, surveyors have established governing lineations across the earth, the ones extending north and south known as principal meridians and those east-to-west as base lines. Having thus cast the main lines of the net of numeration across half a continent, so to speak, they further divided the area into an ever smaller mesh, first of Ranges measured westward from the meridians and then of townships measured from the base lines. Each township is six miles square, thus totaling thirty-six square miles, and—attend closely for just a few moments more—it is these townships, wherein the individual homesteader takes up his landholding, that the American penchant for systemization fully flowers. Each square mile, called a section, is numbered, in identical fashion throughout all townships, thusly:*

6	5	4	3	2	1
7	8	9	10	11	12
18	17	16	15	14	13
19	20	21	22	23	24
30	29	28	27	26	25
31	32	33	34	35	36

As can be seen, the continuousness of the numeration is reminiscent of the boustrophedon pattern a farmer makes as he plows back and forth the furrows of his field—or, indeed, of the alternate directions in which earliest Greek is written! Thus does the originality of the American experiment, the ready granting of land to those industrious enough to seek it, emulate old efficacious patterns!

Rob's remark at the time was that Crofutt himself verged to Greek here. But upon the land itself, there on the great earthen table of the American experiment, the survey system's lines of logic wrote themselves out so clearly they took your breath away. Why wasn't the rest of humankind's ledger this orderly? Filing our homestead claims of 160 acres apiece, the allowable amount one person could choose out of a square-mile section of 640 acres, amounted merely to finding section-line markers—Ninian Duff could stride blindfolded to every one of them in the North Fork valley—and making the journey to the land office at Lewistown and putting a finger on the registrar's map and saying, this quarter-section is the patch of earth that will be mine. The land has been made into arithmetic indeed. On the Declaration of Applicant there in front of me my land's numbers were registered as *SW ¼ Sec. 31, Tp. 28 N, Rge. 8 W*, on Rob's they were *NE ¼ Sec. 32, Tp. 28 N, Rge. 8 W*, and with our grins at each other we agreed that ink had never said anything better.

Here then is land. Just that, land, naked earthskin. And now the due sum: from this minute on, the next five years of your life, please, invested entirely into this chosen square of earth of yours.

Put upon it house, outbuildings, fences, garden, a well, livestock, haystacks, performing every bit of this at once and irrespective of weather and wallet and whether you have ever laid hand to any of these tasks before. Build before you can plan, build in your sleep and through your mealtimes, but build, pilgrim, build, claimant of the earth, build, build, build. You are permitted to begin in the kind delusion that your utensils of homestead-making at least are the straightforward ones—axe, hammer, adze, pick, shovel, pitchfork. But your true tools are other. The nearest names that can be put to them are hope, muscle and time.

"Ay, Robert, you will eat your fill of wind up here," Ninian Duff brought along as a verdict one forenoon when he rode up to inspect our house progress.

Rob's choice of land was lofty. His homestead claim lay high as it could across the south slope of Breed Butte itself, like a saddle blanket down a horse's side. Those early summer days when we were building his house—we bet the matter of whose to build first on which of a pair of magpies would leave their snag perch sooner, and would you not know, Rob's flew at once—those summer-starting days, all of the valley of the North Fork sat sunlit below Rob's site; and if you strolled a few hundred yards to the brow of the butte each dawn, as I did, you even saw the sun emerge out of the eastward expanse of plains all the way beyond the distant dunelike Sweetgrass Hills.

Rob found Ninian's decree worth a laugh. "Is there somewhere in this country that a man wouldn't have wind in his teeth?"

Even while we three stood gazing, the tall grass of the valley bottom was being ruffled. A dance of green down there, and the might of the mountains above, and the aprons of timber and grazing land between; this would always be a view to climb to, you had to give Rob that. Even Ninian looked softened by it all, his prophetic beard gently breeze-blown against his chest. I was struck enough to announce impromptu: "You did some real choosing when you found us the North Fork, Ninian."

The beard moved back and forth across the chest. "None of us has bragging rights to this country yet."

After Ninian had ridden away and Rob and I climbed up to resume with raftering, there still was some peeve in Rob. He aimed his chin down at the Duff and Erskine homesteads, one-two there beside the creek at the mouth of the valley. "By damn, I didn't come all the miles from one River Street to live down there on another."

"You can see almost into tomorrow from up here, I will say that," saying it against my own inclination in the matter. For, unlike me as it was to be in the same pulpit with Ninian, to my way of thinking, too, this scenery of Rob's had high cost. By choosing so far up onto the butte he was forfeiting the meadow of wild hay that meandered beside the North Fork the full length of the valley, hay that seemed to leap from the ground and play racing games with the wind as we went back to hammering together Rob's roof. And more serious than that, to my mind, he was spurning the creek itself, source for watering livestock. True, at the corner of his land nearest to mine a spring lay under a small brow of butte, like a weeping eye, and Rob gave me to know that I would see the day when he built a reservoir there. But we live in the meantime rather than the sometime and to me a nearness to the creek was the way to begin the world at the right end, in a land as dry as this Montana. Which was why my own homestead selection, southwest from Rob's and just out of view behind the dropping shoulder of Breed Butte, was down into the last of the North Fork valley before foothills and mountains took command of the geography. There at my homestead meadows of wild hay stood fat and green along both sides of the creek, and the bottomland was flat enough beside the clear little stream to work on my house-to-be and its outbuildings in level comfort; for all the open glory of Rob's site, you always were trudging up or down slope here.

But try telling any of this, as I had, to Rob, who assured me in that Barclay future-owning style: "In the eventual, a dab of hay or water more or less won't make the difference. What counts, see now, is that no one can build to the west of me here," and the timbered crest and long rocky shoulder of Breed Butte indeed made that an unlikelihood. "Angus, this butte will be the high road into all the pasture there ever was and I'll be right here on it, am I right?"

There he had me. *Crofutt* notwithstanding, anyone with an eye in his head could see that the key to Scotch Heaven was not our homestead acreage, because no piece of land a half mile long and wide is nearly enough to pasture a band of a thousand sheep on. They'll eat their way across that while you're getting your socks on in the morning. No, it was the miles and miles of free range to the west, the infinity of grass in the foothills and on up into the mountains, that was going to be the larder for our flocks of fortune. Ninian Duff had seen so, and Rob and I, not to mention our treasurer Lucas, could at least puff ourselves that we glimpsed Ninian's vision.

"Our woolly darlings," Rob broke these thoughts now, "can you spot them up there?"

"Just barely. They're grazing up over the shoulder of the butte. One of us is going to have to, again. You know I'd gladly tell you it's my turn, except that it isn't."

Rob swore—sheep will cause that in a man, too—and went down the ladder, the fourth time that morning one or the other of us had to leave off roof work to ride around our zestful new band of yearling ewes and bring them back within safe view.

"Angus, I wish we had oakum to do the chinking with. Make nice dark seams against the logs instead of this clay."

"Toussaint told you how to darken it."

"Considering the cure, I'll accept the ill, thank you just the same." The Toussaint Rennie formula for darkening the chinking clay was: *You take horse manure. Mix it in nice with that clay.*

A buckboard was coming. Coming at speed along the road beside the North Fork, past Duffs' without slowing, past Erskines' just short of flying. It looked like a runaway, but at the trail which led up the butte to us, the light wagon turned as precisely as if running on a railroad track. Then Rob and I saw one of the two figures wave an arm. Arm only, no hand to be seen. Lucas. And Nancy was driving.

The rig, one of Dantley's hires, clattered to a stop just short of running over us and the house. The horses were sweat-wet and appeared astounded at what was happening to them. Behind their reins Nancy seemed as impervious as she did in the kitchen. Lucas was as merry as thick jam on thin bread.

"By Jesus, there's nothing like a buggy ride to stir the blood," he announced as the buckboard's fume of dust caught up with the contingent. "Air into the body, that's the ticket. Angus, lad, you're working yourself thin as a willow. Come to town for some buttermilk one of these evenings." Both arms cocked winglike for balance, Lucas bounded down from the wagon. "So this is your castle, Robbie. I've seen worse, somewhere, sometime."

"You're a fund of compliments," Rob said back, but lightly. "This will do me well enough until I have a house with long stairs."

"And a wife and seven sons and a red dog, ay? That reminds me, lads, Gros Ventre has progress to report," announced Lucas. His stubs were in his coat pockets now, he was wearing his proprietor-of-Montana demeanor. "A stagecoach line! Direct from up there where they're building the Great Northern railroad, to us. What do you say to that? I tell you, our town is coming up in the world so fast it'll knock you over."

There was more than a little I didn't know about stagecoaches, but I had a fair estimate of the population of Gros Ventre and its surroundings. Helena had more people on some of its street corners. "What, they're running a stage line just to Gros Ventre? Where's their profit in that?"

"Oh, the stage goes on to Choteau too," Lucas admitted, "but we'll soon have that place out of the picture."

"Up here we have news of our own," Rob confided happily in turn. "Ninian has had word of three families from the East Neuk of Fife on their way to here."

"Grand, grand," exulted Lucas. "The Scotch are wonderful at living anywhere but in Scotland. I suppose they'll all be Bible-swallowers like Ninian, but nobody's perfect." Lucas rotated himself until he stood gazing south, down the slope of Breed Butte to the North Fork and its clump of willows. Beyond, against the sky, stood the long rimrock wall we now knew was named Roman Reef, and then a more blunt contorted cliff called Grizzly Reef, and beyond Grizzly other mountains stood in rugged file into the Teton River region. "By Jesus, this is the country. Lads, we'll see the day when all this is ranches and farms. And Robbie, you're up in the place to watch it all." A whiff of breeze snatched at Lucas's hat and he clamped an arm stub onto the crown of it. "You'll eat some wind here, though."

While we toured our visitors through the attractions of the homestead and Lucas dispensed Gros Ventre gossip—Sedge and Lila were very nearly ready to open the hotel but couldn't agree what sign to paint on it; Wingo had another new niece—I tried to watch Rob without showing that I was. He was an education, this first time he had been around Nancy since Lucas's bargain made homesteaders of us. So far as Rob showed, Nancy now did not exist. His eyes went past her as if she was not there, his every remark was exclusive to Lucas or to me or to the human race with the exception of one. It was like watching the invention of quarantine.

Nancy's reaction to this new Rob, so far as I could see, was perfectly none. She seemed the exact same Nancy she had been at the first moment Rob and I laid eyes on her in the doorway of Lucas's kitchen, distinct but unreadable. That always unexpected flash of front teeth as she turned toward you, and then the steady dark gaze.

Meanwhile Lucas was as bold as the sun, asking questions, commenting. "Lads, you're a whole hell of a lot further along with all this than I expected you'd be. Do you even put your shadows to work?" Nearly so. Never have I seen a man achieve more labor than Rob did in those first homestead months of ours, and my elbow moved in tandem with his.

Rob gave a pleased smile and said only: "You're just seeing us start."

"I know this homesteading is an uphill effort. At least Montana is the prettiest place in the world to work yourself to death, ay?" Lucas paused at a rear corner of the long low house, to study the way Rob's axework made the logs notch together as snug as lovers holding hands. While Lucas examined, I remembered him in the woodyard in Nethermuir, choosing beech worthy for an axle, ash for shafts, heart of oak for the wagon frame. I could not help but wonder what lasts at the boundaries of such loss. At his empty arm ends, did Lucas yet have memory of the feel of each wood? Were the routes of his fingers still there, known paths held in the air like the flyways of birds?

"And the woollies," Lucas inquired as he and Nancy returned to the wagon. "How are the woollies?"

That was the pregnant question, right enough. The saying is that it takes three generations to make a herdsman, but in the considerable meantime between now and the adept grandson of one or the other of us, Rob and I were having to learn that trying to control a thousand sheep on new range was like trying to herd water. How were the woollies? Innocently thriving when last seen an hour ago, but who knew what they might have managed to do to themselves since.

Rob looked at me and I at him.

"There's nothing like sheep," I at last stated to Lucas.

Lucas and Nancy climbed into the buckboard, ready for the reversal of the whirlwind that brought them from Gros Ventre.

"Well, what's the verdict?" Rob asked in a joking way but meaning it. "Are we worth the investment?"

Lucas looked down at him from the wagon seat.

"So far," he answered, "it seems to be paying off. Pound them on the tail, Nancy, and let's go home."

That first Montana summer of ours was determined to show us what heat was, and by an hour after breakfast each day Rob and I were wearing our salt rings of sweat, crusted into our shirts in three-quarter circles where our laboring arms met our laboring shoulders. Ours was not the only sweat dripping into the North Fork earth. In a single day the arrival of the contingent from Fife almost doubled our valley's population—the Findlater family of five, the young widower George Frew and his small daughter, and George's bachelor cousin Allan. Two weeks later, a quiet lone man named Tom Mortensen took up a claim over the ridge south from my place, and a week after that, a tumbleweed family of Missourians, the Speddersons, alit along the creek directly below Rob. As sudden as that, the valley of the North Fork went from almost empty to homesteaded.

"Who do you suppose invented this bramble?" Barbed wire, that was meant. Neither of us liked the stuff, nor for that matter the idea of corseting our homesteads in it. But the gospel according to Ninian Duff rang persuasive: *If you don't fence, you will one morning wake up and find yourself looking into the faces of five hundred Double W cows.*

"Never mind that, why didn't they invent ready-made postholes to go with it?"

Rob and I were at my homestead. We had bedded the sheep on the ridge and come on down to wrestle a few more postholes into my eternal west fenceline before dark. There were occasional consequences from nature for decreeing lines on the earth as if by giant's yardstick, and one of them was that the west boundary of my homestead claim went straight through a patch of rock that was next to impossible to dig in. Small enough price, I will still tell you all these grunted postholes later, to have the measures of the earth plainly laid for you; but at the time—

"Now, you know the answer to that. A homestead is only 160 acres and that's nowhere nearly enough room to pile up all the postholes it needs."

"Dig. Just dig."

Can a person be happy while he's weary in every inch of himself? Right then, I was. I entirely liked my homestead site. Maybe you could see around the world and back again from Rob's place on Breed Butte, but mine was no blinkered location. Ridges, coulees, Roman Reef in the notch at the west end of the valley, the peak called Phantom Woman, the upmost trees on Breed Butte—all could be seen from my yard-to-be. The tops of things have always held interest for me. Rob's house was just out of view behind the shoulder of the ridge. Indeed, no other homesteads could be seen from mine, and for some reason I liked that, too.

"Digging holes into the night this way—back in Nethermuir they'd think we're a pair of prime fools."

"We're the right number for it, you have to admit."

Dusk slowly came, into this country so appropriate for dusk—the tan and gray of grass and ridge looking exactly right, the soft tones a day should end with. This time of evening the gullies blanked themselves into shadow, the ridgelines fired themselves red with the last sunset embers. But we were here to make homesteads, not watch sunsets. And by the holy, we were getting them made. Just as soon as Rob's house was done we began on our sheep shed, at the lower end of my homestead for handiness to the creek. The shed work we interrupted with the shearing crew for our sheep. We finished the wool work just in time to join with Ninian and Donald in putting up hay for the winter. Any moment free from haying, we were devoting to building fencelines. And someway amid it all we were hewing and laying the logs of my house, to abide by the spirit of the homestead law, even though I was going to share the first winter under Rob's roof; we were reasonably sure President Harrison wouldn't come riding over the ridge to check on my residency.

Full dark was not far from being on us but we wanted to finish my fenceline. Between bouts with shovel and crowbar and barbed wire, we began to hear horses' hooves, more than one set.

"Traffic this time of day?" Rob remarked as we listened. "Angus, what are you running here, an owl farm?"

We recognized the beanpole figure of Ninian Duff first among the four who rode out of the deep dusk, long before he called out: "Robert and Angus, good evening there. You're a pair who chases work into the night."

"It's always waiting to be chased," Rob said back. I ran a finger around the inside leather of my hat, wiping the sweat out. Besides

Ninian the squadron proved to be Donald Erskine and the new man Archie Findlater and a settler from the South Fork, Willy Hahn. Every kind of calamity that could put men on saddle leather at the start of night was crossing my thoughts. Say for Ninian, you did not have to stand on one foot and then the other to learn what was on his mind.

"Angus, we've come to elect you."

I blinked at that for a bit, and saw Rob was doing the same. *What was I, or my generation,/that I should get such exaltation?* "Elected, is it," I managed at last. "Do I get to know to what?"

"The school board, of course," Ninian stated. "There are enough families herearound that we need a proper school now, and we're going to build one."

"But—but I'm not a family man."

"Ay, but you were a teacher once, over across, and that will do. We want you for the third member of our school board."

"Together with—?"

"Myself," Ninian pronounced unabashedly, "and Willy here." Willy Hahn nodded and confirmed, "You are chust the man, Anguss."

"The old lad of parts!" Rob exclaimed, and gave my shoulder a congratulatory shove. "He'll see to it that your youngsters recite the rhyming stuff before breakfast, this one."

"That fact of the matter is," Ninian announced further, "what we need done first, Angus, is to advertise for a teacher. Can you do us a letter of that? Do it, say, tomorrow?"

I said I could, yes, and in the gathering dark there at my west fenceline the school was talked into shape. Because of their few years' headstart in settlement, the South Fork families had a margin more children of schoolable age than did Scotch Heaven, and so it was agreed to build the schoolhouse on their branch of the creek.

"You here in Scotch Heafen will haff to try hard to catch up with uss," Willy Hahn joked.

"Some of us already are," came back Ninian Duff, aiming that at the bachelorhood of Rob and me.

"The rest of us are just saving up for when our turn comes," Rob contributed. That drew a long look from Ninian, before he and the other three rode away into the night.

It was morning of the third week of August, still a month of summer ahead on the calendar, when I came in from the outhouse with my shoes and the bottoms of my pantlegs damp.

Yawning, Rob asked: "What, did you miss your aim?"

I almost wished I had, instead of the fact to be reported: "Frost on the grass."

That forehint of North Fork winter concentrated our minds mightily. In the next weeks we labored even harder on Rob's out-buildings and fences, and when not on those, on the schoolhouse or on my house; and when not any of those, we were with the sheep, keeping a weather eye on the cloudmaking horizon of the mountains. Soon enough—too soon—came the morning when the peaks showed new snow like white fur hung atop.

On the day when Donald Erskine's big wagon was to be borrowed for getting our winter's provisions in Gros Ventre, we bet magpies to see which of us would go. Mine flew first from the gate. "Man, you're sneaking out here and training them," Rob accused. But off he went to the sheep and I pointed my grin toward Gros Ventre.

The Medicine Lodge was empty but for Lucas. "Young Lochin-var is come out of the west," he greeted me, and produced an instant glass between his stubs and then a bottle.

"What's doing?" I inquired.

"Not all that much. People are scarce this time of year, busy with themselves. We'll soon have snowflakes on our heads, do you know, Angus."

"We will and I do," I answered, and drank.

"You and Robbie are ready for old winter, are you?"

"Ready as we'll ever be, we think."

"Winter can be thoroughly wicked in this country. I've seen it snow so that you couldn't make out Sedge's flagpole across there. And my winters here haven't been the worst ones by far. Stories they tell of the '86 winter would curl your dohickey."

"I'll try not hear them, then."

"You and Robbie have worked wonders on those homesteads of yours, I have to say. Of course I could tell from the moment the pair of you walked in here that you were going to be a credit to the community."

"Credit. Do you know, Lucas, there's the word I was going to bring up with you."

"Angus, Angus, rascal you." Shaking his head gravely, Lucas poured a drink for himself and another for me. His toast, odd, was the old one of Scottish sailors: "Wives and sweethearts."

After our tipple, Lucas resumed: "What do you and Robbie do, sit up midnights creating ways to spend my money? What's the tariff this time?"

"Pennies for porridge. We need groceries enough to get us through the winter, is all."

"All, you say. You forget I've seen you two eat."

"Well, we just thought if you maybe were to mortgage the Medicine Lodge and your second shirt—"

"I surrender, Angus. Tell Kuuvus to put your groceries on my account. By Jesus, you and Robbie would have to line up with the coyote pups for supper on the hind tit if I didn't watch over you."

"We might yet, if half of what you and Ninian keep saying about winter comes true."

"Put me in the same camp with Ninian, do you. There's a first time. How is old Jehovah Duff? Still preaching and breeding?"

"In point of fact, Flora does have a loaf in the oven. As does Jen Erskine. As does Grace Findlater. If our neighbors are any example to the sheep, we're going to have a famous lamb crop come spring."

"Lambs and lasses and lads," Lucas recited with enthusiasm. "By Jesus, we'll build this country into something before it knows it." I raised an eyebrow at his paternal "we" there. Lucas raised it a good deal higher for me by declaring next: "Angus, I believe you need to think of a woman."

"I do, do I." Truth known, on my mind right then was the visit I was going to make to Wingo's niecery as soon as I was finished with other provisioning. "Along any particular lines, do you recommend?"

"I'm talking now about a wife. All right, all right, you can give me that look saying I'm hardly the one to talk. But the situation of Nancy and myself is—well, not usual." That was certainly so. "You're young and hale and not as ugly as you could be," he swept on, "and so what's against finding a wife for yourself, ay? I tell you, if I were you now—"

"Just half a moment, before you get to being me too strenuously. What brings this on?" It wasn't like Lucas to suddenly speak up for womanhood at large. "Is this what you're prescribing today for all your customers?"

"Just the redheaded ones." My eyebrow found a new direction

to cock itself. Why was I the subject of this sermon instead of Rob? He was the one Lucas had needed to negotiate away from Nancy.

"Oh, I know what you're thinking," and as usual, he did. "But that's another case entirely, our Robbie. The first bright mare who decides to twitch her tail at Robbie, she'll have him. He's my own nephew, but that lad is sufficiently in love with himself that it won't much matter who he marries. Whoever she is, she'll never replace him in his own affections. You though, Angus. You're not so much a world unto yourself. You, I'd say, need the right partner in this old life."

I hoped the Lucas Barclay Matrimonial Bureau was about to close for the day. "I'm already in partnership with a pair of Barclays," I pointed out, "which seems to keep me occupied twenty-five hours a day eight days a week."

"Mend your tongue," Lucas answered lightly, but with a glance that seemed to wonder whether I'd heard any word he'd been saying. "Robbie and I'll have you so prosperous you can take your pick of womanhood. But who's that going to be, ay? It wouldn't hurt you a bit to start thinking in that direction."

"And was Lucas in fettle?" asked Rob as we unloaded the wagon of groceries.

"Lucas was Lucas," I attested, "and then some."

Was it a long winter Rob and I put in together, that first homestead one? Yes, ungodly so. And no, nothing of the sort. How time can be a commodity that lets both of those be equally true, I have never understood.

November and December only snowed often enough to get our attention, but the North Fork had ice as thick as a fist and we were chopping a water hole for the sheep and our workhorses each morning. Of course that was the time of the year the bucks were put with the ewes to breed spring lambs, and so at least there was warm behavior in the pastures, so to speak.

"See now, McAngus, don't you just wish it was spring? To watch those lambs come—man, it'll be like picking up money along the road."

"That's what it had better be like, or we're going to be in debt to Lucas down to our shoe soles."

You might not think it, but with winter we saw more of the other homesteaders than ever. People neighbored back and forth by horse and sled to escape cabin fever, and no more than a few weeks ever passed without Scotch Heaven having a dance that brought out everyone, for even the Duffs and Erskines were not so skintight they could resist waving a foot to a tune. I thought many a time that to watch Ninian on the dance floor was like hearing a giggle out of God.

Not, let me say, that Ninian got all that much of my watching that winter, nor Rob's nor George Frew's nor Allan Frew's nor old Tom Mortensen's either. We of the bachelor brigade were too busy appreciating that Scotch Heaven's balance sheet of men and women was less uneven than it had been, with the teacher Mavis Milgrim and Archie Findlater's sister Judith, newly come from Scotland, now on hand. Miss Milgrim always had a starch to her that she thought a schoolma'am had to have, and Judith Findlater had a startling neck that was not so much swanlike as goose-like, but they helped the situation of the sexes, they helped. Most especially Judith. She was a sweet, quiet woman, of the kind in the old saying *she's better than she's bonny*, and there were moments at those dances when I had to wonder whether she was that prescription of Lucas's for me. Along those lines, the single time I found a decent chance to get Judith aside and coax a kiss out of her, she delivered one that I could feel all the way to my ears.

Something to put away for spring, although whenever I looked in a mirror I still was not seeing anything that resembled marriage.

When the last day of the calendar came—no Hogmanay commemorative portrait of Rob and myself this year, except the one that memory draws—we were invited down to see out the eve at the Duffs', together with the five Erskines and the six Findlaters, as many people as could breathe in one house that size. The right way to bridge years, in company with those we had come to know best in our homestead effort. Donald Erskine was a fretful man, who changed his mind so often he went around half-dizzy. Yet Donald would leap a mile to your aid, letting his own work stand while he pitched in on yours. Ninian Duff on the other hand would think three times before offering to lend you the sleeves of his vest, but there was no one more sound in advice than God's solemn brother Ninian. Their wives Jen and Flora were equally broad women, grown wide as wagons in childbearing, and each as capable as a mother lion. Archie Findlater was a plump man, like a grouse—I admit, his roundness caused me to wonder what Judith's future shape would be—but sharp in his head, a calculator. Grace Findlater did the talking of their household, but as she was the one person in Scotch Heaven who could quote more verse than I could, I figured she had every right.

As midnight neared, there was acclamation from all these, led by Judith with a bit more enthusiasm than I was comfortable with that I of course had to be one to first-foot the new year in for Ninian and Flora.

"Can't I wait for a year when the weather is better out there?" I protested. But at a minute before 1891, out I went into the cold blustery middle of the night.

I stood alone there in the mountainous dark where weather comes from, where years come from. Then turned myself around to the homestead house.

"Now there's a year's worth of good luck if I ever saw him," announced Rob after I stepped back in across the Duff threshold without a word, strode to the stove and poked the fire into brisker flame. Not that any of us at all believed the superstition about a tall unspeaking man who straightway tended the hearth fire being the year's most propitious first foot, but still.

"He will do," granted Ninian, while Flora handed us steaming cups of coffee with just a tip of whiskey therein. "Warm yourselves, you may need it riding home."

"What do you make of this weather, Ninian?" I wondered. By the sound of it the wind was whooping harder every minute. "A squall, is this?"

"It may be. Or it may be the start of winter."

For the next eight days, all the wind in the world tore at Scotch Heaven. We had wind that took the hay as we struggled to feed the sheep, wind that coated us and the workhorses with snow, wind every breath of the day and wind in our sleep.

And then came cold. Probably Rob and I were lucky not to know until later that from the tenth of January until the twenty-second, Donald Erskine's thermometer never rose above fifteen below zero.

"Angus, you're my favorite man, but there are times when I wish your name was Agnes."

This was ribald from Rob. I gave him back: "What times are

those, I wonder? January can't be one, surely. A month of snow-white purity—"

"You say snow one more time and you'll be out in it."

Winter engines, us now. The pale smoke of Rob's breath as he chopped ice from the waterhole, I could see from the top of the haystack two hundred yards away. As our workhorses Sadie and Brandy pulled the haysled in a great slow circle in the snow while we fed the hay off, they produced regular dragonsnort. Our exertions were not the only ones there in the air; there was the whacking sound of Tom Mortensen at his woodpile over the ridge from my place, and the spaced clouts of George Frew next down the creek breaking out the water hole for his livestock. It was a new way to live, bundled and laborious and slow, oddly calm, and you had to wonder how Eskimos put up with it all the time.

A Saturday of February. The day had been blue and still. Rob's whistling was the liveliest element around. We had not been to Gros Ventre since Christmas, and we were preparing to remedy that. Haircuts had been traded, baths had been taken, boots blacked with stovelid soot. Mustaches were our winter project, which meant meticulous trimming. We were putting on our clean shirts when a white gust was flung past the south windows, as if someone had begun plucking geese.

"Don't be that way," Rob told the weather.

"Probably it's only a flurry."

"It had better be."

It was not. The snow drove and drove, sifting out of the silent sky as if to bury the planet. In minutes the west window to the mountains was caked white.

"That's that, then," Rob admitted at last. "Goodbye, Gros Ventre."

"We'll go twice next time." That was brighter than I felt, for I was as keen as Rob for a meal cooked by Lila Sedge, for a drink poured by Lucas, for talk in the air of the Medicine Lodge, for what waited at Wingo's.

"Next time is the story of homesteading, I'm beginning to think," Rob gloomed.

"You're coming down with winter fever. Elk stew is the only known antidote." Or at least the only supper we had now that Lila Sedge's cuisine was out of the picture.

"Lord of mercy, man. No town, and now Ninian's elk that bends forks?"

"The same famous one." The bull elk shot by Ninian was so elderly he had a set of antlers that would have scaffolded Canterbury Cathedral. "Old Elky, grandfather of beasts."

"And enemy of teeth. Tell me again the price of mutton."

I raised my thumb to him. "One, the cost of a sheep herself." Then extended my first finger. "Two, the cost of the hay she's eaten so far this winter." Next finger. "Three, the loss of her lamb next spring." Next finger. "Four, the loss of her fleece next summer." Final finger. "Five, explaining to Lucas that we've been sitting out here eating an animal he put up good money for."

Rob studied my display. "McAngus, if you had more fingers on that hand, you'd have more reasons too. All right, all right, the sheep are safe again. Elk stew by popular demand."

To cheer him up while I heated the familiar stew, I resorted to: "Surely you've never heard the story about Methuselah and his cook?"

"This weather has me to the point where I'll listen to anything. Tell away."

"Well, Methuselah's cook got tired of cooking for that houseful. All those begattings, more and more mouths at every meal—a couple of hundred years of that and you can see how it would start to get tiresome. So she went to Methuselah and said, 'What about some time off, like?' 'No, no, no,' he tells her, 'we can't possibly spare you, you're too good a cook. In all these years have I ever complained once about your food?' She had to admit he hadn't. 'No, nor will I,' he says. 'If you ever hear me complain, I'll do the cooking myself, for the rest of my life.'

"The cook went away thinking about that. Methuselah was only around four hundred years old at the time, still doing all that begatting, and he looked as if he maybe had another five hundred years or so in him. The cook kept thinking, five hundred years off from all that cooking if she could just get Methuselah to complain. So the next morning for breakfast, the first thing she does is put a handful of salt in Methuselah's coffee and send it out to the table. Methuselah takes a big swallow and spews it right back out. The cook starts to take her apron off. *'By Jehovah!'* he says, and she can hear him coughing and sputtering, *'the coffee is full of salt!'* She's just ready to step out of that kitchen forever when she hears him say: '*Just the way I like it!*'"

After laughter, Rob went quiet during the meal. I was hoping that after the last bite of elk he might put down his fork and proclaim *Just the way I like it,* but no, the evening was not going to be that easy. He pushed back his chair and said instead: "Angus, do you know what I think?"

"When it starts out that way, probably not."

"I think we need more sheep."

"What, so we can eat some? Rob, it won't be elk forever. As soon as we can get to town—"

"I'm serious here," Rob attested. "More sheep would be just the ticket we need, is what I think."

"If I understand right what those bucks were doing to those ewes, we're pretty soon going to have more."

"Not just the lambs, man. We ought to be thinking about buying more ewes. Another five hundred, maybe another thousand. It can't be that much more trouble to run two thousand sheep than it is a thousand."

"It's twice the hay, though." My meadows were just enough to get us through a winter such as this, if we were lucky. "Where's that going to come from?"

"We can buy it. Jesse Spedderson would a lot rather sell us his hay standing in the field than exert himself to put it up, I'll bet you this kitchen table on that."

"Say he does, then. What do we use to buy these famous further sheep with?" Although I thought I knew.

"We'll get Lucas to back us."

"Rob, we're already in debt to Lucas a mile deep."

"Angus, look at it this way: if we're going to be in debt, Lucas is our best choice anywhere around. Naturally there's a bit of risk, taking on more sheep. But if you're going to homestead, you have to take risk, am I right?"

I peered over at him, to be sure this was the same Rob who had been ready to spurn the North Fork for going in with Fain in the blacksmith shop.

"These sheep we have now can be just the start of us, man," he galloped right on. "That's why it was worth coming from Scotland. Worth even finding Lucas—the way he is. His hands maybe are gone but none of his head went with them. No, Lucas has the fact of it. This Two Medicine country will grow. It's bound to. And we're in on the ground floor."

I directed his attention to the white outside the window. "Actually we may be down in the cold cellar."

"Angus, Angus. By damn, I wish it was spring. You'd be in a brighter mood, and you'd see in a minute what I'm talking about here."

If my ears were to be trusted, he was talking about the theory of sheep, which is the world's best. In theory a band of sheep is a garden on legs. Every spring a crop of lambs, every summer a crop of wool. Feed us and clothe us, too; not even potatoes yield so beneficially. But the fleecies are a garden that wanders around looking for its own extinction, and in the Two Medicine country there were many sources willing to oblige their mortal urge. Coyotes, bear, cliffs, blizzards, death camas, lupine. Not least, themselves. I can tell you to this moment the anguish when, the second day after we had trailed our yearlings home to the North Fork from their former owner in the Choteau country, Rob and I found our first dead sheep. A fine fat ewe on her back, four legs in the air like hooved branches. In her clumsy cocoon of wool she had rolled helplessly onto her back when she lay down to scratch a tick itch and couldn't right herself again. Rob was shocked, and I admit I was a bit unsettled myself. And as any sheep owner must, we began thinking the terrifying arithmetic: what if we lose another ewe two days from now . . . Lord of mercy, what if we lose one again *tomorrow* . . . A little of that and in your mind you soon not only have no sheep left, you possess even fewer than that—cavities of potential loss of however many sheep you could ever possibly buy to replace the ones that right now are out there searching for ways to die. Thus you draw breath and try to think instead of the benefits of sheep. Watch them thrive on grass a cow wouldn't even put its head down for. Watch the beautiful fleeces, rich and oily to the touch, unfold off them as they are sheared. Dream ahead to when you can watch your first crop of lambs enlarge themselves week by week. As Rob was doing now in his winter rhapsody about more sheep. But I didn't want that tune, expensive as it promised to be, to get out of hand, and so I responded:

"Rob, I see that we don't even know yet if we're going to get through this winter with *these* sheep alive, let alone twice that many that we don't have."

"With an attitude like that," he retorted a bit quick and sharp, "you're not looking ahead beyond the end of your nose, you know."

And you're looking right past all the precipices there are, I thought but managed not to say. This was new. Usually when Rob and I disagreed it was about some speck of a matter that was gone by the next day. Even during our months here in the white cave of Montana winter, our most spirited argument had been over whose turn it was to bring in the firewood. But I knew too well that if Rob Barclay decided to believe in a thing as if it were fairy gold, words weren't an antidote. I shook my head now, both at Rob and at the silliness of us filling the kitchen with debate about phantom sheep. "You're working hard on the wrong source here," I pointed out to him. "It's Lucas's wallet you're going to have to persuade."

"I can see winter isn't the season to reason with you," he gave me back. "Let's talk this over in the spring, what do you say."

"I say, knowing you, we're sure to talk it over, all right."

That at last drew a smile and a short laugh from him, and he got up and went to the south window. The snow no longer was flailing past, but clouds covered the mountains, and more storm was only minutes away.

"McAngus, who of your old poets called clouds the sacks of heaven?"

"*Undo the silver sacks of heaven,/seed the sky with stars./See every gleam grow to seven,/*something something *Mars.* I can't think now, which."

"He ought to be shot," Rob stated.

Then in March, this.

"There. Hear that?" We were feeding the sheep their hay beside the North Fork, on a morning as icy as any of the winter had been.

"Hear what? The sound of me pitching hay and you standing there with your ears hanging out?"

"There, that rushing sound up in the mountains. That's new."

"Just the wind."

"What wind? There isn't a breath of one."

"Running water, then?"

"That creek is frozen stiffer than I am."

"Creature, maybe?"

"Making a noise that size? We'd better hope not."

The sheep began to raise their heads from the hay, nosing the air.

"They hear it, too."

"Listen. Isn't it getting louder?"

Off came our flap caps, not just for keener listening but because the air strangely no longer seemed chilly. In minutes the great flowing sound was dispensing itself down from the peaks and crags as a sudden stiff breeze, but a breeze warm all through. A day that had been firmly fifteen degrees below zero began to feel tropical. As we finished the pitchfork work we had to shed our scarves, then our coats. Not until Rob and I talked with Ninian a few days later, the snow already gone from every south slope and elsewhere retreating down into its deep coulee drifts, did we learn the word of that miracle wind, which was chinook. But driving the haysled home from the sheep on that chinook day, our gloves next off, the two of us kept flexing our pale winter hands, one and then the other as if shedding old skin, in that astonishing blowing air of springtime.

In the after years, Rob always made the jest that the winter with me was what caused him to marry Judith Findlater.

"Your cooking, of course I mean to say, Angus. Every recipe you knew was elk, do you remember. Judith brought one of her mince pies to a dance and I was a gone gosling."

I laughed ritually each time, but what Lucas had forecast about Rob's route into marriage always tinged the moment. For I did see it come, Judith's quiet sorting of us during her husband-looking winter—me too wary and waitful, George Frew so gawkishly silent, Allan Frew too irresponsible, Tom Mortensen too old and bachelorly, but Rob bright and winnable, Rob always pleased to find himself reflected back in someone's attention. When Archie Findlater came that March to ask Rob for a few days' skilled help in building lambing pens, work which anybody who could fit fingers around a hammer could do, and mentioned "Take your meals with us too, why not, and save yourself the ride back and forth," he may as well have brought Judith and the marriage license with him.

The wedding, in almost-warm-enough weather you could step into blindfolded and know it was May in Montana, was in Rob's front yard. All of Scotch Heaven assembled there under the crest of Breed Butte for the valley's first matrimony, and as best man I had the closest look of anyone except the minister at how Rob and Judith gleamed for each other. He was newly dismustached and his smile seemed all the fresher. Judith already looked wifely, quietly natural beside Rob. He'd teased her beforehand that when the major question came he was going to respond, "Can I toss a coin to decide that?" But when the moment arrived, Rob spoke out "I do" as if telling it to generations before and aft.

Afterward we ate and danced and talked and danced and drank and danced. As evening came on, before heading home I got Rob and Judith aside to congratulate them one last time.

"For people who just got married beyond redemption, you both look happy enough about it," I assessed for their benefit.

"You're the best best man there could be," Judith nicely assured me and rose on tiptoes to kiss my cheek while Rob warned merrily, "Not too much of that, now."

Riding toward home with the bunch from the wedding, I took full notice that the May dusk was telling us the lengthened days of summer were truly on their way, but otherwise I heard with only half an ear the jokes and chat that were being passed around. Until silent George Frew and I swung off together on the trail to our homesteads. Then George, who was sloshing a bit with the amount of wedding drink in him, jerked his head back toward Breed Butte and blurted: "They're at it now."

No doubt Rob and Judith were. I'd have been, in Rob's place. But George's whiskeyed words set off something in me. I rode home thinking over whether I ought to have made the maneuvers— maybe I flattered myself, but I believed it would not have taken any too many—that would have put me in Rob's place. And decided again, no. The same voice in me that said all winter about Judith, *not yet, not this one,* was saying even stronger now, *wait, let time tell.* Oh, I knew that all you can count on in life is your fingers and toes, but I was determined to do marriage as right as I could when I did it at all. Did I have an enlarged sense of carefulness, where weddings were concerned? Maybe, but I felt it had grown naturally in me. My parents' case, a marriage locked in ice whenever it wasn't shaking with thunder, was not anything I intended to repeat. No, there had to be better than that. And the matrimonial exchange I had just witnessed on Breed Butte: Judith bagging a husband, Rob pocketing a wife. I hated even to think it of two people I so prized, but there had to be better than that, too. A high idea, maybe, but the North Fork valley around me and the strong mountains over me seemed the place for such a thought. If better could not be done here, on new land on a new continent, myself a new version of a McCaskill—the American version—where could it ever be done?

Say you are a stone that blinks once a year, when the sun of spring draws the last of winter from you. In the wink that is 1891, you see nine houses in the valley of the North Fork where there had been but those two of the Duff and Erskine homesteads. You note the retreat of timber on Wolf Butte where Rob and myself and Archie Findlater and Jesse Spedderson and old Tom Mortensen and the Frew cousins George and Allan sawed lodgepole pines to build those houses. You notice lines of new fence encasing each of Scotch Heaven's homesteads, straight and taut as mesh. You see Vinia Spedderson's laundry flying from a hayrack, to the disgust of the other wives. You see the Erskine boy Davie riding his pony along the creek as if in a race with the breeze-blown hay.

Your next glimpse, 1892, shows you newborn Ellen, the first of Rob and Judith's girls. You see slow-grazing scatters of gray which are the sheep of one or another of us, maybe mine and Rob's working the grassy foothills west of my homestead, maybe the new band belonging to Rob and Lucas there on the slope of Breed Butte. (Were not stones famously deaf, you would have heard Rob try to the end to persuade me to come in with him and Lucas on that second thousand of sheep, *Angus, you're thinking small instead of tall, I'm disappointed in you, man;* and from me, to whom deeper debt did not look like the kind of prosperity I wanted, *Rob, if this is the first time or the last I disappoint you, you're lucky indeed.*) You see rain booming on the roofs in the rare two-day May downpour that brought the North Fork twice the crop of hay any of us had expected or imagined. You behold Ninian Duff coming home from town with a bucket of calcimine, and you watch as every Scotch Heaven household, mine included, quickly whitens a wall here or there.

And now in your third blink, 1893, you notice an occasional frown as we lords of sheep hear how the prices are beginning to drop in the distant wool and lamb markets. You see my life as it was for the rest of that year, achieveful yet hectic as all homestead years seemed to be, tasks hurrying at each other's heels: turn out the last bunch of ewes and their fresh lambs onto new pasture and the garden needs to be put in; do that, and fence needs mending; mend that, and it is shearing time; shear the beloved woollies, and it is haying time. You see me look up, somewhere amid it all, to a buck-board arriving, drawn by Ninian Duff's team of matched bay horses.

On the seat beside Ninian perched Willy Hahn. School board business, this could only be.

Ninian pulled his bays to a halt and announced down to me: "News, Angus. We've lost our teacher. George Frew is marrying her." With the school year so close on us, Ninian was saying what was in our three minds in the last of his pronouncement: "Maybe she can teach him to speak up sooner."

"So we've a fast advertisement to write, have we?" I responded. "Come down and come in, I'll—"

Ninian interrupted, "In point of fact, Willy and I already have located a replacement teacher. Haven't we now, Willy?" Willy dipped his head yes. "More than that even," Ninian swept on, "we've voted to hire." Willy dipped again.

I was peeved to hear this. By damn, I was more than that. These two old puffed-up whiskerheads. "Well, then. Since the pair of you are running the school board so aptly without me, we haven't anything more to talk about, now have we. Don't let me keep you here, busy persons like yourselves."

Ninian winked solemnly to Willy. "The man doesn't see it."

"What's to see?" I blazed. "You two parade in here and—"

"Anguss," Willy put in mildly. "It iss you we voted to hire."

Ordain me here and now as the Lord High Kafoozalum and I would be no more surprised than I was to be made the South Fork schoolteacher. Not that there was ever any supposition I was the pedagogical genius the world had been seeking since Jesus went upstairs; after all, back there in Nethermuir I had only ever been the pupil-teacher assisting Adam Willox, never the actual master of a schoolroom. What designated me now, as Willy and Ninian cheer-fully made plain, was that time was short and I was nearest.

"Temporary, just for the year," Ninian assured me as if school-teaching could be done with my little finger.

"Can't Flora fill the situation as well as I can?" I astutely retorted to him, citing the only other person in the vicinity who had experi-ence at standing at the front of a classroom. Willy tittered, cast a glance toward Ninian on the wagon seat beside him, then looked

down at me severely. Which caused me to remember that Flora
Duff was currently a prominent six months in the family way.

Ninian and Willy proceeded to argue qualm after qualm out of
me. Yes, they would see to it that I had help with my homestead
tasks as needed. Yes yes, they would put in a word with Rob about
the necessity of adjusting our sheep arrangement if I took the
school. Yes yes yes, they would find someone more suitable for the
position next year.

"There is of course the matter of the teacher's wage," Ninian at
last found around to, and there he met me coming, I do have to
admit. That year of 1893 was the sour kind that we hadn't known
was in the calendar of America. Prices of wool and lambs both were
falling through the floor while I still was trying to climb out of
Lucas's wallet. And be it said if it needs to, no homesteader was
ever his own best paymaster. Besides, I had come across the bend
of the world looking for a different life, had I? The one thing certain
about a year as the South Fork teacher was that it would be different.

"All right, then," I acquiesced to my electors. "If you haven't
come to your senses in the last minute, I'm your schoolkeeper for
this year."

"Anguss, you are chust the man," Willy ratified, and I swear
Ninian very nearly smiled at me.

That first South Fork morning. The Hahn brothers were the
earliest to trudge down the road toward the waitful school and
waitful me, dragging with them the invisible Gibraltar of burden
of having a father on the school board. The children from the
other families of that branch of the creek as well, the Petersons
and Roziers and Van Bebbers, all lived near enough to walk to
school and soon they were ricocheting around outside in those
double-quick games that erupt before the class day takes everyone captive. I turned from the window for one last inventory of
my schoolroom. Desk rows across the room. Blackboard and a
roll-down map of the world fastened above. Framed portraits of
Washington and Lincoln, men whose lives I knew only the
vaguest of, staring stoically at each other on the far wall. I hammered days of nails when this schoolhouse was built, I came here
many a time with Ninian and Willy to tend to our teacher, I had

danced on this schoolroom's floor, mended its roof. Yet I tell you, it was a place foreign to my eyes as I waited for the minute when it would fill with pupils. My pupils.

For the dozenth time I looked at the alarm clock ticking on my solitary desk at the front of the schoolroom. This time it told me I had to ring the bell to begin school, even though a significant half of my pupil population hadn't yet appeared.

Ring I did.

In trooped the South Fork boys and girls.

I hemmed and hawed and had them take temporary seats until the others arrived.

But still no others.

Accident? Boycott? Jest of the gods? Possibilities trotted around in me until I needed to do what I had been resisting, retreat out onto the porch and peer up the North Fork road. With me went the echo of Lucas's reaction to my new and quite possibly stillborn career: *By Jesus, Angus, you're the first swamper the Medicine Lodge ever had that's turned out to be a schoolmarm.* Maybe I was in over my head, trying to be schoolkeeper as well as homesteader as well as sheep partner with Rob. Maybe . . .

Here they came, the child cavalry of Scotch Heaven. The three Findlaters on a fat white horse named Snowy. Susan Duff regal on one of Ninian's blood bay geldings. Jimmy Spedderson on a beautiful blazeface black worth more than the rest of the Speddersons' homestead combined. George Frew's daughter Betsy on an elderly sorrel. Davie Erskine on his fast-stepping roan with small sister Rachel clinging behind him.

I let out a breath of thanks. But to show them I did not intend for tardiness to become habit, I stood conspicuously waiting while they put their horses on picket ropes. Already there on a length of grazing tether was the Dantley mare Patch that I still rode, and with all our horses picketed around the schoolhouse, the scene suddenly hit me as one of life's instants I had been through before—Rob and I gawking at the Floweree outfit's cow camp the day we arrived green as peas into Gros Ventre. I reminded myself how greatly more veteran in life I was by now, and tried to believe it in the face of what advanced on me here, Susan Duff.

She poised below me as if bearing a message from Caesar. "We cut through our lower field and couldn't get the gate open and the top loop was too tight and barbwire besides," she reported in funereal tones. "My father will need to fix that gate." Unaccountably my spirits rose as I thought of Ninian having to deal with this daughter. "Meg Findlater's nose is running and she doesn't have a hanky, and Davie Erskine forgot to bring his and Rachel's lunch." This seemed to conclude Susan's docket, and up the porch steps and into the schoolhouse she marched with the other Scotch Heaven children in a straggle behind her.

I kick myself yet for not anticipating the next snag of that morning, although I am not sure what I could have done about it. My gender. In Scotland schoolmasters were thick on the ground. But here, having a man teacher proved to be an unexpected thought to pupils accustomed to Miss Milgrim. The larger boys were plainly restless about me, and I was afraid little Meg Findlater's eyes would pop from her head every time I leaned far down to bring my handkerchief to the rescue of her nose.

My predecessor still governessed that schoolroom in another way, too. After I had everyone sorted and seated and the littlest ones were more or less occupied with the new things called desks and books, I started on my upper grades in what I thought was peerless emulation of Socrates, "Tell me, anyone please, the presidents from Washington to Lincoln."

I drew back stares.

There I stood wondering what had taken their tongues, until Susan Duff informed me that it was the practice of Miss Milgrim to tell the pupils such matters as the presidents to Lincoln, while they listened.

"That's as may be, Susan. But I look very little like Miss Milgrim, don't I, and so I need to do things my own way. Now who'll tell the presidents, Washington to Lincoln?"

A silence deep as a corner of eternity. As the silence yawned on, my only immediate hope was Susan again. But a look at her told me she had lent me all the instruction she currently intended to.

This tiny box of school, on the universe's ocean. How could we in here ever hope to know enough to get by on, let alone improve the race at all? I despaired and was starting to reach for the chalk and begin listing presidents, anything to stir this congealed schoolroom, when I heard:

"Hickory Jackson."

I turned, blinking. Davie Erskine was regarding me with a helpfulness that managed to be vague and earnest at the same time. I'd

made mental note to share my lunch with him and his little sister
Rachel; this opening effort of Davie's resolved me to give them it
all. Taking my surprise for encouragement, the boy visibly
searched around in his head some more. After a while:

"Quincy Adams."

Yet another Davie spell of thought—Shakespeare could have
written a couple of acts during this one—and:

"Some other Adams."

I was desperately debating within myself whether to shut off this
random trickle of presidents, try to suggest some order into it, or
what, when Davie's thought-seeking gaze lit on the wall portraits.

"Abe Lincoln," he announced to us. "George—"

It was too much for Susan Duff. Up shot her hand. "Washington-
johnadamsjefferson," she launched, "Madisonmonroejohnquincy-
adams—"

My pupils, my minnow school of new Montana. It was like having tailor's samples, swatches, of Scotch Heaven's families all
around you daylong. Susan Duff had bones longer than they knew
what to do with themselves, in the manner of Ninian, so that her
elbows stuck over the aisle the way his poked wide when he cut his
meat. The Findlaters all were marvels at arithmetic. The Hahn
boys had cherubic lispy voices like Willy's, you would never suspect
that one or more likely both of them had just been in a blazing
fistfight during recess. Yet I always needed to watch out not to peg
a child according to his parents or older brothers and sisters. Along
came small Karen, of the cog-at-a-time Petersons, and she had a
mind like a magic needle. It penetrated every book I managed to
find for her, and of my bunch in that schoolroom Karen was the one
spellbound, as I had been at her age, by those word rainbows called
poems.

And so there I stood before these sons and daughters of the
homesteads, their newly minted teacher of such topics as the history
of the United States of America, with my Scottish schooling which
had instructed me thoroughly in the principal events from Robert
the Bruce to the Union of the Crowns. My daily margin of American history over my various grades was the pages I'd scurried
through the night before. Fortunately, not all the subjects were as
lion-sized as history. Even in America lessons in handwriting were
lessons in handwriting, and reading was reading. And spelling was

spelling except when *harbour* arrived to this side of the ocean as *harbor, tyre* as *tire,* and sundry other joggled vowels. But geography. The grief of American geography. When it came to geography, my pupils and I had to be strange pickles together. In that schoolroom of mine were children born in Bavaria and Scotland and Norway and Alsace-Lorraine, and others who never had been farther in the world than ten miles down the creek to Gros Ventre. Our sole veteran traveler of the continent we were on was Jimmy Spedderson, seven years of age, who had lived in Missouri, Kansas, North Dakota, Manitoba, and now Montana—a life like a skipping stone. Whatever the roll-down map of the whole world proclaimed, every one of us there came from a different earth and knew only the haziest about anyone else's. For me, terra incognita was the 99% of Montana where I had never been. I could instruct my pupils perfectly well that Thomas Carlyle—he of *I don't pretend to understand the universe; it's a great deal bigger than I am*—originated at Ecclefechan, pronounced Eckle-FECK'n, county of Dumfries in southmost Scotland, near to Carlisle and the Solway Firth. But I had to learn along with them the sixteen counties of Montana and the mysterious town names of Ekalaka, Ubet, Saco, Missoula, Shawmut, Rimini, Ravalli, Ovando . . .

One geographic inspiration I did have. The piece of the planet that stayed with me as no other, the Atlantic. Vivid as this minute, that time of Rob and myself on the *Jemmy*, down in Steerage Number One, deep there in the hole in the water. The Hahn boys and the three Findlaters and Daniel Rozier and Susan Duff and Davie Erskine also all remembered crossing the ocean to America. I strived to have them make the other pupils understand that feat of crossing, and to hold it in their own minds ever and ever. And got more than I bargained for when Jenny Findlater hesitantly raised her hand and asked if when I was on the ocean, was I scared any?

"Jenny, I was," I said to Daniel's smirk and the careful gazes of all the others. "An ocean is dangerous enough to be afraid of. As are the rear hooves of our horses out there, and blizzards, and just a number of things in life. But we try to use our judgment and be afraid only when it's worth it, don't we, and then only as much as we have to be. Is that how it was with you, Jenny, when you were on the ocean?" Jenny's vigorous nod carried me from that trouble.

Thank heaven arithmetic is a neutral country. At least I could put addition and subtraction and multiplication and division into my pupils like nails into a shingle roof, pound pound pound pound. Here was once when old Scotland came back to help me out, for when I had been pupil-teacher under Adam Willox in Nethermuir he made arithmetic my particular topic. *They can become literate from me, Angus, and learn to be numerate from you.*

So maybe it was numbers alone that kept me, that school year, from ever riding into the Duff homestead and saying "Ninian, start advertising for someone else, this is beyond me." Instead, day upon day I ransacked my brain for how Adam Willox had done things. Then amended nearly all of that, for Adam never had the situation of the Hahns' dog Blitzen following them to school and howling by the hour; of keeping track of whose turn it was among the big boys to go to the creek and fill the water bucket; of Einar Peterson's perpetual tendency toward nosebleed and Jenny Findlater's toward hiccups; of having to watch for ticks on everyone, including myself.

Of having to deal with Daniel Rozier about the issue of the girls' outhouse.

A country school such as South Fork was not an individual receptacle of knowledge, it was an educational trinity. You saw all three as you came to where the streambed of the North Fork met that of the South Fork and made the main creek; just upstream within a willow-thick bend, the white schoolhouse and behind it the white twin toilets, girls' to the left, boys' to the right. Each waiting to do its duty, they sat there like an attentive hen and two pullets. My problem, or more accurately the girls' problem, was Daniel Rozier's fascination with the possibilities of that left-hand outhouse.

It all began with garter snakes. Most of the girls were not normally afraid of them, but go seat yourself appropriately and glance down to find restless green reptiles beside you, and see what you think.

I heard out the girls' lamentations, and made my threats about what would happen to whomever I caught at snakework. But the Rozier homestead was just down the creek from the school, near enough for Daniel to sneak back before or after the rest of us, and try as I did I never could convict Daniel.

Susan Duff, rather than I, ended the snake episode the recess time when she stormed out of the girls' toilet grasping a writhing foot-long serpent by the tail, carried it around to the side of the schoolhouse where Daniel Rozier was in a game of ante-I-over, and whapped him across the bridge of the nose with the thing.

Even if she was the avenging figure of justice, Daniel was livid about being hit by a girl.

"SUSAN-DUFF-YOU'RE-WORSE-THAN-SNOT!" he screeched.

"The next snake I find in there I'll hit you with twice," she vowed in return.

And so only two of the trinity were standing when I rode into sight of the South Fork the morning after that. The casualty naturally was the girls' outhouse, flat on its back as a dead beetle. The bad fact now was that even Daniel Rozier at his most indignant wasn't strong enough to tip over a two-hole outhouse. He'd had help from the other boys. It took Daniel and Davie Erskine and the Hahn brothers, conscript labor all, and me to lift the structure upright.

Two mornings later, the girls' outhouse was horizontal again.

By then I knew Daniel Rozier was the sort you could punish until he was jelly and he'd still behave the same. Instead, I opened school that day with the observation: "A freak of nature seems to have struck the girls' outhouse." Smirk from Daniel to Susan Duff, glower from her to him. "Until it comes along again and puts the toilet back up, chivalry will have to be in force. Who'll tell me the spelling of chivalry? Daniel, crack at it, please."

The smirk went and confusion came. "Unngg, ah, is it s-h-o-v-u-l-r-y?"

"Closer than you might think," I granted. "Susan, enlighten Daniel as to chivalry, please." Which she did as fast as the letters could prance out her mouth.

"Thank you, Susan. Now the definition, at least in this case. The boys will yield their toilet to the girls."

Little Freddie Findlater, a lad with a nervous kidney, had his hand up in an instant. "Where will the boys go, then?"

I directed attention to the willow thicket along the creek. "Like Zeus on Mount Olympus, Freddie, all of outdoors is your throne." Looks were cast toward Daniel Rozier, but the boys sat firm, so to speak, on their outhouse position.

Montana weather being Montana weather, I didn't have to wait long for the day I needed. Squalls were getting up speed in the mountains as I reached into my cupboard that morning, and by noon hard wind and blasts of sleet shot against the schoolhouse windows.

"My eyes must have been big this morning, I brought more than

I can eat," I confessed during lunchtime. "Daniel, pass those around please," handing him the big bag of prunes. In groped his paw for the first haul, then the fruit began its fist-diving circle among the other boys.

When the prunes had time for full effect, and boy after boy trooped back in from the bushes as if dragging icicles behind, I decided here was my moment. "I've been meaning to ask, how many of you can stay after and put the outhouse back up?"

Where it then held.

"A coyote can too run faster than a dog, Fritz Hahn." Jimmy Spedderson's contention wafted in through an open window as I was at my desk cramming that afternoon's American history.

"Can't either. Our dog Blitzen runs after coyotes all the time, see."

"Your dog can't catch coyotes! That's a fat lie. Liar, liar, pants on fire!"

"Didn't say he catches them."

"See, then."

"He'd have to run *faster* to catch them. What he does is he *keeps up* with them. So a dog and coyote run the same, see."

"They don't, either. After recess we'll ask McAsker."

"All right then. McAsker will know."

McAsker, was I now. It could have been worse.

For all the daily tussle of schooling, there were distinct times when I wished the rest of the world were made of children as well. I had wondered what some of the community thought of having me as a teacher, and I found out when the first dance of the year was held in the schoolhouse. Just after I had done a schottische with Rob's Judith, Allan Frew called out to me in a high girly voice: "Angus, aren't you afraid your petticoat will show when you kick up your heels like that?"

I stepped over within arm's reach of Allan, which made him blink and think.

"Ask me that outside," I urged him, "and I'll answer you by hand."

That ended that.

Then there was the matter that fists have never been able to settle. Of course it had to be Ninian to bring me word of this, and I give him full due, he looked nowhere near happy to be performing it.

"Angus, this business about the universe being too big to understand and so on. I'm hearing from a few folks that they would like a bit more orthodox view of things told to their children."

Of anything to be scanned and poked and sniffed in the making of education, this. So far as I could see I was doing the job of teaching as well as I knew how. Probably better. To have it all snag on a sentence from Carlyle, himself a God-wrestler right in there with the most ardent—it put my blood up.

"Ninian, I can't get into that. You can say all day long you just want a bit of orthodoxy, but there's my-doxy, your-doxy, this-doxy, that-doxy. They're all *somebody's* orthodoxy. I don't notice Willy being here with you. Has he been saying I don't trot Martin Luther into the classroom often enough? Then there are the Roziers. I can invite the Pope to visit from Rome to please them, too, of course?"

"Angus, I am troubled myself with this. The matter was simpler when we were over across in Scotland."

"Oh, was it? Then you don't hold with the fellow who said the history of Scotland is one long riot of righteous against righteous."

"Now Angus, don't start."

"Ninian, you and the others can fill your children with funnels of religion at home, as far as I'm concerned. But I won't do it for you here at school. If you want a kirk school, then you'd better sack me and find yourself a preacher."

Ninian by now looked more bleak than I'd ever seen him, which is saying a lot.

"Ay, well. That's your last word, then?"

"It's even the one after that."

"Angus, we will leave this where it was. I have to go and tell them I told you." The long beard moved on Ninian's chest as he shook his head at me. "They don't need to know how hard of hearing you can be."

And then there was Rob.

"You know you're demented to be spending yourself there in the school." He said it smiling, but I could tell he more than half meant it. "Of course," he swept on, "that goes without saying, about anyone as redheaded as you are. But—"

"—you'll be glad to say it for me even so," I finished for him.

"And here I thought you'd be relieved to know there's a solid mind at the school, what with all the Barclays that seem to be on their way to the place," I said, Judith being notably along then toward their second child. You had to wonder, with the wives of Scotch Heaven as fruitful as they were, was there a permanent pregnancy that simply circled around among them?

"Solid is one word for it. Thick is another. Angus, man, you're missing a golden chance by not coming in with Lucas and me on more sheep. With prices down where they are, we can buy enough woollies to cover this country from here to there."

We. *Lucas and thee and his money make three*, I thought to myself. But said: "If you and Lucas want to be up to your necks in sheep, that's your matter. I have all I can handle and still take the school."

"You're a contrary man, McAngus, is what you are. Give you bread and roses and I swear you'd eat the petals and go around with the loaf in your buttonhole." Rob shook his head as if clearing it of vapors caught from me. "You're missing serious opportunity," he reiterated, "passing up Lucas's pocket this way when he has it open. Don't say I never told you."

"Rob, I never would."

"I can only hope you're saving up your brains to contend with this horse dealer," Rob switched to with a laugh, and quick as that, the how-many-sheep-are-enough? debate was behind us one more time and he was the other Rob, the sun-bright one. A Saturday, this, and the pair of us were pointing our horses across the divide of Breed Butte and down, north, to Noon Creek. Our mission was a new horse for me, poor old mare Patch no longer having enough step in her for my miles back and forth to the school and out and around our band of sheep when I took them from Rob each weekend—I seemed to use the saddle for a chair anymore. Patch's plodding pace here beside Rob's strong roan reinforced my conviction that buying another horse from Dantley's stable in Gros Ventre would be like throwing the money in the stove, so we were resorting to elsewhere. I say we; Rob was avidly insistent, when I mentioned to him my rehorsing intention, that Patch's successor be a partnership horse. *Angus, man, you'll be using him on the band of sheep we own together, so it's only logical I put up half the price of him. He can be the horse of us both, why not.* In fine, going in with me on the purchase of the horse was Rob's roundabout way of helping me to juggle the school along with the homestead and the sheep, without having to say out loud that it was something worth juggling. Maybe the right silences are what keep a friendship green?

Isaac Reese's horse ranch was as far up Noon Creek as mine was along the North Fork, comfortably near the mountains without having them squat on you. As we approached the place Rob now asked, "Do you know this geezer Reese at all?"

"Only by hearsay."

Isaac Reese, long-mustached and soft-eyed, had been issued the right face for a horse trader, for he showed no twitch of anticipation when I stepped off the Dantley nag as if I was a plump hen seeking a chopping block. When I told him my purpose, he only asked in some accent my ears were not prepared for: "How much horse?"

I took that to mean how much was I willing to pay for a horse, and began the sad hymn of my finances. But Isaac Reese meant what he said. He studied me, eyeing my long legs, and judged: "You vant about him high," holding his arm out at a height considerably more lofty than the back of old Patch.

Plainly this was a man who knew horses. What else he knew was as unclear to me then as his version of English, which had Rob covering a smile as he witnessed our conversational free-for-all. By common report, this Isaac Reese was a Dane who alit in America as a penniless teamster—likely about the time of Rob and me ourselves, for he looked to be only a few years older than us—and soon had horse crews of his own at work on the railroad that was being built north of the Two Medicine River. My bet is that he learned his English, to call it that, from someone else who didn't speak it as an original language. It was Isaac who made famous a Noon Creek winter day when the temperature rose from twenty below to zero by observing, "Der t'ermometer fall up dis morning."

What Isaac Reese led out for me was a high horse, no question about that. A tall young gelding of a strong brown color odd in a horse, remindful of dark gingerbread. Maybe Rob and I were no great equinists, but at the wheel shop in Nethermuir we had seen enough horses pass through to fill a corner of Asia, and with a quick look at each other we agreed that here was a strikingly handsome animal. Both of us stepped closer to admire the steed and began companionably rubbing his velvet neck while I asked Isaac: "What's his name?"

"Skorp Yun," Isaac informed me. That had a pensive homely Scandinavian ring to it, and I was on the verge of asking what it translated to. When it came clear to me, and Rob at the same instant.

Both of us stepping with great promptness back to where we had begun, I gulped for verification: "His name is Scorpion?"

There ensued from Isaac a scrambled-egg explanation that the horse was titled not for his personality but for the brand on his right hip. Rob and I looked: yes, a spidery long-tailed script M brand— *M* . Isaac's explication of the brand sounded to me as if the horse originated on a ranch which belonged to the Mikado. Later Lucas clarified that the *M* was the mark of the Mankato Cattle Company in North Dakota, and *No, Angus, I wouldn't know either what a Mankato horse is doing six hundred miles from home, nor would I ask into the matter as long as I had a firm bill of sale from Isaac.*

There in the Reese corral I cast a glance at Rob. Studying the big brown horse gravely, he told me: "It's your funeral, McAngus." But I knew from the way his head was cocked that he would be pleased to own half of this lofty creature.

While I was making up my mind about Scorpion, Isaac Reese was eyeing my colossal saddle on the Dantley nag. He inquired dubiously, "Do you came from Texus?"

"No, not quite that bad. How much do you want for this fanciful horse?"

> *Flow gently, sweet Afton, among thy green braes,*
> *Flow gently, I'll sing thee a song in thy praise;*
> *My Mary's asleep by thy murmuring stream—*
> *Flow gently, sweet Afton, disturb not her dream.*

Songtime in the schoolroom each week hinged on whatever Burns was in my mind just then and wherever Susan Duff's fine clear lilt led us. Neither premise was much my choice. But a thousand hymns had built Susan a voice, even I had to admit, and I'd found it was like pulling teeth to draw song suggestions from my other pupils, even though the schoolyard often rang with one chant or another. Children are their own nation and they hold their anthems to themselves. Ritually, though, I tried to pry music out of them:

"You're like a school for the mute today. Now who'll tell, please, what we can sing next?"

"I know one, Mr. McCaskill," piped Davie Erskine, standing and swallowing a number of times. Here was surprise.

"Do you, Davie? Can we hear it now?"

Another salvo of swallows. Then out quavered:

> *I came down from Cimarron, alooking for a job*
> *riding for the outfit they call the Jinglebob.*
> *The boss told me "Stranger, let's have ourselves some fun.*
> *Come and throw your saddle on our horse called Zebra Dun."*
> > *Oh, that old zebra dun,*
> > *that bucking son of a gun,*
> > *a-pitching his walleyed fit,*
> > *while upon him I did sit.*
> *The punchers came and gathered, laughing up their sleeves*
> *counting on their zebra bronc to do just what he pleased.*
> *And when I hit the saddle, old Dunny quit this earth*
> *went right up to try the sky, for all that he was worth.*

Susan Duff was wrinkling her nose at Davy's minstrelsy. But as soon as I gave her a severe look, she joined in the chorus with Davie and me, and the rest of the children followed her. Onward Davie warbled with his verses:

> *Old Dunny pawed the moon and passed right by the sun*
> *He chased some clouds a while then came down like a ton.*
> *You could see the tops of mountains under our every jump*
> *But I stayed tight upon his back just like the camel's hump.*
>
> *We bucked across the prairie, scattered gophers as we went*
> *kicked the cook and stewpot right through the boss's tent.*
> *But when the fray was over and Zebra done all he did*
> *No doubt was left in this world: that outlaw I had rid.*
>
> *The boss whooped hurrah! and threw the hat high off his head.*
> *He shook my hand until it ached and here is what he said:*
> *"If you can toss the lasso like you rode old Zebra Dun*
> *You're the man I have looked for since the year of one."*

"Davie Erskine, that was—remarkable." It was more than that. There were days when Davie was so drifty he could scarcely remember how many fingers he had. "And where did you learn that tune?"

"From Mr. Fox and Mr. Mitchell." I had to expend a long moment to translate Mr. Fox and Mr. Mitchell: the riders Perry and Deaf Smith. "They took supper with us, when they were riding for strays. They said it's a song from Texas," Davie reported as if the place was blue heaven. "Texas is where I'm going when I grow up."

"That may be, Davie. But for now you're going to arithmetic. Davie and Susan and Daniel and Einar, your book is page 132. Karen, show the others where they're to read, please."

At the close of school that day, I stepped out as always to watch the children start for home, the walkers up the South Fork, the riders up the North Fork. The white horseload of little Findlaters, Susan Duff aboard her blood bay and Jimmy Spedderson on his black pony with the blaze face and Betsy Frew atop her old sorrel, Davie Erskine urging his roan with Rachel tight behind him. It was Davie I was seeing most of all. Seeing older Davies, although their names were Rob and Angus, hearing their own tunes of a far place.

A late afternoon near the end of the school year, Ninian Duff appeared in the schoolroom as I was readying to go home.

"Angus, I've been by to see Archie and Willy and we have made our decision on next year's schoolteacher."

"Have you, now?" I'd been more and more aware that my time at the South Fork was drawing to a close, but it made me swallow to hear the fact. "I hope you've found a right one."

"Ay, we do too," he delivered right back. "It is you again. Temporary, of course, just for another year."

Three times more in the next three years, Ninian made that same ay-it-is-you-again call on me at the schoolhouse. "Ninian," I at last inquired of him, "did you ever happen to have a look at the word *temporary* in a dictionary?" But he knew as well as I did that the teaching job pleased me, and I was more than glad, too, to have its wage, because in that set of years spawned by the economic crash of 1893 the rewards of raising sheep were more aptly counted in small coins than in major currency. Even our prophet of profit Lucas looked perturbed, as if the sun had begun coming up in the wrong end of the sky. I don't know who among us in Scotch Heaven said in 1894 or 1895 or 1896 that despite the calendar, it still seemed to be 1893. But ever after, we spoke of this hard time as the years of '93.

In truth, though, the years of '93 were most harsh not in their lamb and wool prices—money is only money—but in abrupt occurrences among our people of the North Fork. Events that might have happened anyway took on darker shadow from the weight of the times. We had an unforgettable lesson when Archie Findlater lost half his band of sheep to a May blizzard, ewes and lambs smothered and frozen by the hundred out on the distant foothills where he had put them a week too soon. We had a heartsickening departure when the Spedderson family simply vanished, abandoning their ramshackle homestead and leaving in the night without a word to any of us. My next several days I taught with a lump in my throat, thinking of small Jimmy in that family that slunk from one piece of earth to the next.

And we had our first deaths. Gram Erskine, Donald's mother who had come with the Erskines and the Duffs on the ship to America when she was nearly eighty, died on a first fine green spring day. Odd, how the old so often last through the winter and then let go. Not a week after Ninian said the words over Gram Erskine, Rob and I had to be the ones to find Tom Mortensen. We were moving a bunch of ewes and week-old lambs over onto a slope of new grass just south of my place, and from there we noticed that, chilly day though it was, no smoke was rising from the chimney of the Mortensen cabin. When the two of us went down to see, a magpie was strutting along the ridgepole of the cabin, watching us cagily. Tom we found sprawled beside his chopping block, on his side, curled up as if napping. I knelt beside him, had a look, and threw up. Rob saw over my shoulder and did the same.

"Lord of mercy, if there is one," Rob choked out after we both retched ourselves dry and I managed to go to the house for a blanket to put over Tom. Rob grabbed up a stone and flung it clattering along the cabin roof toward the black and white bird, causing the magpie to swim away silently through the air. "I'll find something here to make a coffin," he said. I said, "And I'll fetch Ninian."

At Ninian's I told him it looked as if Tom's heart had given out. He started to the house for his Bible, saying "I'll come in the wagon with Flora, she can help lay out the body."

"No. Don't bring Flora."

"Ay? Whyever not? Flora has seen a man dead before."

"Not like this one. Ninian, the magpies have been at his eyes."

Death had been to Nethermuir, too. I remember bringing out the letter, small taut handwriting on it I did not recognize, when I came back from a grocery trip into Gros Ventre, and Rob at the wagon ripping it open as quick as he saw that writing. The news was on his face, although he read all the letter before passing it to me with the words, "My father's dead." Vare Barclay in the woodyard of the wheelshop, my father and Lucas beside him; Vare who had given me work as his clerk—the letter was from Rob's sister Adair, telling that her mother could not bring herself to write yet, that the Barclay house on River Street had been sold for what little they could get, that she and her mother would live now with Rob's oldest brother, who was closing down the wheelwrighting but would try to stay in business by making wheelbarrows and suchlike small stuff. As much sadness as paper can absorb was in that letter.

Rob set his jaw to go into the house to tell Judith and then make the ride into town to tell Lucas. But first he put a hand on my shoulder. "We were right to come, Angus. Hard as times ever can get here, we're better off than them over across in Scotland." I thought of Rob's mother and young Adair, being seen to in a household not their own. Being seen to. Not much of a prospect in life, not much at all. I had sheep waiting and school preparation waiting, but I stood and watched the erect American back of Rob as he took the news of his father's death into the house on Breed Butte. And watched again not half a year later, when word came that his mother, too, had passed away, dwindled away really. The strangest news there is, death across a distance; the person as alive as ever in your mind the intervening time until you hear, and then the other and final death, the one a funeral is only preliminary to, confusedly begins.

"By Jesus, the woollies do make a lovely sight," intoned Lucas. "If we could just sell them as scenery, ay?"

The time was September of 1896, a week before shipping the lambs, and Lucas and Rob and I were holding a Saturday war council on the west ridgeline of Breed Butte where we could meanwhile keep an eye on our grazing bands. By now Rob and Lucas's sheep had accumulated into two oversize bands, nearly twenty-five hundred altogether, as Rob kept back the ewe lambs each year since '93 rather than send them to market at pitiful prices. The band he and I owned in partnership I always insisted keeping at a regular thousand, as many as my hay would carry through a winter. So here they were in splendid gray scatter below us, six years of striving and effort, three and a half thousand prime ewes and a fat lamb beside each of them, and currently worth about as much as that many weeds.

"Next year is going to be a bit tight," Rob affirmed, which was getting to be an annual echo out of him.

"These tight years are starting to pinch harder than I'm comfortable with," he was informed by Lucas. Lucas's Jerusalem, Gros Ventre, was not prospering these days. Nowhere was prospering these days. I noticed how much older Lucas was looking, his beard gray now with patches of black. The years of '93 had put extra age on a lot of people in Montana. "So, Robbie lad, we have sheep galore. Now what in the pure holy hell are we going to do with them?"

"Prices can't stay down in the well forever," Rob maintained. "People still have to wear clothes, they still have to eat meat."

Lucas squinted at the neutral September sun. "But how soon can we count on them getting cold and hungry enough?"

"All right, all right, you've said the big question. But Lucas, we've got to hang onto as many sheep as we can until prices turn around. If we don't, we're throwing away these bands we've built up."

"Robbie," said Lucas levelly, "this year we've got to sell the ewe lambs along with the wether lambs. Even if we have to all but give the little buggers away with red bows on them, we've just got to—"

"I'll meet you halfway on that, how about," Rob put in with a smile.

"Halfway to what, bankruptcy?" retorted Lucas in as sharp a tone as I had ever heard from him.

I saw Rob swallow, the only sign of how tense a moment this was for him. Then he brought it out: "Halfway on selling the lambs, Lucas. I'm all for selling the ewe lambs, just as you say. But this year let's keep the wether lambs."

"Keep the wethers?" Lucas stared astounded at Rob. "What in the name of Christ for? Are you going to make history by teaching the wethers"—which was to say, the castrated male sheep whose sole role was mutton—"how to sprout tits and have lambs?"

"We'd keep them for their wool," Rob uttered as rapidly as he could say it. "Their wool crop next summer. Lucas, man, if we keep the wethers until they're yearlings they'll shear almost ten pounds of wool apiece. And if wool prices come back up to what they were—"

Lucas shook his head to halt Rob and brought up a stub to run vigorously along his beard. "I never listen to a proposition beyond the second *if*."

"Lucas, it's worth a try. It's got to be." If conviction counted, Rob right then would have had the three of us in bullion up to our elbows. "See now, the man McKinley is sure to be president, and that'll be like money in the bank for the sheep business." True, there was talk that McKinley could bring with him a tariff on Australian wool. If he did, prices for our fleeces then could climb right up. Pigs could fly if they had wings, too.

"Angus, what do you say to this new passion of Robbie's for wethers?"

"Maybe it's not entirely farfetched," I conceded, earning myself a mingled look from Rob.

Lucas still looked skeptical. "Here's the next thing you can enlighten me about, Robbie—how in holy hell do you handle that many sheep next summer? Tell me that, ay?" I knew it already was costing dear on them to hire herders for their two bands while Rob and I shared the herding of our one, and for them to add a third herder—

He was ready, our Rob. "I'll herd the wether band myself. Judith will have kittens about my doing it." And well she might, because with Rob herding in the mountains all summer she would need to manage everything else of the homestead, not to mention three daughters. "But she'll just have to have them, she married Breed Butte when she married me."

I regarded Rob for a waitful moment, Lucas glancing uncomfortably back and forth between us. Finally I said what was on my mind and Lucas's, even if it didn't seem to be within a hundred miles of Rob's:

"That leaves just one band of sheep unaccounted for."

"Yours and mine, of course," Rob spoke up brightly. "And

there's where I have a proposition for you, Angus. If you'll take our band by yourself next summer, I'll give you half of my half."

I made sure: "On the wool and the lambs both?"

"Both."

Translated, half of Rob's half meant that I would receive three-fourths of any profit—wool and lambs both, the man had said it—on our band of sheep next year. And if wool went up as Rob was betting on . . . if lamb prices followed . . . Never listen to a proposition beyond the second *if*, ay, Lucas?

"Done." I snapped up Rob's offer, which would make me money while he made money for himself and Lucas on the wethers. "That is, if Lucas agrees to your end of it."

Lucas studied the two of us, and then the three-about-to-be-four bands of sheep below.

"There are so goddamn many ways to be a fool a man can't expect to avoid them all," he at last said, as much to the sheep as to us. "All right, all right, Robbie, keep the wethers. We'll see now if '97 is the year of years, ay?"

Let me give the very day of this. The twentieth of April, 1897. Here in the fourth springtime that I had watched arrive outside the windows of the South Fork school, I perched myself on the water-bucket stand at the rear of the classroom while Karen Peterson, small but great with the occasion, sat at my big desk reading to us from the book of stories.

"One more sun," sighed the king at evening, "and now another darkness. This has to stop. The days fly past us as if they were racing pigeons. We may as well be pebbles, for all the notice life takes of us or we of it. No one holds in mind the blind harper when he is gone. No one commemorates the girl who grains the geese. None of the deeds of our people leave the least tiny mark upon time. Where's the sense in running a kingdom if it all just piffles off into air? Tell me that, whoever can."

"If you will recall, sire—"

In the trance of Karen's reading, even Daniel Rozier squirmed only ritually, and I took quiet pleasure in seeing those still rows of oh so familiar heads in front of me. I swear to heaven Susan Duff could have ruled France with the crown of her head. How such chestnut luster and precise flow of tress had derived from old dust-mop Ninian was far beyond me. But Davie Erskine's crownhair

flopped in various directions and no definite one, and that seemed
distinctly Erskinian. But then there was the bold round crown of
Eddie Van Bebber, so that you'd have thought half the brains of the
human race were packed under there, and Eddie Van Bebber was
only barely bright enough to sneeze.

*"Why is it that the moon keeps better track of itself than we manage
to? And the seasons put us to shame, they always know which they are,
who's been, whose turn now, who comes next, all that sort of thing. Why
can't we have memories as nimble as those? Tell me that, whoever can."*

"Sire, you will recall—"

Each of those South Fork and Scotch Heaven heads in front of
me, a mind that I as teacher was to make literate and numerate.
The impossibly mysterious process of patterning minds, though.
How do we come to be the specimens we are? Tell me that, whoever can.

*"Oblivion has been the rule too long. What this kingdom needs in the
time to come is some, umm, some blivion. There, that's it, we need to
become a more blivious people. Enough of this forgettery. But how to do
it, it will take some doing. What's to be done? Tell me that, whoever
can."*

"If you will recall, sire, this morning you named a remembrancer."

*"Eh? I did? I mean, I did. And what a good idea it was, too. For a
change things are going to be fixed into mind around here. Send me this
remembering fellow."*

"Bring forth the king's remembrancer!"

In time to come, during what the fable king would call blivion, I
always remembered Daniel Rozier more vividly than Karen Peterson, and in no way under heaven was that fair.

In time to come, when Susan Duff had grown and herself become
a teacher in Helena—I've always been sure that Helena is the better for it—I could wonder if I truly affected that in any meaningful
way.

In time to come, when Davie Erskine—

But that was waiting some hundreds of days to come, Davie's
time. Memory still had everything to make between here and there.

This was a full-fledged spring day in the Two Medicine country,
breezy along with sunny, melt and mud along with greening grass
and first flowers. The afternoon was better than my afterschool
chore, which was to call on the replacement teacher newly arrived

at Noon Creek. Old Miss Threlkeld, who held forth there since Cain and Abel, toward the end of winter had suffered palpitation of the heart, and about this sudden successor of hers I more than half knew what to expect and fully dreaded it.

"Ramsay is her name," Ninian Duff reported, "they are a new family to here, down from Canada. Man and wife and daughter. The Mrs. seems to be something of an old battle-axe, I do have to say." Coming from Ninian, that was credential for her indeed. "They bought the relinquishment up there to the west of Isaac Reese," he went on, "with a bit of help from Isaac's pocket from what I hear."

Given the basis that Isaac Reese headed the Noon Creek board as Ninian did ours, I couldn't let pass the opportunity to declare: "Now there's the way for a school board to operate."

Ninian broadly ignored that and stated, "When you find a spare moment, Angus, you would do well to stop by the schoolhouse over across there and offer hello. Our schools are neighbors and it would not hurt us to be."

"Maybe not severely," I had to agree, and now Scorpion and I were descending from the divide between our valleys to Noon Creek, a prairie stream twice as twisty as the North Fork ever thought of being. Scorpion was pointed to the country where I bought him—the Noon Creek schoolhouse was within easy eyeshot of Isaac Reese's horse ranch—and I wondered if he held horse memories of this stretch of territory. "Skorp Yun, lad, what about that?" I inquired of him and patted his rich-brown velvet neck. Scorpion's ears twitched up and I suppose that was my answer, as much as the horse clan was willing to tell a man.

A quick how-do here and home was my intention. This schoolhouse was much like mine—for that matter, so was its attendant pair of outhouses—except for standing all but naked to the wind, Noon Creek providing only a thin sieve of willows instead of the South Fork's broadback clumps of cottonwoods. Ask any dozen people passing and thirteen of them would tell you my school site was the obvious superior.

Pleased with that and armored with the thought that, however howlingly formidable Mrs. Battle-Axe Ramsay might try to be, I was the senior teacher hereabout, I tied Scorpion beside the Noon Creek teacher's horse and strode to the schoolhouse.

"Hello, anyone," I called in, and followed my words through the doorway.

A woman did look up from the teacher's desk. A woman whose shoulders drew back nobly and whose breasts came out nobler yet. A woman my age or less. A woman with the blackest of black hair done into a firm glossy braid, and with perfect round cheeks and an exactly proportionate chin and a small neat nose, and with direct blue eyes. A glory of a woman.

She granted me an inquiring half-smile, the rest of her expression as frank as a clock. "Hello," she enunciated, although what was being said was And What Is Your Business Here, If Any?

I told her me. And made about as much impression as a mosquito alighting on a stone fence.

"I am called Anna Ramsay," she stated in return, and I was going to need to ask Ninian what he thought a battle-axe talked like. Hers was a liltful voice which may have paused in Canada but only after fully flowering in Scotland.

"I'm the teacher at the South Fork school, over across, Mrs. Ramsay," I hurried to clarify.

"I am the teacher here," said she, "and it is Miss Ramsay."

Rob, Lucas, my unhearing father, my sorrowful mother, all who have ever known me, and generations yet to come: did you feel any of this catchbreath instant together with me, this abrupt realization in the throat that said here was the end to all my waiting, this surprise swale of time while I traced step by step back to the brain of Ninian the Calvinian? Ninian Duff had told me Mrs. Ramsay was an old battle-axe. He had told me the new Noon Creek teacher could stand a cordial look-in. He had never bothered to tell me those two formulations did not add up to the same person.

"Yes, well. Miss Ramsay, now. I, ah, seem to have been misinformed," I understated. "In any case, I came by to say hello"—her look told me that had been more than amply done by now, and not in ribbon-winning fashion—"and to see if there's any help I can offer."

"That's kind," she decided. "But I know of none."

In that case, Miss-not-Mrs. Ramsay, help me and my dazed tongue. What do you think the price of rice in China will reach? And are you the absolute lovely thing you appear to be under the crust?

"I'm trying to place your voice," I managed, true enough in its way: trying to coax the sound of it into my ears for as long as possible. "Your town in Scotland is—?"

"My town was Brechin." Brechin! Not all that far from my own Nethermuir, in the same county of Forfar. The magic that life is. She and I must have grown up sharing the same days of sun, the same storms from the sea.

I at once told her of my Nethermuir nativity, which did not noticeably set her afire with interest. "This Montana is different from old Scotland, isn't it," I imparted.

She regarded me steadily as ever. "Yes."

"Although," I began, and had no idea where to head from there.

"Mr. McCaskill, you've just reminded me, there is one matter you may be able to help me with." Anything, anything. Wheelbarrowing a mountain from here to there. Putting socks on snakes. "I find I'm in short supply of Montana geography books. Mr. Reese promised me more, but he's away buying horses."

"I have loads extra," I offered as fast as I could say it. Later would be soon enough to calculate whether or not I actually had any. "You're more than welcome to them."

Anna Ramsay shook that matchless head of hers, but in general perturbance at men who would see to horses before geography, rather than at my offer. "I've had to put the pupils to making their own."

I was as flummoxed now as a duck in thunder. "You've—?"

"Yes, they're a bit makeshift but better than nothing," she said, and gestured to the stack of them at the corner of her desk. They were pamphlets of as many colors as a rainbow, bound with yarn, with My Montana Book and each pupil's name bold on the cover. More than just that, the pamphlets were scissored into the unmistakable shape of the state of Montana, twice as wide as high and the entire left side that curious profile of a face looking down its bent nose at Idaho. I opened the pamphlet proclaiming Dill Egan, grade four, to be its author. Intently—not only was I curious but I was not going to forfeit this opportunity to hover in the near vicinity of Miss Anna Ramsay—as I say, intently as I could manage with so much distraction so close, I started through the pamphlet pages. PRODUCTS OF MONTANA, and Dill Egan's confident map of where gold, copper, cattle, sheep and sundry grains each predominated. AREA AND POPULATION OF MONTANA, 147,138 square miles and 132,159 persons respectively, and his enstarred map showing

Helena, Butte, Bozeman, Missoula, Great Falls, Billings, Miles City and the now twenty-four county seats. MOUNTAINS OF MONTANA and another map showing the western throng of ranges, Bitterroot and Cabinet and Garnet and Mission and Flathead and Swan and Tobacco Root and on and on until the Little Rockies and Big Snowys outposted the eastern majority of the state. DRAINAGES OF MONTANA and yet another map of all the rivers and what must have been every respectable creek as well, with the guiding message *The Continental Divide separates the Atlantic and the Pacific slopes of America.* MINERALS OF MONTANA. RAILROADS OF MONTANA. I had a sudden image of this brisk, beautiful woman beside me as the goddess of geography, fixing the boundaries of this careless world as unerringly as Job's prosecutor or even the U.S. General Land Office. Anna Ramsay's ten-year-olds all too evidently knew more about Montana than I did. Every one of them a Crofutt in the bud.

I swallowed hard. I took a look around me. High on the blackboard behind us was chalked the majestically handwritten single word:

chilblain

Other than it, the blackboard was not only freshly cleaned, it shone black. The best I could scrape together to remark was: "Your chalk keeps talking after school, does it?"

"Yes, that's tomorrow's word in the air," she explained. "I write a different one up there for each day. That way, when the pupils' eyes go wandering off into air, they at least are looking at how one word of the language is spelled."

"A sound principle," I vouched sagely, wishing I'd thought of it the first day I stepped into my South Fork classroom. Contemplate the miracle of *chilblain* spelling itself, even approximately, into the mind of Daniel Rozier. My eyes moved on from the blackboard. Her schoolroom gleamed like the Queen's kitchen. This Miss Ramsay seemed to be a stickler about everything.

"You, ah, you were a teacher in Scotland, were you?" I entirely unnecessarily asked.

"In a dame school, back in Brechin." It seemed to me a magnificent beneficence when she tilted her head ever so slightly and decided to add: "As you say, this is different."

I wanted to sing out to her, so are you, so are you. I wanted to hang Ninian Duff from a high tree by his beard. I wanted to go back out that schoolhouse door, turn myself around three times, and start this anew. I wanted—instead I managed to draw in enough breath to clear my head and free up my tongue: "I'll fetch the geographies to you. Tomorrow, I even could. And if there's anything else whatsoever you need—"

"Mr. Reese will be back from his beloved horses any day. It is his job to see that I have what the school needs." Again that first half-smile of hers and the simultaneous clocklike frankness, in which I desperately tried to discern a momentworth more of warmth than when I arrived. "Mr. McCaskill, I do appreciate that you came."

"It's been my pleasure, Miss Ramsay."

Riding home, I was the next thing beyond giddy. Scorpion must have compassed his own route around the west shoulder of Breed Butte and down to my homestead, or he and I would be circling there yet.

Astonishment. That was my word in the air. The coming of dusk was an astonishment, the last of this April day coloring a blue into the gray of the mountains as if sky had entered rock. My homestead was an astonishment, in expectant welcome there beside the North Fork like the front porch to the future. The greening grass, the dabbed yellow of buttercups, the creek rattling mildly over smooth stones, the rhythm of Scorpion's hooves against the earth, the ever-restless air of the Two Medicine country traveling over my skin, the pertinent Burns: *my heart was caught/before I thought,* astonishments all. For that matter, I was an astonishment to myself, how fertile for love I was. Is this life? Just when you have lived long enough to think you know yourself, behavior such as this crops out?

But the braided marvel that touched alive all these others. Anna Ramsay. Where, really, did I stand with her, after an acquaintance that would have barely boiled an egg? I didn't know. I didn't even know how to know. Thunder tumbling out of an absolute clear sky, was the way this had fallen on me. The one certainty I held was that the women I had met in my life so far were no training for this one.

Oh, I tried to tell myself whoa and slow. And by the time I'd cooked supper twice—my first try burned conclusively—I had myself half-believing I was somewhere near to sane again. Steady, Angus, don't rush in brainless. For that matter, Miss Anna Ramsay did not look anything like a person who tolerated rushing.

But I did go to bed with the thought that tomorrow, nothing known on earth could keep me from delivering those geography books to her.

"This was kind of you"—she, even more glorious on second inspection. "To make the ride over here so soon again."

"Not at all"—myself, earnest without even trying. "If one schoolkeeper can't lend a hand to another schoolkeeper, the world is a poor place."

Just over Anna's head as she stood behind her desk was her blackboard word for today, *accommodate*, which for the first time in my life I noticed contains more than one *m*.

"Mr. McCaskill, before you go"—I had no thought of that—"I do have something further I wonder if you might advise me about."

"Miss Ramsay, if I can I will. What?"

"How do you keep the big boys from playing pranks that have to do with"—she never blinked—"the girls' outhouse?"

With teacup delicacy I outlined to her the curative effects of the boys having to go in the brush. Throughout, she regarded me steadily. Then she swung to the schoolroom window and studied the willow supply along the creek. As I watched her at this it came to me that she was very much a practitioner of the Scottish verdict, Not Proven, this Anna Ramsay. Guilty or Innocent could stand on either side of a matter until their tongues hung out, but she was going to do justice firmly from the middle ground of proof and nowhere else. I also stored away forever the fact that her braid gloriously swung almost all the way down her glorious back.

Evidently she judged the Noon Creek willows ample to their duty, sufficient thatch of them to screen a boy but not enough to thwart the chilly seeking nose of the wind, for she turned around to me and nodded with spirit. "Yes, that should do it. Thank you for that advice, Mr. McCaskill. Well. I have grading—"

"As do I," I put in, as accommodating as can be imagined. "But now there's a question I need to put to you. I've visited your school, and I'd much like you to visit mine. We're holding a dance, Saturday next week. Could I see you there?"

She grew as intent as if I'd thrown her a major problem in multiplication. "It's early to say." Seeing my hope plummet, she provided me a half-smile to grapple it back up. "But possibly—"

"I could come for you."

"That won't be necessary."

"Oh, no trouble."

"But it would be." She was looking at me a bit askance, as if wondering how a grown man could not see that an extra stint on horseback equaled an inconvenience for himself. Anna Ramsay plainly could out-teach me in spelling and geography, but there was at least one variety of arithmetic she didn't yet understand.

"I'm sure others from Noon Creek will be attending," she elucidated for me, "and I can come with them."

Come in a congregation, come by your lovely lone self, come dogback or come in a purple carriage with wheels of gold, but just come. Aloud, I granted: "A sensible solution. I'll see you at South Fork then, on the night."

When I went to the lambing shed to relieve Rob that evening, he greeted me with: "And how is life among all you schoolkeepers?"

Already. The way news flew in a country with so few tongues to relay it, I never would comprehend.

Stiff as a poker, I retorted to Rob: "You seem to know at least as much about my doings as I do."

"Angus, Angus. Just because there's a fresh path worn this deep"—he indicated to his knee—"between the South Fork schoolhouse and the Noon Creek schoolhouse, I thought I might inquire."

"Well, you've done." But I couldn't stay miffed where Anna was concerned. "She needed a bit of help on a geography matter."

"Geography," Rob mused. "That's the word for it these days, is it."

"Rob, aren't you on your way home to supper?"

"You're certain sure you know what you're getting into with all this geography business? From what I hear, Miss Noon Creek is a bit of a snooty one."

I was outraged. "Speaking of snoots, you can just keep your own damn one out of—"

"All right, all right. If you're not in a mood to hear wisdom, you're not." The words were light enough, although behind them Rob still seemed peeved. But a day in overshoes in the muck of a lambing shed will do that to a man, and he sounded thoroughly himself when he went on: "Probably this is nothing you'll find near so interesting as geography, but Lucas brought out word today that wool is up to 12½ cents and lambs are climbing fine, too. This is the year we've been looking for, man." Rob had it right, the world and its price of wool and lambs was not what I wanted to think about, only Anna. However far gone he thought I was down romance's knee-deep road, he didn't know half of it. I was Anna dizzy, in an Anna tizzy. These days there seemed to be fresh blood in my veins, brewed by the maker of harem potions. But the relentless fact of Anna always in my mind also startled me constantly, if it can be said that way, and I will admit that it was a bit scaring, too.

At the end here of what I thought was perfectly normal lambing shed conversation, Rob cocked his head and asked: "Are you off your feed this spring, McAngus? You'd better come by and let Judith tuck a few solid suppers into you."

I said I would, soon, whenever that was, and Rob gave me one last askance glance and departed.

You could have counted the next ten days on my face. I went from remorse at how long it would be until I laid eyes on Anna again, to fevers that I wouldn't be prepared when I did. One morning I was gravely giving arthmetic when Susan Duff pointed out that I already had done so, not an hour before. And I suppose all my South Fork pupils were startled by the onslaught of Montana geography that befell them.

One thing I did know for dead-certain, and this was that my schoolhouse was going to be grandly ready to dance. At the close of class that Friday I prevailed on Davie Erskine to stay after and help me, and we moved the rows of desks along the walls and pushed my desk into a corner. Davie took out the stove ashes while I filled lanterns and trimmed wicks. There never has been a boy enthusiastic about a broom, so I next swept the floor myself in solid Medicine Lodge swamping style and put Davie to wiping the windows with old copies of the Choteau *Quill*.

"But Mr. McCaskill, it'll be dark out, why do the windows need to be clean?"

"On account of the moonbeams, Davie. You've got to let the moonbeams in on a dance, or people's feet will stick to the floor. Did you not know moonbeams are slick as soap, Davie?"

Davie gaped at me as if I already was askate on moonbeams, but he did the windows fine. Next I had him wash the blackboard, then fill our bucket with fresh drinking water from the creek. I swept and hummed, dusted and hummed, I even straightened the pictures of George and Abraham and gave them each a hum of joy, they always looked as if they needed cheer.

"Do you know this old tune, Davie?" I asked, for it seemed to me an impossibly dim prospect that anyone should go through this wonderful thing, life, knowing only songs of Texans and horses. "You don't? That's odd, for it seems to be addressed to you."

"Me?"

"Surely. Listen to it."

> *Dancing at the rascal fair,*
> *try it, Davie, if you dare,*
> *hoof and shoe, stag and mare,*
> *dancing at the rascal fair.*

Davie whipped through the last of his tasks as if afraid my lunacy might be catching. "Is there anything more, Mr. Mc-Caskill?"

"You've more than earned supper, Davie. And thank you the world, for your help here." I fished in my pocket and handed him a coin. From the size of Davie's eyes it was more of a coin than I'd intended, but no matter.

There was a thing more I wanted done, but I needed to be the doer. I went to the freshly washed blackboard and in my best hand, which was an urchin's scrawl compared to Anna Ramsay's, wrote large the next verse to come:

> *Dancing at the rascal fair,*
> *moon and star, fire and air,*
> *choose your mate and make a pair,*
> *dancing at the rascal fair.*

By last light of Saturday, the sun behind the peak called Phantom Woman and dusk graying the valley, people came. Rob and Judith. The Duffs and Erskines. I scattered oatmeal on the floor to help the moonbeams with our gliding. George Frew as ever was our fiddler, and the night began with the high beautiful tune of *Green Glens of Strath Spey*. I took a diplomatic first turn with

George's Mavis, toward convincing her that while I might never run a school the way she did, my dancing made up for it.

The first time we earliest dancers stopped to blow, Rob glanced over his shoulder to be sure Mavis Frew née Milgrim was nowhere in hearing and declared, "This place definitely dances better since you're the schoolkeeper, McAngus. What, have you put bed springs under the floor?"

I was gazing around fondly, awaiting what—who—I knew would come. Must come. "Owe it to George, not me. He fiddles better as a married man."

Judith put in, "There's a lesson there for you, Angus."

"You mean if I married, I'd be able to play the fiddle? Judith, that's surprising. What would I need to do to be able to play the piano?"

Rob chortled and batted my shoulder while Judith mocked a huff and declared: "Angus McCaskill, you are just impossible." Ah, Judith, but I no longer was. I was purely possible. I was possibility with its wings ready, these days. "You have me right," I mollified Judith though, "yet would you dance with me anyhow? Rob, there's paper and pen in my desk there, if you'd care to jot down for yourself how Judith and I do this."

"I'm lending her to you with two sound feet, so bring her back unbroken, hear?" he stipulated.

"Unbroken, nothing. She'll be downright improved." And Judith and I swung away together, Rob's two closest people in this world, who once had kissed hotly at one of these gatherings and could grin a little rue at each other that we never would again.

Archie and Grace Findlater came. *The Shepherd's Schottische*. The Hahns and Petersons and Van Bebbers came. *The Herring Lasses' Reel*. The Roziers from down the main creek, the Kuuvuses and Sedgwicks from town, they came and came.

"Angus, lad, you can hear this schoolhouse of yours a mile down the road." Lucas! And Nancy on his arm. This major night had brought even them.

"What, did you turn the Medicine Lodge over to the customers?" I asked incredulous.

"The same as. Toussaint showed up in town today, and so he's tending the saloon for me tonight. If you can call that tending—giving away a drink to anybody who has a story Toussaint wants to hear, which is to say everybody." Nancy, brown beside Lucas's ruddiness, already was making heads turn here and there in the dance crowd. "But there's more to life than what you can put in your pocket, ay?" concluded Lucas, squaring himself and casting a resolute look around my thronged schoolroom. "Good evening there, Ninian," he called as that lanky figure capered past, "you're as spry as King David up on his hind feet." I thought the beard was going to drop off Ninian when he saw Lucas here. Then Rob and Judith were beside us, a last dab of startlement on Rob's face as he said: "You didn't tell me we were going to have this pleasure, Lucas."

"I didn't want to spoil the surprise, Robbie. Nancy and I thought we'd come learn how to shake a leg."

When that didn't bring anything from Rob except a smile as neutral as he could make it, I rapidly inserted, "This is definitely the learning place and they tell me I'm the teacher. Nancy, may I have the first honor?" And next quick thing, out on the floor Lucas was paired with Judith, one handless sleeve on her back and the other meeting the grasp of her hand in the musical air, while Nancy went into the swirl with me—she did not really dance but moved quietly with me, a dark-eyed visitor from an earlier people.

After that tune, Lucas regathered Nancy and took her across to greet Sedge and Lila just as if he hadn't seen them a dozen times that day. Evening proceeded toward night. On and on the music flowed and the sweat rolled. Thank heaven George Frew's fiddling left arm was as oaken as the rest of him. Sedge taught us a square dance called *Bunch to the Middle* and we danced it until the floor would remember every step of it.

By the holy, I loved these people. This night I loved all of Scotch Heaven, the Two Medicine country, Montana, America, the sky over and the earth under. Who could not?

What I loved strongest of all entered now through my schoolroom doorway in a dark blue skirt and white shirtwaist and an ivory brooch at her throat. Anna. And her mother and father—surprisingly unprepossessing, for a pair who had given mankind such a gift—and others from Noon Creek, the Wainwrights and Egans and and Isaac Reese, all come in one wagon, and now entering our tuneful school eager for the reward of that ride.

"Welcome across the waters to Scotch Heaven," Rob called out to this delegation and drew a laugh from all. The South Fork and

North Fork and Noon Creek taken together, you could still skim your hat across.

"Brung the Ramsays along to translate for us," gruffed the rancher Thad Wainwright. "I damn well might've known, the only heaven I'd get into I need to learn to talk Scotch to do it."

Hoping for battle-axe avoidance this first night, I waited until Anna's mother and father took a dance together, then seized my chance to go over and greet Anna alone. "I see your chalk keeps talking after school, too," she said of my rascal fair verse in white on the blackboard. Which I took as approval, on the grounds that it didn't seem to be disapproval.

"That chalk must have caught the habit somewhere. Do you know, it took me by the hand as I was walking past and made me write that?"

"I suppose you objected strenuously all the while?"

"Objecting is a thing I try not to believe in, particularly the strenuous kind. Just for example, Miss Ramsay, I'm hoping you won't object to a turn around the floor with me right now? *Sir Patrick MacWhirr* wasn't meant to be stood to."

A flicker went through her steady eyes, but if that was hesitation I'll never mind a dose so small. Here came something else I'd hoped, her sidelong half-smile. Then up came her hand, writing in the air between us as if onto her Noon Creek blackboard. I waited, yes, astonished, while whatever it was got elaborately spelled into the atmosphere of my schoolroom. When done, she pronounced for me with vast amused deliberation: *"unobjectionable."* And onto the dance floor I pranced with her.

> *To Noroway, to Noroway!*
> *To Noroway over the foam!*
> *The King's fair bride from Noroway—*
> *oh, Sir Pat, Sir Pat, Sir Pat, Sir Pat!—*
> *'Tis thee must sail and bring her home!*

"I'll need to see whether there's a floor left for my pupils, after tonight."

"If there's not, you will have to teach outside as did the ancient Greeks."

"Outside, were they. Small wonder all they ever knew how to talk was Greek. Think the tongues they'd speak if they'd gone to school to the pair of us." She had to smile fully at that, and so did my heart. Anna was alive with loveliness, she was mine in my arms for as long as I could make the moment. "And what would they think of this at the Brechin dame school?"

I saw the new moon, late yester e'en,
with the old moon in her arm!
If we go to sea, oh my dear queen—
oh, dear queen, dear queen, dear queen, dear queen!—
I fear we must come to harm!

"They would think this Scotch Heaven of yours is a shameless place." My heart keeled sideways. "Cavorting in a place of learning. See up there, even your presidents think so." The jounce of the dancing had tilted Washington and Lincoln toward each other, and they did look like two old streetcorner solemns, confiding the world's latest waywardness to each other.

"I hope that's not what you think," I hoped desperately.

"If a schoolhouse is the only place big enough for a dance," she postulated, "then the schoolhouse should be used."

"My own thought, exactly. And so we'll be dancing next at Noon Creek, will we?"

I particularly meant the two of us. She only granted, "The school board has the say of any dance. But I'll not object."

The sails were hoist on Mononday morn,
the wind came up on Wenensday!
It blew and blew and blew so forlorn—
oh, Sir Pat and Queen, Sir Pat and Queen!—
blew Sir Pat and Queen from Noroway!

I bided my time for a small eternity—it must have been fully the next two tunes' worth—before dancing with her again. But the wait was worth it, for during this circuit of the floor she sanctioned my suggestion that "Miss Ramsay" and "Mister Mc-Caskill" might just as well be discarded to give "Anna" and "Angus" some wear. My aim this night was to dance with Anna enough times to begin to ratify us as a couple, yet not so many as to alarm her. So I didn't mind—much—when Allan Frew took a turn with her. From his doggish look toward me I knew that Al-

lan knew I would pound him back to milkteeth if he tried seriously to get in my way with Anna. She even went a few rounds
with Isaac Reese and made him and his drooping mustache look
almost presentable. Then Rob danced with Anna to *Brig of Dee*
while I did with Judith, and I saw Judith's eyebrow inch up at
Rob's nonstop chat there, but I knew that was just him being him. I
thanked my stars that Rob was not in the running with me for
Anna. Indeed, peer along the lovelit road ahead as far as I could, I
saw no one else who was. Which was wondrous and sobering and
exhilarating and bewildering and intimidating and sublime all in the
same pot together.

So spirited was *Brig of Dee* that it made Thad Wainwright come
by and announce, "Angus and Rob, I got to hand it to you. You
Scotchmen sure do know how to make feet move. Only one thing
missing from tonight, so far's I can tell. How come no bagpipes?"

Lord of mercy, when was the rest of mankind going to quit thinking of us as wild Highlanders? Past Thad I caught Rob's eye-rolling
look, and if Lucas hadn't been across the room trading sheep
theories with Willy Hahn, I knew he'd have given a response that
would rattle the room. The soul of moderation, I only told Thad:
"We thought there's enough wind in this country without making
more."

"It's kind of disappointing though, you know? With all you
Scotchmen here under one roof, the rest of us figured we were going
to see some real flinging." The Noon Creek rancher chuckled a regret and moved on.

*Moon and star, fire and air,/choose your mate and make a
pair,/dancing at the rascal fair,* my verse on the blackboard spoke to
me over Thad's retreating shoulder. It made me remember aloud to
Rob: "Fergus the Dervish!"

Rob roared a laugh. "Fergus and his Highland whoops! He'd
show old Thad some steps."

"Why don't we? The two of us saw Fergus enough times at the
rascal fair."

"You think we can?"

"Man, is there something we can't do?"

"We haven't found it yet, have we. You're right, you're right, it
will take Barclay and McCaskill to show these Noon Creek geezers
what dancing is."

"McCaskill and Barclay," I set him straight, "but you're correct enough other than that. See if our man Geoge can play *Tam Lin*, why not, while I tend to the rest."

Apprehensively, Judith began: "Now, you two—"

"No, love, it's we three, you're into this, too. And whoever Angus can inveigle into risking her—"

I was across the room before my feet knew they were moving. I hadn't a wisp of a clue as to how this person Anna would react to a dancing exhibition. Here was the time of times to find out.

"It's all for the cause of education, of course," I prattled to her while those direct blue eyes worked on me. "Instruction for the world at large, think of it as."

The smile I wanted began to sidle onto her face. "I'll believe you," granted Miss Anna Ramsay, and lightly grasped the arm I proffered, "but thousands would not."

With Anna gloriously beside me, I hadn't even a qualm about attempting the next impossibility across the room.

"SING?!" Lucas repeated as if I'd asked him to shed all his clothing. "Angus, what in goddamn hell"—he stoppered that because of Anna's presence, but there still was considerable flame in his next try. "Angus, lad, I hate to say that your common sense flew out the hole in your hat, but asking for singing from me . . ."

"Lucas, you're the only other one of us here who's been to the rascal fair and watched old Fergus. If Rob and I are going to step out here and show how it's done in Nethermuir, we need you to sing the tune of it."

Lucas was shaking his head vehemently when Anna spoke in firm fashion: "Mr. Barclay, we in Brechin always heard that the men of Nethermuir are brothers to the lark."

That halted his head. "Well, yes, I know that was always said," Lucas confirmed without undue modesty. "We once in a while even said something of the sort ourselves. *Tam Lin*, did you mention, Angus?" I nodded. Lucas swallowed as if to be sure he had a throat there, then looked at Nancy. If answer passed between them I never saw it, but Lucas now said: "All right, all right, if I can remember any word of it."

> *Oh, you must beware, maidens all,*
> *who wear gold in your hair*
> *don't come or go by Linfield Hall*
> *for young Tam Lin is there.*

> *Dark and deep lay the wood of night*
> *and eerie was the way*
> *as fair Janet with hair so bright*
> *toward Linfield Hall did stray.*

I grant that other nationalities are known to dance, but it is my hypothesis that they must have learned how from the Scots. You can't but admit that a land of both John Knox and Robert Burns is nimble, and we like to think that quality comes out on us at both ends, head and feet. Earlier that night I danced a reel with Flora Duff, who was wide as any other two women there, and she moved like a rumor. And now Rob and Judith and Anna and I were the four-hearted dancer of all dancers, gliding to and from, following the weave of the tune, answering Lucas's unheavenly but solid voice with the melody of ourselves, saluting the night and life with our every motion and capping them all with the time-stopping instant when Rob and I faced one another, each with a hand on a hip and the other arm bent high above head, and our two throats as one flung the exultant Highland cry, *hiiyuhh!*

> *Her skirt was of the grass-green silk,*
> *her cloak of velvet fine.*
> *Around her neck so white as milk*
> *her fox-red furs entwine.*

> *About the dead hour of the night*
> *she heard Tam's bridles ring.*
> *Her maidenly heart beat with might,*
> *her pulse began to sing.*

Put away geography and numeration and the presidents from yon to hither, pupils of mine and of my partner in whirl Anna, and write for us books of that dance. Scissor her lovely profile down the left of your pages and in eternal ink say how forthright she is even when set to music. *Miss Ramsay seems to look into the face of the tune in the air and say, yes, you are what music should be.* Make an exact report of the way she and I blend into a single dancing figure and then shift swiftly into two again and next meld with

Rob and Judith. You will please find a line somewhere there, too, for the heady Scotch Heaven serenade this schoolroom has never heard before tonight: *hiiiyuhhh!*

> *She heard the horseman's silv'ry call,*
> *'Come braid your golden hair*
> *in the fine manse of Linfield Hall*
> *for I, Tam Lin, am there.'*
>
> *She went within that hall of Lin*
> *fair Janet on her ride*
> *and now you maidens know wherein*
> *dwell Tam Lin and his bride.*
> *HiiiiYUHHHH!*

Our final whoop, Rob and I agreed, could have been heard by old Fergus the Dervish himself wherever he was cavorting in Scotland just then.

The crowd too gave us whoops and hoots and claps of commendation as we two pairs of flingers vacated the floor to merely mortal dancers and Lucas accepted bravos from all directions. Escorting Anna off—I could have made a career of just that—I asked, "Don't you suppose that changed their minds any about schoolhouse dances, over across in Brechin?"

Where she held my arm I felt a lightest affirming squeeze. "If anything could," was her voice's lilting version.

When I reluctantly left Anna's side, I saw Rob gesture for me to come over where he and Judith were catching their breath between chat with Archie and Grace Findlater. Rob had a strange distant smile on him. As I came up, he gripped my shoulder. "I have to hand it to you, Angus, you do get an idea now and again."

I must have grinned like a moonchild, for Rob's head went from side to side and he expostulated, "No, no, I don't mean her. Any man with one eye that'll open could get that idea. What I mean is our Fergus fling. Angus, it made me think back to all our rascal fairs together and Nethermuir."

"What, are you growing sentimental in your old age?"

He gave me the caught smile of a mildly guilty boy. Whatever this was about, it had put that joyous shine on him of the day we stood on the Greenock dock. But he said only, "The surprises of this thing life. A person just never does know, does he." George Frew's fiddle began *The Soldier Lad's Love's Lament.* "And now that I've danced with you, McAngus, do you mind overmuch if I take a turn with my wife?"

I got myself beside Anna one last time as the goodbyeing was going on, and began: "You know, of course, tonight was a mark your Noon Creek dance will have to match."

"We will strive," she answered.

"It'll not be easy. Much of the music of the world got used up here tonight."

"We will dust off any that's left, you needn't worry. By now I know you are not a man for standing."

"There, you see? A mere few hours in my schoolroom and you've already learned a thing." Her parents were waiting at the door, I was drawing heavy looks from that mother of hers.

"Well. Goodnight, Anna," I finally had to say.

"Yes." A bit slow from her, too, I noted with hope. "Goodnight, Angus."

But before she could turn, I blurted: "Anna, I'd like to call on you."

That direct look of hers. "Then why don't you?"

A fly buzzed uselessly against the window of the Ramsay parlor, herald of my audience thus far with Anna's parents.

"So, Mr. McCaskill, you too are of Forfar," speaks the main dragon. "That surprises me."

Margaret Ramsay, mother of Anna, looked as if she could out-general Wellington any day of the week. A drawn, bony sort of woman with none of Anna's adventurous curves, she seemed to have room in herself only for skepticism toward the male race. Beside her sat probably her prime reason for that. Peter Ramsay was a plump, placid man who sat with his hands resting on his belly, the first finger of his right hand gripped in his left, in the manner a cow's teat would be grasped. Ready to milk one hand with his other and evidently content to spend a lifetime at it. It stretched my imagination several ways beyond usual, as to how these two beings could have made Anna.

I was trying to be extra careful with my tongue, but: "I'd be interested to know, Mrs. Ramsay, in what aspect I look so different from other Forfar folk. My face, is it? I should have put on my other one."

If vinegar can smile, Margaret Ramsay smiled. "Of course I meant surprised to find someone else from Forfarshire so near at hand here in Montana." She paused a mighty moment to let me comprehend the utter justice of her viewpoint. Next she needed to know: "You were schooled where?"

"At a 'venture school in Nethermuir."

"I see. Anna and I both matriculated from the dame school in Brechin."

"So I understand." *I am a famous scholar, see./ Graddy-ated and trickle-ated, me./I've been to Rome in Germany/and seen the snows of Araby.* I swallowed that safely away and put forth: "Education is the garment that never wears, they say."

"And what of your family?"

I looked squarely at her. "Dead," I said.

Margaret Ramsay regarded me. "I mean, of course, what of them in life."

My father the ironhand, encased in his deafness; my mother the mill worker; myself the tall alone boy treading the lightless streets of old stone town Nethermuir . . . try sometime to put those into parlor speech. Anna was interested and encouraging—Anna could do me no wrong—but it was uphill all the way, trying to tell of the wheelshop years.

Sun lightened the room a half-minute, cloud darkened it, the day's weather restlessly coming and going up there on the divide of the continent. This Ramsay place all but touched the mountains. Until humans learned to hang to the side of a crag with one hand and tend livestock with the other, here was as far as settlement could go. I hoped these Ramsays knew what they were in for when winter's winter, which is to say January and February, howled down off the Rockies onto them. From where I sat I could look right up into the granite face of Jericho Reef through the curtain, the window where the fly was haplessly zizzing.

"You've seen the Bell Rock lighthouse," I thought of abruptly, "off from Arbroath?"

"I passed it close on a schooner once," spoke Peter Ramsay, his most extensive contribution to that day's conversation. "Surprising."

Well, he didn't know the half of it yet. I began telling of Alex-

ander McCaskill of the Bell Rock. Of his day-by-day fear of his
ocean workplace, of his daily conquer of the fact that a boat is a
hole in the water. Of he and the other Arbroath stonemen encircling
the engineer Stevenson as the first foundation block of the lighthouse was laid and its dedication recited, *May the Great Architect of
the Universe complete and bless this building.* Of the fog-pale day the
boat did not come and did not come, the floodtide rising to take the
Bell Rock, dry-mouthed Stevenson drinking poolwater like a dog to
try to say bravery to his men, the random pilot boat at last. Of the
three-year materializing of the round beacon tower there beside the
verge of Scotland, a single bold sliver of brightwork in the sea. And
if the impression was left that my great-grandfather had been the
right hand of the colossal Stevenson throughout that feat of bringing
fire to the sea, I didn't mind.

"Interesting," granted Margaret Ramsay. "Interesting indeed."

"I'll walk out with you," Anna said when it came my time to go.

Air was never more welcome to me. Whoof. Picklish Meg Ramsay was going to be something to put up with. But Anna was worth
all.

As soon as we were out of sight around a corner of the house, I
put her hand on the back of mine and urged, "Quick, give me a
pinch."

She lightly did and inquired, "And what was that for?"

"I needed to be sure my skin is still on me."

Anna had to smile. "You did well. Even Mother thought so, I
could tell."

"Well enough to be rewarded by my favorite teacher?"

Anna let me kiss her. Not as boundlessly as I wished, but amply
enough for a start. Then she gave my arm a squeeze, and went
back to the house.

A recess soon after that, I stepped from my classroom into the
mud room for something from my coat. The outside door had been
left open, and in from the girls' field of play was wafting the clear
lilt of Susan Duff.

> *The wind and the wind and the wind blows high,*
> *the rain comes scattering through the sky.*
> *He is handsome, she is pretty,*
> *boy and girl of the golden city.*

I smiled at all that brought back, song of every schoolyard in Scotland. I bent to my coat search and hummed along as Susan sang on.

> *The wind and the wind and the wind blows high,*
> *the rain comes scattering through the sky.*
> *Anna Ramsay says she'll die*
> *if her lover says goodbye.*

That took care of my humming. What was coming next verse, I could guess all too definitely.

> *The wind and the wind and the wind blows high,*
> *the rain comes scattering through the sky.*
> *A bottle of wine to tell his name—*
> *Angus McAsker, there's his fame.*

I wondered whether everybody on this cheek of the earth knew the future of Anna and me except the pair of us. Maybe it was time we found out, too.

Those next honeyed weeks. Anna and I, as spring wove itself around us in leaf and bud and the recess-time sounds of scamper by our unpenned school flocks. In mid-May the dance at her schoolhouse, where it all but took a pardon from the governor for anyone other than myself to be permitted a whirl on the floor with Anna. Evenings, as many as we could possibly find, of kissing and fondling and the talk that was the spring air's equivalent of those. And before I was even done wishing for it to happen, the momentous gift out of the blue, the departure of those parents of hers. They went north with Isaac Reese and a great aggregation of his workhorses—Anna said it was like seeing a lake decide to move itself, the flow of manes and the slow patterned swirl of the herd—for a summer of building railroad crossings and plowing fireguard strips along the route of the Great Northern Railway. Peter Ramsay, wherever he hid the knack for it, was to be Reese's horse tender, and Anna's mother was to cook for the crew of teamsters. The single bit of grit for me in this fine news was that it encompassed Anna. As soon as school was out, she was to go up and join her mother as second cook. "This is our chance to get something ahead at last," she told me frankly of the rare

Ramsay bonanza of three good wages at once. As I was to do much the similar myself by going into the mountains with my and Rob's sheep, there was no arguing the case, really. I put aside pangs about a summer apart as best I could and concentrated on gaining every possible moment with Anna until then.

When May granted us its last Saturday night and the end-of-school dance at my schoolhouse, it was a roaring one even for a South Fork event, as if everyone was uplifted by the green year grinning at us. The hour went to late and then rounded midnight into early, and jigged on from there.

When the dance at last called itself done at nearly three in the morning, I was to see Anna home—we were a lovely distance past that essential rung of the courting ladder—as soon as my schoolhouse had been set to rights.

"Swamping is to sweeping what whaling is to fishing," I was enlightening her as I displayed my broom style.

"And where were you so fortunate as to learn the art of swamping?" she asked from where she was closing and locking the schoolroom windows. Lovely, to see that woman stretch to the window locks, her braid swaying free as a black silk tassel when her head tilted back.

"There's a standard answer to that among swampers," I informed her, "which I'll take refuge in: 'At my mother's knee and other low joints.'" This in fact wasn't a time when I particularly wanted to recount Rob and me arriving into the Two Medicine country and my subsequent career in the Medicine Lodge. I had seen again tonight what I'd begun to notice at the other dances, that while Anna plainly prized Lucas for the rare specimen he was, she was impervious to Rob. I knew I was going to have to sort that out at some soon point, but for now it merely seemed to me Rob's hard luck.

She turned enough from her chore to throw me a bright frank look. "I do have to say, Angus, history has a strange ring to it in your schoolroom."

Broom and I veered to her, and I leaned down and kissed her quickly but thoroughly.

"Is this part of swamping?" she wanted to know.

"When it's done right."

Banter and chores went along that way together as they should, until the South Fork school was tidier than it had ever been and the one task left was to take down the coal-oil lanterns from their ceiling hooks. I stood on a chair to reach each one down to Anna, and finally I was down myself with the last lit one, so we could find our way out to where our horses were tethered.

All night until then I had not bothered to see anything beyond Anna, so the moonbeams at the windows and across the schoolroom floor shone new to me. "Let's not go out just yet," I suggested to Anna before we were at the door. "We need to study this." I turned out the lantern and we were in the night's own soft silver illumination. In the moonwashed windows of the schoolhouse, the wooded line of the creek loomed like a tapestry of the dark. Above the trees stood the long level rampart of benchland between the North Fork and Noon Creek, and above that firm horizon flew the sky, specked with the fire of stars.

After a minute Anna uttered, "This country can be so beautiful, when it tries a little."

With my arm around her and the moon's exhibition in front of us, she seemed in no hurry to go. I was in none myself.

"Anna," I began, trying to find how to say it the best possible, better than anyone had said the great words before, "I want to marry you. More than I've ever wanted anything, I want that. Will—"

Her fingers stopped my lips, as if they had come to trace a kiss there. "Angus, wait. Please. Wait with that—that question."

"Anna, love, I've been making a career of waiting."

"You've certainly waited in a hurry where I'm concerned," she maintained lightly but seriously. "We've only known each other a little more than a month."

Forty days! I thought indignantly, but let her go on. "What I really mean to say"—rare difficulty for her, making real meaning known—"you don't know me all that well. The person I'd be for you, I mean, Angus, for the rest of your life."

"You can let me worry about that."

"You don't show any sign of making an effort at it," she said gently. "You seem to regard me as the first woman you've ever seen."

"That's more or less the case," I vouched.

"Angus, we can see at the end of the summer. You know I need to go be with Them"—my term for her mother and father—

"for this summer, and you have your own obligations with your sheep, don't you."

"Woman," I said to her as if she truly was the first, the only, of the species, "let's say to hell with the obligations and go get ourselves married. Right now, this very morning. We'll point the horses toward Gros Ventre and go roust the minister out of bed. The man'll need to climb out soon anyway to fluff up his sermon. Anna, what do you say?"

Do you know, for a long moment I almost won her to that. I could feel the halt of all she had been setting forth until now, the stop of her thought as this new proposal opened, enormous as the future, before her.

But after that teetering moment:

"I have to say life isn't that simple, Angus. It's a stale way to say it, but there are others we have to think of."

"Anna, just tell me this. While you're being dutiful daughter this summer, will you think about what I'm going to ask you the instant you get back?"

"Yes."

"*Yes!*" I shouted and the reverberation *yes . . . es . . . es* filled the darkened school. "Do you hear that, world? Miss Anna Ramsay knows the word *yes!*"

"You great gowk," she laughed, and this time laid a single finger across my lips. "They'll hear you everywhere along the creek."

I kissed that finger of hers three times and proclaimed: "I hope they hear it down in China. I hope every ear there is knows now that at the end of the summer I have this romantic prospect to cash in—"

"Cash in?" She gave me her half-smile, her straightforward way of teasing. "Is that your idea of the language of romance?"

"—and that this timid maiden—"

"Timid! Angus, you are absolutely—"

"—will have spent her every spare moment rehearsing the word *yes!* and come to the not illogical conclusion that having said it once in her life, she can say it again. And again and again and again, as many thousand times as I ask her to be mine."

She was looking at me bright-eyed, half ready to burst into even more laughter, half ready to fondly kiss me or be kissed. We could catch up on the laughter in our old age. I reached her even closer to me.

The darkness, the moonsilver, the night-morning that was both and neither, the two of us a chime of time together and yet about to be separated for an abyss of months; maybe because everything including ourselves was between definitions just then, bodily logic began to happen. Our kisses asked ever more kisses. Our clothing opened itself in significant places. Hands and lips were no longer enough.

I whispered huskily to Anna *wait*—entire new meaning to the word she had so recently used—and went out to Scorpion and fetched my sheepskin coat that was tied behind the saddle and then the coat was under us, *us,* on the schoolroom floor. I undid more of her dress while she was slowly and wonderfully busy at my neck and back with her arms, hands, fingers. Wherever I caressed her skin it was white elegance. Except where the bold twin pink nipples and their rose circles now bloomed.

You unforgettably feel the ache, the sweet ache. The deliciousness of thighs finding their way to thighs, the soft discovery of her body's cave place, the startling silkiness my hand was stroking there at the join of her, the curly tangle and stalk where her hand was searching out my own center. There was no eyes-closed mooniness: we were both watching this.

"Anna," my voice thick. "If I'm the first, you know this may hurt a bit."

"It won't," she spoke with surprising clarity.

Atop the piled softness of the wool coat we moved as slowly as we could hold ourselves to. Anna knew things. I was not the first. I didn't care. I was the one now. Her eyes into mine. Mine into hers. All below, our locket of bodies. Slow was far too wonderful to last, now my straining to touch her as deep inside as love can thrust, her clutching to gather me in, us and the husking cries from our throats mingling.

After, I felt perfect. It seemed the perfect echo of the delirium we had just been through to murmur in a fond gabble to her beside me on the coat, "They must be wondering in China what's going on up here with the two of us this morning."

Anna laughed and perfected it with a gentle poke of me. "You do have to admit, it's unusual behavior even in a schoolroom of yours."

"I wish it was absolutely customary," I said, and kissed between her perfect breasts.

An evening of middle June, Rob poked his head in on me. "Angus, sharpen your ears. I've a proposition for you."

"It'd be news if you didn't."

"Now don't be that way. I'm here to offer you an excursion, free gratis for nothing, and all you have to provide is your own matchless self for company. What this is, I've to go up to the railroad—Judith's new cream separator came in by train. Ride along with me in the wagon, why not. It's our last chance for an outing before we turn into shearers and sheepherders."

Rob was expansive these days because commerce suddenly was. Prices of wool and lambs had sprung back to what they were before all the buckets fell in the well of 1893. With their abundance of wethers to be shorn, Rob and Lucas were looking at a real payday ahead, just as my lamb crop would raise me to comfort; to where I wanted to be for Anna and me to begin our married life.

I said my first thought: "Why don't you just have the next freight wagon bring the thing?"

"That'd be weeks yet, and I want this to be a surprise for Judith. I'm telling her you and I are going up to talk sheep with the Blackfeet Agency people. Come along, man. You've been keeping yourself scarce everywhere but Noon Creek. See some more of the world for a change. This'll be the ride of your life." Rob smiled that blame-me-if-you're-heartless-enough-to smile of his. "Well, maybe not quite. *Men*," he pulled his chin into his neck for the croaking tone of the freighter Herbert seven years before, *"there's no hotel like a wagon. Warm nights your room is on the wagon—"*

"—Stormy nights it's under it," I couldn't help but complete the chorus. Our first prairie night out from Helena was beginning to seem another life ago. I still wasn't ready to relent to Rob. Jaunting for jaunt's sake was not something I was in the mood for, having better moods to tend to, and to the railroad and back was a journey of three days. "So your clinching argument is the opportunity to sleep out with the coyotes, is it?"

"Angus, Angus. Trust me to carry more than one motive at a time. I thought we could spend the going-up night there on the Two Medicine at Toussaint Rennie's place. You won't pass up the chance for a dose of Toussaint, now will you? The two of you can gab history until you're over your ears in it."

As Rob full knew it would, this cast a light of interest. Visiting Toussaint on his home ground would be like seeing where they put the music into fiddles. Besides, Rob was indubitably right that after shearing next week there would be a long summer in the mountains, stretched all the longer by Anna being away. The two weeks since she left had taken at least twice that much time to pass. Anna and the railroad, though. Here now, as Lucas would have put it, was a pregnant thought. Maybe, if I had the luck that love ought to have, just maybe the Reese crew plowing fireguard strips would be somewhere on the section of railroad where Rob was headed. A bonus chance to see Anna, however slight—

"You'll come, certain sure?" Rob specified. When I agreed so, he assured me: "Herbert would be proud of you."

"You know that Nancy," said Toussaint in making the introduction of his Blackfeet wife Mary Rides Proud to us the next night. "This is another one."

I am sure as anything I saw a flick of curiosity as Mary looked at Rob. About a heartbeat's worth. Then she moved to the stove and the fixing of supper, as if she were a drawing done of her niece at that moment in the kitchen of Lucas's house, but with blunter pencil.

The household's indeterminate number of leather-dark children eyed Rob and me with wariness, but Toussaint himself seemed entirely unsurprised at the sight of us, as if people were a constant traffic through this remote small reservation ranch. I see now that in Toussaint's way of thinking, they were. In his mind, time was not a calendar bundle of days but a steady unbroken procession, so that a visitor counted equally whether he was appearing to Toussaint at the very moment or long past.

"Toussaint, this reservation opened my eyes for me today," Rob said as we sat to supper. "There's a world of grass up here."

"The buffalo thought so," agreed Toussaint. "When there were buffalo."

"Now there's a thing you can tell us, Toussaint," Rob the grazier speaking now. "Where did those buffalo like to be? What part of this country up here was it that they grazed on?"

"They were here. There. About. Everywhere." Another Toussaint chuckle. "All in through here, this Two Medicine country."

The knit of Rob's brow told me he was having some trouble with a definition of *here* that took in *everywhere*. I tried another angle for him. "What, Toussaint, were they like the cattle herds are now?" I too was trying to imagine the sight the buffalo in their black thousands made. "Some here and there, wherever you looked?"

"The buffalo were more. As many as you can see at one time, Angus."

Supper was presented on the table to us the men, but Toussaint's wife Mary ate standing at the stove and some of the children took their meals to a corner and others wandered outside with theirs and maybe still others went up into the treetops to dine, for all that Rob or I could keep track of the batch. Domestic arrangements interested me these days, but this one was baffling. So far as I could see, Toussaint and Mary paid no heed to one another. That must have had limits, though, because somehow all these children happened.

The supper meat was tender but greasy. After a few thoughtful forkfuls Rob let fall: "Now you have me asking myself, Toussaint, just what delicacy is this we're eating?"

"Bear."

Rob cocked an eyebrow to me. Then swung half around in his chair and called to Toussaint's yokemate in life, "Absolutely the best bear I've ever eaten, Mary."

"This cream separator," wondered Toussaint about our tomorrow's cargo, "is it a Monkey Ward one?"

Rob took a slow sip of coffee, in what I knew was his way of hiding a smile, then exclaimed: "The exact very make, Toussaint. See now, Montgomery Ward and anything else in the world is right out on our doorstep with this railroad. What a thing it's going to be for this country," he went on, sounding more and more like the echo of Lucas. "Homesteaders can come straight from anywhere to here, they can hop from the train into a buckboard and go find a claim without even needing to set foot on the ground. Not quite like when you and I hoofed in all the way from Augusta, Angus."

"Jim Hill's haywagons," Toussaint summed the Great Northern railroad and its builder, and chuckled. "One more way people will bring themselves."

People and what they are. As Rob and Toussaint talked I was thinking of the expanse of country-to-be-peopled that Rob and I had come through that day, I was thinking of Anna out there somewhere under its waiting horizon, summerlong her erect presence beside the fresh steel road of rails, I was thinking of the intricate come and go that weaves us and those around us, of how Toussaint inexplicably was partnered in existence with Mary Rides Proud, Rob now with Judith, Lucas with Nancy. "The winter of '86, Toussaint," I suddenly found myself at. "What was that like, up here?"

"That winter. That winter, we ate with the axe."

Rob made as if to clear an ear with his finger. "You did which?"

"We ate with the axe. No deer, no elk. No weather to hunt them in. I went out, find a cow if I can. Look for a hump under the snow. Do you know, a lot of snowdrifts look like a cow carcass?"

Rob was incredulous. "Toussaint, man, you mean you'd go out and find a dead cow to eat?"

"Any I found was dead," Toussaint vouched. "Chop her up, bring home as much as the horse can carry. West wind, all that winter. Everything drifted east. You had to guess. Whether the horse could break snow far enough to find a cow." Toussaint seemed entertained by the memory. "That winter was long. Those cattlemen found out. I had work all summer, driving wagon for the cowhide skinners. That was what was left in this country by spring. More cowhides than cows."

"A once in a lifetime winter," Rob summarized, "and I'm glad enough I wasn't here to see it. Now we know to have hay and sheds, anyway. It's hard luck that somebody else had to pay for that lesson, but life wasn't built even, was it."

Mary Rides Proud rose from her chair by the stove and went out, I supposed to the outhouse, if there was one. *By now Nancy is part us and part them,* Lucas's voice that day we arrived to Gros Ventre, and all this, *and you never quite know which side is to the front, when. They say when Toussaint rode into town with her, the two of them wrapped in buffalo robes, they had so much snow on them they looked like white bears.*

"That winter must've made it hard to get to Gros Ventre," I said to Toussaint. He gave away nothing in his look to me. Rob glanced over at me, curious about my curiosity, nothing more. "If you ever had to," I added.

"When I had to, I did that ride," said Toussaint. "One time was all."

Setting out from Toussaint's to the railroad the next morning, Rob and I traveled the brink of the Two Medicine River's gorge for several miles to where the main trail crossed it by bridge. It was as if the earth was letting us see a secret street, the burrowing route of its water.

"Now why do you suppose they put a river all the way down there, Angus? It'd save us a lot of hill grief if it was up here with the rest of the country." The Two Medicine would have needed to flow in the sky to match Rob's lofty mood this morning.

"Talk to the riverwright about it," I advised him. Below us in its broad canyon the Two Medicine wound and coiled, the water base for all the world that could be seen. The sentinel cottonwoods beside the river rustled at every touch of wind. Up where we were and out across the big ridges all around, pothole lakes made blue pockets in the green prairie. Anna, you need to see this with me, I vowed that June morning on the green high bluffs of the Two Medicine. Sometime we must come, just the two of us, and on a morning such as this watch summer and the earth dress each other in light and grass.

"No help for it that I can see," Rob announced as he peered down the long slope to the river and up the longer one on its north side. "Here's where our horses earn their oats." Down we went and across, beside sharp stark bluffs.

The buffalo cliff, Toussaint had indicated the rock-faced heights along the river here with a nod. *It was a good one. These Blackfeet put their medicine lodge near. Two times. The river got its name.* Looking at the gray cliff I could all but see the black stampede in the air as the Blackfeet drove the buffalo over. Eyes whitely mad with flight, legs stiff for shock they could never withstand, the animals would have been already dying in midair. Lucas's little recital off a tombstone that first-ever night Rob and I spent in Gros Ventre, in the Two Medicine country: *I fell through life.* . . . That had been one of the sagas here too, in a time of other people, other creatures. Maybe epitaphs were the same everywhere.

At the summit of the lofty grassy ridge above the Two Medicine, the land opened again into billowing prairie with mountains filling the western horizon. It took some looking as we rattled along in the wagon to spot our destination. This was before Browning was a town, and before it was even Browning. Willow Creek, the site had been dubbed for its stream, and what differentiated it from the absolute prairie was the depot and the buildings of the Blackfeet Indian Agency. Those and the railroad, a single thin iron trellis across all this prairie, bringing the world to Montana, taking Montana to the world. From here at wan Willow Creek, Browning-to-be, now you could go straight by train to either ocean.

Rob may have been thinking of the wool that would travel these tracks to the mills of Massachusetts in a few weeks, of the lambs that would go to Chicago at summer's end. For once he did not speak his thoughts, but sat there next to me looking royally satisfied. I was the opposite of that, for nowhere along the miles of railroad in sight was there any dark turned earth of plowed fireguards, no crew of teamsters. No cook tent. No Anna. She was somewhere east beyond the grass horizon, at Havre, Harlem, Malta, places as distant as they sounded. Had I known to a total certainty that there would be no sight of her, I would have passed up this wagon jaunt with Rob as if it was cold gravy. But even love can't see clearly over the curve of the earth. Rob clucked to the team and we headed for the depot.

Now that there was no prospect of Anna, I was anxious to head home and begin using up the days of this summer of waiting. Rob was showing impatience, too, at the lack of whoever ought to be in charge of railroad freight.

"What do they do, put coats of vanishing paint on depot agents?" he pronounced annoyedly. "McAngus, give a look for the rascal inside and I'll try the freight room, why not."

I stepped quickly into the waiting room. The sole person there was a young woman, auburn-haired and bright-cheeked, likely the out-of-place daughter or very young and trying-not-to-be-abject wife of some Blackfeet Agency clerk. A fetching enough girl, but not a fraction of Anna. "Hello," I tossed with some sympathy, still glancing around for the depotman, and then turned my eyes back to this other to ask whether she'd seen him lately. She was looking at me pertly, as if expecting answer from me instead. And then uttered:

"Hello yourself, Angus McCaskill with a mustache."

Nethermuir. Nethermuir in the voice. That shined-apple complexion and her gray eyes. She had to be, but couldn't possibly—

"Adair?" I got out. "Are you, you can't—"

Uproar burst in on us then, Rob laughing and hooting and hugging his sister and pounding me, "He never guessed! Adair, we did it to the man! It was perfect as can be, he never had a clue you'd be here! Angus, wait until they hear in Scotch Heaven how you let a slip of a girl sneak up on you all the way from Scotland!"

By now I had enough wit and wind back to enlist in the laughing, and Adair gave me a quick timid hug and asked, "Do you mind the surprise, Angus? It was this dickens Rob's doing, he insisted we not tell you."

"Mind, how could I mind. It's a thing I never expected, is all—finding you in a Montana train station, Dair Barclay. But, but what're you doing here?"

"What, you can't tell by the sight of me? Adair is a tourist," she defined herself with a self-mocking small smile. Of course I knew in my mind that Adair had grown from the scrap of a girl she was when Rob and I left Nethermuir. She was, what, twelve then. But knowing that was different from understanding, as my eyes were having me do, that she now had reached nineteen and was certifiably more than a girl in every way that I could see. "It was Rob's notion for me to come spend a bit of time. To see this famous Montana of yours."

"Rob is definitely a wonder," I said with a trickle of suspicion beginning in me. "And so how long are you here for?"

"The summer," was Adair's all innocent answer, "to keep Judith company while Rob and you are out being shepherds." But Rob had his own expanded version as he gave his sister the fifth hug of the past minute: "She's here for as long as we can keep her. The lads of Nethermuir will just have to cry at the moon."

The former lad of Nethermuir who was me looked those words over, looked over their source as thoroughly as I could and still keep a reasonably pleasant face for Adair. I had major questions to put to Rob Barclay as soon as I could get him alone and he knew it, he oh most definitely knew it.

"See now, McAngus, I did bring you along for a reason," he said brightly, "to help load Adair's things. Then we'd better make miles before dark, hadn't we?"

"One of your better thoughts recently," I told him, and set off for the luggage. As I went I heard Adair ask, "What, we won't reach Scotch Heaven by tonight?" and Rob answer, "No, not quite." So far, Dair Barclay and I were even in the day's surprises.

After we started across the prairie, Adair kept up with the first rush of talk from Rob while I *mmm*ed and *hmm*ed in the spots between, but I could see her glancing around restlessly at the land, the grass, the Indians, and for that matter at Rob and myself. Time and again she turned her head toward the mountains. After a bit she said of herself: "Forgive Adair for the amount of green in her, but she has to ask. You don't mean those are the mountains where the two of you will be with the sheep?" Myself, I thought the Rockies looked particularly stately this calm sunlit day, purple old widows at tea.

"The very ones," Rob and I chorused.

"But they're nothing but cliffs and snow. Where is there even a place for you to find a foothold?"

"Just the country for sheep and Scotchmen," Rob assured her. "Angus and I will come down from the top of the world there in a few months with our fortunes trotting in front of us."

Adair continued to study the vast jagged line of mountains as if they might pounce out at us. Well, well. This sister of his whom Rob thought was a Montanian in the making might hold a surprise for him as well.

"Do the full recitation of them for her," Rob urged me. "Adair, what this person on the other side of you doesn't know about the Two Medicine country isn't worth knowing."

Adair turned to me with a wisp of a smile. "Are you guilty of all that?"

"He's greatly worse," Rob declared. "I've only told you the top part about him. This is a coming man, this McCaskill person. Even I have to say so."

"I am in trouble," I agreed feelingly with Adair, "if I'm in the good graces of our Rob. But our mountains, now, since you're keen to know." I took her through the catechism of the peaks and crags rising above Scotch Heaven: Jericho Reef, Guthrie Peak, Phantom Woman Mountain, Rooster Mountain, Roman Reef, Grizzly Reef.

By the time I finished, Adair had turned from the mountains toward me again. "You say them as if they were lines of verse," she remarked almost in a questioning way.

"Now you've gone and done it, Adair. You have to watch your step all the time around this man," Rob enjoined, "or you'll give him the excuse to start spouting—"

"—Burns, did I hear someone start to say?" I thrust in. "*Beware a tongue/that's smoothly hung,* for instance? Now there's a major piece of advice, Dair, for being around this brother of yours." Pick the bones out of that for a while, Rob, why don't you.

Adair laughed, a pretty enough sound, fully half as melodious as Anna's. "You mean you haven't been able to change him at all in seven years?"

"Thank heaven I can recognize jealousy when I hear it," Rob gave us equably, and slapped the reins lightly on the team's rumps. "It's time to let the wheels chase the horses," he emulated our stagecoach driver from Craig to Augusta those years ago. "Next stop, Badger Creek."

At least I knew better than that. Any schoolteacher could have informed Rob that unless girls of Nethermuir grew up with iron bladders these days, a stop was imminent somewhere in the hours before we would reach Badger Creek. Nor did Rob help his own cause by being too busy with talking, when we crossed the Two Medicine, to think of offering Adair a pause within its sheltering grove. So when we topped the Two Medicine gorge's southern rim and Adair took her first look at the naked world ahead, no concealment higher or thicker than a spear of grass for miles in any direction, I truly believe I discerned her first squirm of realization. *Forgive me this, Dair Barclay*, I thought to myself, *but you may as well meet the bare facts of this country sooner than later.* And both of us were going to be the better off the quicker I could get Rob alone and wring out of him what he was up to in bringing her here.

Grant Adair a good high mark, she did about as well as could be done with the situation. "Coachman," she eventually ventured to Rob with only a minimum tone of embarrassment, "are there any conveniences at all along this route of yours?"

He looked startled and cast hurriedly around for a coulee. There was one about half a mile ahead, which he promised her. "They're, ah, they're of an airy construction in this neighborhood."

When we reached the brow of the coulee and I stepped off to help Adair down from the wagon, I saw her nipping her lower lip against having to ask the next question. That fret at least I could spare her. "No snakes in this grass," I assured her.

"Except," I began on Rob the instant Adair had passed down from view, "maybe one major one. Just out of curiosity, Mister Rob, how long have you had this little visit of Adair's in the works?"

"Not all that long."

"Not all how long?"

"Not long at all."

"How long is that?"

"Angus, I don't carry a calendar around in my hand."

"No, anyone with your armload of schemes of course couldn't. Just tell me this: you thought it up back this spring before I met Anna, now didn't you?"

"Angus, Angus. Which would you rather hear—yes, no or maybe?"

I could have throttled him there on the wagon seat. An instructive scene for Miss Adair Barclay of Old Scotland when she came up out of the coulee, mayhem on the wild prairie. "Your idea was to get Adair over here and marry her off to me, wasn't it?"

"If it worked out that way, I wouldn't mind, now would I. Though I do have to say, Angus, your attitude this afternoon is starting to make me have second thoughts about you as a brother-in-law."

"For God's sake, man! Do you think you can just take lives and tie them together that way?" Whatever his answer was I didn't give him a chance to polish it and bring it out. "At least why didn't you let her know about Anna and me? Why'd you let Adair come, after that? Now here she is, looking at me the way a kitten looks at her first mouse, and there's nothing in it for her."

"You and Anna, that did arrive as a surprise after I'd already written to Adair," he admitted. "But who knew, maybe you'd fall off a horse and come to your senses." Rob must have seen the incitement that was going to bring down on him, because he quickly put in, "Just joking, Angus. Man, I know how you feel about Anna. It's written all over you six inches high. But if you're not the one for Adair, there are other possibilities wearing pants in this world, aren't there. What harm can it do to bring her here for the summer and let her find out what her prospects are? You and I found our way out of that used-up life over across there. Adair deserves the chance, too, doesn't she?"

"Damn it, Rob, her chance at life here is one thing. Her chance at me is totally another. You're going to have to tell her that."

"And I will, I will. But just let me get the girl home to Breed Butte in peace, can't you? Is that so much? Whup, here she comes, looking improved. You could stand to, too, do you know."

The dusk began to catch us as we came down into the broad bottomland beside Badger Creek, and we quickly chose a willow-sheltered bend with the trickle of the creek close by. In the slow sunset of that time of year, the mountains stood out like silver-blue shards of rare stone. The western half of the sky was filled with puffy clouds the same shade as the mountains, but with their bottoms ember-lit by the setting sun.

"Angus and I ordered that up special for you," Rob was quick to assure Adair.

"You're a pair of old profligates then," she retorted, gazing at the emberglow sky and the miles and miles of mountains.

We rapidly made a fire of our own, for Montana has a chill in its night air even in summer.

"You ought to have seen where Angus and I spent last night," Rob now at suppertime was reporting to Adair, about Toussaint's household. "The crowd there was enough to make you thankful this prairie is so empty."

"This isn't as empty as it looks," I put in purely out of peeve at Rob. "We're camped near history here."

Rob cocked his head and peered into the last of the dusk. "What color is it, Angus, I don't seem to see it."

"Actually it ended up red," I said, "which history seems to have a bad way of doing."

"You mean the man Lewis that Toussaint was on about?" *Meriwether Lewis. Do you know of him, Angus and Rob? He was a bad sign for these Blackfeet. Came up the Marias, looking. Came to the Two Medicine, looking some more. There where Badger Creek runs in, he found something, do you know. These Blackfeet. Eight in a party, horse takers. Lewis and his were four. Lewis smokes the pipe with those Blackfeet, nothing else to do. They all camp together that night near Badger and Two Medicine.* "Adair, this one," Rob inclined his head toward me, "will teach at you day and night if you don't watch out for him."

She was watching me with curiosity. "Lewis was the first white man to explore through here," I tried to explain. If she was here to taste Montana, she had better be aware of its darker flavors. "He and another led a group across this part of the country almost a hundred years ago. Burke? Not quite it. Clark, that was the other with Lewis." *In the night, do you know, the Blackfeet grab guns from*

Lewis and his three. Everybody fights. These Blackfeet knew how to fight then. But Lewis and another get their guns back. BOOM! One Blackfeet dead. BOOM! One more Blackfeet dead. But they say that one combed Lewis's hair with a bullet first. The rest of the Blackfeet ran off, go away to think it over a while. Lucky for Lewis they did, or maybe no more Lewis.

"McAngus," Rob proclaimed, "you're a great one for yesterdays."

"They've brought us to where we are," I retorted with an edge to it. Noticing Adair blinking at this session between Rob and me, I toned matters down a bit. "But Rob's right, you didn't come across the ocean for a history lesson, did you."

"No, it's all interesting," Adair insisted. "Go on, Angus." But go on to what. I gave a lame version of Lewis and the Blackfeet struggling in the night, then shrugged. "Toussaint has it more or less right, this reservation we're on grew out of that and these Indians have had to give way ever since."

"To the likes of us," Rob intoned. "Peaceable men of attainment, in pursuit of cream separators."

A round of laughter for that which I made myself join, promising Rob a time soon when he would have to laugh out the other side of himself. But then Adair said: "So much land here, and"—she sent me an apologizing look—"so empty. It's hard to think of men killing each other over it."

"A great mighty struggle," Rob said solemn as a knell, "with two casualties."

"I suppose they died as dead as any," I observed to him. *Man at war is maggots' meat/dished up in his winding sheet.* Adair at once sided with me—but then she'd have to, wouldn't she, I reminded myself—chiding Rob, "What if we were the Indians and they were us? Who'd be joking then?"

"Anyway it wasn't the Battle of Culloden, now was it, you two," Rob closed off that direction of conversation. "Angus, have you ever seen anything like this grass up here. If we could ever manage to get sheep onto this, we'd have found the front gate to heaven." He was not wrong, the grassland of the Blackfeet reservation indeed was a grazier's dream. Led by Rob, our talk turned now to the Two country's prospects this bountiful year, our prospects as sheepmen. There but not spoken were also Adair's prospects as a Montana wife, although I doubted those more and more as I watched her try to keep a brave face to this overwhelming land.

Eventually bedtime, and Rob telling her, "The lodgings are simplicity itself, Adair. Ladies upstairs"—he indicated the wagon, with its bed of robes—"and others downstairs."

As we settled in for the night, a coyote sent its song to the moon. "We hired music for the occasion, too," Rob said up through the wagon to Adair.

"Cayuse," we heard her try very softly to herself. Then: "Coyote. Rob, Angus," she raised her voice, "is our serenade coming from a coyote?"

"Nothing else," we assured her, and then the night went still, as if the song dog had simply come by to test whether Adair could name him.

I had just begun to drowse when Rob's snoring started. Then came a cascade of giggles overhead, and my own grudging laughing as I was reminded of so many other nights of Rob's nose music, from the steerage bunks of the *Jemmy* to now.

I moved where I lay so that my head was out from under the wagon and spoke softly upstairs to Adair, "You ought to have heard him when the pair of us were on the old ocean. He drowned out the whales and all other challengers."

"Do you remember our tall narrow house, Angus?" I did, although I had not thought of cramped River Street in a long while. "When I was little and sleeping in the gable room, I would wake up and hear Rob sawing the dark below me and know that nothing had carried us off during the night," she said fondly.

And now he's carried you off here, under a misapprehension at least as big as any Scottish night. But I said only, reassuringly, "He's vital here, too. We need him to give singing lessons to our coyotes."

She giggled again, then went quiet. I was remembering now that first vast black pit of Montana night when Rob and I started for the Two Medicine country with Herbert and his freight wagon, six, no already seven years before. This time of year Adair at least ought to be safe from waking into a snowstorm as Rob and I did, although in Montana you couldn't be entirely sure ever. I hoped, too, that she would not be too hurt by the disappointment of this "visit," this bedamned misbegotten matrimonial outing Rob had got her into; I hoped that this Adair would find at the end of the dark the life she wanted, as I had now that Anna was in my life.

To be saying something in that direction without alarming Adair, I brought out: "None of this is exactly Scotland, is it?"

"No. But then I thought that's why you and Rob are here."

"Goodnight then, Dair Barclay."

"Goodnight yourself, Angus."

The next day's miles went back and forth between fleet and slow—the team and wagon urged snappily toward home and Rob's confession to Adair whenever it was my turn at the reins, lapsing into a determined saunter whenever Rob held them. At whichever pace, our passenger between us in her clothes of Scotland and her larklike smallness looked like someone unexpectedly being carriaged along the banks of the Congo. But true to yesterday Adair still responded avidly to any word I said, on those occasions when Rob managed to gouge one out of me, and that was what led to it.

Rob had the reins when we came south out of the cattle-spotted hills of Double W rangeland to the shallow valley of Noon Creek and that strange bold view of Breed Butte, so gradual but so prominent, ahead on the divide between this valley and Scotch Heaven's, and Rob would not have been Rob if he hadn't halted the horses to begin extolling his homestead pinnacle there to Adair. She seemed to be listening to her brother a thousand percent, but suddenly she was pointing west along Noon Creek to where two small white dots and a less small one stood out. This Adair had eyes that could see. "Angus, there. Is that your schoolhouse?" she asked as if already deeply fond of it.

"No," I answered, not looking toward her, not looking toward Rob. "No, that one is my fiancée's."

All but true, that word *fiancée*. I propped it up with the others I had been wanting to say into the air all of this journey from the depot. "Her name is Anna Ramsay. We met early this spring." In me, *And I love her beyond all the limits*, but Adair did not need that added to this necessary revelation. At the tail of my eye I could see her make herself hold steady, make herself keep that defending look she had had when she first saw this land of raw mountains and unpeopled vastness. From beyond Adair I could feel Rob's hot dismayed—betrayed?—gaze on me. But fair is fair, square is square, Rob. I had waited with it until we were within sight of home, I had held it in despite every doubt about when and how and if and whether you ever were going to say it to Adair yourself.

"Why, Angus," Adair managed, after a long moment. "I hadn't heard." Nothing was ever more true. "Congratulations to you. And her."

The source of guilty silence beside Adair spoke now in a strained version of Rob's voice, "Our lad Angus has had a busy spring."

Past that as if it never existed, Adair queried: "When is the wedding then?"

"We haven't named the date," I responded, and explained the circumstances of Anna's absence. "But at summer's end."

"You sound so happy," spoke Adair. Then again: "Congratulations to you." Plucky. Every Barclay ever made was that.

Done and done, at least my part of it.

"Rob," I said innocent as a choir note, "hadn't we better move on to Gros Ventre? Adair has yet to meet Lucas."

Apprehension comes in various sizes, and Rob had his next quantity of it by the time we came down off the benchland to Gros Ventre and could see past the trunks of the cottonwoods the sky-blue sign proclaiming MEdICINE LOdGE.

"Adair, I'd better tell you," from him as if this was a hard day in the business of telling, "Lucas is not quite what a person expects an uncle to be."

Adair gave him a look of *what next?* "You mean because of his hands? But we at home have known about that for years."

"No," answered Rob, "I just mean Lucas."

"So now Montana can boast another Barclay!" boomed Lucas when Rob fetched him out of the Medicine Lodge. I swear, Lucas had figured out the situation to the last zero, just by the look on Rob's face, and for Dair's sake was being twice as hearty as usual. "Come down here for a proper hug, lass!" and she did, stepping gamely from the wagon into an embrace between Lucas's arm stubs. "Adair, welcome to Gros Ventre," he bestowed on her with enough hospitality for several towns this size. "By Jesus—excuse my Latin—you can't know how pure glad I am to lay eyes on my very own . . . niece!"

If Lucas hadn't been facing down the street toward Wingo's; if his last word hadn't shot out with an unexpected ring as the years of habitual talk about Wingo's "nieces" chimed in him; if Lucas hadn't started roaring, I never would have laughed. And Rob wouldn't have reddened into resemblance to a polished apple if it hadn't been for the uncontrollably chortling two of us.

Adair blinked in mystification.

"Nothing, nothing, lass," Lucas assured her. "Just a private joke. Maybe Robbie can explain it to you when he has time, ay, Robbie?"

There ensued a fast stew of family chitchat, ardent questions from Lucas and mettlesome tries at response from Adair and infrequent mutters from Rob, which I carefully stayed out of. If I knew anything by now I knew that the Barclays were going to be the Barclays, and the rest of the race may as well stand back.

"Now you have to come around to the house," Lucas ultimately reached, "and meet Nancy."

"Nancy?" responded Adair, further bewildered.

"Sometime, we can," Rob inserted rapidly. "But we need to head home just now, Angus and I have chores and more chores waiting."

"No matter." Lucas waved an arm stub that Adair's eyes could not help following. "We'll be out to see you shear next week. It's past time all of us in the sheep business got a chance to watch something that'll make us money instead of taking it from us. We can have a Barclay gathering and welcome you proper then, Adair. In the meantime, make this awkward squad treat you right."

"And how is Adair taking to Scotch Heaven?" I sweetly asked that famous matchmaking brother of hers a few days later when he and I had to begin readying the sheep shed for shearing.

"Fine, fine," Rob attested stoutly. "She's having just a fine time."

"Getting used to the wind, is she?" I asked with solicitude. The last of our wagon journey home from Gros Ventre after Adair's niecehood coronation by Lucas had been into a bluster which steadily tried to blow the buttons off the three of us, and at the creek crossing sent Adair's sunhat sailing. I had gallantly held the team's reins while Rob waded to retrieve the hat from its port of willows fifty yards downstream.

"She never even notices the old breeze any more," Rob responded, and impatiently waited for me to lift my end of the next shearing-pen panel to be carried into place.

"I imagine seeing shearing will be a major thrill for her," I went on, straight as a poker but enjoying myself immoderately, "don't you think?"

"I'm sure as anything it will," responded Rob as we grunted and carried. "And that reminds me of a thing," he galloped to the new topic, "the Leftover Day. I'm going to keep back a bunch of yearling wethers for it, enough to make a real day of shearing. Why don't you pair with me?"

This startled me twice at once. First, that Rob was asking me to pair-shear, so soon after making myself less than popular with him by unfurling my news of Anna to Adair before he could prepare. But one of the problems of a partnership is the difficulty of staying steadily angry at someone you have to work side by side with, and I supposed Rob's peeve at me simply had worn out in a hurry. The further unexpectedness, though, was that Rob intended a big event of what was usually merely the do-whatever-is-left-to-be-done final day of shearing. It of course had been Ninian Duff, back when we all entered the sheep business, to discern that if we ourselves did the last odds and ends of shearing—the lambless ewes who hadn't borne that spring, our bellwether Percy and the handful of less fortunate wethers destined to be mutton on our own tables, the crippled sheep and the lame sheep and the ill sheep and the black sheep, all the "leftovers" there ever are at the fringe of raising sheep—if we ourselves did Leftover Day we saved a full day of paying the hired shearing crew. Too, Leftover Day had come to be not just the finale of shearing but also as much of a bit of a festival as you can make from an occasion such as the undressing of sheep, with four of us taking up the wool shears ourselves, and the rest of Scotch Heaven to wrangle the sheep remnant and provide commentary. But this was new, that some of Rob and Lucas's fine healthy yearling wethers would be in with the hospitalers and other raggletaggles of Leftover Day.

I studied Rob. It was a clear economy for the Barclays, to get those wethers shorn free by neighbors instead of the hired crew. But as to how Rob was going to justify this to those neighbors—

"What it is," he enlightened me without delay, "I thought maybe Adair would enjoy seeing a real shearing contest. So I challenged

George and Allan Frew to one on Leftover Day. They went for that like a pair of fetching pups."

I had to hoot. "You're a generous man, to show your sister how you get the whey beat out of yourself"—and myself too; I didn't miss that interesting implication—"shearing against the Frews. I can hear Allan crow now." I could, too. Other shearing times Rob and I had paired to try, Ninian and I had tried, Ninian and Rob had tried, every set of Scotch Heaven men with any contest blood in them had tried and fully failed to tally more sheep than the Frew cousins on Leftover Day. The damn man Allan simply was a wool-making machine and George was almost as bad.

"This is the year we'll put a plug in Allan Frew," maintained Rob. "What do you say to that?"

"I'll say the plain fact, which is that we've never even managed to come close yet. Rob, the two of us have about as much chance of outshearing the Frew boys as we have of jumping over this sheep shed."

He smiled and then shook the smile at me. "This year, we've got a card in our hat."

"Do we. And what's that?"

"These."

Rob stepped over to where his coat was hanging, reached under, and with a beam of triumph brought forth two gleaming sets of wool shears.

I had seen my share of wool shears before. But not these. Each of these shears had a pair of elongated triangular blades which faced each other with sharp expectancy, their bottoms linked in graceful loops of handle.

"Just listen to these lovelies sing," Rob urged me. Experimenting dubiously I put my hand around the grip of the shears he'd handed me and squeezed the hafts of metal. The faces of the blades moved across each other like very large scissors that had just been dipped in oil, steel crooning ever so gently against steel. *Zzzing zzzing*, they chimed a soft chorus with the identical blades Rob was clasping and releasing, *zzzing zzzing*. Truly, here was a shears that seemed to coax my hand to keep working it, keep discovering the easy buttered whet of the blades as they met. Here was just the thing to make wool fly, right enough. I made my hand stop eliciting the whicker of the blades, so that I could read their tiny incut letters:

MANUFACTURED IN SHEFFIELD, ENGLAND.

"Finest steel in the known world," proclaimed Rob. "Sheffield stuff holds an edge like a razor."

"These don't grow on trees. Where'd you get them?"

"I had Adair bring them. See now, McAngus, these're our ticket over the Frew boys."

I saw, and then some: saw through Rob here as an open window. The winning shearing team were the heroes of Leftover Day, which was to say, stolid and effacing as George Frew was, Allan Frew was the perpetual hero of Leftover Day. But this time, this time Rob wanted me up there on the woolly cloud of triumph, for Adair to see up at. The damn man was still trying to fan up ardor between her and me, exactly as if Anna did not exist. You had to credit him for persistence, moments when you didn't want to wring his stubborn Barclay neck. But rather than spend the rest of the day in steaming argument with Rob, I held myself to pointing out the hole in the bottom of his scheme:

"Rob, it's a clever notion and all. But I can't say I'm going to be that much faster a shearer even with blades such as these. Allan came out of his cradle shearing faster than I can even dream about."

"Fast isn't it, man. Come on now, think sharp." He paused significantly. "The afternoon recess. Do you see the idea now, or am I going to have to paint it red for you?"

I saw again, this time with my every pore, down to the small of my back. I can swear that there was not a shearing muscle in me not alarmed by what Rob was proposing. Yet it might work. Outlandish enough, it just might. More than that, even. Gazing at Rob there in the shed, as innocently luminous with scheme as he had been when he lured me to the depot and Adair, I had the thought that Allan Frew was not the only one eligible for getting a plug put in him, come Leftover Day.

Life missed a major step in efficiency by putting fleece onto sheep instead of directly onto us. There is no other harvest like shearing, the crop directly from the living animal, panting and squirming, the shearers stooping daylong in sweat and concentration as they reap greasy wool. Everyone had work. Most often I was gate man, scurrying to operate all the waist-high swinging doors in the cutting chute that sluiced the sheep into the shearers' catch pens six at a time, each penful the pantry the shearer went to for sheep, so to say. Behind me, Rob and Allan Frew customarily were the wranglers, wrangling consisting of steadily shoving the band of sheep to the end of the corral where they funneled single file into my cutting chute, but as Rob and Allan performed it, lengthy wrangles about theories of sheep and sheepdogs and sheepherders also went on between them as if it was coffee-time conversation. If you think of shearing as an hourglass of work, Rob and Allan and I and the unshorn sheep were the supply bell of sand grains at the top. The hired crew of shearers who traveled from job to job of this sort—my back ached to think of their season of stooped-over labor—made the neck of the hourglass: from the shearing floor where twelve or fifteen of them did their clipwork, naked sheep and fleeces of wool steadily trickled. Then on the other side of the shearing crew, the catch-chamber of all this effort of shearing: Archie Findlater the tallyman, Donald Erskine the brander who daubed the sheep owner's paintmark onto each ewe's newly naked back, one boy or another as doctor—Davie Erskine had just enough concentration to manage it—who swabbed on disinfectant whenever a sheep was nicked by the blades; and finally, ultimately, Ninian Duff as wooltromper, stomping the fluffy fleeces down into the long woolsack hung like a giant's Christmas stocking through a hoop in the high little tromping tower. It always seemed to me fittingly festive that as each woolsack filled with its thirty-five or forty fleeces, Ninian within the sack gradually emerged out its top like a slow, slow jack-in-the-box.

All this to undress a sheep, you may say. But it wasn't the naked affronted ewe, stark as glass knickers, that was the product of this. No, it was the rich yellow-white coat she had been separated from. Wool. The pelt that grows itself again. I for one could readily believe that when man started harvesting his clothes from tamed animals instead of shopping wild for furs, then true civilization began. The wool of our sheep went off to eastern mills with abracadabra names such as Amoskeag and Assabet and transformed into cloth for shirts, dresses, trousers, everything. You cannot overlook the marvelous in that.

"Man, this is the year we've been looking for under every rock." Rob was built on springs, this shearing time. A tremendous wool crop at a good price, Adair on hand, the Sheffield shears waiting to trim Allan Frew down to size—every prospect pleased.

"The sky is about to rain gravy," I agreed with him, and grinned. I was in great spirits myself, Anna and our future always right there at the front of my mind. Adair I was aware of only at meals, when the entire shearing gang of us trooped into my house to eat off the long plank-and-sawhorse table Rob and I had put up. Odd to see, there in my kitchen, her and Judith—particularly Judith, whose presence there always reminded me that with a small veer of fate those years ago she might be in my kitchen all the time—but odd is part of life, too. Yet I wondered what Adair made of all this, our Two country and its infinity of sheep and its mountains the size of clouds.

I had my one chance to find out midway through that shearing time. We had just finished with the Erskine band and I was helping Davie drive them west from the shed, toward the start of their summer in the mountains. As we shoved them past my house and buildings, the bare sheep blatting comparisons of indignation to each other and Davie and I and our dogs answering them in full, out from the house came Adair to empty a dishpan. She stopped to witness the commotion, as who wouldn't. Once the sheep were past the buildings I called out, "They're yours, Davie," and dropped away to return to the shearing shed. But my spirits were so thriving, with how well the shearing was going and, yes, with thoughts of Anna someday standing there in my yard where Adair now stood, that I veered over to Adair to joke: "Whatever you do, don't count these sheep as they go past or you'll be asleep a year."

"They look so—so forlorn without their wool."

"They'll have a fine fresh coat of it by the end of summer. By the time you go back to Scotland, you won't recognize these ladies." Or by the time, Dair Barclay, I am the husband of Anna and you're married to some Montanian conspicuously not me. One or other. But not that result which Rob dreamed up and still was trying to puff life into, not that result for which he brought you innocent from Nethermuir: not the altar halter tying together Angus and Adair, thank you just the same.

"Yes, I know they'll get new wool," Adair answered. "It's just that they're so plucked right now. Like poor old chickens ready for the pot."

I noticed she was flinching from the wind trying to find its way into her through her eyes. "What you have to do, girl," I instructed as I moved around to stand between her and the breeze's direction, "is learn to get in the lee of it. I make an A Number One windbreak, if I say so myself."

"That helps," Adair concurred. "Thank you." She took the chance to look past me to the mountains, high and clear in the June air, and then around at my house and outbuildings and down the creek to the sheep shed. While she was at that I did my own bit of inventory. Not so bad a looker, this Adair, actually. Slim and small-breasted, but I had seen less consequential examples. Then those Barclay rosettes in her cheeks, and the auburn crinkle of her hair, like intricately carved ornamentation. Anna of course was an Amazon cavalcade all by herself, but in the rest of womanhood's rank and file this Adair was no worse than midway. Something I had forgotten from her face when she was a Nethermuir tyke; under each eye she had a single dark freckle, specks that repeated the pupils just an inch above. As if there had been an earlier near-miss try at siting her eyes in her face. Interesting. Odd. Now in that recital way of hers, as if providing information to herself, Adair was saying: "You and Rob have built all this, here and at Breed Butte."

"And the others their own places, Ninian there and Donald and Archie." I thought to scrupulously add, "And the Frew boys, they're as solid as people come, too. But yes, we had to build ourselves."

"For you it must be like being born a second time, is it? Coming into the world again, but already grown."

"Something of that sort, I suppose. If you can call me grown." Standing a foot taller than she did, I meant this to cheer her with a chuckle. She only smiled the minimum and went on, as if still trying to get to the fact of the matter: "I don't see how you could do all this, you and Rob."

"Main strength and ignorance," I said. "Dair, I hope you're taking to Scotch Heaven all right."

She gave me a glance in which she seemed to be seeing

something of herself instead of me, not a Barclay declarative look at all. "Adair is not to be fretted about," she quietly advised.

Leftover Day. The morning of it was sheer hospital work, George and Allan and Rob and I laboring our way with our clippers through ill and lame sheep, trying to be as tender as they were fragile, poor old dears. Life perked up measurably just before noon, when we reached the first few of Rob and Lucas's big yearling wethers. It was always the case, that older sheep who had been through the shearing process before knew what lay in store for them and did not like it one least bit. Even that morning's wheezers and geezers squirmed and writhed to the best of their ability. Yearlings on the other hand, virgin wool on their broad young backs, were greatly easier to shear because of their undefiled ignorance. Even as you held a yearling wether down and began working the shears over his body, he had a dazed disbelief that what was happening could be happening. And being wethers they had on them no hazards of udder and teats for us to be extra careful of; the easy of the easy, these innocent sheep who now were meeting our shearing blades.

"Those were just enough to get us going," Rob announced to the world and Frews at large, and with a wink to me, when we halted for noon dinner, "Barclay and McCaskill can hardly wait until we start counting." I grinned, but only half meant it. Already shearing was taking a toll on my back and whatever other parts of me it could reach. The afternoon ahead looked long.

Allan Frew of course was as fresh as froth. "You're ready for the shearing lesson this afternoon, then?" he piped out, with a particular glint my way to remind me I was a schoolteacher. But it wasn't news to me that Allan had beef where his brains ought to be, and so I let pass everything of that noon hour except the constant thought that my shears were going to have to do a lot of talking the rest of the day.

"Ay, you're ready, both pairs?" declaimed Ninian from on high, atop his woolsack platform. "As you know, Archie will tally and call out the totals of each team every hour. Set then, are you, Allan and George? Angus and Robert?"

Receiving our four nods, Ninian lowered himself into the

woolsack until just his head and half his beard showed, and
boomed his starting call:

"MORE WOOL!"

We dove to the work. Four amazed sheep emerged from the
woolsack curtains between our catch pens and the shearing floor,
being dragged by us and then before they knew it being half sat
up, half held against our bodies, like stunned cats press-ganged
into a children's game. Worse came next, as the suspicious sound
of snipping started circling their bodies and did not stop. Here
was the moment for each sheep to declare its character. Some
bleated in consternation and tried to wriggle free, which earned
them only a tighter clamp of the shearer's legs and a possible
gash if they did their worming while the blades were moving to
meet them. Others seemed to try to sink through the shearing
platform, ooze away from the alarming problem. Either case, the
unfleecing relentlessly proceeded to happen to them, and their
eyes became like doublesize marbles, hard glaze of fatal
acceptance there now. As the yellow-white wool, oily and rich,
began to fall away like a slipping gown, you could all but feel the
young sheep's innocence of life sliding off with it.

Both Allan and George were left-handed. With them opposite
that way to Rob and myself, the two pairs of us down in labor
must have been like a mirror reflection. Except that the left-side
image little by little, inexorably and inevitably, produced a
greater number of shorn sheep than did my and Rob's version.
Leave the pairs of us there shearing for centuries and it would go
on and on that way, always the left-side Frews manufacturing a
few more naked sheep than we ever could. From experience and
all else, Rob and I knew this would be the case. I am overtall to
be any kind of an ideal shearer, having to get through the endless
stoopwork in whatever spurts I could manage. Rob, as a person
lower to the ground, could go about it much more ably, and with
his deft hands he was a proficient workman with the shears, fine
to watch. But George Frew was as relentlessly regular as do-re-
mi-fa-so-la in disposing of a catch pen of six sheep, while the
damnable Allan had several rhythms, all of them casually swift,
for undoing the fleeces off his animals. Spirited infantry in the
attack on wool, Rob and myself; the saber cavalry, those damn
Frews.

As was confirmed by Archie Findlater's tally at the end of the first hour: "The Frew boys, ahead by two sheep." Actually, Rob and I could take heart from that. Other times, they outsheared us by twice that in the opening hour.

"We've got them just where we want them," Rob imparted to me in an undervoice as he dragged his next wool victim past me. Maybe so, but my muscles had elsewhere they wanted to be.

The next hour Allan and George gained another two sheep on us, again a heartening loss for Rob and me in that it could have been so much greatly worse. By now the women were arriving from the house to watch the finale. Rob tossed a wave to Judith and Adair between finishing one wether and diving into his catch pen for the next. I wasn't sure I could lift an arm high enough for a wave, so I called out—panted out, really—my greeting. Long since had these big broadbacked wethers, absolute fields of wool, stopped being the easy of the easy of shearing.

"By Jesus, lads, we could see the wool flying from a mile off," Lucas called out, now arriving grandly, Nancy's brown inquisitive face beside his broad bearded one. "Angus and Robbie, a little faster if you can stand it, ay?" Not even Rob could muster the retort that deserved. It had to come instead from the squirmy dismayed sheep between my knees: BLEAGH!

Half an hour until the momentous mid-afternoon recess. My arm and wrist and hand were becoming a sullen rebel band from the rest of my body. I wondered how many other parts of myself there were to be contended with in the half of an afternoon still ahead.

At last, it seemed days, Ninian climbed up out of his wool-sack and called, "Recess, both pairs. Time to see to your blades."

From the corner of my eye I could see Allan and George stretch and arch their backs, then walk over to the grindstone to bring an edge back onto their blades, while Rob and I labored to finish the sheep we were on. A streak of sparks flew as a Frew bladeface met the whirling stone, *kzzzkzzzkzzz*. Rob released his shorn sheep, straightened for a glance at the Frews in their leisure of shear-sharpening and a quick cocked glint of reassurance at me, then dove to his catch pen and brought out a next sheep. I swallowed hard and followed his example.

"Angus, Robert, have you lost your ears?" came the next call from Ninian. "It's afternoon recess. Time to take a rest halt and sharpen your blades."

"Work is all the whetstone we need, Ninian," Rob answered in gulps of breath as he clipped rapidly around his sheep. I saved air and wordlessly labored ahead on my own wether. The Sheffield shear in my hand still felt nearly as sharp and gliding in its clipping as when we'd started.

Here now was the famous card in the hat, the bone for the craw of those Frews. Now we were gambling, Rob and I, that by forfeiting the stop to rest and sharpen we could gain enough sheep to offset George and Allan's skill and speed. The thought was that by keeping stoplessly at it we might just eke in ahead of them—one sheep, a half a sheep, any portion of a sheep would be pure victory—by the end of the day. The thought was that Barclay and McCaskill were hardy enough specimens to withstand a recessless afternoon. The thought was . . . I tried not to think further about our forfeit of blessed rest.

From beside the skreeking grindstone Allan Frew hooted to us. "You pair had better hope your fingernails are sharp, so you can use them when those shears get dull as cheese."

"Up a rope, Allan," Rob gritted out, sulphurous for him, the rest of that phrase involving an unlikely hydraulic feat by Allan.

We sheared like fiends. Meanwhile George and Allan with apparent unconcern went on with their blade-sharpening, interrupting to refresh themselves with swigs of water, which from Allan's lip-smacking testimonial you would have thought was the king's brandy.

At recess end, Archie announced the new tally: "Rob and Angus are ahead by three sheep." I thought I saw Allan's eyebrows lift a fraction of an inch at that, but immediately he was mauling wool off a sheep and George was, too, and Rob and I set ourselves to be chased.

But across the next hour the Frews not only did not catch us, they gained only a sheep and a half. With one last hour of sheep left, that pace by both pairs of us would make the outcome as narrow as a needle. Rob was shearing valiantly, even-steven with George's implacable procession of fleeces. I wasn't faring that well with Allan, or rather my hand wasn't. Going into this day I thought my hands were hard as rasps, toughened by every kind of homestead work since I took off my winter mittens months before. But shearing is work of another magnitude and I was developing a blister the size of a half dollar where the haft of the Sheffield shears had to be gripped between my thumb and first finger. Between sheep I yanked out my handkerchief and did a quick wrap around my palm to cushion the blistered area—Allan seemed to gain half a dozen swooping strokes on me in just that time—and then flung myself back to shearing.

In the effort of that final hour, I swear even my mustache ached with weariness. My shearing arm grew so heavy that the labor of dragging each fresh sheep from the catch pen was perversely welcome. Even through the wrap of the handkerchief I could still feel the hot blotch of pain that was the blister. And I noticed Rob lurch a little—yes, you can imbibe too much work just as you can too much liquid leisure—in his trips past me to his catch pen. Our salvation was that the Frew cousins were having the blazes worked out of them, too, challenged more mightily this day than they had ever been before.

The afternoon and the supply of sheep drew down together. Our audience beyond the shearing floor had not uttered a word for many minutes. The snick of four sets of blades was the only sound now. *I thought maybe Adair would enjoy seeing a real shearing contest.* She was seeing, right enough, Rob. Nethermuir eyes were going to get a Montana education this day, if it killed me. Which it just maybe was about to.

Finishing with yet another mammoth sheep, I lurched groggily to my catch pen. The fog of work was so heavy in me that I had an instant of muddle when wool did not meet me everywhere there in the pen. Only one sheep, looking defiant and terrified and indignant and piteous, was there. Rob's pen next to mine was empty. George's next to his was empty. Allan's had one sheep left.

Dear God. This close. This far.

I sucked breath. Grabbed the lone last sheep and dragged.

As I burst out through the woolsack curtain with my sheep, I saw Allan hurl past me to catch his final wether.

I had mine's head shorn and was working desperately along the top of his back when I heard the coarse slicing sound of Allan's blade go into action.

"Good, good, Angus," from Rob with hoarse glee. "You're almost there, man. Just keep on and you've got it made."

My yearling seemed vast, long as a hog, enough wool on him to clothe an orphanage. Sweat streamed into my eyes. My hand seemed to work the clippers without me.

I turned the sheep for the final side. Only moments later, I heard Allan grunt as he turned his own sheep.

Now I had to do this just so.

Hand, keep your cunning. Do as bid. Slow yourself just enough, while seeming to speed for all you are worth. Work less than you know you can, aching faithful hand, for the first time this day.

As my shearing hand was performing its curtain scene, the tail of my eye caught a movement of Allan's head—he was throwing a desperate glance to see how much wool was left on my sheep. I met his eye with mine, and did what I could not have resisted for a thousand dollars: I gave Allan the briefest instant of a wink. And then nearly regretted it, for it made him falter in surprise between his mighty strokes with the shears. But hand, you were in on the wink, too, you were ever so little less busy than you made yourself seem, and now, there, cut air instead of wool, now the fleece again, what little is left, drive the blades but not too—

A scrape of steel on steel. No wool between in that noise. Allan's shout of it, "Done!"

As his word finished in the air, my own blades shaved free the last of my wether's fleece.

I stood up, as far as my outraged skeleton would let me, and met the face of supreme disappointment that was Rob.

"Angus, Angus," he shook his head in a mix of consternation and commiseration. "I'd have bet every nickel that lummox wasn't going to catch you on that last sheep."

"You'd be on your way to the poorhouse if you had, then," I managed to provide, trying to look properly downcast. Now that we were being joined by the Duffs and Erskines and Findlaters and Lucas and Nancy and Judith and most of all Adair, I spoke out with what I wanted in all their minds and that last one in particular: "Did you ever see a man shear the way of that Allan? He can't be beat, I'm here to tell you." I caught the instant of regret, condolence, in Adair's gray eyes as I waved widely to my conqueror. "Come over here, man. Let me shake that hand of yours."

Which I did, blister and all, with the last shred of fortitude in me. Allan by then had convinced himself he hadn't seen a wink from me, I must have been merely blinking sweat from an eye, and by the time I found an excuse to get away from the throng, much was being made of him, not a little of it by himself.

And so it went later, too, at the dance that put away Leftover Day for another year, where I assiduously romped the floor with Judith, with Flora Duff, with Jen Erskine, with any and everyone other than Adair. Not that I maybe had to be that circumspect, for by then she was being squired to the hilt by Allan.

Dearest Anna— Although they are no competition to a certain lovely product of Brechin, I can tell you that a few thousand ewes and lambs do provide absorbing company. In point of fact, they absorb time from me as if it was water and they were sponges. One minute the band will be grazing on the mountainside as peaceful as picnickers and I think to myself, now here is the way herding is done—the sun mothering the fresh grass, the ewes butting and nuzzling their lambs in an epidemic of affection. Then the next minute, reality intrudes when one of the rearmost sheep is spooked by her own shadow, she bolts in alarm, alarming the next few around her, they race pell-mell into the others, and before I can say an appropriate word or two, the tail-end of the band is wrapped around its lead, a sudden colossal knot of sheep . . .

Dear Angus— Here where we are is called the High Line, in deference to the Great Northern as the northernmost, "highest," of railroads. The towns along the railroad have been named out of a gazetteer: Havre, Malta, and such. Considerably eastward there is even a prairie version of Glasgow. . . .

Try as I did to give them their due for scenery and the healthy hermit life, the days of that mountain summer were merely stuffing between the too-short time Anna and I had had together and the rest of our life together that would begin in autumn. In telling her goodbye, I made her pledge that we would write copiously to each other throughout the summer. "A number of times a day," I stipulated earnestly. "As often as possible," she concurred, and with one last kiss—remarkable how much more a kiss means when the two of you have done all it promises—we had gone our ways for the vast months of summer.

Dearest Anna— I have been doing my utmost to make this a monumental summer. By now I have built several of them— sheepherder's monuments, cairns about as tall as I am, to serve as landmarks and boundary points between the area of the mountain where I graze my band and the one where Rob is herding his wethers. So, Miss Noon Creek Schoolkeeper, the topic is history: did old Alexander McCaskill, stone mason of the Bell Rock, ever have the thought that a great-grandson of his would be piling stones into miniature towers in far America? . . .

Dear Angus— It would be gratifying to tell you that I can look out from this cook tent to the distant Rockies and imagine you there at work on your monuments, but the actuality is that the mountains are not within sight from this section of the High Line. All is prairie here. This is quite another Montana from your Scotch Heaven or my Noon Creek, and I wonder how many Montanas there are, in all . . .

Everything of life we ever find or are given ends up in the attic atop our shoulders, it is said. I have no cause to doubt it. During those high summer weeks my head stored away new troves all the time. My final season alone, this. The point at which the trade was to be made, my solitary wonderment at life and where it was taking a person, for becoming half of two. *You, I'd say, need the right partner in this old life, Angus.* You spoke it first, Lucas, and now it was on its way to happening. Even after the marriage there would be the everlasting astonishment of how Anna and I had coincided, from a handful of miles apart in Scotland, where we had not met and may well never have, to coming together in this far place. And now there would be McCaskills derived of Nethermuir and Brechin. I could imagine waking beside Anna every morning the rest of our lives and gazing at her face and thinking, how did this come to be? And then she would blink awake—

"McAngus, do you let a visitor onto your cloud?"

Rob had ridden so near he could have tossed his hat onto me, that noontime in early August, without my noticing.

"Some of us are intent on our flocks," I maintained, with a

gesture to my band serenely shaded up in a stand of lodgepole pine, "while others of us have nothing better to do than go around sneaking up on people."

"A choir of geese could sneak up on you these days," he said with a mighty smile down at me.

I doubted that he had ridden all the way across the mountainside just to test my alertness. No, he admitted, he saw this as an errand of mercy. He had come to see if I wanted to take a turn at camptending. "Man, from the look of you, you'd better go down for air," Rob urged.

Well, why not. The day's ride down to Breed Butte and back up with a pack horse laden with our groceries would stir the blood around in me, right enough. When I told Rob I'd do it, he suggested with a straight face that I take along a second pack horse for my High Line mail.

When I rode in to Breed Butte that next day, it didn't take a bushel of brains to figure out that mine wasn't the only well-being Rob had in mind when he suggested I come instead of him. Ordinarily Judith wasn't the kind to get nettled unless she sat in them. But one look at her told me she had been storing up opinions for Rob about his absence from the homestead's remorseless summer tasks. All she said to me—it somehow sounded like a lot more—was: "How quick will you two be bringing the sheep down?"

"Another three weeks," I proffered as if it was overnight, and began lugging groceries out of range of her. And almost waltzed over Adair, coming up onto the porch as I was starting to step off it.

"Hello you," I sang out brightly, and received a lot less than that in exchange. As I went on over to the pack horse, she stood on the porch steps and watched.

"So. How are you liking this country of ours by now?" I asked her across the yard.

"It's—different," I heard back.

"Getting acquainted some, are you, with this Scotch Heaven tribe?"

"A bit." Not exactly bright as a bangle, a report of that sort. I sallied on anyway:

"Seen or heard anything of our champion shearer?"

Those gray eyes of hers sent me a look as direct as a signpost. "Angus," she said levelly, "you know as well as I do that Allan Frew is stupid as a toad."

I made my retreat from the Breed Butte garrison of women and headed gratefully back to mountains and sheep. The Barclays. What an ensemble. Rob ought to have his head examined for plopping Adair over here from Nethermuir in the first place. It would be saner all around when she wrote off this visit of hers as one of Rob's follies and returned to Scotland at summer's end. Well, I at least had done what I could to pair Adair with a Montana mate, so long as it wasn't me. I couldn't help but agree with her about Allan Frew, though.

The last day of August, down I came from the mountains with fat lambs and plump profit everywhere in front of me, and beyond those the precious prospect that waited for me at Noon Creek. As soon as the sheep were putting their noses to the first bouquets of grass on the slope above my homestead, I aimed Scorpion north as fast as he could trot. On hunch, I went not to the Ramsay place but to the Noon Creek schoolhouse. With the beginning of school so near, I'd have bet hard money, Anna, that you would be readying your classroom. And I'd have won, three times doubly. I patted your sorrel saddlemare rewardfully as I stepped past and toward the schoolhouse door.

"Is this where a person comes to learn?" I called in.

You turned around from the blackboard so quickly your braid swung forward over your shoulder, down onto the top of your breast. "Angus! They said you were still in the mountains, I wasn't expecting you yet!" I'll tell you again now, that braid was the rope to my heart.

"Yet?" I answered. "It's been forever, whatever the calendar says." I went to you and held you at arm's length and simply looked, drank you in. Your gaze was steady on mine, then you put your face against my shoulder. "You look as if the mountains agreed with you," you said warmly. After my summer of not hearing it, your voice was as rich as a field of buttercups.

"They were good enough company, but I desperately need to hear a Brechin voice."

"You do, do you."

"I do. And I want it to tell me every minute of itself since I last heard it, back in Napoleon's time."

"That's an extravagant expectation," you said, giving me the half-smile.

"A mighty word, extravagant. What's the spelling for it? Write it for me, Miss Noon Creek Schoolkeeper."

"You are the Angus McCaskill who can read the air, are you? We shall see." You began tracing lovely maneuvers of alphabet before my eyes.

"An unfair advantage," I protested. "You can't expect me to read your old word backwards." I moved around behind you, peering down over your right shoulder, my cheek against the black silk of your hair, my hands along the twin bone thresholds so near to where your breasts began. "Now then. Write your utmost, Anna Ramsay."

You stood stock-still. Then, "Angus . . ."

Suddenly what we were saying to each other was with lips, but words were nowhere involved. Our kissing took a wild blind leap. The next thing I knew my lips had followed your neck down, the top of your dress was open and the feminine undergear was somehow breached—your breasts were there, bare as babes, and I was kissing the beautiful whiteness and twin budding nipples. Your hand was under my shirt, your fingers spread and moving back and forth on my spine.

I looked up at you and your other hand came to my face, to the corner of my mouth. You looked intent, Anna, ready to say something. My urge was to keep on with the kissing and the divesting of clothing, and yours evidently was, too. But instead, "Angus, we can't. Not—not here."

"We can," I answered gently. "And sooner or later we will. But for now just let me hold you." Your hands hesitated where they had begun to close the front of your dress; and then they were clutching my back again, the two of us snug together, just being there clasped. We rocked gently against each other or the schoolroom floor was swaying on a gentle tide, we didn't care which. Out of my spell of sheer happiness I heard myself say: "Talk, we were mentioning. It seems to me a poor second-best to this, but yes, let's talk some more. I'll even begin. Anna, marry me now."

I felt you tighten even more against me, the twin globes of your breasts wonderful in their pressure. You said into my shoulder: "I have to tell you, Angus, you're not the first to ask."

"I suppose not. If the male half of the world has any sense at all, it's been trooping to you in regimental file with that question since you were the age of twelve. But Anna, love, first isn't what I had in mind—I just want to be the last."

While I was saying it all you pushed yourself just far enough away to look me in the eye. You didn't smile, not even the half-smile I loved so. "Isaac has asked me."

I nearly chuckled and asked how many words of how many different tongues he did it in. But your face stopped me. Lord of mercy, Anna, had you been so overkind as not to tell Isaac Reese outright no?

"Angus," you said.

"Angus," you said, "I've told Isaac yes."

I rode away doomed.

Not around Breed Butte toward home, because I could not face the new everlasting canyon of emptiness waiting for me there. Down the Noon Creek road toward Gros Ventre I reined Scorpion. In ordinary times it was a pleasant straight-as-a-rope route along the benchland, roofs of the Noon Creek cattle ranches below, but this day I wouldn't have given them a glance if they were the castles of the moon. The tatters that were left of me had all they could do to cling there onto Scorpion's back, hang in the saddle and be a sack for the disbelief. *Angus,* Anna saying, there in the schoolhouse and endlessly in my mind, *I am fond of you, I enjoy you. You know I find you attractive*—the memory of her open dress came into the air between us. *You know how we were, Angus, that last night there in your schoolroom. I have to tell you. Isaac and I have been that way together all this summer.* The moment of pause as that news pierced every inch of me. Then even worse words. *Angus, I'm afraid it's Isaac I feel actual love for.*

Scorpion's ears pricked, his horse view of life alert to the stark lone outline standing ahead of us on the benchland. The pole gateframe of the Double W ranch, gallows-high. As we passed the lofty gate I turned my head to the other side and looked back to where the misery began. The Noon Creek schoolhouse was a square white speck now, under the mountains with their evening roof of cloud and beside the longsail rise of Breed Butte and nearest of all to a spacious creekside ranch that was Reese horseland.

Angus, I'm afraid it's Isaac I feel actual love for. Just that way. As if we two men were jars of jam on the table and she was saying, this is strawberry, this is plum, I'll have plum from now on. Anna was marrying him for the sake of those parents of hers, to tie the leaky boat of Ramsay finances to the ark of Isaac. She was marrying him because she felt sorry for him, damned Dane gabbler him. She was marrying him because she had temporarily lost her mind. Amnesia. A blow on the head she couldn't recall. The instant she came out of this sad mad drift of her senses . . .

She was marrying Isaac because she chose to. Because she wanted to. Because some form of the love infection that had happened to me had now happened to her. I knew that, to the bone. Knew it indelibly and with no possible mistake because Anna Ramsay in her honesty made plain the difficulty of her decision. *Angus, you are a rare man. Maybe the rarest I've ever met.* Her half-smile seemed wistful, or did I imagine. The frank faction of her, though, the Not Proven verdict-giver, went right on to say: *But I think you don't know yet what you want of life.* But I did, did, did. Everything I wanted was standing here telling me she was marrying someone else.

And you do, I raged, *and his name is Isaac?*

How can I ever say it as well as you deserve? Angus, you are one who wants to see how many ways life can rhyme. I just—I just want it to add up as sensibly as I can make it do. And while I didn't at all intend it to, this summer told me how much I want to be with Isaac. Her perfect face looked at me with steady regret. *Angus, I'm so sorry. I am sorrier for you than can ever be said.* She put her hand gently on my wrist, half a grasp which she must have thought was better than none. *I can tell you this. If I ever see that Isaac and I are not right for each other, I'll know where to turn for better. Any woman would do well to marry you, Angus.*

Scorpion was snorty and nervous, our shadow a restless one on the road in front of us from his head-tossing and twitching. If truth could show itself as sunlight throws down our outlines, there would have been a third form there in our composite shadow—the dread that rode me. There is nothing else to call it, a dread as harsh and bottomless as the smothering one I had felt in the steerage bunk those first Atlantic nights out from Scotland. For what was tearing at me was not simply that Anna had turned me down. No. No, the greatly worse part was that even now I could not stop myself from siding with her, defending her against myself even as I derided her reasons in favor of mumblejumble Isaac. I still loved that woman. And if this day had not changed that fact, what ever could?

"By Jesus, Angus, you look as if the dog ate your supper."

I gave Lucas an answering eyeshot that sent his stubs reaching for a large glass for me. Lucas Barclay, author of my homesteading venture, commandant of the Medicine Lodge and the tall house behind and Nancy in that house. All this without even having hands. Isaac Bedamned Reese barely had approximate English. Yet here was I, supposedly complete but womanless. Less the exact one woman I wanted.

I explained to Lucas in the one word: "Anna." Misunderstanding the situation as something that could be mollified he said: "A spat, ay? Don't be so down, lad, you're not the first—"

"She told me to go chase myself," I told him. I told him about the Anna–Isaac wedding-to-be, told him my bafflement, told him a couple of rapid drinks' worth.

"Bad," he agreed. "But you will mend, you know."

I wanted to blaze to him that this wasn't like Rob being infatuated with Nancy, he'd sing a different tune if he were me right now. For that matter, something of the sort must have flared, because Lucas now was steering me to the weaning corner of the bar and casting keep-away looks at the few other customers as they drifted in. "Another glass or so will do you more good than harm, Angus, but that's the end of the night for you then."

Harm, did I hear him say. From that day when Rob and I walked into this Medicine Lodge and Lucas laid his lack of hands before us to see, I had wondered what so harmed a life was like, how Lucas must feel, true and deep, about enduring the rest of existence as less than he had been. Now Lucas was the one who did not, could not, know anything near the full sum of damage I felt. Come put on my bones, Lucas. Come and wear Angus McCaskill like borrowed clothes, let our hearts pump in tune, our eyes sight together at this rascal thing life. Come stand here under my skin and find what this is like, I will learn your loss and you mine.

"Angus, Angus. Take it slow, now. Both on this whiskey and yourself."

Slow, is it. My whole life is slow as anything can be now, indeed it's halted, bogged, stranded . . . This was my Bell Rock. My time of stone, with obliteration all around. The ocean was coming to cover me, ready to put salt pennies on my eyes, and it may as well, why live if this was what living amounted to. *I'm here to tell you. No boat on the reef and none in sight anywhere.* Land stood a dozen miles distant from the Bell Rock; yes, that was the ever same unswimmable distance, from here in the Medicine Lodge to that Noon Creek schoolroom where Anna had told me no, Isaac yes.

"Angus, man, you're full. No more of the wet stuff for you tonight. Sedge and Toussaint, each grab an end of him, can you, and take him around to the house. Angus, here now, just let the lads lift you, there's the way. You'll be different in the morning."

Let the tide come. The Atlantic, the Annalantic. Take my ankles, shins, knees, rise, damn you, bless you, sweep me off this reef, blanket me with water, arms and throat and eyes and higher yet, the whole hopeless thing I am.

What followed, an exact month from that day Anna said no to me, even yet seems the kind of dream a puppet must have, each odd moment on its own string of existence, now dangled, now gone, no comprehension allowed between. Around the wedding pair a cloud of faces, high nimbus and low, years-married couples remembering with faint smiles and their children curious but fidgety. Inevitable breeze, blowing the few strands of the Gros Ventre minister's gray hair down into his eyes as he begins to read the ceremony, *We are gathered . . .* Mountains up over the valley in their eternal gather. The couple, in voices as brave as they can make them, reciting vows for life. The thought caught up with me: *Life. That could be a long time.* Then moved on through my slowly registering mind. Here the last of the dreambead instants, this tardy and this soon, the ring being handed by the brightfaced best man.

I shifted slightly, turning to the woman beside me. Onto Adair's finger I slipped the ring warm from Rob's grasp and it was done. We were wed.

The minister gave out that last intonation to us. "You may kiss the bride." Leaning my head down to Adair's, I saw she had her eyes closed, as if casting a wish. It all revisited me, the pieces of time that had never really passed, simply drifted from corner to corner within me, dreamlike yet never with a dream's innocence. Rob's voice beginning by saying *Her Highness gave you a flick of her handkerchief, I hear,* when I rode home the morning after my night of forlorn souse and found him there, crossing the yard to feed my indignant chickens. *Those Ramsays think they're God's first cousins, though where they get it from I can't see. Angus, she's not the only woman in this world.* No. There was another. In three days, when I hoped I was some semblance of a human again, I rode to Breed Butte, asked Adair to walk with me to the brow of the butte, and there my words came out with cloppety boots on, but they came out. *Dair, you know what's happened with me.* She: *I know about Anna, Angus, and I'm sorry for you.* She did not entirely know, though, nowhere nearly all. Could not know how thoroughly the lovespell for Anna still gripped me, that neither disappointment nor anger nor reason nor laughing at myself nor crying with myself nor anything else among the storms going through me seemed to loosen at all. Nor did I dare even try to bring out my hopelessness for Adair to see, because the bargain we needed to make could not withstand full truth. I spoke fact instead: *That's the past now, Dair. And I'm asking you not to go back to Scotland. I'm asking you to stay and marry me.* Further fact silent but plain behind each line aloud: I no longer could stand to face life by my solitary self, could not reverse myself into the awaiting watcher I was before Anna changed me; Adair who had come across an ocean believing I was awaiting her did not want to return empty-handed to a stone Scottish town: we two together at least were a different sum than either of those awkward results. *She made her choice, more pity to her,* Adair said softly without touching Anna's name. Then said the rest in that lofty little way as if outside herself, speculating. *And Adair has made hers. Angus, I'll marry you any number of times over.* I: *We can start with once.* And Rob again, exultant: *McAngus, man, this is the best news in the world! Have the wedding here on Breed Butte, what do you say? We'll throw you two a shindig that'll not be forgot.*

Someone of the crowd calling out now, "That kiss ought to more than do the job, you two. You'll be married a couple of hundred years on the strength of that!"

Adair looked as if I had taken every bit of breath from her, she looked as if she'd heard a wild rumor prove true. In front of us the minister hemmed and hankered as he wished us well. Faces of my pupils had been astounded into giggles.

"I thought all the kissing had to be done at once," I alibied to the world at large and drew Adair snug against my side. "You mean to tell me there's more of that to come, Dair Barc—" I stopped and laughed with the rest until I could manage the correction—"Dair *McCaskill?*"

I heard more giggles, shushes, whispered bulletins, as if echoing ghostly up the butte from my schoolroom. Then unmistakably Susan Duff announcing, "We have a song for Mr. and Mrs. McCaskill." I turned and Adair with me, to the every-sized choir that had crept behind us; my pupils in slicked-down hair and stiff Sunday clothes, descending in grinning disorder around the central figure of Susan Duff, Susan long and tall, Susan princess of my classroom, Susan of that silvered voice that now soared out and coaxed the wavery others:

> *Dancing at the rascal fair,*
> *Adair Barclay, she was there,*
> *gathering a lad with red hair,*
> *dancing at the rascal fair.*
> *Angus McCaskill, he was there,*
> *paired with a lass named Adair,*
> *dancing at the rascal fair.*
> *Feel love's music everywhere,*
> *fill your heart, fill the air,*
> *dancing at the rascal fair.*

"Some people," I declaimed after the applause died and Adair and I thanked Susan Duff to the limit, "will try anything to get on the good side of their teacher." Laughter met that, Adair met my pupils one and all, and after them it would be their parents and everyone. The song had helped, I told myself. Maybe I did know what I was doing, maybe Adair did, too, maybe we were going to be a good fit. But tell myself whatever I would, the other refused to leave my mind. I tried and tried not to think any of it, which only incited the factions up there all the more. *Anna, come today. No, don't come, not this day that is by every right Dair's day.*

Married life was proceeding from there. Congratulations from the men filling my ears, Adair receiving bushels of advice from the women about how to perfect me. Lucas at one point provided me brief rescue with a generously full glass captured between his stubs. "Have a drop of angel milk," he directed. "You look as though you need it, ay?"

It was a lovely whiskey, like drinking the color off a ripe wheat field. "This is the house brand in the Medicine Lodge now, is it?" I advocated.

"Don't get wild ideas, lad. It happens to be a bottle that's a precious commodity. Only the advent of good sense in you, marrying a Barclay, makes me crack it open."

Lucas's face did not live up to our banter, either; he was eyeing me in a diagnosing way. And so he knew, knew for certain that my tongue had just vowed for one woman but my thoughts still chose another.

I waited for words from this man who always could see through me and out the other side. For once, there were none. Lucas gravely nodded—was it simply acknowledgment? or lodge greeting of the maimed?—and left Adair and me to our congratulators.

Scotch Heaven was here without exception, and nearly everyone from the South Fork and down the main creek as well, and many from Gros Ventre and several from Noon Creek, although not the two most on my mind. Seven days ago, Anna and Isaac had gone through this same ceremony at Fort Benton on one of his horse-merchant trips. *Anna, come. No, stay away. Anna, I just want to see you, before Adair and I make our life, to ease you from my mind. No, I want to see you because that is what I always want, the hunger I always have, and so Anna, don't—*

I felt Adair startle, startling me. A round walnut-colored face, crinkles of amusement permanently at the corners of its eyes, regarded the two of us as if we held the secrets it had forever wanted to know.

"I came to see the cream separator," spoke Toussaint. "She looks like the good kind."

All simultaneously I was exclaiming in relief and shaking hands hello with Toussaint and introducing him to Adair, who was looking as if she'd encountered a feathered Zulu. When Toussaint had paid us his chuckling respects and gone she asked, "Who on earth was that?"

"The king's remembrancer, except that the Two Medicine country doesn't have the king. I'll try to explain Toussaint later."

As much to herself as to me she said softly, "Adair has much to get used to in your Montana."

"And she will," I said with a heartiness based on my own need to believe that. "First, though, she has to meet all these Montanians who admire my taste in wives." Countless more introductions were undergone to the tune of *Angus, we wondered who you've been waiting for.*

When the next chance came I asked her, low, "Dizzy with names yet?"

"At least," she said, close to breathless again. She looked a bit abstracted, too, as if having stepped off a sudden little distance from the proceedings. Deciding that since I was now a husband I'd better undertake to be husbandly, I announced to our assemblage: "Time for our first war council. We'll be back before you can get your whistles wet." I led her up the butte a little way, just far enough to be by ourselves.

Adair asked in wonder, "Do people flock out this way for every wedding?"

"Only the ones I'm in," I vouched.

"Angus." She put her hand on my arm. "Angus, I'll try with whatever's in me to be a good wife. I don't want you disappointed in me."

"Dair, what's this about?" The unexpected note of doubt in her voice hit deep in me, colliding with my own fears. But I made the words light enough to float away. "It's been most of an hour already since the vows and I'm not ready to trade you in yet."

"I want you to know. I'll be all I can for you."

"Then that ought to be more than enough."

"A person just doesn't know . . ." Her words faltered. "Or least this one doesn't know."

In my chest the sound thudded in echo: *know . . . know . . . know . . .* or was it *no . . . no . . . no . . .* I made the fatal little round sound become her word again: "Know? Know what, Adair?"

"I don't know how I'll be. Amid all of this." She swerved from my staring quiz of her, and the two of us looked out over as much of all as eyes can ever see. The homesteads along the creek, the unpopulated miles all around, the cluster of wellwishers for this occasion, our occasion—Rob with Judith, Lucas and Nancy, Ninian Duff and Flora, Toussaint, the children of my school, people and people and people—and the mountains patiently propping the sky.

"We have the rest of our lives to find that out, Dair," I at last offered. "Let's not worry about ourselves until we have to."

Our public was calling to us from the tables of wedding supper. *Here now, the lovey-dovey stuff just will have to wait a bit . . . Angus, you've got the ring on her finger now, you can afford to share her with us . . .* Rob's voice emerging over the others: *We're moving on to important matters such as food and drink, you two, so bring yourselves on down here.*

"Hadn't we better?" Adair said, and tried to give me a smile. I manufactured one in return and confirmed, "By popular demand." And in me that desperate double chorus I could not be rid of. *Anna, come. No, don't.*

Anna.

And Isaac. Just arriving. The sight of Adair and me coming down the butte to join the wedding crowd halted the two of them at the far edge of the throng as though it was a wall.

There wasn't a chance in this world to know what Isaac Reese was thinking above that drooping mustache, behind those horse trader's eyes. As well go read a fencepost as try to decipher that Dane. But Anna registered on me exactly, instantly as a mirror reflection. I saw in Anna a great judiciousness, a careful holding back as she met my gaze with hers, and understood at once that this was the total of our meeting today, these exacting looks across the wedding crowd: a man beside his yet-to-be-known bride, casting every glance he can toward the woman he knows every inch of. Propriety was delivered now by Anna and Isaac being here, now there could be no behind-back talk as to why schoolkeeper Anna was absent the day of schoolkeeper Angus's wedding, *weren't they seeing one another, for a time? You don't suppose . . .*

And now I had my private answer as to whether the sight of Anna here, unattainable, the past in a glorious glossy braid, would begin to heal my pang for her or make it worse. Seeing her did absolutely neither. Not a candleworth of difference one way or the other in the feeling for Anna that burned like a sun in me. That heartfire had persisted past her choice of Isaac for a husband, it was persisting past my vow to this new presence at my side, my wife. But it couldn't persevere on and on in the face of all the rest of life to come, could it? Could it, Angus? I drew breath. I had to hope not. I had to make it not.

I put my hand in a reassuring clasp over Adair's, where it held hard to the corner of my arm. "That brother of mine," she was saying, "you never know the next from him."

Rob had climbed onto a chair. He stood amidst all of us of the wedding crowd, half again as tall as anyone. A glass of Lucas's magic whiskey was raised in his hand. "A toast!" he called out. "In fact, many more than one toast before this day is nearly done, but this one first."

Rob turned toward Adair and me, his eyes met mine and our looks locked as they had so many times. Of everyone there on Breed Butte—Adair, his own Judith, Lucas, Nancy, the many of Scotch Heaven and Noon Creek and Gros Ventre—of this day's entirety of people, Rob was speaking straight to me. "Angus, man, you and I have been all but family." He held his glass as high in the air now as he could reach, as if toasting the sky, the earth, all. "And now we're that."

THE 'STEADERS

The Great Herdsman Above must have thrown up his hands over the territory of bald plains between here and North Dakota and ordained it to be eternally stampede country. First of all, He turned loose the buffalo there; next the cattle herds in the days of open range; and now the homesteaders are flocking in by the thousand. Nearest us, a Paris of the prairie called Valier already exists on the maps the irrigation company is providing to hopeful immigrants, and there can even be found in the townsite vicinity occasional buildings which, if rounded up and bedded down, may constitute some sort of a town eventually.
—GROS VENTRE WEEKLY GLEANER,
MAY 13, 1909

I MEAN this better than it will sound. Adair was the biggest change my life had known since sheep came into it.

"Dair? You don't snore."

She stopped the work of her fork, that breakfast time in the early weeks of our marriage, and gazed across at me curiously. "Such high praise so early in the day."

"All I meant was—it's a nice surprise." Surprise and cause for wonder, this small woman silent in the dark as if she wasn't there in the bed beside me. My years of alone life had made me think that adding a second person to a household would be like bringing in a crowd. Whenever you looked up, there would be a presence who hadn't been, now at the stove, now at the window, now in the chair across from you, now in the blanket warmth next to you. But not so, with Adair. She was not what could be called a throng of wives. No, instead she was proving to be a second solitude on the homestead, a new aloneness daily crisscrossing my own. Constantly now I had to try to fathom this sudden young gray-eyed woman with my name joined onto hers. This quietly-here newcomer from the past. This afterthought bride in the lane of time where I foresaw only Anna.

That was the parallel I meant with the sheep: the saying is that to be successful with sheep, even when you're not thinking about them you had better be thinking about them a little. Now that I was coupled into life with Adair, even when I was trying not to wonder I had to wonder whether I was up to this.

I was letting this be seen bald by remarking to the presence across the breakfast eggs from me about her snorelessness, wasn't I. Figuring I had better get out of the topic before damage was done, I deployed: "You're sure you're related to Rob Barclay, the Scotch Banshee?"

"Would you like me to ask Rob for lessons in sawing with my nose?" she said back, lightly enough.

"No, no, no. I can step out and listen to the coyotes whenever I feel too deprived."

My wife lifted her chin at me and declared softly, "Adair has the same news for you, old Angus McCaskill. You aren't a snorer, either."

"Where do you get the evidence for that?" For if she was asleep as she seemed while I lay there searching the night—

"I wake up early, well before you do. And you're there, quiet as a gatepost."

So Adair and I were opposite wakefulnesses, were we, at either end of the night. The dark quiet between, we shared.

"I always knew marriage would agree with you," Rob accorded me. "You don't have that bachelor look on you any more." He sucked his cheeks into hollows and meanwhile crossed his eyes, just in case I didn't happen to know what abject bachelorhood looked like.

Adair had barely come across the threshold when Rob and I had to trail his wethers and my lambs to the railhead for shipping. Quick after that, school began again and I was making the daily ride from homestead to the South Fork and then back. In weekends and other spare minutes, winter had to be readied for.

It sometimes seemed I saw more of Scorpion than I did of my new wife.

She said nothing of my here-and-gone pace, just as I said nothing of her beginning attempts at running a household. Accustomed to tea, Adair applied the principle of boiling to coffee and produced a decoction nearly as stiff as the cup. Her meals were able enough, but absentminded, so to speak; the same menu might show up at dinner and at supper, then again at the same meals the next day, as if the food had forgotten its way home. Courage, I told my stomach and myself, we'd eventually sort such matters out; but not just yet. There already was a problem far at the head of the line of all others. Adair's lack of liking for the homestead and, when you come all the way down to it, for Montana.

Again, her words were not what said so. I simply could see it, feel it in her whenever she went across the yard to fling out a dishpan of water and strode back, all without ever elevating her eyes from her footsteps. The mountains and their weather she seemed to notice only when they were at their most threatening. I counted ahead the not many weeks to winter and the white cage it would bring for someone such as Adair, and tried to swallow that chilly future away.

Before winter found its chance to happen, though, there was a Friday end-of-afternoon when a session of convincing Ninian on the need for new arithmetic books—*ay, are you telling me there are new numbers to be learned these days, Angus?*—didn't get me home from the schoolhouse until suppertime. During my ride, I had watched the promise of storm being formed, the mountains showing only as shoals in the clouds by the time I stepped down from Scorpion.

"Sorry, Dair," I said, providing her with a kiss, and headed sharp for the washbasin while she put the waiting food on the table. "It's just lucky I didn't end up arguing with Ninian by moonlight."

"The old dark comes so early these days," she said, and took the glass chimney off to light the lamp wick.

"We get a little spell of this weather every year about now," I mollified her as I craned around to peer out the window at the clouds atop the mountains, hoping they would look lessened, "but then it clears away bright as a new penny for a while. We'll be basking in Indian summer before you know what's hap—" The sound of shatter, the cascade of glass, spun me to Adair.

She was staring dumbstruck at the table strewn with shrapnel of the lamp chimney, shards in our waiting plates and in the potatoes and the gravy and other food dishes as if a shotgun loaded with glass had gone off. In her hand she still held a glinting jagged ring of glass, the very top of the chimney.

I went and grasped her, wildly scanning her hands, arms, up the aproned front of her, up all the fearful way to her eyes. No blood. *Mercy I sought, mercy I got.* Adair gazed back at me intact. She did not look the least afraid, she did not look as if she even knew what the fusillade of glass could have inflicted on her. Tunnels of puzzle, those eyes above the twin freckle marks. She murmured, "It just— flew into pieces. When I went to put it back on the lamp."

"That happens the rare time, the heat cracks it to smithereens. But what matters, none of it cut you? Anywhere? You're sure you're all right, are you, Dair?"

"Yes, of course. It surprised me, is all. And look at poor supper." Adair sounded so affronted about the surprise and the stabbing of supper that it could have been comical. But my heart went on thundering as I stepped to the shelf where I kept a spare lamp chimney.

In the morning I said what had lain in my mind through the night.

"Dair? You need to learn to ride a horse today."

She thought it was one of my odder jokes. "I do, do I. What, do I look like a fox-hunting flopsie to you? Lady Gorse on her horse?"

"No, I mean it. As far back in here as we are, no one else near around, it'd be well for you to know how to handle a horse. Just in case, is all." In case lamp chimneys detonate in innocent moments, in case any of the accidents and ailments of homestead life strike when I am not here with you, I was attempting to say without the scaring words. "I'm living proof that riding a horse isn't all that hard. Come along out, Scorpion and I'll have you galloping in no time." I got up from my breakfast chair and stood waiting.

"Now?"

"Now. Out to the barn." I put my arm in hers, ready escort. "Scorpion awaits."

Her gaze said *all right, I will humor you, show me what a horse is about if you must.*

At the barn I demonstrated to her the routine of saddling, then unsaddled Scorpion and said: "Your turn."

"Angus. This is—"

"No, no, you don't do it with words. Hands and arms are unfortunately required. They're there at the ends of your shoulders if I'm not wrong." No smile from her. Well, I couldn't help that. "Just lift the saddle onto him and reach slowly under for the cinch."

Beside the big gingerbread-colored horse, Adair was a small pillar of reluctance.

"Now then, Dair," I encouraged. "Saddle him and get it over with."

She cast me a glance full of *why?*

"Please," I said.

The saddle seemed as big as she was, but she managed to heave it onto Scorpion. Then in three tries she struggled the cinch tight enough that I granted it would probably hold.

"There," she panted. "Are you satisfied?"

"Starting to begin to be. Now for your riding lesson. *Over Pegasus I'll fling my leg / and never a shoe will I need to beg.*" Verse didn't seem to loft her any more than the rest of my words. "What you do is put your left foot in the stirrup," I demonstrated with myself, "take hold of the saddle horn, and swing yourself up this way." From atop Scorpion I sent my most encouraging look down to Adair, then swung off the horse. "Your turn. Left foot into stirrup."

"No." She sounded decisive about it.

"Ah, but you've got to. This isn't Nethermuir. Montana miles are too many for walking, and there are going to come times when I'm not here to hitch up the team and wagon for you. So unless you're going to sprout wings or fins, Dair, that leaves you horseback."

"No, Angus. Not today. I have this dress on. When I can sew myself a riding skirt—"

"There's nobody around to see you but me. And I've glimpsed the territory before, have I not?" I hugged her and urged her, wishing to myself that I knew how to snipper Barclay stubbornness into five-foot chunks to sell as crowbars. "You can do this. My schoolgirls ride like Comanches."

"I'm not one of your wild Montana schoolgirls. I'm your wife, and I—"

"I realize that makes your case harder, love, but we'll try to work around that handicap." She didn't give me the surrendering smile

I'd hoped that would bring, either. By now I realized she wasn't being stubborn, she wasn't being coy, she was simply being Adair. At her own time and choosing, riding skirt newly on, she might announce her readiness. Fine, well, and good, but this couldn't wait. "I'm sorry, Dair, but there's no halfway to this. Come on now," I directed. "Up."

"No."

I suppose this next did come out livelier than I intended.

"Dair, lass, you came across the goddamned Atlantic Ocean! Getting up into a saddle is no distance, compared. Now will you put your foot here in the stirrup—"

"No! Angus, I won't! You're being silly with all your fuss about this." Adair herself wasn't quite stamping that foot yet, but her voice was. She sounded as adamant as if I'd wakened her in the middle of the night and told her to go outside and tie herself upside down in the nearest tree.

The only thing I could think of to do, I did. I stepped to Adair and lifted her so that she was cradled in my arms. Surprised pleasure came over her face, then she giggled and put her arms rewardfully around my neck. The giggling quit as I abruptly took us over beside Scorpion.

"Angus, what—"

"Upsy-daisy, lazy Maisie," I declared. "Whoa now, Scorpion," and with a grunt I lifted Adair, feet high to clear the saddle horn and I hoped aiming her bottom into the saddle.

"Angus! AnGUS! ANGUS, quit! What're you—"

"Dair, let yourself down into the saddle. Whoa, Scorpion, steady there, whoa now. Don't, Dair, you'll scare the horse. Just get on, you're all but there. Whoa now, whoa—"

Her small fists were rapping my back and chest, and not love taps, either. But with no place else but midair to go, at last she was in the saddle, my arms clasped around her hips to keep her there. Scorpion gave us a perturbed glance and flicked his nearest ear. "Dair, listen to me. Sit still, you have to sit still. Scorpion isn't going to stand for much more commotion. Just sit a minute. You have to get used to the horse and let him get used to you."

She was gulping now, but only for breath after our struggle; her tears were quiet ones. "Angus, why are you doing this?"

"Because you have to know how to handle a horse, Dair. You just absolutely do, in this country." I buried my face in her dress while the sentences wrenched themselves out of me. "Dair, I'm afraid for you. I could never stand it if something happened to you on account of marrying me. An accident, you here alone, this place off by itself this way . . ." The ache of my fear known to both of us now. I had lost one woman. If I lost another, lost her because of the homestead— "But this place is all I've got. We've got. So you have to learn how to live here. You just have to."

A silent time, then I raised my head to her. She was wan but the tear tracks were drying. "Hello you, Dair Barclay. Are you all right?"

"Y-yes. Angus, I didn't know—how much it meant to you. I thought you were just being—"

I cleared enough of the anxiety out of my throat to say: "Thinking will lead to trouble time after time, won't it. Now then, all you need do is to take these reins. Hold them in your right hand, not too slack but not too tight either, there's the way. Don't worry, I'll be hanging tight onto Scorpion's bridle and first we'll circle the yard. Ready?"

You won't find it in the instructions on the thing, but for the first year of a marriage, time bunches itself in a dense way it never quite does again. Everything happens double-quick and twice as strong to a new pair in life—and not just in the one room of the house you'd expect.

Here, now, in the time so far beyond then, when I see back into that winter after Adair and I were married, it abruptly is always from the day in May. The day that stayed with us as if stained into our skins. Take away that day and so much would be different, the history of Adair and myself and—

Even on the calendar of memory, though, winter must fit ahead of May, and that first winter of Adair and myself outlined us to one another as if we were black stonepiles against the snow. After the first snowfall the weather cleared, the air was crisp without being truly cold yet. Being outside in that glistening weather was a chance to glimpse the glory the earth can be when it puts its winter fur on, and Rob and I tried any number of times to talk Adair into bundling up and riding the haysled with us as we fed the sheep. "Come along out and see the best scenery there is. They'd charge you a young fortune for an outing like it in the Alps." But nothing doing.

Adair quietly smiled us away, brother as well as husband. "Adair can see the winter from where she is," she assured us.

For a while my hope was that she was simply content to be on the inside of winter looking out, the way she paused at any window to gaze out into Scotch Heaven's new whiteness. That hope lasted until a choretime dusk soon after the start of the snow season when George Frew, quiet ox in a sheepskin coat and a flap cap, trooped behind me into the house. "Anything you'd like from town besides the mail, Dair?" I asked heartily. "George is riding in tomorrow."

"Yes," she responded, although you couldn't really say it was to George or myself. Times such as this, conversing with her was like speaking to a person the real Adair had sent out to deal with you. Wherever the actual mortal was otherwise occupied at the moment, the one in front of us stated now: "Adair would like a deck of cards."

George positively echoed with significant silence as he took those words in. Flora Duff might want darning thread, Jen Erskine might want dried peaches for pie, but what did Adair McCaskill want but a—

"You heard the lady, George," I produced with desperate jollity. "We're in for some fierce cribbage in this household, these white nights. Kuuvus's best deck of cards, if you please. I'll ride down and pick it up from you tomorrow night."

Thereafter, Adair would indeed play me games of cribbage when I took the care to put my reading aside and suggest it in an evening. But her true game was what I had known she intended. Solitaire. After the deck of cards arrived, I began to notice the seven marching columns of solitaire laid out on the sideboard during the day. Aces, faces, and on down, the queues of cards awaiting their next in number. Adair amid her housework would stop and deal from the waiting deck to herself, play any eligible card where it belonged, and then go on about whatever she had been doing, only to stop again her next time past and repeat the ritual.

But I soon was repeating my own silent ritual that winter, wasn't I. My own solitary preoccupation. Against every intention in myself, I was soon doing that.

The schoolhouse dances brought it on. At the first dance in my schoolroom, fresh silver of snowfall softening the night, I was in mid-tune with Adair when I caught sight of Anna and Isaac Reese entering. The sensation instantly made itself known within me, unerringly as the first time I ever saw Anna. Toussaint Rennie once told me of a Blackfeet who carried in his ribcage an arrowhead from a fight with the Crow tribe. That was the way the feeling for Anna was lodged in me: just there, its lumped outline under the skin same and strong as ever. *Dair, here in my arms, what am I going to do with myself and this welt inside me? Marrying you was supposed to cure me of Anna. Why hasn't it?* Until that moment of Anna entering from the snow-softened dark, not having laid eyes on her since the day Adair and I were married, I was able to hope it was my body alone, the teasing appetite of the loins, that made me see Anna so often as I waited for sleep. *I am not inviting any of this, Dair, I never invited it.* Her in the midst of this same music, that first night of glorious dancing here in my schoolroom. Her in the Noon Creek school, turning to me under a word in the air, her braid swinging decisively over her shoulder to the top of her breast. *Dair, I wish you could know, could understand, could not be hurt by it.* Anna beneath me, watching so intently as we made the dawn come, arousing each other as the sun kindled the start of morning. Double daybreak such as I had just once shared with a woman, not the woman I had wed. Night upon night I had been opening my eyes to explode those scenes, driving sleep even farther away. Beside me, Adair who slept as if she was part of the night; there in the dark was the one place she seemed to fit the life I had married her into. But this other inhabitant of my nights—I knew now, again, that whether she was Anna Ramsay or Anna Reese or Anna Might-Have-Been-McCaskill, every bit of me was in love with the woman as drastically as ever.

How many times that winter, to how many tunes, was I going to tread the floor of my South Fork schoolroom or her Noon Creek one, glimpsing Anna while Adair flew in my arms? I couldn't not come to the dances, even if Adair would have heard of that, which she definitely would not have. To her, the dances were the one time that Montana winter wasn't Montana winter.

"She's another person, out there in the music." This from Rob. He meant it to extol, but that he said anything at all about an oddness of Adair was a surprise.

"She is that," I couldn't but agree. Dancing with Adair you were partnered with some gliding being she had become, music in a frock, silken motion wearing a ringleted Adair mask. It was what I had seen when she danced with Allan Frew after the shearing, a tranced person who seemed to take the tunes into herself. Where this came from, who knew. At home she didn't even hum. But here from first note to last she was on the floor with Rob or me or occasional other partners, and it was becoming more than noticeable that she never pitched in with the other wives when they put midnight supper together. To Adair, eating wasn't in the same universe with dancing.

"Angus, you look peaked," Adair remarked at the end of that first schoolhouse dance. "Are you all right?"

"A bit under the weather. It'll pass."

But then the Monday of school, after that dance. A squally day, quick curtains of snow back and forth across the winter sun, the schoolroom alight one minute and dimmed the next. By afternoon the pupils were leaning closer and closer over their books and I knew I needed to light the overhead lanterns. Yet I waited, watching, puzzled with myself but held by the mock dusk that seemed to find the back of the schoolroom and settle there. Davie Erskine in the last desk gradually felt my stare over his head toward that end of the room. He turned, peered, then at me. "Is something there, Mr. McCaskill?"

"Not now there isn't, Davie." Of all the tricks of light, that particular one. Slivers of cloud-thinned sunshine, so like the moonsilver when Anna and I lay with each other on the floor there. *You've got to let the moonbeams in on a dance, Davie.* The silvered glim had come and gone in the past half-minute, a moment's tone that I had seen in this schoolroom any number of times without really noticing, that now I would always notice.

"Davie!" I called out so sharply his head snapped up. "Help me light the lanterns, would you please."

That winter, then. Adair and I so new to each other, and the snow-heavy valley of the North Fork so new to her. I at least believed I could take hope from the calendar. Even as the year-ending days slowed with cold and I fully realized that Adair's glances out into the winter were a prisoner's automatic eye-escapes toward any window, even then I still could tell myself that with any luck at all she would not have to go through a second Scotch Heaven winter with only cards for company. Any luck at all, this would be our only childless winter. Children, soon and several, we both wanted. Adair seemed to have an indefinite but major number in mind—it came with being a Barclay, I supposed—while I lived always with the haunt of that fact that my parents had needed to have four to have one who survived. It would be heartening to think the world is growing less harsh, but the evidence doesn't often say so, does it. In any case, the next McCaskill, the first American one, was our invisible visitor from the winters to come.

It was a morning in mid-March when Rob and I declared spring. Or rather when the sheep did, and he and I, fresh from the lambing shed, came into the kitchen bearing those declarations, a chilled newborn lamb apiece.

"Company for you, Adair," sang out Rob.

She gave a look of concern at our floppy infants, who in their first hours of life are a majority of legs, long and askew as the drone pipes of a limp bagpipe. "But whatever's wrong with them?"

"A bit cold, is all," I told her. "Bring us that apple box, would you please."

"Poor things." She went and fetched the box. "What are you going to do with them?"

"Put them in the oven, of course."

"The oven?"

"A cold lamb's best friend," vouched Rob.

"In—this oven? The oven of my cookstove?"

"It's the only oven there is," I replied reasonably.

"But—"

"They'll be fine," I provided instruction to her as I dropped the oven door and Rob arranged his little geezer in the box next to mine, "all you need do is set the box behind the stove when they come to. In you go, tykes." With their amplitude of legs out from sight under them, the lamb babes in the open oven now looked like a pair of plucked rabbits close to expiration, their eyes all but shut in surrender and the tips of their tongues protruding feebly. "They're not as bad off as they look," I encouraged Adair. "They'll be up and around before you know it."

"But, but what if they climb out of the box?"

"In a situation like that, Adair," Rob postulated, "I'd put them back in. Unless you want designs on your floor."

"How long are they going to be in here?"

Rob gawked around studiously. "Do you have an almanac? I can never remember whether it's the Fourth of July or Thanksgiving when we take the lambs out of the kitchen. McAngus, can you?"

"You know better than to listen to him," I counseled her. "He'll be up to get these lambs when they thaw out in an hour or so. Dair, the lambs are our living. We've got to save every one we can, and when they're chilled, as a lot of them are always going to be, this is the only way to do it."

"How long did you say lambing goes on?"

"Only about six weeks."

So May was a double event for Adair, an end to lambs in the oven and the beginning of weather that wasn't winter. Her spirits rose day by day, taking mine with them. Compared with how we had wintered, Adair and I were next things to larks the afternoon when we were to go to Gros Ventre for provisions.

"You're ready for town, are you?" I called in through the doorway to her. "Or can you stand to be away from the company of lambs for that long?"

"Adair is more than ready for town," she informed me.

"If she's that eager she can practice her driving, can't she. I'll go see whether Jupiter and Beastie are agreeable to you handling their reins."

"Tell them they'd better be if they know what's good for them."

The day was raw, despite the new green of the grass and the fact that the spring sun was trying its best. We were a bit late starting because I'd had to take a look at the last bunch of ewes and lambs that had newly been put out to graze. Even so, how fine it felt to have a change from the muck of the lambing shed.

"This must be what they mean by the civilized life," I said with my arm around Adair as she handled the reins. "A carriage and a driver and the kind of day that makes poets spout. Have you heard this one: *My life your lane, my love your cart/Come take my rein, come take my heart?*"

"I've heard it now, haven't I. Depend on you and your old verses." We were almost at the side road up to Breed Butte. "Had we better see if Rob and Judith want anything from town?"

"Rob was in just yesterday, there'll be no need. Let's make up the time instead. Poke the team along a little, Dair, what about. Then I'll take a turn driving after we cross the creek."

Jupiter and Beastie stepped along friskily as we passed meadow after meadow of half-grown hay beside the North Fork. I never tired of reviewing Scotch Heaven, the knob ahead where I first gazed down into this valley, Breed Butte and the south ridges on either side of us and the plains opening ahead through the benchland gap made by the creek.

"A halfpenny for them," spoke up Adair eventually. "Or are you too lost in admiration for my driving to have any thoughts."

"Actually, I've been watching that horse." Considerably distant yet, the stray animal was moving along the fenceline between the Findlater place and Erskines' lower pasture. It acted skittish. Going and stopping, going again. Shying sideways. Too early in the season for locoweed. Odd.

"Dair, stop the team. I need to see over there."

With the buckboard halted, I stood up and peered. The distant horse shied once more, and the inside of me rolled over in sick realization. That stray horse had a saddle on.

"Angus, what—" Adair let out as I grabbed the reins and slapped the team into a startled run.

"Something's happened over there, we've got to go see what. Hang on, Dair." She did, for dear life. We left the road behind and went across the Findlater pasture at a rattling pace.

The wire gate into the Erskine field was closed: it would be. I saw the scene in my mind as Adair held the team and I flung the gate aside. The rider starting to remount after having come through the gate and closed it, his foot just into the stirrup, the horse shying at the sudden flight of a bird or a dried weed blowing, then in alarm at the strange struggling thing hanging down from its stirrup . . .

I swerved our team from the worst rocks and dips in the ground but we could not miss them all and keep any speed, so we jolted, banged, bounced, Adair clinging part to me and part to the wagon seat, closer and closer ahead the antsy saddlehorse and the figure dragging below its flanks.

By the time I got our own horses stopped they were agitated from their run.

"Dair, you've got to get down and hold them by their heads. Don't let go, whatever happens. Talk to them, croon to them, anything, but hold onto those halters. We can't have a runaway of our own."

"Good Beastie, good Jupiter, yes, you're good horses, you're good old dears . . ." Her words came with me as I slowly approached the restless saddlehorse, my hands cupped as if offering oats. I was halfway when there was a sharp jangle of harness and a clatter behind me; I looked fearfully around to where our team had jerked Adair off her feet for a moment, but she still clung to their heads, still recited "Beastie . . . Jupiter . . . be good horses now," still bravely holding a ton and a half of animals in her small hands.

"Are you all right there, Dair?" I called with urgent softness, not to startle the saddlehorse off into another dragging of its victim.

"Yes," she said, and resumed her chant to Jupiter and Beastie.

"Easy now," my voice added to Adair's horse chorus as I turned back to the saddlehorse, "easy now, fellow, easy, easy, easy . . ."

The false offer of oats got me to within a few steps before the saddlehorse snorted and nervously began to turn away. I lunged and caught the rein, then had both hands clinging to his bridle.

"Whoa, you son of a bitch, whoa, you demented bastard, whoa . . ."

The worst wasn't done yet, either. Somehow I had to hold his head rock-firm and at the same time sidle along his side until I could reach the stirrup and the ankle and foot trapped in it. For once I was glad of the long bones of my body as I stretched in opposite directions to try this rescue.

When I managed to free the ankle and foot I had time to look down at the dragged and kicked rider.

The battering he had undergone, it took a long moment to recognize him.

"Dair," I called. "It's Davie Erskine. He's alive, but just. You'll have to lead the team and wagon over here. Slow and easy, that's the way."

Adair caught her breath when she saw how hooves and earth had done their work on Davie. "Angus. Is he going to live?"

"I don't know that," I answered, and tried to swallow my coppery taste of fear for poor Davie. He was a bloodied sight it made the eyes pinch together in pain just to look at. "He looks as if he's hurt every way he can be. The best we can do is get him home to Donald and Jen."

Now our ride to the Erskine homestead had to be the reversal of the careening dash we had just done; as careful as possible, our coats under Davie in the back of the wagon while Adair held his head steady, the saddle horse docilely tied to the tailgate.

By the time the doctor had been fetched to the Erskine place and delivered his verdict of Davie to white-faced Donald and Jen, his news was only what Adair and I expected. Oh, it is hindsight, there is no way she and I could have known as we conveyed him home in the creeping but still jolting wagon, that the places of shatter in Davie could never entirely true themselves, that he would lead the limping half-atilt life he had to afterward. But I still feel we both somehow did know.

Two days after that, Adair had the miscarriage.

"Angus, you dasn't blame yourself."
Seeing me silent and long-faced, Adair herself brought the matter into words. "We had to help Davie. That's just the way it happened. You heard the doctor say it's not even certain the wagon ride caused it. Maybe so, maybe no. Isn't that the way everything is?"

I had heard. And as best I could divine, Adair entirely meant it when she said there was no blame on me. As well blame the rocks for jarring the wagon wheels, or the wheels for finding the rocks. No, I knew where Adair put the blame. On Scotch Heaven itself, on Montana, on a land so big that people were always stretching dangerously to meet its distances and season-long moods. Not that she came out and said so. Another case of dasn't; she did not dare lay open blame on our homestead life, for she and I had no other footing of existence together.

You would have to say, then, Adair took the loss of our child-to-be as well as a person can take a thing such as that. Not so, me. To me, a double death was in that loss. The child itself, the packet of life, we had withheld from us; and the miscarriage also had cost us a possible Adair, Adair as she could be, Adair with the son or daughter she needed to turn her mind from the homestead, the isolation. I had lost my own best self when Anna spurned our life together. How many possibles are in us? And of those, how many can we ever afford to lose?

"Angus." Adair by me now, touching me, her voice bravely bright. As if the ill person had climbed from bed to dance and cheer up the mourning visitor, she was doing her best to bolster me. "We'll have other children," she assured me. "You're definitely a man for trying."

That December, Adair miscarried again. This time, four months into her term.

I see that second winter of our marriage as a single long night. A night in the shape of the four walls of a bedroom. The man Angus with thoughts hammering at him from the dark. *How has it turned out this way? I saw where my life ought to go, to Anna. Why then this other existence, if that is what it is, of Adair and me not able to attain the single thing we both want?* The woman Adair this time the one staying grievous, silent as the frost on the window and as unknowable. A pair patternless as the night, us.

I turn onto my side, to contemplate again the sleeping stranger who is my wife. And am startled to meet her awake, her head turned toward me.

"Angus. Angus, what—what if we can't have any children."

Silence of darkness, our silence added into it. Until she says further: "If *I* can't have any children."

"You don't seem anything like a stone field to me." I move my hand to her. "Or feel like one either."

"I need to know, Angus. Do you still want me for a wife, if?"

How to answer that, in the face of *if?*

"Dair, remember what the doctor keeps saying. 'There's not that much wrong; as young and strong as you are, there's every chance . . .'"

"Every chance. But none has come yet, has it." She didn't add but it is there anyway: *will it ever?*

Suddenly I was angry with life. Not in the spit-against-the-wind way of exasperation, but vexed all the way up from my core, from whatever heartpit of existence I have. For life to be against this marriage of ours was one matter. Adair and I could answer for that, we *were* answering for it. But why begrudge us our child, life? A child would be the next link of time, the human knot woven from all McCaskills and Barclays there ever have been, the new splice of Scotland and America and Montana and what was and what needs to be. But here where our child ought to fit—by your own goddamn logic of us, life—the only strands of time in sight to us were the old harsh ones of winter and night. Well, you haven't done us in yet, I vowed silently to the winter thorns of frost on the window and the faceless night, we will stave you off a while yet. Adair did her utmost to bolster me after the wagon ride cost us our first child. My turn now.

"Dair, listen to me." I touch to her, stroking the gentle horizon of her body. "Dair," I say with the kind of declaration that can be said only in bed, "we'll get you a baby."

We . . . I rise over her and kiss her lips . . . *will* . . . next kiss for the point of her chin . . . *get* . . . now down to her throat for the next kiss and the tender unbuttoning . . . *you* . . . this kiss on her breastbone . . . *a* . . . kissing back and forth on her breasts now . . . *baby* . . . as she lifts to me with her quickening breath.

It was one of those May mornings which could have just as well saved itself the trouble of posing as spring and simply admitted it was leftover February. A wash day, too, and Adair was hard at it when I pecked her cheek and went out into the day. In the gray chilliness of the barn I had untied my sheepskin coat from behind Scorpion's saddle and gratefully put it on, and was ready to swing onto the horse when I heard Adair, calling from the house: "Angus! Come look!"

I wrapped Scorpion's reins and hurried out of the barn. Snow had begun to fall, a fat and feathery May squall, so that I saw Adair as if through cloud tufts. I strode across the yard calling to her, "What's happened?"

"Just look around you! It's snowing!"

I peered at her, then had to laugh. "Either that or it's awful early for dandelions to fly."

Laugh was the least thing this wife of mine was in a mood to hear. She was the closest I had ever seen her to despair when she fastened her gaze on me and demanded: "But how can it snow? This is May! Almost summer!"

"Dair, in this country it snows any time it takes a sweet notion to."

She scrutinized me as if I'd told her the sun was due to go cold. Then she was reminded of her basket of wet laundry. "My poor wash, though. What'll I do about—"

"Hang it as usual. If nothing else it'll freeze dry."

"Angus, you really don't care that it's snowing in May?"

If I couldn't say truth about the weather, then what could I. "Worse than that, Dair. I'm glad to see it."

"*Glad?*" As if I'd said treason. "But what will this do to the grass? And the lambs?"

"I was on my way to shed up the ewes and newest lambs. They'll be fine, under roof. And a spring snow is just exactly what the grass wants. After an open winter such as we had, the country needs the moisture."

Adair blinked steadily against the snowflakes as we stood looking at each other. "A strange way to get it," she told the country and me.

The next did not surprise me. I had only wondered when it would come.

Two days after the snow, when slush and mud were everywhere and spring was reluctantly starting over, Adair asked:

"Angus, do you ever have any feeling at all to see Scotland again?"

"No, Dair. It never occurs to me." We might as well have the next into the open. "But it does to you, doesn't it."

"I don't mean going back for good. But for a visit."

"If it's what you want, we can get the money ahead some way for you to go."

"But you won't come?"

"No."

"Is it the ocean? Adair doesn't really like the old Atlantic, either."

"No, it's not the ocean, at least not just. Dair, everything I have is here now. Scotland is an old calendar to me." To hear that from me who once stood pining up the Clyde to yesterday. *Angus, are we both for it?* And to have the sister of Rob the America prophet turning back like a compass needle toward Nethermuir and all its defeats. Straight paths simply are not in people.

Adair at least deserved to have the terms between us made clear, here. "If you feel you want to, you can go—for however long you like."

She did the next clarifying. "Do you want me to, Angus?"

"No." The full answer was greatly more complicated than that, but that was the uppermost edge of how I felt. I wanted not to be alone in life, and whatever else marriage with Adair wasn't, it was not utter aloneness. My way of saying so came out now as: "What would I do without you?"

She answered as simply as those gray eyes gave their knowledge of me: "You would still have a life to look ahead to."

Time to be honest, said the thief in the noose. Since the moment of my wedding vow to this inexplicable woman, I had spent four-thirds of my time imagining how I might ever be found out, and here when it happened, it was nothing at all like the rehearsed versions. Time and again in those, out of somewhere it would come, Adair's question *Angus, after all this while, haven't you been able to forget Anna?* There we would be at last. On the terrible ground of truth that I had hoped we could avoid. Adair would be staring at me in appeal. *Convince me otherwise,* her look would be saying. And I would ready myself to begin at it. *Dair, you are imagining. There is nothing between Anna and me any more, there has not been for—for years. You are my wife, you are the one woman I hold love for.* The disclaiming would marshal all of itself that way in my head, ready to troop along my tongue. And instead I would look at Adair and in eight words give up all I had. *Dair, you're too right. I still love Anna.*

But now it had happened, and not that way at all. Whether Adair saw it in the manner I tried not to watch Anna at the dances, or whether it simply stuck out all over me as I tried to be a husband, she knew my love for Anna was not changing. More than that. In her distance-from-all-this way of doing so, Adair had just told me she knew that Anna maybe was possible for me yet, in time. And more than that again. By invoking Scotland, Adair was saying that our marriage need not be a lasting barrier keeping me from Anna.

Straight paths are not in people: amidst all my relief that Adair knew, and granted, my helplessness about Anna, I was sad that the knowing had to cost her. She was carefully not showing so, she was staying at that slight mocking distance from herself as she calmly answered my gaze with her gray one. But cost surely was there, in her and in our marriage from here on.

Our marriage, if that was what it was going to continue to be. Wedding vows are one thing; the terms of existing together are another language altogether. "Dair, where are we coming out at here? *Are* you going back to Scotland?"

My wife shook her head, not meaning no, she wouldn't like to go, just that she wasn't deciding now. "I'll see." We both would.

"Adair seems a bit drifty lately," Rob remarked when he rode by the next day.

"Does she," I acknowledged without really answering.

His head went to one side as he studied me. "Angus, you know I only ask this because Adair is my sister and you're all but my brother. Is life all right between you two, these days?"

"Right as ever," I provided him, and managed to put a plain face over my quick moment of irk before I added: "But you didn't come all the way to take the temperature of Adair and me, I know."

"You're right, you're right, there's other news. I've been up looking at the grass"—he gave a head toss toward Roman Reef, where we grazed our sheep each summer—"and there's no reason we can't trail the sheep in a week or so." A good early start toward fat lambs in the fall, and I nodded in satisfaction with his news. Or rather, with that much of it. "We've got a new neighbor up there," Rob went on. "The Double W."

My turn to cock a look at him. "With how many cows?"

"No more than a couple of hundred head, is all I met up with. I gave them a dose of dog and pushed them north off where we've been pasturing. But that damn Williamson," Rob said in what almost might have been admiration. "The man has already got cattle on every spear of grass he owns on Noon Creek, he 'borrows' on the reservation, and now he's putting them up in the mountains. Old Wampus Cat must have invented the saying, 'all I want is all I can get,' ay?"

"We'd better hope he doesn't make a major habit of putting cattle up there."

Rob shook his head. "They're big mountains. No, Angus, I don't like having Double W cows within mouth distance of our summer grass any better than you do. But Williamson will have to put enough cows up there to tip over the world, before he makes any real difference to us. That's what brought us here, wasn't it—elbow room when we need it?"

True enough, Rob. But as you gave me a lifted hand of goodbye and rode away that day, Montana even then did not seem to me the expanse it had been.

At first I thought it was bad pork. Just an evening or two after our inconclusive circle of Scotland, Adair took her opening bite of supper and then swiftly fled outside, where I could hear her retching as if her toenails were trying to come up.

I pushed my plate back. Even our meals could not go right.

When a marriage begins to come apart, the stain spreads into wherever it can find. The thunder between my father and mother within the stone walls of River Street. The worse silences between whatever Adair sought of life and the unattainable, the Anna shadow, that I wanted. Those mindblind days before Adair and I said the vow there on Breed Butte, why had I ever, why had she ever—

The screen door slapped again. Adair leaned against the doorway, one hand cupped onto her stomach. She still appeared a bit weatherish, but strangely bright-eyed, too. Fever next?

"Dair, are you all right?"

Her heart of a face had on the damnedest expression, a smiletry that wasn't anything like a Barclay smile; a nominated look that seemed a little afraid to come out. Adair gazed at me with it for a considerable moment. Then she moved her cupped hand in a small arc out and down over the front of her stomach, as if smoothing a velvet bulge there.

I can only hope my face didn't show the arithmetic racing through me before I stood and went to my wife-with-child. *May-June-July-August-September-October-November?-December?* That calendar of pregnancy could not have been worse. If we lost this child as we had the other two, it would be with Scotch Heaven winter staring Adair in the face again.

"McAngus, the third time is the charm," Rob proffered with a hearty smile but worried eyes.

"Something grand to look forward to, Angus, pure grand," from Lucas, his eyes not matching his words either.

We count by years, but we live by days. Rightfully, we should do both by seasons. Even now, looking back, it makes greater sense to me to recall how that springtime, when the baby was yet invisible in her, nurtured Adair's hope along cautiously, as a sun-welcoming tree unobtrusively adds a ring of growth within itself. That summer, when the creekside meadows became mounded with haystacks, Adair began to round out prominently. Then as autumn came and remorselessly wore on toward worse weather, a gray strain began to show on Adair as well. But so far so good, we said to each other in our every glance. Each season in the procession had handed her along without jolt, without fatal jostle to the life she was carrying.

Drawing ever nearer to the birthtime, I cosseted her every way I could think of. The oldest Findlater daughter, Jenny, for months now had been on hand as hired girl to do our washing and other work of the house. Adair was the first to declare of herself, "Adair has the life of a maharanee these days." I knew it was put somewhat differently by others in Scotch Heaven. "Adair is still feeling delicate, is she?" I was queried by Flora Duff, who marched babies out of herself as if they were cadets. Elbows of the neighbors I didn't care about; Adair and her inching struggle to bring us a child were all that counted. She had become a kind of season herself, a time between other times. I noticed that once in a while now she would lay a game of solitaire, but only seldom. Almost all of her existence now was waiting. Waiting.

One single day of that time stands out to be told. The day of Isaac.

It came courtesy of Ninian Duff. "I am here to borrow a favor," he announced straight off. "We have a wagon of coal coming for the school." Ninian stopped to glance sternly at the sky. This was late October now; first snowfall could come any hour. "But Reese's man can only deliver Sunday or never. Ay, he's busy as the wind these days. Everyone in Gros Ventre has caught the notion they can't live without coal now. A Sunday, though. You see my dilemma, Angus."

I did. Any hard breathing on Sunday that wasn't asthma was frowned upon by the Duffs and Erskines.

"Angus, I will trade you whatever help you need around your place when Adair's time comes, if you'll handle this."

I agreed to be the welcomer of Sabbath coal, and on the day, the big wagon and its team of horses were no sooner in sight on the road from Gros Ventre than I knew. Isaac Reese himself was the teamster today.

"Annguz," he greeted when he had halted the wagon. "You vish for coal?"

"Isaac," I reciprocated, my throat tight. "I'll see if your shovel fits me."

Not much more was said as we began unloading the coal. I suppose we were saying without words, letting our muscles talk. Coal flew from our two shovels. I wondered if he had any least idea of my love for his wife. Of those words of hers to me, *If I ever see that Isaac and I are not right for each other, I'll know where to turn for better.* Those were words with only the eventual in them, though. The ones with the actual in them had been the ones that counted: *You know how we were, Angus, that last night there in your schoolroom. Isaac and I have been that way together all this summer.* I sent a glimpse at him as we labored. Since when did Denmark manufacture Casanovas? Isaac Skorp Yun Reese. Scarecrow of sinew and mustache and unreadable face. If you had tried to tell me the day I bought Scorpion from him how this man was going to figure in my life, I would have laughed you over the hill. Yet, maybe Isaac in turn was living in silken ignorance of me and what I might someday—in the eventual—do to his life with Anna. Wasn't that more than possible? With an ordinary human, yes, but with a horse dealer . . . I would have given a strip of skin an inch wide to know what Anna's mate in life knew. In that mustached face, though, there was no sign I ever would. Through everything, I had never managed to hate Isaac Reese. Not for lack of trying; with him as a target my despair about Anna would have had a place to aim. But Isaac was not a man who could be despised. Calm, solid, entirely himself in the way a mountain is itself; that, and nothing else, so far as could be seen. I had might as well despise the coal we were shoveling. No, all I ever felt when I was around Isaac was a kind of abrupt illness. An ache that I was myself instead of him.

Exertion greatly warmed the chilly day, and as soon as Isaac stopped to peel off his coat, I did, too. As we stood and blew, he asked, "How are your missus?"

I told him Adair was fine, hoping as ever that our history of misfortune wasn't making a liar of me at that precise moment. Then I was privileged to ask: "And your better half. How is she, these days?"

Isaac Reese gave me a probable smile under that mustache, nodded skyward and gabbled out:

"Ve got a stork on de ving."

I held my face together not to laugh, and cast a glance into the air around for the hawk or heron that Isaac was trying to name. Then his meaning came.

"So, congratulations," I got our, trying not to swallow too obviously. Anna now with child, now of all times? Now as I watched Adair grow with our own creation, Anna with this man's—"When does the baby arrive?"

"Sometime of spring." He gave me a twinkling look, unquestionably grinning under his handlebars now. "Foalz, calfs, lamps," he recited, as if the busyness of the animal kingdom then was contagious. I stooped to more shoveling, more pondering. But Isaac's hand came down onto the haft of my shovel. When I peered up at him I found he had something more he wanted to say. It came out: "Ve vill be feathers of our country, Annguz."

I had to hope Isaac was right even if his corkscrew tongue wasn't. I had to hope he and I indeed would be fathers of children whose dangerous voyages into life somehow would do no harm to the women we were each wed to.

On the eleventh of November, 1899, Adair's baby came—weeks early but alive, whole, healthy, squalling for all he was worth.

"It's a wonder a son of yours didn't come out spouting verse," Flora Duff tendered to me when she had done the midwifing.

In our bed with the tiny red storm of noise bundled beside her, Adair was wan except in her eyes. I leaned over her and said low and fervent, "He's the finest there ever was. And so is his mother." She smiled up while I smiled down. Our son found higher pitch. We didn't care. He could yell for a year, if that was the fanfare it took to bring us a child. Softly Adair asked, "Whatever time of day is it?"

"Early. Flora is fixing breakfast and right after I'll need to feed the sheep. And you're going to have a feeding of your own to do, with a prettier implement than a pitchfork."

When I went out into that day and its start-of-winter chores I felt as exultant as any being ever has, I felt that this was the morning the world was all possibilities. Adair and I and in the frosty November daybreak this miracle of a baby, our son of the sun.

To balance this boy of ours, Adair and I gave him a name from each side of the family. *Varick* because it was her father's, and then the traditional McCaskill *Alexander* for a middle, in spite of it being my father's.

I measure the next span of years by you, Varick. You who were born into one century, one era of Scotch Heaven and the Two Medicine country, and by the time you were approaching eight years of age, a different epoch and place had been brought around you. Or so it very much seemed to me, as sentinel called father.

You were not past your first birthday before your mother and I knew by doctor's verdict that you were the only child there was going to be for us. You weren't past your second before our hearts ticked on the fact that keeping you in life was never going to be simple. Every winter from then on you worried us, coming down with alarming coughs and fevers and bouts of grippe, as influenza was called then, for which spring seemed to be the only cure. Strange, the invalid ghost of yourself that you became as soon as cold weather cooped you in the house. As if your vitality dwindled when the length of daylight did. But in your hale seasons you more than made up for that; you sprouted long and knobbly, like me, and rapidly you were out and roaming into every corner of the homestead. The first major talking-to I ever had to give you was about wanderlust, the spring afternoon I found you in the barn: down under the workhorses at their oat trough, crooning happily amid those hooves that with a casual swipe could have smashed you as if you were a pullet egg. Had your mother seen you there innocent among the feet of death, she would have forfeited years of her life. My own heart pounded several months' worth before I managed to sidle among the big horses and snatch you. Snatch only begins to say it, for I also gave three-year-old you a shake that rattled your eyeballs, and the appropriate gospel: "If I ever again catch you anywhere, ANYWHERE, around the hoof of a horse, I'll lather you black and blue! DO YOU UNDERSTAND ME? Varick? DO YOU?" You looked downright shocked—at me rather than realization of your peril. But you piped apologetically, "I unnerstand," and lived up to it.

You went on, in the next year or so, to your lasso period of trying to rope the chopping block, the dog, the cat, the chickens, and fortunately got over that. But horses you did not ever get over. By the time you were five you could ride as well as I could, and by six you were twice the person I was on the back of a horse. The more horseman you became, the more worrisome it was for your mother; that hauntful day of our finding Davie Erskine bloody as a haunch of beef was ever there in her eyes when she watched you rollicking full-tilt across a meadow aboard Scorpion or some other mount. But she braced herself, as a person will when there seems nothing else to be done, and like a person who has simply decided to suffer—there is no less way to say it—she watched you out of sight the school morning when you proudly set off toward the South Fork on the back of your own pony Brownie now.

To say the truth, I had my own overwhelming fret about you. The dread deep as the bloodstream in me. What I feared for you, from the time you began to toddle, was what I had until then always prized. The water of the North Fork and its easy nearness to the house. I who would never swim was determined for you to become complete tadpole; water and the McCaskills were already several generations late in coming to terms with each other. And so the minute you were old enough I got Rob to teach you the water, your small strokes dutifully imitating his there in the North Fork's beaver ponds beneath Breed Butte, until he was saying, and meant it: *See now, McVarick, they couldn't drown you in a gunnysack.*

Did it lead on from there, the alliance between you and Rob? "Unk" as you called him from the time you were first persuaded to try your tongue on "uncle." No, even without the swimming you and he would have doted on one another, I have to believe. The two of you made a kind of inevitable league against your girl cousins, Rob's daughters Ellen and Dorothy and Margery and Mary, who for all that he treasured them like wealth were unmistakably four versions of Judith. Your tenet of those years, *girls are bossy,* fit snugly with his customary joke about unexpectedly running a convent on Breed Butte, and it was your Unk more often than not who enlisted you into riding the gutwagon with him during lambing time or a buckrake during haying, you little more than a tyke but the reins taut in your small hands as Rob taught you to tug the workhorses into their necessary routes.

You just don't know how lucky you are, Angus, I heard from your Unk regularly in that time, *having a Varick.*

I maybe have some idea of it, Rob.

I did not take the school that first South Fork year of yours, on the doctrine that you ought to be spared the awkward load of having your own parent everlastingly up there at the teacher's desk. But when that first year produced as little in you as it did, I tossed away doctrine and became schoolmaster as quick as the annual offer came again from Ninian. And found out for myself that as a pupil, you were reminiscent of the fellow who declared that his education simply hadn't happened to include reading, writing and 'rithmetic. Oh, you could do well enough to scrape by in the schoolroom, and did, with prods from me. But the main parts of you were always outside the walls rather than in. Riding beside you to and from the schoolhouse, I saw day by day what made you absentminded above a book. Absent to the mountain canyons like crevices in the wall of the world, absent to the warm velvet back of Brownie, absent to the riffles and trout holes of the North Fork—you already were a fishing fiend—absent to anywhere your volition could be your own, rather than an arithmetic book's or a teacher father's. Those were points at which, as maybe all parents ever have, your mother and I wondered where we got you. Except in the lines of your body, there was much about you that did not necessarily seem to be my son. Except in your annual war with winter and a certain habit of drifting quietly into yourself, there was considerable about you that did not seem to be your mother's son. You seemed to be the Two Medicine country's son. Your chosen curriculum, even then, was with Rob and me in the year's rhythm with our band of sheep, lambing-shearing-summering-shipping-wintering. With us as either Rob or I rode up atop Roman Reef once each summer week to tend the camp of our sheepherder, Davie Erskine, whom I had hired as soon as he grew from twisted boy into twisted man. With us as we more and more discussed—*cussed and discussed,* as Rob put it—the jumping total of Double W cattle on the mountains' summer grass after the Blackfeet reservation finally was fenced against the Williamsons of the world. With us, jackknife in your earnest small hand, skinning the pelts off our bad loss in the winter of 1906, when almost a quarter of our sheep piled up and smothered during a three-day blizzard. With us to every extent a boy could be in his greenling years.

A last thing that needs saying of those earliest years of yours, Varick. In all that was to come, I hope it was not lost to you that some supreme truces were made of those years. Your mother's with the homestead. Mine with the everpresence of the shadow between your mother and me, the shadow named Anna; Anna now with children of her own, Lisabeth born half a year after you and Peter a few years after that, children who might have been mine, instead of you. Truce, yes: your mother's and mine with each other, for I believe—I hope with all that is in me—that you grew through these years without yet having to know that a truce is not a full peace.

In the spring of the year that Toussaint Rennie ever after spoke of as *that 19-and-7,* you at rambunctious seven-going-on-eight. A Saturday morning amid lambing time you were helping me at the sheep shed, watering the jugged ewes with as much as you could carry in a bucket while I suckled a freshborn lamb onto its reluctant mother. As you were making one of your lopsided trips from the creek, outside the shed door I heard a voice with Missouri in it say to you:

"Hullo, mister. Funny how water turns heavy when you put a bucket around it, ain't it."

"Uh, yeah, sure is, I guess." I could hear, too, the startlement in your question back to the Missouri voice: "Who is it you're looking for, my dad?"

"If he's the sheep boss of your outfit here, yeah, I'd kind of like to talk to him about something."

You plunged into the shed as nearly running as a person can with a bucket of water tilting him sideways. "Daddy!" you called out, your face still lit from having been mistered for the first time in your life, "Daddy, there's some man—"

"I hear, son. As soon as little Fiddlesticks here gets his breakfast, I'll be there. Tell our visitor so, will you please?"

But you lurched on toward me with your water bucket until near enough to whisper in scared thrill, "Daddy, he's wearing a badge!"

An added fact such as that does take the slack out of a person's behavior. I finished with the lamb quicker than I'd have thought possible and stepped out of the shed, you close as a shadow to my heels, Varick.

And both of us very nearly tromped on the nose of a chestnut-colored saddle horse with so much white on his head he was the sort called an apron face, chewing the tall new grass beside the shed.

"Hullo," the figure atop the big horse greeted. "Sorry to pull you off of your work this way." The man wore a campaign hat and a soft brown leather vest, and was lazing on the horse with one knee hooked over the saddle horn in an easy way I knew I would never learn. His face had good clean lines but only a minimum of them: a sparse, almost pared look to this rider. And while the badge on his vest seemed to say he was a lawman, he was more casual about it than any I'd ever seen. He was asking me now, "You the gent of this enterprise?"

"I am."

"Myself, I carry the name Meixell. Stanley Meixell." He put down a hand and I responded with mine and my own name. The restlessness behind me was close enough to feel, and I added: "This bundle of fidgets is my son Varick."

"Him and me has met just now, though we didn't get quite as far as names. Pleased to know you, Varick," and the rider put down his hand again. While your small one was going into his large work-brown one I snatched the chance to look hard at the man Meixell's badge. Not a law star; not anything I had ever seen: a shield with a pine tree embossed in its middle.

Stanley Meixell moved his head to take in the ridgeline above the creek valley, the summit of Breed Butte above that. "This's a pretty valley in here. Kind of up toward the roof of the world, though. Get some snow in the winter, do you?"

"A bit," I submitted. "Then a few feet more for sauce on that."

"Winter," he repeated, as if it were an affliction of the race. Meanwhile the chestnut saddle horse chewed on at the high grass, the only one of us getting anything accomplished. Whatever this Meixell's business was he seemed to have forever to do it in, but I had a maternity ward of sheep waiting.

"Your badge isn't one I'm familiar with. What, have the trees elected you sheriff?"

"Not exactly the trees. A character named Theodore Roosevelt. I'm what's called a forest ranger." He went on in his same slow voice, "The country up west of you here is gonna be made a national forest." Meixell shrugged in what seemed a mildly regretful way. "They sent me to make it."

"Mr. Meixell, I have to ask you to trot that past me again. A which forest?"

"A national one." He began giving me an explanation of the new United States Forest Service, and then I remembered that what were called forest reserves existed a number of places, mostly west of the Divide where trees grew big enough to be made into lumber.

"Mr. Meixell, I'm afraid you've got your work cut out for you if you're looking for timber to reserve anywhere around here. It reserves itself on this dry side of the mountains. No self-respecting logger would bother with these little pines of ours for anything but kindling, now would he?"

Meixell's gaze had been all around our valley and up the pinnacle of Breed Butte and back and forth across the mountains we were talking of, and now it casually found me, and stayed.

"No, I don't guess he would, Angus—if I can go ahead and call you that?"

I had to nod; civility said so.

"But actually it ain't just the trees I'm supposed to be the nurse-maid of," Meixell went on, "it's the whole forest. The soil and water, too, a person'd have to say."

He contemplated me and added in a slower voice yet:

"Yeah, and the grass."

I felt as if a tight rope suddenly was around my insides. It was then I blurted to you, Varick, "Son, you'd better get on with your watering, before those ewes come looking for you."

"Aw." But you went as promptly as a reluctant boy ever can. And I have regretted since that I sent you, for if you had stayed and heard, the time ahead might have come clearer to you. You who were born in the Two Medicine country with its rhythms and seasons in you had a right I did not manage to see just then, there in the welter of apprehensions instantaneously brought on me by Stanley Meixell's words, a right to witness what was beginning here. We both knew it was not the worst you could ever hold against me, but if I had that exact moment back . . . Instead, as soon as you were out of earshot, I spun around to the man Meixell. "But we summer our sheep up there. Everybody here, on both forks of the creek. That's free range and always has been."

"Always is something I don't know that much about, Angus. But I just imagine maybe the Blackfeet who used to have free run of this country had their own notion of always, don't you suppose? And if there was anybody here before them, they probably knew how to say always, too." Meixell shook his head as if sorry to be the herald of inescapable news. "As I get it—and I'm the first to admit that the Yew Ess Forest Service ain't the easiest thing in the world to savvy—the notion is we can't go on eating up the land forever. As the lady said to the midget, there's a limit to everything."

I could feel the homestead, seventeen years of labor, hours incalculable spent on the sheep, all slip beneath my feet as if I were on a 160-acre pond of ice. With surprising quickness now, the forest ranger spoke to my wordless dismay:

"Don't take on too hard about the national forest, though. More'n likely you're still gonna be able to summer your sheep up there. There's gonna be grazing allotments and permits I'll be doling out, and prior use is something I'm supposed to take into account." Up there on his chestnut horse he began outlining to me how the permit system was to work, every inch of it sounding reasonable in his

laconic tone, but I was still unready to let myself skid back to hope.
I broke in on him:

"But then, if we can still use the range, why bother to—Mr.
Meixell, just what in holy hell is it you and President Teddy have in
mind for us?"

"The idea ain't to keep the range from being used," Meixell said
as if it was a catechism. "It's to keep it from being used to death."

Now the summer mountains filled my mind, the rising tide of
Double W cattle we sheep graziers were encountering in each grass
season up there, Wampus Cat Williamson's chronic imperial complaint, *You people would sheep this country to death.* The awful echo of
that in what this—what was the word for him, *ranger?*—had just
said. Prior use. But *whose* prior use of that mountain range? Suddenly cold with suspicion, I studied the hardworn lean face above
the badge, beneath the campaign hat: had he come as agent of the
Wampus Cat Williamsons of the world, those who had the banks
and mills and fortunes in their white hands? *Ruin's wheel drove over
us/in gold-spoked quietness.* I had thought it wouldn't be like that in
America. I clipped my next words with icy care:

"I hope while you're so concerned against grass being sheeped
out, you'll manage to have an eye for any that's being cattled out,
too."

From his saddle perch Meixell gave me a look so straight it all but
twanged in the air. "Yeah," he spoke slowly, "I figure on doing
that."

Maybe so, maybe no. I kept my gaze locked with his, as if we
were memorizing each other. Say for this Meixell, he did not look
like anyone's person but his own. Yet even if he was coming here
neutral, that eternal seep of Double W cattle to wherever Williamson's eye alit . . . "You may as well know now as later," I heard
myself informing the man in the saddle, "there'll be some who have
their own ideas about your government grass."

"Oh, they won't have no real trouble telling the difference between the forest grass and their own," Meixell offered absently.
"There's gonna be a bobwire fence for the boundary. And I'll
pretty much be on hand myself, if the fence ain't enough." Still
absently, he tacked on: "And if I ain't enough, then Assistant
Ranger Windchester likely'll be." The butt of his Winchester rifle

stuck out of its scabbard as casually ready as this forest ranger himself.

"Fellow there in the saloon in town," Meixell resumed as I was striving to blink all that in, "he told me you're the straw boss of the school up here. I wonder if I could maybe borrow your schoolhouse for a meeting, just in case anybody's got any questions left over about the national forest." Meixell paused and scanned the long stone colonnade of Roman Reef atop the western horizon. "The Yew Ess Forest Service is great on explaining. Anyway, next Saturday wouldn't be any too soon for me about your schoolhouse, if it wouldn't for you."

I answered, "I'll need to talk to our school board," which meant Ninian. "But I can tell you the likelihood is, people here are going to have questions for you, yes."

Meixell nodded as if that was the fairest proposition he'd heard in years. "Well," he concluded, "I better get to getting. Figured I might as well start here at the top of the valley with my good news and work on down. Noticed a place on that butte." He inclined his head an inch toward the summit of Breed Butte. "I suppose you maybe know the fellow's name up there?"

Only as well as I knew my own. And although this forest ranger was a stranger to me, and maybe a dire one, I felt impelled to tell him at least the basic of Rob Barclay. "He has a mind of his own, especially where his sheep are concerned."

Meixell cast me another look from under his hat, a glance that might have had a tint of thanks in it. "There's some others of us that way. Be seeing you, Angus." Before he swung the chestnut saddle horse away, he called into the shed to you: "Been my day's pleasure to meet you, Varick."

While the man Stanley Meixell rode away, I stood staring for a while at the mountains. National forest. They did not look like a national anything, they still looked just like mountains. A barbed wire fence around them. It did not seem real that a fence could be put around mountains. But I would not bet against this Meixell when he said he was going to do a thing. A fence around the mountains not to control them but us. Did we need that? Most, no. But some, yes. The Double W cattle that were more and more. It bothered me to think it in the same mental breath with Wampus Cat Williamson, but even Rob's penchant for more sheep was a formula the land eventually would not be able to stand. And without the land healthy, what would those of us on it be? The man Meixell's argument stood solid as those mountains. But whether he himself did . . . Not Proven.

I heard you come out of the shed with your bucket and start your next dutiful journey to the creek. When I glanced around at you, I found that you had taken a sudden new interest in your hat. You were wearing it low to your eyes as the forest ranger did. I registered then, Varick, that from the instant he reached down to shake your hand, you looked at Stanley Meixell as if the sun rose and set in him. And I already was telling myself that you had better be right about that.

"What in goddamn hell"—Rob, full steam up—"are we going to do about this national forest nonsense?"

"You're of the opinion there's something to be done, are you."

"Man, you know as well as I do that's been our summer grass up there ever since we set foot into this country. We can't just let some geezer in a pinchy hat prance in here and tell us how many sheep we can put on this slope, how many on that one. What kind of a tightfart way is that to operate, now I ask you?"

"There's maybe another piece to the picture, you know," I had to say. "Those grazing allotments could mean Williamson can't pour every cow on earth up there any more, too."

"Williamson has never managed to crowd us off those mountains yet."

"Yet."

"Angus, are you standing there telling me you're going to swallow the guff this man Meixell is trying to hand us? Just because he wears a goddamn tin badge of some kind?"

"I'd say it's not the worst reason to pay the man some attention. And no, I'm not swallowing anything, just yet. I do think we all need to do some chewing on the matter, though."

Rob shook his head slowly, deliberately, as if erasing Meixell and the heresy he called a national forest. "I'll tell you this: I can't stand still and accept that any sheep I own has to have a permit to eat grass that doesn't belong to a goddamn soul."

"Rob, there's a fair number of sheep you own one side of and I own the other."

That drew me a sharp look. I had not seen Rob so het up since our ancient debates over how many sheep we ought to take on.

Yet why wouldn't he be; this matter of the national forest grass was the same old dogfight, simply new dogs.

Rob must have realized we were fast getting in deep, for he now backed to: "All right, all right, I might've known you're going to be as independent as a red mule. If it'll keep peace in the family, you can go around daydreaming that we can run sheep with reins on every one of them." He cocked his head and made his declaration then and there: "But if that forest ranger of yours thinks he's going to boss me, and a lot of others around here, he has his work cut out for him."

When I made a quick ride down to the Duffs' after supper, Ninian was bleak, even for Ninian. "Ay, we can open the schoolhouse next Saturday and give a listen to the man Meixell," he granted. "But if what he has to say isn't against our interests as sheepmen, I'll be much and pleasantly surprised."

That night at bedtime, I told Adair: "I think we'd better make a trip to town, after school Monday."

She glanced over at me in surprise. Any town trip other than a periodic Saturday was rare for us, and during lambing time it was unheard of.

"Davie can handle the lambing shed until we get back," I elaborated. "That way, we can take our time a bit, have supper with Lucas and Nancy."

She still gazed at me. She knew as well as I did that my elaboration was mere fancywork, not revelation.

"Dair, I need to talk to Lucas about this national forest."

"Rob has made his opinion clear."

"Rob isn't Lucas."

At least that turned off her gaze. "No," she said. "No one is anyone else."

Gros Ventre these days was a growing stripling of a town, all elbows and shanks. The main street was beginning to fill in; fresh buildings for the *Gleaner* newspaper, for a new saloon that called itself the Pastime, for the stagecoach office next to Dantley's stable, for an eating place that had opened beside the Medicine Lodge— *pure convenient*, as Lucas put it, *whenever the notion of a meal happens to strike one of my customers.* But it still had plenty of room to go.

In every conceivable way, though, I was assured by Lucas in the next breath after I stepped into the Medicine Lodge, the town was advancing grandly. "We're even about to get ourselves a bank, Angus. It's bad business to let such places as Choteau and Conrad keep our money in their pockets." All this he tendered to me as I was noticing that now that a bridge of bright new lumber hurdled the creek ford, by weathered comparison the Northern Hotel looked as if it had been in business since Lewis and Clark spent the night there. And Rob and I preceded the Northern, and Lucas preceded us . . .

I took a sip from the glass Lucas had furnished me, and speculated, "Then if we were to put the royal mint next to the bank, with a chute between for the money to flow through, and spigots on the front of the bank . . ."

Lucas had to laugh. But he came right out of it with: "Angus, you'll see the day this town of ours is the county seat, and of our own county, too. Gros Ventre is a coming place."

I could agree with that. It had been coming for nearly twenty years that I knew of personally. Before I could say anything to that effect, Lucas produced a glass for himself, between his stubs, then the whiskey bottle, freshening my drink after he had poured his own. "But enough progress for one day. Lad"—for a change that was not me but Varick, who had wanted to tag along with me rather than endure while his mother and Nancy were fixing supper— "what would you say to a fine big glass of buttermilk?"

"Uh, no thanks," uttered Varick with that eloquent dismayed swallow only a boy can perform.

Lucas peered over the bar at him. "It's a known fact that buttermilk will grow a mustache on you practically overnight. How do you think this father of yours got his? I'm telling you, this is your chance to get yourself a cookie duster." Varick grinned up at him and gave out a skeptical "aw."

Lucas shook his head as if dubious. "If you're going to pass up perfectly good buttermilk, I'm afraid the only choice left is root beer." That resolved, while Varick happily started into his rich brown glassful, Lucas remarked all too casually in my direction: "It's not usual to see McCaskills in town on a school night."

"I thought we ought to talk, Lucas. You just maybe can guess what about."

"Angus, Angus." Lucas's great face behind the bar, his bald

dome and his kingly beard, and those gray Barclay eyes regarding me; how many times had I known this moment? "Life was a lot simpler before this man Meixell, wasn't it," Lucas was saying.

"You've met up with him, I understand."

"The day he hit town. I believe this was the exact next place he found after the Northern."

"And?"

"And once I'd picked my jaw up off the floor after hearing the words *national forest* and what they meant, I stood him a few drinks while I tried to figure him out. That, I have to say, didn't even come close to working." It was an admission chipped in stone, the chilly way Lucas said that, then this: "Our Meixell definitely is a man with a hollow leg, and by the time he strolled out of here I was the one wobbling."

Lucas stopped and cocked a look Varick's direction. Then, soul of discretion, said: "That was Meixell's first half hour in town, Angus, and his second was a visit to Uncle Bob," which was to say Wingo and his "nieces." A fellow who attends to priorities promptly, this Meixell, ay, Lucas?

All of this Varick was taking in avidly. The first Montana Mc-Caskill, trying to hear beyond his years. Even to myself I couldn't have specified why, but I now wanted my son to know as many sides as there were to this thing called the Two Medicine National Forest, this matter of the land and us on it, and the sudden forest ranger on whom our future pivoted. I asked Lucas straight: "Other than Meixell's social capacities, what've you concluded about him?"

To my surprise, Lucas Barclay hedged off to: "The talk I hear, this national forest notion is about as popular around here as a whore in church."

"I've heard similar, just recently. But unless our conversation walked out the door while I wasn't looking, Lucas, we're talking now about Meixell himself and what we can expect from him."

"Angus, Robbie is not wrong about what this national forest can do to us and the way we're used to going about things. I know as well as you do that Robbie can be the quickest in the world to get a wild hair up his"—Lucas's eye caught the attentive face of Varick below—"nose. But this notion of divvying the grass as if it was the oatmeal and we were the orphans. By Jesus, I don't know why that should have to be, Angus, I just don't. What I do know is that we've always run whatever sheep we could manage to, up on that grass, and we've built ourselves and Scotch Heaven and Gros Ventre and the entire Two country by doing it, ay?"

"That's been the case, yes," I had to agree. "But how long can any piece of ground, even one the size of those mountains, keep taking whatever sheep get poured onto it?" I studied Lucas to see how he would ingest this next: "Or cattle either, for that matter."

Lucas rubbed a stub across his beard as if reminded of an untidiness there. "You mean Williamson. Our dear friend Wampus Cat. I don't have the answer there either, Angus, any more than I do this geezer Meixell. I'm as fuddled about this as the old lady when she was told that astronomers had found planets named Mars and such up there among the stars. 'I've nae doubt they can see those things with their long glasses and all,' she said, *'but how did they find out their names?'"*

And that proved to be Lucas's say on planetary matters this night. Even after the lilt of that joke, though, I was certain of this much: certain that I saw come back into Lucas the same bleakness I had found in Ninian Duff two evenings ago. *Ay,* the one of them beginning dourly about Meixell, and the other concluding dourly, *ay?* Not pleasant to be squeezed between, Ninian and Lucas. If these two old stags of the country set their minds and horns against Meixell; if they led the many others who would listen to them into rank behind Rob's anger . . . A fence could be built around a forest, but a fence could be cut, too. Grass could be allotted, but sheep could forever stray onto the unallotted, too. A forest ranger could be sent to us, but that forest ranger could rate early replacement if everything he touched turned to turmoil.

I looked down at my son and had the sudden wish for him to be twice or three times his not-quite-eight years, to be old enough, grown enough, to help me think through what I ought to do. To bring his native attunement to the land into my schoolmasterly mind.

Lucas, too, now put his attention on the inquisitively watching boy. Leaning across the bar, he announced:

"Varick, I happen to know for a fact that Nancy has ginger cookies in oversupply at the house. Go tell her I said to give you the biggest one, ay?"

Varick couldn't help blurting his astonishment at such unheard-of fortune: "This close to supper?"

"I know just who you mean by that, lad," sympathized Lucas.

"But tell that mother of yours that I've known her since she was just an idle notion up my brother's leg"—I'd wanted Varick to have full education tonight, had I—"and I don't want to hear any whippersnap arguments out of her about when a cookie can be eaten. Tell her that for me if she needs it, ay?"

Varick scooted out of the saloon for the house and I sat wondering if the Barclays maybe constituted an entire separate human race. It would explain a lot. Lucas now turned his magnanimity my way and proclaimed: "We've just time to top off these drinks before supper." He poured and toasted, "Rest our dust."

As we put our glasses down, Lucas asked: "And how is life treating its schoolkeepers?"

Schoolkeepers. That *s* whispering *more than just yourself and you know who I mean by more, Angus.*

I studied my glass while all the other whispers of Anna whizzed in me, years of accumulated echoes of not having her, a chorus of whispers adding and adding to themselves until they were like the roar of a chinook wind. *Angus, I've told Isaac yes . . . Angus, Angus, take it slow now, both on this whiskey and yourself. . . . Angus, man, this is the best news in the world! . . . Angus, I'll try with whatever's in me to be a good wife. . . . Annguz, ve got a stork on de ving.* And ever around to first words again: *I am called Anna Ramsay. And it is Miss Ramsay.*

The swarm of it all was too much. If I ever once began letting it free . . . Even here now to Lucas, I could stand only to say the utter minimum of my Anna situation:

"We get by, Lucas. That seems to be the story of schoolkeepers."

"And that's enough, is it?"

"I try to make it be."

George and Abraham traded their eternal stoic stares along the schoolroom wall, and the bunch ranged below seemed to have caught their mood. If faces could somehow be said to be sitting there with crossed arms, these of Scotch Heaven's sheepmen on Saturday morning were.

Stanley Meixell half-perched half-leaned on the corner of my big desk in front of us. By years, he was the youngest person in this gathering. But with his hat off, the start of a widow's peak suggested itself there in his crow-black hair, and the lines webbed in at the corner of his eyes by wind and sun and maybe personal weather as well made his face seem twice as old as the rest of him.

Having just given us the full particulars of the land he was bound-arying to create this Two Medicine National Forest of his, Stanley paused to let it all sink in, and it definitely sank.

"Why don't you just arrange your goddamn boundaries to the North Pole and the Atlantic Ocean while you're at it?" spoken lividly by Rob.

To say the truth, the empire of geography the forest ranger had delineated to us was stunning. Grizzly Reef. Roman Reef. Rooster Mountain. Phantom Woman Mountain. Guthrie Peak. Jericho Reef. Anywhere in the high stone skyline to our west, name a rimrock bow of mountain or a sharp flange of peak, and it sat now within the Two Medicine National Forest. And its foothills below it, and its neighbor crags behind it, all the way up to the Continental Divide. All the way up to the moon, may as well say. And Stanley hadn't only tugged his indelible boundary west to the Divide and north to the Two Medicine River. To the startlement of us all, he already had put a Forest Service crew to building his ranger station here on the east edge of Scotch Heaven, at the juncture where the North Fork and the South Fork met to form the main creek. The narrow panhandle of national forest boundary he had drawn from the mountains down here to the station site took in only hogback ridges of rocks and stunted pine that could never be of use to any-one, but still. Everyone of Scotch Heaven and the South Fork both would need to pass by the ranger station and the bold flag atop its pole, whenever they traveled to or from town. Like having an unex-pected lodger living on the front porch of our valleys, although I knew from Stanley's own lips why he had done it: *You're asking me if I absolutely have to bring the national forest all the way down to the forks of the creek, Angus, and yeah, I figure I do. If I hide the ranger station way to hell and gone out of sight somewheres, that's not gonna do either side of the situation any good. This station and the forest have got to be facts of life around here from now on. People might as well get used to them as quick as they can.* My answer, *Some aren't going to like your station out there so prominent.* I didn't much myself. *Me and the forest got plenty of time,* said Stanley, *for them to change their minds.*

Changing of minds wasn't the fad yet, if this schoolroom audience was any evidence. In the seat next to me Rob was tight-jawed, fired up as a January stove. On the other side of him, Lucas was the definition of skeptical. Around us, a maximum Ninian frown and variations of it on Donald Erskine, Archie Findlater, the two Frews . . . the only unperturbed one in the room was Stanley.

He wasn't going to stay that way if Rob had anything to do with it. "Christ on a raft, man! You're taking every goddamn bit of the country we use for summer range!"

"I ain't taking it anywhere," Stanley responded quietly. "It's still gonna be there."

"What makes you think," Rob spoke up again, "you can parade in here from nowhere and get us to swallow this idea of a national forest and like it?"

"I wouldn't necessarily say you got to like it, Bob," answered Stanley. "If you just got used to it, that'd be plenty to suit me."

"But man, what you're asking of us"—pure passionate Rob, this—"is to get used to limiting our sheep on all that mountain grass. That's the same as limiting our livelihoods. Our lives, too, may as well say."

"I'm not here to fool you any," Stanley responded. "You're probably not gonna be able to put any more sheep into those mountains than you've already had up there, and maybe some fewer." Glower from Rob, on that. His look changed to bafflement as he realized the ranger didn't intend to expand that response. Rob burst out:

"You mean you're flat-out telling us there isn't anything we can do about you and your goddamn grazing allotments?"

"Me personally," Stanley said to Rob, "I guess you could get rid of someway. Or at least you could try." The schoolhouse filled with consideration of that. "But about the grazing allotment system, no, I don't really see nothing for you to do."

Before Rob's fury found a next tangent, the forest ranger went along us from face to face with his eyes. "But none of what we been saying so far here today goes through the alphabet all the way from A to Why, does it. I've told you what the national forest is gonna be, you've told me what you think about it. Seems to me we both better take a look at just why I got sent here to make the Two Medicine National Forest."

I shifted drastically in my chair, not just for the exercise. Was this going to work? Was I several kinds of a fool for abetting Meixell as I had? The night after my visit to Lucas in town, another visit,

this one in the lambing shed after supper: Stanley Meixell appearing again where Varick and I first laid eyes on him. *Found your note
under my door, Angus.* I almost hadn't gone to the Northern and left
that message, when I announcedly got up from Lucas and Nancy's
table to go harness the team for our drive home to Scotch Heaven.
Yet I did, yet I had to make the effort to give Stanley the words,
the thoughts, for fitting this national forest onto the Two Medicine
country with as little woe as possible to all concerned. My words to
him there in the lantern light of the shed, that the national forest
was actually the pattern of homesteading, the weave of land and
utility, writ large: lines of logic laid upon the earth, toward the pattern of America. A quiltpiece of mountains and grass and water to
join onto our work-won squares of homestead. The next necessary
sum in trying to keep humankind's ledger orderly. Those words of
mine, Stanley's tune of them now to listening Scotch Heaven: "I
guess you're all familiar with the term public domain. It's the exact
same bunch of land you were all able to homestead on . . ." Land,
naked earthskin. America. Montana. *We can be our own men there,*
the Rob of then to the me of then. Maybe so, maybe no. What can
you have in life, of what you think you want? Who gets to do the
portioning? Stanley's voice going on, low, genuine: "The national
forest is a kind of pantry for tomorrow, for your youngsters when
they grow up and inherit all this you've got started . . ." In the
lambing shed as Stanley and I met, our one witness: Varick. *Your
mother doesn't need to know about this, son;* one more item put into
that category, sorry to say. But Rob and Lucas already were more
Barclays than any sane man ought to have to contend against, without an Adair salient, too. I hated for Varick to see me sneak. But I
wanted him there that night, to absorb whatever he could of the
words of the land as Stanley and I knew them.

"My life maybe don't count up as much in years as some of
yours, but I been quite a number of places in it." No one of us in
his audience could doubt that. Stanley definitely had the look of a
man with a lot of befores in his life. "Every one of those places," he
went on, "I seen some pretty sad behavior toward the country." I
watched him twice as carefully as I had been. There was none of
me in these words, this was undiluted Stanley now. "I used to ask
people about that. What was gonna happen when the land wore out.
And they always said that when they'd used the country up, they'd
just move on. But I don't know of anything you can just keep on

using up and using up and using up, and not run out of. And that's all the Forest Service is saying with this Two Medicine National Forest. You can use it, but not use it up."

The schoolroom was quiet. Stanley was finished with that part of the task. But now the next.

I wanted not to be the one to ask it. Yet no one else was. I would have to; Stanley had to have the chance to answer. Before I got my mouth to agree, though, I heard my intended words coming out of Lucas:

"What about cattle? Do your grazing allotments take in the fact that cattle eat grass, too?"

"I guess I know what you got on your mind, Mr. Barclay. Its initials are Double W, ain't they." Stanley paused to gather his best for this. "I went and did some riding around in the mountains, taking a look at the ground wherever the snow was off. Trying to figure out for myself just what the country up there can carry. How many sheep. And how many cattle." *There's one thing you've utterly got to do,* my last words to him in the shed those nights ago. *Somehow prove you're going to put a rein on Williamson as well as on the rest of us. If you're going to have people of Scotch Heaven accept the notion of this national forest, prove to them it's not just going to be another honeypot for the Williamsons of the world.* Prove it to me, for that matter. And Stanley easing away then out of the lantern light, saying only, *Been a interesting evening. Good night, Angus, and thanks.* And to the watching boy not much higher than our waists: *My pleasure one more time, Varick.* Now I waited with the rest, waited for proof.

"Arithmetic never was my long suit," Stanley was saying unpromisingly. "But I do savvy that old formula, which I guess all of you know better than I do, that you can run five sheep on the same ground it takes for one cow. Now, each of you in this room has got a band of a thousand sheep, by yourself or in partner with somebody"—here a Stanley glance along the line from me to Rob to Lucas—"or whatever. So, the fairest thing I can think of to do is what I went ahead and did. Let Williamson know I'm allotting him a grazing permit the equal of a band of sheep. Two hundred cows."

A massive thinking silence filled the schoolroom.

Stanley spoke again. "If it'll help your own arithmetic along any, I figure he's been running a couple of thousand cows up there the last summer or so. Fact is, I came across some bald places around springs and salt licks where it looks like he's been running a couple million." Came across such places, yes, with my guidance. It would take a man weeks to ride an inspection of those mountains, and Stanley had had only days; I'd cited him chapter and verse, where to see for himself the overuse and erosion from Williamson cramming the land with Double W cattle. "Manure to your shins, and the grass worn away just as deep," as Stanley was saying it now. "I asked our friend Williamson about behavior like that. He told me any overgrazing up there was done by you sheep guys. I kind of hated to have to point out to him I do know the difference between cowflops and sheepberries when I see them on the ground."

Ninian now, starkly incredulous—it was worth being here today just for this. "Ay? Am I hearing you right, that you've already instructed Williamson you're cutting him to just two hundred head of cattle in those mountains?"

"Yeah." Stanley peered out the window toward the mountains, as if for verification.

"And then—?" demanded Ninian.

"Some other stuff got said, is all. Mostly by him." Stanley still studied the mountains. "As long as I'm the ranger here, though, he ain't gonna get treated any different than the rest of you."

Now Stanley Meixell looked out among us.

"None of us needs any more trouble than we already got," the man at my desk with a face older than himself offered. "For my part, I can always be worked with if you just keep one thing in mind. It's something they"—the jerk of his head eastward, to the invisible church of the Forest Service in Washington—"claim President Roosevelt himself goes around saying, 'I hate a man who skins the land.'"

Deep silence again. Until Stanley cleared his throat and said: "Just so we all know where we're coming out at here, can I get a show of hands on how many of you go along with the idea of grazing allotments the way I intend to do them?"

I raised my hand.

No other went up.

Indecision was epidemic in the room. Stanley had said much sense. But the habit of unrestricted summer grass, the gateless mountains, the way life had been for the two decades most of these men had put into their homesteads, those said much, too. Skepticism and anger and maybe worse weren't gone yet. I could feel

Rob's stiff look against the side of my head. My hand stayed lonely in the air, and was getting more so.

Then, from the other side of Rob:

"Will a slightly used arm do?"

Lucas's right sleeve, the stub barely showing out its top, slowly rose into the air.

The next assent that went up was that of Ninian Duff. Then Donald Erskine's hand vaguely climbed. Archie Findlater's followed, and George Frew's, and Allan Frew's. Until at last Rob's was the only hand not up.

The expression on Rob was the trapped one of a man being voted into exile. I felt some sorrow for him. The horizon called Montana was narrower for Rob after today.

But you never wanted to be too quick to count Robert Burns Barclay out. As if by volition of all the other assents there in the air, Rob's hand at last gradually began to rise, too. For better or for worse, in trepidation and on something a bit less than faith, all of Scotch Heaven had taken the Two Medicine National Forest for a neighbor.

There was not a one of us who stepped out of that South Fork schoolroom into the spring air and put a glance to the mountains of the new Two Medicine National Forest who didn't think he was looking at a principal change. But those of us that day weren't even seeing the first wink of what was coming. In the next few years, change showed us what it could do when it learned the multiplication table. Change arrived to the Two Medicine country now not in Stanley Meixell's mountain realm west of us but onto the prairies everywhere to our east, it arrived wearing thousands of farm boots and farm dresses, and it arrived under the same name we ourselves had come with, homesteaders.

Overnight, it seemed, the town Lucas had always said Gros Ventre was going to be was also arriving. But it was arriving twenty miles away, at a spot on the prairie which had been given the name Valier. A town made from water, so to speak, by a company fueled by water. *Irrigation* was the word wetting every lip now. The water-flows coursing from the Rockies would be harnessed as if they were clear-colored mares, and made to nurture grainfields. Dam to canal to ditch to head of wheat was going to be the declension. And soon enough it began to be. Scotch Heaven simply watched, because the valley of the North Fork was narrow and slanted to the extent that only a smidgen of hayfield irrigation could be done, or, honestly, needed doing. But a water project such as the one around the townsite called Valier, seventy-five thousand acres of irrigation being achieved and homesteaders pouring off every train, was reason enough to rethink the world and what it was quick becoming.

Yet you have to wonder. If someone among those prairie homesteaders, Illinoisan or Missourian or Belgian or German, if some far-eyed soul of 1908-9-10 who had come to plaid himself or herself into this Montana land could have taken an occasional moment to watch Scotch Heaven, would even we up here have seemed as fixed in a rhythm of life as we assumed we were? Riffle through us in those years, and you find Scotch Heaven's first automobile—Rob's Model T Ford. *See now, McAngus, I haven't laid eyes on one of these contraptions yet that has a wheel worth the name. But the thing is an amazement, am I right? To be able to go down the road without horses . . .* You find a fresh new wire atop the fenceposts beside the road to town, the Forest Service telephone line from the ranger station to the world. You find in my schoolhouse a long-boned boy named Samuel Duff, son of inimitable Ninian and brother of inimitable Susan—Samuel, my first pupil whose dreams and passions are of airplanes and wireless messages that fly between ships at sea.

So, no, even spaces of time that seem becalmed must be riding a considerable tide.

I knew I was. Season by season, those nearest around me were altering. Varick was ever taller, like a young tree. His quiet beyond-the-schoolbook capabilities grew and grew; he had a capacity for being just what he was and not caring an inch about other directions of life. A capacity that I could notice most in one other figure, when I did my wondering about it. Was it in any way possible that Varick somehow saw the knack he wanted for his own, began to practice it in himself even then, that first time the two of us laid eyes on Stanley Meixell?

My son, then, was steadily becoming some self that only he had the chart of. And as he did, my wife just as surely began glimpsing ahead to the time when Varick would leave us. Several years yet, yes, but Adair saw life the way the zoo creature must see the zoo; simply inexorably there, to be paced in the pattern required. The requirement beyond raising Varick through boyhood was losing him to manhood, was it? That being life's case, she would go to the only other manner of pacing that she knew. She was preparing herself to be childless again, while I watched with apprehension. Not that Adair was in any way ending, yet, the companionable truce that was our marriage. We had our tiffs, we mended them. We still met each other in bed gladly enough. The polite passions of our life together were persevering. But in the newly watchful gazes she sent to the mountains now, in how the deck of cards occasionally reappeared and she would be absorbed into the silent game of solitaire, I could more than notice that this was beginning to be the Adair of our first winters of marriage again, the Adair of *Angus, I don't want you disappointed in me.* The Adair of *A person just doesn't know . . . Or at least this one doesn't know.*

So there were shades of change anywhere I looked in those years—except within me. This person me, permanent in the one way I ought not to have been: in silent love with a woman not my wife, not the mother of my son; seeing her at dances, thinking across the divide of the North Fork and Noon Creek to her. Angus the Hopeless. If I could have changed myself from that, would I? Yes, every time. For it was like having a second simultaneous existence, two sets of moments ticking away in me at once, one creating the Angus who was husband to Adair and father to Varick and partner to Rob in sheep and schoolmaster to my pupils and all other roles to the community, the other the mute Angus who did nothing but love Anna Reese. One existence too many, for the amount of me available. It was cause enough to wonder. Was everyone more than the single face they showed the world? It periodically did seem so. The side of Adair I could not get to. Angles within Rob that could catch me by surprise even after twenty years. And were these divisions in people relentlessly at war with each other, as mine were? Or did I alone go through life in the kind of armistice that my South Fork pupils used as time-out in their games at recess, thrusting up crossed fingers and calling out *King's X?*

Nineteen-ten was our year of fire. A summer that would have made the devil cough. We of Scotch Heaven had seen hot before, we had seen dry before, we had even seen persistent forest fire smoke before. But this. This was unearthly.

What seemed worse than the acrid haze itself was that the great source of it lay far beyond the horizon to the west of us, all the way over in the Bitterroot mountains along the Idaho border, halfway to Seattle. Every splinter of that distant pine forest must have caught aflame, for its smoke seeped east to us day after day as if night was drawing over from the wrong side of the world. Somebody else's smoke, reaching across great miles to smear the day and infect the air, it rakes the nerves in a way a person has never experienced before.

And next, as if our own mountains were catching the fire fever from the Bitterroot smoke, in mid-August a blaze broke out in the Two Medicine National Forest. From the shoulder of Breed Butte the boil of gray-black cloud could be watched, rising and spreading from the timber gulches north of Jericho Reef. Stanley Meixell rounded up crews and fought that fire for weeks, but it burned and burned. *We'd might as well been up there spitting on the sonuvabitch, Angus, for all the goddamn good we ended up doing,* Stanley told me after. With the Two Medicine smudge added into the Bitterroot smudge, the sky was saturated with smoke. The day the Northern Hotel caught fire and burned like a tar vat—by a miracle of no wind, not quite managing to ignite the rest of Gros Ventre along with itself—none of us in Scotch Heaven even noticed any smoke beyond usual in the murky direction of town.

On the homestead we went through the days red-eyed, throats and noses raw, nerves worse yet. I felt a disquiet in myself even before the season of smoke honestly arrived. Somehow I had smelled the smoke coming, a full day before the sky began to haze. An odor of char, old and remindful of something I could not quite bring back into mind. No other aroma so silky, acidic. . . . It hung just there at the edge of being remembered, pestering, as each dusklike day dragged past.

By turns, Varick was wide-eyed and fretful—"It can't burn up all the trees, can it, Dad?"—and entranced by the fire season's un-dreamt-of events—"Dad, the chickens! They went back in to roost! They think this is night!"

Adair looked done in. How else could she look, these days of soot, of smoky heat seeming to make the air ache as the lungs took it in?

A suppertime in our second or third week of smoke, she said across the table to me:

"How long can this last?"

At first I thought her words were ritual exasperation, as a person will wonder aloud without really wondering, *Isn't this day ever going to end?* But then I saw she was genuinely asking.

"Dair, I'd rather take a beating than tell you this. But a couple or three times since I've been in this country, it didn't rain enough in August to disturb the dust. And it'll take a whopping rain to kill fires as big as these." I had delivered that much bad news, I might as well deliver worse. "They might go on burning until first snow in the mountains, Labor Day or so."

"Really?" This out of Varick, as he tucked away yet another un-heard-of prospect. After he went outside to his daily woodpile chore, his mother turned her face to me again. "And yet this is the one place you want to be."

"Times like this, I could stand to be somewhere else a minute or two."

"Angus. I don't want this to sound worse than I mean it. But this country never seems to get any easier."

And anywhere else in life does, does it? Famous places of ease, Adair, such as Scotland and Nether—

Abruptly I knew the smell, the disquieting connection that had been teasing in my mind these weeks of the forest smoke. *Angus, is your sniffer catching what mine is?* That unvarying question from Vare Barclay, Adair and Rob's father, to me there in the Nether-muir wheelshop. *It is,* I reply. *Better see to it, Angus, best to be sure than sorry.* Out I go into the woodyard to inspect for fire, the wheel-shop's worst dread. But as ever, the sawyers merely have halved an ash tree. It is the black heart of an ash when it is split, an inky streak the length of the tree, that gives off the smell so much like burning; like a mocking residue of char. And now in the air of Scotch Heaven and much of the rest of Montana, that old odor from Nethermuir. I wondered if Adair, daughter of that wheelshop, somehow was recognizing the freed aroma of the ash's heartwood, too, in this latest dismay of hers against Montana. I was in no mood to ask.

Instead, levelly as I could:

"Dair, this isn't a summer you can judge by. I know the country is so damn full of smoke you can cut it with scissors. But this is far out of the ordinary. None of us has ever seen a worse fire season and we're not likely to."

"I'm trying not to blame the country for how awful these days are, Angus. I truly am."

I wonder if you are, ran in my mind. It'd be new of you. But that was smoked nerves squeaking. I made myself respond to her:

"I know. It's just a hard time. They happen. You're perfectly entitled to throw your head back and have a conniption fit, if it'll help."

"Adair would do that," she went that mocking distance from herself, from the moment, "if she thought it would help."

It helped matters none either that a few days later I had traveling to do. With school to begin in not much more than a week and the flood of pupils from the homestead influx that was upon us, the county superintendent was calling all country-school teachers to a meeting in new Valier.

"I'll be back the day after tomorrow," I told Adair. "Any stray rain I see, I'll bring home with me."

"Varick and I will do our best not turn into kippers in the meantime," she gave me in return.

Riding into Gros Ventre just before nightfall—although it was hard to sort dusk from haze any more—I stayed over with Lucas and Nancy, and in the small hours got up and resaddled Scorpion and rode eastward.

The face of the land as dawn began to find it took my breath away. The land I had ridden across so gingerly when Rob and I first came to Gros Ventre, the bald prairie where I had met only the one Seven Block rider in my three days of scouting, now was specked with homestead cabins. Built of lumber, not our Scotch Heaven logs. This was as if towns had been taken apart, somewhere distant, and their houses delivered at random to the empty earth. *The rainbow eyes of memory/that reflect the colors of time.* My remembering of a hawk hanging on the wind, steering me with his wings to this prairie that was vacant of people then; these people now in these clapboard cabins, would they in twenty years be recalling when their plump farms were just rude homesteads? And the memories-to-come of the next McCaskill: what tints of any of this change in the land were waiting to happen in Varick's mind? For that matter, if people continued to flock in, if the scheme of earth called Montana grew ever more complicated, where was there going to be room, land, for Varick to root his life and memories into?

With more and more light of the morning, which was tinted gray-green even this far from our smoke-catching mountains, I could see the upsloping canal banks of the irrigation project, and machinery of every kind, and then, not far from the Valier townsite, the whitish gray of several tents near a corral.

As I passed that encampment the many colors of horses grew apparent, muted a bit by the hazy air but still wonderfully hued; big workhorses standing like dozens of gathered statues. Quickly I began to meet and greet men walking in from homesteads to their day's work of teamstering, another session of moving earth from here to there in the progress of canals.

I rode on trying not to dwell on those tents and the brand on the hips of those workhorses, Isaac Reese's Long Cross.

At Valier, or what was going to be, a three-story hotel of tan brick sat mightily above the main intersection of almost houseless streets, as though lines had been drawn from the corners of the world to mark where the next civilization was to be built. The other main enterprises so far were lumberyards and saloons. There was something unsettling about coming onto this raw abrupt town sprung from the prairie, so soon after Gros Ventre nestling back there in its cottonwood grove. Valier did not possess a single tree—no, there, one: a whip being watered from a wash tub that a tan-faced woman had just carried out and dumped. I touched my hat brim, the washerwoman gave me a solemn Toussaint-like "Morning," and we went our ways. Say this for the fledgling town, Valier was only half as smoky as anywhere else I had been in recent history; the other half of its air was an enthusiastic wind. Squinting, I saw through the scatter of buildings to where the schoolhouse sat alone, and directed Scorpion that way.

The rural teachers from nearer were already there and of course the Valier ones, six in total, more than Gros Ventre's school had. The rounds of hello revealed that four of the Valier contingent were young single women, none so pretty as to make a man break down the door but each unhomely enough that in all likelihood four marriage proposals were around not very distant corners.

If the Valier maiden teachers wanted a lesson in loveliness, she was the next to arrive after me. Anna.

I knew she had been spending the summer here where Isaac's horsework was. For how many years now had I had ears on my ears and eyes on my eyes with the sole specialty of gathering any news of Anna, and the early-June item in the Gros Ventre *Gleaner* had shot out of the page of print at me: *Anna Reese has joined Isaac at*

Valier. *Isaac's crew will be the fortunate beneficiaries of her provender the duration of the summer, as they engage in canal construction on the irrigation project and grading streets in the forthcoming metropolis.* She was in the cook tent of that corralside assemblage I rode past, she was here in front of me now as the county superintendent solemnly joked, "Mrs. Reese, you and Mr. McCaskill maybe already have made each other's acquaintance. If not, it is past time you did." For the benefit of the Valier teachers, he further identified us: "These two have been the pillars of education at Noon Creek and the South Fork ever since the foundations of the earth were laid."

"Angus, how are you?" Her half-smile, glorious even when she was being most careful with it.

"Hello again, Anna." *And you know how I am. We both know that, Anna.*

I but half-heard the morning's discussions of school wagons to bring children from the nearest homestead farms into Valier, of country schools to be built east and south of town for the more distant pupils, of the high school to be begun here next year. My mind was ahead, on noon.

When that hour came, picnic dinner was outside in the wind because every new Montana town tries to defy its weather. I got myself beside Anna as we went out the door into the first gust.

"Wouldn't you say we've eaten enough wind at our own schools," I suggested, "without having to swallow this place's?"

The truth of that brought me a bright glance from her, and then her words: "I could say that even without any prompting."

We stepped around the corner of the schoolhouse out of the wind and seated ourselves on the fire-door steps there. Promptly a high-collared young man, more than likely a clerk at the hotel or a lumberyard, strolled by with the most comely of the Valier teachers. There went one.

As Anna and I began to eat, we resorted to conversation confined to our schools.

"Three of my pupils this year are children of some of my first pupils," she noted.

"I have that beginning to happen, too." *And after them will it be these children's children in our schoolrooms, and the two of us still separate? By all evidence.* I stood up abruptly. Seeing her look, I alibied, "Just a cramp in my leg."

I drew a breath and hoped it had as much resolve in it as it did smoke and dust, then sat down beside Anna Ramsay Reese again. Even from our low set of steps, Valier and the irrigation future could be seen being built, a steam dragline shovel at continuous work in the near distance. It was like a squared-off ship, even to the smoke funnel belching a black plume at its middle. Its tremendous prow, however, was a derrick held out into the air by cables, and from the end of the derrick a giant bucket was lifting dirt, swinging and dropping it along a lengthening dike for the lake that would store irrigation water. Handfuls of earth as when a child makes a mud dam, except that the handfuls were the size of freight wagons.

"People come from miles just to watch it work," Anna said.

"It does dig like a banker who's lost a nickel down a gopher hole," I had to grant. "Turning a prairie into Holland. You need to see it to believe."

"Yes. A town built from a pattern," she announced as if storing away the spelling of a fresh word. "They say they are planning for ten thousand people here."

"They've got a ways to go."

"And you don't think they'll get there?" Not disputing me, merely curious to hear so minority an opinion; her instinctive interest in Not Proven.

"Who knows?" Things are famous for not turning out the way I think they will, aren't they. "Maybe all this time we've been living in the Two Medicine grainfield and never realized it."

I forced my attention back into my plate. It was as much as I could do not to turn to Anna, say *Here's something ten thousand Valierians ought to be here to cheer for*, wrap her in my arms and kiss her until her buttons burst.

"Isaac thinks you are right."

I instantly was staring at her, into those direct eyes.

"To have stayed with sheep as you and the others in Scotch Heaven have and not be tempted off into farming or cattle," she went on. "He tells our Noon Creek neighbors that if they want to go on being cowboys, they had better buy some sheep so they can afford their hats and boots."

"Isaac"—my throat couldn't help but tighten on the name—"has always been the canny one."

Now Anna's plate was drawing diligent attention. After a bit she gazed up again and offered, carefully casual: "With Isaac out and around in his work so, we don't see much of Scotch Heaven anymore. Except at dances, and there's never any real chance to visit during those. I don't feel I even much know Adair and Varick." She paused, then: "How are they this fire summer?"

"They're as well as can be. Varick gets an inch taller every hour."

Her voice was fond of the thought. "Lisabeth and Peter, too. They're regular weeds at that age." But when she turned her face directly to me to ask this next, I saw she was starkly serious. "And you yourself. You really didn't answer when I asked this morning. How is Angus?"

"The same." We looked levelly into each other's eyes, at least we always were capable of honestly seeing each other. "Always the same, Anna."

She drew a breath, her breasts lifting gently. Then:

"How much better if we had never met." What would have been simpering apology in any other woman's mouth was rueful verdict from hers. "For you, I mean."

"Anna, tell me a thing. Do you have the life you want?"

She barely hesitated. "Yes. Given that a person can have only one, I have what I most want. But you don't at all, do you."

I shook my head. "It's never as simple as do and don't. The version I walk around in, there's nothing to point to and say, 'this is so far wrong, this can't be borne.' Adair and Varick, they're as good as people generally come. It's the life I don't lead that is the hard one."

I turned to her, that face always as frank as it was glorious. She *had* hesitated, before answering my question about her life. There was something there, something not even the remorseless honesty of Anna wanted to admit. More than the accumulated firesmell of this summer was in the air around the two of us now. A feel, a tang, of sharpest attention, as if this moment was being devoutly watched to see how it would result.

Anna's intent stillness told me she was as aware of it as I was. I needed to know. Was I alone in the unled life of all these years? Or not alone, simply one separate half and Anna the other?

"I wonder when I'll get used to it," I suddenly was hearing Anna say. But this was not answer, I hadn't yet asked, she had slipped her eyes away from my gaze, past my shoulder to a chugging noise down the street. "Every automobile still is a surprise," she continued. If this coming one was any standard, Valier was going to be a clamorsome town. With no patience I waited for the racketing machine to pass by the school.

It didn't pass. The automobile yanked to a stop and sat there clattering to itself while the driver flung himself out. And with a lift of his goggles became Rob.

"Angus!" he tumbled his words out as he came, "there's been— you have to come. There was an accident."

Anna and I were onto our feet without my having known we'd done so, side touching side and her hand now on my arm to help me stand against Rob's words. He stopped halfway to us, the realization of Anna and me together mingling with what he had to report. Dumbly I stared all the questions to his tense bright face: Adair or Varick, Varick or Adair, how bad, alive or—

"It's Varick. He was chopping wood. We got him in to Doc Murdoch. You have to come." He jerked his head almost violently toward the chattering automobile.

"I'm coming." But to what. I pressed Anna's hand in gratitude for her touch, in gratitude for her. "Goodbye."

"One of Isaac's men will bring your horse home for you," Anna said before echoing my goodbye. I climbed into one side of the Ford while Rob banged shut the door of the other, and in a roar we hurled away.

On the rattling ride to Gros Ventre Rob provided me the basic about Varick's accident, and then we both fell silent. In those miles of fire haze and dust from the Ford's tires, I seemed already to know the scene at the homestead that morning, before Adair's words told it to me. *I was just ready to bake bread, before the day got too hot. And I heard the sound.* An *auhhh*, a low cry of surprise and pain. Then the awful silence in her ears told her Varick's chopping at the woodpile had stopped. *I ran out*, the screen door flying open and crashing shut behind her like a thud of fear. She knew there would be blood somewhere, but she was not ready for the scarlet fact of it on our son's face, on the edge of the hand he was holding over his left eye as he stood hunched, frozen. *Varick, let me see, I've got to see*, Adair lifting his red wet hand far enough away for the eye to show. *Hold still, darling. Perfectly still.* The blood was streaming from the outer corner of the tight-shut eye, there was no telling whether the eyeball was whole. *The stick of wood*, Varick was gasping. *It flew up.* She carefully put his hand back in place to staunch the flow. *Sit. Sit right here on the chopping block, Varick, and don't touch your eyeball at all while I go*—with water and clean rags she tended the bloody mess, then half-led half-carried the boy big as her into the house. *Listen to me now. You have to lie here on the bed until I get back. Hold the rag there against the cut, but don't touch your eye itself. Varick, no matter how it hurts, don't touch that eye.* Varick ice-still as she left him on the bed holding back the red seep, as she went to the barn silently crying and saddled Varick's mare Brownie and swung herself up and still was silently crying when she halted the horse on Breed Butte in front of Rob. Then the Ford journey to Gros Ventre with Varick, past the fenceline where she and I had found Davie Erskine being dragged by his horse, where she and I first learned of the impossibly unfair way life can turn against its young.

"We'll just have to wait," judged Doc Murdoch to Adair and me that night. "To see whether those eye muscles are going to work. I do have to tell you, there's about an even chance they won't." Precisely what we wanted not to hear: flip of the coin, whether Varick would be left with one powerless eye, a staring egg there in its socket. "But the eyeball looks intact," the doctor tried to relent, "and that's a piece of luck."

Luck. Was there any, and if so, where? Had the chunk of wood flown a fraction farther away Varick would have only a nicked cheek or ear, one quick cry and healed in a few days. But a fraction inward and the eyeball would have been speared. The tiny territory between, the stick struck. That must be luck, the territory between.

In the big guest bed at Lucas's house, the same bed where Rob and I had spent our first dazed night in Gros Ventre, Varick lay as still as an eleven-year-old boy ever has for a week. Then the doctor lifted the bandage to examine the left eye and its eyelid as Adair and I and Lucas and Nancy wordlessly clustered to watch.

"Blink for us now," the doctor directed. And Varick did. "Open wide. Close it now. Excellent. Look this way. Good. The other. Good again. Now bat your eyes, that's the boy." All those, too, Varick performed.

"If that eye was any better, my boy," the doctor eventually stepped back and announced, "you'd be seeing through these walls."

Varick regarded him, and the others of us, with his two good eyes. This can only be retrospect, but I swear I already was seeing a Varick considerably further in years than the one I left when I rode off to Valier the week before; a boy who knew some of the worst about life now, and who was inserting some distance, some gauging space, between it and him. Because, when all at once Varick was grinning up at the doctor, the smile maybe was as boyish as ever but that left eyelid independently dropped down to half-shut. As it ever did thereafter when something pleased him; my son's wise wounded squint of amusement and luck.

"Varick is twice the son you deserve, McAngus," Rob acclaimed when I went by Breed Butte to tell him and Judith of Varick's mend. More, he clapped me on the shoulder and walked out with me to the gate where I'd tied Scorpion.

"The fact is, I wish I'd managed to sandwich in a son along with the girls," Rob went on confidentially when we were far enough from the house not to be heard. He gave a laugh and added in the same low tone: "I still could, of course, but I'd have to do it without Judith, she tells me."

"Man, think of all the husky sons-in-law ahead," I assuaged him. "Pretty soon you'll have them wholesale." His and Judith's oldest girl, Ellen, already was out in the world of swains, working at the millinery shop in Choteau.

"They aren't the real item, though, are they," Rob mused in a lamenting way that wrote off any future husbands of Barclay daughters. I was opening my mouth to point out that he and I were real enough in-laws, of the brother-in-law sort, when he went on: "Whether or not you know it, there's no substitute for having a Varick."

"I at least know that much," I affirmed to him lightly. Rob could brood if he wanted to, but on a day such as this my mood was topnotch. I stood there at the gate a moment with Rob beside me, just to enjoy all around. *I didn't come all the miles from one River Street to live down there on another.* This day supported those lofty homestead-building words of Rob's. The first fresh fall of snow shining in the mountains had sopped the forest fires, the air was cleansed and crisp with autumn now, and the view from Breed Butte was never better nor would be. My own outlook was just as fresh as the moment. Varick's restored eye, another year in my schoolroom about to begin, the Valier minutes spent with Anna so significant in my mind—I felt as life had shed a scruffy skin and was growing a clean new one.

Absorbed, I was about to swing up onto Scorpion when Rob stopped me with:

"Angus, I think it's time you had a talking to."

I turned to him with the start of a grin, expecting he had some usual scold to make about my taking the school again.

"About Anna Reese," he said, destroying my grin.

"Rob. She's not a topic for general discussion."

"But she's one that's generally on your mind, isn't she. Angus, this is no way to be."

"Is that a fact?" It was and it wasn't. By choice I would not be the way I was toward Anna, carrying this love through the years. But choice was not in this. "Rob, who the hell do you think you are, my recording angel?"

Rob had the honesty to look uncomfortable. "I know you maybe think I'm poking my nose in—"

"You're right about that, anyway."

"—but Angus, listen, man. Adair is my sister. I can't just stand by and see you do this to her."

"You're going to have to." My eyes straight into Rob's eyes six feet away, suddenly a gap the size of life. "Dair and I are managing to live with it, it shouldn't be a major problem for you."

"Living with it, are you? That's what you call this, this infatuation you won't let go of?"

I wanted to shout in his face that there had been a time when he was the expert on infatuation, right enough. That if Lucas had not outwitted him and sent Nancy out of reach and us here to the North Fork, Robert High-and-Mighty Barclay would have taken his own uncle's woman. What had been a quick infection in him had escaped every cure I could try on myself but it was the same ill. Why couldn't he of all people see so, why—

Rob was resuming, "I kick myself—"

"You needn't," I tossed in on him, "I'll be glad to help you at it."

"—Angus, serious now. I kick myself that I didn't see this earlier, why you and Adair aren't more glad with each other. It wasn't until I saw you with Anna there in Valier that I put two and two together."

"Rob, you have a major tendency, when you put two and two together, to come out with twenty-two."

Rob surged on: "I've known you forever but I can't understand this Anna side of you. How is it that you're still smitten with her?" Smitten? I was totally harpooned, and this man was not willing to make himself understand that. Rob stood planted, earnest, waiting. "All I'm asking is how you can let a thing like this go on and on." He meant for this conversation to work as a poultice, I knew. But it wasn't going to.

I had to be sure: "Do you hear any complaints out of Adair about me?"

"She's not the kind to. But—"

"Let me understand this, Rob. You're telling me I owe you more about this than my own wife is content with?"

"Adair is not content with this, how can she be? You moping like a kicked pup, another man's wife always on your mind. What woman can accept that?"

What Barclay? was his real question, wasn't it. Now that I saw where this storm had come from I was sad as well as angry. The old great gulf, life as it came to the McCaskills and as the Barclays expected it to come to them.

But Rob, you. You who indeed had known me forever. You, now, who would not listen and then say, *yes, I see, you have a friend in me for always, if I can help I will and if not I'll stand clear.* You who instead stood here in-lawing me relentlessly. I got rid of sad in a hurry and stayed with angry.

"Rob, I'm telling you. This isn't yours to do. You can't interfere into my life and Adair's this way. So don't even start to try."

"Interfere? Angus, you're not taking this in the spirit it's meant. All I want is for you and Adair not to come apart over—over Anna. Can you at least promise me that?"

"Promise—? Where in all hell do you think you get a right like that—that I have to promise you anything about my own marriage? Listen to yourself here a minute. This is idiots out at play, the pair of us yammering on and on at this, is what this is."

I swung up onto Scorpion and looked down at Rob. "If it'll close you on this topic, I'll tell you this much: Adair and I are not coming apart over Anna Reese. All right?"

Rob as he studied up at me was a mixture of suppressed ire and obvious discomfiture. I at least thought the decent side, discomfiture, won out when he spoke:

"All right, Angus. We'll leave this at what you just said."

I let my breath out slowly over the next several days. But it seemed to have passed, that notion of Rob's that he had a say in how Adair and I were to manage our marriage. Rob being all he was to me, I was able to forgive him the incident, although not forget it.

One last waft of that summer of smoke did not pass. Instead, it began to spread in the benchland country to the south of Scotch Heaven and Gros Ventre; the wind-blown and slope-skewed landscape where Herbert's freight wagon tilted its way through, twenty years earlier, while a pair of greenlings named Angus McCaskill and Rob Barclay trudged behind. The dry and empty bottom edge of the Two country, which now, who would have ever thought it, was drawing in people exactly because it was dry and empty.

They were a few families at first, and then several, and then more. Homesteaders who were alighting on dry-land claims instead of the irrigated acres of Valier and the other water projects. It took Stanley Meixell to dub them so sadly right. After riding past one or another of their shanties optimistically sited up a wind-funneling coulee or atop a shelterless bench of thin soil and plentiful rock, Stanley bestowed: "Homestead, huh? Kind of looks to me like more stead than home." And that is what they became in Scotch Heaven's askance parlance of them. The 'steaders.

Settlers who were coming too late or too poor to obtain watered land and so were taking up arid acres and trusting to rainfall instead.

Men and women and children who had heard of Montana's bonanza of space and were giving up their other lives to make themselves into farmers instead.

Investors of the next years of their hopes into a landscape that was likely to give them back indifference instead.

Watching the 'steaders come, the first few in 1910 and more in the next summer and the summer after that, I couldn't not ask, if only to myself: Was this what that dry land was meant for—plowed rows like columns on a calendar, a house and chicken coop every quarter of a mile? In homesteading terms, it indubitably was. But

when can land say, *enough?* Or *no, not here?* We of Scotch Heaven
believed we were doing it as right as could be—you can't live anywhere without some such belief, can you—but then we had the
North Fork, water bright and clear on the land. At Valier and the
other irrigation projects, those settlers too had water, ditch water.
But these ones out on the thirsty benchlands . . . I grant that Rob
and I knew next to nothing about homesteading when we came to
undertake it. But we were royal wizards compared to many of these
freshcomers. Here were people straight from jobs in post offices and
ribbon stores, arriving with hope and too little else onto the
benchlands and into the June-green coulees. Entire families down
to the baby at the breast, four-five-six people living in a shanty the
size of a woodshed or in a tent while they tried to build a shanty.
And meanwhile were struggling too to break the sod and plant a
crop, dig a well, achieve a garden. I suppose these 'steaders had to
be as Rob and I were when we began in Scotch Heaven, not daring
to notice yet that they were laboring colossal days and weeks for a
wage of nothing or less. I suppose there is no other way to be a
homesteader. Yet, bargaining yourself against the work and the
weather is always going to turn out to be greatly more difficult than
you can ever expect. Even in Scotch Heaven we had the absences
around us, the Speddersons and Tom Mortensen, to remind how
harsh and unsure a bet homesteading was. Yet and again, agog as I
might be at the numbers of these incomers and aghast as I often was
at how little they knew of what they needed to, I could not deny
that the 'steaders on their raw dry quarter-section squares were
only attempting the same as we had, trying to plaid new lives into
this proffered land.

This was bright June. Winter waited four or five months away
yet. Nonetheless I began saying a daily prayer to it: be gentle with
these pilgrims.

Not many days later, Rob and Lucas waylaid me when I was in
my lower meadow making a peaceful reconnaissance of the hay
prospect there. Angling a look into the Ford as it halted briskly
beside me, I couldn't help but put the query:

"What's this, now—a war council of Clan Barclay?"

Out they climbed, here they were. "Mark this day, McAngus,"
Rob proclaimed, Lucas equally sunny beside him. "We're here with
the proposition of a lifetime for you."

"Wait. Before I hear it"—patting each appropriate neighborhood of my body I recited: "*Testicles, spectacles, wallet, watch.* There's proof I had all my items before the two of you start in on me, just remember."

"Angus, Angus," chided Lucas. "You're as suspicious as one deacon is of the other. Just hear what we've got in mind, ay?"

"That shouldn't take all day. Bring it out."

"There's hope for you yet, Angus," Rob averred with a great smile. "Now here's the word that's as good as money in the bank: 'steaders." He cocked his head in that lordly way and waited a moment for my appreciation before proceeding. "You know as well as we do that they're starting to come into this end of the Two country by the hatful and they can barely recognize ground when they're standing on it."

"And?"

Rob's smile greatened more yet. "And we can be their land locators."

Lucas broke in: "Angus, it's something I ought to've listened to when I first came, when I was mining." Into his coat pockets went his stubs, as if he was whole again there at the start of Montana life. "Someone asked old Cariston there in Helena, the same geezer you worked for in his mercantile, Angus, what he did for a living. Do you know what he said? 'I mine the miners, there's where the real money is.' And it's pure true. Every word of it and then some. In a new country the one thing people need is supplies. And what's the supply every homesteader needs first of any? Land, Angus. You and Robbie know all this land around here by the inch. You're just the lads to supply homestead sites."

I studied from Lucas to Rob, back to Lucas again. Usually Lucas was as measuring as a draper, but Rob plainly had him entirely talked into the gospel of land locating. Rob alone I would have given both barrels of argument at once, but for Lucas's sake I went gentler. "Just how does this rich-making scheme work?"

"Simple as a dimple," Rob attested. "I'll meet people right at the depots, in Valier and Conrad and Browning—you know they're pouring in by the absolute trainload." They were that. Just recently an entire colony of Belgians came to the Valier land; men, women, children, grandparents, babes, likely cats and canaries, too! The Great Northern simply was throwing open the doors of freight cars in St. Paul, and Montana-bound families were tossing in their belongings and themselves. "I'll ferry them out to here in the Lizzie," Rob strategized, "and here's where you come in, Angus. You're the man with the eye for the land. You'll locate the 'steaders onto the claims, mark the claim for them, tell them how to file on it, all but give them their homestead on a china plate. Lucas just said it, really. What we'll be is land suppliers, pure and simple."

The arguing point to all this couldn't be ignored any longer. "If we had the goods, I could see your supply idea," I told Rob. Then with a nod toward the south benchlands: "But what land is left around here is thin stuff for homesteading." I paused and gave him a look along with this next: "Concentrate a bit and you'll maybe remember what we thought of it ourselves, when you and I walked into this country behind Herbert."

"By our lights, maybe it isn't the best land there ever was," Rob granted. "But to these 'steaders it's better than whatever to hell they've had in life so far, now isn't it? Man, people are going to come, that's the plain fact of the matter. Whether or not we lead them by the hand, they're going to file homestead claims all through this country. They might as well be steered as right as possible, by knowledgeable local folk. Which is the same as saying us. In that way of looking at it, McAngus, we'll be doing them a major favor, am I right?"

"And charging them a whack for it," I couldn't help saying of Rob's version of favor.

"Are you so prosperous you can do it for free?" came back at me from him. "Funny I don't notice the bulges in your pockets."

"Lads, now," Lucas interceded. "Angus, we're not asking for your answer this very minute. Just put the idea on your pillow for a few nights, ay?"

Had they been asking my answer right then, it would have been No, in high letters. But. The prosperous problem. The perpetual problem with homesteads, with livestock, or maybe just with McCaskills. Working yourself gray, year after year, and always seeing the debt years eat up most of the profit years. To now, Adair had never said boo about the fact that where money was concerned we were always getting by, hardly ever getting ahead. So the dollar thoughts were delaying my No a bit, and I

decided to leave matters with the Barclays at: "I'll need to do a
lot of that pillow work, and to talk it over with Dair."

"You can save your breath there," Rob tossed off. "She's thoroughly for it."

I gave Rob a look he would have felt a mile away. "You know
that already? From her?"

"I happened to mention it to Adair, yes. Angus, she is my sister. I do talk to her once in a blue moon. Not that I'd particularly
have to in this case. She's bound to be for anything that'll fetch
money the way this will. Who wouldn't be?"

"Angus, I know how you feel about this country and the
'steaders," Adair said that night. By then we had been thoroughly through it all. Adair's point that here was a plateful of
opportunity on Varick's behalf, as easy a chance as we would
ever have at money for his future, his own start in life and land
in the years not far ahead now. My lack of any way to refute
that, yet my unease about the notion of making myself into a
land locator. "But change always has to happen," she was saying, "doesn't it?"

"The big question is whether it happens for the better or the
worse."

"Either case, what can you really do about it?" she responded.
"You and Rob came here as settlers. So are all these others."

"If they were bringing their own water and trees and decent
topsoil, I'd say let everybody and his brother come. But good
Christ, this dry-land craziness—Dair, they say there are 'steaders on the flats out north of Conrad now who haul all their water a
couple of miles, a barrel at a time on a stone boat. They strain
that cloudy water through a gunny sack as they bucket it into the
barrel. My God, what a way to try to live. And these have been
wet summers and open winters. What are those people going to
do when this country decides to show them some real weather?"

"I suppose some will make it and some won't," she answered
in all calmness. "It's their own decision to come here and try. It's
not ours for them." The deep gray eyes were steady on me, asking me to reason as she was.

I could do that. What I wasn't able to manage was the waiting
conclusion: that I ought to join in, bells, tambourines and all,

with Rob and Lucas in putting people onto land that ought not to have to bear any people.

"There's something more, Angus," my wife offered now. "It's not just Varick we need to plan for. It's each other as well."

Her silence, my waiting. Then from her:

"Adair doesn't know if she can stay, after Varick is grown and gone."

So here it was, out. Adair and how long she would reconcile herself to Scotch Heaven, once it became a childless place to her again, had been in my mind with Anna at Valier and so I could not call this an entire surprise. Stunning, yes, now that it was here, openly said. But all the years since *Angus, do you ever have any feeling at all to see Scotland again?*, since *Do you still want me for a wife, if?*, all those years led here, if you were Adair.

I reached her to me, but there was too much in me to speak straight to what she had just said. Adair herself, myself, Anna, past, future, now. It all crowded in me beyond any saying of it. No, only the one decision, the one I had to do at once rather than let the next years take care of, came to my tongue. If there were three Mc-Caskill lives ahead that needed finance—mine of Scotch Heaven, Varick's of the Two Medicine country, Adair's of Scotland or wherever—then I had to find money.

"All right, Dair," I whispered. "We're in business with a couple of Barclays."

Squint as hard as you will, you can't see to tomorrow. Had I been told in the wheelwright shop in Nethermuir, *Angus, the day will arrive when you trace the hopes of homesteaders onto the American earth with a wagon wheel . . . when the turns of that wheel become the clock that starts dew-fresh families on years of striving . . . when the wheel tracks across the grass single out another square of earth for the ripping plow . . .* I would have looked around from my own dreams and said skeptically, *You have the wrong Angus.* Yet there I was, that summer and the next, on the wagon seat with a white handkerchief tied around a wheelspoke to count revolutions by, counting the ordinations of wheelspin. *Fifty.* Seeing the craft of my unhearing father, the band of iron encircling the spokes, holding all together to write the future of 'steaders onto prairie acres. *That's a hundred.* Conveying, in a single day, lives from what they had abandoned to where they had dreamed of being. *A hundred fifty.* Here is your first corner of your claim, Mr. and Mrs. Belgium. Mr. Missouri bachelor. Miss Dakota nurse. Mrs. Wisconsin widow. Then to the next corner, and the next, and the next, and the square was drawn, here was your homestead utter and complete: *SE¼ Sec. 17, Tp. 27 N, Rge. 8 W: the land has been made into arithmetic.* A sort of weaving, wasn't it, these numerated homestead squares, the lives threaded in and out. But these bare dry-land patches amid the mesh of homesteading . . . It was said there were twice as many people in Montana now as five years ago. The growth, the 'steader-specked prairies and benchlands and coulees, the instant towns, they were what Lucas dreamed of and Rob calculated on, and I was earning from. If I could dance ahead into time yet to come, what would I see in this procession of 'steaders that ought not have been let to happen, and what ought to have been encouraged instead? But we never do dance ahead into time; every minute is a tune-step of ours to the past. Say it better, the future is our blindfold dance, and a dance unseen is strangest dance of all, thousands of guesses at once. That was what my 'steaders amounted to, after all. Say that each of these people beside me on the wagon seat was a flip of the coin. Half would turn up wrong. And so for two summers I watched the 'steaders, Rob and Lucas's 'steaders, my 'steaders, and wondered just which of them were wrong tosses, which would meet only distress and failure and maybe worse here on this dry land which was free but not costless, not nearly.

It was a Saturday early the next May that there was the Hebner occurrence.

The family of four was Rob's first delivery to me in this new season of 'steaders. As Rob and the Ford receded back down the road to further depot duty, the newcomers and I sized each other up.

The man was loose-jointed, shambly, with a small chin, a small mouth, small nose, and then a startlingly high and wide forehead. The woman was worn, maybe weary after their journey from wherever to Montana, maybe just weary. Two children thin as sticks, the boy a replica two-thirds the size of his father, the girl small yet. Both children and the man stared at me as openly as hawks. As to what they saw in all this eyework on me, I do not really know, do I.

I introduced myself, and received from the man in just less than a shout: "Our name's Hebner, but you got to call me Otto."

I invited them into the wagon, and after an odd blank little pause while the rest of the family glanced at him and he fidgeted an untrusting look at me, up they came.

The ride into the south benchlands was a few miles, and would be longer than that without conversation. I inaugurated:

"Where is it you're from?"

The man peered at me in dumb dismay. Hard of hearing, the poor pilgrim must be. Deaf and a 'steader too ought to be more hardship than any one soul rated. I squared around to the fidgeting Hebner and repeated my question louder and slower.

Relief came over him. In a braying voice, he responded: "Couldn' cut through your brogue, there that first time. A feller gets so used to hearin' American he gets kind of spoiled, I reckon."

I gazed at Hebner, hoping that was what passed for a joke wherever to hell he had been spawned, but no. He rattled on: "Anyhow, we come from Oblong, Illinois. Ever hear of it?"

"Illinois, yes."

Having had my fill of conviviality Otto Hebner style, I whapped the team some encouragement with the reins. Delivering this man and his wan family to their 160 acres of delusion couldn't come too soon for me.

Atop the rim of the benchland, I halted the wagon. Beside me Hebner kept his head turned in a gawk toward the mountains and the North Fork for so long that I truly wondered if he and I both belonged in the human race. Now he gesticulated for his family's benefit to the hay-green valley of the North Fork, the newly lambed bands of sheep on its ridges around, the graceful wooded line of the creek and its periodic tidy knots that were our houses and outbuildings.

"Hannah, honey, those're what I been tellin' you about," he resounded to his wife. Noticing that the boy's stare was still fixed in my direction rather than onto the Scotch Heaven homesteads, Hebner added sharp to loud in telling him: "Garland! You listen up to what I'm sayin' here, you hear?" The boy's gaze slowly drifted from me to the North Fork. His father by now had reached his proclamation point: "Those're what our homestead is goin' to be like before you know it."

Bring that moment around to me again and I would utter what I furiously kept myself from uttering at the time. *Hebner, you major fool, you're looking at twenty years of stark work down there. Twenty years of building and contriving and fixing and starting over again. Twenty lambing times, twenty shearings, twenty hayings. Twenty Montana winters, each of them so long they add far beyond that. You're looking at the stubborn vision of Ninian Duff, you're looking at the tireless ambitions of Rob Barclay, you're looking at the durable routes Scorpion and I have worn into the ground back and forth between sheep and schoolchildren, you're looking at choreworn wives who put up with more isolation and empty distance than anyone sane ought to have to. You cannot judge this country by idle first glance. I am here to tell you, you cannot.* But no, I was there to guide the Hebners of the world to available acres, such as they were now. Try to dike this 'steader flood with myself and all I would get was reputation for being all wet.

I drew a steadying breath. My own gaze down into Scotch Heaven helped. On the shoulder of Breed Butte between Rob's homestead and mine, a rider had come into motion: Varick, on his way up to check our sheep, while I was in the midst of this Hebnerian episode. Varick on a horse now looked as big as a man. Already his first year of high school was nearly behind him. His school year of boarding in town with Lucas and Nancy and returning to Adair and me only on weekends was his first footprint away from home, and this summer would bring his next. He had asked Stanley Meixell for, and received, the job of choreboy at the ranger station until school began again in the fall. Not many years now, not many at all, Angus, until this son of yours would need to find his own foothold in this country, and so I swung back to the task of delving with 'steaders.

"Those of us in Scotch Heaven do have a bit of a head start on you, Mr. Hebner, so there's—"

"Otto," he corrected me with a bray.

"Otto, then. As I was setting out to say, there's no real resemblance between a settled creek valley and a dry-land homestead. So I don't want to startle you, but here we are at the available land for you to have a look at."

Hebner hopped down and gawked south now, across the flat table of gravelly earth sprigged with bunchgrass, his son duplicating the staring inspection while I took the girl down from his wife and then helped her out of the wagon. We stood in a covey at the section marker stone, the wind steadily finding ways to get at us under and around the wagon, until Hebner strode off twenty or so paces to-

ward the yawning middle of the benchland as if that was the favored outlook. After a long gander and kicking his heel into the soil,
what there was of it, a number of times, he marched back and took
up a stance beside me. Still scrutinizing the benchland, the shanties
and chicken coops and pale gray-brown furrows of the Keever and
Reinking and Thorkelson homesteads, he demanded: "You're
dead-sure this here is the best piece of new ground?"

Anyone with an eye could see that the benchland was equally
stark, stony, unwelcoming, wherever a glance was sent. "None of it
is fair Canaan, is it," was all I could answer Hebner. "But if here in
this dry-land end of the Two country is where you truly want to
homestead, right where we're standing is as good as any."

Not a lot of satisfaction for him to find in my words. He leaned
away from me and turned a bit so his silent wife would see the
shrewdness of what he asked next: "How deep is it to water?"

The question I had been dreading. "I can only tell you this
much. The Keevers and the Reinkings and the Thorkelsons all dug
about forty feet to get their wells."

"*Forty!* Back in Illinois we could dig down ten feet anywhere and
get the nicest softest vein of wellwater there is!"

"Then you ought to have brought one of those matchless wells
with you." I faced around to his wife, on the chance she might not
be so hopeless a case as him. "Mrs. Hebner, you had better know,
too—the water up here is hard." She made no reply. "Just so you
know, come first washday," I tried to prompt, "and you won't cuss
me too much." Still nothing from her except that abject or defeated
gaze at her husband. By the holy, if she could stand here wordless
and let this Hebner commit her to a homestead eternity of clothes
washed out stiff as planks and of a sour grayness in every teaspoon
of water she ever used, why then—

"Seems like you ain't overly enthusiastic about this here
ground," Hebner now gave me with a suspicious frown.

"Mr. Hebner, listen—"

"Otto," the man insisted thunderously.

"Otto, then. Listen a minute. None of this is going to be easy or
certain, for you and your family. Even at its best, homesteading is a
gamble, and it's twice that in these benchlands. A dry-land homestead is just what it says it is, dry."

"I didn' notice as how you left us any room back down there

along the creek," he retorted, making only small attempt to smile around the resentment.

Roust yourself twenty years ago from Lopside or wherever it is that spawned you, and there was room along the North Fork, along the South Fork, room everywhere across the Two Medicine country. And in the same thinking of that I knew that I would not have welcomed Otto Hebner even then; that anyone who did not come accepting that the homestead life was going to be hard, I did not want at the corner of my eye.

"Let's call this off," I said abruptly. "We're not doing each other any good here."

"Call it off!" Hebner blinked at me, thunderstruck. "This's a funny doggone arrangement you're pullin' on us, seems like," he brayed. "Leadin' us out to this here ground and then givin' us the poormouth about it. This's doggone funny exchange for the money we paid, is what I say."

"I thought you might want to know what you're in for, trying to homestead country such as this. I was obviously wrong. I'll give you your money back and take you in to Gros Ventre. If you're still set on finding a site, someone in town can do your locating for you."

"Nothin' doin'." Hebner did not look toward his wife and children, did not look around at the land again. He fixed his gaze onto my face as if defying me to find any way to say him nay. "This here's what I'm goin' to claim, right where we're at."

"Even against my advice, you want me to mark off the claim?"

"That's what we come all the way out here for."

I wrote HEBNER on four corner stakes, climbed into the buggy and counted the one hundred and fifty wheel revolutions south, east, north, and finally west to the section stone again.

By the time that day was done, I knew my craw could not hold any more Hebners, ever. All 'steaders from here on were going to have to dry-land themselves to death without my help.

In bed that night, I said as much to Adair.

"We're back where we started, then," she said as the fact it was. "Back to just getting by, and putting nothing ahead."

"There may be a way we can yet," I offered to her in the dark. "Dair, if I'm going to get us and Varick anywhere in life, it's going to have to be some way where I savvy and believe in what I'm doing. Something I know the tune of." I could feel her waiting.

"Sheep," I announced. "If we were to take on another band of sheep, the profit from that we could set aside for Varick."

Silence between us. Until Adair spoke softly: "You've never wanted to take on more than the band you and Rob run."

"I'll need to try stretch my philosophy, won't I." Try, for Varick. For you, Dair. For myself?

"Do we have the money for another band of sheep?"

"No. Half enough, maybe."

"Lucas would have it," she contributed.

"Lucas took his turn in backing me with sheep, long since. Besides, he's in up to his neck in land dealings these days. No, I think I know who would be keener than Lucas for this." Although I didn't look forward to hearing it from him: *I never thought I'd see the day, McAngus, when you'd start sounding like me—'More sheep, that's the ticket we need.'* "Dair, I thought I'd see if Rob will partner with us on another band."

Adair spoke what I was counting on, from her, from her brother. "He will."

What I had not counted on was Rob's notion of where we ought to put a new band of sheep. "Angus, I won't go for putting any more sheep up there in Meixell's hip pocket, even if the damn man would let us." If not on the national forest, then we'd have to rent grazing somewhere else, I pointed out to him. Maybe in the Choteau country, not that there was that much open range left there or anyplace, for that matter.

"Give me a couple of days," Rob said. "I just maybe know the place for those sheep, where Meixell or some Choteau geezer either one won't have a hoot in hell to say about them."

The couple of days later, Rob's announcement was pure jubilation.

"The reservation! Angus, you remember that Two Medicine grass. Elephants could be grazed on it! The Blackfeet don't know anything to do with it but sit and look at it."

I stirred. "Rob, hold your water a minute here. You know as well as I do why the Agency fenced the cow outfits out. That old business of 'borrowing' reservation grass—"

"'Borrowing,' who said anything about 'borrowing'? We'll be paying good lease money to the Blackfeet. You can ask your pocket whether there's any 'borrowing' to this. No, this is every-dot legal, Angus. The agent will let us on the big ridge north of the Two Medicine River with the sheep the first of the month. Man, you can't beat this with a stick! A full summer on that grass and we'll have lambs fat as butter."

I gave it hard thought, sheep on the Blackfeet grass. Sheep were not plows that ripped the sod; sheep with a good herder were not cattle casually flung Double W style. Prairie that had supported buffalo herds vast as stormclouds ought to be able to withstand a careful load of sheep. If Rob saw this band as a ladle to get at the cream of reservation grass, so be it. With Davie Erskine as herder, I could see to it the summer of leased grazing was kept civil and civic. I wanted it begun right, too.

"Those are some miles, from here to the Two Medicine," I pointed out. Forty or more, in fact.

"Sheep have feet," retorted Rob. As I knew, though, the days it would take to trail the sheep were not going to be his favorite pastime. "I hate like the dickens to lose that many days from the locating business. But I suppose—"

Without needing to think, I said: "I'll take the sheep up. Varick and I can, with Davie along."

I felt Rob study me. Probably it was all too plain that I didn't want to see his next crop of 'steaders. Then from him:

"Angus, you're made of gold and oak. If you can handle the reservation band until shearing, I'll make it right to you when we settle up this fall."

They were a band of beauties, our new sheep; the top cut of ewes and their eight-week lambs from the big Thorsen sheep outfit in the Choteau country. And confident grazers, definitely confident. The morning Varick and Davie and I bunched them to begin the journey from Scotch Heaven to the reservation, making them leave the green slopes above the North Fork was sheer work. You could all but hear their single creed and conviction in the blatting back and forth, *why leave proven grass for not proven?* That first hour or so it seemed that every time I looked around, a bunch breaker was taking off across the countryside at a jog trot, her lamb and twenty others in a scampering tail behind her. Relentlessly Varick and

Davie and I dogged that foolishness out of them, and the band at last formed itself and began to move like a hoofed cloud toward the benchland between the North Fork and Noon Creek, toward the road to the Two Medicine River.

Telling Varick and Davie I'd be with them shortly, I rode back down to the house.

"Varick and I ought to be no more than a week, Dair. Four days to get the sheep there, a day or two to help Davie settle in, and then the ride home."

"I'll look for you when I see you coming," she said.

"We're going a famous route, you know. A wife of mine came into this country by way of it," I said from high spirits. "My expectation is that there'll be monuments to her every mile along the way."

Adair smiled and surprised me with: "I hope there's not one at a certain coulee south of the Two Medicine River." *Coachman*, a so-young Adair to Rob at the reins, *are there any conveniences at all along this route of yours?* Myself ready to throttle Rob as she disappeared to piddle: *Your idea was to get her over here and marry her off to me, wasn't it?* The inimitable Rob: *If it worked out that way . . .* Rob's was the way it had worked out, although whether life after the wedding vow was working out for Adair and me seemed ever an open question.

"Dair?" The impulse of this felt deeper, truer, even as I began to speak it. "Come along with us, why not. To the Two Medicine."

Now the surprise was hers. "To christen the monuments?" she asked lightly.

"I'm talking serious here. You can ride the wagon with Davie, or have a turn on Scorpion whenever you feel like. But just come, why don't you. See all that country again." With me who is your husband, even if the country and I are not what you came expecting. With our son of this country and its namesake Two Medicine River. Come and make us the complete three, the McCaskills of Montana, America.

She watched me as if sympathetic to what I was saying, but then shook her head. "I suppose I think I saw the country as much as I am able to that first time, Angus. No, I'd better stay." She lifted her head in the self-mocking way and pronounced: "Adair will take care of here while you and Varick have to be there."

"Well, I tried. But if you can't be budged without a crowbar—"

Surprising again, how strong my pang that she wouldn't be sharing this Two Medicine journey with me. "Goodbye, Dair."

This wife of mine came up on tiptoes and kissed me memorably. "Goodbye yourself, Angus McCaskill."

The bell of the lead wether, the latest Percy, led us all. A thousand ewes and their thousand lambs, and Varick and Davie and I and two sheepdogs to propel them across forty miles to the northern grass. By all known rules of good sense there was much that I ought to have been apprehensive about. Weather first and last. The very morning we started, the mountains looked windy, rain-brewing; one of those restless days of the Rockies when a storm seems to be issuing out of every canyon, too many to ever possibly miss us. Well, we of Scotch Heaven had seen weather before. The under-the-sky perils that sheep invite on themselves were another matter. Fatal patches of death camas or lupine could be hiding ahead amid these grass miles that neither Davie nor I had local knowledge of. Alkali bogs that lambs could wander into, which would be their last wander. Of course, coyotes. *Cayuse . . . Coyote. Rob, Angus, is our serenade coming from a coyote?* Badger Creek two days ahead, and Birch Creek a day before that, creeks usually lazily fordable but if spring runoff was still brimming them . . . Things left, right and sideways all could go wrong, but they were going to have to do it over the top of me. I had never in my life felt so troubleproof. *This I know the tune of,* conviction sang in me from the first minute of that sheep drive. This band of sheep was Varick's future, his foothold into Two Medicine life when he would need it. For his sake, if it ended up that I had to carry each and every last wonderful woolly fool of a sheep on my back these forty miles, *this I know the tune of.*

As the first hard drops of rain swept onto us we were shoving the sheep across the short bridge over Noon Creek. In less time than it takes to tell, Varick and Davie and I in our slickers were wet yellow creatures, the ewes and lambs were gray wet ones, as we pressed across creek water through storm water. But the rain was traveling through so swiftly that the lambs did not stay chilled and begin to stiffen too much to walk, and there was the first woe we hadn't met.

This I know the tune of. All of life seemed fresh, sharp, to me as we spread the sheep into a quick grazing pace. The mountains from an angle different than the one I had known every day for more than twenty years were somehow an encouraging chorus up there, news that the world is more than the everyday route of our eyes. I could even look west to the Reese ranch nestled in the farthest willow bends of Noon Creek and not crush down under the weight of what my life and Anna's could have been, much. After a last glance west I swallowed away the thought of her, at least away as far as it would ever go, and dogged my wing of the band of sheep into quicker steps, and pointed us north.

Now the rise of the long hills beyond the Double W, their pancake summits the high flat edge of the Birch Creek country ahead. I called out to Davie, and to Adair in my imagination, that these bare ridgelines were in dire need of our sheepherder monuments. But there are monuments not just of stone, aren't there. When the sheep were topping that first great ridge north of where the buildings of the Double W lay white and sprawling, there on that divide I climbed off Scorpion, unbuttoned my slicker, and pissed down in the direction of Wampus Cat Williamson.

Overnight at Birch Creek, and then across the ford of the creek at dawn and through the gate of the reservation fence and into the first of the Blackfeet reservation and a land immediately different. Drier, more prairielike, the benchlands flatter and more isolated. Here toward the northern heart of the Two country, every distance seemed to increase, as if giving space to the Blackfeet grassland. The mountains no longer were head-on and near, but marching off northwestward toward the peak called the Chief, which stood out separate as if reviewing them. Benchlands here were bigger and higher and more separate than we were used to, so that cattle and horses looked surprisingly small in the Indian pastures we passed, and when I rode ahead a mile or so to be sure of water for noon, our band of sheep was hard to spot at all.

This I know the tune of. But did I. At the end of that day, bridgeless Badger Creek. Bridgeless and brim full. Time to turn sheep into fish. I had Varick lead Percy across, the wether uneasy about the creek water up to his belly but going through with his leadership role. His followers were none. For an endless hour there on the brink of dark, we relearned that making sheep wade water is a task that would cause a convent to curse in chorus. At last by main strength Varick and I half-led half-hurled enough sheep into the water to give the others the idea, and the community swim began. There was a last mob of lambs, frantic about not being across with their mamas but also frantic about the rushing water. Varick and Davie and the dogs and I fought them into the creek, lambs splashing, thrashing, blatting, and when there were no more kinds of panic to invent, swimming. *This I know the tune of.*

From dawn of the next day, with not a stormcloud in the Black-feet sky and a fine solid bridge ahead of us at the Two Medicine River, I could feel our great journey as if it already had happened, as if now we, Varick and I and our poor bent Davie, we incompara-ble three had only to walk steadily in its tracks. Hour on hour, life sang out to me. Any moment that my eyes were not on the sheep and the land, they were on Varick. More and more he was growing to resemble me. The long frame, the face that was a mustacheless version of mine, probably of all McCaskills back to old Alexander hewing the Bell Rock lighthouse into the sea. *The job was there . . . it was to be done.* We still were living resemblances of old Alexander McCaskill in that, too, this son of mine born attuned to this coun-try's work and I who had spent every effort I knew to learn it. Time upon time that day, I stood in my stirrups and gazed for the sheer pleasure of gazing. The land rolled north with grassy promise in every ridge. The pothole lakes we were passing, with clouds of ducks indignantly rising at the sight of us, seemed a wondrous ad-vent. Even old Scorpion under me seemed more interested in being a horse. By the holy, I was right. Right to have brought these sheep, for Varick's sake. Right, even, to have married Adair and persisted through our strange distanced life together if this strong son was our result.

We came to the Two Medicine River in sunny mid-afternoon and were met by gusts of west wind that shimmered the strong new green of the cottonwood and aspen groves into the lighter tint of the leaves' bottom sides, so that tree after tree seemed to be trying to turn itself inside out. In the moving air as we and the sheep went down the high bluff, a crow lifted off straight up and lofted back-wards, letting the gale loop him upward. I called to Varick my the-ory that maybe wind and not water had bored this colossal open tunnel the Two Medicine flowed through. And then we bedded the sheep, under the tall trees beside the river.

When morning came, I was sorry this was about to be over. All the green miles of May that we had come, the saddle hours in com-pany with Varick, the hand-to-hand contest with the sheep to impel them across brimming Badger Creek, yesterday's sight of the Two

Medicine and its buffalo cliffs like the edge of an older and more patient planet. Every minute of it I keenly would have lived over and over again. This I knew the tune of.

The sheep crossed the bridge of the Two Medicine in a series of hoofed stammers. Up the long slope from the river Varick and Davie and the dogs and I pushed them. When they were atop the brow of the first big ridge north of the river, we called ourselves off and simply stood to watch.

On the lovely grass that once fed the buffalo, the sheep spread themselves into a calm cloud-colored scatter and began to graze, that first day of June of 1914.

TWO MEDICINE

*With water projects abounding from the Sun River
in the south to the Two Medicine River in the
north, it is evident that the current creed of our
region of Montana is "we'll dam every coulee, we'll
irrigate every mountain." But the betterment of
nature goes on apace in other ways as well. Anna
Reese and children Lisabeth and Peter visited
Isaac Reese at St. Mary Lake for three days last
week, where Isaac is providing the workhorses for
the task of building the roadbed from St. Mary to
Babb. Isaac sends word through Anna that the summer's work on this and other Glacier National Park
roads and trails is progressing satisfactorily.*

—GROS VENTRE WEEKLY GLEANER,
JULY 2, 1914

"*P*RRRRR PRRRRR. Right along, Percy, that's the way, into the
chute, earn a brown cracker. *Prrrrr prrrrr.* Bring them for their
haircut, Percy. *Prrrrr.*"

It stays with me like a verse known by heart, that first ever
Two Medicine day of shearing and all it brought. Our site of pens
and tents atop the arching grass ridge above the river was like
being on the bald brow of the earth, with the sunning features of
the summer face of the land everywhere below. Three weeks before, Varick and I had left Davie here with his browsing cloud of
sheep; when I returned with its shearing crew, the reservation
grass had crisped from green to tan, the pothole lakes now were
wearing sober collars of dried shore, the bannerlike flow of the
Two Medicine River had drawn down to orderly instead of headlong. Even the weather was taking a spell of mildness, a day of
bright blue positively innocent of any intention to bring cold rain
pouncing onto newly naked and shelterless sheep, and with that
off my mind I could work at the cutting gate with an eye to other
horizons than the storm foundry of those mountains to the west.

A long prairie swooped from our shearing summit several miles north to Browning and its line of railroad, iron thread to cities and oceans. The chasm of the Two Medicine River burrowed eastward to graft itself into the next channel of flow, the Marias, and next after that the twinned forces of water set forth together to the Missouri. Every view from up here was mighty.

Not that any scenery short of heaven's was ever going to ease the hard first hours of shearing. The crew of shearers laboriously re-learning the patterns of the work from the year before. The sheep alarmed and anarchic. But I could grin at all that and more. The troubleproof mood I brought here to the Two Medicine when Varick and Davie and I trailed the sheep was still in command of me, still the frame of all I saw and thought as the swirling commotion of a thousand ewes was being turned into the ritual of wool. Life and I still were hand in hand, weren't we, life.

Past noon, whenever I found chance to gaze up from my cutting gate, it was south, the direction of Scotch Heaven and home, that needed my watching. Up from the great trench of the Two Medicine River the Gros Ventre-to-Browning road wove itself in a narrow braid of wheel tracks worn into the ground, but Rob still had not appeared on that road as promised. *First thing after breakfast that first day, Angus, I've got a 'steader to take out to see his claim. But I'll drive up in the Lizzie the minute after that's done. You can get the shearers under way and then I'll be there by afternoon to pitch in. You and the sheep can gimp along without me for that long, can't you?* Aye, yes and yea, Rob. We could do that and were. It was plain as noonday that these Two Medicine sheep were nowhere near Rob's central enthusiasm this summer, but I didn't mind. In the eventual, these sheep were not for his benefit anyway nor for mine, but for Varick's. I thought of my son, man of employment now at the ripe age of fifteen, somewhere beside Stanley Meixell there on distant Phantom Woman Mountain or Roman Reef or other venue of the Two Medicine National Forest, hard at the tasks of summer. *He'll have misfortunes great and small/He'll be a credit to us all.* In summers to come, if Adair and I could make our financial intention come true, Varick could have his own sheep in those mountains, could be as much a master of flocks as Rob or I ever were. So it was befitting that I was here amid earnful sheep, seeing across the miles from the Two Medicine to Varick's future.

What I still was not seeing any clue of was Rob. This was unlike

Rob Barclay, to not be where he said he would. As time kept passing, it more than once brought the thought, Rob, is that automobile of yours on its side in a gully somewhere and you under it? I would give him until suppertime, and then serious searching would need to commence.

"*Prrrrr*, Percy, bring them, that's the lad. Follow Percy, ladies. Time to get out of those winter coats. *Prrrrr*."

As the end of the afternoon neared I at last saw a wagon begin to climb the road from the river toward our shearing operation. This now was possibly Rob, resorting to hoof and wheel if his automobile had disgraced itself in some way, and so I kept watch between my chute duties. Before long, though, I could make out that there were three people on the wagon seat. Most likely a family of Blackfeet going in to Sherburne's trading post at Browning. I dismissed my attention from the ascending wagon and went back to sluicing sheep into the shearers' catch pens.

When I happened to glance down the ridge again, the wagon was less than a quarter of a mile away and it was no Blackfeet rig, not with that pair of matched sorrels and the freshly painted yellow wheelspokes. A gaping moment before I could let myself admit it, the shoulders-back erectness of the driver made me know definitely.

Anna at the reins. Her daughter and son on either side of her.

She brought the wagon to a stop near the shearing pen. I went over to her flabbergasted.

"Anna!" I greeted with more than I wanted to show in front of Lisabeth and Peter, but couldn't help. They were just going to have to take my warm tone as surprised hospitality; in their lack of years, how could they know it as anything more? I made myself speed on to: "You're no small distance from Noon Creek."

"Angus, hello again." Anna provided me her life-giving half-smile. "That husband of mine is even farther," she divulged. "Isaac is building roads in the national park. He'll be away most of the summer, so we're going up to St. Mary to spend some days with him." Except for the light veil of time that had put a few small wrinkles into her forehead and at the edges of those forthright eyes, she could have been the glorious young woman gazing back at me that first instant I stepped into her schoolhouse. Except for whatever propriety that had managed to find me now that I was a husband and a father, I still was the surprised smitten caller who was perfectly ready to rub my nose off kissing her shadow on that schoolroom wall.

Our eyes held. Was I imagining, or were we both watching this moment with greatest care?

"Angus"—how many thousands and thousands of times, across the past seventeen years, had I missed her saying my name—"how far is it into Browning for the night?"

Eight or ten miles, and I of course put it at ten. This sudden wild chance thumped in me as I said what civility would say but with greatly more behind it: "That's a lot of wagonwork yet, before dark. You're welcome to stay here, do I even need to say." I indicated the shearing camp, our impromptu little tent town, oasis amid the grassy miles if she would just see it that way. "Mrs. Veitch is cooking for the crew. You could share the cook tent with her and have proper company for the night, why not."

"Mother, let's!" from the boy Peter, craning his neck toward the hubbub of the wrangling corral and the rhythmic motions of the shearers at work.

Anna cast her look north across the expanse of prairie to Browning, the girl Lisabeth so much like her in face and bearing as she gauged the miles to Browning, too.

Anna, stay. That same desperate chant in me from the day when Adair and I were wed, yet not the same. This time there was no division in the chorus. This time it wanted only one outcome. *Stay, Anna. I want to see you, here, now, in this least likely place.*

When Anna stated, "It is a distance—I suppose we had better stay here for the night," Lisabeth nodded firmly, a separate but concurring decision. I breathed a thanks to Montana's geography for its helpful surplus of miles. Young Peter yipped his pleasure and asked to go watch the shearing, could he please, and was away.

I helped Lisabeth down from the wagon, then her mother, aware as deep as sensation can go that I was touching the person who might have been my daughter and then the person who might have been my wife.

"We'll of course lend Mrs. Veitch a hand with supper," Anna was detailing to Lisabeth now, "but I don't feel we should impose on her for the night. Under the wagon served us perfectly fine last night and there's no reason why it won't again." Anna sent her gaze around the shearing camp, her eyes eventually coming back across my face and lingering a bit there. Or was I imagining? "Beth," she spoke to her daughter, "why don't you go see the shearing with Peter, before we pay our respects to the cook tent. Mr. McCaskill can help me with our things from the wagon."

The girl's eyes, the same direct sky-source blue as her mother's, examined the bedrolls and other travel gear in the back of the wagon, then Anna and myself as if weighing the capability of adults in such matters. Evidently satisfied that the tasks were not beyond us, she gave that decisive nod again and went to join Peter at the shearing pen. I watched her go in a gait of grace that was more than a girl's. Lisabeth was, what, fourteen now, and womanhood had its next priestess arriving.

As I lifted out the Reese traveling larder, a venerable chuckbox with cattle brands singed into every side of it, I said to Anna, "She resembles you so much it must be like meeting yourself in the mirror."

"People think we're as alike as eggs, yes. Beth has a mind of her own, though." Anna glanced at me. "But then I suppose there are those who would say an independent child serves me right."

"Send me anybody who says so much as word number one against you and I'll pound the tongue out of him for you."

Her gaze stayed on me. "You would, too, wouldn't you, Angus. In spite of everything, you would."

Yes and then some. I would defend her in any arena, even the one within myself. Every instant of the next few minutes, as I helped Anna unhitch the sorrel team and situate her family's night gear under the shelter of the wagon, and then accompanied her to the shearing pen a discreet adult distance from where Lisabeth and Peter were engrossed in watching the clipwork, it was beyond belief to me that, yet and now, this still could be so. But I felt as thundershook by love for this woman as that first giddy ride home from the Noon Creek schoolhouse when it was all I could do not to fall off the back of Scorpion. Not to fall off the planet, for that matter.

Like a dozen marionettes, the shearers made their patterned motions, stooping, clipping, rising to begin over again. The sheep, betrayed and dismayed, gave up their buttery fleeces with helpless blats. While I was there beside Anna assiduously spectating the shearing pageant, my mind was everywhere else.

I knew I had only moments in which to contrive, before she gathered Lisabeth and they marched off to the cook tent. Yet she wasn't showing great sign of going, was she. Watching wool depart from sheep seemed the most absorbing activity either of us could imagine.

"Anna," I finally began, then found nowhere to alight next but onto: "The times we meet up are few and far between."

"Yes, they are. And now you're busy here. I mustn't take up your time, Angus."

"No, I thoroughly wish you would." I signaled to Davie to come up and work the cutting gate for the next batch of ewes into the catch pens. "I've had my fill of wool today, the crew can get along fine without me a bit." As I said it I wondered: did she know I would be here, handy beside her road north? By now everyone in the Two country above nipple age would have heard of the McCaskill-Barclay advent of sheep onto the Blackfeet reservation. But granting that Anna knew, did she come because I would be here on her plausible route to Isaac? Or in spite of it?

I tried to test that water now. "It's glorious to see you. But what's Isaac going to think of you"—I didn't want to say spending the night—"stopping over here?"

"Isaac knows me." I questioned how thoroughly true that could be. How much any skinsack of existence ever can know of what is in another. She went on: "If it'll relieve your conscience, he'll at least know nothing out of order could happen with so many people around." Yes, two of them his own—your and his—children. That was unfortunately so, my yearning told me. Yet I was aware there was something else here with us. Her tang of interest toward me. The air's taste of about-to-happen, that I had caught so clearly during our noon hour together the time in Valier. I was every inch conscious of it again, and so was Anna. She was making every effort to say lightly: "Counting the sheep into the situation, Angus, we have chaperones by the hundred, don't we."

Sheep or not sheep, sentinels were going to have to get up before early to stop me from seeing this woman. *The liquid fire/of strong desire.* I gathered it all behind my words and asked her rapidly:

"Anna. Will you do a thing for me?"

She scrupulously kept her eyes on the wool brawl in front of us. "If I can, I will. You know that, Angus. What?"

"See the dawn with me tomorrow."

A blue flash of eyes from her, quicker than quick, then away. I reasoned to her profile: "It'd be our one time to talk alone."

There was that same narrow hesitation she had shown when I asked her four years before, *Do you have the life you want?* Now her answer:

"Yes. Show me a Two Medicine dawn."

Rob pulled in just before suppertime, the automobile gray with mud halfway up itself like a pig that has been wallowing, Rob himself more than a little dirt-freckled as well.

"See now, McAngus," he called out, "I'm the only land merchant who carries his real estate on his person."

I had to grin a bit. Even when he was abominably late, the man arrived the way olden travelers might have been announced by a drum.

Rob waved a hand toward his automobile.

"Badger Creek," he explained ruefully. "The Lizzie got stuck in the crossing and I had to troop off and find the nearest Blackfeet to pull me out. You can just about guess how involved an enterprise that turned out to be, Angus. A person might as well dicker with the creek, at least it has some motion to it. How those people manage to—" He broke off. The girl Lisabeth was stepping out of the cook tent with a kettle to fill from our milk cans of drinking water. Like the wraith of Anna stepping out of years ago.

Rob rid himself of his look of confoundment as fast as he could, then offered speculatively: "Company, have we. I thought Isaac was somewhere north, contracting roads or some such."

"He is," I affirmed.

Rob scanned around until he found the Reese wagon, plainly parked for the night, and for once seemed not to know what to say. Which of course did not stop him from coming out with: "A girl that age isn't kiting around the country by herself, I hope."

"No," I solemnly assured him.

He gave me a close look that had me on the verge of answering him by hand. By the holy, how did this man think he was the clerk in charge of my life?

"Angus," he began, "I don't savvy what in the hell—" and I didn't want to hear the rest.

"Her brother is with her, Rob. And her mother. She's thoroughly chaperoned," as if I still meant Lisabeth, although we both knew that I meant Anna. I enlightened him about their journey onward to

Isaac in the morning, and he unruffled considerably. But couldn't help adding:

"It's just a bit odd to have overnight guests in a shearing camp, is all I meant."

"Don't worry about your reputation, Rob," I gave him. "I'll vouch for you."

He cocked his head and ajudged, "You're a trifle touchy, McAngus," which I thought made two of us by that description. "Well, I'd better wash this Blackfeet real estate off me. Supper guests and all that, a person needs to keep up his appearance, doesn't he?"

Steel on grindstone and whetstone, the keen-edged chorus of the shearers sharpening for the day. A wisp of wind, the grass nodding to it.

I leaned over into the corral where the sheep had been wrangled up against the chute mouth by Davie and the shearing crew's choreboy, and felt the wool on three or four ewes' backs for dew. Dry enough to shear, now that the sun had been up for a few hours.

But before beginning the shearing day I cast a look to all the directions, lingering on north and the road to Browning that had taken a wagon with bright yellow wheels and a team of sorrel horses from sight a bit ago. The morning was bright as yesterday and so was I.

"*Prrrrr*, Percy, you're ready to bring them through, are you? Let's start making wool, Percy, what do you say."

The bellwether blinked idly at me in reproach and stayed where he stood in the mouth of the chute. Well, he was right. I needed to live up to my end of the proposition if I expected him to enter into his, didn't I. Life has its rules of bargaining.

"Here you are, Percy, half a brown cracker. *Prrrrr*, Percy, come get the rest here at the cutting gate. *Prrrrr*, sheep, follow Percy, that's the way. Everybody into the chute, *prrrrr, prrrrr*."

All the while that I was shunting sheep from the chute into the shearers' catch pens, all the while that the crew was taking their places and beginning the snipwork of taking the fleeces off the ewes, all the while I was not truly seeing any of it, but the scene at dawn instead. The barest beginning of light in the east, and Anna materializing from the direction of the shearing camp and joining me under the brow of the ridge, out of sight to all but each other.

Anna, you need to see this with me, that vow from another June morning, the first time I saw this green high bluff above the Two Medicine River, the precipice of the buffalo cliff, the prairie heaven of grass emerging from the sky's blue-and-silver one. Then as the warming colors of morning came, our words back and forth, my hope and her ver—

I felt the hand drop onto my shoulder just as I finished filling the catch pens. The clamping touch alone told me this was Rob, back from his start-of-day chore of spreading yesterday's shorn sheep along the slope of the ridge to graze. I glanced around at him inquisitively, for I'd assumed he would be taking his place behind the sheep to help Davie with the wrangling.

The face on Rob Barclay was thunderous. He grated out: "What in Christ's name is it between you and her, man? Out there this morning, like a couple of slinking collie dogs."

Again, was this. Rob patrolling my life again, Rob the warden of my marriage again. And again no more able than ever to understand the situation between Adair and me, and therefore Anna and me.

"Put it in the poorbox, Rob," I told him flatly.

But plainly he didn't intend to be dissuaded from giving me what was on his mind. He persisted: "You're not answering—"

"Oh, but I am. I'm telling you what I told you before, Anna isn't a topic of discussion between us. So just save yourself the trouble of trying, all right?" Save us both it. The two of us had been through this backwards and forward, after Valier. That outbreak of in-law from you was more than enough, Rob. Neither of us had one damn least iota of a thing to gain by—"Neither of us has a thing to gain by getting into this again," I kept to. "You know my opinion by heart, and yours is stamped all over you."

"You'd like the trouble saved, all right, wouldn't you. Well, not this time. You're going to hear me on this, goddamn it." Beyond Rob I saw that Davie was watching us wide-eyed, Rob's words loud enough to carry anger above the sounds of sheep and shearing.

"Then it better be away from here," I informed Rob, and I went off enough distance from the chute and corral, him after me.

We faced each other again. Still determined to carry me by the ears, Rob began: "You just won't make yourself stay away from her, will you. Even after that last talking-to I gave you—"

"Try giving me a leaving-alone, why not," I answered. "Anna

and I are still none of your business, Adair and I are still none of your business, and climbing out of your bed this morning to spy on me was none of your business either, Rob." Oh, I had known even while it was happening that Anna and I were seen. But not by these Barclay gray eyes that were auguring into me now. No, it was when Anna returned first from our dawn, went to the wagon and had a look at her sleeping children, and then headed on toward the cook tent to begin helping toward breakfast; and I meanwhile came up over the ridge from a deliberately different direction. Beneath the wagon, Lisabeth's head suddenly was up out of the bedroll. She watched her mother go. Then she turned enough to watch me come. Across that distance, I knew she knew. The steady attitude of her head, the gauging way she looked at us both, and then conclusion. That lovely young face in its frame of black hair, like a portrait of Anna gazing from the past, seemed to have seen through the ridge to where her mother and I were together. And there was no explaining I could do to the girl. It was a situation I would make worse if I so much as tried to touch it; Anna would have to be the one to handle it if Lisabeth brought out the question. The truth would have to handle it. The truth, Lisabeth, that I had asked your mother: *Anna, when Lisabeth and Peter and Varick are grown and gone . . . if Adair takes herself back to Scotland then . . .* if and when, Anna, is there the chance then of our lives fitting together? Of you answering my love with yours, if and when? And her, *Angus, you know how I am. Beyond anyone else, really, you grasp the kind of person I am. So you know all too well, I can only decide as far as I see a situation.* The judging hesitation, the click as she gauged. *But I can't see ahead to forever, can I. Whether Isaac is there in my life, after the children go—or whether . . .* Her eyes honestly telling me the same as her words. *I'm sorry the words aren't any better than they were, those years ago. You more than deserve better ones from me. But they're the same, Angus. If I ever see that Isaac and I have become wrong together, I'll know in the next minute to turn to you.* Again and yet and still: Isaac was not lastingly innocent of the hazard of losing Anna: I was not irredeemably guilty of loving her hopelessly. Not Proven, the verdict one more time. Well, we had life ahead yet to see if proof would come, didn't we. I had lost no ground since our meeting in Valier, I could stay on the compass setting Adair and I had agreed to, getting on in life as best we could for Varick's sake, hers, mine, ours.

"You've utterly got to stop this infatuation of yours," Rob was delivering urgently to me now. "It was one thing when you were just mooning around like a sick calf over her. But this is the worst yet. Meeting her out there to go at it in the grass."

I stared at Rob as if some malicious stranger had put his face on. *Go at it in the grass?* On the one hand, this slander was the worst thing that had come out of him yet today, which was saying a lot. On the other hand, the random stab of what he had just said showed that at least he hadn't slunk out after us this morning close enough to count our pores. All during our meeting of dawn, Anna and I had not so much as touched. We knew we didn't dare. Starved as I was for her—and I recognized, from another morning, long ago, that she was more than a little hungry for me—we didn't appease those cravings. Anna was still Isaac's, I was still Adair's; until those facts managed to change, we did not dare make the remembered touches we wanted to on each other's body, for families and lives would tumble with us.

"Rob," I uttered flat and hard. "You're going way too far."

"Somebody finally has to tell you what a lovesick sap you're looking at in the mirror every morning," he retaliated. "Adair has been too easy on you, all these years."

"Who made you the world's expert on Dair and me?" I burst out. "Man, just what is it you want from the two of us—doves and honey every blessed minute? She and I have what life together we can manage to. And we have Varick. Those are worth whatever Dair and I have cost each other."

The Barclay face bright with anger wasn't changed by my words. I took a last try.

"Rob. Will you just remember that your sister and I are a pair in life you devised yourself. Dair and I knew from early that we weren't perfect for each other, and it's damn far past time for you to accept that fact, too."

"I'm not accepting that you can sniff off after her"—he jerked his head north toward Anna's route to Isaac—"whenever you get the least little chance. Angus, how is it you can't see that when you're the way you are about Anna, you're only half a husband to Adair. And that's not enough."

"ANGUS AND ROB!" Davie had limped halfway our direction to call out worriedly to us. "The shearers are hollering for more sheep."

I gave Davie a wave of reply. And then I answered Rob, one last time. "It'll have to be enough. It's as good as I can ever do."

Rob shook his head stonily, at me, at my answer, at the existence of Anna. Each of us had said our all, and we hadn't changed each other a hair. That was that, then. I turned from him to go to the shearing pens, but had to let him know this useless argument couldn't go on perpetually.

"Rob, don't ever give me any more guff about something that's none of your business, all right?"

Behind me, his tone was tighter than ever. "I'm telling you this. I'll give you more than guff if you don't get her out of yourself."

For the rest of the shearing, speaking terms between us were short and narrow. When Rob announced, as soon as we were done loading the woolsacks for hauling to the depot at Browning, that he'd like to get on back to Breed Butte immediately, I nodded and silently applauded. The three or so days before I finished the wool-hauling and made my ride back to Scotch Heaven would give us both some time to wane from the argument about Anna. I just wondered what year it would be on the calendar when Rob Barclay decided he had to get huffy in a major way again.

The third day later, I was atop the divide between Noon Creek and the North Fork when I decided to veer past the ranger station on my way to home and Adair. There was no telling how soon I'd see Varick if I didn't snatch this chance to drop in on him at his summer employ, and I much wanted him to hear the news that as far as our Two Medicine sheep and shearing was concerned, the world was wagging its tail at us.

When I rode over the crest into sight of the ranger station, I was double glad I'd come by. Varick was out behind the building boiling fire camp utensils in a huge tub of lye water, a snotty job if there ever was one, and good news would sound even better amid that.

By the holy, I swear the son I was seeing ahead of me had put another inch on himself during the week and a half I'd been at the Two Medicine. Growing so fast his shadow couldn't keep up with him.

Varick's fire under the lye tub was crackling crisply—odd to hear, this warm almost-July afternoon—and he was judiciously depositing into the boiling murky water a series of camp pots as black as tar buckets. I got down from Scorpion and went over to him. With a grin I said, "When the Forest Service washes dishes, it really means it, ay?"

My tall son stayed intently busy with his lye cauldron until all the pots were drowned, then turned around to me. And delivered:

"You and Mrs. Reese. Is that true?"

The inside of me fell to my shoetops.

Varick's face showed all the strain behind the asking, all the confoundment of a fifteen-year-old not wanting to believe the world was askew. I made myself look back at him steadily before I said: "I suppose that depends on what you've heard."

"What I hear is that you and her get together any chance you can. Out in the grass along the Two Medicine, say."

Mercy I sought, mercy came not. Where had this squall dropped on us from, besides out of the vasty blue? Abruptly my mind saw again the face of the girl Lisabeth, up out of the bedroll beneath the wagon, gazing levelly toward her mother, turning that gaze toward me. No accusation in her look, only judgment: choosing among the three verdicts, innocent or guilty or not proven. But even if she accounted me guilty, why would she have sought out Varick with poison such as this? *Your father and my mother* . . . A person with any of Anna in her, destructive and vindictive to this degree? In that young Anna-like face beneath the wagon, I just could not see—

Accusation still stood here staring at me, waiting, wearing its painful mask of Varick. Pushing the echo of that question at me: *Is that true?*

"Son," a confused sound I added to the thudding of my heart, "I did see Anna, yes, but not—"

Varick's next was on its way: "Is that why you put sheep on the reservation? So you'd have a way to sneak off to her?"

"For Christ's sake, no!"

"Unk says it was."

Disbelief filled me now.

And in a sick terrible surge after it, belief.

The voice I knew as well as any but my own, following me across the Two Medicine prairie. *I'll give you more than guff if you don't get her out of yourself.* But Rob, why this? Why drag Varick into the middle between Anna and my helpless love for her? Why in all hell did you ever resort to this, Rob?

I struggled to concentrate through my fury at Rob and my anguish toward Varick, fight one welter of confusion at a time.

"Varick. You've heard the worst possible version. Nothing anywhere near wrong happened between Anna and me at the Two Medicine."

"Then what were the two of you doing out there alone that morning?"

"I asked her to watch the dawn with me."

Varick's look said this confounded him more than ever. He swallowed and asked shakily, "What, are you in love with her?"

Truth, were you going to be enough in this situation? Maybe so, maybe no.

"Yes." An answer that needed to go back seventeen years had to start somewhere. "This is hard to find the words for. But yes, I've always been in love with her, in spite of myself. Varick, this goes back farther in my life than you. Farther than your mother, even. She's known how I feel toward—"

"She *knows?* Mother *knows?*"

"Ask her. If you're intent on the history of this, you'd better get all sides of it." Not just that meddling bastard Rob Barclay's version. I tried again to swallow Rob away and say what was needed to make Varick understand. "Son, your mother and I—"

"I don't savvy any of this!" he blurted.

"Listen to me half a minute, will you. What—"

"You and Mother aren't—" the words broke out of him. "You don't—"

"If you're trying to say your mother and I don't love each other, all I can tell you is we come close enough. Otherwise you wouldn't be here." Wouldn't be here challenging the years we had spent trying to have you, and then to raise you, Varick. "Let's get a grip of ourselves here, and I'll try again to make you see how this is. What I feel for Anna Reese has nothing to do with your mother. That's the utter truth, son. It began before her, and nothing she or I have ever been able to do has changed it any. It's something I have to live with, is all. And I pretty much do, except when that goddamned uncle of yours shoves his size twenty nose into the situation."

My words didn't have effect. There wasn't a semblance of understanding on Varick's face. A hurt bafflement instead. My son who could so readily comprehend the land and its rhythms and its tasks, could not grasp my invisible involvement with a woman not his mother. Those stormy countries of the mind—love, loss, yearning—were places he had not yet been. And what words were strong enough to bring him there, make him see.

"Varick, there is just no way to undo the way I've always felt for Anna. I know you're upset about your mother and me, you've every right in the world to be. But we'll go on as we have been. She and I will stay together at least until you're grown and gone from home, I promise you that on all the Bibles there are."

But I could see I was losing. I could see from Varick's pained stare at me that whatever I said, my son was going to look on me from here forward as someone he had not really known. Even that realization, though, nowhere near prepared me for what came now from him.

"You don't have to stay together on my account. Not any more, you don't."

I eyed Varick and tried not to show how his words made me come undone inside. "Meaning what, son?"

"I'm not coming home at the end of this summer. Or any other time."

The clod of realization choked my throat. Any other boy-man, man-boy, whichever this son of mine was, might have been pretending the determination behind that statement. But you could collect all the pretense in Varick on an eyelash; he was like Adair in that. He meant his declaration.

He had gulped in enough breath for the rest, and now was rushing it out: "I'll board in town for school, but weekends and summers I'm going to be working here for Stanley."

"Varick, you're making this a whole hell of a lot worse than it needs to be."

"I'm not the one who started making it worse, am I. I don't want to be"—his gaze said *be around you*—"be part of this situation, as you call it."

If only the tongue had an eraser on the end of it as a pencil does, this terrible set of minutes wouldn't need to be called anything. Rob would unsay his monstrous slur, Varick would never need to blurt, *Is that true?* I would not have to frantically search for how to keep what little was left after my son's declaration. "You can't just walk out on your mother"—I swallowed miserably—"and me."

"I don't see how you're going to stop me from it."

"By stirring your head with a stick, if I have to. Varick, behave toward me the way you feel you need to. But not your mother. Go to her and tell her you take her side in all this, tell her you're on the outs with me, tell her whatever the hell. But don't pull away from her." I tried to will into him the urgency of what I was saying, tried to hold in the loss this was costing me. "If you'll keep on terms with her, stay the same as ever with her, you can ignore me or throw rocks at me when you see me coming or whatever will make you feel any better. If you'll do that, I won't stop you from staying on with Stanley as much as you want." Until you get your dismay at me out of your system. If you ever do.

With a wordless nod, my son took that bargain. And turned away from me to his boiling task.

He was on his porch waiting when I rode to Breed Butte.

I climbed down from Scorpion and tied his reins to the gate while Rob came across the yard to me.

"McAngus, you've got a face on you that would curdle cream," he began on me. "But man, something had to hammer it home to you about your foolishness over that woman. Maybe this will finally do the job."

The *job*? As if the life of my family was some task for him to take into his hands, bang us this way and that, twiddle our parts around—

"If I know you," his words kept soiling the air, "you're going to drag out that old argument of yours that I don't have any right to do anything about the mess you're making of your marriage. But I told you before, and I'll tell you till the cows come home. Adair is my sister and she's my right to stop you from making a fool of yourself, any way it takes to do that."

Any way? Even by costing me my son? Was that the crazy gospel you still believed, Rob—sonless yourself, you were wishing on me the worst spite you could by tearing my son out of my life? After you had returned from the Two Medicine and hotly spilled your words to Varick, didn't you want them back, want them unspoken? Want yourself not to have been the tool of anger that jealously ripped between Varick and me? I stared into you, needing to know.

Your face again now had as much anger as it could ever hold. But Rob, your eyes did not have enough of red emotion. Or of any other. Your tranced look, your helmeted mood when you had put yourself where it all could not but happen. And so I knew, didn't I. Your own belief in your sabotage wasn't total now, you had to trance yourself now against the doubt. Not let yourself bend now, from the angle you had talked yourself into. And now was too late. Doubt and trance didn't count in your favor now. Nothing did.

"You sanctimonious sonofabitch." My fist following my words, I swung to destroy that Barclay jaw.

Rob was ever quick, though. My haymaker only caught him pulling away, staggering him instead of sending him down. Which only meant he was still up where I could hammer at him. The single message thrummed in me, it had built in my blood from the instant I left Varick to come here and fight Rob. *Will I kill him? How can I not, deserving as he is.* He tried to set himself to return my blows, but I was onto him like fire, punching the side of his head, his shoulders, forearms, any available part of him. I beat that man as if he was a new drum. He took it grimly and struck back whenever he could manage. We struggled there, I see now, and fought through the years into our pasts, into the persons we had been. A Rob stands lordly and bright-faced on the Greenock dock, and my Angus of then pummels him in search of the being who hides inside that cocked stance. Rob on the sly with Nancy, and in Lucas's behalf the me whirling in from my first-ever North Fork day pounds him with the hands for both of us. The exultant Rob of the depot at Browning, *He never guessed! Adair, we did it to the man!* and the Angus who only ever has wanted Anna smashes the words back down his throat. The Rob of his homestead site aloof above the rippling North Fork, of ever more sheep, of the 'steaders, I at last was finding them all with my fists. The final one, the monster Rob who had betrayed by turning my son against me, I wanted to butcher with my bare hands. In that Rob's eyes, here, now, amid the thuds of my blows bringing blood out of him, there was the desperate knowledge that I was capable of his death.

How many times Rob Barclay went down from my hitting of him, I have no idea. Not enough for my amount of rage against him and what he had done. Eventually he stayed down, breathing brokenly. The sound of him, ragged, helpless at last, came up to me as if it was pain from a creature trapped under the earth.

A corner of my mind cleared and said, "You're not worth beating to death. You're worse off living with yourself."

I left him there in the dirt of his Breed Butte.

"I wish Rob hadn't bothered."

"Bothered? Dair, bothered doesn't begin to say it. The damn man has set Varick against me. Nobody has the right to cost me my son."

"I suppose Rob thought he was doing what he did for my sake." Her glance went from me to the rimline of mountains out the window. "As when he brought me over here from Scotland."

"That's as may be." I drew a careful breath. "In both cases he maybe thought he had you at heart, I give him that much. But he can't just glom into our lives whenever something doesn't suit him. We're not his to do with."

"No." She acknowledged that, and me, with her gray eyes. "We're our own to do with, aren't we." She stayed her distance from me across the kitchen, but her voice was entirely conversational, as if today's results were much the same as any other's. I almost thought I had not heard right when she quietly continued: "I'll have to live in town with Varick when school starts." Then, still as if telling me the time of day: "We'll need to get a house in town."

Her words did worse to me than Rob's fists ever could. On every side, my life was caving in. Varick. Rob. Now her. Our marriage had never been hazardless, but abrupt abandonment was the one thing we had guarded each other against.

Suddenly my despair was speaking. Suddenly I desperately had to know the full sum against me, even if it was more severe than I had imagined.

"Dair. Are you leaving me? Because if you are, let's—let's do the thing straight out, for once."

"Leaving?" She considered the word, as if I had just coined it. "All I've said is that I had better live in town with Varick during the school year." She looked straight at me now. "Angus, in all these years you've never really been able to leave Anna. So do you think leaving is something that can be done, just like that?"

"What do you call this, then, whatever it is you intend?"

"I call it living in town with our son while he goes to school, so that he has at least one of us in his life."

My wife, the ambassadress to my son. How does a family get in such kinks? Trying to keep the shake out of my voice, I asked Adair next: "And summers?"

"Summers I'll come back here with you, of course." Of course? Seventeen years with Adair and I still didn't recognize what she saw as the obvious. She was adding: "If you want me to."

"I want you to," I answered. And heard myself add: "Of course."

Lucas tried to invoke peace. The first time I stopped in at the Gros Ventre mercantile after Rob and I divided, the message was there that Lucas needed to see me. That didn't surprise me, but his absence at the Medicine Lodge when I went across to it did. "Luke just works Saturday nights now," I was told by the pompadoured young bartender. Around to the house I went for my next Barclay war council.

"Angus, I'll never defend what Robbie did to you. We both know there was a time he was half into the honey jar himself."

Lucas inclined his head to the kitchen doorway. Nancy could be heard moving about in there, the plump woman of middle age who had been the curvaceous girl at the stove when I walked in on Rob and her. Her lifted front lip, inquiring my verdict on them. Rob quick to ask my hurry, to blur the moment with his smile. So long ago, yet not long at all. "That lad needs some sense pounded into him every so often," Lucas was going on, then paused. "As I hear you undertook to do, ay?"

"I was too late with it."

"Maybe more of it sank in than you think," Lucas speculated behind a puff of his pipe. Does humankind know enough yet, Lucas, to determine what has and hasn't sunk into a Barclay skull? Enough of that thought must have come out in my gaze at him, for Lucas now went to: "None of this has to be fatal, Angus. It's one pure hell of a shame Varick got dragged into this, but he'll get over it sooner or later, I hope you know."

"I don't know that at all. Nothing I've tried to say to him does a bit of good. He has that edge to him. That way of drawing back into himself, and the rest of the world can go by if it wants."

"But in the eventual, Angus, he'll—"

Lucas, Lucas. *In the eventual* was time I could not spare. *In the eventual* lay the only possible time-territory of Anna and myself, when our lives would find their way together if they were ever going to. No, it was in the *now*, in these years before the possibility of Anna and myself, that I had to regain my son. To have him grow up understanding as much of me as he could. But the impossibly knotted task of that, so long as Varick refused to come near me in mind or self. My father, in his iron deafness. Myself, encased in my love for Anna. They look at us, our fleeceless sons do, and wonder how we ever grew such awful coats of complication. To understand us asks so much of sons—and for all I knew, daughters—at the precise time when they least know how to give.

"Angus, I know that what's between you and Varick, the two of you will have to work out," Lucas was onto now. "But maybe I'm not without some suasion where Robbie is concerned. Or where you are either, I hope." He peered at me in his diagnostic way, and wasn't heartened by the signs. "By Jesus, lad"—Lucas threw up his hands, or what would have been his hands at the empty ends of those arms—"I tell you, I just don't see how it helps the situation any for you and Robbie to be reaming the bones out of each other this way."

I shook my head. No, it helped nothing for Rob and me to be in silent war, and no, I would do nothing to change it. The hole in my life where Varick had been was a complication I wouldn't have but for Rob. In exchange, he could have my enmity.

Lucas's last try. "Angus, all those years of you and Robbie count for something."

I looked steadily at Lucas, the age on him gray in his beard and slick on his bald head. Here was a man who knew time, and I wanted to answer him well about those years of Rob and myself: our lives, really.

"The trouble is, Lucas, they don't count for the same in each of us. Maybe they never have, with Rob and me. He sees life as something you put in your pocket as you please. I never find it fits that easily."

"That's as may be, Angus," he said slowly, deliberatingly, when I was done. "But those differences weren't enough to put you at each other's throats, in all the time before." He gave me one more gaze that searched deep. "I just can't think it's forever, this between the two of you."

"If it's not forever, Lucas," I responded, "it's as close as can be."

In less time than is required to tell it, Rob and I took apart twenty-four years of partnership.

With Adair and Judith, each of them silent and strained, on hand to restrain us, everything went. He took my share of the Two Medicine sheep, I took his share of the band we had in the national forest. I bought his half-ownership in the sheep shed we had built together at the edge of my homestead nearest his. Oh, I did let him know he still had watering freedom on my portion of the North Fork whenever he had sheep at Breed Butte—my grudge was not against his animals, after all—if he wanted, and while he most definitely did not want so, he had no choice when the situation was water or no water. But of all else, we divvied everything we could think of except Scorpion. There, Rob would not touch the money I put on the table for his long-ago grand insistence that he stand half the price of my saddle horse. Bruised and scabbed as he was from my beating of him, Rob still wore that disdainful guise. There could not be more contempt than in the wave of his hand then, and his banishing words: "Keep your goddamn Reese horse, as a reminder."

Or so I thought, about the limits of disdain, until that September. When there was the morning that I looked up from my ride to school and saw teams of horses and earth equipment coming across the shoulder of Breed Butte. It seemed too many for road work, but then who knew what royal highroad Rob Barclay had to have to travel on.

Riding home at the end of that schoolday, I saw what the project was. The soil was being scraped, hollowed, beneath the spring at the west edge of Rob's homestead.

"Rop's ressavoy," Isaac Reese confirmed to me when I went up to see closer. "Ve build him deep."

Rob had always said I would see the day he would build a reservoir here. As I stood beside Isaac, watching the fresnoes and teams of big workhorses with the Long Cross brand on their sides as they scraped the hillside down into a dam, it seemed to me one last barrier was going up between Rob and myself. Spurning my offer that he could use my portion of the North Fork for his sheep, he was choosing to store up the spring's trickle instead. Choosing to create water of his own. That was Rob for you.

As the reservoir rose, it changed the face of the North Fork valley. A raw dirt pouch beneath the silver eye of the Breed Butte spring; a catchment inserted into a valley built for flow. Then when Rob brought the Two Medicine sheep home from the reservation for the winter, each few days I would see him on horseback pushing the band back and forth across the top of the earthen dam to pack down the dirt, a task which the sharp hooves of sheep are ideal for. Him and his gray conscript column, marching back and forth to imprison water. I know I had an enlarged sense of justice, where Rob Barclay was concerned. But that private earthen basin of his up there on Breed Butte only proved to me, as if I needed any more proof, the difference in the way he saw the planet and the way I did.

As those sheep tamped and tamped the Breed Butte reservoir into permanence, I tried to settle myself into the long seasons without Adair and Varick that Rob had inflicted on me. Back across time's distance, when America and Montana began for me at the Greenock dock, I thought the Atlantic was worth fear. But the Atlantic was a child's teacup compared to the ocean that life could be. The unexpected ferocities of family I now was up against, their unasked hold on me, were as implacable in their way as the seawater ever was. This too was a sick scaredness of the kind that gripped me in the steerage compartment of the *Jemmy*, down in the iron hole in the water. Suddenly again my life was not under my own control, now that everyone I had tried to stretch myself toward had yanked away from me. I felt so alone on the homestead that if I had shouted, I would have made no echo. When I tried to occupy myself with tasks and chores, even time was askew. Hours refused to budge, yet days went to no good use. I did not even have the usual troublesome company of sheep, for after Rob and I went our separate ways, that autumn at shipping time I sold my band of the sheep to provide for Adair and Varick living in town; somehow two households cost three times as much to run as one did. I told myself I would soon have heart enough again to go back into the sheep business, but I did not. Back there in my ocean fear, the worst that could happen was that my life might promptly end that way. Now the worst was that my life, without Varick at all, without Adair most of the time, without Anna yet, my so-called life might go on and on this way.

I believe this: my South Fork schoolhouse saved my sanity, gave me a place to put my thoughts and not have them fly back shrieking into my face. Day after day I was mentally thankful for the classroom distraction of Paul Toski and his tadpoles in a jar; thankful, too, that he hadn't quite figured out how to jug up skunks, coyotes, bears. There was the slow circling intelligence of Nellie Thorkelson to watch, and to wonder where it would alight. There was Charlie Finletter's war cry at recess-time disputes with Bobby Busby, *you whistledick!* There was the latest generation of Roziers, none as lethal as Daniel but formidable enough, formidable enough.

During that school year and then next after that, Scotch Heaven saw Adair ensconced in a rented house in town with Varick and of course assumed that she and I had had a falling out and Rob was aloof to me because of that. But then glance out some sunny start-of-summer day and here Adair was, like the turn of the calendar from May into June each year, at the homestead with me again, wasn't she. And Varick nearby, working for Stanley at the ranger station or up in the national forest.

The McCaskills dwelt in some strange summer truce, did they? I knew not much more of it than you did, Scotch Heaven. I turned my brain inside-out with thinking, and still none of it came right. Varick, Adair, Rob, Anna as ever—each had extracted from my life whatever portions of themselves it suited them to, and I knew nothing to do but try to trudge along with whatever was left.

These were years, 1915 and 1916, when it seemed downright unpatriotic not to be thriving. I could stay as sunk as a sump if I wanted, but the homestead boom was rollicking along. 'Steaders were not only retaining those dry-land footholds of theirs that I thought were so flimsy and treacherous, they were drawing in more 'steaders; Montana in these years attracted like a magnet amid iron filings. And while the dry-land acres of farming extended and extended, even the weather applauded. The winters were open and mild. Each spring and summer, rain became grain. There was even more to it: thanks to the endless appetite of the war in Europe, the price of anything you could grow was higher than you had ever dreamed. I had been dubious about whether prairie and benchland ought to be farmed, had I? Obviously I didn't know beans from honey.

The other person who did not join in the almost automatic prosperity was named Rob Barclay. Not for lack of trying, on his part. But to my surprise, he sold the Two Medicine band of sheep even before lambing time of the next spring after our split. Rob's decision, I learned by way of Lucas, was to put all his energy into land-dealing. *See now, there's just no end to people wanting a piece of this country:* I could hear him saying every letter of it. His misfortune in deciding to become a lord of real estate was that the buying multitudes had their own ideas. When Rob took the plunge of purchasing every relinquished homestead he could lay his hands on, under the notion of selling land to 'steaders as well as delivering them onto it, he then found that the next season's seekers were seeking elsewhere, out in the eastern sweeps of the state where there still was fresh—"free"—land for homesteading. When he decided next to enter the sod-breaking business, buying a steam tractor half the caliber of a locomotive and the spans of ripping plows and hiring the considerable crew for the huge apparatus, that was the season he discovered he was one of many new sodsters, so many that there wasn't enough 'breaking business to go around. No, the more I heard of Rob's endeavors in these years, the more he sounded to me like a desperate fisherman trying to catch a bait grasshopper in his hat—always at least one jump behind, and sometimes several.

Hearsay was my only version of Rob Barclay now, and that was plenty for me. He and I had not spoken to one another since the day of severing our partnership, we tried not even to lay eyes on each other. This was the other side of the mirror of the past twenty-five years; the two of us who had built ourselves side by side into the Two Medicine country now were assiduously separate existences.

"Angus, it's not for me to say so," Ninian began once, "but it seems unnatural to see Robert and you—"

"—then don't say it, Ninian," I closed that off.

"Angus, lad," from Lucas toward the end of that time, "Robbie is losing his shirt in his land dealing, and he'd go all the way to his socks if I'd let him. By Jesus, I don't mind telling you it's time I straightened his head around for him again. So I'm going to back him in buying maybe fifteen hundred head of prime ewes. These prices for wool and lambs are just pure glorious. If I can talk Robbie into it, I wonder if you'd consider coming in with us on the deal."

"You can stop wondering, Lucas," I said, "because I won't do any considering of that sort."

And then it was our own war year, 1917. Wilson and America had been saying long and loud that they never would, but now they were going into Europe's bloody mud with both feet. That first week of April, I put down the *Gleaner* with its declaration-of-war headline, I thought of the maw of trenches from Belgium all across France, and I felt as sick as I ever had. This was the spring Varick would finish high school in Gros Ventre. If the war did not stop soon, a war that had so far shown no sign it would ever stop, Varick in all soldier-age inevitability would go to it or be sent to it.

"Angus?" from Adair, one of that year's first summer evenings, the dusk long and the air carrying the murmur of the North Fork flowing high with runoff from the mountains. Her first evening at the homestead with me, now that the school year was done. Now that our son no longer had the safety of being a schoolboy. "I need to tell you. There's something terrible I wish. About Varick."

This was new. I have to truthfully say that each other June, Adair reappeared here in this house just as if she had never been away from me. The homestead simply seemed to take on a questioning air, the same as it had when she first came here, straight from our Breed Butte wedding. But this was open agitation of some sort.

"What's this now, Dair? I don't believe the terrible in anything you could—"

"I wish he'd lost that eye." She gazed at me steadily, her voice composed but sad. "When the stick of kindling flew up, that time, I wish now it had taken his eye, Angus."

"Because, because of the war, you mean."

"Is that wrong of me, Angus?" To wish a son saved, from the army, from the trenches, from metal death? When Samuel Duff enlisted, Ninian subscribed to the daily newspaper from Great Falls and the war news came to us in that, the battle for some French hill in one headline, the sinking of half a convoy in another, in pages worn from reading as they traveled up the North Fork valley. As if tribes were fighting in the night, and messengers were shouting guesses at us. A person had to wonder. Was this what all the effort, the bringing of yourself around the bend of the world to another life, the making of homesteads, raising of children, was this what it all came to? Our armies trading death with their armies?

"No," I answered my wife. "No, I can't see that you're wrong at all, Dair. You brought him into the world. You ought to have every right to wish the world wouldn't kill him."

Only a night later, Adair and I had just gone to bed when the scuff of hooves arrived in the yard, then the creak of a saddle being dismounted from. I pulled clothes on, went and opened the door. To Rob.

Our stiff looks met one another. "I have something to say to Adair," was as much as he let me know.

From behind us, Adair's voice: "Anything you ever say to me, you say to Angus as well."

Rob stepped in around me, toward his sister. He began huskily, "Lucas—"

His voice cut off, swallowed by the emotion of his news. He did not really need to wrench out the rest; Adair and I knew the sentence.

"Do you know, Angus," Lucas's death spoke itself in Toussaint's words the afternoon of the funeral, "we thought he was funning us. Saturday night, everybody in the Medicine Lodge. Luke pouring drinks left, right, sideways. All at once, he says: 'My hands hurt. They're like fire.' We didn't know. To laugh or not. He rubbed both his stubs slow on his chest, like so. Then he fell. Doc was right there. But no use. Luke's heart went out, Doc says."

Lucas's funeral brought everyone. In its way, Gros Ventre itself seemed to attend, the town and its tree columns of streets at a respectful distance from the green graveyard knoll. Around me at his graveside, the years' worth of faces. Anna and Isaac. Rob and Judith. Duffs, Erskines, Frews, Findlaters, Hahns, Petersons, the rest. Varick arrived with Stanley Meixell, a faded but clean workshirt on each of them, and strode across to join his mother and me, saying nothing to me. Nancy with us, too, not wearing widow's weeds . . . All of us, except the one whom death had chosen for this first whittle into us, Lucas's slit in the earth.

I blinked when Ninian Duff stepped from amid us to the head of the grave.

"I have asked Robert whether I may say some words over Lucas," he announced. The feedbag beard looked even mightier now that it had cloudswirls of gray in it. I could see in my mind how that asking went. Not even Rob could turn down Ninian.

"It is no secret that Lucas and I did not see eye to eye about all of life." *Lad*, Lucas's voice to me in the Medicine Lodge that year

Rob and I arrived to Gros Ventre and the Two Medicine country, *how many Bibles do you suppose old Ninian's worn the guts out of?* "I bring no Bible here today," Ninian was all but thundering now, "yet there is one passage that I believe even Lucas would not overly mind to hear, if said in its proper light. It is of sheep, and those of us who make them our livelihood. One of the most ancient livelihoods, for as you will remember, Adam's first son Abel was a keeper of sheep." *Ninian, you're as spry as King David up on his hind feet.* "The old treasured words come to us from ancient Israel, where the tending of sheep was a work far different from the sort we know. The flocks of that ancient time were small in number and each sheep possessed its own name, and answered to that name when the familiar voice of his shepherd called forth." *May we all go out with the timbre of a Ninian accompanying us; a voice such as that would shut down Hell.* "Ay, and a shepherd of Israel did not herd his little flock from behind, as we do with our bands of a thousand and more. Rather, that shepherd of old went before his flock, finding out the safer ways, and his sheep followed him in confidence, depending upon him to lead them to safe watering places and to good pasturage." *The North Fork there, that's sinfully fine country. I'll tell you lads what may be the thing, and that's sheep. As sure as the pair of you are sitting here with your faces hanging out, sheep are worth some thinking about.* "And too, that same shepherd of Israel carried certain items necessary to the guarding and care of his sheep. His rod was a club of some heft, nailed through at one end, and was used for fighting off wild creatures and robbers. His staff was a longer, lighter tool, used to beat down leaves from trees and shrubs for his sheep to eat when the grass was short, and it had too a crook in one end, for the rescuing of sheep caught in the rocks or tumbled in a stream. Ay, very like our own sheephooks, they were." *I'll go with you on them. I'll partner the two of you in getting sheep. What do you say to the idea, Angus? Can I count on you both?*

Ninian paused, as if to let the wind carry his words where it wanted before he gave it more to transport. Then he resumed:

"Lucas was stubborn as a stone. They seem to be like that in Nethermuir. But he was no bad man. And like the others of us, all of us who draw breath, he is part of the flock who in one way or another speak through time in the words of the Twenty-third Psalm." Ninian's beard rose as he put his head back to recite:

"The Lord is my shepherd. I shall not want. He maketh me to lie down in green pastures. He leadeth me beside the still waters . . . Yea, though I walk through the valley of the shadow of death, I will fear no evil; for Thou art with me. Thy rod and thy staff, they comfort me."

By Jesus, the woollies do make a lovely sight. If we could just sell them as scenery, ay?

As the funeral crowd began to disperse, and Adair was taking condolences, I singled out Rob. I would rather have been made to pull my own toenails out one by one, but this I needed to do.

"Rob," I stepped in while several others were around him and his family, so that he had no private chance to ignore me, "see you a minute, I need to."

He aloofly followed down the slope of the graveyard after me, far enough where we wouldn't be heard.

I began with it. "I've a thing to ask of you."

"You can always try," issued back from him, wintry.

"The remembrance of Lucas for the *Gleaner*. I, I'd like to write it."

"You would, wouldn't you." It didn't come from Rob as any kind of commendation. "When all is done, you come prissing around wanting to have the saying of it, don't you. That's been a failing in you since—" Since the dock at Greenock, Rob, do you mean? Since the moment you and I put foot into Helena? Gros Ventre? Scotch Heaven? Where and when did I become something other than the Angus you have known the length of your life? Specify, Rob. If you can, man, specify. I'm here waiting.

He didn't finish, but went to: "Well, you've asked. And I'm telling you no, in big letters. I'll write that remembrance myself. It's for a Barclay to have final say about a Barclay. And Christ knows, you've never even come close to being one."

Two days from then, in the lawyer Dal Copenhever's office up over the First National Bank of Gros Ventre, Rob sat at one end of the arc of chairs in front of the lawyer's desk, I at the other with Adair and Nancy between us. Gros Ventre's streets of cottonwood trees had grown up through the years until they now made a shimmering green forest outside this second-story window, and I stared out into the lace of leaves while trying to collect my mind. The reading of Lucas's will was just over, and its effect was beginning.

"Dal, is this some sort of joke lawyers make?" Rob broke out. "To see if they can rile up the audience? If so, you've damn well succeeded in that."

The lawyer shook his head. "I've only read you what's on the paper. It's an unusual document, I'm the first to admit."

Unusual, he said.

I, Lucas Barclay, being of sound and disposing mind and memory and mindful of the uncertainty of human life . . . do hereby make, publish and declare this to be my last will and testament . . .

First: I give and bequeath to Nancy Buffalo Calf Speaks my residence in Gros Ventre, Teton County, Montana, and all my household furniture, linen, china, household stores and utensils, and all personal and household effects of whatsoever nature. Further, I direct that my business property, the Medicine Lodge Saloon, shall be sold, at public or private sale, by my executor; and that said executor shall pay over the proceeds of that sale, together with all funds on deposit under my name in the First National Bank of Gros Ventre, to Nancy Buffalo Calf Speaks in such monthly sums as may reasonably be expected to sustain her for the remainder of her life . . .

Well and good, Lucas. Even Rob, after his involuntary grimace at the news of all that was being bequeathed to Nancy, did not seem unduly surprised. But the rest of that piece of paper.

Second: I direct that my share of the sheep, approximately one thousand five hundred head, either owned outright by me or with my personal lien upon them, that are operated in partnership with Robert Burns Barclay, shall be conveyed thusly: said sheep I give and bequeath to Robert Burns Barclay, Adair Sybil McCaskill née Barclay, and Angus Alexander McCaskill, share and share alike, provided that they operate said sheep in partnership together for three years from the effective date of this will. I expressly stipulate that within that same period of time said sheep cannot be sold by the beneficiaries, nor the proceeds of any such sale derive to them, unless all three beneficiaries give full and willing agreement to such sale. In the event that said beneficiaries cannot operate in partnership and cannot agree unanimously to sell said sheep, my executor is directed to rescind said sheep and all rights thereunto from said beneficiaries and sell said sheep forthwith, with all proceeds of that sale to be donated to the

*municipality of Gros Ventre, Montana, for the express purpose of
establishing a perpetual fund for the care and upkeep of the Gros
Ventre cemetery.*

*. . . I hereby nominate and appoint Dalton Copenhaver to be the
executor and trustee of this my last will.*

"The three of us couldn't pet a cat together," from Rob now,
thoroughly incredulous, "and Lucas full well knew that! So how
in the hell are we supposed to run fifteen hundred head of
sheep?"

With the supreme patience of a person being paid for his
time, the lawyer stated: "If it's indeed the case that you can't
cooperate in a partnership, then Lucas left you the remedy here
in plain sight. The three of you only need to agree to sell, and the
money from the sheep holdings can be split among you in equal
shares."

From his face, Rob evidently didn't know which to be at this
prospect of getting only a third of what he'd been anticipating,
enraged or outraged. But at least he could be quickly rid of me
by agreeing on sale of the sheep. "That's readily enough done,"
he spoke with obvious effort not to glare in my direction. I nodded sharp agreement. With all that lay between us, there was no
way known to man by which the two of us could work as sheep
partners again.

"No."

That from Adair. Rob cast her an uncomprehending glance and
asked what my mind was asking too: "No what?"

"Just that." She returned Rob's gaze, gray eyes to gray eyes.
"No."

Silence held the law office. Then the three male tongues in the
room broke into wild chorus.

"Dair," I chided—

"Adair," Rob blurted—

"Mrs. McCaskill," the lawyer overrode us, "we must be very
clear about this. You refuse to divide these sheep?"

Adair gave him a floating glance as if he was the biggest silly in
the world, talking about dividing sheep as if they were pie
pieces. "I refuse, yes, if that's what it has to be called."

In any other circumstance, I would have sat back and admired.

My wife looked as though she had a lifetime of practice at being an intractable heiress. Small, slim, she inhabited the big round-backed chair as if it were a natural throne. Not a quiver in the ringlets above her composed face. How many times had I seen this before. Wherever Adair was in that head of hers, she was firmly planted there. But as rich as the value was in watching Rob goggle at his sister, this was going to be expensive entertainment. Unless her *no* could be turned around, neither she nor I nor Rob was going to get so much as a penny from the sale of Lucas's sheep.

Rob gamely began on her. "Adair, what's this about? Unless you agree, the cemetery gets it all when the sheep are sold." Try his utmost, the look on Rob and the strain in his voice both told what a calamity he saw that as. *Robbie is losing his shirt in his land dealing, and he'd go all the way to his socks if I'd let him.* Well, well. The skin of Rob's feet were closer to touching disaster than I'd even thought. He was urging Adair now, "And surely to Christ that isn't what you want to happen, now is it?"

"Of course it isn't," she responded. "And you don't either." She regarded Rob patiently. "We can keep that from happening by the three of us running the sheep."

That brought me severely upright. Rob and I exchanged glances of grim recalcitrance.

"See now, Adair"—credit him, Rob sounded valiantly reasonable under the circumstances—"we can all grant that Lucas intended well with this piece of paper of his. But you know better than anyone that Angus and I—we'd just never jibe, is all. The two of us can't work together."

"You did," she said, cool as custard. "You can learn to again."

"Dair, it'd be craziness for us to even try," I took my turn at reasoning with her, past my apprehensions that reasoning and Adair weren't always within seeing distance of each other.

"Trying is never crazy," she reported as if telling me the weather. "Lucas wished us to try this together, and that's what we're going to do."

Rob shifted desperately around in his chair to confront the lawyer again. "Give us a bit of mercy here, why not. All that rant in the will about 'sound mind' and what is it, 'disposing memory' and such; surely to Christ this sheep mess Lucas came up with can't be called sane, am I right?"

"It was up to Lucas to dispose of those sheep as he saw fit," responded Copenhaver. "All I can tell you is, this will is plainly legal in its language." He pushed the paper toward Rob. "And here's Lucas's signature validating it." Even from where Adair and I and Nancy sat, that royal coil of signature could be recognized. Lucas's stubs propelling a pen, proudly saying to Scotland, *This place Gros Ventre is a coming town,* leading Rob and me from Helena with its loops and swirls. *Why did I write it, after these years? Matters pile up in a person. They can surprise you, how they want out.* They were out now, weren't they, Lucas. You saying with this last signature of yours that Rob and Adair and I must make ourselves look at reconciliation, must face it if only to reject it.

"Moreover," the lawyer was asserting to Rob, "the will has been attested by the requisite two witnesses"—he glanced closer at the pair of much smaller ragged scrawls—"Stanley Meixell and Bettina Mraz."

Rob shot the accusatory question to Adair and me, but neither of us knew the name Bettina Mraz either.

"Bouncing Betty," said Nancy quietly.

The other four of us swung to Nancy in stupefaction. Her dark eyes chose Rob to look back at. The lifted middle of her lip made it seem as if she was curious to know what he would make of her news to him. "Wingo's 'niece,' once. A year, two, ago. Stanley's favorite. Young. Yellow hair. And—" Nancy brought her hand and arm up level with her breasts, measuring a further six inches or so in front of them. "Bouncing Betty," she explained again.

Rob was out of his chair as if catapulted now, his knuckles digging into the lawyer's desktop as he leaned forward to half-demand half-plead: "Dal, man, a will witnessed by a forest ranger and a whore can't be valid, can it?"

Adair faced around to Rob reproachfully. "Really now, Rob. Just because Stanley Meixell is a forest ranger doesn't give you reason to question—"

"Mrs. McCaskill," the lawyer put up a hand to halt her, "I imagine your brother has reference to the competency of Miss"—he checked again the bottommost signature on the will—"Mraz as a witness. But unless she has ever been convicted of practicing her purported profession, she is as competent to witness as any of us. And convictions of that sort are hardly plentiful in Montana, I would point out to you. No, there really isn't much hope of contesting this will on the basis of its witnesses, in my opinion. Nor on any other that I'm aware of."

Rob looked as if he'd been kicked on both shins. "Adair," he intoned to her bleakly, "you've got to get us out of this sheep mess Lucas put us in."

"You know how much I hate to admit it, Dair," I chimed in at my most persuasive, "but for once in his life Rob happens to be right."

She stated it for us once more. "No."

There was a long moment of silence except for the rattle of the breeze in the cottonwood trees. But everything in my mind was as loud as it could be and still stay in there. *Adair,* it banged again and again, *what now?*

"Gentlemen," the lawyer summed, "Mrs. McCaskill is entirely within her rights. If and when you three heirs decide to divide the sheep, I can draw up the necessary papers. But until that decision is reached, you are in the sheep business together."

At home that night, I tried again.

"Dair, I don't know what it is you want, in this matter of Rob and me."

"I want the two of you to carry out Lucas's wish."

"It's not as if I want to go against something Lucas had his heart set on."

"Then you won't," she said.

"If you want us back in the sheep business so badly, I'll find the money somewhere to buy a band of our own."

"We already have sheep," she instructed me, "as of today."

"Dair. Dair, you know as well as I do that there's every reason under the sun for me to say a *no* of my own." *No* to her hopeless notion that Rob and I together could ever run that band of sheep, *yes* to the perpetual upkeep of the green bed, ay, Lucas? *Yes* to a ruination of Rob, as glad a *yes* as I could utter.

"I'm hoping you won't. I'm asking you not to."

"Because why?"

"Because this is another chance, for each of the three of us. Angus, I've never asked you these words before, but I am now. Will you do this for me?"

Put that way, this notion of hers resounded. Put that way, it had an inescapable echo. Here was the other end of the bargain she quietly broached to me those years ago: *You would still have a life to look ahead to.* Her acceptance, her grant, all through our marriage that I still loved Anna. And now this asking, that I make a demented try to partner with Rob again. Because why? Because for better or worse, Adair and I had each other, our marriage, until time told us otherwise. The Atlantic itself was a field of battle now; there could be no Scotland for Adair until the war wore itself out. Anna's Lisabeth was grown now, I had heard that she was going away to the teachers' college at Dillon in the fall, but Peter was still a few years from homeleaving. All the hinges that life turns on. And in the meantime Adair at last asking a thing of me, repeating it gently as if wondering aloud to herself:

"Will you, Angus?"

How many times had I seen this, now. A Barclay locked into an iron notion. Lucas becoming a builder of the Montana that had torn his hands from him. Rob so outraged toward me about Anna that he pried my son away from me. And now Adair bolting Rob and me into impossible partnership.

"Dair, I don't even want to be around the man. How under thunder am I supposed to run sheep with him?"

"The sheep won't care whether you and Rob have anything to say to one another."

I studied her. "Does Adair? Do you care?"

"In my way, I do."

I went to Breed Butte to begin lockstep sheep-raising.

The sheep were grazing complacently on the shoulder of the butte nearest Rob's reservoir. As I rode Scorpion across the narrow top of the dam I saw that Rob had been packing its dirt down again with the sheep, their small sharp hoofprints leaving every inch of it as pocked as a grater. The damn man and his damn dam.

Rob came out into his yard looking baleful in the extreme. I planted myself to face his harsh silence.

Nothing, from either of us.

Then some more of it.

Eventually I asked:

"How are we going to do this, by signal lamp?"

"Don't I wish."

"Rob, wishing isn't going to help this situation."

"You're one to tell me not to toss away life by wishing, are you. Surprising."

"We'd better stick to the topic of sheep."

Rob looked bleakly past me, down the slope of Breed Butte to the sheep shed that had been ours and now was mine. Then he shifted his gaze to the contented cloud of sheep. I followed his eyes there with my own. At least neither of us was new to the sheep part of this; after nearly thirty years, we could be said to have commenced at starting to make a stab at a beginning toward knowing a thing or two about the woollies.

After enough stiff silence, he made himself say it. "What brings you? Shearing?"

I confirmed with a nod.

He rapped back, "You know my thoughts on it. Or at least you goddamn ought to, after all these years."

"That doesn't mean I agree with them a whit," I pointed out. "I'm for shearing at the end of this month, to be as sure as possible of the weather."

"That's just the kind of pussyfoot idea you'd have, right enough. I say shear now and get the sheep up on the forest grass."

"You've said it, and I don't agree."

The next jerked out of him savagely, not simply at me but at the situation. "Goddamn it all to hell, this can never work. We both know Adair means well, but a half-assed situation like this, neither of us able to say a real yes or a real no—how to hell are we ever going to settle anything about the sheep?"

He was right about one matter. Nothing he or I could provide was going to ordain anything to the other. I reached in my pocket and showed him what Adair had handed me before I left the house.

Rob stared down at my hand, then sharply up into my eyes. "What's this, now?"

"What it looks like. A deck of cards. Adair says when we can't agree, we're to cut for who gets to decide."

"Jesus' suffering ass!" Rob detonated. "We couldn't run a flock of chickens on that basis, let alone fifteen hundred goddamn sheep!"

"Adair has one more stipulation," I informed him. "Low card always wins."

You never know. Adair's second stipulation so dumbfounded Rob that his howl of outrage now dwindled to the weary mutter, "It'd take that sister of mine to think of that."

"Anyway it's a change from letting magpies decide," I reminded him. Turning around to Scorpion, I used the seat of his saddle to shuffle the cards on three times, then held the deck toward Rob: "Your cut."

He produced the five of diamonds.

Grabbing the deck as if he wanted it out of sight of him, he shuffled it roughly, then thrust it out to me.

I turned up the ten of clubs.

"Well, then," Rob ground out. "We'll shear now, won't we."

I nodded once, and left.

The summer went that way. The thousand and a half sheep and Rob and I and our goddess of chance, also known as Adair. To ask myself how I had got swallowed into all this was to bewilder myself even more, so I tried instead to set myself to wait it through. Waiting was what I had practice in by now.

The deck of cards did me one inadvertent favor. In early August, when I was trying to finish the last of haying, Rob and I cut cards to see who had to camptend Davie that week, and I lost. Nothing to do but pocket my exasperation and begin the journey on Scorpion up into the national forest with the pack horse of Davie's supplies behind.

It was one of those mornings of Roman Reef looming so high and near in the dry summer air that my interest wandered aloft with it rather than toward the barbwire gate of the boundary fence I was nearing. When I came to earth and glanced ahead and discovered the person off his horse at the gate, performing the courtesy of waiting for me to ride through too before he closed it, at first his brown Stetson made me hope it was Varick. I saw in my next minute of riding up, no, not quite that tall and far from that young. Stanley Meixell.

"Hullo, Angus," the ranger spoke up as I rode through and stopped my horses on the other side of the gate. "What do you know for sure?"

Never nearly enough, Stanley. But aloud: "I know we could use rain."

"That we could. There's never enough weather in Montana except when there's too much of it."

Both of us knew I had stopped for more than a climate chat. I threw away preamble and asked:

"How's Varick doing for you?"

"Just topnotch. He's about a man and a half on anything I put him to. Regular demon for work, and what he can't do a first time he learns before a next time gets here. I tell you, the Yew Ess Forest Service is proud of him." Stanley paused, then casually tacked on: "You maybe heard, he's getting to be just quite a bronc stomper, too."

I had heard, unenthusiastically. The Sunday gatherings of young riders at the Egan ranch on Noon Creek were no longer complete without Varick atop a snorty horse, the report was.

Stanley studied me, then Roman Reef, as if comparison was his profession. "I guess you'd kind of like to know his frame of mind about you, Angus. It ain't real good."

"I wish that surprised me." What I went on to say did startle myself: "You know what it's about, this between Varick and me?"

"I do, yeah. Him and me had a session right after the blowup first happened between you two." Stanley regarded me thoughtfully for a moment before saying: "The ladies and us. Never as tidy as you'd think it ought to be, is it."

Definitely not for some of us, Stanley. Others of us, and I could name you one quick, the Bouncing Bettys ricochet soundlessly off of and never leave a whisper in the world.

"Angus, I've tried and tried to tell Varick to let it drop, the ruckus between him and you. And I'll keep on trying. But I've got to say, Varick ain't easy to budge, wherever he gets that from." Stanley paused again, then: "This probably don't help none, but my guess is it ain't just you that's burring him, Angus. It's him wanting to be away from home, get out in the world a little."

"He can be out in the world and still have a father."

"Yeah, I suppose. It's a whole hell of a lot easier for you and me to see that than it is for him, though."

It was my turn to glance away at Roman Reef. This deserved to be said, Stanley in his Stanley way had earned the hearing of it:

"Stanley. If I can't have Varick around me at this time of his life, there's nobody I'd rather he was with than you."

The only answer from under the brown hat was a brief session of throat-clearing. After a considerable moment: "Yeah, well, I better get on up the mountain. See you in choir practice, Angus."

At shipping time that fall, for once in our yoked partnership Rob and I did not need to cut the cards to find a decision.

"Ones like these, I'm going to take leave of my senses and go up to 17½ cents on," the lamb buyer offered. "However you Scotchmen manage to do it, you grow goddamn fine lambs."

While keeping a careful straight face Rob glanced at me. I was already glancing implacably at him. When we both nodded and got out ritual admissions that we supposed we could manage to accept such a sum of money, the flabbergasting deal was done. Eighty-five pounds per lamb × 1500 lambs × 17½¢. In the years of '93, Rob and I and all other sheepmen would have gone through life on our knees to get three cents a pound for our lambs instead of two, and now these unasked lofty prices of wartime. Life isn't famous for being evenhanded, is it.

"This doesn't mean one goddamn bit that I want to go through another year of this with you," Rob lost no time in imparting to me outside the stockyard as we were pocketing our checks. "If you had the least lick of sense, you'd go home right now and ask Adair if she won't let us sell the ewes this fall, too."

"I already asked," I gave him in identical tone. "She won't."

The next two months of numbers on the calendar, I hated to see toll themselves off. Why can't time creep when you want it to instead of when you don't. I stood it for half the toll, then on a mid-October Sunday afternoon I told Adair I was riding up into the foothills to see where our firewood was for this winter and instead rode across the shoulder of Breed Butte to Noon Creek.

Elderly Scorpion being pointed now to the country where I bought him: *Skorp Yun, lad, what about that?* What about it indeed. A woman looking up from the teacher's desk, a woman with the blackest of black hair done into a firm glossy braid, a glory of a woman: *I am called Anna Ramsay.* How long had it been in horse years, Scorpion? How long since Anna, at her schoolhouse or at the old Ramsay place, began being my automatic destination at Noon Creek? My destination anywhere in life, for that matter. But not

now, not today, not yet, when I was reining Scorpion instead toward the round corral at the Egan ranch.

He was there atop a corral pole with the other young Sunday
heroes when I arrived. Varick, whom I had come to lay eyes on
before the eleventh day of the next month made him eighteen years
of age. Before he became war fodder.

He saw me across the corral as I dismounted. I gave him a hello
wave, he nodded the minimum in return, and with public amenities
satisfied, we left it at that. Maybe more would eventuate between
us later, but I did not really expect so. No, today I simply was
bringing my son my eyes, the one part of me he could not turn
away from on such a public afternoon as this.

As I tied Scorpion where he could graze a little, I heard a chuckle
from the passenger on a horse just arriving. "You are here to ride a
rough one, Angus?"

I looked up, at the broad-bellied figure in the saddle. "That I'm
definitely not, Toussaint. A bronc has to bring me a note of good
behavior from his mother before I'll go near him. But you. What
fetches you down from the Two Medicine?"

"The riding. The young men riding." As if such a sight was worth
traveling all distances for. Well, I had come no small way myself,
hadn't I, to peruse Varick.

I chatted with Toussaint about the fine green year, his job as
ditch rider on the reservation's new Two Medicine irrigation canal—"Did you know a man can ride a ditch, Angus?"—the war in
Europe—"those other places," he called the warring countries—until I saw the arrival of a buckboard drawn by a beautiful team of
sorrels. My breath caught. But this time the Reese wagon was not
driven by Anna but by Isaac, with the boy Peter beside him. I
might have known that wherever horses were collected, here would
be Isaac.

"Toozawn, Annguz," he greeted us benignly, and headed on toward the corral. Peter's eyes registered me but didn't linger, flew
on to the happenings within the circle of poles. I felt relief that he
didn't dwell on me. Yet some pang, too, that the immensity of the
past between his mother and me did not even generate a specu-
lative gaze from this boy. Add inches to him for the next year or
two, 1918, 1919, and he would be out into life. About the time when

Adair and Rob and I would have done our duty to Lucas's will and could all go our separate ways. I had thought through the arithmetic of these next few years a thousand times: the Reese nest would be empty and Anna would be able to judge just on the basis I had waited so long for, Isaac or me.

"That Isaac," declared Toussaint. "He knows."

I could feel my face going white or red, I couldn't tell which. I stared at Toussaint. "Knows?"

"He knows horses like nobody's business, that Isaac."

I recovered myself, told Toussaint it was time I became a serious spectator and found a place along the corral. Men *hello*ed and *Angus*ed me in surprise as they passed. Quite a crowd in and on the corral by then. Besides Varick and Pat Egan's son Dill and other local sons, riders from the Double W and Thad Wainwright's Rocking T abounded here today, and just now, the last one they had been waiting for before starting was arriving with a whoop and a grin, young Withrow from the South Fork.

"Angus, good to see you here," Pat Egan called out as he came over to me. "Heard about the special attraction, did you?"

When my blank look said I'd heard no such thing, Pat told me that after the bronc riding there was to be a bucking exhibition of another sort. "Some guy from Fort Benton brought over this critter of his. Claims he's trained the thing to toss any rider there is. Our boys are going to have to show him how real riding is done, don't you think?"

Away went Pat, as he said, to get the circus started. Across the pole arena from me, the Withrow lad had climbed onto the fence beside Varick. "How you doing, Mac?"

"Just right, Dode. How about you?"

"Good enough, if they got some real horses here for us."

"They're rank enough, probably. I see you're dressed for the worst they can do, though." Withrow was always the dressiest in a crowd, and for today's bronc riding he sported a pair of yellow-tan corduroy trousers with leather trim at the pockets, new as the moment. Except for his habit of dressing as if he owned Montana, he was an engaging youngster, of a sheep-ranching family that had moved to the South Fork from the Cut Bank country in the past year or so. I perched there, watching Varick and Dode, listening to their gab of horses. Aching at the thought of how much of Varick I had not been able to know, these years of his climb into manhood.

Shortly the afternoon began to fill with horsehide and riders. Even just saddling each bronc was an exercise in fastening leather onto a storm of horse. The animal was snubbed to a corral post by a lasso tight around his neck while the saddlers did their work. Any too reluctant horse or a known kicker was thrown onto his side in the corral dirt and saddled while down. The rider would poise over him and try to socket himself into the saddle and stirrups as the horse struggled up. It looked to me like a recipe for suicide.

My throat stoppered itself when I saw that Varick had drawn one of the saddle-in-the-dirt rides.

"Watch out for when this sonofabitch starts sunfishing," I heard Dode counsel him, "or he'll stick your head in the ground."

Varick nodded, tugged his hat down severely toward his eyes, and straddled with care across the heaving middle of the prostrate pinto horse. Then said to the handlers: "Let's try him."

The pinto erupted out of the dirt, spurts of dust continuing to fly behind his hooves as he bucked and bounced, querulously twisting his spotted body into sideway crescents as if determined to make his rump meet his head. While the horse leapt and crimped, Varick sat astride him, long legs stretched mightily into the stirrups. My blood raced as I watched. What son of mine was this? Somehow this bronc rider, this tall half-stranger, this Sunday centaur, was the yield of Adair and me. I was vastly thankful she was not here to see our wild result.

When Varick had ridden and the other braves of the saddle tribe had taken their turns at rattling their brains, Pat Egan hollered from beside the corral gate: "Time for something different, boys!"

Pat swung the gate open and in strolled a man and a steer.

At first glimpse, the Fort Benton critter looked like a standard steer. Red-brown, haunch-high to a horse, merely beef on the hoof. But when you considered him for a moment, this was a very veteran steer indeed, years older than the usual by not having gone the route to the slaughterhouse. An old dodger of the last battle, so to say. He was uniquely calm around people, blinking slow blinks that were halfway toward sleep as the onlookers gathered around him. The circle gave way considerably, however, when he lifted his tail like a pump handle and casually let loose several fluid feet of manure.

For his part, the Fort Benton man was a moonface with spectacles; a sort you would expect to see behind the teller's wicket in a bank instead of ankle deep into a corral floor. The fiscal look about him was not entirely coincidental. He was prepared, he announced, to provide twenty-five dollars to anyone who could ride this steer of his. He also would be amenable, of course, to whatever side bets anybody might care to make with him about his steer's invincibility.

At once, everybody in the corral voted with their pockets. All the young riders wanted a turn at the steer, or professed to. But the Fort Bentonian shook his head and informed the throng that was not how steer riding worked, it was strictly a one-shot proposition. One steer per afternoon, one rider per afternoon: what could be more fair? Then he set forth the further terms of steer riding, Fort Benton mode: the rider had to stay astride the steer for a total of three minutes in a ten-minute span. Naturally this Sunday assortment of bronc conquerors was free to choose the best rider among them—the bland spectacles suggested there had been a lot of other claims of "best" that came and went—and if the rider could stay on the steer the required sum of time, the twenty-five dollars was his.

Somebody spoke up: surely the steer impresario didn't mean three minutes straight, uninterrupted, aboard the animal, did he?

He did not. The rider could get off and on again any hundred number of times he wanted to during the overall time span. Did he need to add, he added, that the steer would be glad to help the rider with the offs.

What about a hazer, to even the odds for the rider getting back on?

The eyebrows lifted above the moonface in surprise. But the Fort Bentonian allowed that one man hazing on foot maybe wouldn't do lasting harm to his cherished pet.

I saw Isaac come into the corral, stoop, sight along the steer's backbone—I could all but hear him mentally compare it to a horse's—and then step over and gabble something to Varick, Dode Withrow and the others. They surveyed the territory for themselves, then somebody put it to the Fort Bentonian. How were they supposed to saddle something with as square a back as that?

Any old which way they desired, came the answer.

The young riders conferred again. Discussion bred inspiration. Could they tie on the saddle as well as cinch it?

They could entwine the steer a foot thick in rope if that was their way of doing things, the steer's spokesman bestowed, but they had better decide soon, as darkness was only hours away.

At last the terms of the contest were as clear as tongue could make them, and all bets were laid. Someone called out the next conundrum:

"Who's gonna climb on the thing?"

Faces turned toward Varick and the Withrow lad. Varick looked at young Withrow, and young Withrow at him. "Toss you for him, Dode," offered my son.

"Heads, Mac. Let her fly."

The silver dollar that spun into the air, I tried to exert to come down heads; not to send danger toward another man's son, simply away from my own. Name me one soul who could have done different. But I had my usual luck where Varick was concerned.

"You got on the wrong pants for riding a male cow anyway," Varick consoled Dode after the coin fell tails. Then, "I guess I'm ready for this if your steer is, Mister Fort Benton."

Varick and his adherents gathered around the steer. The steer blinked at them. As Dode Withrow approached with the saddle, someone moved from behind the steer to watch. The steer's right rear leg flashed, the hoof missing the pedestrian by an inch.

"Now, now, McCoy," the Fort Bentonian chided his pet. "That's no way to act towards these boys." He scratched the steer between its broad eyes as if it were a gigantic puppy, and it stood in perfect tranquility while Dode and the others saddled and trussed. The kick had done its work, though, as now both Varick and Dode, who was going to be his hazer, knew they would have to avoid the steer's rear area during the corral contest.

When the saddlers had done, a rope ran around the steer's neck and through the forkhole of the saddle. Two further ropes duplicated the route of the saddle cinch encircling, if that was the word for such a shape, the steer. And it had been Dode Withrow's ultimate inspiration to run a lariat around the animal lengthwise, chest to rump and threaded through the rigging rings of the saddle, like the final string around a package. "You people over here sure do like rope," observed the Fort Bentonian.

Dode Withrow gripped the halter with both hands at the steer's jaw while someone passed the halter rope up to Varick. He took a wrap of it in his right hand and put his left into the air as if asking an arithmetic question in my classroom. He called to Pat Egan and the Fort Bentonian, the two timekeepers: "Let's try him."

The moonface boomed out, "GO, McCOY!" and the steer writhed

his hindquarters as if he were now a giant snake. A giant snake with horns and hooves. Varick's head whipped sideways, then to the other side, like a willow snapping back and forth. Then the steer lurched forward and Varick whipped in that direction and back.

MURRRAWWWW issued out of McCoy, a half-bellow, half-groan, as he and Varick began storming around the circle of the corral. It was like watching a battle in a whirlwind, the steer's hooves spraying the loose minced dirt of the arena twenty feet into the air.

I watched in agony, fear, fascination. So I wanted to know about Varick's Sunday life, did I. We spend the years of raising children for this, for them to invent fresh ways to break their young necks?

At about McCoy's dozenth MURRRAWWWW, Varick continued left while the steer adjourned right.

"That was fifty-one seconds!" Pat Egan shouted out as Varick alit in the corral earth.

His words still were in the air when Dode dashed beside the steer to grab the halter rope. As he reached down for it, the animal trotted slightly faster, just enough to keep the rope out of reach. Dode speeded up. McCoy speeded up even more, circling the corral now at a sustained pace that a trotting horse would have envied. As the seconds ticked by in this round race between Dode and McCoy, it became clear what they used for brains in Fort Benton. Before the considerable problem of climbing onto McCoy and staying on, there was going to be the trickier problem of catching him each time.

Varick by now had scrambled to his feet and joined the chase. "I'll cut across behind the sonofabitch, you run him around to me," Dode strategized in a panting yell.

He started his veer behind McCoy. Sudden as a clock mechanism reaching the hour, McCoy halted in his tracks and delivered a flashing kick that missed Dode by the width of a fiddlestring.

But while McCoy was trying to send his would-be hazer into the middle of next week, Varick managed to lay hands on the halter rope and hold the steer long enough for Dode to gain control of the halter. Time sped as Dode desperately hugged McCoy by the head and Varick remounted, then the writhing contest was on again. The steer bounced around the arena always in the same direction, with the same crazy seesaw motion, and I thought Varick was beginning to look a bit woozy. Then MURRRAWWWW again and my son flew into the dirt another time.

"Another forty-six seconds!" shouted Pat. "That's five and a half minutes," chimed the Fort Bentonian. Away went McCoy, away went the puffing Dode after him, in a repeat race until Varick managed to mount again and the bucking resumed.

They rampaged that way, McCoy and McCaskill, through three further exchanges, man onto steer, steer out from under man. Each time, Varick's tenancy atop McCoy was briefer; but each time added preciously toward the three minute total of riding, too.

Now McCoy sent Varick cloudchasing again, and I half-hoped my stubborn son would find enough sense to give up the combat, half-wished his heavy plummet into the arena would conk him hard enough that he had to quit. But no, never. Varick was one long streak of corral dust, but he was onto his feet again, more or less. Gasping as if he'd been running steadily in tandem with McCoy ever since their bout began, he cast a bleary look around for his adversary. Over by the corral gate Dode Withrow had McCoy by the halter again, snugging the animal while urging Varick: "Now we got the sonofabitch, Mac! One more time!"

The steer casually studied young Withrow, then tossed his head and slung Dode tip over teakettle into the expanse of fresh green still-almost-liquid manure he had deposited just before the riding match commenced. The dazzling corduroy trousers and most other fabric on Dode abruptly changed color. While he slid and sloshed, the steer started away as if bored. But Varick had wobbled close enough to grab the halter rope as it flew from Dode, and now somehow he was putting himself aboard McCoy again.

The steer shook him mightily, but whatever wild rhythm McCoy was cavorting to, Varick also had found. The clamped pair of them, creature and rider, MURRRAWWWW and gritting silence, shot around the corral in a steady circle, if up-and-down isn't counted. Varick grasped the halter rope as if it was the hawser to life. McCoy quit circling and simply spun in his tracks like a dog chasing its tail. Varick's face came-went, came-went . . .

"Time!" yelled Pat Egan. "That's three minutes' worth! And still half a minute to the limit!"

"Whoa, McCoy," the Fort Benton man called out sourly. At once the steer froze, so abruptly that Varick pitched ahead into its neck. With a great gulp of air, Varick lowered himself from McCoy's back, held out the halter rope and dropped it.

Blearily my son located the figure, manure-sopped but grinning, of young Withrow.

"Dode," Varick called out, "you're awful hard on a pair of pants."

It is now one year, a year with blood on it, since America entered the war in Europe. Any day now, the millionth soldier of the American Expeditionary Force will set foot into France. Nothing would be less surprising, given the quantities of young men of Montana who have lately gone into uniform, than if that doughboy who follows the 999,999 before him in the line of march into the trenches should prove to be from Butte or from Hardin, from Plentywood or from Whitefish—or from here in our own Two Medicine country. We can but pray that on some future day of significance, a Pasteur or a Reed or a Gorgas will find the remedy to the evil malady of war.

—GROS VENTRE WEEKLY GLEANER,
APRIL 11, 1918

"As sure as thunder falls into the earth and becomes stone," cried the king the next morning, "I am struck dumb by what you are saying, Remembrancer! You can stand there in truth's boots and say time will flee from us no matter what we do? The sparks as they flew upward from the fireplace last evening were not adding themselves into the stars? The whipperwhee of the night bird did not fix itself into the dark as reliably as an echo? The entire night that has just passed is, umm, past? Where's the sense in all this remembering business, then?"

"Those things yet exist, sire. But in us now, not in the moments that birthed them."

"If that is so, we'll soon overflow! Puddles of memory will follow us everywhere like shadows! Think of it all, Remembrancer! The calm of a pond lazing as it awaits the wink of a skipping stone. The taste

*of green when we thumb a summer pea from its pod. The icicle
needles of winter. The kited fire of each sunrise. How can our poor heads
hold the least little of all there is to remember? Tell me that, whoever
can.*"

"Let's stop there for today, Billy, thank you the world," I called
out from my perch at the rear of the classroom to the boy so earnestly reading aloud at my big desk.

Blinking regretfully behind his round eyeglasses, like a small owl
coming out of beloved night into day, Billy Reinking put the place
marker carefully into the book of stories and took his seat among
my other pupils. "Now tomorrow," I instructed the assortment of
craniums in front of me, "I want your own poor heads absolutely
running over with arithmetic when you walk into this schoolhouse,
please." Then out they went, to their saddle horses or their shoe-
worn paths, Thorkelsons and Keevers and Toskis and the wan
Hebner girl and the bright Reinking boy to their 'steader families in
the south benchlands, the Van Bebber and Hahn girls up the South
Fork, the Busby brothers and the new generation of Roziers and
the Finletter boy down the main creek.

After watching them scatter like tumbleweeds, I picked my own
route through the April mud to my new mount, a lively bay mare
named Jeannette. Scorpion I'd had to put out to pasture, he was so
full of years by now. I felt a little that way myself—the years part,
not the pastured one—as I thought of the lambing shed duties waiting for me before and after supper. Of Rob, scowling or worse, telling me in fewest words which of the ewes were adamant against
suckling their newborn and needed to be upended so their lambs
could dine. I would like to see the color of the man's hair who could
look forward to ending his day with stubborn ewes to wrestle and
Rob Barclay as well.

Prancy Jeannette and I entered the wind as soon as we rounded
the base of the knob hill and were in the valley of the North Fork,
but it was not much as Montana breezes go. Reassuring, in a way.
The waft felt as if it was loyally April and spring, not a chilly leftover of winter. My mood went up for the next minutes, until I rode
past the Duffs', where Ninian was moving a bunch of ten-day lambs
and their mamas up the flank of Breed Butte onto new grass. Across
the distance I gave him a wave, and like a narrow old tree with one

warped branch Ninian half-lifted an arm briefly in return and let it
drop.

I rode on up the North Fork, in the mix of fury and sorrow that
the sight of Ninian stirred in me. Scotch Heaven now had its first
dead soldier, Ninian and Flora's son Samuel. Long-boned boy fascinated with airplanes and wireless. Little brother of the immortal
Susan. Heir to all that Ninian and Flora had built here in the North
Fork the past thirty years. Corpse in the bloody mud of France. *A
life bright against the dark/but death loves a shining mark.* Samuel was
our first casualty but inevitably not our last. Suddenly every male
in Montana between milkteeth and storeteeth seemed to have gone
to the war. Was it happening this drastically in all of America? A
nation of only children and geezers now? Why wouldn't Europe sink
under the Yankee weight if our every soldier-age man was arriving
over there? Of my own generation, only Allan Frew was young
enough to enlist, and he of course figured on settling the war by
himself. But our sons, our neighbors, boy upon boy upon boy who
had been pupils of mine, were away now to the war. Maybe that
was my yearfull feeling, the sense of being beyond in age whatever
was happening to those who were in the war. Yet, truthfully, who of
us were not in it? Here at our homestead that I was riding into sight
of, Adair would be in her quiet worry for Private Varick A. Mc-
Caskill of Company C, 361st Regiment, 181st Brigade, 91st Division, in training at Camp Lewis in the state of Washington. And
Anna, invisible but ever there, on the other side of Breed Butte
from me Anna was doubtless riding home now from the Noon Creek
school just as I was from mine, maybe with her own thoughts of
pupils who already were in the trenches of France but definitely
with the knowledge that her own son Peter was destined into uniform, too, if the war went into another year. Like the inescapable
smoke of the summer of 1910, the war was reaching over the horizon to find each of us.

"Hello, you," I gave to Adair as spiritedly as I could when I
came up from the lambing shed to supper.

She knew my mood, though. She somehow seemed to, these
days. The winter just past was the first that Adair and I had spent
together since Varick turned his face from me. The first, too, of
trying to live up to this horn-locked partnership with Rob. To my

surprise, when he and I had begun feeding hay to the sheep, she insisted on getting into her heavy clothes and coming with us. *I can drive the sled team for you,* she said, and did. Of course the reason was plain enough. She was putting herself between the slander Rob and I could break into at the least provocation. And it had worked. Seeing her there at the front of the hayrack, small bundled figure with the reins in her hand, seemed to tell both her brother and me that we may as well face the fact of her determination and plod on through this sheep partnership. At least that was my conclusion. I could never speak for Rob these days. By midway through the winter I was able to tell Adair she could abstain from her teamstering. *Rob and I are never going to be a duet, but we can stand each other for that long each day.* She scrutinized me, then nodded. *But you'll let me know if you need me again?* I hoped it would never be again that I needed her between myself and Rob, but I answered, *Dair, I'll let you know. I most definitely will.*

"How many today?" Adair asked as she began putting supper on the table.

"Forty," I gave the report of the day's birth of lambs.

She gave me a smile. "I'm just as glad you didn't bring them all in for the oven at once." I had to laugh, but I was still hearing her *how many?* question. This was the first lambing time Adair had ever asked that, night after night, the first time she had shown interest in the pride and joy of any shedman, his daily tally of new lambs. A new ritual, was this. Well, I would take it. Anything that emphasized life, I would gladly take.

At the end of May came our news of where Varick would be sent next by the army.

It's going to look just a whole lot like where I've been, he wrote in the brief letter to Adair. *Maybe because it's the same place.*

He was staying stationed at Camp Lewis, he explained, in a headquarters company. *They think they found something I can do, without me jeopardizing the entire rest of the army, so for now they're going to keep me here to do it. So here I stay, for who knows how long. I sure as h——don't, and I think maybe the army doesn't either.*

As they did each time, Varick's words on the paper brought back the few that had passed between him and me before he went off to the army. He had ridden into the yard just after I had come home from the school. I stepped out of the house to meet him. He dismounted and said only, *I came to see Mother.*

Unless you close your eyes quick, you'll see me, too, I tried.

No grin at all from him. Well, that could be because of the war rather than just me. But for three years it hadn't been.

Your mother's out at the root cellar, I informed him. But I couldn't stand this. Since time out of mind, Varick was the first McCaskill to wear the clothes of war. A ticket of freedom had let my great-grandfather shape the blocks of stone at the Bell Rock rather than face the armies of Napoleon. Neither my Nethermuir grandfather nor my deaf father were touched by uniform, nor was I. Which led inexorably to the thought that Varick was bearing the accumulated danger for us all.

*Varick. Son. Can't we drop this long enough to say goodbye? Who knows when—*if, I thought—*I'll see you again.*

Sure, we can say that much. And that was going to be all, was it. Varick held no notion that this could be our last occasion. He was at that priceless age where he thought he was unkillable. He drew a breath, this man suddenly taller than I was, and came to me and thrust out his hand. *Goodbye then.*

Goodbye, Varick. Your mother . . . and I . . . you'll be missed every moment.

I saw him swallow, and then he went off around the house to the root cellar. I felt my eyes begin to stream, tears that have been flowing since the first man painted blue fought the first man painted green and still have not washed away war.

Now Adair was putting Varick's letter in the top drawer of the sideboard with his others. Without turning, she asked, "And which do we hope for now, Angus? That they keep him and keep him in that camp, or that they ship him to France?"

I knew what was in her mind, for it was abruptly and terribly at the very front of mine as well. The army camps were becoming pestholes of influenza. Generally that was not something to die of, but people were dying of it in those camps. We had heard that the oldest son of the Florians, a 'steader family south of Gros Ventre, was already buried at a camp in Iowa before his parents even had word that he was ill. And now there in the midst of it at Camp Lewis was going to be our son, the child who came down with something in even the mildest of winters; Varick would be a waiting candidate for influenza as the months of this year advanced. But to wish him into the shrapnel hell of the fighting in France, no, I never could. Twin hells, then, and our son the soldier being gambled at their portals.

In earliest June, Rob and I met to cut the cards for a shearing time. This year mine was the low card, contradictory winner in Adair's order of things, and so we would shear later in the month, when I thought the weather was surest. Rob looked as sour as usual at losing, but before I could turn away to leave, he broke out with: "Any word from the Coast lately?"

By that he meant the Pacific Coast and Camp Lewis and Varick, and I stood and studied him a moment. We would never give each other the satisfaction of saying so, but he and I at last did have one thing we agreed on, the putrid taste of the war. *They're rabid dogs fighting in a sack, England and Germany and France and all of them*, I had heard him declare in disgust to Adair. *Why're we jumping in it with them?* Yet I knew, too, that the war's high prices for wool and lambs were the one merit he found in this partnership of ours. Well, nobody ever said Rob Barclay was too insubstantial to carry contradictions.

"Nothing new," I said shortly, and turned from him.

In the Fourth of July issue of the *Gleaner* was published the Two Medicine country's loss list thus far in the war.

> THE MEN WHO GAVE ALL

Adams, Theodore, killed in action at Cantigny.

Almon, John, fought in the taking of Boureches, died of wounds.

Duff, Samuel, killed by a high explosive shell in the Seicheprey sector.

Florian, Harold, contracted influenza and died at Camp Dodge, Iowa.

Jebson, Michael, while returning from a furlough, was killed in a train wreck between Paris and Brest.

McCaul, George, saw service in France, taken ill with influenza, died in hospital of lobar pneumonia.

Ridpath, Jacob, killed in action at Château-Thierry.

Strong Runner, Stephen, entered the service at Salem Indian Training School in Oregon, died of tuberculosis at the Letterman General Hospital, San Francisco.

Zachary, Richard, killed in action at Belleau Wood.

A hot noon in the third week of August, the set of days that are summer's summer. I had my face all but into the washbasin, gratefully swashing off the sweat of my morning's work with cupped handfuls of cool well water, when Adair's hand alighting on my back startled me.

"Angus," she uttered quietly, "look outside. It's Rob coming. And Davie."

The first of those was supposed to be taking his turn at camptending our herder with the sheep up in the mountains, and the other was that herder. They could not possibly both be here, because that would leave the sheep abandoned and—yet out the west window, here they both came, slowly riding.

I still was mopping myself with the towel as I flung out to see what this was, Adair right after me. At the sight of us, Rob spurred his horse ahead of the lagging Davie and dismounted in a hurry almost atop Adair and myself.

"Davie's come down ill," he reported edgily. "I didn't know what the hell else to do but bring him out with me. It's all he can do to sit on that horse." Rob looked fairly done in himself, showing the strain of what he'd had to do. His voice was rough as a rasp as he went on: "Davie has to be taken on home to Donald and Jen, but one of us has got to get up there to those sheep, sharp. Do we cut to see who goes?"

"No, I'll go up. You tend to Davie." I stood planted in front of Rob, waiting for what he would be forced to tell me next.

"The sheep are somewhere out north of Davie's wagon, a mile or so more. I threw them into the biggest open patch of grass I could." He told it without quite managing to look at me. If you ever wanted to see a man cause agony in himself, here he was. Leaving a band of sheep to its own perils went against everything in either of us. I could all but see the images of cliff, storm, bear, mountain lions, coyotes, stampeding in Rob's eyes; and for a savage moment I was glad it was him and not me who'd had to abandon that band to bring Davie.

I went over to the sagging scarecrow on the horse behind Rob's. "Davie, lad, you're a bit under the weather, I hear."

His feverish face had a dull stricken look that unnerved me more than had his bloody battered one beneath the horse's hooves, the day of that distant spring when Adair and I jolted across the Erskine field to him; that day. Now Davie managed in a ragged near-whisper, "Couldn't . . . leave the . . . sheep."

"I'm going up to them this minute. The sheep will be all right, Davie, and so will you." If saying would only make either of those true.

As Rob and his medical burden started down the valley toward Davie's parents' place, I headed for the barn to saddle the bay mare. I hadn't gone three steps when I heard: "Angus. I'm coming with you."

I turned to my wife, to the gray eyes and auburn ringlets that had posed me so many puzzles in our years together. "You don't have to, Dair. I'll only be a day or so, until Rob can fetch another herder up."

"I'm coming anyway."

I hesitated between wanting her along and not wanting her to have to face what might be waiting up there, a destroyed band of sheep. The wreck of all our efforts since the reading of Lucas's will. "The sheep are a hell of a way up onto the mountain, Dair." I jerked my head to indicate Roman Reef standing bright in the sun, its cliffs the color of weathered bone. "It's a considerable ride."

"Adair knows how to ride, doesn't she."

True. But true enough? The saddle hours it would take to climb Roman Reef, through the sunblaze of the afternoon heat, to the grim search for adrift sheep—I recited the reasons against her coming, then asked: "Do you still want to?"

I swear she said this, as if the past twenty-one years of her avoidance of the Two Medicine country's mountainline were unceremoniously null and void. She said, "Of course I want to."

All afternoon Adair and I went steadily up and up, not hurrying our saddlehorses but keeping them steady at the pace just short of hurry. At midpoint of the afternoon we were halfway up Roman Reef, the valley of the North Fork below and behind us, Scotch Heaven's log-built homesteads becoming dark square dots in the distance. Our own buildings looked as work-stained as any. Then a bend of the trail turned us north, and the valley there was Noon Creek's, with the Reese ranch in easy sight now. Easy sight to where Anna was. Anyone but me would not have known the years and years of distance between.

At the next climbing turn of the trail I glanced back at Adair. She had on Varick's old brown Stetson he had left home when he went away to the army, and her riding skirt, and a well-worn blouse that had begun as white and now was the color of cream. My unlikely wife, an unlikely mote of light color against the rock and timber of the mountain. I wondered if she at all had any of the division of mind I did on this journey of ours. Part of me saw, desperately, that if the sheep had found a way to destroy themselves since Rob left them atop this mountain, Adair and I would possess what we had on our backs and that homestead down there and the rest you could count in small coins. Yet if the sheep were gone, stampeded all over the hemisphere, eaten, dead a myriad of ways, that also would mean the end of my teeth-gritting partnership with Rob. As we climbed and climbed, there was a kind of cruel relief for me in the fact that the sheep in their woolheaded way were doing the deciding, whether this enforced pairing of Rob and myself was to be the one thing or the other.

Atop, with the afternoon all but gone, Adair and I urged our horses toward where Davie's sheepwagon showed itself like a tall canvas igloo on wheels. Rob had shut Davie's dog in the sheep-wagon so that he wouldn't follow down the mountain. When I un-jailed him he came out inquisitive as to why I was not Davie, but otherwise ready to participate. I climbed back on my horse, leaned down from the saddle and called, "Come up, Scamp. Come up, boy."

The dog eyed me a moment to see if I really meant such a thing, then crouched to the earth and sprang against my leg and the stir-rup leather, scrambling gamely as I boosted him the rest of the way into my lap. There across my thighs between the saddle horn and my body he at once lay quiet, exactly as if I had told him to save all possible energy. If the sheep were not where Rob had left them, this dog was going to have to work his legs off when we found them. If we found them. If we found them alive.

Adair and I and my border collie passenger in about a mile found what I was sure was the meadow Rob had described, and no sheep. An absence of sheep, a void as stark as a town empty of people. We sat on our horses and listened. Except for the switching sounds of our horses' tails, the silence was complete. I put the dog down. "Find them, Scamp." But the sheep had been over so much of the meadow that the dog could only trace out with his stymied dashes what I already knew, that some direction out of this great half-circle of grass they had quit the country.

Below us the last sunshine was going from the plains, the shadow of these mountains was now the first link of dusk. This meadow in the fading light looked like the most natural of bedgrounds for sheep. Tell that to the sheep, wherever the nomadic bastards had got to. Here Rob had made his decision that flung the sheep to their own wandering. Now I had to make mine to consign them to their own perils for the night.

"We'll take up the looking in the morning, Dair. It won't help anything for us to tumble over a cliff up here in the dark."

Back at the sheepwagon, Adair began fixing supper while I picketed our horses and fed Davie's dog. Then I joined her in the round-topped wagon, inserting myself onto the bench seat on the opposite side of the tiny table from the cooking area. That was pretty much the extent of a sheepwagon, a bench seat along either side, cabinets above and below, the bunk bed across the wagon's inmost end and the midget kitchen at its other. I suppose a fastidious cook would have been paralyzed at the general grime of Davie's potwear and utensils. Adair didn't seem to notice. She gave me a welcoming smile and went on searing some eggs in a black-crusted frying pan.

I sat watching her, and beyond her, out the opened top half of the wagon's Dutch door, the coming of night as it darkened the forest trees. So here we are, Dair. The McCaskills of Montana. After twenty-one years of marriage, cooped in a mountaintop sheepwagon. Sheepless. All the scenery we can eat, though. Not exactly what you had in mind for us when you contrived that will of yours, ay, Lucas? Somewhere out there in the prairie towns, Rob was scouring for a herder in these hireless times, at Choteau or Conrad if none was to be had in Gros Ventre, as there likely wasn't. Everyone in the war effort, these days. It was an effort, they were most definitely right about that.

After we had eaten, I leaned back and looked across at this wife of mine. Those twin freckles, one under each eye, like reflections of the pupils. Flecks of secondness, marks of the other Adair somewhere within the one I was seeing. I asked, "How do you like sheepherding, so far?"

"The company is the best thing about it."

"You have to understand, of course, this is the deluxe way to do it. Usually there are a couple of thousand noisy animals involved."
Sheep sound like the exact thing to have, Rob responding to Lucas's suggestion of our future in my newfound valley called the North Fork. *Now if we only had sheep.*

"Tomorrow will tell, won't it," she answered my spoken and unspoken disquisitions on sheeplessness.

Well, if today was its model for revelation, it would. Adair volunteering herself into these mountains: I could have predicted forever and missed that possibility.

My curiosity was too great to be kept in. "Dair, truth now. Coming up here today where you could see it all, what did you think of it?"

In the light of the coal-oil lantern, her eyes were darker than usual as she searched into mine.

"The same as ever," she told me forthrightly, maybe a bit regretfully. "There is so much of this country. People keep having to stretch themselves out of shape trying to cope with so much. Distance. Weather. The aloneness. All the work. This Montana sets its own terms and tells you, do them or else. Angus, you and Rob maybe were made to handle this country. Adair doesn't seem to have been."

"For someone who can't handle that"—I inclined my head to the sweep of the land beneath our mountain—"you gave a pretty good imitation today."

"Such high praise," she said, not at all archly, "so late at night."

"Yes, well." I got up and stepped to the door for one last listen for the sheep. The dark silence of the mountains answered me. I turned around to Adair again, saying "Night is what we'd better be thinking about, isn't it. That bed's going to be a snug fit."

Adair turned her face toward me in the lanternlight. She asked as if it was the inquiry she always made in sheepwagons: "Is that a promise?"

The buttons of that creamy blouse of hers seemed to be the place to begin answering that. Then my fingers were inside, on the small pert mounds of Adair's breasts, and eventually down to do away with her riding skirt. Her hands were not idle either; who has said, *the one pure language of love is Braille?* If no one else, the two of us were inscribing it here and now. We did not interrupt vital progress on one another even as I boosted Adair into the narrow bunk bed and my clothes were shed beside hers. Two bodies now in the space for one, she and I went back and forth from quick hungers of love, our lips and tongues with the practice of all our years together but fresh as fire to each other, too, to expectant holidays of slow soft stroking. Maybe the close arch of canvas over us cupped us as if in a shell, concentrating us into ourselves and each other. Maybe the bachelor air, the sheepwagon's accumulated loneliness of herders spending their hermit lives, fed our yearning. Maybe the desperation of the day, of the marriage we somehow had kept together, needed this release. Who knew. It was enough for Adair and me that something, some longing of life, had us in its supreme grip. Something drives the root, something unfolds the furrow: its force was ours for each other, here, now.

As ever, Adair's slim small body beneath mine was nothing like Anna's the single time it had been under mine; as ever, our love-making's convulsion was everything like Anna's and mine. Difference became sameness, there in our last straining moments. This was the one part of life that did not care about human details, it existed on its own terms.

At first hint of dawn, we had to uncoil ourselves from sleep and each other. No time for a breakfast fire, either; the two of us ate as much dried fruit from Davie's grocery supply as we could hold, and then we were out to our saddle horses and the eager dog. As we set off into a morning that by now was a bit fainter than the darkness of night, my hope was that we were getting a jump on the sheep of maybe an hour.

That hour went, and half of another, before we had sunrise. Adair and I tied the horses and climbed up to an open outcrop of rock where we could see all around. As we watched, the eastern sky converted from orange to pink. Then there was the single moment, before the sun came up, when its golden light arrived like spray above a waterfall. The first hot half of the sun above the horizon gave us and the rock outcroppings and the wind-twisted trees long pale-gray shadows. Scrutinize the newly lit brow of the mountain as we did, though, there were no shadows with sheep attached to them.

"All this," Adair said as if speculating, "you'd think something would move. Some motion, somewhere."

I took her arm to start us down from the vantage point. "We're it, Dair. Motion is our middle name until we catch up with those goddamn sheep."

We worked stands of timber. Sheep sifted out of none of them.

We cast looks down over canyon cliffs. No wool among the harsh scree below.

We found at least three meadows where the grass all but shouted invitation to be eaten by sheep. All three times, no least trace of sheep.

Two hours of that. Then another. Too much time was passing. I didn't say so, but Adair knew it, too. The day already was warm enough to make us mop our brows. If we didn't find the sheep by ten o'clock or so, they would shade up and we would lose the entire hot midpart of the day without any bleats of traveling sheep to listen for.

Now Adair and I were ears on horseback, riding just a minute or two and then listening. How could there be so much silence? How could the invisible ligaments that bound the sky to the earth not creak in tense effort at least once in a while?

But nothingness, mute air, answered us so long and so steadily that when discrepancy finally came, we both were unsure about it.

I shot a glance to Adair. She thought she had heard it, too, if you could call that hearing. A sliver of sound, a faintest faraway *tink*.

Or more likely a rock dislodging itself in the morning heat and falling with a *clink*?

The dog was half-dozing in my lap. One of his ears had lifted a little, not enough to certify anything.

Adair and I listened twice as hard as before. At last I had to ask, low and quick, "What do you think, Dair?"

She said back to me in a voice as carefully crouched as my own: "I think it was Percy's bell."

By now we were past mid-morning, not far short of ten. We could nudge our horses into motion toward the direction where we imagined we'd heard the *tink* and risk losing any repeat of it in the sounds of our riding. Or we could sit tight, stiller than stones, and try to hear through the silence.

With her head poised, Adair looked as if she could sit where she was until the saddle flaked apart with age. I silently clamped myself in. I say silently. Inside me my willed instructions to the bellwether clamored and cried. *Move, Percy,* I urged. *Make that bell of yours ring just once, just one time, and I promise I'll feed you graham crackers until you burst. If you're up, don't lie down just yet. If you're down, for Christ's sake get up. Either case, move. Take a nice nibble of grass, why not, make that bell—*

The distant little clatter came, and Davie's dog perked up in my lap. I put him down to the ground and away he went, Adair and I riding after him, in the direction of the bell.

But for the dog, we still would have missed the sheep. They were kegged up in a blind draw just beneath a rimrock, as if having decided to mass themselves to make an easy buffet for any passing bear. The dog glided up the slope and over into the draw, we followed, and there they were, hundreds of gray ghosts quiet in the heat, contemplating us remorselessly as we rode up.

Adair anxiously asked, "Is it all of them?"

"I can't tell until I walk them. Make the dog stay here with you, Dair."

I went slowly on foot to the sheep, easing among them, moving ever so gradually back and forth through them, a drifting figure they did not really like to accept but did not find worth agitating themselves about. All the while I scanned for the band's marker sheep. Found Percy, with his bell. Found nine of the ten black ewes, but not the tenth. Found the brownheaded bum lamb with the lop ear, but did not find the distinctive pair of big twin lambs with the number brand 69 on their sides.

When I had accounted for the markers that were and weren't there, I went back down the slope to Adair.

"Most of them are here," I phrased it to her, "but not quite all."

It was noon of the next day before Rob appeared with a herder in tow, a snuff-filled Norwegian named Gustafson. "And I had to go all the way to Cut Bank even to come up with him," Rob gritted out. His eyes were on the sheep, back and forth across them, estimating. "Much loss?"

"At least a couple of hundred, maybe a few over."

"Lambs, do you mean? Or that many ewes and lambs together? Spit it out, man."

And so I did. "That many of each, is what I mean."

Rob looked as if my words had taken skin off him in a serious place. In a sense, they had. He knew as well as I did that such a loss would nick away our entire year's profit. But dwelling on it wasn't going to change it, was it. I asked him, "How's Davie?"

"Sick as a poisoned pup." Rob cast a wide gaze around, as if hoping to see sheep peeking at him from up in the treetops, out the cracks in rocks, anywhere. "Let's don't just stand here moving our mouths," he began, "we've got to get to looking—"

"Dair and I have done what looking we could," I informed him, "and now that you're here, the three of us can try some more. But there hasn't been a trace of the rest of the sheep. Wherever the hell those sheep are, they're seriously lost."

We never found them. From that day on, the only existence of those four hundred head of vanished sheep was in the arithmetic at shipping time; because of them, our sheep year of 1918 subtracted down into a break-even one. Not profit, not loss. Neither the one thing nor the other.

"Sweet suffering Christ," Rob let out bitterly as we stuffed the disappointing lamb checks into our shirt pockets. "What does it take, in this life? I put up with this goddamn partnership Adair keeps us in, and for no pay whatsoever?"

"Just think of all the exercise we get out of it, Rob," I answered him wearily.

By that September day when we shipped the lambs and turned toward the short weeks before winter, Davie had recuperated. His malady stayed on among us, however. Doc Murdoch could not account for how the illness had found Davie, as remote and alone on his mountainside as a person could ever be, but he was definite in his dire diagnosis: this was the influenza which had first bred in the army camps. Here in its earliest appearance in Scotch Heaven, it let Davie Erskine live, barely, while it killed his father.

From all we heard and read, the influenza was the strangest of epidemics, with different fathoms of death—sudden and selective in one instance, slow and widespread in another. Donald Erskine's fatality was in the shallows, making it all the more casual and awful. One morning while he and Jen were tending Davie, he came down with what he thought was the start of a cold, and by noon he was feeling a raging fever. For the first time since childhood, he went to bed during the day. Two days after that, the uneasy crowd of us at the Gros Ventre cemetery were burying that vague and generous man.

Man goeth to his long home, and the mourners go about the streets. Donald Erskine and Ninian Duff were the first who homesteaded in Scotch Heaven, and now there was just Ninian. I only half heard Ninian's grief-choked Bible words, there at graveside. I was remembering Adair and myself, our night together in Davie's sheepwagon, our slow wonderful writhe onto and into each other, there on his bedding. Davie had not been in that wagon, that bed, for some days before his illness, tepeeing behind the sheep as he grazed them on the northern reach of the mountain. Had he been, would one or both of us now be down with the influenza? Or be going into final earth as Donald was? *Ever the silver cord be loosed, or the golden bowl be broken . . .* My thoughts went all the way into the past, to my family's house of storm in Nethermuir. To Frank and Jack and Christie, my brothers and sister I never really knew, killed by the cholera when I was barely at a remembering age. To the husk that the McCaskill family was after that epidemic; my embittered and embattled parents, and the afterthought child who was me. Thin as spiderspin, the line of a family's fate can be. *Or the pitcher be broken at the fountain, or the wheel broken at the cistern . . .* And now another time of abrupt random deaths? What kind of a damn disease was this influenza, a cholera on modern wings? With everything medicine can do, how could all of life be at hazard in such a way? Maybe Ninian had an answer, somewhere in the growlings of John Knox that a fingersnap in heaven decided our doom as quick as we were born. I knew I didn't have one. *Then shall the dust return to the earth as it was . . .*

Adair and I were silent on our wagon ride home from Donald's funeral. I supposed her thoughts were where my own were, at

Camp Lewis. Winter was not far now, Varick's frail season. What chance did he have, there in one of the cesspools of this epidemic?

What chance did anyone have, the question suddenly began to be. You couldn't turn around without hearing of someone having lost an uncle in Chicago, a cousin in Butte, a sister on a homestead east of Conrad. Distant deaths were one thing. News of catastrophe almost next door was quite another. At a homestead on the prairie between Gros Ventre and Valier a Belgian family of six was found, the mother and four children dead in their beds, the father dead on the floor of the barn where he had tried to saddle a horse and go for help.

People were resorting to whatever they could think of against the epidemic. Out on the bare windy benchlands, 'steader families were sleeping in their dirt cellars, if they were lucky enough to have one, in hope of keeping warmer than they could in their drafty shacks. Mavis and George Frew became Bernarr Mcfadden believers, drinking hot water and forcing themselves into activity whenever they felt the least chill coming on. Others said onion syrup was the only influenza remedy. Mustard plasters, said others. Whiskey, said others. Asafetida sacks appeared at the necks of my schoolchildren that fall. When a newspaper story said masks must be worn to keep from breathing flu germs, the Gros Ventre mercantile sold out of gauze by noon of that day. The next newspaper story said masks were useless because a microbe could pass through gauze as easily as a mouse going through a barn door.

During all the precautions and debates, the flu kept on killing. Or if it didn't manage to do the job, the pneumonia that so often followed it did. Not more than ten days after our burial of Donald Erskine, it was being said that more were dying of the flu than of combat on the battlefields in Europe.

Odd, what a person will miss most. As the flu made people stay away from each other, Adair and I had our end of the North Fork valley to ourselves. Except for my daily ride to the schoolhouse, we were as isolated as if the homestead had become an island. An evening when Adair had fallen silent, but in what seemed a speculating way, I waited to see whether she would offer what was on her mind.

When Adair became aware I was watching her, she smiled a bit and asked: "Worth a halfpenny to you, is it?"

"At least," I answered, and waited again.

"Angus, I was thinking about our dances. And wondering when there will ever be one again."

Adair in the spell of the music, light and deft as she glided into a tune. Yes. A sharp absence to her, that the epidemic had made a casualty of the schoolroom dances. I missed them, too, for they meant Anna to me. Seeing her across the floor, gathering her anew each time in the quickest of looks between us, remembering, anticipating.

I looked across the room at Adair. If our senses of loss were different, at least they were shared. I got to my feet.

"We'd better not forget how, had we," I said to my wife. My best way to carry a tune is in a tub, but I hummed the approximate melody of *Dancing at the Rascal Fair* and put out my hands to Adair.

"Angus, are you serious?"

"I'm downright solemn," I said, and hummed another batch.

She gave me a gaze, the Adair gray-eyed glint that I had encountered in the depot at Browning all the years ago. Then she came up into my arms, her head lightly against my shoulder, the soft sound of her humming matching itself to mine, and we began the first of our transits around the room, quiet with each other except for the tune from our throats.

Less than two weeks after the beginning of school that autumn, every schoolhouse in the county had to close because of the influenza peril. It seemed that the last piece of my life that I could count on to be normal was gone now. At the homestead the next week or so, I went restlessly from chore to chore, rebuilding my damnable west fence that always needed it, patching the sheep shed roof, anything, everything, that could stand to have work done to it.

How Adair was managing to put up with me, I don't know. It must have been like living with a persistent cyclone, and one whose mood wasn't improved by how achy and stiff he felt from all his labors.

She persevered with me, though. "There's just one item on the place you haven't repaired lately," she told me one noon, "and that's you. Let me give you a haircut."

"What, in the middle of the day? Dair, I've got—"

"Right now," she inserted firmly, "while the light is best. It won't take time at all. Go get yourself sat, while I find the scissors."

I grumpily took my place by the south window. The mountains were gray in the thin first-of-October light. The year was waning down toward winter every day now. Toward another season of feeding hay with Rob, ample justification for gloom if I needed any further reason.

Over my head and then up under my chin came a quick cloud of fabric, Adair snugly knotting the dish towel at the back of my neck. "Stop squirming," she instructed, "or the lariat is next." From the edge of my eye I could see the dark-brown outline of the barn, and impatiently reminded myself I'd better go repair harness as soon as Adair had trimmed me to her satisfaction.

Her scissorwork and even the touch of her fingers as she handled my hair were an annoyance today. After I flinched a third or fourth time, Adair ruffled my hair with mock gruffness as she used to do to Varick when he was small and misbehaving, and said questioningly, "You're a touchy one today."

"It's not your barbering. I've got a bit of a headache, is all."

The scissors stopped on the back of my neck, the blades so cold against my skin I felt their chill travel all through me. "Angus, you never get headaches."

"I'm here to tell you, I've got a major one now," I stated with an amount of irritation that surprised me. But it genuinely did feel as if a clamp was squeezing the outer corner of each of my eyes, the halves of my head being made to press hard against each other.

"Dair, let's finish making me beautiful," I managed to say somewhat more civilly. "I need to get on with the afternoon work."

It wasn't an hour from then when she found me in the barn, sitting on a nail keg with my head down, trying to catch my breath.

When Adair asked if I was able to walk, I sounded ragged even to myself when I told her of course I could, any distance.

"The house, Angus," she answered that, her voice strangely brave and frightened at once. "Hold onto me, we're going to the house."

House, the distant echo of the woman's voice said. But we were in a wagon, weren't we, at the edge of a cliff. River below. *Those*

340

Blackfeet, Angus. The Two Medicine. Those Blackfeet put their medicine lodge near. Two times. Wait: the horses didn't answer to the reins. I yanked back but they were beginning to trot, running now. The cliff. *I fell through life* . . . The woman beside me clung to my arm. Bodies below. Bigger than sheep, darker. Cows, no, bigger. Buffalo. *The buffalo cliff, Angus. It was a good one.* The river was so far, so far down. Harness rattling. She clung to me. The cliff. I could see down over the edge, the buffalo were broken, heaped. *Fell through life.* She clung to me, crying something I couldn't hear. The horses were going to run forever. Our wagon wheels were inches from the cliff, I had to count the wheelspoke with the white knot of handkerchief *one* as it went around *two* count the wheelspin *three* as the ground flew . . . What. She was crying something. Hooves of the horses, wagon bumping. *Hang on,* I tell the woman, *we've got to* . . . Count the wheelspoke, start over. *One,* no, *two.* Tell the woman, *you count. While I* . . . what. Helpless. They don't answer the reins. Quiet now, horses run silently. But so close to the cliff. Two Medicine. *Those Blackfeet. Two times. Count,* I tell her. Too late. The spoke is coming loose. Rim breaking from the wheel. *Can't,* I tell her. *A wheel can't just* . . . Wheel breaking apart now, nearest the cliff. Iron circle of the rim peeling off, the spokes flying out of the hub. *Hold on,* tell the woman. Tipping, falling. I shout into her staring face: Anna! *Anna!* ANNA!

The bedroom was silent except for the heaviness of my breathing. "You decided to wake up, did you."

Adair's voice. Her face followed it to the bed and me. The back of her small hand, cool and light, rested on my forehead a long moment, testing. "You're a bit fevery, but nothing to what you were a few days ago. And if you're finally well enough to wonder, the doctor says you don't have any pneumonia." Adair sat on the side of the bed and regarded me with mock severity. "He says you're recovering nicely now, but it'll be a while before you're up and dancing."

I felt weak as a snail. "Dair," I croaked out. "Did I . . . shout . . . something?"

A change flickered through her eyes. And then she was looking at me as steadily as before. "You do know how to make a commotion." She got up from the bedside and went out of the room.

My head felt big as a bucket, and as empty. It took an effort to lick my lips, an exertion to swallow.

In a minute or several, Adair was back, a bowl of whiteness in her hands.

"You need to eat," she insisted. "This is just milk toast. You can get it down if you try a bit."

The spoon looked too heavy to lift, the bowl as big as a pond. I shook my head an enormous inch. "I don't want—"

"Adair doesn't care," stated Adair, "what you don't want. It's what you're going to get." And began to spoonfeed me.

In a few days I was up from bed in brief stints, feeling as pale as I looked. My body of sticks and knobs was not the only thing vigor had gone out of. It was gravely noticeable how quiet Scotch Heaven seemed. No visiting back and forth, no sounds of neighbors sawing wood for winter.

As my head cleared, thoughts sharp as knives came. Donald Erskine being put into his grave, gone of the same illness I had just journeyed through. Those reports of the epidemic's efficient carnage in the army camps. Varick. No, Adair would have told me if— yet could she have, deeply ill as I was, wobbly as I still was? She had said nothing about our son, was saying nothing. That was just Adair. Or was it what I could not be told.

"Dair," I at last had to ask, "this influenza. Who else—?"

The gray eyes of my wife gave me a gauging look. "I've been keeping the newspaper for you. Maybe you're as ready to see it as you'll ever be. It has the list."

I pushed the prospect away with a wince. "If it's so bad they have to have a list, I don't want to see it."

Adair gauged me again. Then she went over to the sideboard, reached deep in a drawer and brought me the *Gleaner*.

VICTIMS OF THE EPIDEMIC

My eyes shot to the bottom of the page.

Munson, Theodore, homesteader. Age 51. Died at his homestead east of Gros Ventre, Oct. 11.

Not anyone I knew; but more *M* names were stacked above

that one. My scan of the list fled upward through them—*Morgan
. . . Mitulski . . . Mellisant*—toward the dreaded *Mc*s:

McWhirter . . .

McNee . . .

McCorkill . . .

McCallister . . .

And then *Kleinsasser . . . Jorgensen . . . Varick was safely absent
from this list, among the living. Mercy I sought, mercy I got.* I was as
thankful as any person had ever been. But while Adair and I still
had a son, a name known to me even longer than Varick's came out
of the list at me.

*Frew, Allan, soldier of the American Expeditionary Force. Age 45.
Died in a field hospital near Montfaucon, Sept. 26.*

Allan in the shearing contest I had let him win. Allan dancing
with Adair afterward, the two of them the melody of my hope that
she would find a husband and a Montana niche for herself, in that
far ago summer, while Anna and I—life isn't something you can
catechize into happening the way you intend, is it. I looked up now
at Adair, whose marriage could have been with Allan, for better or
for worse but surely for different than all she had been through with
me. "It's too bad about Allan," I offered to her, and she nodded a
slight nod which was agreement but also instruction for me to look
at the list again.

Erskine, Jennie, widow of Donald, mother of David . . . "Not Jen,"
I squeezed out of my constricted throat. "Not old Jen, too, after
poor Donald . . ."

"Yes. It's an awful time, Angus," Adair answered in a voice as
strained as mine.

My thoughts were blurred, numb, as my eyes climbed the rest of
the list. *Benson . . . Baker . . .* Between them would have been
Rob's slot, if Barclays were susceptible to the mere ills of the rest of
the world. What would I be feeling now, if his name stood in stark
print there? Or he, if mine was in rank back down there in the *Mc*s?
I did not know, you never can except in the circumstance, but I
could feel it all regathering, the old arguments, the three angry
years apart from Rob after the Two Medicine and the angry time
with him since then in this benighted damn sheep partnership—I
was too weary, done in, to go where that train of thought led. I fast

read the rest of its list to the first of its names, *Angutter, Hans, homesteader* . . . and put the *Gleaner* away from me.

"Angus." I heard Adair draw a breath. The newspaper was back in her hand, thrust to me.

"Dair, what?" I asked wearily. "I read the damn list once, I'm not going to again."

Then I saw. Beside Adair's thumb there on the page, was that name at the bottom of the list, *Munson, Theodore;* but there was also the small print beneath that. *List continues on p. 3.*

"Angus," my wife said with a catch in her voice, "you have to."

No.

No no no.

But I did have to. Did have to know. The newspaper shook in my hands as I opened it to the third page, as I dropped my eyes to the end of the remainder of the list and forced them, the tears already welling, back up to the *R*s.

Reese, Anna, wife of Isaac, mother of Lisabeth and Peter. Age 44. At the family ranch on Noon Creek, during the night of Oct. 12.

1919

Times are as thin in Montana as they can get. No one needs telling that this has been a summer so dry it takes a person three days to work up a whistle. But we urge our homesteading brethren to hold themselves in place on their thirsty acres if they in any way can, and not enlist in the exodus of those who have given up heart and hope. As surely as the weather will change from this driest of times, so shall the business climate.

—GROS VENTRE WEEKLY GLEANER,
AUGUST 21, 1919

LET IT tell itself, that season of loss.

By first snowfall, as much of me as could mend was up and out in the tasks of the homestead, of the sheep, of the oncoming winter. Had I been able, I would have filled myself with work twenty-four hours a day, to have something in me where the Anna emptiness always waited. Yet even as I tried to occupy myself with tasks of this, that, and the other, I knew I was contending against the kind of time that has no hours nor minutes to it. Memory's time. In its calendarless swirl the fact of Anna's death did not recede, did not alter. Smallest things hurt. A glance north to read the weather, and I was seeing the ridge that divided the North Fork from Noon Creek, the shoulder of geography between my life and hers. A chorus of bleats from the sheep as they grazed the autumn slope of Breed Butte, choir of elegy for the Blackfeet grass and the moment when I recognized Anna at the reins of the arriving wagon. And each dawn when I went out to the first of the chores, the slant of lantern light from the kitchen window a wedge between night and day—each was the dawn of Anna and myself and the colors of morning beginning to come to the Two Medicine country. Each time, each memory, I told myself with determination that it would be the last, that here was the logical point for the past to grow quiet. But no known logic works on that worst of facts, death of someone you loved, does it.

By Armistice Day, when the war pox in Europe finally ended, the influenza epidemic was concluding itself, too. In the Gros Ventre cemetery the mounded soil on the graves of Anna and its dozens of other victims was no longer fresh. When the schools reopened and Ninian came to ask if I was well enough to resume teaching, I told him no, he would need to make a new hire. Whether it was my health or not that lacked the strength, I could not face the South Fork schoolroom just then. Anna dancing in my arms there the first time ever, my voice asking, *And we'll be dancing next at Noon Creek, will we?* and hers answering, *I'll not object.* Before Ninian could go, I had to know: "What's being done about the Noon Creek school?" He reported, "Mrs. Reese's daughter is stepping in for them there." Lisabeth. In younger replica, the same beautiful face with an expression as frank as a clock, still in place at Noon Creek. But not.

By Christmas week, Rob and I were meeting wordlessly each day at a haystack to pitch a load onto the sled and feed the sheep. Maybe the man knew how to keep a decent silence in the face of a sorrow. Maybe he thought the hush between us added cruel weight to his indictment of me and my hopelessness about Anna. Who knew, and who cared. Whatever I was getting from Rob, cold kindness or mean censure, I at least had mercy from the weather. There was just enough snow to cover the ground, and only a chill in the air instead of deep cold. Day upon day the mountains stood their tallest, clear in every detail, cloud-free, as if storm had forgotten how to find them. Any number of times in those first days of feeding, I saw Rob cock his head up at this open winter and look satisfied.

On New Year's Day of 1919, Varick came home.

He was taller, thinner, and an eon older than the boy-man I had fearfully watched ride the Fort Benton steer. To say the truth, there was a half-moment when I first glanced down from the haystack at the Forest Service horse and the Stetsoned person atop it, that I thought he was Stanley Meixell.

" 'Lo, Dad," he called up to me. His gaze shifted to Rob, and in another tone he simply uttered with a nod, "Unk."

"Varick, lad," Rob got out. I watched him glance at me, at Varick, confusion all over him. When no thunderbolt hit him from either of us, he decided conversation could be tried. "You're looking a bit gaunt. How bad was the army life?"

Varick gave him a flat look. "Bad enough." It was not until the weeks ahead that I heard his story of Camp Lewis. *Christamighty, Dad, the flu killed them like flies. Whole barracks of guys in quarantine. You'd see them one day, standing at the window looking out, not even especially sick, and the next day we'd be packing them out of there on stretchers to the base hospital. And a couple of days after that, we'd be burying them. A truckload of coffins at a time. I didn't figure you and Mother needed to know this, but I was doing the burying. They found out on the rifle range this eye of mine only squints when it takes a notion to, so they decided I wasn't worth shipping to France to get shot. Instead they put a bunch of us guys who knew which end of a shovel to take hold of onto the graveyard detail. The Doom Platoon, we were called. That was the war I had, Dad. Digging graves for all the ones the flu got.* But now, in the first moments of his homecoming, Varick moved his gaze from Rob, not saying anything more to him but somehow making a dismissal known. My breath caught, as I waited for the version I would get from him.

Varick swung down from the borrowed horse. Reins at the ready to tie to the haystack fence, he called up to me: "Can you stand a hand with that hay?"

"Always," I said.

When the sheep were fed and Rob went off alone and silent to Breed Butte, Varick rode home with me on the hay sled, his horse tied behind, and we talked of the wonderful mild winter, of his train journey from Seattle to Browning with his discharge paper in his pocket, of much and of nothing, simply making the words bridge the air between us. I am well beyond the age to think all things are possible. I had been ever since Anna's name on the death list in the *Gleaner.* But going home, that first day of the year, my son beside me unexpected as a griffin, I would have told you there is as much possibility in life as not.

As the crunching sounds of our sled and the team's hooves halted at the barn, Varick cupped his hands to his mouth and shouted toward the house:

"MOTHER! YOUR COOKING IS BETTER THAN THE ARMY'S!"

Adair flew out and came through the snow of the yard as if it wasn't there. She hugged the tall figure, saying not a word, not crying, not laughing, simply holding and holding.

Ultimately Varick said down to the head of auburn ringlets, "You better get in out of the weather. We'll be right along, as soon as I help this geezer unharness the horses."

Amid that barn chore, Varick's voice came casual above the rattle and creak of the harnesses we were lifting off. "I hear we just about lost you."

"As near to it as I care to come." I hung my set of harness on its peg. When my throat would let me, I said the next painful words: "Others didn't have my luck."

"Dad, I heard about Mrs. Reese." Varick stood with his armful of harness, facing me. His eyes were steady into mine. They held no apology, no attempt at reparation for the years he had held himself away from me; but they conceded that those years were ended now. The Varick facing me here knew something of the storm countries of the mind, latitudes of life and loss. Now he said with simple sympathy: "It must be tough on you."

"It is," I answered my son. "Let's go in the house to your mother."

At long last now, Varick's life took its place within comfortable distance of mine and his mother's. Stanley Meixell provided him work and wage at the ranger station through the next few months of that shortest and mildest of winters, then in calving time the job of association rider for the Noon Creek cattlemen came to him.

"I don't remember raising a cow herder," I twitted Adair. "He must be yours."

"And I don't remember doing him by myself," she gave me back, with a lift of her chin and a sudden smile.

The other climate kept getting warmer, too. Spring came early and seemed to mean it. By lambing time the last of the snow was gone from even the deepest coulees. Rob and I shed our overshoes a good three weeks earlier than usual, and the nights of March and on into April stayed so mild that Adair did not even have to have lamb guests in her oven.

So if I was never far from the fact that Anna was gone, that fact which stood like a stone above all tides, at least now I had the

shelter of Varick and Adair. What I did not have, as spring hurried
its way toward the summer of 1919, was any lessening of Rob.

At first I figured it was simply a case of seasonal bachelorhood.
Now that their girls were grown and gone, Rob had installed Judith
and himself in a house in Gros Ventre—or quite possibly Judith in
her quiet way had done the installing—and so during the feeding
time of winter and the start of lambing, Rob had been staying by
himself at the Breed Butte place. With just one more year ahead of
us to the fulfillment of Lucas's will and the sale of the sheep, you'd
have thought he would have been gritting hard and putting all his
energy into enduring the next dozen months. You'd have been as
wrong in that expectation as I was. A day soon after lambing began
in mid-March, when I asked him something he at first didn't answer
at all, simply kept on casting glances out the shed door to the valley
and the ridges around. Eventually he rounded on me and declared
as if lodging a complaint: "There isn't enough green in this whole
goddamn valley this spring to cover a billiard table."

Despite his tone, I forbore from answering him that the wan
spring wasn't my fault, that I knew of. "It's early yet," I said instead. "There's still time for the moisture to catch up with the season."

But when the rest of March and all of April brought no moisture,
I became as uneasy as he was. It ought to have been no bad thing,
to have us joined in concern about the scantiness of the grass and
the grazing future of the sheep. The air around us could stand a rest
from our winter of silent antagonism. But Rob took that spring's
lackings as an affront to him personally.

"Sweet Jesus!" he burst out in early May when we were forced to
throw the sheep back onto a slope of Breed Butte they had already
eaten across once, "what's a man supposed to do, pack a lunch for
fifteen hundred sheep?"

Before thinking, I said to him the reassurance I had been trying
on myself day after day. "Maybe we'll get it yet."

It. A cold damp blanket of it, heavy as bread dough. It had happened before; more than a few times we had known mid-May snow-
falls to fill this valley above our shoe tops. Normally snow was not a
thing Scotch Heaven had to yearn for, but we wildly wanted it now,
one of May's fat wet snowstorms, a grass bringer. Let that soak the
ground for a week, then every so often bestow a slow easy rain, the

kind that truly does some good, and the Two country's summer could be salvaged.

Not even so much as a dour retort from Rob. He simply sicced the dog after a lagging bunch of ewes and their lambs and whooped the rest of the sheep along. I swung another look to the mountains, the clear sky above them. What was needed had to begin up there. No sign of it yet.

On through the moistureless remainder of May, I wanted not to believe the mounting evidence of drought. But the dry proof was everywhere around. Already the snowpack was gone from the mountains, the peaks bare. Hay meadows were thin and wan. The worst absence, among all that the drought weather was withholding from the usual course of spring, was of sound from the North Fork. The rippling runoff of high water from the mountains was not heard that May.

The creek's stillness foretold the kind of summer that arrived to us. With June the weather turned immediately hot and stayed that way.

The summer of 1918 had been dry. This one of 1919 was parched.

"Fellows, I hate like all hell to do it," Stanley Meixell delivered the edict to Rob and me when we trailed the sheep up onto our national forest allotment. "But in green years when the country could stand it I let you bend the grazing rules a little, and now that it's a lean year we got to go the other way. I like to think it all evens out in the end."

Rob looked as if he'd been poked in a private place. I did a moment of breath catching, myself. What the forest ranger was newly rigorous about was the policy of moving our band of sheep onto a new area of the scant grass every day. Definitely *moving* them, not letting them graze at all in the previous day's neighborhood.

"We can't fatten sheep by parading them all over the mountains every day!" Rob objected furiously. "What you're asking is damn near the same as not letting them touch the grass at all. So what in the goddamn hell are we supposed to do, have these sheep eat each other?"

"It's a thought," Stanley responded, looking at Rob as if in genial agreement. "Lamb chops ought to taste better to them than grass as poor as this."

"Just tell me a thing, Meixell," Rob demanded. "If we can't use this forest for full grazing now when we most need it, then what is it you're saving it for?"

"The idea is to keep the forest a forest. Insofar as I can let you run sheep on it—or Wampus Cat Williamson or the Noon Creek Association run cattle on it—I do. But I think I maybe told you somewhere before along the line, my job is to not let any of you wear it out."

"Wear it out?" burst from Rob. "A forest as far as a person can see?"

"It all depends," answered the ranger, "how far you're looking."

What do you do when the land itself falls ill with fever?

Throughout that summer in Scotch Heaven and the rest of the Two country, each day and every day the heat would build all morning until by noon you could feel it inside your eyes—the wanting to squint, to save the eyeballs from drying as if they were pebbles. And the blaze of the sun on your cheekbones, too, as if you were standing too near a stove. Most disquieting of all, the feel of the heat in your lungs. Not even in the fire summer of 1910 had there been this, the day's angry hotness coming right into you with every breath.

Then after the worst of the heat each day, the sky brought the same disappointment. Clouds, but never rain. Evenings of July, as sundown neared, the entire sky over the mountains would fill with thick gray clouds. While the clouds came over us they swirled into vast wild whorls, as if slowly boiling. Then there would be frail rainlike fringes down from the distant edges of the cloud mass; if those ever reached the ground, it was not in the valley of the North Fork or anywhere else near. Ghost showers.

The first to be defeated by the hot brunt of the summer were the 'steaders. With no rain, their dry-land grain withered day by day. The high prices of the war were gone now, too; last year's $2-a-bushel wheat abruptly was $1-a-bushel or less. By the first of August, the wagons of the 'steaders and their belongings were beginning to come out of the south benchlands. The Thorkelsons were somehow managing to stay, and to my surprise, the Hebners;

but then there was so little evidence of how the Hebners made a living that hard times barely applied to them. The others, though, were evacuating. The Keevers, family and furniture. A wagonload of the Toskis. Billy Reinking rode down to return the copy of *Kidnapped* I had lent him and reported that his family was moving into Gros Ventre, his father was taking a job as printer at the *Gleaner* office.

I watched the wheel tracks of the 'steaders now undoing the wheel tracks from when I had marked off their homestead claims. And I watched Rob for any sign that he regretted the land locating we had done. I saw none in him, but by now I knew you do not glimpse so readily into a person.

It was midsummer when I rode up onto Roman Reef on a camp-tending trip and heard a dog giving something a working-over. The barking was not in the direction of our herder and sheep, but farther north; unless I missed my guess, somewhere in the allotment of the Noon Creek cattle. At the next trail branch in that direction, I left the pack horse tied to a pine tree and rode toward the commotion.

I met the red-brown file of Double W cattle first, lolloping down the mountainside. Then the dog who was giving close attention to their heels. Then the roan horse with Varick in its saddle.

My son grinned and lifted a hand when he saw me. "That's enough, Pooch," he called to the dog.

"That's not very charitable of you," I observed as I rode up and stopped next to Varick. "All Warren Williamson wants is your grass as well as his."

"We go through this about once a week, Dad," he told me with a laugh. "Wampus Cat sends somebody up to sneak as many cattle as he can here onto the Association's allotment. As soon as I find them, I dog them back down the countryside onto his allotment. Those cows are going to have a lot of miles on them before the summer's over."

Watching the last tail-switching rumps disappear into the forest, I was doubly pleased—at the thought of Wampus Cat Williamson having to contend with a new generation who pushed back as quick as he pushed, and at this impromptu chance to visit with Varick. "Other than having the Double W for a neighbor, how is cow life?"

"About as good as can be expected." Varick's tone was a good deal more cheerful than the words. In fact, he looked as if this was high summer in Eden instead of stone-dry Montana. He lost no time in letting me know why.

"Dad, there's something you better know about. I'm going to marry Beth Reese."

Everything in me went still, as if a great wind had stopped, gathering itself to hurl again. Across the plain of my mind the girl—almost woman—Lisabeth looking at me in that steady gauging way, the Two Medicine morning. Knowing there had been something between her mother and me, something, but having no way to know that from my direction it was deepest love. Maybe worse if she did know, if she had asked Anna, for Anna would have told her it all. That springtime pairing, Anna and I, that had come unclasped. And now the two resemblances of us, about to clasp?

I managed to say to Varick: "Are you. When's all this to happen?"

He grinned. "She doesn't quite know it yet."

I stared at this son of mine. Doesn't any generation ever learn the least scrap about life from the—

"Don't give me that look," Varick said. "Beth and I aren't you and—her mother. All this got started at a dance last spring when we kind of noticed each other. I didn't know what the hell else to do, so I just outright tried her on that. Told her that I hoped whatever she thought of me it was on my own account, not anything that had to do with our families. She told me right back she was born with a head with her own mind in it, so there was no reason why she couldn't make her own decisions. You know how she has that Sunday voice when she gets going." Like Anna. "Christamighty," Varick shook his head, "I even love that voice of hers."

Varick won where I had not. Beth said yes to his proposal, they were to be married that autumn after shipping time. Alongside my gladness for the two of them was my ache where Anna had been. Solve that, Solomon. How do you do away with a pang for what you have missed in life, even as you see it attained by your son?

If you are me you don't do away with it, you only shove it deeper into the satchel of that summer's hard thoughts. The latest worry was waiting for me in the hay meadows beside the trickle of the North Fork. I knew this was the thinnest hay crop I'd ever had, but until I began mowing it there was no knowing how utterly paltry it was. This was hay that was worth cutting only because it was better to have little than none. I could cover the width of each windrow with my hat.

I stood there with the sweat of that summer on me, dripping like a fish, and made myself look around at it all. The ridges rimming the valley, the longsail slopes of Breed Butte, the humped foothills beneath the mountains, anywhere that there should have been the tawny health of grass was instead simply faded, sickly-looking. The stone colonnades of the mountains stood out as dry as ancient bones. There was a pale shine around the horizon, more silvery than the deeper blue of the sky overhead. The silver of heat, today as every other day.

But the sight that counted was the one I was avoiding looking down at, until at last I had to again. The verdict was written in those thin skeins of dry stalks that were purportedly hay. Now the summer, the drought, had won. Now there was a *yes* I absolutely had to get.

When I came into the house for supper at the end of that first day of cutting hay, Adair looked drained. Cooking over a hot stove on such a day would boil the spirit out of anybody, I supposed. I took a first forkful of sidepork, then put it back down. I had to say what I had seen in the scantiness of the hayfield.

"Dair, Lucas's sheep. We've got to sell them this fall."

"The lambs, you mean. But we always—"

"I mean them all. The ewes too, the whole band."

She regarded me patiently. "You know I don't want us to."

"This isn't that. This time I don't mean because of Rob and me. I can go on with it for as long as he can and a minute longer, you know that. No, it's the sheep themselves. There's just not enough hay to carry them through the winter. We won't get half enough off our meadows. We can buy whatever we can find, but there isn't any hay to speak of, anywhere, this summer." She still looked at me that same patient way. "Dair, we dasn't go into winter this way. That band of sheep can't make it through on what little feed we're going to have, unless we teach them to eat air."

"Not even if it's an open winter?"

"If it's the most open winter there ever was and we only had to feed the least bit of hay, maybe, they might."

"Last winter was an open one, Angus."

"That was once, Dair. Do you really want to bet Lucas's sheep on it happening twice in a row?"

She studied her plate, and then gave me her grave gray-eyed look. "Those sheep will die?"

"Dair, they will. A whole hell of a bunch of them, if not all. They and the lambs in them. We've never had so poor a grass summer, the band isn't going to be as strong as it ought to be by fall. And you know what winter can be in this country. I realize this is sudden, but I figured if I pointed it out to you now we'd still have time to get out of this sheep situation with our skins on. All I ask is that you start thinking this over and—"

"I don't need to," she answered. "Sell the sheep, Angus."

"Sell the sheep now?" Rob repeated in disbelief. "Man, did you and Adair check your pillows this morning, to see whether your brains leaked out during the night?"

He may have been right. Certainly I felt airheaded at this reaction of his to my news of Adair's willingness to sell. This person in front of me, Robert Burns Barclay as far as the eye could attest, from the first minute in the lawyer's office had been the one for selling Lucas's sheep, and now—

"There's not money to be made by selling while prices are as low as they are," he was saying to me contemptuously. "A babe coming out of his mother could tell you that. No, we're not selling."

"Christ on a raft, Rob! You don't remember the years of '93? Four years in a row, and prices stayed sunk the whole while."

"That was then, this is now." When that didn't brush me away, he gave the next flourish. "I remember that we hung on without selling, and we came out of it with full pockets."

"We didn't start off with a summer like this."

"Will you make yourself look at the dollars of this situation?" he resorted to. "For once in your life, will you do that?" He cocked his head, then resumed: "The first year of these goddamn sheep of Lucas's, we made decent money. Last year, we only came out even. This year we're not making a penny on the wool or the lambs, either, and if we sell the ewes at these prices we're all but giving them away, too. It'd mean we've spent three years for no gain, man. And I want a hell of a lot better pay than that, for having to go through this goddamn partnership with you."

"You can want until you turn green with it and that still doesn't mean it'll happen. Rob, for Christ's sake, listen—"

"Listen yourself," he shot back. "Prices are bound to come back up. All we've got to do is wait until next year and sell the whole outfit, ewes and lambs and all."

"And what about this winter, with no more hay than we've got?"

"We've never seen a winter in this country we couldn't get through. I even got through one under the same roof with you, somehow. If we have to buy a dab of hay, all right, then we'll trot out and buy it. You'd worry us into the invalids' home if you had your way."

I shook my head and took us back around the circle to where this had begun. "Adair and I want to sell now."

"Want all you please. I'm telling you, I'm not selling. Which means you're not."

I had pummeled him down to gruel once, why not pound him again now? And again every day until he agreed to sell the sheep? I was more than half ready to. But the fist didn't exist that could bring an answer out of Rob that he didn't want to give. I withheld my urge to bash him and said: "Rob, you're not right about this. I hope to Christ you'll think it over before winter gets here."

"Try holding your breath until I do, why don't you." He looked both riled and contemptuous now. "In the meantime, I'm not hearing any more mewling from you about selling the sheep."

What walloped me next was Ninian Duff's decision to leave the North Fork.

"Ay, Angus, I would rather take a beating with a thick stick." For the first time in all the years I had known this man he seemed embarrassed, as if he was going against a belief. "But I know nothing else to do." Ninian stared past me at the puddled creek, the scant grass. "Had Samuel not been called by the Lord, I would go on with the sheep and say damn to this summer and the prices and all else. But I am not the man I was." Age. It is the ill of us all. "So, Flora and I will go to Helena, to be near Susan."

That early September day when I rode home from the Duffs' and the news of their leaving, the weather ahead of me was as heavy as my mood. Clouds lay in a long gray front, woolly, caught atop the peaks, while behind the mountains the sky was turning inky. All the way from the South Fork to Jericho Reef, a forming storm that was half a year overdue.

Despite the homestead houses and outbuildings I was passing as I rode, the valley of the North Fork seemed emptier to me just then than on the day I first looked down into it from the knob hill. Tom Mortensen and the Speddersons, gone those years ago. The Erskines taken by the epidemic. The year before last the Findlaters had bought a place on the main creek and moved down there. Allan Frew, gone in the war. And now the Duffs. Except for George Frew, Rob and I now suddenly were the last of Scotch Heaven's homesteaders; and George, too, was talking of buying on the main creek whenever a chance came.

A person could count on meeting wind at the side road up Breed Butte to Rob's place, and today it was stiff, snappy. In minutes it brought the first splatting drops of rain. The first real rain in months and months, now that the summer of 1919 had done us all the damage it could.

Beside me on the wagon seat Adair said, "I wish they had a better day for it."

I put an arm around her to help shelter her from the wind. Only the start of October, and already the wind was blowing through snow somewhere. Above the mountains the sky looked bruised, resentfully promising storm. It had rained almost daily ever since that first September gullywasher, and today didn't seem willing to be an exception. Below Adair and me now as our wagon climbed the shoulder of Breed Butte before descending the other slope to Noon Creek, we could see Rob's reservoir brimming as if it had never tasted drought; a glistening portal of water in the weary autumn land.

By the time we were down from the divide and about to cross Noon Creek, clouds like long rolls of damp cotton were blotting out the summits of the mountains. Weather directly contrary to Adair's wish. She'd had her original moment of staring startlement, too, about the daughter of Anna Reese being spliced into our family. But as quick as she could, she granted that if Lisabeth was Varick's choice in life, so be it. I tried to muster cheer for her against the sky's mood: "If you can remember so far back, the night of this counts for more than the day."

Her arm came inside my sheepskin coat and around my back, holding me. "Adair remembers," she declared.

How dreamlike it seemed, when we arrived at the old Ramsay place and stepped into the wedding festivities of Varick and Lisabeth. I had not put foot in that house since my time of courting Anna. In my memory I saw again the vinegar cruet that was Meg Ramsay. *So, Mr. McCaskill, you too are of Forfar. That surprises me.* Plump Peter Ramsay, silent as a stuffed duck. Not only were they gone now, but so was the one I saw everywhere here: Anna.

She came to the door now on the arm of Varick to greet Adair and me. She was in every line of Lisabeth, Anna was; the lovely round cheeks, the eyes as blue and frank as sky, the lush body, even the perfect white skin hinting down from her throat toward her breastbone. *Beauty bestowed upon her full receipt,/vouching her in every way complete.*

"Mother, Dad," Varick greeted us. "You came to see if Beth is going to come to her senses before the knot gets tied, I guess?"

"We came to gain Beth," Adair said simply and directly. Our daughter-in-law-to-be gave her a gracious enough look, but in an instant those steady blue eyes were gauging me. I got out some remark I hoped wasn't damaging, then Adair and I were moving on into the house out of the way of the other wedding-comers arriving behind us.

Glad as I was for Varick and Beth, this event of theirs was a gauntlet I had to make myself endure. Over there was Isaac. Despite the efforts of that concealing mustache and the unreadable crinkles around his eyes, the year since Anna's death was plainly there in the lines of his face. His son Peter was hovering near him, still too young to quite believe marriage was a necessity in life but enough of a man now to have to participate in this family day. Then over here was Rob, with Judith beside. For once he was not as brash as brass, whatever was on his mind. I saw him glance every so often toward Varick and Beth. I hoped he was seeing the past there, too, and I hoped his part of it was gnawing in him. Probably remorse would break its teeth if it even tried to gnaw him, though.

Then through the throng of the wedding crowd I saw with relief that Stanley Meixell had come in. While Adair was occupied accepting congratulations for the union of the McCaskills and the Reeses, I crossed the room to him.

Stanley was at the window that looked west to the mountains, a glass in his hand. Since the inanity called Prohibition, we were reduced to bootleg whiskey; I had to admit, whoever Isaac's source was, the stuff wasn't bad.

After we had greeted, I asked Stanley: "What's this I hear about you aiding and abetting matrimony here today?"

"Yeah, when Mac asked me to be best man I told him I would." He paused and resumed his window vigil. "Though it's closer to a preacher than I promised myself I'd ever get."

"Maybe it's not catching," I consoled him.

"I'm trying to ward it off with enough vaccine," Stanley remarked a bit absently with a lift of his glass. The major part of his attention was still gazing outside, away from the hubbub of the room. He said, "Angus, take a look at this, would you."

I stood beside Stanley at the window and saw what he was keeping vigil on. The mountains by now were entirely concealed under clouds, but along the ragged bottom of the curtain of weather occasional patches of the foothills showed through. Patches of startling white. First snow.

"It's christly early for that, seems to me," Stanley mused. "You ever know it to come already this time of year?"

"No," I had to admit. "Never."

Stanley watched the heavy veil of weather a long moment more, then shrugged. "Well, I guess if it wants to snow, it will." He started to lift his glass, then stopped. "Actually, we got something to drink to, don't we." He looked across the room toward Varick and Beth, and my eyes followed his. I heard the clink of his glass meeting mine, then Stanley's quiet toast: "To them and any they get."

I was returning around the room to Adair when the picture halted me. Just inside the open door into the bedroom, it hung on the wall in an oval frame the size of a face mirror. I had never seen it, yet I knew the scene instantly. The wedding photo of Anna and Isaac.

I stepped inside the bedroom to see her more closely. A last visit, in a way. She was standing, shoulders back and that lovely head as level as ever, gazing forthrightly into the camera. Into the wedded future, for that matter. I stood rooted in front of the photo, gazing now not only at Anna but at the pair there, Isaac seated beside and below her in the photographic studio's ornate chair and seeming entertained by the occasion, and I thought of the past that put him in the picture instead of me.

The presence behind me spoke at last. "It's a good likeness of them, isn't it," Beth said.

I faced around to her. My words were out before I knew they were coming.

"Beth, I'm glad about you and Varick."

She regarded me with direct blue eyes. Her mother's eyes. Then said: "So am I."

Operas could be made from all I could have told this young woman, of my helpless love for her mother, of what had and had not happened that morning above the Two Medicine when she registered her mother and then me. Of her mother's interest in me, of the verdict that was never quite final. But any of it worth telling, this about-to-be Beth McCaskill already knew and had framed her own judgment of. She was thoroughly Anna's daughter, after all.

By her presence in front of me now, was Beth forgiving me for having loved her mother? No, I think that cannot be said. She would relent toward me for Varick's sake, but forgive is too major. Probably more than anyone except Anna and myself, Beth knew the lure I was to her mother. The daybreak scene at the Two Medicine would always rule Beth's attitude toward me.

Hard, but fair enough. For twenty-one years I endured not having Anna as my wife. For however long is left to me, I can face Beth's opinion of me.

"Beth. I know we don't have much we can say to each other. But maybe you'll let me get this in. To have you and Varick in a life together makes up for a lot that I—I missed out on." I held her gaze with mine. "May you have the best marriage ever."

She watched me intently for another long moment, as if deciding. Then she gave me most of a familiar half-smile. "I intend to."

Beth and Varick said their vows as bride and groom ever do, as if they were the first to utter those words. The ritual round of congratulations then, and while those were still echoing, George Frew was tuning his fiddle, the dancing was about to begin. Adair here on my arm in a minute would be gliding with me, so near, so far, as the music took her into herself. Music and Adair inside the silken motion I would be dancing with, the wife-mask with auburn ringlets on the outside. Well, why not. There was music in me just now as well, the necessary song to be given our son and daughter-in-law, in the echoing hall of my mind.

> *Dancing at the rascal fair,*
> *Lisabeth Reese, she was there,*
> *the answer to Varick's prayer,*
> *dancing at the rascal fair.*
> *Varick's partnered with her there,*
> *giving Beth his life to share,*
> *dancing at the rascal fair.*
> *Devils and angels all were there,*
> *heel and toe, pair by pair,*
> *dancing at the rascal fair.*

Winter was with us now. The snow that whitened the foothills the day of Varick and Beth's wedding repeated within forty-eight hours, this time piling itself shin-deep all across the Two country. We did the last of autumn chores in December circumstances.

That first sizable snowstorm, and for that matter the three or four that followed it by the first week in November, proved to be just the thin edge of the wedge of the winter of 1919. On the fifteenth of November, thirty inches of snow fell on us. Lacelike flakes in a perfect silence dropped on Scotch Heaven that day as if the clouds suddenly were crumbling, every last shred of them tumbling down in a slow thick cascade. From the windows Adair and I watched everything outside change, become absurdly fattened in fresh white outline; our woodpile took on the smooth disguise of a snow-colored haystack. It was equally beautiful and dismaying, that floury tier on everything, for we knew it lay poised, simply waiting for wind the way a handful of dandelion seeds in a boy's hand awaits the first flying puff from him. That day I did something I had done only a few times in all my years in Scotch Heaven: I tied together lariats and strung them like a rope railing between the house and the barn, to grasp my way along so as not to get lost if a blizzard blinded the distance between while I was out at the chores.

The very next day I needed that rope. Blowing snow shrouded the world, or at least our polar corner of it. The sheep had to be fed, somehow, and so in all the clothes I could pile on I went out to make my way along the line to the barn, harnessed the work-horses Sugar and Duke, and prayed for a lull.

When a lessening of the blizzard finally came, Rob came with it, a plaster man on a plaster horse. He had followed fencelines down from Breed Butte to the North Fork, then guided himself up the creek by its wall of willows and trees. Even now I have to hand it to him. Here he was, blue as a pigeon from the chill of riding in that snow-throwing wind, yet as soon as he could make his mouth operate he was demanding that we plunge out there and provide hay to the sheep.

"Put some of Adair's coffee in you first," I stipulated, "then we'll get at it."

"I don't need—" he began croakily.

"Coffee," I reiterated. "I'm not going to pack you around to-day like a block of ice." When Adair had thawed him, back out we went into the white wind, steering the horses and hay sled along the creek the way Rob had done, then we grimly managed to half-fling half-sail a load of hay onto the sled rack, and next battled our way to my sheep shed where the sheep were shelter-ing themselves. By the time we got there they were awful to hear—a bleated chorus of hunger and fear rending the air. Not until we pitched the hay off to them did they put those fifteen hundred woolly throats to work on something besides telling us their agony.

That alarming day was the sample, the tailor's swatch, of our new season. The drought of that summer, the snow and wind of that winter: the two great weathers of 1919. Through the rest of November and December, days were either frigid or blowy and too often both. By New Year's, Rob and I were meeting the mark of that giant winter each day on our route to the sheep's feedground. At a place where my meadow made a bit of a dip, snow drifted and hardened and drifted some more and hardened again and on and on until there was a mound eight or ten feet deep and broad as a low hill there. "Big as the goddamn bridge across the Firth of Forth," Rob called it with permissible exag-geration in this case. This and other snow bridges built by the furrowing blizzards we could go right over with the horses and hay sled without breaking through, they were so thickly frozen. *Here winter plies his craft,/soldering the years with ice.* Yes, and his-tory can say the seam between 1919 and 1920 was triple thickness.

Thank heaven, or at least my winning cut of the cards, that we had bought twice as much hay as Rob wanted to, which still was not as much as I wanted to. Even so, every way I could calculate it now—and the worried look on Rob said his sums were coming out the same as mine—we were going to be scratching for hay in a few months if this harsh weather kept up.

It kept up.

As the chain of frozen days went on, our task of feeding the sheep seemed to grow heavier, grimmer. There were times now when I would have to stop from pitching hay for half a minute, to let my thudding heart slow a bit. The weariness seemed to be accumulating in me a little more each new time at a haystack; or maybe it was the sight of the hay dwindling and dwindling that fatigued me. In those catchbreath pauses I began to notice that Rob, too, was stopping from his pitchfork work for an occasional long instant, then making the hay fly again, then lapsing quiet for another instant. Behavior of that sort in him I at first couldn't figure. To look at, he was as healthy as a kettle of broth. No influenza had eroded anything of our Rob. But eventually it came to me what this was. Rob's pauses were for the sake of his ears. He was listening, in hope of hearing the first midair roar of a chinook.

From then on, my lulls were spent in listening, too. But the chinook, sudden sweet wind of thaw, refused to answer the ears of either of us.

Maybe I ought to have expected the next. But in all the snip and snap that went on between Rob and me, I never dreamt of this particular ambush from him.

Usually I drove the team and sled to whatever haystack we were feeding from and Rob simply met me there, neither of us wanting to spend any more time than necessary in the company of the other. But this day Rob had to bring me a larger horse collar—Sugar's was chafing a sore onto his neck, which we couldn't afford—before the team could be harnessed, and so he arrived into my barn just as I was feeding Scorpion.

No hellos passed between us these days, only dry glances of acknowledgment. I expected Rob to pass me by and step straight to the workhorses and their harness, but no, anything but.

He paused by Scorpion's stall. "This horse has seen his days, you know."

What I knew was the hateful implication in those words. To close off Rob from spouting any more of it, I just shook my head and gave Scorpion's brown velvet neck an affectionate rub as he munched into the hay.

Rob cocked a look at me and tried: "He's so old he'd be better off if you fed him your breakfast mush instead of that hay."

I turned away and went on with my feeding of Scorpion.

"The fact is," Rob's voice from close behind me now, "he ought to be done away with."

So he was willing to say it the worst he could. And more words of it yet: "I can understand that you're less than keen to have him done away with. It's never easy. The old rascals get to be like part of us." They do, Rob, my thought answered him, which is why I am keeping Scorpion alive this winter instead of putting the bullet you suggest into the brainplace behind his ear. "But," that voice behind me would not stop, "I can be the one to do away with the old fellow, if you'd rather."

"No. Neither of us is going to be the one, so long as Scorpion is up and healthy. Let's put a plug in this conversation and go feed the sheep."

But Rob blocked my way out of the stall. "Do you take telling?" he snapped. "We can't spare so much as a goddamn mouthful of hay this winter, and you're poking the stuff into a useless horse as if we've got worlds of it. Give yourself a looking-at, why don't you, man. This winter is no time for charity cases. Any spear of hay that goes into Scorpion doesn't go into one of those ewes half-starving, out there."

I knew that. I knew, too, that our hay situation was so wretched that Scorpion's daily allowance mattered little one way or the other. We needed tons of the stuff, not armfuls. We needed a chinook, we needed an early spring, we needed a quantity of miracles that the killing of one old horse would not provide. I instructed Rob as levelly as I could:

"I know the word doesn't fit in your ears, but I've told you no. He's my horse and you're not going to do away with him. Now let's go, we've got sheep waiting for us."

He didn't move. "I have to remind you, do I. He's the horse of us both."

Then I remembered, out of all the years ago. The two of us pointing ourselves down from Breed Butte toward Noon Creek on my horse-buying mission; that generous side of Rob suddenly declaring itself, clear and broad as the air. *Angus, you'll be using him on the band of sheep we own together, so it's only logical I put up half the price of him, am I right?*

And now the damn man demanded: "Get out the cards."

Those cold words of his sickened me. How could he live with himself, as sour as he had become? None of us are what we could be. But for Rob to invoke this, to ask the sacrifice of Scorpion and all the years this tall horse had given me, when it was his own blind gamble that delivered us into this hay-starved winter—right then I loathed this person I was yoked to, this brother of Adair's whom I had vowed to persist with because she wanted it so. Enduring him was like trying to carry fire in a basket.

I choked back the disgust that filled me to my throat. I turned so that Scorpion was not in my vision, so that I was seeing only this creature Rob Barclay. I slowly got out the deck of cards.

Rob studied the small packet they made in the palm of my hand. As if this was some teatime game of children, he proclaimed, "Cut them thin and win," and turned up the top card. The four of diamonds.

I handed the deck to him. He shuffled it twice, the rapid whir of the cards the only sound in the barn. Now the deck lay waiting for me in his hand.

I reached and took the entire deck between my thumb and first finger. Then I flipped it upside down, bringing the bottom card face-up to be my choice.

The two of us stood a moment, looking down at it. The deuce of hearts.

Rob only shook his head bitterly, as if my luck, Scorpion's luck, was an unfair triumph. As we turned from the old brown horse and began harnessing the workhorses, he stayed dangerously silent.

Near the end of January I made a provisioning trip into town. Every house, shed, barn I passed, along the North Fork and the main creek, was white-wigged with snow. Gros Ventre's main street was a rutted trench between snowpiles, and no one was out who didn't have dire reason to be. All the more unexpected, then, when

I stomped the white from my boots and went into the mercantile, and the person in a chair by the stove was Toussaint Rennie.

"What, is it springtime on the Two Medicine?" I husked out to him, my voice stiff from the cold of my ride. "Because if it is, send some down to us."

"Angus, were you out for air?" he asked in return, and gave a chuckle.

"I thought I was demented to come just a dozen miles in this weather. So what does that make you?"

"Do you know, Angus, this is that '86 winter back again." *No deer, no elk. No weather to hunt them in. West wind, all that winter. Everything drifted east. I went out, find a cow if I can. Look for a hump under the snow. Do you know, a lot of snowdrifts look like a cow carcass?* "That '86 winter went around a corner of the mountains and waited to circle back on us, Angus. Here it is."

"As good a theory as I've heard lately," I admitted ruefully. "Just how are your livestock faring, up there on the reservation?"

Toussaint's face altered. There was no chuckle behind what he said this time. "They are deadstock now."

The realization winced through me. Toussaint had not been merely making words about that worst-ever winter circling back. Again now, humps beneath the vast cowl of whiteness; carcasses that had been cattle, horses. The picture of the Two Medicine prairie that Toussaint's words brought was the scene ahead for Scotch Heaven sheep if this winter didn't break, soon.

I tried to put that away, out of mind until I had to face it tomorrow with a pitchfork, with another scanty feeding of hay by Rob and me. I asked the broad figure planted by the warm stove: "How is it you're here, Toussaint, instead of hunkered in at home?"

"You do not know a town man when you see him, Angus?"

I had to laugh. "A winter vacation in temperate Gros Ventre, is this. Where are you putting up?"

"That Blackfeet niece of Mary's." Nancy. And those words from Lucas, echoing across three decades: *Toussaint didn't know whether he was going to keep his own family alive up there on the Two Medicine River, let alone an extra. So he brought Nancy in here and gave her to the DeSalises.* "She has a lot of house now," Toussaint was saying. "That Blackfeet of mine"—Mary—"and kids and me, Nancy let us in her house for the winter." He chuckled. "It beats eating with the axe."

Before leaving town I swung by Judith's house for any mail she wanted to send out to Rob. She handed me the packet and we had a bit of standard conversation until I said I'd better get started on my ride home before the afternoon grew any colder. The question came out of Judith now as quietly as all her utterances, but it managed to ask everything: "How are you and Rob getting by together?"

To say the truth, the incident over Scorpion still burned like a coal in me. But I saw no reason to be more frank than necessary in answering her. "It's not good between us. But that's nothing new."

Judith had known Rob and me since our first winter in Scotch Heaven, when I still thought the world of him, so it was not unexpected when she said in an understanding voice, "Angus, I know this winter with him is hard for you." What did surprise me was when this loyalest of wives added: "It's even harder for Rob with himself."

February was identical to the frigid misery of January. At the very start of the last of its four white weeks, there came the day when Rob and I found fifteen fresh carcasses of ewes, dead of weakness and the constant cold. No, not right. Dead, most of all, of hunger.

Terrible as the winter had been, then, March was going to be worse. Scan the remaining hay twenty times and do its arithmetic every one of those times and the conclusion was ever the same. By the first of March, the hay would be gone. One week from today, the rest of the sheep would begin to starve.

A glance at Rob, as we drove the sled past the gray bumps of dead sheep, told me that his conclusion was the same as mine, with even more desperation added. He caught my gaze at him, and the day's words started.

"Don't work me over with your eyes, man. How in hell was I supposed to know that the biggest winter since snow got invented was on its way?"

"Tell it to the sheep, Rob. Then they'd have at least that to chew on."

"All it'd take is one good chinook. A couple of days of that, and enough of this snow would go so that the sheep could paw down and graze a bit. That'd let us stretch the hay and we'd come out of this winter as rosy as virgins. So just put away that gravedigger look of yours, for Christ's sake. We're not done for yet. A chinook will show up. It has to."

You're now going to guile the weather, are you, Rob? Cite Barclay logic to it and scratch its icy ears, and it'll bounce to attention like a fetching dog to go bring you your chinook? That would be like you, Rob, to think that life and its weather are your private pets. Despite the warning he had given me, I told him all this with my eyes, too.

The end of that feeding day, if it could be called so, I was barning the workhorses when a tall collection of coat, cap, scarf, mittens and the rest came into the yard atop a horse with the Long Cross brand. If I couldn't identify Varick in the bundle, I at least knew his saddlehorse. I gave a wave and he rode through the deep snow of the yard to join me inside the barn's shelter.

"How you doing?" asked my son when he had unwrapped sufficiently to let it out.

"A bit threadbare, to say the truth. Winter seems to be a whole hell of a lot longer than it ever used to be, not to mention deeper."

"I notice the sheep are looking a little lean." Lean didn't begin to say it, Varick. They were getting to resemble greyhounds. "You got enough hay to get through on, you think?"

"Rob and I were just discussing that." I scanned the white ridges, the white banks of the North Fork, the white roof of the sheep shed. Another week of this supreme snow sitting everywhere on us and we had might as well hire the coyotes to put the sheep out of their hungry misery. "Neither of us thinks we do have anywhere near enough, no."

Varick was plainly unsurprised. He said, part question and part not, "What about that Dakota spinach they've got at Valier?" Trainloads of what was being called hay, although it was merely slewgrass and other wiry trash, were being brought in from North Dakota to Valier and other rail points and sold at astounding prices.

"What about it?" I nodded to the east, across more than thirty miles. "It's in Valier and we're here."

"I could get loose for a couple days to help you haul," offered Varick. "Even bring my own hay sled. Can't beat that for a deal, now can you?"

I said nothing, while trying to think how to tell him his generosity was futile, Rob and I were so far beyond help.

Eyeing me carefully, Varick persisted: "If you and Unk and me each take a sled to Valier, we can haul back a hell of a bunch of hay, Dad."

"Varick, our workhorses can't stand that much journey. This winter has them about done in." *As it about has me, too,* I kept to myself.

"How about if I get you fresh horses?"

Well and good and fine but also impossible. Every horse in Scotch Heaven and anywhere around was a sack of bones by now. There wasn't a strong set of workhorses between here and—abruptly I realized where Varick intended to get fresh teams.

"Yeah, they'd be Isaac's," he confirmed.

Isaac. My nemesis who was never my enemy. In a better world, there would have been an Anna for each of us.

"Don't worry, Dad. He'll loan you the horses."

Why would he? Although I said it to Varick as: "What makes you so sure of that?"

"I already asked him. The old boy said, 'I hate for anyvun to get in a pince. Tell Annguz the horses is his.'"

A pinch definitely was what winter had us in, you were purely right about that, Isaac. I stared east again, to the white length of Scotch Heaven, the white miles beyond that to the railroad cars of hay in Valier. Why try, even. A sled journey of that sort, in a winter of this sort. *There is so much of this country, Angus.* That quiet mountaintop declaration of Adair's. *People keep having to stretch themselves out of shape trying to cope with so much. This Montana sets its own terms and tells you, do them or else.*

Or else. There in the snow of the valley where Rob and I had just pitched to them half the hay they ought to have had, the sheep were a single gray floe of wool in the universal whiteness. I remembered their bleating, the blizzard day we were late with the feeding; the awful hymn of their fear. Could I stand to hear that, day after day when the hay was gone?

Finally I gave Varick all the answer I had. "All right, I'm one vote for trying it. But we'll need to talk to Rob."

"He'll be for it. Dead sheep are lost dollars to him. He'll be for it, Dad."

In the winter-hazed sky, the dim sun itself seemed to be trying to find a clearer look at our puzzling procession. A square-ended craft with a figurehead of two straining horses was there in the white nowhere, plowing on a snow sea. Then an identical apparition behind it, and a third ghost boat in the wake of that.

Three long sleds with hay racks on them, Varick at the reins of the first, myself the next driver, Rob at the tail of this sled-runner voyage toward Valier, our convoy crept across the white land. But if slowly, we moved steadily. The big Reese horses walked through the snow as if they were polar creatures. Copenhagen and Woodrow, my pair was named. Even Isaac's horses had the mix of his two lands. Horse alloys, strong there in the dark harness in front of me.

We stopped at the Double W fenceline, half the way between Gros Ventre and Valier, to eat from the bundle of lunch Adair had fixed us. Rob and I stomped some warmth into ourselves while Varick cut the barbed wire strands so we could get the sleds through. Of the four-wire fence, only the top two strands were showing above the snow. While Varick was at that, I gazed around at the prairie. Cold and silence, stillness and snow. Once upon a time there were two young men, new to Montana, who thought they were seeing snow. *This is just a April skift,* was the freighter Herbert's croaking assessment. That April and its light white coverlet sounded like high summer to me now. That flurry that had taken the mountains and the wheel tracks from our long-ago trek toward Lucas and his nowhere town was a pinch of salt compared to this. And Rob and I of then, how did we compare with what we are now? The journeys we had made together, across thirty years. Steamship and railroad and horse and foot and every kind of wheel. And by ash sled runners, enmity accompanying us. What, were we different Rob and different Angus, all the time before? Else how did the enmity manage to come between us? In all likelihood I am not the best judge of myself. But I can tell you, from trudging through the days of this winter beside the unspeaking figure known as Rob Barclay, that this was not the Rob who would throw back his head and cockily call up to the hazed sun, *Can't you get the stove going up there?*

Onward from the fence, the marks of our sled runners falling away into the winter plain behind us. Silence and cold, snow and stillness. The murmurs within myself the only human sound. Adair asking, when Varick and I went into the house with his offer to make this hay trip: *Do both of you utterly have to go?* Reluctant *yeah* from her son, equally involuntary *yes* from her husband. From her:

Then I have to count on each of you to bring the other one back, don't I.
Toussaint, when I arranged for him to feed the sheep while we were
gone, saying only: *This winter. You have to watch out for it, Angus.*
And myself, here on this first ground I ever went across on horseback, scouting for a homestead site. Did I choose rightly, Scotch
Heaven over this prairie? That farmhouse there on the chalky horizon. If I had chosen that spot those years ago, I would right now be
in there drinking hot coffee and watching hay-hungry sheepmen ply
past on their skeleton ships. No, not that simple. In the past summer of drought and grasshoppers and deflated prices, that farm, too,
was bitter acres. The year 1919 had shown that farming could be a
desperate way of life, too. Maybe everything was, one time or another.

It was dusk when we came around the frozen length of Valier's
lake and began to pass the stray houses of the outskirts. Valier did
not have as much accumulation of winter as Scotch Heaven or Gros
Ventre, but it still had about as much as a town can stand. The
young trees planted along the residential streets looked like long
sticks stuck in to measure the snowfall. The downtown streets had
drifts graceful as sand dunes. Stores peeked over the snowbanks.
Pathways had been shoveled like a chain of canals, and at the eastern edge of town we could see the highest white dike of all, where
the railroad track had been plowed.

Along the cornices of the three-story hotel where we went for the
night, thick icicles hung like winter's laundry. When we three numb
things had managed to unharness the teams at the stable and at last
could think of tending to ourselves, Varick gave his sum of our journey from Scotch Heaven: "That could've been a whole hell of a lot
worse."

And Rob gave his. "Once we get those sleds heavy with hay, it
will be."

At morning, the depot agent greeted us with: "I been keeping
your hay cool for you out in the icebox."

When no hint of amusement showed on any of the three of us, he
sobered radically and said: "I'll show you the boxcar. We can settle
up after you're loaded."

We passed a dozen empty boxcars, huge husks without their
cargo, and came to a final one with a stubbly barricade of hay behind its slatted side. The agent broke ice from its door with a black-

smith hammer, then used a pinch bar to pry the grudging door open. "All yours," he stated, and hustled back inside the warmth of the depot.

The railroad car was stacked full of large bales like shaggy crates. Rob thrust a mitten under his armpit, pulled out his hand and thrust it into a bale. The handful he pulled out was brown crackly swamp-grass, which only in a winter of this sort would qualify as hay at all. "Awful stuff," Rob proclaimed.

"The woollies won't think it's as awful as starving," I told him. "Let's load and go." The weather was ever over our shoulder, and this was a lead-colored day that showed no intention of brightening. First thing of morning, I had taken a look out the hotel window to the west for the mountains and they were there, white-toothed as if they had sawed up through the snow prairie. As long as the mountains stayed unclouded we had what we needed from the weather today, neutrality.

Our work was harsh, laboring the bales from their stacks in the boxcar to the sleds alongside, as if we were hauling hundreds of loaded trunks down out of an attic. Oftener and oftener, Rob and I had to stop for breath. The smoke of our breathing clouded between us, two aging engines of work. To say the truth, without Varick's limber young strength I do not know how we ever would have loaded those three hay sleds.

When the last bale was aboard, even Varick looked close to spent, but he said only, "I guess that's them." A marker in our journey, that final bale; with it, the easy half of our hay task was over. Now to haul these loads, and ourselves, all the miles to Gros Ventre before nightfall, and on to Scotch Heaven the next day. Rob and I headed for the depot with our checkbooks to pay an outland-ish price for this god-awful hay that was the only hay there was, and then we would have to get ourselves gone, out onto the prairie of winter.

We had our own tracks of yesterday to follow on the white plain west of Valier, smooth grooves of the sled runners and twin rough channels chopped by the horses' hooves. The Reese horses strained steadily as they pulled our hay loads. With every step they were rescuing us a little more, drawing us nearer to Scotch Heaven and out of this width of winter.

All was silence except for the rhythm of the horses' labor, muscle against harness, hooves against snow. Existence crept no faster than our sleds, as if time had slowed to look gravely at itself, to ponder what way to go next, at what pace. I know I had thoughts—you can't not—but the lull we were traveling in held me. Keeping the team's leather reins wrapped in my mittened hands was the only occupation that counted in the world just then.

The change in the day began soon after we were beyond Valier's outlying farms and homesteads, where our tracks of yesterday went on into the prairie of the Double W range. At first the mountains only seemed oddly dimmed, as if dusk somehow had wandered into midday. I tried to believe it as a trick of light, all the while knowing the real likelihood.

In front of me I could see Varick letting only his hands and arms drive the team, the rest of him attentive to those dimming mountains. Behind me Rob undoubtedly was performing the same.

So the three of us simultaneously watched the mountains be taken by the murk. As if a gray stain was spreading down from the sky, the mountains gradually became more and more obscure, until they simply were absorbed out of sight. We had to hope that the weather covering the western horizon was only fog or fallow cloud and not true storm. We had to hope that mightily.

The wind, too, began faintly enough. Simply a sift along the top of the snow, soft little whiffs of white dust down there. I turtled deeper into the collar of my sheepskin coat in anticipation of the first gust to swoosh up onto the sled at me. But a windless minute passed, then another, although there were constant banners of snow weaving past the horses' hooves. I could see Varick and his sled clear as anything; but he and it seemed suspended in a landscape that was casually moving from under them. A ground blizzard. Gentle enough, so far. A breeze brooming whatever loose snow it could find, oddly tidy in its way. Another tease from the weather, but as long as the wind stayed down there at knee-high we were out of harm.

I believed we were nearly to our halfway mark, the Double W fence, yet it seemed an age before Varick's sled at last halted. I knew we were going to feed our teams, and for that matter ourselves, at this midpoint. But when Rob and I slogged up to Varick, we found he had more than replenishment on his mind.

"I don't know what you two think," he began, "but I figure we better just give up on the notion of going back the same route we came by."

Rob gave a grimace, which could have been either at Varick's words or at the sandwich frozen to the consistency of sawdust which he had just taken first bite of. "And do what instead?" he asked skeptically.

"Follow this fence," Varick proposed with a nod of his head toward it, "to where it hits the creek." Half a fence, really, in this deep winter; only the top portions of the fenceposts were above the snow, a midget line of march north and south from our cluster of hay sleds and horses. "Once we get to the creek," Varick was postulating, "we can follow that on into Gros Ventre easy enough."

"Man, that'd take twice as long," Rob objected. "And that's twice as much effort for these horses, not to mention us."

Varick gave me a moment's look, then a longer gaze at Rob. "Yeah, but at least this fence tells us where the hell we are," he answered. He inclined his head to the prairie the other side of the fence, where the wind's steady little sift had made our yesterday's tracks look softened. "It won't need a hell of a lot more of this to cover those tracks."

"Even if it does, Varick, we know that country," Rob persisted. "Christ, man, the hills are right out there in plain sight." The benchlands north of Noon Creek and the Double W were like distant surf above the flow of the blown snow.

"We won't know an inch of it in a genuine blizzard," Varick insisted. "If this starts really storming and we get to going in circles out there, we'll end up like the fillyloo bird."

Rob stared at him. "The which?"

"The fillyloo bird, Unk. That's the one that's got a wing shorter than the other, so that it keeps flying in littler and littler circles until it disappears up its own rear end."

Rob gave a short harsh laugh, but credit him, it was a laugh. I chortled as if I was filled with feathers. Were we all going giddy, the cold stiffening our brains? Would they find us here in the springtime, with ice grins on our faces?

"All right, all right," Rob was conceding, as much to the notion of the fillyloo bird as to Varick. If I had been the one to broach the fence route to him, Rob would have sniffed and snorted at it until we grew roots. But here he was, grudging but giving the words to Varick. "Lead on to your damn creek."

We began to follow the Double W fenceline south. The low stuttered pattern of the fenceposts could be seen ahead for maybe a quarter of a mile at a time, before fading into the ground blizzard. Occasionally there was a hump, or more often a series of them, next to the barbed wire—carcasses of Double W cattle that had drifted with the wind until the fence thwarted them. I wondered if Wampus Cat Williamson in his California money vault gave a damn.

A tiny cloud caught on my eyelash. I squinted to get rid of it and it melted coldly into my eye.

I blinked, and there were other snowflakes now, sliding across the air softly.

The stillness of their descent lasted only a few moments, before the first gust of wind hit and sent them spinning.

Quickly it was snowing so hard there seemed to be more white in the air than there was space between the flakes. In front of me Varick's sled was a squarish smudge.

The wind drove into us. No longer was it lazing along the ground. From the howl of it, this blizzard was blowing as high as the stars.

The Reese horses labored. Varick and I and Rob got off and walked on the lee side of our hay sleds, to lessen the load for the teams and to be down out of the wind and churning whatever warmth we could into ourselves. I had on socks and socks and socks, and even so my feet felt the cold. This was severe travel, and before long the ghostly sled in front of me halted, and Varick was emerging from the volleys of wind and snow to see how we were faring. Rob promptly materialized from behind. A gather seemed needed by all three of us.

The wind quibbled around our boots even in the shelter of my hay sled. There we huddled, with our flap caps tied down tight over our ears and scarves across our faces up to our eyes. Bedouins of the blizzard. One by one we pulled down our scarves and scrutinized each other for frostbite.

"We're doing about as good as we can, seems to me," Varick assessed after our inspection of each other. In the howl of the wind, each word had to be a sentence. "I can only see a fencepost or two at a time in this," Varick told us, "but that'll do. Unk, how's it going with you, back there?"

"Winterish," was all Rob replied.

"How about you, Dad—are you all right?"

That question of Varick's was many in one. I ached with cold, the rust of weariness was in every muscle I used, I knew how tiny we three dots of men, horses and hay were in the expanse of this winter-swollen land. But I took only the part of the question that Varick maybe had not even known he was asking: was I afraid? The answer, surprise to myself: I was not. Certainly not afraid for myself, for I could make myself outlast the cold and snow as long as Rob Barclay could. If one of us broke, then the other might begin to cave. But our stubbornnesses would carry each other far. We would not give one another the satisfaction of dying craven, would we, Rob.

"I'm good enough," I answered my son. "Let's go see more snow."

Trudge and try not to think about how much more trudging needed be done. Here was existence scoured down as far as it could go. Just the flecked sky, filled with fat snowflakes and spiteful wind; and us, six horse creatures and three human. Hoofprints of our horses, sliced path of our sled runners, our bootprints, wrote commotion into the snow. Yet a hundred yards behind Rob you would not be able to find a trace that we had ever been there. Maybe winter was trying to blow itself out in this one day. Maybe so, maybe no. It had been trying something since October. I felt pity for Woodrow, the horse of my team who was getting the wind full against his side. But being a Reese horse, he simply turned his head and persevered with his work.

I pounded my arm against my side and trudged. The wind whirled the air full of white flakes again. *Old mad winter/with snow hair flying.* This must be what mesmerism is, every particle of existence streaming to you and dreamily past. A white blanket for your mind. A storm such as this blew in all the way from legendary times, other winters great in their fury. The winter of '83. *The Starvation Winter, these Blackfeet call that, and by Jesus they did starve, poor bastards them, by the hundreds. Pure gruesome, what they went through.* Gruesome was the apt word for such winters, Lucas, yes. The winter of '86, Toussaint's telling of it. *That winter. That winter, we ate with the axe.* And Rob saying, *A once in a lifetime winter.* It depended on the size of the lifetime, didn't it.

The wind blowing, the snow flowing. Try to pound another arm's worth of warmth into myself and keep trudging. Every so often Varick, tall bundle of dimness ahead in the blowing snow, turned to look for me. I did the same for Rob. Rob. Rob who was all but vanished back there. Say he did vanish. Say he stumbled, sprawled in the miring snow, could not get up in time before I missed him, next time I glanced back. Say Rob did vanish into the blizzard, what would I feel? Truth now, Angus: what? As I tried to find honest reply in myself, a side of my mind said at least that would end it once and all, if Rob faltered back there in the snow and Varick and I could not find him, the poisoned time that had come between us— this entangled struggle between McCaskill and Barclay—would at last be ended. Or would it.

Whether it was decision or just habit, I kept watching behind me periodically to Rob. The team he had were big matched grays, and against the storm dusk they faded startlingly, so that at a glance there simply seemed to be harness standing in the air back there, blinders and collars and straps as if the wind had dressed itself in them. And ever, beside the floating sets of harness, the bulky figure of Rob.

We were stopped again. Varick came slogging to me like a man wading surf, and reported in a half shout that the fenceline had gone out of sight under a snowdrift that filled a coulee. We would need to veer down and around the pit of snow, then angle back up once we were past it to find the fenceline where it emerged from the coulee.

"If we've got to, we've got to," I assented to Varick, and while he returned to his sled I beckoned for Rob to come up and hear the situation. He looked as far from happy as a man could be, but he had to agree that the detour was all there was to do.

The horses must have wondered why they had to turn a corner here at the middle of nothingness, but they obediently veered left and floundered down the short slope.

Now the problem was up. The slope on the other side of the coulee was steep and angling, the top of it lost in the swirling snow, so that as the horses strained they seemed to be climbing a stormcloud. This was the cruelest work yet, the team plunging a few steps at a time and then gathering themselves for the next lunge, all the while the loaded sled dragging backward on them. It hurt even to watch such raw effort. I sang out every encouragement I could, but the task was entirely the horses'.

Up and up, in those awful surges, until at last the snow began to level out. The horses' sides still heaved from the exertions of getting us here, but I breathed easier now that we were atop the brow of the coulee and our way ahead to the fenceline would be less demanding.

Varick had halted us yet again. What this time?

One more time I waved Rob up to us as Varick trudged back from the lead sled.

"This don't feel right to me," Varick reported. He was squinting apprehensively. "I haven't found that fenceline yet and we ought've been back to it by now."

"We must not have come far enough to hit it yet, is all," Rob said impatiently, speaking what was in my mind, too.

Varick shook his head. "We've come pretty damn far. No, that fence ought to be here by now. But it isn't."

"Then where to Christ is it?" demanded Rob belligerently into the concealing storm. Our faces said that each of the three of us was morally certain we had come the right way after veering around the coulee. Hop with that first leg of logic and the second was inevitable: we ought to have come to the fence again. But no fence, logical or any other kind, was in evidence.

For a long moment we peered into the windblown snow, our breath smoking in front of our faces like separate small storms. Without that fence we were travelers with nowhere to go. Nowhere in life, that is. Bewilderment fought with reasoning, and I tried to clear my numb mind of everything except fence thoughts. Not even a blizzard could blow away a line of stoutly set posts and four lines of wire. Could it?

"There's just one other place I can think of for that fence to be," Varick suggested as if he hated to bring up the idea. "The sonofabitch might be under us."

With his overshoe he scuffed aside the day's powdery freshfall to show us the old hardened snow beneath. Rob and I stared down. Oh sweet Christ and every dimpled disciple. A snow bridge, was this? If it was, if we were huddled there on a giant drift where the snow had built and cemented itself onto the brow of the coulee all winter, fenceposts and barbed wire could be buried below us, right enough. Anything short of a steeple could be buried down there, if this truly was a snow bridge. And if we were overshooting the fenceline down there under the winter crust, we next were going to be on the blind plain, in danger of circling ourselves to death.

"Damn it," Rob seemed downright affronted by our predicament, "who ever saw snow like this?"

Varick had no time for that. Rapidly he said, "We can't just stand around here cussing the goddamn situation. What I'd better do is go out here a little way"—indicating to the left of us, what ought to be the southward slope of the long hump of drift we were on, if we were—"and take a look around for where the fence comes out of this."

His words scared my own into the air. "Not without a rope on you, you won't."

"Yeah, I'm afraid you're right about that," Varick agreed. The three of us peered to the route he proposed to take. Visibility came and went but it was never more than a few dozen strides' worth. I repeated that Varick was not moving one step into the blizzard without a rescue rope to follow back to us, even though we all knew the cumbersome minutes it would cost us to undo the ropes that were lashing the hay to the sled racks, knot them together, affix them around his waist—"It won't take time at all," I uttered unconvincingly.

Hateful as the task was, stiff-fingered and wind-harassed as we were, we got the ropes untied from each of our hay loads. Next, the reverse of that untying chore. "Rob, you're the one with the canny hands," I tried on him. He gave me a look, then with a grunt began knotting the several ropes together to make a single lifeline for Varick. One end of the line I tied firmly around Varick's waist while Rob was doing the splice knots, then we anchored the other end to Varick's hay rack.

"Let's try it," Varick said, and off he plunged into the blizzard. Rob and I, silent pillars side by side, lost sight of him before he had managed to take twenty effortful steps.

With my son out there in the oblivion of winter, each moment ached in me. But I could think of no other precaution we might have done. If Varick didn't come back within a reasonable time, Rob and I could follow the rope into the blizzard and fetch him. I would do it by myself if I had to. It might take every morsel of energy left in me, but I would get Varick back out of that swirling snow if I had to.

The rope went taut.

It stayed that way a long moment, as if Varick was dangling straight down from it instead of out across a plain of snow. Then the line alternately slackened and straightened, as Varick pulled himself back to us hand over hand.

His face, strained and wincing, told us before his words did. "I didn't make it to the fence. Ran out of rope."

Rob swore feelingly. I tried to think. We needed more rope, more line of life, to explore again into that snow world, and we did not have more rope. We just had ourselves, the three of us.

"Varick," I began. "Can you stand another try at it?"

"Floundering around out there isn't really anything I want to make a career of," he admitted, breathing as if he'd been in a race. "But yeah, I can do it again if I have to."

"Then this time I'll go out with you, for however far he can still see me." I jerked my head to indicate Rob. "You give us a yell when we're just about out of sight, Rob. Then you go out beyond me, Varick, while I hold the rope for you. What do you think? It would gain us that much distance"—I nodded to the edge of visibility out there—"for looking, at least."

"That sounds as good as any," Varick assented. Rob only bobbed his head once; we McCaskills could take it for yes if we wanted.

Varick and I set out, the wind sending scythes of snow at us. The cold sawed at us through every seam in our clothing. Quickly we were up to our knees in a fresh drift. Varick broke the way and I thrashed after him. A drift atop a drift, this latest dune of snow would be. And other layers beneath that as we slogged. October snow. November on top of that. And December atop that, and January, and February . . . How many tiers of this winter could there be. This wasn't a winter, it was geologic ages of snow. It was a storm planet building itself layer by layer. It was—

Abruptly I stopped, and reaching a hand ahead to Varick's shoulder brought him to a halt, too. When he turned, the apprehension in my manner made words unnecessary.

We looked back. Nothingness. The white void of snow, the blizzard erasing all difference between earth and sky. No glimpse of Rob. No sound in the air but the wind.

We stood like listening statues, our tracks already gone into the swirling snow we had come out of. Again, yet, no voice from the safety of there.

The bastard.

The utter betraying triple-slippery unforgiving bastard Rob had let us come too far. I ought to have killed him with my own hands, the day we fought there on Breed Butte, the day it all began. He was letting the blizzard eat us. Letting Varick and me vanish like two sparks into the whirl of this snow. Letting us—

Then sounds that were not quite the wind's.

. . . *arrr* . . .

. . . *ough* . . .

The blizzard swirled in a new way, and the wraith figure of Rob was there, waving both arms over his head.

"*Far enough,*" his voice faintly carried to us. "*Far enough.*"

Varick's heavy breathing was close to mine. "He always was one to press the luck, wasn't he," my son uttered. "Particularly when it's somebody else's."

We breathed together, marking the sight and sound of Rob into our senses, then turned ahead to squint for any sign of the fenceline. None.

"You ready to go fishing?" asked Varick, and away he plunged again, the rope around his waist and in my mittened hands.

Through my weariness I concentrated on the hemp in my hands. *To see a world in a grain of sand* . . . Would grains of snow do? By the dozens and hundreds they fell and fell, their whiteness coating my sleeves and mittens. . . . *Hold infinity in the palm of your hand* . . . Would mittened palms be deft enough, for that? I had to force my cold claw of a hand to keep making a fist around the moving line of rope. The rope paying out through my grip already had taken Varick from sight, into the snow cyclone. Thoughts swarmed to fill his absence. What if he stumbled out there, jerking the rope out of my stiff hands? Hold, Angus. Find a way to hold. I fumbled the end of the rope around my waist, clutching it tightly belted around me with my right hand while the left hand encircled the strand going out to Varick. If he fell I would fall, too, but nothing would make me let go of this rope. I would be Varick's anchor. Such as I was, I would be that much. A splice knot caught in my grip an instant before I let it belly out and away. The knots. Rob's knots. Lord of mercy, why hadn't I done them myself? What if he hadn't tied them firmly, what if just one began to slip loose? No. No, I could trust Rob's hands even if I couldn't trust him.

Only a few feet of rope left. If Varick did not find the fenceline now, we never would. My heart thundered in me, as if the enormity of clothing around it was making it echo. A quiver of chill went through me each time the wind clasped around my body. If we couldn't go on we would need to try to hide ourselves in caves of the hay, try to wait out the blizzard. But if this cold and wind went on through the night, our chances were slim. More likely they were none. If any one of us could live through, let it be Var—

Tugs on the rope, like something heavy quivering at the end of the hempen line. Or something floundering after it had fallen.

"VARICK!" I shouted as loud as I could. The wind took my words. I might as well have been yelling into a bale of that Dakota hay.

The tugs continued. I swallowed, held firm, clutching the jerking rope around me. I resisted a hundred impulses to plunge forward and help Varick in his struggle. I resisted another hundred to whirl around in search of Rob, to see whether he still was there as our guidemark. The distance back to him and the hay sleds was the same as it ever had been, I had to recite to my bolting instincts, only the snow was in motion, not the white distance stretching itself as it gave every appearance of. Motion of another wild sort at the invisible end of this rope, the tugs continuing in a ragged rhythm that I hoped had to be—

Varick suddenly coming hand over hand, materializing out of the whirl. A struggling upright slab of whiteness amid the coiling swirl of whiteness.

He saved his breath until he was back to me, my arms helping to hold him up.

"It's there!" he panted. "The fenceline. It comes out of the drift about there"—carefully pointing an angle to our left, although everything in me would have guessed it had to be to our right. "The sleds are actually on the other side of the sonofabitch. We about went too far, Dad."

Fixing ourselves on the figure whose waves and shouts came and went through the blowing flakes, we fought snow with our feet until we were back beside Rob. Varick saved him the burden of asking. "We got ourselves a fence again, Unk."

Laboriously we retied the ropes across the hay loads, as well as men in our condition could. Then Varick turned his team to the left—they were glad enough to, suffering in the wind as they had been—and I reined Woodrow and Copenhagen around to follow them, and Rob and his grays swung in behind us. Once our procession was down off the mound of snow, the tops of fenceposts appeared and then the topmost single strand of barbwire, the three strands beneath it in the accumulated white depth. This white iron winter, with a brutal web in it. That single top strand, though. That was our tether to the creek, to survival. I had never known until then that I could be joyously glad to see barbed bramble.

Now how far to the creek? We had to keep going, following the line of fence, no matter what distance it was. There was no knowing the hour of the day, either. The storm had made it all dusk. The complicated effort of trying to fumble out my pocket watch for a look, I couldn't even consider. Slog was all we needed to know, really. But how far?

Another laborious half-mile, mile. Who knew. This day's distances had nothing to do with numbers.

Then thin shadows stood in the snowy air.

Trees, willows of the creek. Dim frieze that hung on the white wall of weather. But as much guidance as if it was all the direction posts on earth, every one of them pointing us to Gros Ventre and safety.

A person is never too weary to feel victory. Blearily exultant, I stood and watched while Varick halted his sled and began to slog back to meet Rob and me. Now that we had the creek, consultation wasn't really needed any more. But maybe he simply had to share success with us, maybe—then as I squinted at the treeline of the creek, something moved in the bottom corner of my vision, there where the fence cornered into the creek.

I blinked and the something still moved, slowly, barely. A lower clot of forms beneath the willow shadows: Double W cattle, white with the snow coated onto them, caught there in the fence corner.

"The two of you go ahead and take your sleds across the creek, why not," my son said as nonchalantly as if our day of struggle was already years into the past. "I'll snip the fence for these cows and give them a shove out into the brush, then catch up with you."

"Man, why bother," Rob spoke bitterly. He still wore that bleak look, as if being prodded along by the point of an invisible bayonet. "They're goddamn Williamson's."

"That isn't their fault," Varick gave him back. "Head on across, you two. I won't be long."

I made my tired arms and tired legs climb atop the hay on the sled, then rattled the reins to start Copenhagen and Woodrow on their last few plodded miles to town, miles with the guarantee of the creek beside us. When we had crossed the narrow creek and made our turn toward Gros Ventre, Rob and his gray team copying behind us, I could hear faintly above the wind the grateful moans of the cattle Varick was freeing from the blizzard.

In the morning, our procession from Gros Ventre west toward home was a slow glide through white peace. New snow had freshened everything, and without the wind the country sat plump and calm.

As we passed the knob ridge at the mouth of the North Fork valley, branchloads in the tops of its pine trees were dislodging and falling onto the lower branches, sending up snow like white dust. The all-but-silent plummets of snow in the pines and the sounds of our teams and sleds were the only things to be heard in Scotch Heaven.

We went past the empty Duff homestead, and then the empty Erskine place, and what had been Archie Findlater's homestead, and the silent buildings of Allan Frew's. The lone soul anywhere here in the center of the valley was George Frew, feeding his sheep beside the creek. George's wave to us was slow and thoughtful, as if he was wondering whether he, too, would soon be making such a journey as we had.

And now we were around the final turn of the valley to my homestead, mine and Adair's, and there on their feedground beside the North Fork were the sheep in their gray gather, and the broad bundled figure of Toussaint distributing dabs of hay. For a long minute he watched our tiny fleet of bale-laden sleds, Varick in the lead, next me, Rob at the tail. Then Toussaint gripped his pitchfork in the middle of the handle, hoisted it above his head and solemnly held it there as if making sure we could see what it was, as if showing us it was not an axe.

We had hay now, but we still had the winter, too.

Each day was one more link in the chain of cold. For the first week after our Valier journey, Rob and I were men with smoke for breath as we fed the sheep in the frozen glistening weather.

Memory takes a fix from landmarks as any other traveler will. That week of bright silver winter after our hay journey was a time when Scotch Heaven never looked better. The mountains stood up as white majesties in the blue and the sun. The long ridgelines wore scarves of fresh snow that made them seem gentle, content. Every tree of the timbered top of Breed Butte stood out like a proud black sprig. Sunshaft and shadow wove bold wild patterns amid the willows along the North Fork. Only an eyeblink of time ago Montana was at its worst, and here it was at its best.

I would like to say that the clear weather and the Dakota hay and our survival of the blizzard made a poultice for the tension between Rob and me. That we put aside the winterlong wrangling—the yearslong enmity—and simply shouldered together toward spring. I would like to say that, but it would be farthest from the truth.

Maybe Rob would have been able to hold himself in if sheep had not continued to die. We found a few every day, in stiffened collapse; weak from the long winter and the short ration of hay, they no longer could withstand the cold and simply laid down into it and died. You could look on the hay journey as having saved the great majority of the sheep, as I did. Or you could look on the fact that in spite of that journey and its expensive hay, some of the sheep still insisted on dying, as Rob did.

It was about the third time he muttered something about "this Dakota hay of yours" that I rapped back, "What, you think we ought to have let the whole damn band just starve to death?"

"Goddamn it, you didn't hear me say that."

"If it wasn't that, it was the next thing to it."

"Up a rope, why don't you," he snapped back. It occurred to me we really ought not be arguing while we had pitchforks in our hands.

Wordlessly we shoveled the rest of the day's hay, and wordlessly I headed home to Adair and he to Breed Butte. By now I was not in my best mood. Overnight the clear weather had faded and gone, today's was a milky indecisive overcast, neither one thing nor another. The feedground wasn't far behind me when I heard the KAPOW of Rob's rifle as he blazed away, as he lately had begun doing, at some coyote attempting to dine on one of our dead sheep. The Winchester thunder rolled and rolled through the cold air, echoing around in the white day that had no horizon between earth and sky for it to escape through. Myself, I was not giving the coyotes any aggravation this winter. As long as they were eating the dead ones maybe they weren't eating the live ones, was my wishful theory. But apparently Rob had to take his frustration out on something, and as a second KAPOW billowed through the winter air, the coyotes were the ones getting it at the moment.

When I reached home with the hay sled, Varick's horse was in the barn. These visits of his through all the deep-drifted country between here and Noon Creek were more than outings, they were major pilgrimages. For Adair's sake, I was greatly glad that he came across the divide to us as often as he did. In full honesty, I was just as glad for my own sake.

Stiff and weary and chilly to the bottom sides of my bones, I clomped into the house. My wife and my son were at the table keeping coffee cups company. "Easy life for some people," I chattered out.

Greatly casual, Varick remarked: "There's news on Noon Creek. I been keeping this table warm for you until you could get here to hear it."

Hot coffee was all I wanted to hear of. Adair reached to the stove for the pot and poured me a cup as I thumped myself into a chair and began to unbuckle my overshoes. "If the news has winter in it," I expelled tiredly to Varick, "I can stand not to hear it."

"Yeah, well, maybe winter had a little something to do with it." Our son grinned all the grin a face could. "Beth's going to have a baby."

Adair stood up. Her face spoke *take care of her*, while her voice was saying: "Varick, that's fine!"

"You're ready to be grandma, are you?"

She hugged him from behind and declared: "It's bound to be easier than raising you ever was."

In her encircling arms our son turned his head to me. "If, ah, if he's a he"—Varick laughed at his word tangle—"Beth and I are going to give him that *Alexander* someplace in his name. Both of us figure maybe we can stand that much of the old country in any son of ours."

A bit dizzily I said, "Thank you both," which of course didn't come within a million miles of saying it enough. Then from Adair: "And if it's a girl?"

Varick paused. "Then we'd name her after Beth's mother."

There was nothing I could say. Not of Anna, not to this family of mine that had put itself through so much because of my love for her. It was Adair who moved us beyond the moment, put something major behind us. "That's an apt name, too," she said quietly to Varick. "You and Beth are honoring both families."

The second week in March, the chinook at last came. It arrived in the night, as if guilty about how tardy it had been, and when I realized from the changed feel of the air that this was a warm gush of wind instead of yet another icy one, I slid out of bed and went to the window.

Already there were trickles of melt, like running tears, down through the frost pattern on the glass. The warm wind outside was a steady swoosh. I looked back to the bed and my sleeping wife. In a few hours, at her end of our shared night, Adair would wake up into spring.

That morning at the feeding, I wished Rob was still in hibernation somewhere.

"Where the hell was this six weeks ago, when it would have saved our skins?" was his bitter welcome to the thaw.

His mood didn't sweeten in the next few days of warmth, either. Now that there was melt and slop everywhere, he grumbled against the thaw's mess as fervidly as he had against the snow it was dispelling. Maybe the chinook air itself was on his nerves—the change from winter coming so sudden that the atmosphere seemed charged, eerie. Or maybe this simply was the way Rob was anymore—resentful against the world.

Whatever his case was, it was not easy to be around. Not far from where we had stacked the Dakota hay there was a pile of dead sheep we had skinned throughout the winter and I had dragged off the meadow when the chinook came, and the boldest of the coyotes sometimes came to eat away at those corpses now that they were thawing. Rob took to bringing the rifle with him on the hay sled, to cut loose a shot if he saw a flash of coyote color there at the dead pile. The first time he yelled at me to hold the team while he aimed and fired, I had all I could do to keep the workhorses under control.

"Why don't you give the artillery a furlough until we're done feeding?" I tried on him. "The horses don't like it, the sheep don't like it, and I hereby make it unanimous."

He didn't even deign to answer, unless you can call a cold scowl an answer. He simply hung the rifle by its sling, back onto the upright of the hay rack where he kept it while we pitched hay, in a way designed to tell me that he would resume combat with the coyotes whenever he damn well felt like it.

Where had this Rob come from, out of the years? Watching him at this kind of behavior, I couldn't help but remember another Rob, of another spring, of another hard time. A lambing time, back in the years of '93. It had been one of those days to wonder why I didn't just walk away from the sheep business and join other certified lunatics in the asylum. The bunch herder we'd hired had lost thirty lambs in the past ten days, and another five had died on him that day. At that rate, by shipping time Rob and I were going to need to buy him a total new supply of lambs if we wanted to have any lambs to ship.

We've got to send this geezer down the road, I had said to Rob that remembered day.

I know, I know, he agreed glumly. *The man is a mortal enemy to sheep. I'll take the band while you trundle him to town, why not. Hire the nearest breathing body in the Medicine Lodge, McAngus. You can't do any worse than we did with this disgrace to the race.*

What if the nearest is Lucas? We both had to laugh.

Then the sheep would hear in a hurry what's expected of them, Rob vouched. *Lads and lasses*, his voice so very like Lucas's, *that's pure wonderful grass you're walking around on, so I want to see your noses down in it, ay? Do you know how much money you're costing me by your silly habit of dying? So let's have no more of that, you woollies, and we'll all get along together grand.*

As I had gone off, still laughing, I stopped to call back: *Rob, do you ever wonder if we're in the right line of work?*

His cocked head, his bright face. *There's an occasional minute when I don't, McAngus.*

In those times I would have walked into fire for Rob, and he for me. Yet that was the Rob who eventually cost me Varick, those years after the Two Medicine. Yet again, that was the Rob who had gained me Adair, all but brought her with frosting and candles on. Done that, and then put a boot through my family because of Anna. Where was the set of weights to measure such things; where was balance when you tried to align the different Robs. If they were different ones.

Going home that day, I heard another clap of Rob's Winchester thunder. He wasn't getting much done in life except trying to ambush coyotes. The man had me worried.

I had some downright dread the next morning. I knew this was the day we were going to have to move the sheep to a new and higher feedground, the chinook having made a soggy mess of where we had been feeding them in my hay meadow. In other times it would have been a task as automatic and easy as scratching an ear, but I could already hear Rob in full bay about having to work the sheep to a fresh site. Then, too, there was the small chore of liberating Scorpion out onto the coming grass, and Rob had already made himself known on the topic of the old horse and his menu.

And so I asked Adair. "What about coming with us today?"

"You want me to, do you?"

I smiled to the extent I could. "It can't hurt, and it might help."

"All right then," she agreed readily. "I'd better come see spring while it's still here, hadn't I."

"Then why don't you ride Scorpion out and we'll turn him loose to graze up there where the sheep are going to be—he and the woollies will be some company for each other, that way. I'll saddle him for you, all right?"

"No," she informed me. "I've known how to saddle a horse ever since five minutes after I married you. You get your old workhorses ready, Scorpion and I will take care of ourselves."

A good sight to see, Adair atop Scorpion as the pair of them accompanied alongside the hay sled and myself. If she pressed me to the hilt, I would have had to say that the day's most enchanting vision was the rivulets of melt running from beneath every snowdrift we passed. Glorious, the making of mud where winter had stood. But definitely this wife of mine and the tall brown horse, elderly and stiff as he was, made the second finest scene today.

Try tell that or anything else to Rob, though.

"What's this, a mounted escort for us on our way to the poorhouse?" he met us with at the haystack.

Degraded as that was, it seemed to be the top of his mood this day. I told him shortly that Scorpion was on his way out to pasture, which drew only Rob's scornful study of the elderly horse. At least he didn't start a recapitulation of how mawkish I was in keeping Scorpion among the living. But then as soon as I suggested that we needed to move the sheep from the muddy feedground in my meadow, the Rob response to that was hundred-proof sarcasm.

"So that hay can be grown to be fed to sheep that are worth less than the hay, do you mean? That definitely sounds like the Mc-Caskill high road to wealth, I can be the first to vouch."

"Rob, there's no sense in being owly about a little thing like this. Christ, man, we always put the sheep onto a fresh feedground after a chinook. You know that as well as I do." Or you would if you'd let your Barclay mind rule your Barclay mouth, for a change. "They can at least get a little grass into them if we move them onto the butte there," I went on, indicating with a nod the slope beside his reservoir, where broad swathes of ground showed themselves amid the melting patches of snow. The earthwork of the reservoir itself was already clear of snow, a chocolate pocket on the mottled slope of Breed Butte.

"Put the bastards up the backside of the moon, for all I care," Rob grumped next, and turned his back on me. He climbed onto the hay rack and hung his rifle by its sling onto the upright. "Let's get this damn feeding done," was his next impatient pronouncement.

Adair's gaze seemed to silence him after that, at least during our effort of loading the hay onto the sled rack. When we were done and standing there puffing, she announced she would drive the team for us now rather than ride Scorpion up the slope. "Adair needs the practice," she stated. Scorpion could follow, his reins tied to the back of the hay rack as they were; no problem to that. The problem anywhere in the vicinity went by the name of Rob, and I knew as well as Adair that the true need for her to be on the sled was to stay between her brother and me when he was this sulphurous.

The sheep were curious about the sled going up the slope instead of toward the meadow and them. *Prrrrr prrrrr,* I purled as loudly as

I could, and the bellwether Percy and the first few ewes began to get the idea and started toward the slope.

The siege of winter was withdrawing but not yet gone. Gray snowdrifts still clutched the treeline of Breed Butte and any swale of the broad slope. The entire country looked tattered and hungry. Up here above the still-white valley our sled runners were passing across as much muddy ground as they were snow, and in those bare damp patches the sickly grass from last year lay crushed, flattened by the burden of a hundred and fifty days of winter. Yet under the old clots of stems there was a faint almost-green blush, even today, after just this half-week of chinook and thaw, that said new grass was making its intentions known.

"Where to, gentlemen?" Adair called back to us from her position at the team's reins.

I asked Rob, "What do you think, maybe here?"

He said acidly, "It's the same muck everywhere, so this is as good as any."

He was going to be thoroughly that way today, was he. Then the thing to do was to get this hay flung off the sled and the sheep up here onto their new venue and be done with the man and his red mood. That curative for today—tomorrow would have to contrive its own Rob remedy as needed—could begin just as soon as Scorpion was turned loose out of the path of the hay, and so I climbed swiftly down to take his saddle and bridle off. I was untying Scorpion's reins from the back of the hay rack when Rob's voice slashed above me.

"*Angus.*"

The first time in years he had used my name. And now it snapped out quick and bitter, as if he wanted to be rid of it.

I swung around to see what this fusillade was going to be.

"Don't turn that geezer of a horse loose yet," Rob directed. "I just saw something I need to do with him."

"What's that, now?" I said up to him in surprise.

"My reservoir. This is a chance to tamp it." There atop the hay, he was gazing in a stony way along the slope to the long narrow mound of the dam and the ice-skinned impoundment behind it. Rob aiming his chin down at the valley and its creek, now and that first time I had watched him do it: *By damn, I didn't come all the miles from one River Street to live down there on another.* "The sheep have got to come up here anyway," he was saying, "the bastards might as well tromp across the dam and do me some good while they're at it. I'm going to ride old horsemeat here down and start shoving them to the reservoir."

"Why don't you wait with that until the next time we move the band," I tried. "The ground will be drier by then and the tamping will go better."

"Rob, yes," Adair interceded. "Angus is right about waiting for another day. Let's just get on with the feeding."

That brother of hers shook his head, his gaze still fixed across at the reservoir and its watery gray disc of ice. So far as I could see, winter and spring were knotted together there, ice and slush in the swale behind the dam versus mud on its sides and top; whatever moment of opportunity Rob Barclay thought he was viewing there made no sense whatsoever to me. But then we had made our separate decisions about water, about Breed Butte and the North Fork, a full thirty years ago, so when had we ever seen with the same eyes?

One thing I was determined to enforce: "Scorpion isn't the best horse for this, after all winter in the barn. You'd be as well off on foot. I'll walk down with you to the sheep, what about, and the two of us can—"

Rob came down off the hay sled. But I saw he hadn't come anywhere toward my line of thinking. His face was tight as a drumhide, and I suppose my own was taut enough. His tone was its most scornful yet, as he unloaded the words onto me:

"Pushing the sheep across that dam is a minute's work, is all. This goddamn horse has been gobbling up hay and doing not one thing to earn it all winter long. And you'd let it be that way." His helmeted look, his high-and-mighty mood when he wouldn't hear any words but his own. He gave me a last lash: "Your heart always has been as soft as your head."

Through it all, he still scanned with determination the reservoir, the sheep, the saddle horse. He would not so much as glance at me. Heart, mind, tongue, and now eyes, the last of Rob that was left to turn from me.

"Rob, Angus," Adair spoke up from the front of the hay sled where she had been waiting for this to abate. "You know how you're supposed to settle these things."

I hated to toss Scorpion to chance one more time. But if that's what it took . . .

"All right," I said with disgusted resignation, "we'll cut the cards for it, then," and reached into my coat pocket for the well-worn deck. "If I draw the low, Scorpion gets turned loose here and now. If you draw it—"

"No."

Before I knew it he had Scorpion's reins out of my hand, snatched into his.

"This horse has been living beyond his time ever since you won that other card cut." The face in front of me was cocked to one side, atilt with anger and the abrupt spill of declaring it. "He can do this one bit of work, and he's by Christ going to." With that, Rob shoved his overshoed foot into the stirrup and swung heavily up onto Scorpion, the horse grunting in surprise at the force of the rider clamping onto him.

I managed to grab hold of Scorpion's bridle and kept Rob from reining the brown head around as he was trying to do.

"Rob, I'm telling you, once," I delivered my own cold anger to this situation. "Behave yourself with this horse or I'll talk to you by hand."

There was a startled whinny from Scorpion as Rob jammed his heels into him and spun the horse out of my grasp, down the slope toward the approaching straggle of sheep.

"Go operate a pitchfork," Rob flung back at me without looking. "It's what you're good for."

So we had reached this, had we. Rob storming off, breaking the last of the terms I knew for enduring him. How in the name of anything were we going to survive lambing, shearing, summering the sheep in the national forest, all the steps that needed decision, if the damn man wouldn't hew to any way of deciding? We had come through the winter and now here was winter coming out of Rob as a white rage.

I climbed onto the back of the hay sled. His coyote rifle hung there on the upright from its sling.

I reached and unslung it, the grip of the wooden stock cold in my hand.

I could feel Adair's eyes on me.

I met her gaze as I jacked the shells out of the rifle one by one and pocketed them. When I had checked the breech to be thoroughly sure the weapon was empty, I hung the Winchester back where Rob had left it. "Just in case that temper of his doesn't know where to quit," I said to Adair.

"I'll talk to him, Angus," Adair said. "Let him get today out of his system, and I'll talk to him."

"I'm afraid his case is more than today, Dair."

"We'll just have to see. Why don't we get on with the feeding. It'll bring the sheep up here that much faster if they see the hay."

She was right. This day and Rob Barclay in it should be sped along, any way possible. I nodded to her to start the team, and began breaking the bales and pitching the dry brown Dakota hay off the sled. I cast glances along the slope as Rob commenced to work the sheep up to the embankment of the reservoir. They were not keen for the scheme. Recalcitrant sheep weren't going to help his mood at all. I would have to try every way in me to steel myself to let this behavior of Rob's pass until tomorrow, as Adair was asking of me. Because I knew, as if it was a memory in my fists, that I would pound Rob if I saw him mistreat Scorpion down there. With the rifle empty, he would be able to do nothing but take my beating, if it came to that. I would try not let it come to fists again, but given the mood the damn man was in, the trend wasn't promising.

I kept a watchful eye on Rob's doings while I kept at the feeding task. At last the sheep were skittishly filing across the top of the dam, a first few, then several, then many, the avalanche of behavior by which they went through life. Even now that the sheep were crossing the dam in maximum numbers, Rob kept reining Scorpion back and forth impatiently close behind the waiting remainder of the band. Scorpion was performing creakily but gamely, like an octogenarian going through remembered steps on a dance floor. The wind blew, the hay flew, and for a bit I had to take my attention from the escapade at the reservoir to feed some bales off the lee side of the sled.

When I looked again, the last of the sheep were halfway across the dam and Rob was right on top of them with Scorpion, shoving them relentlessly. Half that much commotion would gain him twice the results. *There are so goddamn many ways to be a fool a man can't expect to avoid them all*, and our Rob was determined to try them all out today, ay, Lucas? By Jesus, I missed Lucas. If he were alive,

Rob would not be down there in a major pout, furiously performing the unnecessary and making an overage horse labor like a—

I saw Scorpion make his stumble, then his hindquarters slip off the edge of the embankment toward the reservoir as he tried to find his footing there at the middle of the dam.

Rob did not even attempt to vault off him to safety. Instead he yanked the reins and stood back hard into the stirrups, seeming to want to stiffen the horse back into steadiness with the iron line of his own body. But Scorpion still was not able to scramble back securely onto the muddy rim of the dam. He tottered. There was an instant of waver, as if the horse's sense of balance was in a contest with his aged muscles. Then Scorpion began to flounder backwards down the brown bank, sliding, skidding.

It took a moment for the sound to travel to me—a crisp clatter, thin iceskin breaking as horse and man tumbled through. The sheep ran, heads up in alarm, never looking back.

"DAIR!" My shout startled her around to me. "Turn the team! Get us to the reservoir!"

She jerked the team and sled in a quick half-loop as I plunged through the hay to the front of the rack. There beside her I grabbed the rack frame with one arm and held Adair upright with my other as she whipped the team with the loose ends of the reins and the hay sled began to trundle and jolt. The sled seemed monumentally awkward, slow, although I knew it was going faster than I ever could on foot through the mud and snow.

Ahead of us there in the reservoir I kept expecting Rob to throw himself out of Scorpion's saddle and lunge or swim his way the eight or ten feet to the embankment. But he and the horse continued to be a single struggling mass amid the shattered ice. Scorpion was thrashing terrifically while Rob clung down onto his back and brown-maned neck. The stubborn fool, to be trying to maul Scorpion out of that water instead of getting himself to the shore.

The top of the reservoir was too narrow for the hay sled. Where the embankment began, Adair jerked the team to a halt and I leaped down from the sled, running as I alit. Adair's cry, "Angus, be careful!" followed me.

Rob and Scorpion were thrashing even worse now, Scorpion tipping far down onto one side with all of Rob except head and arms under him, struggling together like water beasts fighting. The goddamn man, why didn't he leave the horse and start toward—Rob's face, shining wet, appeared for an instant between Scorpion's jerking neck and the murky water. His expression was perplexed, as if the world had rolled over beneath him and left him hanging horizontal this way. Then I heard his hoarse gasped shout of the word.

"STIRRUP!"

Good Christ, he's caught in the stirrup, those overshoes of his. Rob was not stubbornly staying with Scorpion, he was trapped on the underside of the off-balance horse.

I ran and ran, slipping, sliding, at last slewing myself on one hip down the bank to where they had tumbled in.

The star-jagged circle of broken ice. Brown roily water. Scorpion's head and neck and side, crazily tilted as if he was trying to roll in a meadow and dark water had opened under him instead.

The water, waiting, welling in steady arcs toward me from the struggling pair. I had to force myself not to back away, up the bank away from the awful water of the reservoir. If Varick were here. If anyone who could swim, could face water without my blood-deep fear of it, were here. It all returned into me—the black steerage gut of the *Jemmy* where I lay in sick scared sweat, the ceaseless waiting sea, the trembling dread of having water over me. *You ask was I afraid,* the McCaskill family voice ever since the treacherous work on the Bell Rock lighthouse. *Every hour and most of the minutes, drowning was on my mind. I was afraid enough, yes.* Out in the water Scorpion floundered in fresh frenzy, Rob's arms clenching his wet-maned neck.

I swallowed as much fear as I could and made myself start to wade.

The reservoir embankment was ungodly steep. My first step and a half, I abruptly was in the cold filthy water up to my waist. Eight feet out from me, no, ten, the splashing fight raged on, Scorpion for all his effort unable to right himself with Rob's weight slung all on one side of him, Rob not able to pull free from the thrashing bulk of the horse angled above him.

"ROB! TRY PULL HIM THIS WAY! I CAN'T REACH—"

I was in the shocking cold of the water to my breastbone now. Down in the hole in the water. Chips of ice big as platters bumped my shoulders. Frantically I pushed them away. The horse and man still were six feet from me. If I could manage another step toward the struggle, if Rob would let go his death grip around Scorpion's neck and reach toward me—"ROB! THIS WAY! REACH TOWARD—"

More sudden than it can be said, they went over, Scorpion atop Rob.

The water-darkened brown of the horse's hip as it vanished. The *W* brand glistening wet there.

Now only the agitated water, the splintered ice.

The reservoir's surface burst again, Scorpion's head emerging, eyes white and wild, nostrils streaming muddy water, ears laid back. I could not see Rob, the horse was between us, I was reaching as far as I could but the water was at my collarbone. I arched my head as high out of the clutching water as I could, struggling to keep my feet planted on the reservoir bottom. If I slid, out there under under them, the water— Scorpion's splashes filled my eyes and mouth. Through that wet new fear I managed to splutter, "Reach around him to me, Rob, you've got to!" Scorpion still could not find footing, could not get upright to swim, could not—abruptly the horse went under again.

The hammering in my chest filled me as I waited desperately for Scorpion to come up.

Neck deep, I waited, waited. The water was not so agitated now. The ice shards bobbed gently.

For as long as I could, I refused the realization that Scorpion was not coming up. Then I made myself suck in breath, and thrust my head under the water.

Murk. Nothing but murk, the mud and roil of the struggle between trapped Rob and burdened Scorpion.

My head broke the surface of the reservoir again and I spewed the awful water. Adair's voice from the embankment was there in the air.

"Angus! You can't! They're gone, you can't—"

I lurched myself backward toward the sound of her, fighting the clawing panic of the water pulling down on me, the skid of my footing on the slant of the reservoir bottom.

Then somehow I was on my side, mud of the reservoir bank under me, the water only at my knees. Adair was holding me with her body, clutching me there to the safety of the embankment. Gasping, shuddering with cold, I still stared out at the broken place in the ice, the silent pool it made.

Seven days now, since Rob's drowning.

More thaw has come. I saw in my ride up to Breed Butte yesterday to check on the sheep that the reservoir has only a pale edge of ice here and there. Today will shrink those, too. From here in the kitchen I have been watching the first of morning arrive to the white-patterned mountains, young sunlight of spring that will be honestly warm by noon.

A week. Yet it seems not much more than moments ago. Stanley Meixell galloping off to summon men from the main creek and the South Fork and Noon Creek, while Adair and I headed on from the ranger station to town with the ugly news for Judith. Then while Adair stayed with her, I returned to the reservoir and the men gathering there. It was Varick who plunged and plunged until he managed, just before dusk, to secure the hook-and-cable around Scorpion's hind leg. Isaac Reese's biggest team of horses, struggling on the muddy footing of the dam to draw their hidden load out of the reservoir. At last the burden broke up through the water and onto the bank, Scorpion's body bringing the other with it. Rob's overshoed foot was jammed through the stirrup so tightly we had to cut the stirrup leather from the saddle. I was the one who put my hat over Rob's face, after closing his eyes forever, while we worked at freeing him.

A person has to sit perfectly still to hear it, but the sound of the North Fork's water rattling softly over stones is in the air these mornings. The creek's lid of ice has fallen through in sufficient places to let the sound out. After so much winter, the constant evidence of spring is a surprise. Grass creeps its green into the slopes and valley bottom of Scotch Heaven noticeably more each day. And the first lambs were born the night before last. The sheep we have left I can handle by myself this lambing time, with a bit of help now and then from Varick. Judith made her decision while still in widow black there at Rob's funeral, asking me to run the sheep until they have lambed and then sell them all for whatever we can get. It was there at the graveside, too, that Judith asked me to write the *Gleaner* remembrance about Rob.

So, here at dawn, the shining mountains up there are the high windows of memory. My night thoughts were a stopless procession, thirty years returning across their bridge of time, to here and now. I was told once I am a great one for yesterdays, and I said back that they have brought us to where we are. In a blue Irish harbor the bumboat women leap away like cats over the side of the steamship, and the rest of us bring our hopes to America. At a nowhere town with the name of Gros Ventre, a saloonkeeper with a remembered face and voice puts on the bar his arms with no hands. Below a stonecliff skyline, a rider with feedbag whiskers looms as the sentry of a calm green valley. A wedding band goes onto an unintended finger. On the trail to the Two Medicine River a thousand lambs go down on their knees to suckle from their thousand mothers, the prayerful noon of the sheep kingdom. A son stands baffled and resentful in a blazing day. Out of all the hiding places in the head, they return.

And so I have thought through the past and words ought to come now, oughtn't they. But which ones. *The word is never quite the deed./How can I write what you can read?* Whichever words will make all the truth, of course. But there is so much of that, starting so far back. The dock at Greenock, where one far figure turns to another with the words *Are we both for it?* and that other makes himself say *Both.* What began there has not ended yet. This autumn, luck willing, there will be Varick and Beth's child. Luck willing, maybe other McCaskills in other autumns. And there will be Adair and me, here where we are. This morning as I began to get up in the dim start of dawn, she reached across the bed and stopped me. I had not been the only one with night thoughts processioning through. Adair's grief for Rob was deep but quick; after all, she is a Barclay, and life hasn't yet found how to make them buckle. Now she has put this winter away. As Adair held me she told me she will stay in Scotch Heaven as long as I do—which I suppose is the same as saying as long as I have breath in me. It makes everything ahead less hard, hearing that decision from her. How long before the sheep business and the Two Medicine country and for that matter Montana recuperate from the drought and winter of 1919, there is just no telling. What is certain is that I will be buying another band of the woollies at the earliest chance. And the teaching job at the South Fork school this autumn is mine for the asking, Fritz Hahn of the school board has informed me. I will ask. It seems that the McCaskills will get by. We start at the next of life in another minute: "Adair will come right out and cook you her famous sidepork for breakfast, old Angus McCaskill," she has just advised me from the bedroom. I am glad she will find this crystal day, the mountains now glistening and near, when she comes.

Lad, at least Montana is the prettiest place in the world to work yourself to death, ay? You were right more often than not, Lucas, handless Lucas who touched my life time upon time.

Angus, you are one who wants to see how many ways life can rhyme. Anna. The divide between our lives, twenty years of divide. It is permanent at last, our being apart, but you were the rhythm in my life I could do nothing about. You still are.

See now, McAngus, it's time you had a talking-to. Rob. My friend who was my enemy. Equally ardent at both, weren't you, bless you, damn you. You I knew longest of any, Rob, and I barely fathomed you at all, did I.

Hard ever to know, whether time is truly letting us see from the pattern of ourselves into those next to us. Rob's is my remembrance that will appear in the clear ink of the *Gleaner* this coming week. But where are the boundaries, the exact threadlines in the weave, between his life and ours? Tell me, tell me that, whoever can.

Acknowledgments

This novel continues the blend I began in *English Creek*—a fictional population inhabiting the actual area along the Rocky Mountain Front near Dupuyer Creek, Montana, the cherished country of my growing-up years. In general I've retained nearby existing places such as Valier, Choteau, Conrad, Heart Butte and so on, but anything within what I've stretched geography to call "the Two Medicine country," I have felt free to change or invent.

For the Scottish background of this book, I'm much indebted to: the Watt Library in Greenock; the St. Andrews University Library and Robert N. Smart, Keeper of Manuscripts and University Muniments; the Mitchell Library in Glasgow; the National Library of Scotland; the General Register Office for Scotland; the Edinburgh Central Library; the Crail Museum; the Angus Folk Museum at Glamis; the Fife Folk Museum at Ceres; the Scottish Fisheries Museum at Anstruther; and the Signal Tower Museum at Arbroath. My particular thanks for their generous help go to Mrs. Couperwhite of the Watt Library, Morag M. Fowler of the St. Andrews University library, and D.L. McCallum of the Mitchell Library's Social Sciences Department.

My version of the Montana period of this novel, 1889–1919, was greatly aided by the historical troves at: the Great Falls Public Library; the Montana Historical Society at Helena; the Mansfield Library of the University of Montana at Missoula; and the Renne Library of Montana State University at Bozeman. I'm indebted to skilled members of all those staffs: Sister Marita Bartholome, Ellie Arguimbau, Dale Johnson, Ilah Shriver, Bob Clark, Richard Gercken, Dave Walter, Howard Morris, Laurie Mercier, Susan Storey, Marianne Keddington, Lory Morrow, Jane Smilie, Kathy Schaefer and Rick Newby.

Other institutions and their members were also vitally helpful: the University of Washington Library at Seattle; the Forest History Society; the Bancroft Library at the University of California, Berkeley; the Shoreline Community College Library at Seattle; and Glenda Pearson, Pat Kelley, Mary Beth Johnson, John Backes, Pete Steen, Carla Rickerson, Melvylei Johnson, Kathy and Ron Fahl, Susan Cunningham, John James, Bob Bjoring, and definitely not least, Jean Roden.

I'm deeply indebted to those who told me, in interview or letter, the everyday details of their lives as youngsters during the Montana homestead boom in the first decades of this century: Florence and Tom Friedt, Dene Reber, Irene Olson, Cecelia Waltman, Georgia Farrington, Eva Farrington, Mary Gwendolyn Dawson, Fern Moore Gregg, Howard Gribble, Margaret Saylor, and Fern Eggers.

It's been of immense benefit to me to be able to draw on the work, encouragement and friendship of Montana's corps of professional historians: Bill Farr, Paula Petrik, Harry Fritz, Duane Hampton, Bill Lang, Merrill Burlingame, Mike Malone, Rich Roeder—and the late Stan Davison, a fellow

Montana kid, who I'm sorry did not live to see this book of the era he was born into. Malone and Roeder's *Montana: A History of Two Centuries* has been my guide as I've tried to make the lives of my characters respond to what might be called the laws of historical gravity; and Rich Roeder deserves full due for his homestead research reflecting the fact that more land was homesteaded in Montana than any other state, and that the peak of the Montana homestead boom was remarkably late in "frontier" history, 1914–1918.

As usual in the long birth of a book, a considerable community of friends and acquaintances provided me encouragement, hospitality, information, advice, or other aid. My appreciation to John Roden, Tom Chadwick, Abigail Thomas, Kathy Malone, Orville Lanham, Howard Vogel, the Lang family of Clancy, blacksmith Richard Connolly, Marilyn Ridge, Richard Maxwell Brown, Gail Steen, Nancy Meiselas, Edith Brekke, the Arnst-Bonnet-Hallingstad-Payton clan of Great Falls, Clyde Milner, Burt Weston, Mick Hager, Kathlene Mirgon, Bob Roripaugh, Solomon Katz, George Engler, Rodney Chapple, Dick Nelson, Sue Mathews, Chris Partman, Marshall Nelson, Ted and Jean Schwinden, Merlyn Talbot, Patti Talmadge, Lois and Jim Welch, Annick Smith, Juliette Crump, Bill Bevis, Joy and Brad Hamlett, Walker Wyman, Mark Wyman, Art Watson, Eric Ford, Bill Kittredge, Caroline and Ron Manheimer, William W. Krippaehne Jr., Mary Farrington, Ken Weydert, Ann Nelson, and Rae-Ellen Hamilton.

My wife, Carol, and her camera captured the Two country and the town of Gros Ventre in the research for *English Creek*, and for this book she added the Scottish backdrop from the Bell Rock to Greenock. For her pictures of what I am trying to say, for her insights into this manuscript during my three years of work on it, and for all else, I can't thank her enough.

Once again, Liz Darhansoff, Tom Stewart, and Jon Rantala in their distinctive inspiriting ways have been entirely essential to bringing this book to life.

"The stillness, the dancing": this book and I have benefited immeasurably from the keen poetic eye of Linda Bierds.

Another sharp-sighted professional who made this a better book than it otherwise would have been: copy editor Elaine Robbins.

The dedication of this book speaks a general thanks to Vernon Carstensen for the past twenty years of knowing him; but I also owe him specific gratitude for so generously sharing his insights into the history of the American West, any time I've ever asked.

Patricia Armstrong, peerless researcher, not only aided me with material about the influenza epidemic but provided me a helpful reading of this novel's opening chapter. Similarly, Ann McCartney's reading of the first three chapters helped me see things I hadn't. For those and for the depth of their friendship with me, thanks one more time to Pat and Ann.

A few words about derivations and inspirations. Scholars of Robert Burns may be mystified by a number of the lines mentally quoted by Angus McCaskill herein. Some of Angus's remembered verse is indeed Burns; some is Burns and Doig; and some is, alas, merely Doig. In all instances, I've used words in their form more readily recognized on this side of the Atlantic—"you" instead of "ye," "old" instead of "auld," for instance. The quote in chapter three from the *"Choteau Quill,"* "You can fight armies or disease or trespass, but the settler never," the *Quill* and I owe to John Clay, *My Life on the Range*. Details of wheelwrighting came from George Sturt's fascinating memoir, *The Wheelwright's Shop*. Whenever I needed to know how the sheep business was doing in any particular year, I had only to resort to Alexander Campbell McGregor's meticulous account of his family's history in the business, *Counting Sheep*. The Crofuttian advice early in chapter one to emigrate "with no divided heart" I fashioned from a similar paragraph in *The Emigrants' Guide*, 1883 edition; the rest of *Crofutt* I made up.

Finally, I wish to thank the National Endowment for the Arts for its grant of a fiction fellowship, and the members of that 1985 selection panel: Alice Adams, David Bradley, Stanley Elkin, Ivy Goodman, Tim O'Brien, Walker Percy, Elizabeth Tallent, and Geoffrey Wolff.

St. Andrews-Glasgow-Edinburgh
Helena-Dupuyer-Seattle, 1983–86

DANCING AT THE RASCAL FAIR

From its opening on the quays of a Scottish port in 1889 to its close on a windswept Montana homestead three decades later, *Dancing at the Rascal Fair* is a passionate and authentic chronicle of the American experience. When we meet the emigrants Angus McCaskill and Rob Barclay—"both of us nineteen and green as the cheese of the moon and trying our double-damnedest not to show it"—they are setting off for a new life in a new land, in America, in Montana, "those words with their ends open." We follow their fortunes in the Two Medicine country at the base of the Rocky Mountains: the building of homes and the raising of families, making a living and making a life.

Here is the tale of the uncertainties of friendship and love; here are sheep-shearing contests and raucous dances in one-room school-houses; here are brutal winters and unrelenting battles of the will; here is a love of delightful and heartbreaking intensity and another love, born of heartbreak, of an equally moving and stoical devotion.

DISCUSSION POINTS

1. At the start of the book, Angus thinks back on his and Rob's decision to emigrate from Scotland and wonders what Rob's "deep reasons" were. What do you think? And how does Lucas serve as a symbol of the West's promise and perils?

2. The novel takes place over thirty years and spans several generations. How does Doig convincingly allow so much time to pass and yet focus on specific events, moments, and exchanges between characters with precision and effect? What narrative methods does he use to create a sweeping saga that is also a nuanced portrait of people and place?

3. The numerous historical events woven into this fictional tale include the influenza epidemic, the establishment of America's national forests, and the First World War. Can fiction bring a milieu alive more vividly than history?

4. Ivan Doig has described the way his characters speak as "a poetry of

the vernacular" and has said that he strives to craft the "poetry under the prose." Find examples of how Doig creates dialogue to show how Angus and Rob become more Americanized over the years.

5. What does Angus's love of verse, and his habit of quoting it, say about his personality? What does he seek by turning to poetry and song? What effect does Doig achieve by peppering the book with Scottish verse? What special significance lies in the lyrics of "Dancing at the Rascal Fair," which the author composed to serve as the book's title?

6. Doig believes that "writers of caliber can ground their work in specific land and lingo and yet be writing of that larger country: life." Yet, setting is anything but a passive backdrop in Doig's fiction. How does the grandeur of Montana dwarf the lives of the characters or make them seem more expansive and dramatic? How does the unpredictable Montana climate parallel the stormy relationships depicted in the book?

7. Angus remarks that "the Atlantic was a child's teacup compared to the ocean that life could be." Discuss the water imagery throughout the book, from Rob and Angus's transatlantic voyage to the droughts the homesteaders suffer to Rob's eventual fate.

8. Throughout the book, Rob and Angus worry over the "perils that sheep invite on themselves." Describe the parallel between the sheep, with all their promise and vulnerability, and the homesteaders who tend them.

9. Do you believe that Anna truly loved both Isaac and Angus, or was she simply sparing Angus's feelings when she told him she would know where to turn if her marriage went awry? If Anna lived through the influenza epidemic, would she and Angus have re-ignited their relationship?

10. Angus calls his marriage to Adair a "truce." Discuss the ways in which Doig explores the interplay of obligation, compromise, loyalty, and affection in their marriage. For which of these two victims of unrequited love do you feel the most sympathy? Considering Adair's knowledge that she is not Angus's true love and her admission that she is ill-suited for homesteading life, why does she stay so long in Montana? In the end, did you find Angus and Adair's relationship practical and companionable or tragic and sad?

11. How does Doig develop Rob and Angus's lifelong friendship? Trace its arc over the decades. How realistically does Doig depict the eventual rift between them? What do you think caused the drastic change in Rob's personality toward the end of his life?

12. In the final chapter, Angus reflects: "Hard ever to know, whether time is truly letting us see from the pattern of ourselves into those next to us." What does this novel say, finally, about the mysteries of human relationships and the human heart?

ABOUT THE AUTHOR

The grandson of homesteaders and the son of a ranch hand and a ranch cook, Ivan Doig was born in Montana in 1939. He grew up along the Rocky Mountain Front that has inspired much of his writing, making it into his own equivalent of Faulkner's "Western Yoknapatawpha," according to reviewers. His first book, the highly acclaimed memoir *This House of Sky* (1978), was a finalist for the National Book Award, and his eight books since then have received numerous prizes.

A former ranch hand and newspaperman, Doig is a graduate of Northwestern University, where he received a B.S. and an M.S. in journalism. He holds a Ph.D. in history from the University of Washington and honorary doctorates in literature from Montana State University and Lewis and Clark College. In the century's-end *San Francisco Chronicle* polls to name the best Western novels and works of nonfiction, Doig is the only living writer with books in the top dozen on both lists: *English Creek* for fiction and *This House of Sky* for nonfiction. He lives in Seattle with his wife, Carol, who has taught the literature of the American West.

Dancing at the Rascal Fair is part of Doig's Two Medicine trilogy, which follows the fate of the McCaskill family in America. *English Creek* resumes the trilogy in 1939, and *Ride with Me, Mariah Montana* leaves the McCaskills in 1989. Doig's latest novel, *Mountain Time,* is a contemporary novel with sisters Mariah and Lexa McCaskill as major characters.

Discover more reading group guides on-line!
Browse our complete list of guides and download them for free at
www.SimonSays.com/reading_guides.html